LOVE (AND) WAR

"A FEISTY ASSORTMENT OF FICTIONAL HEROES AND HEROINES. The Hazards, a wealthy Pennsylvania industrialist family, and the Mains, prosperous plantation owners from South Carolina, fight and intermarry with fiery abandon."
—*People*

"IN DELICIOUS DETAIL ARE THE WICKED AND TAW-DRY DOINGS OF A MEMORABLE CAST OF CHARAC-TERS." —*The Washington Post Book World*

John Jakes

LOVE AND WAR

"AT THE VERY HEART OF EVERY JAKES SAGA IS A STORY THAT THROBS TO THE BEAT OF HISTORY."
—*The Plain Dealer* (Cleveland)

"WHAT [HE] CAN DO THAT HISTORY BOOKS CAN'T IS DRAW THE READER INTO THE MID-1800s, letting us feel the emotions of participants and helping us to understand on a personal level what led Americans to the bloodiest conflict this nation has ever faced." —*Detroit Free Press*

"JAKES SPECIALIZES IN CREATING CHARACTERS YOU CARE ABOUT AND SKILLFULLY MERGING THEIR LIVES WITH THE HISTORY OF THEIR TIMES."
—*The Charlotte Observer*

BY JOHN JAKES

Homeland
In the Big Country
North and South
Heaven and Hell
The Kent Family Chronicles

The Bastard
The Rebels
The Seekers
The Furies
The Titans
The Warriors
The Lawless
The Americans

LOVE (AND) WAR

John Jakes

A DELL BOOK

Published by
Dell Publishing
a division of
Bantam Doubleday Dell Publishing Group, Inc.
1540 Broadway
New York, New York 10036

If you purchased this book without a cover you should be aware that this book is stolen property. It was reported as "unsold and destroyed" to the publisher and neither the author nor the publisher has received any payment for this "stripped book."

For Julian Muller
No writer ever had a better friend

Copyright © 1984 by John Jakes

All rights reserved. No part of this book may be reproduced or transmitted in any form or by any means, electronic or mechanical, including photocopying, recording, or by any information storage and retrieval system, without the written permission of the Publisher, except where permitted by law. For information address Harcourt Brace Jovanovich, Inc., Orlando, Florida.

The trademark Dell® is registered in the U.S. Patent and Trademark Office.

ISBN: 0-440-15016-7

Reprinted by arrangement with Harcourt Brace Jovanovich, Inc.

Printed in the United States of America

Published simultaneously in Canada

Two previous Dell Editions

October 1988

30 29 28 27 26 25 24 23

RAD

With the exception of historical figures, all characters in this novel are fictitious, and any resemblance to living persons, present or past, is coincidental.

*Two things greater
than all things are,
The first is Love,
and the second War.*

KIPLING

PROLOGUE: ASHES OF APRIL

The house burned an hour before midnight on the last day of April. The wild, distant ringing of the fire bells woke George Hazard. He stumbled through the dark hallway, then upstairs to the mansion tower, and stepped outside onto the narrow balcony. A strong, warm wind blew, strengthening the flames and intensifying their light. Even from this height above the town named Lehigh Station, he recognized the blazing house—the only substantial one remaining in the seedy section near the canal.

He raced down to his dimly lighted bedroom and grabbed clothing with hardly more than a glance. He tried to dress quietly but inevitably woke his wife, Constance. She had fallen asleep reading Scripture—not her own Douay version but one of the Hazard family Bibles, into which she'd slipped her rosary before closing the book and kissing George good night. Since the fall of Fort Sumter and the outbreak of war, Constance had spent more than her usual time with the Bible.

"George, where are you rushing?"

"There's a fire in town. Don't you hear the alarms?"

Still sleepy, she rubbed her eyes. "But you don't chase the pump engines whenever the bell rings."

"The place belongs to Fenton, one of my best foremen. There's been trouble in his household lately. The fire may be no accident." He bent and kissed her warm cheek. "Go to sleep. I'll be back in bed in an hour."

He turned off the gas and moved swiftly downstairs and to the stable. He saddled a horse himself; it was far faster than waking a groom, and concern spurred him to haste. This acute involvement puzzled him, because, ever since Orry Main's visit two weeks ago this very night, George had been submerged in a strange, numb

9

state. He felt at a distance from most life around him and especially from that of the nation, one part of which had seceded and attacked the other. The Union was sundered; troops were mustering. As if that somehow had no bearing on his existence, or any impact on his emotions, George had resorted to self-willed isolation.

On horseback, he raced from the rear of the mansion he'd named Belvedere and down the twisting hillside road toward the fire. The strong wind gusts blew like blasts from one of the furnaces of Hazard Iron; the foreman's house must have become an inferno. Was the volunteer company on the scene? He prayed so.

The road, high-crowned and bumpy, required tight control of his mount. The route took him by the many buildings of the ironworks, generating smoke and light and noise even at this hour. Hazard's was running continuously, rolling out rails and plate for the Union war effort just commencing. The company was also about to sign a contract to cast cannon. Just now, however, business was the farthest thing from the mind of the man riding swiftly past the terraces of the better homes, then into the flat streets of the commercial district toward the heat and glare of the fire.

The trouble in Fenton's house had been known to George for some time. Whenever a worker had a problem, he usually heard about it. He wanted it so. Occasionally discipline was required, but he preferred the remedies of discussion, understanding, and advice, wanted or no.

The previous year, Fenton had taken in his footloose cousin, a muscular, energetic chap twenty years his junior. Temporarily without funds, the young man needed a job. The foreman found him one at Hazard's, and the newcomer did well enough for a month or two.

Though married, Fenton was childless. His handsome but essentially foolish wife was nearer the cousin's age than his own. Soon George noticed the foreman losing weight. He heard talk of an atypical listlessness when Fenton was on duty. Finally George received a report of a costly mistake made by the foreman. And a week later, another.

Last week, both to prevent new errors and to help Fenton if he could, George had called him in for a talk. Usually easygoing—responsive in conversation, even with the owner—Fenton now had a cold, tight, tortured look in his eyes and would make only one statement of substance. He was experiencing domestic difficulty. He emphasized the two words several times—domestic difficulty. George expressed sympathy but quietly said the errors had to stop. Fenton promised to ensure it by remedying the difficulty. George asked how. By insisting the cousin move out of his house, the foreman said. Uneasily, George left it there, suspecting the nature of the *domestic difficulty.*

Now, silhouetted ahead, he saw spectators, and figures dashing to and fro in front of the blaze, and jets of water spurting ineffectually over the already collapsed residence. The red light reflected on the metalwork of the outmoded Philadelphia-style pump engine and on the black coats of the four horses that had pulled pumper and hose wagons to the site; they pawed and snorted like fearsome animals from hell. George thought of hell because the scene suggested nothing else.

As he jumped from the saddle, he heard a man screaming in the dark street to the left of the burned house. George worked quickly through the spectators. "Stay back, damn you," the volunteers' chief shouted through his fire horn as George emerged from the crowd. The chief lowered his horn and spoke an apologetic "Oh, Mr. Hazard, sir. Didn't recognize you."

The statement really meant he hadn't recognized the richest man in town, perhaps in the entire valley, until he saw him clearly; everyone knew stocky George Hazard, thirty-six this year. George's windblown hair already showed the beginnings of the sun-streaking that lightened it in the spring and summer; it showed some permanent gray, too. The ice-colored eyes, common in the Hazard family, reflected the fire without and George's anxiety within. "What happened here?"

The words brought a stammering summary from the chief while the volunteers, who years ago had named their company the Station Stalwarts and gilded its motto, *Officium Pro Periculo,* on every piece of equipment, continued to work the front and back pumping brakes. The water was wasted on the demolished house. All that could be done was protect the nearby hovels and shanties from the spreading effect of the wind. So the chief had time to speak to the most important man in town.

He said it looked like Fenton had discovered his wife in bed with his cousin earlier in the evening. The foreman had taken a large kitchen knife and stabbed his wife and her lover before setting fire to the house. During that time, the mortally wounded

11

cousin managed to turn the knife back on his attacker, stabbing him four times. Tears filled George's eyes, and he scrubbed at them with hard knuckles. Fenton had been the politest of men; well read, industrious, intelligent, kind to those he supervised.

"That's him yelling," said the chief. "But he don't figure to live long. The other two was dead when we got here. We dragged them out and covered them up. They're lying over there if you want to look."

Somehow, George was compelled. He walked toward the two bodies, foul-smelling beneath a square of canvas in the middle of the street. The screaming went on. The wind fanned the fire, gave it a whooshing voice, and swirled embers and glowing debris upward. The volunteers continued to pump furiously, two rows of men on each brake, one row on the ground, the other on the platform running the width of the engine. The riveted leather hoses, brought in two coffinlike wagons, ran clear across the abandoned canal to the river for water. The matched black horses, trained for this work, continued to behave strangely, pawing and throwing their heads, and flashing their red-reflecting flanks.

George stopped a foot short of the canvas and lifted it. He had lately been investigating the cost of a modern Latta steam pumper for the town, hence knew something of fires and their effects. That didn't prepare him for the sight of the dead lovers.

Of the two, the wife was charred worse, her blackened skin split and rolled back upon itself in many places. The cousin's burned-away clothing revealed hundreds of blisters weeping a shiny yellow fluid that mirrored light. The faces, necks, protruding tongues of both victims had swollen in the final agonies of wanting air and drawing only scorching fumes into the lungs. Ultimately, the throats had swollen, too, though in the wife's case it was hard to tell whether flames or asphyxiation had killed her. With the cousin there was less doubt; his eyes bulged, big as new apples.

George let the canvas fall and managed to suppress vomit as it reached his throat. What he had seen conjured strange specters. Not merely fire. Death. Suffering. Loss. And, in overpowering summation, war.

Shuddering, he walked back to the chief, feeling deep, unexpected things stirring within him.

"Can I be of help, Tom?"

"Mighty good of you to offer, sir, but it's too late to do anything except wet down them places next door." A fireman ran up

12

to say Fenton had died. George shivered again; why did he still hear screaming? He shook his head. The chief went on. "It was too late when we got here."

George nodded sadly and walked back to his horse.

What happened to George as he left the scene, mounting and letting the horse walk, was the result of tragedy encountered, of horror witnessed. The numbed state in which he'd lately been drifting vanished.

He had known there was—would be for many weeks, possibly months—a civil war. But knowing was not the same as understanding. He had known and not understood, and that was true even though he'd fought in Mexico. But the Mexican campaign was a long time in the past. As he rode slowly back up the hillside with wind-driven ash blowing overhead, he at last came to grips with reality. The nation was at *war.* His younger brother, Billy, an officer in the Corps of Engineers, was at *war.* His dearest friend in all the world, West Point classmate, comrade in Mexico, sometime financial partner, was at *war.* He didn't remember the writer, but he remembered the passage: No man is an island—

He cast his thoughts back over the past two weeks, attempting to discover in the national mood an explanation of his own. To many, perhaps most, citizens in the North, the final relieving of three decades of tension by the bombardment of Fort Sumter on the twelfth of this month of April, 1861, had been a welcome, if not a joyous, event. George's principal reaction had been sadness; the guns said that men of good will had failed to solve a grievous human problem conceived the first day white traders sold black men and women on the coast of the American wilderness.

Sadness because the problem had been so long deemed insoluble—and, toward the last, not even capable of examination, so thick were the barbicans of rhetoric surrounding the opposing camps. For others, the forever self-occupied and self-serving, the issues were not threatening, or even serious, merely nuisances to be stepped around—treated as invisible, as one would treat beggars sleeping in some gutter.

But in the years in which the war cauldron came to the boil, America had not consisted of two classes only—the fanatical and the indifferent. There were men and women of decent intention. George thought of himself as one of them. Might they have kicked the cauldron over and soaked the coals and called a council of the reasonable? Or were the divisions so deep, so pervasive, that the hotheads on both sides would never have permitted that? Whatever the answer, the men of good will had not prevailed, had let the rest take charge, and the cloven nation was at *war*.

Sadness. Orry Main had shared it when he visited Lehigh Station. Just two weeks ago, it was. His courageous journey from South Carolina to Pennsylvania was laced with menace, and the visit itself had become a night of desperate danger when George's sister, Virgilia—extreme abolitionist, obsessive hater of all persons and things Southern—had betrayed Orry's presence to a mob that George held off at gunpoint until he could get his dear and honorable friend out of town.

After that had come—what? Not lassitude, not quite. He had coped with daily problems: contract proposals; uneasiness about Fenton's plight at home; a hundred things, small and large, with one excepted. Until tonight, he had somehow walled out understanding of the meaning of the war. The fire and the knife had destroyed that wall and retaught a basic lesson. The hell with fools who blithely predicted "only" a ninety-day conflict. You needed nothing but brief moments for death and ruin.

His head pounded. His stomach felt vile. Beyond the leveled wall he saw the threat from which he'd been trying to hide these past two weeks. It was a threat to the lives of those for whom he cared most in the world, a threat to the slowly forged bond between his family and that of the Mains of South Carolina. He'd been hiding from the truth about those lives, that bond. The fire had shown him they were perilously fragile. Fragile as Fenton, and the other two, and the house that had held them with all their passions, imperfections, dreams. Of them, that house, those emotions, nothing remained but that which followed George on the wind, spotting his collar, flicking his ear—ashes; blowing, blowing all around him.

Riding up the Pennsylvania hillside after midnight on the first of May, he could turn his back on the glow of a small, soon-to-be-forgotten domestic tragedy—a cliché in its commonness; so goddamn horrifying and heartbreaking in its specifics. He could turn his back but not his mind. His inward vision swept beyond the past two weeks to embrace two decades.

The Hazards, ironmasters of Pennsylvania, and the Mains, rice planters of South Carolina, had formed their first ties when a son

14

from each house met by chance on a New York City pier on a summer afternoon in 1842. George Hazard and Orry Main became acquaintances on a northbound Hudson River boat that day. As soon as they left the boat, they became new cadets at West Point.

There they survived much together, much that strengthened their natural affinity for one another. There was the skull work—easy for George, who had no great desire for a military career; hard for Orry, who wanted nothing else. They managed to endure the hazing of a deceitful, some said lunatic, upperclassman named Elkanah Bent, even conspired to get him dismissed after a series of particularly heinous acts on his part. But influence in Washington had returned Bent to the Military Academy, and he had graduated promising George and Orry a long memory and full accounting for their sins against him.

The Mains and Hazards got to know one another, as Northern and Southern families often did in those years while the long fuse of sectionalism burned down to the powder of secession. There had been visits exchanged, alliances formed—hatreds, too. Even George and Orry had seriously quarreled. George was visiting at the Main plantation, Mont Royal, when a slave ran away, was caught, then cruelly punished on orders from Orry's father. The argument of the two young men afterward was the closest they ever came to seeing their friendship destroyed by the divisiveness dripping into the country's bloodstream like a slow poison.

The Mexican War, which found the two friends serving as lieutenants in the same infantry regiment, finally separated them in unexpected ways. An encounter with Captain "Butcher" Bent sent George and Orry into action on the Churubusco Road, where a shell fragment destroyed Orry's left arm and his dreams of a career. Not long after, news of the death of the senior Hazard called George home, because his mother, with sound instincts, could not trust George's older brother, Stanley, to be a wise steward of the immense family business. Soon after taking charge of Hazard's, George wrested control of the ironworks from his ambitious, irresponsible brother.

Amputation of Orry's left arm put him in a brooding, reclusive mood for a time. But as he trained himself to run the plantation and perform two-handed tasks with one, his outlook revived and the friendship with George renewed itself. Orry stood up as best man when George married Constance Flynn, the Roman Catholic girl he'd met in Texas while en route to Mexico. Then George's

15

younger brother, Billy, decided he wanted to attend the Academy, while Orry, desperately seeking some way to save his orphaned young cousin Charles from a wastrel's life, persuaded him to seek an Academy appointment. The friendship of Charles Main and Billy Hazard, already acquainted, soon replicated that of the two old grads.

In the last decade of peace, many Northerners and Southerners, despite ever fiercer rhetoric, ever sharper threats from political leaders and public figures on both sides, remained personal friends. It was so with these two families. Mains came North, Hazards traveled South—though not without difficulties in each case.

George's sister, Virgilia, who had carried her passionate abolitionism across an invisible line into extremism, had nearly undone the friendship. During a Hazard family visit to the Main plantation, she'd met a slave belonging to the man who later married Orry's sister, Ashton. Virgilia encouraged the slave to run away. When he did, he succeeded.

Ashton Main, beautiful and unprincipled, had fancied Billy for a while, but he soon saw the fine and genuine qualities of Ashton's younger sister, Brett. As headstrong and crazed as Virgilia in some ways, the rejected Ashton had waited for her moment of vengeance; she conspired to have Billy murdered in a trumped-up duel not two hours after he married Brett at Mont Royal. Cousin Charles had dealt with that plot in his direct cavalry officer's way —rather violent, it was—and Orry banished Ashton and her fire-eater husband, James Huntoon, from Main land forever.

Virgilia's black lover, the slave whose escape she'd assisted, had been slain with others of John Brown's murderous gang at Harpers Ferry. Virgilia, at the scene and panic-stricken, had fled back home and was thus at Belvedere the night Orry made his perilous visit. It was this visit and the circumstances leading to it that a grieved and thoughtful George pondered as he rode up the last bit of steep road to Belvedere.

Orry's iconoclastic older brother, Cooper, had usually disagreed with most Southerners regarding their peculiar institution. In contrast to an economy based on the land, and the working of it by human property, he pointed to the example of the North— not perfect by any means, but in step with the new world-wide age of industrialism. In the North, free workers were speeding into a prosperous future to the hum of machines, not dragging a load of

16

rusty methods and ideologies as heavy as wrist cuffs and leg manacles, and fully as hampering. As for the traditional apology of Cooper's state and region—that slaves were more secure, therefore happier, than Northern factory workers fastened by invisible chains to huge, hammering machines—he laughed that off. A factory worker might indeed starve to death on what the owners paid him. But he could not be bought or sold like mere chattel. He could always walk away, and no posse would ride in pursuit; no laborer would be recaptured, flogged, and hung from the flywheel of his great engine.

Cooper sought to establish a shipbuilding industry in Charleston and had envisioned, even started to construct, a huge iron vessel patterned after one designed by the British engineering genius Brunel. George had put capital into the venture, as much for the sake of friendship and belief in Cooper's principles as for the possibility of quick profit, which was slim.

In the final days of Sumter's survival as a Union bastion, with war no longer a doubtful question, Orry had gathered up as much cash as he could by mortgaging family property. It amounted to six hundred fifty thousand dollars of the original one million nine hundred thousand George had invested. Despite Orry's pronounced Southern accent, he had undertaken to carry the money to Lehigh Station in a small, plain satchel, by train. The risk was enormous, yet he came. Because of his friendship and because of a debt of honor.

The night the two friends met, Virgilia furtively summoned the mob—most certainly to lynch the visitor. But the attempt failed, and Orry had gotten safely on a late train and now was—where? South Carolina? If he had reached home safely, he had at least one chance for happiness. Madeline LaMotte, the woman whom Orry had loved, as she had loved him despite her imprisonment in a disastrous marriage, had rushed to Mont Royal to warn of the conspiracy against Billy's life. Once there, in defiance of the husband who had deliberately and systematically mistreated her for years, she stayed.

The aftermath of Sumter forced other decisions, however uncertain or emotional. Charles had enlisted in a South Carolina legion of cavalry after resigning from the United States Army. His best friend, Billy, remained with the Union engineers. And Billy's Southern-born wife, Brett, was living in Lehigh Station. The per-

17

sonal world of the Mains and the Hazards hung in a precarious balance as massive, threatening, unpredictable forces gathered.

It was that fact which George had been shunning these past fourteen days. Life was fragile. Friendship the same. Before parting, he and Orry had pledged that the war would never sunder the bonds between them. In this night's remembered ugliness, shrieks of pain, geysers of fire, George wondered whether they were naïve. He felt, almost wildly, that he must do something to reaffirm his dedication to defending the ties.

He stabled his horse and went directly to Belvedere's library, a vast room with smells of leather and fine book papers. It was as silent as the night house.

When he crossed toward his desk, he spied a memento always kept on an otherwise bare refectory table. It was a conical object, rough-textured, measuring six inches from apex to base. The dark brown color indicated heavy iron content.

He realized why it had attracted his eye. Someone—a maid, probably—had moved the object from its customary position. He picked up the meteorite and continued to hold it while he envisioned the place in the past where he'd found it—the hills around West Point during his cadet days.

What lay in his hand was a piece of a much larger meteorite that had traveled through starry dark, and distances beyond his power to comprehend. Star-iron, the old men of the trade—his ancestors—called it. Known since the pharaohs ruled the Nile kingdoms.

Iron. The most potent stuff in the universe. The raw material for building civilization, or leveling it. From iron came the immense death weapons George planned to cast for a whole battery of reasons: patriotism, hatred of slavery, profit, a paternal responsibility for those who worked for him.

What lay in his hand was, in its way, war. He replaced it on the table precisely where it belonged, but he did so quickly.

He lit the gas mantle above the desk. Opened the lower drawer in which he had put the small, plain satchel—for remembrance. He looked at the satchel a while. Then, out of profound emotion, he inked a pen and wrote with great speed.

My dear Orry,
   When you returned this valise, you performed an act of supreme decency and courage. It is one I shall hope to repay in

kind someday. But in case I do not—cannot—I place these words herein so you will know my intentions. Know most of all that I want to preserve the bonds of affection between us and our families which have grown and strengthened for so many years—want to, and have striven to, despite Virgilia, despite Ashton—despite the lessons about war's nature which I learned in Mexico but forgot until tonight. I know you believe in the worth of this bond as much as I do. But it is fragile as a stalk of wheat before the iron scythe. If we fail to preserve what so richly merits preservation—or if some Hazard or Main falls, as, God pity us, some surely may if this conflict is anything other than brief—you will know I prized friendship to the last. Prized and never abandoned it. As I know you have not. I pray we meet when it ends, but if we do not, I bid you— from my deepest heart—an affectionate good-bye.

Your friend—

He started to inscribe the initial letter of his first name but then, with a swift, sad smile, wrote instead his West Point nickname. *Stump.*

He slowly folded the sheets; slowly placed them in the satchel and latched it; slowly closed the drawer and arose to the accompaniment of several irritating noises from his joints. Windows were open throughout Belvedere because of the warm night. He smelled the diminishing fetor of burning carried by the high wind. He felt cold and old as he put out the gas and wearily climbed the stairs.

BOOK ONE

A VISION
FROM SCOTT

*The flag which now flaunts the breeze
here will float over the dome of the old
Capitol at Washington before the first
of May.*

CONFEDERATE SECRETARY OF WAR
LEROY P. WALKER, *speaking in
Montgomery, Alabama,* APRIL 1861

1

Morning sunshine drenched the pasture. Suddenly, at the far side, three black horses burst into sight at the summit of a low hill. Two more followed them over and down into the windblown grass, splendid coats shining, manes and tails streaming. Close behind the five appeared two mounted sergeants in hussar jackets heavy with braid. Riding at the gallop, great grins on their faces, the sergeants hallooed and waved their kepis at the black horses.

The sight immediately distracted Captain Charles Main's troop of young South Carolina volunteers walking their matched bays in file along a road that meandered through the woods and farmlands of Prince William County. The three-day field exercise had taken them well north of their camp between Richmond and Ashland, but Charles felt a long ride was needed to sharpen the men. They were born riders and hunters; Colonel Hampton wanted no other kind in the cavalry units of the legion he'd raised in Columbia. But their reaction to the Poinsett *Tactics,* the unofficial name for the manual that had been the cavalryman's textbook ever since '41, ranged from restrained indifference to loud contempt.

"Deliver me from gentlemen soldiers," Charles muttered as several of his men turned their mounts toward the rail fence separating road and pasture. The black horses veered, galloping beside the fence. The sweating sergeants chased them hard, speeding past the long line of troopers in trim gray jackets decorated with bright gilt buttons.

"Who are you, boys?" shouted Charles's senior lieutenant, a stocky, cheery young man with red curls.

On the June breeze, blurred by hoofbeats, the answer came back: "Black Horse. Fauquier County."

"Let's give 'em a run, Charlie," First Lieutenant Ambrose Pell yelled to his superior.

To stave off chaos, Charles reacted with a bellowed order. "Form twos—trot—*march!*"

The execution of the maneuver was so sloppy as to defy belief. The troop managed to straggle into a double file at the proper gait, then responded with whoops and much kepi-flourishing when Charles gave the order to gallop. But they were too late to catch the sergeants, who drove the five black horses away to the left, crossing the pasture and vanishing in a grove.

Envy stung Charles. If the noncoms indeed came from the Black Horse Cavalry he'd heard so much about, they had found some fine animals. He was dissatisfied with his own mount, Dasher, bought in Columbia. She came of good Carolina saddle-horse stock, but she was frequently balky. So far she didn't live up to her name.

The road curved northeast, away from the fenced pasture. Charles reduced the gait to a trot, ignored another frivolous question from Ambrose, whom he had the professional misfortune to like, and wondered how in heaven he could forge a fighting unit from this assortment of aristocrats who called you by your first name, disdained all graduates of West Point, and tried to knock you down if you gave an order to which they objected. Twice since arriving at the bivouac down in Hanover County, Charles had resorted to his fists to curb disobedience.

In the Hampton Legion, his was a kind of misfit troop, consisting of men who'd come in from all parts of South Carolina. Nearly every one of the foot and mounted units in Hampton's command had been raised in a single county, or even a single town. The man who put a company together generally won the election by which the volunteers chose their captain. There was no such familiarity and friendship to produce a similar outcome in Charles's troop; his roster included boys from the mountains, the piedmont, even his own low country. This assortment called for a leader who possessed not only good family background but also plenty of experience with military organization. Ambrose Pell, who'd opposed Charles in the election, had the former but not the latter. And Wade Hampton had indicated his clear choice before the balloting. Even so, Charles won with only a two-vote

23

margin. He was beginning to wish he'd electioneered for Ambrose.

With the sweet summer breeze bathing his face, and Dasher moving smoothly under him, however, he felt he might be too concerned with discipline. Thus far, the war was a lark. One Yankee general, Butler, had already been trounced in a sharp fight at Bethel Church. The Yankee capital, presided over by the Western politician many South Carolinians called "the gorilla," was said to be a terrified village as deserted as Goldsmith's. The main problem in the four troops of Hampton Legion cavalry seemed to be an epidemic of bellyaches brought on by too many fetes in Richmond.

All the volunteers had signed on for twelve months, but none of them believed this muss between the two governments would last ninety days. Inhaling the fragrance of sun-warmed grass and horseflesh, Charles, twenty-five, tall and ruggedly handsome and deeply browned, found it hard to believe there really was a war in progress. He had even more trouble remembering the watery feel of the gut when a man heard bullets fired in anger, though he'd dodged his share before he resigned from the Second U.S. Cavalry in Texas early in the year and came home to join the Confederacy.

"Oh, young Lochinvar is come out of the west—" Charles smiled; Ambrose was singing the poem in a monotone. Others quickly joined in. *"—through all the wide border his steed was the best."*

Liking for these high-spirited youngsters tempered Charles's professional reservations. He shouldn't let them continue singing, but he did, relishing in silence his own separateness. He was only a year or two older than most of them, but he felt like a parent.

"So faithful in love and so dauntless in war—there never was a knight like young Lochinvar!"

How they loved their Scott, these Southern boys. The women were no different. All of them worshiped Scott's chivalric vision and endlessly read every novel and poem he'd written to give it life. Maybe that odd devotion to old Sir Walter was one of the clues to this decidedly odd war which as yet had not quite begun. Cousin Cooper, considered the heretic of the Main family, often said the South looked back too much, instead of concentrating on today—or the North, where manufactories like the great ironworks of the Hazard family dominated the physical and political landscapes. Looking backward worshipfully to the era of Scott's plumed knights was a custom Cooper excoriated passionately and often.

Suddenly, ahead, two shots. A shout from the rear. Twisting to look back, Charles saw that the trooper who'd cried out was still upright—surprised, not hit. Swinging front again and silently cursing his inattention, he focused on a thick walnut grove down the road to the right. Flashes of blue amid the trees confirmed the source of the musket fire.

Ambrose and several others reacted to the sniping with grins. "Let's go catch that bunch," a private whooped.

You idiot, Charles thought as his midsection tightened. He glimpsed horses in the grove and heard the pop of other muskets, overlaid by the roar of his own voice bellowing the order to charge.

2

The charge from the road to the trees was ragged but effective. The sunlit blue flashes, bright as plumage, became the trouser legs of a half-dozen patrolling enemy horsemen. The Yanks galloped off when Charles's men cantered into the grove, assorted shoulder weapons ready.

Charles went in first, his double-barrel shotgun cocked. The Academy and Texas had taught him that successful officers led; they didn't prod. No one exemplified that more than the rich and physically powerful planter who'd raised the legion. Hampton was one of the rare ones who didn't need West Point to teach them to soldier.

Among the walnut trees, with shotguns booming, muskets

snapping replies, smoke thickening, Charles's troop scattered. The men went skylarking off every which way, taunting the retreating enemy, now barely visible.

"Where you Yankee boys goin' so fast?"

"Come on, turn around and fight us!"

"They aren't worth our time, lads," Ambrose Pell cried. "Wish our niggers were here. They could chase 'em."

A single musket shot from a dark part of the grove punctuated the last of his sentence. Charles instinctively ducked down close to Dasher's neck. The bay seemed nervous, uncertain, even though, like all of the legion's horses, she'd been drilled to the sound of shotgun and artillery fire in camp in Columbia.

A ball whizzed past. Sergeant Peterkin Reynolds yelled. Charles fired both barrels into the trees. Immediately, he heard a cry of pain.

He yanked Dasher's head hard, turning back. "Reynolds—?" The sergeant, pale but grinning, held up his cadet gray sleeve to show a tear near the cuff and only a small spot of blood.

Friends of Reynolds treated the wounding less lightly. "Goddamn tailors and shoemakers on horseback," one man shouted as he galloped past Charles, who vainly ordered him back.

Through a gap in the trees Charles saw a laggard from the Union patrol, a plump blond fellow with no control of his horse, one of the heavy draft plugs typical of the hastily assembled Northern cavalry. The man kicked the animal and cursed. German.

The Dutchman was such a poor horseman, the trooper who'd shot past Charles had no trouble riding up to him and pulling him sideways. He fell out of his saddle and hit the ground, wailing till he freed his boot from the left stirrup.

The young man from South Carolina had drawn his forty-inch, six-pound, two-edged, straight-bladed sword, bigger than regulation and forged in Columbia to the colonel's specifications. Hampton had equipped his legion using his own money.

Ambrose rode up beside Charles. He pointed. "Look at that, will you, Charlie? Scared as a treed coon."

Ambrose didn't exaggerate. On his knees, the Yank trembled as the trooper climbed down, took a two-handed grip and raised the blade over his head. Charles yelled, "Manigault! No!"

Private Manigault turned and glared. Charles shoved his shotgun into his lieutenant's hand and dismounted in a leap. He dashed to the trooper, seizing the still-raised sword arm.

"I said no."

Defiant, the trooper struggled and strained against Charles's grip. "Let go of me, you damned puppy, you damned West Point son of a bitch, you damned—"

Charles let go, then smashed his right fist into Manigault's face. Bleeding from his nose, the young man crashed backward into a tree trunk. Charles wrenched the trooper's sword away from him and turned to confront the glowering men on horseback. He stared right back.

"We're soldiers, not butchers, and you'd better remember that. The next man who disobeys my order or curses me or calls me by my first name goes up for court-martial. After I deal with him personally."

He let his eyes drift past a few hostile faces, then threw the sword down and reclaimed his shotgun. "Form them up, Lieutenant Pell."

Ambrose avoided his eyes but got busy. Charles heard plenty of grumbling. The joy in the morning was gone; he'd been stupid to believe in it anyway.

Discouraged, he wondered how his men could survive in a real battle if they considered a skirmish somewhat less serious than a fox hunt. How could they win if they refused to learn to fight as a unit—which first of all meant learning to obey?

His long-time friend from his West Point days, Billy Hazard, of the federal engineers, knew the importance of taking war seriously. Cousin Orry Main and his closest friend, Billy's older brother George, knew it, too. All Academy men did. Maybe that explained the gulf between the professional officers of the old regular army and the amateur hotspurs. Even Wade Hampton sometimes mocked men from the Point—

"No worse than bees buzzing, was it?" Charles overheard a trooper say while Ambrose re-formed the troop by twos on the road.

Charles withheld comment and rode to the soiled, cringing prisoner. "You'll have to walk a long way back with us. But you won't be harmed. Understand?"

"*Ja, versteh'*—onderstand." The Dutchman pronounced the English word with difficulty.

The troopers considered all Yankees mere mudsills or mechan-

27

ics; unworthy opponents. Studying the poor tun-bellied captive, Charles could understand the viewpoint. Trouble was, there were hundreds of thousands more mudsills and mechanics in the North than in the South. The Carolina boys never considered that.

The North reminded him of his friend Billy. Where was he? Would Charles ever lay eyes on him again? The Hazard and Main families had grown close in the years before the war; would they ever be close again, even with Cousin Brett now married to Billy?

Too many questions. Too many problems. And as the double column headed south again, the sun was all at once too cool for summertime. A half mile from the site of the skirmish, Charles heard and felt Dasher cough. Saw her nostrils excessively damp when she turned her head.

A discharge beginning? Yes. The coughing persisted. God, not the strangles, he thought. It was a winter disease.

But she was a young horse, more susceptible. He realized he had another problem, this one potentially disastrous.

3

Each of the young man's shoulder straps bore a single bar of silver embroidery. His coat collar displayed the turreted castle within a wreath of laurel, the whole embroidered in gold on a small black velvet oval. Very smart, that uniform of dark blue frock coat and stovepipe trousers.

The young man wiped his mouth with a napkin. He had eaten a delicious meal of beefsteak, browned onions, and fried oysters, which he was just topping off with a dish of blancmange—at ten after ten in the morning. You could order breakfast here until eleven. Washington was a bizarre town. A frightened town, too. Across the Potomac on the Arlington Heights, Brigadier General McDowell was drawing up war plans in the mansion the Lees had abandoned. While awaiting new orders, the young man had hired a horse and ridden over there day before yesterday. He had not been encouraged to find army headquarters a crowded, noisy place with a distinct air of confusion. Awareness that Confederate pickets stood guard not many miles away seemed very real there.

Federal troops had crossed the Potomac and occupied the Virginia side in late May. Regiments from New England crowded the city now. Their presence had partially lifted the burden of terror Washington had borne during the first week after Fort Sumter fell; then, telegraph and even rail connections to the North had been cut for a time. An attack had been expected any hour. The Capitol had been hastily fortified. Some of the relief troops were presently bivouacked there; a military bakery operated in the basement. Tensions had lessened a little, but he still felt the same confusion he'd detected at McDowell's headquarters. Too many new and alarming things were happening, too fast.

Late yesterday, he had picked up his orders at the office of old General Totten, the chief of engineers. Brevet First Lieutenant William Hazard was assigned to the Department of Washington and instructed to report to a Captain Melancthon Elijah Farmer for temporary duty until his regular unit, Company A—all there was of the United States Army Corps of Engineers—returned from another project. Billy had missed the departure of Company A because he'd been recuperating at his home in Lehigh Station, Pennsylvania, where he'd taken his new bride, Brett. He'd married her at the Main plantation in South Carolina and then nearly been murdered for it by one of her former suitors.

Charles Main had saved his life. Billy's left arm occasionally ached from the derringer ball that could have killed him but didn't. The ache served a useful purpose. It reminded him that he would forever be Charles Main's debtor. That was true even though the friends had taken opposite sides in this peculiar, half-unwanted, still-unstarted war.

The breakfast had appeased his hunger, but it hadn't relieved his foreboding. Billy was a good engineer. He excelled in mathematics and liked the predictability of equations and such things as standard recipes for construction mortar. Now he faced a future neither neat nor predictable.

What's more, he faced it in isolation. He was cut off from his fellow engineers; from his wife, whom he loved deeply; and, by choice, from one of his older brothers. Stanley Hazard lived in the city with his disagreeable wife, Isabel, and their twin sons. Stanley had been taken along to the War Department by his political mentor, Simon Cameron.

Billy loved his older brother George, but toward Stanley he felt a certain nameless ambiguity that had no respect in it but plenty of guilt, and—shamefully—no affection. He didn't know a single person in Washington, but that wouldn't force him to see Stanley. In fact, he'd chosen to eat breakfast here at the National Hotel because a large part of its clientele was still pro-Southern, and there was little chance of encountering Stanley, who was anything but.

He paid his bill and handed a tip to the waiter. "Thank you, sir —thank you. That's much more than I ever get from all those cheap Westerners traipsing into town to get jobs from their nigger-loving President. Luckily, we don't get many of the Western crowd here. They scarcely drink, I doubt they fornicate, and they all carry their own bags. Some of my friends at other hotels can't earn—"

Billy walked away from the complainer, whose accent suggested he'd migrated from a Southern or border state. There seemed to be plenty like him in the capital. Yankees, but only nominally. If the city fell, as well it might, they'd be in the streets waving the Stars and Bars to welcome Jeff Davis.

Outside, on the corner of Sixth and Pennsylvania, he discovered that the muggy gray sky had produced a drizzle. He put on his dress hat of black felt; one side of its braided brim was turned up against the crown and held by a bright brass eagle. The drizzle wouldn't impede a brisk walk.

Billy, a year older than his friend Charles, was a powerfully built young man with the dark hair and pale, icy eyes that ran in the Hazard family. A blunt chin lent him an air of dependability, a look of strength. He'd recently succumbed to the new craze for mustaches; his, from which he now flicked a crumb of breakfast roll, was almost black, thick and darker than his hair.

Since Billy suspected this Captain Farmer of being a political appointee, he wasn't anxious to report early. He decided to spend a few more hours exploring the city—the parts of it well removed

30

from the north side of Pennsylvania Avenue, the respectable, fashionable side.

He soon regretted his decision. War had swollen the town's population of forty thousand to three times that number. You couldn't cross a main street without dodging omnibuses, rowdy soldiers reeling drunk, teamsters beating and cursing their mules, flash gentlemen slipping up to whisper the address of some quack who cured the French pox in twenty-four hours—even stray hogs or a flock of noisy geese.

Worse, the town smelled. The worst odors came from sewage floating in slimy lumps in the City Canal, which Billy came upon by walking straight south on Third. He paused on one of the footbridges leading across to the southwest section known as the Island. He looked down on someone's dead terrier floating among spoiled lettuce leaves and excrement.

He reswallowed some bit of his breakfast and got away fast, heading east to the Capitol, which still lacked its dome. Soldiers and politicians swarmed on the grounds and along the porticoes. Workmen scurried around stacks of lumber, piles of iron plates, and huge blocks of marble littering the area. Billy rounded the corner of one such block and bumped into an old overweight whore in dirty velvet and feathers. She offered him a choice of herself or her gray-faced daughter, no more than fourteen, who huddled at her side.

Billy strove to be polite. "Ma'am, I have a wife in Pennsylvania."

The whore failed to appreciate the courtesy. "Kiss my ass, shoulder straps," she said as he walked on. He laughed, but not heartily.

A few minutes later he gazed across the canal to the weeds around the monument to President Washington, unfinished due to a lack of interest and subscriptions. A cattle herd pastured near the forlorn obelisk. The drizzle turned to rain, fell harder, so he gave up. He struggled past some noncoms loudly singing "Sweet Evelina" and headed north across the avenue into the crowded area where he'd taken a boardinghouse room. On the way, he bought a copybook at a stationer's, paying for it with silver half-dimes.

Later, while twilight deepened, he whittled a point on a pencil. In shirt sleeves, he bent over the first blank page of his copybook

31

lit by a lamp whose flame never wavered in the heavy air. He inscribed the day and date, then wrote:

My dear wife—I begin this journal, and will keep it, to let you know what I have done, other than miss you constantly, on this day and those to come. Today I explored the national capital —not a pleasant or heartening experience, for reasons which delicacy prevents me from conveying to this page—

Thinking of Brett—her face, her hands, her ardor in the privacy of their bed—he felt the physical need of her. He closed his eyes a moment. When he was again in control, he scribbled on.

The city is already heavily fortified, which I would take as a sign of a long war were there not such a pervasive general opinion that it will be short. A short war is greatly to be desired for many reasons—not the least of which is the most obvious, viz., my desire for us to live together as husband and wife wherever duty takes me in time of peace. Speaking not of personal matters but political ones, however, a war of short duration will make it easier to restore things as they were. Today on a public thoroughfare I encountered a negro—either a freedman or a contraband, General Butler's term for a Southern runaway. The black man would not vacate the sidewalk to permit me to pass. Memory of the incident has unsettled me all day. I am as fervent as any citizen about ending the disgrace of slavery, but the black man's liberty is not license. Although I know my long-lost sister would contradict me, I do not consider myself unjust or immoral for holding that belief. To the contrary—I feel I reflect a majority view. Speaking only of the army, I know that to be absolutely true. It is said that even our President still speaks of the urgent need to resettle freed blacks to Liberia. Hence my fear of a protracted war, which could well bring the havoc of too many rapid changes in the social order.

He stopped, pencil poised on the same level as the steady flame. How wet, how weighty the air felt; drawing deep breaths took great effort.

What he had just written produced unexpected flickerings of guilt. He was already coming to loathe the war's ideological confusion. Perhaps by the time he and Brett were together again and she read all of the journal, including passages yet unwritten, answers, including his own, would be clearer than they were this evening.

Do forgive the strange philosophizing. The atmosphere of this place produces curious doubts and reactions, and I have no one with whom to share them save the one with whom I share all—you, my dearest wife. Good night and God keep you——

Closing the passage with a long dash, he shut the copybook. Soon after, he undressed and blew out the lamp. Sleep wouldn't come. The bed was hard, and his need of her, his lonesome longing, kept him tossing a long time, while hooligans broke glass and fired pistols in nearby streets.

"Lije Farmer? Right there, chum."

The corporal pointed out a Sibley tent, white and conical, one of many. He gave Billy's back a cheery slap and went away whistling. Such breaches of discipline among the volunteers were so common Billy paid no attention. At the entrance to the tent he cleared his throat. He folded his gauntlets over his sash and, orders in his left hand, walked in.

"Lieutenant Hazard reporting, Captain—Farmer—"

Astonishment prolonged and hushed the last word. The man was fifty or better. Pure white hair; a patriarchal look. He stood in his singlet, with his galluses down over his hips and a Testament held in his right hand. On a flimsy table Billy saw a couple of Mahan's engineering texts. He was too stunned to notice anything else.

"A hearty welcome, Lieutenant. I have been anticipating your arrival with great eagerness—nay, excitement. You discover me about to render thanks and honor to the Almighty in morning prayer. Will you not join me, sir?"

He dropped to his knees. Dismay replaced astonishment when Billy realized that Captain Farmer's question was an order.

4

While Billy reported for duty in Alexandria, another of the government's continual round of meetings took place in the War Department building at the west side of President's Park. Simon Cameron, former boss of Pennsylvania politics, presided at his unspeakably littered desk, thought it wasn't the secretary who had called the meeting but the elderly and egotistical human balloon who purported to command the army. From a chair in a corner where Cameron had ordered two assistants to sit as observers, Stanley Hazard watched General Winfield Scott with a contempt he had to work to hide.

Stanley, approaching forty, was a pale fellow. Paunchy, yes, but a positive sylph compared to the general long ago nicknamed "Old Fuss and Feathers." Seventy-five, with a torso resembling a swollen lump of bread dough, Winfield Scott hid most of the upper part of the largest chair that could be found in the building. Braid crusted his uniform.

Others at the gathering were the handsome and pompous Treasury secretary, Mr. Salmon Chase, and a man in a plainly cut gray suit who sat in the corner opposite Stanley's. The man had barely spoken since the start of the meeting. With a polite, attentive air, he listened to Scott hold forth. When Stanley had first met the President at a reception, he had decided there was but one word to describe him: repulsive. It was a matter of personal style as well as appearance, though the latter was certainly bad enough. By now, however, Stanley had assembled a list of other, equally apt, descriptions. It included clownish, oafish, and animal.

34

If pressed, Stanley would have admitted that he didn't care for any of those present at the meeting, with the possible exception of his superior. Of course his job demanded that he admire Cameron, who had brought him to Washington to reward him for a long record of lavish contributions to Cameron's political campaigns.

Though a departmental loyalist, Stanley had quickly discovered the secretary's worst faults. He saw evidence of one in the towers of files and the stacks of Richmond and Charleston newspapers—important sources of war information—rising high from every free section of desk or cabinet top. Similar collections covered the carpet like pillars erected too close together. The god who ruled Simon Cameron's War Department was Chaos.

Behind the large desk sat the master of it all, his mouth tight as a closed purse, his gray hair long, his gray eyes a pair of riddles. In Pennsylvania he'd carried the nickname "Boss," but no one used it any longer; not in his presence, at least. His fingers were constantly busy with his chief tools of office, a dirty scrap of paper and a pencil stub.

"—too few guns, Mr. Secretary," Scott was wheezing. "That is all I hear from our camps of instruction. We lack the matériel to train and equip thousands of men who have bravely responded to the President's call."

Chase leaned toward the desk. "And the cry for going forward, forward to Richmond, grows more strident by the hour. Surely you understand why."

From Cameron, dryly, but with hinted reproof: "The Confederate Congress convenes there soon." He consulted another tiny scrap, discovered inside his coat. "To be exact—on the twentieth of July. The same month in which most of our ninety-day enlistments will expire."

"So McDowell must move," snapped Chase. "He, too, is inadequately equipped."

Discreetly, Stanley wrote a short message on a small tablet. *Real problem is vols.* He rose and passed the note across the desk. Cameron snatched it, read it, crushed it, and gave a slight nod in Stanley's direction. He understood McDowell's chief concern, which was not equipment but the need to rely on volunteer soldiers whose performance he couldn't predict and whose courage he couldn't trust. It was the same snide pose common to most regular officers from West Point—those, that is, who hadn't deserted after being given a fine education, free, at that school for traitors.

Cameron chose not to raise the point, however. He replied to the commanding general with an oozy deference. "General, I continue to believe the chief problem is not too few guns but too many men. We already have three hundred thousand under arms. Far more than we need for the present crisis."

"Well, I hope you're right about that," the President said from his corner. No one paid attention. As usual, Lincoln's voice tended to the high side, a source of many jokes behind his back.

What a congress of buffoons, Stanley thought as he wriggled his plump derrière on the hard chair bottom. Scott—whom the stupid Southrons called a free-state pimp but who actually needed to be closely watched; he was a Virginian, wasn't he? And he'd promoted scores of Virginians in the prewar army at the expense of equally qualified men from the North. Chase loved the niggers, and the President was a gauche farmer. For all Cameron's twisty qualities, he was at least a man of some sophistication in the craft of government.

Chase chose not to answer but to orate. "We must do more than hope, Mr. President. We need to purchase more aggressively in Europe. We have too few ordnance works in the North now that we have lost Harpers Fer—"

"European purchasing is under investigation," Cameron said. "But, in my opinion, such a course is unnecessarily extravagant."

Scott stamped on the floor. "Damn it, Cameron, you talk extravagance in the face of rebellion by traitorous combinations?"

"Keep in mind the twentieth of next month," added Chase.

"Mr. Greeley and certain others seldom let me forget it."

But the waspy words went unheard as Chase roared ahead: "We must crush Davis and his crowd before they assert their legitimacy to France and Great Britain. We must crush them utterly. I agree with Congressman Stevens, from your own state. If the rebels won't give up and return to the fold—"

"They won't." Scott handed down the word from on high. "I know Virginians. I know Southerners."

Chase went right on: "—we should follow Thad Stevens's advice to the letter. Reduce the South to a mudhole."

At that, the Chief Executive cleared his throat.

It was a modest sound, but it happened to fall during a pause, and no one could ignore it without being rude. Lincoln rose,

36

thrusting hands in his side pockets, which merely emphasized how gangly he looked. Gangly and exhausted. Yet he was only in his early fifties. From Ward Lamon, a presidential crony, Stanley had heard that Lincoln believed he would never return to Springfield. Anonymous letters threatening his murder came to his office every day.

"Well—" Lincoln said. Then he spoke quickly; not with volume but with definite authority. "I wouldn't say I agree with the Stevens response to the insurrection. I have been anxious and careful that the policy of this government doesn't degenerate into some violent, remorseless struggle. Some social revolution which would leave the Union permanently torn. I want it back together, and for that reason, none other, I would hope for a quick capitulation by the temporary government in Richmond. Not," he emphasized, "to satisfy Mr. Greeley, mind. To get this over with and find some accommodation to end slavery."

Except in the border states, Stanley thought with cynicism. There, the President left the institution untouched, fearing those states would defect to the South.

To Cameron, he said, "I leave purchasing methods in your hands, Mr. Secretary. But I want there to be sufficient arms to equip General McDowell's army *and* the camps of instruction *and* the forces protecting our borders."

They all understood the last reference: Kentucky and the West. Lincoln refused to risk a chance misunderstanding. "Look into European purchasing a little more aggressively. Let Mr. Chase mind the dollars."

Spots of color rose in Cameron's shriveled cheeks. "Very well, Mr. President." He wrote several words on the grimy paper and stuffed the scrap in a side pocket. God knew whether he'd ever retrieve it again.

The meeting ended with Cameron promising to assign an assistant secretary to contact agents of foreign arms makers immediately.

"And confer when appropriate with Colonel Ripley," the President said as he left. He referred to the chief of the Army Ordnance Department headquartered in the Winder Building; like Scott, Ripley was an antique left over from the 1812 war.

Chase and Scott left, each in a better mood because of Cameron's pretense of pliability. Also, the news from western Virginia

37

was good lately. George McClellan had whipped Robert Lee out there early in June.

The men who had convened today represented two different theories of victory. Scott, who could be seen wincing and growling from the pain of gout induced by his gluttony, some weeks ago had proposed a grand scheme to blockade the entire Confederate coastline, then send gunboats and a large army straight down the Mississippi to capture New Orleans and control the gulf. It was Scott's intention to isolate the South from the rest of the world. Cut off its supply of essential goods that it couldn't produce for itself. Surrender would follow quickly and inevitably. Scott capped his argument by promising that his strategy would assure victory with minimum bloodshed.

Lincoln had liked some sections of the design; the blockade had become a reality in April. But the complete plan, which the press had somehow learned about and christened "Scott's Anaconda," drew sharp fire from radicals like Chase—they were numerous in the Republican party—who favored a swift, single-stroke triumph. The kind summed up in "Forward to Richmond!"—the slogan heard everywhere, from church pulpits to brothels, or so Stanley was told. Although he constantly craved sex and his wife seldom granted it to him, he was too timid to visit brothels.

Would the Union press on to the Confederate capital? Stanley had little time to speculate because Cameron returned quickly after seeing his visitors out. He gathered Stanley and four other assistants around him and began pulling oddly shaped little papers out of every pocket and rattling off orders. The scrap on which the secretary had jotted the President's firm command fluttered to the floor unseen.

"And you, Stanley—" Cameron fixed him with those eyes gray as the winter hills his Scottish forebears trod—"we have that meeting late today. The one in regard to uniforms."

"Yes, Mr. Secretary."

"We're to meet that fellow at—let's see—" He patted his hopsack jacket, hunting another informative scrap.

"Willard's, sir. The saloon bar. Six P.M. is the time you set."

"Yes, six. I don't have the head for so many details." His vinegar smile said he wasn't excessively concerned.

Shortly before six, Stanley and the secretary left the War Department and crossed to the better side of the avenue. Yesterday's rain had changed the street to a mud pit again. Though he tried to walk carefully, Stanley still got a few spatters on his fawn trousers, which displeased him. In Washington, appearances counted for more than the reality beneath. His wife had taught him that, just as she'd propounded so many other valuable lessons during their married life. Without Isabel, Stanley well knew, he'd be nothing but a mat for his younger brother George to step on whenever he pleased.

The secretary swung his walking stick in a jaunty circle. In the amber of the late afternoon, the shadows of the strollers stretched out ahead. Three boisterous Zouaves, each in scarlet fez and baggy trousers, passed them, trailing beer fumes. One of the Zouaves was a mere boy, who reminded Stanley of his twin sons, Laban and Levi. Fourteen now, they were more than he could handle. Thank God for Isabel.

"—dictated a telegraph message after our meeting this morning," he heard Cameron say.

"Oh, is that right, sir? To whom?"

"Your brother George. We could use a man of his background in the Ordnance Department. If he will, I'd like him to come to Washington."

5

Stanley felt as though he'd been kicked. "You telegraphed—? You want—? My brother George—?"

"To work for the War Department," the secretary said with a trace of a smirk. "Been mulling the notion for weeks. That drubbing I took this morning settled it. Your brother is one of the big dogs in our state, Stanley. Top of his field—I know the iron and steel trade, don't forget. Your brother makes things happen. Likes new ideas. He's the kind who can pump some fresh air into Ordnance. Ripley can't; he's a mummy. And his assistant, that other officer—"

"Maynadier," Stanley whispered with immense effort.

"Yes—well, thanks to them, the President's handing me poor marks. Those two say no to everything. Lincoln's interested in rifled shoulder weapons, but Ripley says they're no good. You know why? Because he's got nothing stored in his warehouses except a lot of smoothbores."

Though Cameron often resisted new ideas as strongly as Colonel Ripley did, Stanley was accustomed to his mentor artfully shifting blame. Pennsylvania politics had made him a master at it. Stanley quickly screwed up his nerve to challenge Cameron from another direction. "Mr. Secretary, I admit there's a need to bring in new people. But why did you telegraph—? That is, we never discussed—"

A sharp glance stopped him. "Come on, my boy. I don't need your permission to do anything. And I already knew what your reaction would be. Your brother grabbed control of Hazard Iron —took it clean away from you—and it's galled you ever since."

Yes, by God, that's right. I've lived in George's shadow since we were little. Now I'm standing on my own feet at last, and here he comes again. I won't have it.

Stanley never said any of that. A few more steps and the men turned into the main entrance of Willard's. Cameron looked merry, Stanley miserable.

The hotel lobby and adjoining public rooms were packed with people, as they were at most hours of the day. Near a roped-off section of wall, one of the Vermont-born Willard brothers argued with a sullen painter. The place smelled of redecorating—paint, plaster—and heavy perfumes. Under the chandeliers, men and women with eyes like glass and faces as stiff as party masks talked soberly, laughed loudly, bent heads so close together that many a pair of foreheads almost touched. Washington in miniature.

Stanley recovered enough to say, "Of course it's your decision, sir—"

"Yep. Sure is."

"But I remind you that my brother is not one of your strongest partisans."

40

"He's a Republican, like me."

"I'm sure he remembers the days when you stood with the Democrats." Stanley knew George had been particularly infuriated by events at the Chicago convention that had nominated the President. Lincoln's managers had needed the votes Cameron controlled. The Boss would only trade them for a cabinet post. So it was with certainty that Stanley said, "He's liable to work against you."

"He'll work *for* me if I manage him right. I know he doesn't like me, but we're in a war, and he fought in Mexico—a man like that can't turn his back on the old flag. 'Sides—" the gray eyes grew foxy—"it's a lot easier to run a man when he's right under your thumb. Even setting aside his experience, I'd sooner have your brother right here than back in the Lehigh Valley where he might do me mischief."

Cameron quickened his step to signal the end of the discussion. Stanley persisted. "He won't come."

"Yes, he will. Ripley's a stupid old goat ready for pasture. He's making me look bad. I need George Hazard. What I want, I get."

With his stick the secretary jabbed one of the swing doors of the saloon bar and passed through. Stanley lumbered after him, seething.

The businessman who had asked for the appointment, some friend of a friend of Cameron's, was a squat, pink-lipped fellow named Huffsteder. He ordered and paid for the expected round of drinks—a lager for Stanley, whiskey for Cameron—and the trio took a table just vacated by some officers. One recognized Cameron and nodded respectfully. Even Stanley drew an intense, almost startled look from a fat soldier at the bar. Cameron had no fears about meeting here. A good part of the time, the government operated from hotel bars and parlors. The smoke and the level of noise pretty well prevented close observations and eavesdropping.

"Let me come right to the point—" Huffsteder began.

Cameron gave him no chance. "You want a contract. You're not alone, I'll tell you that. But I wouldn't be sitting here if you didn't deserve—oh, call it an accommodation." His eyes met those of the other man. "Because of past courtesies. Let's be no more specific than that. Now, what do you sell?"

"Uniforms. Delivered fast, at the right price."

"Made where?"

"My factory in Albany."

41

"Oh, that's right. New York. I remember."

The contract-seeker reached into his coat for a square of coarse fabric dyed dark blue and laid the sample on the table. Stanley picked it up with both hands and easily tore it in two. "Shoddy," he said. It wasn't a judgment but the familiar name of material made of pressed wool scraps. Huffsteder said nothing. Cameron fingered one of the pieces. He knew, as did Stanley, that any uniform made of the material would last two or three months; less if the wearer happened to be caught in a heavy rain. Still, it was wartime; the actions of the rebel combinations dictated certain compromises.

Cameron quickly made that evident: "In procurement, Mr. Hoffsteder—" The contractor muttered his correct name, but Cameron ignored him—"the law's clear as crystal. My department obeys that law. Operates on the bid system—the bids are sealed if the contract's advertised. On the other hand, I have certain funds at my personal disposal, and I can disburse that money to authorized agents of the War Department for discretionary purchases not dependent on bids. You catch my drift?" Huffsteder nodded. "When our brave boys need overcoats or powder, we can't be too finicky about law. With the rebs right over there in Virginia, liable to swoop down any minute, we can't wait for sealed bids to come in, can we? So—" Cameron raised an eloquent hand—"special agents with special funds."

To be handed to special friends. After just a few months, Stanley understood the system well.

Cameron dropped his pose of eloquence. "Stanley, write the names and addresses of our New York State agents for this gentleman. See either one of them, and I'm sure you can do business."

"Sir, I can't thank you enough."

"But you already did." Again he fixed the nervous man with those gray eyes. "I recall the amount of the donation exactly. Handsome, handsome indeed. The sort of donation I'd expect from someone anxious to help the war effort."

"I'd better write our agents," Stanley put in.

"Yes, take care of it." Cameron didn't need to warn his pupil to use vague language; Stanley had written over a dozen letters of the same type. Cameron rose. "Well, sir, if you'll excuse me now, I'm off to have supper with my brother. He, too, is serving the cause. Commander of the Seventy-ninth New York. Mostly Scots,

42

those fellows. But you wouldn't catch me in a Highlander's kilts. Not with my knees."

Cameron was away from the table by the time he uttered the jovial remark. Huffsteder remained seated, smiling in a dazed way. Stanley hurried after his boss, thinking a not infrequent thought. If some of the department's practices ever came to light —Well, he did his best to stay clear of the worst illegalities. He wanted to be in Washington, the center of power, and if the price was the risk of soiled hands, he'd pay it. Besides, Isabel insisted.

In the lobby, he made a final attempt with Cameron. "Sir, before you go—please reconsider about George. Don't forget he's one of those West Point peacocks—"

"And I don't like them or the institution any better than you do, my boy. But I reckon I've got to take the squall if I want the baby."

"Mr. Secretary, I beg you—"

"That's enough! Don't you hear me?"

Several heads turned. Reddening over his outburst, Cameron grabbed Stanley's sleeve and yanked him toward an empty settee. "You come over here. James will be sore when I'm late, but I want to get something straight."

Oh, my God, he's going to discharge me—

Cameron's expression certainly suggested the possibility. He shoved Stanley down on the cushions. "Now listen here. I like you, Stanley. What's more, I trust you, and I can't say that about many who work for me. Quit worrying about your brother. I'll handle him. You'd be a damn sight smarter if you forgot about the past and took advantage of the present."

With a dull look, Stanley said, "What do you mean?"

Calmer, Cameron sat down. "I mean take a leaf out of the book of that thief we just met. Find an opportunity and capitalize on it. I run my department strictly according to the law"—Stanley was too upset to laugh at the absurdity—"but that doesn't mean I'm unwilling to see trusted associates prosper. Many little jobs must be done if we're to accomplish the big one."

It dawned then. "You mean I should seek a contract?"

Cameron slapped his knee. "Yessiree."

"For what?"

"Anything our boys need. These, for instance." Reaching down, he poked his left shoe, then rested his gaze on the newly painted ceiling while he mused. "The shoe industry's the second biggest in the North, only it's fallen on hard times lately. Bet there are a lot of small factories for sale in New England."

"But I know nothing about the shoe indus—"

"Learn, my boy." Snakelike, Cameron's head shot toward him. *"Learn."*

"Well, I suppose I could—"

"Sure." Affable again, Cameron gave Stanley's knee a second slap and stood. "Shoes are in damn short supply. It's a fine opportunity for somebody."

"I appreciate the suggestion. Thank you."

Cameron beamed. "Good night, my boy."

"Good night, sir."

After the secretary left the hotel, Stanley sat staring at his feet for more than a minute. He always had trouble with decisions, but tonight was worse because of George. He had no more say in that matter. Could he withstand Isabel's fury when she learned that the man who'd forced them out of Lehigh Station was now being invited to become Stanley's rival once again?

6

"Wouldn't have this war if it wasn't for the niggers."

"You're wrong. It's them rebs pulling out of the Union that started it. I say fight for the flag but not the darkies."

"I'm with you there. Way I see it, the best way to solve the problem would be to shoot 'em all."

The comment generated loud agreement from several other civilians at the Willard bar. The solitary officer held the same opinion, but since he was in uniform, he made no comment. Some pro-nigger toady from the government might take notice.

The officer weighed two hundred and thirty pounds. A paunch inflated his spotless dress coat. In a dead white face that bright sunlight could broil red in half an hour, dark eyes shifted toward a corner table. One man still seated had been left by two others a moment ago. Of the pair departing, the younger man had a tantalizingly familiar face.

The officer sipped his whiskey and cudgeled his memory. He was thirty-seven, but his black hair had begun to show gray streaks six months ago. He applied dye every day to hide them and preserve a youthful appearance. Brevet Colonel Elkanah Bent only wished he could conceal his awareness of them as easily.

In that gray, he found intimations of his own mortality and a heightened sense of frustration with his career. He'd suffered career frustration during most of his adult life. But this past month it had worsened as he idled through the days in this benighted pro-Southern city. Bent hated Southerners almost as much as he hated blacks. He hated one Southerner, named Orry Main, most of all; Main and his Yankee classmate George Hazard. On top of that, Washington was the home of the only human being for whom Bent had any affection, and he was forbidden to see him.

The face of the departed stranger lingered in his mind. Bent motioned for the barkeep. "Did you see that gentleman who just left?"

"Secretary Cameron."

"No, the one with him."

"Oh, that's one of his flunkies. Stanley Hazard."

Bent's hand clenched. "From Pennsylvania?"

"I suppose. Cameron brought a lot of political pals to the War Department." A nod to the empty glass. "Need another?"

"Yes, I do. A double."

Stanley Hazard. George Hazard's brother, surely. That would explain the familiarity despite the soft, sagging face. For a moment such overwhelming emotions buffeted him that he felt sick, dizzy.

Orry Main and George Hazard had been one year behind Elkanah Bent at the Military Academy. From the start, they had despised him and conspired to turn others against him. He held them directly responsible for his failure to win promotions and commendations. That had been true at West Point and again during the war in Mexico.

In the late fifties, Bent had been posted to the Second Cavalry in Texas. There, Orry Main's cousin Charles, a brash new lieutenant in the regiment, had further besmirched his record.

In this war, the Mains naturally sided with the Southern traitors. George Hazard had left the army years ago, but his younger brother, Billy, was in the Union engineers. Bent didn't know the whereabouts of any of them, but this he did know beyond doubt: Elkanah Bent was destined for greatness. Supreme power. All of his adult life he'd believed he would emerge as the American Bonaparte, and he still believed it, even though an upstart Academy classmate, George McClellan, lately returned to the army, had somehow persuaded the gullible press to confer the title on him.

Never mind. What mattered was the power itself. It would bring recognition and reward for Bent's military genius and, just as surely, the opportunity to destroy the Mains and the Hazards.

He gulped whiskey and fixed a clear image of Stanley's present appearance in his mind. After he emptied the glass, he pulled out his watch. Past seven already. Soon it would be dark, and when it was, the steets were unsafe. Unlike the daytime police, those on duty at night were paid by the government, principally to protect public buildings, not citizens. He ought to be leaving. Though he wore his dress sword, he didn't care to invite the attention of the thugs and robbers who hunted for victims when the sun went down. Men like that terrified him.

One more drink, then he'd go. He sipped it, struggling to summon satisfying visions of throttling Stanley Hazard or stabbing his sword into Stanley's belly. The effort did him no good. The one he wanted to hurt was George. George and that damned Orry Main.

Clutching the hilt of his sword, he lurched out of Willard's. He could feel and smell dampness in the air; another pestilential fog would soon be rising from the river. He bumped into an oyster-seller giving one last toot of his horn as he wheeled his cart away. Bent cursed the blurred figure and wove on through twilight shadows from which strange, taunting voices whispered to him. Real voices? Phantoms? He wasn't sure. His walk approached a run.

Three blocks of this torment brought him to the safety of the boardinghouse. Panting, he climbed steps to the lighted veranda and huddled there until his tremors of relief subsided. Then he went into the parlor, where he found another boarder with whom he'd struck up an acquaintance. Colonel Elmsdale, a jug-eared New Hampshireman, chewed a cigar as he pointed to some papers on a table.

"Picked up my orders today. Yours, too. There they are. Not the best of news."

"Not—the best—?" Licking lips already moist, Bent snatched the orders. The handwriting, typically ornate, seemed to writhe, as if snakes were somehow imprisoned in the paper. But he understood every word. He was so frightened, he passed wind uncontrollably. Elmsdale didn't laugh or smile.

"Department of—Kentucky?"

A grim nod. "Army of the Cumberland. Do you know who's in command? Anderson. The same slave-owning bungler who hauled the flag down at Sumter. I know a lot of people called him a hero, but I'm hanged if I do."

"Where's this Camp Dick Robinson?"

"Near Danville. Camp of instruction for volunteers."

Incredulous, Bent said, "I've drawn line duty—in secesh country?"

"Yes, and I've drawn the same. I'm no happier than you are, Bent. We'll have greenhorns to command—bushwhackers behind every tree—nobody fighting by the book. I'll bet the plowboys we're supposed to train can't even read the goddamn book."

"There's been some mistake," Bent whispered, wheeling and stumbling to the stairs.

"There certainly has. The army kind." Elmsdale sighed. "Not a thing we can do about it."

Lumbering upstairs, Bent didn't hear. Down a dusty, gas-lit hall reeking of stew beef and onions—the dining-room supper he was too sick to eat—he found his room. He slammed the door. Sank to the edge of the bed in the dark. Line duty. Commanding illiterates in a wilderness where a man ran a high risk of dying from the bullet of some Southern sympathizer.

Or from the inattention of superiors who had all but forgotten his potential—his very existence—

What happened? In the stale dark, smelling of uniform wool and his own sweat, he was nearly crying. Where was his protector? From Bent's earliest days that man had labored secretly on his behalf. Secured the Academy appointment from Ohio, and

47

then, after the machinations of Hazard and Main brought dismissal, his protector had won reinstatement for him by an appeal to the Secretary of War. Except for unavoidable service in the Mexican War and that one posting to Texas, he'd always been given safe duty. He'd been kept in the army, out of danger—

Until now.

My God, they were sending him into exile. Suppose he wound up leading combat troops? He could die. Why had his protector let him down? Surely it was unintentional. Surely no one knew of these orders except a few army clerks. That had to be the explanation—

Still shaking, he decided on what he must do. It was a violation of the clear and long-standing agreement that he must never contact his protector directly. But this crisis—this absolute disaster—took precedence over the agreement.

He ran out of the room and down the stairs, startling Elmsdale, who was just coming up. "Fog's gotten mighty thick out there. If you have to go somewhere, take your revolver."

"I don't need advice from you." Bent shoved him. "Stand aside." He lurched out the front door, sword scabbard swinging wildly. Elmsdale swore and said to himself, How has a lunatic like that managed to stay in the army?

7

The hired hack turned north into Nineteenth, where the homes were few in number. The wealthy built in this remote section to avoid the dirt and dangers of the central city.

"Which house between K and L?" the driver called.

"There's only one. It takes up the whole block."

Bent hung from the inside hand strap as if it were a life line in the ocean. His mouth felt hot, parched, the rest of his body cold. The Potomac fog hung drapes of dirty gauze over even the brightest windows.

Bent's destination was the residence of a man named Heyward Starkwether. An Ohioan, Starkwether had no profession in the traditional sense, no office, no visible source of income, though he'd lived in the city twenty-five years. The only term to describe his circumstances during the last sixteen was opulent. Reporters new to Washington—young men, usually, and long on nerve, short on wisdom—sometimes described him as a lobbyist. The totally foolhardy substituted the words *influence peddler*. Elkanah Bent didn't know a great deal about Starkwether's affairs, but he did know that calling the man a lobbyist was the same as calling Alexander of Macedon a common soldier.

Starkwether was rumored to represent huge New York money interests, men almost Olympian in their wealth and influence. Men who could ignore any law if it suited them and shape government policy to fit a personal purpose. In their behalf, it was said, Starkwether had maintained friendships at the highest levels of government for more than two decades, through a succession of administrations, a fact that had long tinctured Bent's affection with awe.

"Turn in here," he exclaimed. The driver had almost missed the great bow-shaped drive in front of the mansion, more Greek temple than house. Fog hid its vast wings and upper floors, and Bent was puzzled by the empty drive and a lack of lighted windows. Several times before this he had driven past at night, always finding many visitors' carriages outside and many gaslights blazing within.

"Wait for me," Bent said, lumbering up wide marble steps to the entrance. He let one of the huge lion's-head knockers fall twice. The sound went rolling away and away inside. Was his protector gone? Thinking of Starkwether, Bent seldom used any other word, especially not the more common but forbidden one.

He knocked again. An elderly servant with reddened eye sockets answered. Before he could speak, the visitor blurted, "I am Colonel Elkanah Bent. I must see Mr. Starkwether. It's urgent."

"I'm very sorry, Colonel, but it's impossible. This afternoon,

49

Mr. Starkwether was unexpectedly—" the old man had trouble saying it—"stricken."

"Do you mean a paralytic seizure?"

"Yes, sir."

"But he's all right, isn't he?"

"The seizure was fatal, sir."

Bent walked back to the hack, seeing nothing, hearing nothing, wondering how to save himself now that he'd lost his father.

8

"He's coming here? With that Catholic bitch who lords it over us as if she's royalty? Stanley, you imbecile! How could you allow it?"

"Isabel," he began in a faint voice as she flounced toward the parlor windows overlooking Sixth Street. She showed him the back of the drab gray hoop skirt and matching jacket she wore for everyday. She groaned, so loudly you might have thought some man was ravishing her. Damn slim chance of her permitting that, Stanley thought pettishly.

His wife kicked her hoops to permit a quick turn, another confrontation. "Why in the name of God didn't you speak against the idea?"

"I did! But Cameron wants him."

"For what possible reason?"

Stanley offered a few of Cameron's explanatory phrases, as best he could remember them. Just the anticipation of this quarrel had exhausted him. He'd spent most of the day rehearsing what he'd say and completely forgotten it when the moment arrived.

Sprawled in a chair, he finished with a lame "There's a strong possibility that he won't come."

"I wish we hadn't either. I detest this cursed town."

He sat silent as she strode around the parlor three times, working off some of her rage. He knew she didn't mean that last remark. She loved being in Washington because she loved power and associating with those who controlled it.

Their current circumstances weren't ideal, of course. With decent quarters hard to find, they'd been forced to rent this dusty old suite in the cavernous National Hotel, a hangout of the secesh crowd. Stanley wished they could move. Quite apart from politics, a hotel was the wrong place in which to raise two headstrong adolescent sons. Sometimes Laban and Levi disappeared in the mazy corridors for hours. God knew what lascivious lessons they learned, listening at closed doors. When Stanley had gotten here at seven, Isabel reported that she'd found Laban giggling in a familiar way with one of the young maids. Stanley had lectured his son—torture for him and boring for the defiant boy. He had then ordered the twins to study Latin verbs for an hour and locked their bedroom door. Mercifully, all sounds of fist-fighting had now stopped; he presumed they were asleep. Small wonder religious Americans considered Washington an immoral place; the first evidence cited was the town's teeming hotel life.

Isabel completed her last circuit of the room and stopped, folding her arms over her small bosom and challenging him with her eyes. Two years older than Stanley, she had grown increasingly forbidding as she aged.

In response to her glare, he said, "Isabel, try to understand. I did object, but—"

"Not strongly. You never do anything strongly."

His back stiffened as he stood. "That's unfair. I didn't want to harm my good standing with Simon. I had the impression you considered it an asset."

Isabel Hazard was an expert manipulator of people, most especially her husband. She saw she'd pushed too hard. The understanding damped her anger. "I do. I'm sorry for what I said. It's just that I despise George and Constance for all the humiliation they've heaped on you."

The truce established, he moved to her side. "And you."

"Yes. I'd like to repay them for that." She cocked her head, smiling. "If they did come here, perhaps I could find a way. We know important people. You have some influence now."

"We might do it at that." He hoped his lack of enthusiasm didn't show. Sometimes he truly hated his brother, but he had also been frightened of him since they were boys. He slipped his arm around her shoulder. "Let me have a whiskey while I tell you some good news."

Isabel allowed him to guide her to a sideboard where fine glass decanters held the best brands of spirits. "What is it? A promotion?"

"No, no—I guess news is the wrong word. It's a suggestion from Simon, a boon to soothe my objections about George." He described the meeting with the contractor and the subsequent conversation with Cameron. Isabel saw the potential instantly. She clapped her hands.

"For that idea, I'd let ten George Hazards come to town. We wouldn't be dependent on the factory—or your brother's whims —for our principal income. Just imagine the money we could make with a guaranteed contract—"

"Simon offered no guarantees," Stanley cautioned. "You don't dare state such things explicitly. But I'm sure it's what he meant. The department operates that way. Right now, for instance, I'm working on a plan to save the government money when it transports soldiers from New York to Washington. The present cost is six dollars a head. By rerouting the troops on the Northern Central through Harrisburg, we can cut that to four."

"But the Northern Central is Cameron's line."

Feeling better with whiskey in him, Stanley winked. "We don't generally advertise that."

Isabel was already planning. "We must travel to New England immediately. Simon will give you time off, won't he?"

"Oh, yes. But, as I told him, I don't know a thing about shoe manufacturing."

"We will learn. Together."

"Give me back my pillow, you little son of a bitch."

The sudden shout from behind the door of the smaller bedroom was followed by more cursing and sounds of struggle.

"Stanley, go stop those boys this instant."

The general had spoken; the subaltern knew better than to argue. He set his drink aside and reluctantly marched off to the sibling wars.

9

Next day, in Pennsylvania, Billy's wife, Brett, left Belvedere to do an errand. A servant could have gone down to Lehigh Station instead, but she wanted to escape the mansion's overheated sewing room and the volunteer work being done there by the ladies of the house. The work for the Union boys bothered her conscience.

Belvedere, an L-shaped stone mansion of Italianate design, stood beside a second residence on the terraced summit of a hill overlooking the river, the town, and the Hazard ironworks. The other residence was twice as large—forty rooms. It belonged to Stanley Hazard and his dreadful wife, who had left a caretaker behind when they went to Washington.

Brett waited on Belvedere's shady veranda until a groom brought the buggy around. Her thank you was perfunctory, and she practically snatched the whip from his hand. She pushed the whip into the dash socket, then off she went in a cloud of dust, mad at herself for her unwarranted surliness.

Brett was twenty-three, an inheritor of the dark hair and eyes common in the Main family. She was attractive but in a fresher, plainer way than her older sister, Ashton, whom everyone, including Ashton, considered a beauty. Ashton's loveliness was suited to evening, to sweet scent and bare shoulders under candlelight. Brett was a child of daylight and the out of doors, most at home in homely surroundings. People introduced to her for the first time quickly sensed that from her manner and especially from her smile. There was nothing of coquetry in it. Instead, it

53

conveyed a kindness, an openness, often lacking in young women her age.

But that seemed to be changing here in her husband's hometown. People knew she came from South Carolina and sometimes treated her with the care given some wilting exotic flower. Not a few, she supposed, considered her a traitor at heart. That annoyed her, and so did the infernal heat of the afternoon. Her sticky white muslin dress clung to her, and the humidity seemed even worse than that of her native low country.

The longer Billy stayed away—the longer the dread uncertainties of this war continued—the more isolated and unhappy she became. She tried not to show those feelings to George and his wife, Constance, with whom she'd been living since Billy returned to duty. But she was far from perfect, and she knew it. So the groom had taken the brunt, just as one of the servant girls had yesterday.

Perspiration quickly soaked through the palms of her net mittens. Why had she worn them? The buggy horse required sharp tugs of the reins to keep him in the center of the high-crowned, bumpy road that wound down the hillside past the factory. The huge Hazard works generated smoke and noise twenty-four hours a day, rolling out rails and plate for the Union war effort. Lately the company had acquired a contract to cast cannon as well.

Above her, the factory's three stone furnaces dominated the laurel-covered mountain nearest the mansions. Below spread the three levels of the expanding town—solid brick or frame homes the highest, then commercial buildings, and finally shanties on the flats near the railroad line and the bed of the abandoned canal next to the river.

Everywhere, she saw evidence of the war. She passed some boys drilling in a vacant lot to the beat of spoons on a pail; not one of the strutting little soldiers was over ten. The front of the Station House, the good hotel, displayed a great amount of red, white, and blue bunting; George was speaking at a patriotic rally inside the hotel this afternoon. And at the intersection where Valley Street met Canal to form a T, hammers and shouts accompanied construction of a plank platform for the coming celebration on Independence Day.

She drove up to Herbert's General Merchandise and tied the horse to one of the six iron posts in front. As she crossed the walk, she noticed two men watching her from a shaded bench outside the lager-beer saloon two doors down. Their muscular arms and drab clothes told her they probably worked at Hazard's.

Watching her, one man said something to the other, who laughed so hard he nearly spilled his tin growler. Despite the heat, Brett shivered.

· The General Merchandise smelled of licorice and rye flour and other items sold by Mr. Pinckney Herbert. The proprietor was a small-boned, bright-eyed man who reminded Brett of a rabbi she'd met once in Charleston. Herbert had been raised in Virginia, where his family had lived since before the Revolution. His conscience had driven him to Pennsylvania when he was twenty; all that he'd brought from the South were his loathing for slavery and the name Pinckney, which he admired and adopted in preference to his real name, Pincus.

"Afternoon, Mrs. Hazard. How may I serve you today?"

"With some heavy white thread, Pinckney. White. Constance and Patricia and I have been sewing havelocks."

"Havelocks. Well, well." He avoided her eyes, which was a second comment on the novelty of a Southern girl fashioning protective flaps for the hats of Union soldiers. When George's wife and daughter began—Constance said most of the women in town were doing similar work—Brett joined in because it didn't seem a partisan act to help another human being protect his neck from rain or sunburn. Why, then, did a subterranean sense of disloyalty persist while she sewed?

She paid for the half-dozen spools and left the store. At the sound of a plank creaking, she turned sharply to her left and wished she hadn't. There stood the two idlers, sloshing beer round and round in their tin cans.

"What d'ya hear from Jeff Davis, lady?"

She wanted to call him an idiot but decided it was safer to ignore the remark. She headed for the buggy, alarmed to notice only one other person in sight: a bonneted matron who vanished around a corner. From the Station House came faint cheering; the rally and the afternoon heat had emptied the streets.

She hurried past her horse, heartbeat quickening. She heard sounds behind her—harsh breathing, boots on the hard-packed dirt—and felt the man near a moment before he grabbed her shoulder and yanked her around.

It was the one who'd taunted her. His beard, bushy red with

white mingled in, held flecks of beer foam. She smelled the dirt on his clothes and the fumes from his drinking.

"Bet you pray Old Abe will get a seizure some night and fall down dead, huh?" The bearded man's companion found that so funny, he brayed. It caught the attention of two men walking on the other side of the street. When they saw who was being bothered, they went right on.

Slurry of speech, the first man said, "Still own some niggers back home in Carolina?"

"You drunken jackass," Brett said. "Take your hands off me."

The second man giggled. "That's the ole reb spirit, ain't it, Lute?"

The first man dug his fingers into Brett's sleeve. Her face contorted. "Somethin's wrong with your eyesight, woman. I'm a white man. You cain't talk to me like I was one of your damn slaves. Get that in your bonnet, an' this, too. We don't want any secesh traitors paradin' around this town." He shook her. "Hear me?"

"Fessenden, let her go, and right now."

Pinckney Herbert had emerged from his store. The second man ran at him. "Get back inside, you old Jew." One hard punch doubled up the merchant and knocked him back through the door. He tried to rise, while Fessenden dropped his growler and grasped Brett's shoulders, shaking and twisting them so as to hurt her and, perhaps, touch her breasts with his forearms, too.

Herbert grasped the door frame and struggled to pull himself up. The second man hit him under the chin. Herbert crashed down on his back with an involuntary yell. Brett knew she could scream for help, but it ran against the grain. Abruptly, fright seemed to defeat her. She sagged in Fessenden's grip, her eyes half shut.

"Please, please let me go!" Were any tears coming? "Oh, please —I'm just a poor female. Not strong like you—"

"Now that's what I 'spect a little Southern girl ought to sound like." Laughing, Fessenden slipped an arm around her waist, pushed her against the buggy wheel, bent near, his beard scraping her cheek. "Say pretty please an' see what happens."

Apparently she didn't understand. "I'm not—big and burly like you—You must be kind—polite—Won't you do that? Won't you?" Small, desperate sighs and gulps fell between the quivering words of the plea.

"I'll think on it, missy," Fessenden promised. His other hand took hold of her skirt and the petticoats beneath and the leg beneath those. That left her hands free.

"You Yankee scum." She raised the leg he wasn't holding and drove it into his privates. While he screamed and turned red, she pushed him. He tumbled into the dust. Though Pinckney Herbert still looked hurt and pale in the doorway, he started laughing over the sudden revival of the wilted flower.

Fessenden clutched his crotch. His friend called Brett a bad name and started for her. She snatched the whip from the socket and laid it across his cheek.

He jumped back as if set on fire, then screamed as he fell over Fessenden behind him. He landed on his head, managing to kick Fessenden's jaw at the same time.

Brett flung her sack of thread on the buggy floor, untied the horse, and clambered up lithely as a tomboy. As she gathered the reins in one mitten, the second bully, back on his feet, came at her once more. She snapped her right hand over her left arm and whipped his face a second time.

By then, two or three conscience-stricken citizens had appeared in doorways along the block, demanding an end to the bullying. *A little too late, thank you.* She raced the buggy away toward the hilltop road, yellow dust rising behind like the evil clouds that preceded summer storms. *How I hate this town, this war—everything,* she thought as fury gave way to despair.

10

On the temporary stage erected at one end of the main parlor of the Station House, George Hazard was being cruelly and unjustly tortured by heat, verbosity, and the hardest chair ever made by human hand. In front of him, moist faces, wagging paper and palm-leaf fans, flags and swags of bunting draping every wall.

Behind George and the other dignitaries hung a large lithographed drawing of the President. Mayor Blane, who worked at Hazard's as an assistant night foreman, had risen from his customary daytime sleep to chair the rally. Blane pounded the rostrum.

"Our flag has been violated! Desecrated! Torn down by Davis and his treasonous mob of pseudoaristocrats! Such mistreatment of the sacred red, white, and blue can be met with but two replies: a volley of shot and a hang-rope for those who dare rend the fabric of this nation and its dear old emblem!"

Godamighty, George thought. How long will he carry on? Blane was supposed only to introduce the two main speakers, of whom George was the reluctant first and a leading Republican from Bethlehem the second. The politician was raising a volunteer regiment in the valley.

The mayor marched on, pausing only to smile and acknowledge whistles, applause, or people jumping on chairs and shaking their fists to approve of some particularly pithy bit of warmongering. In the weeks since federal flags had been hauled down, spat on, and burned throughout the South, the North had experienced an epidemic of what the newspapers called star-spangled fever.

58

George didn't have the disease. He would have preferred to be at his desk, supervising affairs at Hazard's, or working on details of his application to start the Bank of Lehigh Station, the first in town.

Banking in Bethlehem had become too inconvenient for Hazard's and most of its employees. George had faith in the usefulness and eventual profitability of a local bank. Conventional thinkers would have shied from such a venture just now—economic conditions were bad, confidence low—but George believed there was never great success without considerable risk.

The new bank would be organized under Pennsylvania's revised Banking Act of 1824, with a twenty-year charter and thirteen directors, all of whom had to be United States citizens and shareholders. He and his local attorney, Jupiter Smith, had plenty to do to prepare all the papers required by the chartering body, the state legislature.

Yet here he was, because he was the only local resident who had fought in the Mexican War, and the audience craved some fiery remarks about the glory of war. Well, he'd serve up the desired dish and try not to feel too guilty. He dared not say what he'd really learned in Mexico when he and Orry Main had campaigned there. War was never glorious, never grand—except in the pronouncements pols and other noncombatants made about it. It was, as he had experienced it, mostly dirty, disorderly, boring, lonely, and, for brief intervals, terrifying.

"Forward to Richmond! Up with Old Glory! Down to the depths, then up to the gallows with the vile combinations of the godless Confederacy!"

George put his palm over his eyes to hide any visible reaction. It was impossible for him to think of his beloved friend Orry as godless or vile. Nor could he apply the description to many of the other Southerners he'd met at the Military Academy and marched with in Mexico. Tom Jackson, the queer duck whose great head for soldiering had been recognized way back, when his cadet nickname, "The General," was bestowed. Was he still teaching at the military school in Virginia, or had he joined up? George Pickett, last reported at a federal garrison in California. Good men, even if unable or unwilling to find a way out of the sectional crisis that had now descended into a fight. Well, he himself was as guilty as any of them of neglectfully surrendering that crisis into the hands of political hacks and barroom bullies. The description

59

wasn't his, but that of Braxton Bragg, another West Pointer from the South.

George wished for a cigar to relieve his mingled annoyance and nervousness. He was to speak next. He unplugged his inner ear a moment to listen.

"—distinguished veteran of the war in Mexico, and the highly successful industrialist many of us know as our trusted friend, good neighbor, and generous employer—"

You won't get a raise that way, Blane.

The moment George thought it, he was ashamed. *What a wretched cynic I've become.* Then something else occurred to him. He leaned over to whisper to the man beside him.

"Had my mind on my remarks. Did he say I went to West Point?" The man shook his head. The omission irked George but didn't surprise him. The school, always falsely perceived as Southern-oriented, was even more unpopular now that so many graduates had left the regular army and gone over to the South.

"—Mr. George Hazard!"

Quickly he cleared his head of the burden of the telegraph message he had received that morning. He waved a fly away from his nose and stepped forward to loud applause, prepared for the sake of the cause to lie splendidly about the joys of war.

11

Halfway up the hill, Brett slowed the buggy. The nerve that had helped her through the encounter with the bullies was leaching away. She felt again, and more stingingly, the absence of the one person whose good sense and physical presence could help her get through these bad times.

She understood that Billy must go wherever duty took him. She'd promised to follow him here, Ruth after Boaz, and wait till he came home again. But her resolve was wearing away faster than ever this afternoon.

She had been the target of hostilities in Lehigh Station before this. Some were sly—little jibes she happened to overhear at social functions. Some were overt—derisive yells when she drove through the streets. Usually they didn't bother her. Like her brother Orry, she took pride in that kind of strength.

But this latest incident somehow pierced the armor. More unwelcome thoughts followed. Thoughts of her sister, Ashton, who had conspired with a would-be suitor of Brett's to have Billy murdered on their wedding day. The memory was too depressing to be held in mind for more than short periods, but now it came back, adding its burden.

She let the horse walk while feelings of defeat and loneliness consumed her. Trembling a little, she felt tears in her closed eyes. She opened them just in time to prevent the buggy's off wheel from slipping over into the drainage ditch.

She stopped the horse and sat motionless in the glaring light. The air was so still that the mountain laurel the Hazards loved so well looked petrified and faintly dusty on the summits above her. She wished the animosity of the local residents didn't upset her, but it did. She couldn't banish the feeling, only contain it.

Control returned in a minute or so. She shook the reins, and by the time she reached the big stable at Belvedere, she was composed again. Determined to say nothing about what had happened, she hoped George wouldn't hear about it by accident.

By the time he got home, the rest of the family had gathered for supper. He entered the dining room as Constance was speaking to their daughter in that friendly but firm tone she reserved for matters of discipline.

"No, Patricia, you may not spend any part of your allowance that way. As you well know, a glass or marble egg has just one purpose—to cool the palms of an overly excited young woman at a dance or a party. It will be a few years before you are in that position."

Patricia stuck out her lip. "Carrie King has one."

61

"Carrie King is thirteen, two years older than you. Furthermore, she looks twenty."

"Acts like it, too, so I hear," remarked William with a salacious grin. George was amused, but the parent in him didn't dare show it. He frowned at his sturdy, handsome son.

Behind his wife's chair, he bent to kiss her cheek. "Sorry I'm late. I stopped at the office." The explanation was familiar in these days of furious war production. He felt her move slightly beneath the affectionate hand he had placed on her shoulder. Damn. She smelled the spirits on him.

"Tell me about your speech," Constance said as he walked to his place at the other end of the long wooden table. "Was it a success?"

"Magnificent." He sat down.

"George, I really want to know." He responded with a tired shrug. "The rally, then. How did it go?"

"Predictably." One of the house girls set terrapin soup in front of him. "The rebs were consigned to perdition, the flag waved verbally several hundred times, then that pol from Bethlehem issued the call for volunteers. He got eight."

Some soup helped him relax and readjust himself to this confined but comfortable domestic universe. The dining room was bright with the shimmer of the gas mantles on fine silver and flocked wallpaper. He peeped at Constance over his spoon. What a lucky fellow he was. Her skin still had the smoothness of newly skimmed cream, and her eyes were the same vivid blue that had enchanted him the night they met, at a dance in Corpus Christi arranged for army officers temporarily stranded en route to Mexico. After the war, he had brought her to Lehigh Station to marry her.

Constance was two inches taller than her husband. He took that as a symbolic incentive to be worthy of her. Though Stanley had once predicted in a sniffy way that her practice of Catholicism would disrupt the marriage, it hadn't. Years of child rearing, intimacies shared, and troubles borne together had deepened their love and kept physical attraction strong in the marriage.

Patricia fidgeted. She stabbed her poached fish with her fork, as if the fish were responsible for her failure to get a hand cooler.

"Did the factory produce a lot of havelocks today?" George asked, addressing the question more to Brett than anyone. She sat on his left, her eyes downcast, her face fatigued. She hadn't said one word to him.

"Quite a few, yes," Constance said, simultaneously shooting out her left arm. She thwacked Patricia's ear with her middle finger. That ended the fish-stabbing.

The meal dragged to its finish. Brett remained quiet. After George gave the customary permission for the children to be excused, he spoke briefly to Constance, then followed his sister-in-law to the library. He closed the doors before he said: "I heard about the trouble today."

She looked up wearily. "I had hoped you wouldn't."

"It's a small town. And, regrettably, you are very much a center of attention."

She sighed, absently brushing her palms across the open *Leslie's* in her lap. George lit one of his strong dark brown cigars as she said, "I suppose I was foolish to think it would all pass unnoticed."

"Especially since Fessenden and his cousin are under arrest for assaulting you."

"Who charged them?"

"Pinckney Herbert. So, you see, you do have some friends in Lehigh Station." After telling her that he had already written orders discharging both of her attackers from their jobs at Hazard's, he said in a gentle voice, "I can't tell you how angry and sorry I am about the whole business. Constance and I care for you just as much as we care for any member of this family. We know how hard it is for you to be so far from home and separated from your husband—"

That broke through. She leaped up, spilling the illustrated paper on the carpet, and flung her arms around his neck like a daughter wanting a father's comfort. "I miss Billy so terribly—I'm ashamed to say how much—"

"Don't be." He patted her back. "Don't be."

"The only salvation is, I'll soon be able to join him somewhere. Everyone says the war won't last ninety days."

"So they do." He released her and turned away so she wouldn't see his reaction. "We'll do our best to see that those ninety days pass quickly—without another incident. I know it wasn't the first. You're a brave young woman, Brett. But don't fight every battle alone."

63

She shook her head. "George, I must. I've always looked after myself." Forcing a smile: "I'll be fine. Ninety days isn't so long."

What more could he do? Frustrated, he excused himself and left, trailing a blue ribbon of smoke.

Upstairs, he found his son marching in the hall and bellowing the popular song about hanging Jeff Davis from a sour-apple tree. George stopped that and ordered William to his room, where he worked with the boy on ciphering lessons for half an hour. He next spent fifteen minutes with Patricia, trying to convince her that she'd have a hand cooler at the proper time. He failed.

In bed in his nightshirt, uncomfortably warm despite the summer breeze blowing in, he reached for the comforting curve of his wife's breast and lay close against her back while he described events at the General Merchandise. "She's counting on a short war to put an end to that sort of thing."

"So am I, George. I haven't heard from Father in months, and I worry about him down there in Texas. You know he never hid his hatred of slavery and slaveowners. Surely it'll all end soon. I can't believe Americans will fight each other for very long. It's inconceivable that they're doing it at all."

"As Orry said, we had thirty years to prevent it, but we didn't. I hate to dash Brett's hopes or yours—" He broke off.

"George, don't do that. Finish what you were going to say."

Reluctantly, he said, "Brett's forgotten that in May, Lincoln called for another forty-two thousand men. But not for the short term. The boys who signed up at the rally are in for three years."

Her voice grew faint. "I forgot it, too. You aren't hopeful about a short war?"

He waited a moment but finally admitted, "If I were hopeful, I'd have thrown away Boss Cameron's telegraph message the minute it arrived."

12

While Brett was encountering trouble in the United States, her brother Cooper and his family were nearing the end of a rail journey in Great Britain.

Smoke and cinders kept flying into the family's first-class compartment because the children, Judah and Marie-Louise, took turns leaning over the sill of the lowered window. Cooper permitted it, but his wife, Judith, considered it dangerous, so she sat forward, her posture tense as she held the waist of one child, then the other.

Cooper Main, forty-one, sat opposite her with a sheaf of naval blueprints unrolled on his knees. He made notes on the blueprints in pencil. Before starting, he'd drawn the curtains of the door and windows on the corridor side.

As usual, Cooper managed to make his fine clothes look untidy. It was his height, his lankiness, his preoccupied scholar's behavior that caused it. He paid almost no attention to the children's sightseeing, which horrified his wife, a flat-bosomed woman with thin arms, a long nose, and a great deal of curly dark blond hair, all of which Cooper found extraordinarily beautiful.

"Pa, there's a river," exclaimed Judah, hanging half in, half out of the compartment as he looked ahead, his hair shining in the hot July sun.

"Let me see, let me see!" Marie-Louise wedged her way into the window beside him.

"Both of you get in here this instant," Judith said. "Do you want that bridge to lop your heads off?" Forceful tugs ensured

65

that it wouldn't. They tumbled back on the upholstery beside her, complaining, while the diamond patterns of the crossed beams began to flicker in the compartment. The express from London rattled over the Runcorn bridge, the river Mersey shining beneath like a field of mirror splinters.

Judah jumped across the aisle and pressed against his father's coat. "Will we be in Liverpool soon?"

"Yes, in half an hour or less." He began to roll the plans in preparation for hiding them in his luggage.

Marie-Louise scrambled over to his right side. "Will we stay for a while, Papa?"

"Several months anyway." He smiled and patted her.

"Captain Bulloch will meet us?" Judith asked.

"That was the meaning of the classified insertion in the *Times*. Of course it's possible that some Union agent did away with him in the past three days."

"Cooper, I don't think you should joke about this work. Secret messages sent by advertisement, enemy spies lurking everywhere —hardly subjects for humor, in my opinion." She glanced from her husband to the children in a pointed way. But they were totally absorbed by the slow-moving shadows.

"Perhaps not. But we can't be grim all the time, and although I take my duties seriously—and I'm sensitive to the cautions Bulloch expressed in his letter—I refuse to let all of that spoil England for us." Leaning forward, he smiled and touched her. "For you most of all."

She squeezed his hand. "You're such a dear man. I'm sorry I snapped. I'm afraid I'm tired."

"Understandably," he said with a nod. They had left King's Cross in the middle of the night and watched the sun rise over the peaceful canals and summer-green countryside, neither admitting that uncertainty, homesickness, and worries about possible dangers beset them.

The family had sailed from Savannah on the last ship that got out before the Union blockade closed the Southern coast. The vessel had called at Hamilton, Bermuda, before steaming on to Southampton. Since their arrival in London, they'd been living in cramped rooms in Islington. Now, however, there was a promise of better, larger quarters in Liverpool, where Cooper was to assist the chief agent of the Confederate Navy Department, who had arrived some weeks earlier. Their mission was to expedite construction of ocean-going raiders to harass Yankee shipping. Behind the program lay a sound strategy. If the Confederacy could destroy or capture enough merchant vessels, insurance rates would rise prohibitively; then the enemy would be forced to draw ships from its blockading squadron to protect its own commerce.

Maritime matters were not new to Cooper. He had a long history of interest in and love for the sea. Unable to tolerate the family plantation or repeated quarrels with his late father on the issues of slavery and states' rights, he had gone to Charleston to manage a frowzy little commercial shipping firm that had come into Tillet Main's possession almost by accident. Through study, determination, and hard work, Cooper had turned the Carolina Shipping Company into the most innovative line in the South and built it to a level of profit only slightly lower than that of its larger but more conservative rival in the port city, John Fraser & Company. That company was now guided by another self-made millionaire, George Trenholm. Its Liverpool cotton-factoring office, operating as Fraser, Trenholm, would secretly channel funds into the illegal work Cooper was to undertake.

Before the war, on a plot of ground overlooking Charleston harbor, Cooper had started to create his great dream—a ship patterned after the immense iron vessels of Isambard Kingdom Brunel, the British engineering genius he had twice visited. He wanted to demonstrate that a Southern shipbuilding industry was a reasonable possibility, that prosperity in the state need not depend entirely on the drip of sweat from black skin.

While the shouters stumped for secession, he worked too quietly—which was one mistake. He worked too slowly—which was another. *Star of Carolina* had scarcely been started when the batteries opened fire on Sumter; he had signed her over to the Confederate Navy, and now, he understood, she had been ripped apart, her metal to be used for other purposes.

It was Cooper's fascination with shipbuilding that helped him shunt aside his doubts about the cause. He had long considered the South to be ignorant and misguided for failing to recognize the world-wide spread of industrialization and for clinging to an agrarian system based on human servitude. He recognized that realistically the problem couldn't be reduced to such a simple statement. But with that caveat, he still contended that a few elitists with wealth and political control had pushed the South to disaster, first by refusing to compromise on slavery and then by

67

promoting secession. The yammering Yankee abolitionists had done their part as well, piling insults on the South for three decades—that the insults had a justifiable base made them no more bearable—and the result was a confrontation decent men, such as his brother Orry and Orry's old war comrade George Hazard, didn't want but didn't know how to prevent. Cooper believed that men of good will on both sides—he counted himself among them —had lacked the power, but they had also lacked the initiative. So the war came.

At that apocalyptic moment, a strange sea change occurred. Much as Cooper detested the war and those who had provoked it, he found he loved his native South Carolina more. So he turned over the assets of his shipping company to the new Confederate government and informed his family that they would be traveling to England to serve the Navy Department.

The situation in Britain vis-à-vis the Confederacy was complex, not to say confused. Nearly as confused, Cooper thought, as the foreign policy of the Davis government. The South needed war and consumer goods from abroad. She could buy those with her cotton, but Mr. Davis had chosen to withhold that from the foreign market because textile mills in Europe and Britain were suffering a severe shortage of their raw material. Thus Davis hoped to force diplomatic recognition of the new nation. All he'd gotten so far was half a pie; while the Cooper Mains crossed the ocean, Britain acknowledged the Confederate States as belligerents in a war with the North.

If full recognition depended on the skills of the three commissioners dispatched to Europe by Secretary of State Toombs, Cooper doubted it would ever be achieved. Rost and Mann were barely adequate mediocrities, while the third commissioner, Yancey, was one of the original fire-eaters—a man so extreme the Confederate government didn't want him. His posting to Britain amounted to exile. An ill-tempered boor was hardly the person to deal with Lord Russell, the foreign minister.

Further, the ambassador from Washington, Mr. Charles Francis Adams, descendant of presidents, had a reputation as a shrewd, aggressive diplomat. He kept pressure on the Queen's government to hold back recognition of the Confederacy. And Cooper had been warned that Adams and his consuls maintained a spy network to prevent the very kind of illegal activity that brought him to Liverpool.

"Lime Street. Lime Street Station."

The trainman moved on to call at the next compartment. Above the stone-sided cut through which the train chugged, Cooper glimpsed the chimneys of steeply roofed row houses stained with dirt, yet reassuring in their solidity. Cooper loved Britain and the British people. Any nation that could produce a Shakespeare and a Brunel—and a Drake and a Nelson—deserved immortality. Duty in Liverpool might have its dangers, but he felt exhilarated as the train jerked and finally stopped in the roofed shed adjoining Lime Street.

"Judith, children, follow me." First out of the compartment, he waved down a porter. While the luggage was being unloaded, a man with more hair on his upper lip and cheeks than on his round head wove through the press of passengers, porters, and hawkers to reach the new arrivals. The man had an aristocratic air about him and was well but not extravagantly dressed.

"Mr. Main?" The man addressed him softly, even though loud voices and escaping steam effectively barred eavesdropping.

"Captain Bulloch?"

James D. Bulloch of Georgia and the Confederate Navy tipped his hat. "Mrs. Main—children. The warmest of welcomes to Liverpool. I trust the journey wasn't too taxing?"

"The children enjoyed the scenery once the sun came up," Judith answered, with a smile.

"I spent most of the time studying the drawings you sent to Islington," Cooper added. They had arrived with a man pretending to be making a delivery of wallpaper samples.

"Good—fine. You-all come right along, then. I have a hack waiting to whisk us over to Mrs. Donley's in Oxford Street. Temporary quarters only—I know you'll want something larger and more suitable."

Turning slightly, he directed the remark to Judith. As Bulloch smiled at her, Cooper noticed his eyes. They moved constantly, scanning faces, compartment windows, trash-strewn corners of the great arched shed. This was no lark.

"You might like the Crosby area," Bulloch continued as he led the family and the porter outside. He flourished his gold-knobbed cane to discourage three sad-faced urchins with trays of old, damaged fruit. The Mains piled into the hack while Bulloch remained on the curb, studying the crowds. Finally he hopped in, rapped the ceiling with his cane, and they were off.

69

"There's plenty to be done here, Main, but I don't want to rush you. I know you need to settle in—"

Cooper shook his head. "The waiting in London was worse than overwork. I'm eager to get started."

"Good for you. The first man you'll meet is Prioleau. He runs Fraser, Trenholm, on Rumford Place. I also want to introduce you to John Laird and his brother. Got to be careful about that meeting, though. Mrs. Main, you understand the problems we contend with here, don't you?"

"I think so, Captain. The neutrality laws don't permit war vessels to be built and armed in British yards if the vessels will go into the service of any power with whom Britain is at peace."

"By Jove, that's it exactly. Clever wife you have, old chap." Cooper smiled; Bulloch was adapting rapidly. He continued energetically. "The laws cut both ways, of course. The Yankees can't build any warships either—but then, they don't need to, and we do. The trick is to construct and arm a vessel without detection or government interference. Fortunately, there's a gap in the laws— one we can sail right through if we have nerve. A solicitor I hired locally pointed it out. I'll explain it in due course."

"Will the local shipbuilders violate the laws on neutrality?" Judith asked him.

"Britons are also human beings, Mrs. Main. Some of them will if there's profit in it. Fact is, they've more offers of contracts than they can handle. There are gentlemen in town who have nothing to do with our Navy but who still want ships built or refitted."

"Ships to run the blockade?" said Cooper.

"Yes. By the way, have you met the man we work for?"

"Secretary Mallory? Not yet. Everything's been done by letter."

"Smart fellow, Mallory. Something of a submissionist, though."

Cooper's nature wouldn't permit deception on such an important point. "So was I, Captain."

For the first time, Bulloch frowned. "You mean to say you'd like to see the old Union patched together again?"

"I said was, Captain. Still, since we're going to work closely, I must be straightforward—" He put an arm around his wriggling daughter to settle her. The hack swayed. "I detest this war. I especially detest the fools on both sides who caused it. But I made

70

my decision to stay with the South. My personal beliefs won't interfere with my duties, that I promise."

Bulloch cleared his throat. His frown faded. "Can't ask for better than that." But he clearly wanted to leave this boggy ground. He complimented the parents on their handsome children, then proudly showed a small, cardboard-framed photograph of his infant nephew Theodore. The boy's mother, Bulloch's sister, had married into an old-line New York family named Roosevelt.

"Expect she has cause to regret it now," he added. "Ah, here's Mrs. Donley's."

He turned away from the oval window as the hack stopped. Bulloch got out first to fold the step down. Cooper assisted Judith and the children while the driver began to unload the trunks and portmanteaus lashed to the roof. They had pulled up in front of Number 6 in a row of brick residences attached to one another and all alike. Suddenly, a decrepit figure in a filthy skirt and patched sweater lurched into sight from the far side of the hack.

Hair that resembled gray broomstraw stuck out from beneath a bandanna. The woman clutched the neck of a smelly rag bag carried over her shoulder and peered at Cooper with an intensity as peculiar as her unlined face.

"Parnmeguvnor," she said, bumping him as she hurried by. Bulloch whipped up his cane and with his other hand seized the ragpicker's hair. The move was so abrupt that Marie-Louise yelped and jumped to her mother's side. Bulloch yanked; gray hair and bandanna came off, revealing cropped yellow curls.

"The hair gave you away, Betsy. Tell Dudley not to buy such a cheap wig next time. Now off with you!"

He waved his cane in a threatening way. The young woman backed up, spitting invective—in English, Cooper supposed, though he couldn't understand a word. Bulloch stepped forward. The woman picked up her skirts, dashed to the corner, and disappeared.

"Who the devil was that?" Cooper exclaimed.

"Betsy Cockburn, a slut, er, woman who hangs out in a pub near Rumford Place. Thought I recognized her. She's one of Tom Dudley's spies, I think."

"Who's Dudley?"

"The Yankee consul in Liverpool."

71

"What was that gibberish she spouted at us?" Judith wanted to know.

"Scouse. The Liverpudlian equivalent of Cockney. I hope none of you understood her." Another throat clearing indicated his concern for delicate sensibilities.

"Not a syllable," Judith assured him. "But I can hardly believe that wretched creature is a spy."

"Dudley hires what he can get. Dock scum chiefly. They are not recruited for their intelligence." Brushing dust from his sleeve, he said to Cooper, "It doesn't matter that we saw through her ridiculous disguise. Its only purpose was to help her get close enough for a good look at your face. Dudley got wind of your arrival somehow. One of my informants told me so yesterday. But I didn't anticipate your becoming a marked man quite this soon—"

The sentence trailed into a disappointed sigh. Then: "Well, it's a lesson in how things operate in Liverpool. Dudley is not a foe to be taken lightly. That drab's harmless, but some of his other hirelings are not."

Judith cast an anxious look at her husband, whose mouth had grown inexplicably dry. How chilly the summer noonday felt. "Don't you think we should go inside and see our quarters?" Judah at his side, he walked to the stoop. He was smiling, but he surveyed each end of the block in turn.

13

Starkwether's burial took place in Washington that same afternoon, in the rain. The location was a small private cemetery in the suburb of Georgetown, beyond Rock Creek and well away from the place seekers and other political canaille.

Water dripped from Elkanah Bent's hat brim and dampened his black-frogged coat of dark blue. He usually enjoyed wearing the coat, with its attached short cloak, adopted in 1851 from a French design; he believed it minimized his fatness and lent him dash. But pleasure was absent this dark, depressing day.

A canvas pavilion protected the open grave and surrounding lawn. Some fifty mourners had gathered. Bent was too far away to identify many of them—he'd tied his horse a quarter of a mile back and walked to his spot behind a great marble cross—but the few he did recognize testified to his father's importance. Ben Wade, Ohio's powerful Republican senator, had come. Scott had sent a senior staff officer, and nigger-loving Chase his pretty daughter. The President's representative was Lamon, the long-haired, mustachioed White House crony.

Bent's mood was one of resentment rather than grief. Even in death, his father prevented closeness. He wanted to stand with the other mourners but didn't dare.

Laborers waited at the head and foot of the heavily ornamented coffin, ready to lift and lower it. The minister was speaking, but Bent couldn't hear him because of the splatter of rain on summer leaves. The cemetery was heavily wooded; dark as a grotto. Dark as he felt.

Late in the morning, so the papers said, his father had been memorialized at a church service in downtown Washington. Bent couldn't go to that either. All arrangements had undoubtedly been handled by Dills, the little old lawyer who stood nearest the grave, flanked by three bland, jowly civilians with the look of moneyed men.

Bent hunched close to the cross, half again as tall as he was. He despised Dills but didn't want to antagonize him by inadvertently showing himself. It was through Dills that Heyward Starkwether had communicated with his illegitimate son and provided him with money. It was Dills to whom Bent appealed in times of emergency. Never in person after their first interview; only in writing.

The solemn minister raised his hand. The coffin went down into the earth, and down, on canvas sling straps. Bent had been invited to meet his father twice in his adult life. At each meeting the conversation was inconsequential and awkward, with many lengthy silences. He remembered Starkwether as a handsome, reserved man, obviously intelligent. He had never seen his father smile.

Rain seemed to get into Bent's eyes as the coffin disappeared. The mourners prepared to leave. Why hadn't Starkwether cared enough about him to acknowledge him? Bastardy wasn't such a great sin in these modern times. Why, then? He hated his father, for whom he cried now, for leaving that and so many other questions unanswered.

Foremost, who was Bent's mother? Not Starkwether's long-dead wife; that much Dills had told him, going on to warn him never to ask a second time. How dare the lawyer treat him that way? How dare Starkwether hide the truth?

During Bent's only talk with Dills, the lawyer had purported to explain why a close relationship with Starkwether was impossible. Those who paid Starkwether wanted him to live in perfect rectitude and never by word or deed draw public attention to himself. Bent didn't believe the smooth story. He suspected Starkwether had a simpler and crueler reason for abandoning him. Starkwether had fathered no legitimate children. He was probably one of those selfish careerists too busy for parenthood.

Bent inhaled sharply. Dills seemed to be watching the stone cross while he conversed with the three moneyed men. Bent began a retreat, careful to keep the monument between himself and the

74

grave. He failed to see a pedestal supporting a looming granite angel. He stumbled against the pedestal and cried out. He kept himself from falling by catching hold of the wet stone drapery.

Had anyone heard him? Dills?

No one came, and the rattle of departing carriages continued. When he got his breath, he lumbered on to the tree where he'd tied his horse. The horse side-stepped when Bent's full weight settled on him.

Soon he was safely away, cantering on a muddy road at the edge of the Georgetown College campus, where forlorn pickets stood guard around the tents of the Sixty-ninth New York militia. His loss continued to hurt, though less and less as his rage intensified. Goddamn the man for dying just now. *Someone* had to intervene to prevent him from being shipped to Kentucky.

Although Bent had eaten a full breakfast, his desperation drove him back to Willard's for a huge dinner in the middle of the afternoon. He stuffed a fork laden with mashed potatoes into his mouth, sopped up chicken gravy with a wad of bread, and stuffed that in, too. Eating had been his narcotic since childhood.

It did little to soothe him today. He kept picturing Starkwether resentfully. He had even refused Bent his own name, insisting the boy take the name of the family with whom he'd been placed for his upbringing.

The Bents were tired, barely literate people who farmed near the Godforsaken hamlet of Felicity in Clermont County, Ohio. Fulmer Bent had been forty-seven when Starkwether's son was delivered to him. Bent had been quite small and didn't remember it. Or maybe he had blotted it from memory; only a very few of the most hurtful scenes from those years remained with him.

Mrs. Bent, who had numerous relatives across the river in Kentucky, was a peculiar woman with a wall eye. When she wasn't dragging him to visit her relations, she forced him to listen while she read the Bible aloud or lectured him in a whisper about the filth of the human body, the human mind, and a majority of human actions and desires. In his thirteenth year she caught him with his hand on himself and whipped him with a rope until he screamed and bled all over the bed sheets. No wonder Fulmer Bent spent more hours out of the house than in it. He was a secretive man whose only source of amusement seemed to be the mating activities of his livestock.

The Felicity years were the darkest of Bent's entire life, not only because he loathed his foster parents but also because he learned at age fifteen that his real father was alive in Washington and unable to acknowledge him. Before, he had presumed his father to be some dead relative of the Bents who had perhaps disgraced the family; they were evasive whenever the boy asked questions.

It was Dills who made the long coach and riverboat journey to Ohio to check on Bent's welfare and tell him the truth, at a time Dills had chosen because he believed the boy capable of receiving and accepting the facts. Dills spoke about Starkwether at length one sunny afternoon on the farm, careful that he and the boy were alone in shade near the well. The lawyer's phrases were tactful, even gentle, but he never guessed how deeply they wounded his listener. Ever afterward, no matter how much Starkwether helped with influence or money, there was submerged outrage in Bent's love for his father.

In Bent's sixteenth year, just before Starkwether secured the boy's appointment to the Military Academy, Fulmer Bent took pigs to market in Cincinnati and died in a shooting incident in a house of ill repute. That same autumn a sweet-voiced young clerk at the Felicity general store had initiated Bent sexually. Bent didn't have his first woman until two years later.

Long before Starkwether secured the Academy appointment, however, Elkanah Bent had begun to dream of a military career. The dream had its genesis in a cluttered Cincinnati bookshop to which the boy wandered one day while Fulmer Bent transacted business elsewhere. For five cents he bought a badly torn, water-stained life of Bonaparte. That was the start.

He saved little bits of the allowance money Dills sent twice a year. He bought, read, and reread lives of Alexander, Caesar, Scipio Africanus. But it was Bony whose heir and American counterpart he came to be in his florid imaginings—

Become a Bonaparte in Kentucky? He was more likely to become a corpse. The state was contested ground; half of its men had joined the Union, half the Confederacy. Lincoln kept hands off the slaveowners so they wouldn't foment secession. He absolutely would not go to a place like that.

Nervous sweat slicking his cheeks, he waved to the waiter. "Bring me another helping of pie." He gobbled it and leaned back, a drip of the sugary filling hanging from his lower lip like a moist icicle. Swollen with food—aching—he felt better, able to

76

think and plan again. One thing he would never deny about Fulmer Bent's wife: she was a splendid cook.

He had attended a country school with a lot of farmers' sons who teased him and conspired to make him the target of pranks. Once, they had filled his lunch pail with fresh cow dung. He had run home and found his foster mother pulling six of her yeasty, yellow-crusted loaves from the iron stove. He had devoured one and begged for another. From that day, she kept him stuffed. When he pleaded for second and third helpings or treats between meals, she was flattered and always gave in.

All the eating made him fatter and fatter. And unattractive to girls. But he learned to use the weight to fend off and punish bullies. He would cringe and cower, and when they thought they had him, he'd push them down and fall on them. Once he did that, they left him alone.

A third piece of pie tempted him now. But his belly hurt, so he concentrated on his problem. He still believed a great military future could be his, but not if he died in Kentucky.

He knew only one man who could intercede now. Bent had been warned against contacting him in person, but a desperate plight required desperate measures.

The office of Jasper Dills, Esquire, overlooked Seventh Street, the city's commercial center. The book-lined room was small, cramped, suggestive of a failing practice. It gave no hint of the wealth and status of its occupant.

Nervous, Bent lowered his buttocks into the visitor's chair to which the clerk had ushered him. He had to squeeze; the fit was tight. He had put on his dress uniform, but Dills's expression said it was a wasted effort.

"I thought you understood you were not to call here, Colonel."

"There are extenuating circumstances."

Dills raised one eyebrow, which nearly devastated his distraught visitor.

"I need your help urgently."

Dills kept a clean desk. In the center lay some sheets of legal foolscap. He inked a pen and began to draw, concentrating on the series of stars that emerged.

"You know your father can't help you any longer." The nib rasped; another star appeared. "I saw you skulking at the cemetery yesterday—come, don't deny it. The lapse is forgivable."

Rasp; scrape. Done with stars, the lawyer inked a blocky *B*. Then he shot a look at his caller. "This one is not."

Bent turned red, frightened and furious at the same time. How could this man daunt him so? Jasper Dills was no less than seventy and no more than five feet one. He had a child's hands and feet. Yet neither size nor age diminished the force he could put into his voice or the intimidating way he could eye a man, as he eyed Bent now.

"I beg—" swallow—"I beg to differ, sir. I'm desperate." In a few jumbled sentences, he described the reason. Throughout, Dills kept drawing: more *B*'s, then a series of finely detailed epaulettes, each smaller than the last. In the hazy yellow light falling through the dirty windowpanes, the attorney looked jaundiced.

At the end of Bent's recital, Dills kept him dangling in silence for ten seconds. "But I still can't understand why you came to see me, Colonel. I have no power to help you and no reason. My sole obligation as your father's executor is to follow his verbal instruction and see that you continue to receive your generous annual stipend."

"The money doesn't mean a goddamn thing if I'm shipped off to die in Kentucky!"

"But what can I do about it?"

"Get my orders changed. You've done it before—you or my father. Or was it those men who employed him?" That scored, all right; Dills stiffened noticeably. Here was the crucial bluff. "Oh, yes, I know something about them. I heard a few names. I saw my father twice, remember. For several hours each time. I heard names," he repeated.

"Colonel, you're lying."

"Am I? Then test me. Refuse to help. I shall very quickly talk to certain people who will be interested in the names of my father's employers. Or my parentage."

Silence. Bent breathed noisily. He'd won. He felt confident of it.

Dills sighed. "Colonel Bent, you have made a mistake. Two, in fact. As I've already indicated, the first was your decision to come here. The second is your ultimatum." He laid his pen on the scrawled stars. "Let me not resort to melodrama, only make this point as clearly as I can. The moment word reaches me that you have attempted to regularize or publicize your connection with my late client—or the moment I hear anything else detrimental to his reputation, including certain names I really doubt that you

78

know—you will be dead within twenty-four hours." Dills smiled. "Good day, sir."

He rose and walked to his bookshelves. Bent burst from the chair, started around the desk. "Damn you, how dare you say such a thing to Starkwether's own—"

Dills pivoted, closing a book with a gunshot sound. "I said good day."

As Bent blundered down the long flight to the street, an inner voice screamed: *He meant it. The man meant it. What shall I do now?*

In the office, Dills replaced the book and returned to his desk. Seated, he noticed his speckled hands. Shaking. The reaction angered and shamed him. Furthermore, it was unnecessary.

Certainly his former client's employers would want their names guarded. But Dills was confident Bent didn't know their identities. Further, Bent was patently a coward, hence could be bluffed. Of course, through certain of Starkwether's connections, Dills could easily have arranged for Bent to take a fatal musket ball. In Kentucky, it could even be made to appear that his killer was a reb. Such a scheme would only work to the lawyer's financial disadvantage, but Bent didn't know that.

That two parents with such positive character traits could have produced a son as weak and warped as Elkanah Bent confounded Dills's sense of order. Born in the meanest poverty in the Western woodlands, Starkwether had been gifted with guile and ambition. Bent's mother had possessed breeding and a background of wealth and eminence. And look at the sorry result. Perhaps force majeure was more than a legal conceit. Perhaps some illicit relationships and their fruit were condemned in heaven from the moment the seed fell.

Unable to compose himself or banish the memory of his visitor, Dills took a small brass key from his waistcoat. He unlocked a lower desk drawer, reached in for a ring of nine larger keys, and used one to enter the office closet. In the dusty dark, another key opened an iron strongbox. He drew out its contents. One thin file.

He examined the old letter which he had first read fourteen years ago. Starkwether, ailing, had given it to him permanently last December. The letter filled both sides of the sheet. His eyes dropped to the signature. The effect of reading that instantly recognizable name was always the same. Dills was stunned, astonished, impressed. The letter said in part:

You used me, Heyward. Then you left me. But I admit I shared a certain pleasure and cannot bring myself to abandon altogether the result of my mistake. Knowing the sort of man you are and what matters most to you, I am prepared to begin paying you a substantial yearly stipend, provided you accept parental responsibility for the child—care for him (although not necessarily in a lavish manner), help him in whatever way you deem reasonable—but most important, diligently monitor his whereabouts in order to prevent any circumstance or action on his part or the part of others which might lead to discovery of his parentage. Need I add that he must never learn my identity from you? Should that happen, whatever the reason, payment of the stipend will cease.

Dills wet his lips with his tongue. How he wished he had met the woman, even for an hour. A bastard would have smirched her name and spoiled her possibilities, and she had been clever and worldly enough to know that at eighteen. She had married splendidly. Again he turned the sheet over to gaze at the signature. Poor vengeful Bent would more than likely crack apart if he saw that last name.

The paragraph above it was the one of most direct interest to him:

Finally, in the event of your death, the same stipend will be paid to any representative you designate, so long as the boy lives and the above conditions are met.

At his desk, Dills inked his pen again, pondering. Alive, Starkwether's son was worth a good deal of money to him; dead, he was worth nothing. Without interfering too directly, perhaps he should see that Bent was spared hazardous duty out West.

Yes, definitely a good idea. Tomorrow he would speak to a contact in the War Department. He jotted a reminder on the foolscap, tore it off, and poked it well down into his waistcoat pocket. So much for Bent. Other duties pressed.

Starkwether's employers had become his, and they were interested in the possibility of New York City seceding from the

Union. It was a breathtaking concept: a separate city-state, trading freely with both sides in a war whose length the gentlemen could to some extent control. Powerful politicians, including Mayor Fernando Wood, had already endorsed secession publicly. Dills was researching precedents and preparing a report on potential consequences. He returned the letter to the strongbox and after three turns of three keys in three locks resumed work.

14

"What the hell did we do wrong?" George said, flinging away the stub of his cigar. It landed in front of the small, plain office building in the heart of the huge Hazard Iron complex.

"I honestly don't know, George," Christopher Wotherspoon replied with a glum look.

George's expression conveyed his fury to the hundreds of men streaming along the dirt street in both directions; the early shift was leaving, the next arriving. George didn't care if they saw his anger. Most would have heard the detonation when the prototype columbiad exploded on the test ground chopped out of the mountainside in a high, remote corner of the property. The big eight-inch smoothbore, cast around a water-cooled core by Rodman's method, had destroyed its crude wooden carriage and driven iron fragments big as daggers into the thick plank barrier protecting the test observers.

"I simply do not know," George's superintendent of works repeated. It was the second failure this week.

"All right, we'll adjust the temperature and try again. We'll try till hell freezes. They're screaming for artillery to protect the East

Coast, and one of the oldest ironworks in America can't turn out a single working gun. It's unbelievable."

Wotherspoon cleared his throat. "No, George, you misapprehend. It is war production. So far as I know, this works has never manufactured cannon before."

"But, by God, we should be able to master—"

"We will master it, George." Wotherspoon weighted the second word. "We will meet the delivery date specified in the contract and do so with pieces that perform satisfactorily." He risked a smile. "I guarantee it because Mr. Stanley helped us win the bid, and I am not anxious to displease him."

"I don't know why," George growled, staring at the faces passing. "You could knock him out with one punch."

"True, but one ought to be frugal with time. That would be a squandering of it."

The dry, donnish jest did nothing to improve George's mood. Still, he appreciated the young Scotsman's effort. And he knew Wotherspoon understood the reason for his impatience. It would be impossible for him to leave Hazard's or even think seriously about Cameron's offer until he was sure the company could fulfill the contract.

He had no doubts about Hazard's doing it, provided the problem wasn't one of method. He and Wotherspoon had repeatedly gone over the calculations together—and Wotherspoon was nothing if not thorough. That was one reason George had promoted the young bachelor so quickly.

Wotherspoon, thirty, was a slender, slow-spoken, sad-eyed sort with wavy brown hair and a merciless ambition concealed behind impeccable manners. He had apprenticed at a dying ironworks run by successors of the great Darby family at Coalbrookdale, in the valley of the Severn, the same part of England from which the founder of the Hazard family, a fugitive, had fled in the late seventeenth century. As the dominance of the Severn's iron trade diminished, Wotherspoon had chosen emigration to America over a shorter journey to the new factories in Wales. He had arrived in Lehigh Station four years ago in search of a job, a wife, and a fortune. He had the first and was still in pursuit of the others. If he solved the riddle of the flawed castings, George knew he could place day-by-day control of Hazard's in the Scotsman's hands and never worry.

He was certain he must leave Lehigh Station and serve; his

quandary was a simple question: Where? By pulling a few wires, he could certainly obtain a field command, lead a regiment. Although he loathed combat, it was not fear that rendered the idea unappealing, but a conviction that his experience would be of greatest use in the Ordnance Department, which meant Cameron and Stanley and Isabel. What a damned, dismal choice.

Wotherspoon broke the glum reverie. "Why don't you go home, George?" Until a year ago, the younger man had addressed him as sir. Then mutual friendship and trust, and George's request, put them on a first-name basis. "I shall spend a while reviewing the Rodman notes once more. Somehow or other, I suspect the fault lies with us. The inventor of the process graduated from your school—"

"That's right, class of '41."

"Then he can hardly be wrong, can he, now?"

This time, George laughed. He lit another cigar and spoke with it clenched in his teeth. "Don't try to sell that opinion in Washington. Half the pols down there think West Point caused the war. Stanley's last letter said Cameron intends to crucify the place in a report he's going to issue. And I'm thinking of working for him. I must be daft."

Wotherspoon compressed his lips, his version of a smile. "No, no—we live in an imperfect world, that's all. You might also consider this: It's conceivable that you could help West Point more there than you could here."

"That's crossed my mind. Good night, Christopher."

"Good night, my friend."

Trudging the dusty street among lines of men flowing in both directions, George heard someone sneer about the test failure. He squared his shoulders and hunted for the offender, but of course couldn't find him. The jibe didn't bother him long; he knew that no owner could be popular with every person who worked for him. Besides, respect mattered more than popularity. Respect and peace with his own conscience. Hazard's paid fair wages. George operated no company store to hold his people in thrall. And he refused to hire children.

A headache started above his eyes. So many problems lately. The bad castings. Brett's unhappiness. The possibility of a War Department attack on West Point—

Stanley's letter, pretending to be informative, had actually been meant as an irritant, and George knew it. Referring to the Academy as a "seedbed of treason," his brother said the secretary had cited lax discipline and a vague but sinister "Southern predisposition" to explain why so many regular officers had defected. He shouldn't even consider working for a hack like that.

Of course Wotherspoon had stated one good reason for a contrary view. George's Washington lawyer stated another. In two recent letters, he'd described the urgent need for men of talent and honor to offset the hordes of incompetents already placed in jobs by their political patrons. Thank heaven he didn't have to decide today.

The climb to Belvedere was tiring in the wet, heavy air of late afternoon. He took off his black alpaca coat, loosened his string cravat, and inhaled and exhaled vigorously as he walked. Occasionally some cigar smoke went scorching down his throat, but he was used to that.

On the dusty path, he stopped to gaze up at the mountains. He recalled the lessons his dead mother had tried to pass on to him. He saw the emblem of the most important one above him on the summits—the mountain laurel, tossing in the wind.

His mother, Maude, had instilled in George her own mystic feeling about the laurel. Hardy, it endured the worst of weathers. So did the Hazards, she said. The laurel was strength born of love, she said. Nothing save love could lift men above the meanness woven through their natures and all their days.

She had talked of the laurel when he wondered about the wisdom of bringing Constance to Lehigh Station, where Catholics were largely scorned. He had repeated her words when Billy despaired of Orry Main's temporary opposition to his marriage with Brett.

Endurance and love. Perhaps it would prove enough. He prayed so.

On Belvedere's long, broad veranda, he caught his breath. Sweat ran on his neck and soaked his shirt. He was home sooner than usual. It was a rare chance to relax in a tepid bath with a cigar. Perhaps he could reason out the cause of the cannon shattering. A frown on his face, he let himself in quietly and started upstairs, stopping in the library for the copybook containing his notes on the Rodman process.

"George? You're early. What a grand surprise."

He turned toward the door.

"I thought I heard you come in," Constance continued as she

entered. Starting to kiss him, she held back. "Darling, what's wrong?"

"The heat. It's infernal out there."

"No, it's something else. Ah—the test. That's it, isn't it?"

He slung his coat over his shoulder, affecting nonchalance. "Yes. We failed again."

"Oh, George, I'm so sorry."

She gave herself then, tightly and closely. One cool arm encircled his damp neck while her sweet mouth kissed. Amazing how it helped. She was the laurel.

"I have a piece of good news," she said presently. "I finally heard from Father."

"A letter?"

"Yes, today."

"Good. I know you've been anxious. Is he all right?"

"I don't know how to answer that. Come along and have a glass of cold cider, and I'll explain. The cider's turned a little—it'll lift your spirits better than cook's lemonade."

"You lift my spirits," he said, closing his fingers as she clasped his hand. He took pleasure in letting her lead him out of the library.

When George read the letter, he understood her puzzling answer. "I can appreciate his disgust with Texas. Patrick Flynn loves a great many things about the South, but slavery isn't one of them. But California? Is that the answer?"

"Not to my way of thinking. Imagine trying to start a new law practice at his age."

"I doubt he'd have a problem with that," George said, picturing the ruddy attorney who'd come to the Gulf Coast from County Limerick. George sat on the yard-square chopping block in the large kitchen, his feet dangling six inches above the floor. The cook and her helpers worked and chatted as if the Hazards weren't there. Constance strove to maintain a relaxed household; except for money matters, there were few secrets.

George sipped the cold cider. It had a bite worthy of a saloon. Noting that his preceding remark hadn't reassured his wife, he said, "He's a tough, adaptable fellow, your father."

"But he'll be sixty this year. And California isn't safe. In this morning's paper, I read a dispatch about Southerners plotting to set up some kind of second confederacy on the Pacific coast."

85

"That's a common rumor these days. One week it's California, the next Chicago."

"I still say the trip would be too long and hard and dangerous. Father's old and all alone."

He smiled. "Not quite. He travels with an eminently dependable guard and companion. I mean that Paterson Colt with the barrel a foot long. I've never seen him without it. Don't you remember when he wore it to our wedding? Furthermore, he's expert at using it."

Constance wouldn't be soothed. "I just don't know what I'm going to do."

George finished the cider and looked earnestly into the blue eyes he loved so well. "Pardon my impertinence, Mrs. Hazard, but I don't believe you can do anything. I didn't notice a request for permission in that letter. It merely says he's going, and he wrote it on April thirtieth. I expect he's halfway across the Sierras by now."

"Oh, good Lord—the date. I was too worried to notice it." She snatched the letter from the chopping block, glanced at the first page, and softly said, "Oh!" a second time. He jumped down and hugged her to help as she'd helped him. They left the kitchen, going upstairs, where he undressed for his bath.

"I'm sorry if I seemed cross downstairs," she said while he peeled off sweaty cotton drawers. Naked, he wrapped his arms around her again.

"Not cross. Understandably concerned. I'm afraid I was sarcastic with you. I apologize."

"We're even." She locked her hands behind his head and gave him a kiss. They held motionless for ten seconds, comfort flowing from one to the other. Such moments were as close as George ever came to understanding the nature of human love.

He took note of the physical side asserting itself. "If we keep this up, I won't get a bath."

She sniffed. "Which you definitely need."

With a mock roar, he flung her backward on the bed, tickling her till she gave her usual plea for mercy. He set off for the bathroom, turned back at the door. "We do have some problems we can do something about. Cameron's invitation, for one."

"The decision's yours, George. I don't want to be any closer to Stanley and Isabel than necessary. But I know you feel there are more important considerations."

"I wish I didn't. Congressman Thad Stevens said Cameron would steal a red-hot stove."

"I have a suggestion. Why don't you go to Washington and talk to some of the Ordnance people? It might help you decide."

"Splendid idea. I can't do it till we solve the problem of the castings, though." He thought a moment. "Do you think I could stand to work near Stanley? I took control of Hazard's away from him, banned his wife from this house—I even hit him once. He hasn't forgotten. And Isabel's vindictive."

"I know that all too well. You must take all of that into consideration. But if you do accept, I'll follow with the children as soon as I can."

His nod showed his troubled state of mind as he walked out of sight. She remained seated on the bed. The room was still; the curtains hung straight; the breeze had died. She understood her husband's uncertainty because she shared it. Old beliefs and relationships had been shattered by this crisis the press had already named "a war of brothers," even though no major battles had been fought. Just as she worried about her father, George feared for the well-being of his friend Orry and for Madeline, the woman Orry loved. How insignificant and helpless they all seemed; single strokes on some giant's canvas whose final design no one could see.

Discussion of the Cameron offer resumed at supper. Looking refreshed in a clean white shirt, George told Brett that Constance had made a very practical suggestion. He would go to Washington before he made up his mind.

"Will you take me with you?" Brett exclaimed. "I could see Billy."

"I can't go immediately." He explained the reason and watched her bright hope tarnish before his eyes. Guilty, he let his thoughts race. It wasn't ten seconds before he continued. "But here's another possibility. I have two important contracts that must go to my attorney down there. I suppose I could find some trustworthy older fellow around the office—he could take them. You could go, too."

"You still won't allow me to go alone?"

"Brett, we disposed of that subject weeks ago."

"Not to my satisfaction."

"Don't get angry. You're an intelligent and capable young woman. But Washington's a cesspool. You don't belong there by yourself—even if we disregard your unmistakably Southern speech, which makes you a target for all sorts of hostility. No, this other way's better. I'll find a man and have him ready to go within a day or two. Pack your valise and stand by."

"Oh, thank you," she said, rushing around the table to hug him. "Can you forgive my bad temper? You two have been so kind, but I've seen so little of Billy since we were married—"

"I understand." He patted her hand. "Nothing to forgive."

She kept thanking him, tears in her eyes. It was one of the rare occasions when Constance saw George flustered.

Later, in their play before love-making upstairs, she said: "Do you really have papers to send to Washington?"

"I'll find some."

She laughed and kissed him and drew him to her breast with great joy.

15

"This carpetbag's heavier than old Fuss and Feathers." Billy groaned as he put it down.

"I brought you a lot of little extras I thought you'd need: books, three havelocks I sewed myself, socks, drawers, a new skillet, one of those small sewing kits for soldiers—"

"In the army they're called housewives." He plucked off his kepi and with his other hand reached back to close the door.

Both kept their voices low, as if wary of listeners. It was three on a sultry afternoon, and they were alone in a room in a boardinghouse. Though they were married, it struck Brett as deliciously wicked.

Stuffy and slope-ceilinged, the small room had but one inadequate window to admit the noise of the unseen street. At that, Billy had been lucky to find any accommodations at all after receiving her telegraph message.

"I've wanted to see you, Brett. See you, love you—" He sounded strange; shy and almost frightened. "I've wanted it so much I ache."

"Oh, I know, my darling. I feel the same. But we've never—"

"What?"

Scarlet, she averted her head. He touched her chin.

"What, Brett?"

She didn't dare meet his eyes. Her face burned. "Before, we've always—made love in the dark."

"I don't want to wait that long."

"No, I—don't either."

He helped with the clothing, rapidly yet without roughness. One by one the layers were shed and tossed anywhere, and there came in the hot gloom that petrifying moment when nothing was concealed, and she knew he'd be revolted by the sight of her body.

The fear melted as he stretched out his hands. He touched her shoulders and slowly slid his palms down her arms, a caress each found tender and exciting. His loving smile changed subtly to a look close to exaltation. Her smile burst into view, radiant, and her joyous laughter accompanied equally joyous tears. Only moments later, she helped him hurry into her for the reunion that was all the sweeter because it was so swift and urgently needed by both of them.

Captain Farmer had given him an overnight furlough. Late in the afternoon, Billy took Brett on a tour of the area near President's Park. The number of soldiers on the streets astonished her. They wore navy, they wore gray, and a few wore such gaudy outfits that they resembled the household troops of some Arab prince. She also noticed a great many blacks wandering.

About an hour before sunset, they crossed a foul-smelling canal to an uncompleted park near the fantastical red towers of the Smithsonian Institution. Several dozen fine carriages had brought well-dressed civilians to watch a retreat exercise conducted by a volunteer regiment, the First Rhode Island. Billy pointed out its commanding officer, Colonel Burnside, a man with magnificent side whiskers. The regimental band played, flags flew, and it was all marvelously exciting and unthreatening; the hour at the boardinghouse had left Brett euphoric.

Billy explained that retreats, parades, reviews, and other public displays were very much a part of the military presence in and around the city. "But there will surely be a battle soon. They say Lincoln wants it, and it looks like Davis does, too. He's got his most popular general commanding the Alexandria line."

"You mean General Beauregard?"

He took her arm and slipped it around his as they strolled. "Yes. Once upon a time this army thought pretty highly of Old Bory. Now everyone calls him a scared little peacock. He didn't help matters when he said our side wanted only two things from the South—booty and beauty. Pretty damned insulting."

Our side. It had become hers by marriage. Whenever that occurred to her, confusion and vague feelings of disloyalty set in. Tonight was no different.

"Does Captain Farmer know when the fighting will start?"

"No. Sometimes I wonder if anyone does—including our senior commanders."

"You disapprove of them?"

"Most of the professionals are all right. The Academy men. But there are generals who got shoulder straps through political connections. They're pretty terrible. Arrogant as it sounds, I'm glad I went to West Point and into the engineers. It's the best branch."

"Also the first into battle."

"Sometimes."

"Scares me to death."

He wanted to confess it scared him, too, but that would only worry her more.

For Brett, the glitter began to fall off the city as they walked to the hotel chosen for supper. They passed a pair of noncoms idling along, thuggish fellows. She heard one snicker and say all officers were shitasses.

Billy stiffened but didn't turn or stop. "Don't pay any attention. If I stepped in every time I heard that kind of remark, I wouldn't have a minute for my duties. Army discipline's terrible—but not in Lije Farmer's company. I'm anxious to have you meet him."

"When will that be?"

"Tomorrow. I'll take you out to camp and show you the fortifications we're building. Plans call for a ring of them, perhaps as many as fifty or sixty, surrounding the city."

"Do you like your captain?"

"Very much. He's an extremely religious man. Prays a lot. The officers and noncoms pray right along with him."

"You? Praying? Billy, have you—?" She didn't know how to complete the question tactfully.

He made it unnecessary. "No, I'm still the same godless wretch you married. I pray for one reason. You don't disobey Lije Farmer. In fairness, I must say men with his kind of deep conviction aren't uncommon in the army."

Abruptly, he steered her away from the curb where two white men were punching a ragged Negro. Billy ignored that, too.

But she couldn't. "I see abuse of slaves isn't confined to the South."

"He's probably a freedman. Slave or free, nigras aren't too popular around here."

"Then why on earth are you going to war for them?"

"Brett, we've argued this before. We're at war because some crazy men in your home state broke the country in half. Nobody's mustering to fight for the nigra. Slavery's wrong; I'm convinced of that. Practically speaking, though, maybe it can't and shouldn't be done away with too quickly. The President feels that way, they say. So do most soldiers."

He felt uneasy attempting to justify his view. He wasn't shading the truth, however. None but a fierce abolitionist minority in the army believed they'd gone to war to dismantle the peculiar institution. They had mustered to punish the fools and traitors who thought they could dismantle the Union.

Brett's pensive frown suggested she wanted to argue. He was glad to see the gaslit entrance to Willard's a few steps ahead.

In the bright, busy lobby, he noticed her still frowning. "Come on, now—no politics and no gloom. You're only here for two days. I want us to have a good time."

"Do we have to pay a call on Stanley and his wife?"

"Not unless you put a gun to my head. I'm ashamed to say it, but I haven't seen them since I reported for duty. I'd sooner face Old Bory's whole army."

She laughed; the evening was back on a better track. At the dining-room entrance, he said, "I'm hungry. Are you?"

"Famished. But we oughtn't to waste a lot of time on supper."

Glancing at him with a smile he understood, she followed the bowing headwaiter. Billy strode after her, straight-backed, straight-faced, jubilant:

"Definitely not."

In the night, Brett woke, alarmed by a distant ominous rumbling. Billy stirred, sensed something amiss, rolled over to face her in the dark.

"What's wrong?"

"What's that noise?"

"Army wagons."

"I didn't hear it before."

"You just didn't notice. If this town or this war has one primary sound, it's the wagons. They go all day and all night. Here —let me curl around you. Maybe it will help you go back to sleep."

It didn't. She lay for over an hour listening to the plodding hoofs, creaking axles, grinding wheels—the thunder below the horizon, warning of inevitable storm.

In the morning she felt tired. A large breakfast, including some passable grits, perked her up a little. Billy had hired a fine barouche to drive across the Potomac. They set out under a threatening sky, and there was real thunder occasionally, muttering counterpoint to the wagons she heard quite clearly now.

As they crossed Long Bridge, Billy told her more about Farmer. He was a bachelor, from Indiana, and had graduated from the Military Academy thirty-five years ago. "Just when a tremendous religious revival swept through the place. The captain and a classmate, Leonidas Polk, led the movement in the corps of cadets. Three years after graduation, Farmer resigned to become a Methodist circuit rider. I once asked him where he lived all those years, and he said on top of a horse. His home's really a little town called Greencastle."

"I think I've heard of Polk, an Episcopal bishop in the South."

"That's the man."

"Why did Farmer rejoin the army? Isn't he too old?"

"No man's too old if he has engineering experience. And Old Mose hates slavery."

"What did you call him?"

"Mose—as in Moses. The captain was put in charge of this volunteer company until the regular engineers return from Florida. The men decided Farmer is a good leader, so they christened

92

him Old Mose. The name suits him. He might have stepped straight from the Old Testament. I still call him Lije—ah, here we are." He pointed. "That's one of the magnificent projects for which I'm responsible."

"Mounds of dirt?"

"Earthworks," he corrected, amused. "Back there we're to build a timbered powder magazine."

"Does this place have a name?"

"Fort Something-or-other. I forget exactly. They're all Fort Something-or-other." They drove on.

Alexandria, a small town of brick homes and numerous commercial buildings, seemed nearly as crowded as Washington. Billy showed Brett the Marshall House, where Lincoln's close friend Colonel Ellsworth had been shot and killed. "It happened the day the army occupied the town. Ellsworth was trying to haul down a rebel flag."

Beyond Alexandria, they came upon tents, a vast white city of them. Around the perimeter, soldiers drilled in trampled fields. Mounted officers galloped in every direction. Bare-chested men dug trenches and dragged logs with chains. Brett could hardly hear Billy for the cursing and the bugling and the ubiquitous wagons.

She observed several squads drilling. "I've never seen such clumsy men. No two are in step."

"They're volunteers. Their officers aren't much better. They stay up all night boning on *Hardee's Tactics* so they can teach next morning. Even then they do a poor job."

"I have no trouble recognizing you as a West Point man," she teased.

On they went, through the vast changing landscape of mess tents smoking, horse-drawn artillery pieces racing and wheeling, regimental and national flags flapping, drums beating, men singing—it was all new, amazing, and festive, though a little frightening, too, because of what it signified.

They passed an unfinished redoubt and stopped before a tent exactly like the others. Billy led her in and saluted. "Sir? If this is not an inconvenient time, may I have the honor of presenting my wife? Mrs. William Hazard—Captain Farmer."

The white-haired officer rose from the flimsy table strewn with diagrams of fortifications. "An honor, Mrs. Hazard. An honor and a privilege."

93

He took her hand and shook it with slow formality. He had a powerful grip. *Billy's right,* she thought, delighted. *He could personate one of the prophets on stage.*

"I am delighted to make your acquaintance and mightily pleased to have your husband in my command. I hope that happy situation will continue indefinitely," the captain said. "Ah, but I am remiss. Please do sit down—here, on my stool." He placed it in front of the desk. "I deeply regret my furnishings are inadequate to the occasion."

Seated, Brett observed the truth of that statement. The tent contained nothing but a table, a camp bed, and five crates, each bearing the words AMERICAN BIBLE SOCIETY. On top of one lay a string-tied packet of tracts. In Charleston, she'd often seen similar four-page leaflets. The one in view was titled "Why Do You Curse?"

Farmer saw her take note of it. "I have thus far lacked the time to conduct Sunday school or evening prayer services, but I am prepared. We must build bridges to heaven even as we raise defenses against the ungodly."

"Sad to say," Brett told him, "I was born among the ungodly."

"Yes, I am aware. Be assured, I meant no personal slight. I cannot deceive you, however. It is my conviction that the Almighty detests all those who keep our black brethren in chains."

His words irked her; they would have irked any South Carolinian. Yet there was a paradox. She found his voice and oratory unexpectedly stirring. Billy looked uneasy, as if thinking, They aren't *my* black brethren.

Brett said, "I respect your forthrightness, Captain. I only regret the issue must be resolved by war. Billy and I want to get on with our lives. Start a family. Instead, all I can see ahead is a period of danger."

Lije Farmer locked his hands behind his lower back. "You are correct, Mrs. Hazard. And we shall confront it because the portion has been passed to us—God's will be done. However, I am persuaded the war will be brief. We shall emerge the victors. As Scripture tells us, the thoughts of the righteous are right, but the counsels of the wicked are deceit. The wicked are overthrown and are not—but the house of the righteous shall stand."

Instantly, she was simmering again. Billy saw, and silently pleaded for restraint while Farmer continued.

"The wicked is snared by the transgression of his lips, but the just shall come out of trouble."

Ready to retort, she didn't because he took her by surprise, defused the tension by stepping to Billy's side and dropping a fatherly arm over his shoulders. Farmer's smile shone.

"If there are perilous days ahead, the Lord God will see this good young man through them. The Lord God is a sun and shield. Even so, I shall look after him, too. When you return to your home, carry my reassurance in your heart. I will do everything I can to see that William rejoins you speedily and unharmed."

At that moment, Brett forgot issues and fell in love with Lije Farmer.

16

Miles away in the South Carolina low country, another man lived with dreams of revenge as vivid as Elkanah Bent's.

Justin LaMotte, owner of the plantation named Resolute and impoverished scion of one of the state's oldest families, yearned to punish his wife, Madeline. She had fled to the Main plantation to expose the plot to kill the Yankee who'd married Orry Main's sister.

But Justin's grudge went back much further. For years, Madeline had disgraced him with her outspoken nature and disregard of accepted female behavior. Except, he recalled with some satisfaction, she had been submissive, if unexciting, when he exercised his connubial rights. He had curbed her offending activities for a while by secretly administering laudanum in her food. Now she was compounding past disgrace by living openly with her lover. The whole district knew she intended to marry Orry the moment she obtained a divorce. She'd never get one. But that wasn't enough. Justin spent hours every day concocting schemes to ruin Orry or imagining scenes in which he punished Madeline with knives or fire.

At the moment he lay submerged in tepid water one of his niggers had poured into the heavy zinc tub in his bedroom. Spirals of dark brown dye coiled away from dampened hair on the back of his head. The absence of any gray had a curious effect of calling attention to, rather than obscuring, his age; the color of his hair, so clearly artificial, lent him the look of a waxwork, though he was oblivious.

Justin was trying to relieve the tension that had bedeviled him lately. His wife wasn't the sole cause. There were problems with the Ashley Guards, the regiment he and his brother Francis were attempting to raise by expanding the home defense unit they had organized in the tense months of the Sumter confrontation.

Brown-spotted white silk, folded into layers and tied vertically, hid the left side of Justin's face. When he had tried to prevent Madeline from leaving Resolute, she had defended herself with an heirloom sword snatched from the wall of the foyer. One stroke of the nicked blade dug a red trench from his left brow through his upper lip to the midpoint of his chin. The scabrous, slow-healing wound hurt emotionally as well as physically. He had reason to hate the bitch.

It was late afternoon; stifling. Shadows of Spanish moss on water oaks outside patterned the bedroom's mildewed pine-block floor. Below the second-story piazza, his brother shouted drill commands. Fed up with trying to train white trash—all the gentlemen of the district except that one-armed scoundrel Main had mustered with other units—Justin had turned today's instruction over to Francis and retired.

His brother had spent lavishly to outfit the regiment. On a stand near the tub hung canary-colored trousers and a smart braided chasseur jacket of bright green, styled after the *habit-tunique* of the French. The outfit was completed by handsome top boots worn outside the trousers; the tops drooped above the knee, in the European manner.

It galled Justin that he and Francis couldn't find more white men who appreciated the value and distinction of such a uniform or what a rare opportunity it was to be led by LaMottes. That damned Wade Hampton had outfitted his legion as drably as cowherds, and men had stampeded to sign up.

Justin loathed the Columbia planter for other reasons, too. LaMottes had arrived in Carolina years before the first Hampton, yet today the latter name was the more honored one. Justin lived on next to nothing, while Hampton appeared to increase his wealth effortlessly; everyone said he was the richest man in the state.

Hampton had refused to attend the secession convention—had even spoken publicly against it—and now he was a hero. He was already in Virginia, with companies of foot, artillery, and cavalry slavishly panting after him while Justin languished at home, cuckolded by his wife and unable to find more than two companies of men—and those ruffians who were always drinking, punching, or stabbing one another or handling their old muskets and squirrel rifles in an unmilitary way.

God, how it depressed him. He sank another half an inch in the water. Then he realized he no longer heard Francis cracking out orders. Instead, the sounds coming up from below were shouts and yelps and unfriendly obscenities. *"Damn them."* The oafs were brawling again. Well, let Francis settle it.

He anticipated a quick end to the noise. Instead, the laughter, the encouraging yells grew louder; so did the swearing and the thump of blows. The bedroom door opened. A black youth named Mem—short for Agamemnon—shot his head in.

"Mr. Justin? Your brother say come, please. They's trouble."

Furious, Justin heaved himself out of the tub. Dye-tinted water dripped from his nose, fingers, half-melon paunch. "How dare you come in here without waiting for permission!" He hit Mem a hard blow with closed fist.

The boy yelled. His eyes opened wide, and for an instant Justin saw such rage he feared an attack. A new, unhealthy spirit was stirring among slaves in the district now that the black Republican Yankees had begun to prosecute their war to rob decent men of their property. Lately there had been an unexplained sharp rise in nigger funerals; some said the coffins being buried contained firearms for an uprising. Old white fears of black skin blew across the low country like the pestilential breezes of summertime.

"Get out," Justin shouted at his slave. Whatever brief rebelliousness Mem had felt was gone now. He ran, slamming the

97

door. From the bed, Justin picked up his stomach-cinching corset. Francis shouted his name; he sounded frightened.

Cursing, Justin flung the corset down and tugged on his tight canary trousers. Patches of dampness immediately appeared on thigh, crotch, and rump. He buttoned his fly as he tore down the main stairs, stopping only to yank the old saber from its pegs.

He rushed into the sunshine and found the fight in progress at one end of the ramshackle house. The Ashley Guards, their fine uniforms carelessly soiled, encircled two men wrestling for possession of an ancient Hall breechloader: the Lemke cousins, ill-tempered cretins who ran a prosperous farm nearby.

Wizened Francis hurried to his brother. "Drunk as owls, both of them. Better fetch some of the niggers—these boys are enjoying themselves too much to help us stop it."

No doubt about that. A couple of the guards sniggered at Justin's sopping pants and the visible quarter-globe of his paunch above. "Christ, can't you discipline them?" he whispered to Francis. "Must I always be the one?"

He wasn't going to be the one this time. Each of the Lemkes had two powerful hands on the contested weapon, and each pulled hard on it. One Lemke rammed his head forward and sank teeth into the other's shoulder, biting deeply enough to bring blood through the uniform. No, thank you, thought Justin, and walked away; he'd find four or five bucks and make them take the risk.

One Lemke changed the position of his hands while the other forced the barrel down. Men near the muzzle backed clear. The piece went off with a smoky boom.

Justin felt a hard hit that began to burn as he pitched toward the ground. He struck chin-first, screaming in pain and outrage. A great red flower bloomed on the yellow field of his buttocks.

17

At Mont Royal, the large rice plantation on the west bank of the Ashley River above Charleston, the present head of the Main family faced a decision similar to the one confronting his friend George Hazard.

From boyhood, Orry Main had wanted to be a soldier. He had graduated in the West Point class of '46 and taken part in some of the hottest action of the Mexican War. At Churubusco, outside Mexico City, he had lost his left arm, partly because of the cowardice and enmity of Elkanah Bent. The injury had forced Orry to abandon his cherished dream of a military career.

Difficult years followed his return to South Carolina. He fell helplessly in love with Justin LaMotte's wife, and she with him, though honor had restricted their long affair to occasional secret meetings without the physical consummation both of them wanted.

Now, tangled events had brought Madeline under his roof to stay. Whether they'd be able to marry legally was another question. The state's divorce law was complex, and LaMotte was doing everything possible to prevent Madeline from gaining her freedom. He was doing that despite a circumstance that would have driven most white Southern men to a directly opposite course. Madeline's mother had been a beautiful New Orleans quadroon. Madeline was one-eighth black, which mattered little to Orry. Though the truth would have been a powerful weapon against Justin, she had lacked the cruelty to use it. But she had certainly imagined the scene of revelation, particularly his reaction, often enough.

In the small office building from which his father and his father's father had run the plantation, Orry sat at the old, littered desk confronting still another issue: papers he must sign if he were to show his loyalty and support the new Confederate government with part of his earnings. It was a humid afternoon, typical for the low country in July. In peacetime, he and Madeline more than likely would have escaped to a summer residence upcountry, where cooler weather prevailed.

Hazy sunshine splashed the office windows. The air smelled of violets and the perfume of the sweet olive, which he could always bring to mind no matter how far from Mont Royal he traveled. Wishing he didn't have to wade through the document in hand, he watched an inch-long palmetto bug scurry along a light-burnished sill near his desk, bound from dark to dark. *As are we all.*

He shook his head, irritated with himself. But the mood refused to pass. Melancholy times brought melancholy feelings.

Conversation, occasional laughter or singing reached him from the nearby kitchen building. He comprehended none of what he heard. His thoughts had turned from the papers to the commission that had been offered to him—staff duty in the Richmond office of Bob Lee, the veteran officer whose loyalty to his native Virginia had forced him to leave the federal army. Lee was presently the special military adviser to Jefferson Davis.

The prospect of desk duty didn't thrill Orry, though he supposed it was unrealistic to expect a field command. Not entirely so, however; not if Richmond was inclined to follow the example of the enemy. An officer Orry had heard about but never met in Mexico, Phil Kearny, had also lost his left arm there—and he was now a brigadier commanding Union volunteers.

Though his sense of duty was strong, he hesitated to accept the commission for a number of other reasons. Davis was said to be difficult. A brave soldier—a West Point man—he was notorious for wanting to lead troops and, in lieu of that, for maintaining tight control of those who did.

Further, Orry's sister Ashton and her husband, James Huntoon, were in Richmond, where Huntoon held some government job. When Orry had discovered the malicious part Ashton played in the near-murder of Billy Hazard, he had ordered her and her husband to leave Mont Royal and never return. The thought of being anywhere near them repelled him.

Next, he had no overseer. Younger men he might have hired had all rushed off to serve. An older one with brains and enough physical strength for the job couldn't be found. He had advertised in the Charleston and Columbia papers and heard from three applicants, all unacceptable.

Most important, his mother was in poor health. And he hated to leave Madeline. That was not merely selfishness. If he were gone, Justin might try to strike at her for the damage she had done to his face and his reputation.

The slaves might pose a threat as well. He hadn't discussed it with Madeline—he didn't want to alarm her unnecessarily—but he had begun to detect subtle changes in the demeanor and behavior of some of the bucks. In the past, harsh discipline had seldom been necessary at Mont Royal and never condoned, except once— a cat-hauling ordered by his late father. In the current situation, Cousin Charles's boyhood friend Cuffey was the most notable offender; he bore watching.

Reluctantly, Orry redirected his attention to the thick, blue-backed document ornamented with seals impressed in wax. If he signed, he would be agreeing to surrender a substantial portion of his rice profits for the year in exchange for government bonds of equal value. This so-called produce loan had been conceived to help finance the war for which Orry, like his friend George, had scant enthusiasm. Orry understood the futility of the South's military adventure because he understood some simple figures first called to his attention, dourly, by his brother Cooper.

About twenty-two millions lived in the North. There, too, you found most of the old Union's industrial plants, rail trackage, telegraphic lines, mineral and monetary wealth. The eleven states of the Confederacy had a population of something like nine million; a third of those, slaves, would never be of use to the war effort except in menial ways.

Dubious, not to say dangerous, attitudes about the war prevailed these days. Fools like the LaMotte brothers snickered at the suggestion that the South could be invaded—or, if it were, that the result could be anything but glorious Confederate victory. From aristocrats to yeomen, most Southerners had a proud belief in their own abilities, which led to an unrealistic conviction that one good man from Dixie could whip ten Yankee shopkeepers anywhere, anytime, world without end, Amen.

In very rare moments of chauvinism, Orry shared some of those beliefs. He would match his younger cousin Charles against any other officer. He saw the same courage in Charles's commander, Wade Hampton. And he found truth—though not the whole of it—in the maxim he had memorized in his young, hopeful years. In war, Bonaparte said, men are nothing; a man is everything.

Even so, to imagine the North had no soldiers to equal those from the South was idiocy. Suicidal. Orry could recall any number of first-rate Yankees from the Academy, including one he had known personally and liked very much. Where was Sam Grant serving now?

No answer to that—and no way to tell which way this strange, unwanted war might go. He forced himself back to the occasionally baffling legalisms of the bond agreement. The sooner he finished work for the day, the sooner he'd see Madeline.

About four, Orry returned from surveying the fields. He wore boots, breeches, and a loose white shirt whose empty left sleeve was held up at the shoulder by a bright pin. At thirty-five, Orry was as slender as he had been at fifteen and carried himself with confidence and grace despite his handicap. His eyes and hair were brown, his face rather long. Madeline said he grew handsomer as he aged, but he doubted that.

He had signed the bond agreement. Having done so, he stopped worrying about repayment. A decision prompted by patriotism oughtn't to have any conditions on it.

He crossed the head of the half-mile lane leading down to the river road. Mossy live oaks hid it from the light most of the day. He walked around the corner of the great house, which faced a formal garden and the pier on the slow-moving Ashley. Light footfalls sounded on the piazza overhead but stopped as he moved out from beneath it. Above him he saw a small, plump woman in her late sixties gazing contentedly at the cloudless sky.

"Good afternoon, Mother."

In response to his call, Clarissa Gault Main glanced down and smiled in a polite, puzzled way. "Good afternoon. How are you?"

"Just fine. You?"

The smile broadened, benign. "Oh, splendid—thank you so much." She turned and drifted inside. He shook his head. He had identified himself as her son, but the prompt was wasted; she no longer knew him. Fortunately, the Mont Royal blacks, with one or two exceptions, loved Clarissa. She was unobtrusively supervised and protected by everyone with whom she came in contact.

Where was Madeline? In the garden? As he studied it, he heard her inside. He found her in the parlor examining a cylindrical package nearly five feet long and heavily wrapped. She ran to put her arms around him.

"Careful," he said and laughed. "I'm dusty and sweaty as a mule."

"Sweaty, dusty—I love you in any condition." She planted a long, sweet kiss on his dry mouth. Refreshing as water from a mountain well. She locked her hands behind his neck while they embraced, and he felt the lushness of her full figure against him. Though legal marriage was as yet denied them, they shared the easy physical intimacy of a couple wed a long time and still in love. They slept without night clothes—Madeline's kind and forthright nature had quickly rid him of sensitivity about the appearance of his stump.

She drew back. "How has the day been?"

"Good. War or no war, these past weeks have been the happiest I've ever known."

She sighed a murmurous agreement, twining her fingers in his as they stood with foreheads touching. Madeline was a full-bosomed woman with lustrous dark eyes and hair and a richly contrasting pale complexion. "Justin has the means to make me a tiny bit happier, I confess."

"I'm sure we'll overcome that obstacle." The truth was, he wasn't sure, but he never admitted it. Over her shoulder he studied the parcel. "What's that?"

"I don't know. It's addressed to you. It came up from the dock an hour ago."

"That's right, the river sloop was due today—"

"Captain Asnip sent a note with the package. He said it arrived on the last vessel into Charleston before the blockade began. I did notice it carries the name of a transshipping firm in Nassau. Do you know what's in it?"

"I might."

"You ordered it, then. Let's unwrap it."

Unexpected panic banished his smile. What if the sight of the contents upset her? He tucked the package under his right arm.

"Later. I'll show you while we have supper. I want to display it properly."

"Mystery, mystery." She laughed as he strode away upstairs.

For the evening, he replaced his bedraggled outfit with a similar but clean one. His dark hair, over which he had poured two pitchers of water before he toweled it, had a soft, loose look. It was dusk as they sat down to dine. Blurry candles, upside-down images of the real ones, glowed in the highly buffed plane of the table. A small black boy stirred the air amiably and whisked flies off with an ostrich fan. Clarissa had eaten in her room, as she usually did, and retired.

"This smells grand," Orry said, touching a fork to the golden crust of the delicacy cooked in half of a big oyster shell. "Blue crab?"

"Netted in the Atlantic yesterday. I ordered two barrels in ice. They came on the packet boat. So much for gastronomy, Mr. Main. I want to see the package." It lay on the floor near him, the outer wrapping gone; oiled cloth was visible.

Studiously digging into the freshly picked and baked crab, he teased her with his straight face and low-voiced "Delicious."

"Orry Main, you're intolerable! Will you show me if I tell you some news about Justin?"

Sober suddenly, he laid his fork aside. "Good news?"

"Oh, nothing concerning the divorce, I'm afraid. Just something funny and a little sad." She relayed what she'd heard from one of the kitchen girls who had done an errand to Resolute earlier that day.

"In the rear," Orry mused. "A direct hit on the seat of the LaMotte family's prestige, eh?"

She laughed. "Your turn now." He broke two red wax seals and unwrapped the package. When she saw what the oiled cloth contained, she gasped.

"It's beautiful. Where is it from?"

"Germany. I ordered it for Charles and hoped it would get through."

He handed her the scabbarded weapon. With great care, she grasped the leather grip wound with brass wire. She drew out the curved blade; the fan boy's eyes grew round as he watched the candlelight reflect on the filligreed steel. Orry explained that it was a light cavalry saber, the approved 1856 design: forty-one inches overall.

Madeline tilted the blade to read the engraved inscription on the obverse: *To Charles Main, beloved of his family, 1861.* She gave him a long, affectionate look, then examined the other side. "I can't read this. Is it Cluberg?"

"Clauberg of Solingen. The maker. One of the finest in Europe."

"There are many tiny engraved flowers and curves—even medallions with the letters C. S. in them."

"On certain versions of this model, the letters are U.S.," he said with a dry smile.

Still treating the sword as if it were glass, she returned it to the gilt-banded scabbard of blue iron. Then, avoiding his eyes, she said, "Perhaps you should have ordered one for yourself."

"In case I accept the commission?"

"Yes."

"Oh, but that's a cavalry sword. I couldn't wear it even if I decided to—"

"Orry," she interrupted, "you're evading. You're evading me and evading a decision."

"I plead guilty to the latter," he admitted with an expression swift to come and go but revealing all the same. He was hiding something from her—behavior not typical of him. "I can't go to Richmond yet. There are too many things standing in the way. Foremost is your situation here."

"I can look after myself splendidly—as you well know."

"Now don't get tart with me. Of course I know it. But there's also Mother to consider."

"I can look after her, too."

"Well, you can't run this plantation without an overseer. The *Mercury* printed my advertisement again. Did the packet boat bring any replies?"

"I'm afraid not."

"Then I must keep searching. I've got to raise a good crop this year if I'm to contribute anything to the government—which I agreed to do by signing those papers today. I won't even think of Richmond till I find the right man to take over."

Later they went to the library. From the shelves Tillet Main had furnished with works of quality, they chose a finely bound *Paradise Lost.* During the years when they had met in secret, they had frequently read poetry aloud; the verse rhythms sometimes

105

became a poor substitute for those of love-making. Living together, they discovered such reading still brought pleasure.

They took places on a settee Orry had moved in just for this purpose. He was always on Madeline's left so that he could hold that side of the book. A dim corner of the room contained the stand on which he had hung one of his army uniforms after he came home from Mexico. The coat had both sleeves intact. Orry seldom glanced at the coat any longer, for which she was thankful.

He leafed through the poem's first book until he found a bit of paper between pages. "Here's the place." He cleared his throat and began in the middle of line 594:

> ". . . As when the sun new ris'n
> Looks through the horizontal misty air
> Shorn of his beams . . ."

Madeline took it up, her voice murmurous in the near-dark:

> ". . . or from behind the moon
> In dim eclipse disastrous twilight sheds
> On half the nations, and with fear of change
> Perplexes monarchs."

"Lesser folk, too," he said. She laid the book in her lap as he continued, "Cooper claims we got into this war because the South refused to accept the changes taking place in the country. I remember in particular his saying that we couldn't deal with either the necessity for change or its inevitability." He patted the book. "It seems John Milton understood."

"Will the war really change anything, though? When it's over, won't things be pretty much as they were?"

"Some of our leaders would like to believe so. I don't."

But he didn't want to spoil the evening with melancholy speculation; he kissed her cheek and suggested they continue reading. She surprised him by taking his face between her cool palms and gazing at him with eyes that shone with happy tears.

"Nothing will change this. I love you beyond life itself."

Her mouth pressed his, opening slightly; the kiss was long and full of sweet sharing. He brought his hand up and tangled it in her

106

hair. She leaned on his shoulder, whispering, "I've lost interest in British poets. Blow out the lights and let's go upstairs."

Next day, while Orry was in the fields, Madeline went hunting for a shawl she needed to mend. She and Orry shared a large walk-in wardrobe adjoining his bedroom; she searched for the shawl there.

Behind a row of hanging frock coats he never wore she spied a familiar package. She had last seen the presentation saber downstairs in the library. Why on earth had he brought it up here and hidden—?

She caught her breath, then reached behind the coats and lifted the package out. Its red wax seals were unbroken. No wonder he hadn't been amused when she teased him about a second sword.

She replaced the package and carefully shifted the coats in front of it again. She would keep her discovery to herself and let him speak to her in his own good time. But there was no longer any doubt about his intentions.

And with fear of change perplexes monarchs. Remembering the line, she stood near the room's single oval window, rubbing her forearms as if to warm them.

18

A sinking sun bled red light through the office windows next evening. Orry sweated at the desk, tired but needing to finish the purchase list for his factor in Charleston. He had been forced to move his business back to the Fraser company, which had served his father, because Cooper had transferred the assets of the family shipping firm to the Navy Department. Cooper held all the CSC stock, and so had a perfect right to do it. But it was damn inconvenient, requiring another adjustment on Orry's part.

There would be more to come, if he could judge from the last letter from Fraser's. It had been stamped with a crude wood-block indicia reading PAID 5¢. It was a splendid example of the annoying little matters of nationhood left over once the shouting stopped. The regular federal service had gone on handling Southern mail right through June first. But now a new Confederate postmaster was scrambling to create an organization and, presumably, print stamps. Till some showed up, states and municipalities produced their own.

Fraser's had owed him a refund from a past transaction. They had sent partial payment in the form of new Confederate bills, all very pretty and bucolic with their engravings of a goddess of agriculture and cheerful Negroes working a cotton field. The bills bore a line of tiny type reading *Southern Bank Note Co.* The letter from Fraser's commented, "The bills are printed in N.Y.—don't ask us how." A clever man could have deduced it from the one-thousand-dollar note enclosed. It carried portraits of John Calhoun and Andrew Jackson. Obviously the damnfool Yankees who designed the bill hadn't read history or heard of nullification.

Cities were printing paper money, too. Orry's representative at Fraser's had enclosed a sample—a bizarre Corporation of Richmond bill bearing a heroic portrait of the governor on pink paper in the denomination of fifty cents. Few secessionists had bothered their addled heads about practical consequences of the deed.

"Orry—oh, Orry—such news!"

Madeline burst into the office, picked up her crinoline-stiffened skirt, and did a wholly uncharacteristic dance around the room while he recovered from his surprise. She was giggling—*giggling*—while she jigged. Tears ran down her face and caught the dark red light.

"I shouldn't be happy—God will strike me dead—but I am. I am!"

"Madeline, what—?"

"Maybe He'll forgive me this once." She pressed an index finger beneath her nose but still couldn't stop giggling. More tears flowed. "I'll—ask Him—if I ever—get over this—"

"Have you lost your senses?"

108

"Yes!" She seized his hand, pulled him up, waltzed him around. "He's dead!"

"Who?"

"Justin! I know it's—shameful—to feel like this. He—" she gripped her sides, rocking back and forth—"was a human being—"

Only by the broadest definition, Orry thought. "You're not mistaken?"

"No, no—one of the housemen saw Dr. Lonzo Sapp on the river road. Dr. Sapp had just come from Resolute. My husband—" calming, she wiped away tears, gulped, and spoke more coherently—"drew his last breath this morning. The gunshot wound somehow spread an infection that poisoned his whole system. I'm free of him." She flung her arms around Orry's neck, leaning back in a great arch of joy. *"We're* free. I am so unbearably happy, and so ashamed of it."

"Don't be. Francis will mourn him, but no one else." He began to feel a mounting elation, an urge to laugh. "God will have to forgive me, too. It's funny in a grim way. The little peacock fatally shot in the ass—excuse me—by one of his own men—"

"There was nothing funny about Justin." Her back was toward the window and the burst of red light, making it hard to see her face. But he had no trouble imagining it as her voice dropped. "He was a vile man. They can fling me into hell, but I won't attend his funeral."

"Nor I." Orry leaned his right palm on the list for Fraser's; it no longer seemed important. "How soon can we be married?"

"It must be soon. I refuse to wait and play the grieving widow. After the wedding we can organize matters so you can accept that commission."

"I'm still determined to find an overseer before I decide." She glanced away as he went on. "Things are too unsettled around here. Geoffrey Bull came over from his place this afternoon very upset. Two nigras he considered to be his most loyal and trustworthy ran away yesterday."

"Did they go north?"

"He presumes they did. Read the *Mercury* and you'll see it's happening all the time. Fortunately, not to us."

"But we don't lack for problems. I can think of at least one— the young man you chose for head driver when Rambo died of influenza last winter."

"Cuffey?"

She nodded. "I've only been here a short time, but I've noticed a change. He's not merely cocky; he's angry. He doesn't bother to hide it."

"All the more reason to put off any decision till I locate an overseer." He drew her against his side. "Let's go to the house, pour some claret, and discuss a wedding."

Long after Madeline went to sleep that night, Orry lay awake. He had minimized the problems with the slaves because he hated to admit a plantation as humanely run as Mont Royal could be experiencing difficulties. Of course Cooper would have scoffed at his naïveté, arguing that no practitioner of slavery could rightly think of himself as kind, just, or morally clean.

Be that as it may, Orry felt a change in the atmosphere on the plantation. It had begun a few days after the start of hostilities. Supervising field work from horseback, Orry heard a name muttered and later decided he was meant to hear it. The name was Linkum.

Serious trouble had struck not long after Madeline's arrival. The trouble had roots in an earlier tragedy. Last November, Cuffey, in his middle twenties and not yet promoted to head driver, had become the father of twin girls. Cuffey's wife, Anne, had a hard confinement; one of the twins lived thirty minutes.

The other, a frail, dark little thing named Clarissa after Orry's mother, had been buried on the third of May this year. Orry had learned of it when he and Madeline returned from a two-night stay in Charleston, where shops and restaurants were thriving and spirits were high in the wake of the fall of the fort in the harbor. Orry drove their carriage back to Mont Royal in a thunderstorm, along a river road almost impassably muddy. They arrived at nightfall to find candles and lamps lit throughout the great house and Orry's mother wandering the rooms with a lost look.

"I believe there has been a death," she said.

Learning some of the details from the house help, he set off to walk the three-quarters of a mile to the slave community. The whitewashed cottages showed lights in the rain, but there was a noticeable absence of activity. Soaked, he climbed to the porch of Cuffey's cabin and knocked.

The door opened. Orry was shocked by the silence of the hand-

110

some young slave and by his sullen stare. He heard a woman crying softly.

"Cuffey, I just learned about your daughter. I am terribly sorry. May I come in?"

Unbelievably, Cuffey shook his head. "My Anne don't feel good right now."

Angered, Orry wondered whether it was because of her loss or something else. He had heard rumors that Cuffey mistreated his wife. Exercising restraint, he said, "I'm sorry about that, too. In any case, I did want to express—"

"Rissa died 'cause you weren't here."

"What?"

"None of them uppity house niggers would fetch the doctor, an' your momma couldn't understand I needed her to write a pass so's I could go get him. I argued and begged her most part of an hour, but she just shook her head like a crazy person. I took a chance and ran for the doctor myself, no pass or nothing. But when we got back it was too late; Rissa was gone. The doc took one look an' said typhoid fever and went away lickety-split. I had to bury her by myself. Little Rissa. Gone just like her sister. You'd been here, my baby would be alive."

"Damn it, Cuffey, you can't blame me for—"

Cuffey slammed the door. The rain dripped from the porch roof. The night pressed close, sticky and full of a sense of watching eyes.

Somewhere a contralto voice began a hymn, barely heard. Orry regretted what he must do but couldn't let the defiance pass, not with so many observing him. He knocked hard the second time.

No answer.

He pounded the door. "Cuffey, open up."

The door creaked back an inch. With his mud-slopped boot, Orry kicked it. Cuffey had to jump to avoid being struck.

"You listen to me," Orry said. "I am deeply sorry your daughter died, but I refuse to have you defy me because of it. Yes, if I'd been here, I would have written the pass instantly or gone for the doctor myself. But I was not here, and I had no way of knowing about the emergency. So unless you want to be replaced as head driver, curb your tongue and don't ever slam a door on me again."

Still silence, filled with rain sounds. Orry grabbed the door frame. "Do you understand me?"

111

"Yes, sir."

Two lifeless words. By the pale gleam of an interior lamp, Orry saw Cuffey's raging eyes. He suspected his warning had been wasted; he only hoped Cuffey would come to his senses quickly. If he didn't, his bad example could cause more trouble. That was why Orry had taken such pains to warn him loudly.

"Extend my condolences to your wife. Good night." He stomped off the porch, sad about the child's death, angry about Cuffey's interpretation of it, guilty about performing as he had for the unseen audience. The part didn't suit him, but he had to take it to preserve order. Cooper had once remarked that the masters and the slaves were equally victimized by the peculiar institution. On this foul night, Orry understood.

And that was the start, he thought, lying with Madeline's thigh soft against his. *That was the first card yanked from the house. That set the others tumbling.*

Four days after the confrontation at the cabin, Cuffey's Anne came to the office at twilight. A nasty welt showed beneath one eye, and the brown skin around it was turning black. She came to Orry hesitantly with a plea: "Please, sir. Sell me."

"Anne, you were born here. So were your mother and father. I know the loss of Rissa has—"

"Sell me, Mr. Orry," she broke in, taking hold of his right wrist, crying now. "I'm so scared of Cuffey, I want to die."

"He hit you? I'm sure he isn't himself either. Rissa—"

"Rissa got nothing to do with it. He hits me all the time. Done it ever since we got married. I hid it from you, but the people know. Last night he whipped me with a stick and his fist, then he hit me with the skillet."

Six feet two, the lanky white man towered above the frail black girl and seemed to grow an inch from anger. "I ran out and hid," she said, still crying. "He would have broke my head open, he was so crazy mad. I tried to take it like a good wife should, but I be too scared any more. I want to leave this place."

The sorry tale done, she let her eyes continue the pleading. She was a good worker, but he couldn't see her destroyed. "If that's your wish, Anne, I'll accept it."

Her face alight, Anne exclaimed, "You send me down to the market in Charleston?"

"Sell you? Absolutely not. But I know a family in the city—

good, kind people—who lost their house girl last autumn and are too hard pressed to buy another. I'll simply give you into their care in the next week or two."

"Tomorrow. Please!"

Her fear appalled him. "Very well. I'll write a letter immediately. Go collect your things and be ready."

She fell against him and clung, her face against his shirt. "I can't go back there. He kill me if I do. I just need this dress, that's all. Don't make me go back there, Mr. Orry. Don't."

He held her, smoothed her hair, calmed her as best as he could. "If you're that fearful, find Aristotle in the house. Tell him I said to give you a place for the night."

Weeping again, this time happily, she hugged him, then drew back in horror. "Oh, Mr. Orry, I was forward. I didn't mean—"

"I know. You did nothing wrong. Go on now, up to the house."

Except for five minutes next morning, when he wrote out the pass for the slave who was to deliver her to the Charleston family along with the letter, it was the last he saw of Anne. She thanked him and blessed his name repeatedly as she drove away down the lane.

The following afternoon, Orry rode out to inspect the squares being prepared for June planting. When Cuffey heard the horse, he raised his head in the glaring summer light and gave his owner a long, penetrating stare. Then he turned and began to badger a buck who wasn't working to his satisfaction. Cuffey hit the buck, making him stagger.

"That will be enough," Orry called. The driver glared again. Orry made sure he didn't blink. After ten seconds, he yanked his horse's head so hard, the animal snorted. The look between slave and master had been explicit. Cuffey had been killing someone, and each man knew who it was.

Orry said nothing about the incident to Madeline, for the same reason he had spared her details of Cuffey's defiance that rainy night. Of course Madeline knew Anne had been sent to Charleston at her own request, and why. She was also chief witness to the fall of the next card.

It happened early in June. Cuffey had taken crews out for the summer planting, put in each year in case the ricebirds or salty river water destroyed the early crop.

High embankments separated each square of cultivated land

113

from those around it. Wood culverts, called trunks, permitted water to flow from the Ashley and from square to square, and drain again when the trunk gates were raised on an ebbing tide. Madeline rode along the embankments, approaching the square where the slaves toiled. The day was clear and comfortable, with a light breeze and a sky of that intense, pure hue she thought of as Carolina blue. As usual when she rode, she wore trousers and straddled the horse; unladylike, certainly, but did it matter? Her reputation in the district could hardly be worse.

Ahead, she saw Cuffey moving among the bent slaves, hectoring and waving the truncheon he carried as his symbol of authority. An older black man working near the embankment did something to displease the driver as Madeline drew near.

"Worthless nigger," Cuffey complained. He hit the gray-haired slave with the truncheon, and the man toppled. His wife, working beside him, cried out and cursed the driver. Losing his temper, Cuffey lunged at her, raising his truncheon. The sudden wild motion frightened Madeline's horse. Whinnying, the gelding sidestepped to the right and would have fallen off the embankment had not another black about Cuffey's age scrambled up the slope, seized the headstall, and let his legs go limp.

The slave's weight and strength together kept the horse from tumbling into the next square. Madeline quickly got control of the skittish animal, but the rescue displeased Cuffey.

"Get back down here an' work, you."

The slave ignored the order. He gazed at Madeline with concern rather than servility. "Are you all right, ma'am?"

"Fine. I—"

"You hear me, nigger?" Cuffey shouted. He had climbed halfway up the embankment and pointed his truncheon at the other black, whose large, slightly slanted eyes registered emotion for the first time. Not hard to tell how he felt about the driver.

"Be quiet while I thank this man properly," Madeline said. "You caused the incident; he didn't."

Cuffey looked stunned, then enraged. At the sound of snickering, he spun, but the black faces below him were blank. He stomped down the embankment, hollering louder than ever.

The blacks resumed work while Madeline said to her rescuer: "I've seen you before, but I don't know your name."

"Andy, ma'am. I was named for President Jackson."

"Were you born at Mont Royal?"

"No. Mr. Tillet bought me the spring before he died."

"Well, Andy, I thank you for your quick action. There could have been a serious accident."

"Glad there wasn't. Cuffey didn't have any call to torment—" With a little intake of breath, he stopped. He had spoken his heart, but it wasn't his place to do such a thing; the realization showed.

She thanked him again. Giving a quick nod, he jumped to the bottom of the embankment; smiles and murmurs from some of the people showed they liked him as much as they disliked the driver. Fuming, Cuffey tapped his truncheon on his other palm. His eye fixed on Andy as he kept tapping.

Andy returned the stare. Cuffey looked away but managed to avoid humiliation by screaming orders at the same time. A bad situation, Madeline thought as she rode on—and that was how she characterized it when she described the incident to Orry later. At dark, he sent a boy to the slave community. Shortly after, a knock sounded at the open office door.

"Come in, Andy."

The barefoot slave crossed the threshold. He wore cloth pants washed so many times they had a white sheen, like his patched short-sleeved shirt. Orry had always thought him a good-looking young fellow, well proportioned and muscular. He knew how to be polite without fawning, and his posture now, straight but at ease, with his hands relaxed at his sides, showed his confidence in his standing with the owner.

"Take a chair." Orry indicated the old rocker beside the desk. "I want you to be comfortable while we talk."

This unexpected treatment disarmed and confused the younger man. He lowered himself with care, sitting tensely; the rocker didn't move an inch one way or the other.

"You saved Miss Madeline from what could have been a grave injury. I appreciate that. I want to ask you some questions about the cause of the mishap. I expect truthful answers. You needn't fear anyone will try to get back at you."

"Driver, you mean?" Andy shook his head. "I'm not scared of him or any nigra who has to push and curse to get his way." His tone and gaze implied he didn't fear that kind of white man either. Orry's favorable impression strengthened.

"Who was Cuffey after? Miss Madeline said the man had gray hair."

115

"It was Cicero."

"Cicero! He's nearly sixty."

"Yes, sir. He and Cuffey—they've had trouble before. Soon as the mistress left the square, Cuffey swore he'd make the old man pay."

"Is there anything else I should know?" Andy shook his head. "All right. I'd like to thank you in some tangible way for what you did." Andy blinked; *tangible* was plainly incomprehensible to him, though he didn't say so. "Do you have a garden? Do you raise anything for yourself?"

"I do, sir. This year I have okra and some peas. And I keep three hens."

Opening a desk drawer, Orry drew out bills. "Three dollars will buy some good seed and a couple of new tools if you need them. Tell me what you want and I'll order it from Charleston."

"Thank you, sir. I'll think on it and speak to you again."

"Can you read or write, Andy?"

"Nigras reading and writing is against the law. I could be whipped if I said yes."

"Not here. Answer the question."

"I can't do either."

"Would you learn if you had the chance?"

Andy estimated the danger before he replied. "Yes, sir, I would. Reading, ciphering—they help a man get ahead in the world." A deep swallow, then he blurted, "I might be free one day. Then I'd need it more than ever."

Orry smiled to relieve the black man's apprehension. "That's a wise outlook. Glad we had this talk. I've never known much about you, but I think you can be of great service on this plantation. You will get ahead."

"Thank you," Andy said, holding up the money. "For this, too."

Orry nodded, watching the strong young man turn toward the door. Some would have whipped Andy for his admission; Orry wished he had a dozen more with similar initiative.

Night had fallen while they talked. In the distance, big frogs made a sound like drums with cracked heads; the cicada obbligato was pleasanter. Andy wasn't tall, Orry observed as he watched the slave walk down the path, but his stride—and his nature— made it seem otherwise.

In the morning, Orry rode to the day's work site to look for Cicero. He didn't see him. Cuffey curbed his ranting until Orry passed by, then doubled the volume. Orry proceeded to the slave cabins and dismounted before that belonging to Cicero and his wife. A naked, merry-faced boy of five was urinating against one of the tabby pillars. Cicero's wife heard Orry shoo the boy away and rushed outside.

"Where's your husband, Missy?"

"Inside, Mist' Orry. He, uh, not working today. He just a little sickly."

"I'd like to see him."

Her response—a burst of nearly incoherent statements amounting to refusal—confirmed that something was wrong. He pushed her aside gently and entered the clean, bare cabin just as Cicero groaned.

Orry swore under his breath. The aging slave lay on a pallet of ticking, arms folded over his stomach, face contorted. Dried blood and matter showed on his closed, discolored eyelids. His forehead bore similar marks. No doubt Cuffey had used his truncheon.

"I'll send for the doctor to look at him, Missy," he said as he rejoined her on the porch. "I'll also see this matter is put to rights before the day's done."

She caught his hand and pressed it. She was crying too hard to speak.

By afternoon, it was broiling. Orry nevertheless built a fire in the iron stove in his office before summoning Cuffey from the fields. When Cuffey walked in—he had his truncheon, as Orry had anticipated—there were no formalities.

"I should have sold you instead of Anne. I'll take this."

He yanked the truncheon from Cuffey's hand, opened the stove door, and threw the stick into the fire.

"You are no longer head driver. You're a field hand again. I saw what you did to Cicero, for God knows what ridiculous reason. Get out of here."

Next morning, an hour after sunup, Orry again spoke to Andy in the office.

"I want you to be the head driver." Andy gave a small, quick nod of consent. "I'm putting a lot of trust in you, Andy. I don't know you well, and these are difficult times. I know some of the people feel a strong pull to run away to Yankee territory. I won't be forgiving if anyone tries that and I catch him or her—as I most likely will. I don't engage in cruelty, but I won't be forgiving. Clear?"

Andy nodded again.

"One more thing. You remember that our former overseer, Salem Jones, whom I caught stealing and discharged, carried a stick. Evidently the late Mr. Jones impressed Cuffey. He adopted the idea. I should have taken Cuffey's truncheon away the first time I saw it."

Andy's lids flickered as he stored the new word in memory. Orry finished by saying, "Carrying a stick shows a man is weak, not strong. I don't want to find you with one."

"I don't need one," Andy said, looking him straight in the eye.

That was how the delicate card house had collapsed. Orry had started to build another when he put Andy in Cuffey's place.

He had soon learned that most of the people liked the change. Orry was well satisfied, too. Not only was Andy quick-witted and hardy enough to work long hours, but he also had a knack for leading rather than driving the others. He was neither craven nor truculent; he had somehow acquired an inner strength in which he had absolute confidence. He didn't need to dramatize it to convince himself of his worth.

The trust Orry had placed in him—on a hunch and an impulse, mostly—created an unspoken but real attachment between the two men. Once or twice Orry had heard his father speak of loving certain of his people as he would love a child of his own loins. For the first time Orry began to have some comprehension of why Tillet Main might have said that.

Much of this flowed through Orry's mind as he lay beside Madeline, but what came last was a disturbing image. Cuffey's face. Wrathful—far more so since the end of his short tenure as driver. Cuffey had to be watched now; he would spread discontent. Orry could easily identify half a dozen of the people who might be receptive.

On balance, the situation, while not ideal, was not as bad as it had been a week ago. Orry believed that if he accepted the post in Richmond, Andy would protect Madeline in the event of trouble. Feeling good about that, he fell asleep.

A week later, he received an unexpected letter.

Deir Sir,
My cozin who resides in Charleston, S.C., shewed me your
advertisement for job of overseer. I have the honr to prezent
myself to your atention, Philemon Meek, age 64 yers but in
the prim of helth and gretly experienced—

"There's a big one he got right." Orry laughed as he and Madeline strolled through the formal garden to the river at twilight of the day the letter came. "He didn't get many of the others."

"Could you take a chance on a man so poorly educated?"

"I could if he's had the right experience. The rest of this seems to suggest he has. He says I'm to get a letter of reference from his present employer, an elderly widower with a tobacco plantation up near Raleigh; no children and no will to keep the place going. Meek would like to buy it but can't afford it. The place is to be broken into small farms."

They reached the pier jutting into the smooth-flowing Ashley. On the other side, in shallows beneath Spanish moss, three white egrets stood like statuary. Orry slapped a mite on his neck. The smack sent the birds swooping away into the river's dark distances.

"There's only one difficulty with Mr. Meek," Orry continued, sinking down on an old cask. "He won't be at liberty until sometime in the fall. Says he won't leave until his employer is properly settled with a sister who's to take him in."

"That kind of attitude recommends him."

"Definitely," Orry agreed. "I doubt I'll find anyone better qualified. I think I should write him and begin salary negotiations."

"Yes, indeed. Does he have a wife or a family?"

"Neither."

Quietly, her eyes on the smooth water specked occasionally by insects too small to be seen, she said, "I've been wanting to ask—how do you feel about the latter?"

"I want children, Madeline."

"Considering what you know about my mother?"

"What I know about you is far more important." He kissed her mouth. "Yes, I do want children."

"I'm glad to hear you say it. Justin thought I was barren,

though I always suspected the fault was his. We should find out soon enough—I can't imagine two people working harder at the question than we've been doing, can you?" She squeezed his arm, and they laughed together.

"I'm so glad you heard from that Mr. Meek," she went on. "Even if you can't leave till autumn, you can write Richmond and accept the commission."

"Yes, I suppose I could do that now."

"So you have decided!"

"Well—" The very way he prolonged it was an admission.

"The bugs are getting fierce down here," she said. "Let's go back to the house for a glass of claret. Perhaps we can even find a second way to celebrate your decision."

"In bed?"

"Oh, no, I didn't mean that—" Madeline blushed, then added, "Right now."

"What, then?"

Impossible to hide her smile any longer. "I think it's time to unwrap the sword you've kept carefully hidden upstairs."

19

"Our Rome," old residents called it. As a girl, Mrs. James Huntoon had preferred the study of young men to that of old cities, but a certain amount of enforced education in the classics enabled her to dismiss the comparison as merely another example of Virginia arrogance. That arrogance permeated Richmond and raised barriers for those from other states. At the first private party to which Ashton and her husband had been invited—to have their persons and pedigrees inspected, she felt sure—a white-haired woman, clearly Someone, overheard Ashton remark crossly that she simply couldn't understand the Virginia temperament.

Someone gave her a smile with steel in it. "That is because we are neither Yankees nor Southerners—the South being a term generally used here to signify states with a large population of parvenu cotton planters. We are Virginians. No other word will suffice—and none says so much."

Ignorance thus exposed, Someone sailed away. Ashton seethed, imagining she'd faced the worst the evening had to offer. She was wrong. James Chesnut's wife, Mary, a South Carolinian with a bitchy tongue and a secure place in Mrs. Davis's circle, had greeted her by name and refused to stop for conversation. Ashton feared that gossip about her involvement with Forbes LaMotte, and the attempt to kill Billy Hazard, had followed the Huntoons to Virginia.

So she had failed two tests in one night. But there would be others, and she was determined to triumph over them. Although she had little except contempt for the well-born gentlemen who ran the government, and for their wives who ruled society, they held power. To Ashton there was no stronger aphrodisiac.

Like the ancient city, Our Rome had hills, but, by comparison, the city was tiny. Even with all the office seekers, bureaucrats, and riffraff swarming in, the population was little more than forty thousand. Richmond had its Tiber, too—the James, looping and winding south and then east to the Atlantic—but surely the air on the Capitoline had smelled of something finer than tobacco. Richmond stank of it; the whole place had the odor of a warehouse.

Montgomery had been the first capital, but only for a month and a half. Then the Congress voted in favor of the move to Virginia—though not without argument. Richmond lay too near the Yankee lines, the Yankee guns, opponents said. Numbers of votes overwhelmed them, as did logic: Richmond was the South's transportation and armament center, and had to be defended whether the government was there or not.

Those who had resided in Richmond a long time spoke with pride of the fine old homes and churches, but never mentioned the teeming saloon districts. They boasted of families of exalted ancestry, but never acknowledged the degraded creatures of both sexes who sauntered the shady walks of Capitol Square in the afternoons, silently offering themselves for sale. The women, a hard lot, and seldom young, were said to be rushing here from Baltimore, even New York, in search of the opportunity a wartime capital offered. God knew from what sewer their male counterparts had crawled.

Old Rome—with Carolina Goths and Alabama Vandals already inside the walls. Even the provisional President—not yet formally confirmed for his single six-year term—was regarded as a Mississippi primitive. He had the further misfortune of birth in Kentucky, the same state that had given the world the supreme incarnation of vulgarity-on-earth, Abe Lincoln.

Although Ashton was glad to be near the center of power, it couldn't be said that she was happy. Her husband, though a competent lawyer and a staunch secessionist—"Young Hotspur," they had called him back home—could find no better job than clerk to one of the first assistants in the Treasury Department. That was in keeping with the contempt shown South Carolinians by the new government. Very few from the Palmetto State had been named to high posts; most were considered too radical. The exception, Treasury Secretary Memminger, wasn't a Carolina native. Fathered by some low-born German soldier, he had been brought to Charleston as an orphan. Never considered one of the so-called fire-eaters, he was the only kind of Carolinian Jeff Davis deemed safe. It was insulting.

Ashton and James Huntoon were squeezed into a single large room at one of the boardinghouses proliferating near Main Street; that, too, displeased her. They would find a suitable house eventually, but the wait was galling—especially because she was required to sleep in the same bed as her husband. He always left her unsatisfied on those rare occasions—initiated by her when she wanted him to do or buy something for her—that she let him maul and heave and poke her with that pitiful flaccid instrument of his.

Richmond might be a tarnished coin, but it was rare and valuable in a few respects. There were important people to be cultivated; power to be acquired; financial opportunities to be seized. There were also quite a few attractive men—in uniform and out. Somehow she would turn all of that to her advantage—perhaps starting tonight. She and James were to attend their first official reception. As she finished dressing, she felt faint from the excitement.

Orry's sister was a beautiful young woman with a lush figure

122

and an innate sense of how to take advantage of those assets. She had insisted they hire a carriage, to create the proper impression from the moment they arrived. James whined that they couldn't afford it; she allowed him marital privileges for three minutes, and he changed his mind. How glad she was when he handed her down from the carriage outside the Spotswood Hotel at Eighth and Main, and she heard approving murmurs from a crowd of loungers on the walk.

The July evening was hot, but Ashton wore everything that fashion dictated for a woman of elegance, beginning with the four tape-covered steel hoops under her skirt; all but the top one had an opening in front, to facilitate walking. A web of vertical tapes held the rig together.

Over this, underskirts, and then her finest silk dress, a deep peach color she offset with little jet spangles on her silk hair net, and with black velvet ribbons tied to each wrist. Fashionable women wore a great amount of jewelry, but her husband's income confined her to a pair of black onyx teardrops hung from her ear lobes on tiny gold wires. So she had arranged her dark hair and chosen her wardrobe to let simplicity and her own voluptuous good looks be her devices for drawing attention.

"Now pay attention, darling," she said as they crossed the lobby in search of Parlor 83. "Give me a chance to circulate this evening. You do the same. The more people we meet, the better— and we can meet twice as many if you don't hang on me constantly."

"Oh, I wouldn't," Huntoon said, with that automatic righteousness that frequently cost him friends and hurt his career. James was six years older than his wife, a pale, paunchy, opinionated man. "Here—down this corridor. I wish you wouldn't treat me as if I were some witless boy."

Her heart raced at the sight of the open doors of Parlor 83, where President Davis regularly held these receptions; he had no official residence as yet. Ashton glimpsed gowned women mingling and chatting with gentlemen in uniforms or fine suits. She fixed her smile in place, whispering: "Act like a man and maybe I won't. If you start trouble now, I'll just kill you—*Mrs. Johnston!*"

The woman about to enter the parlor ahead of them turned with a polite though puzzled expression. "Yes?"

"Ashton Huntoon—and may I present my husband, James?

James, this is the wife of our distinguished general commanding the Alexandria line. James is in Treasury, Mrs. Johnston."

"A most important position. Delightful to see you both." And away she went into the parlor. Ashton was glad they'd exchanged words out here; Joe Johnston ranked the other general on the Alexandria line—the one who captivated everyone—but his wife was not one of Mrs. Davis's intimates.

"I don't think she remembered you," Huntoon whispered.

"Why should she? We've never met."

"My God, you're forward." His chuckle conveyed admiration as well as reproof.

Sweetly, she said, "Your backwardness demands it, dear—Oh, Lord, look. They're both here—Johnston and Bory." Thus, on a wave of unexpected joy, Ashton swept into the crowd, nodding, murmuring, smiling at strangers whether she knew them or not. On the far side of the packed room, she spied the President and Varina Davis. But they were surrounded.

Memminger greeted the Huntoons. The Dutchman brought Ashton champagne punch and then, responding to her request, introduced her to the officer everyone wanted to meet—the wiry little fellow with sallow skin, melancholy eyes, and an unmistakably Gallic cast to his features. Brigadier General Beauregard bent over her gloved hand and kissed it.

"Your husband has found a treasure, madam. *Vous êtes plus belle que le jour!* I am honored."

Her look deprecated the flattery and at the same time acknowledged the truth of it; Carolina women knew coquetry, if nothing else. "The honor's mine, General. To be presented to our new Napoleon—the first to strike a blow for the Confederacy—I know that will be the high point of my evening."

Pleased, he replied, *"Près de vous, j'ai passé les moments les plus exquis de ma vie."* Then, with a bow, the Creole general slipped away; many more admirers waited.

Huntoon, meantime, anxiously eyed the crowd. He feared someone had overheard Ashton. Was she so stupid that she didn't know the high point of the evening should be an introduction to President and Mrs. Davis? In such states of terror over small things did James Huntoon pass most of his life.

Huntoon's study of the crowd soon generated a new emotion—anger. "Nothing but West Point peacocks and foreigners. Oh-oh, that little Jew's spotted us. This way, Ashton."

124

He tugged her elbow. She jerked away and, with a glare and a toss of her head, sent him off to mingle. This left her free to greet the small, plump man approaching with a genial smile and a hand extended.

"Mrs. Huntoon, is it not? Judah Benjamin. I have seen you once or twice at the Treasury building. Your husband works there, I believe."

"Indeed he does, Mr. Benjamin. I can hardly believe you'd take notice of me, however."

"It's no disloyalty to my wife, presently in Paris, to say that the man who has never noticed you is a man who has never seen you."

"What a pretty speech! But I've heard the attorney general is famous for them."

Benjamin laughed, and she found herself liking him—in part because James didn't. A good deal of opposition to the President and his policies had already arisen; Davis was especially scored for allegedly favoring foreigners and Jews in his administration. The attorney general, who presided over a nonexistent court system, was both.

Benjamin had been born in St. Croix, though raised in Charleston. For unexplained offenses said to be scandalous, he had been expelled from Yale, which her brother Cooper had attended. A lawyer, he had moved with ease from the United States Senate, where he had represented Louisiana, to the Confederacy. His critics called him a cheap and opportunistic machine politician— among other things.

Benjamin escorted her to the buffet table and gathered little dainties on a plate, which he handed to her. She saw James, in the act of sidling up to the President, throw her a furious look. Delightful.

"An ample repast this evening," Benjamin commented. "But not first quality. You and your husband must join me some other night and sample my favorite canapé—white bread baked with good Richmond flour and spread with anchovy paste. I serve it with sherry from Jerez. I import it by the cask."

"How can you possibly get Spanish sherry through this blockade?"

"Oh, there are ways." Benjamin smiled, an innocent, airy dismissal. "Will you come?"

"Of course," she lied; James wouldn't.

125

He asked for their address. Reluctantly, she gave it. It was clear he recognized the boardinghouse district, but it didn't seem to diminish his friendliness. He promised to send a card of invitation soon, then glided away to pay court to General and Mrs. Johnston. They stood by themselves, displeased by the fact and by the crowd around Old Bory.

Ashton thought of following Benjamin, but held back when she saw Mrs. Davis approach the attorney general and the Johnstons. She didn't have nerve enough to join a group that formidable; not yet.

She studied the First Lady. The President's second wife, Varina, was a handsome woman in her mid-thirties, presently expecting another child. It was said that she was a person without guile, plain-spoken and not hesitant to state opinions on public questions. That was not traditional behavior for a Southern woman. Ashton knew Mrs. Johnston had called her a Western belle behind her back, and not to compliment her. Still, she'd give anything to meet her.

With a delicious start, she saw that she stood a far better chance of meeting Davis himself. James had somehow engaged him in conversation. Ashton started through the maze of scented feminine and braided male shoulders.

She passed near three officers greeting a fourth, a spirited-looking chap with splendid mustaches and curled hair whose pomade was almost as strong as her perfume. "California's a long way from here, Colonel Pickett," one of the other officers was saying to him. "We're glad you made the journey safely. Welcome to Richmond and the side of the just."

The officer thus addressed noticed Ashton and favored her with a gallant, mildly flirtatious smile. Then he frowned, as if trying to place her. One of Orry's classmates had been named Pickett. Could this be the same man? Could he have seen a resemblance? She moved on quickly; she had no desire to discuss a brother who had banished her from her childhood home.

James saw her coming, turned his back. Bastard. He wouldn't present her; it was her punishment for talking with the little Jew. He'd pay.

She sought a familiar face and finally located one. She forced herself on Mary Chesnut, caught alone and unable to escape. Mrs. Chesnut seemed friendlier tonight, and inclined to gossip.

"Everyone's crushed that General and Mrs. Lee are absent—

126

and without explanation. A domestic spat, do you suppose? I know they're a model couple—they say he never curses or loses his temper. But surely even a man of his high moral character occasionally lets down. If he were here, we'd probably have an impromptu West Point reunion. Poor old Bob—flogged by the Yankee press when he resigned and joined our side."

"Yes, I know." They said the woman kept a diary and that it was prudent to speak guardedly in her presence.

Smirking, Mrs. Chesnut tapped Ashton's wrist with her fan. "You'd think that would make him popular with the troops, wouldn't you?"

"Doesn't it?"

"Hardly. Privates and corporals from fine families call him the King of Spades because he sent down orders that they must dig and sweat like the commonest field hands."

Hanging on her words with feigned interest, Ashton had not failed to see a tall, well-set-up gentleman in blue velvet studying her from the punch table. He let his gaze drift down to the peach silk spread tightly between her breasts. Ashton waited till he met her eye again, then turned away. She left Mary Chesnut and drew nearer her husband and the President.

Jefferson Davis looked several years younger than fifty-one; his military bearing and his slim figure helped create the impression, as did his abundant hair. Worn long at the back of his neck, it showed almost no white. Nor did his tuft of chin whiskers.

"But Mr. Huntoon," he said, "I do insist that a central government must institute certain measures mandated by its existence in a time of war. Conscription, for example."

They had fallen into an amiable philosophic discussion, Huntoon and the soft-spoken President and a third man, Secretary of State Toombs. Toombs was said to be a malcontent, already spreading disaffection in the administration. He particularly criticized West Point because Davis, class of '28, placed a great trust in some of its graduates.

"You mean you would enact it into law?" Huntoon challenged. He had strong beliefs and relished the chance to make them known.

"If it became necessary, I would urge that, yes."

"You'd order men out from the several states, the way that nigger-loving baboon has done?"

Davis managed to sound annoyed when he sighed. "Mr. Lincoln has asked for volunteers, nothing more. We have done the same. On both sides, conscription is at this point purely theoretical."

"But I submit, sir—with all respect to you and your office—it is a theory that must never be tested. It runs counter to the doctrine of supremacy of the states. If they should be forced to surrender that supremacy to a central power, we'll have a duplication of the circus in Washington."

Gray eyes flashed then; and the left one, nearly blind, looked as wrathful as the right. Huntoon had heard gossip about the President's temper; they worked in the same building, after all. It was said that Davis took any disagreement as a personal attack and behaved accordingly.

"Be that as it may, Mr. Huntoon, my responsibility's clear. I am charged with making this new nation viable and successful."

Equally hot, Huntoon said, "How far will you go, then? I've heard that certain members of the West Point clique have suggested we enlist the darkies to fight for us. Will you do that?"

Davis laughed at the idea, but Toombs exclaimed, "Never. The day the Confederacy permits a Negro to enter the ranks of its armies—on that day, the Confederacy will be degraded, ruined, and disgraced."

"I agree," Huntoon snapped. "Now, as to conscription itself—"

"Theoretical," Davis repeated sharply. "It is my hope to win recognition of this government without excessive bloodshed. Constitutionally, we were entirely right to do what we did. I will not behave, or prosecute a war, as if we were in the wrong. Nevertheless, a central government must be stronger than its separate parts, or else—"

"No, sir," Huntoon interrupted. "The states will never tolerate it."

Davis seemed to pale and blur; then Huntoon realized his metal-rimmed spectacles were steaming.

"If that be so, Mr. Huntoon, the Confederacy won't last a year. You may have the doctrine of states' rights, pristine and scrupulously enforced, or you may have a new country. You can't have both without some accommodation. So take your choice."

Giddy with anger, Huntoon blurted, "My choice is not to be a party to autocratic thinking, Mr. President. Further—"

"If you will excuse me." Spots of color showed in the President's cheeks as he pivoted and left. Toombs followed.

Huntoon fumed. If the President resented disagreement about fundamental principles, the devil with him. The man was very definitely the wrong sort. He gave mere lip service to the ideals of Calhoun and the other great statesmen who had endured the calumnies of the North for a generation and exhausted themselves fighting for man's right to own what property he pleased. Huntoon was glad he had told Davis—

"You blundering, simple-minded—"

"Ashton!"

"I can't believe what I overheard. You should have flattered him, and you spouted political cant."

Scarlet, he seized her wrist, crushing the velvet band under sweaty fingers. "People claim he acts like a dictator. I wanted to confirm that. I did. I expressed my strong convictions about—"

By then she was leaning close, smiling her warmest smile, flooding him with the sweet odor of her breath. "Shit on your strong convictions. Instead of introducing me so I could help you —ease you through a prickly situation—you blathered and argued, and sounded the knell for your already insignificant career."

She exploded into swift motion, bumping guests and drawing stares as she stormed toward the refreshments, tears in her eyes. *Idiot.* She clutched a chilled punch cup between her hands; she had removed her gloves because sweat had soaked them. *The idiot. He's wrecked everything.*

Anger quickly gave way to a feeling of depression. A fine social opportunity had been ruined; large groups of people were already starting to leave. As she sipped punch, she wanted to sink into the floor and die. She had come to Richmond in search of the power she had always craved, and in a few sentences he had guaranteed he would never get it for her.

Very well—she would find someone else. Someone to help her rise. An intellectual ally, or, better, a man on whom she could use certain skills she knew she possessed. A man more intelligent and tactful than James; more dedicated to success and adept at achieving it—

Thus, in a minute or less, in Parlor 83 of the Spotswood, Ashton made up her mind. Huntoon had never been much of a husband; her secret box of special souvenirs validated that. Henceforth, he'd be a husband in name only. Perhaps he wouldn't even be that if she could find the proper replacement.

She lifted the empty cup. "Might I have regular champagne?" Gaily smiling again, she handed it to the Negro behind the table. "I can't abide punch that's gone flat."

The tall man in the blue velvet frock coat extinguished his long cigar in a sand urn. Having asked a few questions to be certain about relationships, he strolled through the thinning crowd toward his target—the perspiring, bespectacled oaf who had just had a ferocious argument with his wife. Earlier, the tall man had noticed the wife enter the room, and within his tight fawn trousers his penis had hardened. Few women did that to him so quickly.

The tall man was thirty-five or so, with a muscular frame and delicate hands. He moved gracefully and wore his clothes well; yet a certain coarseness communicated itself, due in part to the presence of childhood pox scars. Smooth, slightly pomaded hair, evenly mixed gray and dark brown, hung to his collar in the Davis fashion. He glided up beside Huntoon. Confused and upset, the lawyer stood polishing and polishing his glasses with a damp handkerchief.

"Good evening, Mr. Huntoon."

The resonant voice startled Huntoon; the man had slipped up behind him. "Good evening. You have the advantage of me—"

"Quite right. You were pointed out to me. Your family's an old and famous one down in our part of the world, I might say."

What was the fellow up to, Huntoon wondered. Promoting some investment scheme, perhaps? He was out of luck there— Ashton controlled the only money they had, the forty thousand dollars that had been her marriage dower.

"Are you a South Carolinian, Mr.—?"

"Powell. Lamar Hugh Augustus Powell. Lamar to friends. No, sir, I'm not from your state, but close by. My mother's people are from Georgia. The family's heavily into cotton, near Valdosta. My father was English. Took my mother as a bride to Nassau, where I was raised, and he practiced law until he died some years ago."

"The Bahamas. That explains it." Huntoon's attempt to smile and be ingratiating struck Powell as insipid and funny. This sod would present no problem. But where—?

130

Ah. Without turning, Powell detected a blur of color moving near. "Explains what, sir?"

"Your speech. I thought I heard Charleston in it—yet not quite." For a moment or two, Huntoon could think of nothing else to say. In desperation, he exclaimed, "Grand party—"

"I didn't introduce myself for the purpose of discussing the party." Stung, Huntoon's grin grew sickly. "To be candid, I am organizing a small group to finance a confidential venture which could prove incredibly lucrative."

Huntoon blinked. "You're talking about an investment—?"

"A maritime investment. This damned blockade creates fantastic opportunities for men with the will and wherewithal to seize them."

He bent closer.

After all the disheartening turns the evening had taken, Ashton at last found some pleasure in the sight of the attractive stranger speaking with her husband. How lamentable James looked beside him. Was the gentleman as prosperous as appearances suggested? As virile?

She hurried toward them. Having punished her, James was now prepared to be polite.

"My dear, may I present Mr. Lamar Powell of Valdosta and the Bahamas? Mr. Powell, my wife, Ashton."

With that introduction, he made one of the worst mistakes of his life.

20

Charles tied Ambrose Pell's bay to the top fence rail. Light rain was falling on him, the bald farmer, and the disappointing horse he had ridden twelve miles to see. The distant Blue Ridge was lost in mist as dreary as his spirits.

"A gray?" Charles said. "Only the musicians ride grays."

" 'Spect that's why I still got him," the farmer replied. "Sold off all my others quick—though if you want to know, I mislike doin' business with you buttermilk cavalry boys. Couple of 'em rode through here last week with papers saying they was Commissary Department men."

"How many chickens did they steal from you?"

"Oh, you know them boys?"

"Not personally, but I know how some of them operate." The thievery, officially called "foraging," contributed to the bad reputation the cavalry had already acquired, as did the widespread belief that all mounted soldiers would use their horses to ride away from a battle. There was an even chance that the men who had visited the farmer had presented papers they themselves had forged.

"About the horse—"

"Already told you the price."

"It's too high. But I'll pay it if the gray's any good."

Charles doubted it. The two-year-old gelding was a plain, undistinguished animal; small—about fourteen hands high—and certainly no more than a thousand pounds. He had the shoulders and long, sloping pasterns of a good racer. But you didn't see many gray saddle horses. What was wrong with this one?

"They don't let you boys ride 'less you can find your own remount, ain't that it?" the farmer asked.

"Yes. I've been minus a horse and hunting a replacement for two weeks. I'm temporarily in Company Q, as the saying goes."

"They give you anything for providin' your own mount?"

"Forty cents a day, food, shoes, and the services of a farrier, if you can find one sober." It was a stupid policy, no doubt invented by some government clerk who had ridden nothing friskier than his childhood hobby-horse. The more Charles saw of army politics, camp life, the new recruits, the less easy it became to decide whether the Confederate Army was comic or tragic. Some of both, probably.

"How'd your other horse die?"

Nosy old grouch, wasn't he? "Distemper." Dasher had succumbed eleven days after Charles first noticed the symptoms. To this hour he could see the bay lying sad-eyed in the isolation the disease required. He had kept her covered with every blanket he could buy or borrow, and while they hid all the ugly abcesses, they couldn't hide her swollen legs or mask the stench of the creamy pus flowing from the lesions. He should have shot her, but he couldn't do it. He let her die and wept with sorrow and relief, off by himself, afterward.

"Um," the farmer said with a shiver. "Strangles is a dirty end for a good animal."

"Just as soon not talk about it." Charles disliked the farmer, and the man had taken a dislike to him. He wanted to conclude the business. "Why haven't you sold the gray? Cost too much?"

"Nah, the other reason. Like you say—only the band boys want grays. I heard you boys try to make the colors match so's one bunch can be told from another."

"That's the theory. It won't last long." His search was proof. "Look, you don't find many horses for sale in this part of Virginia. So what's wrong with him? He's broken, isn't he?"

"Oh, sure, my cousin broke him good. That's where I got him —off my cousin. I'll be straight with you, soldier—"

"Captain."

The farmer didn't like that. "He's a good, fast little thing, but something about him doesn't please. Two other boys like you

133

looked him over and found him kind of plain and, well, disagreeable. Maybe it's the Florida blood."

Instantly, Charles perked up. "Is he part Chickasaw?"

"Ain't got nothing to prove it, but my cousin said so."

Then the gray might be a find. The best Carolina racers combined the strains of the English thoroughbred and the Spanish pony from Florida. Charles realized he should have suspected Chickasaw blood when he saw the gray frisking in the pasture as he rode up.

"Is he hard to ride?"

"Some have found him so, yessir." The farmer was growing tired of the questions. His belligerence told Charles to hurry up and decide; he didn't care which way.

"Has he got a name?"

"Cousin called him Sport."

"That could mean lively, or it could mean an animal too different to be any good."

"I didn't ask about that." The farmer leaned over and blew a gob of saliva into the weeds. "You want him or not?"

"Put that headstall on him and bring him over here," Charles replied, unfastening his spurs. The farmer went into the pasture, and Charles observed that Sport twice tried to bite his owner while the headstall was being placed. But the gray followed tractably when the man led him to the fence.

Charles walked to Ambrose Pell's bay and pulled his shotgun from the hide sheath he had cut and stitched together. He checked the gun quickly. Alarmed, the farmer said, "What the hell you fixin' to do?"

"Ride him a ways."

"No saddle? No blanket? Where'd you learn to do that?"

"Texas." Tired of the old man, Charles gave him an evil grin. "When I took time off from killing Comanches."

"Killing—? I see. All right. But that shotgun—"

"If he can't handle the noise, he's no good to me. Bring him closer to the fence."

He barked it like an order to his men; the farmer instantly became less troublesome. Charles climbed to the top of the fence, slid over, and dropped down on the gelding gently as he could. He wrapped the rope around his right hand, already feeling the gray's skittish resistance. He raised the shotgun and fired both barrels. The sound went rolling away toward the hidden mountains. The gray didn't buck, but he ran—straight toward the fence at the far side of the pasture.

Charles gulped and felt his hat blow off. Raindrops splashed his face. All right, he thought, show me whether your name signifies good or bad.

The fence rushed at him. *If he won't jump, I could break my damn neck.* With his light mane standing out above the fine long line of his neck, Sport cleared the fence in a clean, soaring leap, never touching the top rail.

Charles laughed and gave Sport his head. The gray took him on one of the wildest gallops he had ever experienced. Over weedy ground. Through a grove where low limbs loomed, and he ducked repeatedly. Up a steep little hill and down to a cold creek; the water driven up by their crossing would finish the soaking the rain had begun. It occurred to Charles that he wasn't testing the gray; the gray was testing him.

Long hair flying, he laughed again. In this wrong-colored, unhandsome little animal, he just might have discovered a remarkable war horse.

"I'll take him," he said when he returned to the fence by the road. He reached for a wad of bills. "You said a hundred—"

"While you was frolicking with him, I decided I can't let him go for less than a hundred and fifty."

"The price you quoted was a hundred, and that's all you get." Charles fingered the shotgun. "I wouldn't argue—you know us boys from the buttermilk cavalry. Thieves and killers."

He grinned again. The deal was concluded without further negotiation.

"Charlie, you were flummoxed," Ambrose declared five minutes after Charles got back to camp with the gray. "Any fool can see that horse has nothing to recommend it."

"Appearances don't always tell the tale, Ambrose." He ran a hand down Sport's slightly arched nose. The gelding nuzzled in a determined way. "Besides, I think he likes me."

"He's the wrong color. Everyone will take you for a damn cornet player instead of a gentleman."

"I'm not a gentleman. I quit trying to be one when I was seven. Thanks for the loan of your horse. I've got to feed and water this one."

"Let my nigger do it for you."

135

"Toby's your manservant, not mine. Besides, ever since I attended the Academy, I've had this peculiar idea that a trooper should care for his own mount. It is his second self, as the saying goes."

"I detect disapproval," Ambrose grumbled. "What's wrong with bringing a slave to camp?"

"Nothing—until the fighting starts. No one will do that for you."

Ambrose found the remark irksome. He stayed silent for some seconds, then muttered, "By the way, Hampton wants to see you."

Charles frowned. "About what?"

"Don't know. The colonel wouldn't confide in me. Maybe I'm not professional enough to suit him. Hell, I don't deny it. I only signed up because I love to ride and I hate Yankees—and I don't want a bundle of petticoats left on my doorstep some night to tell everybody I'm a shirker. I thought I'd earn the respect of my friends by taking a legion commission, and instead I've lost it." He sighed. "Remember we're dining with old princey-prince this evening?"

"Thanks for reminding me. I forgot."

"Tell Hampton not to keep you, because his highness expects us to be prompt."

Charles smiled as he led Sport away. "That's right, in this army it's dinner parties before duty. I'll be sure to remind the colonel of that."

Though Camp Hampton was the bivouac of an elite regiment, it was still succumbing to familiar afflictions, Charles noticed on his way to regimental headquarters forty minutes later. He saw human waste left on the ground instead of in the sinks dug for the purpose. The smell was worse because the late afternoon was windless.

He saw a pair of privates stumbling-drunk from the poisonous busthead sold by the inevitable sutler in the inevitable tent. He saw three gaudily dressed ladies who were definitely not officers' wives or laundresses. Charles hadn't slept with a woman in months, and he could tell it. Still, he wasn't ready to take up with beauties like these; not with so many complaints of clap in the encampment.

In contrast to the busy sutler, the gray-bearded colporteur had

136

no customers at all and made a forlorn sight seated against the wheel of his wagon reading some of his own merchandise. One of the Bibles he sold? No, it was a tract, Charles observed; possibly *A Mother's Parting Words to Her Soldier Boy*, eight pages of cautionary moralizing in the form of a letter. It was a hot seller throughout the army, though most of the better-educated legionnaires jeered at it.

He passed two young gentlemen whose salutes were so brief as to border on insulting. Before Charles finished returning the salutes, the men were once again arguing over the price to pay a substitute when it was inconvenient to stand guard. Twenty-five cents per tour was the customary rate.

The next unpleasantness he came upon was a large pavilion with its sides raised because of the sweltering heat and dampness after the rain. Inside lay those already felled by the shotless war. Sickness was everywhere; bad water made men's bowels run and constrict with ghastly pain; balls of opium paste did little to alleviate the suffering. Surviving dysentery in Texas had not kept Charles from spending another week with it in Virginia. Now there was a new epidemic in the army: measles.

He hated to wish for combat but, as he entered the headquarters area, he couldn't deny he was sick of camp life. Mightn't be long before he got his wish, at that. Some old political hack, General Patterson, had pushed Joe Johnston and his men out of Harpers Ferry, and word was circulating that McDowell would shortly move at least thirty thousand men to the strategic rail junction of Manassas Gap.

Barker, the regimental adjutant, was finishing some business with the colonel, so Charles had to wait. He scratched suddenly. God, he had them, all right.

About six, the captain came out and Charles reported to the colonel he greatly admired—Wade Hampton of the Congaree: a millionaire, a good leader, and a fine cavalryman in spite of his age. "Be at ease, Captain," Hampton said after the formalities. "Sit if you like."

Charles took the stool in front of Hampton's neat field desk, one corner of which was reserved for a small velvet box with its lid raised. In the box stood an easeled frame, filigreed silver, containing a miniature of Hampton's second wife, Mary.

The colonel rose and stretched. He was a man of commanding appearance, six feet tall, broad-shouldered, obviously possessed of immense strength. Though a splendid rider, he never indulged in the kind of equestrian pranks that were common in the First Virginia, commanded by Beauty Stuart, whom Charles had known and liked at the Academy. Jeb had dash, Hampton a forceful deliberateness. No one questioned either man's courage, but their styles were as disparate as their ages, and Charles had heard their few meetings had been cool.

"I'm sorry I was gone when you sent for me, Colonel. Captain Barker was aware of the reason. I needed a remount."

"Find one?"

"Luckily, yes."

"Very good. I wouldn't care to lose you to Company Q for too long." Hampton drew a paper from a pile on the desk. "I wanted to see you about another discipline problem. Earlier today, one of your men absented himself without leave. He was present for morning roll call but gone by breakfast call a half hour later. He was apprehended ten miles from here, purely by chance. An officer recognized the legion uniform, hailed him, and asked where he was going. The young idiot told the truth. He said he was on his way to participate in a horse race."

Charles scowled. "With some First Virginia troopers, perhaps?"

"Exactly." Hampton brushed knuckles against his bushy side whiskers, dark as his wavy hair; the whiskers met and blended into a luxuriant mustache. "The race is to be held tomorrow, within sight of enemy pickets—presumably to add the spice of danger." He didn't hide his scorn. "The soldier was returned under guard. When First Sergeant Reynolds asked why he'd gone off as he had, he replied—" Hampton glanced at the paper—" 'I went to have some fun. The First Virginia are a daring bunch, with good leadership. They know a trooper's first responsibility is to die game.' " Chilly gray-blue eyes fixed on Charles. "End of quote."

"I can guess the man you're talking about, sir." The same one who had wanted to kill the Union prisoner they took some weeks ago. "Cramm?"

"That's right. Private Custom Dawkins Cramm the third. A young man from a rich and important family."

"Also, if the colonel will forgive me, an aristocratic pain in the rear."

"We do have our share of them. Brave boys, I think, but unsuited to soldiering. As yet." The addition declared his intent to change that. He slapped the paper with the back of his other hand. "But this foolishness! 'To die game.' That may be Stuart's way, but I prefer to win and live. Regarding Cramm—I'm empowered to convene a special court-martial. He's your man, however. You deserve the right to make the decision."

"Convene it," Charles said without hesitation. "I'll serve, if you'll permit one."

"I'll place you in charge."

"Where's Cramm now, sir?"

"Confined to quarters. Under guard."

"I believe I'll give him the good news personally."

"Please do," Hampton said, his eyes belying his dispassionate expression. "This man's come to my attention too often. Examples must be made. McDowell will move soon, and we can't mass our forces and overwhelm the enemy if each soldier does exactly as he wishes, whenever he wishes."

"Exactly right, Colonel." Hampton had no formal military training, but he understood that part of the lesson book. Charles saluted and went straight to Private Cramm's tent. Outside, a noncom stood guard. Nearby, Cramm's black body servant, old and hunchbacked, polished the brass corners of a trunk.

"Corporal," Charles said, "you will hear and see nothing for the next two minutes."

"Yes, sir!"

Inside, Private Custom Dawkins Cramm III reclined among the many books he had brought to camp. He wore a loose white silk blouse—nonregulation—and didn't rise when his superior entered, though he gave him an annoyed stare.

"Stand up."

Cramm went off like a bomb, hurling down the gold-stamped volume of Coleridge. "The hell I will. I was a gentleman before I joined your damned troop, I'm still a gentleman, and I'm damned if you'll continue to treat me like some nigger slave."

Charles took hold of the fine blouse, ripping it as he yanked Cramm to his feet. "What I'm going to do, Cramm, is chair the special court-martial to which Colonel Hampton appointed me five minutes ago. Then I'll do my utmost to give you the maximum penalty—thirty-one days of hard labor. You'll serve every minute of it unless we go up against the Yankees first, in which case they'll punish you by blowing your head off because you're too stupid to be a soldier. But at least you'll die game."

He pushed Cramm so hard that the young man sailed into his little wooden library cabinet, bounced away, and knocked down the rear tent pole. On one knee, gripping the pole, Cramm glared.

"We should have elected a gentleman as our captain. Next time we will."

Red-faced, Charles walked out.

"Here we come, gentlemen. Nice hot oysters Creole. Got 'em fixed crispy and jus' right for you."

With a politeness so exquisite it approached mockery, Ambrose Pell's slave Toby bent forward to offer a silver tray of appetizers on small china plates; Toby had been dragooned to assist the host's hired servants, a couple of rascally looking Belgians. Toby was about forty, and in contrast to his servile posture, his eyes shone with a sly resentment. So Charles thought, anyway.

Privately, he termed that kind of behavior putting on old massa. He had a theory that the more expert a slave became at the deceptive ritual, the more likely it was that he hated those who owned him. Not that Charles blamed any black very much for such feelings; four years at West Point, and exposure to people and ideas not strictly Southern, had begun a change in his thinking, and nothing since had stopped it or reversed it. He considered all the rhetoric in defense of slavery so much spit in the wind and probably wrong to boot.

The large striped tent belonging to their host was ablaze with candles and filled with music—Ambrose performing some Mozart on the better of his two flutes. He played well. One side of the tent was raised and netted to bar night insects but allow entry of an occasional breeze. Bathed and outfitted in clean clothes, Charles felt better. The trouble with Cramm had put him in a bad mood, but discovery of a parcel from Mont Royal had helped to relieve it. The sight of the inscription on the light cavalry saber touched him. The gilt-banded scabbard rested against his left leg now. Though the sword lacked the practicality of Hampton's Columbia-made issue, Charles would treasure it far more.

With a tiny silver fork, he broke the lightly spiced breading on the oyster. He ate a morsel, then swallowed some of the good whiskey from the Waterford goblet provided by their host and new friend, Pierre Serbakovsky. He and Ambrose had met the stocky, urbane young man during a tour of Richmond's better saloons.

Serbakovsky had the rank of captain but preferred to be addressed as prince. He was one of a number of European officers who had joined the Confederacy. The prince was aide-de-camp to Major Rob Wheat, commander of a regiment of Louisiana Zouaves nicknamed the Tigers. The regiment contained the dregs of the streets of New Orleans; there wasn't a unit in Virginia more notorious for robbery and violence.

"I believe this will be enough whiskey," the prince declared to Toby. "Ask Jules whether the Mumm's is chilled, and if so, serve it at once."

Serbakovsky liked to be in charge, but his manner was too lofty even for a slave. Charles watched Toby swallow twice and compress his lips as he walked out.

He took more whiskey to relieve feelings of guilt. He and Ambrose shouldn't be lolling at supper, but conducting school for their noncoms, which they did almost every night so that the noncoms could attempt to re-teach the lessons on the drill field. The devil with guilt for one evening, he thought. He'd drink it away now and let it return tomorrow.

Abruptly, Ambrose jerked the flute from his lips and scratched furiously under his right arm. "Damn it, I've got 'em again." His face grew as red as his curls. He was a fastidious person; this was humiliation.

Serbakovsky leaned back in his upholstered chair, amused. "Permit me a word of advice, *mon frère,*" he said in heavily accented English. "Bathe. As frequently as you can, no matter how vile and strong the soap, how cold the stream, or how repugnant the notion of standing naked before one's inferiors."

"I do bathe, Princey. But the damned graybacks keep coming."

"The truth is, they never leave," Charles said as Toby and the younger Belgian entered with a tray of fluted glasses and a dark bottle in a silver bucket of flaked ice, a commodity so scarce in the South it might well have cost more than ten times the champagne. "They're in your uniform. You have to give the vermin a complete discharge."

"What, throw this coat away?"

"And everything else you wear."

"Replacing 'em at my own expense? Damned if I will, Charlie.

Uniforms are the responsibility of the commandant, not gentlemen who serve with him."

Charles shrugged. "Spend or scratch. Up to you."

The prince laughed, then snapped his fingers. The young Belgian stepped forward at once, Toby more slowly. Was Charles the only one who noticed the slave's resentment?

"Delicious," he said after his first drink of champagne. "Do all European officers entertain this handsomely?"

"Only if their ancestors accumulated wealth by means better left unmentioned."

Charles liked Serbakovsky, whose history fascinated him. The prince's paternal grandfather, a Frenchman, had held a colonelcy in the army Bonaparte led to Russia. Along the invasion route, he met a young woman of the Russian aristocracy; physical attraction temporarily overcame political enmity, and she conceived a child, born while the colonel was perishing on the infamous winter retreat. Serbakovsky's grandmother had given her illegitimate son her last name as a symbol of family and national pride, and never married. Serbakovsky had been a soldier since his eighteenth birthday, first in his mother country, then abroad.

While Ambrose vainly tried to drink and scratch at the same time, in came the first course—local shad, baked. This was to be followed by a specialty of the older Belgian, three chickens stewed with garlic cloves in the style of Provence.

"Wish we'd get out of this damn camp and see the elephant," Ambrose said as he prepared to attack the shad.

"Do not ask for that which you know nothing about, my good friend," the prince said, somber suddenly; he had been blooded in the Crimea and had told Charles of some of the horrors witnessed there. "It's an idle wish anyway, I believe. This Confederacy of yours—she is in the same happy position as my homeland in 1812."

"Explain that, Prince," Charles said.

"Simple enough. The land itself will win the war for you. It is so vast—so spread from here to there—the enemy will soon despair of conquering it and abandon the effort. Little or no fighting will be necessary for a victory. That is my professional prediction."

"Hope it's wrong," Charles said. "I'd like one chance to wear this to accept the surrender of some Yanks." He touched the scabbard. The various drinks had combined to banish what he knew about the nature of war and create a pleasant sense of invulnerability.

"The sword is a gift from your cousin, you said. May I examine it?"

Charles drew the saber; reflections of the candles ran like lightning along the blade as he passed the weapon to Serbakovsky. He inspected it closely. "Solingen. Very fine." He returned it. "Beautiful. I would keep a sharp eye on it. Serving with these Louisiana guttersnipes, I have discovered that soldiers in America are like soldiers everywhere. Whatever can be stolen, they will steal."

Drunk, Charles managed to forget the warning right away. Nor did he hear the sound of one man, perhaps more, moving on again after stopping in the dark beyond the netting.

21

From the valise on the dirty floor, Stanley took the samples and set them on the desk, which was clean and bare of so much as a single piece of paper. The factory had no business; it was shut down. A property broker had directed the Hazards there shortly after they arrived in the town of Lynn.

The man at the desk was temporarily acting as a sort of caretaker for the factory. He was a husky, ruddy fellow, white-haired and broad about the middle. Stanley put his age at fifty-five. The man picked up the samples, one per hand, with a quickness suggesting he hated his idle state.

"The Jefferson style," he said, tapping a free finger on the moderately high quarter of the shoe. "Issued to the cavalry as well as the infantry."

"You know your business, Mr. Pennyford," Stanley said with a smarmy smile. He distrusted New Englanders—people who spoke with such a queer accent couldn't be normal—but he needed this man on his side. "A contract for bootees of this type would find a broad and lucrative market."

"In heaven's name, Stanley, call them by their right name. They're shoes," Isabel said from near the window. The light of a dark day through a filthy pane didn't flatter her; outside, a late June storm pounded the roofs of Lynn.

Stanley took pleasure in retorting, "The government doesn't use the term."

Pennyford backed him up. "In military circles, Mrs. Hazard, the word *shoe* signifies footwear for a lady. Mighty odd, if you ask me. Strikes me there's plenty that's odd in Washington."

"To the point, Mr. Pennyford," Stanley broke in. "Could that rusty machinery downstairs manufacture large quantities of this item and do it quickly and cheaply?"

"Quickly? Ayah—once I effect some repairs the present owners couldn't afford. Cheaply?" He flicked one of the samples with a finger. "Nothing could be cheaper than these. Two eyelets—only pegs twixt the sole and upper—" One wrench of his strong hands separated the two parts of the right shoe. "These are a disgrace to the cordwainer's trade. I'd hate to be a poor soldier boy wearing them in mud or snow. If Washington sees fit to issue such trash to our brave lads, Washington is more than odd; Washington's contemptible."

"Spare me your moralizing, please," Stanley said, seeming to inflate as he did so. "Can the Lashbrook Footwear Company turn out this kind of bootee?"

Reluctantly: "Ayah." He leaned forward, startling Stanley. "But we can do much better. There's this fellow Lyman Blake who has invented the greatest advance in factory equipment I've ever seen, and I have been in the trade since I apprenticed at age nine. Blake's machine sews the uppers and sole together swiftly—cleanly—securely. Another man will soon be manufacturing the machine—Blake lacked capital and sold his design—but I'll wager that within a year his invention will bring this industry and the entire state back to life."

"Not quite, Mr. Pennyford," Isabel countered with a smile meant to put him in his place. "What will bring prosperity back to Massachusetts and the shoe industry is a long war and contracts that can be obtained by well-connected men like my husband."

Pennyford's cheeks grew dark as ripe apples. Alarmed, Stanley said, "Mr. Pennyford was only trying to be helpful, Isabel. You will stay on, won't you, Dick? Manage the factory as you did before it closed?"

Pennyford stayed silent quite a while. "I would not like to do this kind of work, Mr. Hazard. But, candidly, I have nine children to house, feed, and clothe, and there are many factories shuttered in Lynn, and few jobs. I will stay—on one condition. You must permit me to run things my own way, without interference, so long as I produce the agreed-upon product, in the agreed-upon quantity, by the agreed-upon date."

Stanley whacked the desk. "Done!"

"I think the whole place can be had for about two hundred thousand," Pennyford added. "Lashbrook's widow is desperate for cash."

"We will locate the representatives of the estate and call on them immediately."

Purchase was arranged by noon the next day, with virtually no haggling. Stanley felt euphoric as he helped Isabel board a southbound train at the grimy depot. Seated in the overheated dining car enjoying eggs and bacon—Isabel loathed his plebeian taste in food—he couldn't contain his enthusiasm.

"We found a treasure in that Dick Pennyford. Now what about buying some of those new machines he described?"

"We ought to weigh that carefully." She meant she would do the weighing. "We needn't worry whether our shoes are durable, only that we deliver enough of them to make money. If the new machines will speed up production—well, then, perhaps."

"We'll make money," Stanley exclaimed as the train swayed around a bend. The whistle howled. The summer storm continued to dash rain against the glass beside their table. "I'm confident of it. Why, do you realize"—he forked eggs into his mouth, speaking while chewing—"you and I will soon be perfect examples of the boss's definition of a patriot?"

"What's that?"

"Someone infused with love of the old flag and an appropriation."

He continued to eat and chew vigorously. Isabel was pensive. She left her broiled fish untouched and sat with gloved hands

145

under her chin, her eyes fixed on the dreary landscape streaming by. "We mustn't confine our thinking to narrow limits, Stanley."

"What do you mean?"

"I heard some fascinating gossip before we left Washington. Certain industrialists are said to be hunting ways and means to trade with the Confederacy in the event of a long war."

Stanley clacked his fork to his plate. His lower jaw had dropped down in front of the napkin stuffed into his collar. "You aren't suggesting—"

"Imagine an arrangement," she went on, low-voiced, "by which military shoes were privately exchanged for cotton. How many shoe factories are there down South? Few or none, I'll bet. Imagine the need—and the price you could get for a bale of cotton if you resold it up here. Multiply the price several thousand times and think of the profit. Enormous."

"But that kind of trade would be—" He sensed someone hovering and glanced up. "We're not finished, boy." He supplemented the remark with a glare at the black waiter, who left again. The table cut into Stanley's paunch as he whispered: "It would be dangerous, Isabel. Worse than that, it would be treason."

"It could also be the way to make not merely a profit but a fortune." Like a mother with a slow child, she patted his pudgy hand. "Don't rule it out, my sweet."

He didn't.

"Finish your eggs before they get cold."

He did.

22

Faint sounds. From far away, he thought in the first seconds of waking in the dark. Across the tent, Ambrose emitted one of his characteristic snores, a malignant mix of whistles and buzzing.

Charles lay on his right side. His linen underdrawers were soaked with sweat. The humidity was fierce. As he thought about reaching over to poke Ambrose and silence him, the sound separated into recognizable elements: night insects and something else. Charles held his breath and didn't move.

Even with his cheek pressed to the camp bed, he could see the tent entrance. Open. A silhouette momentarily blocked the glow of a guardpost lantern. He heard the intruder breathing.

He's after the sword.

It lay in its oiled-paper wrapping on top of the small trunk at the foot of the bed. *Should have found a safer place.* He prepared himself as best he could, fear edging into him. It was a hard position from which to rise suddenly, but he did it, bolting up from the waist. As he gained his feet he let out a growl he hoped would confuse and frighten the thief.

Instead, it woke Ambrose. He uttered a wild yell as Charles lunged at the shadow-man who was picking up the sword. "Give me that, damn you."

The thief drove an elbow into Charles's face. Blood spurted from his left nostril. He staggered, and the thief dove into the street of neatly spaced tents and raced left, away from the picket post where the lantern shone. Bleeding and swearing, Charles went after him.

He could pick out a few details of the thief's appearance. He was heavy and wore white gaiters. One of Rob Wheat's Tigers, by God. Serbakovsky's warning came to mind. That evening he dined with the prince, Charles had been feeling too good to detect or even worry about the presence of someone outside, someone who must have spied on the party through the netting, seen the saber—

His arms and legs pumped. Blood trickled down his upper lip; he spat it away. Stones and burrs hurt his bare feet, but he kept gaining. The thief looked back, his face a round blur. Charles heard Ambrose hollering just as he hurled himself forward, his feet leaving the ground a second before his hands caught the waist of the thief's blue-and-white sultan's bloomers.

The man screamed an obscenity; both fell. Charles landed on the back of the man's legs, badly jarred. The thief dropped the sword and struggled to turn beneath Charles and get free, kicking all the while. A gaitered boot knocked Charles's head back. The Tiger jumped up.

Dazed, Charles grabbed the man's left leg and pulled him down again—along with the huge bowie knife he had yanked from a belt sheath. Charles whipped his head aside to avoid a cut that would have sliced away most of one cheek.

The Tiger pushed Charles over. His head hit a rock. "Corporal of the guard! Corporal of the guard!" Ambrose was bellowing. Charles could well be dead before help arrived; he had gotten a look at the thief, so it would be safer for the man to leave a corpse.

He dropped on Charles's chest with both knees. He had a round face, pug nose, curly mustachios. He smelled of onions and dirt. "Fuckin' Carolina fop," he grunted, holding the bowie with both hands and forcing the point down toward Charles's throat.

Frantic, Charles locked his hands under the thief's wrist and pushed up—*pushed*. God, the bastard was strong. He shifted a knee into Charles's groin and put weight on it. Blinded by sweat and the pain, Charles almost couldn't see the knife blade as it dipped to within three inches of his chin.

Two inches.

One—

"Jesus," Charles moaned, tears in his eyes because of the knee crushing his balls. One more moment and his throat would be slashed. He gambled he could hold the thief's wrist with one hand, thrust the other upward—

His left hand moved. The knife edged down. Charles found the thief's hair and pulled. The man shrieked, his attack thrown off. Slippery fingers released the bowie. Falling, it raked Charles's left ribs lightly. As the thief tried to stand, Charles grabbed the knife and buried three inches of it in a thigh.

The Tiger screamed louder. He toppled over and crashed in the weeds some yards beyond the last tent, the knife sticking from his fine striped pantaloons.

"You all right, Captain Main?"

Rising, Charles nodded to the noncom, first to reach him; other men poured down the dark tent street and surrounded him. The thief moaned and thrashed in the weeds.

"Take him to the surgeons to have that leg tended. Make sure someone fastens a ball and chain on his other ankle so he's around when his regiment court-martials him."

The noncom asked, "What did he do, sir?"

Charles wiped blood from his nose with his bare wrist. "Tried to steal my dress sword." No honor code among these recruits, he thought with bitterness. Maybe I'm a fool, hoping for a rule-book war. He picked up the scabbarded blade from where it had fallen and trudged away.

Wide awake and excited, Ambrose wanted to discuss the incident. Charles held a scrap of rag to his nose until the bleeding stopped, then insisted they turn in. He was spent. Barely asleep, he bolted up again.

"What in the name of God—"

The nature of the noise registered. Men, right outside, singing "Camptown Races" loudly enough for Richmond to hear it.

"They're serenading you, Charlie," Ambrose whispered. "Your own boys. If you don't go out and listen, they'll be insulted."

Groggy and skeptical, Charles pushed the tent flap aside, then shivered with an unexpected emotional reaction to the tribute. A wind had sprung up, blowing from the direction of the seacoast. The mist was gone and the moon was visible; so were faces he recognized. The men must have heard of the thief's capture. They were honoring him in a traditional way.

Some were honoring him, he amended; he counted eleven.

Ambrose danced up and down like a boy, breaking out his flute to accompany the singers. Over his shoulder, Charles said, "They'll expect the usual reward for a serenade. Haul out our private stock of whiskey, will you?"

"Glad to, Charlie. Yes, indeed."

The men liked him for a change. While it lasted, he might as well enjoy it.

23

On July 1, a Monday, George arrived in Washington. He checked into his hotel, then took a hack to an area of huge homes set far apart on large lots. The driver pointed out the residence the Little Giant had occupied for such a short time. Stephen Douglas had died in June, strongly supporting the President he had opposed as a candidate last year.

Housing was scarce in Washington. Stanley and Isabel had been fortunate to hear of an ailing widow no longer able to keep up her home. She packed off to live with a relative, and Stanley signed a year-long lease. He had provided this information and the address in a recent note so stiffly worded that George felt sure Cameron had insisted Stanley write it for purposes of departmental harmony. Why had the old bandit meddled? George thought irritably. The note had forced this response—a duty call with all the charm of a tumbril ride in the French Revolution.

"Mighty fine place," the hackman called as they drove up. "Mighty fine" hardly covered it. Stanley's home, like those nearby, was a mansion.

A butler informed him that Mr. and Mrs. Hazard were in New England. The servant had a snide and condescending manner. Maybe Isabel gives them demonstrations, George thought with cheerful spleen.

Inside, he spied unopened packing crates. Evidently they had

150

just moved in. George left his card and jumped in the hack again, smiling. No need to call a second time; not this trip.

He ate alone in the hotel dining room, where he overhead some speculative talk about old General Patterson, said to be ready to march from Harpers Ferry into the Shenandoah. In his room, George tried to read the latest *Scientific American* but couldn't concentrate. He felt nervous about the interviews scheduled for next morning.

At half past nine, he arrived at the five-story Winder Building on the corner of Seventeenth Street across from President's Park. The original brick had been brightened up by a coat of plaster and an ironwork balcony on the second floor. George studied this and found it wanting in style. He couldn't manufacture every piece of iron in America, but he often wished he could.

He moved past sentries on duty to protect the important government officials headquartered here; one was General Scott. Entering the building was like diving under the sea on a sunny day. Going up the gloomy iron stairs, he noticed the bad state of the woodwork and paint peeling everywhere.

Civilians with portfolios or rolled-up plans packed the benches in the second-floor corridor. Clerks and uniformed men traveled from doorway to doorway on mysterious errands. George stopped a captain and was directed through another door into a stone-floored office of appalling disorder. At rows of desks, other clerks wrote or shuffled papers. Two lieutenants argued over a clay model of a cannon.

George and Wotherspoon had found the flaw in the casting process, and organization of the bank was proceeding smoothly, so he had a clear conscience about this visit—though at the moment he had a wild urge to flee.

A middle-aged officer approached, radiating importance. "Hazard?" George said yes. "The chief of Ordnance is not here as yet. I am Captain Maynadier. You may sit and wait—there, next to Colonel Ripley's desk. I regret I have no time to chat. I have been in this department fifteen years and have never once caught up with my paperwork. Paper is the curse of Washington."

He waddled off and went exploring among several mountains of it landscaping his desk. Someone had told George that Maynadier was an Academy man. Though all West Point graduates were supposed to be brothers, friends, George would be happy to make an exception.

151

He took a chair. After twenty minutes, he heard shouting in the hall.

"Colonel Ripley!"

"If you'll only give me a moment—"

"May I show you this—?"

"Han't got time."

The irascible voice preceded an equally irascible lieutenant colonel, a sharp-featured old fellow from Connecticut, Academy class of '14. The chief of the Ordnance Department carried his official burdens and his sixty-six years with notable displeasure.

"Hazard, is it?" he barked as George rose. "Han't got much time for you, either. Do you want the job or not? Carries the rank of captain till we can get you a brevet. All my officers need brevets. Cameron wants you in here, so I guess it's cut and dried if you say yes."

Hat and dress gauntlets were slapped on the desk during the foregoing. Ripley's verbal tantrum would have been funny to anyone not connected with the department—or thinking of being connected. A distinct silence—fear?—had descended on the high-ceilinged room the moment Ripley entered.

"Sit down, sit down," the colonel said. "The Hazard works has a contract from this department, don't it?"

"Yes, sir. We'll meet it on schedule."

"Good. Better than a lot of our suppliers can say. Well, ask me questions. Talk. We're due in the park in half an hour. The secretary wants to see you, and since he's the one who put me in this job two months ago, I reckon we'll go."

"I do have one important question, Colonel Ripley. You know I'm an ironmaker by trade. How would that help me fit in here? What would I do if I worked for you?"

"Supervise artillery contracts, for one. You also run a huge manufactory, which I presume takes organizational skill. We can use it. Look at the mess I inherited," he cried with a sweeping gesture. Maynadier, whose desk was adjoining, renewed his attack on the paper peaks with a haste approaching frenzy.

"I'd welcome your presence, Hazard—long as you don't bother me with newfangled proposals. Han't got any time for those. Tested weapons are the best weapons."

Another Stanley. Foursquare against change. That was a definite negative. George began to understand why the colonel's critics called him Ripley Van Winkle.

They discussed pay and how soon he could report—details he considered secondary. He was in a mood as sour as Ripley's when the colonel consulted a pocket watch and proclaimed them two minutes late to meet Cameron.

Out they dashed through the barricades of bodies. Several contract seekers followed Ripley downstairs, shrill as gulls chasing a fishing boat. One man, yelling about his "remarkable centrifugal gun" that would hurl projectiles "with the fury of a slingshot," knocked George's hat off with brandished plans.

"Inventors," Ripley fumed as he crossed the avenue. "Ought to ship every last one back to the madhouses they came from—"

Another innovation no doubt infuriating to the colonel floated above the trees of President's Park. Guy ropes secured its empty observation basket to the ground. George recognized *Enterprise,* the balloon featured in last month's illustrated papers. It had been exhibited in this same location not many days ago, and Lincoln was said to have been interested in its potential for aerial observation of enemy troops.

The balloon fascinated George because he had seen only one other, at a Bethlehem fair. *Enterprise* was made of colorful gored sections of pongee, the whole filled with hydrogen. Farther back in the trees, beyond the crowd of mothers, children, government officials, and a few blacks, he saw the wagon with wooden tanks in which sulphuric acid and iron filings combined to produce the gas.

Ripley paraded through the crowd in a manner that said he was a person of authority. They found Simon Cameron talking with a thirtyish fellow in a long linen coat. Before introductions could be finished, the young man pumped George's hand.

"Dr. Thaddeus Sobieski Constantine Lowe, sir. An honor to meet you! Though I'm from New Hampshire, I know your name and high standing in the world of industry. May I describe my plan for an aerial spy corps? I hope interested citizens will support it so the commanding general will be persuaded—"

"General Scott will give the scheme due consideration," Cameron broke in. "You needn't arrange any more exhibitions of this kind." Behind the smile of the old pol lay a hint that they wouldn't be tolerated on government land, either. "If you will excuse me, Doctor, I have business to discuss with our visitor."

And he drew George away as if they had always been political partners, not opponents. Ripley dogged them as they strolled.

153

"Have a good chat with the colonel, George?"

"I did, Mr. Secretary."

"Simon. We're old friends. Look here—I know you and Stanley don't always get along. But this is wartime. We have to set personal matters to one side. I never think of the past. Who worked and voted against me back home and who didn't—" After that sly dig, Cameron began to preach. "Ripley urgently needs a man for artillery procurement. Someone who understands ironmakers, who talks their language—"

He faced George, squinting against the hot July light. "Unless we wish to see this nation fail, we must all shoulder part of the burden of preserving it."

Don't spout homilies at me, you damned crook, George thought. At the same time, curiously, he responded to the appeal. The words were true, even if the man wasn't.

Ripley harrumphed, intruding. "Well, Hazard? Any decision?"

"You've been very forthcoming with practical information about the job, sir. But I'd like the rest of the day to consider everything."

"Only fair," Cameron agreed. "I look forward to hearing from you, George. I know your decision will be good news." Once again he clapped the visitor on the shoulder, then rushed off.

The fact was, George had already decided. He would come to Washington, but he would bring a load of reservations as baggage. He didn't feel noble, merely foolish and, consequently, a little depressed.

Ripley whirled at the sound of a commotion—Dr. Lowe chasing some urchins from beneath the bobbing balloon basket. "Han't got time for such nonsense in wartime," Ripley complained as they left President's Park. Whether he meant balloons or children, George didn't bother to ask.

Later that day, George hired a horse and rode across the Potomac, following directions Brett had provided. He couldn't find Captain Farmer's pick-and-shovel company. Since business required that he take a 7:00 P.M. train, he reluctantly turned back. All around the fortifications he saw fields of tents and men drilling. It reminded him of Mexico, with one difference: the soldiers obliquing or clumsily marching to the rear were so young.

24

Several days later in the mansion on I Street, Isabel took tea in a room she had claimed for herself during their first inspection of the house. For one hour, starting at four, she forbade anyone to disturb her while she sipped and read the newspapers.

It was a daily ritual, and one she considered vital to success in this labyrinthine city. A quick study, Isabel already knew certain fundamentals of survival. It was better to be devious than forthright. Never reveal one's true opinion; the wrong person might hear it. A sensitivity to shifting power balances was also important. Stanley was about as sensitive as a wheel of cheese; so his wife, a step removed from the daily activities of the government, relied on newspapers. One could learn only so much at balls, receptions, and salons—or from Stanley.

Today she discovered the reprinted text of the President's Independence Day message to Congress. It was largely a reiteration of the causes of the war. Lincoln put all the blame on the South, naturally, and stated again that the Confederacy hadn't really needed to take Fort Sumter for any strategic reason. Hotheads had created a false issue of patriotic pride, and as a consequence, the South was rashly testing *whether a constitutional republic, or a democracy—a government of the people, by the same people—can, or cannot, maintain its territorial, integrity against its own foes.*

Isabel loathed the apelike Westerner, but never more so than when she read his declaration that he was seeking *the legal means for making this contest a short, and a decisive one.*

Legal, when he had just asked Scott to suspend habeas corpus in certain military districts between Washington and New York? The man's pronouncements were twaddle. He was already behaving like an emperor.

Two sections of the message did please her. Although Lincoln hoped for a short war, he had asked Congress to place four hundred thousand men at his disposal. Isabel saw eight hundred thousand Jefferson boots.

Further, the President didn't spare the military academies:

It is worthy of note that in this, the government's hour of trial, large numbers of those in the army and navy who have been favored as officers have resigned and proved false to the hand which had pampered them.

Splendid. When her egotistical brother-in-law arrived, perhaps she could make capital of the rising anti–West Point sentiment. News that George would be coming to town had been waiting when she and Stanley returned from New England. She had also learned that he had called at the mansion, a sham courtesy resulting from Cameron's insistence that Stanley write a conciliatory note welcoming the brother who had once knocked him down. The whole incident infuriated her.

George remained a West Point loyalist, but many influential people wanted the institution abolished. Most with that goal belonged to a new clique that was forming: an alliance of senators, congressmen, and cabinet officers from the extreme pro-abolition wing of the Republican party. Kate Chase's father belonged, it was said; so did the clubfooted old wreck from Isabel's home state, Congressman Thad Stevens. How she would use this information to hurt George was still nebulous. But use it she would.

Isabel had been watching the new radical clique slowly coalesce. She already knew certain facts, one of the most important being that the foxy Mr. Cameron carried no weight with the group.

The radicals favored an aggressive war and harsh terms when it was won. Lincoln held different views on the war and on slavery. He didn't want all the Negroes freed to rampage and rape and rob white men of jobs. Neither did Isabel. But that wouldn't prevent her from cultivating the wives of the radicals if doing so offered some advantage.

At dinner that evening, she brought up Lincoln's message. "He is saying exactly the same thing we've heard from certain congressmen. West Point trained traitors at public expense and should be closed. That sentiment might be useful against your brother."

Stanley's unusual good cheer infuriated her—he had been grinning ever since he got home—and so did his obtuse, "Why should I want to hurt George now?"

"Have you forgotten all of his insults? And those of his wife?"

"No, of course not, but—"

"Suppose he comes here and starts asserting himself in that pushy way of his?"

"What if he does? Ordnance reports to the War Department. I outrank him. And I'm close to Simon, don't forget."

Did the fool believe that was a safe spot? Before she could snap at him, he continued, "Enough about George. I received two pieces of good news in today's mail. Those attorneys we hired in Lynn—absolute charlatans, but they reached and paid off the right people. The property transfer will be pushed through quickly. I heard from Pennyford, too. He'll have the factory ready for double-shift operation within the month—and no problem about help. There are two or three applicants for every job. We can hire children even more cheaply."

"How wonderful," she sneered. "We have everything we need. Except a contract."

He shot his hand into his pocket. "We have that, too."

Isabel was seldom speechless, but she was now. Stanley handed her the ribbon-bound document as if he had captured it in battle. "How—very fine." She said it weakly because she didn't mean it; he had obtained the contract on his own. Was this city or his job somehow changing him into what he had never been before? A real man? The mere possibility was profoundly upsetting.

25

Serbakovsky was dead.

In the first week of July, fellow officers laid him in a coffin of raw yellow pine. Two bearded men in heavily braided uniforms appeared with a wagon and civilian driver. The Russians, who spoke only rudimentary English, carried safe-conduct papers signed by Union as well as Confederate authorities. The ease with which they had traveled from Washington in response to a courier message confirmed something Charles had heard repeatedly: going through the lines in either direction was not hard.

The blithe prince, who had missed death on so many battlefields, had been killed by a child's disease. It was killing soldiers in epidemic numbers. Victims got up too soon, thinking themselves over the measles, and relapsed into fatal fevers. The surgeons seemed helpless.

The wagon creaked away into the hot dusk, and Ambrose and Charles went to the sutler's to get drunk. After four rounds, Ambrose insisted on buying copies of *The Richmond Songster,* one of many such compilations being sold throughout the army. Charles put the songbook in his pocket and noticed a black smear on his thumbs. Damp ink. Everything was speed and opportunism these days.

A harsh surprise awaited them in their tent. Toby had disappeared, taking his master's best boots and many personal effects. Furious, Ambrose went straight to legion headquarters, while Charles, on a hunch, rode to the Tiger encampment not far away.

158

Sure enough, the prince's pavilion was gone, and so were his servants.

"Bet you my pay for the year that Toby and that pair left together," he said to Ambrose later.

"Absolutely! The Belgies can pretend Toby's their nigra and sneak him right across the Potomac into Old Abe's lap. The colonel granted me permission to leave and try to recover my property. But he said I needed your permission, too." His look said Charles had better not withhold it.

Charles sank down on his bed, unbuttoning his shirt. The death, the thefts, the waiting—all of it depressed him. He didn't believe Toby could be found—wasn't even sure the recovery attempt should be made—but he wanted a change of scene.

"Hell, I'll go with you if I can."

"By God, Charlie, you're a real white man."

"I'll speak to the colonel first thing tomorrow," he promised, anxious to sleep and forget.

"I don't object to your undertaking to assist Pell," Hampton said next morning, "provided your other subaltern and your first sergeant can handle drills."

"Easily, sir—though I wouldn't want to be away if we might be called up for an engagement."

"I don't know when we'll fight, or if we will," Hampton replied with uncharacteristic choler. "No one tells me anything. If you ride north, you'll be closer to the Yankees than I am—perhaps you'll see some action. Have Captain Barker write a pass and be back as soon as you can."

Fatigue shadows ringed Hampton's eyes, Charles noticed as he left. Handling a regiment all day and attending Richmond levees every night took a toll.

He and Ambrose set out at eight o'clock. Charles had donned the dress shako he seldom wore and took his shotgun, the light cavalry saber, and rations for two days. Sport frisked through the cool morning. The gelding was rested and healthy; the legion had an abundance of dry corn and plenty of pasturage near the encampment.

Charles had never thought himself capable of loving anyone or anything deeply, but he was developing a strong and unexpected liking for the quirky little gray. He knew it when he used drinking money to buy molasses to mix with Sport's feed; molasses gave a horse extra energy. He knew it when he spent an hour rubbing down the gray with a folded piece of the softest blanket he could find; fifteen minutes would have sufficed. He knew it when he devoted free time to currying and brushing the horse and trimming his mane. He knew it especially when a careless noncom put Sport in with the troop's bay mares at feeding time. A fight broke out, and Charles dashed among the snorting horses to lead the gray to safety. He cursed out the noncom, then lectured him on the importance of feeding like with like, never mixing mares and geldings.

The air today was mild and breezy, too sweet for there to be war anywhere. They inquired about the fugitives at hamlets and farms, and found the trail easy to follow. Several patrols demanded to see their passes, and Charles insisted they stop often to water the horses; an animal needed twelve gallons daily, minimum, in the summer. Charles made sure Sport stood in the shade, with hooves in water to help prevent cracking. The gray seemed nearly ready to speak when, after teasing motions toward his pocket, Charles would finally pull out the salt block and let Sport nibble and lick contentedly.

On they rode, the Blue Ridge and the sundown on their left. When Ambrose began his monotone version of "Young Lochinvar," Charles joined in with enthusiasm.

Next morning they crossed into Fairfax County, drawing closer to Old Bory's base at Manassas Junction, a small depot stop of no intrinsic value but considerable strategic significance; there, the Manassas Gap rail line came in from the Shenandoah to meet the Orange and Alexandria line. The trail had simply run out. They met no one who had seen two white men and a black answering the descriptions; there were just too many glens, woods, windy little roads, and hiding places up here near Linkumland.

About two, Charles said, "No use going on. We've lost them."

Ambrose sighed. "Damned if I like to admit it, but I think you're right." He squinted into the glare. "What do you say to a stop at that farm up by the bend? My canteen's empty."

"All right, but then we turn around. I thought I saw a flash of blue on that ridge a minute ago." He didn't know how close they were to the Yankee lines and couldn't have marked their position if it had been given to him. Reliable maps didn't exist.

They rode the last quarter mile to the neat white house with a big green wood behind. Fine fields spread on the north side.

Charles slowed Sport to a walk. "Look sharp, Ambrose. There's another visitor here ahead of us."

He bobbed his head toward the horse and buggy tied to an elm shading the rear of the house. As they turned into the front door-yard and dismounted, Charles thought a window curtain stirred. His neck began to itch.

He tethered Sport and carried his shotgun up to the porch, spurs clinking in the summer stillness. He knocked. Waited. Heard movement inside; muffled voices.

"Stay to one side and keep that piece ready," he whispered. Ambrose slid up by the wall, hands on his shotgun, cheeks popping with sweat. Charles pounded the door.

"What the devil you mean, makin' such racket?" said the poorly dressed old farmer who answered. He crowded into the opening as if to hide whatever the shadows behind him contained.

"Beg your pardon, sir," Charles said, keeping his temper. "Captain Main, Wade Hampton Legion. First Lieutenant Pell and I are searching for a fugitive Negro and two white men, Belgians, who may have passed here on their way to Washington."

"What makes you think so? This road takes you to Benning's Bridge, but there's plenty of others close by."

Warier each second, Charles said, "I fail to understand your lack of civility, sir. Whose side are you on?"

"Yours. But I got chores waitin'." He stepped back to shut the door.

Charles rammed his shoulder against it. The old man fell back, exclaiming. A woman uttered a little piping scream out of all proportion to her size. An elderly person with the shape and bulk of a small whale, she lumbered into the parlor entrance to block Charles's view. He was too tall.

Terrified, the woman said, "We're caught, Miz Barclay."

"We shouldn't have tried to keep him out. Unless it's McDowell in disguise, he's one of our own."

The soft, tart words of the second speaker startled and confused Charles for a moment. She sounded like a Virginian, but what he saw of the young woman was decidedly suspicious. Her outer skirt was hoisted to reveal a second one, crinoline-stiffened and divided into small pockets, each of which bulged slightly. On a chair he saw four oilskin packets tied with string. All at once it dawned, and he almost laughed. He had never met a smuggler, let alone an attractive one.

"Captain Charles Main, ma'am. Of—"

"The Wade Hampton Legion. You have a loud voice, Captain. Are you trying to bring the Yankees down on us?"

Saying it, she smiled, but without friendliness. He had trouble knowing what to make of her. Her clothing wasn't poor, but it was plain and wrinkled from travel. She was about his age and four or five inches shorter, with wide hips, a full bosom, blue eyes, and blond curls; a young woman who managed to look both robust and pretty as hell. For a few seconds he felt light-hearted as a boy. Then he remembered his duty.

"I'd better ask the questions, ma'am. May I present First Lieutenant Pell?" Ambrose entered the parlor. The old man huddled beside his wife.

"I saw him preening in the hall mirror. I'd have suspected you were South Carolina boys even if you hadn't announced it."

"And just who are you, if you please?"

"Mrs. Augusta Barclay of Spotsylvania County. My farm is near Fredericksburg, if that's any of your concern."

He began, "But this is Fairfax—"

"My. A student of geography as well as bad manners." She leaned over to pluck packets from the underskirt. "I haven't time to waste with you, Captain. I fear there are horsemen not far behind me. Yankees." *Plop* went another packet on the chair, and *plop*.

"The widow Barclay's been to Washington City," the farmer's wife said. "A secret errand of mercy for—"

"Sssh, don't say no more," the old farmer interrupted.

"Oh, why not?" snapped the young woman, whipping out packets. "Perhaps if he knows what we're doing, he'll help us instead of standing there like some stately pine, waiting to be admired."

The blue eyes shot Charles a look so scornful it left him unable to speak. To the old couple, the young widow continued: "I was wrong to arrange a rendezvous this close to the Potomac. I feared someone was on to the scheme when they took ten minutes to examine my papers at the bridge. One sergeant's eyes kept boring holes in my skirt—and I'm not that attractive."

"I want to know what's in the packets," Charles said.

"Quinine. Plentiful in Washington, but scarce in Richmond. It will be desperately needed once the real fighting starts. I'm not the only woman doing this work, Captain. Far from it."

162

Spurs jingling, Ambrose crossed the parlor. The widow Barclay's prettiness and patriotism pleased Charles but not her sharp tongue. He was reminded of Billy Hazard's sister Virgilia.

He had been a mite rough on the old couple. To the woman he said, "You may certainly help her if you wish." The woman lumbered past, knelt behind Augusta Barclay and put her head under the widow's outer skirt. Packets appeared twice as fast.

Addressing Charles, and still with sarcasm, the young woman said, "Generous of you. I was serious when I said there might be pursuit."

"Damn if there isn't," Ambrose exclaimed from the parlor's north window. Tense, he motioned for Charles, who peered over his shoulder and saw dust rising behind a hill a mile or two down the road.

"Must be Yanks, riding that fast." He let the curtain fall. To the women struggling with the packets he said, "I regret my sharp words, ladies—" He hoped the widow Barclay understood he meant that for her; a slight lift of her head said perhaps. "I don't want this commendable work undone, but it will be if we don't move quickly."

"Just a few more," the fat woman panted. Packets flew right and left.

Charles signaled for the farmer to gather them, asking: "Where's the safest place to hide those?"

"Attic."

"Do it. Ambrose, go out and take that buggy into the trees. If you can't get back before those horsemen come into sight, stay put. You finished, Mrs. Barclay?"

She smoothed down her outside skirt as the farmer's wife loaded her husband's arms with packets. "It only takes two eyes to answer that, Captain."

"Kindly spare me the banter and go out to the woodshed in back. Get inside and don't utter a syllable. If that's possible." Surprisingly, she liked the sally and smiled.

The farmer tottered up the hall stairs. Outside, wheels creaked as Ambrose moved the buggy. Augusta Barclay hurried out.

Charles ran to the north window again. He saw the riders clearly now, approaching at a gallop. Half a dozen men, all wearing dark blue. Under his cadet gray jacket, sweat began to pour.

The farmer came down again. "Is there water in the kitchen?" Charles asked the woman.

"A bucket and a dipper."

"Fill the dipper and bring it here. Then both of you keep still."

He tossed his shako aside and moments later strolled out to the porch, shotgun hanging in the crook of his left arm, dipper in his right hand. He saw the riders react to the sight of him by drawing swords and side arms. The lieutenant in charge of the detail held up his hand.

The moment in which Charles could have been shot passed so quickly, it was over before he realized it. He leaned on one of the porch pillars, the beat of his heart pounding in his ears.

26

The horsemen spilled in from the road, raising dust that blew away on the breeze. The barrels of several army revolvers pointed at Charles's chest.

Red as an apple in the heat, the lieutenant walked his horse to the porch. Charles drank from the dipper, then let his hand fall laconically. He pressed his right sleeve against his ribs to hide a tremor. He had seen the young Union officer before.

"Good day, sir," the lieutenant said. His voice broke into a squeak as he spoke. Charles didn't laugh or smile. A nervous man —or one humiliated—often reacted without thinking.

"Good day," he answered with a pleasant nod. His gaze drifted from face to face. Four of the Yanks were barely old enough to use razors. Two refused to meet his eye; they would be no threat.

By waiting, Charles forced the first identification: "Second Lieutenant Prevo, Georgetown Mounted Dragoons, Department of Washington, at your service."

"Captain Main, Wade Hampton Legion. Your servant."

"May I inquire, sir, what a rebel officer is doing so near the Potomac?"

"I don't care for the term rebel, sir, but the answer to your question is simple. My nigra bond servant, whom I brought all the way from South Carolina, ran away day before yesterday—heading for the blessed freedoms of Yankee territory, I presume. I have now concluded I can't catch him. Trail's gone cold."

The lieutenant indicated the two tethered horses. "You didn't undertake the pursuit by yourself, I see."

"My first lieutenant is inside, napping." Where the devil had he met this green youngster?

"You say your nigger slave ran away—?"

"These rebs got all the luxuries, don't they, Lieutenant?" said a toothy corporal with a huge dragoon pistol. Bad eyes on that one, and a side arm that could blast Charles to pieces. Had to watch him.

Charles's tactic was to ignore the corporal and say to the officer, "Yes, and I'm goddamn angry about it."

The corporal persisted. "That's what the war's all about, ain't it? You boys don't want to lose your boot polishers or them nigger gals you can fuck anytime you—"

The lieutenant started to reprimand the noncom. Before he could, Charles flung the dipper in the dirt. "Lieutenant Prevo, if you'll ask your man to step down, I'll reply to that remark in a way he'll understand." He stared at the corporal while reaching across to his saber hilt. It would be stupid to bluff his way into a fight. But if they smelled fear and dismounted and spread out, Mrs. Barclay was a goner.

"Not necessary, sir," Prevo said. "My corporal will keep his mouth shut." The toothy noncom grumbled, glaring at Charles.

The Yank officer relaxed somewhat. "I confess I'm not entirely unsympathetic to your feelings, Captain. I hail from Maryland. My brother had two slaves on his farm there, and they've run away, too. When this militia unit was mustered, about a third of the boys refused to take the loyalty oath and resigned. I was tempted. Since I didn't, I must carry out my duty." Like a weathervane in a gale, his mood swung again. "But I can't escape a feeling we've encountered one another before."

"Not in Maryland." His memory suddenly made the connection. "West Point?"

"By God that's it. You were—?"

"Class of '57."

"I reported just before you graduated." Prevo paused. "I had to take the Canterberry Road after my plebe year. Couldn't handle the studies. I wish I'd been able to last the course. I loved the place—Well, the mystery's cleared up. If you'll pardon us, we'll get on with our job."

"Surely."

"We're pursuing a female smuggler. We believe she brought contraband medicines out of the district and came this way. We're searching every farm along this road." He prepared to dismount.

"Female smuggler?" Charles hoped his stifled laugh sounded convincing. "Save yourself, Lieutenant. I've been here an hour, and I give you my word, there's no such person inside this house."

Prevo settled in his saddle again, hesitating. The gun muzzles remained trained on Charles, the toothy corporal's steadiest.

"My word as an officer and Academy man," Charles said in an offhand manner that, he hoped, lent conviction to the carefully delimited truth.

Seconds passed. Prevo took a breath. *It didn't work. Now what will they—?*

"Captain Main, I accept your word and thank you for your gentlemanly cooperation. We have more ground to cover, and you've saved us time."

He sheathed his sword, shouted orders, and the detachment wheeled back to the road and moved on southward. The corporal's disappointed face disappeared in dust. Charles retrieved the dipper and leaned against the post, momentarily dazed with relief.

27

Charles waited ten minutes in case the soldiers returned, then called Augusta Barclay from her hiding place and whistled Ambrose out of the woods. "Leave the buggy there. Those Yankees might take the same road home."

"I gather your eloquence was persuasive, Captain," Augusta said as she brushed wood splinters from her skirt.

"I gave them my word there was no female smuggler in the house." He gauged the distance between the white building and the woodshed. "It missed being an outright lie by about seven feet."

"Clever of you."

"That compliment just makes my day, ma'am."

He didn't mean to be biting, but it came out that way as the tight-wound tensions of the last half hour let go. He turned and quickly bent over the water trough to splash his face. Why did he give a damn what she said or didn't say?

A touch on his shoulder. "Captain?"

"Yes?"

"You have a right to be irked. I spoke out of turn earlier. And more than once. You acted bravely and performed a valuable service. I owe you thanks and an apology."

"You owe me neither one, Mrs. Barclay. It's my war, too. Now I suggest you go indoors and stay there till it gets dark." Responding with a small nod, she let her blue eyes hold his a moment. He felt a deep and unfamiliar response; unsettling—

About four, he was watering Sport and Ambrose's bay at the

167

trough when noise and dust signaled the approach of northbound riders. Prevo's detachment galloped by. The lieutenant waved. Charles waved back. Then the house hid the blue horsemen.

The farmer and his wife invited the cavalrymen to stay for supper. They agreed, the more readily because Augusta Barclay seconded the suggestion. Charles washed up as the sun sank and the heat went out of the day. A refreshing breeze blew through the house when they sat down to a plain but tasty meal of cured ham, potatoes, and pole beans.

He kept glancing at Augusta there beyond the chimney of the table lamp. Tonight she kept her eyes averted, like any proper girl from a proper Southern family. A delicate femininity was cultivated by such women and prized by their suitors; some females, the best example he could think of being Ashton, even playacted shamelessly to convince others of their conformity to the ideal. This yellow-haired widow didn't conform. She was too outspoken. Too robustly built, when you came right down to it. He wondered about the size of her feet. Any girl with big feet was done for socially and romantically.

Shyly trying to strike up a conversation, the old farmer said to Ambrose, "That's a fine-looking horse you ride."

"Yes, sir. South Carolina saddle horses are the best in the world."

"Don't say that to a Virginian," Augusta told him.

"Amen," said Charles. "I get the feeling some people in this part of the country think Virginia invented the horse."

"We're mighty proud of men like Turner Ashby and Colonel Stuart," the farmer's wife said, passing the beans. It was her only statement during the meal.

Ambrose finished a second potato. "I do agree with Charlie, though. Virginians are pretty good at making you feel like an outsider with no more than a word or a look."

Augusta smiled. "I know the type. But as the poet says, Lieutenant, to err is human, to forgive, divine."

"You like Shakespeare, do you?" asked Charles.

"I do, but I was quoting Alexander Pope, the Augustan satirist. He's my favorite."

"Oh." Smarting from his show of stupidity, Charles lunged for more ham with his fork. "Always did confuse those two. Not much of a reader of poetry, I'm afraid."

"I own a copy of nearly everything Pope wrote," she said. "He was a magnificent wit, but sad in many ways. He was only four feet six inches tall, with a deformed spine. Curved like a bow is the phrase used by his contemporaries. He knew life for what it is, but he could push away the pain by mocking it."

"I see." The two murmured words hung in the silence. He didn't know Pope except by name, but now he thought he knew her better. What pain did her jibing conceal?

The fat woman served a pear tart and coffee while her husband asked Augusta when and how the quinine would be taken to Richmond. "A man should be here for it in the morning," she replied.

"Well, your bed's made up in the spare room," the wife called from the kitchen. "Captain, will you and your lieutenant stop overnight with us, too? I can fix pallets on the floor of the parlor."

Augusta turned in his direction. Her face, bisected by the lamp chimney, seemed expectant. Or did he merely imagine that?

He felt duty and personal desire pulling against each other.

Ambrose awaited guidance from his superior. None being forthcoming, he said, "I wouldn't mind a good night's rest. 'Specially if you'll permit me to try that melodeon in the parlor."

"Yes indeed," the farmer said, pleased.

"All right, then," Charles said. "We'll stay."

Augusta's smile was restrained. But it seemed real.

The farmer's wife produced a stone jar of excellent apple brandy. Charles took some, and so did Augusta. They sat in facing chairs while Ambrose experimented with the old squeeze-organ. Soon he started a lively tune.

"You play well," Augusta said. "I like that melody but don't recognize it."

"The name is 'Dixie's Land.' It's a minstrel piece."

"They played it all over the North when Abe stood for election last fall," the farmer added. "The Republicans marched to it."

"Might be so," Ambrose agreed, "but the Yankees are losing the song as fast as they'll lose this war. Everybody is singing and playing it in the camps around Richmond."

The lively music continued. Augusta said, "Tell me something about yourself, Captain Main."

He chose words with extreme care, wary of being spiked again by some smiling sarcasm. He mentioned West Point, and how he had gone there at his cousin's urging and with his help; in a few

169

sentences he covered his service in Texas, his friendship with Billy Hazard, and his doubts about slavery.

"Well, I have never believed in the institution either. When my husband died a year ago last December, I wrote manumission papers for both his slaves. They stayed with me, thank heaven. Otherwise I would have been forced to sell the farm."

"What do you raise?"

"Oats. Tobacco. The eyebrows of the neighbors. I do some of the field work, which my husband always forbade because it wasn't feminine."

She leaned back in the old rocker, her head resting on an embroidered pillow. How fair and soft she looked in the lamplight. One of Charles's fingers tapped, tapped his glass of apple brandy. Not feminine? Had she married a crazy man?

"Your husband was a farmer, I gather?"

"Yes. He lived on the same property all his life—and his father before him. He was a decent man. Kind to me—although he was definitely suspicious of books, poetry, music—" She inclined her head at Ambrose, who was lost in some sweet classical air Charles couldn't identify. Augusta continued. "I accepted his proposal seven months after his first wife died. He went the same way she did. Influenza. He was twenty-three years older than I."

"Even so, you must have loved him—"

"I liked him; I didn't love him."

"Then how could you marry him?"

"Ah—another disciple of the romantic Sir Walter. Virginians worship him only slightly less than the Lord and George Washington." She finished her brandy quickly. The combative glint had returned to her eyes. *He had a deformed spine. He could push away the pain by mocking it.*

"The answer to your question is very plain and unromantic, Captain. My father and mother were dead, and my only brother, too. A hunting accident took him when he was sixteen and I twelve. I had no other kin in Spotsylvania Leonard County, so when Barclay came to propose, I thought it over for an hour and said yes." She gazed in the empty glass. "I felt no one else would ever ask me."

"Why, of course they would," he said at once. "You're a handsome woman."

She looked at him. Feeling leaped like lightning between them. The little mouth curl, the smile of defense, slipped back as she

170

broke away from his steady gaze, standing abruptly. Her big breasts swelled the bosom of her dress, which she tugged self-consciously. "That's gallant of you, Captain. I know I'm not, but I always wanted to be. Hope springs eternal. That, too, is Mr. Pope. Now, whatever else I am, I'm tired. I will thank you again for saving the quinine and ask you to excuse me. Good night."

He rose. "Good night." When she was out of sight, he said to Ambrose, "Damnedest female I ever met."

Ambrose laid the melodeon aside and grinned. "Don't get smitten, Charlie. Colonel wants you to tend to business."

"Don't be an idiot," he said, hoping he sounded convincing.

Charles slept well and woke at dawn, filled with an unusual eagerness to be up and doing. He left Ambrose snoring, stole outside and whistled "Dixie's Land" softly while he fed and watered Sport and the bay. He studied the upstairs windows of the farmhouse. Which was the spare room?

A red sun rose over the gentle hills and woodlands east of the road. Birds sang, and Charles stretched, exhilarated. He hadn't felt so fit and good in months. He hoped the change would last a while. He didn't need to speculate about the cause.

Wood smoke, pale and pungent, rose from the kitchen chimney; breakfast working. He was starved. Going in, he remembered he must unpack his personal pistol from his camp trunk. With a battle surely coming soon, he must clean and oil it. He hadn't worn the weapon since he returned from Texas. It was an 1848 army Colt, six shots, .44 caliber, to which he had added several expensive options, including walnut grips, a detachable shoulder stock, and a cylinder engraved with a depiction of dragoons attacking Indians. With the revolver, his shotgun, and the regulation legion sword, he had everything he needed to whip Yankees —a task he was eager to undertake this morning.

Augusta was in the kitchen helping the farmer's wife fry eggs and slabs of ham. "Good morning, Captain Main." Her smile seemed cordial and genuine. He replied in kind.

Soon they all sat down. Ambrose was handing Charles a warm loaf of heavy homemade bread when they heard a horseman in the dooryard. Charles overturned his chair in his haste to rise. Augusta, seated on his right, touched his wrist.

"I suspect it's the man from Richmond. Nothing to worry about."

Her fingers, quickly withdrawn, left him with a quivery feeling. *Acting like a damn schoolboy,* he thought as the farmer went to admit the visitor. Augusta stared at her plate as if it might suddenly fly away. Pink showed in her cheeks.

The man from Richmond knew her name but didn't give his. He was slim, middle-aged, clerkish, in a brown suit and flat-crowned hat. He accepted the farmer's invitation and hauled a chair to the table, saying, "The quinine's here, then? Safe?"

"In the attic," Augusta said. "It's safe thanks to the quick work of Captain Main and Lieutenant Pell." She described yesterday's events. The man from Richmond responded with praise and gratitude, then started on his food. He didn't say another word and ate enough for six men his size.

Charles and the widow conversed more comfortably than they had the night before. In response to questions about Billy, he described the unhappiness of the Hazards and the Mains when they found themselves on opposite sides of the war. "Our families have been close for a long time. We're tied by marriage and West Point, and just by the way we feel about one another. If the Hazards and the Mains hope for any one thing right now, I guess it's to stay close, no matter what else comes."

A gentle tilt of her head acknowledged the worth of the wish. "My family is split by the war, too."

"I thought you said you had no kin."

"None in Spotsylvania County. I have one bachelor uncle, my mother's brother, in the Union army, Brigadier Jack Duncan. He went to West Point. He graduated in 1840, as I remember."

"George Thomas was in that class," Charles exclaimed. "I served under him in the Second Cavalry. He's a Virginian—"

"Who stayed on the Union side."

"That's right. Let's see, who else? Bill Sherman. A good friend of Thomas named Dick Ewell—he's a general on our side. He's just been given one of the brigades at Manassas Junction."

"My," she said when he paused, "West Point does keep track of its own."

"Yes indeed—and we aren't too popular because of it. Tell me about your uncle. Where is he?"

"His last letter was posted from a fort in Kansas. But I suspect he's back in this part of the country now. He expected reassignment. In a paper I picked up in Washington, I read a piece about

172

high-ranking army officers who are Virginians. Nine have joined the Confederacy. Eleven stayed. One is Uncle Jack."

Ambrose shot his hand out, beating the Richmond courier to the last ham slab. After everyone finished, Ambrose brought Augusta's buggy to the front while Charles carried her travel valise to the porch. As he stowed the valise in the buggy, she finished tying a yellow veil over her hair.

"Will you be safe going the rest of the way alone?" he asked.

"There's a pistol in that bag you just put away. I never travel without it."

He welcomed the chance to take her hand and help her up to the seat. "Well, Captain, again I express my gratitude. If your duties ever bring you along the Rappahannock to Fredericksburg, please call on me. Barclay's Farm is only a few miles outside town. Anyone can direct you." She remembered herself. "The invitation extends to you, of course, Lieutenant Pell."

"Oh, certainly—I knew that's how you meant it," he said with a sly glance at his friend.

"Good-bye, Captain Main."

"It's a little late, but please call me Charles."

"Then you must call me Augusta."

He grinned. "That's pretty formal. We had nicknames at West Point. How about Gus?"

It was one of those things quickly said because it came to mind the same way and seemed clever and inconsequential. She sat up as if touched by something hot.

"As a matter of fact, my brother always used that name. I detested it."

"Why? It suits you. Gus would work in her own fields, but I doubt Augusta would."

"Sir, I admit your gen'ral rule—"

"How's that?" Then he realized she must be quoting that damn Pope. Sweet and dangerous, her smile shone.

"—that every poet is a fool. But you yourself may serve to show it, that every fool is not a poet. Good-bye, Captain."

"Wait, now," he called, but the chance for apology left as fast as the buggy. She whipped up the horse, jolted out of the dooryard, and turned south. On the porch, the farmer nudged his wife. Ambrose approached with an air of mock gloom.

"Charlie, you put both feet in your mouth clear to the ankles that time. Had a nice spark struck with that little widow, too.

173

'Course, I don't think a gal's very feminine if she hoes a potato patch or has a vinegar tongue or a name like Gus, for that mat—"

"Shut the hell up, Ambrose. I'll never see her again, so what difference does it make? She can't take a joke, but she sure can hand 'em out. The hell with Mr. Pope. Her, too."

He saddled Sport, touched his shako to salute the farm couple, and rode like a Tatar toward the south. Ambrose had to hold his shako and spur his bay just to keep Charles in sight.

After about five miles, Charles cooled down and slowed down. During the next hour he silently examined details of his various conversations with Mrs. Damned Highbrow Widow Augusta Barclay, whom he continued to find devilishly attractive despite the poor note on which they had parted. She shouldn't have been so quick to pounce on an innocent gaffe. She was no more perfect than anybody else.

He wished he could see her again, patch things up. Impossible to do that any time soon, not with a battle brewing. The actions of the Yankee lieutenant, Prevo, had restored his faith in the possibility of a gentleman's war, conducted with gentleman's rules. Maybe one huge affray would get it over with, and then he could look up the young widow, whom he could no longer think of, unfortunately, by any name except Gus.

28

The thirteenth of July fell on a Saturday. Constance had one more day to finish packing for the trip to Washington.

George had gone earlier in the week, with obvious reluctance. The night before his departure he had been restless, finally jumping up and leaving for ten minutes. He returned with several sprigs of mountain laurel from the hills behind Belvedere. He slipped the laurel into a valise without explanation, but Constance needed none.

Brett would remain in charge of the household, Wotherspoon of the ironworks, and George's local attorney, Jupiter Smith, would push the bank organization ahead. All three had been urged to telegraph at once in case of emergency, so Constance had no fear of leaving important matters to drift.

Yet on this sunny Saturday, she was cross. There was too much to pack, and her two best party dresses, neither of which she had tried on for a month, fit too tightly. She hadn't realized it, but in her contentment, and despite the war, she had enjoyed life too much lately and put on weight. Usually blunt on other subjects, George hadn't said a word. But the despicable evidence—the small melon bulge of her stomach, the new thickness of her thighs—confronted her when she inspected herself in a mirror.

Late in the morning, Bridgit hesitantly entered the luggage-strewn bedroom to find Constance muttering and attempting to jam folded garments into an overflowing trunk. "Mrs. Hazard? There is"—the normally outgoing girl was whispery and strangely pale—"a visitor in the kitchen asking for you."

"For heaven's sake, Bridgit, don't bother me about some tradesman when I'm busy with—"

"Ma'am, please. It—isn't a tradesman."

"Who is it? You're acting as though you've seen Beelzebub himself."

Hushed: "It is Mr. Hazard's sister."

Save for the unexpected death of George or one of the children, no more stunning blow could have fallen on Constance. As she rushed downstairs, strands of red hair flying, her customary calm crumbled. She was astonished, baffled, outraged. That Virgilia Hazard dared to return to Belvedere almost defied belief. How could it be—*how*—after all she had done to embarrass the family and create friction between the Hazards and the Mains?

Virgilia's history was one of warped independence. Involving herself in the abolition movement—as Constance had done by operating an underground railroad stop in a shed on the grounds of Hazard Iron—Virgilia had gravitated to the movement's most

175

extreme wing. She had appeared in public with black men who were not merely friends or associates in her work but lovers.

On a visit to Mont Royal, she had betrayed the hospitality of the Main family by helping one of their slaves escape. She had later lived in poverty with the man, whose name was Grady, in the stews of Philadelphia; both were social outcasts because of it. She had helped her common-law husband take part in the raid on Harpers Ferry led by the infamous John Brown, who had held and expressed views as extreme and violent as her own.

Virgilia hated all things Southern, and never was that better demonstrated than when Orry made his dangerous trip to Lehigh Station to repay part of the ship-construction loan. Virgilia had summoned the mob to Belvedere, and only George and a gun had held them off. That very night, George had ordered his sister away forever. Now, incredibly, she was back. She deserved—

Stop, Constance thought, standing still in front of the closed kitchen door. Control. Compassion. *Try.* She smoothed two stray wisps of hair into place, steadied her breathing, prayed silently, then crossed herself and opened the door.

The kitchen, where the daily bread was baking and a pink loin of pork lay half trimmed on the block, was empty except for the visitor. Through a back window Constance glimpsed William shooting at a target bale with his bow and arrows.

The bread fragrance, the loin and cleaver, the hanging utensils and polished pots, all the homely furniture of family sustenance seemed desecrated by the creature standing near the door with a carpetbag so dirty its pattern could not be seen. Virgilia's dress was nearly as filthy. The shawl around her shoulders had holes in it. *How dare you,* Constance thought, momentarily out of control again.

Virgilia Hazard, thirty-seven, had a squarish face lightly marred by a few pox scars left from childhood. Buxom in the past, she was thin now, almost emaciated. Her skin had a yellow pallor, and her eyes were dumb lumps in the center of dark, sunken sockets. She smelled of sweat and other abominable things. Constance was glad Brett was down in Lehigh Station with cook, shopping. She might have torn Virgilia to pieces. Constance felt like it.

"What are you doing here?"

"May I wait for George? I must see him."

How small her voice sounded. It had lost the perpetual arrogance Constance remembered with such distaste. She began to see the hurt in Virgilia's eyes. Joy ignited like a flame inside her, burning till shame and her own better nature put it out.

"Your brother has gone to Washington to work for the government."

"Oh." She squeezed her eyes shut a moment.

"How is it possible that you're here, Virgilia?"

Virgilia tilted her head forward to acknowledge the accusation in the question and the anger Constance couldn't keep out of her voice. "May I sit down on that stool? I really am not feeling well."

"Yes, all right, go ahead," Constance said after hesitating. Without thinking, she moved to the great wood block and put her hand on the cleaver. Virgilia sank to the stool with the slowness of a person much older. With a shock, Constance saw what she was touching and pulled her hand back. Outside, William whooped and ran to the target to pull three arrows from the bull's-eye.

Constance pointed at the carpetbag. "Is that the one you took in April? The one you filled with my best silver pieces? You disgraced this family in nearly every conceivable way and then you found one more. You stole."

Virgilia folded her hands in her lap. How much weight had she lost? Forty pounds? Fifty? "I had to live," she said.

"That may be a reason. It isn't a justification. Where have you been since you left?"

"Places I'd be ashamed to tell you about."

"Yet you presume to come back here—"

Glinting tears appeared in Virgilia's eyes. Impossible, Constance thought. She never cried for anyone but her black lover.

"I'm sick," Virgilia whispered. "I'm hot and so dizzy I can barely stand. Coming up the hill from the depot I thought I'd faint." She swallowed, then gave the ultimate explanation. "I have no place else to go."

"Won't your fine abolitionist friends take you in?"

The disfiguring sneer came unconsciously, and in its wake, more shame. *You must stop.* This time the warning served. There was no humanity in venting such feelings and nothing to be gained. Virgilia was a beaten creature.

Answering at last, she said, "No. Not any longer."

"What do you want here?"

"A place to stay. Time to rest. Recover. I was going to beg George—"

"I told you, he's taken an army commission in Washington."

"Then I'll beg you, if that's what you want, Constance."

"Be quiet!" Constance spun and covered her eyes. She was stern but composed when she again faced Virgilia after a minute. "You can stay only a short time."

"All right."

"A few months at most."

"All right. Thank you."

"And George mustn't know. Did William see you arrive?"

"I don't think so. I was careful, and he was busy with his archery—"

"I'm leaving to join George tomorrow and taking the children. They mustn't see you. So you'll stay in one of the servants' rooms until we go. That way, I'll be the only person required to lie."

Virgilia shuddered; it was cuttingly said. Try as she would, Constance couldn't dam everything inside. She added, "If George were to discover you're here, I know he'd order you out again."

"Yes, I suppose so."

"Brett is staying here, too. While Billy's in the army."

"I remember. I'm glad Billy's fighting. I'm glad George is doing his part, too. The South must be utterly—"

Constance snatched the cleaver and slammed the flat of it on the block. "Virgilia, if you utter so much as one word of that ideological garbage you've heaped on us for years, I will turn you out myself, instantly. Others may have a moral right to speak against slavery and slaveowners, but you don't. You aren't fit to sit in judgment of a single human soul."

"I'm sorry. I spoke without thinking. I'm sorry. I won't—"

"That's right, you won't. I'll have trouble enough persuading Brett to let you stay at Belvedere while I'm gone and she's in charge. If she weren't a decent person, I'd have no chance of doing it. But you mustn't question my terms—"

"No."

She struck the block with her palm. "You must accept every one."

"Yes."

"—or you'll go out the same way you came. Do I make myself clear?"

"Yes. Yes." Virgilia bowed her head, and the word blurred as she repeated it. "Yes."

Constance covered her eyes again, still confused, still wrathful. Virgilia's shoulders started to shake. She cried, almost without sound at first, then more loudly. It was a kind of whimpering; animal. Constance, too, felt dizzy as she hurried to the back door and made certain it was shut tightly so her son wouldn't hear.

29

"I require and charge you both, as ye will answer at the day of judgment—"

Other voices suddenly rose to compete with that of the Reverend Mr. Saxton, rector of the Episcopal parish. Standing beside Madeline in the finest, and hottest, suit he owned, Orry looked swiftly toward the open windows.

Madeline wore a simple but elegant summer dress of white lawn. The slaves had been given a free day and invited to listen to the ceremony from the piazza. About forty bucks and wenches had gathered in the sunshine. The house men and women, being, and expecting to be treated as, members of a higher caste, were permitted in the parlor, though only one person was seated there now: Clarissa.

"—that if either of you know any impediment why ye may not be lawfully joined together in matrimony—"

The quarrel outside grew noisier. Two men, with others commenting. Someone yelled.

"—ye do now confess it. For be ye well assured—"

The rector faltered, lost his place in the prayer book, coughed twice, exhaling a whiff of the sherry taken beforehand in company with the nervous bride and groom. Before bringing Madeline to the parlor, Orry had jokingly said that Francis LaMotte might show up to object to their marrying so soon after Justin's funeral.

"Be ye well assured—" the Reverend Mr. Saxton resumed as the volume of the shouting increased. A man started to curse. Orry recognized the voice. His face dark red, he bent toward the rector.

"Excuse me for a moment."

His mother gave him a bright smile as he strode past and out into the hot sunshine. A semicircle of blacks faced the combatants in the drive. Orry heard Andy.

"Leave him be, Cuffey. He did nothing to—"

"Hands off me, nigger. He pushed me."

"Was you that pushed me," a weaker voice replied, a slave named Percival.

Unnoticed behind the spectators, Orry shouted: "Stop it."

A pigtailed girl screamed and jumped. The crowd shifted back, and he saw Cuffey, ragged and sullen, standing astraddle Percival's legs. The frail slave had fallen or been pushed to a sitting position against the wheel of a cart. In the cart, beneath a tarpaulin, were eight pairs of candlesticks and two sets of hearth irons, all brass; Orry was sending them to a Columbia foundry in answer to the Confederacy's appeal for metal.

Andy stood a yard behind Cuffey. He wore clean clothes, as did all the others. It was a special day at Mont Royal. Orry strode straight to Cuffey.

"This is my wedding day, and I don't take kindly to an interruption. What happened here?"

"It's this nigger's fault," Percival declared, indicating Cuffey. Andy gave him a hand up. "He came struttin' in after the preacher had already started and the rest of us was listenin'. He got here late, but he wanted to see better so he pushed and shoved me."

Cuffey was caught, which made him all the madder. Hate shone before he averted his eyes, trying to soften or prevent punishment by mumbling, "I din't push him. Haven't been feelin' good—kind of dizzy, like. I just stumbled an' knocked him down. Haven't been feelin' good," he repeated in a lame way.

Over derisive groans from some of the others, Percival said, "He's been feelin' snake-mean, like every other day. Nothin' else wrong with him." As protocol demanded, Orry glanced at his head driver for a verdict.

"Percival's telling it right," Andy said.

"Cuffey, look at me." When he did, Orry continued. "Two tasks each day for a week. A task and a half every day for a week after that. See that he does them, Andy."

"I will, Mr. Orry."

Cuffey fumed but didn't dare speak. Orry wheeled and stomped back to the house.

Soon after, he and Madeline joined right hands while the rector said, "That ye may so live together in this life that in the world to come ye may have life everlasting. Amen."

In their bedroom that night, Madeline reached through the dark to find him. "My goodness, you'd think the bridegroom had never been with the bride before."

"Not as a husband he hasn't," Orry said, sitting beside her; his hair-matted thigh touched the smoothness of hers. A bright, cloudless night filled the room with light that spilled softly over them while they sat kissing and touching. The tips of her breasts were as dark as her hair and eyes; the rest of her was marble.

She laid both arms over his shoulders and clasped her hands. Kissed him. "Lord, but I do love you."

"I love you, Mrs. Main."

"It is real, isn't it? I never thought it would be—" She laughed low. "Mrs. Main. How grand it sounds."

Another long, ardent kiss, his hand on her breast.

"I'm sorry that muss happened during the ceremony. I ought to sell Cuffey. I don't want him causing trouble when I go to Richmond."

"Mr. Meek will be here to handle him then."

"Hope so." No reply had arrived from North Carolina as yet. "I trust Meek won't live up to his name. Cuffey needs a strong hand."

Madeline caressed his cheek. "As soon as you're settled in Virginia, I'll join you. Till then, everything will be fine here. Andy's a good, trustworthy man."

"I know, but—"

"Darling, don't worry so." Saying that, she turned herself. The bed creaked as she brought the white of belly and breast into the pale glow from outdoors. They lay back gently; she touched him with her hip. Mouth against his face, she murmured, "Not to-night. A husband must attend to certain duties, you know."

Drowsing afterward, both woke to a wild, raw sound out in the night.

"Dear God, what's that?" She started up, bracing her hands on the sheet.

The cry came again, then went echoing away. They heard birds roused in the night thickets. Downstairs a house woman called an anxious question. The sound wasn't repeated.

Madeline shuddered. "It sounded like some wild animal."

"It's a panther cry. That is, an imitation of one. Now and again the nigras will use it to frighten white people."

"There's no one here who would want to do such a—"

She stopped and pressed against his back, shivering again.

30

A momentous excitement filled Washington that night. The city resounded with the grind and rumble of wagons moving, the thuds and flinty ring of horsemen galloping, the shouted songs of regiments marching to the Virginia bridges. It was Monday, the fifteenth of July.

George had spent the day trying to get a hundred personal details in order—it seemed that many, anyway—in preparation for the arrival of Constance and the children. At half past nine, he entered Willard's main dining room. His brother waved from a table near the center.

George felt stiff and ridiculous carrying the French chapeau, with its clutter of devices, authorized for general staff officers: gold strap, extra braid, brass eagle, black cockade. He had purchased the cheapest regulation sword available, a tinny weapon good only for show. That was all right; he would wear it as seldom as possible. The damned hat, too.

It seemed queer to be back in uniform, queerer still to be greeting his own brother in a hotel in wartime. George had sent a message over to Alexandria suggesting supper, and it had gotten through.

"God preserve us—what elegance!" Billy said as George sat down. "And I see you outrank me, Captain."

"Let's have none of that or I'll put you on report," George growled good-naturedly. He found it hard to arrange himself and the sword on the chair without embarrassing contortions. "I'll probably be a major in the next month or so. Everyone in the department is due to move up one or two grades."

"How do you like Ordnance so far?"

"I don't."

"Then why on earth—?"

"We must all occasionally do things we don't like. I think I can be useful to the department. I wouldn't be there otherwise." He lit one of his cigars, which induced a coughing spasm in the hovering waiter. George barked selections from the menu, inwardly amused when he realized he sounded like a West Point upper classman hectoring a plebe. He had never cared for soldiering, but it came easily. The waiter's pencil flew.

"I'll have the veal chops too," Billy said. The waiter left, and the brothers sipped their whiskeys. "You know, George, maybe you won't have a chance to do anything in the department. One sweep to Richmond and it could be all over. McDowell's moving tonight."

Nodding, George said, "You'd have to be dumb and blind not to notice. I had advance warning from Stanley. We had dinner this noon."

Billy looked guilty. "Should we have invited him tonight?"

"Yes, but I'm glad we didn't. Besides, Isabel probably wouldn't let him out."

"Your note said Constance will arrive in the morning. Do you have rooms?"

"Right here. A suite. Expensive as hell, but I couldn't get anything else."

"Willard's is packed. How did you manage it?"

"Cameron managed it somehow. I gather the secretary can rig or arrange anything." He puffed the cigar. "Are you as fit as you look?"

"Yes, I'm doing well—except for missing Brett a lot. I have a splendid commanding officer. Much more religious than I am, but a fine engineer."

"On speaking terms with God, is he? Got to keep track of fellows like that. We may need all available help. I watched some volunteers drilling on the mall this afternoon."

"Bad?"

"Incredibly."

"How many men is McDowell marching into Virginia?"

"I heard thirty thousand." Another puff. "I'm sure the correct figure will be in print tomorrow. We can write Old Bory for confirmation. I'm told he gets the local papers delivered by courier every day."

Billy laughed, amazed. "I've never been in a war, the way you have. But I never imagined it would be carried on this way."

"Don't fool yourself. This isn't war, it's—well, who knows what to call it? A carnival. A convocation of zealous amateurs led by a lot of politicians everybody trusts and a few professionals they don't. Maybe it's an exhibit fit for Barnum's Museum—it's that bizarre." The waiter brought steaming bowls of fat oysters in a milky broth.

"Tell you one thing," George continued as he put his cigar aside and spooned up stew. "To speed the end of the war, I'd certainly arm all the blacks pouring in from the South."

"You'd arm the contrabands?"

George was put off by Billy's disapproving expression. He shrugged. "Why not? I suspect they'd fight harder than some of the white gentlemen I've seen skylarking around town."

"But they aren't citizens. The Dred Scott case said so."

"True—if you believe the decision was right. I don't." He leaned over the table. "Billy, secession is the powder that blew up to start this war, but the fuse was slavery. It's the moral heart of all this trouble. Shouldn't black men be allowed to fight for their own cause?"

"Maybe. I mean, you may be right politically, but I know the army. There'd be violent reactions if you introduced Negro troops. The change would be too drastic."

"You're saying white soldiers would have no faith in colored ones?"

"No, they wouldn't."

"Including you?"

Concealing his embarrassment behind a faint defiance, Billy answered, "Yes. I may be wrong, but that's how I feel."

"Then perhaps we'd better change the subject."

They did, and the rest of the meal proved pleasant. Afterward they walked out to the avenue in time to watch a regiment of foot ramble by, bayoneted muskets pointing every which direction. The drummers might as well have tapped their cadence on the moon.

"Take care of yourself, Billy," George said in a quiet voice. "The big one is coming—maybe within the week."

"I'll be all right. I'm not sure our unit would be sent on to Richmond with the others anyway."

"Why is everyone so confident of reaching Richmond? People act as if the rebs are all fools and fops. I know some of the West Point men who went south. They're the cream. As for the rank and file, Southern boys are accustomed to the fields, to rough living out of doors. Their way of life favors them. So don't underestimate them. And heed my advice. Be careful. For Brett, if for no one else."

"I will," Billy promised. "I'm sorry we differed over the nig— the other question."

"I needn't agree with my brother's dunderheaded opinions to care about him."

George put his arms out. They embraced, and Billy went away into the dark, following the spiky glitter of bayonets, the tap-tapping of unseen drums.

Constance and the children arrived safely. They brought stacks of luggage, and a package of food and reading material Brett had prepared for Billy.

Patricia was excited to see the capital and elated by the thought of attending school there in the fall. Her brother, older by exactly ten months, shared the former enthusiasm but stuck out his tongue at the latter—in the Willard lobby. His forceful opinion earned him a whack and a reprimand from his mother.

George said they all might be back home by autumn. The coming battle would give some indication, anyway. Prices for hiring

185

horses and renting vehicles had escalated wildly in the past couple of days; hundreds of people planned to drive into Virginia to view the stirring event from some safe vantage point. Although George knew the real nature of war, he too had succumbed; they had a barouche available if they wanted it.

"If I told you what it cost, Constance, you might turn me out."

Wednesday evening, George returned to the hotel suite after long hours of attempting to wade through the quixotic confusion of Ripley's department. Looking grim, Constance handed him a *carte de visite.*

"Someone delivered it while I was shopping. I thought we might be fortunate enough to have Stanley and Isabel snub us."

He turned the card over and, with dismay, read Isabel's handwritten invitation to dinner the following night. He scowled at the message for some time before he said: "Let's go this once and be done with it. Otherwise she'll keep inviting us, and we'll keep suffering and dreading it the way you dread an appointment to have teeth yanked."

Constance sighed. "I suppose I can endure it if you can, though we both know who's probably behind the show of friendliness. Old Simon wants to keep you content."

He shrugged to acknowledge the likelihood, then said, "Perhaps Isabel actually enjoys entertaining us."

"George, do be serious."

"I am. It gives her a chance to show off to newcomers." He scratched his chin. "Wonder what she'll choose to brag about this time?"

A whole menu of items, as it turned out. The appetizer was the rented mansion on I Street. They were forced to tour it for fifteen minutes; Isabel alternately called attention to its expensive appointments and commiserated: "I feel so sorry for you, cramped into Willard's. We were ever so fortunate to escape the National and get into this place, don't you think?"

"Oh, yes." Constance was impeccably polite, her smile imperviously genuine. "It was kind of you to invite us, Isabel."

"Bygones should be bygones—especially in times like these." Isabel thrust that one at George, who didn't swallow it. He suddenly felt tired, cranky, and overdressed—a toy soldier. The hilt of the ridiculous staff sword kept knocking against his sash.

At dinner, the knives were brought out. Stanley and Isabel larded their talk with names of important persons, implying they

186

were intimate with all of them—Chase, Stevens, Welles, General McDowell, and of course Cameron.

"Did you see his latest monthly report, George?"

"I am in no position to see it, Stanley. I read about it."

"The remarks about the Academy—?"

"Yes." It took control merely to admit that.

"Exactly what did he say, dear?" Isabel asked, causing George to hear a phantom door go *bang;* he was in their trap.

"Why, merely that the rebellion wouldn't have been possible—at least not on such a large scale—without the treason of the officers educated at West Point at public expense. Simon concluded by asking whether such treason was not directly due to some radical defect in our national system—namely, the mere existence of the elitist institution."

Elitist. Public expense. Treason. It was the same old crowd of ragpickers, given new respectability by their new red, white, and blue suits. "Balderdash," he said, longing to use a stronger word.

"Permit me to differ, George," Isabel said. "I've heard the same view from any number of the congressional and cabinet wives. Even the President expressed it in his July fourth message."

Stanley feigned a mournful air, shaking his head. "I'm afraid your old school is in for hard times."

George shot his wife a seething glance over the tureens of turtle soup. Her eyes mirrored his misery but pleaded for patience.

The next knife appeared as the table servants offered platters of broiled tilefish and roast venison. Smiling, Isabel said, "We have another bit of good news. Tell them about the factory, Stanley."

Like a schoolboy reciting a rote lesson, Stanley did so.

George said, "Army shoes, eh? I presume you already have a contract?"

"We do," Isabel said. "Profit isn't the chief reason we purchased Lashbrook's, however. We wanted to help the war effort."
George couldn't help a glance at the ceiling. Fortunately, Constance missed it.

Isabel continued, "I will admit to one selfish consideration. If the factory succeeds, Stanley will no longer be exclusively dependent on income from Hazard's to supplement the pittance paid by the War Department. He will stand on his own feet."

He'll rest in Boss Cameron's pocket, more likely.

Infernally insincere, Isabel continued to smile as she went on. "If each of you manages his own business, it should promote

187

family harmony—something I would find refreshing. Of course we assume the income from Stanley's ownership interest in Hazard's will continue to be paid—"

"You needn't worry that anyone will defraud you, Isabel." Constance heard the growl in her husband's remark and touched his wrist.

"We mustn't stay late. You said tomorrow would be busy."

False politeness settled over the table again. Isabel was in fine spirits for the rest of the meal, as if she had played a trump—or several—and won.

In the hack returning to the hotel, George burst out: "Stanley's shoe contract makes me feel like a damn profiteer, too. We're selling iron plate to the navy and eight-inch columbiads to the War Department I work for—"

Constance patted his hand and kept patting, trying to relieve his tension. "Oh, I think there are differences."

"Too subtle for me to see."

"What would you do if the Union desperately needed cannon but couldn't afford to pay? What if you were asked to manufacture guns on that basis?"

"I'd kick like hell. I have an obligation to the people who work for me. They expect wages once a week."

"But if you could manage to meet the payroll, you'd say yes. That's the difference between you and Stanley."

Dubious, George shook his head. "I don't know whether I'm as saintly as all that. I do know our cannon are probably a damn sight better made than Stanley's bootees."

Constance laughed and hugged him. "That's why Stanley may turn into a profiteer, but you'll be—always and forever—George Hazard." She kissed him on the cheek. "For which I'm thankful."

At Willard's, she was relieved to find their son safely back from the encampments over in Virginia. She hadn't wanted him to go by himself, deeming him too young. George had persuaded her not to be so protective. The boy seemed none the worse for the experience.

"McDowell's on the march," he told them with great enthusiasm. "Uncle Billy says we'll probably fight the rebs on Saturday or Sunday."

Stanley had announced plans to drive out to view the spectacle. Undressing for bed, George and Constance discussed the possible

188

risks of such an outing. She wanted to go and, counting on his consent, had ordered a lunch in a hamper from Gautier's. George marveled silently; in her short time in the city, his wife had learned any number of things, including the fact that one simply didn't do business with any other, less prestigious, caterer.

"All right," he said. "We'll go."

That night, Billy wrote in his journal.

Today my nephew and namesake came over from the city. Securing the captain's permission, I took him to Fairfax Courthouse to watch the advance. It was a grand sight, with colors waving, bayonets sparkling, drums throbbing. The volunteers displayed high spirits because a fight is now virtually certain. Some units, not engineers but designated so, have already drawn the fire of hidden batteries as they labor to clear the roads of trees felled by the rebels. Our company is to stay behind with the District forces, which disappoints me. Yet I also confess to a measure of relief. The battle may not be easy and sportive—though the volunteers behave as if they expect such. At M.R. this spring, C. told me that prior to a fight, soldiers grow nervous and joke a lot. It's true; so much whooping and joshing I never heard as I did today. They sang, too— one song, "J. Brown's Body"—and were so busy with the music and merriment they forgot all else. They do not keep in orderly ranks or follow instructions well. No wonder McDowell is mistrustful. Returning several miles to the encampment by shank's mare—we found no supply wagons bound this way— William and I passed Capt. F.'s tent and heard him praying in full voice: "Behold the day of the Lord cometh. He shall destroy the sinners." What is that? asked my startled namesake. To which I replied, "I think it is Isaiah." When I recovered from my mistake—he wanted to know the speaker's identity— he confounded me by asking whether God had turned away from our friends the Mains. I gave him the most honest answer possible, viz.—Yes, according to our side. But I explained that our enemy counted upon His favor with equal confidence. Young William is quick, like his father; I believe he understood the paradox. Capt. F. invited him to join our mess and treated him most cordially, complimenting him on intelligent questions. William stayed till watch fires shone across the

*countryside, then mounted his hired horse to go back to Wash-
ington, where, I am told, great excitement also prevails. As I
write, I can still hear the army in the distance—wagons, cavalry, singing volunteers, and all. Though I have not seen the
elephant and would be scared, I now wish I were going, too.*

31

Brett missed Constance. The longing was sharpened because another woman had replaced her at Belvedere. A woman Brett
strongly disliked.

A number of times in the days after Constance left, Brett tried
to draw her sister-in-law into polite conversation. Each time Virgilia answered with monosyllables. She didn't act righteous or
angry, as she had before the war, but she had found a new way to
be rude.

Yet the younger woman felt a responsibility to be kind. Virgilia
was not only a relative by marriage; she was a wounded creature.
The night after George and Constance dined at Stanley's, Brett
decided to approach her again.

She couldn't find her. She asked the house girls. One said, with
evident distaste, "I saw her go up in the tower with the newspaper, mum."

Brett climbed the circular iron stair George had designed and
manufactured at Hazard's. She opened the door from the book-
lined third-floor study to the narrow balcony encircling the tower.
Below were the lights of Lehigh Station, glowing in the summer
dusk, the dark ribbon of the river, and the sun-etched mountains

beyond. Smoke and a dirty red glare overlay the noisy immensity of Hazard's to the north. The factory work never stopped these days.

"Virgilia?"

"Oh. Good evening."

She didn't turn. Strands of unpinned hair flew in the breeze; she might have been mistaken for Medusa in the failing light. Brett saw, tucked under her arm, a copy of the *Lehigh Station Ledger*, which had recently transferred its patriotism to the masthead and become the *Ledger-Union*.

"Is there any important news?"

"They say a battle will be fought in Virginia in a few days."

"Perhaps it will bring a quick peace."

"Perhaps." She sounded indifferent.

"Are you coming to supper?"

"I don't think so."

"Virgilia, do me the courtesy of looking at me."

Slowly, Billy's sister complied; her eyes caught light from the sky, and Brett imagined she saw a flash of the old Virgilia— martyred, angry. Then the eyes grew dull. Brett forced a gentleness she didn't feel.

"I appreciate that you've undergone some terrible experiences—"

"I loved Grady," Virgilia said. "Everyone hates me because he was a colored man. But I loved him."

"I can understand how lost you must feel without him." It was a lie; it was beyond her to understand a white woman's love for a Negro.

Virgilia sank into self-pity. "This is my own home, and no one wants me here."

"You're wrong. Constance took you in. I'd like to help you, too. I know"—how difficult this was—"we'll never be warm friends, but, even so, we needn't behave as if the other person doesn't exist. I would like to make you feel better—"

At last, the old Virgilia—scathing: "How?"

"Well—" Desperate, Brett seized a straw. "For one thing, we must do something about that dress. It doesn't become you. In fact, it's horrid."

"Why bother? No man wants to look at me."

"No one's trying to rush you to the altar or into the social whirl"—the light reply drew another hard stare—"but you might

191

feel better about yourself if you discarded that dress, took a long bath, and fixed your hair. Why don't you let me help you with your hair after supper?"

"Because it won't make any difference."

How foolish to think she'd accept help, Brett said to herself. She's as stupidly ungrateful as—

The thought went unfinished as Brett studied the other woman. Virgilia's hair blew this way and that, and she had grown round-shouldered. Though she had lost weight, she still had a full bosom. But it sagged, like a crone's. Her eyes picked up light from the fading day again. Hurt. So hurt.

"Come—let's try." Like a mother with her child, she grasped Virgilia's wrist. Feeling no resistance, she tugged gently.

"I don't care," Virgilia said with a shrug. But she let the younger girl lead her inside and down the iron stair.

After supper, Brett sent two girls to pour kettles of hot water into a tub. When the girls realized the reason, they looked at her as if they suspected lunacy. But she pressed on, urging a limp and unresisting Virgilia upstairs.

She shut her in the bathroom. "Throw out your clothes. Everything. I'll find something else for you to wear."

She sat in the gloomy bedroom—Virgilia had closed all the drapes—and let five minutes pass. After ten, her irritation changed to alarm. Had the mad creature done away with herself? She pressed her ear to the door. "Virgilia?"

Her heart hammered. Finally she heard sounds. She stepped back as the door opened. A hand extended a wad of clothing Brett didn't want to touch. She marched it downstairs at arm's length.

"Burn this," she said to one of the girls. To another: "Find a nightdress and robe Miss Virgilia can wear. Mine are too small." The order horrified the girl. "I'll pay you twice what the clothes are worth. You can buy new ones."

That got action. Upstairs again, she laid the gown on the bed and handed the old linen robe through the bathroom door. She turned all the gas mantles up full so that the bedroom was bright when Virgilia finally emerged, stepping out almost shyly, the robe tightly wrapped and tied. Her skin and hair were damp, but she was clean.

"You look splendid! Come sit here."

Virgilia took the embroidered seat Brett had placed in front of the large oval mirror. With a fresh towel, Brett dried Virgilia's hair vigorously—it was indeed like grooming a child—then began to ply a silver-backed brush inlaid with pearl. She stroked down and down while a clock on the fireplace mantel ticked. Down and down. Virgilia remained rigid, staring in the mirror, seeing God knew what visions.

When she finished the brushing, she parted Virgilia's hair in the current style—down the center—then wound a strand on her finger and pinned it above Virgilia's left ear. She repeated the procedure on the other side. "Those will shape into attractive loops." She lifted the rest: Virgilia did have beautifully thick tresses. "We'll gather the rest in a net in the morning. You'll be very fashionable."

She saw her own smiling face in the glass, above Virgilia's lifeless one. Discouraged, she tried not to show it.

"There's a nightgown on the bed. First thing tomorrow, we'll drive into town and buy some new clothes."

"I have nothing to wear."

"We'll borrow a dress."

"I don't have any money."

"Never mind. I do. Consider it a present."

"You don't have to—"

"Yes, I do. Hush. I want you to feel better. You're an attractive woman."

That finally fetched a smile—of contemptuous doubt. Vexed, Brett turned away. "Rest well. I'll see you in the morning."

Virgilia remained motionless, like a piece of garden statuary. Brett decided she had wasted her evening.

For a long while after the door closed, Virgilia sat with her hands in her lap. No one had ever used the word *attractive* to describe her. No one had ever come close to saying she was pretty. She was neither, and she knew it. And yet, staring at the gaslit image, she saw a woman marvelous and new. A not-unpresentable woman with hair modishly arranged. Even her complexion looked better; scrubbing her cheeks had brought some color, which helped to hide the pox scars of which she had always been ashamed. A lump formed in her throat.

When Brett had said she wanted to help her, Virgilia's first reaction had been suspicion, her second exhausted indifference. Now, before the mirror, something stirred in her. Not happiness; she was seldom capable of that, and not now especially. Call it interest. Curiosity. Whatever its name, it was a little bud of life that unexpectedly broke through hard ground.

She rose, unfastened the robe, and opened it to see herself.

Corseted, her breasts would become her. The near-starvation she had endured after selling the last of the stolen silver had slimmed her. Perhaps the agony of those weeks of hunger would have a positive side.

She let the robe fall. Suddenly overwhelmed, she took a small step forward. One hand, not steady, came up—reached out—touched the wondrous reflection. *"Oh."* Her eyes filled with tears.

She found it hard to sleep that night. Around midnight she opened the curtains so the morning light would wake her. Wearing both the gown and the robe, she was seated in the dining room waiting when Brett appeared for breakfast.

32

George woke at five on Sunday morning. He slipped from bed—but not quietly. His activity soon roused Constance and the children. "You're as excited as a boy," she said, yawning as she struggled into her clothes.

"I want to see the battle. Half the town expects it to be the first and last of the war."

"Do you, Pa?" his son asked, acting as cheerfully jittery as his parent.

"I wouldn't venture a guess." He wrapped the old army-issue gun belt around his waist and made sure the 1847-model Colt repeater rested securely in the holster. Constance took note of the preparation but limited her comment to a frown. George gestured.

"William, fetch my flask of whiskey and take care of it. Patricia, help your mother with the lunch hamper. I'll get the carriage."

Patricia made a face. "I'd rather stay and read and feed the cows on the mall."

"Now, now," Constance said as George left. "Your father made all the arrangements. We're going."

So was a large part of the population of Washington, it appeared. Even at this early hour, a line of riders and vehicles waited at the city end of Long Bridge while sentries checked passes. Among the sightseers there was a great deal of animated conversation, laughter, and the displaying of opera glasses and telescopes bought or borrowed for the occasion. It promised to be a warm, lovely day, the scents of summer earth and air mingling with the aromas of horse droppings and perfume.

Finally the Hazards reached the head of the line. George showed his War Department pass. "Plenty of traffic this morning."

"Plenty more ahead of you, Captain. They've been passing for hours." Saluting, the sentry signaled the barouche forward.

They crossed the river, George smartly handling the two plugs rented as part of the rig that had cost him an outrageous thirty dollars for the day. He had paid without protest and deemed himself lucky; among the phaetons, hacks, and gigs on the rutted road, he spied even more unusual conveyances, including a dairy wagon and another with the name of some city photographer blazoned on it.

The trip was not short; they had to travel roughly twenty-five miles southwest to find the armies. As two hours became three and the miles rolled on, they drove past cornfields, small farms, and ramshackle cabins. White and black people watched the cavalcade with equal astonishment.

McDowell's advance had torn up the road. Constance and the children constantly swayed and bounced; Patricia loudly lamented the discomfort and the long distance.

A stop near a patch of woods was necessary for all of them. Constance and her daughter retired first, then George and William after they returned. George folded down the calash top so they could enjoy more of the scenery and sunshine. That mollified

195

William a little, but Patricia continued to express boredom and annoyance. George spoke to her and put a stop to that.

A horseman sped around the left side of the barouche; George recognized a senator. He had already seen three well-known members of the House. They were still a couple of miles this side of Fairfax when William tugged George's sleeve, excited. "Pa, listen!"

Amid all the cloppings and creaking, George had missed the faraway rumbling. "That's artillery, all right." Constance put her arm around Patricia. George's spine prickled, and he remembered Mexico. Shells bursting. Men toppling. The raging screams of wounded; the lost cries of the dying. He remembered the shell that blew away the hut on the Churubusco road—and his friend Orry's arm in the bargain. He shut his eyes to blot out the memories—

With a shiver, he straightened and concentrated on driving. The shelling beyond the horizon excited travelers all along the road. Horses were urged to greater speed. But some difficulty ahead slowed movement. Huge dust clouds billowed. "Good God, what's this?" he said as Union troops, marching toward Washington, forced vehicles, including the barouche, over to the shoulder.

"Who are you?" George yelled at a corporal driving a high-piled baggage cart.

"Fourth Pennsylvania."

"Is the battle over?"

"Don't know, but we're going home. Our enlistments ran out yesterday."

The corporal drove on, followed by clots of ambling volunteers who laughed a lot and handled their shoulder weapons as if they were toys. Purple berry stains ringed the mouth of more than one young soldier. Wild flowers stuck from the muzzle of more than one musket. The Pennsylvanians straggled through the fields on either side of the road, picking flowers, pissing, doing whatever they pleased, while the guns grumbled in the south.

Past Fairfax, the Washington picnickers pressed on toward a thin blue haze drifting above ridge lines still miles distant. The boom of artillery grew louder. About noon, George began to hear the crackling of small arms, too.

The countryside here was rolling and wooded, though it had open stretches as well. They drove through Centreville and down the Warrenton Turnpike until they came upon great numbers of carriages and horses lined up on high ground on both sides of the road. An army courier galloping to the rear shouted that they had better go no farther.

"I can't see anything, Pa," William complained as George turned the horses left, behind the line of spectators with their picnic blankets and baskets spread among the trees. In front of them a hillside sloped to a creek called Cub Run, with smoke-muddied fields and woods beyond.

Hunting an open spot, George noticed enough foreign uniforms and heard enough different languages to furnish at least one diplomatic ball. He continued to see Washingtonians, too, including Senator Trumbull, of Illinois, present with a large party.

He winced when he came upon a familiar group. "Good morning, Stanley," he called, driving on. He was thankful there was no room on either side of Stanley's phaeton.

"Three hampers and a champagne bucket—what wretched excess," Constance said as William directed his protest to her:

"I can't see anything."

"That may be, but we're going no closer," George said. "Here's a place." He pulled into vacant space at the end of the line of vehicles, tired and hot. His watch showed ten past one. Their view of the battle consisted of a panorama of distant clouds of thick smoke.

"They're not firing." Constance sounded relieved as she unfolded and spread their blanket. Could it be over already? George said he would try to get some information. He set off on foot toward the turnpike.

Courtesy forced him to stop a moment with his brother's family. The twins were busy bashing each other behind a tree. Sweaty Stanley looked cross-eyed from champagne. Isabel declared that the artillery fire had been "fearsome" until a few minutes ago and that the rebs certainly must be on the run to Richmond. George touched his hat brim and left in search of more reliable sources.

He passed several loud groups and found himself irked by their jollity—maybe because he had a grasp of what was probably happening beneath and behind the smoke. He reached the turnpike and scanned it for anyone who appeared trustworthy. In three or four minutes, a gig came rattling up the hill from the suspension bridge spanning Cub Run.

The gig pulled off the opposite side of the road. A portly civilian, well dressed, put on eyeglasses hanging from a chain. From under the seat he took a hard-backed writing pad and pencil. George crossed the road.

"Are you a reporter?"

"That's correct, sir." The proper British accent startled George. "Russell's the name." He awaited a reaction and was cooler when he had to add, "The *Times* of London."

"Yes, of course—I've seen your dispatches. Have you been forward?"

"As far as prudence allows."

"What's the situation?"

"Impossible to be sure, but the Federals appear to be carrying the day. The troops on both sides are spirited. One Confederate general distinguished himself in a hot contest around a farmhouse close by the Sudley Road. A Union action vedette gave me particulars, and the chap's name—" he leafed back two pages—"Jackson."

"Thomas Jackson? Is he a Virginian?"

"Can't say, old fellow. Really—I must get on here. Both sides are resting and regrouping. There'll be more soon, I don't doubt." He dismissed his questioner by bending over his pad to write.

George felt sure the hero of the farmhouse must be his old friend and West Point classmate; the strange, driven Virginian with whom he had shared study hours and hashes and conversation in sunny cantinas after Mexico City fell. Jackson had been teaching at some military school before the war, and it was logical that he would join up and stand out. Even back at the Academy, there had been two distinct opinions about Tom Jackson: he was brilliant, and he was crazy.

George tramped back to his family. Around two, while they ate, the lull ended. Ground-shaking cannonading began, exciting William and terrifying Patricia. Hundreds of spectators peered through spyglasses, but little could be seen except occasional fiery glares in the roiling blue clouds. An hour went by. Another. The rattle of small arms never stopped. Since the best soldier couldn't fire a muzzleloader much faster than four times a minute, George knew that continuous fire meant great numbers of men were volleying.

Suddenly horses burst from the murk hanging over the turnpike. One wagon emerged, followed by two more. All sped toward the Cub Run bridge—too rapidly; the spectators heard unseen wounded screaming at every jolt.

Constance leaned near. "George, there's something vile about all this. Must we stay?"

"Definitely not. We've seen enough."

That was confirmed when a carriageload of officers with horse tails on their elaborate helmets pulled out of line, heading for the turnpike. One officer stood, swayed drunkenly, and fell out. The carriage stopped. As his comrades helped him back in, he vomited on them.

"Yes, definitely this isn't—"

A commotion interrupted George. He turned and followed the pointing fingers of people nearby. A private in blue came running along the turnpike, heading for the bridge. Then another. Then more than a dozen. George heard the first man screaming unintelligibly. Those behind were throwing away kepis, haversacks—God almighty—even their muskets.

And then George understood the cry of the boy on the bridge. "We're whipped. *We're whipped.*"

George's stomach spasmed. "Constance, get in the carriage. Children, you too. Forget the food." He slipped the nose bags off the horses; he had wanted to water them in the creek, but now there was no time. He smelled something vague and terrible in the powder-laden air. He shoved his son and daughter. "Hurry."

His tone alarmed them. Down the line, two horsemen were mounting, but no one else acted concerned. George maneuvered the barouche into the open and started toward the road, aware of soldiers running up the hill while more poured from the smoky woods beyond Cub Run on a steadily widening front. One youngster in blue shrieked, "Black Horse Cavalry. Black Horse Cavalry right behind us!"

George had heard about that feared regiment from Fauquier County. He shook the reins to speed the stable plugs, passing Stanley and Isabel, who seemed puzzled by his haste. "I'd get going if you don't want to be caught in—"

The whine of a shell muffled the rest of the warning. Craning, George watched another ambulance reach the suspension bridge just before the shell hit. The horses tore against leather, the wagon rolled over—the bridge was blocked.

More vehicles and men appeared on the Warrenton Turnpike and in the flanking woods. Geysers of smoke and dirt erupted as projectiles fired by distant artillery struck the slope and creek banks. The Union volunteers were fleeing; the bridge was impassable; ambulance and supply wagons piled up in the smoky vale behind; and quick as brush fire, the terror spread to the spectators.

A civilian leaped into the barouche and tried to grab the reins. His nails raked the back of George's hand, drawing blood. George squirmed sideways and booted the man in the groin. He fell off.

"Black Horse, Black Horse!" the running soldiers screamed, the turnpike thick with them now; most were soaked from wading the creek to avoid the bridge. Constance cried out softly and hugged the children as a shell burst in the field to their right. Dirt came down all over them.

George drew his Colt, transferred it to his left hand, and struggled to turn the nervous animals using only his right. Not easy, but he was determined to get his family to safety. He stayed off the turnpike; too many retreating men made it impossible to travel with any speed. Uniforms were mingled, regulation blue with gaudy Zouave outfits—the entire Union force must have collapsed into disorder.

"Hold on," he yelled as he plunged the team through a stubble field south of the road, then swerved wildly to avoid a tuba thrown away by some musician. In a quarter of a mile, hundreds of men caught up with them and passed them. George was outraged by the rout, the fleeing soldiers, and the spectators. Beyond the turnpike, he saw three women thrown from their buggy by two men in civilian clothes. He raised his Colt to fire at them, then realized the futility of it and didn't.

He began to ache from the rough transit of the fields. Smoke made his eyes smart; shells landed close behind them. Crossing another small stream, the barouche's rear wheels sank into ooze on the bank. George ordered the family out and gestured William to the off rear wheel. Just then he saw Stanley's rig race by, straight down the middle of the turnpike. Soldiers had to leap out of the way. Isabel spied the barouche, but her fear-stricken face suggested she didn't recognize anyone.

A sergeant and two privates splashed toward the mired vehicle. George was wary of the sergeant's glazed look. Standing in muddy water halfway up his thighs, George drew the Colt's hammer back.

"Help us push it out or get the hell away."

The sergeant called him a name and motioned his men on.

200

Almost blinded by sweat, George put his shoulder against the wheel and told his son to do the same. "Push!"

They strained and heaved; Constance dragged at the headstall of the near horse. Finally the barouche sprang free of the mud. Dirty, angry, and fearful, George resumed the drive toward Washington, wondering if they would ever see it again.

Men and wagons, wagons and men. The summer light slanted lower, and the smoke hampered visibility. The smells grew intolerable: urine-stained wool, bleeding animals, the bowels of an open-mouthed dead youth in a ditch.

The woods ahead looked impassable; George put the barouche back on the road. He heard weeping. "The Black Horse Cavalry tore us to pieces!" Soldiers repeatedly tried to climb in the carriage. George handed the Colt to Constance and armed himself with the whip.

Under drooping trees, the stable nags were slowed to a walk, then stopped completely. A bleeding cavalry horse had fallen in the center of the road. It blocked the retreat of about a dozen men in stained Zouave uniforms. All but one double-timed around the dying animal; the last soldier, young and pudgy and displaying a deeply gashed cheek, halted and stared at the animal. Suddenly he raised his muzzleloader and brought the butt down on the horse's head.

Crying and cursing, he hit the horse again. Then twice more, with increasing ferocity. Ignoring his wife's plea, George jumped from the barouche. The boy had already broken open the horse's skull. While the animal thrashed and George's outraged yell went unheeded, the soldier raised his musket for another blow. Tears washed down into his wound.

George shouted, "I am giving you a direct order to—"

The rest got lost in the boy's sobbed obscenities and the scream of the horse taking the next blow. George ran around the animal, glimpsing its head by chance; the sight brought vomit to his throat. He tore the muzzleloader out of the hands of the demented youth and menaced him with it.

"Get out of here. Go on!"

Indifferent to the anger, the boy gave George a vacant look, then stumbled down the shoulder to the ditch and turned in the direction of Washington. He was still crying and muttering to himself. George quickly checked the musket, found it was loaded, and fired a shot to end the horse's agony. He stopped three running men, and the four of them dragged the dead animal to the side of the turnpike.

Breathing hard and still tasting vomit, he searched for the barouche. He spied Constance standing in the road, an arm around each child and the Colt dangling in her right hand. George saw the barouche moving away toward Centreville, packed with men in blue.

"They took it, George. I couldn't shoot our own soldiers—"

"Of course not. It's my fault for leaving you—Patricia, crying won't help. We'll get out of this. We'll be all right. Give me the gun. Now let's walk."

In Mexico, George had learned that a battle was inevitably larger than what the individual soldier perceived and experienced; even generals sometimes failed to discern the larger patterns. George's knowledge of the battle at Bull Run consisted of what he saw from the spectator site and on the retreat in the hot, insect-ridden hours of a waning Sunday. For him, Bull Run would forever be a road of wrecked wagons and discarded gear, a stream bed for a blue torrent that overflowed both sides and crashed by them, impelled by the melting of some unknown grand plan.

Constance tugged the sleeve of his uniform. "George, look there—ahead."

He saw Stanley's carriage lying on its side. The horses were gone; stolen, probably. Isabel and the twins huddled around George's brother, who sat on a roadside stone, his undone cravat dangling between his legs. Stanley's hands were pressed to his face. George knew why; he had experienced a similar moment years ago.

"Christ, do I have to take care of him again?"

"I know how you feel. But we can't leave them there."

"Why not?" said Patricia. "Laban and Levi are hateful. Let the rebs get them." Constance slapped her, turned red, hugged her, and apologized.

George refused to look at Isabel as he stepped in front of his brother. "Get up, Stanley." Stanley's shoulders heaved. George seized Stanley's right hand and jerked it down. "Get on your feet. Your family needs you."

"He just—collapsed when the carriage overturned," Isabel said. George paid no attention, pulling and hauling till he got his brother up and pointed in the right direction. George pushed; Stanley started walking.

So the shepherd and his flock went on. Men continued to pass them, most dirty with powder and grime, many bloodied. They encountered a few volunteer officers bravely trying to keep a small squad formed up, but these were the exception; the majority of officers had no men and walked or ran faster than their subordinates.

Stanley's breakdown infuriated his wife but, oddly, her anger focused on George. The twins complained and muttered disparaging remarks about George until near-darkness separated them from the others in a field. After five minutes of frantic shouting, the twins found the adults again. Henceforth they walked directly behind George, saying nothing.

The detritus of defeat lay everywhere: canteens, horns and drums, shot pouches and bayonets. Darkness came down, and the eerie cries of the hurt and dying made George think of an aviary in hell. In the shadow tide flowing by, the voices rose and fell:

"—fucking captain ran. *Ran*—while the rest of us stood fast—"

"—my feet are bleeding. Can't—"

"—Black Horse. They was nigh a thousand of—"

"—Sherman's brigade broke when Hampton's *voltigeurs* hit—"

Hampton? George plucked the name out of the babble of voices, the creak of wheels, the complaints of his children. Wasn't Charles Main riding with Hampton's Legion? Had he fought today? Had he survived?

The rising moon provided scant light; translucent clouds kept floating across it. The air smelled of rain. George guessed it to be ten or eleven o'clock; he was so weary, he could have crawled in a ditch and slept. That told him how tired the others must be.

At Centreville, they finally saw lights again—and wounded everywhere. Some New York volunteers with a supply wagon noticed the children and offered to drive them on to Fairfax Courthouse. They had no room for the adults. George spoke earnestly to William, whom he knew he could trust, and when he was sure his son knew the rendezvous point, he and Constance helped the youngsters into the wagon. Isabel uttered objections; Stanley stared at the rainy moon.

The wagon disappeared. The adults resumed their walk. Along the roadsides beyond Centreville they passed more casualties, sleeping or resting or still. The sight of hurt faces, bloodied limbs,

203

the moonlit eyes of lads too young to be asked to look at death, continually reminded George of Mexico, and of the burning house in Lehigh Station.

It was small consolation to know he had not been imagining danger then. The fire bells had signaled a greater conflagration, and now they were all trapped in it. Trapped in war's folly and madness. Chicane seducing honesty. Ruin replacing plenty. Fear banishing hope. Hatred burying amity. Death canceling life. This fire was the mortal foe of everything the Mains and Hazards wanted to preserve, and it would not be extinguished quickly, like that at home. This day—this night—had shown him the fire was out of control.

"Stanley? Don't fall behind." The shepherd's eyes began to water with dust and fatigue. The moon melted, and streaks of it dripped down the sky. Instead of the dim road, he saw the soldier striking the fallen horse. An unbelievable act. A change had begun that he couldn't comprehend. Some terrible change.

"Isabel? Are you all right? Come on, now. You must keep up."

BOOK TWO

THE DOWNWARD ROAD

Nobody, no man, can save the country. Our men are not good soldiers. They brag, but don't perform, complain sadly if they don't get everything they want, and a march of a few miles uses them up. It will take a long time to overcome these things, and what is in store for us in the future I know not.

COL. WILLIAM T. SHERMAN, *after First Bull Run,* 1861

33

All night long, rumors of disaster swept the city. Elkanah Bent, like thousands of others, was unable to sleep. He lingered in bars or in the streets where quiet crowds awaited word. He prayed there would be news of a victory. Nothing else would save him.

Around three, he and Elmsdale, the New Hampshire colonel, gave up the vigil and returned to the boardinghouse. Bent dozed rather than slept and heard the rain start sometime before daybreak. Then he heard men in the streets. He dressed quickly, went out to the boardinghouse porch, and in a vacant lot in the next block saw eight or ten soldiers resting in the weeds. Three others, visibly filthy, dismantled a board fence to make a fire.

Yawning, Elmsdale joined him with a supply of cigars. With a nod at the vacant lot, he said, "Looks bad, doesn't it?" Bent felt a silent hysteria rising.

The two colonels hurried toward Pennsylvania Avenue. An officer's horse walked by; the man in the saddle was asleep. At another boardinghouse, Zouaves begged for food. A civilian in a white suit staggered through the drizzle with several canteens and a musket. Battlefield souvenirs? Bent tried to control his trembling.

On the avenue, they saw the ambulances, the wandering men with defeated expressions. Dozens more lay sleeping in President's Park. Bent saw bloodied faces, arms, and legs. He and Elmsdale separated for a short time. Then Elmsdale rejoined him.

"It's what we feared. A rout. I knew it last night. If McDowell had won, the President would have sent word from the telegraph room. Well—" he lit a cigar under his hat brim, out of the drizzle —"it's a taste of what's in store for us in the West."

Never religious, Bent had implored God yesterday for a Union victory. He and Elmsdale already had train tickets to Kentucky. Now he would have to use his. The war might last for months. He might perish in Kentucky, his trove of genius untapped, wasted—

He wanted to escape that fate but didn't know how. He didn't dare appeal to Dills again; the lawyer might make good on his threat. Short of desertion, which would definitely bring his dreams of military glory to an end, he saw no alternative but to use the ticket.

The child inside him screamed in futile protest. Elmsdale took note of his companion's queer, strained expression and, muttering some excuse, once more strode away in the rain.

The day after Manassas, Charles and his troop encamped with the legion not far from Confederate headquarters at the Lewis house, which was named Portici. This was quite near the center of the field of battle and less than a mile from Bull Run, whose pink-tinted brown water still held dead bodies from both sides.

As the light faded, Charles set about rubbing and currying Sport. He was elated by the victory but angry with the circumstances that had denied him a part in it. On Friday, following his return from Fairfax County, the legion had been ordered to come up from Ashland and reinforce Beauregard. But the Richmond, Fredericksburg, & Potomac rail line had only enough cars for Hampton and his six hundred foot. There were none for his four troops of horse or his flying artillery battery.

After numerous delays, Hampton reached Manassas on the morning of the battle; his cavalry was still laboring across a hundred and thirty miles of winding road, fording the South Anna, North Anna, Mattapony, Rappahannock, Aquia, Occoquan, and many lesser streams. Despite maddening slowdowns caused by two heavy rainstorms, Charles had brimmed with unexpected confidence on that long ride. He believed his men, once in action, would be all right; in spite of their resistance to discipline, they were riding well as a unit. Most could sit the dragoon seat respectably, if not as perfectly as the already fabled Turner Ashby.

Charles never had a chance to verify his new feeling; the troopers arrived after the day was won. They learned the colonel had distinguished himself, sustaining a light head wound while leading his infantry against crumbling federal regiments. That did little to soothe some of Charles's young gentlemen, who complained of missing not only the scrap but also the chance to pick through the weapons and accoutrements dropped by the fleeing Yankees. Charles sympathized with his men and mentally prepared for the next fight. It was already clear that this one wouldn't end matters.

President Davis had ridden the cars from Richmond personally to congratulate the various commanders, including Hampton, whom Davis and Old Bory called on in Hampton's tent. By late Monday, however, Charles and many others were hearing of complaints from certain members of the government; Beauregard had failed to press his advantage, drive on to Washington and capture it.

Charles kept his counsel. Lard-assed bureaucrats who sat at desks and carped had no comprehension of warfare or the limits it imposed on men and animals. They had no grasp of how long you could drive a soldier or a horse to fight fiercely and expend maximum energy. It was not a long time, relatively speaking. Battle was hard work, and even the greatest courage, the hardest will, the strongest heart must give in to overwhelming exhaustion.

Complaints aside, Manassas had been a triumph, the proof of a long-held belief that gentlemen could always whip rabble. Charles shared some of that euphoria in the pleasant hours following the battle and tried not to take undue notice of certain stenches drifting on the summer wind or the ambulance processions passing in silhouette against the red sundown.

There had been losses less impersonal than those represented by the passing vehicles. The legion's second-in-command, Lieutenant Colonel Johnson, of Charleston, had been killed by the first volley he and his men faced. Barnard Bee, one of Cousin Orry's friends from the Academy, had been mortally hit just after rallying men to the colors of that reportedly mad professor from the Virginia Military Institute, Fool Tom Jackson. Bee had praised Jackson for standing like a stone wall near the Henry house, and it appeared that "Fool Tom" had now been replaced by a more complimentary nickname.

All the members of Hampton's family who were serving had gotten through unscathed: his older son, young Wade, on the staff of Joe Johnston, whose valley army had come in on the cars of the Manassas Gap line; and Wade's younger brother, Preston, a smart-looking twenty-year-old famous for wearing yellow gloves.

Preston was one of his father's aides. Hampton's brother Frank, a cavalryman, had also escaped injury.

While Charles was using a pick to remove dirt and bits of dead tissue from Sport's hooves, Calbraith Butler, another troop commander, drifted up. Butler was a handsome, polished fellow, exactly Charles's age. He was married to the daughter of Governor Pickens and had given up a lucrative law practice to raise the Edgefield Hussars, one of the units Hampton had absorbed into the legion. Though Butler had no military experience, Charles suspected he would be fine in a fight; he liked Butler.

"Ought to have a nigra do that for you," Butler advised.

"If I were as rich as you lawyers, I might." Butler laughed. "How's the colonel?"

"In good spirits, considering the loss of Johnson and the casualties we took."

"How high?"

"Not certain. I heard twenty percent."

"Twenty," Charles repeated, with a slight nod to show satisfaction. Best to think of the dead and injured as percentages, not people; it helped you sleep nights.

Butler crouched down. "I hear the Yankees not only ran from our Black Horse, but they ran from the mere thought of them. They ran from bays, grays, roans—any color you care to name. Called 'em all the Black Horse. Sure sorry we missed that. One nice development—whether we fought or not, we're to taste the fruits of victory in a week or so. Those of us who can manage to get back to Richmond, anyway."

He went on to explain that grateful citizens had already announced a gala ball to which favored officers from Manassas would be invited. "And you know, Charlie, cavalry officers are the most favored of all. We needn't tell the ladies we were miles from the battle. That is, you needn't. Out of respect for my wife, I don't suppose I'll attend."

"Why not? Beauty Stuart's married, and I bet he'll be there."

"Damn Virginians. Have to be in the forefront of everything." During the battle, Stuart had led a much-discussed charge along the Sudley Road, further enhancing his reputation for bravery— or recklessness, depending on who told the story.

"A ball. That does have a certain tempting ring." Charles tried to keep his gaze away from more ambulances moving in slow file along the ridge, past the blazing disk of the sun.

"Charming female guests from miles around are to be invited. The sponsors don't want our brave boys to suffer a shortage of dance partners."

Thoughtfully, Charles said, "I just might go if I can scrounge an invitation."

"Well! There's a sign of life in the weary trooper. Good for you." Butler strolled off, and Sport nuzzled Charles's arm as he resumed his work. He found himself whistling, having realized that with a touch of luck he might find Augusta Barclay at the ball.

34

They had arrived in the capital at seven in the morning, soaked and on the verge of sickness. George, Constance, and the children went straight to Willard's; Stanley, Isabel, and the twins to their mansion, with not so much as a syllable of good-bye exchanged.

George washed, shaved—cutting himself twice—drank two fingers of whiskey, and reported to the Winder Building in a daze. So widespread was despair over the defeat that nothing got done all morning; Ripley shut the office down at half past eleven. George heard that the President was in another of his depressive states. Small wonder, he thought as he staggered through crowds of army stragglers on his way to the hotel.

He fell into a stuporous sleep, from which he was gently shaken around nine that night. Constance felt he should take some nourishment. In Willard's dining room, which was packed yet unnaturally quiet, George questioned those at nearby tables and winced at the answers. He asked more questions next day. The scope and consequences of the tragedy at Bull Run became clearer.

Everyone spoke of the disgraceful behavior of the volunteers and their officers, and of the ferocity of the enemy troops, especially something called the Black Horse Cavalry. George got the impression the rebs had no other kind, which couldn't be true. Yet even Ripley spoke as if it were.

Casualty figures were vague as yet, though some losses were certain; Simon Cameron's brother had died leading a Highlander regiment, the Seventy-ninth New York. Scott and McDowell were the identified culprits. While George snored away most of Monday, McDowell had been relieved and George's old classmate McClellan was summoned from western Virginia to command the army and, presumably, organize and train it into something more nearly worthy of the name.

On Tuesday, office work resumed. George received orders for a flying trip to acquaint himself with activities of the Cold Spring Foundry across the river from West Point. His father had visited the foundry during George's cadet years. Even back then, it had been turning out some of the finest ironwork in America. The foundry was now manufacturing great iron-banded artillery pieces designed by Robert Parker Parrott. The Ordnance Department's on-site officer was a Captain Stephen Benét.

Tuesday night, after George packed, the high-command change took up most of the conversation before he and Constance fell asleep.

"Lincoln and the cabinet and the Congress all pushed McDowell. They forced him to send poorly trained amateurs into battle. The volunteers failed to behave like regulars, and McDowell's been punished for it—by Lincoln and the cabinet and the Congress."

"Ah," she murmured. "The first girl on the President's card proved clumsy, so he's changing partners."

"Changing partners. That says it very well." George hoisted his nightshirt to scratch an itch on his thigh. "I wonder how many times he'll do it before the ball is over?"

George was thankful to exchange Washington's air of hopelessness for the beauty of the Hudson River valley, all the more vivid because of the glorious sunshiny weather he found there. Old Parrott, class of '24, ran the plant, and he insisted on showing the

211

visitor every part of it personally. Bathing in the foundry's heat and light was a kind of joyous homecoming. George was fascinated by the precision with which the workers bored out the cannon and heated, coiled, and hammered four-inch-square bars of iron to form the bands that were the maker's mark on Parrott guns.

Parrott seemed to appreciate the presence in the Ordnance Department of someone who understood his problems as manufacturer and manager. George liked the older man, but the real find, personally as well as professionally, was Captain Stephen V. Benét, whom George remembered from the class of '49.

A Florida native, so dark as to be mistaken for a Spaniard, Benét divided his time between the foundry and West Point, where he taught ordnance theory and gunnery. Together, the two men crossed the river to roam their old haunts one afternoon. They discussed everything from their own classes to the mounting attacks on the institution.

Over supper at the post hotel, Benét said: "I admire the patriotism that inspired you to accept a commission. As for being in Ripley's department—that calls for condolences."

"That place is an infernal mess," George agreed. "Lunatic inventors in every cranny, piles of paper a year old, no standardization. I'm trying to compile a master list of all the types of artillery ammunition we're using. It's a struggle."

Benét laughed. "I should imagine. There are at least five hundred."

"We may defeat ourselves and save the rebs the job."

"Working for Ripley would discourage anyone. He looks for reasons to reject new ideas. He seeks their flaws. I'd rather look for strengths. Reasons to say yes." Benét paused, twirling his glass of port. He gave his visitor a level look and decided to trust him. "Perhaps that's why the President now sends prototypes directly here for evaluation." He sipped. "Did you know about that—bypassing Ripley?"

"No, but it doesn't surprise me. Taking the other side, I must tell you Lincoln's very unpopular in the War Department because of his constant interference."

"Understandable, but—" another searching look—"how will we whip the Ripleys without it?"

George carried the pessimistic question back to the city unanswered.

July sweltered away, and George hunched at his desk late into the evenings. He seldom saw Stanley, but he saw Lincoln often. The storklike, vaguely comical Chief Executive was always dashing from one government office to another with bundles of plans and papers and memoranda and a spare joke or two, some very bawdy. Gossip said the dumpy little woman to whom he was married refused to hear the stories repeated in her presence.

Occasionally Lincoln turned up at the Winder Building in the late afternoon, wanting one of the staff to join him in target practice over at Treasury Park. Once George was tempted to volunteer, but he held back, not because he was in awe of the Chief Executive—Lincoln was usually gregarious and eminently approachable—but because he feared he would let his frustrations spill out. As long as he worked for Ripley, he owed him silence as a measure of loyalty.

Although procedure outweighed performance in the departmental scheme of things, Ripley's record was not all bad. George discovered the old man had pleaded for purchase of a hundred thousand European shoulder weapons more than three months ago to supplement the antiquated stores in federal warehouses. Cameron had insisted the army use only American-made weapons, which suggested to cynical George that some of the secretary's cronies must have firearms contracts. The Manassas debacle darkened the cloud over Cameron, and his purchasing decision was now being denounced as a blunder. The war wouldn't end with the summer, and there weren't enough guns to train and arm recruits who had already reported to camps of instruction from the East Coast to the Mississippi.

George was pulled from drafting a mortar contract and assigned to rewrite and polish a new Ripley proposal for purchase of a hundred thousand foreign-made weapons. The proposal went to the War Department bearing half a dozen signatures, the most prominent after Ripley's being George's. After three days of silence, he walked over personally to check on the fate of the proposal.

"I found it sitting on some desk," he reported when he returned. "Marked rejected."

Without stopping his eternal movement of papers, Maynadier snapped, "On what grounds?"

"The secretary wants the proposal resubmitted with the quantity cut in half."

Ripley overheard. "What? Only fifty thousand pieces?" He exploded into invective that made his typical tantrums pale; work was impossible for nearly an hour.

That night, George told Constance, "Cameron authorized the rejection, but Stanley signed it. I'm sure he took great pleasure in it."

"George, you mustn't sink into feelings of persecution."

"What I'm sinking into is regret that I took the damn job. I was a fool to ignore the warning signs."

She was sympathetic and tried to tease him out of his mood. "See here, you're not the only one suffering. Look at my waist. If I don't stop gaining, I'll soon be bigger than one of Professor Lowe's balloons. You must help me, George. You must remind me to hold back at mealtimes." The problem wasn't fictitious, but it was certainly a less significant worry than his. He replied with a mumbled promise and a vague look that made her fret about him all the more.

Ripley informed George and certain others that they would all receive brevets in August, Ripley himself rising to brigadier. George would be wearing three loops of black silk braid on his coat-cloak and the gold star of a major. The department's crimes of omission and commission, unfolding daily like the petals of a rose, left him too disheartened to care.

Ripley let contracts to virtually any middleman who said he could obtain "foreign arms." The mere claim was enough to induce faith and an outpouring of funds. "You should see the frauds who pass themselves off as arms merchants," George exclaimed to Constance during another late-evening complaint session; they were becoming chronic. "Stable owners, apothecaries, relatives of congressmen—they all promise on the Bible to deliver European arms overnight. Ripley doesn't even question them about sources."

"Do you have similar problems with artillery?"

"I do not. I interview at least one would-be contractor a day, and I weed out the charlatans with a few questions. Ripley's in such a panic, he never bothers."

Duties frequently took George to the Washington Arsenal on Greenleaf's Point, a jut of mud flats at the confluence of the Potomac and the Anacostia south of the center of town. There, neatly ranked beneath the trees around the old buildings, were artillery pieces of all sorts and sizes. Prowling the arsenal storage rooms in search of ammunition, George discovered a curiously designed gun with a crank on the side and a hopper on top. He asked Colonel Ramsay, the arsenal commandant, about it.

"Three inventors brought it here early this year. The official name on our records is .58-caliber Union Repeating Gun. The President christened it the coffee mill. It fires rapidly—the ammunition's loaded into that hopper—and after the initial tests, Mr. Lincoln wanted to adopt it. I'm told he sent memoranda on the subject to your commanding officer," Ramsay finished pointedly.

"With what result?"

"There was no result."

"Any more tests?"

"Not to my knowledge."

"Why not?" George already suspected the answer, which Ramsay provided in a vicious imitation of the new brigadier general:

"Han't got time!"

Discussing the gun, George said to Constance, "So a promising weapon molders while we waste our time with lunatic schemes and their equally deranged proponents." He said this because he was often diverted from important tasks and forced to interview inventors.

One August afternoon when he was already late for a mortar test at the arsenal, Maynadier insisted he speak with the cousin of some congressman from Iowa.

The man wanted to sell a protective vest. Unfortunately, his sample had been delayed in shipment. "But it should be here tomorrow. I know you'll be impressed, General."

"Major."

"Yes, your excellency. Major."

"Tell me about your vest," George snarled.

"It's crafted of the finest blued steel and certified to stop any projectile fired by an enemy's shoulder or hand weapon."

With a feline smile, George smoothed his mustache. "Oh, you're a steelmaker. Delighted to hear it. That's my trade also. Tell me about your facility in Iowa."

"Well, Gen—Major—actually—the prototype was crafted by a supplier in Dubuque. I am—" the man swallowed—"a hatter by profession."

Faint with fury, George repeated, "A hatter. I see."

"But the prototype was made to my specifications, which I assure you are metallurgically precise. The vest will do everything I claim. One test will prove it."

George experienced déjà vu. Vendors of body armor visited the department in regiments these days. "Would you be willing to stay in Washington until a test can be arranged?"

The encouraged hatter beamed. "I might, if the omens for a contract were favorable."

"And, of course, since you're confident of the performance of your prototype, I presume you're willing to wear it personally during the test, allowing a sharpshooter to fire several rounds at you, so we may verify—"

The hatter, with hat and diagrams, was gone.

"What a terrible thing to do, George," Constance said that night. But she giggled.

"Nonsense. I have learned one of the primary lessons of Washington. One of the surest remedies for the madness of the place is laughter."

Laughter was no antidote for the next bad news to reach Ripley's office. Cameron's decision against foreign arms had given Confederate purchasing agents some ninety days in which to snatch up all the best weapons for sale in Britain and on the Continent. When a few samples of what remained arrived at the Winder Building, gloom was instantaneous.

In the steamy dusk, George took one sample down to the arsenal. The weapon was a .54-caliber percussion rifle carried by Austrian jaeger battalions. Designed on the Lorenz pattern of 1854, it was ugly, cumbersome, and had a brutal recoil. After he fired three rounds at the targets normally used for testing artillery— five thick pilings planted ten feet apart in the middle of the Potomac—his shoulder felt as if a mule had kicked it.

He heard a carriage. He was at the end of one of the arsenal piers, so he walked back to see who was arriving. The carriage remained indistinct for some while, moving among trees near the U.S. Penitentiary, which shared the mud flats with the arsenal.

Beneath the hazy pink sky, the carriage finally approached the pierhead. George knew the driver, one of Lincoln's secretaries, William Stoddard. His office stockpiled sample weapons that inventors sent directly to the President in the hope of by-passing Ripley.

Carrying some sort of shoulder gun, the President stepped out of the carriage while Stoddard tied the team to a cleat. In the dusky light Lincoln's pallor looked worse than usual, but he seemed in good humor. He plumped his stovepipe on the ground and nodded to George, who saluted.

"Good evening, Mr. President."

"Evening, Major—I apologize, but I don't know your name."

"I do," Stoddard said. "Major George Hazard. His brother Stanley works for Mr. Cameron." Lincoln blinked and appeared to stiffen slightly, suggesting that George's relationship to one, possibly both, men did nothing for his status.

Still, Lincoln remained cordial, explaining, "It's my habit to go shooting in Treasury Park, although the night police hate the racket. Couldn't go there this evening because there's a baseball game." He peered at the piece George had been firing. "What have we here?"

"One of the jaeger rifles we may purchase from the Austrian government, sir."

"Satisfactory?"

"I'm no small-arms expert, but I would say barely. I'm afraid it's about the best we can get, though."

"Yes, Mr. Cameron was a mite slow to enter the quadrille, wasn't he? We could substitute this type of weapon"—Lincoln's big-knuckled hand lifted the gun he had brought as if it were light as down—"but your chief doesn't care for breechloaders, never mind that a scared recruit in the thick of action can have a peck of trouble with a muzzleloader. Maybe he forgets and slips the bullet down in before the powder. Maybe he forgets to pull the rammer, and there she goes, fired off like a spear—"

He puckered his lips and whooshed as he swept his free hand up and out to suggest an arc over the pink-lit river. George studied the breechloader. He could just discern the maker's name on the right lock plate: C. Sharps.

"I also realize that *new* and even *recent* are words unwelcome in the brigadier's vocabulary," Lincoln continued with a smile. "But I'm reliably informed that breech-loading pieces were known and demonstrated in the time of King Henry the Eighth, so we don't exactly have a brand-new thingamajig, do we now? I favor single-shot breechloaders, and, by Ned, the army's going to have some."

Stoddard asked George, "Are there any on order in Europe?"

"I don't believe—"

"There are none," Lincoln interrupted, sounding more melancholy than irked. Then the thunder blow: "That is why I recently sent my own buying agent over there with two millions of dollars and free rein. If I can't get satisfaction from Cameron and Company, I shall have to get it another way, I guess."

Awkward silence. Stoddard cleared his throat. "Sir, it will be dark soon."

"Dark. Yes. The hour for dreams—best I get on with shooting."

"If you'll excuse me, Mr. President—" George feared that he sounded strange; the bad news had dried his mouth.

"Certainly, Major Hazard. Happy to see you down here. I admire men who like to learn all they can. Try to do that myself."

Lugging the Austrian rifle, George retreated into the gathering night. He mounted his horse and rode up past the brightly lit penitentiary to the sounds of firing from the pier. He felt as if someone had hit him over the head. Cameron and Company was in worse trouble than he had imagined. And he worked for Cameron and Company.

It had pleased Stanley to reject the proposal prepared by his brother. Stanley had a few clear memories of the long, horrible walk back from Manassas—he had none of crying at the roadside; it was Isabel who frequently reminded him of it—but those that remained included one of George pushing and bullying him as if he were some plantation nigger. If he could slight George or make his job more difficult, he now had one more reason for doing so.

Stanley was worried about his position as Cameron's creature. Saloon gossip said the boss's star was already falling. Yet nothing in the department appeared to change. The secretary had spent several days away from his desk, mourning his brother, but after that, it was business—and confusion—as usual.

Important congressmen had begun to inquire orally, by letter, and through press pronouncements about the purchasing methods of the War Department. Lincoln's dispatch of his own man to Europe on a gun-buying trip showed no great faith in them, to say the least. Complaints about shortages of clothing, small arms, and equipment continued to pour in from the camps of instruction. It was stated with increasing openness that Cameron was guilty of mismanagement and that the army, which little McClellan would attempt to whip into fighting trim, had not half of what it needed.

Except for bootees, Stanley could note with self-congratulation. Pennyford was producing in quantity, on schedule. Lashbrook's profit figures, projected out to year-end, staggered Stanley and delighted Isabel, who claimed to have expected the bonanza.

Regrettably, Stanley's personal success couldn't help him weather the departmental crisis. The written and oral demands for information now contained barbs in them. *Scandalous shortages. Reported irregularities.* If an impropriety was actually alleged, Cameron didn't deny it. He didn't even acknowledge it. One day Stanley overheard two clerks discussing this technique.

"Another sharp letter came in this morning. Treasury this time. Got to admire the way the boss handles them. He stands silent as a stone wall—same as that crazy Jackson at Bull Run."

"I thought the battle was fought at Manassas," said the second clerk.

"According to the rebs. According to us, it's Bull Run."

The other groaned. "If they start naming battles for places and we start naming them for streams, how the devil will schoolboys figure it out fifty years from now?"

"Who cares? I'm worried about today. Even the boss can't put up a stone wall forever. My advice is, bank your salary and—" He noticed Stanley lingering over a bound volume of contracts. He nudged his companion and both moved away.

The clerks epitomized the desperation beginning to infect the department. Cameron's precarious position was no longer a secret known only to a few. He was in trouble and, by extension, so were his cronies. When Stanley returned to his desk, the thought made it impossible for him to concentrate.

He needed to put distance between himself and his old mentor. How? No answer came to mind. He must discuss the problem with Isabel. He could count on her to know what to do.

That evening, however, she wasn't in a mood to discuss it. He found her seething over a newspaper.

"What's upset you, my dear?"

"Our sweet conniving sister-in-law. She's ingratiating herself with the very people we should be cultivating."

"Stevens and that lot?" Isabel responded with a fierce nod. "What's Constance done?"

"Started her abolition work again. She and Kate Chase are to be hostesses at a reception for Martin Delany." The name meant nothing—further cause for wifely fury. "Oh, don't be so thick,

219

Stanley. Delany's the nigger doctor who wrote the novel everyone twittered over a couple of years ago. *Blake;* that was the title. He runs around in African robes, giving lectures."

Stanley remembered then. Before the war, Delany had promoted the idea of a new African state to which American blacks could, and in his opinion should, emigrate. Delany's scheme called for the blacks to raise cotton in Africa and bankrupt the South through competitive free enterprise.

Stanley picked up the paper, found the announcement of the reception, and read the partial list of guests. His moist dark eyes reflected the bright gas mantles as he said carefully, "I know you can't abide the colored and those who champion them. But you're right, we need to speed up our own—cultivation, as you call it, of the important pro-abolition people attending that party. Simon is about to go down. If we aren't careful, he'll take us with him. He'll ruin our reputations and dam up the river of money that's flowing into Lashbrook's." There was a hint of uncharacteristic strength in his voice as he finished. "We must do something and do it soon."

35

The hot haze of August settled on the Alexandria line. Encamped north of Centreville, the legion awaited replacements and the Enfields the colonel had paid for with personal funds. The rifles were to come from Britain on a blockade runner.

The legion reorganized to compensate for its losses at Manassas. Calbraith Butler, promoted to major, took command of the four troops of cavalry. Charles reacted to the change with initial resentment, which he was sensible enough to keep to himself. When he thought about it, the choice wasn't so surprising. Butler was a gentleman volunteer, without the taint of professionalism Charles carried. Being married to the governor's daughter didn't hurt, either.

Also, Charles knew his own cause hadn't been helped by his insistence on discipline and his occasional anger with offenders. He had a less violent temper than many an Academy graduate—a Yankee hothead named Phil Sheridan came to mind—but he still yelled in the approved West Point style.

The hell with it. He had enlisted to win a war, not promotions. Butler was a fine horseman and by instinct a good officer; he led men the right way—by example. Charles congratulated his new superior with unfeigned sincerity.

"Decent of you, Charles," said the new major. "In terms of experience, you're more deserving than I." He smiled. "Tell you what. Since I have all these new responsibilities and am married to boot, you must hie yourself to Richmond and represent me at that ball. Take Pell along if you like."

Charles needed no further invitation. He spruced up his uniform and hurried completion of the most important of his current tasks. Sometimes, he thought, the duties were more a father's than a soldier's. He finished the work just in time for evening review. At the ceremony, the colonel formally received the regiment's newest battle flag, sewn by ladies at home. A palmetto wreath and the words *Hampton's Legion* decorated the scarlet silk.

Afterward, Charles made final preparations for travel to Richmond. He was interrupted by a trooper named Nelson Gervais, who had a long letter from a girl back home in Rock Hill. The nineteen-year-old farmer shifted his weight back and forth and rattled the letter paper as he explained.

"I've pressed my suit with Miss Sally Mills for three years, Captain. No luck. Now all of a sudden she says—" *rattle* went the paper—"she says my joining up and going away made her wake up to how much she cares for me. She says here that she'd entertain a marriage proposal."

"Congratulations, Gervais." Impatient, Charles missed the point of the trooper's imploring look. "I don't believe you'd be permitted a furlough anytime soon, but that shouldn't stop you from asking for her hand."

"Yes, sir, I want to do that."

"You don't need my consent."

"I need your help, sir. Miss Sally Mills writes real well, but—" his face turned red as the new flag—"I can't."

"Not at all?"

"No, sir." Long pause. "Can't read, either." *Rattle.* "One of my messmates, he read this for me. Where Sally said she loved me and all—"

Charles understood, gently tapped the desk. "Leave that, and as soon as I'm back from Richmond, I'll compose a letter of proposal and we'll go over it till it meets with your approval."

"Thank you, sir! I really thank you. I can't hardly thank you enough."

Private Gervais's effusions floated in the humid night for some moments after his departure. Charles smiled to himself and blew out the light in his wall tent, feeling remarkably middle-aged.

The night ride on the cars of the Orange & Alexandria proved exhausting due to unforeseen and unexplained delays en route. Charles dozed on the hard seat, doing his best to ignore Ambrose's attempts at conversation. His friend was annoyed that they were segregated from Hampton and other senior officers in the car ahead.

Charles was worn out and dirty when they arrived in Richmond late next morning. Quarters had been arranged with a Mississippi unit, so he had a chance to jump into a zinc tub, then find a pallet and try to catch an hour's sleep. Excitement made it impossible.

The Spotswood ballroom glittered with braid and jewels and lights that shone on yards of Confederate bunting. Hundreds packed the room and the adjoining parlors and corridors. Soon after Charles entered, he glimpsed his cousin Ashton on the far side of the dance floor. She and her pale worm of a husband were hovering near President Davis. Charles would avoid coming anywhere near them.

Young women, many quite beautiful and all vivacious and handsomely gowned, laughed and danced with the officers, who outnumbered them three to one. Charles wasn't anxious for companionship unless he found the right person. He didn't see her anywhere. His hopes had been far-fetched, he supposed. Fredericksburg was miles away.

But there were unexpected diversions. A burly first lieutenant with the beginnings of a great beard left a group around Joe Johnston and hurled himself over to give Charles a bear hug.

"Bison! I suspected you might be here."

"Fitz, you look grand. I heard you were on General Johnston's staff."

Fitzhugh Lee, nephew of Robert E., had been a close friend at West Point and in Texas. "Not so grand as you, Captain." He loaded the last word with mock deference. Charles laughed.

"Don't hand me that. I know who's superior here. You're regular army. We're still just state troops."

"Not for long, I'm sure. Oh-oh—there's another gorgeous phiz you should recognize. And precisely where you'd expect it, too—in the middle of a bevy of admiring females."

Charles looked, and his heart leaped at the sight of an old friend who was in theory his colonel's rival. Jeb Stuart's russet beard was full and resplendent. Gauntlets were artfully draped over his sash. A yellow rose adorned his buttonhole. His blue eyes flashed as he teased and flattered the ladies pressing close to him.

The commander of the First Virginia Cavalry had been a first classman when Charles entered the Academy. Stuart had given the callow plebe a haircut—or half of one—that Charles would never forget. Together, he and Fitz worked their way toward Stuart. He spied them and excused himself from the disappointed ladies just as Charles saw a major from the First Virginia request a dance from a full-bosomed blonde wearing pale blue silk. It was Augusta.

Away from the crowd, Stuart's boots were visible; there were the gold spurs everyone talked about. "Bison Main! Now the party's perfect!"

Charles's greeting was restrained and correct. "Colonel."

"Come, come—you don't say hello to your old barber that way."

"Very well, Beauty. It's grand to run into you. You and General Beauregard are the heroes of the hour."

"I do hear those Yankees think we all ride black stallions that squirt fire and brimstone from their nostrils. Good! We'll whip 'em that much sooner if they stay scared. Come along and have a whiskey."

The three walked to the refreshment bar, where black men deferentially filled the orders. Stuart couldn't help crowing a little.

"Hear you boys missed the muss the other day. Luck of the game. How do you find your commander?" He indicated Hampton, some distance away. The colonel was engaged in conversation with one man in civilian clothes; there were no admirers.

"None better."

"Never make a cavalryman. Too old."

"He's a superb horseman, Beauty. Strong as any of us."

Stuart's flashing smile relieved the brief tension. Whiskey helped, too. The three were soon chatting about Fitz's uncle, who had been superintendent at West Point for a time; Lee was scrapping with the Federals in the western reaches of the state.

Charles's glance kept returning to Augusta. She was dancing a gallopade with the same major, who in Charles's jealous imagination had become an exemplar of boring pomposity.

Fitz startled him by saying: "Handsome little morsel."

"Know her?"

"Certainly. She's a rich woman—modestly rich, anyway, thanks to her late husband. Her mother's people, the Duncans, are one of the oldest families on the Rappahannock. One of the finest, too."

"Except for her damned traitorous uncle," Stuart said. "He sold out to the Africanizers, just like my father-in-law."

"But you named your son in honor of old Cooke," Fitz said.

"Flora's changed the boy's name at my insistence. He's no longer Philip; he's James—now and forever more." There was ice in Stuart's smile, and the light of the true believer in his eyes. It bothered Charles.

Stuart had other admirers waiting. His departure, though friendly, left Charles with the feeling that rivalries of rank and state now divided them, and they both recognized it. The result was a kind of melancholy, enhanced when the orchestra started a new piece and the major once more claimed a dance from Augusta.

"If she's the one you want, go after her," Fitz whispered.

"He outranks me."

"No self-respecting Southerner would consider that an obstacle. Besides"—Fitz's voice went lower still—"I know that man. He's a fool." He thumped Charles on the shoulder. "Go on, Bison, or the night'll be over and you'll have nothing to show for it."

Wondering why he felt anxious and hesitant, Charles maneuvered his way around the edge of the floor where couples whirled and stirred the air. He caught Augusta watching him—with pleasure and relief, unless he was imagining things. He quickly planned his strategy, waited till the music ended, then went charging to her side.

"Cousin Augusta! Major, do excuse the interruption—I had no idea I'd see my relative here tonight."

"Your relative?" the First Virginia officer repeated in a voice that seemed to echo from a barrel. He frowned at his partner. "You said nothing about relatives in the Palmetto State, Mrs. Barclay."

"Didn't I? The Duncans have a host of them. And I haven't set eyes on dear Charles for two—it must be three years now. Major Beesley—Captain Main. You will excuse us, Major?" She smiled, taking Charles's arm and turning him away from the scowling Virginian.

"Beastly, did you say?" he whispered. The whiskey was bubbling in him; he felt hot and reacted to the touch of her breast against his sleeve.

"That should be his name. Feathers for brains and feet of lead. I thought I was doomed for the rest of the night."

"Feathers and lead—that isn't Mr. Pope, is it?"

"No, but you certainly have a good memory."

"Good enough so I remember not to call you Gus."

She whacked his hand lightly with her fan. "Be careful or I'll go back to Beastly."

"I'll never allow that." He glanced over his shoulder. "He's hovering. Let's get some food."

Charles handed Augusta a cup of punch, then started to fill two small plates. Several girls crowded in beside him. With stagey gestures and exaggerated diction, one was loudly reciting a satiric piece Charles had heard in camp. The *Richmond Examiner* had originally printed the so-called fable of the orang-outang named Old Abe:

"The orang-outang was chosen king, and this election created a great disturbance and revolution in the Southern states, for the beasts in that part of the country had imported from Africa a large number of black monkeys and had made slaves of them. And Old Abe the orang-outang had declared that this was an indignity offered to his family—"

Augusta said, "Oh, I'm so sorry," an instant before she ap-

225

peared to stumble. She dumped punch all over the speaker's beige silk skirt.

The performer and her friends squealed and fumed. Augusta didn't show her wrath till she had pulled Charles away. "Witless little fools. I swear, I love the South, but I surely don't love all Southerners. She'd never utter such remarks in my home. I'd take a horsewhip to her. My nigras are fine men."

Charles carried the plates to a small balcony overlooking the busy street. Augusta sighed. "I really don't belong at this party. The trip's too long, and most of the company intolerable." She took a small toast wedge from the plate; the caviar glistened. "Most," she said again, gazing up at him; his height made it necessary.

"Why did you come, then?"

"They said they needed a good supply of women. I decided—" she paused—"it was my patriotic duty to attend. One of my freedmen made the trip with me. Not that I couldn't have driven alone —Why are you smiling?"

"Because you're so damned—uh, blasted—"

"That's all right, I've heard the word damn before."

"So confident. You have more brass than Jeb Stuart."

"And it isn't proper in a woman?"

"I didn't say that, did I?"

"Then why take note of it?"

"Because it's—surprising."

"Is that the best you can do—surprising? How do you really feel about it, Captain?"

"Don't get prickly with me. If you must know, I like it."

She blushed, which stunned him. She stunned him a second time by saying, "I didn't mean to be prickly. It's a bad habit. As I think I told you when we met, I was never much of a belle, and I don't always conduct myself in the approved manner."

"Nevertheless, I approve. Wholeheartedly."

"Thank you, dear sir." The barrier was up again. Did he unsettle her with his attentions? His own attraction to this pretty but unconventional widow definitely unsettled him.

Yet he wouldn't have left for anything. They stood in shy silence, watching the wagons and foot traffic below. Richmond swarmed with strangers these days, and he had heard that street crime was out of control. Robberies, murders, sexual assaults—

The orchestra resumed. "Will you dance with me, Augusta?"

226

The way he blurted it, with a slight hoarseness, alarmed her again. *Well, we both have reason to be cautious. It's the wrong time and place for anything but light conversations and casual friendships.*

She felt soft and exactly right in his arms. He had been so long without a woman, he consciously had to maintain distance between them or she would feel the result of his deprivation. They waltzed past a group of officers; Fitz Lee applauded him in pantomime. They waltzed past Huntoon, who stared; Charles nodded. They waltzed past the First Virginia officer, whom Charles acknowledged by calling out a greeting: "Major Beastly."

On they danced, Augusta laughing and limp against him for a moment. He felt her body through their clothing; slight plumpness made the contact more sensual.

With her eager consent, Charles kept her as a partner the rest of the evening, then walked her back to the boardinghouse where she had secured a room. Her freedman had been waiting outside the Spotswood with the buggy, but she had sent him on to sleep. Charles was glad for the extra time alone with her. His train left at three, nearly a whole hour yet.

The presentation saber bumped his leg lightly as they walked. The streets were quiet, empty of all but a few furtive figures or occasional carriages bound home from the ball. In some noisy saloons they passed, crowds of civilians and soldiers still roistered. But no one bothered them; Charles's height and obvious strength deterred that sort of thing. Augusta seemed to like sheltering on his arm.

"I must tell you the truth, Charles," she said when they reached the dark stoop of the boardinghouse. She took a step up, bringing her eyes level with his. "This evening we have talked about everything from my crops to General Lee's character, but we've missed the one subject we ought to discuss."

"What's that?"

"The real reason I traveled so far. I am a patriot, but not that much of a one, thank you." She drew a breath, as if ready to dive into water. "I hoped you might be here."

"I—" *Don't entangle yourself.* He ignored the inner warning. "I hoped the same about you."

"I'm forward, aren't I?"

"I'm glad. I couldn't have said it first."

"You have not struck me as a shy type, Captain."

"With men like Beastly, no. With you—"

In a far steeple, a bell chimed the quarter hour. The night was still warm, but he felt warmer. Her right hand closed on his left, tightly.

"Will you come visit me at the farm when you can?"

"Even if I forget and call you Gus?"

She looked at him; bent to him. Blond curls bounced softly against his face. "Even then." She kissed him on the cheek and ran inside.

He strode off toward the rail station, whistling. The inner voice persisted. *Be careful. Cavalrymen must travel light.* He knew he should heed it, but he felt tall as a house, and he didn't.

36

At Treasury, James Huntoon came out of an emergency meeting convened by the secretary to discuss the counterfeiting problem. Huntoon sank into the pool of autumn light dappling his desk and laid before him a ten-dollar note that looked authentic but was not. He had been assigned to show it to Pollard, editor of the *Examiner,* so the paper could warn readers about all the bogus notes in circulation—notes printed more expertly, alas, than those from Hoyer and Ludwig, the government's official engraving firm.

Pollard would love the story, and Huntoon relished the thought of reporting it; he shared the editor's dislike of the President, his policies, and the administration as a whole. The paper's current target was Colonel Northrop, commissary-general of the army, rapidly becoming the most hated man in the Confederacy because of his mishandling of food procurement and distribution. Pollard's anti-Northrop editorials never failed to mention that, once again, Davis was siding with a West Point crony. The only Academy graduate the *Examiner* supported was Joe Johnston; that was because the general and the President were wrangling bitterly over the rank to which Johnston felt entitled.

When speaking privately, editor Pollard was even more vindictive. He called Davis "a Mississippi parvenu." Accused him of taking orders from his wife—"he is wax in her hands." Reminded listeners that Davis had vetoed the congressional decision to move the capital to Richmond—"Does that not tell you how he feels about our beloved Old Dominion?"—and had appeared "stricken with grief," according to his wife's statement, when informed he had been chosen president.

Pollard was not an isolated case. A cyclone of enmity, some of it expressed in extreme and violent language, was rising in the South. Stephens, the elderly vice president, openly referred to his superior with words such as *tyrant* and *despot.* Many were demanding Davis's removal—and the election to ratify his provisional presidency would not be held until November.

Huntoon's disenchantment with the administration was one reason for his depressed state. Ashton was another. She spent all her time trying to maneuver herself higher on the social ladder. Twice she had forced him to attend dinner parties hosted by that shifty little Jew, Benjamin. They had much in common, those two. They trod warily, pleasing all, offending none—because who could tell from which direction the cyclone would be blowing next week?

One genuinely savage quarrel had marred Huntoon's summer. Two weeks after the reception at the Spotswood, the flash gentleman with connections in Valdosta and the Bahamas had called at the residence into which Huntoon and Ashton had moved a few days earlier. The gentleman offered to sell Huntoon a share in what he termed his maritime company. On the Merseyside, at Liverpool, he said, he had located a fast steamer, *Water Witch,* that could be refitted at reasonable cost to run the blockade between Nassau and the Confederate coast.

"What would she carry?" Huntoon asked. "Rifles, ammunition, that sort of thing?"

"Oh, no," Mr. Lamar H. A. Powell replied. "Luxuries. There's much more money to be made from those. Risks to the vessel would be considerable, as you know. So we are looking to the short rather than the long term. My figures suggest that if the cargo is selected carefully, just two successful runs can produce a profit of five hundred percent—minimum. After that, the Yankees can sink the vessel whenever they please. If she continues her runs, the potential earnings of shareholders approach the astronomical."

Just then, Huntoon noticed his wife closely watching the visitor. Huntoon feared handsome men because he wasn't one, but he couldn't tell whether it was the aloof stranger's scheme or his good looks that titillated Ashton. Either way, he wanted nothing to do with Mr. L. H. A. Powell, whose background he had looked into after Powell had sent a note around requesting this meeting.

It was said Powell had been a mercenary soldier in Europe and, later, a filibuster in South America. Government records showed he claimed exemption from any military service by virtue of a rule excusing those who owned more than twenty slaves; Powell's declaration claimed seventy-five on his family's plantation near Valdosta. A telegraph message from Atlanta replying to one of Huntoon's stated that the "plantation" consisted of a dilapidated farm cottage and outbuildings occupied by three people named Powell: a man and woman in their seventies and a forty-year-old hulk with a brain of an infant. A third brother had run off to the West. Hardly impeccable credentials, but they justified Huntoon's response to his caller.

"I want no part of any such scheme, Mr. Powell."

"May I ask the reason?"

"I have several, but the principal one will suffice. It's unpatriotic."

"I see. You'd rather be a poor patriot than a rich one, is that it?"

"Importing perfumes and silks and sherry for Secretary Benjamin is not my idea of patriotism, sir."

"But, James, darling," his wife began.

Goaded by some ill-defined but clearly felt threat the flash gentleman represented, he cut in, "The answer is no, Ashton."

After Powell had gone, they screamed at each other long into the night.

Huntoon: "Of course I meant what I said. I'll have nothing to do with such unprincipled opportunism. As I told that fellow, I have any number of reasons."

Ashton, fists clenched, teeth, too: "Name them."

"Well—the personal risk, for one. Imagine the consequences of discovery."

"You're a coward."

He went red. "God, how I hate you sometimes." But he had turned away before he said it.

Later, Ashton again, wilder than before: "It's my money we live on, don't forget. *Mine.* You scarcely make as much as niggers who pick cotton. I control our funds—"

"By my sufferance."

"You think so! I can spend the money any way I wish."

"Would you care to test that in court? The law says those funds became my property the moment we married."

"Always the smug little attorney, aren't you?" She tore blankets from their bed, opened the door, and hurled the bundle into the hall. "Sleep on the settee, you bastard—if you're not too fat to fit."

She pushed him out. Eyes watering behind his spectacles, he raised a placating hand. "Ashton—" The slamming door struck his palm. He leaned against the wall and shut his eyes.

They had made up the next day—they always made up—although she denied him physical contact for a period of two weeks. After that her mood improved remarkably. She was cheerful, as if Powell and his scheme didn't exist.

But the memory of that quarrel existed and wouldn't go away; it was one more troubling cloud on a horizon that seemed to be filling with them. Huntoon sat at his desk with the forged note, his eyes vacant, his expression unhappy. The clerk he worked for had to tell him pointedly to get going to the paper.

Richmond's normal business day ended at three, with a large dinner, the main meal, served shortly thereafter. The schedules didn't apply to households of those who worked for the government, however. Ashton seldom had to worry about planning menus with her black cook—a blessing, since it bored her. Most weekdays, James arrived home well after seven-thirty, the customary hour for a light supper.

On this particular autumn afternoon, Ashton again did not expect him until late. She spent an entire hour making herself attractive and was ready to leave at two; one hour remained of the period reserved for formal calls. Homer brought the carriage around, and they left the two-and-a-half-story house on Grace

Street, in a respectable area which was nevertheless a bit too far from downtown to be fashionable.

The day was mild, but Ashton sweltered. The risk she ran was enormous, but she had been driven to it by a number of things, including her husband's timidity and her growing frustration with their inability to penetrate Richmond society. She knew two reasons: they lacked position, and they lacked real wealth. James had failed her on both counts, just as he failed her whenever he tried to satisfy her with his wretched little instrument.

She leaned back against the velvet of the closed carriage, staring out the window into the dazzle of the day. Did she dare go through with this? It had taken a week merely to locate the man's address, then another to phrase and properly polish a note announcing the date and time of her call "regarding a commercial matter of mutual interest." She could imagine the amusement in his eyes when he read that.

If he read it. She had received no reply. What if he were out of town?

She had sent the note via an anonymous black boy she had hired on a corner opposite Capitol Square. How did she know the boy had delivered the wax-sealed envelope? Preoccupied with these doubts and with anticipations of disaster, she didn't hear the clopping rhythm of the carriage horse slow, then stop.

Over the hoot of a train at the Broad Street depot, Homer called: "Here's the corner you wanted, Miz Huntoon. Shall I pick you up in an hour?"

"No. I don't know how long I'll be shopping. When I'm finished, I'll catch a hack or stop and see Mr. Huntoon and come home with him."

"Very well, ma'am." The carriage pulled out behind a white-topped army wagon. Briskly, Ashton entered the nearest store. She hurried out a few minutes later with two unwanted spools of thread. After a quick survey of the area to assure that Homer was gone, she hailed the first passing hack.

Perspiring, her heart racing, she got out in front of one of the lovely high-stooped houses on Church Hill. It was located on Franklin, a few doors from the corner of Twenty-fourth. The imposing residence looked closed against the warmth of the afternoon, asleep under the maples just starting to lose their green.

Glancing neither right nor left for fear she would see someone

232

watching, she climbed the stoop and rang. Would there be servants—?

Lamar Powell answered personally. She nearly swooned from excitement.

He stepped back into the shadow. "Please come in, Mrs. Huntoon." She did; the door closed with a tick like that of a clock.

The foyer was cool. Rooms were visible through doors on either side, rooms with opulent woodwork, furniture, pendant crystal. One night recently, James had again brought up Powell's name, saying he had made inquiries about him. "It appears the fellow lives on nerve, self-promotion, and credit." If the snide remark had any truth to it, Powell's credit must be enormous.

He smiled at her. "I confess I was surprised to receive your note. I wasn't sure you'd keep the appointment. On a chance, I sent my houseman off fishing and stayed home. There's no one else here." He gestured with one of those slender, curiously sensual hands. "So you needn't worry about being compromised."

Ashton felt awkward as a child. He was tall—so very tall—and appeared perfectly relaxed in his dark breeches and loose white cotton shirt. He was barefoot. "It's a splendid house," she exclaimed. "How many rooms do you live in?"

Amused by her nervousness, he said, "All of them, Mrs. Huntoon." He grasped her arm gently. "When we were introduced at the Spotswood, I knew you'd come here eventually. You look lovely in that dress. I suspect you'd look even lovelier without it."

Never hesitating, he took her hand and led her to the stairs.

They ascended silently. In a room where slatted blinds striped the bed with light—she noticed the top coverlet was already turned down—they began to undress; he calmly, she with jerky movements generated by her nerves. No man had ever put her in this state before.

The silence lengthened. He helped with her bodice buttons, kissing her left cheek with great gentleness. Then he kissed her mouth, slowly moving his tongue over her lower lip. She felt as if she were sinking into a bonfire. Began to hurry, fumble—

He pushed at the lace straps on her shoulders, baring her from the waist upward. His touch careful, tender, he lifted first one breast, then the other, gently pressing his thumb against each nipple. He bent forward, still smiling in that curiously remote way. She flung her head back, eyes closed, loins damp, expecting to feel his tongue.

He smashed his open palm against her head, knocking her onto the bed. She was too terrified to scream. He stood with one leg against the tangle of her skirt, smiling.

"Why—?"

"So there is no doubt about authority in this liaison, Mrs. Huntoon. I knew when we met that you were a strong woman. Reserve your displays of that quality for others."

Then, swiftly, he bent and began to strip her of the rest of her clothing.

Her terror transformed itself to an excitement that was so intense it resembled insanity. She ran wet as a river when he slipped off his cotton drawers. He was oddly shaped, smaller than she had expected, given his stature. He pulled her legs apart and bored into her without closing his eyes.

She couldn't believe what began to happen to her. She beat the twisted damp sheets, excited to frenzy by his having struck her. She began to cry as he quickened the tempo; that had never occurred with other lovers. Tears flowed down her cheeks, and when he gave her the last ramming thrust, she sobbed, screamed, and fainted.

He lay propped on an elbow, smiling, when she woke. She was sweaty, spent, frightened by her loss of consciousness. "I passed out—"

"La petite mort. The little death. You mean it's the first time—?"

She swallowed. "Ever."

"Well, it won't be the last. I've been watching you sleep almost twenty-five minutes. Enough time for a man to renew himself." He pointed. "Put your mouth on me here."

"But—I've never done that with any—"

He seized her hair. "Did you hear what I said? Do it."

She obeyed.

They came to the next consummation a long time later. She slept again, and on the second wakening found herself free of earlier terrors. She thought vaguely of collecting the souvenir of this occasion but was too drowsy; she preferred to rest comfortably against his side.

The barred light changed, darkened. The afternoon was running out. She didn't care. What had transpired in this room, the

234

secret things, had transfigured her emotionally but at the same time had destroyed a long-cherished sense of her own sexual enlightenment. She had had more than her share of lovers. Her souvenir collection proved that. But Lamar Powell had taught her she was a novice, a child.

Slowly, however, the second reason for the visit asserted itself. "Mr. Powell—"

His laughter boomed. "I should think we know each other well enough to use first names."

"Yes, that's true." Scarlet, she flung a wet strand of black hair off her forehead. His humor had cruelty in it. "I wanted to speak to you about business. I control the money in my household. Do you still have room for another investor in your maritime syndicate?"

"Possibly." Eyes like opaque glass hid whatever he was thinking. "How much can you put in?"

"Thirty-five thousand dollars." Investing that amount would leave only a few thousand in the event the scheme failed. But she didn't believe it would fail, any more than she had believed Powell would not bed her if she called on him.

"That sum will give you substantial equity position in the vessel," he said. "And in her profits. Does your decision mean your husband changed his mind?"

"James knows nothing about this, and he won't until I decide it's appropriate to tell him. He will also know nothing about my calling here today—or in the future."

"If there are any calls in the future." That was meant to make her squirm and worry. She didn't care for it.

"There will be if you want the money."

He leaned back, smiling. "I need it. As soon as I have it, we'll be in a position to proceed."

"I'll bring a draft next time we meet."

"Bargain. By God, you're a find. There are damn few men in this town with your nerve. We're a matched pair," he said, rolling over and bending to kiss her bare belly. This time, he was the one who fell asleep afterward.

Ashton had a box her husband had never seen. Into it went mementos of romantic liaisons lasting a month or a week or a night. The box, from Japan, was lacquered wood with designs inlaid in cleverly cut bits of pearl. On the lid, a couple sipped tea.

The inside of the lid pictured the same couple, but they had doffed their kimonos and were copulating with broad smiles. The artist had composed the design so that the genitals of both partners were distinctly shown. Considering the size of the gentleman's machine, Ashton could understand the woman's happy expression.

The souvenirs she kept in the box were trouser buttons. She had started her collection long before the war, after visiting Cousin Charles when he was a cadet at West Point. It was the custom in those days for a girl to exchange a little gift for her cadet escort—sweets of some kind were the most common—for a prized button from his uniform tunic. Ashton entertained not one but seven cadets in a single evening in the smelly darkness of the post powder magazine. From each she demanded an unconventional souvenir: a button from the fly of his trousers.

Now, while Powell slept, she crept from bed, found the pants he had flung on the floor, and silently tugged and twisted till one of the buttons popped free. She put this into her reticule and slipped back into bed, pleased. When the button was safely in the box, her collection would number twenty-eight—one for each man who had received her favors. This did not include the boy who had initiated her when she was a mere girl, one other boy, and a highly experienced sailor with whom she had had relations before her West Point visit inspired the collection. The only other partner not represented by a button was her husband.

236

37

Washington had scapegoat weather that autumn. McDowell continued to be castigated, but Scott now shared the blame for Bull Run. And almost nightly Stanley came home with some new Cameron horror story. The boss was being universally scourged by bureaucrats, press, and public.

"Even Lincoln's joined the claque. Our spy in the Executive Mansion saw some notes made by his secretary, Nicolay." He pulled out the scrap on which he had penciled the alarming quotes. *"President says Cameron utterly ignorant. Selfish. Obnoxious to the country. Incapable of either organizing details or conceiving and executing general plans."* He gave her the scrap. "There was more, in the same vein. Damning."

They were taking supper by themselves; it was their custom, because, by day's end, Isabel was exhausted from dealing with the hostility of her twin sons, their resistance to discipline, and the near-lethal pranks meant to drive off the tutor she had engaged when it became evident they would never behave in a private schoolroom. She generally packed the twins off to eat in the kitchen—which suited them perfectly.

She studied the paper, then said, "We've waited too long, Stanley. You must disassociate yourself from Cameron before they lop off his head."

"I'm willing. I don't know how."

"I've thought and thought about it. I believe we can be guided by what happened to that fool Frémont." The famous Pathfinder, military commander in St. Louis, had independently declared all slaves in Missouri free. The declaration had pleased the congressional radicals, but Lincoln, still treating border-state whites with extreme deference for fear of losing them, had countermanded the order. "There is a definite schism, and we must gamble on one of the sides winning."

Baffled, Stanley shook his head and plied his fork. "But which?" he said with his mouth full of lobster.

"I can best answer by telling you who I entertained this afternoon. Caroline Wade."

"The senator's wife? Isabel, you constantly astonish me. I didn't know you were even acquainted with her."

"Until a month ago I wasn't. I took steps to arrange an introduction. She was quite cordial today, and I believe I convinced her that I'm a partisan of her husband and his clique—Chandler, Grimes, and the rest. I also hinted that you were unhappy with Simon's management of the War Department but felt helpless because of your loyalty to him."

Instantly pale, he said, "You didn't mention Lashbrook's—?"

"Stanley, you are the one who commits blunders, not I. Of course I didn't. But what if I had? There's nothing illegal about the contracts we obtained."

"No, just in the way we obtained them."

"Why are you so defensive?"

"I'm worried. I hope to Christ those bootees hold up in winter weather. Pennyford keeps warning me—"

"Kindly cease your foul language and stick to the subject."

"I'm sorry—go on."

"Mrs. Wade didn't say so explicitly, but she left the impression that the senator wants to form a new congressional committee, one that would curb the dictatorial powers the President is assuming and oversee conduct of the war. Surely a committee like that would make Simon's removal one of its first orders of business."

"Do you think so? Ben Wade is one of Simon's staunchest friends."

"Was, my dear. *Was.* Old alliances are shifting. Publicly, Wade may stand fast in support of the boss, but I'll wager it's a different story behind the scenes." She leaned closer. "Is Simon still out of town?"

He nodded; the secretary had gone on a tour of the Western theater.

"Then it's the perfect opportunity. You won't be watched too

238

closely. Go see Wade, and I'll order the invitations for a levee I'm planning for his wife and the senator and their circle. I may even invite George and Constance, for the sake of appearances. I suppose I can stomach her arrogance for an evening."

"All very fine, but what am I supposed to say to the senator?"

"Keep quiet and I'll explain."

Their meal forgotten, he sat listening, scared to the marrow by the thought of approaching the toughest and most dangerous of the radicals. But the more Isabel said—first urging, then insisting —the more convinced he became that Wade represented their means of survival.

Next day he secured the appointment, though it wasn't until the end of the week. The delay upset his digestion and ruined his sleep. Several times fear prodded him to plead for a different strategy. Wade was too close to Cameron; it would be smarter to approach the President's senior secretary, Nicolay.

"Wade," Isabel insisted. "He'll be receptive, because it's always possible to do business with scoundrels."

So it was that Stanley turned up on a bench in Senator Benjamin Franklin Wade's antechamber on Friday. His stomach hurt. He clutched the gold knob of his cane as if it were some religious object. The hour of the appointment, eleven, went past. By a quarter after, Stanley was sweating heavily. By half past, he was ready to bolt. At that moment Wade's office door opened. A small, stocky man with spectacles and a magnificent beard strode out. Stanley was too terrified to move.

"Morning, Mr. Hazard. Here to take care of some departmental business?"

Say something. Cover yourself. He was positive his guilt showed. "It's—actually, it's personal, Mr. Stanton." The small but intimidating man who stood polishing his wire-frame glasses was, like Wade, an Ohioan; a Democrat who had long been one of the best and most expensive Washington lawyers, and, more recently, Buck Buchanan's attorney general. He was also Simon Cameron's personal attorney.

"So was mine," Edwin Stanton said. His whiskers exuded a strong smell of citrus pomade. "I apologize that my appointment ran over into yours. How is my client? Back from the West yet?"

"No, but I expect him soon."

"When he returns, convey my regards and say I'm at his disposal to help draft his year-end report." With that, Stanton van-

239

ished into the Capitol corridors, which still stank of greasy food cooked while volunteer troops were quartered in the building, sleeping in the Rotunda and lolling at congressional desks and conducting mock legislative sessions when the hall was empty.

"Go in, please," Wade's administrative assistant prompted from his desk.

"What? Oh, yes—thanks." Numb from the unexpected encounter with Stanton and mortally afraid of the encounter to come, he entered and shut the door. His palms felt as if they had been dipped in oil.

Ben Wade, once a prosecutor in northeastern Ohio, still had that air about him. He had come to Washington as a senator in 1851 and remained for a decade. During the crisis of Brown's raid, he had carried two horse pistols to the Senate floor to demonstrate his willingness to debate Mr. Brown's behavior in any manner his Southern colleagues chose.

Stumbling toward the senator's big walnut desk, Stanley was intimidated by the scornful droop of Wade's upper lip and the gleam of his small jet eyes. Wade was at least sixty but had a kind of tensed energy that suggested youth.

"Sit down, Mr. Hazard."

"Yes, sir."

"I recall we met at a reception for Mr. Cameron earlier this year. But I've seen you since. Bull Run, that was it. Paid two hundred dollars to rent a rig for the day. Disgraceful. What can I do for you?" He fired the words like bullets.

"Senator, it's difficult to begin—"

"Begin or leave, Mr. Hazard. I am a busy man."

If Isabel was wrong—

Wade locked his hands together on the desk and glared. "Mr. Hazard?"

Feeling like a suicide, Stanley plunged. "Sir, I'm here because I share your desire for efficient prosecution of the war and appropriate punishment for the enemy."

Wade unclasped his hands and laid them on the burnished wood. Strong hands; clean, hard. "The only appropriate punishment will be ruthless and total. Continue."

"I—" It was too late to retreat; the words tumbled forth. "I don't believe the war's being managed properly, Senator. Not by the executive"—Wade's eyes warmed slightly there—"or by my

240

department." The warmth was instantly masked. "I can do nothing about the former—"

"Congress can and will. Go on."

"I'd like to do whatever I can about the latter. There are"—his belly burning, he forced himself to meet Wade's black gaze—"irregularities in procurement, which you surely must have heard about, and—"

"Just a moment. I thought you were one of the chosen."

Baffled, Stanley shook his head. "Sir? I don't—"

"One of the Pennsylvania bunch our mutual friend brought to Washington because they helped finance his campaigns. I was under the impression you were in that pack—you and your brother who works for Ripley."

No wonder Wade was powerful and dangerous. He knew everything. "I can't speak for my brother, Senator. And, yes, I did come here as a strong supporter of our, ah, mutual friend. But people change." A feeble grin. "The secretary was a Democrat once—"

"He is ruled by expediency, Mr. Hazard." The pitiless mouth jerked—the Wade version of a smile. "So are all of us in this trade. I was a Whig until I decided to become a Republican. It's beside the point. What are you offering? To sell him out?"

Stanley paled. "Sir, that language is—"

"Blunt but correct. Am I right?" The frantic visitor looked away, his cheeks damp with cold sweat. "Of course I am. Well, let's hear your proposition. Certain members of Congress might be interested. Two years ago, Simon and Zach Chandler and I were inseparable. We made a pact: an attack on one would be considered an attack on all, and we'd carry retaliation to the grave if necessary. But times and attitudes—and friends—do change, as you have sagaciously observed."

Stanley licked his lips, wondering whether the unsmiling senator was mocking him.

Wade went on: "The war effort is foundering. Everyone knows it. President Lincoln's dissatisfied with Simon. Everyone knows that, too. Should Lincoln fail to act in the matter, others will, much as they might regret it personally." A brief pause. "What could you offer to them, Mr. Hazard?"

"Information on contracts improperly let," Stanley whispered. "Names. Dates. Everything. Orally. I refuse to write a word. But I could be very helpful to, let's say, a congressional committee—"

A verbal sword slashed at him. "What committee?"

"I—why, I don't know. Whichever has jurisdiction—"

Satisfied by the evasion, Wade relaxed slightly. "And what would you ask in return for this assistance? A guarantee of immunity for yourself?" Stanley nodded.

Wade leaned back, brought his hands up beneath his nose, fingertips touching. The jet eyes bored in, pinning his caller, expressing contempt. Stanley knew he was finished. Cameron would hear of this the instant he returned. Goddamn his stupid wife for—

"I am interested. But you must convince me you're not offering counterfeit goods." The prosecutor leaned toward the witness. "Give me two examples. Be specific."

Stanley burrowed in his pockets for notes Isabel had suggested he prepare to meet such an eventuality. He served Wade two small helpings from his tray of secrets, and when he finished, found the senator's manner distinctly more cordial. Wade asked him to speak to the assistant outside and arrange a meeting at a more secure location where Wade could receive the disclosures without fear of interruption or observation. Dazed, Stanley realized it was all over.

At the door, Wade shook his hand with vigor. "I recall my wife mentioning a levee at your house soon. I look forward to it."

Feeling like a battle-tested hero, Stanley lurched out. Bless Isabel. She had been right after all. There was a conspiracy to unseat the boss, either through congressional action or by presentation of damning information to the President. Was it possible that Stanton was in the scheme, too?

No matter. What counted was his deal with the old crook from Ohio. Like Daniel, he had walked among lions and survived. By midafternoon he was convinced it was all his doing, with Isabel's role incidental.

38

His name was Arthur Scipio Brown. He was twenty-seven, a man the color of amber, with broad shoulders, a waist tiny as a girl's, and hands so huge they suggested weapons. Yet he spoke softly, with the slight nasality of New England. He had been born in Roxbury, outside Boston, of a black mother whose white lover deserted her.

Early in his acquaintance with Constance Hazard, Brown said his mother had sworn not to surrender to the sadness caused by the man who had promised to love her always, then left, or by the way her color impeded her even in liberal Boston. She had spent her mind and her energy—her entire life, he said—serving her race. She had taught the children of free black men and women in a shack school six days a week and given different lessons to pupils in a Negro congregation every Sunday. She had died a year ago, cancer-ridden but holding her boy's hand, clear-eyed and refusing laudanum to the end.

"She was forty-two. Never had much of a life," Brown said. It was a statement, not a plea for pity. "No braver woman ever walked this earth."

Constance met Scipio Brown at the reception for Dr. Delany, the pan-Africanist. In his splendid dyed robes, Delany circulated among the fifty or sixty guests invited to the Chase residence, enthralling them with his conversation. It was Delany who had brought young Brown to the reception.

Falling into conversation with Brown, George and Constance were fascinated by his demeanor as well as his history and his views. He was as tall as Cooper Main, and though he was not well dressed—his frock coat, an obvious hand-me-down, had worn lapels and sleeves that ended two inches above his wrists—he didn't act self-conscious. The clothes were probably the best he owned, and if people were scornful, the problem was theirs, not his.

When Brown said he was a disciple of Martin Delany, Constance asked, "You mean you'd leave the country for Liberia or some equivalent place, given the chance?"

Brown drank some tea. He handled the cup as gracefully as anyone present. "A year ago, I would have said yes immediately. Today, I'm less certain. America is viciously anti-Negro, and I imagine it will remain so for several generations yet. But I anticipate improvements. I believe in Corinthians."

Standing with his head back a few degrees, which was necessary when George conversed with extremely tall men, he said, "I beg your pardon?"

Brown smiled. His head was long, his features regular but unmemorable. His smile, however, seemed to re-sort those features into a shining amber composition that was immensely attractive and winning. "Paul's first letter to the Corinthians. 'Behold, I shew you a mystery. We shall not all sleep but we shall all be changed. In a moment, in the twinkling of an eye, the dead shall be raised incorruptible, and we shall all be changed.'" He drank more tea. "I just hope we don't have to wait until the last trump, which is a part of the verse I left out."

George said, "I grant that your race has suffered enormous tribulation. But wouldn't you say that you personally have been fortunate? You grew up free, and you've lived that way all your life."

Unexpectedly, Brown showed anger. "Do you honestly think that makes any difference, Major Hazard? Every colored person in this country is enslaved to the fears of whites and to the way those fears influence white behavior. You're fooled because my chains don't show. But I still have them. I am a black man. The struggle is my struggle. Every cross is my cross—in Alabama or Chicago or right here."

Bristling slightly, George said, "If you consider this country so wicked, what's kept you from leaving?"

"I thought I told you. Hope of change. My studies have taught me that change is one of the world's few constants. America's hypocritical picture of the freedom it offers has been destined to change since the Declaration was signed, because the institution of slavery is evil and never was anything else. I hope the war will hasten abolition. Once I was foolish enough to think the law would accomplish the task, but Dred Scott showed that even the Supreme Court's tainted. The last resort and shelter of despotism."

George refused to surrender. "I'll grant much of what you say, Brown. But not that remark about American freedom being hypocritical. I think you overstate the case."

"I disagree. But if so"—the smile warmed away any antagonism—"consider it one of the few privileges of my color."

"So it's hope of change that keeps you here—" Constance began.

"That and my responsibilities. It's mostly the children who keep me here."

"Ah, you're married."

"No, I'm not."

"Then whose—?"

A call from Kate Chase interrupted. Dr. Delany had consented to speak briefly. The secretary's attractive daughter wanted the guests to refill their cups and plates and find places.

At the serving table, where a young black girl in a domestic's apron gave Brown an admiring glance, George said, "I'd like to hear more of your views. We live at Willard's Hotel—"

"I know."

The statement astonished Constance, though it seemed to pass right by her husband.

"Will you dine with us there some night?"

"Thank you, Major, but I doubt the management would like that. The Willard brothers are decent men, but I'm still one of their employees."

"You're what?"

"I am a porter at Willard's Hotel. It's the best job I could find here. I won't work for the army. The army's running its own peculiar institution these days: hiring my people to cook and chop wood and fetch and carry for a pittance. We're good enough to dig sinks but not good enough to fight. That's why I'm a porter instead."

"Willard's," George muttered. "I'm dumbfounded. Have we ever passed one another in the lobby or the hallways?"

Brown led them toward chairs. "Certainly. Dozens of times.

245

You may look at me, but you never see me. It's another privilege of color. Mrs. Hazard, will you be seated?"

Later, realizing Brown was right, George started to apologize, but the lanky Negro brushed it away with a smile and a shrug. They had no further opportunity to talk. But Constance remained curious about his reference to children. Next afternoon at the hotel, she searched until she found him removing trash and discarded cigar butts from sand urns. Ignoring stares from people in the lobby, she asked Brown to explain what he meant.

"The children are runaways, what that cross-eyed general Butler calls contrabands. There's a black river flowing out of the South these days. Sometimes children escape with their parents, then the parents get lost. Sometimes the children don't belong to anyone, just tag along after the adults making the dash. Would you like to see some of the children, Mrs. Hazard?"

His eyes fastened on hers, testing. "Where?" she countered.

"Out where I live, on north Tenth Street."

"Negro Hill?" The soft intake of breath before the question gave her away. He didn't react angrily.

"There's nothing to fear just because it's a black community. We have only our fair share of undesirables, same as down here—I take it back, you have more." He grinned. "You also have the politicians. Truly, you'll be perfectly safe if you'd care to come. I don't work Tuesdays. We could go during the day."

"All right," Constance said, hoping George would agree to it.

Surprisingly, he did. "If anyone could protect a woman anywhere, I have a feeling it's that young chap. Go visit his community of waifs. I'll be fascinated to know what it's like."

George paid a livery to bring a carriage to Willard's front door on Tuesday. The lout delivering it glowered when he saw Brown and Constance sit side by side on the driver's seat. The Negro was a companion, not a servant. The lout muttered something nasty, but one glance from Brown cut it short.

"When did you come to Washington?" Constance asked as Brown drove them away from the hotel into the perennial congestion of omnibuses, military wagons, horses, and pedestrians.

"Last fall, after Old Abe won."

"Why then?"

"Didn't I explain at the reception? The resettlement plan is in abeyance because of the war, and I thought this might be the

246

cockpit of change. I hoped some useful work might find me, and it has. You'll see—*Hah!*" He bounced the reins over the team.

Soon they were rattling through the autumn heat to the overgrown empty lots far out on Tenth. Negro Hill was a depressing enclave of tiny homes, most unpainted, and hovels built of poles, canvas, and pieces of old crates. She saw chicken pens, vegetable patches, flowerpots. The small touches could do little to relieve the air of festering poverty.

The Negroes they passed gave them curious, occasionally suspicious looks. Presently Brown turned left into a rutted lane. At the end stood a cottage of new yellow pine bright as sunflower petals.

"The whole community helped build this," he said. "It's already too small. We can feed and house only twelve. But it's a start, and all we could afford."

The shining little house smelled deliciously of raw wood and hearth smoke and, inside, of soap. The interior, brightened by large windows, consisted of two rooms. In the nearer one, a stout black woman sat on a stool, Bible in hand, with twelve poorly dressed waifs of all shades from ebony to tan encircling her feet; the youngest child was four or five, the oldest ten or eleven. Through the doorway arch, Constance saw pallets laid in precise rows.

One beautiful coppery girl of six or seven ran to the tall man. "Uncle Scipio, Uncle Scipio!"

"Rosalie." He swept her up and hugged her. After he put her down, he walked Constance a short distance away and said, "Rosalie escaped from North Carolina along with her mother, stepfather, and her aunt. Near Petersburg a white farmer with a rifle caught them in his haymow. He killed the mother and stepfather, but Rosalie and her aunt got away."

"Where's the aunt now?"

"In the city, hunting for work. I haven't seen her for three weeks."

More children came clamoring around his legs. He patted heads, faces, shoulders, offering just the right encouragement or question to each as he worked his way to the old iron stove where a soup pot simmered; mostly broth and bones, Constance observed.

She ate with Brown and the lost children and the black woman, Agatha, who tended them while Brown was away at his job. Most of the youngsters laughed and wiggled and poked each other in a childlike way, but there were two, sad and grave, who didn't speak at all, merely sat spooning up broth in the slow, exhausted manner of the elderly. She had to turn away to keep from crying.

In spite of that, the place and the youngsters fascinated her. She hated to see the visit end. On the way back to Willard's, she asked, "What's your plan for those children?"

"First, I must feed and shelter them so they don't starve. The politicians will do nothing for them; I know that."

"You do have strong feelings about politicians, Mr. Brown."

"Why not Scipio? I'd like us to be friends. And, yes, I do despise the breed. Politicians helped put the shackles on black people and, what's worse, they have kept them there."

The carriage bumped on for a minute. Then she said, "Beyond helping the children survive, do you have anything else in mind for them?"

"From the necessary we move to the ideal. If I could locate another suitable place for the twelve you saw—a place to house and teach them till I can find homes for them—I could take in twelve more. But I can't afford to do it on what they pay me to empty the spit from brass pots." Eyes on the yellow and red leaves over the street, he added, "It would be possible only with the help of a patron."

"Is that why you brought me to Negro Hill?"

"Because I had hopes?" He smiled at her. "Of course."

"And of course you knew I'd say yes—though I'm not sure how we'll work out the details."

"Don't do it just to ease your white guilt."

"Damn your impertinence, Brown—I'll do it for whatever reason I please. I lost my heart to those waifs."

"Good," he said.

They drove another block, past the first white residence. Two children were petting a pony on the side lawn. Constance cleared her throat. "Please excuse my language a moment ago. Occasionally my temper shows. I'm Irish."

He grinned. "I guessed."

Constance didn't know how George would react to her desire to help Brown. To her delight, he went far beyond mere consent. "If he needs a place for the children, why don't we provide it? And food, clothing, books—furnishing everything would hardly make a nick in our income, and the work sounds eminently worthwhile. God knows little black children shouldn't be made to suffer for past and present stupidities of their white elders."

Lighting his cigar, he squinted through the smoke in a way that lent him a familiar piratical air, made even stronger by his new mustache. That look effectively hid a sentimental streak Constance had discovered years ago and loved ever since. With his thumbnail George shot the match straight into the hearth. "Yes, I definitely believe you should invite Brown to set up his facility back home."

"Where exactly?"

"What about the shed above Hazard's? The site of the old fugitive depot?"

"The location's good, but the building is small."

"We'll expand it. Add a couple of dormitories, a classroom, a dining room—The company carpenters can do the work."

Reality intruded on enthusiasm when she said, "Will they?"

"They work for me—they damn well better." He reflected a moment, then frowned. "I don't understand why you even asked the question."

"The children are black, George."

His reply was ingenuous. "Do you think that would matter?"

"To many, maybe most, of the citizens of Lehigh Station, yes, I think it would. Very much so."

"Mmm. Never occurred to me." He paced to the mantel, turning his cigar in his fingers as he often did when working on a problem. "Still—that's no excuse for rejecting the idea. It's a good one. We'll do it."

She clapped her hands, delighted. "Perhaps Mr. Brown and I could travel home for a few days to get things started. We might even take a child or two."

"I can arrange a short leave and go with you."

She started to say that would be splendid but caught herself. Vivid as a railway warning lantern in the night, there was a name: Virgilia.

"That's generous, but you're busy. I'm sure Mr. Brown and I can survey the property."

"Fine." His words and his shrug relieved her. "I'll write Christopher a letter to authorize whatever work you want done. Speaking of letters, have you seen this?" From the mantel he took a soiled, badly crumpled missive sealed shut with wax.

"It's from Father," she exclaimed when she saw the handwriting. She tore it open, sank to the sofa, read a few lines with a strained expression. "He's reached Houston—wearing his revolver constantly, he says, and constantly biting his tongue because of the hot rebel sentiments expressed everywhere. Oh, I hope he makes the rest of the journey safely."

George walked to her side, gently placing a hand on her shoulder. *We are all on a journey now. God knows who among us will come through it safely.* He stood patting her and smoking his cigar while she finished reading.

Constance and Brown left Washington a few days later. Brown had chosen three children to go with them: Leander, a sturdy eleven-year-old with a belligerent manner; Margaret, a shy, coal-black child; and Rosalie, the pretty little one whose merriment filled the silences of the others.

The fear she had expressed to George was not without substance, she discovered. A conductor at the Washington depot insisted that Brown and the children ride in the second-class car reserved for colored. Brown's eyes revealed his anger, but he didn't provoke a scene. Leading the youngsters up the aisle, he said, "I'll see you farther up the line, Mrs. Hazard."

When they had left the car, the conductor said, " 'S that nigger your servant, ma'am?"

"That man is my friend."

The conductor walked off shaking his head.

After changing at Baltimore, they journeyed on toward Philadelphia through golden autumn landscapes. Men around Constance thumped their newspapers and crowed over the superiority of Yankee soldiers. At a place called Cheat Mountain in rugged western Virginia, the enemy general once considered America's best soldier had taken a drubbing.

"It says down in Richmond folks call him Evacuating Lee. There's one reb star that's sinking mighty fast."

The Lehigh valley, fired with the reds and yellows of fall, seemed refreshingly peaceful to the tired adult travelers. On the station platform, the children gaped at the homes rising in terraced levels, the looming ironworks with its smoke and noise, and the great scene-drop of mountains and evening sky. Little Rosalie whispered, "Lordy."

Constance had telegraphed ahead. A groom was there with a

carriage. She didn't miss the brief change in his expression when he realized Brown and the children were her companions.

The rig rattled up the inclined street. The two little girls squealed and hugged Brown as the wind ruffled their hair and clothes. Pinckney Herbert waved from the door of his store, but the faces of some other citizens, notably a discharged Hazard's employee named Lute Fessenden, showed hostility. Giving the youngsters a murderous stare, Fessenden whispered to a companion as the carriage passed.

Western light poured over the mansion at the summit. Brett was waiting on the veranda, together with a woman Constance didn't recognize until they were in the driveway. The carriage stopped; Constance alighted and ran up the steps. "Virgilia? How lovely you look! I can't believe my eyes."

"It's the handiwork of our sister-in-law," Virgilia said, nodding toward Brett. She spoke as if the change were unimportant, but a vivacity in her expression gave her away.

Constance marveled. Virgilia's dress of rust-colored silk with lace cuffs flattered her figure, which loss of a great deal of weight had reshaped into voluptuous, billowy curves. Her hair, neatly bunned at the back of her head, gleamed with a cleanliness Constance had never seen before. There was color in Virgilia's cheeks, but rouge and powder had been applied subtly and expertly; they rendered her old scars nearly invisible. Virgilia would never qualify as a pretty woman, but she had become a handsome one.

"I'm neglecting my duties," Constance said. She performed introductions, and in a few sentences explained why she had brought Scipio Brown and the children to Belvedere.

Brett was polite to Brown, but cool; nor had he missed her accent. Constance watched Virgilia's eye draw a languorous line from Brown's face to his chest. He quickly busied himself with the children, kneeling and fussing over them. Seeing Brown embarrassed was a new experience for Constance. Recalling Virgilia's fondness for Negro men, she realized George's sister had not changed in certain fundamental respects.

The visitors were taken into the house, fed, and settled for the night. Next morning, while Virgilia looked after the children and vainly tried to draw Leander into conversation, Constance and Brown drove to the main gate of Hazard's and up to the remote site of the shed that had functioned for a time as a stop on the underground railroad to Canada.

Brown poked around inside, then came out. "With some fixing, it will be perfect." They discussed specifics while they drove back down to the gate. Workers respectfully stepped out of the way of the carriage, but most registered silent disapproval of a black man appearing in public with the owner's wife.

By noon they had spoken with Wotherspoon, and he had dispatched men to knock out one wall of the shed and patch and whitewash the other three. Late in the day, Constance and Brown went to check on progress. The head of the painting crew, a middle-aged fellow named Abraham Fouts, had worked for Hazard's fifteen years. Always friendly, this afternoon he merely gave Constance a nod and no greeting. That night, while the adults and children ate supper, someone threw a stone through the front window.

Leander spun toward the noise, tense as a cat whose whiskers touched something threatening in the dark. Virgilia rose in wrath. To the surprise of George's wife, it was Brown who sounded a note of tolerance.

"Some of that's to be expected when a man like me comes into a house like this—and through the front door."

"That's true, Mr. Brown," Brett responded. It was not said unkindly, but it produced an angry glance from the visitor. Tired all at once, Constance realized she had overlooked a potential problem here. Brown couldn't be expected to like Southerners any more than a South Carolina native could readily accept a black at the dinner table.

Up early, she drove alone to the shed, arriving simultaneously with Abraham Fouts and his crew of four. Fouts and a second man suppressed smirks at the sight of big, crude letters someone had slashed onto the side of the shed with black paint: WE ARE FOR THE WAR BUT WE AINT FOR THE NIGGER.

Saddened and angry, Constance hoisted her skirts and stormed to the wall. She rubbed her thumb across the last letters as if to wipe them out. They were dry. "Mr. Fouts, please paint over this obscenity till it can't be seen. If the message or anything like it appears again, you will do the same thing, and keep doing it until the nastiness stops or this building collapses under a hundred coats of whitewash."

The pale man poked nervously at his upper lip. "They's a lot of talk about this place among the men, Miz Hazard. They say it's gonna be some kind of home for nigger babies. They don't like that."

"What they like is immaterial to me. My husband owns this property, and I'll do whatever I please with it."

Goaded by glances from the others, Fouts stuck out his chin. "Your husband, he might not—"

"My husband knows and approves of what I plan to do. If you care to keep working for Hazard's, get busy."

Fouts dug a toe in the dirt, but another man was bolder. "We ain't 'customed to takin' orders from a female, even if she is the wife of the boss."

"Fine." Constance was melting with anger and uncertainty but didn't dare show it. "I'm sure there are any number of manufactories where it isn't necessary. Collect your pay from Mr. Wotherspoon."

The stunned man raised his hand. "Wait a minute, I—"

"You're done here." She pointed to the man's hand, stained between thumb and index finger. "I see you used some black paint last night. How courageous of you to state your views under cover of darkness." Her voice broke as she took swift steps forward. "Get out of here and collect your pay."

The man ran. Anxiety replaced her fear; she had certainly exceeded the authority George had granted her. Well, it was too late to worry. Besides, Brown's shelter would never be secure unless she made sure of it.

"I regret this incident, Mr. Fouts, but I stand fast. Do you want to whitewash the building or quit?" She saw three men with carpenter's tools trudging up the hill; she would have to ask the same of them.

"I'll work," Fouts grumbled. "But for a bunch of nigras? It ain't right."

Returning to Belvedere, she tried to purge herself of her rage. The North was no pristine fount of morality—a fact that had infuriated Southerners subjected to abolitionist rhetoric for three decades and more. Fouts no doubt believed with perfect sincerity that the Negro was inferior to the white man; George said Lincoln had been known to express the same view. She could understand that Fouts was a product of the times, comfortable and safe in sharing the opinions of a majority.

But condone those views or join that majority—or let it intimidate her? The devil she would. She was the wife of George Hazard. She was the daughter of Patrick Flynn.

"Abominable," Virgilia said when Constance told her about the painted message. "If we had proper leadership in Washington, things would be different. I believe they will be soon."

"Why is that?" Brett asked from across the table laden with a huge lamb roast and five other dishes, comprising the typically gargantuan midday meal. Rosalie, Margaret, and Leander didn't eat; they devoured. Even Brown couldn't seem to get enough.

"The President's a weakling." Virgilia handed down the pronouncement in much the same tone that had caused so much trouble in the past. "Look at the way he responded to Frémont's manumission order in Missouri. He cowers and caters to the slave masters of Kentucky and the other border states—"

"He does that for military reasons, I'm told."

Virgilia paid no attention to Constance. "—but Thad Stevens and some others show signs of wanting to bring him to heel. With the right Republicans in control, Lincoln will get what he richly deserves. So will the rebs."

"Please excuse me," Brett said, and left the room.

After the meal, Constance gathered her nerve to speak to Virgilia in private. "I wish you wouldn't make—pronouncements in front of Brett. You said she extended herself to help you, that she's responsible for the wonderful change, and—"

"Yes, she helped me, but that has nothing to do with the truth or—" She took a breath, finally comprehending that Constance was furious with her.

Virgilia's new vision of herself, her increased confidence, had begun to change her perceptions in a number of other ways. Sometimes it was necessary to be tactful with opponents. She forced a sigh. "You're perfectly right. While I can never abandon my beliefs—"

"No one asks that of you."

"—I do understand that Brett's entitled to some deference."

"Not to mention plain everyday courtesy."

"Certainly. She's become part of the family, and, as you say, she was kind to me. I'll try harder from now on. Still, under the present arrangement, there are bound to be disputes."

Quietly: "Since you brought up what you call the present arrangement, suppose we discuss it."

Virgilia nodded. "I know that my grace period here is running out. I'm anxious to leave. Anxious to get back into the stream of things. I don't know how. Where can I go to earn a livelihood? What can I do when I have no training and very little education in practical things?"

Virgilia slowly walked to the parlor window. A shower was in progress. Rain clung to the glass, casting patterns on her face like new pox scars. In a small, sad voice, she said, "Those are the questions I've never had to ask before. To wait for answers that don't come is frightening, Constance."

She stared into the rain. Constance thought, *Don't wait—search!* But the pique passed, and she again felt pity for George's sister. Virgilia appeared a changed woman, but did the changes go any deeper than her skin? She began to doubt it.

Two points clarified themselves as a result of the brief conversation. Virgilia had to leave Belvedere before George discovered her presence or Brett, goaded to anger, told him. But she was incapable of finding her way alone, so part of that burden, too, fell on Constance.

39

In late October, Mrs. Burdetta Halloran of Richmond was a woman distressed.

Two years a childless widow, she was thirty-three, statuesque, with gorgeous auburn hair, a stunning derrière, and breasts that were, in her opinion, merely adequate. But the package had been sufficiently enchanting to captivate the wine merchant who had wed her when she was twenty-one. Sixteen years her senior, Halloran had died of heart failure while struggling to satisfy her strong sexual appetites.

Poor fellow, she had liked him well enough, even though he lacked the technique and stamina to keep her happy physically. He had treated her well, however, and she had only cuckolded him twice: the first liaison had lasted four days, the second a single night. His passing had left her in comfortable circumstances—or she had thought so until this wretched war came.

Today, when the rest of the town was euphoric about a victory at some spot near the Potomac called Ball's Bluff, she was upset by her tour of retail stores. Prices were climbing. Her pound of bacon had cost fifty cents, her pound of coffee an outrageous dollar and a half. Only last week the freedman who supplied her from the country with stove and firewood had announced that he wanted eight dollars for the next cord, not five. With such inflation, she would not long survive in her accustomed style.

Born a Soames—the family went back four generations in the Old Dominion—she deplored all the changes in her city, her state, and in the social order. Bob Lee, finest of the fine, was being mocked with the name "Granny" because of his military failures; she had heard he would soon be shipped to one of the benighted military districts of the cotton South.

Queen Varina was outraging members of local society by forming a court made up chiefly of those who were not. Oh, Joe Johnston's wife belonged, but Burdetta Halloran suspected she did so to advance her husband's career; she certainly had nothing in common with the rest of the upstarts who surrounded and influenced the First Lady: Mrs. Mallory, a flaming papist; Mrs. Wigfall, a vulgar Texan; Mrs. Chesnut, a Carolina bitch. Beneath contempt, every one. Yet they were favored.

The city was too crowded. Harlots and speculators poured off every arriving train. Hordes of niggers, many undoubtedly fugitives, swelled the mobs of idlers in the streets. Captured Yankees filled the improvised prisons, like Liggon's Tobacco Factory at Twenty-fifth and Main. Their unprecedented arrogance and contempt for all things Southern outraged solid citizens like Burdetta Halloran, who courageously bore the cross of Jeff Davis and spent every free hour knitting socks and more socks for the troops.

She had stopped knitting two weeks ago, when her distress

reached crisis proportions. This afternoon, covertly nipping on whiskey from a flask in a crocheted cozy, she was traveling in a hack to Church Hill. She had been contemplating the visit for days. Sleeplessness and mounting despair had finally pushed her to act.

The hack slowed. She sipped again, then hid the covered flask in her bag. "Shall I wait?" the driver asked after he parked near the corner of Twenty-fourth. Some dismal premonition caused Mrs. Halloran to nod.

She darted along the walk and up the stoop, so nervous she nearly fell. She had drunk the liquor for courage, but it only dulled her mind and sharpened her anxiety. She raised the knocker and let it fall.

Her heart beat hurtfully. The slanting October light foretold winter—sadness and loneliness. God, wasn't he here? She knocked again, harder and longer.

The door opened six inches. She nearly fainted from happiness. Then she looked more closely at her lover. His hair was uncombed, and a wedge of skin showed between sagging lapels of claret velvet. A dressing gown at this hour?

At first she assumed he was ill. Soon she realized the truth and the extent of her stupidity.

"Burdetta." There was no surprise and no welcome in the way he said her name. Nor did he open the door wider.

"Lamar, you haven't answered a single one of my letters."

"I thought you'd understand the significance of silence."

"Dear Lord, you don't mean—you wouldn't simply cast me out —not after six months of unbelievable—"

"This is an embarrassment," he said, his voice lower and hard as his instrument when he took her in various ways, satiating her only after four or five hours. His eyes shunted past her to the curious hackman on his high seat. "For both of us."

"Who have you got now? Some young slut? Is she inside?" She sniffed. "My God, you have. You must have soaked in her perfume." Tears filled her eyes. She extended her hand through the opening. "Darling, at least let me come in. Talk this out. If I've wronged or offended you—"

"Pull your hand back, Burdetta," he said, smiling. "Otherwise you'll get hurt. I'm going to shut the door."

"You unspeakable bastard." Her whisper had no effect; the sun-splashed door began to close. He would have broken her wrist or

257

fingers if she hadn't withdrawn her hand quickly. The door clicked. Six months of risking her reputation, of performing every conceivable wickedness for him, and this was how it ended? With indifference? With the sort of dismissal a man would give a whore?

Burdetta Soames Halloran had been schooled in Southern graces, which included courage and the maintenance of poise in the face of social disaster. Although it would take days or weeks to compose her emotions—Lamar Powell had spoken to some animalistic side of her, and she had never loved any man more or more completely—it took less than ten seconds for her to compose her face. When she turned and carefully stepped down the first tall riser, her hoops raised in her gloved hands, she was smiling.

"Ready?" the hackman asked, unnecessarily, since she was waiting for him to jump and open the door.

"Yes, I am. It required only a moment to conclude my business."

In fact, she had only begun it.

40

Turmoil swept the Carolina coast that autumn. On the seventh of November, Commodore Du Pont's flotilla steamed into Port Royal Sound and opened fire on Hilton Head Island. The bombardment from Du Pont's gunboats sent the small Confederate garrison retreating to the mainland before the sun set. Two days later, nearby, the historic little port of Beaufort fell. There came reports of burning and looting of white homes by rapacious Yankee soldiers and revengeful blacks.

Each day brought new rumors. Arson would soon raze Charleston, which would be replaced by a city for black fugitives; Harriet Tubman was in the state, or coming to the state, or thinking about coming to the state, to urge slaves to run or revolt; for failure in western Virginia, Lee had been banished to command the new Department of South Carolina, Georgia, and East Florida.

The last proved true. Unexpectedly, the famous soldier and three of his senior staff appeared on horseback in the lane of Mont Royal one twilight. They spent an hour with Orry in the parlor before riding on to Yemassee.

Orry had met Lee once, in Mexico; yet because of the man's reputation, both military and personal, he felt he knew him well. What a jolt, then, to confront the visitor and find he no longer resembled his published portraits. Lee was fifty-four or fifty-five, but his seamed face, shadowed eyes, white-streaked beard, and general air of strain made him appear much older. Orry had never seen a picture of Lee with a beard, and said so.

"Oh, I brought this back from the Cheat Mountain campaign," Lee said. "Along with a portfolio of nicknames I'd be happier to discard." His staff men laughed, but the mirth was forced. "How is your cousin, young Charles?"

"He's well, the last I heard. He enlisted with the Hampton Legion. I'm surprised you remember him."

"Impossible to forget him. While I was superintendent, he was the best rider I saw at the Academy."

Lee fell to discussing the point of his visit. He wanted Orry to accept the commission in Richmond, even though he was no longer headquartered there and could not employ him directly. "You can be of great service to the War Department, however. It isn't true, as the backbiters would have it, that President Davis constantly interferes or that he's the person who actually runs the department." Lee paused. "It is not completely true, I mean to say."

"I plan to go as soon as I can, General. I've just been awaiting the arrival of a new overseer to run the place. He's due any day."

"Good news. Splendid! You and every West Point man like you are of infinite value to the army and the conduct of the war. The great failing of Mr. Davis, if I may in confidence suggest one, is his belief that there's nothing wrong with secession. Perhaps in the South there is not. In Washington, I assure you, they consider it treason. I am not enough of a constitutionalist to state positively that the act was illegal, but I consider it a blunder whose magnitude is only now being perceived. But no matter what personal feelings you or any of us have about secession, one of its consequences is immutable. We shall have to win our right to it—our right to exist as a separate nation. When I say win, I am speaking of military victory. Mr. Davis, regrettably, believes the right will be awarded us if we merely press our claim rhetorically. That is the dream of an idealist. Laudable, perhaps, but a dream. What we did was heinous to a majority of our former countrymen. Only force of arms will gain and hold independence. Academy men will understand and fight the war as it must be fought, unless we plan to quit or be defeated."

"Fight," one of the staff men growled. Orry nodded to agree.

"That's the proper spirit," Lee said, rising; his knees creaked. He shook Orry's hand, passed a social moment on the piazza with Madeline, then rode away to the duties of his obscure command. Orry put his arm around his wife and pulled her against him in the chill of the darkening sky. Parting was inevitable now. It hurt to think of it.

Next morning, further news came. Nine blacks from Francis LaMotte's plantation had used basket boats, woven in secret, to float down the Ashley on the ebb tide. They had abandoned the boats above Charleston and fled south, presumably to the Union lines around Beaufort.

Along with that report, the day brought the overseer from North Carolina, Philemon Meek, mounted on a mule.

Orry's first reaction was disappointment. He had expected a man in his sixties, but not someone with the stoop and demeanor of an aged schoolmaster; Meek even wore half-glasses down near the tip of his nose.

Orry interviewed Meek for an hour in the library, and the impression began to change. Meek answered his new employer's questions tersely but honestly. When he didn't know or understand something, he said so. He told Orry that he didn't believe in harsh discipline unless slaves brought it on themselves. Orry replied that, except for Cuffey and one or two others, few at Mont Royal were troublemakers.

Meek then made clear that he was a religious man. He owned

and read only one book, the Scriptures. Any kind of reading was hard for him, he admitted, which perhaps contributed to his strongly stated opinion that secular books, and especially fiction, were satanically inspired. Orry made no comment. It wasn't an unusual attitude among the devout.

"I'm not sure about him," Orry told Madeline that night. In a week, he formed more positive opinions. Despite Meek's age, he was physically strong and brooked no nonsense from those who worked for him. Andy didn't appear to like Meek but got along with him. So Orry packed his trunks and the Solingen sword, ready at last.

The day before his train left, he and Madeline went walking. It was a dying November afternoon around four o'clock. The sun was slightly above the treetops, ringed by spikes of light. In the west the sky was a smoky white, shading away to deep blue in the east. Somewhere in the far squares of the rice acreage, a slave with a fine baritone sang in Gullah: spontaneous music of a kind seldom heard at Mont Royal any more.

"You're anxious to go, aren't you?" Madeline said as they retraced their route from the great house.

Orry squinted against the cruciform light around the sun. "I'm not anxious to leave you, though I feel better about it now that Meek's here."

"That doesn't answer my question, sir."

"Yes, I am anxious. You'll never guess the reason. It's my old friend Tom Jackson. In six months, he's become a national hero."

"You surprise me. I never thought you had that kind of ambition."

"Oh, no. Not since Mexico, anyway. The point about Jackson is, we were classmates. He rushed to do his duty, while I've taken half a year to answer the call. Not without good reason—but I still feel guilty."

She wrapped both arms around his and hugged it between her breasts. "Don't. Your waiting's over. And in a few weeks, when Meek has settled in, I'll be on my way to Richmond for the duration."

"Good." Peace and a sense of events moving properly for a change settled on him as they drew near the house, long shadows stretching out behind them. Orry fingered his chin. "I saw a lithograph of Tom last week. He has a fine bushy beard. All the officers seem to have them. Would you like it if I grew one?"

"I can't answer until I know how badly it scratches when we—"

She stopped. The houseman, Aristotle, was waving from a side entrance in a way that conveyed urgency. They hurried toward him. Orry was the first to see the rickety wagon and despondent mule standing at the head of the lane.

"Got two visitors, Mr. Orry. Uppity pair of niggers. Won't state their business to nobody but you and Miss Madeline. I packed 'em off to the kitchen to wait."

Orry asked, "Are they men from another plantation?"

The irritated slave grumbled, "It's two females."

Puzzled, Orry and Madeline turned toward the kitchen building, the center of a cloud of savory barbecue smells. Nearing it, they recognized the elderly Negress seated in an old rocker near the door. Her right leg, crudely splinted and bound with sticks and rags, rested on an empty nail box.

"Aunt Belle," Madeline exclaimed, while Orry speculated about the identity of the octoroon's companion, just coming outside. She wore field buck's shoes; the right side of one upper had been pulled away from the sole. Her dress had been washed so often, all color had been lost. She was an astonishingly attractive young girl, nubile and dark as mahogany.

Madeline hugged the frail old woman, exclaiming all in a rush, "How are you? What happened to your leg? Is it broken?" Aunt Belle Nin had practiced midwifery in the district for a generation, living alone and free back in the marshes. She and Madeline had met at Resolute, where Aunt Belle came occasionally to assist with a difficult birth. It was to Aunt Belle that Madeline had taken Ashton when Orry's sister got herself in a fix and begged Madeline's help.

"That's a lot of questions," Aunt Belle said, grimacing uncomfortably. "Yes, it's broke in two or three places. When you're my age that's no blessing. I fell trying to climb into our wagon last night." Bright eyes deep-set in flesh of mottled yellow studied Orry as if he were a museum exhibit. "See you got yourself a different husband."

"Yes. Aunt Belle, this is Orry Main."

"I know who he is. He's a sight better than the one you had before. This pretty thing is my niece, Jane. She used to belong to the Widow Milsom, up on the Combahee, but the old lady perished of pneumonia last winter. Her will gave Jane her freedom. She's been living with me since."

"Pleased to meet you," Jane said, with no curtsy or other demonstration of deference. Orry wondered if he could believe Aunt Belle. The girl might be a fugitive, gambling that no one would check her story in these disordered times.

In the ensuing silence, someone dropped a pot in the kitchen. One girl spoke sharply to another. A third intervened; soft laughter signaled restored harmony. Jane realized the white people were awaiting an explanation.

"Aunt Belle's health has not been good lately. But she wouldn't give up the marsh house till I convinced her there was a better place."

"You don't mean here?" Orry asked, still not certain what they wanted.

"No, Mr. Main. Virginia. Then the North."

"That's a long, dangerous journey, especially for women in war-time." He nearly said black women.

"What's waiting is worth the risk. We were just ready to start when Aunt Belle broke her leg. She needs doctoring and a safe place to rest and heal."

To the midwife, Orry said, "Your house isn't safe any longer?"

Jane answered; her presumption rather annoyed him. "A week ago Friday, two strangers tried to break in. Colored men. There are a lot of them wandering the back roads. I drove them off with Aunt Belle's old hunting musket, but it was scary. Yesterday, when she had the accident, I decided we should find another place."

Aunt Belle said to Madeline, "I told Jane you were a good Christian person. I told her I thought you'd take us in for a while. We have all our goods in the wagon, but they don't amount to much. Neither of my husbands left me with anything but good and bad memories."

Orry and his wife questioned one another with their eyes; each knew the problems the appeal presented. Since Orry was leaving, Madeline decided she must be the one to resolve them. "We'll surely help you all we can. Darling, would you find Andy, so he can take them to the cabins?" Orry seemed to understand that she had another purpose in asking; he nodded and walked off, leaving her free to speak.

"Aunt Belle, my husband is going to Richmond in the morning.

263

He's going into the army. I'll be in charge here until I join him. I'm only too glad to give you refuge, with one reservation. Right or wrong, the people at Mont Royal aren't free to go north, as you plan to do. They might resent you or cause trouble for me."

"Ma'am?" Jane said, to get her attention. Madeline turned. "There is no right in slavery, only wrong."

Madeline's reply had sharpness. "Even if I agree with you, the practical solution is another matter."

Jane reflected on that with a visible defiance Madeline admired yet couldn't tolerate. At last Jane uttered a small sigh. "I don't think we can stay, Aunt Belle."

"Think once more. This lady is decent. You be the same. Don't butt in like a billy goat. Bend."

Jane hesitated. Aunt Belle glared. The younger girl said, "Would an arrangement like this be agreeable, Mrs. Main? I'll work for you to earn our keep. I won't tell any of your people where we're going or do anything to stir them up. As soon as Aunt Belle can travel, we'll pack and go."

"That's fair," Madeline said.

"Jane keeps her word," Aunt Belle said.

"Yes, she impresses me that way." Eyes on the girl, Madeline nodded as she spoke. Neither woman smiled, but in that moment, liking began. "Our new overseer may not care for the arrangement, but I believe he'll accept—"

Voices in the dusk interrupted her. Orry and the head driver stepped into the orange halo of the lantern beside the kitchen door. "I've explained matters to Andy," Orry said. "There's an empty cabin available. That is—" The pause asked a question.

"Yes, we've worked out the details," Madeline told him. "Andy, this is Aunt Belle Nin and her niece, Jane." She described the bargain she had struck with them.

"All right," Andy said. Taken with the girl, the young driver smiled in his friendliest way. Madeline felt sorry for him. The girl was in love with an idea.

"Mr. Orry says you have a wagon," Andy continued. "I'll drive you to the cabin."

"Pick up some barbecue in the kitchen," Orry said. "You two are probably hungry."

"Starved," the tiny octoroon said. "I don't know you, Mr. Main, but you're beginning to sound like a good Christian person, too."

As the wagon proceeded slowly to the slave community, Andy peeked over his shoulder at Jane. When he had first approached the kitchen porch and saw her there, gathering and reflecting the orange light, he had caught his breath in wonder. He had never set eyes on anyone more beautiful.

He worked up courage to say, "You speak mighty well, Miss Jane. Can you read?"

"And write," she replied from the wagon bed, where she sat with Aunt Belle's legs resting on top of hers. "I can cipher, too. A year before Mrs. Milsom died, she knew she was going and started to teach me."

"That was against the law."

"She said the devil with the law. She was a feisty old lady. She said I had to be ready to make my way alone." The mule plodded; the axle creaked. "Can you read and write?"

"No." Then, desperate to make a good impression, he blurted, "I'd like to know how, though. Yes, indeed. A man can't better himself unless he has learning."

"And a man can't better himself when he's the property of—" Aunt Belle whacked her niece's wrist with her fingers. Jane looked chastened as she finished, "I'd be happy to give you lessons, but I couldn't do it without asking Mrs. Main's permission."

"Maybe we could do that sometime."

"Let's eat first," Aunt Belle said irritably. "Let's remember who needs attention here, is that all right?"

"Just fine," Andy said, jubilant.

The wagon rolled into the lane between the slave cottages. At the gnarled base of a mammoth live oak rising between two of them, Cuffey sat with his spine against the bark, a twig in his teeth, and his right hand down between his legs, scratching lazily. Spying the unfamiliar girl in the wagon, he sat up. He had heard nothing about purchase of any new slaves. Who was she? He surely wanted to find out.

Giving a nasty glance at Andy, who paid no attention, Cuffey watched the wagon pass. His eyes returned to the lush line of the girl's bosom, and his hand grew busier in his crotch.

In bed, naked beneath a comforter, Orry said, "I liked that little nigra girl. Peppery; just like the old woman. But I have a feeling you can trust her to keep her word."

"I wouldn't have let her stay otherwise," Madeline touched him. "Everything will be fine. Let's not spend your last night worrying that it won't."

"Lord, I'm going to miss you these next two or three months."

"Show me how much."

In the morning, in a hat and frock coat and cravat suitable for a funeral, Orry kissed his vaguely smiling mother. "Thank you for visiting, sir. Do come again, won't you?" she said.

As he kissed his wife she held him fiercely, whispering: "God keep you safe, dearest. One day when I was small, a moment came when I suddenly understood the meaning of the word *death*. I started crying and ran to my father. He took me in his arms and said I shouldn't let it frighten me too much, because we all shared the predicament. He said it eased the mind and heart to remember we are all dying of life. It took me years to understand and believe him. I do, but—I don't want it to happen to you any sooner than necessary. Life's become too sweet."

"Don't worry," he reassured her. "We'll be together before long. And I don't think anyone fires at officers who sit behind desks."

He kissed and embraced her once more and went away down the lane, with Aristotle driving.

41

Certain American civilians remembered that two of the chief destroyers of the British Army in the Crimea were dirt and disease. Not long after Sumter fell, these civilians decided to prevent, if they could, a repetition in the Union encampments of those mistakes of half a dozen years ago and half a world away.

As soon as the plan became public, army surgeons began to scoff and call the civilians meddling amateurs. So did most government officials. The civilians persisted, forming the United States Sanitary Commission. By midsummer, the organization had a chief executive, Frederick Law Olmsted, the man who had designed New York City's Central Park in 1856 and described slavery in unfavorable terms in a widely read travel memoir.

Lincoln and the War Department didn't want to sanction the commission but were forced to do so because important people were connected with it, including Mr. Bache, a grandson of Ben Franklin, and Samuel Gridley Howe, the famous Boston doctor and humanitarian. Even after official recognition, members didn't forgive the President for saying they were a fifth wheel on the coach.

Whether the nay-sayers liked it or not, the commission intended to supply soldiers with items they lacked and to police the camps and hospitals to keep them clean. Some of the opposition to this work softened after Bull Run; sixteen commission wagons had driven there to bring out wounded when most of the Union soldiers were fleeing the other way.

The commission recruited and united great masses of women all across the North, giving focus and direction to volunteer work that had been largely individual during the early weeks of the war. In Lehigh Station, as elsewhere, ladies organized the first of many Sanitary Fairs to raise money and gather goods for the organization.

While Scipio Brown was bringing the rest of his waifs to the newly expanded building and settling them in with a Hungarian couple hired to supervise the place, Constance was busy planning a Sanitary Fair for the second Friday and Saturday in November. The site was Hazard's shipping and receiving warehouse down by the railroad tracks beside the canal.

Wotherspoon kept crews working two days and nights to clear the building by loading huge shipments of iron plate onto a series of special trains. Virgilia helped as a committee member and so did Brett, who justified it on two grounds: her husband was a Union officer and, even if he weren't, humanitarian concerns in this case outweighed partisan ones. The ultimate aim of the fair and the commission was the saving of lives. Brett's real problem in connection with the fair was working with Virgilia. It was difficult.

From the first hour, the fair was a success, drawing huge crowds from the valley. Great loops of patriotic bunting decorated the walls and rafters of the warehouse. The most popular display featured posed photographs of some of the brave boys of Colonel Tilghman Good's Forty-seventh Pennsylvania Volunteers, the valley's own regiment, together with a greatly enlarged newspaper likeness of General McClellan. The sketch artist for the local paper exhibited satiric portraits of Slidell and Mason, the reb commissioners to Europe who had been dragged off the British mail packet *Trent* early in the month; the pair was presently imprisoned in Boston, which outraged the Queen's government and provoked threats from Lord Lyons, British minister in Washington.

There were military exhibits—stacked arms, contents of a typical haversack, an authentic canteen authentically pierced by a ball —and booths for collection of food, reading material, and clothing. Virgilia manned the clothing booth. A committee member had somehow obtained a regulation army tunic of dark blue shoddy, from which small squares had been cut. Every fifteen minutes, Virgilia would gather a crowd, then conduct her demonstration. Holding a square of shoddy over a bowl, she poured water on the material. The shoddy disintegrated into little pellets, which she distributed to the outraged spectators, coupling this with a request for decent clothing to be deposited in the barrels provided.

The work excited her; she was striking a small but useful blow against the South. She also felt quite pleased with her appearance. Constance had loaned her a shawl and Brett a cameo brooch to pin it at the bosom of her dark brown dress. She had done her hair in a silk net and put on teardrop earrings of iridescent opal, also borrowed. Because of her speaking skills, polished by appearances at abolitionist rallies, she was by far the best demonstrator in the hall. She earned a compliment from her sector chairman and a more important one from a man she didn't know.

He was a major from the Forty-seventh. While Virgilia tore the shoddy apart verbally and literally, he watched from across the aisle, in front of the cologne booth; soldiers were begging for perfume to defend against the stench of camp sinks and open drains.

The officer studied Virgilia during the demonstration. She lost her train of thought and faltered when his eye dropped from her face to her breasts, then shifted back. He left supporting the arm of a woman, perhaps his wife, but those few moments in which he looked at Virgilia were immensely important to her.

Always before, feeling and looking ugly, she had never appealed to any men except outcasts, like poor Grady. But there had been a sea change, and the major of volunteers had found her, if not beautiful, at least worthy of notice. The profundity of the change couldn't be denied; realizing it left her euphoric.

Virgilia experienced a letdown following the final day of the fair. She roved the house and town, knowing she must leave, must find a direction for herself. The days passed, and still she couldn't.

Nearly two weeks after the fair, Constance brought a letter to the dinner table. "It's from Dr. Howe, of the Sanitary Commission. He's an old friend."

"Is he? From where?" Virgilia asked.

"Newport. He and his wife summered there when we did. Don't you remember?" Virgilia shook her head and bent to her plate; she had managed to forget almost everything about those years.

Brett spoke. "Does the doctor say anything about the fair?"

"Indeed he does. He says ours was one of the most successful thus far. At a dinner party, he reported the fact to Miss Dix herself—here, read it." She passed the letter to Brett, seated on her right.

Brett scanned the letter, then murmured, "Miss Dix. Is she the New England woman I've read about? The one who's worked so hard for reform of the asylums?"

Constance nodded. "You probably saw the long piece about her in *Leslie's*. She's very famous and very dedicated. The article said Florence Nightingale inspired her to go to Washington when war broke out. Miss Nightingale landed at Scutari, in the Crimea, with thirty-seven Englishwomen, and they saved scores of lives that might have been lost otherwise. Miss Dix has been superintendent of army nurses since the summer."

Virgilia looked up. "They are using women as nurses?"

"At least a hundred," Brett replied. "Billy told me. The women get a salary, a living allowance, transportation—and the privilege of bathing soldiers, most of whom are pretty unenthusiastic about the idea, Billy said."

"I understand the surgeons are violently opposed to the nurses," Constance added. "But that's a doctor for you—guarding his little scrap of territory like a dog." She hadn't missed Virgilia's sudden animation. She turned to her. "Would nursing work interest you?"

"I think it might—though I don't suppose I'd qualify."

Constance considered it a kindness to withhold certain details from the piece in *Leslie's*. Miss Dix required no medical or scientific training from her recruits; all she asked was that they be over thirty and not attractive. So Constance could truthfully say, "I disagree. You'd be perfect. Would you like me to write Dr. Howe for a letter of introduction?"

"Yes." Then, more strongly, "Yes, please."

That night, Virgilia was sleepless with excitement. Perhaps she had found a way to serve the Union cause and strike at those responsible for the death of her lover. When she finally closed her eyes, she dreamed lurid dreams.

Grady's grave opened. He rose from it, bits of earth falling from his eyes and nose and mouth as he held out his hand, pleading for someone to avenge him.

The picture blurred, replaced by an unfamiliar plantation where dreamy black figures bucked up and down, impregnating moaning colored girls to beget more human chattels.

Then, a long row of men in gray; she watched each being shot, shot again, shot a third and fourth time, blood spatters multiplying on the breasts of their tunics while one man in Union blue fired endlessly. She knew the slayer. She had nursed him in a field hospital till he was once more fit for duty.

She awoke sweating and excited.

In the note included with his letter of introduction, Dr. Howe offered two pieces of advice: Virgilia should not dress too elaborately for her interview with Miss Dix, and although the superintendent of nurses would be quick to detect raw flattery, a discreet bit of praise for *Conversations on Common Things* would not be out of order. Miss Dix's little book of household advice had sold steadily ever since its publication in 1824. It was in its sixtieth printing; the author was proud of her child.

Virgilia reached Washington during an early December warm spell. When she stepped down to the sunlit train platform, she wrinkled her nose at the odor arising from eight pine crates on a baggage wagon. Water stained the wood, seeped from the joints, and splashed on the platform. She asked a baggage man what the boxes contained.

"Soldiers. Weather like this, the ice don't hold."

"Has there been a battle?"

"Not any big ones that I know about. These boys likely died of the flux or something similar. You hang around a while, you'll see hundreds of them boxes."

Swallowing back something in her throat, Virgilia moved away, carrying her own portmanteau. No wonder the commission considered its work so necessary.

At ten the next morning, she entered the office of Dorothea Dix. Miss Dix, a spinster of sixty, was neat and orderly in her dress, her gestures, and her speech. "It is a pleasure to meet you, Miss Hazard. You have a brother in Secretary Cameron's department, do you not?"

"Two of them, actually. The second is a commissioned officer working for General Ripley. And my youngest brother is with the engineers in Virginia. It was his wife who recommended your book, which I thoroughly enjoyed." She prayed Miss Dix wouldn't ask a question about the contents, since she hadn't bothered to buy or borrow a copy.

"I am happy to hear it. Will you see your brothers during your stay in the city?"

"Oh, naturally. We're very close." Did it sound too exaggerated, making the lie apparent? "It's my hope that my stay will be permanent. I would like to be a nurse, though I'm afraid I have no formal training."

"Any intelligent female can quickly learn the technical aspects. What she cannot acquire, if she does not already possess it, is the one trait I consider indispensable."

Miss Dix folded her hands and regarded Virgilia with gray-blue eyes whose sternness seemed at odds with the femininity of her long neck and her soft voice.

"Yes?" Virgilia prompted.

"Fortitude. The women in my nurse corps confront filth, gore, depravity, and crudity that good breeding forbids me to describe. My nurses are subjected to hostility from patients and also from the doctors, who are, in theory, our allies. I have definite ideas about the work we do and how it must be done. I tolerate no disagreement—a characteristic that further alienates certain poli-

271

ticians and surgeons. Those are challenges we face. Yet the greatest one remains the challenge to human courage. What you will do if you join us, Miss Hazard, is what I have done for many years, because someone must. You will not merely look into hell; you will walk there."

Virgilia breathed with soft sibilance, trying to conceal the sensual excitement seizing her again. In blinding visions that hid Miss Dix, windrows of young men in cadet gray fell bleeding and screaming. Grady grinned at the spectacle, showing the fine artificial teeth she had bought to replace the ones pulled out to mark him as a slave—

"Miss Hazard?"

"I'm sorry. Please forgive me. A momentary dizziness."

A frown. "Do you have such spells frequently?"

"Oh, no—no! It's the heat."

"Yes, it is excessive for December. How do you respond to what I told you?"

Virgilia dabbed her upper lip with her handkerchief. The bright light through the windows showed the scars on her cheeks; she had worn no powder. "I was active in abolitionist work, Miss Dix. As a consequence, I often saw—" she forced more strength into her voice—"the ravaged bodies of escaped slaves who had been whipped or burned by their masters. I saw scars, hideous disfigurement. I bore it. I can bear the rigors of nursing."

At long last the woman from Boston smiled at the visitor. "I admire your certainty. It is a good sign. Your appearance is suitable and Dr. Howe's recommendation enthusiastic. Shall we turn to particulars of your compensation and living arrangements?"

42

Lieutenant Colonel Orry Main's first forty-eight hours in Richmond were frantic. He found temporary quarters in a boardinghouse, signed papers, took the oath, bought his uniforms, and presented himself to Colonel Bledsoe, in charge of operations at the War Department offices, on the Ninth Street side of Capitol Square.

A clerk named Jones, a Marylander with a sour, secretive air, showed Orry his desk behind one of the flimsy partitions that divided the office. Next day Secretary Benjamin received him. The plump little man had replaced Walker, the blunt-spoken Alabama lawyer blamed for the failure to capitalize on the Manassas victory, as well as for recent military inaction.

"Delighted you're with us at last, Colonel Main." The secretary exuded camaraderie, except in his unreadable eyes. "I understand we're dining together Saturday night."

Orry expressed surprise. Benjamin said, "The invitation is probably at your lodgings now. Angela Mallory sets a superb table, and the secretary's juleps are renowned. Mr. Mallory is full of praise for the work your brother and Bulloch are doing in Liverpool—ah, but I imagine you are more interested in hearing about your own duties."

"Yes, sir."

"The spot you're to fill has been empty too long. It is a job both necessary and, I regret to say, difficult, because it requires contact with a person of odious disposition. Does the name Winder mean anything?"

273

Orry thought a bit. "At West Point, they used to talk about General William Winder. He lost the battle of Bladensburg in—1814, was it?" Benjamin nodded. "Now it's coming back. Winder fought from a superior position with superior forces, but the British whipped him anyway, then marched unopposed to Washington and burned it. Later, I understand, they named a building after him when they rebuilt the town, but professionals always cite him as one of the bunglers who prompted reform in the army by means of reform at West Point. I suppose you could say Sylvanus Thayer was appointed because of him."

"It is Winder's son to whom I refer. He was a tactical officer at West Point for a period."

"That I didn't know."

With noticeable care in selection of his words, Benjamin continued, "He was, in fact, an instructor when President Davis attended the institution. Thus, when Major Winder came here from Maryland earlier this year, the President had good memories of him. Winder was appointed brigadier general and provost marshal. His offices are close by. I will try to prepare you by explaining that Winder is nominally charged with apprehending military criminals and aliens. In other words, he's a glorified policeman—which in itself would not be a problem were he not also one of those persons in whom advancing age induces inflexibility. Finally, and regrettably, he is a martinet. Yet, in spite of it all, he enjoys the President's favor." Benjamin gave him a level look. "For the time being."

Orry nodded to signify understanding. He now had a clue as to why the word difficult had been used to describe his new duties.

Benjamin told him that the provost marshal had recruited a number of men listed on his personnel roster as professional detectives. "I characterize them as plug-uglies. Imported ones at that. Yankee scum who neither understand nor behave like Southerners. They appear more suited for ejecting hooligans from saloons and ten-pin alleys than for careful detective work. But, as I indicated, they are responsible for investigation of military as well as civil wrongdoing. Because of the general's, ah, character, they tend to exceed their authority. However, regardless of the nature of the case or the severity of the offense, I will not have them acting against the best interest of the army. I will not have them usurping the powers of this department. When they try, we curb them. Of course someone must be in charge of that effort.

The last man was not up to the responsibility. Hence my pleasure at your arrival."

Again, that direct stare. Orry, not a little intimidated by what was in store for him, got a shock when Benjamin revealed something else.

"Also, I regret to say, Winder is assuming authority for local prisons. If he does not enforce humane standards of treatment for captives, it could hurt us in the diplomatic sphere, especially with European recognition still in doubt. In short, Colonel, there are any number of ways the general can harm the Confederacy, and we must prevent him from doing so."

It struck Orry that the secretary was reaching into questionable areas; he was responsible for military, not foreign, policy, yet his treatment of Winder was designed to affect both. Benjamin must have seen the doubt on Orry's face. He leaned back and continued.

"You will discover that lines of authority in this government are not clear. The government, in fact, often resembles a maze at an English country house: difficult to picture in total and difficult to negotiate because there are so many passages that cross and look alike. You let me worry about interdepartmental problems; you deal with the general."

"The secretary will permit me to observe that General Winder out-ranks me."

"So he does—until such time as he presents a direct threat to the welfare of this department. Then we shall see who ranks whom." Benjamin brought his chair forward and gave Orry a look that revealed the iron beneath the silk. "I'm confident you will handle your duties with tact and skill, Colonel."

Not a hope, that; an order.

Next morning Orry paid his courtesy call on the provost marshal, whose office was an ugly frame building on Broad Street near Capitol Square. The moment Orry entered, negative impressions began to accumulate. A couple of Winder's plug-uglies, civilians wearing muddy boots and slouch hats, lounged on benches and stared at him as he approached the clerks. Orry didn't miss the huge revolvers worn by the detectives.

He had trouble gaining the attention of the clerks. They were engaged in loud argument and swearing at each other. He rapped on the railing separating the benches from the work area. The clerks ceased their shouting. With odors of beer and overflowing spittoons swirling around him, Orry stated his business.

Brigadier General John Henry Winder kept him waiting one hour. When Orry was finally admitted, he saw a stout officer who looked much older than sixty. Pure white hair jutted from his head in tufts that appeared to have gone uncombed, untrimmed, and unwashed for some time. Winder's skin was flaking from dryness, and the permanent inverted U of his mouth showed he didn't make smiling a habit.

Orry strove to introduce himself pleasantly and stated his hope for a good working relationship. The provost wasn't interested.

"I know your boss is a friend of Davis, but so am I. We'll get along all right if you follow two rules: don't get in my way and don't question my authority."

Less friendly, Orry said, "I believe the secretary also has rules, General. In matters that affect the army in any way, I am instructed to make sure proper procedure is fol—"

"Hell with procedure. This is war. There are enemies all over Richmond." Eyes like those of some ancient turtle fixed on Orry. "In uniform and out. I shall uproot them and not care a damn about *procedure*. I'm busy. You're dismissed."

"Your servant, General." He saluted, but Winder had already bent over a file and didn't acknowledge it. Red-faced, Orry stalked out.

Work had emptied the department offices of everyone except a few clerks, Jones among them. Orry described his meeting, and Jones sneered. "Typical behavior. There isn't a man in the government I detest more. You'll soon feel the same way."

"Damned if I don't already."

Jones sniggered and returned to writing in some kind of journal. Sometime later, Orry saw Jones return the book to a lower desk drawer with a surreptitious look around. *Does he keep a diary? Better watch what I say in front of that fellow.*

Still reacting to Winder, he felt in need of a drink when the day ended and he started home through the December dark. He stopped at a rowdy, cheerful place called Mrs. Muller's Lager Beer Saloon. With a schooner in front of him, he leafed through the *Examiner,* which was once again excoriating the Davis administration, this time for the state of the South's rail system. The paper denounced it as incapable of moving large numbers of troops between the east and the Kentucky-Tennessee theater.

The complaint was not an unfamiliar one. Orry knew the South's rolling stock was old and many sections of rail worn out —and there was no manufactory in the South capable of replacing either. It was Cooper Main's decade-old warning about the inadequacy of Southern industry coming true. Davis's journalistic foes were now saying it might doom the war.

He finished his beer and with a touch of guilt called for another. He wanted to forget the work Benjamin had given him. Here he was, a trained soldier, assigned to spy on another soldier. He supposed he had accepted the possibility of rotten duty when he took the commission. There was nothing to be done except carry out orders.

The longer he stayed at the crowded bar, the more depressed he became. He overheard conversations full of gloom and invective. Davis was a "damned dictator," Judah Benjamin a "pet of the tyrant," the war "fool's business." No doubt many of these same men had cheered the news of the bombardment of Sumter, Orry thought as he left.

A more positive air pervaded the Saturday-night dinner party at the home of Navy Secretary Stephen Mallory. A Floridian born of Yankee parents, Mallory had the good luck—or the misfortune, depending on how you looked at it—to head a department that Jefferson Davis ignored almost completely. The secretary quickly made his strong views known to his guest.

"I never regarded secession as anything but a synonym for revolution. But now that we're fighting, I intend to extend myself and my department to beat the enemy, not win his approval or his recognition of our right to exist as a nation. On that and many other matters, the Chief Executive and I differ. Another julep, Colonel?"

Orry's head was already whirling from the first one and from the glitter of the gathering. The brightest jewel was Mallory's Spanish wife, Angela, a gracious and gorgeous woman. She praised Cooper—she kept track of navy matters—and introduced Orry to her little girls before bundling them away to bed.

During the superb meal there was much toasting of the Confederacy, and especially, its imprisoned representatives, Mason and Slidell, both favorites of the archsecessionist faction. So was Benjamin, Orry discovered after some table conversation. Orry admired the sleek little man's aplomb but wondered about the sincerity of his convictions; he struck Orry as more of a survivor than a zealot. Still, the secretary brought wit and jollity to the gathering. The table was so amply supplied with fine food and drink and china and crystal that Orry had trouble remembering it was wartime. For a very short while he even forgot how much he missed Madeline.

As the party broke up, Benjamin invited him to come along to one of his favorite haunts: "Johnny Worsham's. I like to go against his faro bank. Johnny runs a fine place. A man can find the sporting crowd there and test himself against lady luck, but he can also be sure of discretion about his presence and an honest deal."

Benjamin said he liked a vigorous stroll in the night air, and Orry didn't object. The secretary sent his driver ahead to Worsham's; Orry had come to Mallory's in a hack. They set out and were just passing the Spotswood when they encountered some noisy people leaving another party. Someone accidentally bumped Orry.

"Ashton!"

Because he was startled, his exclamation sounded friendlier than it might have otherwise. His sister clung to the arm of her porcine husband and gave him a smile with all the warmth of a January freeze. "Dear Orry! I heard you were in town—married, too. Is Madeline here?"

"No, but she'll join me soon."

"How splendid you look in your uniform." Ashton's smile for the secretary was noticeably warmer. "Is he working for you, Judah?"

"I am happy to say he is."

"How fortunate you are. Orry, my dear, we must take supper when all of us can find time. James and I are positively dizzy with the social whirl. Some weeks we scarcely have five minutes to ourselves."

"Quite right," Huntoon said. His glasses steamed in the cold; the two words were his contribution to the conversation. Ashton waved and flirted with her eyes at Benjamin as her husband helped her into their carriage.

"Attractive young woman," Benjamin murmured as they

278

moved on. "I was charmed the moment we met. It's pleasant for you to have a sister in Richmond."

No point hiding what would eventually be public knowledge. "We are not on good terms, I'm afraid."

"Pity," said Benjamin, with a smile of condolence that was small, perfect, and hollow. I am sailing with a master navigator of the political seas, Orry thought. He knew he would never hear from Ashton about supper. That suited him perfectly.

"Ashton?"

"No."

Turning away from his hand and his pleading whine, she moved her pillow to the edge of the bed, as far from him as possible. She puffed the pillow and buried her left cheek in it. Just as delicious thoughts of Powell stole into her head, he bothered her again.

"Quite a surprise, seeing your brother."

"An unpleasant one."

"Do you really plan for the three of us to dine together?"

"After he banished me from the home where I was raised?" A contemptuous monosyllable answered the question. "I wish you'd be quiet. I'm worn out."

Worn out with him, anyway. Of Powell she could never get enough—not enough of his skilled lovemaking or his decidedly unconventional personality, which she was beginning to discover and appreciate.

Ashton saw Powell at least once a week, twice if Huntoon's schedule worked in her favor. The assignations took place on Church Hill. Although there was still risk in going to his front doorstep, she preferred it to sneaking in through the back garden. In fact, she rather liked the danger of arriving on Franklin Street in the daylight; once inside, she was completely safe, which wouldn't have been true at some tawdry rooming house.

James never questioned her about the dalliance. He didn't even know about her mysterious absences from their house. He was too stupid, too preoccupied with his petty tasks at the Treasury Department, which kept him working till eight or nine every night.

Powell not only fulfilled Ashton with his occasionally cruel lovemaking, he also fascinated her as a person. He was a hot patriot, yet ruthless in his devotion to his own cause. There was no paradox. He loved the Confederacy but hated "King Jeff." He believed in secession but not in this secessionist government. He intended to survive the doomed war and prosper.

"I have a year or so to do it. Davis will blunder along unchecked for some time yet. Our cause is just—we should and we could win. With the right man leading us, I could become a prince of a new kingdom. Under present circumstances and the present dictator, I'm afraid all I can become is rich."

A patriot, a speculator, an incomparable lover—she had never met a man quite as complex, and surely never would again. By comparison, Huntoon suffered even more than he had in times past.

No matter. The marriage, frail from the beginning, had now perished. The past few months had convinced Ashton that Huntoon couldn't provide social or financial advancement because he lacked the slyness, the nerve, and the brains. In that one short argument with Davis, he had fashioned his own noose and sprung the trap. Weekly, her loathing grew, as did her certainty that she was in love with Lamar Powell.

In love. How strange to realize the familiar words could apply to her. She had experienced the same emotion only once before. Then Billy Hazard had rejected her in favor of Brett, starting the chain of events that ended with her damned brother banishing her from Mont Royal.

Ashton doubted that Powell loved her. She judged him incapable of loving anyone except himself. It didn't concern her. She had enough to give for both of—

"Ashton?"

Her back was still to her husband. She snarled a vile word and pounded her fist on the pillow. Why wouldn't he leave her alone? "What is it?"

A soft, repulsive hand crept over her shoulder. "Why are you so cold to me? It's been weeks since I was permitted my marital rights."

God, even when he whined of love he sounded like a lawyer. He was going to pay for disturbing her. She rolled away, tossing her hair, found a match and struck it. She jerked the chimney from the bedside lamp, lit the wick, and slammed the chimney back. Braced on her elbows, she pulled her nightdress above her hips.

"All right, come on."

"Wh—what?"

"Get that smelly nightshirt off and take what you want while

280

you can." The lamp set small fires in her eyes. She bent her knees, spread them, clenched her teeth. *"Come on."*

He struggled with the long flannel garment, his voice muffled inside. "I'm not sure I can perform on command—" As he dropped the shirt beside the bed, exposing his white body, she saw he was right. Huntoon looked ready to cry. Ashton laughed at him.

"You never can. Even if that scrawny thing does show a little life, it's no better than a thimble inside me. How did you ever expect to keep a wife content? You're pathetic."

And she snapped her legs together, jerked her nightdress down, seized the lamp, and left the bedroom.

Huntoon listened to her marching downstairs. "You mean bitch," he shouted, momentarily not caring whether Homer or any of the other house people heard him. Serve her right if they did.

The anger wilted as quickly as the slight stiffness, all he had been able to manage while she yelled at him. Her cruelty did something more than hurt him. It confirmed a suspicion that had been with him for some days. There was another man.

Huntoon flung himself back in bed and put his forearm over his eyes. Everything in Richmond was awry. He was trapped in menial work for a government he had first distrusted and now despised. He felt the same about Davis, whose foes no longer formed a company or a regiment, but a small army. Important men: Vice President Stephens; Joe Johnston; Vance of North Carolina and Brown of Georgia, governors who said Davis was usurping their powers; Toombs, the former secretary of state, to whom Davis had been forced to hand over a brigadier's commission to stop his scathing attacks.

The President dictated to the army and truckled to the Virginia clique, as if that were the only way to make his shabby pedigree acceptable. He was botching the war, mismanaging the nation, and—an easy extension in a distraught mind—thwarting Huntoon's ambition, thereby causing the rift with Ashton.

For an hour, he lay imagining her naked with another man. Some officer perhaps? That wily little Jew with his cabinet post and his fine manners? Or could it be a man like that sleek, patently untrustworthy Georgian, Powell? Dry-mouthed, Huntoon pictured his wife coupling with various suspects. He wanted to know the man's identity. He would confront her; demand that she give him the name of—

He stopped thinking that way. He couldn't do it. Knowing would probably kill him.

When two hours had gone by, he heaved himself out of bed, donned his robe, and went downstairs. The house had grown cold. His breath plumed visibly against the glow of a lamp in the parlor. He stepped into the doorway.

"Ashton? I came to apologize for—"

The sentence trailed away. He grimaced. She breathed lightly and evenly, curled in a large leather chair, fast asleep. Her legs were drawn up near her bosom and her arms clasped around them. On her face a smile of dreams, sensually contented.

He turned and stumbled toward the staircase, his ears ringing, that smile acid-etched on his memory. Tears came. He hated her but knew he was powerless to do anything about it, which only worsened the feeling. He climbed the stairs like an old man as the hall clock tolled three.

43

At Belvedere, Brett continued to fight her own daily war with loneliness.

One consolation: Billy's letters sounded more cheerful. His old unit, Engineer Company A, had returned to Washington and was quartered on the grounds of the federal arsenal along with two of the three new volunteer companies congressionally approved in August—B from Maine and C from Massachusetts.

Billy still maintained a starchy pride in belonging to "the old company." But he wrote that most of the regulars accepted the new recruits and were attempting to make them overnight experts in every skill from pontoniering to road building.

The newly constituted Battalion of Engineers incorporated the old cadre of corps regulars, and was now attached to McClellan's Army of the Potomac and commanded by Captain James Duane, '48, an officer Billy respected. In order to stay with the battalion, Billy's friend Lije Farmer had been required to resign as captain of volunteers and take a regular army commission as a first lieutenant. *Oldest one in the Potomac Army, he claims, but he is content, and I am glad he's with us.*

Brett was happy her husband was back where he wanted to be. With winter bringing military hibernation, she hoped he would be relatively inactive and thus out of danger for several months. She wondered about chances for a leave. She missed him so; there was many a night when she slept only an hour or two.

She helped around the house as much as she could, but that still left great stretches of empty time. Constance had gone back to Washington to be with George. The strange, ill-tempered colored man, Brown, was there, too, gathering more strays. Virgilia had won a place among Miss Dix's nurses and wouldn't be returning. Brett was by herself, moody and lonesome.

One steel-colored December day, she bundled up, walked to the gate of Hazard's, then up the hill to Brown's building. She found two of the children, a boy and a girl, studying at a board with Mr. Czorna, the Hungarian. His wife was stirring soup at the stove. Brett greeted each of them.

"Morning, madam," the gray-haired woman replied, deferential but not especially friendly. Each had an accent: Mrs. Czorna's heavily European, Brett's heavily Southern. Brett knew the couple didn't trust her—not exactly a novelty in Lehigh Station.

She started to say something else but noticed a child in the adjoining room. Sitting on a cot beside the partition dividing the area, the little coppery girl stared at her hands with her head bowed.

"Is the child ill, Mrs. Czorna?"

"Not sick, not that kind of ill. Before he go, Mr. Brown bought her a turtle in a store. Two nights ago, when we had the snow, the turtle crawled out the window and froze. She won't let me take it and bury it. She won't eat, she won't speak or laugh—I miss her laugh. It warms this place. I don't know what to do."

283

Touched by the sight of the forlorn figure in the other room, Brett followed her impulse and spoke. "May I try something?"

"Go ahead." The statement, the shrug, said a Carolina plantation girl didn't seem the right person to deal with a runaway black child. It was a familiar canard.

"Her name's Rosalie, isn't it?"

"That's right."

Brett walked to the dormitory and sat down beside the little girl, who didn't move. In the open palm at which the child was staring lay the dead turtle, on its back—not smelling good at all.

"Rosalie? May I take your turtle and give him a warm place to rest?"

The child stared at Brett, nothing in her eyes. She shook her head.

"Please let me, Rosalie. He deserves to be warm and snug while he sleeps. It's cold in here. Can't you feel it? Come help me outside. Then we'll go to my house for some cookies and cocoa. You can see the big mama cat who had kittens last week."

She folded her hands, waiting. The child stared at her. Slowly, Brett reached out to grasp the turtle. Rosalie glanced down but didn't say or do anything. After Brett found the child's coat, she asked Mrs. Czorna for a large spoon, and they went out behind the whitewashed building. Brett knelt and used the spoon to chisel a hole in the wintry ground. She wrapped the turtle in a clean rag, laid him away, and replaced the soil carefully. She looked up to see Rosalie crying, emotion shaking loose at last in silent heaving sobs, then audible ones.

"Oh, you poor child. Come here."

She stretched out her arms. The little girl ran to her. While the sharp wind blew, Brett held the trembling body. She stroked Rosalie's hair and, with a small start, made a discovery. In her years of helping on the plantation, she had picked up bundled black babies or held the hands of older children many a time, yet always stopped shy of the ultimate giving—an embrace.

Had she been guided by some unexpressed belief that Negroes were somehow unfit for a white woman to touch? She didn't know, but this moment in the gray morning jarred her to awareness. Rosalie felt no different from any other child hurting.

Brett hugged her tight and felt the little girl's hands slip around her neck and then the cold wetness of her cheek pressing hers for warmth.

44

Aunt Belle Nin died on the tenth of October. She had been sinking for days, the victim of what the Mains' doctor termed a poison in the blood. She was alert to the end, smoking a cob pipe that Jane packed for her and commenting on dreams that had shown her scenes of the afterlife. "I don't feel bad about going, except for one reason," she said through the smoke. "I'll probably meet my two husbands on the other side, and I could do without that. I'm leaving a better world than I was born into—the light of the day of jubilo will be breaking next year or soon after. I know it in my heart."

"So do I," said Jane. They had agreed for a long time that if war came, the South would fail and fall. Now freedom was a scent on the wind, like that of rain before a heat spell broke. Aunt Belle took several more puffs, smiled at her niece, handed her the pipe, and closed her eyes.

Madeline readily consented that Aunt Belle be buried at Mont Royal the next day—the same day a fire swept Charleston. There was scorched earth for blocks, six hundred buildings lost, billions of dollars' worth of property. Black arsonists were blamed. The news reached Mont Royal the evening after the funeral; a courier galloping to the Ashley plantation warned of possible uprising.

While the courier was speaking to Madeline and Meek, Jane was walking alone in the cool moonlight by the river. A creak of boards at the head of the dock alarmed her. Cuffey was always watching her these days, and the moment she turned and saw the dark, threatening silhouette of a man, she thought he had followed her. She stood motionless, filled with fear.

"Just me, Miss Jane."

"Oh, Andy. Hello." She relaxed, pulling at her shawl. The early winter moon lit his face as he turned his head slightly, approaching in a cautious, shy way.

"Wanted to say how much your aunt's passing grieved me. Didn't think it was my place to speak to you at the burial."

"Thank you, Andy." To her surprise, Jane found herself gazing at him slightly longer than politeness dictated. She had recently grown much more aware of him.

"Like to sit down a minute? Visit?" he asked. "Don't get much of a chance to see you, working all day—"

"Aren't you chilly? You have nothing but that shirt."

"Oh, I'm fine." He smiled. "Perfect. Here, let me help you—"

He grasped her hand so she wouldn't fall as she sat on the edge of the dock. A fish leaped, scattering liquid moonlight. When it struck him that he had been forward when he touched her, a look of mortification appeared on his face. That made her think all the more of him.

Truthfully, Jane was as nervous as he was. She had never had much contact with boys in Rock Hill. Too independent, for one thing. Too scared, for another. She was a virgin and had been sternly advised by Widow Milsom to keep herself in that state until she found a man she loved, trusted, and wanted to marry. She knew she was attractive, or anyway not ugly. But none of the gentlemen around Rock Hill had marriage in mind when they attempted to court her.

"Terrible about that fire in Charleston."

"Terrible," she agreed, though she felt no sympathy for the white property owners. She had no desire to see lives lost, but if every plantation in the state burned down, she wouldn't mind.

"Reckon you'll be starting north soon."

"Yes, I suppose. Now that Aunt Belle's buried, I'm—" She checked, not wanting to say free, in case it would hurt him. It was a potent word, *free*. "—I'm able to do that."

He examined his fingers, searched the bright river, finally exploded. "Hope you don't mind me saying something else."

"I won't know till you say it, will I?"

He laughed, more at ease. "Wish you'd stay, Miss Jane."

"You don't have to call me miss all the time."

"Seems proper. You're a fine, pretty woman—smarter than I'll ever be."

"You're smart, Andy. I can tell. You'll do even better when you learn to read and write."

"That's part of what I mean, Mi—Jane. Once you leave, won't be anyone here who could teach me. Nobody to teach any of us." He leaned closer. "Jubilo's coming. The soldiers of Lincoln are coming. But I can't get along in a white man's world the way I am now. White people write letters, do sums, carry on business. I'm no better fixed for that, I'm no better fixed for freedom than some old hound who lies in the sun all day."

It was not a plea so much as a summation of the plight of a majority in the South: the black people. With Andy, she believed the day of freedom was rapidly approaching. How could slaves meet and deal with the change? They weren't prepared.

She felt a prick of anger then. "You're trying to make me feel ashamed because I won't stay and teach. It isn't my task. It isn't my duty."

"Please don't be angry. That isn't all."

"What do you mean, it isn't all? I don't understand you."

He gulped. "Well—Miss Madeline, she'll be leaving soon to join Mr. Orry. Meek isn't a mean overseer, but he's a hard one. The people need another steadying hand, another friend like Miss Madeline."

"And you think I could replace her?"

"You ain't—aren't a white woman, but you're free. It's the next best thing."

Why the rush of disappointment, then? She didn't know. "I'm sorry I misunderstood, and I thank you for your faith in me, but —" She uttered a little cry as he snatched her hand.

"I don't want you to go, because I like you."

He spoke so fast, it sounded like one long word. The instant he finished, he shut his mouth and looked ready to die of shame. She could barely hear him when he added, "I apologize."

"No, don't. What you said is—" how tongue-tied she felt— "sweet." Inclining her head, she brushed his cheek with her lips. She had never been so bold. She was as embarrassed as Andy; churning. She pushed against the dock. "It's chilly. We ought to go."

"May I walk along?"

"I'd like it if you did."

287

The three-quarters of a mile to the cabins was traversed in silence, a silence so strained it hurt. They reached the slave street, the far end washed by lemon lamplight from the overseer's house Meek had repainted inside and out. Andy said, "G'night, Miss Jane," in a strangled voice. He veered away toward his own cabin without breaking stride. A last sentence floated behind. "Hope I didn't make you too mad."

No, but he had unsettled her. Mightily. She had developed a strong romantic interest in Andy; it had crept over her with stealth. Tonight, while drops of light fell from the jumping fish, she had come square up against it. It was a powerful pull against the magnet of the North.

Lord. After crying at the burial, she had been certain of her next step. Now she was all topsy-turvy and unsure—

"Boss nigger's the only one good enough for you, huh?"

"What's that?"

Alarmed by the voice from the dark, she searched and saw a form break from an unlit porch to the left. Cuffey ambled to her, took that admire-me stance of his, and said, "Guess you know who." With his tongue pressed against the back of his upper teeth, he made a scary little hissing sound. "I was head driver once. That make me good enough to walk you in the moonlight? I know all the ways to pleasure a gal. Been learnin' since I was nine or ten."

She started around him. He grabbed her forearm with a hand that hurt. "I asked you somethin', nigger. Am I good enough for you to go walkin' with or not?"

Jane struggled to hide her fright. "Nothing on earth would make you good enough. You let go of me or I'll go after your eyes with my fingernails, and while I'm at it, I'll yell for Mr. Meek."

"Meek's gonna die." Cuffey pushed his face near hers, his mouth spewing a fetid odor. "Him an' all the white folks who kicked and beat and bossed us all our lives. Their nigger pets gonna die, too. So, bitch, you better figure out which side—"

"Let go, you ignorant, foul-mouthed savage. A man like you doesn't deserve freedom. You're worthless for anything but spitting on."

She had listeners on various dark porches. A woman hee-heed, a man laughed outright. Cuffey spun left, then right, the whites of his eyes catching moonlight through the trees. His search for his unseen mockers left Jane free to tear loose and run. She dashed into her cabin and stood with her back against the door, panting.

She pulled her pallet against the door and on top of it laid the one Aunt Belle had used. She decided to leave the lamp burning as a further defense. The cabin was uncomfortable; oiled paper in the window frames didn't bar the cold. She pulled two thin blankets over herself and pressed her back against the door. She would feel it move if an intruder tried to open it.

She watched the lamp wick burning, saw the faces of two men in the flame. She would go as soon as she could.

Tomorrow.

During the night she dreamed of country roads choked with thousands of black people, wandering aimlessly. She dreamed of great malformed doors opening to reveal a room she had seen before. The room radiated blinding light; from its white heart, calling voices summoned her—

She woke to the crow of roosters and memories of Cuffey flooding her mind. She pushed these aside and seized on the swiftly fading dream images. Aunt Belle had always put stock in the importance of dreams, though she always said a person had to work hard to figure out the meanings. Jane did this and in an hour reached a decision.

It would be harder to stay than to leave. Despite Cuffey, there would be compensations. One was the help she could give her own people to prepare them a little for the jubilo she believed to be certain.

Another compensation might be Andy. But even without him, there was the call of conscience. She wasn't a Harriet Tubman or a Sojourner Truth; not a great woman; but if she did what she could, she could live with herself. She dressed, fixed her hair, and hurried to the great house to find Madeline.

Orry's wife was at breakfast. "Sit down, Jane. Will you have a biscuit and jam? Some tea?"

She was stunned by the invitation to share the table with the white mistress. She thanked Madeline, sitting opposite her but taking no food. She caught the scandalized look of a house girl returning to the kitchen.

"I came to discuss my leaving, Miss Madeline."

"Yes, I assumed that. Will it be soon? Whenever you go, I'll miss you. So will many others."

"That is what I wanted to speak to you about. I've changed my mind. I'd like to stay at Mont Royal a while longer."

"Oh, Jane—that would make me so happy. You're a bright young woman. I hope to start for Richmond before the end of the month. After I go, you could be of great assistance to Mr. Meek."

"The people I want to help are my own. They must be ready when jubilo comes."

Madeline's smile vanished. "You believe the South will lose?"

"Yes."

Madeline glanced toward the door to the kitchen; there were only the two of them in the dining room. "I confess I have the same dire feeling, though I don't dare admit it because it would destroy Meek's authority. And God knows how my husband would operate this place without—"

She broke off, dark eyes seeking Jane's. "I've said too much. I must trust you not to repeat any of it."

"I won't."

"What could you do to help the people get ready, as you call it?"

It was too soon to speak of teaching; a first concession must be won. "I'm not sure, but I know a place to look for the answer. Your library. I'd like your permission to take books and read them."

Madeline ticked a tiny spoon against the gold rim of her teacup. "You realize that's against the law?"

"I do."

"What do you hope to find in books?"

"Ideas—ways to help the people on this plantation."

"Jane, if I gave you permission, and if your reading or your actions caused any harm to this property and, more important, to anyone who lives here, white or black, I wouldn't deal with you through Mr. Meek. I'd do it with my own two hands. I'll have no unrest or violence stirred up."

"I wouldn't do that." Jane held back the last of the thought. *But someone else might.*

Madeline looked at her steadily. "I take that as another promise."

"You can. And the first one still stands. I won't encourage any of the people to run away, either. But I will try to find ideas to help them when they're free to go or stay, as they choose."

290

"You're a forthright young woman," Madeline said; it was far from a condemnation. She stood. "Come along."

Jane followed her to the foyer patterned with sunshine through the fanlight. Madeline reached for the handles of the library doors. "I could be flogged and run out of the state for this." But she seemed to take pride in opening the doors in a theatrical way and standing aside.

It was the room in her dream. Slowly, Jane walked in. Madeline slipped in after her and shut the doors soundlessly.

"Ideas have never frightened me, Jane. They are the chief salvation of this planet. Read as much of what's here as you want."

Leathery incense swirled from shelves without so much as an inch of empty space. Jane felt herself to be in a cathedral. She continued to stand silently, like a petitioner. Then she tilted her head back and raised her gaze to the books, all the books, while a radiance broke over her face.

45

"George, you mustn't rave so. You'll bring on a fit."

"But—but—"

"Have a cigar. Let me pour you a whiskey. Every night it's the same. You come home so upset. The children have noticed."

"Only a statue could stay calm in that place." He ripped his uniform collar open and stamped to the window, where snowflakes touched the glass and melted. "Do you know how I passed the afternoon? Watching this nitwit from Maine demonstrate his water-walker: two small canoes fitted onto his shoes. Just the thing for the infantry! Cross the rivers of Virginia in Biblical style!"

Constance held a hand over her mouth. George shook a finger. "Don't you dare laugh. What makes it worse is that I've interviewed *four* inventors of water-walkers in the last month. What kind of patriotic service is that, listening to men who ought to be committed?"

He pushed at his hair and gazed at the December snowfall without seeing it. Darkness lay on the city, and discouragement; an uneasy possibility of the war lasting a long time. The one shaft of light was McClellan, busy organizing and training for a spring campaign.

"Surely some intelligent inventors show up occasionally," Constance began.

"Of course. Mr. Sharps—whose breechloading rifles Ripley refuses to order, even though Colonel Berdan's special regiment was willing to pay the slight extra cost. The Sharps is newfangled, Ripley says. An army ordnance board tested the gun and praised it a mere eleven years ago, but it's newfangled." He kicked the leg of a stool so hard that it dented the toe of his boot and made him curse.

"Can nothing be done to overrule Ripley? Can't Cameron step in?"

"He's beset by his own problems. I don't think he'll last the month. But certainly something can be done. It was done in October. Not by us, however. Lincoln ordered twenty-five thousand breechloaders."

"He bypassed the department?"

"Do you blame him?" George sank to the sofa, his uniform and disposition in disarray. "I'll give you another example. There's a young fellow from Connecticut named Christopher Spencer. Been a machinist at Colt's in Hartford, among other things. He's patented an ingenious rapid-fire rifle you load by inserting a tube of seven cartridges into the stock. Do you know Ripley's objection to it?" She shook her head. "Our boys would fire too fast and waste ammunition."

"George, I can hardly believe that."

His hand shot up, witness fashion. "God's truth! We dare not equip the infantry with guns that might shorten the war. Ripley's had to give on the breechloaders—we're ordering a quantity for the cavalry—but he's adamant about the repeaters. So the President continues to do our work. This afternoon Bill Stoddard told me ten thousand Spencers are being ordered from the Executive Mansion. Hiram Berdan's sharpshooters will have some to try by Christmas."

George stormed up again, trailing smoke from a new cigar. "Do you have any notion of the damage Ripley's doing? Of how many young men may die because he abhors the thought of wasting ammunition? I can't take it much longer, Constance—thinking of the deaths we're causing while I pretend to be interested in some village idiot's water-walker—"

He lost volume toward the end. He stood smoking with his head bowed in front of the window framing the slow downdrift of the snow. She had often witnessed her husband's explosions of temper, but they were seldom mingled with this kind of despair. She slipped her arms around him from behind, pressed her breast to the back of his dark blue coat.

"I don't blame you for feeling miserable." She clasped her hands and leaned her cheek against his shoulder. "I have a piece of news. Two, actually. Father's in the Territory of New Mexico, trying to stay out of the way of the Union and Confederate armies maneuvering there. He feels confident he'll reach California by the end of the winter."

"Good." The reply was listless. "What else?"

"We've been invited to a levee for your old friend the general of the armies."

"Little Mac? He probably won't even speak to me now that he's top man." McClellan had been promoted November first; Scott was finished.

"George, George—" She turned him and looked into his eyes. "This isn't the man I know. My husband. You're so bitter."

"Coming here was a catastrophe. I'm wasting my time—doing no good at all. I should resign and go home with you and the children."

"Yes, I'm sure Ripley makes you feel that way." Soothingly, she caressed his face; the day had produced a rough stubble below the waxed points of his mustache. "Do you remember Corpus Christi, when we met? You said you wished the steamer for Mexico would leave without you—"

"That's right. I wanted to stay and court you. I wanted it more than anything."

"But you boarded with the others and sailed away."

"I had some sense of purpose then. A hope of accomplishing something. Now I'm just a party to bungling that may cost thousands of lives."

"Perhaps if Cameron's forced to resign, things will improve."

"In Washington? It's a morass of chicanery, stupidity, witless paper shuffling—but self-preservation has been raised to a high art. A few faces may change, nothing more."

"Give it a little longer. I think it's your duty. War is never easy on anyone. I learned that lying awake every night fearing for your safety in Mexico."

She kissed him, the barest tender touch of mouth and mouth. Some of his strain dissipated, leaving a face that was almost a boy's despite the markings of the years.

"What would I do without you, Constance? I'd never survive."

"Yes, you would. You're strong. But I'm glad you need me."

He clasped her close. "More than ever. All right, I'll stay a while longer. But you must promise to hire a good lawyer if I break down and murder Ripley."

On Monday, December 16, Britain was in mourning for the Queen's husband.

News of Albert's death the preceding Saturday had not yet crossed the Atlantic, but certain pieces of diplomatic correspondence, authored at Windsor Castle shortly before the prince consort's passing, had. Though not overly belligerent in tone, Albert continued to press for release of the Confederate commissioners.

Stanley knew it was going to happen, and soon, although not for any of the high-flown, moralistic reasons that would be handed out as sops to the press and the public. The government had to capitulate for two reasons: Great Britain was a major supplier of niter for American gunpowder, but she was currently withholding all shipments. Further, a second war couldn't be risked, especially when the latest diplomatic mail said the British were hastily armoring some of their fighting ships. The smoothbore guns placed to defend American harbors would be useless against an armored fleet.

December became a nexus of hidden but genuine desperations for the government. They threatened Stanley's little manufacturing empire, which had increased his net worth fifty percent in less than six months. Mounting panic drove him to extreme measures. Late at night, he jimmied drawers of certain desks and removed confidential memoranda long enough to read them and copy key phrases. He had frequent meetings with a man from Wade's staff in parks or unsavory saloons below the canal; at the meetings he turned over large amounts of information, without actually knowing whether his actions would help his cause. He was gambling that they would. He was laying all his bets on a single probability, said by some to be certainty: Cameron's fall.

Even Lincoln was threatened by the militancy of Wade and his crew. The new congressional committee was to be announced soon. Dominated by the true believers among the Republicans, it would curb the President's independence and run the war the way the radicals wanted it run.

For all these reasons, the atmosphere in the War Department had grown tense. So, on that Monday morning, having just received another bad jolt, Stanley thankfully absented himself. He hurried through a light snowfall to 352 Pennsylvania, where, above a bank and an apothecary's, three floors housed the city's and the nation's premier portrait studio, Brady's Photographic Gallery of Art. Stanley's watch showed he was nearly a half hour late for the sitting.

On Brady's first floor, a dapper receptionist sat among images of the great framed in gold or black walnut. Fenimore Cooper peered from a fading daguerreotype; rich Corcoran had been photographed life-size and artistically colored with crayon, a popular technique; and Brady still kept a hot-cyed John Calhoun on display.

The receptionist said Isabel and the twins were already in the studio. "Thank you," Stanley gasped as he rushed up the stairs, quickly short of breath because of his increasing weight. On the next floor he passed craftsmen decorating photographs with India ink, pastels, or the crayons Isabel had chosen for the family portrait. Before he reached the top floor, he heard his sons quarreling.

The studio was a spacious room dominated by skylights. Isabel greeted him by snapping, "The appointment was for noon."

"Departmental business kept me. There's a war in progress, you know." He sounded even nastier than his wife, which startled her.

"Mr. Brady, my apologies. Laban, Levi—stop that instantly." Stanley swept off his tall, snow-soaked hat and smacked one twin, then the other. The strapping adolescents froze, stunned by their father's uncharacteristic outburst.

"Delays are to be expected of someone in your position," Brady said smoothly. "No harm done." He hadn't become successful and prosperous by insulting important clients. He was a slender, bearded man nearing forty, expensively outfitted in a black coat, smart gray doeskin trousers, a sparkling shirt, and a black silk cravat that flowed down over a matching doeskin vest. He wore spectacles.

With crisp gestures, Brady signaled a young assistant, who repositioned the big gold clock against the red drapery backdrop. The clock face bore the name Brady, as did almost everything else in his business, including his published prints and his field wagons, one of which Stanley had seen overturned along the Bull Run retreat route.

"The light's marginal today," Brady observed. "I don't like to make portraits when there is no sun. The exposures are too long. Since this is a portrait for Christmas, however, we shall try. Chad?" He snapped his fingers, gestured. "To the left slightly." The assistant jumped to move the tripod bearing a white reflector board.

Brady cocked his head and studied the truculent twin sons of Mr. and Mrs. Hazard. "I believe I want the parents seated and the boys behind. They are active young fellows. We shall have to clamp their heads with the immobilizers."

Laban started to protest, but a growl from Stanley cut it short. The sitting lasted three-quarters of an hour. Brady repeatedly dove under the black hood or whispered instructions to the assistant, who slammed the huge plates into the camera with practiced haste. At the end, Brady thanked them and suggested they speak to the receptionist about delivery of the portrait. Then he hurried out. "Evidently we're not important enough to see him more than once," Isabel complained as they left.

"Oh, for God's sake, can't you ever worry about anything except your status?"

More in surprise than anger, she said, "Stanley, you're in a perfectly vile temper this morning. Why?"

"Something terrible's happened. Let's send the boys home in a hack, and I'll explain over some food at Willard's."

The sole with almonds was splendidly prepared, but Stanley had no appetite for anything but pouring out his anxiety. "I managed to get hold of a draft copy of Simon's annual report on departmental activities. There's a section they say Stanton drafted. It states that the government has the right and perhaps the obligation to issue firearms to contrabands and send them to fight their former masters."

"Simon proposes to arm runaway slaves? That's bizarre. Who's going to believe the old thief has suddenly turned into a moral crusader?"

"He must think someone will believe it."

"He's lost his mind."

Stanley eyed the tables around them; no one was paying attention. He leaned toward his wife and lowered his voice. "Here's the grisly part. The entire report has gone to the government printer —but not to Lincoln."

"Does the President usually review such reports?"

"Review them and approve them for publication, yes."

"Then why—?"

"Because Simon knows the President would reject this one. Remember how he overturned Frémont's emancipation order? Simon's desperate to get his statement into print. Don't you see, Isabel? He's sinking, and he thinks the radicals are the only ones who can throw him a line. I don't think they'll do it, for the very reason you sensed. Simon's ploy is transparent."

"You've been helping Wade—won't that save you if Cameron goes down?"

He pounded a fist into his other palm. "I don't know!"

She ignored the outburst and pondered. In a few moments, she murmured, "You're probably right about Simon's motive and the reason he doesn't want Lincoln to see the report until it's printed. Whatever happens, don't be lulled into speaking in support of that controversial passage."

"For God's sake why not? Surely Wade will endorse it. And Stevens, and I don't know how many others."

"I don't think so. Simon is a trimmer, and the whole town knows it. The mantle of the moralist looks ludicrous on him. He'll never be allowed to wear it."

She was right. When an early copy of the report reached the President, he ordered an immediate reprinting with the controversial passage removed. The day it happened, Cameron stormed about the department speaking in a shout. He sent a messenger to the offices of Mr. Stanton at half past nine. He dispatched the same boy to the same destination shortly after noon and again at three. It didn't take great intelligence to guess that Cameron's lawyer, now acknowledged as the writer of the passage, was, for whatever reason, not answering his client's appeals for help.

"The damage is done," Stanley said to Isabel the next evening. Ashen, he handed her a copy of Mr. Wallach's *Evening Star,* the city's strongly Democratic—some said pro-Southern—paper. "Somehow they got hold of the report."

"You told me the passage had been removed."

"They got the original version."

"How?"

"God knows. It would be just my luck for someone to accuse me."

Isabel ignored his guilt fantasies, musing, "We could have passed the report to the papers ourselves. It's a rather nice touch. Sure to heat the bipartisan fires. Neither party wants to see guns passed out to the darkies—yes, a nice touch. I wish I'd thought of it."

"How can you smile, Isabel? If the boss goes down, I may be dragged along. I don't know whether Wade found any of my information useful or whether I gave him enough. I haven't seen him since the party here. So nothing's assured—" He thumped the dining table with his fist; his voice rose, shrill. "Nothing."

She closed her fingers on his wrist and let him feel her nails. "The ship is in a storm, Stanley. When a ship is in a storm, the captain ties himself to the wheel and rides it out. He doesn't run whimpering belowdecks to hide."

The scorn—the comparison—humiliated him. But it did nothing to relieve his fears. He fretted and tossed in bed, getting little more than three hours of solid sleep.

Next morning, he jumped in his chair when Cameron shot into his office with a file of footwear and clothing contracts he had just approved. The haggard secretary disposed of business in a few sentences, then asked, "Haven't seen Mr. Stanton anywhere about town, have you, my boy?"

Stanley's heart hammered. Did it show? "No, Simon. It isn't likely that I would. He and I don't move in the same circles at all."

"Oh?" Cameron gave his pupil an odd stare. "Well, I can't seem to locate him, and he won't answer messages. Curious. The

298

fellow who wrote the very words that got me in the soup won't say a damn thing in defense of them. Or me. I've shown myself to be on the side of Wade's bunch, but they don't want me. Stanton acts as if he's on the President's side, but last week I heard him call Abe the Original Gorilla. Understand Little Mac got quite a chuckle out of that. I'm still trying to find out how the report reached the *Star*—" His eye fixed on Stanley again. He knows. *He knows.*

Cameron shook his head. There was something sad about him now. He seemed less competent, less sure. A mere mortal, and a tired one. A bitter smile appeared. "I'd call it all mighty queer business if I didn't know its real name. Politics. By the bye—did you and Isabel receive an invitation to the President's levee for McClellan?"

"Y-yes, sir, I believe Isabel mentioned that we did."

"Hmm. I failed to get mine. Fault of the postal service, don't you suppose?" Looking as if he had alum in his mouth, he darted another look at his subordinate. "Must excuse me, Stanley. Got a lot to do before I surrender my portfolio. They'll be asking for it any day now."

He went out with a sprightly step. Stanley pressed his palms to the desk and shut his eyes, dizzy. Had he pulled it off? Had Isabel pulled it off?

46

I am, George thought, too damned much of a cynic.

Not so, argued a second side of him. You have just become, in short order, a Washingtonian.

The hack's back wheels bumped into a splattery mudhole, lurched out again. A few more blocks and he'd be back at Willard's, where a small dinner was being given to honor the visitor from Braintree.

A light snow fell. The town George sometimes referred to as Canaille on the Canal looked pretty as an engraving. Shining Christmas lights temporarily obscured the vapid minds behind the eyes of the bureaucrats; the deep, piney smell of greens temporarily masked the stink of fear, damp, and cavelike cold pervading everything this December. Despite the splendor of the martial reviews General McClellan had staged here and in Virginia throughout the autumn, and despite the general's frequent predictions of forthcoming victory, George wondered whether any substance supported the show. He hated his own faithless attitude, but he wondered.

He had just come from the arsenal, where Billy was encamped with his battalion—happy enough, though displaying a certain shortness of temper. George knew that to be a common symptom of winter quarters. Yesterday Constance had returned from another short trip to Lehigh Station; Brown had gone up with her and planned to stay a few more days to settle in some more children. Brett had sent Christmas packages with Constance. Delivering Billy's was the excuse that had taken him to the arsenal.

The brothers had discussed the visitor from Braintree. Billy had heard about the private party but hadn't been invited. In an effort to make him feel better about that, George said, "Hell, I'll probably be the most junior shoulder strap in attendance. I was warned that half of Little Mac's staff would be there, though not the general himself."

"Have you ever met the guest of honor?" Billy hadn't.

"Once, after a graduation. Can't claim I know him."

At the hotel, George rushed to the suite, kissed his wife, hugged his children, brushed his hair and mustache, then dashed downstairs again, late for the reception preceding the dinner for Superintendent Emeritus Sylvanus Thayer. Seventy-six and long retired, Thayer had come down from Massachusetts to attend the levee for McClellan.

A formidable quantity of brain and brass filled the parlor: sixty or seventy officers, most of them colonels or brigadiers. The West Point bond minimized boundaries between ranks. Protected from the curious by closed doors, the old grads enjoyed generous portions of port or fine bourbon poured by black men in hotel livery. George was thankful Brown had quit his job as porter and accepted a salary arrangement the Hazards had proposed so he could devote full time to the children.

A large crowd surrounded the slender and exceptionally fit-looking Thayer, so George fell into conversation with another major and a colonel, both of whom he remembered from Mexico. Half the regular officers in the army had served there.

Two brigadiers joined the group—men George knew from the class ahead of his. Baldy Smith and Fitz-John Porter both had divisions. Smith seemed irked by the surroundings, the refreshments, the lighting—he had that kind of disposition—but George still liked him better than Porter. Even in his Academy days, Porter had struck George as showy and prone to boasting—like the general to whose staff he now belonged.

Bourbon relaxed the men; they were soon reminiscing as equals. Thayer walked to the group, warmly greeting each officer. He had a phenomenal memory; it was a vast permanent file of the names and careers of every graduate, even those like George and the brigadiers who had gone through the place long after his tenure.

"Hazard—yes, certainly," Thayer said. "Where are you now?" George told him. "Pity. You had an excellent record at the Academy. You belong in the field."

Not wanting to offend the guest, George responded with care. "I never felt I had a talent for soldiering, sir." What he meant was a taste for it.

Baldy Smith snorted. "What we're doing in Virginny isn't soldiering; it's cattle droving."

To the abattoir? George thought; he still had nightmares about Bull Run. He smiled and shrugged. "I went where I was asked to go."

"You don't sound happy about it." Directness was Thayer's style.

"I don't believe I should comment on that, sir."

"That kind of answer qualifies you to be a general," said another brigadier, a jovial Pennsylvanian named Winfield Hancock whom George was glad to have join the group. Presently they all sat down at a great horseshoe table for a huge meal centered around capon and prime steer beef. The whiskey and port flowed, and various dinner wines; by the time Thayer was introduced,

George was ready to slide under the table. He couldn't hold back a belch. On his right, Fitz-John Porter cleared his throat and silently disapproved.

Thayer's voice was thin, but he spoke with passion. He stated a fact already known to those in the room: West Point was once again under attack. This time, however, the attack carried special danger because of the effort to fix blame on the Academy for the resignation of all the officers who had gone south. Thayer pleaded for each man to make a personal pledge to defend the school if, as he feared, Congress attempted to destroy it by removing its appropriation.

"I am cheered," he said, "to see so many of you serving the nation that educated you and gave you a proud profession. I know you have the stamina to stay the course. I was dismayed by many newspaper articles I read before the great battle in July, articles that said the struggle would be quickly concluded. Knowing our brother officers from the states in rebellion—their intelligence, their courage, their records, which remain as fine as yours except in one fatal respect—I would counter every one of those assertions with one of my own."

No sound then except the gas hissing. The frail old man held every eye. Thick layers of cigar smoke gave the speaker and the scene a kind of infernal unreality.

"An assertion that you know as a principle and a truth. It requires three years to build an efficient army. Even then, when such an army is in place, it must endure great tribulation in order to win. War is not a Sabbath rest or a summer picnic. Those of you who campaigned in Mexico remember. Those of you who campaigned in the West remember. War extracts a mighty toll in human life and human sorrow. Be ever mindful of that. Be strong. Be patient. But be certain, too. You shall prevail."

When he sat, the stamping and shouting were thunderous. They sang "Benny Haven's, Oh!" and even George the Cynical had moist eyes by the last verse. Later, for Constance, he quoted as much of Thayer's speech as he could remember. The closing passage haunted him in the sleepless small hours of the night.

The great levee for Major General George Brinton McClellan took place as the year wore away in a continuing atmosphere of doubt and hidden struggle. Gossip flew; pronouncements abounded. The *Trent* captives would be released because the

Union could not afford to do without niter. Formation of the new Joint Congressional Committee on the Conduct of the War would be announced at any hour. McClellan would crush the Confederacy in the spring. Didn't he issue frequent statements to that effect? McClellan's detractors said he had intrigued to have gouty old Scott removed so the post of general-in-chief would also be his.

The Executive Mansion shone with lights, hummed with conversation, resounded with the holiday airs played by a string ensemble as the privileged guests arrived. George promised to introduce Constance to his old classmate, but only after he had surveyed the territory from afar, so to speak.

McClellan looked hardly older than when he and George had boned for exams together. He had grown a dramatic auburn mustache but was otherwise much the same stocky, assured fellow George recalled from the class of '46. Everything about him, from his fine, bold nose to his wide shoulders, seemed to make a single statement. Here is strength; here is competence. He had returned to the army from the railroad business in Illinois, and his brilliant ascendancy made George feel more than slightly inferior.

Brilliant was the word, all right. An aura of celebrity surrounded the McClellans as they circulated in the crowd. Close after the general trotted two of his numerous European aides, the merry young French exiles the Comte de Paris and the Duc de Chartres. Silly hostesses had renamed them Captain Parry and Captain Chatters.

It was McClellan to whom all the eavesdroppers listened when he and his wife engaged the President and Mrs. Lincoln in conversation. Since establishing himself in an H Street house in defiance of those who said he should live in camp, McClellan had left no doubt about which person, President or general-in-chief, was the more important. The town still talked of a November incident. One evening Lincoln and another of his secretaries, young John Hay, had gone to H Street on government business. The general wasn't home yet. An hour later he arrived. He went straight upstairs without seeing the visitors, was informed the President was waiting, and went to bed. Some said Lincoln was infuriated, but he tended to cover such emotions with a blend of Western modesty and good humor. Unlike McClellan, arrogance was not his style.

"Plenty of politicians here," George said to Constance from the

303

side of his mouth. "There's Wade—he's to run the new committee. There's Thad Stevens."

"His wig's crooked. It's always crooked."

"Are you playing Isabel tonight?"

She whacked his braided sleeve with her fan. "You're horrid."

"On the subject of horrid—I see the lady herself. And my
brother."

Stanley and Isabel had not as yet noticed George and Constance. All their attention was given to Wade, then to Cameron,
who showed up alone and was circulating with an air Stanley
could only characterize as conspiratorial. How had he gotten an
invitation? Cameron saw them but avoided them. What did that
signify?

Stanton spoke tête-à-tête with Wade, not even acknowledging
the presence of his client. Stanley felt less like a Judas; others were
selling, too, it appeared. But what? To whom? For what purpose?
He felt like an ignorant child who knew he was ignorant.

"I'll bet Stanton wants Simon's job," Isabel said behind her
unfolded fan. "That would explain why you saw him skulking
around Wade's office and why he failed to defend or even take
responsibility for the original report."

The thought, wholly new, left Stanley dumbfounded.

"Close your mouth. You look like a cretin."

He obeyed, then said, "My dear, you constantly astound me. I
think you may be right."

She drew him to a more private corner. "Let's suppose I am.
What sort of man is Stanton?"

"Another Ohioan. Brilliant lawyer. Strong abolitionist."
Stanley's eyes darted here and there. He bent close. "Willful, they
say. Devious, too. Very much to be feared."

She seized his arm. "Their conversation's over. You must speak
to Wade. Try to find out where you stand."

"Isabel, I can't simply walk up to him and ask—"

"We will go greet him. Both of us. Now."

There was no argument. Her hand clawed shut on his and she
pulled. By the time they reached Ben Wade, Stanley feared his
bladder might let go. Isabel smiled in her best imitation of a stage
coquette. "How delightful to see you again, Senator. Where is
your charming wife?"

"Here somewhere. Must find her."

304

"I trust all's going well with the new committee we hear so much about?"

Isabel's question was an irresistible prompt. "Yes indeed. We'll soon put the war effort on a more solid footing. A clearer course."

The slap at Lincoln was obvious, so she said quickly: "A purpose I support, as does my husband."

"Oh, yes." Wade smiled; Stanley felt there was contempt in it, meant for him. "Your husband's loyalty and—" the slightest pause to heighten effect "—devoted service are known to many of those on the committee. We trust your cooperative spirit will continue to prevail, Stanley."

"Most definitely, Senator."

"Good news. Good evening."

As Wade strode off, Stanley almost fainted. He had survived the purge. His vision blurred. He saw the machines of Lashbrook's cutting, sewing, spewing bootees that piled up in hills, then foothills, then mighty mountains washed with gold light.

He pulled himself from the delicious reverie, prideful as a boy who has hooked a big fish. "Isabel, I think I may get drunk tonight. With or without your permission."

The inevitable meeting of the brothers and their wives took place a few minutes later, near the glittering glass punch bowls. Greetings were polite on both sides, but nothing more; George found it hard to put feeling into a wish that Stanley and Isabel would enjoy a fine Christmas.

"Met our young Napoleon yet?" Stanley slurred the question; he was consuming rum punch rapidly, George noticed.

"Haven't spoken to him so far this evening, but I will. I know him from Mexico and West Point."

"Oh, you do?" Isabel's face briefly suggested she had lost a point in some game.

"What's he like? Personally, I mean," Stanley asked. "I gather he has a fine pedigree. But he's a Democrat. Soft on slavery, they say. Odd choice for the President to make, don't you think?"

"Why? Aren't politics supposed to be set aside during a crisis?"

Isabel sniffed. "If you believe that, you're naïve, George."

He saw pink rising in his wife's cheeks. He picked up her hand and curled her arm around his; gradually her hand unclenched. "To answer your question, then—McClellan's extremely bright. Graduated second in our class. He was brevetted three times in Mexico for gallantry. Billy told me the troops love him. They

305

cheer when he rides by. We needed a man the rank and file would trust, and I'd say we have one. Strikes me the President made an intelligent choice, not a political one."

"The President couldn't have said it better himself."

Isabel looked ready to sink into the floor at the sight of the speaker behind George. Lincoln's long arm lifted; his hand came to rest on George's shoulder. "How are you, Major Hazard? Is this attractive lady your wife? You must introduce me."

"With pleasure, Mr. President." George presented Constance, then asked whether Lincoln knew his brother and Isabel. The tall man with the scarecrow look politely said yes, he believed they had met, but George got an impression that Lincoln had not found the meeting memorable in a positive way. Isabel caught that, too. It clearly irked her.

Constance was properly deferential to the Chief Executive but relaxed, not grimacing or fidgeting with her lace gloves as Isabel was. "My husband said he encountered you one evening at the arsenal, Mr. President."

"That's right. The major and I discussed firearms."

George said, "I hope I'm not being disloyal to my department if I tell you I was pleased to hear of the purchase of some Spencers and Sharps repeaters."

"Your chief wouldn't buy them, and someone had to. But we mustn't bore the ladies with sanguinary talk tonight." He changed the subject to Christmas, which recalled an anecdote. Telling it with visible glee, he did different voices and dialects. The laughter at the end was genuine except for Isabel's; she brayed so loudly, people stared.

"Tell me something about yourself, Mrs. Hazard," the President said. She did; they chatted about Texas for a minute. Then a remark of hers prompted another anecdote. He had just started it when his pudgy, overdressed wife bore down and swept him away. That gave Isabel an opportunity to leave. Stanley followed without instruction.

"George, that was one of the most thrilling things I've ever experienced," Constance said. "But I felt so humiliated—I've put on so much weight. It makes me ugly."

He patted her hand. "The extra pound or two may be real, but the rest is in your head. Did you see how Lincoln heeded your every word? He has an eye for handsome women—which is why

306

his wife swooped down that way. I'm told she hates for him to be alone with another female. Ah, there's Thayer. Come meet him."

Constance charmed the retired superintendent, too. The trio approached McClellan, temporarily without a crowd around him. "An old classmate of yours—" Thayer began.

"Stump Hazard! I saw you across the room a while ago—knew you instantly." McClellan's greeting was hearty, yet George thought he detected artificiality. On second thought, perhaps it existed mostly in his imagination. McClellan was now a national figure; George knew that changed the way people perceived and treated him. His own self-conscious reply demonstrated it.

"Good evening, General."

"No, no—Mac, always. Tell me, what's become of that fellow you were so tight with? Southerner, wasn't he?"

"Yes. Orry Main. I don't know what's become of him. I last saw him in April."

McClellan's wife, Nell, joined them, and the four fell to talking about Washington and the war. McClellan grew grave. "The Union is in peril, and the President seems powerless to save it. The savior's role has fallen to me. I shall perform it to the best of my ability."

Not even a hint of lightness leavened the statement. George felt his wife's hand tighten on his sleeve; was her reaction the same as his? In a moment the McClellans excused themselves to join General and Mrs. Meade. Constance waited till they were out of earshot.

"I have never heard anything so astonishing. There's something wrong with a man who calls himself a savior."

"Well, Mac isn't your average fellow and never was. We shouldn't be too quick to judge. God knows the task they handed him is formidable."

"I still say there's something wrong with him."

George silently admitted McClellan had left the same impression with him.

He could no longer fool himself into thinking he was having a good time. As the currents of the party flowed and mingled, he and Constance found themselves in a circle with Thad Stevens, the Pennsylvania lawyer who would be the most powerful House member of Wade's oversight committee. Stevens struck most everyone as peculiar, with his clubfoot and his head of thick hair cocked fifteen degrees off the vertical. A certain sinister air was only enhanced by his cold passion.

"I do not agree with the President on all subjects, but I agree on one. As he says, the Union is not some free-love arrangement which any state can dissolve at will. The rebels are not erring sisters, as Mr. Greeley so tenderly termed them, but enemies, vicious enemies, of the temple of freedom that is our country. There can be only one fate for vicious enemies. Punishment. We should free every slave, we should slaughter every traitor, we should burn every rebel mansion to the ground. If those in the executive lack the grit for the job, our committee does not." The eye of the zealot swept the awed group. "I give you my solemn promise, ladies and gentlemen—the committee does not." He limped away.

"Constance," George said, "let's go home."

Madeline and Hettie, a house girl, were wiping out a mildewed trunk when feet pounded on the attic stair. "Miss Madeline? You better come quick."

She dropped the damp rag and went instantly. "What is it, Aristotle?"

"Miss Clarissa. She went for her walk after breakfast, and they found her in the garden."

Dread pierced her, sharp as the air of the winter morning. The sun had not risen high enough to burn the white rime from the lawn. They ran down to the garden, where Clarissa lay on her back between two azalea bushes. Clarissa stared at Madeline and the slave with glittering eyes.

Her left hand reached toward them, imploring. Her right lay unnaturally limp. Tears in her eyes, she tried to form words and produced nothing but thick glottal sounds.

"It's a seizure," Madeline said to the anxious black man. She wanted to cry; she wouldn't get away before New Year's after all. She couldn't go until Clarissa recovered. "We must make a litter and move her inside." Aristotle dashed for the house. When the litter was ready, lifting Clarissa revealed melted rime in the shape of her body—a shadow on a snowfield.

The doctor emerged from Clarissa's bedroom at half past eleven. Outwardly calm, Madeline received the news that paralysis of the right side was nearly total, and recovery might take most of next year.

47

Christmas Eve fell on a Tuesday. George couldn't shake the bad mood that had been with him since the McClellan reception. The war, the city, even the season depressed him for reasons he couldn't completely explain.

A fragrant fire brightened the hearth of the parlor after supper. Patricia had resumed her music lessons with a local teacher, but a regular piano wasn't practical in the crowded suite, so George had bought a small harmonium. Patricia opened a carol book, pumped the pedals, and played "God Rest Ye Merry, Gentlemen."

Constance came out of the bedroom with three large presents. She placed the packages near similar ones at the base of the fir tree decorated with cranberry strands, gilt-painted wood ornaments, and tiny candles. Buckets of water and sand waited behind the tree. All the gas had been shut off in the room; the light was mellow and pleasant—quite unlike George's state of mind.

"Sing with me, Papa," his daughter said between phrases. He shook his head, remaining in his chair. Constance went to the harmonium and added her voice to Patricia's. The young girl resembled her mother in her prettiness and her bright hair.

Singing, Constance glanced occasionally at her husband. His despondency worried her. "Won't you, George?" she asked finally, motioning.

"No."

William wandered in and sang "Joy to the World" with them. Puberty put a crack in his voice; Patricia giggled so hard Constance had to speak to her. After the carol William said, "Pa, can't each of us open one present tonight?"

"No. You've nagged me about that all evening, and I'm sick of it."

"George, I beg your pardon," Constance said. "He hasn't nagged. He's mentioned it only once."

"Once or a hundred times, the answer's no." He addressed his son. "We shall attend our church in the morning, and your mother will go to mass, then we'll have our gifts."

"After church?" William cried. "Waiting that long isn't fair. Why not after breakfast?"

"It's your father's decision," Constance said softly. George paid no attention to her slight frown.

William wouldn't be persuaded. "It isn't fair!"

"I'll show you what's fair, you impertinent—"

"George!" He was halfway to his son before Constance stepped between them. "Try to remember it's Christmas Eve. We are your family, but you act as if we're enemies. What's wrong?"

"Nothing—I don't know—Where are my cigars?" He leaned on the mantelpiece, his back to the others. His eye fell on the sprig of laurel he had brought from Lehigh Station and kept on the mantel. The sprig was withered and brown. He snatched it and flung it in the fire.

"I'm going to bed."

The laurel smoked, curled, and vanished.

He slammed the bedroom door and splashed cold water on his face, then searched till he found a cigar. After raising the window, he crawled into bed with a stack of contracts he had brought home. The fine loops and flourishes of the copyists blurred before his eyes, meaningless. He felt guilty about his behavior, angry with everyone and everything. He dropped the contracts on the floor, stubbed out the cigar, extinguished the gas, and rolled up under the comforter.

He never knew when Constance came to bed. He was lost and far away, watching exquisitely slow shellbursts on the road to Churubusco, watching a great malevolent India-rubber head— Thad Stevens—loom steadily larger, the shouting mouth huge as a cave. *Free every slave. Slaughter every traitor. Burn every mansion.* In the ravening maw he saw Mont Royal afire.

He watched the road from Cub Run. The fallen horse. The young Zouave, crashing his musket down on the only target he could find for his fear and fury. The horse peeled its lips back from its teeth, demented by pain. The Zouave struck once more. The head opened like some exotic fruit, spilling its red pulp in pumping spurts that became a flow. Which was the animal? Which was the man? The guns changed everything.

The Zouave, the horse, the scene exploded as if struck by a shell. Deep in dreams, the dreamer retreated, whimpering with relief—only to see the Zouave approach the horse again, raise the musket again, bring the butt down again, the cycle restarting—

"Stop it."

"George—"

"Stop it, stop it." He flailed at soft things wrapped around his body. He kept screaming "Stop it."

A young voice called out fearfully: "Pa? Mama, is he all right?"

"Yes, William."

"Stop—" A great, long gasp from George, and realization. Faintly: "—it."

"Go back to bed, William," Constance called. "It's just a nightmare."

"Jesus Christ," George whispered in the dark, shuddering.

"There." Her arms were what he had attempted to fight off. "There." She brushed hair from his wet forehead, kissing him. How warm she felt. He slid his hands around her and held her, ashamed of his weakness but thankful for the comfort. "What were you dreaming? It must have been horrible."

"Mexico, Bull Run—it was. I'm sorry I was so rotten tonight. I'll speak to the children first thing in the morning. We'll open gifts. I want them to know I'm sorry."

"They understand. They know you're hurting badly. They just don't know why. I'm not sure I do either."

"God; they must hate me."

"Never. They know you're a good father. They love you and want you to be happy, especially at Christmas."

"The war makes Christmas a mockery." He pressed his face to hers; both cheeks were cold. The room was freezing; he had opened the window too far. The air smelled of old cigars and of his sweat.

"Is it the war that's troubling you so badly?"

"I guess. What a little word, *war,* to bring so much misery. I can't stand the dishonesty in this town. The greed behind the flag-waving rhetoric. Do you know something? At the rate Stanley is

311

selling bootees to the infantry, he'll have an enormous profit within a year. Practically a small fortune. And do you know that the shoes he's delivering will fall apart after a week of use on hard roads in Virginia or Missouri or wherever the damned disgraceful things are sent?"

"I'd rather not know things like that."

"What bothers me most is something Thayer said at the dinner. You don't build an effective army in ninety days. It takes two or three years."

"You mean he thinks the war may last that long?"

"Yes. The springtime war—short, sanitary—that was a cruel delusion. War's not like that. Never has been, never will be. Now everything's changing. Other men are taking charge, men like Stevens, who want slaughter. Can Billy survive that? What about Orry and Charles? If I ever see Orry again, will he speak to me? Long wars make for long hatreds. A long war will change people, Constance. Wear them out. Destroy them with despair, if it doesn't kill them outright. I finally faced that—and look what it's done to me."

She hugged him to her breast. Her silence said she understood his fears and shared them and had no answers for his questions. Presently he went to shut the window. Outside, it was snowing again.

48

Charles had fired his shotgun in anger just three times during the autumn. Each time he had led a scout detachment well past the rifle pits Hampton's infantry had dug as part of the Confederate defense line; each time the targets were fleeing Yanks on horseback. He had wounded one but missed the rest.

That typified the months since Manassas: uneventful except for the spirit-lifting victory at Ball's Bluff in late October. In the North the engagement had produced accusations of bungling, even treason, directed against the Union commander who had led the Potomac crossing, then seen his men shot or drowned as Confederate fire repelled them. Shanks Evans, a South Carolinian who had ridden against Charles in horse races in Texas, had distinguished himself at Ball's Bluff, just as he had at Manassas. Promotion looked doubtful for him, though; he drank too much and had a violent temper.

The colonel's elevation to brigadier, on the other hand, looked certain. He was in favor with Johnston, who had been given the whole Department of Virginia in the reorganization after Ball's Bluff. Old Bory had lost out and was now relegated to command of the Potomac district, one of several in the department. As a practical matter, Hampton had been carrying the responsibilities of a brigadier since November, with three more regiments of foot, two from Georgia, one from North Carolina, placed under him. Calbraith Butler was commanding the cavalry, which did everything from probing Yankee positions to guarding paymaster wagon trains.

During the fall, Charles had found just one period of two days when he was free to visit Spotsylvania County. After a fast, exhausting ride, he had located Barclay's Farm easily, only to find the owner absent. The older of her two freedmen, Washington, said she had gone to Richmond with the younger one, Boz, to sell the last of her corn crop and a few pumpkins, eggs, and cheeses. Charles rode back to the lines in a bitter mood, made no better by hours of drenching rain.

The legion had hutted for the winter near Dumfries. Tonight, Christmas Eve, Charles was alone in the log-and-daub cottage he and Ambrose had put together with axes, sweat, and no Negro labor. Except for a few holdouts such as Custom Cramm III, most of the troopers had sent their slaves home rather than see them run away.

Tattoo had been sounded half an hour ago, and the final call for quiet would be skipped because of tomorrow's holiday. Ambrose had drawn patrol duty, riding out before dark in the direction of Fairfax Courthouse to conduct a routine surveillance of the Union lines. His detachment included Private Nelson Gervais, for whom Charles's epistolary skills had won a promise of the hand of Miss Sally Mills; the couple planned a wedding when Gervais got his first leave.

A small fire burned in the hut fireplace, constructed of bricks foraged in the finest cavalry tradition by First Sergeant Reynolds. The bricks ran to a height level with the top of the door; above, the chimney was mud and sticks. On the mantel, a plank resting on pegs, sat a cased ambrotype of Ambrose's parents and a photograph of Ambrose and Charles with ferns, columns, and the Confederate national flag in the background; such properties were a standard part of the kit of photographers who worked the camps.

The hut measured twelve feet on each side and included a pair of built-in bunks at opposite ends of the room, a rack for sabers and shotguns, and comfortable handmade furniture: a table of thick boards nailed to a keg; two chairs with curved backs created from flour barrels. Ambrose was a fine woodworker, though he complained that it was slave's work. He had carved the sign hanging outside above the door and insisted that doing so gave him the right to name the hut. But Charles had vetoed Millwood Mansion as too obvious an attempt to flatter Hampton. Ambrose settled on Gentlemen's Rest. Charles would have preferred something less sententious; he rather liked the name of the eight-man hut where Gervais lived, Phunny Phellows.

Though the fire made the hut cozy, Charles's mood was not the best. The evening had started badly when the salt horse served at supper proved inedible. Despite pickling, it was purplish and slimy. They had made do with teeth-dullers and whippoorwill peas.

Turkey, sweet potatoes, and fresh corn bread were promised for Christmas. He would believe a feast when he saw it. Charles's men hated the Commissary Department. They cursed its head man, Northrop, as floridly as they cursed Old Abe—sometimes more. The beef was getting so tough, Colonel Hampton had remarked last week, he was thinking of requisitioning some files for sharpening teeth.

Parcels from home helped to offset the recent and noticeable decline in the quality of rations. Charles had one such package, or the remains of it, on the table in front of him. It had arrived from Richmond this afternoon, preceded by a letter from Orry, who reported that he was now a lieutenant colonel in the War Department and stuck in a job he disliked.

As a precaution, Orry had written out a list of the contents of the package and sent it with the letter: two oranges—all he could locate; they had arrived squashed but edible. Two copies of the *Southern Illustrated News;* one featured a lengthy article about the victory at Ball's Bluff. The list showed four paper-covered novels, but these had been stolen from the badly torn parcel.

The damage probably accounted for the green mold forming on the two dozen baking-powder biscuits. With his knife, Charles scraped off some of the mold and ate a biscuit. They would do. He wiped the knife blade on his sleeve, which, like the rest of his uniform, had acquired a dirty cast no amount of washing would remove.

Orry had also sent three small crocks of jam for the biscuits; all arrived broken, the contents oozing around pieces of the containers. Charles had thrown the whole mess away. Finally, the package included a dark chocolate cake which looked as if a cannonball had dropped on it. That could be salvaged, crumbs and all. Charles knifed out a large wedge and gobbled it.

He pulled out his pocket watch. Half past eight. He had duties tonight, some official, some not; he supposed he might as well start. He scratched his beard, which he was permitting to grow because it kept his face warm. It was already more than an inch long, thus a convenient home for graybacks, but so far he had managed to avoid a serious infestation. Unlike many of his troopers, he washed as often as possible. He hated feeling dirty, and beyond that, if he were ever lucky enough to be alone with Gus Barclay, and if she were receptive to an advance, he damn well didn't want any crab lice in residence around his privates. That would scotch romance forever.

Her face came into his thoughts often these days. It had a special vividness tonight. He felt lonely and wished he were at Barclay's Farm, perhaps listening to her read Pope over cups of heated wine.

He shook his head. Mustn't let anyone else see his state; others in his care surely felt the same way or worse, and were less experienced at dealing with it. It was his duty to look after them.

He rose and plopped his hat on his head as a nearby tenor voice began "Sweet Hour of Prayer." He liked the melody and hummed along as he strapped on his revolver and took his gauntlets from

315

their peg. He saw his breath as he ducked out the door; a light snowfall had begun. Ambrose planned to return by midnight, after which they were going to open a bottle of busthead bought from the sutler. Maybe they should organize a snowball fight first; the men were growing quarrelsome from inactivity.

Three messmates from down near the Savannah River came out of their winterized tent to gaze in wonder at the white flakes falling between great dark trees. Charles approached. "First you've ever seen, boys?"

"Yes, sir."

"Better look sharp, Captain Main," said another. "A snowball just might pop that hat off your head 'fore you know it."

Charles laughed and walked on down the row of winterized tents; the lower walls were palisaded logs, the roofs canvas, flat or peaked. The unseen tenor began "Away in a Manger." Two deeper voices joined. A burst of laughter from a card game briefly drowned out the carol. Charles kept walking, his boots crunching snow. It already covered the ground.

From a narrow lane between tents came a familiar sputtering sound. Angry, he turned into the lane. Sure enough, there was the malefactor with his pants and drawers down around his calves and his rear jutting over a soiled patch of snow.

"Goddamn you, Pickens, I've told you before—use the sinks. It's men like you who spread sickness in this camp."

The frightened boy said, "I know what you said, Cap'n, but I got a ter'ble case of the quickstep."

"The sinks," Charles said without pity. "Get going."

The trooper clumsily tugged up his clothing and limped away with a kind of sideways crab step. Charles returned to the street and walked toward the camp entrance, two elaborate pillars and an arch, fashioned of peeled saplings woven together. Quite a work of art, that gate. It would stand till spring, when they would surely take the field to fight McClellan.

Charles passed men standing guard and returned each salute without really seeing it or the man who gave it. Gus Barclay's face filled his thoughts. Outside a hut twice the size of his own, he said to the corporal on duty, "How's the prisoner?"

"He cussed a blue streak for 'bout a half hour, Captain. When I dint pay no attention, he shut up."

"Let's go in and release him. No one should stand punishment on Christmas Eve."

The corporal nodded, brushed snowflakes from his eyebrows and the bill of his kepi, and ducked into the hut. Charles followed. A certain reluctance mingled with his kinder impulse; the man put here just before supper call was the perennially rebellious Private Cramm. First Sergeant Reynolds had issued another order Cramm didn't like, and as the sergeant was moving away, Cramm hawked and spat loudly. Charles ordered him bucked and gagged for the night. Sometimes he wished Cramm were a Yankee, so he could shoot him.

Cramm sat on the dirt floor of the guardhouse, a single bare room feebly lit by a lamp. Above the stick tied in his mouth, sullen eyes watched Charles. Cramm's wrists were roped together behind his drawnup knees; a thick length of pine pole had been slipped between knees and forearms.

"You don't deserve it, Cramm, but I'm going to release you because it's Christmas Eve." While Charles said this, the guard knelt and unfastened the gag. "Escort him to his tent, Corporal. Stay there until reveille, Cramm. Understand?"

"Yes, sir." Cramm made a great show of grimacing and twisting his head as if badly hurt. No gratitude was visible on his face; just his eternal contempt. Feeling his temper start to rise, Charles quickly left.

The snow fell like pillow down. The most important call of the night was yet to be paid. He would go right now. The thought relieved the anger Cramm always caused.

Passing the winterized tents again, he stopped. Inside a tent whose sign announced it was the home of The Fighting Cocks, a name chosen in honor of Sumter, the hero of the Revolution, Charles heard a young voice: "Lord God. Oh, Lord God. Oh, oh."

He recognized the speaker; it was Reuven Sapp, nineteen-year-old nephew of the doctor who had drugged Madeline LaMotte with laudanum for so long. The boy had the makings of a good cavalryman if he could get over letting his louder but less competent comrades intimidate him.

"Oh, Lord—oh." Charles tapped on the door and pulled it open without waiting for permission. Seated on one of the four bunks, the straw-haired boy jerked his head up. A letter dropped from his lap. "Captain! I didn't know anyone was close by—"

"I wouldn't have come in, but I heard a voice that sounded pretty low." Charles removed his hat, shook snow from it, walked down three plank steps to the dirt floor, which was excavated to a depth of three feet below ground level for added warmth. The hearth was dark, the tent freezing. "Where are your messmates?"

"Went out to see if they could club some rabbits." Sapp struggled to sound normal, but his eyes betrayed him. "That was pretty scrummy food tonight."

"Rotten. May I sit down?"

"Oh, certainly, Captain. I'm sorry—" He jumped up as Charles took a chair. He waved Sapp back to the bunk and waited, suspecting the boy would eventually tell him why he felt bad. He was right. Sapp picked up the letter. He spoke haltingly.

"Last August, I worked up the nerve to write a girl I like real well. I asked her whether she could ever look favorably on me as a suitor. She sent me a Christmas greeting." He indicated the fallen letter. "Said she's sorry but I can't be a suitor because I'm not respectable. I don't go to church."

"That makes two of us who aren't respectable then. It's a damn shame you got the news at Christmas. I wish there was something I could—"

Bursting tears interrupted him. "Oh, Captain, I'm so homesick. I'm ashamed of feeling so bad, but I can't help it. I hate this damn war." He bent forward from the waist, hiding his face in his hands, down near his knees. Charles twisted his hat brim, drew a breath, walked to the bunk, and squeezed the shoulder of the crying boy.

"Listen, I feel the same way myself, and often. You're no different from any other soldier in that respect, Reuven. So don't get after yourself so hard." The boy raised his wet red face, gulping. "I suggest we forget this and forget the rules about enlisted men drinking with officers, too. Stop by my hut after a while, and I'll pour you something to brace you up."

"I don't touch spirits, but—thank you anyway, sir. Thank you."

Charles nodded and left, hoping he had done some good.

He resumed his walk toward the shelters, built with sloping roofs and walls on one side to protect the horses from the worst of the weather. He heard the animals before he saw them. They were upset. His belly tightened as he spied someone crouching next to Sport, where he didn't belong. The man reached for something.

Three long strides, and Charles was on him. He caught the man by the collar, recognizing him; he was an aide to Calbraith Butler.

"That's my property you're trying to steal, Sergeant. I foraged those boards so my horse wouldn't stand on wet ground all winter. Go find some firewood for Major Butler somewhere else—and thank your stars I don't report you to him."

Taking a two-handed grip on the collar, Charles flung the thief away from the nervous horses, then booted him in the butt for good measure. The noncom fled through the falling snow without a backward look.

Sport recognized him. Charles peeled off his gauntlets, straightened the heavy gray blanket, and knelt in the mud to be sure the gelding's feet were squarely on the boards. He stepped to the trough holding the evening fodder. Almost all of it was gone. No surprise there; a cavalry horse would eat another horse's tail if he was hungry enough.

Charles fingered a bit of fodder left in the trough: coarse, dry straw; poor stuff. Winter pasturage was already scarce; thousands of cavalry and artillery horses were rapidly chewing away all the grasslands of Virginia. At least there would be another review tomorrow. Calbraith Butler ordered them frequently to keep the animals fit and the men busy.

Charles rubbed Sport affectionately. Taking a lantern from a nail, he lit it and walked along slowly behind the horses. They were growing quiet now that the forager was gone. Holding the lantern high, he checked for signs of disease. He saw nothing alarming. A minor miracle.

What an assortment of nags the troop rode these days. The fine notion of color matching had broken down before the summer ended. Most of the bays in that first springtime skirmish were gone, lost to disease, poor care, and, in four cases, to enemy fire. They had been replaced by browns, roans, Charles's gray, even a couple of conjugates, including one piebald with the ugly lines of a draft horse. But the Yanks still lived in fear of the satanic and largely nonexistent Black Horse Cavalry. Funny.

Thinking about the horses kept drawing him back to the spring, so distant and different. It might have been part of another year, another life, so rapidly had changes come. He hadn't heard Ambrose sing "Young Lochinvar" for a month. Men no longer read Scott for lessons in chivalry, only for entertainment. The behavior of the Yankee officer who had led the search for the quinine smuggler seemed quaint and foolish. He wished Ambrose would return early so they could get to drinking.

He inspected the rest of the troop's shelters; empty spaces here and there belonged to the men patrolling with Ambrose. The color situation was the same in every shelter, proving what was said so often lately: in Virginia a cavalry horse was good for six months.

"We'll prove them wrong, won't we?" he asked Sport when he went back to say good night. He stroked the gelding's head. "By God we will. I'd throw away my fine sword and everything else I own before I'd let you go, my friend."

A passing picket halted. "Who goes there?"

"Captain Main." Embarrassed, Charles kept his head averted, in shadow.

"Very good, sir. Sorry." The footsteps faded. The snow fell, silent and beautiful against the lights of camp.

Charles trudged back to his hut and set out the bottle of busthead. Eleven o'clock. Still in his clothes, he wrapped up in blankets, sure that Ambrose would bound in before long. He slid into his bunk for a short nap, and dreamed of Gus. He woke with a start, rubbed his eyes, and pulled out his watch.

Quarter past three.

"Ambrose?"

Silence.

He rolled out, stiff from the cold. He knew the other bunk was empty before he looked. The busthead stood where he had put it.

He couldn't go back to sleep. He bundled up, finishing by wrapping a scarf round and round his neck, and made a tour of the picket posts. He found one youngster asleep, an offense punishable by execution. But it was Christmas morning. He nudged the boy, reprimanded him, and walked on. Worry infected him like a disease.

At the sapling arch, he asked a guard if there had been any sign of Lieutenant Pell's detachment.

"None, sir. They're late, aren't they?"

"I'm sure they'll be here soon." Some bone-deep instinct said it was a lie.

He rechecked the horse shelters, did a second tour of the picket posts. The snow had stopped while he slept and lay thickly everywhere. He waited and watched till he saw the first glimmer of icy orange daybreak. The sapling gate remained empty, the dirt lane beyond leading to pale distances, smoky with cold, where nothing moved. Ambrose wouldn't be back. None of them would be back.

Who should he recommend for promotion before someone began electioneering for it? His junior lieutenant, Wanderly, was a nonentity; his first sergeant, well intentioned, was not smart enough. He recalled that Nelson Gervais had gone out with Ambrose. Along with the letters to the families of the men in the detachment, there was another to write, to Miss Sally Mills.

The changes were coming, steady as the seasons. Old Scott had been pushed aside. McClellan was waiting. First thing you knew, one of his troopers would go to Company Q and come back with a mule. He felt like hell.

Safe from observation in his hut, he bowed his head, swallowed several times, then straightened up. He walked to the mantel, gazed a while at the photograph of himself and his merry lieutenant, both of them looking so confident among the ferns and columns in front of the great proud flag. He turned the photograph face down.

Without removing his gauntlet he picked up the busthead and pulled the cork with his teeth. He emptied the bottle before reveille.

BOOK THREE

A WORSE PLACE
THAN HELL

*The people are impatient; Chase has no
money; the General of the Army has typhoid
fever. The bottom is out of the tub. What
shall I do?*

ABRAHAM LINCOLN TO QUARTERMASTER
GENERAL MONTGOMERY MEIGS, 1862

"Mounted men up ahead, sir."

Charles, seated on Sport beneath a dripping tree where they had halted to await the scout's report, drew a quick breath. There were six of them, returning from Stuart's headquarters on this third day of 1862: Charles; the lieutenant shipped in to replace Ambrose; the junior lieutenant, bland Julius Wanderly; two noncoms; and the scout, Lieutenant Abner Woolner, who had just ridden out of the white murk to utter those five words and set Charles's stomach churning.

He tugged down the scarf tied around the lower part of his face. The Virginia winter was proving cruel—snow, winds, drizzle. Though it was above freezing this morning, the cold somehow struck through all his layers of clothing. The time was a little after seven. Visibility was down to a few yards. The world consisted of muddy ground, the wet black pillars of tree trunks, and the fog, luminous because the sun shone above but could not penetrate.

"How many, Ab?" Charles asked.

"Couldn't see them in this soup, Cap, but I reckoned it to be at least a squad." The scout, a lanky man of thirty, wore cord trousers, covered with mud, a farmer's coat, and a crushed soft hat. He wiped his dripping nose before continuing. "Moving nice and quiet, right on the other side of the tracks."

The Orange & Alexandria. Charles's party had to cross the right of way on this return trip from Camp Qui Vive. "Which way are they headed?"

"Toward the Potomac."

Hope took a tumble. The direction almost certainly meant Yanks. Perhaps they had slipped through the lines to tear up stretches of track during the night. He was depressed by the possibility of a scrap, perhaps because it was the last thing he had expected.

Calbraith Butler had sent the detachment to Stuart's camp for three reasons. Two were military, one personal. The cavalry had run short of corn, and the major wanted the loan of some; he guessed that a request carried by an old friend of the brigadier—Stuart now had his promotion; Hampton was still awaiting his—might get more prompt and positive attention than a letter by courier.

The detachment stayed two nights, and Beauty, who seemed jollier than ever, thriving in the atmosphere of war, entertained Charles at the small house in Warrenton where he had installed his wife, Flora, and his son and daughter. Of course he could spare some corn for fellow cavalrymen in need; he had brought back a whole wagon train of fodder from Dranesville in the autumn, though not without a price. He had maneuvered too boldly, as was his wont sometimes. Pennsylvania infantry had ambushed and threatened him in a two-hour battle, in which the wagon train had almost been lost.

But it hadn't been after all, so wagons would quickly be on their way to Major Butler, compliments of Brigadier Stuart, who asked politely about the health of Colonel Hampton. From that, Charles knew nothing had changed; Stuart had a professional regard for the older officer, but no affection.

Calbraith Butler's second reason concerned the replacement for Ambrose Pell. The new man had come from Richmond two days before New Year's, having waited sixty days to be posted to the lines, so he said. Butler wanted to know how he would behave in the field. The day after his arrival, Butler spoke privately to Charles.

"He was foisted on us because he's somehow connected with Old Pete or his family"—Old Pete was Major General Longstreet, a South Carolinian by birth—"and, after I reported Pell missing, he showed up so fast I suspect someone was just waiting for an opportunity to get shed of him. I have talked with your new man no more than a half hour, but I received two strong impressions.

He's a dunce and a schemer. A bad combination, Charles. I suggest you be on your guard."

First Lieutenant Reinhard von Helm was a German from Charleston, eight or nine years older than Charles. He was a small, slim man, bald except for an encircling fringe of dark hair. His artificial teeth fit badly. Twice already, Charles had spied him standing alone in the open staring off to some private hell. Each time, he remained motionless for about half a minute, then bolted off like a rabbit.

Von Helm said he had given up a law practice to answer the call to arms. This, together with the names of noted Charlestonians he dropped into his conversation, greatly impressed Wanderly. The young lieutenant and von Helm became a chummy pair the first day they met.

On New Year's Day, an officer from another troop, Chester Moore, from Charleston, had invited Charles to his hut for a drop and the purveying of additional facts about Lieutenant von Helm.

"He was a lawyer, all right, but not much of a one. It was his father who had the successful practice, with three partners. He forced 'em to take sonny into the firm. Bad mistake. All the inherited money and high life ruined him. It does that to some. When he wrote a brief or was permitted to argue some unimportant case, he was usually drunk. The moment his father went to his grave, the partners showed von Helm the door. No other firm would touch him. That of your cousin's husband, Huntoon, rejected him in a trice. Only his money kept him from sinking out of sight. He's worthless, Charles. What's more, he knows it. Failures are often vindictive. Be careful."

The personal reason for the mission was Charles's own state of mind; gloom had possessed him ever since Christmas Eve, and Calbraith Butler recognized it. But the famed festivity of a Stuart encampment had done little to dispel this mood, even though Charles had been personally entertained by the brigadier, and he and his two lieutenants had received a cordial welcome at the officers' mess. Charles soon learned that the famed Black Horse, the Fourth Virginia, now rode horses of different colors.

The South Carolinians found innumerable visitors of the fair sex bustling around the camp at all hours; Stuart's frequent parties and his reputation for gaiety attracted them. One to whom Charles was introduced was Miss Belle Ames of Front Royal. In cold need of a woman, he arranged a rendezvous at a nearby country inn where Miss Ames was staying the night.

Miss Ames had forgotten to put away the certificate the prettiest visitors received. The certificates named them Honorary Aides-de-Camp to General Stuart, and each was authenticated by his signature and an impression of his signet ring in wax. After Charles and Miss Ames made love twice in a vigorous but essentially empty way, they found the certificate crumpled under her thin buttocks. He laughed, but she was vexed. Miss Ames never suspected her lover was astonished and disturbed because, right in the middle of things with her, he had seen a vision of Gus Barclay.

"Sir?" the scout said. "Want me to ride back and try to get a close look at 'em?"

"Why?" von Helm said, pushing his horse up beside theirs. "Can't be any boys but ours."

Charles felt tired, colder than ever. "Sure of that, are you, Lieutenant?"

Von Helm's oddly vacant eyes fixed somewhere beyond him. "Of course. Aren't you?" The question implied stupidity on Charles's part. "Best thing is to hail them, so they don't fire at us by mistake. I'll do it."

"Just a minute," Charles said, but von Helm was already spurring into the fog.

Second Lieutenant Wanderly beamed admiration. "Has a touch of the Stuart dash, doesn't he?"

Charles had no chance to express an uncomplimentary opinion. Von Helm's voice rang from the white murk hiding the tracks. Other voices, none Southern, answered the hail, overlapping almost too quickly for comprehension.

"Who goes there, a reb?"

"Sure he's a reb. Can't you tell?"

"Hey, how many nigger wives you got?"

Gunfire then. Charles yanked his shotgun up and didn't allow himself the luxury of even one curse. "Trot—march." He led, ducking, dodging, the fog and low-hanging branches dangerous impediments to speed.

Behind him, Wanderly let out a long yipping cry of excitement or released tension. A ball snipped off a twig that nicked Charles's eye and further hampered his vision. Ahead, von Helm's rifle boomed. Charles took a fearful risk in view of the fog and the terrain but felt compelled to do it to save the witless lieutenant.

"Gallop—*haaaa!*" In a fight, niceties of pronunciation disappeared.

Sport took the touch of spur and the knee pressure perfectly. Charles heard von Helm cursing, trying to reload, he assumed. Damn fool, he thought. Hampton would never fight this way, unsure of the enemy's strength—

He bent beneath branches flying past overhead. Glimpsed squirts of ruddy light in the fog. Heard explosions whose rapidity defied belief. Unless they had run into a much larger body of men than Woolner estimated, some Yank was shooting almost without pause.

He had broken his concentration, failed to see the fallen trunk of an immense elm directly ahead. Because of his speed and his position in the lead, it was too late to turn. The scout galloped behind him, reins in his teeth, a revolver in each hand. "Woolner, veer left!" he shouted. "There's a tree down ahead."

Charles and Sport were nearly on the obstacle. None of the pages in the tactics manual on leaping the ditch and the bar by trooper and by platoon would help; he had to rely on instinct and faith in the gray. He signaled by bunching his thighs and calves in tight, reining slightly.

Jesus, that trunk's five feet high—

Charles leaned forward as Sport readied to spring. He raised his buttocks off the saddle, and suddenly, up from the ground and away, man and animal sailed over, stirring the murk. At the top of the arc his heart nearly burst with love. He was riding the strongest, bravest horse on God's earth.

Down they came, striking, jarring Charles's teeth. Woolner's hurrah said the scout had heeded the warning and avoided the obstacle in time. Wanderly, a mediocre rider, reined in too fast before he reached the elm and shot forward over the head of his mount. The two noncoms, frightened, just galloped by, one passing each end of the log.

Riding hard, Charles saw the Yanks between Sport's laid-back ears. Three or four, off their horses, fired from behind the raised roadbed. Von Helm, likewise dismounted, had taken cover and alternately shot with rifle and revolver.

Whoever commanded the Yankees abruptly ordered them to mount and retreat. A ball whizzed past Charles's ear; a noncom

328

following him cried out, slapped his other arm, and almost fell off before he caught the dropped reins again. The wounded man just hung on as his horse galloped away to the left oblique.

Charles searched the line of enemy soldiers, mounted now, for the source of the rapid firing. He found it; the single marksman was within range. He reined Sport to a trot and with the shotgun steadied discharged both barrels. The blast hurled the Yank backward. His eyes rolled up in his head, horrifyingly white, the instant before he dropped.

Woolner blew down two more Yanks and von Helm a third. The rest, their total number still a mystery, quickly vanished in the fog.

As the hoofbeats faded, von Helm stamped toward the track embankment, brandishing his rifle and shouting: "Go tell the Gorilla we ignore our nigger wives when there are Yanks to be whipped!"

"Whoo-ee!" the corporal cried approvingly. He slapped his kepi on his leg and doubled back to find his fallen comrade. Clearly the enlisted man was impressed with the Dutchman's bravado—even though his rashness could have gotten them all killed.

Charles slid from the saddle, laid the hot shotgun against a tree, and tried to fight away shivers of shock setting in as he realized how close he had come to a fatal spill. He should check on his wounded trooper; but he was distracted by a thought of the shoulder weapon fired with such speed; was distracted from that by the sight of von Helm turning his back and bobbing forward, like some drinking bird. Charles glimpsed a silver flash and something slipped back into a side pocket.

Turning to the rear, Charles shouted into the fog, "How's Loomis?"

"Just nicked, sir. I'm tying it up."

Charles walked toward the embankment. The fog was whiting out, thinning as the sun climbed. "Fortunate that we weren't really facing a platoon or a troop, though it sounded like it," he said to von Helm, who started moving forward at the same time he did, evidently with the same idea.

"But we weren't." The Dutchman sounded belligerent.

They found three Union cavalrymen dead and a fourth, a sergeant, groaning from a gory belly wound. They would have to

329

take him back for treatment, but he wouldn't last long; stomach wounds usually proved fatal.

Woolner and the unhurt trooper came racing forward, ready to scavenge. The first time Charles had indulged in it, after a skirmish last fall, he had felt like a ghoul. Now, scarcely bothered at all, he went after anything that would help him fight harder or longer.

He stepped onto the crossties. The trooper knelt on the chest of one dead man, busily went through jacket and pants pockets. He found nothing except some tobacco and a pipe, and said, "Shit." Simultaneously, Charles saw what he wanted lying in dead yellow weeds beyond the embankment. Von Helm saw it, too, tried to hurry past his captain. Charles pivoted, nearly causing the lieutenant's shiny head to crash against his jaw.

"Mine," Charles said. "And one more thing. Next time, wait for my orders, or I'll have you up on charges."

Von Helm clenched his denture-filled jaws and wheeled away; Charles had already smelled the spirits. All the warnings were right. He had a bad one on his hands.

"Just proves what they say," the trooper complained, bending over the feet of the dead soldier. "Damn Yanks ain't worth nothing but a pair of shoes." He stripped off the right one, swearing when he saw the upper separated from the sole. He peered inside. "Lashbrook of Lynn. What's that mean?"

No one bothered to answer him. Calming a little, Charles slipped down the side of the embankment and retrieved the weapon from the weeds. The look of the piece was completely new. About four feet long, it had a mysterious aperture in the butt of the stock. It bore the maker's name on top of its receiver.

SPENCER REPEATING-RIFLE CO.
BOSTON, MASS.
PAT'D. MARCH 6, 1860

A memory door clicked open, showing Charles a paragraph from one of the many Washington papers read behind Southern lines. A specially commissioned corps of marksmen led by some famous New York sharpshooter had received or was to receive a new type of rapid-repeating rifle. Could he be holding one—perhaps stolen? The sharpshooters were still in Washington, so far as he knew.

Death had relaxed the bodies of the Yanks; the stench was ripening over the roadbed. But he refused to leave without the ammunition for the piece. He found the dead man who had fired it. Woolner had already carried off his shoes and pocket items but left behind three odd tubular magazines. Charles plucked one from the weeds where it lay beside a stiffening hand. He opened it and discovered seven rim-fire copper cartridges, one behind the next. He now understood the function of the opening in the butt.

Woolner appeared. "That the piece that was bangin' away so fast? Never seen one like it."

"Let's hope we don't see many more. I recovered some of the ammunition. I want to fire it."

The sun broke through the fog in long shining shafts. They slung the wounded Yank across the back of Loomis's horse and, leaving the dead, proceeded on toward camp. Julius Wanderly had missed the brief action, so von Helm rode beside him, describing it.

The Yank's belly bled all over the horse. When they arrived in camp, Loomis reached around and touched the man—"Hey, Yank, wake up."—and found him dead. Loomis suddenly paled, fainted, and fell off his horse.

Exhausted and still a little shaken, Charles arranged for disposal of the Yank's body, dismissed the men, then saw to Sport: the unsaddling, rubbing down and brushing, feeding, and watering. In casual, slipshod fashion, von Helm put up his mount in a third of the time.

Finished at last, Charles patted the gray and went to the mess to fill his growling stomach. Von Helm had headed for the quarters he now shared with Charles. Their first few days as hut-mates had included little except remarks required by duty or politeness. Henceforth there would be even fewer exchanges if Charles had anything to do with it.

It was late in the day before he found Calbraith Butler and reported on the trackside fight. "It was a totally pointless action, in my opinion. One we should have avoided."

Butler leaned back in his camp chair, silhouetted against the sun now shining brightly outside. "You're not telling me everything. Ab Woolner's been by. He seconded your opinion, but he also described the way the detachment got into the muss. The Dutchman dragged you."

"First and last time, sir," Charles promised.

"I warned you," Butler said, not to reprimand but to sympathize. "Maybe I can get the little rodent transferred again. I must say he made quite an impression on Wanderly. Your second lieutenant is singing hosannas and comparing the new man to Stuart. He's telling everyone von Helm exemplifies Stuart's first axiom—gallop toward your enemy, trot away—and never mind that there may not be anyone left to trot after you gallop."

"I'll handle Lieutenant von Helm," Charles said, though with less confidence than his tone demonstrated. "Any further word from headquarters about Ambrose?"

"No, nothing again today. I honestly don't think we'll ever know what happened."

Unsmiling, Charles bobbed his head to agree. He then described the shoulder weapon he had confiscated. "I want to take it to the drill ground tomorrow and test it. It'll be no use to me later—there's no ammunition beyond those three tubes. Twenty-one rounds."

"I should like to be there for the test."

"I'll let you know when I go, sir." A weary salute, and he left his commanding officer, who stared at the fallen tent flap for some moments after Charles disappeared. Then Butler shook his head in a melancholy way and went back to work.

Still reluctant to rejoin von Helm in the hut, Charles trudged back to the horse shelters, to be sure Sport was properly blanketed and standing on the planks instead of the soggy ground. He rubbed his hand slowly over the gray's warm neck. He felt terrible, sorrowful and angry at the same time.

Well, that was the soldier's portion after almost any engagement. No one could explain why the reaction was so common, but experience had taught him that it was. To see Gus Barclay might pull him out of it. Even as the wish welled up, he reminded himself that it wasn't a wise one. War was no time for liaisons, except the sort he had had with Stuart's Honorary Aide-de-Camp.

About one variety of love he had no reservations. He flung his arm around the gray head of the animal who had saved his life and pulled it close. Sport nipped his other wrist, which was rubbing the gelding's muzzle. But the nip was careful, inflicting no pain. Nothing mattered then except that affection. One thing sure: he and this incredible horse must survive the strange slippage, impossible to understand but equally impossible to miss, that seemed to be taking place in his life.

The report went roaring away through the woodlands. The paper target pinned to the tree snapped in the pale afternoon light, hit dead center.

Charles levered the trigger guard downward, springing the spent cartridge from the breech. Lever up, cock the piece manually, fire. Lever down, up, cock, fire. Half a dozen men lounged about, watching. With each round, their jaws fell a little lower. Ab Woolner pulled at his crotch to loosen his underwear, muttering, "Sweet God."

Thickening smoke drifted upward. Calbraith Butler had been counting by tapping his silver-mounted riding whip against his leg. As the sound of the final round faded, the bottom part of the target fell away and fluttered to earth. Butler looked at Charles.

"I make it seven rounds in approximately thirteen seconds."

A couple of the watchers picked up the spent copper cartridges for souvenirs. Charles butted the piece on the cracked toe of his boot and nodded glumly. The heat of the blued barrel seeped through his gauntlet.

It was the scout who spoke for all of them: "Let's hope them Yanks don't get too many rifles like that. They could load 'em on Monday and shoot at us the rest of the week."

Charles trudged back to his hut, where he laid the repeater in the gun rack. Von Helm was absent—all to the good, given the renewed gloom that followed the test. Charles stored the two remaining tubes in his field trunk, recalling Cousin Cooper's warnings about the North's industrial superiority. Wasn't this new rifle more evidence of that superiority? Why the hell had no one listened?

Or was he the man out of step? The negative thinker? The cynic who couldn't subscribe to the belief that was widespread in the army—the absolute certainty that nerve and spirit would prevail over numbers and better weapons? That might be true occasionally. But every time?

He lit a vile cigar bought from the sutler at three times the fair price. Hanged if he knew who was right, the skeptic who haunted his head or all his braggy troopers who discovered great omens in

333

week-old Yankee newspapers. Because McClellan had failed to move, certain Republicans were already calling for his replacement.

Encouraging rumors reached the camp from Norfolk, too. Some awesome new dreadnought was nearly off the ways. This *Virginia* was a rebuilt Union vessel, *Merrimack,* which the Yanks had tried to scuttle when they abandoned the navy yard. She had been raised and refitted with a sheathing of plate; an ironclad, they were calling her. Men spoke as if she might end the war by firing one or two salvos. The skeptic in Charles's head looked askance.

Next day's delivery of the mail brought a pleasing surprise, a package posted in Fredericksburg late in November. Inside it Charles found a small leather-bound book: *An Essay on Man* by Alexander Pope. On the flyleaf she had written:

> *To Captain Charles Main*
> *= = At the Front = =*
> *Christmas, 1861*

She had signed herself *A. Barclay* and tucked in a separate card that read: *I am very sorry I missed your visit and hope you will return soon.* He could see her vividly in the lines and loops of her graceful hand.

Many soldiers carried small Testaments in their coats or shirt pockets. That gave Charles an idea. He scrounged a piece of soft leather and with his sewing kit fashioned a small bag with a drawstring. He added a longer thong to slip over his head and put the little volume in the bag. He carried it beneath his shirt against the flat of his chest. It felt good there.

The gift buoyed him for several days, even given the presence of von Helm. The Dutchman bustled in and out of the hut with barely a word, though he seldom lost that demented glint in his eye. One evening, when Charles had a stomach complaint and didn't feel like attending a performance of *Box and Cox* being presented by some camp thespians, his first sergeant unexpectedly called on him.

"What brings you here, Reynolds?"

"Sir, it's just—" the man blushed—"I feel it's my duty to speak to you."

"Go ahead."

"It's Lieutenant Wanderly and Private Cramm, sir. Those two are spending a lot of their own money at the sutler's, treating the other boys. They're, uh, campaigning."

"For what?"

The sergeant answered first with a huge gulp. "For Lieutenant von Helm."

Tired, his middle hurting, Charles was cross. "I still don't understand. Goddamn it, man, say it plainly."

Peterkin Reynolds gave him a miserable look. "They want to elect him captain, sir."

An hour later, von Helm returned, trailing fumes of bourbon. "Missed a fine show this evening. Those actors—" His brown eyes grew vacant, then surprised, as he perceived the condition of the hut. "What's happened here? Where are my things?"

"I had them moved." Charles lay in his bunk, speaking around the smoldering cigar stub jammed between his teeth. "To the hut of your campaign manager."

"My—?" Von Helm blinked. "Oh." Somehow, Charles's eyes didn't intimidate him; perhaps he was too drunk. His mouth tucked up at the corners as if pulled on puppet strings. "Very well. Good evening, Captain." He left.

Charles yanked the cigar from his mouth and indulged in a string of oaths whose fervor concealed his sense of tired defeat. He was still in his twenties and felt twice that. He stood for a while, feeling the book in the pouch under his shirt. At least the battle lines were clear now. Captain Main against the posturing schemer from Charleston.

He remembered something, went outside, and pulled and pried until the small sign came loose. He threw it into the fireplace and watched the flames slowly consume *Gentlemen's Rest*. The words might be appropriate to some other army, but they no longer fit this one.

50

Stanley knocked and entered the secretary's office in a state of nerves. He was sure he had been accused and would be demoted or dismissed.

He was astonished to find the boss in a sunny mood, stepping around the office inspecting boxes and barrels packed with personal files and mementos. Cameron's cheeks had a pink sheen, left by a fresh shave; he smelled of lavender water. His desk was bare, which was unprecedented.

"Stanley, my boy, sit down. I'm clearing out in a hurry, but I wanted a chat with you before I leave." He waved the younger man to a seat while he took his regular place behind the desk.

Trembling, Stanley lowered his heavy body to the chair. "I was shocked when I heard the news of your resignation last Saturday, sir."

Cameron put the tips of his thumbs together and touched his index fingers above them, creating a triangle through which he peered at his visitor. "Even in this building, it can be Simon again —or Boss. I'm not particular. The one thing that won't fit any more is Mr. Secretary."

"That's a tragic loss for the war effort, sir."

The lame remarks brought a tight smile to Cameron's mouth. He snickered. "Oh, yes, any number of contract holders will say so. But a loyal fellow goes where his superiors think he can do best. Russia's a mighty long way from home, but I'll tell you the truth, Stanley—I won't miss the hurly-burly and backbiting of this town."

A lie, Stanley thought; the boss had bitten with the best. But all the departmental irregularities had finally forced Lincoln to act, although Cameron was allowed the face-saving fiction that becoming United States minister to Russia was a promotion.

"I imagine you'll get along with the new man," Cameron continued in a relaxed way. "He won't be as loose as I've been. He's a champion of the colored people"—Cameron's brief fling as an apostle of abolition had been forgotten by virtually everyone, including himself—"and pretty hard on those who don't come up to expectations. Now you take me—I was more inclined to overlook a mistake or a slight." The smile hardened ever so little. "Or an act of will. Yes, sir, you'll have to toe the mark for the next occupant of this office."

Stanley gnawed his bottom lip. "Sir, I'm in the dark. I don't even know the name of the new secretary."

"Oh, you don't?" Up flew the white brows. "I thought Senator Wade would have confided in you. If he didn't, I spose you'll just have to wait for the public announcement."

And there he left it, while Stanley twisted on the hook Cameron had snagged into him. Surprisingly, the older man laughed before he went on.

"I don't blame you too much, Stanley. I'd have done the same thing in your position. You turned out to be an apt pupil. Learned how to apply each and every lesson I taught you. 'Course, now I look back and reflect that maybe I taught you one too many."

The smile spread, infected with a jolly malice. "Well, my lad, let me give you one final bit of advice before we shake hands and part. Sell as many pieces of footwear as you can, for as much as you can, for as long as you can. And save the money. You'll need it, because in this town someone is always waiting. Someone who wants to sell you out. Someone who *will* sell you out."

Stanley felt he might have a heart seizure. Cameron sprang around the desk, clasped Stanley's hand so hard it hurt, then said, "You must excuse me now," and turned his back. Stanley left him rummaging cheerfully among the packed ruins of his empire.

The next night, George came home with news for Constance. "It's Stanton."

"But he's a Democrat!"

"He's also a zealot who can please the radicals. Those who favor him call him a patriot. If you're on the other side, the

337

descriptions include dogmatic and devious. They say he's willing to gain his ends by any means. And likely to use the suspension of habeas corpus—I mean use it widely. I wouldn't want to be a dissenting newspaper editor or an advocate of a soft peace and come to Mr. Stanton's attention. He may be Lincoln's appointee, but he's the creature of Wade and that crowd." A bemused smile softened his severity. "Did you know Stanton once tried a case involving McCormick's reaper, and Lincoln went along as a junior counsel? Stanton snubbed him as a bumpkin. Incredible how people change. This lunatic world, too—"

"Not you and I," she said, kissing him gently.

General McClellan recovered from his severe case of typhoid but remained the victim of another disease, for which all but his fiercest partisans excoriated him. Lincoln called the malady the slows. Under increasing internal and external pressures, the President issued Special War Order Number 1 on the last day of January. The order commanded the general-in-chief to get the Army of the Potomac moving toward Manassas by February 22, no later.

The February issue of the *Atlantic* printed new verses for "John Brown's Body" written by Mrs. Howe; George and his wife and son sang the stirring "Battle Hymn" while Patricia played. The song fit the new, more aggressive mood of the capital. The figure of Stanton, small and fierce, was being widely seen at all hours in the buildings on President's Park. George observed him several times in the Ordnance Department but had no reason to speak with him.

From the Western theater came a burst of news so glorious it produced mobs and drunken jubilation outside the newspaper offices, where long sheets summarizing the latest telegraphic dispatches hung. A combined river and land offensive had brought the surrender of Fort Henry, a key rebel bastion on the Tennessee, just below the Kentucky border.

Ten days later, Fort Donelson, on the Cumberland, fell. Both victories were theoretically the work of the departmental commander, General Halleck. But the man given the hero's wreath by the correspondents was an Academy graduate who had been out of George's thoughts a long time. As a West Point first classman, Sam Grant had once taken Orry's part when Elkanah Bent was deviling him.

338

Sam Grant. Astonishing. He and George had drunk together in cantinas after the Mexico City campaign. A likable officer and brave enough. But a soldier without the stamp of brilliance that was now on Tom Jackson, for example. The last George had heard, Grant had failed in the army out West and resigned because of problems with drinking.

Now here he was, just promoted from brigadier to major general of volunteers and nicknamed "Unconditional Surrender" because, when answering a request for terms from Donelson's commander, he said he would accept nothing less. *I propose to move immediately upon your works,* he wrote Buckner—and then he did it, breaking the Confederacy's hold on western Kentucky, western Tennessee, and the upper Mississippi. The South reeled, the North rejoiced, and Grant's name became known to every schoolboy whose parents read a paper.

Offsetting this, bad rumors continued to seep from the Executive Mansion. The President suffered from depression so profound some said it bordered on insanity. He roamed sleeplessly at night or lay motionless for hours, to rise and tell of queer prophetic dreams. The Washington gossip chefs, whom Constance said must be nearly as many as the uniformed men in town, had a variety of tidbits to offer, something for every political or emotional palate. Lincoln was going mad on behalf of the Union. Mary Lincoln, who acknowledged a lot of rebel relatives in Kentucky and the Confederate Army, was a spy. Twelve-year-old Willie Lincoln was fighting typhoid. That turned out to be true; the boy died two days before McClellan was to take Manassas.

McClellan did not; the army stayed put. And Lincoln did not show up at any of the official observances of Washington's birthday, although the armies on both sides celebrated the holiday, as was the custom before the war.

Billy paid a surprise visit one night. The brothers fell to exchanging complaints over whiskey before supper.

Billy: "What the devil's wrong with Mac? He was supposed to save the Union—week before last, wasn't it?"

George: "How should I know what's wrong? I'm nothing but a glorified clerk. All I hear is street talk. You should know more than I; he's your commander."

"He's your classmate."

"What a sarcasm. You sound like a Republican."

"Staunch."

"Well," George said, "all I hear is this. Little Mac outnumbers the enemy two or three to one, yet he keeps asking for postponements and reinforcements. Otherwise, he says, he can't be certain of success—which, he then repeats in the next breath, is guaranteed once he does move. God knows what goes on inside his head. Tell me about your new men."

"They've had nearly seven weeks of training, but of course good work in training is no yardstick of performance in a fight. Last week the battalion built a big floating raft on the canal—the next best thing to a pontoon bridge, which we've yet to try. The President came down to watch. He did his best to show interest in the work, but looked worn out. Positively ancient. He—"

Both looked up as Constance came in, pale.

"There's an orderly from your battalion at the door."

Billy rushed from the room. George paced, trying to overhear the muted voices. His brother returned, settling his cap on his head. "We're ordered to camp to prepare for departure on the cars."

"Where are you going?"

"I don't know."

They embraced hastily. "Take care of yourself, Billy."

"I will. Maybe Mac's finally moving."

And out Billy went into the dark.

51

Charles knew it meant trouble when Calbraith Butler summoned him after tattoo and he found the colonel as well as the major waiting.

"Please sit if you wish, Charles," Hampton said after Charles presented himself formally. He found Hampton's sober tone ominous.

"No, thank you, sir."

Hampton continued. "I rode here because I wanted to speak to you personally. I am faced with a thorny situation in Major Butler's command."

Butler said, "Sir, I prefer the word nasty."

Hampton sighed. "I'll not deny the rightness of that."

Charles marveled at how fit the colonel looked in a winter that was ruining the health of much younger men. He noticed the colonel's sword—slimmer, not the one he usually wore. Could it be the one Joe Johnston had given him in token of friendship—and until the rank of brigadier could be offered in fact?

"There is no point wasting words, Charles. Major Butler is in receipt of a petition from members of your troop. They request a new election of officers."

His cheeks numbed suddenly. Once aware of the electioneering, he had tried to monitor it discreetly. Von Helm wanted the captaincy and had promised Julius Wanderly a promotion if he got it. Peterkin Reynolds remained deferential to Charles but had grown less friendly. Was he to be raised to second lieutenant?

"Signed by how many men, sir?" Charles asked.

Embarrassed, Butler said, "Over half the troop."

"God above." Charles managed a laugh. "I knew I wasn't well liked, but that downright makes me sound like a Yankee. I had no idea—"

"You are an exceptionally good officer—" Hampton began.

"I agree," Butler said.

"—but that isn't the same as being a popular one. As you know, Charles, the men are not entitled to hold new elections until their one-year enlistments come up for renewal. However, I thought I should advise you of how matters stood and ask—"

This time he interrupted Hampton. "Let them go ahead. Tomorrow—I don't care." He did but hid it, standing rigidly straight.

Frowning, Butler asked, "But what if you lose?"

"Begging the major's pardon—why do you state it that way? You know I'll lose. The number of signatures on the petition guarantees it. I still say let them hold the election. I'll find some other way to serve."

The senior officers exchanged looks. Charles realized this had been planned with some care, and not solely to administer bad medicine.

Hampton spoke quietly: "I appreciate the spirit in which you said that, Charles. I appreciate all the qualities that make you a fine officer. Your bravery is beyond dispute. You have a father's concern for your men. I suspect it's your discipline that precipitated this, since so many in the legion still fancy themselves Carolina gentlemen, rather than soldiers awaiting the sanguinary pleasure of General McClellan. Also, your Academy training may have worked against you."

It hadn't worked against Stuart or Jackson or a score of others, Charles reflected with bitterness. But it was stupid to blame anyone else for his own shortcomings.

Hampton's voice rose emphatically. "I do not want you lost to this command. Nor does Major Butler. Therefore, if you don't care to campaign against your, ah, opponent—"

"I wouldn't waste a minute on that stupid Dutchman!" Charles caught his breath. "I'm sorry, sir." Hampton waved the apology aside.

"We have another arrangement to propose," Butler said. "You're a loner, Charles, but that can be valuable. Would you consider leading Abner Woolner and a few more of my best men in a squad of scouts?"

Hampton leaned forward, half his face in darkness. "It's the most necessary and most dangerous of all mounted duty. A scout is constantly at hazard. Only the best can handle the job."

Charles pondered, but not long. "I'll accept on one condition. Before I start, I'd like a short furlough."

That brought another frown from the major. "But the whole army's moving, or soon will be."

"To the rear, I'm told. To the Rapidan and the Rappahannock. The lady lives near the Rappahannock. Fredericksburg. I can rejoin the legion quickly if necessary."

Hampton smiled. "Request granted. Do you concur, Major Butler?"

"Yes, sir."

"Then," said Charles, "I accept duty as a scout. With pleasure."

Even though the rejection hurt, and would for a long time, he felt, at the same time, set free. He was happy. Did a manumitted black man experience similar feelings, he wondered as he walked back to his hut at a brisk pace, whistling.

His military passport, countersigned in Richmond, noted his age, height, complexion, hair and eye color, and stated that he had permission to travel to the vicinity of Fredericksburg, subject to the discretion of the military authorities. If that discretion had somehow proved an obstacle, Charles would have put the spurs to Sport, jumped over the authorities, and taken his chances.

As he crossed the miles to Spotsylvania County, first through rainstorms, then a cold snap that whitely crisped the dead fields and bare trees, his eagerness to reach Barclay's Farm increased, together with anxiety that he would find her gone again. At last he saw the sturdy stone house and wooden barns and outbuildings on the north side of the narrow road.

"And smoke coming out of the chimney," he yelled to the gelding.

It was a fine farm, well maintained despite the war. From the appearance of the fields, he judged that her property spread on both sides of the road. The main house had a look of great age and strength, fortresslike behind a pair of ninety-foot red oaks that must have sprung up wild, hunting the sun they needed. Since the house was old, the trees had probably been saplings when it was built. Now they had grown and spread until their thick limbs hung over the wooden roof shakes and touched the front dormers of an upstairs floor or attic. Wonderful trees, made for climbing and making him wish he was a boy again.

As he reined in, in the dooryard, he heard a squeak and whine. Away to his right he glimpsed a jet of sparks in the dark interior of an outbuilding. He dismounted, and the pedals of the grinding wheel stopped squeaking. A Negro of about twenty emerged from the building. He wore heavy plow shoes, old pants, a mended shirt. He had both hands on the curved scythe he had been sharpening.

"Something we can do for you, sir?"

"This man's all right, Boz."

The new voice belonged to another Negro, older, moon-faced, with few teeth; he appeared from behind the house, a sack of henhouse feed over his shoulder. Charles had met him in Richmond the night of the ball.

"How are you, Captain?" the older black asked. "You look like you rode through eighty acres of mud."

"I did. Is she home, Washington?"

He let out a kind of hee-hee laugh. "Indeed she is. It's early for a social call, but don't you mind that—she's always up before daylight. Probably frying our morning ham right now." Washington jerked his head to the right. "Back door's quicker."

Charles walked past him and up the wooden stoop, spurs jingling. "Put the captain's horse in the barn, Boz," the older freedman said to the younger. Charles knew he should look after Sport himself, but all he wanted to do was rap on the door, hoping he didn't appear or smell filthy. He could scarcely believe his own excited state.

The door opened. Gus gasped, and a flour-white hand flew to her chin. "Charles Main. It *is* you?"

"So my passport says."

"You confused me for a moment. The new beard—"

"Is it all right?"

"I'll get used to it."

He grinned. "Well, it's warm, anyway."

"Are you on your way somewhere?"

"I didn't realize the beard was that repulsive."

"Stop that and answer me." She had liked his retort.

"I am responding, ma'am, to your kind invitation to visit. May I come in?"

"Yes, yes—certainly. I apologize for making you stand in the cold."

Her old cotton dress, much laundered and nearly bleached of its yellow dye, still became her. She looked a trifle sleepy, yet pleased and excited. He noticed a button missing in the row rising over the swell of her breast and saw flesh in a momentary gap. He felt faintly wicked and fine.

She had been stirring batter. She laid the spoon aside and put her fist against her hip. "One question before we get down to visiting in earnest. Are you going to insist on calling me by that wretched name?"

"Most probably. This is wartime. We all have to put up with a few unpleasantries."

He had tried to mimic her tart style. She picked that up and smiled again. "I shall make a patriotic effort. Breakfast will be

344

ready shortly. There's plenty. I'll heat some water if you want to wash first."

"I'd better, or your house will look like a mudhole."

She surprised him by grasping his left sleeve. "Let me look at you. Are you all right? I hear there may be heavy fighting soon. You've survived the winter so far—so many men haven't, they say." She responded to his reaction with an annoyed shake of her head. "Are you laughing at me?"

"No, ma'am. But I counted about half a dozen statements and questions whizzing by. Which shall I take first?"

She blushed, or so he thought. It was hard to be sure because only the fire in the great stone hearth illuminated the room, and the day was dark.

The kitchen was huge, peg-floored and furnished with tables, chairs, a work block on thick legs. All were simply but well designed, with an appearance of strength that matched the house. Like Ambrose, Barclay must have been a good woodworker, Charles thought with a jealous twinge.

"First?" she repeated, lifting and turning pieces of frying ham in a black iron skillet. "This. How are you? I didn't hear from you. I was worried."

"Didn't I ever tell you I'm a bad letter writer? I especially lack the nerve to write someone as well educated as you. Another thing—the army mails are slow as glue. Your gift arrived late. I thank you for remembering me."

"How could I not?" Then, hastily averting her head: "At Christmas."

"The book's handsome."

"But you haven't read it."

"No time yet."

"That's a hedge, if I ever heard one. How long can you stay?"

Underneath the lightness of the question he believed he heard something different, unexpected, vastly pleasing. "Until tomorrow morning, if it won't compromise you. I can sleep in the barn with my horse."

Hand on hip again: "With whom would it compromise me, Captain? Washington? Bosworth? They're both discreet, tolerant men. I have a spare room with a bed and no neighbors closer than a mile."

"All right, but I still have reason to worry about you. There's liable to be fighting around here, and you're—"

A soft clunk. He glanced down. A lump of mud had dislodged from his pants and lay on the floor. Sheepish, he picked it up. She waved the spoon.

"Off with those things, then we'll eat and talk. Go into my room—straight down there. I'll send one of the men with water for the tub and a nightshirt that belonged to Barclay. Some of his things are stored in the attic. Leave your uniform in the hall, and I'll brush it up." Through all this urging, she prodded him with the spoon, determined as any sergeant drilling a recruit. A last prod—"Now scat." He left, laughing.

Gus Barclay's mere presence drew him out of the dank inner places where he had dwelled of late. He sank into hot water in the zinc tub and scrubbed himself with a cake of homemade soap, having first removed the thong from around his neck and laid the leather bag where it couldn't get wet.

He put on the nightshirt and returned to the kitchen, where she filled him with plain, hearty food. The freedmen ate, too. They regularly took their meals in the kitchen, she explained. "Though they always come and go by the back door. Some of my neighbors —fine religious folk, church every Sunday—would probably burn me out if they saw black men crossing my threshold at all hours. Washington and Boz and I talked it over, and we decided we could all stand a bit of injury to our pride if that's the price of keeping the roof over our heads."

The freedmen smiled and agreed. The two of them and Gus were a family, Charles realized; one into which he was immediately welcomed.

After he dressed in his cleaned-up clothes, she showed off her fields and buildings in a leisurely ramble on foot. The frost melted, the temperature rose, bare earth oozed moisture and scents of a coming spring. They spoke of many things. Of Richmond, where she had sold produce from the farm twice in the fall. "It was my impression that every person in that city is engaged in swindling every person in some fashion."

Of his disillusionment with the army. "Staff officers are a pretty busy lot. I calculate they spend fifty percent of their time politicking, fifty percent fiddling with pieces of paper, and fifty percent fighting."

"That's a hundred and fifty percent."

"That's why there hasn't been much fighting."

346

Of her uncle, Brigadier Jack Duncan. She wished she knew his whereabouts so that she could write him. Unofficial couriers—smugglers—could carry almost anything across Confederate and Union lines, using a combination of forged passports and bribes.

Then, without prompting, she spoke of things past. "I wanted a child, and so did Barclay. But I became pregnant only once, and then only with extreme difficulty."

They were strolling along a lane bordering a small apple orchard. The lowering sun threw a web of branch shadows down upon them. She was bundled in an old hip-length coat, a coat for chores, and had crossed her arms over her breast and tucked her hands under her sleeves. She didn't look at him while she discussed the subject of childbearing, but otherwise there was no sign of embarrassment. Nor did he feel any.

"I was sick almost constantly for the first four and a half months. Then one night I lost the child spontaneously. I would have had a fine son if he'd lived. I may be able to quote Pope, but I'm not as good at simple things as the old cow in the barn who keeps us in milk and calves."

She made a joke of it, but she kept her head down, kicking at stalks of long grass beside the lane.

For the evening meal she spit-roasted a round red roast of beef. Washington said he and Boz had chores and so would not be able to join the others for supper. Gus accepted the fiction without question. She and Charles ate by the light of the kitchen hearth—one of the best meals he had ever tasted. Thick slices of browned potatoes grown on her land. Hot corn bread unlike the army's; no wiggling visitors revealed themselves when he broke a piece in half. And the juicy, tender beef, free of the stink of brine and the Commissary Department.

She brought a jug of rum to the table and poured a cup for each of them.

He shared more of his thoughts about the war. "Independence is a fine, laudable quality in a man. But an army that wants to win can't accommodate it."

"Seems to me the government is caught in the same dilemma, Charles. And suffering. Each state puts its own wishes and welfare ahead of every other consideration. The principle we're fighting for may turn out to be what destroys us. But here—we're getting too gloomy. Will you have some more rum? Tell me about your command."

347

"Shrunk considerably since we danced in Richmond." He mentioned the petition and his reassignment to Butler's scouts.

Solemnly, her blue eyes fixed on his. "I've read about the duties of scouts. Very dangerous."

"But less trying than leading men who want to go fifty ways at once. I'll be all right. I value my horse and my hide—in that order."

"My, you're in a good mood."

"It's the company, Gus."

"Odd—" A log broke in the hearth; fire and shadow moved sinuously over the walls, the stove, the handmade shelves holding her dishes. "I can almost listen to that name without cringing. As you say"—eyes on him again, briefly—"the company."

Each felt, then, the isolation of the house, the sex and rising emotion of the other. Charles brought his legs together under the table. She began to fuss with dishes, forks, spoons, clearing things. "You must be worn out—and you have a long ride tomorrow, don't you?"

"Yes and yes." He wanted to follow her as she moved away, sweep his arms around her, let only one bedroom in the dark house be occupied tonight. It wasn't propriety that prevented him, or fear that she would say no, though she certainly might. It was a self-spoken warning from the silences of his mind, one he had heard before. A warning about time and place and the circumstances that had brought them together.

He pushed away from the table. "I suppose I had better turn in." He did feel pleasantly tired, his muscles loose, his body warm, his heart content except in one regard. "It's been a wonderful day."

"Yes, it has. Good night, Charles."

Going to her, he leaned down and gently kissed her forehead. "Good night." He turned and walked to the spare bedroom.

He lay under the comforter an hour, reviling himself. *I should have touched her. She wanted it. I saw it in her eyes.* He flung the cover off. Strode to the door. Listened to the night house, the tiny creaks and shifts. Reached for the knob. Stopped with his fingers an inch from it. Swore and went back to bed.

He wakened with his heart beating fast and caution gripping him. He heard noise in the hall, sounds not normal for a house at rest. Light flashed under the door. Barefoot, in the borrowed nightshirt, he jerked the door open. Augusta Barclay stood in a listening attitude near the foot of the attic stairs. She wore a cotton flannel bed gown with an open throat, and had braided her yellow hair.

"What's wrong?" he said.

She hurried along the hall, an old percussion rifle in one hand, a lamp casting tilting shadows in the other. "I heard something outside." Saying this, she stopped close to him. He clearly saw her nipples raising the soft flannel. Restraint and good sense deserted him. He put his right hand on her breast and leaned down, inhaling the night warmth of her skin and hair.

She pressed to him, eyes closing, lips opening. Her tongue touched his. Then knocking began.

She pulled back. "What have you done to me, Charles Main?"

The knocking grew louder, overlaid by Washington's urgent voice. Charles fetched his revolver from the bedroom and ran after her to the back door, where he found the two freedmen, obviously upset.

"Powerful sorry to wake you in the middle of the night, Miz Barclay," Washington said. "But they's all sorts of commotion on the road." Charles heard it: axles creaking, hoofs clopping, men cursing and complaining.

Gus motioned with the rifle. "Come inside and close the door." She put down the lamp and cocked the weapon.

Charles strode through the dark to the parlor, crouched by the window, and returned presently with reassurance. "I saw the letters CSA on the canvas of two wagons. They're moving toward Fredericksburg. I don't think we'll be bothered."

Back in the parlor, standing side by side at the window but careful not to touch, Charles and Gus watched the train of heavy vehicles pass in bright moonlight. When they were gone and the bellowed complaints of the teamsters, too, Charles saw daylight glinting. There was no time to go back to bed, for any reason.

Washington and Boz said they were cold. Gus began brewing coffee. So the night and the visit ended. He left after breakfast. She walked to the road with him. Sport, well rested, was frisking, eager to be off.

She touched his gauntleted hand where it lay on his left leg. "Will you come again?"

"If I can. I want to."

"Soon?"

"General McClellan will have a lot to say about that."

"Charles, be careful."

"You, too."

She lifted his hand and pressed it to her lips, then stepped away. "You must come. I haven't felt so happy in years."

"Nor I," he said, and gigged Sport into the road the wagons had rutted with their wheels.

He waved as he spurred away, gazing over his shoulder at the dwindling figure against the backdrop of the stone house and the two red oaks. Impossible to deny his feelings any longer.

You'd better try. In wartime no man could make a promise to a woman with any certainty of keeping it.

He remembered the warmth of her bosom, her mouth, her hair, that exquisite touch of tongues before Washington knocked.

He mustn't become entangled.

He *was* entangled.

He wasn't falling in love—

It had already happened.

What the hell was he supposed to do now?

52

On the first Saturday in April, the mood in James Bulloch's Liverpool office was light as the spring air. Captain Bulloch had lately returned from a swift but uneventful dash through the blockade; at Savannah he had conferred with some of Mallory's men, though he had imparted no details to Cooper.

The office still basked in the success of its first project. On March 22 the screw steamer *Oreto* had slipped away from the

Toxteth docks without crown interference; two of Consul Dudley's detectives had watched and cursed from the dockside, but that was all.

Bulloch had invented the name *Oreto* to confuse the authorities. While she was under construction at William Miller's, the yard had listed her as a Mediterranean merchantman, and when she cleared to sea her destination was shown as Palermo. In fact, it was Nassau. The British captain hired for the transatlantic run would there hand over command to Captain Maffitt of the Confederate Navy, for *Oreto* was far from a humble freighter. Her design and engineering followed standard plans for gunboats; two seven-inch rifles and half a dozen smoothbores were on their way to Nassau separately, on the bark *Bahama.* When *Oreto* was armed, she would be a formidable fighting ship.

How long this scheme to foil British law would work, no one could be sure. It must be long enough for their second vessel to be launched. Bulloch had said this when he and Cooper retired to their safest meeting place—Bulloch's parlor—a few nights after the captain's return.

A mail pouch just in from the Bahamas had brought an urgent message, he told Cooper. The second gunboat must be rushed to completion, because Lincoln's plan to bottle up the South was rapidly changing from a contemptible paper blockade to a real and damaging one as more and more Yankee warships went on line. *Florida*—that would be *Oreto*'s name when she was commissioned—had a clearly defined mission: to capture or sink Northern merchant vessels, thus causing a steep rise in the cost of maritime insurance. Next, according to Confederate assumptions, Lincoln would hear howls from commercial shipowners and demands for increased protection. He would be forced to pull vessels from the blockade squadrons for this duty.

A second fast, armed raider could increase the pressure. They had such a ship nearing completion over at Laird's. Though resembling *Oreto,* she was superior in several respects. Bulloch's code name for her was *Enrica.* On the shipyard books she was Number 290—the two hundred ninetieth keel laid down at Laird's, whose founder, old John, had moved into politics while sons William and John Junior looked after the enormous business that had grown from a small ironworks making boilers.

Work on *Enrica* must be speeded; that was the message Cooper had to deliver this spring Saturday. It was not as easy as it sounded, because neither he nor Bulloch nor anyone from the office dared step onto Laird property. Dudley had spies everywhere. If they saw Southerners at the yard, or even meeting openly with one of its owners, the Yankee minister, Adams, would press for an investigation and the game would be up. That was the reason the contract for *Enrica* had been negotiated in clandestine meetings at Number 1 Hamilton Square, Birkenhead, the residence of John Laird, Junior.

Cooper rather enjoyed the intrigue. Judith called it dangerous and his zest for it foolhardy. Well, perhaps, but it lent his days a sense of purpose and put an edge of excitement on them. As the hour for departure neared, he could feel a not unpleasant tingling on his palms.

The office remained unusually cheerful this balmy afternoon. Yesterday's pouch had brought several papers from home, including a *Charleston Mercury* for March 12. In it, Cooper read details of THE GREAT NAVAL BATTLE IN HAMPTON ROADS, as it was headlined. On March 9, a Confederate steamer plated with iron had exchanged fire with a strange-looking Union ship alternately referred to as an Ericsson Battery, after the inventor of her revolving turret, and *Monitor*.

Thrilled, Cooper read of the "sharp encounter" between *Virginia* and the Yankee ironclad; they had dueled with only thirty to forty yards of water separating them. The paper said *Virginia* had achieved a "signal victory." The naïve writer failed to grasp the real significance of the meeting.

With a shiver up his spine, Cooper reread the piece, remembering Brunel, the great British engineer whose ship designs he had studied and attempted to duplicate in South Carolina. Brunel would have understood and seen what Cooper saw: the last rites of wood and sail; the accelerating ascendancy of steam-driven iron on the oceans and the continents as well. Brunel had predicted it years ago. It was an incredible time in which to live, a time of marvels amidst the perils.

He checked his pocket watch, collected his things, and started for the stair. Bulloch emerged from the partitioned space that formed his tiny office.

"Convey my regards to Judith."

"And mine to Harriott."

"I trust you'll have a restful Sabbath."

"I shall after I go to church."

"You have our donation?"

"Yes." Cooper tapped his tall hat. Looks and half-smiles during the exchange conveyed a second set of questions, responses, meanings. Two of the clerks in the office were new; one couldn't be perfectly sure of loyalties.

Going downstairs, he tipped his hat to Prioleau, the manager of Fraser, Trenholm, who was just returning to the building. Cooper crossed the shadowed cobbles of the court and hurried through the short tunnel beneath the offices fronting Rumford Place. He turned left as the bells of the Church of St. Nicholas rang the quarter hour. He would be able to make the 4:00 P.M. ferry easily.

At the corner he checked to the left, to the right, then to the rear. He saw no one suspicious among those hurrying or idling in the spring sunshine. He turned right toward the Mersey. The sun was sinking over the Wirral, and the span of water between the city and Birkenhead dazzled him with thousands of moving splinters of light. A freighter passed, outbound. He heard the faint ring of the ship's bell.

Cooper missed South Carolina now and then. But with Judith and the children and his job all here, he had concluded he was better off and probably happier in Liverpool. Except for Prioleau and two others at Fraser, Trenholm, no one in the city knew his history, hence no one remarked on the inconsistency of working for a cause in which he did not entirely believe. He himself couldn't adequately explain this dualism, in which one Cooper Main continued to loathe slavery, while another loved and served the South with a new, war-born fervency.

He wasn't even sure the Confederacy would survive. Recognition by the two most important European nations, Britain and France, was still a hope, nothing more, and little seemed to be happening militarily except for the stunning triumph at Hampton Roads. A prudent man, a man who wanted to retain his sanity, did as he was doing now: he concentrated on the task of the moment, not the dour issues beneath.

"England off'ring neutral sauce to goose as well as gander"—he softly sang the Southern doggerel put to the old tune as he proceeded across the landing stage from the ticket booth to the ferry —"was what made Yankee Doodle cross and did inflame his dander." Relaxed by the warm sunshine, he found a spot at the rail and leaned there, thinking of his wife and other pleasant subjects. The ferry, packed with families, shoppers, and workers whose offices closed early on Saturday, left the city stage at a minute past four, bound for the Woodside stage across the Mersey.

Cooper had succumbed to Liverpool as he had long ago succumbed to the charms of Charleston, though the two cities could not have been more unlike. Charleston was a pale lady who napped away the hot afternoon, Liverpool a freckled girl who poured the beer at a public house. But he had come to love the second as much as the first.

He loved the bustle of the port. Into the Mersey poured the commerce of the empire, and out of it went old ships freshly loaded and new ones freshly launched. He loved the banter of the seafaring men who came and went like the tides. Whether they were Liverpudlians or lascars from the East Indies or even would-be shipbuilders from the Carolinas, they spoke a common tongue and belonged to the same restless, frequently lonely brotherhood.

Cooper loved Liverpool's dark, square buildings, as solid as the good-humored people who inhabited them. He loved the comfortable town house he and Judith had found, directly across Abercromby Square from Prioleau's. He had even learned to eat black pudding, a local specialty, though he would assuredly never love that.

He did love the people, a fascinating, cross-grained lot, from the magnates who sent men sailing around the storm capes with a pen stroke to lesser mortals such as Mr. Lumm, his greengrocer, who had abruptly been made a childless widower at thirty-seven and never remarried because he had discovered the world's enormous population of willing women, a population unknown to him when he wed at fifteen.

Now seventy-four, Mr. Lumm continued to operate his shop a full six days each week and boasted to Cooper, man to man, of the enormous resources of his goolies. "Nuff ter popyoulate an ole country, assa fack." While still in his fifties, he had discovered that the secret of keeping his nudger in trim was to exercise it often, with any quim but a House of Commons. Cooper loved the roguish old fellow as much as he loved the white-haired vicar of the parish, who bred bull terriers, led wildlife walks in the Wirral, and took pains to visit the Mains at least once a week because he knew strangers in a foreign land lacked friends. The vicar strongly opposed slavery and the South, but on a personal basis that made no difference.

Of an evening, Cooper liked to stroll the Toxteth docks and

gaze at the stars above the Mersey and the Wirral hills, and tell himself it was a good time, a good place, even if he was far from home. "Dirty old town," Mr. Lumm often said in a tone of great affection. Cooper understood perfectly.

His mind drifting and his eye on the panorama of docks and coaling floats on the Liverpool shore, he suddenly had a tight-drawn feeling. He turned, and saw the man for the first time.

About fifty, Cooper judged. Bulbous nose. A mustache of heroic proportions. Cheap suit, too heavy for the weather. Paper sack in one hand. The man stubbornly occupied one end of a bench overloaded with a thin woman and her five children. From the sack the man drew a leek. He bit the white bulb with great relish.

Chewing and chewing, the man gave Cooper a glance—not unfriendly, merely curious. But Cooper was by now experienced at spotting those who might be Dudley's thugs. He checked the width of the man's shoulders. Very possibly this was a new one.

He felt jittery as Birkenhead's yards and old, soot-black buildings rose ahead. The ferry bumped in, and Cooper was one of the first to get off, moving quickly but not at a pace to suggest panic. He wove through the rank of lounging hackmen and climbed the cobbled street to a lane tucked behind Hamilton Square. He darted in and, halfway down, turned around. He watched the mouth of the lane, but there was no sign of the man who ate leeks.

Relieved, he entered the public house, the Pig and Whistle, where the lane dead-ended.

As usual, only a few sailors and dockworkers were in the place at this hour. Cooper took a seat at a small, round table, and the landlord's gray-haired wife soon brought him a pint of ale without receiving an order. "Afternoon, Mr. Main. Evensong is delayed two hours."

"That late?" He couldn't suppress anxiety. "Why?"

"I know nothing about the reason, sir."

"All right, Maggie, thank you."

Damn. Two hours to kill. The man on the ferry and now this—was there trouble? Had Charles Francis Adams somehow convinced the crown to seize the 290? A flock of alarming fantasies flew around in his head and robbed the ale of its savor. He jumped when the bell over the door jangled. A bulky figure filled the rectangle of light.

The man with the sack of leeks came straight to his table. "Mr.

355

Cooper Main, I believe?" A smarmy smile; a pudgy hand extended. "Marcellus Dorking. Private inquiry agent." He withdrew his hand. "Mind if I sit and have a word?"

What the devil was the game? Matt Maguire, Broderick—none of Dudley's other detectives operated this boldly. Heart hammering, Cooper said, "I don't know you."

Dorking slid onto the long seat beneath the window of dirty bottle glass. He laid the much-handled sack on the table, called for a gin, took a leek from the sack, and began to toy with it, his huge smile unwavering.

"But we know you, sir. Bulloch's chap—right, eh? No problem there. We admire a man of conscience."

"Who is we?"

"Why, the parties who requested me to approach you, sir." He bit the leek in half, masticating noisily. From the bar, a small man with coal-dusted hand complained about the stink. Dorking glared, then shone his smile on Cooper again. He ate as he spoke. "Parties discomforted by Captain Bulloch's interpretation of the Foreign Enlistment Act."

Cooper sensed he was in trouble, perhaps caught. Would he be searched? The message in his hat discovered? Unwise to put that sort of thing on paper, he realized belatedly, but no one in Bulloch's office was a professional spy.

Would he be arrested? Jailed? How would he notify Judith?

Dorking reached for another leek. "You're on the wrong side, sir. This nigger slavery stuff—m' wife's very strong against it. So 'm I."

"Does your conviction spring from your conscience or your pocketbook, Dorking?"

The man scowled. "I wouldn't joke, sir. You are a foreign national, involved in serious violations of the Enlistment Act. Oh, I know the dodge, sir—shipyards cannot arm and equip vessels of war for belligerents with whom Great Britain is at peace. But nothing in the act says it's illegal to build a ship *here*"—he waved the green stem near Cooper's nose—"and buy guns and powder and shells *there*"—the leek flew away as he extended his arm—"and bring 'em together three or more nautical miles from our coastline. Not illegal, but it is definitely a Jesuitical interpretation of our law, wouldn't you say, sir?"

Cooper stayed silent. Dorking leaned in again, intimidating. "Very Jesuitical indeed. In your case, however, it could be over-

356

looked—even a small stipend paid—if my clients received one or two brief reports as to the purpose and status of a certain vessel sometimes identified as the 290 and sometimes as *Enrica*—Still sailing the same course, aren't we, sir?"

Pale with rage despite his fright, Cooper said, "You are offering me a bribe, is that it, Mr. Dorking?"

"No, no! Merely a little more financial security, sir. Just for a few helpful facts—such as an explanation of the odd behavior of some sailor boys lately seen on Canning Street. They were marching along with fife and drum, playing a tune called 'Dixie's Land.' The same sailor boys had been spotted at John Laird's not long before. Spotted inside the gate. Do I make myself clear? Now what does that say to you, Mr. Main?"

"It says they like the tune of 'Dixie's Land,' Mr. Dorking. What does it say to you?"

"That Laird's might be hiring a crew, sir. For the proving run of a new Confederate States war vessel, could it be?" The inquiry agent flung his half-eaten leek on the table, roaring at Maggie. "Where's my damn gin, woman?" He then gave Cooper time to observe his narrowed eyes and clenched teeth before he said, "I shall be candid with you, sir. There's more than a fee if you help us. There's assured safety for your wife and little ones."

Maggie had reached the table. Cooper snatched the glass from her hand and dashed the gin in Dorking's face. The man cursed, dripping and wiping. Cooper grabbed his throat with his left hand.

"If you touch my wife or my children, I'll find you and personally kill you."

"I'll fetch Percy," Maggie said, starting away. "Me husband. He weighs seventeen stone."

Hearing that, Dorking bolted to the door, pausing long enough to shout back, "Slave-owning nigger-beating bastard. We'll stop you." He shook the paper sack. *"Rely on it!"* Jangle went the bell, vibrating long after the door slammed.

"You all right, sir?" Maggie asked.

"Yes." Cooper swallowed; shock set in. He couldn't believe he had seized Dudley's man so violently. It was the threat against his family that had provoked him—without thought or hesitation. The Confederate banners could sink to oblivion, Jeff Davis and all the rest could die and go to glory—he wouldn't care so long as nothing harmed the three human beings he held dear.

357

The incident left him shaken, and not solely because of the personal aspect. It showed him the hour was growing later, the stakes larger, the mood more desperate on both sides of the table. He finished his ale and drank a second, and still felt church-sober; no relief there.

Shadows heavied in the lane, and finally it was time to leave for the Church of St. Mary, Birkenhead. The church was situated near the Mersey, practically next door to Laird's and the ship he had never seen. "Want Percy to tag after you for safety's sake?" Maggie whispered before he went out. He did, desperately, but he shook his head.

The walk to the church was tense. The narrow streets of the Birkenhead waterfront struck him as peculiarly empty for a fine early evening. He kept glancing behind but reached the church, a cruciform structure of Gothic design built early in the century, without incident.

A nondescript man stepped away from the side of the building. He offered an apology and brief explanation for the delay. Then, after both checked the surrounding area for possible observers once more and saw none, Cooper removed his hat and passed the folded message to the man, who walked quickly away, and that was all.

Cooper ran most of the way to the ferry stage but missed the boat by three minutes and had to wait an hour for the next. The terminal smelled of dust and sausages and the odors of a drunk snoring on the floor in a corner. The short trip in the gathering evening was far less sunny than the earlier one. Cooper again leaned on the rail, seeing not the water or the city but the eyes and mustache and chomping teeth of Marcellus Dorking.

We'll stop you.

Into his mind there stole a question that, even a week ago, would have revolted him and brought derisive laughter. But now—

"Sir?"

"What's that?" He started, then showed embarrassment; the person who had stolen up behind him was a crewman.

"We've docked, sir. Everyone else has got off."

"Oh. Thank you."

And away he went, frowning in the spring dusk, silently repeating the question that was ludicrous no longer: Should I get a gun?

53

"Take the regiment, Colonel Bent."

Over and over, he heard the command in his head. Heard it despite the crashing of artillery in the cool Sunday air. Heard it despite the clatter of guns and limbers wildly wheeling up to defend the line. Heard it despite the hurt or frightened cries of the untrained Ohioans he was to rally and hold in position. Heard it despite all the hell-noise of this April morning.

"Take the regiment, Colonel Bent."

The division commander's eye had fallen on him at staff headquarters near the little Shiloh Meeting House, an hour after the first faint firing and the return of the first patrols to confirm its dire meaning. Albert Sidney Johnston's army was out there to the southwest and had caught them by surprise.

Bent was in this spot because the division commander disliked him. The commander could have ordered a junior officer to lead the Ohio regiment when its colonel, lieutenant colonel, and adjutant were all reported killed. Instead, he sent a staff colonel—one to whom he had been curt and unpleasant since their first meeting.

Had any officer ever served in worse circumstances? The general was a besotted incompetent, the division commander a little martinet, who last fall had been prostrated by an attack of nerves brought on by fear of Albert Sidney Johnston. Bent was convinced William Tecumseh Sherman was a madman. Vindictive, too. "Take the regiment, Colonel Bent."

After that, Sherman said something that made Bent hate him as he had never hated anyone except Orry Main and George Hazard: "And don't let me hear of you standing behind a tree with your hand out, feeling for a furlough. I know about you and your Washington connections."

Those connections had rescued Elkanah Bent. Or so he thought till this Sabbath morning. The day he boarded the westbound train with Elmsdale, he wrote and posted a polite, apologetic letter—a last appeal—to lawyer Dills. When he arrived in Kentucky, he found new orders, reassigning him from line command to staff duty with Anderson.

Then commands were shuffled, as they were endlessly shuffled. Anderson left, replaced by Sherman, whose brother was an influential Ohio senator. Had the little madman somehow gotten wind of wire-pulling? Bent didn't know, but he knew the division commander had been waiting for an opportunity to punish him.

Squinting into the smoke, Bent saw his fears made visible: a new assault wave forming down there in the woods. Hardee's men, a dirty rabble, many in shabby butternut-dyed uniforms. At the summit of the gentle slope the rebs would climb, Bent's green Ohioans lay behind trees or clumps of weeds. The Federals had been caught over their breakfast fires, no entrenching done, because General Grant had neglected to order any. Brains Halleck had good reason for distrusting Grant.

Trembling, Bent saw the rebel charge beginning. "Hold your positions, boys," he called, forcing himself to step clear of a thick oak and raise his field glasses. He wanted to crouch behind the tree and cover his head.

The first gray wave commenced firing. Bent winced and jumped back to the protection of the tree. The butternut rabble began to utter wild yells, the yells that had become a staple of Confederate charges, though no one quite knew when or why. To Bent they sounded like the howling of mad dogs.

He heard balls buzzing all around. To his left, a kneeling soldier stood suddenly, as if lifted under the arms. A slice of his right cheek sailed away behind him, then he toppled backward as the ball entered his brain.

On they came, up the hill in a wide line, the bank ranks firing when the men in front knelt to load and fire a second time from that position. Then the whole line swept forward again, bayonets fixed, officers screaming as loudly as enlisted men.

The rebs were within fifty yards, butternut and gray; beards

360

and tatters; huge fierce eyes and huge open mouths. Shell bursts speckled the blue sky; smoke bannered from the treetops; the earth shook, and Bent heard an even louder scream.

"Oh, no, my God—no."

The first rebs reached the Ohioans, who had never fought a battle—seen the elephant—until this morning. Clumsily, they fended off the stabbing bayonets of the attackers. Bent saw one length of steel bury in a blue coat and pierce through the other side, red. The scream sounded again.

"Oh, God, *no!*"

With his saber he beat at the back of an Ohio soldier. He whacked and he flailed, lumbering through long grass, right on the heels of the fleeing private. The rebs were pouring along the hilltop, the Ohioans breaking and scattering, their position over-run. Bent beat at the private's blue coat until the man stumbled and dropped. Bent sped past, fleet now despite his bulk.

He threw away his field glasses and his sword. Hundreds were running through the trees in the direction of Pittsburg Landing on the Tennessee River. Regiment after regiment was crumbling. He had to save himself even if every other soldier in the command perished; he was worth all of them combined.

Those who had fled ahead of him had already trampled out a path. Following it made Bent's progress easier until he caught up with someone blocking the path—a tiny soldier, limping and holding tight to the blue-enameled rim of a drum. Bent reached for the narrow shoulders of the drummer boy, caught hold, flung the boy to one side, but not before he saw the glare the youngster gave him, scared and scathing at the same time. The boy lost his balance and pitched to the ground beside the path. Bent ran on.

His panic grew worse as he plunged through thicker trees and across a creek. He heard a shell whining in. He leaped to a tree, flung his arms around it, closed his eyes, and buried his face. The instant before everything blew up, he realized who had screamed "Oh, God, no" just before the line broke.

He was the one who had screamed.

He awoke, pelted with rain. In the first incoherent moments he imagined he was dead. Then he began to hear the cries in the dark. Moans. Sudden shrieks. Snuffling, he groped everywhere from his ankles to his groin to his throat, feeling for injuries. He was soaked, stiff, hideously sore. But whole. *Whole.* God above. He had survived the day.

Lightning flashed above budding tree limbs. As the thunder followed, he started to crawl. He bumped his head against a trunk, went around it, then through some vicious briars. The ground in front of him sloped downward. He thought he smelled water. Crawled faster.

Lightning again; thunder; and with it the constant chorus of the injured. Thousands must be lying in the meadows and woodlands round about Shiloh Meeting House. Who had won the battle? He didn't know or care.

His hands sank in mud. He reached out and plunged them into the water. His mouth was parched. He scooped water in both palms, drank, retched, and nearly threw up. What was wrong with the water?

Lightning glittered. He saw bodies bobbing. Red liquid trickled out of his cupped hands. He doubled over and gagged. Nothing came up. He was confused. *I am in Mexico. This is Mexico.*

He staggered up, crossed the little stream, gagging at each gentle bump of the floating dead against his legs. He ran through more trees, tripped over a rock, went down with a gasp. One outflung hand struck something, tightened on it, helped check his fall.

From the feel, he believed it to be a bayonet socket. Strings of hair in his eyes, he struggled to his knees. Lucky he hadn't grabbed the bayonet itself.

White light lit everything. The bayonet had pinned another drummer boy to the earth, through the neck. Bent screamed until he had no more strength.

He started on. The shocks piled one upon another began to have a reverse effect: mental clarity returned. He didn't want that. Better to be numb, unaware. It happened anyway, forcing him to examine the realities.

Though he had behaved exactly like the Ohioans—broken, and fled—his was the greater crime because he was in command. Worse, he had been among the first to bolt. He knew the Ohioans would spread the story. The stigma would ruin him. He couldn't let that happen.

Snorting, soaking his trousers with his own urine and not caring, he doubled back in the dark, searching the underbrush. He found the wrong body the first time—put his hand deep into a blown-open chest, a reb's this time, and shrieked. When he was able, he went on and located the little drummer.

I can't, he thought, gazing at the impaled throat in a flicker of lightning.

There's no other way to save yourself.

Sweating and panting, he grasped the bayonet and gently pulled, gently twisted, gently freed it from the boy's flesh. Then, bracing his back against a tree, he steadied himself and gathered his nerve.

Once more he turned his head to the side and shut his eyes. By feel, he placed the point of the bayonet against the front of his left thigh.

Then he pushed.

Both sides claimed victory at Shiloh. But Grant had conducted the offensive on the second day, and ultimately the Confederate Army retired to Corinth, with one of its great heroes, Albert Sidney Johnston, a fatality of the battle. Those facts said more than the declarations of either side.

In the hospital, Elkanah Bent learned that the behavior of the Ohioans was not an isolated instance. Thousands had run. Pieces of regiments had been found all along the bank of the Tennessee, lounging in safety and listening to the pound and roar of the Sunday battle that was a defeat until the Union turned it around on Monday and produced a victory.

None of that alleviated the threat confronting Bent, however. He was soon under investigation for his conduct while in command of the regiment. He grew expert at repeating his story. "I was indeed running, sir. To stop my men. To stop the rout."

To the question about the place where he had been found unconscious—a small tributary of Owl Creek, nearly a mile from the regiment's position—he would reply: "The reb I fought—the one who bayoneted me—caught me right near our original line. I was facing him, not running away. The location of my wound proves that. I have few recollections of what happened after he stabbed me, except that I cut him down, then ran to stop the rout."

The inquiry went all the way to Sherman, to whom he said, "I was running to stop my men. To stop the rout."

"The allegation of some witnesses," said the general coldly, "is that you were among the first to break."

"I did not break, sir. I was attempting to stop those who did. If you wish to convene a general court-martial, I will repeat those statements to that body—and to any witnesses called to accuse me. Let them step forward. The regiment to which you assigned me consisted of men never before in battle. Like many others at Shiloh, they ran. I ran to stop them. To stop the rout."

"God above, will you spare me, Colonel?" Cump Sherman said, and leaned over to spit on the ground beside his camp desk. "I don't want you in any command of mine."

"Does that mean you intend—?"

"You'll find out what it means when I'm ready for you to find out. Dismissed."

Bent saluted and hobbled out on his padded crutch.

His nerves hurt worse than his wound. What would the little madman do to punish him?

On the peninsula southeast of Richmond, McClellan was sparring with Joe Johnston with little result. In the Shenandoah, Stonewall Jackson was maneuvering brilliantly, whipping the Yankees and expunging some of the shame of Shiloh. Down the Mississippi, Admiral Farragut ran past Confederate batteries to New Orleans. Virtually unprotected, the city surrendered to him on April 25. Within a week—almost a month after his thorny meeting with Sherman—Bent was reassigned.

"Staff duty with the Army of the Gulf?" said Elmsdale when Bent told him the news during a chance meeting. "That's principally an army of occupation. A safe berth, but it won't do much for your career."

"Neither did this," Bent growled, pointing at his trouser leg. Some seepage from the dressing stained the fabric.

Elmsdale shook his hand and wished him well, but Bent saw a smugness in the colonel's eyes. Elmsdale had taken a shoulder wound at a section of the battlefield christened the Hornet's Nest; he had received a citation in general orders. Bent had been plunged into new ignominy, for which he held others responsible, everyone from Sherman, the little madman with the scrubby beard, to the drab, drunken architect of the Shiloh victory, Unconditional Surrender Grant.

Elkanah Bent felt his star was descending, and there was little he could do about it.

54

"Bring those wagons up," Billy yelled. "We need boats!"

In mud halfway to his boot tops, Lije Farmer bumped the younger man's arm. "Not so loud, my lad. There may be enemy pickets on the other side."

"They can't see me any better than I can see you. How wide is this benighted stream anyway?"

"The high command does not favor us with such information. Nor do they issue topographical maps. Just orders. We are to bridge Black Creek."

"Hell of a good name for it," Billy said, a scowl on his stubbled face.

The bridging train—pontoon wagons, balk, chess and side-rail wagons, tool wagons, and traveling forge—had labored along gummy roads as rain started at nightfall. It had slacked off a while but was now pouring down again, and the wind had risen. Billy surveyed the unfinished bridge by the light of three lanterns swaying on poles planted in the mud. It was risky to reveal their position that way, but light was necessary; the creek was deep, the water high and swift.

The bridge extended halfway across the broad creek. Pontoon boats spaced by twenty-seven-foot balks were anchored on the upstream side, and every other one by a second, downstream, anchor. Work parties were running out chesses and laying them on the balks while others placed and lashed the side rails where the cross planks were already down. It was rough work, made more difficult because the whole structure heaved under the push of a wind approaching gale force.

No one answered Billy's hail, nor could he see any more boat wagons in the darkness. "I suspect they are mired," Farmer said. "I suggest you go see. I'll handle matters here." He snugged his old musket down in the vee of his left elbow. The infantrymen detailed for this kind of duty were responsible for guarding the construction area. But those in the Battalion of Engineers, Army of the Potomac, had more confidence in themselves than in greenhorns, and they seldom worked without a weapon. Billy's revolver rode in a holster with the flap tied down.

Covered with mud and growing numb, he slopped up the bank past a tool wagon. He was not certain of the date; the tenth of April, maybe. General McClellan's huge army, said to outnumber the combined Confederate forces of Joe Johnston and Prince John Magruder two to one, had come down by water to Fort Monroe at the low-lying tip of the peninsula between the York and James rivers. The embarkation began March 17, six days after Little Mac was stripped of his duties as general-in-chief. To explain the demotion, some cited his refusal to move against Manassas. Others merely mentioned the name Stanton; the generals now reported directly to him.

Though McClellan's command had been reduced to the Department and Army of the Potomac, he fought on for what he wanted: more artillery; more ammunition; McDowell's corps, which was being held to defend Washington. When the administration refused most of the demands, McClellan decided to besiege Magruder instead of attack him, a decision to which some, including Lije Farmer, had objected.

"What is wrong with him? They say he takes the number of enemy troops supplied by his Pinkerton spies and doubles it—but even then, our forces are superior. Of what is he so afraid?"

"Losing his reputation? Or the next presidential election maybe?" Billy said, not entirely in jest.

The campaign against Yorktown began April 4. The tasks of the Battalion of Engineers included corduroying roads and bridging creeks so men and siege artillery could advance toward Magruder's line, which stretched almost thirteen miles between Yorktown and the Warwick River. Scouts brought back reports of sighting many big guns in the enemy works.

The peninsula was a maze of unmapped roads and creeks. Movement in the maze became increasingly hard as rainy weather set in. But the engineers were prepared. When Billy left Washington so hastily that winter night, the battalion had been sent up the Potomac to test the training of their seven-week recruits. The successful test, construction of a complete pontoon bridge, had renewed the engineers' almost arrogant pride. Now Billy felt none of it. Nights sleeping in damp tents and eighteen-to twenty-hour stretches of work in ceaseless rain had beaten it out of him. He merely existed, pushing himself and his men through one minute, then the next, to complete one job in order to move to another.

He reached the line of pontoon wagons, stalled a good half mile above the bridge. Each wagon carried one long wooden boat and its gear: oars and oarlocks, anchors and boat hooks and line. As they had suspected, the problem was mud; the first wagon sat hub deep in it.

He surveyed the situation by the light of a teamster's lantern. He suggested unhitching the oxen, moving them forward, and running lines from their yoke over a thick overhanging limb and down again to the wagon to provide a lifting action. The lines were rigged, and the teamster hit his oxen with his quirt. Instead of pulling straight ahead, they headed away at the right oblique. The limb cracked ominously.

"Slack off!" Billy shouted, jumping to knock the teamster out of the way moments before the limb broke and dropped onto the prow of the boat, smashing it and snapping the wagon's front axle with its weight.

Furious with himself, Billy climbed from the mud. The wrecked wagon would prevent the others from coming up; there was no room to pass on the muddy road. "All right, you drivers—I'll send you some men, and we'll carry the boats to the launching site. We're behind schedule."

Away in the dark, some phantom shouted, "Whose fault is that?"

Billy scowled again. Someone else complained. "Carry them? From the last wagon that could be damn near a mile."

"I don't care if it's fifty," Billy said, and stormed back to Lije, full of self-disgust.

On the unfinished bridge, the weary infantrymen had fallen idle. Nothing more could be done until the next boat was floated down and pushed out twenty feet from the last one placed. "I need men to carry the boats, Lije. I tried to free the wagon that's stuck and wrecked it instead. No one can pass."

Standing with his musket in his arms, Farmer gave a majestic slow nod. "I saw. Don't take the guilt so deeply into your soul. There is not an engineer breathing who has not miscalculated in his time—and these are not the best of conditions for sharp thinking. Be thankful you lost a wagon and not a life."

The younger man stared at the older, thinking that when he and Brett raised children, he hoped they could counsel them as wisely and humanely as Farmer counseled those who served with him.

A musket flashed in the woods beyond the stream. On the bridge, a soldier yelled and grabbed his leg. He started to topple into the water, but others pulled him back. Simultaneously, Farmer grasped his musket by the barrel and clubbed the nearest lantern from its pole. Billy leaped for another as musketry and gibbering hoots and cries issued from the dark. They put all the lanterns out, retreated up the bank, and returned fire. In fifteen minutes the rebel sniping stopped. Fifteen minutes after that, Billy and Lije relit the lanterns and work resumed.

By half past two they had launched enough boats and laid enough balks and chesses to reach the opposite bank. Billy wrote a brief dispatch reporting completion of the bridge and sent it back to headquarters with a courier. Lije ordered a rest. The men slept in the open, finding the best available cover for themselves and their gunpowder. Troubling thoughts strayed through Billy's mind as he lay against a tree trunk, a soggy blanket over his legs. Water dripped on him. He sneezed for the fourth time.

"Lije? Did you hear what they said about the Shiloh casualties before we started out tonight?"

"I did," came the answer from the far side of the tree. "Each army is said to have lost a quarter of those engaged."

"It's unbelievable. This war's changing, Lije."

"And will continue."

"But where's it going?"

"To the eventual triumph of the just."

I am not too sure all of us will live to see that, Billy thought as he shut his eyes. His teeth chattered, and he started to shake. Somehow, though, he slept, sitting in the rain.

In the morning the engineers secured the last cables on the bridge, scouted the woods beyond for rebs and found them gone, and settled down to wait. They would be sent somewhere else soon enough.

Bivouacked one night near Yorktown, Charles said to Abner Woolner, "We've ridden together for a few weeks, but I still don't know much about you."

"Hardly a thing worth knowin', Charlie. I don't read good, I spell worse, and I can't cipher at all. Ain't married. Was once. She died. Her and the baby." The straightforward way he said it, devoid of self-pity, made Charles admire him.

"I farm up near the North Carolina line," the scout went on. "Small place. Right near where my grandpa fought the redcoats. King's Mountain."

"What do you think about this war?"

Ab pushed his tongue back and forth between front teeth and upper lip for a minute. "Might hurt your feelin's if I told you."

Charles laughed. "Why?"

" 'Cause I don't like you plantation nabobs and your godless high life down on the coast. You dragged us into this muss. There's a few of you who are all right, but not many."

"Do you own slaves, Ab?"

"No, sir. Never have, never would. I can't say I 'specially favor the black folk, though if you pressed me, I'd prob'ly say no man ought to be chained up against his will. I know some judge said Dred Scott and the rest of the darkies wasn't persons, but I know some who are fine persons, so I'm not sure how I feel about the nigra question that's a part of all this. I do know which folks I like. You. Major Butler. Hampton—I could tell he din't think I was enough of a gentleman to be in one of his regular troops when I signed up, but he didn't say that and make me feel bad. He just acted real happy that I'd scout for him. I'll take him over that flashy Jeb Stuart any day."

"So will I. Beauty's an old West Point classmate of mine, but I don't have the regard for him that I once did. I share your feelings about Hampton. About most of the planters, too, matter of fact."

Ab Woolner smiled. "I knew there was a reason I liked you, Charlie."

In his journal, Billy wrote:

The general is a paradox. He requires us to emplace his siege artillery, all seventy-two pieces, to bombard a position many feel could be taken in a single concerted attack. The derrick and roller system required to unload the guns would take a page to describe. We must fling up ramps to move each gun into place. A layman would be led to believe that here is a siege destined to last a year.

Questions are asked. Why is this being done? Why is Richmond the objective and not the Confederate Army, whose defeat would force a surrender beyond all question? Be it noted that such questions, though common, are not voiced within hearing of any of the ultra-loyal officers the general has gathered about him.

The paradox of which I wrote is this. The general does little, yet is loved greatly. The men molded by his hand into the most superb fighting force ever seen on the planet lie idle—and continue to cheer him whenever he comes into their sight. Do they cheer because he keeps them safe from the hazards of a conclusive engagement?

Brett, I am becoming bitter. But so are the factions in this army. Some call the general "McNapoleon." It is not meant as praise.

When the Confederates pulled back from the Yorktown line early in May, the engineers were among the first into the empty fortifications. Billy raced to a gun emplacement, only to curse what he found. The great black fieldpiece jutting into the air was nothing more than a painted tree trunk with a dummy muzzle cut in one end. The emplacement contained five similar fakes.

"Quaker guns," he said, disgusted.

Lije Farmer's white beard, grown long, snapped in the May breeze. " 'Thou has deceived me, and I was deceived. I am in derision daily—every one mocketh me.' "

"Prince John's a master artillerist. Loves amateur theatricals, too. A deadly combination. I wonder if there are more of these?"

There were. Compounding the insult, a deserter said Magruder had paraded a few units up and down at Yorktown to convince the enemy that he was holding the line with many more than the thirteen thousand he had now withdrawn. While Magruder held his foes at bay with tricks and nerve, the main rebel army slipped away to better defense positions being secretly prepared farther up the peninsula. McClellan's huge guns, three weeks in the placing, were now trained on worthless targets. Little Mac's dallying had given Johnston a second advantage—additional time to summon reinforcements from the western part of the state.

"This blasted war may last a while," Billy said. "Our side may have more factories, but it strikes me the other side has more brains."

For that, Lije had no ready Scriptural reply.

In May, on the Pamunkey River, Billy wrote:

Last night I saw a sight that will stay with me until I die.

Shortly after tattoo, duties took me on a course leading back across one of the low hills close by. There before me, unexpectedly, spread the whole of the Cumberland Landing encampment beneath a sky shedding light red as that from any furnace at Hazard's. Struck dumb with wonder, I knew at last what Lije means when he says, ever paraphrasing the Bible, that we have come here with an exceeding great army.

I saw below the hill rows of Sibley and A tents numerous as the tipis of some migratory tribe. I smelled the smoke of cooking fires, the homely stinks of the horses, the worse one of the sinks. I heard the music of war, which is more than song or bugling; it is a varied strain of courier horses and artillery; the lowing of our great cattle herd; the hails of pickets, the called-back countersigns; arms rattling and clicking as they are cleaned and stacked; and voices, always the voices, speaking of homes, families, sweethearts, in English, Gaelic, German, Hungarian, Swedish—the many and varied tongues of man. Two units of our "aeronautic corps," tethered for the night like beasts, rode the air above the holy of holies—the tents of those who lead us, surrounded by the chosen of the headquarters guard. Adding brightness were the flags—our own, whose integrity we fight for, and all the regimental banners, rainbows of them, handed to so many proud colonels by so many pretty girls at so many martial gatherings in so many cities and hamlets. All the arrayed flags I saw, and watched their hues all melting to the scarlet of the sundown, and then to gray.

371

There is much of this war I am not clever enough to under-stand—and much I do not like. Nor do I refer solely to physical hazards. But as I stood watching the May wind snap the flags and ripple the white tops of five hundred wagons in their park, I had a sense of our purpose. We are here engaged in something vast and noble, and things will change because of it, though exactly how, I have not the wisdom to predict. Overcome by this feeling of epochal time and place, I lingered a while and then moved on. I soon came upon a civilian seated on a stump completing a sketch of our boys at bayonet drill. He introduced himself as Mr. Homer, said he had observed the drill earlier and was touching up his artwork for inclusion in a composite picture he will later prepare for Harper's, *which sent him here. He commented on the beauty and majesty of the evening scene. He said it made him think of the migration of the children of Israel.*

But we are not many tribes bound to dwell peaceably in some promised land—we are many regiments bound to Richmond, to burn and kill and conquer. Behind the evening scene lay that truth, of which I said nothing to Mr. Homer as we walked down from the hill in companionable conversation.

The May woods smelled of rain. Charles, Ab, and a third scout, named Doan, sat motionless on their horses, hidden by trees, watching the detachment pass on the country road: twelve Yankees in double file, moving at a walk from the direction of Tunstall's Station toward Bottom's Bridge on the Chickahominy. Johnston had withdrawn to the other side of the river. Pessimists in the army were given to observing that at several points the watery demarcation line was little more than ten miles from Richmond.

The three scouts had been on the Yankee side of the Chicka-hominy for two days, with inconclusive results. They had checked the Richmond & York rail line for signs of traffic, found none, doubled back, and were heading for the low, boggy land near the river when they heard the Yanks approaching. The scouts immediately hid in the woods.

A yellow butterfly darted in and out of a shaft of sun a yard to Charles's left. He had his .44 Colt drawn and resting on his right thigh and his shotgun within reach. He wanted a fight far less than he wanted to know the identity of these Yanks and their purpose on this road.

"Mounted rifles?" he whispered, having seen that the pair of officers in the lead wore orange pompons on their hats.

"Not likely 'cept for them two shoulder straps," Ab answered. "If any of the rest of them boys has been on horses more than two hours in their whole lives, I'm Varina Davis."

Doan leaned close. "Who the devil are they, then? Their uniforms are so blasted dirty, you can't tell."

Charles stroked his beard, which now reached to an inch below his chin. He connected mud to riverbanks and riverbanks to his friend Billy. "Bet anything they're engineers."

"Might be," Ab said. "Doin' what, though? Scoutin' the swamps?"

"Yes. For bridges. Places to cross. This may be the first sign of an advance."

Sport shied. Charles steadied the gray with his knees as a far part of his mind noted a queer whispery sound on the ground. He didn't ponder its meaning because Doan was talking.

"Can we shoot 'em up a little, Cap?"

"I wouldn't mind, but I suspect it would be smarter to ride on to the next road. The sooner we're over the river with news of this, the better."

"Rattler," Ab whispered, louder than he should have. The snake tried to slither past the forehoofs of his horse. The horse danced back and whinnied, long and loud.

"That's done it," Charles said. He heard halloos on the road; someone yelling orders. The snake, more frightened than any of them, disappeared. "Let's ride out of here."

Ab had trouble with his spooked mount. "Come on, Cyclone, damn you—" Accustomed to gunfire but not reptiles, the scout horse reared and nearly unseated its rider. Charles grabbed the headstall, the forehoofs crashed down, and Ab kept his seat. But seconds had been lost, and the horse's erratic behavior had placed it in one of the shafts of light falling through the trees. Two Yankees at the tail of the column spotted Ab and aimed shoulder weapons.

Charles pulled his shotgun, discharged both barrels, then fired his revolver three times with his right hand. As the fusillade faded, the Yanks skedaddled, shouting, "Take cover."

"Come on, boys," Charles cried, leading the way. The Yanks

373

would likely go to ground in the roadside ditches, giving the scouts a margin of time. He spurred Sport through the trees, not away from the road, as he had first intended, but toward it, up the side of an imaginary triangle that should bring them out well ahead of the detachment.

After some hard riding, he burst onto the road, Ab a length behind, Doan bringing up the rear. A glance behind showed him two Yanks standing in the road. The rest were hidden.

Both Yanks fired at the scouts. A ball flipped the side brim of Charles's hat. Another few seconds and they were safely out of range of the enemy muskets. Charles shoved his revolver into the holster and concentrated on riding. The road serpentined through woods where swampy pools glittered.

Another quarter of a mile and the sheets of water were solid on both sides. The trees appeared to rise from a surface fouled by green scum and speckled by tiny insects. A mile or less should bring them to the crossing.

The road behind them erupted in a single jet of flame and a fountain of shrapnel. Ab was so unnerved, he nearly galloped off into the water. Charles reined around, saw a smoking hole and Doan dragging himself from under his fallen horse.

Round-eyed, Doan made choking sounds. The horse was finished. The buried columbiad shell triggered by a friction primer had hurled lethal fragments into the animal's shoulder, chest, and crest.

Doan struggled free of the left stirrup. His horse slid tail first into the hole. Doan walked in a little circle like a confused child. Hidden by the looping curves of the road, the Yanks could be heard coming at a gallop.

Charles began to sweat. He urged Sport to the edge of the hole, but the gray shied from the dying horse, shuddering down there and blowing out its breath in great sad gasps. "Get up," Charles said, reaching behind to slap Sport's croup. Doan's confusion continued. Ab excitedly fired a shot up the road, though no Yankees were in sight.

Suddenly Doan began crying. "I can't leave him."

"He's a goner, and Company Q is a better post than some Yankee stockade." The first blue horseman came around the bend. Charles seized Doan's collar. "Get up, damn it, or we'll all be caught."

Doan managed to climb onto the gray and take hold of

374

Charles's waist. Charles pulled Sport's head around, and they broke for the Chickahominy. Ab stepped his horse to one side to let the gray go by, then emptied his side arm at the oncoming horsemen. He had little chance of a hit, but the firing slowed the pursuers.

Even carrying double weight, Sport performed valiantly, leading the escape to the river. Charles could feel Doan trembling. Suddenly the scout yelled, "Goddamn savages."

"Who?"

"The Yanks who buried that infernal machine in the road."

"You'll have to blame Brigadier Rains or somebody else on our side. Before we pulled out of Yorktown, Rains planted those torpedoes all over the streets and docks. How we doing, Ab?" he called to the scout riding alongside.

"We're way ahead of them thimble merchants and ribbon clerks. Look yonder—there's the bridge."

The sight stopped the shouted discussion of the torpedo that had killed Doan's mount. General Longstreet called the devices inhuman and forbade their use. Lot of good that did. What shook Charles as they raced to Bottom's Bridge was realizing that the slain horse could just as easily have been Sport. A buried bomb didn't differentiate.

The gray hammered across the river bridge, hoofs pounding a rhythmic litany. *Just as easily. Just as easily.*

Jealousy had as much to do with it as politics, Billy later decided. He had been primed for a scrap when he walked into the sutler's tent that evening toward the close of May.

A dour nervousness had gripped the peninsular armies for days. The rebs were dug in beyond the Chickahominy, prepared to die for Richmond. On the Union side, instead of expectancy or a giddy sense that one fierce blow could end it, there was uncertainty. The high command suffered from it, and the leakage spread. Rumor simmered with fact in a stew of negativism. Jackson was humiliating the Union in the Shenandoah. McDowell, holding near Fredericksburg, might be diverted to meet that threat. Little Mac continued to insist he had not nearly enough men, though he had over a hundred thousand. He also insisted the hounds of Washington were tearing at him, led by the rabid Stanton.

Cliques had formed, holding and arguing each side. Little

375

McNapoleon's detractors claimed that his cadre of senior officers, Porter and Burnside among them, would execute any command of the general's without question and would support and promote his policies and reputation in defiance of Washington and at the expense of a victory.

All of this, together with the normal weariness induced by long hours on duty, wore Billy away, as it wore away many others, and primed him for trouble.

The night he visited the sutler's, a junior officer was present whom he didn't know personally but nevertheless disliked. The young man, another Academy graduate, belonged to staff; Billy had seen him dogging behind Little Mac on horseback. The officer was pale as a girl and bore himself with the relaxed arrogance of a clubman. Even the fellow's uniform irritated Billy. In a season of mud, it was immaculate. So were the sparkling boots. With long, light-colored curls and a red scarf knotted around his throat, he resembled a circus performer more than a soldier.

Most galling to Billy, hunched there at one end of the plank counter with a dirty glass in hand, was the officer's attitude. He was three or four years younger than Billy and wore no shoulder straps at all because of his junior rank. But he behaved like a senior man.

A loud one.

"The general would win posthaste if it weren't for the abolitionist scoundrels in Washington. Why he tolerates them, I don't know. Even our revered President humiliates him. He dared to call the general a traitor last week. To his face!"

Billy drank; it was his second glass. The sutler piously proclaimed that he served only cider. That cider, however, was harder than a New Hampshireman's head. Even so, it was safer to drink than some of the misbegotten combinations—brown sugar, lamp oil, grain alcohol—purveyed as whiskey.

But the cider—the sutler's name for it was oil of gladness—wasn't very good on the gut or the disposition if you hadn't eaten since noon. Superintending a detail making gabions, a routine job of the battalion, Billy had somehow been too busy for food.

The officer paused to toss off a double glass of cider. He had a lithe build and knew how to hold the stage the way actors did. His little coterie, five other officers, captains and lieutenants, waited expectantly for him to resume and paid close attention when he did.

376

"Have you heard the latest outrage? The estimable Stanton is attacking the general's honor and questioning his bravery—behind his back, of course—while influencing the Original Gorilla to withhold the men we desperately need."

"Sounds like a conspiracy," another lieutenant muttered.

"Exactly. You know the reason for it, don't you? The general likes and respects the Southern people. So do many in this army. I do. The estimable Stanton, however, favors only a certain class of Southerners—those with dark complexions. He's like all the Republicans."

Billy whacked his glass on the counter. "But he's a Democrat."

The long-haired lieutenant parted his group like Moses parting the sea. "Did you address a comment to me, sir?"

Back off, Billy said to himself. For some reason he couldn't. Damn strange that he, no partisan of the colored people, was defending one who was.

"I did. I said Mr. Stanton is a Democrat, not a Republican."

A cold smile from the junior officer. "Since this is an informal meeting place, may I have the pleasure of knowing who is offering such valuable information?"

"First Lieutenant Hazard. Presently assigned to B Company, Battalion of Engineers."

"Second Lieutenant Custer, headquarters staff, at your service." There was no service or respect in it, only conceit and contempt. "You must be from the Academy, then. But a few years before my time. I was in the four-year bunch graduated last June. Last of the lowest—thirty-sixth among thirty-six." He seemed to relish that. His cronies snickered dutifully. "As to your statement, sir, it is only narrowly correct. Shall I set aside considerations of rank and tell you what Stanton really is?"

The young officer walked toward Billy. His hair smelled of cinnamon oil. Behind Custer, his coterie hung on each word. A mangy dog, yellow and muddy, trotted into the tent. There were scores of dogs in camp, pets and stray; this one went straight to Custer and rubbed against his boot. A dozen other officers at flimsy tables stopped their own conversations to listen to the second lieutenant.

"Stanton is a man so vile, a hypocrite so depraved, that if he had lived in the time of the Saviour, Judas would have been respectable by comparison."

Several of the eavesdropping officers reacted angrily. One

started to stand, but his companion held him back. Only Billy, with alcohol boiling in his empty stomach, was irked enough, rash enough, to answer.

"That kind of talk doesn't belong in the army. There's too much politicking already."

"Too much? There isn't enough!" The coterie responded with nods and knuckles rapped on the plank.

Billy persisted. "No, Lieutenant Custer, it's winning we should worry about, not whether—" an example flashed into mind "—whether a singing group can or cannot perform in our camps."

"Oh, you mean that damn Hutchinson Family?"

"I do. My brother's in the War Department, and he wrote me that it was a bad decision. Trivial in the first place, and it offended some important cabinet members and congressmen who heard about it."

Over Custer's shoulder, a captain blustered, "Your brother's entrenched behind a War Department desk, is he? Brave fellow."

Billy's self-control weakened. "He's a major in the Ordnance Department. The work he does is damned important."

"What is that work?" asked Custer with a droll smile. "Blacking Stanton's boots? Serving refreshments to Stanton's darky visitors?"

The captain said, "Kissing the secretary's fundament on demand?"

"Damn you," Billy said, and went for him.

Even Custer reacted with dismay. "Captain Rawlins, that goes a bit beyond—" Billy pushed Custer aside and flung a fist at the captain, who was a head taller. It glanced off the man's chin. Others in the tent were up and shouting like cockfight spectators.

"Give the gentlemen room!"

"Not in here," the sutler protested, waving a billy. Everyone ignored him. The captain unfastened his collar, a loose grin pushing up his cheeks. Stupid of me, Billy said to himself as he clenched and unclenched his hands. Plain stupid.

Someone entered the tent and called his name. But he was focused on the captain sidling forward.

"I'll accommodate you, you little piece of Republican dung." His fist zoomed up, landing in the center of Billy's face while Billy was still raising his hands.

He spun away, fell across the counter, blood threads trickling from each nostril. The bigger man aimed another punch. Billy pushed upright, locked his hands, and struck the forearm of the fisted hand, diverting the blow. The captain drove a knee into Billy's crotch, and he went down on his back. Grinning, the captain raised his boot over Billy's face.

"There you are," the familiar voice said from behind the other men crowding in.

Custer exclaimed, "That's plenty, Rawlins. He may be a nigger Republican, but he deserves fair treatment."

"The hell you say." Down came the boot. Billy started to roll, knowing he was too slow.

Suddenly, mysteriously, Rawlins tilted backward. The boot intended to stomp Billy's face made funny, jerking motions in midair. Billy elbowed himself from the dirt, blinked, and saw the reason. Lije Farmer was holding the captain's shoulders, his face full of fury. He flung Billy's adversary. Captain Rawlins sat down so hard he squealed.

Lije pulled Billy to his feet. "Conduct yourself out of this iniquitous establishment." No one smiled. Given Lije's size and the way he let his eye rove around the ring of McClellanites, no one had the nerve. To Rawlins he said, "It would be foolish to invoke rank in this matter. If you try, I shall testify against you."

Billy took his kepi from the counter and walked out. A few steps from the tent, he heard Custer laugh again, joined by his friends and even by his barking dog.

Billy's bruised, bloody face felt hot. Lije touched his sleeve. " 'But whosoever shall smite thee on thy right cheek, turn on him the other also.' "

"Sorry, Lije, I couldn't do it. He hit low, then tried to mash my face with his boot. 'Course, it might have improved my looks—What do you think?"

Farmer neither smiled nor answered. Billy sobered and probed some tender spots. "Officers like that are tearing this army to pieces. I'd heard others say it, but I didn't believe it until tonight."

"It's to be expected. The general possesses a profound knowledge of the military arts, but he also possesses a profound and raging ambition. It can be read in his orders, heard in his orations to the troops, seen in the nature and demeanor of his staff."

"That curlylocks lieutenant is one of them."

"Yes. I have noticed him before. One cannot help it. He dresses to draw attention."

"I know I was a fool to fly off that way. But they made remarks about my brother George that I couldn't tolerate. I thank you for pulling that captain off me. One minute longer and there wouldn't have been much left of my face. Your timing was remarkable."

"It was not entirely coincidence. I have been searching for you. We are ordered to move out before daylight. Let the others fight the political wars. We've our own to wage, and it will keep us busy enough."

Thinking of the tangly forests through which they had hacked a path with axes, of the roads they had planked and the streams they had bridged, Billy said a heartfelt, "Yes. I still thank you, Lije." He felt the same warm regard for Farmer that he had felt for his late father. The older man bucked him up with a clap on the back, then fell to humming "Amazing Grace."

No wonder the atmosphere on the peninsula was poisoned, Billy thought. They were practically at the door of the Confederate capital, which was defended by inferior numbers, yet the campaign dragged on, indecisive and costly. Tonight he had run smack into one of the reasons. Billy feared that before the campaign ended, scores of men might be sacrificed needlessly because of the general's ambition and feelings of persecution. He would not care to be one of them.

55

By the last week in May, the end seemed near. Each morning Orry confronted that fact as he rose and drank the foul brew of parched corn the boardinghouse served in lieu of coffee. Since New Orleans fell, there wasn't even sugar to sweeten it.

Like everyone in Richmond, while he went about his daily routine Orry listened for resumption of the heavy artillery fire that shook windowpanes all over town. He was glad Madeline had so far been unable to join him; his mother was recovering too slowly. News of her seizure had struck him hard when he first read it in a letter. McClellan's guns had magically changed a sorrow to a blessing.

How ironic to recall that in February local papers had bragged about military success in the Southwest and the creation of the Confederate Territory of Arizona, whose boundaries not one person in a hundred thousand could define. Of what earthly use was a southwest bastion after Forts Henry and Donelson fell—and Orry's friend and superior, Benjamin, slid over to the State Department because someone had to be blamed. Benjamin had survived, but barely.

George Randolph replaced him. An earnest man, a Virginian with impeccable family background, an outstanding legal reputation, and recent military experience—he had commanded artillery under Magruder—Randolph held the War Department portfolio but could do little with it. By now everyone knew the real secretary of war lived in the President's mansion.

Island No. 10 had gone last month, a major weakening of control of the lower Mississippi. The Yankees had Norfolk, too; in desperation, the navy had sunk the already legendary *Virginia* to prevent her capture.

April had brought another, even more dire, indication of the Confederacy's plight. Davis approved a bill conscripting all white males from eighteen to thirty-five for three years. Orry knew it was a needed measure and grew angry when the President was cursed by street vagrants and state governors alike. Two of the latter said they would withhold as many men as they pleased for home defense, law or no law.

McClellan was close now, feinting toward the city. Though his strategic plan was not apparent, his mere presence plunged Richmond into a time of trial. Davis has already packed his family off to Raleigh. Jackson was still performing brilliantly in the valley, but that did little to mitigate Richmond's fear of the pincers that might snap shut from the peninsula and from the north at any moment.

The terror had become acute on a Thursday in mid-May. Five federal vessels, including *Monitor,* steamed up the James to Drewry's Bluff, within seven miles of the city. Winder's thugs dragged men off the street and out of saloons to build a temporary bridge to the fortified side of the James. The windows of Richmond rattled from cannonading that eventually drove the federal vessels away. But the city had whiffed the winds of defeat for a few hours, and no one could forget the smell.

After Drewry's Bluff, Orry had trouble sleeping more than an hour or two each night. With the crisis building, he questioned whether his duties were appropriate to a supposedly sane man. As a favor to Benjamin, he went to General Winder in search of a house servant who had disappeared while Winder's bullies were recruiting bridge builders at gunpoint. The provost marshal denied such tactics and shelved Orry's inquiry without answering it or bothering to hide his animosity, which was now deep and vicious. The two had quarreled at least once a month ever since Orry's arrival.

Refugees poured into the city on foot and in every conceivable kind of conveyance. They slept in Capitol Square or broke into the homes of those who had already left by train, carriage, or shank's mare. Orry heard that Ashton was one of those refusing to leave. It leavened his dislike of her, but not much.

Soldiers swelled the population, too. Wounded sent back from the Chickahominy lines; deserters who had shot or stabbed themselves—who could say which were which? Specters in torn gray, they walked or limped everywhere, thin from hunger, hot-eyed from fever, befouled by dirt, and covered with bandages stained by blood and pus. Some women of the town aided them, some turned away. All night and all day, the wagons and buggies and carts rumbled in and rumbled out, and the windowpanes hummed and cracked, and sleep became impossible.

Orry had another bad experience in the pine building housing Winder and his men. This time he called at the request of Secretary Randolph, who operated a large family farm near Richmond. Randolph had a friend, also a farmer, who had refused to sell his produce at the lower prices fixed by the provost marshal. In a polemical letter to the *Richmond Whig,* the farmer called Winder a worse threat to the populace than McClellan. Having expressed that opinion, he was snatched right out of the Exchange Bar one night. Away he went to the foul factory on Cary Street where Winder was now locking up those whose utterances he deemed seditious.

Orry went to the pine building to request an order freeing the prisoner. He sent his name in, but the general wouldn't see him. Instead he had to speak with one of the civilian operatives, a tall, lanky man dressed completely in black save for his linen.

The man's name was Israel Quincy. Looking more like a Massachusetts parson than a Maryland railroad detective, he clearly enjoyed having someone of Orry's rank in his shabby little cubicle as a supplicant. He was quick to answer the request.

"There'll be no release order from this office. That man made General Winder angry."

"The general has made Secretary Randolph angry, Mr. Quincy, as well as most of Richmond, because of his absurd tariffs. The city desperately needs food from outlying farms, but no one will sell at the prices set by this office." Orry drew a breath. "Your answer is no?"

His dark eyes benign, Quincy smiled at the visitor. Then the smile seemed to crack and reveal the venom beneath. "Unequivocally no, Colonel. The secretary's friend will stay in Castle Thunder."

Orry rose. "No, he won't. The secretary has the authority to go over the general's head and will do so. He preferred to follow protocol, but you've made it impossible. I'll have the prisoner out of that pesthole within an hour."

Leaving the cubicle, he was stopped by Quincy's sharp, hard, "Colonel. Think twice before you do that."

Disbelieving, Orry turned and saw arrogance. He boiled over. "Who do you people think you are, terrorizing free citizens and stifling any opinion that differs from yours? By God, we'll have no damned Pinkertons operating in the Confederacy."

Low-voiced, Quincy said, "I caution you again, Colonel. Don't defy the authority of this office. You might need a favor from us one of these days."

"Threaten me, Mr. Quincy, and with this one hand I'll beat you into the ground."

Forty-five minutes later, Castle Thunder lost one inmate. But there were many more for whom he could do nothing. As for the warnings of the power-drunk guttersnipe in the black suit, he never gave them another thought.

At the War Department, Orry supervised the packing of box after box of ledgers, files, records, as May twisted down to its fearsome end, which brought the battle of Fair Oaks, virtually on the doorstep of the city. McClellan clumsily repulsed the Confederate attack, which saw Joe Johnston seriously wounded and replaced in twenty-four hours by the President's former military adviser, back from exile.

Granny Lee took charge of the Army of Northern Virginia for the first time. Confidence in him was not high. Boxes were packed with even greater haste, and a special train kept steam up around the clock to haul off Treasury gold if the final assault broke through Lee's lines. Orry sweated and packed more boxes and picked up a rumor of a plan afloat in Winder's department. He heard no details, only that he was the target. Quincy's forgotten threats came to mind again, increasing the tension he felt. He thanked the Almighty that Madeline wasn't here to face the danger and feel the madness.

"Please," the woman said.

Scarcely thirty, she looked much older. She smelled of the mud bespattering her clothes. Three children, starved gray mice, hunched against her skirt, and over her shoulder peered an adolescent black girl with decayed teeth and a red bandanna on her head.

The heavily planted garden rustled and dripped. The shower had stopped an hour ago, about half past six. The garden was twenty feet square, wild and green—almost too lush. Ten steps led down to it from the house. At the top, Ashton stood behind Powell, one of her palms pressing the back of his fine linen shirt.

In reply to the woman, he cocked his revolver. The potent sound aroused Ashton unexpectedly.

"Please," the woman repeated, freighting the word with her tiredness, her desperation. "We came in from Mechanicsville. The Yanks were too close. My man's with Old Jack in the valley, and we have nowhere to go. The gate was open—"

"Some niggers forced it last night, hunting a place to squat. I wouldn't have them, and I won't have you. Go out the way you came."

One of the youngsters tugged the woman's skirt. "Ma, where can we stay?"

"Ask President Davis," Powell said. "He hustled his wife out of town in a hurry—maybe he has a spare bed." Powell flourished the gun at them. "Get out, you goddamn vermin."

The woman managed a look of loathing as she herded her brood into the lowering June twilight. The faraway sky reverberated with a sound like tympani. Powell thrust the gun into his pants, walked down the stairs, and kicked the gate shut. "Find me some rope," he said without turning around.

Ashton darted inside and was back within a minute. He lashed the gate shut and secured it with several knots. Leaves dripped in the silence. Then the sky drummed again.

Upstairs, with all the windows open on the steamy evening, he reclined on his elbows and let her work him to a huge erection, in the fashion he enjoyed. Then he bored into her like a bull. They tore the bedclothes loose and pushed them all over the place with their rolling and straining. He was splendid, inducing, as he always did, a joy she could only express and relieve by screaming.

Overcome by a satiated exhaustion, she fell asleep. She woke presently to find Powell reading a book he kept at the bedside: Poe's *Tales*. He had told her that the fantastical stories and the character Dupin were favorites of his. It was fitting to reread them in Richmond, where Poe had edited the *Literary Messenger* for a period.

In perspiring lassitude, they lay together, Powell speaking in a reflective way, as he liked to do after making love.

"I was discussing the Conscription Act with some other gentlemen yesterday. There was unanimity that it's an outrage. Are we apes, to be prodded into a cage anytime Jeff says jump? At least there are ways around the law."

Ashton rested her cheek on the bristly hair of his chest and circled one of his nipples with her nail. "What ways?"

"The exemption for owning a hundred and twenty slaves, for one. I doubt King Jeff will entrain for Valdosta in order to discover that a hundred and eighteen of mine are imaginary." He chuckled.

"I love you," Ashton whispered, "but I surely don't understand you sometimes."

"How so?"

"You carry on about conscription and King Jeff as you call him, yet you've stayed in Richmond when most of the permanent residents are running for their lives."

"I want to protect what's mine. Which includes you, partner dear."

"A successful partner, I might add."

385

"Very successful."

"You're the reason I've stayed, Lamar." That was true, but there was more to it. Sometimes the artillery fire frightened her to death, and she wanted to board the first outbound train. She didn't do it because she believed that if she showed the slightest weakness, Powell might throw her over.

She needed him too much to let that happen. In Lamar Powell she had at last found a man who would rise in the world, ultimately wield great power and control great wealth in the Confederacy if it survived—or somewhere else if it didn't. She refused to risk a separation.

She planted a light kiss on the nipple she had been touching and continued. "Poor James wants to rush me to the depot all the time. I'm always inventing excuses."

He kissed her cheek. "Good for you. I wouldn't want you spineless, like the wife of the tyrant."

Spineless? she thought. What a rich jest. Ashton had always been absolute mistress of those with whom she had dallied. Every man but Powell had willingly bent to her wishes. That she couldn't dominate Powell was one of his great attractions.

"You really hate Davis, don't you, Lamar?"

"Kindly don't make it sound so peculiar. Yes, I hate him—and there are enough men who share my view to form a division or two right here in Richmond. If he were strong—a dictator, even —I'd support him. But he's weak. A failure. Do you need more proof than the presence of General McClellan less than a dozen miles from this bed? King Jeff will preside at the South's funeral unless he's stopped."

"Stopped—?"

"That is what I said." Moist dark had claimed the bedroom, a dark redolent of the garden. Despite its passion, Powell's voice remained controlled. "And it won't be oratory that saves the Confederacy and ends the blundering career of Mr. Davis. It will be something more decisive. Final."

Naked against him, Ashton had a sudden vision of the revolver he had shown the refugees from Mechanicsville. Surely he didn't mean anything like that.

Surely not.

Like the man whose existence he suspected but whose name he didn't know, James Huntoon hated the President of the Confeder-

386

ate States of America. He would have liked to see him out of office, if not dead. The way things were going this June, the Yankees might achieve both objectives.

Huntoon lived in a state of constant nervous exhaustion, unable to sleep soundly, unable to take cheer from reports of Jackson's feats in the valley or of Stuart and twelve hundred men riding completely around McClellan's army—a spectacular stunt, certainly, but one of small practical benefit to the besieged capital.

At Treasury, too, boxes were being packed. Huntoon had to sweat like a slave, which angered him. Adding to his unhappiness were speculations about Ashton's absences. They were frequent these days, usually long, and always unexplained.

What a lunatic world this had become. The Grace Street house was defended against refugees and military stragglers by a musket Huntoon had placed in the hands of Homer, the senior houseman. Never would he have imagined that he would arm a slave, but with rabble skulking everywhere and mobs rushing to the hilltops to listen for firing or watch the Union balloons at all hours, what choice had he?

He listened for the gunfire, too. He listened to the drums and fifes of relief units marching out to the earthworks. And, unwillingly, he listened to the ceaseless creak of ambulances coming in —long lines of them, deceptively festive at night when they were bedecked with lanterns. There was nothing festive about the noises that issued from them. Nothing festive about the church foyers and hotel lobbies where the wounded and dying were laid in rows because the hospitals couldn't hold them.

Huntoon desperately wanted to escape the city. He had purchased a pair of railway tickets—wheedled, schemed, even bribed one man for the privilege of paying triple the regular price—but Ashton flatly refused to leave. She implied he was a coward simply because he possessed the tickets. Did she believe that or was it subterfuge? From whence came this new courage, this patriotism she had never exhibited before? From her lover?

Early one evening, while she was still out, he went quite innocently to the desk where she wrote personal notes to ladies of her acquaintance. Searching for a pen nib to replace his, which had broken, he found the packet of statements and letters.

"What is this bank account in Nassau?" In shirt sleeves, wet rings showing under his arms, he thrust the packet at her an hour later. "We have no bank account in Nassau."

She snatched the packet. "How dare you invade my desk and pry into my belongings?"

He winced and retreated to tall open windows overlooking Grace Street. The street was filled with Southern Express Company wagons doing duty as ambulances. "I—I didn't pry or spy or anything like that. I needed a pen—Damn it, why must I explain to you?" he shouted with uncharacteristic bravery. "You are the one cheating on me. What do those papers mean? I demand you explain."

"James, calm yourself." She saw she had pushed him too far. This had to be handled delicately lest it threaten her liaison with Powell. "Please sit down, and I will."

He fell into a chair that crackled as if it might break. Homer's shadow passed the open windows. The slave made her nervous with that musket. High in the eastern sky, a signal shell exploded. A flat report followed the shower of brilliant blue light-streamers. She began carefully.

"Did you read through all the statements? Study the numbers?" Flushed with heat and tension, she extracted one paper from the packet, unfolded it, and handed it to him. "That shows the balance in our account as of last month."

The fine, looping handwriting blurred. He knuckled his eyes. *Our* account, she said. Still, he was baffled. "These are pounds sterling—"

"Quite right. At present exchange rates, we have a quarter of a million dollars—sound Yankee dollars, not Confederate paper." Skirts whispering, she ran to him and knelt—humiliating, but it might divert him when she reached the trickiest part. "We have earned a profit of approximately seven hundred percent from just two voyages between Nassau and Wilmington."

"Voyages?" He goggled. "What in God's name are you talking about?"

"The ship, darling. The swift little steamship Mr. Lamar Powell wanted you to invest in, don't you remember? You refused, but I took the risk. She was refitted in Liverpool last fall, sailed to the Bahamas by her British captain and crew—and she's already made us what some would consider a fortune. If she goes to the bottom tomorrow, we've recouped our investment many times over."

"Powell—that worthless adventurer?"

"A shrewd businessman, dearest."

388

His tiny eyes blinked behind the wire spectacles. "Do you see him?"

"Oh, no. Disbursement of profits takes place in Nassau, and we receive these reports by mail that comes in on blockade runners. *Water Witch* has done so well because she doesn't carry any war cargo. She brings in coffee, lace—niceties that are scarce and command huge prices—and when she goes out again, she's loaded with cotton. There, I've explained everything, haven't I? It just addles my poor head to do so, but I want you to retire for the evening assured and comforted. You can fall asleep dreaming of your new-found—"

"You defied me, Ashton," he broke in, shaking the paper at her. Still heavy weather ahead. "I said no to Powell, and secretly, behind my back, you took our nest egg—"

She let the sweet belle's smile go now; it hadn't worked. "The money, I remind you, was mine to start with."

"Legally it's mine. I am your husband."

Creak and *creak,* the express wagons passed, lanterns bobbing like skiffs in a rough sea. A man shrieked; another wept; two more signal lights burst, cascaded, and died behind the rooftops. "James," she said, "what is the matter with you? I have increased our wealth—"

"Illegally," he shouted. "Unpatriotically. What else have you done that's immoral?"

Instinct said she must attack, and quickly, or he would suspect. "What do you mean by that insulting remark?"

"Noth—" He pushed at hair straggling over his greasy forehead. "Nothing." He turned away.

Ashton jerked him around. "I demand a better answer than that."

"I just—" he avoided her eye—"wondered—is Powell in Richmond?"

"I believe so. I can't swear. I told you, I don't see him. I delivered the initial investment to an attorney handling formation of the syndicate. Powell was there, but I have not met him since."

Her breast felt fiery, painful because her heart beat so fast. But she had learned long ago that successful deception depended on strong nerves, a controlled expression, and eyes that never wavered from the person to be deceived. She knew Huntoon's emotional temperature was falling when his shoulders returned to

389

their customary droop. His attempt at masculinity had been brief and unsuccessful.

"I believe you," he said, then noticed her dark eyes fixed behind him. Turning, he saw Homer on the terrace, drawn by the shouting.

Ashton lashed him. "Get back to your rounds!" He disappeared.

"I believe you," Huntoon said again, "but do you realize the stigma you've put on yourself? You're a speculator now. They're a scorned breed. Some say every one of them should be arrested, tried, and hung."

"Too late to worry about that, my sweet. If anyone calls for a noose, two will be needed in this family. So I suggest you follow my example and be discreet about the subject of *Water Witch.* You might also be glad I had the foresight you lacked."

It was harsh and slipped out, but she was tired of dealing with a child. This child deserved whipping, not coddling. Fortunately, he could no longer summon anger, just his customary whine:

"But, Ashton—I don't know whether I can accept money from—"

"You can. You will." She pointed to the packet. "You already have."

Suddenly he squeezed his eyes shut and clutched the edge of the tall window as the last ambulance rolled out of sight. There came sudden rumblings and boomings. Rooftops flickered red. Responding to pent-up fear, people poured into nearby streets, shouting questions. Was the invasion at hand?

Oblivious, Huntoon whispered, "Jesus, you're so hard." Tears trickled from the corners of his eyes. "So hard—You leave me nothing. I feel—You make me feel like a man not worthy of the name."

How shortsighted and pathetic he was. It made her angry all over again, with no desire to spare him.

"Is the word you want *castrated,* darling?"

Trembling, loathing her, he watched her affirm her own question with a small, neat nod. Businesslike, she continued. "In this matter and in some others we might name, you're exactly that. We've known it for years, haven't we?"

Red flashes; cannon fire. "You bitch."

Ashton laughed at him.

Huntoon's face changed from red to a color close to purple. He blinked, and again, and kept blinking as he rushed to her, grasping and stroking her hand repeatedly. "I'm sorry. I'm sorry, sweetheart. Will you forgive me? I'm sure your decision is an intelligent one. Whatever you want is agreeable. God, I love you. Please say you forgive me?"

After letting him writhe a few moments longer, she did. She even let him fondle and attempt to make love to her when they went to bed. She was relieved when he was unable to finish and withdrew, flaccid, but saying how happy he was that she had forgiven him.

Simpleton, she thought, smiling in the dark.

56

"Never in my life have I spent a more peculiar Independence Day," George said to Constance.

William was leaning from the parlor window, hauling in bunting he and Patricia had hung the night before. "Why, Pa?"

"Because," George said, folding the tricolored material and putting it in a box, "the speeches were so brave and full of hope" —in the afternoon they had attended a long public ceremony— "and down on the peninsula we're whipped."

"It's really over?" Constance asked.

"Nearly. The departmental telegraph reports the army's withdrawing to the James. McClellan almost had Richmond in his hand and couldn't take it."

"Because Lee brought Stonewall marching to help him," William said. George responded with a somber nod. His son sounded like an admirer of Old Jack.

There were none at the Winder Building. How often had George listened to departmental blowhards mock Jackson because he held his arm in the air before or during a battle so the blood would flow properly? How often had he heard it said that some of Jackson's own subordinates declared him certifiably insane? George was often pressed to provide anecdotes of Jackson's bizarre behavior from their cadet days, but, although there were plenty, he declined. The mockery disgusted him because its source was fear. Tom Jackson was smart and relentless as a Joshua. His foot cavalry had quick-marched all the way from the valley and helped save Richmond.

For a full week, the battle for the Confederate capital had seesawed through a series of hot engagements. Mechanicsville—there, inexplicably, Jackson was late to come up to reinforce General A. P. Hill, and his reputation suffered; Gaines's Mill; Savage Station; Malvern Hill. Despite mistakes and minor successes on both sides, at the end of the seven days, the Richmond defense perimeter, which Bob Lee had worked a month to set and strengthen, still held. Old Bob had outthought and outfought Little Mac and his commanders at every turn. He had slipped and slid in the early months of the war, and suffered for it. But the seven days wiped out all that. George feared for the Union's fate if Lee took charge.

Organization of the Bank of Lehigh Station hit a snag. Attorney Jupiter Smith rushed to Washington to report that the legislature respectfully suggested the state participate in the bank's profits, if any. "What they're proposing, George, is that we give the state shares amounting to forty thousand dollars and a ten-year option to buy an equal amount at par."

George barked, "Oh, is that all?"

"No, it isn't. A donation of twenty thousand dollars to the road and bridge fund would be welcome. But I repeat—the suggestions were made very respectfully, George. The legislators realize you're an important man."

"I'm a man with a big club over his head. Goddamn it, Jupe, it's bribery."

The lawyer shrugged. "I prefer to call it accommodation. Or standard practice. The Philadelphia and Pittsburgh banks entered into similar arrangements to get their charters. Whether you want to do it is up to you, of course. But we've bought the building, and if you say no, we'll have to put it up for sale. If you do say no, it won't bother me. I'll be shed of huge amounts of paperwork."

"And huge fees."

Smith looked aggrieved.

George chewed his cigar. "I still say it's bribery." More chewing. "Tell them yes."

George proved a poor prophet of military affairs. McClellan stayed on, evidently for want of a competent replacement. The only West Point officers who seemed capable of winning were those who had gone south. This renewed the outcries against the Academy. In mid-July, George received a letter asking him to serve on West Point's Board of Visitors as a replacement for a member suddenly deceased. The mounting attacks inclined him to accept, so he requested an interview with Stanton. The secretary gave him permission to serve so long as it didn't interfere with his assigned duties.

George was mired in work, but he assured Stanton there would be no problem. From the brief conversation, he gained not the slightest hint as to the secretary's opinion about the Academy. Mr. Stanton, he concluded, was by design a circular fortress—safe from attack from any direction.

Though the Board of Visitors appointment meant more pressure, George was thankful to have it. His job had grown so frustrating he hated to open his eyes in the morning, because that meant donning his uniform and going to the Winder Building. His work with artillery contracts was constantly interrupted by interminable meetings. Should the department recommend adoption of rifle shells—Minié balls with time fuses that exploded after firing? Should the department test shells containing liquid chlorine, which would turn to a heavy, deadly gas when released? George also continued to interview inventors of patently insane weapons. One day he wasted three hours examining drawings of a two-barrel fieldpiece designed to fire a pair of cannonballs linked by a chain. The chain was supposed to decapitate several soldiers when the balls landed.

"We court the lunatics, and the sane inventors stay away," he protested to Constance. "They can get a better hearing from a bootblack than they can from us."

"You're exaggerating again."

"Think so? Read this." Into her hands he thrust the latest *Scientific American* whose editorializing had sent Ripley into a rage:

We fear that the skill of our mechanics, the self-sacrifice of our people, and the devoted heroism of our troops in their efforts to save the country will all be rendered futile by the utter incompetency which controls the war and navy departments of the government.

"They deem us fools, and they're right," he growled when she finished. She had nothing to say. He went off to see the children in a grumpy, abrasive mood that was becoming a constant in their lives.

Only one thing helped him survive in the Winder Building. It was not possible for Ripley to interfere with everything, and he now seemed inclined to refrain from meddling with the artillery program. The turnabout had come in April when Parrott rifles had proven their worth by quickly reducing Savannah's Fort Pulaski to ruins. Still, George felt like a man hanging from a ledge. How much longer his hands would hold out he didn't know.

Interwoven with his work and the war were the no less important events of day-to-day family life, some amusing, some troublesome, many just mundane and tiring. Constance by some miracle had found a small, snug house for rent in Georgetown, near the college. By mid-July they were into the upheaval of moving. For a week George roared around the place unable to locate his underdrawers, his cigars, or any other necessities of life.

One morning Patricia found the bedclothes reddened, and though her mother had prepared her with information about young womanhood, she wept for an hour.

William was growing rapidly, and his attitude toward girls was changing from loathing to interest tinctured with suspicion. Early in the war he had often said he couldn't wait to grow up, enlist, and have a grand time fighting for the Union. The long day and longer night after Bull Run had put an end to those declarations.

No letters came from Billy—another cause for concern. Often at night, when George had worried all he could about Old Ripley and the army, he would lie awake fretting about his younger brother or his old friend Orry.

Except for Brett, living in Lehigh Station, ties between the Hazards and the Mains were broken. Where was Orry? Where was Charles? A letter smuggler might be hard put to find either of them, though George supposed it could be done if absolutely necessary. What mattered was not that they exchanged letters but that they all came through this dark passage unhurt.

He never worried about Stanley. His older brother was dressing well and living lavishly. Stanley and Isabel were intimate with Washington's most powerful men and seen at the city's most prestigious social gatherings. George couldn't understand how it could happen to someone as incompetent as Stanley.

"There are seasons, George," Constance said by way of answer. "Cycles for all things—the Bible says that. Stanley stood in your shadow for a long time."

"And now I'm to be hidden in his?"

"No, I didn't mean to imply—"

"It's the truth. It makes me mad."

"I feel a bit jealous myself, if you must know. On the other hand, I'm sure Isabel is the chief architect of their success, and I'd hang myself before I'd change places with her."

George puffed his cigar. "You know, I can't forget that I hit Stanley after the train wreck. Maybe this is justice. Maybe it's my punishment."

"Did you notice how friendly the secretary was?" Stanley exclaimed one Saturday night in July. Their carriage was taking them home from a Shakespearean performance at Leonard Grover's new theater on the site of the old National on E Street. "Did you notice that, Isabel?"

"Why shouldn't Stanton be cordial? You're one of his best employees. He knows he can trust you."

Stanley preened. Could it be true? The evidence certainly pointed that way. He was on good terms with the dogmatic but unquestionably patriotic secretary, at the same time maintaining friendly relations with Wade, to whom he occasionally passed bits of information about confidential War Department matters. Lashbrook's was prospering beyond all expectations, and Stanley was now anticipating a trip to New Orleans, there to establish additional trading contracts of a sensitive but potentially lucrative nature. He was making the world not merely his oyster but a whole plate of them. Strange how a savage war could change a man's life so greatly.

There were only a few aspects of Stanley's role of fierce Republican that he didn't like. He mentioned one to Isabel when they got to bed that night.

"The Confiscation Act's to be signed this week. The slaves will be freed in captured territory, and use of colored troops approved. But there's more coming. Stanton told me so during the second intermission, while you were in the toilet."

"Don't utter that word in my presence. Tell me what you learned from Stanton."

"The President's drafting an executive order." Stanley paused to achieve an effect. "He wants to free all the slaves."

"My God. Are you sure?"

"Well, all of them in the Confederacy at least. I don't believe he'll touch slavery in Kentucky or the other border states."

"Ah. I didn't think he was that much of an idealist. It won't be a humanitarian measure, then, but a punitive one." She continued, grudgingly, "Lincoln has all the charm of a pig, but I'll give him this: he's a shrewd politician."

"How can you say that, Isabel? Do you want mobs of freed niggers swarming into the North? Think of the unrest. Think of the jobs decent white men will lose. The whole idea's scandalous."

"You'd better keep that opinion private if you want to keep the friendship of Stanton and Ben Wade."

"But—"

"Stop, Stanley. When you dine at the devil's house, you can't choose the menu. Play your part. The loyal Republican."

He did, although it galled him to hear all the talk of emancipation suddenly flying through the offices and corridors, the parlors and saloon bars of official and unofficial Washington. Lincoln's radical proposal offended many whites who got wind of it, and it was sure to cause social upheaval if it were implemented. Stanley obeyed his wife, however, and kept his views to himself.

Except on one subject. He invited his brother to dine at Willard's, so he could gloat.

"I wouldn't devote much time to that Board of Visitors, George. If Ben Wade and some others have their way, this time next year West Point will be nothing but abandoned buildings and memories."

"What the hell are you talking about?"

"There will be no more appropriations to operate that place. It's provided a free education to traitors, but what has it given our side? One general reportedly drunk as a lord at Shiloh, another so egotistical and inept he couldn't win against an army half the size of his. I could also mention—a host of—lesser—"

The sentence became mumbling; George had laid his fork next to the slab of venison and was glaring.

"You said this was a social occasion. No politics. I should have known better than to believe you."

He walked out, leaving Stanley with the bill.

Stanley didn't mind. He felt expansive that day; affluent—even handsome. He had just achieved a nice little triumph. His strutting brother's precious institution was doomed, and there was not one damn thing he could do about it.

* She was black and beautiful. Coppered oak, over two hundred feet long from bowsprit to stern. A single low stack amidships enhanced her rakish appearance. The red of her shield figurehead and the gilt of her stern carvings were her only vivid colors.

Cooper knew her intimately and loved her without reservation. She was a steam barkentine, a thousand and fifty tons, with two oscillating engines of three hundred and fifty horsepower driving a single propeller that could be raised from the water to reduce drag. Her three masts could be donkey-rigged with plenty of canvas. She lay in the Mersey this twenty-ninth day of July with everything from bedding to galley stores in place and her full crew aboard.

A stream of carriages discharged passengers on the cobblestones of the pier. Bulloch greeted each local businessman or officeholder by name; all had been invited—hastily—for an afternoon's excursion on Number 209.

Captain Butcher, lately second officer on the Royal Mail vessel *Arabia,* had steam up and was waiting for the last few guests. They might or might not arrive before the order that Bulloch's spies had reported to be on the way from Whitehall: the ship was to be prevented from sailing because her ultimate mission violated British law.

Bulloch maintained a fine front, smiling and chatting as he saw guests to the gangway and directed them to refreshments on trestle tables beneath a striped awning. Cooper paced the pier, snapping his watch open every couple of minutes. If they didn't get away—if Charles Francis Adams succeeded—this beautiful, invaluable commerce raider would be lost to the Confederacy.

A clerk hovering close to Bulloch showed him a list. "All but these two gentlemen are present, sir."

"We shall go without them."

Up the gangway he went, past the seamen recruited from Cunard and other lines to sail Number 209 on the first leg of her voyage. Suddenly, beyond some dockworkers, Cooper saw a hack careen through Canning Street, heading for the ship. From the foot of the gangway, he called, "Our last guests may be here, James."

Quickly, Bulloch stepped to the helm and spoke to young Captain Butcher, whose light whiskers danced in the Mersey breeze. The hack rattled along the pier, slowing. Before it came to a stop, a man jumped out. Cooper's stomach wrenched as he recognized Maguire. Preceded by the smell of leeks, Marcellus Dorking also appeared.

The sight of the man enraged Cooper. Since that afternoon in the Pig and Whistle, he had been followed intermittently by several different spies, all of whom undoubtedly worked for Tom Dudley. Of Dorking, however, he had seen no sign. The threat against Cooper's family had been nothing but air; a coward's way of inspiring fear. That lowered Dorking even further in Cooper's estimation.

Maguire and Dorking bolted toward Cooper, who barred the gangway. Dorking's right hand dipped into the pocket of his garish plaid coat. "Little pleasure cruise, sir?" he asked with his familiar smarmy smile.

"That's right. As you can see, we have local dignitaries on board."

"Be that as it may, we must request that you delay your departure. A train should be arriving at Lime Street right about now bearing a gentleman who wishes to speak with the captain about certain improprieties that—"

"You'll have to excuse me," Cooper interrupted. He started up the gangway.

"Just a minute." Dorking grabbed Cooper's shoulder and roughly turned him around. A couple of seamen called warnings to Butcher. The invited guests murmured and frowned.

Bulloch started down to help Cooper, too late. Marcellus Dorking produced a small silver pistol and shoved it into Cooper's stomach, indenting his waistcoat half an inch.

"Stand aside while we speak to the master of this vessel."

Cooper had never been so scared or so directly confronted with the threat of violent death. Yet that was somehow less important than the need to get Number 209 to her destination. Dorking realized his pistol was in view and tried to hide it from those on deck. As the muzzle dipped down, Cooper stamped on Dorking's shoe.

"Bleeding Christ," Dorking cried, staggering. Maguire tried to strike Cooper, who pushed him, then gave Dorking a knee in the crotch. Consul Dudley's agents spilled onto the cobbles like ill-trained acrobats.

Energized by his success in the face of danger, Cooper loped up the gangway, shouting at Dorking and Maguire, "Invited guests only on this cruise, gentlemen." He passed seamen at the rail. "Take up the gangway."

Captain Butcher bellowed orders. The dockworkers who had watched the fray with puzzled amusement cast off the lines on the double. There was consternation among the guests.

Brown water began to show between the hull and the pier. Maguire regained his feet, then Dorking, who went for the pistol again. "My word," said a guest behind Cooper. There were other, less polite oaths.

Dorking raised the pistol, a flicker of silver in the summer sunshine. Maguire dragged his arm down. Dorking glared at Cooper, who gripped the rail and yelled, "It never pays to brag, Mr. Dorking. It never pays to say you'll do something when you can't. I hope you didn't tell Dudley you'd stop us."

"Keep quiet," Bulloch said behind him. Red, Cooper turned, ready to apologize. Only he could see Bulloch's smile or hear him whisper, "Sharp work." Swiftly, he returned to the guests, who swarmed around him asking questions.

The figures of Maguire and Dorking receded. Cooper relaxed at the rail, surprised at the quickness of his reactions. He was pleased with himself.

The river shone like gold; the air was salty and not too hot; a perfect afternoon. Bulloch promised to answer all questions shortly but first urged the guests to help themselves to French champagne and the delicacies he had ordered to support the illusion of an innocent outing. When a measure of calm returned, he politely asked for attention and stepped into the sunshine just beyond the awning shadow. From there he addressed the passengers.

"We trust you will all enjoy your cruise on the vessel variously known in Liverpool and Birkenhead as *Enrica* or Laird's 209. She will have her real name soon. We want you to be perfectly comfortable this afternoon. Eat and drink as much as you like and try not to let that unpleasantness on the pier bother you. I must be honest and confess that your return journey will be aboard a tug awaiting us down the coast at Anglesey."

"What's that?"

"Dammit, Bulloch, what subterfuge are you—?"

"Bloody trick, that's what it—"

"A regrettable necessity, gentlemen," Bulloch said, his deep Georgian voice overriding the protests. "On Sunday we were warned that if this ship remained in the Mersey another forty-eight hours, she'd be impounded. Lost to our cause. You'll have no trouble with the authorities if you simply tell the truth. You were invited on a cruise, which you are now taking. The only difference is, your cruise ship won't be the vessel taking you back to Liverpool. For that, I accept all blame."

"Are the rumors true, then? Was this vessel built illegally?"

"She was built in scrupulous conformity with British law, sir."

"That's no answer," someone else said. "Where's she bound?"

"Up the Irish Channel and then to a port I am not at liberty to name. Ultimately, she will sail in American waters with a different crew."

Cooper felt a strange thrill up his spine—unexpected as his own clumsy bravery at dockside. What a remarkable change had come over him, scarcely noticed, since those days when he had debated the folly of secession and war with anyone who would listen. He was proud of this ship and proud of his part in getting her to sea. He was proud of her name, which Bulloch had confided to him; it was to be *Alabama*. He was proud to stand on her spanking new deck as she headed down the glittering Mersey to the destination Bulloch quietly announced to the stunned guests.

"She is going to war."

While the Confederate ship escaped to the Isle of Anglesey, George was en route to Massachusetts, having first stopped at Lehigh Station for a day and a half. He had conferred with Jupe Smith, who informed him that the legislature now looked on the bank charter application with great favor—"What a surprise," George muttered—and spent seven hours with Wotherspoon inspecting the books, the manufacturing areas, and samples of Hazard's current output. Before he left, he saw the Hungarian couple and their black charges—fifteen of them now. To relieve her loneliness, Brett said, she sometimes helped Mr. and Mrs. Czorna care for the children. It was the only time during the visit that George saw a sign of animation in his sister-in-law.

After unsuccessfully trying to doze while sitting upright on the train all night, George was exhausted when he reached Braintree. Old Sylvanus Thayer allowed him three hours in a comfortable bed, then woke him and served a breakfast more like a banquet. Usually a Spartan eater, George put away six fried eggs, four slices of ham, and six biscuits at five o'clock of a hot summer afternoon. While he ate, Thayer talked.

"Scapegoats, George. Men need them most—they are driven to find them—when matters are out of control and somehow cannot be set right. The human animal is willful and frequently stupid. Blame is often placed where it doesn't belong simply because any explanation of chaos, however ludicrous, is better than none, and people would go mad without one. I do not claim that is always the case. In the war, the army was the focus of blame, and rightly so." For Thayer, there was always and only one war: the last fought against Britain. "Now, however, I believe the tide's flowing the other way. I take your brother's warning seriously."

He tapped a copy of *Harper's* pulled from under recent issues of the *New York Tribune*. "This noxious rag—and Greeley's paper—are both demanding the Academy close forever. Great men have come from our school, but that's of no consequence. The army is failing again, and someone or something must be put up on the cross."

George finished his coffee and lit a cigar. "I get so damn sick of them saying we trained the enemy."

"I know, I know." Thayer's hands, white as the fine linen cloth covering the table, clenched. Dark blue veins rose up on the backs of them. "We have also trained many accomplished officers who have remained loyal. Alas, for all his effort and sincerity, the President can't seem to utilize them properly. Perhaps he interferes too much, as they say Davis does. That is an observation, not an excuse for inaction. We cannot avoid the inescapable, George. West Point is at war."

He plucked the cigar from his mouth. "What's that, sir?"

"At war. Those of us who love the place must campaign as if

the enemy has formidable leadership—which it does—" He whacked Greeley's newspaper. "We must fight with intelligence, zeal, our whole soul—and never admit to even the remotest possibility of defeat. We shall not cower. We shall not wait passively to have our position overwhelmed. We shall mount an offensive."

"I'd agree with that strategy, Colonel. But what are the tactics?"

The old man's eyes sparkled. "We do not hide our light under a bushel. We promote our past—our performance on behalf of the republic in Mexico and on the frontier. We trumpet our case and our cause. We whisper into influential ears. We twist reluctant arms. We knock resistant heads. We attack, George—"

Thump went the fist on the table.

"Attack. Attack. Attack!"

They talked on into the night. Graduates and friends of West Point had to be recruited to speak or write in defense of it. George would send letters to six members of the Board of Visitors, and Thayer would do the same with the other ten. On the spot, George decided to visit the Academy on his way home. He didn't put his head down till half-past three, but Thayer was up an hour ahead of him, at six-thirty, and saw him to the station. Even on the noisy platform, Thayer's mind kept working.

"What influential allies have we in the Congress. Any at all?"

"The chief one I can think of is Wade's fellow senator from Ohio—Cump Sherman's brother, John. He and Wade don't particularly like each other."

"Cultivate Senator Sherman," Thayer urged as he pumped George's hand. George felt as though he had received marching orders. Thayer was still bobbing along beside the car calling suggestions as the train pulled out.

After a brief stop at Cold Spring and some mutual complaining with Benét, George crossed the Hudson to the Plain and began campaigning there. Professor Mahan promised to step up his writing about the institution. Captain Edward Boynton, a classmate of George's and Orry's who had returned as adjutant, said he would rush completion of the manuscript of his history of West Point, incorporating rebuttals of its critics into the final text. Washington-bound again on a crowded, sooty train, George felt a little better; the offensive was under way.

He hoped it hadn't been launched too late. The appropriation

402

would come up in Congress early next year. They had less than six months to conduct and win their small war while the larger one rumbled along a murky road whose end no one could see.

Returning to duty, George found criticism of the army more ferocious than ever. Old Brains Halleck had been summoned from the West to be supreme commander. McClellan still had the Army of the Potomac, largely a Washington defense force now, and John Pope had been given the Army of Northern Virginia as a consequence of his success at Island No. 10. Pope quickly alienated most of his men by observing that soldiers in the western theater were tougher and fought harder. He then remarked that he was a commander who could be counted on to take the field; he would keep his headquarters in the saddle. Wags turned headquarters into hindquarters.

Lincoln's Negro policies were causing fights in saloons and army camps. The only part of the Confiscation Act anyone seemed to like was that encouraging emigration of freedmen to some unspecified country in the tropics. "There's all this talk of emancipation, and we're not ready for it," George said to his wife. "No one believes in it."

"They should."

"Yes, of course. But you know the realities, Constance. Most Northerners don't give a damn for the Negro, and they certainly don't think he has the same rights as a white man. This war is still being fought for one reason only—love of the Union and the grand old flag. I'm not saying it's right. I'm saying it's a fact. If emancipation comes, I fear the consequences."

Late August brought a second major battle near Bull Run and a second outcome like the first. Beaten Union armies withdrew to Washington, where fear of a direct attack spread like fire on a prairie. Critics of the war stepped up their attack, saying the whole thing was misbegotten and negotiated peace should be sought at once.

The secretary called Stanley to his office on a stormy day in early September. Stanton had relinquished direct control of the armies to Halleck, but he was quietly gathering the lines of control of other areas into his hands. Once scornful of Lincoln, he had now ingratiated himself with the President and become a trusted adviser and professed friend. Not yet fifty, Edwin McMasters Stanton—small round spectacles, perfumed beard, and Buddha face—was said to be the second most powerful man in the country.

He had emphatic views about the mounting dissent:

"We must stamp it out. We must curb these peace Democrats and their milksop cronies and make it evident that if they continue to attack the government and its actions, they face arrest, prison, even charges of treason. The war must be prosecuted to its conclusion."

Rain spattered the office windows; the noonday was dark as twilight. Thinking of the busy production lines at Lashbrook's, Stanley gave a fervent nod. "I definitely agree, sir."

"Secretary Seward formerly had responsibility for matters of government integrity and security—" Seward's prosecution of those duties was legendary. It was said he had kept a little hand bell on his desk and boasted that if he rang it, any man anywhere could be put behind bars indefinitely. "But I am in charge now."

Stanley wondered why the secretary was stating the obvious. Stanton laced his plump hands together on the desk. "I need a deputy whom I can trust. One who will be zealous in seeing that my policies as well as my specific orders are executed with dispatch and without question."

Stanley gripped the arm of the visitor's chair to steady himself. Rain hit the office window. The vista of power Stanton spread before him in a sentence or two was awesome.

"We must organize the security function more completely and begin to take vigorous action against enemies in our own camp."

"No doubt of that, sir. None. But I wonder how easily the goal can be accomplished. Just the habeas corpus matter has created a storm of debate and outcries about violations of Constitutional rights."

Up jerked the ends of Stanton's mouth, a sneer. Stanley's knees shook. Hoping to demonstrate his grasp of the situation, he had instead enraged the secretary.

"Was the country made for the Constitution, Stanley? I think not. The reverse, rather. Still, I know the warped view of our enemies. If the country sinks to oblivion, they will no doubt take extreme comfort in knowing the Constitution is still safe."

Quickly, Stanley leaned toward the desk. "People like that are not only misguided, they're dangerous. That is all I meant to say, sir."

Stanton leaned back, stroking his beard. Today it was perfumed with lilac. "Good. For a minute I thought I might have misjudged you. You've served me loyally, and absolute loyalty is one qualification for the job I am proposing. I need a man who can be discreet but firm about silencing our critics—and keep any onus from falling on this office."

A plump hand rose to indicate a large inked diagram hanging on one wall. The diagram consisted of many connected circles and boxes, each with its neat legend inside or below. "For example, the official descriptive charts illustrate the structure of this department. Should we find it wise to establish a special unit to suppress treasonous activity, it must never appear on the chart."

"I can make sure of that, sir. I can do everything you ask, and I will."

"Excellent," Stanton murmured. Then, slyly, he peeked at Stanley over his round spectacles. "I should think that if you go about your new duties efficiently, you will still have ample time to sell footwear to the army."

Stanley sat still, not daring to reply.

The secretary murmured on for another fifteen minutes, and toward the end gave Stanley a folder containing his confidential plan for strengthening the police arm of the War Department. At Stanton's suggestion, Stanley took a few moments to leaf through the half-dozen pages of the document, paying special attention to the philosophic preamble.

"This opening statement is exactly right, sir. We need to tighten up. It will be even more important if the President goes through with his plan to free the nig—the black people in the rebelling states."

"He's adamant about doing so. As I see it, in his mind the step has undergone a change from a punitive measure to a moral imperative. Just yesterday he told the cabinet that although he has doubts about a great many things, from generals to weapons, he has none in regard to the rightness of emancipation. However, Seward and I and some others have convinced him to withhold the proclamation until the time is more propitious." He seemed to hunch, his face and form darkening along with the clouds outside. From the dark mound came the intense voice. "The policy change the President proposes is so unusual, not to say radical, we dare not make it public when the war's going against us. For the proclamation to meet even minimum acceptance, it must be an-

405

nounced at a peak of public confidence and euphoria. We must have a victory."

Stanley closed his hand on the folder—his key to expanded authority and power. The secretary had made it clear. He didn't want a brilliant thinker but an obedient soldier. Stanley had learned that kind of soldiering under one of the best, now in exile.

"Most definitely, sir," he said with an excess of sincerity, even though he loathed the thought of all those strange, hostile, dark-skinned people being set free to roam the North at will. "A victory."

After scouting around Frederick, Maryland, Charles and Ab turned back toward White's Ford on the Potomac. It was the fourth of September, autumn coming on.

The scouts, both dressed as farmers, proceeded at a slow trot along a rutty road between steep, heavily treed hillsides. The leaves had not begun to change color, but Charles was already afflicted with the melancholy of the coming season. Despite his aversion to writing letters, he had sent three to Barclay's Farm in recent months and received no replies. He hoped that was just another example of the wretchedness of the army mails, not a sign Gus had forgotten him.

Light through overhanging branches flashed and flickered over the bearded men. Charles had his wool coat open, his revolver within reach. They had found good forage at a stable near Frederick last night. Sport acted livelier today. So did Ab's horse, Cyclone. Of late the army had provided only green corn.

Before hunting up the stable yesterday, they had ventured into Frederick itself—a nervous two hours for Charles because his accent demanded that he remain mute and let Ab do the talking. He poked about the town by himself for a while, speaking to no one and arousing no suspicion. Ab visited a saloon and came back with a disconcerting report.

"Charlie, they ain't a damn bit interested in bein' liberated. You think Bob Lee got the wrong information? I was told we could expect a big uprisin' of locals to help us out when we invaded this here state."

"I was told the same thing."

"Well, most of them boys in that grogshop acted like they didn't care whether I was from hell or Huntsville. I got a few stares, one offer to sit in a card game, a glass of whiskey I bought myself, and a good look at a lot of backs. The people hereabouts aren't gonna feed us or fart on us, either one."

Charles frowned. Had the army miscalculated again? If so, it was too late; the advance was under way. Mr. Davis and the generals did appear to be at odds on the status of Maryland. The President insisted the state belonged to the South, and they would come as liberators—a judgment Ab's report contradicted. Camp talk said they were marching to strike a blow on enemy soil for a change: invading Yankee territory to strip it of cattle and produce and, not incidentally, give the farmers of Virginia a chance to harvest their crops without fear of bluebellies pouring over their rail fences and trampling their fields.

Whatever the answer, they had finished their mission. After leaving Frederick and stopping at the stable, they had slept in a secluded grove, halter tie-ropes fastened to their wrists and shotguns laid across their bellies.

Now Ab said, "Ask you somethin', Charlie?"

"Go ahead."

"You got a girl? Been curious about it because you never say."

He thought of Private Gervais and Miss Sally Mills. "This is the wrong time and place for a man to have a girl."

The other scout laughed. "That's sure-God true, but it don't answer my question. You got one?"

Charles tugged his dirty felt hat down over his forehead, watching the road. "No."

It was an honest answer. He didn't have a girl except in his imagination. If you had a girl, she wrote to you. Gus had kissed him, but how much did that mean? A lot of females gave away their kisses as if they were no more special than pieces of homemade pie.

The terrain changed rapidly. The hills were higher, steeper. There were no cottages or shanties in the few clearings and level places because there was no way to subsist on the land. Charles suspected they were close to the river and soon heard distant sounds to confirm it—the noise of the army of fifty-five thousand men leaving Virginia by way of the ford.

He saw insects in a shaft of sun and then Gus Barclay's face. *Oughtn't to be muddling your head that way.* He blinked; the insects returned. The noise grew louder. When Little Mac got word of the invasion, the Yanks would come out from Washington and fight. Scouting for the cavalry on the peninsula, Charles had done his share of fighting and had had two close scrapes, but he would never grow accustomed to it or regard it lightly.

They reached the river in time to watch the coming of the cavalry—five thousand horse, Ab claimed, including new brigades that contained old comrades. His old friend Beauty Stuart, the golden-spurred, plume-hatted, was major general of the division —and not yet thirty. Hampton was his senior brigadier, Fitz Lee his junior. Charles's old friend had risen rapidly; from lieutenant to general in fifteen months.

Stuart's innovative flying artillery batteries went rolling and crashing through the water. Then Ab let out a shout, spying Hampton's men on the Virginia side. The brigade included the newly formed Second South Carolina Cavalry, put together around the nucleus of the four original troops of the legion.

Calbraith Butler was colonel of the regiment. He saw the two scouts hunched on their horses in the shallows and greeted them with a wave of his silver-chased whip. With Butler rode his second-in-command, Hampton's younger brother Frank.

Charles felt like the schoolroom dunce. He was still a captain, and this was one of the occasions when it hurt. On the other hand, he couldn't deny that he had come to prefer the dangerous but more independent life of a scout.

He reminded Ab that they should find Stuart's headquarters and report. Suddenly spurring into the Potomac from the Virginia shore, came Hampton. He spied the scouts and rode toward them, scattering sunlit water. He took their salutes with a warm smile and shook each man's hand.

Hampton's color was good. He was a massive, martial figure on his prancing horse, even if his uniform did look shabby, like everyone else's. Charles noticed three stars on his collar—the same insignia Stuart wore. You couldn't tell one kind of Confederate general from another.

"I hear you like what you're doing, Captain Main."

"I'm better at it than I was at leading a troop, General. I like it very much."

"Happy to hear it."

"You look fit, sir. I'm pleased you've made such a fine recovery." Commanding infantry at Seven Pines, Hampton had been on horseback when an enemy ball struck his foot. Fearing he would be unable to remount if he climbed down for treatment, he remained in the saddle while a surgeon yanked off his boot, probed and cut until the lump of lead was found and removed. With the wound bandaged, the boot shoved back on, and the bullet hole plugged, he stayed with his men until dark ended the fight and he could be lifted down. His boot was full of blood, which ran out over the top.

"I'm glad to run into you this way," the general said to him, "because it allows me to bring you two bits of news you may regard as vindications." Puzzled, Charles waited for him to continue. "In attempting to drill his men recently, Captain von Helm fell off his horse and cracked his neck. He was intoxicated at the time. He died within the hour. Further, your favorite, Private Cramm, has disappeared without leave."

"He's probably twenty miles behind with a few hundred others."

"Cramm is not a straggler. He deserted. He left a note informing us he had enlisted to defend Southern soil, not to campaign in the North."

"God above. I'm surprised he didn't hire a lawyer to write up his explanation." Charles stifled laughter. So did Ab.

"I thought the news would be of some comfort."

"Shouldn't admit it, General, but it surely is."

"Don't be ashamed. The shame was that a leader as good as you lost that election. If we had only Cramms and von Helms, we'd be finished. Godspeed, Captain. I'm sure I'll be calling for your services and Lieutenant Woolner's quite soon." He galloped off to rejoin his staff.

After presenting their report, Charles and Ab spent the evening awaiting new orders. They didn't get any. They ate, tended their horses, tried to sleep, and in the morning went down to watch Old Jack lead his men into Maryland.

In the mind of Charles Main and many others, Stonewall Jackson had undergone a transformation during the past year. His fame was so enormous, his feats so Olympian, that you tended to think more and more of Jackson as merely a name—a legend that couldn't possibly be connected with a real human being, especially not one like the shy bumpkin Cousin Orry had befriended in his plebe year. But Jack was real, all right, smartly sitting his cream-colored mount as he crossed over the river to the trees while a band blared "Maryland, My Maryland" to welcome him.

Ab gave Jackson some attention, but was more interested in the long column of infantry following him. Jackson's men looked as if they had marched and fought and slept in their clothes for years without washing them. They carried weapons but little else. Gone were the bulging knapsacks and haversacks of '61.

These were the fabled soldiers known as Jackson's foot cavalry because they could march sixty miles in two days, and had. Charles stared in amazement at rank on rank of wild beards, crazy glinting eyes, cheeks and foreheads burned raw by exposure to sun.

"My God, Ab, a lot of them don't have shoes."

It was true. Whatever footwear he saw was torn or in separate pieces kept together by snippets of twine. Watching the column pass, Charles estimated that fifty percent of Jackson's men marched on bare feet that were cut, bruised, stained with old blood, stippled with scabs, covered with dirt. A man might learn to tolerate such misery in warm weather, but when winter came—?

Studying one wrinkled, mean-faced private sloshing through the shallows, Charles presumed the soldier was forty, then saw he was wrong. "They look like old men."

"So do we," Ab said, hunching over Cyclone's neck. "Taken notice of the gray in your beard lately? They say Bob Lee's is almost white. A powerful lot of things have changed in a year, Charlie. And it ain't the end."

Unexpectedly, Charles shivered. He watched the dirty feet marching into Maryland and wondered how many would march back.

57

Ninth of September. Hot light of late summer hazing the rolling country. The green yellowing now, drying and withering. The time of gathering a harvest.

The cavalry strung out a line nearly twenty miles long. Behind it, Lee's divisions maneuvered, ready to strike clear to Pennsylvania, some said. Below the line, over the blurry hills—McClellan, surely. Coming out in force from Washington. Slow as ever, but coming out. Bogus rustics on horseback had been spied along the Potomac, watching the movement through White's Ford. Scouts for the other side.

Hampton encamped at Hyattstown, a few miles south of Urbana. Charles packed all but essential possessions into the field trunk holding his original legion sword and the Solingen blade. Out of the trunk he took his gray captain's coat. It didn't take many brains to conclude that the invasion would lead to some heavy fighting. He wanted his own side to be able to identify him. He watched his trunk lifted into one of the baggage wagons as if for the last time.

He bundled his coat and tied it behind his saddle—his well-worn McClellan model, bought new in Columbia. The saddle had been adapted from a Prussian design by the man so earnestly trying to destroy them. Queer war, this.

Hungry war, too. Ab Woolner complained half the evening. "Nobody around here gonna feed us. It's more green corn for the two-legged as well as the four-legged. We ought to name this the green corn campaign, Charlie boy."

411

Charles said nothing, seeing to his powder and ball so he could get some sleep. They might need it, wish for it, pray for it soon.

Tenth of September. Charles and eight other scouts out after nightfall, probing. They damn near rode into blue-coated videttes. They charged the videttes on the white-drenched road and heard no yells about *Black Horse, Black Horse!*

Gunfire. One scout blown down—and luckless Doan lost another mount. The scouts galloped off carrying two wounded; Charles carried Doan, hot wind in his face under the moon. Had they met Pleasonton's men, he wondered. Those boys had shot straight and ridden better than any Yankees he had seen so far. Maybe the shoe salesmen and machinery operators were learning how to fight on horseback. Maybe the Union cavalry would be something to worry about one day.

At Urbana, quite a few hurt Hampton riders went for treatment at a hilltop academy that General Stuart had lit up for the evening. A goddamned ball, of which the vainglorious Virginian couldn't seem to get too many. The sight of bleeding men sort of spoiled the festivities. Most of the girls went home; some—a few —stayed to help. But even their pretty round eyes glared in the candlelight, fearful of the dirt and odors of the strange wild men who had ridden in to say a great force was moving beyond the night horizon.

Ninety thousand, it was, although straggling quickly bled it to less. Bob Lee did not yet know the strength of his opponent. And that army, for a change, did not have the usual McClellan slows. It was not exactly prancing along, but it didn't have the slows. Old Bob didn't know that, either.

Twelfth of September. Westward, Lee boldly, crazily split his army—that much Charles learned, guessing at the rest. Old Bob wanted his supply line down to Winchester open and secure before he struck fiercely north to Hagerstown; hell, maybe even to Philadelphia. That meant nullifying the Harpers Ferry garrison. That meant dividing his forces. The order had been written on the ninth, but Charles didn't know it then.

He had met Lee in Texas, dined with him, talked with him at length—but that wasn't battle, just field duty with occasional Indian skirmishing. Besides, Lee had been away a lot, leaving the command to subordinates. So now, as others did, Charles got reacquainted by sixth-hand hearsay.

Old Bob was universally acknowledged as a polite fellow, slow to anger—and who had ever heard him curse or seen him do a discourteous or ungentlemanly deed? But the sound of guns got his blood up, and when he was making military bets, he sometimes pushed in all the chips he had, like a flash gambler on a Mississippi boat. Charles and Ab decided he had done it again. He had figured he could split his forces—the very idea of which would produce foam on the mouths of writers of strategy texts—and put them back together with time to spare. Because Little Mac, as always, would have the slows. The general had also politely, eloquently asked Marylanders to rise up and embrace their deliverers. Nobody paid attention to that, unfortunately.

Stuart went west out of Frederick, behind Lee, the morning of the twelfth. Charles and Ab and Hampton's troopers lingered behind, the rear guard, looking for men in blue—And God, there they came, marching at incredible speed. What had cured Mac's slows? A cup of Bruised Ego Tea, brewing since the peninsula? A promise of a dose of Dr. Lincoln's Elixir of Demotion?

No time or means to answer that now. Away the rear-guard troopers went across the Catoctin Ridge, Charles already fevered with the tiredness he knew would not pass or be relieved, except slightly, for days, possibly weeks.

The threat, the sense of building forces, rose up like the temperature. Something was wrong, but what?

Not many signs of great joy greeted the deliverers. Near Burkittsville, with blue riders clearly visible, chasing them, raising dust, Charles sped past a tiny girl with yellow braids who hung on a farm fence waving a tiny Stars and Bars, but that was the extent of any patriotic uprising he witnessed. Doan, who had appropriated the horse of a dead man, screamed at the girl to get out of the obscene way of the obscene bluebellies coming over the near hill. The child kept waving her tiny flag.

Hampton's boy Preston held his father's overcoat at Burkittsville in a swirling little fight. Charles shotgunned a Yankee from the saddle—he never did such a thing but that it wrenched his stomach—and got his left cheek shaved by another's saber before they were away.

413

Thirteenth of September. Old Marse Bob's men moving swiftly through the cuts in the beautiful heights of the northern spur of the Blue Ridge, which the locals called South Mountain. Now the army was split for fair, Old Jack whipping around one way, over the Potomac and hooking back, his scab-footed demons marching and marching to invest Harpers Ferry from the southwest, while McLaws's division aimed for the Maryland heights and Walker's for Loudoun Heights, a triangle of force closing upon the point of land at the confluence of the Potomac and the river of that sweet-song name, Shenandoah.

Charles and the scouts exchanged fire with some marching men they thought to be Jacob Cox's Ohioans, but of course there was no way for a man riding fast, hungry, and sleepy, but needing to watch and shoot, to know for certain. The heat grew, and the tiredness.

And that was the day of the cigars, which changed everything. Charles learned of it only later.

Three cigars—found by some dumb-luck Yankee on ground where Daniel Harvey Hill's men had encamped at Frederick. More interesting than the cigars was the paper in which they were wrapped: a beautifully scripted, apparently authentic copy of Order 191. Who left it nobody knew. Who read it was soon clear. McClellan read it and knew Lee had split his army. Fueled with that information, Little Mac began to move like a blue storm. Surprise, initiative, time all began to run like water between Old Bob's fingers.

Fourteenth of September. In the morning, Charles emptied his revolver four times in forty-five minutes of fighting at Crampton's Gap, southernmost of the three mountain passes the Confederates sought to hold. Out of ammunition for the Colt and starting to worry, really worry, that Sport would be hit, he drew his shotgun. Running low on ammunition for that, too.

Stuart ordered Hampton away hastily to support and protect McLaws, with Lee in desperate need of time to reassemble the split army lest Little Mac eradicate its separate parts with hardly any effort. Orders: dig in; hold the passes.

But the passes slowly gave, the shells coming in true and blowing holes in the hillsides and in the gray lines, and all it gained Lee was a day.

Galloping horsemen sped for Harpers Ferry. Nobody knew

what would happen next. Charles was uneasy. Had the advantage been lost? As they rode on through the night, he sometimes shut his eyes to sleep ten minutes, trusting Sport to carry him without falter or fall.

Then, soon after dawn, in mist the color of a reb's sleeve, Charles and Ab and Doan and a fourth scout circled back and exchanged shots with more videttes in dark blue jackets that looked black in the foggy gloom—Yanks who had forced through Crampton's Gap and were coming on—coming on—to squeeze them between their guns and the garrison at Harpers Ferry. The passes were lost, surely. The advantage, too. Could Lee save anything now, including his army?

Fifteenth of September. No danger waiting at Harpers Ferry. Instead, they found singing, cheering, feasting. Old Jack had gotten unconditional surrender.

The victors smashed the doors of magazines and granaries. There were thirteen thousand small arms and federal fodder for the starved horses. Eleven thousand men taken, two hundred serviceable wagons, cannon numbering seventy or more. And ammunition in plenty, some for Charles's Colt.

A curious thing happened when Old Jack went abroad late in the day. He wore his dirtiest, seediest coat and filthy old wool hat. He didn't smile. He looked like some ignorant, smelly, mad-eyed Presbyterian deacon from the hills of western Virginia as he rode by. His men saw him and threw their hats in the air and cheered. The captured Yankees cheered him, too. Red-faced, they cheered him. Uttering yells as wild as any reb's, they cheered him. Sitting on Sport, hunched and dizzy-tired, Charles could only shake his head as one boy whooped it up in the improvised prison pen, screaming, "By damn, good for you, Jack! You're something. If we had you, we could whip you boys for sure."

As night came on, Charles tied Sport to his wrist and sat down against the wall of the arsenal and slept. After half an hour Ab woke him.

"I think they're gettin' ready to go at it some place north of here. Jack's ordered rations cooked for two days."

A calm descended with the dark. The peculiar peace of those hours when battle became a certainty. Awaiting orders, Charles went here and there and saw bits of it. Some butternut boys— literally that; eighteen, seventeen—broiling meat and joking and

415

chattering and nudging one another in the cook-smoke. Charles knew they had not seen the elephant before. Troops who had were quieter. They dozed while they had a chance. Wrote letters. The devout Christians meditated, reading little Testaments, readying for a possible journey up the bright stairs to their certain heaven.

Around eleven, the issuing of ammunition began, done late to keep the powder as dry as possible. Fifty rounds of powder and ball per man, someone told Charles, though whether that was true he couldn't say. But the drums would sound the long roll for immediate assembly soon, that he could tell as he continued to walk here and there; now Ab was napping with both horses tied to his wrist.

At huge fires built beside the bubbling rivers, colonels were following the custom of addressing the veterans and the untried alike.

"Remember, men, it is better to wound than to slay, since it takes time to carry an injured man to the rear and sometimes requires two of the enemy rather than one."

In the dark, Charles walked on.

"—and when we are deployed upon the field of Mars, we shall achieve decisive victory and conquer the egalitarian mercenaries dedicated to despoiling your liberties, your property, and your honor. Do not forget for one moment that the eyes and hopes of eight millions and more rest upon you. Show yourselves worthy of your race and your lineage. Of your wives, of your mothers, of your sisters, of your sweethearts—of all Southern womanhood, which is dependent upon you for protection. With such incentive and firm trust in your leaders and in God the most high, you shall succeed. You cannot fail."

In the dark, Charles walked on. Waiting.

Sixteenth of September. Jackson sounded the drums and marched at one in the morning.

Up in the saddle went Charles and the others. Brigadier Hampton looked fresh and fiery-eyed as he organized his regiments for deployment behind the main column. How did he do it at his age, Charles wondered, feeling Sport friskier again, fed and rested. *Wish I were.*

"Where we goin', Charlie?"

"Tagging after Old Jack. Protecting his backside again."

"I know that. Where's he goin'?"

416

"Frank Hampton told me Sharpsburg. Little town fifteen, sixteen miles up the road. When Old Jack won, I guess Old Bob decided to dig in and fight."

"Way we was all divvied up, 'twas either that or be buried, strikes me." Charles agreed. After a pause, Ab said, "The foot cavalry looks wore out."

"The foot cavalry has plenty of company."

Sharpsburg proved a small, green village in pleasant countryside with a few hills but none of the peaks found along the Potomac. Lee's headquarters was Oak Grove, a short distance southwest of town. His main line, nearly three miles long and attenuated, ran north from the center of Sharpsburg, roughly following the Hagerstown Pike. Stuart's cavalry shifted all the way up to the extreme left, Nicodemus Hill, near a bight of the river. John Hood had two brigades and Harvey Hill five, digging in and peering eastward through high corn in a forty-acre field to the hilly land along Antietam Creek, which, like the pike, ran roughly north and south, though on a course much less straight. From the east Little Mac would come with his seventy-five thousand. Little Mac had stragglers, too, but he was the player with the most chips; he could throw them away by the handful and still dominate the table.

While Old Jack placed his troops to brace the northern sector of the line, Charles was kept busy bearing orders to Stuart and other orders for outposts along Antietam Creek above and below the place where the pike to Boonsboro crossed it. He saw dust in the autumn sky eastward. The outposts pulled back, and Hunt's blue batteries began shelling, answered by those of Pendleton and Stuart, from his relatively higher ground. Booming fieldpieces flashed red light into the darkening day.

Returning to headquarters, southbound on the pike at a gallop, Charles saw pickets slipping forward through the field of corn. When he next encountered Ab, outside headquarters an hour later, the other scout told him, "They say the pickets is so close to each other out there that when one side breaks wind the other side feels it."

There had been sporadic skirmishing, which Charles had heard but not seen, and heavy bombardment throughout most of the twilight hours. At dark Lee's army lay quietly along the Sharpsburg Ridge, with McClellan's off by Antietam Creek and who knew where else; some woods at the left of the line had looked especially ominous to Charles in the daylight. They were thick, dark woods, fine for hiding preparations for an advance.

Things settled down to an occasional shout or bang of a musket. In the small hours of the night it started to drizzle. When daylight broke, the hell began.

Seventeenth of September. The blue waves appeared early, rolling from those suspicious woods Charles had spied. Shoulder weapons showing in the gray mist, banners unfurling, they trotted forward, double line of skirmishers first, then the main force, firing and loading, firing and loading—coming on. A Southern soldier cried, "Joe Hooker!"

Joe Hooker, handsome and a hell of a fighter, raised a hammer of two Union corps and let it fall on the Confederate left flank. Charles was dispatched up through Hood's position, west of the pike in some trees around a small white Dunker church, carrying instructions for the Nicodemus Hill gunners. The Union troops coming out of the woods opened fire on Hood, and Yankee artillery out of sight beyond those same woods let loose, shot coming in, and shell, and the Yankee foot pushed through the corn with heads down or turned aside as if to avoid a rain shower.

The fighting began at six, and by nine the sides had thrown each other back and forth across the cornfield several times. The waving cross of St. Andrew, the South's battle ensign, had gone down in the noise and smoke and been raised several times. The battle was so huge and swiftly shifting that Charles saw only threads, never the pattern.

Coming back from Nicodemus Hill, head down, revolver in hand, he was caught in a driving charge of federals against Old Jack's men, who lay waiting amid trees on rocky ridges. A colonel who had lost several officers ordered Charles off Sport at gunpoint and screamed, "Hold this position at all hazards."

So he fought in the woods with two squads of the foot cavalry for fifteen incredible minutes, shooting at Yankees who came running over the pike, bayonets gleaming steadily brighter as the sun burned off the mist and hot, cheerful light broke over the battle.

In the midst of Old Jack's men, Charles fired, reloaded, shouted, encouraged—helped repulse the charge that cost the Yankees almost five thousand men in under half an hour. When the jubilant foot cavalry went hollering and countercharging toward the cornfield, Charles, feeling that his duty to the anony-

418

mous colonel had been discharged, ran back, untied Sport, and went on his way, shaking from nerves and excitement.

As he rode out from the rocks behind the Dunker Church, a bloodied figure in blue rose up and rammed a bayonet at Sport. Charles shot the soldier—in the face, as it happened; he had been aiming lower. He saw beardless flesh and red tissue and an eye fly away as the boy went down. The sight did something to Charles's sensibilities, set some unwholesome process in motion.

Shells burst; the ground trembled. He shook himself like a wet dog and pressed on, fearing Sport wouldn't survive the morning.

Along about eleven, the cockpit of the battle had shifted to a sunken road east and slightly south of the cornfield, which Charles passed through about this time. In the last three hours at least a dozen charges had gone screaming and lurching and shooting back and forth where the stalks could no longer be seen. Head high yesterday, they were gone, beaten and stamped and crushed down by living men, and dead.

He sensed he was staring into some demonic kaleidoscope, each gory scene a new variation in horror. Seeing them, Charles felt his self-control slipping. He gripped the rein more and more tightly. While turtle's instinct brought his head down beneath another billowy burst in the sky, he thought of a face. A name. Anchored himself to both.

He had an impulse to dismount and hide. It passed, and he kept going in the direction of the sunken road, where Old Bob's officers and men were not just scrapping to save the army now but maybe the whole Confederacy, too.

Charles forced Sport ahead. He was a man adrift on a vast, destructive sea. No cause could save his life; no slogan. Just scraps of memory.

Name.

Face—

Her.

Near the sunken road, he was among madmen—soldiers in gray seeing the elephant for the first time and berserk with fear. He watched one throw his canteen away; another pound one, two, three, four balls down his rifle muzzle without counting, without noticing; a third standing with clenched fists, squalling like an abandoned child. A sky-borne chunk of exploded iron cut off his left leg and his yell in one neat slice. Blood pattered the ground like the earlier drizzle.

"Get up, get up, damn you!"

Charles saw the shouter, a red-faced, red-bearded lieutenant booting a fallen horse. The lieutenant's men crouched around a three-inch Blakely gun foundered in a rut. The lieutenant kept kicking the horse. Charles bent low as another shell burst, then slid from the saddle, found a rock, put it on the loose end of the rein. He ran forward at a crouch and pushed the hysterical officer with both hands.

"Get away. That horse can't pull anything. That leg's broken."

"But—but—this gun's needed up by the road. I was ordered to move it to the road." The lieutenant wept now.

"Stand aside. You men"—Charles pointed—"cut the traces. We'll pick it up by the trail handle and pull it. Some of you push each wheel. One of you watch my horse."

Through Minié balls thick as bee swarms, shell bursts scattering shrapnel, they hauled the little rifled field gun, cursing like dock hands, sweating ferociously, pulling it forward yard by yard till they found a major, who flourished his saber to salute them. "Good for you, boys! Wheel her right up there."

"The captain done it," said one of the horse artillerymen pushing a wheel. "Our lieutenant couldn't. He's scairt out of his pants."

"Who are you, Captain?" the major asked.

"Charles Main, sir. Scout for Hampton's Brigade."

"I'll write up a commendation for this if any of us survive the day."

Charles turned and ran doubled over back through the field to the soldier guarding Sport. The bearded lieutenant sat on the ground beside the lamed horse. Charles put a bullet into the animal to end its suffering. The lieutenant stared at him with wet eyes, as if he wished for the same mercy.

"Come on, Sport," Charles whispered in a raw voice. He must get back to headquarters.

Going was hard. The federal artillery cannonaded from behind a smoke wall on the heights above the creek. Charles never saw the man who shot him. Something struck his chest, and he jerked sideways, nearly falling from the saddle.

Bewildered, he looked down and found a round hole to the left of a shirt button. He opened his shirt and lifted the leather bag. It too had a hole, though not on the reverse side. A ball, maybe partly spent when it struck him but deadly anyway, had been stopped by the book.

He got snarled in Anderson's Brigade, which was being rushed to the sunken road in an attempt to save the position. They made slow progress, and so did he against their flow. What began to effect some permanent change in him wasn't death, which he had seen before, but the staggering multiplication of it. Bodies propped one another up. One, the spattered jacket gray, had no head; green flies crawled on the meaty stump. Bodies hung belly down over farm fences. Bodies of enemies lay twined in accidental embrace.

An artillery piece and its limber were being raced along the Hagerstown Pike for some unknown purpose, and Charles was near it on the lower perimeter of the cornfield, where bodies in blue and gray and butternut had fallen so closely there was hardly any ground visible. Sport had to slip and pick through a terrain of dead backs, lifeless heads cocked at strange angles, groping hands wet with the flow from mortal wounds, mouths that howled for succor, water, God to stop the pain.

He tried to cross the pike in front of the racing artillerymen, wasn't fast enough, reined to the side. He heard the shell coming in, saw the horses hit and blown apart.

Smoke shrouded him. Sport reared, whinnying for the first time all morning. Horse bone, horse flesh, horse entrails, horse blood rained down on Charles in a quarter-minute of baptism. He yelled in rage, saw a wounded Yankee, unarmed, rise to his feet a yard away, started to shoot him, and instead leaned to the right and threw up.

Next thing he remembered, he was again riding toward the northern edge of Sharpsburg. Suddenly, in the reddened grass to the right, he spied a fallen man whose form seemed familiar. The man was prone, and by some happenstance his face had landed or been forced into the inverted crown of his wide-brimmed hat.

Shaky, Charles climbed down. "Doan?"

The scout didn't stir. There were bodies strewn along both sides of the road, but Doan's horse was nowhere visible. "Doan?" This time he said it softly, as if in recognition of what he knew he would find when he rolled the scout over.

It was worse than he expected. A ball had entered Doan's left cheek, in and out, and there had been plenty of bleeding. Doan's whole face dripped when Charles lifted the head. Blood ran off his eyeballs and out his nostrils and over his tongue and lower teeth. His hat was full. Doan had drowned in it.

Eighteenth of September. In the dark of the night, Bob Lee's army went back over the Potomac to Virginia.

Twenty-three thousand had fallen in the battle that had lasted till nightfall on the seventeenth, rolling east across Antietam Creek. Little Mac's plan had lacked a vision of what might be accomplished that day. Attacks had been piecemeal, savage but seemingly unconnected. As a direct consequence, Lee had been unable to seize the initiative, was forced instead to rush masses of men from danger point to danger point, all over the field. He had in effect conducted a series of hasty and relatively disorganized rescue operations, rather than an offensive based on a grand strategic design. The desperate defense efforts had been carried out at enormous cost; a massed frontal assault on Union positions could hardly have been less bloody.

There were moments when everything looked lost. In the afternoon, the Yankees had been within half a mile of Sharpsburg, half a mile from swinging around and cutting Lee's escape route. There were moments to be proud of—as when A. P. Hill's gray-clad Light Division arrived late that same afternoon, Hill having been busy with details of the Harpers Ferry surrender until he found himself urgently needed up where the corn and the boys from both sides lay together in a red harvesting. So Hill came up; forced march—an incredible, legendary seventeen miles in seven hours.

Politicians who had never led troops or even tasted combat often carped because generals slacked off a fight late in the day and failed to pursue an advantage all night long. The carpers were men who did not understand and could not imagine the awesome burden of battle. It was not only mortally frightening but cursedly hard work. It left the combatant drained—starved, thirsty, ready to lie down anywhere there wasn't a corpse.

So the battle day had ended with both sides exhausted but still facing the long, dreadful night of screams and moans and searching for survivors. Candles moved across the fields and through the woods, like the last of summer's fireflies. Pickets held their fire; both sides were searching.

That night Charles saw the ambulances roll with their wailing cargoes. He saw the improvised pavilions where surgeons pushed

422

up their sleeves, took out their saws, and amputated mangled arms and legs by the hundreds. He saw corpses growing huge, ripening with the gasses of death. Near dawn, he saw one explode.

Next day, the eighteenth, assessments began to emerge.

McClellan had assumed a defensive posture, or he might have buried the Confederacy forever. Presented with an opportunity to destroy Lee's army, he merely stopped the invasion. Lee hadn't been whipped, but neither had he won. He had simply rushed his defensive units from one place to another, repelling in succession five apocalyptic attacks between daybreak and dark: at the west woods and cornfield three times; at the sunken road, leaving a lane of the dead six, seven, eight deep in one thousand-yard stretch; and, lastly, at the lower bridge on Antietam Creek.

Reinforced during the early hours of the eighteenth, McClellan chose to stand fast. The Confederate high command chose to withdraw. By now Charles had only fragmentary recollections of the day before. He couldn't remember all the places he had been sent or how many men he had shot at. Several times he had been on his own an hour or more, isolated from his objective or any familiar faces—a not uncommon happening in a battle that slid from here to there like mercury. He knew he would forever carry memories of his constant fear for Sport and his feeling that the September afternoon was eternal, the sun nailed to the sky, never to fall and force an end.

On the retreat, more segments of the tapestry—one an afternoon incident whose site he could not recall, though the images were burned into his mind. Three men in gray, one very young, with drool in the corners of his cracked lips, moved across Charles's line of vision thrusting their bayonets deep into the bodies of dead Union soldiers.

A wisp of a lieutenant colonel, perhaps a schoolmaster or attorney once but now a blood-covered casualty, managed to lift himself in the sunshine and indicate by raising a hand that he was pleading for—anticipating—mercy. The split-lipped boy was the first to stab him, through the bowels. The others stabbed his upper chest, then all lurched on, the smile of a pleased drunkard on each face.

That single memory planted a new conviction in Charles's heart and mind. It would be a longer war than anyone had dreamed and henceforward would be fought without the punctilio of that remote day when Union riders pursued Gus, and the Yankee lieutenant, Prevo, accepted his word as an officer and West Point graduate that she wasn't in the farmhouse. Gentlemanly conduct had disappeared along with the black horses and the brave, shouting lads he had led in that springtime he wanted to remember but could not because of the slain animals, the butchered or bloating bodies, the gray trio with their bayonets and grins.

Who had won, who had lost—who gave a damn? he thought in the strange, light-headed mood that came over him as he and Ab, reunited, rode toward the Potomac in the long procession that stretched away and away, forward and behind, over the hills of Maryland. They were about a mile to the rear of the troopers of the Second South Carolina, who were relatively fresh because they had been held in reserve on the extreme left during the entire battle.

In moonlight, near the river, they passed some infantrymen who had fallen out to rest. One, bitterly jocular, called to them, "Bet you two boys didn't see the scrap, bein' in the critter cavalry."

"That's right," said another, "bein' in the critter cavalry is jes' like havin' an insurance policy nobody will ever cash in."

Ab looked bleak and feverish. He pulled his side arm and cocked and aimed it at the last speaker, who yelped, "Hey, now," and jumped up to run. Charles grabbed Ab's arm and pulled it slowly, steadily, down. He felt Ab's trembling.

The next day, Charles became like many of those who went into a great battle and came out again. He didn't smile; he hardly spoke. He felt his soul clasped by a deepening depression. He could function, obey orders, but that was about all. And when someone asked Ab Woolner why his friend had such a remote look in his eyes, Ab explained.

"We was at Sharpsburg. Charlie still is."

58

Of the battle his army called Antietam, Billy wrote but one line in his journal:

Horror beyond believing.

A sense of it began to infect him on the advance to what became the battlefield. The engineers found it hard to march on the Maryland roads because those roads were jammed with ambulances. From the ambulances came sounds Billy had heard before, though he could never grow accustomed to them.

He saw the smoke and heard the firing from South Mountain but didn't reach the summit of Turner's Gap until after dark on the fifteenth. Reveille roused the battalion at four, and when the light broke they found they had bivouacked among fallen dead from both sides. Even men with strong stomachs lost everything they had eaten for breakfast.

From Keedysville, late in the afternoon, the battalion was rushed to the front. By five Billy and Lije were organizing detachments to search the surrounding farmland for every available stone. Other men carried these to Antietam Creek. Shirtless, Billy worked till the sun sank, seeing to the paving of soft spots in the creek bottom, creating a ford where the artillery could cross. A similar one was prepared for the infantry.

When the tool wagons arrived—late—grading of the approaches commenced. At half past ten the work was finished. Though Billy was yawning and ready to drop, nervousness kept him awake most of the night. Tomorrow there would be a battle. Would Bison be in it? He had thought of Charles frequently in the last few days. Was he still alive?

As was customary, the engineers were issued ammunition—forty rounds for the cartridge box, twenty for the pockets—and rations, but they were withheld from the actual fighting. Billy and Lije and the others sat out the bloody day on a ridge overlooking the fords constructed the night before. In view of what he saw, Billy wished he had been elsewhere. The sight of the dead and wounded induced a disloyal reaction in him for a time; how could any cause be worth so many human lives?

Rushed forward next day, the engineers acted as infantry support for a battery near the center of the line. Sporadic Confederate sniping harassed them, but caused no casualties. The day after that, the battalion withdrew toward Sharpsburg across the lower creek bridge, already being called Burnside's in honor of the general who had stormed it during the battle's final phase.

The federal pontoon bridge at Harpers Ferry had been wrecked by the rebels, so the engineers marched there, and late on the twenty-first fell to rebuilding it. Billy found the work restorative; with hands and backs and minds and a lot of sweat, the battalion created things instead of destroying them. He built a mental barrier and behind it hid the purpose of those creations.

From the shallows they dragged pontoon boats that could be salvaged and repaired them with wood from boxes in which rations of crackers were shipped. By now Billy's beard was two inches long. He existed in a perpetual bleary state and sometimes fell asleep on his feet for five or ten seconds. He longed for Brett.

During the night of the twenty-second, wagons arrived with the regular pontoon train and additional men—the Fiftieth New York Volunteer Engineers. He worked until dawn, frequently wading in chilly water, and at first light on the twenty-third was relieved to sleep a while. He covered himself with a blanket. The long separation from his wife produced night dreams and embarrassing evidence afterward.

After four hours, he woke and ate, feeling he could go on now. Some of the engineers formed a betting pool; each man drew a slip with a date on it. The date was understood to be that on which McClellan would be relieved. Choices were offered all the way through the end of December.

Billy heard no great condemnation of the commanding general,

426

just acceptance of a fact. Little Mac had failed to pursue and destroy Lee's army when he had the opportunity, and the Original Gorilla would not like that.

Two days later came news of what Lincoln had announced publicly on the twenty-fourth. Over the evening fires, men argued and, in the time-honored tradition of armies, garbled the details.

"He signed this paper freeing every goddamn coon in the goddamn country."

"You're wrong. It's only them in the states still rebelling come the first of January. He didn't touch Kentucky or places like that."

"Well," said one of the New York pick-and-shovel volunteers, "the thing is still an insult to white men. No one will back him up. Not in this army."

Much agreement there.

Unsure of his own reaction, Billy went to Lije's tent and poked his head in. His bearded friend was kneeling, hands clasped, head bowed. Billy withdrew, waited five minutes, coughed and scuffed his feet before entering again. He asked Lije what he thought of the proclamation.

"A month ago," Lije said, "Mr. Lincoln was still meeting with some of our freed brethren, urging them to search out a place in Central America to colonize. So the conclusion cannot be escaped. He has promulgated a war measure, nothing more. And yet—and yet—"

Lije's index finger ticktocked, as if admonishing caution from a pulpit. "I have read books about Washington and Jefferson and foul-mouthed Old Hickory which hint of powers in events—in the presidency itself—that sometimes transmute base metal to gold. It could be so here, with the deed and with the man."

"He exempted any state that comes back in the Union by January."

"None will. That is why it is a war measure."

"Then what's the worth of it, except to make the rebs mad and maybe start uprisings that won't amount to much?"

"What is the worth? The worth is in the core of it. The core of it—however equivocated, however compromised—is right. It creates, at last, a moral spine for this war. Henceforward we fight for loosing the shackles on fellow human beings."

"I think it'll bring down a hell of a lot of trouble—inside the army and out."

427

He hadn't changed his mind at dusk when he went for a stroll along the Potomac. He wanted to shake off lingering revulsion for the sights of the campaign and confusion over this newest twist in the war's course. He concentrated on thoughts of Brett.

A melancholy bugle call sounded beneath the bluffs—a new call, played for the first time down in Virginia in June or July. Who had composed it and where, he didn't know. A last salute to a soldier.

Who was it for, who had died, he wondered. And what had died with the stroke of Lincoln's pen? What had been born? All were questions appropriate to the gathering autumn darkness.

He stood motionless, listening to the river's purl and the familiar camp noises and the fading of the final notes of "Taps."

In Virginia, Charles showed Ab *An Essay on Man*. Touching the lead ball embedded in the center, then the book itself, Ab asked, "Who give you this?"

"Augusta Barclay."

"Thought you told me you didn't have a girl."

"I have a friend who sent me a Christmas present."

"Is that right?" Ab fingered the flattened bullet again. "You was saved by religion, Charlie. You didn't get a Testament wound"—every month or so you heard of someone's life being spared because a shot hit his pocket Scripture—"but it's near as holy."

Silence.

"You got a Pope wound. Says so right here."

Charles didn't smile, just shook his head. Ab looked embarrassed and unhappy. Charles replaced the book, pulled the drawstring, and hid the bag under his shirt.

Cooper took his wife out of the house to tell her.

It was the hour of soft gray, with stars sparkling and a bar of orange light narrowing over the Wirral. Autumn breezes swept Abercromby Square, sending the swans to their sleeping places under the willows around the pond. A few leaves, already crisped and reddened, spun around the black iron bases of the street lamps.

"They want us home again. The message arrived in today's pouch from Richmond."

Judith didn't reply immediately. Hand in hand, husband and

wife crossed the square to a bench where they liked to sit and discuss decisions or the events of the day. A part of Cooper never surrendered fatherhood; he had given Judah permission to run a while, on the condition he not stray too far. He repeatedly glanced toward the fence for a sign of the boy returning.

They reached the bench. The wind was sharp. The Mersey smelled of salt and some newly berthed spice ship. "That is a surprise," Judith said at last. "Was a reason given?"

Across the way, an elderly manservant emerged from Prioleau's house to trim the gas lamps flanking the front door. On the second floor, centered in a window lintel, a single star in bas-relief declared Prioleau's loyalty.

"The war isn't going well for the Yankees, but neither is it going well for our side. The toll in Maryland was dreadful."

And lives were not the only loss. When reports of the battle reached Europe, the outcome was construed as a defeat for the Confederacy. Despite false cheer and pretense to the contrary, those in Bulloch's section knew the silent truth of Sharpsburg. The South would never gain diplomatic recognition.

"I'm wanted in the Navy Department," he told her. "Mallory needs help and evidently believes I'm the one to provide it. James has matters well in hand here, and I know he sent a favorable report on my work after we launched *Alabama.*"

Bulloch had officially commended Cooper's clumsy but effective defensive action on the pier. Cooper had stayed aboard the ship until the middle of August, when she was joined in the remote Bay of Angra, on the island of Terceira in the Azores, by two other vessels. One was *Agrippina,* a bark that Bulloch had purchased; aboard were a hundred-pound Blakely rifle, an eight-inch smoothbore, six thirty-two pounders, ammunition, coal, and enough supplies for an extended cruise. *Bahama* brought twenty-five Confederate seamen and Captain Semmes. The new ship was armed, coaled, commissioned, and christened, and Cooper felt another unexpected thrill of pride when the small band blared "Dixie's Land" in the hot tropical afternoon.

The secret mission completed, he returned to Liverpool by passenger steamer. Judith was grumpy the day he told her about his feelings during the ceremony. One of their rare quarrels developed. How could he feel pride in a cause he had once derided? Caustically, he replied that she would have to forgive his lack of perfection. The statements and counterstatements rapidly grew incoherent. It took them a day to patch things up.

Now she asked softly, "How do you feel about Secretary Mallory's request?"

He pressed his shoulder to hers. The wind was cold; the stars shone; the orange horizon-glow was nearly gone. "I'll miss this old town, but I've no choice. I must go."

"How quickly?"

"As soon as I finish a couple of current projects. I would hazard that we'd be on our way by the end of the year."

She lifted his arm and placed it around her shoulders for warmth and because she loved his touch. "I worry about a winter crossing."

What worried him more was the last leg of the trip, the run from Hamilton or Nassau through the blockading squadron. But he refused to upset her by saying it aloud. Instead, he sought to reassure her with a squeeze, a press of his lips to her cold cheek, a murmur.

"As long as the four of us are together, we'll be fine. Together we can withstand anything."

She agreed, then pondered a moment. "I do wonder what your father would say if he saw you so devoted to the South."

He hoped they wouldn't argue again. He answered cautiously. "He'd say I wasn't the son he raised. He'd say I've changed, but so have we all."

"Only in some respects. I loathe slavery as much as I ever did."

"You know I feel the same way. When we win our independence, it will wither and die naturally."

"Independence? Cooper, the cause is lost."

"Don't say that."

"But it is. You know it in your heart. You talked of resources in the North, and the lack of them in the South, long before this horrible war started. You did it the first day we met."

"I know, but—I can't admit defeat, Judith. If I do, why should we go home? Why should I take any risks at all? Yet I must take them—The South's my native land. Yours, too."

She shook her head. "I left it, Cooper. It's mine because it's yours, that's all. The war is wrong, the cause too—Why should you or Bulloch or anyone keep fighting?"

The lamplight fell on her face, so beautiful to him, so beloved. For the first time, sitting there, he admitted her to the small inner chamber where he kept the truth she had already identified, the truth made manifest by the dispatches about Sharpsburg. "We must fight for the best conclusion we can get. A negotiated peace."

"You think it's worth going home to do that?"

He nodded.

"All right, my dearest. Kiss me, and we will."

A gust set leaves chuckling around their legs as they embraced. They were still kissing when a constable coughed and walked by twirling his truncheon. They separated with muddled, chagrined looks. Since Judith wore gloves, the disapproving officer couldn't see her rings. He probably thought she was misbehaving with a lover. It made her giggle as they hurried back across the square. Full dark had come. It would be good to be inside.

In the gaslit foyer, Cooper paled and pointed to a drop of blood on the tile floor. "Good God, look."

Her eyes rounded. "Judah?"

Marie-Louise popped her blonde head out of the parlor. "He's hurt, Mama."

Cooper flew up the stairs, his belly tied up like a sailor's knot, his head hammering, his palms damp. Had his son fallen into the hands of some thief or molester? The slightest threat to either of his children was like a barbed hook in his flesh. When they were ill, he stayed up with them all night, every night, until the danger passed. He ran toward the half-open door of the boy's room. "Judah!"

He thrust the door open. Judah lay on the bed, clutching his middle. His jacket was ripped, his cheek bruised, his nose bloodied.

Cooper ran to the bed, sat, started to take his son in his arms but refrained. Judah was eleven and deemed such contact sissified. "Son—what happened?"

"I ran into some Toxteth dock boys. They wanted my money, and when I said I hadn't any, they swarmed on me. I'm all right." He made the subdued declaration with evident pride.

"You defended yourself—?"

"Best I could, Pa. There were five of them."

Uncontrollably, he touched Judah's brow, brushed some hair back, fighting his own trembling. Judith's shadow fell over his sleeve. "He's all right," Cooper said as the fear began to run out of him like an ebbing tide.

59

In the occupied city of New Orleans, the weather was warm that morning. So was Colonel Elkanah Bent's emotional temperature. It matched that of the local citizens with whom he shared the corner of Chartres and Canal streets, watching the tangible evidence of General Ben Butler's radicalism.

The limpid air smelled as it always did, predominantly of coffee but laced with the Mississippi and the toilet water of gentlemen who had to be out because they were in commerce; gentlemen who had lived off cotton once and were perhaps doing so again, less covertly every day. Those of the better classes were still indoors. Perhaps they had received a hint of what they might see if they ventured out. Most on the corner had been caught there by chance, like Bent, though undoubtedly one or two watched by choice, to keep hatred stoked.

Fatter than ever and puffing a cigar, Bent was fully as angry as the civilians, though he dared not show it. The drums tapped, the fifes shrilled, and with limp colors preceding them, the First Louisiana Native Guards came parading up Canal.

Major General Butler had raised the regiment in late summer in the wake of other outrages, which included hanging Mumford, the man who dared to pull down an American flag from the mint building, and an order of May 15 stating that women who spoke or gestured to Union soldiers in an insulting manner would be arrested and treated as prostitutes.

Those were schoolboy pranks compared to this, Bent thought. He found the mere existence of the guards, officially mustered on

432

September 27, both unbelievable and repulsive. He pitied the officers chosen to command this regiment of ex-cotton pickers and stevedores.

The town was abuzz with rumors generated by aspects of the Butler style. The Yankee general who pillaged private homes for salable silver pieces would be replaced because of such crimes against the civilian population. Lincoln would not allow the guards to serve in the federal army, wanting nothing to upset the delicate potentialities—the chance that a wayward sister might return—before the fateful proclamation deadline. Bent had heard those and many more.

The Negro regiment wasn't a rumor; it was right in front of him—yellow faces, tan faces, sepia and blue-ebony faces. How they grinned and rolled their eyes as they pranced past their old oppressors, who were standing still as statues, paralyzed by disbelief and disdain.

The fifes struck up the "Battle Hymn" to heighten the insult. The black unit, one of the first in the army, tramped on toward the river. Bent flipped his cigar into the street. The sight was enough to turn a man into a Southerner—a breed he had always hated but now regarded with a deepening sympathy.

Bent's hands began to itch as he thought of a glass of spirits. Too early. Much too early. But he couldn't banish the desire, to which he gave in with increasing frequency these days. He had no friends among his fellow officers in the occupying army; few even spoke to him except in the line of duty. He cautioned himself not to give in to the temptation, knowing full well he would. Only a drink, or several, would relieve his misery.

Pittsburg Landing had sent his life spiraling downward. He had reached Butler's headquarters in New Orleans after a difficult journey to the East Coast and a steamer voyage around the tip of Florida to the reopened port. After a two-minute meeting with the cockeyed little politician from Massachusetts, Bent found himself attached to the provost's department. The duty was ideal, because it allowed him to give orders to civilians as well as soldiers.

Bent had been in New Orleans before. He enjoyed the city's cultured atmosphere and the delights it offered to gentlemen with money. It was in the bordellos of the town that he had gained a certain limited passion for equality; he would pay a high price to fornicate with a nigger girl, especially a very young one. He had enjoyed that experience last night.

He peered down the street after the regiment—the Corps d'Afrique, the presumptuous darkies styled themselves. White officers had to be coaxed, bribed with brevets, or threatened with a general court before they would accept command of so much as one company of a new Negro regiment—of which there were several.

What a remarkable about-face General Butler had done in organizing them. Initially he had declared himself against the idea. In August he changed his mind, persuaded, it was said, by his wife, his friend Secretary Chase, and perhaps by belated realization that the appearance of black regiments would make local whites apoplectic. At first Butler said he would recruit only the semitrained members of a black unit formed to defend the city before it fell. He reversed himself on that, too, and was soon signing up plantation runaways.

Bent started toward the old square, encountering unfriendly faces on the walks shaded by charming iron balconies. Ah, but the civilians did step aside for him. Indeed they did.

His thoughts drifted to the brothels again. There was one house he particularly wanted to visit at an opportune moment. He had chanced on the place before the war, on his way back from the hellish duty in Texas. In the madam's quarters there hung many fine paintings, including a portrait of a woman connected with the Main family in some way he did not as yet understand. The connection itself was certain. In Texas, in Charles Main's quarters, he had seen a photograph of a woman with virtually identical features.

What stimulated Bent's imagination were facts conveyed to him by the owner of the bordello, Madame Conti. The painting depicted a quadroon who had once worked in the establishment. In other words, a nigger whore.

That painting was one of the few positive aspects of Bent's current exile. He believed it to be a weapon he could use eventually against the Mains. He never forgot or abandoned his desire to harm members of that family; only set it aside periodically because events forced him. He knew the bordello was still operating under Madame Conti's management. He assumed the painting was still there.

By the time he reached Bienville, he knew he must have a drink soon. Just then he noticed a well-dressed white woman alighting from a barouche beyond the intersection of narrow streets. She dismissed the driver and, like Bent, walked in the direction of the cathedral. Two black soldiers were coming the other way, laughing and jostling each other. Yellow stripes on light blue breeches showed they belonged to the cavalry Ben Butler had raised.

The woman stopped. So did the soldiers, blocking the walk. Bent saw the woman's hat bob as she said something. The soldiers replied with laughter. Bent drew his dress saber and lumbered across Bienville.

"You men stand aside."

They didn't.

"I gave you a direct order. Step into the street and let this lady pass."

They continued to block the walk. It was a kind of disobedience not unknown to him, but it angered him more than usual because of their color. They wouldn't have dared defy him if it weren't for Butler and Old Abe. In the wake of the President's proclamation, the darkies thought they ruled the earth.

The tableau held. Bent heard one of the troopers mutter something about white officers, and both eyed him in a speculative way. Foolish of him to interfere with such brutes. Suppose they attacked him?

Then he saw his salvation: three white soldiers coming into sight down at the corner of Conti. The sergeant wore a side arm. Bent waved his sword. "Sergeant! Come here this instant."

The trio hurried. Bent identified himself. "Take these two insubordinate rascals to the provost, and I'll follow to charge them." His breathing slowed; he could ooze contempt on the niggers. "If you hope to be part of the Union Army, gentlemen, you must behave like civilized human beings, not apes. Dismissed, Sergeant."

The noncom drew his revolver. He and his men began to enjoy their assignment. They poked the two blacks and kicked their shins. The cavalrymen looked frightened.

As well they might, Bent thought. They would be tied by their thumbs, with stout cord, to a suitable beam or limb and left to hang with their toes just touching the ground. An hour of it was standard punishment in cases of insubordination. For them he would order three or four hours.

"Colonel?"

He swept off his hat; the woman was middle-aged, attractive. "Ma'am? I do apologize for the way those—soldiers harassed you."

"I am most grateful for your intervention." Her accent was that of the city, melodious and warm. "I trust you won't take offense if I remark that you are not typical of members of the army of occupation. Indeed, I would find it more natural for a man of your sensibilities to be wearing gray. Thank you again. Good day."

Overwhelmed, he muttered, "Good day," as she swept into a doorway that was her destination.

It had been so long since anyone had complimented him about anything that he flew along toward the cathedral square in a euphoric state. Perhaps the woman was right. Changing sides was unthinkable, of course, but her insight couldn't be faulted. Perhaps his lifelong loathing for Southerners was misguided. It might be that in certain ways he was more reb than Yank. Pity to learn it too late.

Under the looming façade of St. Louis Cathedral, Bent halted suddenly, attention arrested by two men in the square. One was the commanding general's brother, an army officer much in evidence in New Orleans lately. The other—

He struggled momentarily, then got it. Stanley Hazard. Bent had seen him last at Willard's over a year ago. What was he doing here?

He hurried on, his craving for drink intense. The sudden sight of Stanley reminded him of George and Orry. Soon old litanies were resounding in his head. He must not forget either family or how much he wanted to repay them. Before he left New Orleans, he had to take possession of the portrait in the bordello.

The table linen was blinding, the silver heavy. The gulf oysters were succulent, the champagne French and cold as January. Most of the liveried waiters had woolly white heads. They bent over the diners with such attention and deference that Stanley could almost imagine Abe and his freedom proclamation were fantasies.

The polite, reserved gentleman sharing the table wore the oak leaves and cuff braids of a colonel, though the source of that rank was a mystery to Stanley and many others. He had done some investigation before leaving Washington. In one group of reports, the officer was consistently called Captain Butler, and it was the captain whose appointment as a commissary the Senate had rejected last winter.

Other reports filed in the War Department referred to him as Colonel Butler, though most of these came from his brother. In other words, in the mysterious ways of wartime, when the gentleman got a job on his brother's staff, he underwent a rapid rise in rank. Whether the promotions were brevets or even legal hardly mattered. Nothing mattered but the man's influence and power. He had plenty of each, so Stanley gladly overlooked the irregularities.

Stanley watched his champagne consumption; difficult negotiation lay ahead. While they ate they kept to safe topics: the question of the length of the war; the question of whether McClellan would be replaced and by whom. On the latter, Stanley knew the answers—yes; Burnside—but feigned ignorance.

Butler asked about his journey. "Oh, it was fine. Sea air is salubrious." He hadn't smelled much of it. He had stayed in his bunk for most of the voyage, rising only to vomit into a bucket. But it was important that business adversaries think him competent in every respect—another of Isabel's little lessons.

"Well, sir"—Stanley's guest leaned back—"a fine repast, and I thank you for it. Since your visit is so short, perhaps we'd better get down to it."

"Happily, Colonel. For background, I might tell you that I own the manufacturing firm of Lashbrook's of Lynn, Massachusetts."

"Army footwear," Colonel Andrew Butler said with a nod. A little shiver chased along beneath Stanley's shirt. The man knew all about him.

He raised his napkin to mop perspiration from his lip. He leaned forward into the shadow of a hanging fern basket. "This is a rather public place. Should we—?"

"No, we're perfectly all right here." Butler touched a match to a large Havana. "Similar, ah, arrangements are being concluded at half the tables in this restaurant. Though none is on the scale of what you propose. Please continue."

Stanley got up his nerve and plunged. "I understand there is a desperate need for shoes."

"Desperate," Butler murmured, blowing smoke.

"In the North, cotton is badly needed."

"It's available. One only needs to know cooperative sources and how to get it into the city and onto the docks." Butler smiled.

"You do understand that in every transaction I receive a commission from the purchaser as well as the seller?"

"Yes, yes—it makes no difference, if you can help me ship shoes to the Con—to those who need them and, at the same time, deliver cotton in sufficient quantity to make its resale worth the not inconsiderable risk. There are laws against aiding and trading with the enemy."

"Are there? I've been too busy to notice." He laughed heartily. Stanley joined in because he thought he should.

They went strolling, working out the details. In the mild sunshine of early winter, Stanley suddenly felt marvelous, unable to believe that, in remote places he would never see, men were living in fear and filth, and laying down their lives for slogans.

On his third cigar, Andrew Butler began to philosophize about his brother. "They nicknamed him Beast because he threatened to treat the townswomen as whores if they made disparaging remarks to our boys, and they nicknamed him Spoons because they say he loots private homes. He's guilty of the former and proud of it, but believe me, Stanley, if Ben wanted to steal, he wouldn't traffic in anything so trifling as spoons. After all, his background is Massachusetts politics—and he's a lawyer besides."

Stanley could have mentioned some things he had heard about the general—that, for instance, he had grown wealthy during his short tenure in New Orleans, though no one could say how. The sources of Andrew Butler's burgeoning fortune were, by contrast, widely known.

Moving toward the riverfront where a paddle steamer lay moored, white as a wedding cake in the sunshine, Butler continued, "The people of this town are wrong to condemn my brother. He's a much more fair-minded and efficient administrator than anyone will admit. He cleaned up pestilential conditions he found when he arrived, he brought in food and clothing when it was badly needed, he reopened the port for business. But all you hear is 'Damn the Beast' and 'Damn Spoons.' Fortunately, in our little commercial venture, you and I will deal with gentlemen who put personal profit ahead of public slogan-mongering."

"You're referring to the cotton planters?"

"Yes. Their desire to be practical was enhanced by the experience of a few who initially refused me their cooperation—and their cotton. Those gentlemen found their slaves absent all at once. When they subsequently consented to, ah, share their crop

438

in the general marketplace, the slaves of course reappeared to do the hard labor."

Working under bayonets held by United States soldiers, Stanley thought. The scandalous stories had reached Washington. But he didn't mention it.

"Even in wartime," Butler concluded, "practicality is often a wiser course than patriotism."

"Yes, definitely," Stanley agreed. The champagne and sunshine and success reached him all at once, generating a sense of self-worth unique in all his life. Isabel should be proud of what he had accomplished today. Damned proud. He was.

By the close of November, most officers in the Army of the Gulf knew they would have a new commander by the end of the year. Protests against Butler's style had grown too numerous, accusations of thievery and profiteering too ripe. The coming of a new commandant usually produced a reorganization and many transfers. Elkanah Bent realized he must retrieve the painting at once.

He observed the entrance to Madame Conti's on three randomly chosen evenings. The observation proved that what he had heard was true: the brothel was popular with officers and noncoms alike, though it was against regulations for them to associate, just as it was for them to visit such a place. Both rules were broken by large numbers of men, who went in quietly and came out rowdily—drunk to the eyes. Within one half-hour period he witnessed two fistfights, which further cheered him.

In his disorderly rented room around the corner from the Cotton Exchange, Bent sat down in his undershirt and devised a plan with the aid of his most helpful companion, a fresh bottle of whiskey. He drank as much as a quart a day—and vile stuff it was, too; little better than sutler's slop. But he needed it to clarify his mind and help him cope with his burden of failure.

The woman who ran the bordello would never sell him the portrait. Nor was he willing to risk burglary late at night; he vividly remembered Madame Conti's black helper. He had to steal the painting while others conducted what was known in military parlance as a diversionary demonstration. With the bordello patrons in a volatile state, it should not be hard to provoke one.

439

It was the best plan he could concoct. He drained the bottle and fell into bed, blearily reminding himself to secure a knife.

The following Saturday night, in full-dress uniform, Bent ascended the beautiful black iron stair he had climbed once before. He found a large, noisy crowd of soldiers in the parlor and didn't recognize one. A touch of luck there.

He ordered bourbon from the old black man behind the small bar. He sipped and listened. When the men weren't boasting to the whores, they maundered about home or muttered anti-Southern sentiments. Ideal.

He ordered a second drink. His neck prickled suddenly. Someone watching—?

He turned. Sure enough, through the press he saw a large, solid woman approaching. She was well into her sixties, and her mass of white hair was as stunningly arranged as it had been the previous time. She wore a robe of emerald silk embroidered with bridges, pagodas, and Oriental figures.

"Good evening, Colonel. I thought I recognized an old customer."

He started to sweat; insincerity lurked behind his smile. "You have a good memory, Madame Conti."

"I just recall your face, not your name." Shrewdly, she didn't bring up their quarrel over the cost of certain special services obtained from the slut he had bedded.

"Bent." On the first visit he had actually called himself Benton, wanting to protect his real name because he believed he could still have a career in the army. At that time, he had yet to learn that the generals never recognized talent, only influence.

And you don't command any. You know who's responsible: your father, who betrayed you in death. The Mains and the Hazards, the General Billy Shermans, and a host of unknown enemies who have whispered and conspired and—

"Colonel? Are you ill?"

A bulging vein in his forehead flattened out of sight. His breathing slowed. "Just a brief dizziness. Nothing alarming."

She relaxed, musing. "Colonel Bent. Certainly, that was it." He missed the flash of doubt in her eyes. He swallowed whiskey and listened to the din in the place. Excellent.

"I recall you had a Negro working for you—a huge, ferocious fellow." *Willing to kill on order.* "I haven't seen him tonight. Is he still here?"

Bitterness: "No. Pomp wanted to join your army. He was a freedman, and I couldn't dissuade him. To business, Colonel. In what may we interest you this evening? You know our range of specialties, as I recall."

He wanted one of her young boys, but in this military crowd dared not ask. "A white girl, I think. One with flesh on her bones."

"Come and meet Marthe. She's German, though she's learning English. One caution: Marthe's younger brother is serving in a Louisiana regiment. I advise Marthe and all the other girls that we run a nonpartisan establishment"—damn lie, that; the madam had several times criticized Butler publicly—"but you can assure yourself of congeniality by avoiding direct reference to the war."

"Certainly, certainly." Anxiety quickened the reply. Could he go through with it? He must.

Madame Conti's hypocrisy helped stiffen his resolve. He ordered a magnum of French champagne for some further stiffening, then waddled along to be presented to the whore.

"Very lovely, dear," Marthe said twenty minutes later. "Very satisfying." She had an accent thick as a sausage and china-blue eyes, which she had kept focused on the ceiling throughout. Plump and slightly pink from her brief exertion, she lay touching and fluffing the corkscrew curls over her ears.

Back turned, Bent struggled into his trousers. Now, he said to himself. *Now.* He picked up the bottle and drained the last inch of flat champagne.

The plump whore rose and reached for her blue silk kimono. Madame Conti's passion for things Asian was evident throughout the house. "It's time to pay, darling. The chap at the bar downstairs will take your mon—"

Bent pivoted. She saw his fist rising, but astonishment prevented an outcry for a moment. He hit her hard. Her head snapped back. She fell on the bed, shrieking in anger and pain.

Turning away to conceal his next action, he raked his nails down his left cheek till he felt the blood. Then he snatched his coat and lurched for the door.

The whore was on him then, pounding with her fists, bellowing German curses. Bent kicked back twice and hurt her enough to stop the hitting. He plunged into the dim hall. Doors opened along it, blurred faces becoming visible. What was the commotion?

He remembered his saber, left behind. *Let it go. You can buy another. There's only one painting.*

Down the stairs he went, staggering, blood dripping from his chin. "Damn rebel slut attacked me. She attacked me!"

He bolted through the arch to the parlor, where his outcry had already generated angry looks among the lounging soldiers. "Look what the whore did to me!" Bent pointed to his bloody cheek. "She called General Butler a pissing street dog—spat on my uniform—then she did this. I won't pay a penny in this nest of traitors."

"Right with you there, Colonel," said a dark-bearded captain. Several men stood up. Marthe bounded down the stairs, heightening the effect of Bent's story by howling her German damnations. Through heavy smoke tinted by the red glass mantles, he saw the barman's hand drop beneath the counter. Madame Conti rushed from a doorway behind him: the office—exactly where he remembered it.

"All of you be quiet, please. I permit no such—"

"Here's what we do to people who insult the United States Army." Bent seized the nearest chair and brought it down on the marble bar, splintering it.

"Stop that, stop it," Madame Conti cried with a note of despair. Several girls fled squealing; others crouched on the floor. The barman produced a pepper-pot pistol. Two noncoms jumped him, one throwing the gun into a spittoon while the other locked hands behind the man's neck and dragged his face down to the marble, swiftly and hard. Bent heard a nose crack.

He picked up another chair and flung it sideways. It struck a decorative mirror; a waterfall of fragments flowed.

The soldiers, half of them drunk, joined the attack like gleeful boys. Tables flew. Chairs crunched. Madame Conti ineffectually pulled at the arms of those wrecking her parlor, gave up and dashed away as demolition commenced in other rooms. An officer caught her, lifted her, and carried her out of sight on his shoulder.

Panting with excitement and fear, Bent ran to the office. There was the red-flocked wallpaper, the array of paintings, including the great Bingham—and there was the quadroon's portrait in its remembered place, among several canvases behind the madam's desk. Bent produced a clasp knife and began to poke and saw the

442

canvas around the inner edge of the frame. In a minute and a half, he nearly had the portrait loose.

"What are you doing?"

Cut, rip—the picture was his. He began to roll it. "You've ruined that," Madame Conti cried, rushing at him. Bent dropped the painting, balled his fist, and hit her on the side of the head. She would have fallen, but she caught herself on the edge of the desk.

Her splendid hairdo undone, she stared at him through straggling gray strands. "Your name wasn't Bent the first time; it was—"

He struck her again. The blow drove her four feet backward and hurled her to the floor. She floundered on her spine and made whimpering noises as he picked up the rolled painting, rushed through the parlor and down the iron stairs, leaving his army comrades to finish their work. From the hurrahs and the sounds of breakage that diminished as he hurried into the dark, they were enjoying the duty.

It had been a good night for everyone.

60

Burnside brought the Army of the Potomac to the Rappahannock in mid-November. The engineers hutted in a huge camp at Falmouth and waited. Seldom had Billy heard such complaining.

"We are delaying so long they will have their best ready to go against us."

"Bad terrain, Fredericksburg. What are we to do, march up the

443

heights like the redcoats at Breed's Hill and be mowed down the same way?"

"The general is a shit-ass, fit for nothing but combing his whiskers. There isn't an officer in the country capable of leading this army to a victory."

Despite Lije Farmer's urgings that he have faith and ignore the malcontents, it was the malcontents Billy was starting to believe. Confidence in Burnside was not enhanced when a story got around that he was asking his personal cook for advice on strategy.

The weather, wet and dismal, deepened Billy's malaise and finally affected him physically. On the ninth of December he started sneezing. Then came queasiness and a headache. The next night, as the pontoon train began its advance to a previously scouted field beside the river, his forehead felt scorching, and he could barely suppress violent shivering. He said nothing.

They moved as quietly as possible. Fog had settled in, helping to muffle sound. At three in the morning, the regular battalion, assisted by the Fifteenth and the Fiftieth New York Volunteer Engineers, unloaded the boats while the teamsters cursed and coddled their horses to minimize noise. Everyone knew the significance of the pale splotches of color in the fog; among the trees and tall houses on the other shore, Confederate picket fires burned.

"Quiet," Billy said every minute or so. The men repeatedly dropped the boats as they labored across the plowed field or blundered into one another and threatened a fight. There was a bad feeling about this campaign so late in the year. It was misbegotten. Cursed.

The fever swirled his thoughts and filmed his vision, but Billy kept on, softly calling directions, maintaining order, lifting and carrying when some weaker man faltered and fell out. A misty drizzle started. Then he began to ache.

During a break in the work, he clasped his arms around his body in a vain effort to warm up. Lije appeared. Touched his shoulder.

"There are plenty to carry on here. Go to the surgeons, where you belong."

Billy jerked away from his friend's hand. " 'M all right."

Lije stood still, said nothing, but Billy knew he was hurt all the

444

same. He started to apologize, but Lije turned and went back to the men.

Shame overwhelmed Billy, then uncharacteristic contempt for his friend. How could Lije believe all that Scriptural twaddle? If there was a compassionate God, how could He permit this nightmare war to drag on?

They kept at the work, continually watching the picket fires on the other side of the river. The drizzle produced heavy smoke from time to time, but the rebs kept the fires replenished with dry wood. One fire directly opposite the bridge site drew special attention because the soldier on picket duty could be seen with some clarity. He was reedy, bearded, and marched back and forth as if he had all the energy in the world.

It was nearly daybreak when the first boats went in. The men dropped one, and it smacked the shallows, loud as a shot. Superintending the work of moving more boats to the shore, Billy heard someone exclaim, "It's all up," then saw the rebel picket pluck a brand from the fire and wave it over his head, an arc of sparks.

Over the picket's cry, Lije shouted, "Press ahead, boys. No need for silence now."

They rushed forward with balks, chesses, and rails as a small signal cannon banged on the opposite shore. Running figures showed against the watch fires. A detachment of infantry came up behind the engineers, sleepy marksmen readying weapons. Artillery wheeled into place on the bluff above. Billy suspected all of it would be scant protection.

They had five boats anchored and two planked by the time enemy skirmishers appeared and opened fire. Looking bilious in the breaking light, Lieutenant Cross and a crew put out in their boats, the first to strike for the enemy shore, which they might or might not reach.

Billy worked on the end of the bridge, soon extended to midstream; he helped to cleat each boat to a pair of balks, then run it out. He heard the guns begin to crackle. A ball plopped in the water to his right; another thunked the gunwale of the pontoon boat over which he was kneeling.

"Wish I had my fucking gun," someone said.

"Stop wasting breath," Billy said. "Work."

Men ran forward with chesses. One of them jerked suddenly, stepped sideways, and tumbled into the Rappahannock.

Consternation. Hands shot down to seize and lift the wounded engineer. Billy had never felt water so icy. Lije ran out on the bridge. "Courage, boys. 'Our soul waiteth for the Lord. He is our help and our shield:' "

Dragging the man to safety—blood and water streaming from his face—Billy twisted around and said, "Shut up, Lije. The Lord our shield didn't help this man, and He isn't going to help the rest of us, so shut up, will you?"

The white-bearded man seemed to shrivel. Anger flashed in his eyes, quickly replaced by sadness. Billy wanted to bite off his tongue. Men stared at him, but only one mattered. He ran to Lije along the slippery bridge and clutched his arm.

"I didn't mean that. I'm eternally sorry for saying something so—"

"Down," Lije yelled as rebs across the river volleyed. He pushed Billy and dropped on top of him.

Billy's head smacked the bridge. He tried to rise, but too much had worn him down. Too much illness, tiredness, despair. Ashamed though he was, he let himself sink into comforting black.

Later the same day—it was Friday, December eleventh—Billy lay in a field hospital at Falmouth. There he learned that the engineers had worked all morning under constant fire and had finished two of five planned bridges across the Rappahannock by noon.

Too weak to return to duty, he spent the hours of Saturday listening to cannonading. On Sunday, Lije came poking among the cots, found his friend, and sat down on a box beside a pole where a lantern hung. He asked Billy how he felt.

"Ashamed, Lije. Ashamed of what I said and how I said it."

"Well, sir," returned the older man a bit formally, "I do confess I took it hard for some length of time."

"You saved me from a wound anyway."

"None of us is a perfect vessel, and the heart of the Master's ministry was forgiveness. You were ill, we were all exhausted, and the situation was perilous. What man can be blamed for a rash word in such circumstances?"

His prophet's face gentled. "You want the news, no doubt. I am afraid the foreboding expressed by you and many others was justified in full. Even my own faith stretches exceeding thin after events of yesterday."

446

Amid the rows of sick, wounded, and dying, Lije told his friend how the federals had crossed the river and what had befallen them.

61

That same Sunday night, three men kept a vigil in Secretary Stanton's office.

Potomac mist drifted outside the windows. The gas hissed, and there were soft clickings from an unseen source. Stanley wished the vigil would end so he could go home. He wanted to examine the latest statements from Lashbrook's, which had doubled its already enormous business thanks to the covert contract arranged by Butler. He tried to conceal his impatience, though unintentionally he shifted farther and farther forward to the edge of the chair. His left foot moved up and down, silently tapping.

Major Albert Johnson, the arrogant young man formerly Stanton's law clerk and now his most trusted aide, strode from the main door to that of the adjoining cipher room, where he about-faced, crossed the office, and began the circuit again.

The President lay on the couch he had occupied most of the day. His unfashionable dark suit had wrinkled. His eyes, focused somewhere far below the carpet, suited a mourner. His color was that of a man poisoned with jaundice.

Lincoln had angrily told them that a Mr. Villard, a correspondent for Greeley's *Tribune,* had returned from the front on Saturday and had been brought to the Executive Mansion at 10:00 P.M. There he had reported what he knew and protested the refusal of the military censor to clear his dispatches about Burnside's futile assaults on Fredericksburg. "I offered him my apology and said I hoped the news was not as bad as he perceived."

None of them knew for certain. The secretary controlled what was published—the military censors reported to him—and he also controlled the telegraph from the front. He had removed the receiving instruments from McClellan's headquarters and installed them in the library upstairs soon after he took office. He had even pirated McClellan's chief telegraph officer, Captain Eckert. Stanley admired the secretary's audacious seizure of the information lines; nothing of substance came into Washington or went out of it without Stanton knowing it first. Stanton used the telegraph like an umbilical cord to tie his department more securely to the Executive Mansion and Lincoln himself. The President continued to profess great trust in Stanton as well as a magnanimous personal admiration for the man who had once snubbed him professionally when both were lawyers. Stanton now termed Lincoln his dear friend, though he had manipulated the relationship so that the President was the dependent, not the dominant, partner.

Stanley, however, continued to regard Abraham Lincoln as a pathetic clod. At the moment, the President was resting on his side on the couch, reminding Stanley of a cadaver or some piece of sculpture by a talentless beginner. Lincoln's secretaries had secret nicknames for various people. Some, such as Hellcat for Mary Lincoln, couldn't be more appropriate. But how could they refer to their chief as the Tycoon unless in mockery? The man would never be reelected, not even if the war reached a swift and successful conclusion, which looked unlikely.

The door of the cipher room opened. Johnson halted. Stanley jumped up. Stanton emerged with several of the flimsy yellow sheets on which decoded dispatches from the front were copied. The secretary smelled of cologne and strong soap, which told Stanley he had been at some large function late in the day. Stanton always scrubbed and anointed himself after contact with the public.

"What is the news?" Lincoln asked.

Reflected gaslight turned the lenses of Stanton's glasses to shimmering mirrors. "Not good."

"I asked for the news, not a description of it." The President's voice rasped with weariness. He shifted higher on his left elbow, his loosened cravat falling over the edge of the couch.

Stanton folded down corners on the first two flimsies. "I regret that it appears young Villard was right. There were repeated assaults within the town."

"What was the objective?"

"Marye's Heights. A position all but impregnable."

Lincoln stared with that bereaved face. "Are we defeated?"

Stanton did not look away. "Yes, Mr. President."

Slowly, as if suffering arthritic pain, Lincoln sat up. Stanley heard a knee joint creak. Stanton gave him the flimsies, continuing quietly, "A dispatch presently being copied indicates General Burnside wished to assault the rebel positions again this morning, perhaps in hopes of compensating for yesterday. His senior officers dissuaded him from that rash course."

Momentary doubts about the worth of the telegraph struck Stanley. Certainly the device was changing warfare in a revolutionary way. Orders could be transmitted to commanding officers at a speed never thought possible. On the other hand, bad news could be returned just as fast, and that had all sorts of ramifications in the stock and gold markets, which tended to fluctuate wildly in response to the war news. Of course, if one had a way to get an early look at key dispatches, then telegraphed appropriate buy or sell orders before the news became known, huge killings could be made. He was delighted with himself for having thought of that. The telegraph was a remarkable creation.

Lincoln leafed through the flimsies, then flung them on the couch. "First I had a general who employed the Army of the Potomac as his bodyguard. Now I have one who celebrates a rout by suggesting another." Shaking his head, he strode to the window and peered into the mist, as if seeking answers there.

Stanton cleared his throat. After a strained silence, Lincoln swung around. His face was a study in aggrieved fury. "I presume the steamers will be bringing us more wounded soon."

"They already are, Mr. President. The first ones from Aquia Creek docked last night. Those flimsies contain the information."

"I didn't read them closely. I can't bear to—instead of numbers, I see faces. I presume the numbers are large and the casualties heavy?"

"Yes, sir, so the first reports would indicate."

Looking paler than ever, the President once more turned to confront the night. "Stanton, I've said it before. If there is a worse place than hell, I am in it."

"We share that feeling, Mr. President. To a man."

449

Stanley made sure he maintained an appropriately sorrowful expression.

Distant cries woke Virgilia on Tuesday morning. She turned her head toward the small window. Black. Not yet daylight.

The window was unbroken, a rarity in the ancient Union Hotel. New-style hospitals—pavilions on the Nightingale plan—were under construction to supply fifteen thousand beds and promote healing rather than impede it. Construction funds had been appropriated a year ago July. Until the work was finished, however, all sorts of unsuitable structures, from public buildings and churches to warehouses and private homes, had to be used—especially in this bleak December when Burnside's bungling had cost over twelve thousand casualties.

The cries kept on. Virgilia sat up hurriedly. Something fell to the floor from her hard, narrow bed. She groped and retrieved the small book, slipping it under a thin pillow. She reread certain passages in *Coriolanus* frequently because they seemed to have relevance to her situation. Ironically, the lines she loved most, from the third scene of the first act, were delivered not by her namesake, the insipid wife of Caius Marcius, but by his mother, Volumnia, the Roman matron whose temperament Virgilia shared.

She reached for the lamp on the floor. She had gone to sleep in her plain gray dress and long white apron with the tabard top. She hadn't known when she would be needed because no one had said whether casualties destined for the Union Hotel Hospital would arrive in Washington by rail or by steamer.

She knew how they were arriving in Georgetown. "Those infernal two-wheelers," she muttered as she lit the lamp. The outcries, characterized by abruptness as well as anguish, told her the wounded were coming in the ambulances that were the curse of the medical service. Some of the patients she had attended since joining Miss Dix's corps said that after riding in one of the tilting, bouncing conveyances, they found themselves wishing they had remained where they had fallen. Better four-wheel models were being tested, but getting them took money and time.

The shimmery lamp revealed the room's tawdry furnishings, warped flooring, peeling paper. The entire hotel was like that, a ruin. But it was where she had been sent. Ironically, she was less than half a mile from the house of George and Constance. She didn't know if her brother knew she was a nurse in Washington, but she had no plans to call and inform him.

She did remain grudgingly grateful to Constance and even to Billy's wife for helping her improve her appearance and showing her a better course. Beyond that, if she never saw any of them again, it wouldn't trouble her.

Virgilia straightened her hairnet, left her room, and strode downstairs with the lamp. A neat, full-bosomed figure, with an aura of authority, she smelled of the brown soap with which she was careful to wash frequently. Already she had been put in charge of Ward One. Virgilia accepted the customary salary of twelve dollars a month, which some of the volunteers did not take. For her it was a necessity, a hedge against some future misfortune.

The hotel was astir. She smelled coffee and beef soup from the kitchen. Soldier nurses, men still convalescing, were rising from none too clean pallets and cots in the halls and ground-floor parlors. Her wardmaster, a youthful Illinois artilleryman named Bob Pip, yawned and squinted at her as she approached.

"Morning, matron."

"Up, Bob, up—they're here."

To confirm it, she stopped at a broken window. A little light showed in the bleak sky, revealing a long line of the two-wheeled horrors snaking through the narrow street to the main entrance. Surveying the hall again, she saw no surgeons. They were customarily the last to arrive, something to do with dramatizing their importance, she had decided.

Despite her dislike of the doctors, she realized that all who worked at the hospital had a common cause—succoring and healing men injured in battle with a detestable enemy. Those crying out from the ambulances had fought in behalf of poor dead Grady, against the vicious army of aristocrats and mudsills Virgilia hated more than anything except slavery itself. That was why she worked so hard to replace dirt with cleanliness, pain with ease, despair with contentment.

She had taken to the work. It was honorable. Favorite lines from the Shakespeare play set five centuries before Christ reinforced her view. Every day or so, she silently repeated Volumnia's scornful speech to Virgilia about the shedding of blood. *It more becomes a man than gilt his trophy. The breasts of Hecuba, when*

451

*she did suckle Hector, looked not lovelier than Hector's forehead
when it spit forth blood.*

Virgilia had the stomach for nursing. Many of the well-meaning volunteers didn't and quickly returned home. She had a person like that in her ward now. In Washington only three days, the young woman was clearly revolted by her duties. Still, Virgilia liked her.

She knocked loudly at the door of a parlor converted to a dormitory for the female nurses; the matrons had small separate rooms, no great blessing.

"Ladies? Get up, please. They've come. Hurry, you're needed immediately."

She heard bustling, soft talk in the parlor. She pivoted with a precision that was unconsciously military and marched toward the flung-back doors of her ward. On one of them a sorry brass sign hung from a nail in its corner. Reading downward at a forty-five-degree angle, the engraved script said BALL ROOM.

The ward consisted of forty beds and a central stove into which Bob Pip was tossing kindling while another soldier nurse lit the mantles. Virgilia marched down the aisles, inspecting to the right and to the left, and when necessary straightening coverlets or the beds themselves. Miss Dix's experiment of employing women had been an unexpected success because the original plan—to place the soldier nurses in charge of the wards—had two flaws: convalescing men tired quickly, and they could not easily and naturally provide the one thing a battle-weary veteran wanted almost as much as he wanted to be well and free of pain—tenderness. Virgilia spent as much time sitting at bedsides, holding hands and listening, as she did changing dressings and assisting surgeons.

As she completed the inspection, her female assistant came in. She was a husky, plain woman, about thirty, with a pleasant face and a great amount of brown hair done up in braids and held by her hairnet. She had told Virgilia she had ambitions as a writer and had already published some articles and verse when patriotic fervor lured her to the volunteer nurses.

"Good morning, Miss Alcott. Please come along and help me bring in our wounded."

"Certainly, Miss Hazard."

With clear command, Virgilia gestured and called out, "Bob—Lloyd—Casey—to the lobby, please."

She marched at the head of her group. A bilious look spread

452

over the face of Louisa Alcott. The lobby was not yet in sight, but they could smell its strong odors—familiar odors that had made Virgilia ill the first time she was exposed to them.

She did hope Miss Alcott would last; something told her the woman had the makings of a fine nurse. She came of a famous family. Her father, Bronson, the Concord educator and transcendentalist, conducted experiments with model schools and communal living. But pedigree wouldn't help her here. Virgilia was dismayed when Miss Alcott gulped and said, "Oh, dear heaven," as the group from Ward One entered the lobby.

Similar groups were arriving from other wards to claim their charges. And there they were, walking unaided or on crutches or being carried, the young, brave boys from Fredericksburg, some so encrusted with mud and bloody bandages it was hard to see their uniforms. She heard Louisa Alcott choke and quickly said, "From now on carry a handkerchief soaked in ammonia or cologne, whichever you prefer. You'll soon find you don't need it."

"You mean you've gotten used to—?"

But Virgilia was off among the litter-bearers, pointing. "Take forty that way, to the ballroom."

Her heart broke as she watched them go. A youth with his right hand sawed off and the stump bandaged. A man about her age, wounded in the foot, struggling with his crutch and staring with eyes like panes of glass. A soldier on a litter, thrashing back and forth, tears trickling into his mud-caked beard while he repeated, "Mother. Mother." Virgilia picked up his hand and walked along beside the litter. He quieted; the anguished lines vanished from his face. She held his hand till they reached the ballroom entrance.

The soap and disinfectant sloshed everywhere last night might have been saved for all the good it did now. Very quickly, the wounded generated a reeking miasma of dirt, festering wounds, feces, vomit. As always, the stench had a strange effect on Virgilia. Rather than disgusting her, it sharpened her sense of being needed and her conviction that the struggle would and must end just one way—with the South reduced to a mudhole, as Congressman Stevens put it so splendidly.

The efficient Bob Pip set out towels, sponges, and blocks of brown soap. A black man brought a kettle from the kitchen and poured steaming water into basins. The ambulance drivers helped their charges to beds, then left. Virgilia saw one sleazy brute eying her. She feigned annoyance and turned her back. Men often noticed her, though it wasn't beauty to which they were responding, merely size. She didn't mind. Once, no one had noticed anything.

"What 'n the divil is this goddamn place?" The booming voice had an Irish lilt. Behind the stove, now radiating heat, Virgilia saw a broad-shouldered soldier in his twenties, red-haired and red-bearded, thrashing about on his cot. "Don't look like Erie, Pennsylvania—nor the old sod neither—"

Pip told the soldier he was in the Union Hotel Hospital. The man started to climb out of bed. Pip restrained him. The soldier cursed and made a second effort. We will begin with him, Virgilia thought. Others were watching, and establishing authority in the ward was important.

She strode to the Irishman's cot. "Stop that foul talk. We're here to help you."

The bearded soldier squinted at her. "Skip the help, woman, an' give me something to eat. Ain't had a thing but hardtack since Burny sent me up that damn hill to die." He wiggled his left foot, wrapped in stained bandages. "Feels like all I did was surrender me toes, or a bit more."

The movement had pained him; that caused anger. "Jasus, woman, don't stand there. I want food."

"You will get nothing until we remove those filthy clothes and wash you down. That is standard hospital procedure."

"An' who the fu— Who's gonna do the washing, might I ask?" The Irishman rolled his eyes around the room, clearly telling her he saw no one capable by sex or training.

"One of my nurses will do it. Miss Alcott."

"A woman bathe me? I should say to God not!"

Above his beard, his cheeks were red. Pip set a bowl of water beside the cot, then handed Miss Alcott two towels, sponge, and brown soap. The soldier attempted to roll away from the women. Virgilia gestured.

"Bob, help me."

She seized the Irishman's shoulders and with some effort kept him in bed. "We do not want to inflict more pain on you, Corporal, and we won't if you cooperate with us. We intend to remove everything except your undergarments and scrub you thoroughly."

"All over?"

"Yes, every inch."

"Mother of God."

"Stop that. Other men besides you need attention. We have no time to waste on the false modesty of fools."

So saying, she ripped his collar open. Buttons flew.

The Irishman didn't struggle much; he was too weak and hurting. Virgilia showed the stupefied Miss Alcott how to ply a soapy sponge, then a towel. The towel was dark gray after two passes over the corporal's skin.

The Irishman kept his body rigid. Virgilia lifted his right arm and washed under it. He wriggled and giggled.

"Let's have none of that," she said, showing a slight smile.

"Jasus, who'd of thought it? A strange woman handlin' me like she was my mother." Sheepish then. "It don't feel too bad after what I been through. Not too bad atall."

"Your change of attitude is very helpful. I appreciate it. Miss Alcott, take over, and I'll start on the next man."

"But Miss Hazard—" she swallowed, pink-faced as the Irishman—"may I speak to you alone?"

"Certainly. Let's step over there."

She knew what was coming but dutifully bent her head to hear the whispered question. She answered with similar softness so as not to embarrass Miss Alcott. "Bob Pip or one of the other soldiers finishes each man. They have a saying: the old veterans wash the new privates."

Miss Alcott was too relieved to be shocked. She pressed a fist to her breast and breathed deeply. "Oh, I'm thankful to hear it. I believe I can handle the other work. I'm getting accustomed to the odors. But I don't believe I could bring myself to—to—" She couldn't even bring herself to say it.

"You'll do splendidly," Virgilia said, giving her an encouraging pat.

Louisa Alcott did do well. In two hours, with the help of a third volunteer nurse who joined them, they had stripped the entire population of the ward of unwearable clothing and all but essential dressings and bandages. Then the orderlies brought in coffee, beef, and soup.

While the men ate, the surgeons began to appear, distinguishable by the green sashes worn with their uniforms. Two entered the ballroom, one an elderly fellow Virgilia hadn't met before. He introduced himself and said he would handle all cases not requiring surgery. She knew the other doctor, a local man who went straight to work inspecting patients on the far side of the ward.

Virgilia found army surgeons a mixed lot. Some were dedicated, talented men; others, quacks without professional schooling, qualified by only a few weeks of apprenticeship in a physician's office. It was those in the latter group who most often acted as if they were eminent practitioners. They were brutal with patients, curt with inferiors, vocal about lowering themselves to serve in the army. She was able to tolerate the pomposity of such quacks only because they shared a common purpose—the healing of men so they could return to their regiments and kill more Southerners.

The surgeon approaching was no quack, but a Washington practitioner of solid reputation. Erasmus Foyle, M.D., barely reached Virgilia's shoulder, but he bore himself as if he were Brobdingnagian. Bald as an egg except for a fringe of oiled black hair, he sported mustachios with points and sweetened his breath with cloves. At their first meeting, he had made it evident that Virgilia interested him for reasons that were not professional.

After an ingratiating bow, he said, "Good morning, Miss Hazard. May I have a word outside?"

The last soldier Foyle had examined, a man with both legs bandaged from knee to groin, began to roll to and fro and moan. The moan slid upward into a high-register shriek. Miss Alcott dropped her bowl, but Pip caught it before it broke.

Virgilia called, "Give that man opium, Bob."

"And plenty of it," said Foyle, nodding vigorously. He slipped his right hand around Virgilia's left arm; his knuckles indented the bulge of her breast. She was about to call him down when something occurred to her.

Men looked at her differently from the way they did in the past. How useful could that be? Perhaps she should find out. She let Foyle's hand remain. He blushed with pleasure.

"Right along here—" He guided her through the doorway and to the left into a dingy hall where no one in the ward could see them. He stood close to her with his small, bright eyes on a level with her breasts. Grady had loved her breasts, too.

"Miss Hazard, what is your opinion of the condition of that poor wretch who's screaming?"

"Dr. Foyle, I am no physician—"

"Please, please—I respect your expertise." He was practically dancing from boot to polished boot. "I have respected and, may I say, admired you since chance first threw us together. Kindly give me your opinion."

The foxy little man reached for her right arm as he said that. He slipped his fingers around and under. *Now he knows how the other one feels.* Amused, she was also slightly bewildered by this unexpected power.

"Very well. I don't believe the left leg can be saved." She hated to say it; she had watched men as they regained consciousness after going under the saw.

"Amputation—yes, that was my conclusion also. And the right leg?"

"Not quite so bad, but the difference is marginal. Really, Doctor, shouldn't you ask your colleague instead of me?"

"Bah! He's no better than an apothecary. But you, Miss Hazard, you have a real grasp of medical matters. Intuitive, perhaps, but a real grasp."

Just as he had a grasp of her arm. His knuckles pressed into her bosom again. "Surgery for that man as soon as possible. Could we perhaps discuss other cases at supper this evening?"

The sense of power intoxicated her. Foyle was no great physical specimen, but he was well off, respected, and he wanted her. A white man wanted her. It couldn't be clearer. She had changed; her life had changed. She was grateful to Dr. Erasmus Foyle.

Not as grateful as he wished her to be, however.

"I should love that, but how would it be construed by your wife?"

"My—? Dear woman, I have never mentioned—"

"No. Another nurse did."

His pink changed to red. "Damn her. Which one?"

"Actually, it was several. In this hospital and also in the one previous to this. Your reputation for protecting your wife's good name is widespread. They say you protect it so zealously, hardly anyone knows she exists."

Taking wicked delight in his reaction, she lifted her right arm, a peremptory signal that he should remove his hand. He was too astonished. She did it for him, dropping the hand as if it were soiled.

"I'm flattered by your attentions, Dr. Foyle, but I think we should return to our duties."

"Attentions? What attentions?" He snarled it. "I wanted a private discussion on a medical matter, nothing more." He jerked down the front of his blue coat, adjusted his sash, and quick-marched into the ballroom. In other circumstances Virgilia would have laughed.

"Well, Miss Alcott?" Virgilia asked when the tired nurses ate their first full meal, at eight that night. They had worked without interruption. "What do you think of the nursing service?"

Worn out and irritable, Louisa Alcott said, "How candid may I be?"

"As candid as you wish. We are all volunteers—all equal."

"Well, then—to begin—this place is a pesthole. The mattresses are hard as plaster, the bedding's filthy, the air putrid, and the food—have you tasted this beef? It must have been put up for the boys of '76. The pork brought out for supper might be a secret weapon of the enemy, it looked so terrible. And the stewed black-berries more closely resembled stewed cockroaches."

She was so emphatic she generated laughter among the women on both sides of the trestle table. She looked tearful, then laughed, too.

Virgilia said, "We know all that, Miss Alcott. The question is—will you stick?"

"Oh, yes, Miss Hazard. I may not be experienced at bathing naked men—at least I was not until today—but I shall definitely stick." As if to prove it, she put a chunk of the beef in her mouth and chewed.

The familiar hospital sounds crept to Virgilia in her room that night. Cries of pain. The weeping of grown men. A woman on duty singing a lullaby.

She was restless, remembering the awkward, seriocomical encounter with Foyle. How marvelous that he had wanted her. Not a field hand, not some fugitive, but a respectable white man. She had today discovered a truth only suspected before. Her body had a power over men, and because of that, she had power as a person. The discovery was as dazzling as a display of rockets on Independence Day.

Sometime in the future, when she met a man more solid and worthy than the randy little surgeon, she would put the new-found power to use. To lift herself higher than she had ever thought possible. To help her find a place to play a truly important part in the final crushing of the South.

In the dark, she slipped her hands down to her breasts and squeezed. She began to cry, the tears streaming while she smiled an exalted smile no one could see.

62

That same Tuesday, the day on which General Banks was to relieve General Butler in New Orleans, Elkanah Bent was summoned before the old commandant at eleven o'clock. He had been steeling himself for an inquiry about the brawl at Madame Conti's but hadn't expected the inquiry officer to be the general himself.

"A fine business to deal with on my last day with the department." Petulant, Butler whacked a file in front of him. Bent was numb. A bad tone was already set, and he hadn't said a word.

Ben Butler was a squat, round man, bald and perpetually squinting. His eyes went different ways, and subordinates joked that if you looked at the wrong one, the bad one, he would demote you. He seemed in that kind of mood now.

"I suppose it never occurred to you that the proprietress of the house would file a complaint with the civil authorities and with me as well?"

"General, I—" Bent tried to strengthen his voice but couldn't. "Sir, I plead guilty to effecting rough justice. But the woman is a prostitute, no matter how grand her manners. Her employees insulted you, then attacked me." He fingered the healing nail marks. "When I and others protested, she provoked us with more insults. I admit matters got somewhat out of control—"

"That's putting a nice gloss on it," Butler interrupted, squinting harder than ever. His voice had the nasal quality Bent associated with New England. "You totally destroyed the place. To go by the book, I should request that General Banks convene a court-martial."

Bent almost fainted. Seconds went by. Then Butler said, "Personally, I would prefer to exonerate you completely." Buoyed, Bent was quickly cast down again: "Can't do it, though. You're one reason, she's the other."

Confused, Bent muttered, "Sir?"

"Plain enough, isn't it? It is because of your record that I can't extend leniency." He opened the file and removed several pages; the topmost ones had yellowed. "It's covered with blemishes, and you have now added another. As for the woman, of course you're right; she's a prostitute, and I know she's vilified me more than once. But if I hanged everyone who did that, there'd be no more hemp in the Northern Hemisphere."

Bent's forehead began to ooze and glisten. With a grunt, Butler launched himself from his chair. Hands behind his back and paunch preceding him, he walked in small circles, like a pigeon.

"Unfortunately, Madame Conti's charges run deeper than inciting to vandalism, which is bad enough. She accuses you of theft of a valuable painting. She accuses you of assault on her person in order to accomplish that theft."

"Both—damned lies." He gulped.

"You deny the charges?"

"On my honor, General. On my sacred oath as an officer of the United States Army."

Butler knuckled his mustache, chewed his lip, stepped in a circle again. "She won't like that. She hinted that if she could get her property back, she might drop the charges."

Something told Bent it was a critical moment. Told him to attack or he'd be finished. "General—if I am not speaking out of turn—why is it necessary to accommodate in any way a woman who is both a traitor and disreputable?"

"That's the point," Butler exclaimed crossly. "She isn't as disreputable as one might expect. Her family goes back generations in this town. Haven't you ever noticed the street in the old quarter that bears her last name?" Of course he had, but he had drawn no conclusions from it. "What I'm telling you, Colonel, is that some of Madame Conti's clients are also friends and highly placed in

460

the municipal government. They're men I dislike but men I was forced to depend upon to keep the city running. General Banks is in the same unfortunate position. So I have to throw her a bone, don't you see?"

That was it, then; accommodation with traitors. In the wake of the realization came rage. Butler, meantime, sank back into his chair, a little comic-opera man. Ludicrous.

But he had dangerous power.

"I suppose I could put you in command of a black regiment"— Bent almost fainted a second time—"but I doubt Madame Conti knows I can't find white officers for that duty. She wouldn't see the nicety of the punishment. Regrettably, I must find a more visible alternative."

From under the contents of the file—the record of humiliations and reversals engineered by others—Butler plucked a crisp new sheet, the ink stark black. He spun the order around and laid it on the desk for Bent to read. The junior officer was too dazed and upset.

"Effective today, your brevet is revoked. That will keep the bitch from barking till I get out of town. Someone from General Banks's staff will speak to you about financial reparations. I am afraid you may spend the rest of your army career paying for this little escapade, Lieutenant Bent. Dismissed."

Lieutenant Bent? After sixteen years, he was to be reduced to the rank he had when he came out of the Academy? "No, by God," he shouted to the disordered room near the mint. He hauled his travel trunk from a cluttered alcove and kicked the lid open. He packed a few books, a miniature of Starkwether, and, last, cushioned by suits of cotton underwear, carefully rolled, wrapped in oiled paper, and tied, the painting. Into the trunk went everything he owned except one civilian suit, a broad-brimmed hat he had purchased an hour after leaving Butler, and all of his uniforms, which he left in a heap on the floor.

Sheets of rain swept the levee, lit from behind by glares of blue-white light. The storm shook the ground, shivered the slippery incline, dimmed the yellow windows of the city.

"Watch that trunk, boy," Bent yelled to the old Negro dragging it up the rope-railed gangway ahead of him. Rain dripped from his hat brim as he staggered aboard *Galena* in the light-headed

461

state which had persisted since his interview yesterday. His military dreams lay in pieces, ruined by jealous, vindictive enemies. He had chosen to desert rather than serve an army that betrayed years of loyalty and hard work with demotion. He was fearful of discovery but awash with hatreds surpassing any experienced in the past.

A terrifying figure with a blue halation blocked him at the head of the gangway. *Calm down, else they'll suspect, you'll be caught, and Banks will hang you.*

"Sir?" rumbled a voice as the halation faded and the thunder, too. Relieved, Bent saw it was merely the purser of the steamship, holding a damp list in the hand protruding from his slicker. "Your name?"

"Benton. Edward Benton."

"Happy to see you, Mr. Benton. You're the last passenger to come aboard. Cabin three, on the deck above."

The wind roared. Bent stepped away from the exposed rail, but the rain found him anyway. He shouted, "How soon do we leave?"

"Within half an hour."

Half an hour. Christ. Could he hold out?

"The storm won't delay us?"

"We'll be bound for Head of Passes and the gulf on schedule, sir."

"Good. Excellent." The wind tore the words away. He groped for the rail of the stair, lost his footing, and almost fell. He spewed obscenities into the storm. The purser rushed to him.

"You all right, Mr. Benton?"

"Fine." The man hovered. Bent wanted no undue notice. "Fine!" The purser withdrew, quickly gone in the dark.

It required both hands on the slippery rail to drag his tired body up the stairs toward the safety of his cabin. What did he have left? Nothing but the painting, hate, and a determination that his enemies would not succeed in destroying him.

No—lightning; his eyes shone like wet rocks as he heaved and pulled himself upward in the rain—*oh, no.* He would survive and destroy them first. Somehow.

Still weak from his sickness, Billy went down to the river again. Under the protection of muskets and artillery, he helped dismantle the bridge he had built. He felt he was committing an act of

462

desecration. He told himself he was taking the military defeat too personally. He couldn't help it.

The pontoon wagons vanished into the winter dark. Encamped at Falmouth again, he wanted to write Brett but feared to do it. He wrote in the journal instead.

Bitter cold again this evening. Someone is singing "Home, Sweet Home," a mournful and curiously ominous refrain, given our place and plight. This week alone, our support regiments have lost a score of men by desertion. It is the same through the entire army. They steal away homeward, disheartened. Even Lije F. prays privately and seldom quotes Scripture any longer. He knows the exhortations and promises ring false. Burnside is done, they say. There is much speculation about his replacement. The bitterest say things like "Oh, don't let your faith waver, boys. They have dozens of equally stupid generals waiting in Washington." Then they reel off a list of mock courses those officers took at West Point: "Principles of Bungling," "Fundamentals of Foolhardiness." It is a terrible medicine to swallow without protest. We might as well be encamped at the rim of the cosmos, so dismal and remote do these huts seem as Christmas nears. Look about and the eye falls upon an unbroken landscape of confusion and cupidity. My men have not been paid for six months. Down in New Orleans, if we may believe the occasional Richmond paper which comes across the river when the pickets make their exchanges—coffee going south, tobacco coming north—General Butler and his brother are busy stealing cotton for personal gain. General Grant occupies himself with ordering all Jews out of his military department—accusing them, as a class, of speculation and lawbreaking. A cabal of Republican senators is said to be agitating for the heads of Mr. Chase and Mr. Seward. Where in God's name is there one iota of concern for this disgraced army? Where is one man whose whole energy is given over to the task of finding generals who can lead us from this swamp of failure in which blunder after blunder has mired us, seemingly for eternity?

If you ever read these scribblings, dear wife, you will know how much I love and need you at this moment. But I dare not try to say it in a missive because other things would surely creep in, and you would be forced to assume part of a burden which is properly mine—the burden of men who feel abandoned, who dare not say aloud that they have no hope.

63

Two nights before Christmas, Charles rode to Barclay's Farm at dusk. A bag made of coarse netting hung from his saddle. The bag held a fine Westphalia ham taken from Yankee stores captured on recent night raids north of the river.

The evening had an eerie quality. The bare limbs, bushes, and roadside fences glittered like glass. It had rained last night while the temperature dropped.

Most of the clouds had gone now; the sky in the west had a purple cast, pale near the tree line, darker above. The moon was visible, a gray sphere with a thin crescent of brilliance on the bottom. There was enough light for Charles to discern the ice-covered farmhouse and the two red oaks standing like strange crystal sculptures.

Sport proceeded at a walk; the road was treacherous. Charles's beard reached well below his collar, and his teeth shone in the midst of it. Anticipation put the smile on his face and helped banish the memories of Sharpsburg that were with him so often. He had never received the promised commendation for helping to move the Blakely gun on the battlefield. Either the major had forgotten Charles's name or unit or, more likely, he had been one of the thousands who had not survived what was the single bloodiest day of the war. This was his first opportunity to visit the farm in months, even though the cavalry had been camped not far away, over in Stevensburg, for several weeks. With his scouts and picked bands of troopers, Hampton had been in the saddle almost constantly since, raiding above the Rappahannock.

Night ghosts, they drifted behind enemy lines and took a hundred horses and nearly as many men at Hartwood Church; rode up the Telegraph Road, cut the enemy wire to Washington, and seized wagons at the supply base at Dumfries; rode again, hoping to go fifteen miles, all the way to Occoquan, only to be forced around when an entire regiment of Yankee horse materialized against them. They escaped with twenty wagons loaded with sutler's delicacies: pickled oysters, sugar and lemons, nuts and brandy, and the hams, one of which he had commandeered as a present for Gus. It would be a hearty Christmas celebration at the encampment, though a short one. Charles had to be back by Christmas night, because Hampton proposed to return to enemy territory the following day.

During the weeks of riding and fighting in snow and thaw, pressure against the town of Fredericksburg had mounted, culminating in savage battle and Burnside's defeat. Charles worried constantly about Gus's safety. If Hampton's lean scavengers crossed the Rappahannock to raid, Union detachments could do the same coming the other way. He had tried to find someone who could tell him whether the Fredericksburg fighting had reached as far as Barclay's Farm, and finally learned it had not.

On the road, he experienced a surge of relief. She was there. Transparent smoke rose up to vanish in the starlight. Unseen lamps brightened the rear of the house and shone from the half-open door of the small barn nearest it.

"Sport," he growled, sharply reining the gelding on a crust of ice, which crackled. Hunching forward, he inhaled the piercing air. Lamplight in the barn at this hour?

Tied to the pump, which had a gleaming stalactite at the spout, were two horses. He supposed there was an innocent explanation, yet the sight of them so close to enemy positions across the river set him on edge. He dismounted in the center of the road, led Sport to the side, and tied him to a fence rail. The gray stamped and blew warm breath that plumed in the cold.

Charles set off on foot for the farmhouse, a short walk of a hundred yards. In the silence, his spurs jingled like tiny bells stirred by a breeze. He crouched and with some difficulty removed them. All of this continued to strike him as slightly foolish; he would say nothing to Gus when her callers turned out to be neighbors.

Still—why was that barn door open? And Washington and Boz nowhere to be seen?

Where the fence ended and the dooryard began, Charles paused to study the horses. Old riding saddles, neither Grimsleys nor McClellans, told him nothing. He stole toward the house, whose ice-covered shakes flashed back the light of the moon for a moment. He was conscious of each crunch and crinkle underfoot; he couldn't avoid a certain amount of noise, no matter how carefully he trod.

The horses grew aware of him, shifted and stamped softly. He held still near the house, listening.

He heard laughter. But not hers. It came from the owners of the horses.

One of the animals stepped to the side, whinnying. Charles held his breath. The laughter stopped. Perhaps that had no connection with the horses. He might be imagining the whole—

The horses had changed position, giving him an unobstructed view of the barn. Inside, outstretched legs projected into his line of sight. The ankles were lashed with rope. The parson and his wife didn't tie people when they called, did they? They didn't visit on a night so brutally cold, did they?

He leaned against the house, his heart beating at frantic speed. Gus was threatened. The woman he cared about was inside— threatened.

Backed against the building, he knew how much he loved her. So deep was the reverse of that emotion, his fear for her, he couldn't move for half a minute. His mind was in confusion. Suppose he took rash action and got her killed?

Another minute went by. Do something, damn you. *Do something.*

He broke free of the numbing confusion and pictured the back porch. He didn't dare enter that way. It would be ice-covered, noisy. He twisted his head toward the road. The red oaks. Great climbing trees. Could he reach one of the dormers and prize it open? If so, he had a chance of surprising the men holding Gus in the kitchen or one of the back rooms. That they were Yankees he now took as a certainty. Everything depended on surprise and silence.

466

He stole to the front of the house and over to the stoop, where he sat and jerked off his boots. Then, crossing the porch, he slowly turned and tested the doorknob.

Locked. All right, it had been a faint hope anyway.

He put his filthy right sock onto the top step, and his whole body tilted wildly. He went flying off the steps; the edge of one cracked him across his spine. He bit back a yell but made a loud bump. He rolled on his side on the hard ground, listening—

After a few seconds, he exhaled. They hadn't heard the noise. He had to be more careful. The ice was everywhere.

Under the tree, he stretched, grabbed, threw a leg over, and pulled himself up on the lowest limb. From there on it wasn't so easy. He wasn't clinging to bark with his knees and elbows, his gauntlets and filthy socks; he was clinging to frozen grease. He went up with excruciating slowness and nearly fell three times. Finally he reached a large branch that hung over the roof.

Taking hold of a thinner one above it, he stood up, then began to move along the icy branch, sliding his right foot toward the house a few inches, then his left one, then his right again. Progress was slow because of the cold; he had lost nearly all feeling below his ankles.

Save for the stars and the crescent moon, the sky was black from horizon to horizon. Balanced on the branch near one of the dormers, he studied the situation. He would have to lean out, grasp the dormer peak, and hope he could hang on. Attempting to stand or kneel on the roof itself would be futile because of the slope and the ice.

He swallowed. Extended his hand. Stretched—

His fingers were three inches short of the peak.

Still holding the limb above, he stepped six inches nearer the house. The branch sagged, began to crack. "Holy hell," he whispered, gambling, letting go and flinging both hands forward. He felt himself falling, caught hold of the peak. The sudden weight shot excruciating pain along his arms. His knees banged the shakes of the dormer. They would hear that all the way to the Floridas.

He hung from the peak by both hands, then removed his right one, reaching downward to the window.

He tugged. Nothing.

Again. Nothing.

Locked, goddamn it. He let out an enraged groan and yanked a third time, thinking he would have to smash his fist through—

The window rose an inch.

His left hand slipped on the peak, but he held on, panting. He slipped his other hand under the window and slowly, slowly pulled it up far enough to allow him to swing through into the dry, chill dark of some cobwebby place. Eyes closed, he rested on his knees. He felt tremors in his quaking left arm.

He waited until a little of that passed. His vision adjusted, and he picked out certain shapes: trunks, an old dress form. This was an attic. A pale oblong showed where the stairs descended to the house proper.

He heard laughter again, then blurred words from Gus. She sounded angry. Next came a smacking sound. She retorted, still angry. A second smack silenced her. He almost felt the blow himself.

He controlled his rage and stood up cautiously, so as not to creak the floor or thump a beam with his head. He stripped off his gloves, blew on his fingers, flexed them, blew again until he felt circulation returning. He unbuttoned his old farmer's coat and eased the loaded Colt from the tied-down holster.

He advanced to the stairs and crept down, a silent step at a time. The anger thickened, possessing him. At the bottom, he took half a minute to twist the handle, ease the door open—no squeak, thank the Lord—and slide through to the warm hall.

To the right, the kitchen doorway. The voices were distinct.

"Meant to ask you, Bud. You ever been with a female?"

"No, Sarge." That voice was light; the speaker sounded younger than the previous one, who seemed to have an accumulation of phlegm in his throat.

"Well, m' lad, we'll change that pretty quick."

Charles moved, sliding toward the kitchen, his back to the wall.

"Ever spied a plumper pair of tits, Bud?"

"No, *sir.*"

"Want to take a look at them 'fore we start the real festivities?"

"If you do, Sarge."

"Oh, yessiree, I do. Sit still, missy."

"Get away from me." Charles was a yard from the door when Gus said that.

"You be quiet, missy. I wouldn't want to bruise up a pretty

468

little reb like you, but I'm gonna open that dress and have a look at them plump things hangin'—"

Charles lunged to the doorway, thumb and finger of his gun hand ready as he spied the two Yanks. Neither wore a uniform—scouts, then, like himself.

The nearest, a blue-eyed youngster with a scraggly yellow mustache, saw him first. *"Sarge!"*

The older Yankee blocked his view of Gus, who was evidently seated in a chair. Charles stepped into the room and thoughtlessly made an error; he jumped a pace to the right to see if she was hurt.

"Gus, are you—?"

Almost too late, he saw what he had missed before—the horse pistol in the waistband of the younger Yank. Out it came, looming huge. Charles fell to his knees and fired at the same time as the younger man.

Only the drop saved him. The Yankee ball passed over his head. His ball flew into the boy's open mouth and through the back of his head, carrying parts of it and splattering them on the wall. Gus screamed. The sergeant goggled at the boy blown backward against the stove. Then he stared at Charles on one knee, his Colt curling out smoke.

The sergeant was scared and consequently slow. Even while he groped for his side arm, he realized he had no time. Wetting himself, he staggered on a crooked path to the back door.

Charles lunged forward, next to Gus's chair, and aimed at the man's back. "You piece of Yankee shit." He squeezed the trigger and simultaneously Gus pulled his arm.

The ball went low, hitting the sergeant's left leg. With a yell he pitched through the door he had opened a moment earlier. He slid belly down across the porch and dropped off the edge, leaving a blood-swath on the ice.

"I'm going to kill the—"

"Charles."

Pale, she gripped his arm and gazed at him, unable to countenance what she saw. The fever in his eyes, the death's-head expression—

"Charles, I'm all right. Let him go."

"But he may—"

They heard a horse whinny, weight on it suddenly. It went clattering toward the road. Boz and Washington shouted from the barn. Slowly, Charles released the hammer of the Colt and laid the gun on the table. He was shaking.

He grasped the shoulders of her plain dress, leaned down. "I've never shot a man in the back, but I'd have shot that one. You certain you're all right?"

A small nod. "Are you?"

"Yes." The madman's glint was dimming; his facial muscles relaxed. He knelt and freed the ropes they had wound around her and the chair. Yes, she said, they were scouts, unable to resist a bit of foraging in a warm place.

"When you stormed through that door, I thought I'd taken leave of my senses." She managed a broken laugh, standing, stretching. "I thought it was a vision. It's been so long since I've seen you."

"I sent letters."

"I got them. I sent some, too. Half a dozen."

"Did you?" The start of a smile.

"You received them, didn't you?"

"Not a one. But that's all right. I'd better go to the barn and untie your men. Sport's down the road—my spurs, too. My gauntlets are in the attic. I came in by the roof. I'm strung out all over this farm." His mood swinging wildly back to elation, he left the house across the bloody ice.

An hour later, down to his long underwear and bundled in three blankets, he rested by the great hearth. The Westphalia ham reposed on the chopping block. Gus had scrubbed the wall, and the boy's corpse was gone; Washington and Boz had seen to that, after repeatedly shaking Charles's hand and thanking him for saving their mistress and them.

Shivering, Charles stared at the fire, still astounded by his own behavior. He had shot a stripling without a qualm about the victim's age. Then he had been ready, even eager, to kill the sergeant with a bullet in the back—and not on a battlefield, but in a kitchen. Those were extreme and alarming changes. What was happening in this damned war? What was happening to him?

He tried to puzzle it out. It was the duty of a soldier to destroy the enemy, but not with pleasure. Not without some human feeling other than rage. The boy with the scraggly mustache wasn't a counter on a board or a figure in a report. There were parents, a home, innocent ambitions, perhaps a sweetheart—none of that had entered his head until this minute. All he had wanted to do

470

was shoot, as casually as if the target were some game bird in an autumn field.

Gus returned to the kitchen, moving straight to his side. "What's wrong?"

"Nothing."

"You looked frightful when I walked in."

"Cold, that's all."

"Can you spend Christmas?"

"If you want me to."

"Want you to—oh, Charles," she cried as the firelight shimmered on the walls, revealing one stain not quite wiped away. "I was so frightened during the fighting in town. I lay awake listening to the guns and wondering where you were." She knelt in front of him, resting her forearms on his blanketed knees, her face soft, damp, no defenses in place. "What have you done to me, Charles Main? I love you—oh, my God, I can't believe how much I love you," she exclaimed, reaching up, pulling him down to a kiss.

With his arm around her, he led her along the hall, worried about his dirty underwear. Her room was cold. They tumbled into bed, groping for one another. "Gus, I need a bath before—"

"Later. Hold me, Charles. I want to forget how that poor boy died."

"He was a damned evil boy."

"He thought he was punishing the enemy."

"There's no manual prescribing the kind of punishment they wanted to inflict on you."

"Well, it was horrible, but it's over, so do stop debating and love me as hard as—what's this?"

Her fingers had found the leather bag. She insisted on lighting a candle while he unbuttoned his underwear and, after some coaxing, slipped the thong over his head and handed her the bag.

Delight spread over her face as she opened it. "You've kept the book with you all this time?" The smile vanished. "The book was hit. You were hit. This is a bullet."

"What's left of it. Mr. Pope saved my life at Sharpsburg."

She burst into tears, seized him, began raining kisses on him. They pulled each other's clothes off. The coupling was quick, almost desperate, with a certain clumsiness because the shock of earlier events still lingered. In less than five minutes he fell away from her and fell asleep.

He woke an hour later to find her jogging his shoulder. "Hot water's in the tub." She had donned a robe, had better color. Her hair, undone, hung nearly to her waist. "I'll wash your back, and we'll go to bed again."

This time, less numb and stunned, Charles lay with her in the cave of warmth beneath the comforter. She kissed his eyes and beard. His hand touched and played with each round breast, then strayed lower. She gripped his wrist and pressed.

Their breathing quickened. Yet there were warnings in his head on this night of shocks and changes.

"Are you sure we should go on? I'm a soldier—I can't get here for months at a time—"

"I know what you are," she said, caressing gently in the dark.

"Do you? I could ride away and never get back."

"Don't say such things."

"Have to, Gus. I'll get out of this bed this minute if you think I should."

"Do you want that?"

"God, no."

"I don't either." Kissing him. Touching him. Rousing him to such rigidity he hurt. "I know the times are fearful and danger-ous. We must accept Pope's advice—" Her mouth slipped across his bearded face, found his lips, opened. Tongues wet and loving touched a moment.

"What's that?"

" 'Whatever is—is right.' " Another deep, long kiss. "Love me, Charles."

He did, and toward the end, she hung her head back and breathed, "I want you always. Always, always."

"I love you, Gus."

"I love you, Charles."

"—love you—"

"—love you—"

"—love—"

The word cycled up the scale like human music as he pushed to the center of her, and she rose and cried her joy in a voice that shook the room.

Still later, deep in the night, she slept against his shoulder, making occasional small sounds. They had shared themselves a

472

third time, and she had closed her eyes afterward. He couldn't seem to doze or even calm down. What he had done tonight, learned tonight, kept his eyes open and his heart beating much too fast for a man in the soft aftermath of love.

He was fearful because his feelings were no longer hidden. He knew he loved her when he stood by the house unable to force himself to action for a few moments because he cared so much.

Then his emotions rendered him mistake-prone. In the kitchen he looked at Gus first, instead of at the young Yank. In the army he had seen men rendered impotent as soldiers by worry over loved ones. The worst cases deserted. He held them in contempt. But after his own near-fatal error, how could he? How was he different?

Finally, and perhaps worst, he had been prepared to kill the coward's way, with a ruthless joy, and to do it in a place supposedly safe from violence and all of the other spreading poisons of the war.

You oughtn't to be here. But how could he be anywhere else? He had been falling in love since he first saw her.

How was it possible to be so fulfilled and so torn? He saw the conflict in a homely little mind picture: two liquids from an apothecary's shelf poured into a mortar and swirled with a pestle.

He loved Gus. She was passion, peace, merriment, contemplation, companionship. He admired her nature, he wanted her physically, she was everything he had ever desired in a woman without expecting to find it.

But there was Hampton, and the Yankees.

The pestle swirled. The hours went by. The apothecary's hopes counted for nothing. The liquids would not mix.

Problem was, he couldn't give up as easily as an apothecary could. Couldn't give up Gus and couldn't give up his duty. Love and war were opposite states, and he was inescapably caught in both. He had no choice except to go forward, wherever the disparate forces might carry him—and her.

Full of foreboding he slipped his arm under her warm shoulders and held her close.

BOOK FOUR

"LET US DIE TO MAKE MEN FREE"

I would like to see the North win, but as to any interest in . . . supporting the Emancipation Proclamation I in common with every other officer and soldier in the army wash my hands of it. I came out to fight for the restoration of the Union . . . and not to free the niggers.

A UNION SOLDIER, 1863

64

"Social suicide," he said when she proposed the idea. "Even for an abolitionist like you."

"Do you think I care about that? It's a fitting place to be tomorrow night."

"I agree. I'll take you."

So here they were, George and his Roman Catholic wife, seated in one of the gold-trimmed pews of the Fifteenth Street Presbyterian Church. Only a third of the candles in the chandeliers had been lit, for this was an hour of meditation, an hour to look backward and ahead. The choir hummed the "Battle Hymn" while the minister stood with head bowed, black hands gripping the marble of the pulpit. His short message to the worshipers, most of them members of the affluent Negro congregation—there were no more than a dozen whites present—had been drawn from Exodus 13: *And Moses said unto the people, Remember this day, in which ye came out from Egypt, out of the house of bondage.*

Midnight was near. Though not a religious man, George was moved by the experience of sitting here and seeing the dark faces upturned, many showing tears, and some with expressions approaching rapture. A shiver down his spine, he reached for his wife's hand and clasped it tightly.

All across the North, similar watch-night services were being held to observe the coming of the new year. In the morning Lincoln would sign the proclamation. George felt tension grow as the final minute passed. The choir fell silent, and the entire church. Then, in the steeple, the first bell note.

The minister raised his head and hands. "O Lord our God, it has come. Thou hast delivered us. Jubilo at last."

"Yes, jubilo." "Amen!" "Praise God!" Throughout the church, men and women proclaimed their joy, and the sound of the bell seemed to swell. The shiver rippled down George's back again. Constance had tears in her eyes.

The bell pealed, soon overlaid by a counterpoint of other bells in other churches ringing through the starry dark. The joyful exclamations grew louder. George felt like shouting too. Then suddenly, sickeningly, like a hailstorm, rocks struck the church. He heard epithets, obscenities.

Several men jumped up, George among them. He and two whites and half a dozen blacks stormed up the aisle. The hooligans were jeering shadows on the run by the time the men reached the steps.

George shoved his dress saber back in its scabbard, listening to the bells chime across the black arch of winter sky. The brief exaltation had passed. The rock-throwing brought him back to the realities of this first day of 1863.

Although the mood of the worship service had been broken, nothing could cancel the power of it. That was clear from the faces of the men and women scattering to the carriages left in the care of little black boys bundled against the cold. Rattling homeward to Georgetown through deserted streets, Constance snuggled close and said, "Are you happy we went?"

"Very much so."

"You looked so grave toward the end of the service. Why?"

"I was speculating. I wonder if anyone, Lincoln included, knows precisely what this proclamation portends for the country."

"I certainly don't."

"Nor I. But as I sat there, I had the oddest feeling about the war. I'm not certain the term war applies any longer."

"If it isn't a war, what is it?"

"A revolution."

Silently, Constance clung to his arm as they absorbed the bite of the wind. George had preferred to drive tonight rather than ask one of their hired Negro freedmen to be absent from his family. The bells kept tolling, ringing their knell of changes across the city and the nation.

Washington had undergone drastic change in the months the

Hazards had lived there. Business had seldom been better, but that was true everywhere in the North. Hazard's was operating at capacity, and the Bank of Lehigh Station, opened in October, was enjoying great success.

Scores of European immigrants, attracted in spite of the conflict—or perhaps because of it; war brought boom times—added to the general overcrowding in Washington. The martial spirit of the early days was gone, washed away by bloodshed in the great battles lost by the Union. No elegant uniforms could be seen on parade on the mall; no military bands performed for the public. At book and novelty stores, people bought Confederate bank notes and kepis picked up by souvenir hunters after Second Bull Run. They paid with government promissory notes; with Treasury-issued fractional currency—green-backed bills in denominations under a dollar, derisively called shinplasterers; or with wartime coins minted by private firms and bearing their advertising. They accepted the presence of black waiters at Willard's—all the white regulars had enlisted—and they accepted the presence of maimed veterans wandering everywhere.

At the start of the war, everyone had agreed that Washington was a Southern city. Only a few months ago, however, Richard Wallach, brother of the owner of the *Star,* had been elected mayor. Wallach was an Unconditional Union Democrat, who wanted the war prosecuted fully to the end, unlike those in the peace wing of his party. Copperheads, some called the peace Democrats; poisonous snakes.

Emancipation had come to the District last April. Stanley and Isabel were in the forefront of those promoting it, although at one of the rare and difficult suppers arranged by the two Hazard wives to maintain a pretense of family harmony, Isabel had stated that emancipation would turn the city into "a hell on earth for the white race." It hadn't exactly worked that way. Almost daily, white soldiers fell on some black contraband and beat or maimed him or her, without subsequent punishment. Negroes weren't permitted to ride the new street railway cars shuttling along Pennsylvania Avenue between the Capitol and the State Department. Isabel deplored such bigoted behavior when paying court to her radical friends.

In the demoralized army, change was certain. Encamped on the Rappahannock, Burnside kept planning winter advances against all advice. He was wild to redeem his failure at Fredericksburg.

On more than one occasion, George had heard senior officers say Burnside had lost his mind.

Fighting Joe Hooker was most frequently mentioned as Burnside's replacement. Whoever took command faced a monumental job of reorganizing the army and restoring pride and discipline. Some regiments refused to march past the Executive Mansion, but would go out of their way to reach McClellan's residence on H Street, where they would cheer as they went by or sing a popular song praising the general. There were some blacks in the army now. Like the contrabands, they were beaten frequently, and were paid three dollars less per month for the same duty than their white counterparts.

In the executive branch, change was likewise a virtual certainty in this new year. The congressional elections had gone badly for the Republicans, and the melancholy President held office in an atmosphere of mounting disfavor. Lincoln was blamed for all the military defeats and called everything from a "country cretin" to a "fawning Negrophile."

So change was in the air—needed, unwanted, immutable. Sometimes, as in the Presbyterian church, just imagining possible futures made George's head ache.

When they reached home, Constance looked in on the sleeping children, then prepared hot cocoa for George. As she waited for water to boil, she reread her father's letter. It had arrived yesterday.

Patrick Flynn had reached California in the autumn. He found a land of sunny somnolence, remote from the war. In '61 there had been rumors of revolt and a Pacific Confederacy, but those had died out. Flynn reported that his new legal practice in Los Angeles brought him virtually no money, but he was happy. How he survived, he didn't say, but his daughter's fears about his safety were eased.

She carried the cocoa to George in the library. She was tired but he, wearing just his uniform trousers with braces and his shirt with sleeves rolled to the elbows, looked exhausted. He had turned the gas up full and spread sheets of paper in front of the inkstand. Some bore writing; some were blank.

She set the cocoa down. "Will you be long?"

"As long as it takes to finish this. I must show it to Senator Sherman tomorrow—that is, today—at the President's reception."

479

"Must we go? Those affairs are horrid. So many people, it's impossible to move."

"I know, but Sherman expects me. He's promised me an introduction to Senator Wilson of Massachusetts. Wilson's chairman of the Military Affairs Committee. An ally we very badly need."

"How soon will the appropriations bill be introduced?"

"In the House, within two weeks. The real fight comes in the Senate. We don't have much time."

Bending over him where he had sunk into a chair, she touched his hair tenderly. "You're a remarkable zealot for a man who never liked soldiering."

"I still don't like it, but I love West Point, though I didn't know it till long after I graduated."

She kissed his brow. "Come to bed as soon as you can."

He nodded absently. He never saw her leave.

He inked his pen and resumed work on the article he had agreed to write for the *New York Times,* one of the Academy's staunch defenders. The piece was a rebuttal of a favorite argument of Senator Wade, namely, that West Point should be abolished because two hundred out of eight hundred and twenty regular officers in the army in 1861 had resigned to join the Confederacy.

If that is sufficient reason to dismantle worthy institutions, George wrote under the gaslight, *we must perforce carry it into other spheres and, recollecting the divers senators and representatives who similarly resigned—among them Mr. Jefferson Davis, whom Senator Wade characterizes as "the arch-rebel, the arch-fiend of this rebellion"—dismantle our national legislative bodies, for they, too, have bred traitors. In this context, Senator Wade's argument can be seen for what it is—specious and demagogic.*

He would make enemies with those last three words. He didn't give a damn. The battle had been joined, and a powerful cabal meant to bury the Academy permanently this year. Led by Wade, the cabal included Lyman Trumbull of Illinois and James Lane of Kansas. Senator Lane was so confident, he was boasting of West Point's demise all over Washington.

Sipping cold cocoa, George wrote on, shivering as the house cooled, yawning against fatigue, firing verbal cannonades in the small war whose outcome he deemed almost as vital to the nation as that of the larger one. He wrote on into the new morning of the new year, until he fell asleep on top of his manuscript around five, a strand of his hair lying across the nib of his discarded pen and getting inky.

"Yes, I'm happy to say she'll be joining me soon," Orry told the President. In his right hand he held a punch cup, but he had declined a plate. Dexterous as he had become, he still could not eat and drink at the same time. "It's entirely possible that she's on her way right now."

The President's appearance disturbed Orry. He was paler than ever, haggard, with the tight, slightly hunched posture of a man in pain. Much more than neuralgia bedeviled Jefferson Davis these days. His cotton embargo was a failure despite a shortage in British mills. Diplomatic recognition in Europe was no longer even a remote hope. Critics sniped at him for continuing to support the unpopular Bragg in the West and for causing shortages at home. In Richmond, coffee had been almost completely replaced by vile concoctions of okra or sweet potatoes or watermelon seeds sweetened with sorghum. Messages were starting to appear, slashed in paint on city walls: STOP THE WAR. UNION AGAIN!

This New Year's afternoon, officers, men in civilian clothes, and many women packed the official residence on Clay Street in the distinguished old Court End neighborhood. Davis strove to fix his entire attention on each guest, if only briefly. Despite his tribulations, his smile and manner were full of warmth:

"Good news indeed, Colonel. You hoped to have her in Richmond long before this, I recall."

"She was to join me early last year, but the plantation was struck with a series of misfortunes." He mentioned his mother's seizure but not the increasing problem of runaways. Davis inquired about Clarissa. Orry said she had regained most of her physical faculties.

Then Davis asked: "How are you getting on with Mr. Seddon?"

"Fine, sir. I'm aware of his outstanding reputation as a lawyer here in Richmond."

That was all Orry would say. James Seddon of Goochland County had replaced General Gustavus Smith as Secretary of War. Smith had served a total of four days after Randolph resigned in November to accept a commission. Orry disliked the gaunt Seddon's somber disposition and strong secessionist views. Seddon and his wife were here somewhere. He changed the subject.

"Permit me a question in another area, Mr. President. The enemy is arming black troops. Do you feel we might benefit by taking the same course?"

"Do you?"

"Yes, possibly."

Davis's mouth straightened to a tight line. "The idea is pernicious, Colonel. As Mr. Cobb of Georgia observed, if nigras will make good soldiers, our entire theory of slavery is wrong. Excuse me."

And off he went to another guest. Orry felt irritated with Davis; it was a harmful weakness, that inability to entertain opinions different from his own.

He sipped the excessively sweet punch, alone in the large crowd in the central drawing room of the mansion people called the White House because of its exterior layer of plaster on brick. It was a splendid residence, bought by the city and presented to Mr. and Mrs. Davis as a gift. There was a drawing room on the west side and a dining room on the east. There, from high windows behind the refreshment tables, Orry had looked out across Shockoe Valley to Church Hill and winter skies dark as the slate roof of the house.

Behind him, some guests discussed a rumored plot to establish yet a third country on the continent, this new one to be combination of states in the Northwest and upper South. The speakers all sounded agitated, even slightly hysterical. The reception was beginning to depress him. He edged toward the door. Suddenly he heard a voice he recognized—Varina Davis's.

"—and henceforward, my dear, I reserve the right of not returning social calls. That is *my* Fort Sumter—and to the devil with the objections of that pipsqueak editor Pollard."

Orry didn't turn to look at the First Lady, but he heard the strain within her sarcasm. Strain infected this crowd and Richmond like a pestilence.

He, too, had fallen victim. The cause was more than loneliness and longing for Madeline exacerbated by the months of delay. He hated his work in the War Department—the constant battle to curb Winder's excesses in the prisons he supervised and to check the reckless arrest of anyone the general deemed an enemy of the state. Currently, Winder was trying to sniff out members of a highly secret peace society, the Order of the Heroes of America.

A report from a reliable source had informed Orry of Israel

482

Quincy and two other plug-uglies jailing and beating three suspected members. Orry's letter of protest had gone unanswered. A personal visit to Winder's office led to nothing but another nasty exchange with Quincy. The suspects had been released from Castle Thunder solely because Winder decided they knew nothing about the peace society.

Orry thought of Dick Ewell, West Point class of '40, who had lost a leg at Brawner's Farm last August but still led troops in the field. At Fair Oaks in the spring, Oliver Howard, '54, had lost an arm, but the Union high command didn't shunt him to a desk. Perhaps it was time he asked for a transfer to the war's cutting edge.

He worked his way slowly to the entrance hall, where he discovered Judah Benjamin with three admiring women. The Secretary of State hailed him cheerfully, as if the recent widely known unpleasantness had never happened. Benjamin had been nabbed when Winder's detectives swarmed into a Main Street gambling establishment. The raid, meant to net deserters, yielded only some chagrined civilians, including a cabinet member.

"How are you, Orry?" Benjamin asked, shaking his hand.

"I'll be better once Madeline's here. She's on the way at last."

"Capital. We must have dinner as soon as she arrives."

"Yes, certainly," Orry muttered, nodding and passing on. A realization had jolted him. After Madeline had struggled for over a year to reach Richmond, it would be damned unfair of him to request a transfer the moment she arrived. She would understand, but it would be unfair. Maybe he would stick it out a few more months. He mustn't blame anyone but himself for failures in dealing with the provost's men. He would try harder.

Passing by the foot of the great staircase, he stiffened at the sight of three people entering the mansion: his sister, beautifully dressed and pink-faced from the cold; Huntoon; and a third man, in the baggy trousers, fine sack coat, and round, flat-crowned hat that identified so many of his breed.

"Good afternoon, Ashton—James," Orry said as the stranger took off his hat. He hadn't seen either one of them in months.

Huntoon mumbled while looking elsewhere. With a wintry smile, Ashton said, "How delightful to see you," and rushed on to Benjamin. They didn't bother to present the handsome, sleepy-eyed chap with them, but Orry didn't care. To judge by his clothing, the man was one of those who infested the Confederacy like

483

parasites: a speculator. Ashton and her husband were keeping peculiar company.

He jammed his hat on his head and left the White House in a foul mood.

65

At last, Madeline's heart sang, at last—the miracle day. For more than a year, it had seemed a day that would never arrive.

Now, on the same New Year's afternoon that found her husband at the Richmond White House, she closed the last ledger, locked the last trunk, checked the strip of green tickets a tenth time, and took her final tour of the house and grounds. She knew the rail trip to Richmond would be long, dirty, and uncomfortable. She didn't care. She would have detoured through the nether regions with Satan as her seatmate if only it would bring her to Orry.

Her tour done, she knocked at Clarissa's door. The spacious, well-furnished room inevitably inspired sadness within Madeline. Today was no different. Clarissa sat at the tilt-top table beside the window, the table at which she had once designed her intricate family trees, one version after another. The mild sunshine fell on a block of paper that bore a charcoal drawing of a cardinal, sketchy and barely recognizable, like child's work.

"Good afternoon." Clarissa smiled politely but failed to recognize her daughter-in-law. Small signs of the seizure remained: a slight droop at the outer corner of her right eye, a certain slowness of speech and occasional thickness of a word. Otherwise she was recovered, though she seldom used her right hand. It lay in her lap, motionless as the bird on paper.

"Clarissa, I am leaving for Richmond shortly. I'll see your son there."

"My son. Oh, yes. How nice." Her eyes, sun-washed, were blank.

"The house people and Mr. Meek will look after your needs, but I wanted to tell you I was going."

"That's kind of you. I have enjoyed your visit."

Tearful all at once, seeing in the older woman her own mortality, her own probable decay into old age, Madeline flung her arms around Clarissa and hugged her. The precipitous act surprised and alarmed Orry's mother; her white brows shot up, the left one a little higher than the right.

The melancholy light of January, the odors of musty clothes pervading the room—the awareness that a whole year of her life with Orry had slipped away—brought the tears more strongly. I am behaving like an idiot at the very moment I should be happiest, Madeline thought as she hid her face from the smiling, quiet woman. She rushed out.

Downstairs, she spoke briefly with Jane, whom she had put in charge of the house people last summer, agreeing to pay her wages. Then she proceeded down the winding walk toward the small building that by turns had been Tillet's, Orry's, and hers. It was now occupied by the overseer.

Sun shafts pierced down through the Spanish moss, lighting the base of a tree where a slave lounged, snapping a piece of bark into small pieces. He gave her an insolent stare. She stopped on the walk.

"Have you nothing to do, Cuffey?"

"No, ma'am."

"I'll ask Andy to remedy that." She swept on. Andy would not be reluctant to discipline Cuffey; the men loathed each other. Cuffey's presence made Madeline uneasy about leaving.

Last May, Hunter, the general in charge of Yankee enclaves on the coast, had issued a military order emancipating blacks in South Carolina. By the time Lincoln annulled it, word had spread, and the tide of runaways was already flowing from up-country plantations. Madeline's letters to Richmond reported each loss at Mont Royal—the total now stood at nineteen—and at Christmastime, Orry had written that he was glad his father

485

hadn't lived to see the defection. Tillet had believed, perhaps with some justification, that his nigras loved him for caring for them and would never repay that love with flight. In Tillet's lifetime, only one had betrayed him that way; Orry had often told the story of how it had nearly undone his father mentally.

Last year, following the proclamation, Cuffey had been one of the first to go. Philemon Meek had already conceived a great dislike of the slave—most of the slaves despised him, too—and had devoted extra effort to pursuit and recapture. Meek, Andy, and three other blacks had found Cuffey unconscious in a marsh, his legs under water. He had a high fever and might have drowned if he had slipped a little farther.

Meek returned Cuffey to Mont Royal in irons. He grew angry when Madeline refused to sanction additional punishment. Recapture and his sickness during flight were enough, she said.

It bothered her that Cuffey had not attempted a second escape. He was attracted to Jane, but Jane couldn't tolerate him, and that was evident. Did Cuffey stay on because he had some labyrinthine plan to harm the plantation after she departed?

Near the office, she glanced back. Cuffey was gone. She immediately changed direction, found Andy and spoke to him. Ten minutes later she knocked at the office door and walked in. Philemon Meek laid his Bible aside—he studied it for short periods every day—and removed his half glasses. How lucky they had been to find him, Madeline thought. Meek was safely past the upper limit of the second conscription act passed in September and should be able to remain at Mont Royal indefinitely—unless, of course, Jeff Davis got desperate enough to draft grandfathers.

"Are you ready, Miss Madeline? I'll call Aristotle to load the luggage."

"Thank you, Philemon. I wanted to say one thing before I go. Should any emergency arise, don't hesitate to telegraph. If that isn't possible, write. I'll come home at once."

"Hope that won't be necessary—least not until you've had an hour or so with your husband."

She laughed. "I hope so, too. The truth is, I'm fairly aching to see him."

"Shouldn't wonder. It's been a hard year for you, what with tending poor old Mrs. Main. Things should run smoothly if the bluebellies don't push any closer. I did hear yesterday that some tax collector read Lincoln's proclamation down near Beaufort.

Big crowd of nigras gathered around a tree they've already named the Emancipation Oak."

She described her encounter with Cuffey. Meek bristled. "Nothing to do, eh? I'll set that to rights."

"No need. Andy will take care of it, at my request."

"Bad one, that Cuffey," Meek declared.

"Orry says it wasn't always so. Cuffey and Cousin Charles were very close as youngsters."

"Don't know a thing about that. I sometimes regret we caught him in the marsh. He bears watching."

"I know you can handle him. You've done a magnificent job, Philemon—with the people and with planting and harvesting the crops. Do write or telegraph if there's anything you want."

He started to speak, held back, then said it. "I'd be pleased if you told Jane she can't teach any more. Learning's bad for nigras, particularly in these times." He cleared his throat. "I strongly disapprove."

"I'm aware of that. You also know my position. I made a promise to Jane. And I think Mont Royal's calmer for having her here, teaching, than it would be if she went north."

"One thing sure—if she left, we'd lose Andy." The overseer peeked from under a scraggly brow. "Still don't like nigras learning to read. 'Gainst the law, for one thing."

"Times are changing, Philemon. The laws must change, too. If we don't help the people improve themselves, they'll go straight to the Yankees at Beaufort. I accept full responsibility for Jane's activity and any consequences."

Meek tried one last sally. "If Mr. Orry knew about Jane, he might not—"

Sharply: "He knows. I wrote him last year."

No sense saying the rest. No sense telling him she believed the Confederacy would lose the war, and the people on the plantation would face freedom in the white man's world without even minimal preparation. That was the strongest reason she wanted Jane here teaching.

Meek gave up. "I wish you a safe journey. I hear the railroads are in mighty bad shape."

"Thank you for your concern." She overcame a hesitation, ran to him, and hugged him, making him cough and blush. "You take care of yourself."

"Surely will. Give my regards to the colonel."

Still scarlet, he left to summon Aristotle for the trip to the little railroad flag stop not many miles distant. Through slanting bars of sunshine and shadow, Madeline drove away, waving to some forty slaves gathered in the drive to see her off.

Standing apart, arms folded over his chest, Cuffey watched, too.

That night, Jane held class in the sick house.

Thirty-two black people crowded the whitewashed room lit by short pieces of candle. Andy sat cross-legged in the first row. Cuffey lounged in a corner, arms crossed, eyes seldom leaving Jane's face. She was uncomfortable with the attention but did her best to ignore it.

"Try, Ned," she pleaded with a lanky field hand. She tapped her writing instrument, a lump of charcoal, on her board, a slat from a crate. "Three letters." She tapped each in turn.

Ned shook his head. "I don' know."

She stamped her bare foot. "You knew them two days ago."

"I forgot! I work hard all day, I get tired. I ain't smart 'nuf to 'member such things."

"Yes, you are, Ned. I know you are, and you've got to believe it yourself. Try once more." She curbed her impatience; this was like pushing stones up a mountain. She tapped the board. "Three letters: *N, E, D*. It's your name, don't you remember?"

"No." Angrily. "No, I don't."

Jane exhaled loudly, wearily. Madeline's departure had affected her more than she realized. It upset the balance at Mont Royal by removing a strong, moderating hand. Meek was fair but stern, and very much opposed to these classes. Others scorned them—like Cuffey, silently standing in the corner. Why didn't he just stay away, as the rest of them did?

"Let's stop for tonight," she said. The announcement brought reactions of dismay. Her eldest pupil, Cicero, protested the most. Recently a widower, Cicero—too old for field work any longer—was a year shy of seventy but swore he would learn to read and write before his next birthday. He said he would die an educated man if he didn't live long enough to die as a free one.

Cuffey, who stood in the same place night after night, finally spoke up. "Ought to stop for good, 'pears to me."

Andy scrambled up. "If you don't want to learn anything, stay away." An older woman mumbled an amen. Cuffey searched the

488

group with murderous eyes, hunting the culprit. The woman was careful to conceal herself behind Cicero.

Jane always took pains to hide her feelings about Andy. He was her outstanding pupil, and no wonder. They met almost every night, late, so she could give him extra work, and the last time Madeline sent him to Charleston, he had managed to secure a book of his own—an 1841 reader in the series prepared by William McGuffey for the white academies.

Proudly, he showed her the book when he returned. He produced it from under his shirt, handling it as if it were a treasure instead of tattered sections held to moldy binding by a few threads and dabs of glue. How he had gotten McGuffey's *First Eclectic Reader* he refused to say, shrugging off her questions about it— "Oh, it wasn't hard." Which she knew to be a falsehood. In South Carolina, a black man who acquired a book placed himself in mortal danger.

Andy was making fine progress in his studies, which was one reason Jane's feelings about him were changing. One, but not the only one. Twice, shyly, he had kissed her. The first time on the forehead, the second on the cheek. This earnest, determined young man was changing her life in ways she didn't altogether understand.

In response to Andy, Cuffey growled, "I jus' may. None of us got to stay on this place. We go down to Beaufort, we be free." Word of Lincoln's proclamation had spread through the district like invisible fire. People at Mont Royal who had never seen a picture of the Union President spoke his name with a reverence usually reserved for divinities.

"Sure enough," Cicero said, shaking a finger at Cuffey. "You go down to Beaufort—you'll starve 'cause you're an ignorant nigger who can't read or write your name."

"Mind your tongue, old man."

Cicero didn't step back or lower his gaze. Cuffey glared and addressed the group. "Won't starve in Beaufort. They gonna give land to the freedmen. Piece of land and a mule."

"So you raise a crop," Andy said, "and the white factors cheat you because you can't understand or add the figures."

Cuffey answered reason with rage. "Somebody raised you to be a real good piece of property, nigger. You ain' got no backbone; you just got yalla there."

Andy lunged. Old Cicero stepped in and barred his way, pushing, panting from the strain of holding the much younger man. Dark hands with candle stubs shook with alarm; shadows wavered violently.

"I hate being property much as you," Andy spat back. "I saw my momma sold off, my baby sister sold off. You think I love the folks who did it? I don't, but I care more about myself than about hating them. I'm going to be free, Cuffey, and I can't make a life for myself if I stay stupid, like you."

Silence.

Eyes shifted from man to man. Shadows leaped on the whitewashed ceiling. Feet shifted, a whispery sound. Cuffey clenched his fist and raised it.

"One of these days, I gonna take that tongue and cut it right out of your head."

"Shame," Cicero said softly but firmly. Others repeated it. "Shame—shame." Cuffey poked his head forward and spat on the floor, a big gob of bubbly white showing his opinion of them.

"I don' want your books," he said. "I don' want your jubilo neither. I want to burn this place. I want to kill the damn people who killed my babies and kep' me chained up all my life. That's my jubilo, you dumb nigger. That's my jubilo."

"You're crazy," Jane said, moving to Andy. The chance positioning, side by side, seemed to heighten Cuffey's anger. "Crazy. Miss Madeline's the best mistress you could have right now. She wants to help everyone in this room get ready for freedom. She's a good woman."

"She's a white woman, an' I'll see her dead. I'll see the whole place burned 'fore I'm done." Cuffey whirled and kicked the door open, stormed out of the sick house and into the dark.

Shaking their heads and muttering "Shame," Jane's pupils drifted away too. Andy stayed. Jane called, "Ned? The two of us can study alone any time you want."

Ned didn't turn or act as if he heard. He just walked straight ahead out the door. She put a hand over her eyes.

Only one candle remained, the one Andy had brought. It flickered in a cracked bowl near their feet. Jane uncovered her eyes and looked at him. "There's no helping Cuffey, is there? He's gone bad inside."

"Think so."

"Then I wish he'd run again. I wish Meek wouldn't go after him. I've never met a nigra who frightens me as much as he does." Hardly thinking of what she was doing, she bent her head against Andy's shirt. He put an arm around her waist, stroked her hair with his other hand. It felt natural and comforting.

"No need for Cuffey to scare you," he said. "I'll look after you. Always, if you'll let me."

"What?"

"I said—always. If you'll let me."

Slowly, he bent and gently kissed her mouth. Something happened within her then, expressed in a bursting, amazed little laugh. She knew they had sealed their future. With just that kiss. She admitted to herself she had been falling in love for weeks—

Visions intruded, staining the moment. Instead of Andy's face, she saw Cuffey's, and, in twisting shadows on the ceiling, Mont Royal afire.

"House Resolution Number 611," Senator Sherman said, tapping the document on his desk. "As you very well know, if it fails to pass both houses, the Academy will have no money to operate."

George sneezed. Outside the senator's windows, snow slashed horizontally. The winter was proving a savage one. George wiped his nose with a huge handkerchief, then asked, "When is the bill to be introduced?"

"Tomorrow. I expect the House will consider it as a committee of the whole."

The office smelled of old cigars. A gold clock ticked. At twenty past ten, most of the town was at home and beneath the blankets. George wished he were. Though he remained bundled in his blue army overcoat with caped shoulders, he couldn't get warm.

"What will the House do with it?" His clogged head lent the question an odd thickness.

"Tinker with it," replied the general's younger brother. "Pare down the ten thousand for roofing the academic buildings. Perhaps strike out the section about enlarging the chapel. The members of the Committee on Finance will want to show their authority, but I doubt they'll do any substantial damage. The hatchets will appear when the bill's reported over to our side."

"Wade is still determined?"

"Absolutely. He's a madman on the subject. You know his hatred of the South."

"Goddamn it, John, West Point is not the South."

"That is your view, George. All members of the Senate don't share it. A considerable number are on the side of Ben Wade, though a few are wavering. Those are the ones to whom I've spoken at some length. I know you and Thayer and the others have made a maximum effort, too—You've gotten sick from it, I'd say."

George waved that aside. "What are the chances of the bill going down?"

"It will depend on who speaks and how persuasively. Wade will hold forth at great length, and he'll offer every imaginable reason for defeat of the measure. Lane will join him—"

"That isn't an answer," George cut in. "What are the odds?"

Sherman stared at him. "At best—even."

"We should have done more. We—"

"We have done everything possible," the senator interrupted. "Now we can only await the outcome." He came around the desk, putting his hand on his visitor's shoulder.

"Go home, George. We don't need officers dying of influenza."

Gray-faced, George shuffled out.

In the snowstorm, it took him three-quarters of an hour to locate a driver willing to make the long trip to Georgetown. He collapsed inside the hack, his teeth chattering. He drove his fist into the side of the hack. "We should have done more!"

"What's going on down there?"

"Nothing," he shouted. By the time he reeled into his house, he was soaked with sweat and half out of his head.

66

Judah leaned across the starboard rail. "Look, Pa. Is that a Yankee?"

Cooper peered into the morning haze and spied the steam cruiser at which his son was pointing. She lay outside the entrance to the roadstead, her sails furled and her men idling on deck. Her ensign hung limp in the bright air. He could see nothing of it except colors—red, white, and a section of deep blue. He doubted it was the national banner of the Confederacy. "I suspect so."

A small boat put the pilot aboard. Soon the sound of the engines increased, and *Isle of Guernsey* steamed slowly into the roadstead. The harbor, protected by small islands to the north, was crowded with vessels driven by steam and sail. Beyond, Cooper saw the pale buildings of tropic latitudes and the green blur of New Providence Island.

The steamer had brought them down through towering seas and winter gales to drowsy warmth. En route, the British supercargo had shown Cooper the essential goods the vessel carried in her packed holds: long and short Enfield rifles, bullet molds, bars of lead, cartridge bags, bolts of serge. Now it must all be unloaded and placed aboard another vessel for the perilous run through the blockade—which extended even to here, Cooper realized when he saw the enemy cruiser.

Judith, pretty and cheerful in the new poke bonnet he had presented as an early Christmas present, joined him with their daughter. "There is another argument for the point I was trying to make last night," Cooper said to his wife. "That's a Yankee vessel standing watch. I would feel much better if you'd let me find a rental house in Nassau town where—"

"Cooper Main," she interrupted, "I have said my final word on that subject."

"But—"

"The discussion is closed. I won't stay here with the children while you sail blithely off for Richmond."

"Nothing blithe about it," he growled. "It's a very hazardous journey. The blockade's tightening all the time. Savannah and Charleston are nearly impossible to get into, and Wilmington's not much better. I hate for you to chance it."

"My mind's made up, Cooper. If you chance it, so shall we."

"Hurrah," Judah exclaimed, jumping and clapping. "I want to get back to Dixie Land and see General Jackson."

"I don't want to go on a boat if they're going to shoot at it," Marie-Louise said. "I'd rather stay here. This place looks pretty. Can I buy a parrot here?"

"Hush," said her mother, tapping her wrist.

Cooper loved Judith for her determination to stay with him, yet he did wish she would follow the more sensible course. He had been debating it with her unsuccessfully since they left the coaling stop at Madeira. He supposed he might as well desist. Perhaps they would experience no difficulty; many runners with good masters and experienced coastal pilots did slip through the net without being fired on or even sighted.

He swept off his tall hat, leaned over the rail, and watched the harbor and the town rise up. These islands had been Spanish first, then British since Stuart times, and always a haunt of pirates. Nassau itself, a colonial capital with a population of a few thousand, had been thrust into sudden prominence by the war.

Gulls hunting garbage began to form a noisy cloud at the stern. The air smelled of salt and peculiar but pleasing spices. Within an hour, *Isle of Guernsey* dropped anchor and a lighter bore the Mains and their trunks and portmanteaus to crowded Prince George wharf.

The wharf swarmed with white sailors, black stevedores with gold earrings, colorfully dressed women of no discernible occupation, seedy vendors hawking pearls amid heaps of sponges and bananas, sparkling mountains of Cardiff coal, and cotton—bales of it, each steam-pressed to half its original volume.

Cooper had never seen so much cotton or heard such polyglot

494

clamor as that surrounding the hired carriage that took them along Bay Street to their hotel. He heard the familiar accents of home; clipped British; and a bastardized English, odd and musical, spoken principally by the blacks. The cobbled waterfront could barely accommodate all the people and traffic. The war might be starving the South, but it had clearly brought wild prosperity to this island off the Floridas.

After installing the family in their suite, Cooper went to the office of the harbor master, where he explained his needs in vague and guarded language. The bewhiskered official bluntly cut through the circumlocutions.

"No runners in port at present. I am expecting *Phantom* tomorrow. She will not transport passengers, however. Just that cargo from *Guernsey.*"

"Why no passengers?"

The harbor master peered at him as if he were mentally defective. "*Phantom* is owned and operated by the Ordnance Department of your government, sir."

"Ah, yes. There are four such ships. I'd forgotten the names. I'm an official of the Navy Department. Perhaps *Phantom* will make an exception."

"You're welcome to speak to her captain, but it's fair to warn you that other diplomatic gentlemen from the Confederacy have attempted to obtain passage on the government runners without success. When *Phantom* weighs anchor, she'll have every inch of deck and cabin space filled with guns and garments."

Next morning, in a steamy drizzle that reminded him of the low country, Cooper and his son proceeded through Rawson Square to the harborside and its yelling vendors, strolling whores, idling journalists, gambling sailors, strutting soldiers from the island's West Indian regiment. Judith still objected to their son's being exposed to the sights and language of a seaport, but Cooper had given Judah a couple of fatherly lectures in Liverpool on the theory that knowledge was a stronger defense against the world's wickedness than was ignorance. Striding beside his father and whistling a chanty, Judah didn't even turn when a seaman lost at toss-penny and cried, "Fucking bloody son-of-a-bitching bad luck." Sometimes Cooper's heart felt ready to burst with love and pride in his fine, tall son.

Phantom had slipped in during the night, flying British colors. Cooper had a short, unsatisfactory talk with her captain. The harbor master was right; even a deputy of Secretary Mallory would not be accommodated as a passenger on an Ordnance Department ship.

"I am responsible for precious cargo," the captain said. "I'll not add responsibility for human lives."

The drizzle stopped, and the sun shone. Two languorous days passed. *Phantom* put out to sea—again at night—and the Yankee cruiser disappeared, no doubt pursuing the smaller vessel. By the end of the week Cooper was sick of waiting and reading old newspapers, even the one that informed him of the stunning Union defeat at Fredericksburg.

The children quickly tired of the sights of the port. The changing of the guard at Government House was diverting once but not twice; the novelty of flamingos vanished after twenty minutes. Hiring a buggy and taking a picnic to the countryside didn't improve the situation. Judith resigned herself to mediating a quarrel between her son and daughter approximately once an hour. Cooper found the dispositions of the children influencing his; he was short-tempered and prone to strike out with the flat of his hand, as he did when Judah took a spoonful of local conch chowder, crossed his eyes, and gagged.

At last, after they had been in town almost a week, the Monday maritime column of the *Nassau Guardian* listed the weekend's arrivals, including *"Water Witch* of New Providence Is., cargo entirely of cotton from St. George's Is., Bermuda."

"She must be a runner," Cooper exclaimed at breakfast. "Cotton isn't exactly a major industry in Bermuda, and Bulloch told me those in the trade pretend to cruise exclusively between neutral islands." So they went off to the harbor again, he and Judah, held up for five minutes by the funeral procession of another of Nassau's numerous yellow jack victims.

They reached the runner's berth. "Strike me," Judah said, back in his Liverpool phase. "Look at all that bleeding cotton."

"Don't use that kind of language," Cooper snapped. But he was equally fascinated. *Water Witch* was a remarkable sight. An iron-plated paddle steamer, she was, by his best estimate, about two hundred feet long and something like three hundred tons. Her masts were short and raked, her forecastle built to resemble a turtle's back, so she could more easily plow straight through a heavy sea. Every inch of her—hull, paddle boxes, stubby masts—was painted lead gray.

496

Every inch he could see, that is. Above the gunwales she looked brown and square because every available deck space held cotton bales piled two and three high. Except for slits to allow visibility, her pilothouse was barricaded behind them.

Cooper and his son dodged aboard, avoiding bales heaved from one pair of black hands to the next. Cooper asked for the captain but found only the mate.

"Captain Ballantyne's ashore. Went first thing. I expect he's already got his nose buried in some chippy's—" He spied Judah behind his father. "You won't find him on board until tomorrow morning when we start loading." A suspicious pause. "Why d'you want him, anyway?"

"I am Mr. Main, of the Navy Department. I'm urgently in need of passage to the mainland for myself, my son here, and my wife and daughter."

The mate scratched his beard. "We'll be bound for Wilmington again. The run's damn dangerous till we're safely under the guns of Fort Fisher. Shouldn't think the captain would want to carry civilians, 'specially young'uns."

The man spoke with the heavy accent Cooper equated with the impoverished farmers of the Georgia coast. Did the mate mean what he said, or was this merely the start of fare negotiations?

"I am under orders to report to Secretary Mallory in Richmond as soon as practicable. I've been waiting nearly a week to find a ship. I'll pay whatever price you ask."

The mate scratched his armpit. "Space is precious on the old *Witch*. We have one cabin, but she's usually stowed full of cut nails, things like that."

"Nails?" Cooper repeated, astonished.

"Sure. They sold at four dollars a keg right after the war started. Then one of the owners of this ship and a few other gentlemen cornered the import market, and now they fetch ten." He grinned, but Cooper's eyes had narrowed with dislike.

"Tell me, Mr.—"

"Soapes. Like the stuff you wash with, but add an e."

"Where's your home, Mr. Soapes?"

"Port of Fernandina. That's in Florida."

"I know where it is. You're a Southerner, then?"

"Yes, sir, same as you and Captain Ballantyne. You said your name's Main?" Cooper nodded. "Any relation to the Mains of South Carolina?"

"I am a member of that family. Why do you ask?"

"Oh, no special reason. Just heard of it, that's all."

Mr. Soapes was lying; Cooper felt certain of it but couldn't guess the reason. Nervous now, the mate shouted at a stevedore teetering down the gangway with a bale balanced on his bare back. "Any of you niggers drop cotton in the water, you'll starve till you pay for it. Sixty cents a pound. Market price."

Cooper cleared his throat. "Tell me, Mr. Soapes, what cargo will you be taking to Wilmington?"

"Oh, you know, the usual."

"But I don't know. What is the usual?"

Soapes scratched his stomach and looked everywhere but at Cooper. "Sherry wine. Havana cigars. Believe we have a consignment of cheeses this time. Then there's tea and tinned meats and plenty of coffee—" As he recited the list, his voice grew fainter and Cooper's cheeks redder. "We've some bay rum—oh, yes, and some London-made bonnet frames."

"When the Confederacy is desperate for war matériel, you're bringing in luxuries?"

"We carry what's profitable, sir." After that retort, the mate's courage wilted. "Anyway, I'm not the supercargo. The captain handles that job. Speak to him."

"I shall, believe me."

"He won't be back from the whorehouse till morning."

Cooper felt like punching Soapes. He had said whorehouse only because he was embarrassed and wanted to strike back by embarrassing Judah.

The boy caught on and grinned. "My pa takes me to those places all the time. Maybe we'll meet him."

Cooper boxed his son's ear. The mate looked stupefied until he realized he was being made fun of. Then he grew as red as Cooper, who marched his son toward the gangway, unamused.

Later that day, Cooper called on J. B. Lafitte, local agent of Fraser, Trenholm. He introduced himself and inquired about Captain William Ballantyne of Fernandina. He learned a good deal.

Ballantyne, a native of Florida, had a reputation as a competent master, though he wasn't a popular one; he drove his crewmen hard. In the past year, Lafitte said, Ballantyne had also become a rich master. In addition to his captain's pay—the customary five thousand, which he demanded in U.S. dollars and banked in Bermuda—Ballantyne conducted some personal speculation on every voyage.

Ballantyne's vessel made only eleven knots at her best—dangerously slow in view of where she sailed. But she hadn't been built for the trade, only refitted, at Bowdler, Chaffer and Company, a Merseyside yard Cooper knew well. Lafitte said *Water Witch* was owned by a consortium of Southerners, a fact no one took trouble to conceal, but the names of the individual owners had never been publicized so far as he knew.

Thus Cooper developed a strong dislike of the ship's captain and owners before he returned next morning. Directed belowdecks, he was overwhelmed by the smell of cured meat. Ballantyne's cabin in the stern reeked of tobacco; small crates filled every spare corner. The crates bore Spanish labels, with the word *Habana* prominent.

"Cigars," Ballantyne said in an offhand way, noticing his visitor's curiosity. "My private venture this trip. Be seated on that stool, and I'll be with you momentarily. I'm just finishing our manifest. It shows us bound for the Bermudas. We never sail anywhere but the port of St. George, or this one."

He beamed like a cherub. William Ballantyne was a moon-faced man with little hair left, except in his ears. He had spectacles and a small paunch and a grating accent that sounded more like the Appalachians than the deep South.

But the need to reach Richmond took precedence over Cooper's conscience; at least it did until he worked out details of the passage. Ballantyne had a fawning manner and an unctuous smile. Cooper silently characterized both as false.

"Well, then, that's done," Ballantyne said at the conclusion of the negotiations. "I'm sorry I wasn't here when you called yesterday. Mr. Soapes told me you have some, uh, quibbles about our cargo."

"Since you raise the subject, I do."

Ballantyne kept grinning but now with a dash of nastiness. "I raised it, sir, because I guessed you would."

"I wouldn't call them quibbles, Captain. They are serious moral objections. Why does this vessel carry nothing but luxury goods?"

"Why, sir, because the owners desire it. Because that's what turns the coin, don't you know?" He brushed his fingertips with his thumb, feeling invisible metal.

"Do you mean to tell me you can make a profit carrying cured meat?"

"Yes indeed, sir. Coming out, we dropped some of our cotton at St. George and in that space put a supply of Bermuda bacon. I think it's to be transshipped to the gulf for the armies in the West, but I wouldn't swear. All I know is, yesterday I sold it to an officer of the Confederate Quartermaster Corps"—beaming now —"for three times what it cost me in Bermuda. It's the finest meat available from New York State. The farmers up there would rather sell to our side than their own. Make a lot more that way." He rubbed thumb against fingers again.

Livid, Cooper said, "You're a damned scoundrel, Ballantyne. Men and boys are dying for want of guns and ammunition, and you carry bacon, cigars, bonnet frames."

"Listen here. I told you I carry what I'm instructed to carry. Plus a little something extra to secure my old age." The smile cracked, showing the creature behind it. "I'm not educated or well off like you, sir. I grew up in the North Carolina mountains. My people were ignorant. I have no schooling except aboard ship —no trade but this—and I must make of it what I can. Besides" —the ingratiating grin slipped back in place—"I don't know why you rail so. This kind of trade's common. Everybody's doing it."

"No, Captain, your own lack of scruples and patriotism are not universal. Not by any means."

Ballantyne's smile vanished. "I don't have to give you passage, you know."

"I think you do. Unless you wish governmental attention directed to the affairs of this vessel. It can be arranged."

Ballantyne rattled the papers in his hand. For the first time, his voice showed unsteadiness. "You try to sink me and you'll be sinking someone near and dear."

"What the hell does that mean?"

"Mr. Soapes said you hailed from South Carolina. So does one of our owners, whose middle name is the same as your last one. She has a twenty percent equity in *Water Witch* and a brother in the Navy Department."

The harbor water lapped the hull. Cooper could scarcely swallow, let alone speak. Finally: "What are you saying?"

"Come on, sir—don't pretend you don't know. One of the owners is a lady named Huntoon—Mrs. Ashton Main Huntoon of Richmond and the Palmetto State. Ain't—isn't she a relative?"

Seeing Cooper's sickened expression, he grinned. "Thought so. Added up the two and two after I spoke with Mr. Soapes. You've booked passage on a family vessel, Mr. Main."

67

George leaned on the rail of the gallery and gazed down at the gilt-and-marble Senate chamber. It was the fifteenth day of January. He had slept badly, waking often, stretched between hope and dread.

Wade, the architect of the attack, rose first.

"I have so often expressed my opposition to bills of this character and to the policy of appropriating money for the establishment and support of this institution that I do not propose to take up time now to argue against it."

In the next sentence, in the universal fashion of politicians, he did exactly what he had just said he wouldn't.

"I know the institution has been of no use to the country. If there had been no West Point Military Academy, there would have been no rebellion. It was the hotbed from which rebellion was hatched. From thence emanated your principal traitors and conspirators."

The debate was joined. It grew sharp, then intemperate, as the minutes lengthened into an hour and the statements to paragraphs, then to orations.

Senator Wilson, the military affairs chairman George had cultivated, took the floor to acknowledge the existence of weaknesses in the Academy but then cited evidence contradicting Wade—the very same figures George had included in his letter to the *Times*.

Wilson thought West Point no "nursery of treason," though he did fault it for "an exclusiveness—a sort of assumption of superiority among its graduates in the army that is sometimes very offensive."

Senator Nesmith tried to blunt the attack by naming graduates who had given their lives for the Union—Mansfield and Reno were two of the best known—and concluded by trying to rouse the emotion of his colleagues by reciting twelve lines of a poem on heroism.

Immediately, Wade charged from the flank. The institution was worthless because it trained engineers, not leaders of a fighting army. Skillfully, he wove a repetitive phrase into his diatribe: *"Traitors to the country—traitors to the country—traitors to the country."*

George's head started to ache. To twist and color the truth as Wade did was abominable. Lee was an engineer but brilliant as a tactician. Why such distortions? Was it the nature of the political beast or just something peculiar to this war, this hour, this special nexus of interests and passions? Did radicals like Wade truly feel the hatreds they expressed? The possibility, by no means new, still had power to terrify him.

There might be a more cynical explanation, of course. If Wade and his crowd railed against the South until it was destroyed, they could step in as a political party and rule it.

On and on Wade went, merciless. "I am for abolishing this institution." Scattered applause. "We do not want any government interposition for military education any more than for any other education."

John Sherman left his desk, began to scurry among his colleagues, sensing a tide flowing the wrong way. Foster of Connecticut spoke in rebuttal. Had not Yale and Harvard educated as many Southerners as West Point?

Wade sneered. "Yale College is not upheld by the government of the United States."

Then there was renewed argument over whether the Academy had or had not produced quality leaders for the Union. This line of debate was interrupted by the cadaverous, mean-visaged Lane of Kansas, whose curt remarks—scarcely a sentence or two—ended with a triumphant repetition of the Academy epitaph he had been jobbing around the city for days: "Died of West Point pro-slaveryism!"

Wade stamped his feet and expressed his approval vocally. Sherman scurried faster.

On it went. Arguments that West Point was a "monopoly." More arguments that it trained men improperly. Here, the powerful Lyman Trumbull spoke for the first time.

"Because they understood the erection of fortifications, they were therefore supposed to be Napoleons? There is the mistake! What we want is generals to command our armies who will rely upon the strength of our armies! Let loose the citizen soldiery of this country upon the rebels! Dismiss from the army every man who knows how to build a fortification and let the men of the North, with their strong arms and indomitable spirit, move down upon the rebels, and I tell you they will grind them to powder!"

The applause, from a good number of gallery spectators as well as from the floor, resounded loudly this time. George's palms were cold and damp, his heart beating too fast. The arguments grew in ferocity.

Lane flashed a whole new set of verbal knives. "This institution for more than thirty years has been under the absolute dominion of your Southern aristocrats. A young man who enrolls at West Point is taught there to admire above all things that two-penny, miserable slave aristocracy of the South—he is taught Southern secession doctrine as a science!"

To George's left, someone clapped. He knew who it was and didn't trust himself to look. Senator Sherman and several of his allies raised their heads; the applause stopped.

Debate continued. Wade put forth his proposal—that West Point be abandoned so a system of separate institutions within the individual states would have room to grow in its place. By this point George felt faint—a lingering effect of the influenza, maybe —and his hands were clenched. The question was called.

"All in favor?"

The yeas were loud, fervent.

"All opposed?"

The nays were even louder but—was it hope playing tricks with his hearing?—fewer.

"I make the count," Vice President Hamlin said, "yeas twenty-nine, nays ten."

Groans in the gallery and from the aisles and desks below. But there was a mingling of hearty applause. John Sherman gave George an exhausted glance, with no sign of pleasure save a spas-

503

modic jerk of his lips. Only then did George dare turn and gaze along the row to pale, fuming Stanley.

George got up, intending to speak some conciliatory word to his brother. Stanley rose, turned his back, and left the gallery while George was still six feet away.

From the Capitol, George rode the street railway to Willard's, where he went to the saloon bar to celebrate. Mentally cursing the trivial work waiting at the Winder Building, he kept buying rounds for other officers at the bar. Presently, all companions gone, he wandered to a table, sat, and began to recite some advertising doggerel which had caught his fancy in a newspaper.

> "Should the weather be cold and the jacket be thin,
> Just take a wee toothful of Morris's Gin."

"I think you should go home, Major Hazard," said the waiter in charge of the table.

> "Should ever the earth be flooded again,
> Let us all hope the rain will be Morris's Gin."

"I very definitely think you should go home," the waiter said, removing George's not yet empty glass.

He went home.

When he had paid the driver and reeled into the house, he said to Constance: "We won."

"But you look so grim. Not to say unsteady. Do sit down before you fall down." She slid the parlor doors shut so the children wouldn't catch sight of him.

"Today I saw the real face of this town, Constance." Holding his head, he watched a marble-topped table separate into two. "I really saw it. Ignorance, prejudice, disregard for the truth—that's the real Washington. Some of those damned rascals in the Senate spouted lies as if they were quoting the Ten Commandments. I can't stand this place any longer. I must get out somehow, some—"

His head lolled back against the chair doily, then fell toward his shoulder. Constance stepped behind him, loving him for an honorable but imperfect man. She reached down to stroke his forehead. His mouth sagged open and he snored.

In contrast, Stanley seemed to thrive in the Byzantine atmosphere of the city. He no longer felt himself a newcomer—quite the opposite—and he relished his growing responsibilities as a trusted aide of Mr. Stanton. Further, he was making vast sums of money on his own for the first time.

Of course, passage of the West Point appropriation bill was a setback, and it left him peevish for several days. The peevishness was enhanced by that of the secretary, which had prevailed ever since General Burnside had begun a movement against Lee on January 20, only to be balked two days later by pouring rains that changed the Virginia roads to bogs.

Burnside's apologists blamed an act of God for the failure of what was sneeringly termed "the Mud March." Those in charge blamed the general and replaced him with Joe Hooker. Fighting Joe announced his determination to reorganize the army, improve every aspect from sanitation to morale—he immediately started granting furloughs—and, above all, annihilate the rebels in the spring.

A further heightening of Stanley's peevishness occurred when Isabel discovered Laban with his drawers down and his sex organ up inside a too-willing maid they employed. Stanley was forced to apply a birch rod to his son's backside—increasingly difficult as the twins grew bigger—then dismiss the sluttish maid, which didn't pain him, and pay her an extra hundred dollars, which did.

On a gloomy day at the end of the month, Stanton called him in. Though he had stayed at his desk all night—he did so frequently—the secretary looked fresh and vigorous. A gray pinstripe drape covered him from the neck down; the War Department messenger who doubled as barber was brushing lather over the secretary's upper lip in preparation for razoring it clean, a twice-weekly ritual.

"Look at this, and I'll be with you momentarily," Stanton said, tossing something metallic onto the desk. The razor rasped.

Stanley picked up the object, which proved to be a dull brown head of Liberty crudely cut or filed from the center of one of the big copper pennies last minted in '57. The messenger finished the job, toweled Stanton's lip, and whipped the sheet off. Stanley

505

turned the penny over and discovered a small safety pin soldered to it.

"The foes of this government are wearing those," the secretary said once the barber was gone. "Openly!" He shouted the word, but Stanley had grown accustomed to Stanton's outbursts. The man was passionate about his beliefs, if about nothing else.

"I heard the Peace Democrats referred to as copperheads, sir. I didn't know a badge like this was the reason. Might I ask where this came from?"

"Colonel Baker supplied it. He says they're numerous. Stanley, the twin abominations of this war are treason and corruption. We can do little about the latter but a great deal about the former. I want you to meet with Baker more frequently. Urge him to step up his activities and monitor his efficiency in carrying out that charge. Baker is an ignorant and headstrong man, but he can be useful. I am personally charging you with the job of increasing that usefulness."

"Yes, sir," Stanley said, enthusiastic. "Is there anyone in particular you want him to move against?"

"Not at this time. But I'm preparing lists. In the case of the worst offenders, dossiers." Stanton stroked his beard. "See Baker as soon as you can. Authorize him to hire more men. We are going to move massively against those attempting to subvert this government—especially those calling for a craven peace. One thing more. The President shall know nothing of this effort. As I've said to you before, Baker's bureau must never appear on our tables of organization. His efforts are vital, however, and we shall support him with all the money he needs." He smiled. "In cash. Untraceable."

"I understand. I'll see Colonel Baker this afternoon."

Stanley left, mildly exhilarated by news of increased covert activity against the new peace societies flourishing in the Northeast and Northwest, as well as those individuals who criticized the administration in speeches or articles. On the other hand, he didn't look forward to more dealings with the crude, enigmatic, and occasionally frightening Lafayette Baker, who had somehow ingratiated himself with Stanton before Antietam. Ever since, the secretary had referred to Baker as the department's provost marshal. He ran his peculiar organization, which Stanton privately referred to as the War Department Detective Bureau, from a small brick building across from Willard's, on the wrong side of Pennsylvania.

Stanley fingered the copper badge. Closer liaison with Baker might have advantages. Perhaps he could surreptitiously lead the bureau to look into the attitudes and actions of his brother George.

In February, George met a man who despised the methods and mazes of the government as much as he did. It happened by accident.

Hazard's had finished casting an order of fifteen-inch Rodman smoothbores for the Rappahannock line. Christopher Wotherspoon saw them aboard a freight train, which eventually shuttled them to the Washington Arsenal for inspection and acceptance. Wotherspoon traveled with them by passenger car.

During two long evenings, he and George conferred about matters at the ironworks. Then Wotherspoon supervised the loading of the immense bottle-shaped guns onto barges that would float them down the Potomac to Aquia Creek Landing. George arranged some time off and traveled downriver on a military gunboat, arriving at the landing in a wet snowstorm typical of the miserable winter. The trip was both a matter of personal interest and a needed escape from a job he could no longer tolerate.

As the temperature rose and rain replaced the snow, George watched Wotherspoon bullying the military crew responsible for moving the fifty-thousand-pound Rodmans from the barges up specially constructed inclines, using block and tackle. Reinforced flatcars waited to roll the guns away down the Richmond, Fredericksburg, & Potomac rail line to the front.

Moving the guns took most of a day. George stamped about in the rain until the work was finished. With unconcealed pride, he stood beside one of the flatcars while men chained down the last gun. A shiny new Mason locomotive had steam up. Gilt lettering on the cab showed its name: GEN. HAUPT. The inscription on the tender read: U.S. MILITARY R. RDS.

Clouds of steam billowed around George while rain dripped from the brim of his hat. Hence he didn't immediately see the dour, mustached man wearing muddy boots, twill trousers, and an old talma who came up to stand beside him. George thought he should know the fellow but couldn't place him.

The man was more than a head taller; occasionally the mere

507

existence of such specimens irked George. That, plus his pride, was the reason he spoke without looking around.

"My guns."

"On my train."

George turned, bristling. He knew him now. "On my rails," he said.

"For a fact? You're Hazard?"

"I am."

"Fancy that. I thought that if there was a real person behind the name, he'd be some paunchy bookkeeper, a man who'd never come near a place like this. The rails you make are good ones. I've laid more than a few."

The whistle hooted, steam hissed. Above the racket, George asked, "Are you General Haupt?"

"No, sir. I am not general anything. When I took the commission last May, it was on the condition that I didn't have to wear a uniform. Last autumn Stanton tried to hoist me to brigadier general of volunteers, but I've never officially accepted. Get to be a general and you spend all your time bowing and scraping and filling out papers. I'm Haupt, that's all."

He peered at George like a prosecutor studying a witness. "You a drinking man? I have a bottle in that building yonder—the cheap one that passes for a yard office."

"I'm a drinking man, yes."

"Well, do you or don't you want a whiskey?"

"If I could bring another person—my works superintendent over there—"

"All right, just quit talking and do it."

And in that way, in the rain, George's friendship with Herman Haupt began.

Haupt was right—the yard office wasn't much more than a shanty. Water dripped through cracks in the plank roof. Droplets glistened in Haupt's beard as he poured liquor into two dirty tumblers. Wotherspoon had declined the invitation, wanting to tour the huge military complex before he left.

"I'm a civil engineer by trade." Haupt's statement was modest; he had a reputation as one of the best in the nation. "I'm supposed to maintain the railroads the army appropriated and build new ones. They make it damn hard with all their rules and procedures. What do you do?"

"I work in Washington."

"Wouldn't wish that on a man I hated. Doing what?"

"Artillery procurement for the Ordnance Department. If you want a more accurate description, I spend most of my time dealing with fools."

"Inventors?"

"They're the least offensive." George drank. "Principally I mean the generals and the politicians."

Haupt laughed, then leaned forward. "What's your opinion of Stanton?"

"Don't deal with him much. He's inflexible politically—a zealot—and some of his methods are suspect. But I think he's more competent than most."

"He learned the lesson of Bull Run more quickly than a lot of them. When this war started, damn few understood that you can move troops faster and easier by rail than by water. Most of the generals are still living in the riverboat age, but old Stanton saw the significance when the rebs brought men from the valley by train and combined two armies to whip McDowell. They did it so fast, McDowell was dizzy."

"Celerity," George said, nodding.

"Beg your pardon?"

"Celerity—it's one of Dennis Mahan's pet ideas. More than ten years ago, he was saying that celerity and communication would win the next war. The railroad and the telegraph."

"If the generals don't lose it first. Have another drink."

"Thanks, no. I must try to find my younger brother. He's in the Battalion of Engineers."

He rose to leave. Haupt thrust out his hand. "Enjoyed our talk. Aren't many in this army as smart and forthright as you." That amused George. He had done little except sit and listen while Haupt expounded—but of course if you did that, a rapid-fire talker always thought you brilliant.

"I am forced to go to Washington occasionally," Haupt went on. "I'll look you up next time."

"Wish you would, General."

"Herman, Herman," he said as George went out.

George checked on the whereabouts of the engineers and early in the afternoon swung aboard an iron-pot coal car, part of the train bound for Falmouth. He tugged his hat down, leaning against the cold metal of the pot and speculating about Haupt. A year ago or so, after the administration had pushed through a bill establishing a military railroad system, Stanton had brought in Daniel McCallum, superintendent of the Erie, to run it. Why McCallum hadn't been satisfactory, George didn't know, but Haupt soon replaced him.

Haupt organized his department into two corps, one to handle operations, the other construction. It was in connection with the latter that Haupt's legend had spread. He was famous for laying track rapidly, building sturdy bridges virtually overnight—and losing his temper as he did it. At least the man accomplished something, which was more than George could say for Ripley. Or for himself.

After jumping off the slow-moving car at Brooks Station, he found Billy supervising construction of a stockade to strengthen the station against attack. They stayed at the work site and talked for an hour. George learned that his brother had just finished a week's leave at Belvedere. Both going home and returning, Billy had passed through Washington in the middle of the night—an inappropriate hour for calling in Georgetown, he explained.

George grinned. "I can understand your eagerness to see your wife but not your haste to get back to duty."

"I want to get this war over with. I'm sick of being separated from Brett. I'm sick of the whole damn thing."

That was the tenor of the reunion: little humor and a pervasive melancholy. George could do nothing to cheer his brother. He felt bad about that as he returned to the city.

To his surprise and delight, before a week went by, Herman Haupt stalked into the Winder Building hunting for him. They went to Willard's for lager and a huge afternoon meal. Haupt had his temper up; he had come from a meeting at the War Department. George asked what had gone wrong.

"Never mind. If I talk about it, I'll just blow up again."

"Well, I had another argument with Ripley this morning, so I don't feel a hell of a lot better. I keep telling my wife that I don't think I can stay here much longer."

Haupt chewed an unlit cigar. "If you decide you must get out, tell me. I'll put you to work building railroads."

"I can manufacture rails, Herman, but I don't know a blessed thing about laying or maintaining them."

"Twenty-four hours in the Construction Corps and you will. I guarantee it."

George smiled abruptly; a weight had vanished. "I appreciate the offer. I may take you up on it sooner than you imagine."

Raw winds, freezing temperatures, sudden snows continued to torment the armies waiting for spring. Everything, including camp life, was harder because of the weather. Charles managed to ride to Barclay's Farm for three overnight visits. The first time he brought two carbines and ammunition taken from dead Yankees, turning the lot over to Boz and Washington, an act that would have gotten him flogged in his home state. But he trusted the freedmen, and they had to be armed if the Yankees crossed the river in force when the weather warmed up.

The second visit almost cost him his life. He came straight from reporting after a two-day ride behind enemy lines with Ab. He was still clad in the uniform he wore for such missions—light blue trousers with broad yellow stripe, confiscated talma of Union blue, kepi with crossed sabers in tarnished metal. It was snowing when he approached the farm. Boz mistook him for the enemy and shot at him. The first round narrowly missed him. By the time Boz fired again, Charles and Sport had taken cover behind a red oak. The bullet hit the tree. Charles yelled to identify himself, and Boz apologized for almost ten minutes.

Charles couldn't get enough of the yellow-haired, blue-eyed widow. Not enough of talking to her, sleeping with her, touching her, or just watching her.

She wanted to know all about his life in the cavalry. Over savory beef soup, from which he plucked the ring bones and sucked the marrow, he told her about the boredom of the winter camps; Jeb Stuart's, south of Fredericksburg, had been nicknamed Camp No-Camp because of the monotony of life there.

Then he talked of Confederate cavalrymen gathering legends around their names. Of Turner Ashby, who had flashed like a comet for a year, displaying a suicidal recklessness when he rode his white charger. Some said he was wild to avenge his slain brother Richard. Ashby had been killed in the valley last summer. Of John Mosby, who had scouted for Stuart on the ride around McClellan, now commanding mounted irregulars in Loudoun, Fauquier, and Fairfax counties, an area rapidly becoming known as Mosby's Confederacy. "The Yanks want to hang him as an outlaw." Out in Kentucky, there was John Hunt Morgan, called the Thunderbolt of the Confederacy. And they were starting to hear fantastic tales of another horseman in the West, a barely literate planter by the name of Bedford Forrest.

"Does he have a nickname, too?"

"The Wizard of the Saddle."

"You've been left out, Charles."

"Oh, no. Ab and the rest of us, we're called the Iron Scouts."

"It sounds like a compliment."

He smiled. "I take it as one."

"If you're that special, the Yankees must consider you prime targets."

He glanced at her as he raised the soup bone to his mouth. There was no lightness in the remark or in her expression.

In the drowsiness after love-making, he liked to share his past with her. He described the way he had been tricked into having half his head shaved the day he arrived at West Point. He told her about the soldiers he had met and admired in the Second Cavalry, among them the Virginian George Thomas, now on the other side. He shared the story of his difficulties with the captain named Bent, who for some reason hated his whole family. And he created pictures of Texas as best he could with inadequate words: the vistas of grass, the blue northers, the pecan trees and post oaks glistening after a rain while larks sang.

"Parts of that state are the most beautiful places on God's earth."

"Would you like to go back there?"

"I thought so once." He took her hand. "Not now."

With cornmeal grits steaming on his breakfast plate, he would admire the soft, still-sleepy beauty of her morning face and, when strong coffee had wakened her a little, tell her of some of the rivalries troubling the cavalry. His old friend Fitz Lee, now an important general he seldom saw, didn't like Hampton because Stuart didn't, and because Hampton would always rank Fitz by ten days, and nothing could change that.

At the end of the third visit, Gus kissed him on the mouth four times before whispering, "How soon will you be back?"

"Don't know. We'll be heading for the lower part of the state soon, to hunt for horses. We've lost a lot of them."

"You tell General Hampton I don't want anything to happen to you."

"And you tell Boz and Washington to sleep with those carbines —loaded."

512

Back in camp, Ab Woolner surprised and annoyed him by joking bitterly, "Lord God, Charlie—you been here a whole hour and you ain't talked about nothing but that gal. You used to talk about Sport some and the war now an' again. You forgotten why we're all here?"

Something flip-flopped in Charles's middle when he heard that and gave him pause.

He had no reply.

68

Virgilia hated to force the visitor to leave. Odd as he was, the patients liked him and counted on his Sunday visits, though sometimes he didn't show up because he couldn't talk his way aboard a military steamer coming down to Aquia Creek Landing.

Whenever he did, he brought pockets sagging with horehound drops and a haversack of cheap pens and writing paper, cut plug tobacco, little pots of jam, and five- and ten-cent bills he distributed so the wounded could buy the fresh milk sold by vendors who came through.

Virgilia suspected that the man impoverished himself to buy the things he gave away. His job couldn't pay much; he was only a copyist in the paymaster general's office. That and his first name were all she knew about him, except that he seemed to have a need to touch and console the wounded soldiers.

It was early afternoon. A feeble February sun shone. The Landing, a vast complex of docks, rail spurs, raw pine structures, tents, and drill fields populated by thousands of soldiers, civilians, and black contrabands, was relatively quiet, as it was every Sabbath.

Patients in this long and narrow hospital building had been either wounded in skirmishes or felled by sickness on the infamous Mud March.

Virgilia could detect a better spirit in the army now. In the spring, General Hooker would lead what might be the final phase of the crusade to crush the rebels. She looked forward to tending the Union wounded and sometimes daydreamed of the suffering of boys on the other side. Every scream from a reb was another penny of repayment for Grady and all his people.

In the reception hall, she heard voices. She approached the Sunday samaritan, who was seated beside a sleeping soldier, holding the young man's hand between his two soft and delicate ones. The visitor, in his mid-forties, was bearded and burly as a dock hand. He had mild eyes and a fair complexion. He always wore a decoration on the lapel of his baggy suit—today, a bedraggled tulip fastened by a pin.

"Walt, the visitors are here."

With slow, bearlike movements, the Sunday man lifted himself from the stool his bulk had completely hidden. The soldier felt the hands leave his, and his eyes flew open. "Don't go."

"I'll be back again," Walt said, bending to place a gentle kiss on the boy's cheek. Some of the nurses called such behavior unnatural, but most of the patients, awaiting the surgeon's saw or suffering horrible internal pain, welcomed Walt's handclasps and kisses. It was all the love some of them would know before they died.

"Next week, Miss Hazard, if I can," the Sunday man promised, settling the haversack strap on his shoulder. He shambled out the doors at one end of the aisle as the dignitaries came in at the other end. The delegation consisted of two women and four men from the Sanitary Commission, plus a seventh individual, to whom the others seemed to defer. Virgilia was glad she and her ward-masters had scrubbed the floor and walls with disinfectant last night; it muted the odors of wounds and incontinence.

"—a typical ward, Congressman. Well maintained by the volunteer nursing staff, as you can see." The speaker, one of the gentlemen from the Commission, beckoned to Virgilia. "Matron? May we have a moment of your time?"

Touching her hairnet and smoothing her apron, she hurried to the visitors. All were middle-aged except the man addressed as Congressman. He was pale and tall, stooped and unprepossessing. Yet he impressed her as he swept off his tall hat—wavy hair

514

gleamed with too much oil, a common fault with gentlemen—and swiftly inspected her face and figure.

The white-whiskered scarecrow who had summoned her said, "You are Miss—?"

"Hazard, Mr. Turner."

"Kind of you to remember me. We have a special guest, who wished to inspect several of our facilities. May I present the Honorable Samuel G. Stout, representative from Indiana?"

"Miss Hazard, is it?" said the congressman, stunning Virgilia. Out of that clerkish body rolled the deepest, most resonant tones she had ever heard—the voice of a born orator or divine, a voice to draw tears and sway mobs. He spoke four words, peering at her with rather small, close-set brown eyes, and sent shivers down her back.

His gaze made her inordinately nervous. "That's correct, Congressman. We're pleased to have you here. A great many dignitaries from Washington pass through Aquia Creek Landing—the President and his party went down to Falmouth on the train recently—but we've not been fortunate enough to have any of them visit our ward until now."

"Next to serving on the lines," Stout said, "this is the most important work of all—restoring our lads to fight again. I don't agree with Mr. Lincoln's contention that we must treat the traitors gently. I am in Mr. Stevens's camp, believing we should punish them without pity. You are helping to hasten that task to its conclusion."

Sententious murmurs of approval came from the others. One woman, huge as a gas balloon, pressed a glove to her vast front and breathed, "Bravo." Virgilia recognized that Stout was behaving like a politician, turning a scrap of casual conversation into a platform statement. Yet his sentiments and his voice continued to touch nerves.

"You are a member of Miss Dix's corps?" he asked, managing to step closer. She said that was true. She smelled the cinnamon oil on his hair.

"Perhaps you'll tell us a little about your charges." Stout smiled. His teeth were crooked—her first impression was correct; he was unimpressive physically—yet she sensed determination and strength in him. "This young lad, for example." Directing her to a bed on the left, he contrived to take hold of her elbow.

Instantly, she experienced a physical reaction so unexpected she was afraid she might be blushing.

The boy in bed stared at the visitors with feverish eyes. "Henry was on picket duty on the Rappahannock," she said. "Rebel scouts crossed near his post. Shots were exchanged." The boy turned his cheek to the pillow and shut his eyes. Virgilia drew the visitors out of earshot. "I'm afraid his right leg can't be saved. It's just a matter of a day or two before the surgeons take it."

"I would take the lives of ten rebels for blighting a young man that way," Stout said. "I would crucify them if that form of punishment were condoned in our society. It ought to be. Nothing is too cruel for those who precipitated this war of cruelty."

One of the Commission members said, "With all due respect, Congressman, don't you feel that's a bit severe?"

"No, sir, I do not. A dear relative of mine, an aide to General Rosecrans, was slain at Murfreesboro not sixty days ago. There were no remains fit to be returned to his wife and little ones. His body was foully mutilated by those who slew him. Certain parts were—"

He stopped, clearing his throat; he knew he had overstepped.

But not so far as Virgilia was concerned. The man excited her as few had since her acquaintance with the visionary John Brown. She led the visitors through the ward in a curious light-headed state, her mind functioning well enough for her to describe each case, yet a part of it reserved for exhilarated contemplation of the congressman. Did he possibly find her as attractive as she found him?

Unwittingly, she lengthened her description of each patient's diagnosis, until Turner started to tap his foot. When that did no good, he pulled out a large gold watch. "I am afraid we shall have to hurry along, Miss Hazard. We are due to inspect the quartermaster's stores."

"Certainly, Mr. Turner." She hesitated, then reminded herself that if Stout walked out unaware of her reaction to him, she might never see him again. "I wonder if I first might have a moment to speak privately with the congressman? This hospital has certain urgent needs. Perhaps he could help with them."

She knew it was flimsy, but she could think of nothing better. Turner and the balloon-shaped female suspected her game and exchanged sharp looks; propriety was being outraged here. Congressman Stout rolled his hat brim in white fingers, unsmiling except in his dark eyes. He understood, too.

Virgilia turned and walked away. The visitors moved in the opposite direction, one grumbling. Stout followed her. Feeling that she must be scarlet, she halted between two beds in which the patients were asleep. No one could hear when she turned and whispered to Stout.

"I lied a moment ago. Our needs are well supplied."

His eyes drifted to her breasts, then upward again. With his back to the others, he permitted himself a smile. "I thought that might be the happy circumstance. Hoped so, to be truthful."

"I—" She hardly believed it was Virgilia Hazard searching for the words, but it was the new Virgilia, conceived the night Brett came to her and brushed her hair. "—I merely wished to express admiration for your remarks about the enemy. I share your loathing of the South, and I can't tolerate the prospect of a soft peace of the kind Mr. Lincoln advocates."

Stout's lips compressed. "There will be no soft peace if certain of us in Congress have our way." He bent forward, his voice as magnificent as the low registers of a pipe organ. "If you have occasion to visit Washington, it would be pleasant to exchange views on the subject at greater length."

"I—would enjoy that, Congressman. I can understand your passion for prosecuting the war, since you had a relative tortured by the enemy."

"My wife's older brother."

He said it and let it hang between them. She felt as if he had hit her. From the slight curl of his mouth and the expression in his eyes, she knew the revelation was not accidental.

"Your—?"

"Wife," he repeated. "Since we came from Muncie, she has been preoccupied with female society—humanitarian committees, that type of thing. I accompany her in public only when some obligation demands it. I say all this to indicate we have little in common."

"Except a marriage certificate."

"That is rather stiff-necked, Miss Hazard. I am not a man given to falsehoods—except when addressing constituents." The effort to produce a smile failed. "Please, don't be angry. I find you exceedingly attractive. I merely wanted to be candid. If I lied and you found out, you'd think the worse of me."

517

Her head began to hurt. A queasy conviction came over her that he had said all this before. It had a practiced smoothness.

"My marriage should not be an obstacle to our meeting discreetly for a meal and some stimulating conversation."

She took a step backward. "I'm afraid it definitely is an obstacle."

He frowned. "My dear Miss Hazard, don't let foolish prudery—"

"You must excuse me, Congressman." She spun and walked away.

Virgilia was furious because she had let her emotions betray her—take her by surprise and humiliate her. She had felt a physical desire for the man stronger than any she had experienced since Grady died. The desire was all the sharper because Stout was a person of power and influence.

The image of his eyes, the memories of his reverberating voice brought a look of pain to her face as she crashed through the swing doors at the end of the ward.

"Damn him, damn him, *damn* him for being married."

69

The taproom was unsavory and in a bad location, down on C Street near Greenleaf's Point. The place teemed with boisterous officers from the arsenal, goatish civilians, loitering thugs, and prostitutes—white, black, even a Chinese. Jasper Dills had gone there with enormous reluctance and only because a meeting could not be held in his usual, respectable haunts. He was, after all, responding to an appeal from an army deserter.

518

Dills's driver, who carried a concealed pistol, waited at the copper-clad bar, which helped to relieve the little lawyer's anxiety. One couldn't be too careful in Washington. Even these once-remote warrens of the island swarmed with new inhabitants—speculators, white refugees who had tossed loyalty aside and fled the war-blasted counties of northern Virginia, contrabands of every age and hue. Dills would never risk himself in such surroundings if it weren't for the stipend.

Across the table, Bent said, "I am desperate, Mr. Dills. I have no means of supporting myself."

Dills tapped manicured nails against his glass of mineral water. "Your somewhat incoherent letter managed to make that clear. I'll speak straightforwardly, and I expect you to heed every word. If I make the arrangements—if I write the note I have in mind—you must not place me at risk. You must deal with the gentleman to whom I propose to introduce you as if the past didn't exist. You must wipe from your mind your difficulties at West Point. Your fancied grievances—"

Bent struck the table. "They are not fancied."

"Do that once more," Dills whispered, "and I will get up and leave."

Shaking, Bent covered his eyes. What a contemptible hulk he was, the lawyer thought. "Please, Mr. Dills—I'm sorry. I can overlook the past."

"You'd better. Because of your actions in New Orleans, no legitimate avenues are open to you. This one is marginal at best."

"How—how did you hear about New Orleans?"

"I have ways. I maintain an interest in your career. It isn't material to our discussion. Now, down to cases. You assure me that, so far as you know, you've never met the gentleman under discussion?"

"No."

"But he is probably familiar with your real name. For that reason, and also because he has access to military records, we must outfit you with another. Let's call it your *nom de guerre.*" The conceit produced a cool smile, the lawyer's first during this encounter.

Nom de guerre. Wonderfully fitting, Bent thought. He was still fighting a war, this one for survival, for life itself.

A tawny whore stroked Dills's shoulder. He lifted her hand and flung it off. She glared and waggled away to someone else. Dills sipped his mineral water.

Then he asked, "What name shall I use?"

Bent fingered his jowl. "Something from Ohio? What about Dayton? Ezra Dayton."

"Bland enough," Dills responded, shrugging. "You will have to go to the War Department for the initial meeting. Can you do that?"

"Is there no other—?" He stopped, seeing Dills's hard stare. "Yes, I'm sure I can."

Dills wasn't, but he said, "Very well. Before your late disappearance from the military rolls, you earned something of a reputation for brutality—Oh, don't gasp and feign innocence. I've seen copies of your records. In this instance, that unpleasant propensity works to your advantage. Write the address of your rooming house on this piece of paper. Tomorrow I'll send a messenger with an envelope addressed to Ezra Dayton, Esquire. The envelope will contain a second, sealed one, which you must not open. That will be my note of introduction, recommending you for employment by the secretary's aide for domestic security, Stanley Hazard."

Two days later, at half past seven in the morning, Bent brushed up the sack coat he had purchased in New Orleans. He deplored its travel-stained condition, but he had nothing else. He planned to walk the whole way to the War Department; he was down to his last few dollars and wouldn't squander them on transportation. The interview might go badly. If it did, he was done. He would be forced to thievery—or worse.

Outside his sleazy rooming house, he turned right, past a weedy lot where contrabands had erected blanket tents and shanties of scrap lumber, undoubtedly stolen. He glared at the colored people squatting around a cook fire.

A mild spell had interrupted the severe February weather. In brightening sunshine, he trudged all the way across the island, over the canal, and through the mall to the columned portico of the War Department building, which looked immense to him: three stories of brick, with chimneys jutting above bare trees.

Inside, an armed soldier demanded to know his business. With a perspiring hand, Bent presented the sealed letter. The soldier directed him upstairs. On his way, he paused to peer into an anteroom where a pudgy gnome with steel-rimmed spectacles stood at a tall writing desk that separated him from a line of petitioners—weeping women, army officers and noncoms, civilians who were probably contractors. The gnome was Stanton, Bent realized with some astonishment. Did he hold public audiences regularly?

In a spacious office on the floor above, an orderly led him to the fine walnut desk of Stanley Hazard. Standing in front of it, he noticed a flake on his left sleeve: some of the hardtack he had munched for breakfast and washed down with a cup of water. He was too nervous to remove the crumb.

He felt the prod of the past. But Mr. Stanley Hazard bore little resemblance to his younger brother. Further, he was plumper and sleeker than Bent remembered. Expensively dressed, too, with a ruffled shirt and a flowing cravat whose color matched his rusty orange frock coat.

Having kept his visitor waiting while he slit open the letter and read it, Stanley at last deigned to wave. "Do sit down. My time is rather short this morning."

Stanley laid the letter in front of him. Bent had to struggle to squeeze his buttocks into the chair. The past overwhelmed him. A blood vessel in his temple started to quiver, but he forced himself to mute thoughts of violence. This man represented his best, perhaps his only, means of saving himself from poverty and total failure. He must forget the man's family.

It became easier the moment Stanley smiled, a slow smile, comfortingly greasy. "This letter from Counselor Dills states that your name's Dayton—but not really."

Bent blinked in terror. "What's that?" Had the lawyer betrayed him?

"You are not aware of the contents of this?"

"No, no."

Stanley read aloud. "Dayton is a pseudonym. His true identity cannot be disclosed because of certain connections with highly placed persons. These must be protected. His enforced anonymity, however, in no wise diminishes his ability to assist you, or my strong commendation of him to your attention."

"Very—very kind of the counselor to say that," Bent gasped, relieved.

Stanley folded his hands and studied his caller. "The counselor presents you as a candidate for what we call special or detached service with a bureau of this department which, officially, does not exist. The bureau involves itself with purging the public sphere of persons whose opinions or actions are inimical to the government. This can be done by direct order of the secretary—"

Bent knew that much; Stanton had a reputation for immense power. He had only to murmur, and a critic of the administration disappeared into Old Capitol Prison, on First Street.

"—although more frequently of late, as enemies become more numerous, action has been initiated by the bureau itself. Chief of the bureau is Colonel Baker, who is also charged with carrying out certain confidential missions behind enemy lines. Occasionally I send him a promising man. Evidently that is what Dills has in mind."

Stanley left it there, awaiting a response. Perspiring, Bent blurted, "It sounds like tremendously important work, sir. Work I could do with enthusiasm. I am staunchly behind the programs of this administration—"

"That always seems to be the case with job seekers." Stanley's smirk made Bent squirm.

A moment later, a new thought struck Bent. This particular member of the Hazard clan might be cut from the same bolt as he was—and perhaps didn't deserve his enmity. Stanley Hazard was haughty, open about his importance. Those were characteristics Bent admired.

"Bear in mind, Dayton, Colonel Baker is the gentleman who says yes or no to hiring an operative. I can, however, add my recommendation to that of Dills."

"It would be very kind if you—"

"I haven't said I would," Stanley interrupted. Another moment of scrutiny. "Why aren't you in the army?"

Terror then. He had prepared himself for the question, but it was as if he hadn't. "I was, Mr. Hazard."

"Of course we can't check on that because of the problem with your identity. Very neat." A faint smile relieved Stanley's severity. "You can at least reveal the circumstances of your separation."

"Yes, surely. I resigned. I refused to accept a transfer to command of a nigger unit."

Stanley closed his fist. "Keep that sort of remark to yourself in this department. The secretary is a devout partisan of emancipation."

Again Bent stared into the abyss of failure. "I'm terribly sorry, Mr. Hazard. I promise—"

Stanley waved a second time. "Take this bit of advice also. Colonel Baker is a strong temperance man. If you drink, don't do it before you meet him."

Bent's hope soared. Stanley continued in a more confidential way. "That caveat aside, the colonel doesn't demand sainthood or even ideological purity. He demands only two qualities. His men must be trustworthy and willing to obey orders. Any orders, no matter how—" a hand fluttered, struggling to convey meaning "—irregular they might appear to certain misguided constitutionalists." He leaned forward so fast he seemed to be swooping down on prey. "Do I communicate clearly, sir?"

"Perfectly." Baker circumvented the law whenever necessary. "I can offer those qualities."

"We need them because we are locked in a vicious struggle. Enemies of the administration abound. But no man or woman is beyond our reach. If helping us achieve our goal—the crushing of domestic treason while our generals crush its military equivalent —is to your taste—"

"Very much so, sir, indeed it is," Bent said, nearly babbling.

"Then I'll add my note of introduction to that of Dills. As I said, Baker will make the final determination. But I'm a good judge of character. I'd say your prospects are excellent."

He reached for his pen and scratched a few swift lines at the bottom of Dills's letter. Then he rang a small hand bell and told his orderly to bring a new envelope. He sealed the amended letter inside.

The visitor was almost delirious. He had completely fooled Stanley Hazard, who didn't connect him with Elkanah Bent. He wanted to ask about George but couldn't think of a pretext that would not arouse suspicion. He forced the vendetta out of his mind; winning Baker's approval came first.

Stanley handed him the sealed envelope. "Take this to Colonel Baker at 217 Pennsylvania Avenue."

"Thank you, sir, thank you." Bent heaved to his feet, extending his hand, only to realize he held the letter. He let it drop. Stanley rose and clasped his hands at the small of his back.

Seething under the rebuff, Bent controlled himself and leaned over. It was hard to pick up the letter; his belly interfered. Sharply, Stanley said, "One more thing."

"Sir?"

"Your name does not appear on my appointment calendar for

523

today. Our conversation never took place, and you will forget you were ever in this building. If you violate that instruction, it could go hard with you." He gestured. "Good morning."

What would they do if he talked? Murder him? The possibility frightened him, but not for long. He could hardly contain his excitement. He had finally found a door, even if open only a crack, to the corridors of power.

He reeled down the stairs, vowing to please Colonel Baker at all costs. He might be able to locate George and Billy Hazard through this special bureau. And the work sounded ideal. He imagined himself interrogating a female suspect. Saw himself tear her clothing. Reach down to touch her. She could do nothing.

Feeling reborn, he launched himself into the sunshine. Clerks and a pair of braid-crusted officers took startled note of an obese man almost dancing along the walks of President's Park.

70

From the starboard rail forward of the pilothouse, Cooper watched the skies. Was it imagination, or was the heavy cloud cover growing luminous? Thinning to permit the rays of the moon to shine through?

Ballantyne had told him that he depended on two conditions for a successful run: the right tide and total darkness. They had the tide, but now, late in the night, an onshore wind had sprung up to push the clouds. The lookout, invisible ten minutes ago, was clearly silhouetted in the crosstrees.

Water Witch had steamed from Nassau in three days without incident. Federal ships were sighted hull down on the horizon, but the runner banked her fires to reduce smoke and slipped past them without detection, aided by her low profile and the gray paint that blurred her lines. Then came the dangerous hours—that short period in which a master earned his five thousand in gold or Yankee dollars. Even as late as an hour ago, however, Ballantyne had acted unconcerned, promising Cooper and his wife the traditional drink of celebration, a champagne cocktail, after they passed Fort Fisher.

Since leaving port, Cooper had repeatedly tried to deal with the revelation that Ashton was part owner of this vessel that so flagrantly ignored the plight of the Confederacy. Ballantyne cautioned him that no one else aboard knew the names of any of the shareholders. He had mentioned Ashton's solely in the hope of stilling Cooper's protests.

It did that, all right, but it also left him in turmoil. He hadn't decided yet what to do about his discovery.

Gripping the rail, Cooper felt the sea breeze on his face. The air was warm for a Carolina wintertime. To port, spectral blue lights hovered, the lanterns of the blockading squadron. How could they not hear the steady slap and thud of the runner's paddle floats. Even though *Water Witch* was proceeding southward dead slow, close inshore in the deepwater channel, her paddles and engines sounded thunderous as she rolled and labored in moderately heavy surf.

"Big Hill to starboard," the lookout called softly. A crewman ran aft to pass the word to the pilothouse. Cooper strained for sight of the landmark on the flat, deserted shore. He saw it suddenly, with alarming clarity, a tall hummock that told runners they were near Fort Fisher and safe water. Overhead, white patches brightened and dimmed between the racing clouds.

Had Judith and the children been able to get to sleep in their cramped berths? He suspected not. The sense of urgent work being done to the vessel in the late afternoon had conveyed itself even to Marie-Louise. The Mains watched Ballantyne's crew cover the engine-room hatchways, drape the binnacle, and haul down all but the lower masts. Special crosstrees were raised on the foremast, and the lookout sent aloft after the perpetually smiling Ballantyne issued a warning to him.

"Remember the rule on my ship. Strike so much as one match for your pipe, and I'll hang you."

Ballantyne and the pilot had agreed on the course of the final dash. They ran some twenty miles north of Cape Fear, then swung around to port, bypassing the northernmost ship on the blockade line. The maneuver accomplished at twilight, they hove to and lay virtually motionless until full dark, then began to slip down the coast toward the mouth of the river.

Slow going, hard on the nerves. Always, off to their port side, the blue lanterns shone. Now, in the growing light, Cooper detected masts and a hull big enough to belong to a cruiser.

How far away? Half a mile? If he could see the Yankee, couldn't its lookout see them?

Once more he craned his head back. Dear God, the clouds were thin as gauze. A few of the larger ones radiated light from fluffy edges, and, between, he spied stars. In a few minutes the freshening wind would completely scour the sky.

He dashed for the pilothouse, forgetting in his haste that the boats had been lowered on their davits to the level of the rail. He banged his head, letting out an exclamation that drew an angry "Keep your goddamn voice down" from a crewman crouched at the gunwale. The man had a wool cap pulled over his ears; his face and hands were blacked with coal dust. Cooper had submitted to the same treatment after questioning the need and having Ballantyne reply, "You'll do it, sir, because it's better to be dirty than dead."

In the pilothouse there was enough moonlight for him to see Ballantyne, the pilot, and the helmsman peering into a large tin cone. The cone shielded the dim light of the compass. Cooper said, "Captain, surely you've taken note of the sky. It's clearing."

"Aye." Ballantyne's grin, his universal defense against all foes and adversities, seemed to waver in the silver light splashing the enclosure. The helmsman and the pilot whispered to each other. "Bad luck, that," Ballantyne added.

"Isn't the passage too risky now? Shouldn't we turn back?"

"What, run for it? If we did, the Yankees'd give chase."

"What if they do? We can get away, can't we? You told me we're fast enough to outrun any of those ships."

"So we are."

"And the closer we get to the river, the heavier the concentration of enemy vessels—isn't that right?"

"It is."

"Then we shouldn't risk it."

"Oh, have you become the master of *Water Witch?*" Ballantyne

526

asked, growing unpleasant. "I think not. You're merely a passenger. It's true we face danger because the clouds broke up unexpectedly. But the owners have given me explicit orders. No unnecessary delays. I am paid to run Cape Fear at all hazards."

Furious, Cooper stepped closer to the captain, whose fear-born sweat he could suddenly smell. "The Confederacy won't fall if a shipment of Havana cigars and bonnet frames is delayed. I'll not allow your avarice and that of my sist—your owners to place my family in jeopardy. Show a little common sense, man! Turn back."

"Get off the bridge," Ballantyne said. "Get off or I'll have you hauled off."

Cooper reached for Ballantyne's arm. "Damn your greedy soul. Listen to—" The captain pushed him. Cooper stumbled and almost fell.

The pilot let out a despairing profanity. "Christ save us— there's the moon."

Flooding white, nearly full, it seemed to sail from behind a glowing cloud. From the pilothouse entrance, Cooper saw the masts and shrouds of four huge vessels light up like stage scenery to port. A baritone voice, amplified by a speaking trumpet, hailed *Water Witch*.

"This is the federal cruiser *Daylight*. On the steamer, heave to and await boarders."

"Hell's fire, stand aside," Ballantyne cried, pushing the helmsman and bending to the engine-room speaking tube. "Engines ahead full. Give me all the steam you can." Cooper could imagine conditions below; with the hatches covered, the stokers would be working in an inferno.

"Oh, my God," he said as a host of little vessels popped into sight from behind the cruiser. Like silvery water bugs, the federal launches chased the blockade-runner. A thousand yards astern of her, they threw off moonlit bow spray.

Standing outside the pilothouse, Cooper looked ahead. Beyond the bow he saw a cluster of blue lanterns he hadn't noticed before. The engines of *Water Witch* grew louder; the rhythm of paddle blades slapping water quickened. A bosun's pipe sounded on the Yankee cruiser. Through the trumpet boomed the great disembodied voice. "Heave to or I will open fire."

"Ballantyne," Cooper began, "you've got to—" Curses and shouts from the scared sailors overlaid his words, as did Ballantyne's loud "Keep him out." The door of the pilothouse slammed, nearly hitting Cooper's nose.

"Steam frigate," the lookout exclaimed. "Dead astern."

And there she was, swung out in pursuit a couple of miles behind them, moonlit smoke billowing, all her square sails set to add an extra two or three knots to the speed generated by her boilers. *Water Witch* began to move faster, leaping free of the heavy surf rolling in to shore on the starboard side.

Cooper's gut hurt. One, two, three sparking trails appeared high above *Daylight*. The moon grew feeble as a trimmed lamp when the Drummond rockets burst, their calcium light whitening everything. Even the muskets of the men in the launches were visible.

A gun on the pursuing cruiser flashed and went *rumph,* then another. The shells fell short, raising geysers that shone like liquid diamonds under the flare light. At the first crash, Cooper ran below, his hair flying.

Their cabin door was open, Judith there, her arms around the children. She tried not to show her fright. Cooper grabbed her damp hand. "Come on, this way."

Another shell exploded, this one much closer. The vessel rocked as she strained ahead.

"Pa, what is it?" Judah exclaimed.

"The moon came out, and Ballantyne wouldn't turn back, the son of a bitch. All he cares about is getting his goods to Wilmington—Come *on.*" He jerked Judith so hard, she cried out. He regretted it, but he had to get them to safety.

"Where are we going?" his daughter said as the hull tilted.

"To the boats. Ballantyne will have them lowered by now. Our only chance is to row ashore."

When the family emerged on deck, Cooper couldn't believe what he saw: every boat still swaying wildly on its davits. He grabbed a passing crewman.

"Put the boats down so we can get off!"

"Nobody's gettin' off, mister. We're runnin' for the river." He dashed on, whirling an alarm rattle. The ratchet sounded loud as pistol fire.

More Drummond lights spread their white glow. A shell came whining in, struck the stern and lifted it. Judith screamed. So did the children. All of them fell against Cooper, tumbling him into the scuppers and crushing him against the rail.

"Papa, I'm scared." Marie-Louise flung her arms around Cooper's neck. "Will the boat sink? Will we be prisoners of the Yankees?"

"No," he gasped, struggling to regain his feet as *Water Witch* rolled again, caught in the heavy surf. Cannon boomed, the glare visible above the rail. Two crewmen turned their heads at a whistling sound. One pushed the other, too late. Scattering grape felled both men and shattered the window of the pilothouse.

Judith ducked and bit her hand to hold back an outcry. A massive detonation went off belowdecks. Someone yelled, "We're hulled."

At once, the runner listed sharply to starboard. Cooper saw Captain Ballantyne on deck, running back and forth in a state of agitation, trying to find men to help him lower one boat. "Bastard," Cooper said. "Greedy stupid bastard. Come on, children—Judith—we're getting in that boat if I have to kill every man on this ship."

Balancing on the steeply tilting deck, they slid to the starboard side, where high waves spent their strength against the shoreline. If all else failed, Cooper thought, they might manage to swim and wade to the beach. Holding his daughter, he worked his way down the slippery incline toward the captain, who had flung himself into the effort to lower a boat.

"Ballantyne—" Before Cooper could shout anything else, another shell hit belowdecks. The explosion was followed by terrifying noise—the howl of metal rupturing, a furious hiss of steam, and some of the worst screams Cooper had ever heard.

Water Witch's port side came up, parallel with the sea. Cooper saw his wife's blonde head rush past him, downward. He saw her form a word—their son's name. Judah's hand had somehow slipped from her grasp. Where was he? Cooper tried to see, still holding fast to Marie-Louise as he himself fell.

In all the noise, the shrieks, the crash of surf and guns, Ballantyne, incredibly, made himself heard. Cooper had a distorted glimpse of the captain, hair standing out from his head, arms flung wide against the moon.

"Boilers have burst. Every man for—" Between Ballantyne's legs, the deck split open and swallowed him, screaming, into clouds of steam.

The mate, Soapes, and two other crewmen fought to be first to jump over the side. Belowdecks, dying men screamed in the engine room. Cooper was flung against the rail with back-breaking force. He started to clamber over, one arm circling his daughter's shoulders, the other groping for Judith's hand and clutching it. The steamer careened farther, its keel rising out of the sea. The Mains fell past the rail into white foam.

Treading water, gasping, Cooper clung to his wife and daughter. "Where's—Judah?"

"I don't know," Judith shouted back.

Then, amidst the debris falling around them as *Water Witch* broke apart, he spied a floating body whose clothes he recognized. He hurled Marie-Louise at his wife and swam the short distance, fighting against the opposing waves. He had a premonition that his son was dead, probably killed when the boilers burst. As he struggled the last few feet, he tried to summon hope that he was wrong.

Judah floated face down. Cooper grabbed for his son's shoulder but miscalculated the distance and caught the boy's head. The head rolled into sight, steam-scalded, bone showing in several places. Judah was barely recognizable. A wave swept between father and son, leaving nothing in Cooper's hand but a piece of skin.

"Judah!" He screamed the name. Away and under went the frail body. "Judah, Judah." He wrenched back, waves battering him, water cascading over his head, choking him, mingling with demented tears. "Judith, he's dead, he's gone, he's dead."

"Swim, Cooper." She seized his collar, jerking him. "Swim with us or we'll all die."

A section of mast fell just beyond her. Cooper started to paddle with his left arm, and kick, while his right hand supported Marie-Louise, crying hysterically now. On the other side of the girl, Judith helped support her. Cooper felt pain in his chest, then in his muscles as he kicked toward the shore, closer to drowning each time the waves broke over them from behind.

A moment more, and he felt himself bumped by floating objects. He spat out salt water and vomit, and saw they had struggled into an area where round, gauze-wrapped disks and small wood casks stenciled in Spanish floated. Sherry and cheese, cheese and sherry—sinking, then bobbing up, on the coast of war—

The sight fused Cooper's thoughts and fears and feelings, locking them in a solid black delirium. He screamed once more and kept swimming. He remembered nothing else.

530

71

In the deep amber dusk, Orry hurried past a wall on which someone had painted three words, only to have someone else attempt
to scrub them away. Just above his head, ghostly white letters
spelled DEATH TO DAVIS.

Neither the message—a not uncommon one these days—nor
anything else, including his odious job, could spoil his mood. He
was rushing because he had taken longer at supper than he intended. He and his old friend George Pickett had drained a forty-
dollar bottle of imported Graves with their meal and packed several years' worth of reminiscences into a little more than an hour.

Pickett, who had been Orry's West Point classmate, looked as
handsome as ever. Scented hair flowed over the collar of his uniform, and his smile shone as brightly as Orry remembered. They
discussed subjects as diverse as their wives and the fat Yankee
Bent, whose hatred of Orry had driven him to plot against Cousin
Charles while both were serving with the Second Cavalry.

Pickett chided his friend for wasting himself in the job of
watchdog over General Winder. "Though the Lord knows the
poor lunatic ought to be watched by someone, so he doesn't disgrace us in the eyes of the world." Orry countered by saying that,
menial and unrewarding as his work might appear, he was finding
it important as carloads of prisoners came to town every few days,
snatched up along the winter lines to swell the populations of
already overcrowded Belle Isle and Libby.

"Winder administers those places, you see. The Yankees would

531

be treated much worse than they are if the War Department didn't go in from time to time and curb the excesses."

Pickett accepted that. When they reached the bottom of the wine bottle, he admitted that despite promotion to major general in the autumn, he was unhappy. During recent months he had commanded the center of the Fredericksburg line, seeing little action. Between the old friends an unspoken truth seemed to hover. The war was not going well for the Confederacy. Soldier and civilian alike felt the stirrings of a poisonous doubt about the outcome. Someone had to be blamed; anonymous malcontents slashed DEATH TO DAVIS on empty walls.

Although the reunion had touches of melancholy, generally Orry enjoyed it, right down to the final cups of real coffee—three dollars apiece, and no questions asked about how the hotel had obtained it. They walked out arm in arm and parted on the street, Pickett to take his wife to see *The Ticket-of-Leave Man* at the smart new Richmond Theater, built where the Marshall had burned last year, and Orry to meet Madeline's train.

He rushed through the crowded, grimy depot, navigating around sad-eyed youths on litters or crutches, yelling peddlers, and strolling tarts. On a large chalkboard, the arriving Richmond & Petersburg train was shown as 1½ HRS LATE.

Night fell. The wait seemed far longer than what the board declared. Finally, out beyond the platform's end, a light appeared on the great trestle sixty feet above the river gorge. The train came in with a squeal of drivers, hissing of brakes, belching of smoke. The weather-bleached cars, most with broken windows, discharged furloughed men returning to duty and civilians of every degree from prosperous to poor. Amid the crowd, Orry stood out because of his height. He saw no one he recognized.

Had she missed a connection? Not been able to get away on schedule? Passengers waved to waiting friends or loved ones. Blurred, happy faces rushed by. His worry and anxiety deepened. Then, stepping down from the last car, there she was.

Her traveling dress had picked up the dirt so common on Southern trains these days. Locks of hair had come undone, straggling over her ears and brow. She looked exhausted and beautiful, and, whether in fact or by the alchemy of imagination, she smelled of the sweet olive of home.

"Madeline!" He shouted and waved like some schoolboy, struggling against the flow of passengers.

"Oh, Orry—my darling. My darling." She dropped a portmanteau and two hatboxes and flung her arms around his neck, hugging him, kissing him, weeping. "I thought I'd never get here."

"I thought you wouldn't either." Happy as a young bridegroom, he stepped back. "Are you all right?"

"Yes, yes—are you? We must collect my trunk. It was shipped in the baggage car."

"We'll get it and catch a hack outside. I hate for you to see my rooms. They're all I could get, and they're dismal."

"I'd sleep on a rubbish heap to be with you. Dear God, Orry—it's been so long—Oh, my. You've lost weight."

The sentences tumbled over one another, happiness cutting through the annoyances of the long, hard journey. Orry tipped a Negro porter, pointed him toward the baggage car, and located a hack. When they were on their way to the quarters he had hired a woman to clean that morning, he sat on Madeline's left so he could keep his arm around her.

"I couldn't wait for you to arrive, but it's a bad time to be in Richmond. People are miserable. Angrier by the day. Everything's in short supply."

"One thing isn't. My love for you." She kissed him.

She treated his accommodations in the rooming house as if they were palatial. Feasting on the sight of her by the light of a single low-trimmed gaslight, he asked, "Are you hungry?"

"Only for you. I brought some books—"

"Hurrah! We can read in the evenings—" Despite the strange, cruel tilting of the world, they might recall at least a little of the past. "Any poetry?"

"Yes, Keats. And a copy of Dickens's *Pickwick Papers,* which I liked very much."

"It's proscribed here. Too vulgar or something." He couldn't control his ebullience, going to her and circling her waist with his arm. He kissed her throat. "You must tell me everything new at Mont Royal. We've hours and hours of catching up to do—" He gazed into his wife's eyes, adding softly, "In many ways."

Madeline smiled. He changed position slightly so that he could touch and warmly close his hand over her breast. He kissed her with such ardor her back began to bow. Laughing, she broke the embrace. She began to unfasten the cloth-covered buttons of her bodice.

Naked with her in the cool bedroom, its door ajar to give them

533

light, he gazed at her hair on the pillow and gently, gently pushed the tip of himself into her, experiencing a happiness almost unbearable. There came back to him then a poem they had read repeatedly during the frustrating years when honor and her marriage vows prevented this kind of consummation. Looking down at her, he spoke some of Poe's *Annabel Lee.*

" 'And this maiden she lived with no other thought than to love and be loved by me—' "

"We'll never be separated again," Madeline cried. "We mustn't be, ever. I would die."

From a second-floor window on Franklin Street, Mrs. Burdetta Halloran watched a hack arrive at the house directly opposite. A bosomy, cheaply attractive young woman with dark hair paid the driver, ascended the stoop, knocked, and waited with a tense air. A moment later, she stepped into a vertical bar of darkness, and the door closed.

Late afternoon light the color of lemons fell through lace curtains into the bay where Mrs. Halloran had kept a vigil on randomly chosen days throughout the past month. To the spinster who owned the house, she had presented herself as the aunt of a young woman suspected of falling into sin with the gentleman living across the way. She needed to be certain before pressing a confrontation, she said. Whatever the elderly spinster thought of the story, the small sum Mrs. Halloran paid each time kept her silent.

Who was the slut? Burdetta Halloran wondered. She didn't know, but she wouldn't forget the face. With short, quick tugs, she pulled on ecru mittens and spoke to the woman hovering in the dusty shadow.

"Thank you so much for the use of your room. I won't be needing it again."

"You saw your niece—?"

"Alas, yes. Going into the house of that Mr. Powell."

"I know him only by sight. He's a very private gentleman."

"He has a foul reputation." She could barely refrain from saying more. She settled her small feathered hat on her head, smiled, and glided to the upper hall. "I shall go out by the back, as usual."

"I have come to anticipate these little visits. I almost regret that your vigil has been successful."

I'm sure you do, greedy old woman.

"If that Powell is as bad as you say, I do hope you can effect a separation between him and your niece."

"I shall, don't worry," the younger woman assured her, hurrying down the stairs because she feared her face would betray her.

Betray—that was the proper word here. Lamar Powell had betrayed her love and trust. Burdetta Halloran had no intention of concerning herself with Powell's current light of love. He was the one who merited her attention. He would get it.

Washington and Boz smelled the approaching spring in wet earth and night wind. A clergyman rode out from Fredericksburg to speak with Gus, and although the freedmen didn't hear the conversation, they guessed the reverend's purpose. He failed to accomplish it.

As the mounds of snow in the dooryard grew smaller, the two blacks began to notice bands of horsemen on the road at all hours. At night, the tree line glittered from artillery fire along the river; occasionally the explosions shook the windowpanes so hard the vibration produced an eerie whining sound. Washington and Boz conferred often about the seriousness of the situation and finally decided to approach their mistress.

They argued for an hour about who should do it. The job fell to the younger man. Boz went to the kitchen at suppertime.

"Ain't no way to get around it, Miss Augusta. Gonna be fighting soon. Union Army might roll straight across this farm. Ain't safe to stay here. Washington and me, we'd fight to the end for you. Die for you. But neither of us wants you killed, an' we don't much want to be killed either if we can help it." He took a deep breath. "Won't you please go to Richmond City?"

"Boz, I can't."

"Why not?"

"Because if he came looking for me, he wouldn't know where to find me. I could write him, but the mails are so poor he might never get the letter. I'm sorry, Boz. You and Washington are free to leave whenever you want. I must stay."

"Stayin's dangerous, Miss Augusta."

"I know. But it would be worse to go and never see him again."

When Billy left Lehigh Station at the end of his short furlough, Brett again found herself adrift in gloom. In part, her mood was a direct result of her husband's preoccupation with the army. He said the sagging morale didn't affect him; he was a professional. But she saw the changes in him—the tiredness, the cynicism, the simmering anger.

Just one medicine seemed to relieve her depression: long hours of helping the Czornas and Scipio Brown care for the lost children. She scrubbed floors, cooked meals, read stories to the smallest, and taught letters and numbers to the older ones. Each day, she worked until she was certain of falling asleep moments after she went to bed.

Late in the bitter winter, Brown took two of the youngsters out to Oberlin, Ohio, by train; he had located a black family who wanted to adopt a son and a daughter. He returned through Washington, bringing three new girls, ages seven, eight, and thirteen. On his first day in Lehigh Station, he took each for a horseback ride. Brown had spent so much time gathering up supplies, some purchased but most donated, and searching the packed refugee camps in Washington and Alexandria that he had found it useful to move faster than he could on foot. He had taught himself to be a competent rider. Horses seemed to sense an innate kindliness in him, as did the children.

That didn't mean he had softened his spine or his militancy. Although Brett had grown to like Brown very much, she felt that he enjoyed provoking arguments with her simply because of who she was and where she came from.

One of these took place on an afternoon in March when she and Brown left the building on the hillside to buy corn meal and some other staples from Pinckney Herbert. Brown drove the buggy, and she sat beside him—something that would have caused no comment around Mont Royal, where it would be presumed that he was a bondsman. In Lehigh Station their appearance together inevitably generated hostile stares and sometimes ugly comments, especially from people like Lute Fessenden and his cousin. Both had thus far evaded military service.

They wouldn't much longer. Lincoln had recently signed an act conscripting able-bodied males twenty to forty-six for three years of duty. A man could hire a substitute or purchase an exemption for three hundred dollars. That escape hatch for the rich had already infuriated the poor of the North—Fessenden and his cousin among them, she suspected.

In good weather the two men were almost always on the street, and that was true today. As Brett and the broad-shouldered black started their return trip up the hillside, the red-bearded Fessenden spied them and shouted an insult.

Brown sighed. "Wonder if this country's ever going to change. I see scum like that, I have my doubts."

"You've certainly changed since we first met."

"How's that?"

"For one thing, you hardly mention colonization any more."

Brown turned to look at her. "Why should the Negro be packed off on ships now that the President's granted us freedom? Oh, I know—the proclamation's really a war measure. Not meant to apply anywhere except down South. But Mr. Lincoln still calls it freedom, and we'll do more with it than even he can imagine. You wait and see."

"I don't believe Lincoln has changed his mind about resettlement, Scipio. The *Ledger-Union* said he has a program to ship a boatload of blacks to a new colony this spring. Nearly five hundred of them. They're going to some tiny island near Haiti."

"Well, Old Abe won't send me there—nor Dr. Delany, either. I saw him in Washington—did I tell you? No more robes for Martin. He wants a uniform. He's trying for a commission in a black regiment."

Over the clop of the walking horses, she said, "Billy told me Negroes aren't being received well in the army. Don't take offense, now—these aren't his words or mine—but most white officers protest that they're being niggered to death."

"Let them. For the first time I feel I'm close to real freedom. Anyone tries to deny it to me, I'll expend every drop of blood in my body. Mr. Lincoln may not have intended his proclamation to say every black man and woman in the land is free now. But that's how I take it."

"That's an extreme view of the proclamation, Scipio."

"You say so because you grew up where it was all right to steal a man's liberty. Own him like you would a side of bacon, a piece of lumber. But it isn't all right. Either the freedom in this country is for every last man or it's a fraud."

"I still say you're being extreme about—"

"Why are you defensive all the time?" he interrupted. "Because I jab a pin into your conscience deep enough to hurt?" He reined in at the shoulder. A baker driving his wagon down the hillside gave them a scornful stare. "Look me straight in the eye, Brett.

Answer one question: Do you think liberty's just for persons of your color?"

"That was the intent of the authors of the Declaration."

"Not all the authors! Anyway, this is 1863. So you answer. Is freedom for the white people and nobody else?"

"I was taught—"

"I don't want to know what you were taught, I want to know what you believe."

"Damn you, Scipio, you're so blasted—"

"Uppity?" Thin smile. "That I am."

"Southerners aren't the only sinners, you know. The Yankees really don't want black people free. Some abolitionists do, but not the majority."

"Too late." He shrugged. "Mr. Lincoln signed his order. And frankly, I don't care much about what *is*. I care about what ought to be."

"Pushing that attitude could set this whole country on fire."

"It's already on fire—or haven't you read the news lately?"

"Sometimes I absolutely detest you, you're so arrogant."

"I detest you for the same reason. Sometimes."

He reached over to pat her hand but held back; he feared she would misconstrue. Calmer, he went on, "I wouldn't bother with you one single minute if I didn't believe there was a sensible, decent woman inside you someplace, twisting and fighting to get out into the light of day. I think the reason you can't stand me sometimes is that I'm a mirror. I make you look at yourself. What you believe—and what you have to become unless you want to mock all the dead of this war."

Quietly, with tension: "You're right. I guess that is why I despise you sometimes. Nobody wants to be shown his errors—be pushed along a path that's hard and dangerous."

"The only other path leads you down to the dark for sure. That the one you want?"

"No—no! But—"

Lamely, she finished there, unable to marshal arguments. Why must he hammer at her conscience all the time? He did, and so did the faces of his flock. Brown or saffron or polished blue-black, they worked on it every day. Worked on it and forced her to question her father's dogmatic belief in the rightness of the peculiar institution. Worked on it so that she asked herself the kinds of questions Cooper had dared to ask their father aloud. What

538

Brown didn't know was that she already felt the pinch and pain associated with dissecting old beliefs. She resented him for fostering the process.

Sensing her mood, Brown said, "We better quit this talk before we stop being friends."

"Yes."

"I wouldn't want to stop being your friend, you know. You're not only a good woman, but we've got two more walls to whitewash at the school. You're mighty fine with a brush. Sure there isn't slave blood in you somewhere?"

Uncontrollably, she laughed. "You're impossible."

"And bound and determined to change you around. That fine husband of yours won't recognize you when he marches home after they disband the army and discharge all those poor suffering white boys who've been niggered to death. Tell you one thing sure—"

Smile gone, he stared into the sunshine. "This country better get ready to be niggered to death, because I won't spend my life as a Dred Scott. Not a person. Nothing. A lot of my people feel the same. Our chains are going to break—the real ones and the invisible ones, too. I swear before God, the chains will break or the land will burn."

"Maybe both will come to pass, Scipio," she said in a small voice.

He, too, was quiet now. "It could be so. I do hope not."

She shivered, knowing suddenly that he was right about liberty. The moment altered her, leaving a small, hard certainty; regret and a sentimental wishing for the old way; and much fear of consequences. She felt as if she had betrayed someone or something but could and would not change the fact. The argument marked a milepost on the road they had talked about. It was a road that allowed no turning back.

He picked up the reins, said "Haw" to the horses, and they went forward.

"So," said the man with the red beard and the holstered pistols under his frock coat. "You believe you could help our special service bureau do the work I've summarized?"

"Very definitely, Colonel Baker."

"I do, too, Mr. Dayton. I do, too."

Bent felt faint. It was not merely because success had finally come after weeks of waiting. It was March now—Baker had postponed the interview three times, pleading emergencies. Bent was light-headed because he was starving. His own money had run out, forcing him to borrow a small amount from Dills. To conserve it, he ate only two meals a day.

Lafayette Baker had the build of a dock hand and the eyes of a ferret. Bent guessed him to be thirty-five. The past hour had consisted of a few questions followed by a rambling monologue about Baker's history: work he had done for the exiled Cameron, his high regard for Stanton's opinions and methods. He spent fifteen minutes on a period in the eighteen-fifties when he had been a San Francisco vigilante, proudly purifying the city of criminals with bullets and hang-ropes. On the desk between Baker and his visitor lay a splendid gold-chased cane, California manzanita wood with a lump of gold quartz set in the head. Nine smaller stones surrounded it, each from a different mine, Baker explained. The cane had been a gift from a grateful San Francisco merchant.

"The chief duty of this bureau, as I cannot stress too often, is the discovery and punishment of traitors. I carry out that task using the methods of the man whose career I have studied and emulated."

Taking the cane, he pointed at a framed portrait on the wall. Bent had noticed it earlier, the sole decoration in the otherwise monastic office. The man in the daguerreotype had a stiff, severe countenance and small eyeglasses perched on his nose.

"The greatest detective of them all: Vidocq, of the Paris police. Do you know of him?"

"Only by name."

"In his early days, he was a criminal. But he reformed and became the hated foe of the very class from which he sprang. You must read his memoirs, Dayton. They are not only exciting, they're instructive. Vidocq had a simple and effective philosophy, which I follow to the letter." Baker slid his palm back and forth over the head of the cane. "It's far better to seize and hold a hundred innocents than to let one guilty man escape."

"I agree with that, sir." Expediency had been replaced by an eagerness to work for Baker.

"I hope so, because only those who do can serve me effectively. We do vital work here in the capital, but we also perform special services elsewhere." Baker's small, unreadable eyes fixed on Bent.

540

"Before employing you in Washington, I would propose to test your mettle. Are you still with me?"

Frightened, Bent had no choice but to nod.

"Excellent. Sergeant Brandt will handle the details of placing you on our payroll, but I shall describe your first assignment now." He stared, intimidating. "You are going into Virginia, Mr. Dayton. Behind enemy lines."

72

For nearly a month, they lived in a single room, a room fourteen by fourteen, which Judith divided by hanging blankets around Marie-Louise's pallet, thus affording her a little privacy.

In the crowded city they had been lucky to get any room at all. A senior officer at Fort Fisher had found this, which had but one good feature—a pair of windows overlooking the river. Cooper sat in front of the windows for hours, a blanket over his legs, his shoulders hunched, his face reduced to gray hollowness by the pneumonia that had kept him near death for two weeks. Learning of Ashton's involvement with *Water Witch* had done something to him, but the demise of his son had done something worse.

On the night Judah drowned, the Mains paddled and floundered through the surf and finally reached shore. They collapsed on a moonlit dune two miles above the earthwork that guarded the river mouth at Confederate Point. There were no other survivors on the beach.

Cooper had vomited everything, all the salty water he had swallowed, then gone wandering up and down the shore calling Judah's name. Marie-Louise lay half conscious in her mother's arms, and Judith kept her tears contained till she could stand it no longer. Then she wailed, not caring whether the whole damn blockade squadron heard her.

When the worst of the grief had worked itself out, she ran after Cooper, took his hand, and led him south, where she presumed they would find Fort Fisher. He was docile and burbling like a madman. The long walk under the moon had a dreamy quality, as though they were on a strand in one of Mr. Poe's enchanted kingdoms. At last they staggered into the fort, and next morning a detail was sent out to search the dunes. Judah's body was not found.

And so they had come twenty-eight miles upriver to the city, where Cooper had fallen ill and Judith had feared for his life. Now he was recovered, at least physically, and he sat by the windows, watching the piers where armed soldiers were on guard to prevent deserters from stowing away on outbound ships.

He spoke only when necessary. Blue-black shadows ringed his eyes as he watched the March sun shimmer on the river. Watched the flatboats of the Market Street Ferry put out for the opposite shore. Watched the little sloops owned by local rice planters darting over the bright water.

Wilmington was a boom town, full of sharps, sailors, Confederate soldiers homeward bound on furlough. The streets, even their room, smelled of naval stores: the pine lumber, pitch, and turpentine busy merchants sold to representatives of the British Navy. Managing to secure a letter of credit from their Charleston bank, Judith purchased new clothing for the three of them from the M. Katz Emporium on Market. Cooper's suit hung in the wardrobe, still wrapped in paper.

Walking at the upper end of their street one day, Judith spied a splendid house with a great many prosperous young men in civilian dress coming and going. From an upstairs window she heard the singing of Negro minstrels. A peddler told her the place was the residence of most of the British masters and mates who ran the blockade. Flush with new money, they held all-night parties, wagered on cockfights in the garden, entertained women of ill repute, and scandalized the town. Judith was glad Cooper wasn't with her; the boisterous house would only make him angrier.

For he *was* angry. His silence told her. So did the queer glitter of his eyes. They shone like metal hemispheres as he sat staring into the March sunshine. They belonged to no man she knew.

At night, Judith often cried for a long time, thinking of Judah; he could not even be given a decent burial. The sorrow was increased by Cooper's remoteness. He no longer put his arm around her or touched her or said a single word when they lay side by side in the hard bed. Judith only cried more, ashamed of the tears but unable to stop them.

One day toward the end of March, Marie-Louise burst out, "Are we going to stay in this awful room the rest of our lives?" Judith wondered that herself. For the first week or so, she had refrained from pushing Cooper about leaving; he was still weak, and tired easily. Prompted by her daughter's question, she suggested to him that she telegraph Secretary Mallory and report their whereabouts. He answered her with a bleak nod and another of his peculiar, indifferent stares.

A few days later, she ran up the stairs of the rooming house with a sheet of flimsy yellow paper. Judith had left Marie-Louise in the parlor with a February number of the *Southern Illustrated News;* she wanted to read the romantic serial and work the word puzzle.

Cooper sat, as usual, watching the piers and darting sloops. "Darling, splendid news," she said. Three steps carried her across the cramped room. "There was a message from the secretary at the telegraph office."

Smiling, hoping to cheer and encourage him, she held out the yellow flimsy. He wouldn't take it. She laid it in his lap. "You must read it. Stephen sends condolences and pleads with you to travel to Richmond as soon as you can."

Cooper blinked twice. His gaunt face, so curiously alien lately, softened a little. "He has need of me?"

"Yes! Read the telegram."

Bending his head, he did.

She almost wished he hadn't when he looked up again. His smile had no humanity and somehow made his glaring eyes appear to sink deeper into their blue-black sockets. "I reckon it is time to go. I must have an accounting with Ashton."

"I know you've been brooding about that. But she isn't really responsible for—"

"She is," he interrupted. "Ballantyne said it explicitly—the owners wanted no delays. They wanted cargo delivered at all hazards. He gambled with Judah's life because of greed. His own and Ashton's. She is very much to blame."

A shiver shook Judith's slim frame. The gay, brightly barbed speech of the old Cooper was gone, replaced by pronouncements, bitterly made. She began to fear the consequences of his rage.

"Help me up," he said suddenly, flinging off the blanket.

"Are you strong enough?"

"Yes." The blanket fell. He wavered and took her arm, grasping so hard she winced.

"Cooper, you're hurting me."

He relaxed his grip without apology, and with a curious, stony indifference. "Where's my new suit? I want to go to the depot for train tickets."

"I can buy them."

"I will! I want to get to Richmond. We've stayed here too long."

"You were ill. You had to rest."

"I had to think, too. Clear my head. Find my purpose. I have. I intend to help the secretary prosecute this war to the full. Nothing else matters."

She shook her head. "I hear you, but I don't believe you. When the war started, you detested it."

"No longer. I share Mallory's view. We must win, not negotiate a peace. I'd like to win at the expense of a great many dead Yankees—and the more of them I can be responsible for, the better."

"Darling, don't talk that way."

"Stand aside so I can find my clothes."

"Cooper, listen to me. Don't let Judah's death rob you of the kindness and idealism that always—"

He slammed the wardrobe open, startling her to silence. Pivoting, his head thrust forward like some carrion bird's, he stared with those awful eyes.

"Why not?" he said. "Kindness couldn't save our son's life. Idealism couldn't prevent Ballantyne and my sister from murdering him."

"But you can't mourn him for the rest of your—"

"I wouldn't be mourning at all if you'd stayed in Nassau with the children as I begged you to do."

The shout drove her back from him. Pale, she said, "So that's it. You must have people to blame, and I'm one."

"Please excuse me while I get dressed." He turned his back on her.

Crying silently, Judith slipped out the door and waited with Marie-Louise till he came down twenty minutes later.

73

Ashton heard the sound, a cry of many voices, before its significance became clear.

She was just entering Franzblau's Epicurean, a fine shop on Main Street that only the wealthiest patronized, never being so indelicate as to ask the sources of its merchandise. Some had come in on the last successful voyage of *Water Witch*. There would be no more such voyages. The steamer had been trapped and sunk near the entrance to the Cape Fear River, Powell said. It didn't matter. The profits already realized were enormous.

Last night, while Huntoon once again worked late, a messenger had brought a note from Ashton's partner. Slyly worded to give an air of courtliness and propriety, it requested that she visit him in the morning so they might give a proper farewell to their late vessel and plan their strategy. Powell loved to tease her with such pretexts—as if she needed any. Already, thoughts of the meeting filled her cheeks with a pink that matched the fluffy dyed marabou trimming the cuffs and collar of her black velvet dress.

Although it was the second of April, a Thursday, the morning was cool. She had arrived at the Epicurean shortly after ten-thirty and now addressed the frail, gray-haired proprietor.

"Mumm's, if you have any, Mr. Franzblau. And a pot—no, two—of that wonderful goose-liver pâté."

As she counted out a hundred and twenty Confederate dollars, Franzblau wrapped the two crocks in butcher's paper, which everyone saved and used for writing letters these days. Again the noise intruded. Franzblau raised his head. So did the black man seated by the door to bar undesirables.

Franzblau put the bottle of champagne beside the wrapped foie gras in Ashton's wicker hamper. "What are those people shouting?"

She listened. " 'Bread.' Over and over—'bread.' How peculiar."

The black man jumped up as Homer bolted through the door. "Mrs. Huntoon, we better get out of here," the elderly houseman said. "There's a crowd comin' round the corner. Mighty big and mighty mad."

Franzblau paled and whispered something in German, reaching under the counter for a six-barrel pepperbox revolver. "I have feared something like this. Will, draw the blind."

Down came the canvas on its roller, hiding Ashton's open carriage at the curb. Homer motioned with urgency. Ashton's heels clicked on the black-and-white ceramic diamonds of the floor. Halfway to the entrance, she heard a crash of glass. She had seen the sullen faces of Richmond's poor and hungry white women, but she had never expected them to take to the streets.

Homer took the hamper and went outside, pausing in the shop's recessed entrance. From that vantage point Ashton saw twenty women, then twice that many, storming down the center of Main Street. More followed. Inside, Franzblau said, "Lock the door, Will." It closed and clicked.

"I run for the carriage," Homer said. Some of the women had the same idea.

"I'll follow you," Ashton whispered, terror-stricken at the sight of hundreds of shabbily dressed women pushing, screaming, hurling rocks and bricks at plate glass, ripping shoes and clothing from the shop windows. "Bread," they chanted, "bread," while helping themselves to apparel and jewelry.

A produce cart trapped in the center of Main was lifted by a pack of women. Its cargo of crated hens tumbled out with a splintering of slats, a fountaining of feathers, a ferocious flapping and squawking. The farmer cowered underneath the wreckage of the cart.

Jumping into the open carriage, Ashton was horrified to see the women drag the man out and swarm over him. They punched, clawed, and kicked. He yelled, but the cries were quickly submerged in the chanting.

More rioters rounded the corner of Ninth Street, some pouring up from Cary, some down from the direction of Capitol Square. They were not all impoverished householders; ratty boys had joined the mob, and some older toughs as well.

Homer fumbled with whip and reins. Half a dozen women rushed the carriage, hands extended, ugly mouths working.

"There's a rich one."

"Got food in that hamper, I bet."

"Hand it over, dearie—"

"Hurry, Homer," Ashton cried, just as a gray-haired woman in smelly rags jumped onto the carriage step. A dirty hand clasped Ashton's wrist and yanked.

"Get her out, get her out," the other women chanted, pressing around the rag woman. Ashton writhed, struggled. It did no good. Marginally aware of Homer flicking the whip at two boys holding the horses, she bent and bit the woman's filthy hand. The woman screamed and fell off the step.

"Bread, bread!" More windows shattered. Women charged the door of Franzblau's Epicurean, broke it, tore down the blind, and jumped through the opening edged with glass. A pistol went off; someone cried out.

Homer whipped one of the white boys, then the other. He got the team started, only to have two women seize the rear of the carriage and hang on. A third attempted to leap in and grab Ashton again. The street was in tumult. "Shoes, shoes!" "Police down there—" "Jeff's coming out to speak." "Let him. We'll cook him for dinner."

"Give me, little Miss Rich," panted the woman as she put her hands on the hamper. Ashton's mouth set. She flipped the hamper open, took the champagne bottle by the neck, and swung it, breaking it squarely across the side of the woman's head.

The woman howled and let go, falling back, covered with foaming champagne and bits of glass. Ashton jabbed the broken bottle at those nearest the carriage. They melted back. Damned dirty cowards, she thought.

Grimacing, she knelt on the seat, reached over, and struck at the hands of the women holding the carriage. She slashed left and right with the bottle neck, cutting veins in the backs of their hands. Blood pumped out. "Homer, goddamn you, get moving!"

Like a wild person, he whipped horses and rioters alike. He turned the carriage and charged another group of women, who scattered. Many were running, Ashton noticed as the carriage careened around a corner into Eleventh Street. She heard shrill whistles, gunshots. The metropolitan detail had arrived.

The unexpected violence wrecked Ashton's schedule for the morning. By the time the carriage reached Grace Street it was twenty past eleven, and another impatient hour went by before she felt she could leave by herself. The servants suspected she had a lover, or so she believed; whenever she went out alone, she was careful not to confirm the suspicion with haste or any kind of outrageous behavior. So she lingered at the house, feigning a case of nerves. Curiously, once she was out of danger, recalling the riot induced a state of arousal.

The war had that same kind of stimulating effect on Ashton. It sharpened every pleasure, from totting up the profits of *Water Witch* to clasping Powell with arms and legs as he drove into her —love was too soft a word for the nearly unbearable sensations he created. In what other time but wartime could she have brought her husband and her lover into the same business enterprise? It was macabre, but it was exhilarating.

Finally, having washed and refreshed herself, she drove to the Queen Anne house on Franklin Street. She arrived at half past twelve, carrying the hamper with the two pots of foie gras.

"I had a bottle of Mumm's, but I had to break it to escape the mob," she explained to Powell in the parlor. He was barefoot, wearing only breeches.

"When you didn't come on time, I decided not to answer the door if you did arrive," he said. "Then I heard a drayman shouting something about a riot downtown. So I forgave you."

"It was the maddest confusion. Hundreds of ugly, utterly filthy women—"

"I'd like to hear about it." He guided her hand. "But not now."

A clock was chiming two when Ashton came swimming up through sleepy satiation. The bedding had been tangled and torn loose. Powell dozed beside her. She brushed hair from her eyes and drowsily studied two surprising objects on a taboret near his right shoulder: a map of the United States and, resting on it, his favorite gun—a rim-fire Sharps pocket pistol whose four blunt muzzles gave it a menacing look. The custom grips were carved

548

with an intricate leaf pattern. She had seen him handling and cleaning it on several occasions.

In a few minutes he woke and asked about the riot. His hand idled between her legs while she described it. "They chanted for bread, but they were stealing anything in sight."

"They'll do more than steal if King Jeff continues to run amok. The situation in Richmond—the whole Confederacy—is disastrous. It can't be borne."

"But we have all the money we need to replace *Water Witch* and perhaps buy a second vessel. We needn't worry about the President."

"We do if we give a damn about Southern principles." He said it softly, yet with passion. Alarmed, she realized she had unintentionally angered him. "I do. Fortunately, there is a way to curb Davis and preserve them."

"What do you mean?"

In the silence, the bedroom clock went *tock-tock.* Iron wheel rims rumbled over cobbled Franklin Street. Powell's thin, strong mouth turned upward at the ends, though his eyes remained chill.

"How much do you love me, Ashton?"

She laughed nervously. "How much—?"

"It's a simple question. Answer it."

"My God—you know the answer. No man has ever made me feel the way you do."

"I can trust you, then?"

"Hasn't the partnership taught you that you can?"

"I believe I can," he countered, "but if I shared a confidence, then found I'd made a mistake—" he snatched the Sharps and pushed the muzzles into her breast "—I'd rectify it."

Ashton's mouth opened as she watched his finger whiten. Smiling, he pulled the trigger. The hammer fell—on an empty chamber.

"What—Lamar—what is—?" Confused, inwardly wild with fright, she could barely form the words. "What's behind all this?"

He put the pistol aside and laid the map on the tangled bedding. In the southwest corner of the map, he had inked a vertical line through the Territory of New Mexico and to the left of it had inscribed several small squares, none overlapping, with dotted lines.

"What you see right here, love. Our inept generals in Texas lost the Southwest. The Union has it all. Including this—" he tapped the section of the map containing the squares "—the new Territory of Arizona. The Yankee Congress created it with the Organic Act, passed in February. A few regulars from California and some New Mexico volunteers are expected to guard this entire area, which of course is impossible. It's too large, and, beyond that, the red savages keep the soldiers dashing hither and yon to protect isolated settlements. The new territory is perfect for a plan conceived by myself and some other gentlemen who realize King Jeff will ruin us if we allow it."

The maddening smile stayed as he rolled up the map and dropped it on the floor. Ashton jumped out of bed on the other side, her buttocks bouncing as she crossed to the window above the garden. She folded her arms over her bosom.

"You're being mysterious to torment me, Lamar. If you won't explain what you mean, I'll dress and go."

He laughed admiringly. "Nothing mysterious about it, love. Those squares on the map are possible sites for a new confederacy."

She whirled, a figure white as milk save for the blackness of her hair. "A new—?" She shook her head. "My God. You mean it, don't you?"

"Absolutely. The idea is certainly not new." She nodded. She had heard discussions of a third country to be formed in the Northwest, and of a Pacific Coast Confederacy. "What I have done is find the ideal location for a new state, small but impregnable. A law unto itself. A place where each can prosper according to his wishes and ability, and where the breeding and holding of slaves will be encouraged."

The idea was so awesome she couldn't quite get hold of it. She padded back to the bed and sat on the edge. "How long have you been hatching this scheme?"

"For over a year. It gained impetus after Sharpsburg, when European recognition became a lost cause."

"But Davis wouldn't have any part of such a plan, Lamar. He'd use every resource of the government to block it."

"My poor, witless Ashton," he said, stroking her cheek and working his thumb into the little valley beside her nose. "Of course he would. Why do you think I had to satisfy myself that you're trustworthy? When we establish our new state, the government here will be headless. Mr. Jefferson Davis will have gone to

550

his reward—in hell, I hope. The first order of business is to send him on his way."

"You mean—assassinate?"

"The President and key members of the cabinet," he concluded. "Those who might rally forces to oppose us."

"How—how many others are involved?"

"You need know only that I'm in charge and that we mean to go forward. Now that you're aware of the plan"—his thumb pressed her cheek; his fingers closed on the back of her neck, turning it ever so slightly, bringing a touch of pain—"you are part of it."

After the first shock passed, questions began to flood her mind. She asked the most obvious first. How would this new state or country be financed? Small as it was, it would have to be defended. How would its army be paid?

Powell circled the bedroom, tense with excitement. "First, with my share of the earnings from *Water Witch.* But it will take much more than that to arm and equip the kind of force we'll need to defend the borders for the first couple of years. Until the Yankees realize they can't overwhelm us, and recognize our sovereignty."

"Where will you get men for an army of that kind?"

"My dear, there are thousands of them in the Confederacy at this moment—in military service and out of it. Disaffected officers and enlisted men. Some of our very best have deserted, disillusioned by all the bungling. We will rally them, adding Westerners who were born in the South or show sympathy for our cause. I have an estimate of at least seven thousand such in Colorado alone. Finally, if need be, we'll hire mercenaries from Europe We'll have no trouble finding soldiers."

"But you still must pay them."

A cat's grin spread again. "We have the resources. Have I ever mentioned my brother, Atticus?"

"In passing. You've never said anything about him."

Powell sat beside her and began to rub her leg. She studied his profile, momentarily wondering about his sanity. He had never struck her as unbalanced, and he didn't now. He spoke passionately but with the lucidity of one who had spent a long time plotting his course. Her doubt passed.

Contempt crept in as Powell explained. "My brother had no loyalty to the South. He left Georgia in the spring of '56, traveling west to the gold fields. A great many Georgians did the same

551

thing. There was quite a colony in Colorado, where Atticus found and staked a claim. He worked it until the summer of 1860, and in all that time he cleared just two thousand dollars—respectable, but nothing more. About the time South Carolina seceded, boredom and wanderlust set in again. Atticus sold the claim for another thousand and started for California with the stake. He got as far as the Carson River diggings at the western border of the Nevada Territory."

"I've heard of the Carson River mines. James once talked of buying shares in one. The Ophir, I think. That was before he found out about *Water Witch.*"

"My brother's timing turned out to be propitious. The year before, some miners, including an obnoxious, half-mad Canadian called 'Old Pancake,' because he ate nothing else, discovered promising sites in two gulches on Mount Davidson. Comstock— that was Old Pancake's real name—Comstock and the others started placer mining in Gold and Six-Mile canyons. They made a decent profit from the beginning. Five dollars a day in gold. That increased to twenty by the time they made the major discovery— two, really. The lode was richer than they dreamed. Ore pockets scattered all through the mountain. Furthermore, mixed in with the gold was something else. Silver."

"Did your brother stake a claim?"

"Not exactly. Miners are a queer, complex breed—always dickering, selling, and trading claims. It amounts to gambling on how much ore remains in a given piece of ground. One of the original finders of metal, fellow named Penrod, owned a sixth interest in the Ophir, which he wanted to sell for fifty-five hundred dollars. My brother couldn't afford that, but Penrod was making a second offering—half interest in a mine called the Mexican for three thousand dollars. Atticus bought it."

Striding across the bedroom again, Powell explained that the mining camp, christened Virginia City by another of the original claimants, Old Virginny Finney, had undergone rapid and dramatic change during the first two years of the war. By agreement among the miners, it became possible for a man to stake a lode claim, which was much larger than the regulation fifty-by-four-hundred-foot placer claim.

"With a lode claim, you can dig down into the mountain for three hundred feet—and you have rights to all the ground on either side where there are offshoots of your lode. The Mexican

552

started with an open pit, then sank shafts, and in spite of smelting and transportation costs—at first the ore had to be carried over the mountains to California—Atticus and his partner were soon clearing three thousand dollars in silver from every ton of ore and a third as much in gold. Last year saw a great influx of Californians, but of course the richest claims were already staked, so the newcomers called Virginia City a humbug. Atticus's partner succumbed to the talk. My brother bought him out at a favorable price. Last summer, when the town had grown to fifteen thousand, poor Atticus met an untimely end."

"Oh, what a pity."

"I can tell you're deeply touched," he said, smiling.

"How did your brother die?"

"Shot," Powell said with a shrug. "A man accosted him in the elevator of the International Hotel. Robbery was presumed to be the motive. The man was never caught or identified. By coincidence, just the week before, Atticus had written a document, which I keep locked up downstairs. It deeds my brother's interest in the Mexican mine to me, his only surviving relative. He wrote the deed and posted it to a contact in Washington. The contact got it to Richmond via one of the regular mail smugglers."

Atticus Powell's act of generosity had been described with a touch of amusement. Ashton suddenly realized the story was a recitation for the credulous. Powell saw the understanding dawn and confirmed it.

"Consider what it means that Atticus and I were the only remaining members of our family. There is no one to come forward and assert that the handwriting on the deed bears only a superficial resemblance to my brother's. I now have a fine foreman superintending work at the mine, and he doesn't care who owns it so long as he's paid well and on time. I'm happy to say the Mexican is producing at a record rate. There's plenty of gold and silver for paying a private army."

He went searching for a cigar, vanishing into another room. Ashton knew Powell had hired the man who shot his brother, just as he had hired some forger to prepare the deed. Rather than being repelled, she felt renewed admiration. He had the kind of ambition and nerve Huntoon would lack through eternity.

"So you see," Powell said when he came back with matches and an unlit cheroot, "what I propose is not so fantastic. Not with the Mexican to finance it. Therefore I must ask you a question."

"What is it?"

He made her wait with elaborate match-striking and puffing. "Would you like to be the First Lady of the new confederacy?"

"Yes. Yes!"

Powell touched her breast; the ball of his thumb circled slowly on the tip. "I thought so." He was unable to keep smugness and a certain faint scorn out of his smile.

In the early afternoon, Huntoon wandered the glass-strewn sidewalks of Main Street. He couldn't go back to his prison at Treasury. Not after what had happened that morning.

Like so many other government workers in the buildings around Capitol Square, he had rushed outside when he learned of the rioting. He watched the gaunt gray President climb onto a wagon and plead for respect for the law. Davis said every citizen must endure hardship for the sake of the cause. People booed him. As a last pathetic gesture, he turned out his own pockets and flung a few coins to the mob.

It made no difference. It required the mayor reading the riot act and the sight of bayonets wielded by the provost's guard to restore order. While the riot was still in progress, Huntoon turned the corner from Ninth to Main and saw a familiar carriage outside a fashionable food and wine emporium. He stopped and huddled by the building, morbidly curious.

His wife was in the carriage. She had a hamper and struggled with several poorly dressed women before the carriage got away; swirling clots of rioters prevented him from seeing more.

But a little was enough. The hamper and the store she had been visiting heightened his certainty, growing for months, that she was involved with someone. Ashton never bought Franzblau's delicacies for their own table. He suspected her lover was Powell, the man who was enriching him, the man he both envied and feared. Huntoon turned and went back to his office but was unable to do any work. So here he was on the streets again.

A lady's shoe lay in his path. He kicked it into the gutter, the afternoon sunshine flashing from his spectacles. He moved like a sleepwalker, brushing aside two harlots who tried to solicit him. The litter of glass and ruined goods in looted windows seemed symbolic of his life and of the Confederacy.

Davis was destroying the dream of a truly free government on the American continent. The man was contemptible. Impotent.

554

He had no ability to inspire people and lacked the wisdom to stop his military meddling and give his best generals their head. His answer to runaway inflation, mounting shortages, universal discouragement was to proclaim special days of fasting and prayer—or throw a few coins to a mob. He deserved impeachment, if not something worse.

Like the nation, Huntoon's personal life was a shambles. In the sleepless hours of many an early morning, with Ashton snoring lightly in the separate bed she now insisted upon, he could no longer deny the truth of that.

Yet he could find no object of blame except Davis. He couldn't bring himself to leave his wife. She had made him wealthy, and, despite the way she treated him, he loved her. The dilemma made him physically and mentally impotent. Over the past months he had lost all appetite and a dozen pounds. In his confused state, the cancerous truth of Ashton's infidelity was mingling and becoming one with the cancer of despair for the government.

His frustration grew worse each day. His eyes hurt whenever he tried to work. He perspired or suffered cold chills for no apparent reason. The top of his head frequently felt as if an auger were being screwed into it. If only he had some way to relieve the bad feelings. Some target to strike—

"What am I to do?" he muttered, wandering amid the glass. "What in God's name am I to do? Murder her? Kill myself? Both?" Two Negro women overheard and stepped off the sidewalk to avoid him.

74

The wind warmed. The earth softened. The season changed. At the brigade encampment in Sussex County, which they had been roaming in search of replacement mounts, Ab looked down. He and Charles were walking their horses across a muddy meadow to the traveling forge. The boots of both men were covered halfway to the tops; the stuff clung to their spurs like some evil yellow plaster.

Ab sighed. "Will you look at that?" He stamped one foot, then the other. None of the mud fell off. "If anybody asks me have I been through Virginia, I can sure to God tell them yes, sir, any number of places."

Charles laughed and put a match to the cob pipe he had taken up now that cigars were scarce. He felt good this morning. Maybe it was the springtime or the fact that Sport had survived the ordeal of winter. He still gave the gray meticulous care, but there wasn't much he could do about shortages of fodder, bad weather, or the filthy conditions of the cavalry camps. Sport had suffered with body lice, then had been struck with a siege of founder that tormented him with two weeks of fever and sweats and nearly caused the loss of his left forefoot. But Charles had rested him— nursed him through—and the gelding was in fine shape again.

Charles felt good for another reason. It was folded and tucked in the pocket of his butternut shirt.

While the farrier finished with some trooper's nag, the two scouts cleaned the feet of their horses with picks and uprooted weeds. The farrier searched for more shoes and nails, then pumped up the firebox mounted on a platform between the limber's two big wooden wheels.

Ab said, "Git your pass all right?" Charles patted his pocket. "You have a care, roamin' up there in Spotsylvany County by your lonesome. You bump into any of that Union horse, go the other way. I have the same feelin' you do about them damn ribbon clerks. They're learnin' to ride and shoot."

The uneasy conviction had been spreading since Sharpsburg. In March, farther north, Fitz Lee had sent one taunting note too many to Brigadier Bill Averell, a New Yorker whom Charles remembered from the class of '55. Fitz dared Averell to bring his boys down across the Rappahannock and fetch along some coffee to be captured. Averell's division of horse struck south like a thrown spear. The raiders killed Stuart's famed artillery officer, gallant John Pelham.

It appeared a small event, speaking relatively, but it wasn't. The passing of any soldier with the legend of glory on him could scar a Southern mind as whole fields of the fallen could not. Pelham's death and Averell's lightning attack convinced Wade Hampton's troopers of one thing: their Yankee counterparts no longer suffered from a fear of being outmatched.

"Let me see that shoe." Charles snatched the tongs from the farrier. "Heat it and put it back in the vise. It isn't wide enough at the heel. His hoof spreads when he puts weight on it."

"I know my job."

Charles stared right back. "I know my horse."

"You plantation boys are all—"

Charles stepped forward, handing Sport's bridle to Ab. The farrier cleared his throat and began to pump the bellows. "All right, all right."

Later that day, Charles bid Ab good-bye and rode north. In Richmond he visited Orry and Madeline, who had found larger quarters—four rooms, the whole upper floor of a house in the Court End district. The owner's mother had lived there, and the quarters became vacant when she died. Orry paid the outrageous rent without complaint, happy to be out of the rooming house.

For Charles's visit, Madeline fried up a dozen fresh farm eggs, never saying how she had gotten them. They all declined to discuss Ashton and her husband, and talked till four in the morning.

Charles told them about Gus, whom he hadn't mentioned before. Orry reacted predictably when he heard the location of Barclay's Farm. Lee was crouched at Fredericksburg with Jackson, but Hooker was just across the river with twice as many men. Orry said it was folly for Gus to remain in Spotsylvania County.

Charles agreed. They talked further. He slept badly, rolled up in a blanket on the floor, and left the city next morning.

North again through the Virginia springtime. Under blue skies, he rode by lemony forsythia and burning pink azaleas growing wild. Cherry blossoms shone like snowfields. The air smelled of moist earth and, here and there, of something else he recognized: rotting horseflesh. It was getting so you could tell where the armies had been just by seeing or smelling the dead horses.

Late that night, he crouched in a grove and watched a troop of southbound cavalry pass. Jackets and kepis looked black in the starlight. Black translated to blue. Union riders were behind Confederate lines again.

Only one aspect of the incident gave him comfort. The Yankees still rode with what he jeeringly called their fortifications—burdensome extra blankets, tools, utensils—as much as seventy pounds of unnecessary gear. The weight was hard on a horse. Charles hoped the Yankees never learned the lesson.

He reached Chancellorsville, a few buildings and a crossroads unworthy of being called a village. Turning right onto the Orange Turnpike, he continued toward Fredericksburg through the Wilderness, an all but impassable forest of second-growth oak and pine entangled with vines. Even in bright sunlight, the place looked sinister.

Where the Wilderness straggled out, he cut to the northeast. The fragile good cheer generated by the weather left him. He was back in the war zone for fair.

The countryside swarmed with Confederate engineer companies, trains of supply wagons, six-horse artillery batteries, slow-moving herds of scrawny cattle. An officer demanded his pass, then asked whether he had seen any Union cavalry between here and Richmond. Charles said he had. The officer told him it was probably Stoneman, reported to be striking at communication lines to the capital.

Gray-clad stragglers wandered through the freshly turned fields, going where and doing what, God only knew. So many soldiers abroad didn't bode well for a woman living alone, even if the soldiers wore the right uniform. It was proven again when he came within sight of Barclay's Farm. A white-topped commissary wagon stood in the road, and two rough-looking teamsters were eying the house as Charles approached. He put his hand on his shotgun, and they decided to drive on.

As he rode into the dooryard, Boz threw down his ax, leaped over some split logs, and ran toward him. "Hello, hello! Miss Augusta—Captain Charles is here."

Boz sounded more than happy. He sounded relieved.

"Something's troubling you," she said. "What is it?"

They lay side by side in the dark. They had supped and talked, hugged and kissed, bathed and made love. Now, instead of feeling a pleasant drowsiness, he was struggling in the web of his own thoughts.

"Where shall I start?" he asked.

"Wherever you want."

"It's going badly, Gus. The whole damn war. Vicksburg's threatened—Grant's in charge there. Orry knew him at the Academy and in Mexico. He says the man's like a terrier with a bone. Won't let go even if the pieces choke him to death. Orry wouldn't say it to anyone else, but he thinks Grant will have Vicksburg by the autumn. Then there's Davis. Still coddling second-rate generals like Bragg. And the cavalry can't find enough horses, let alone the grain to feed them."

"The farms around here are stripped bare. The war doesn't help anyone catch up, either. You plow an acre, ten minutes later a battery of artillery gallops across it, and you start over."

"The superstitious boys say our luck's turned bad. Sharpsburg might have been a victory instead of a stand-off if the Yankees hadn't found those cigars wrapped in a copy of Lee's order. Courage doesn't count for much against bad luck—or the numbers the other side can muster."

But Cooper had spoken of the numbers long ago, hadn't he? Warned of them. Charles shivered in the dark. She stroked his bare shoulder, soothing. "I'd say those are all eminently respectable worries."

"There's one more."

"What is it?"

He rolled onto his side, able to see her only as a pale shape. "You."

"My darling, don't squander a single minute fretting about me.

559

I can take care of myself." There was pride in the statement, and reassurance. But he heard anger, too.

"Well, I do fret. Can't sleep half the time, thinking of you stuck here by yourself."

And that's why no man should let himself fall in love in wartime. The conviction lay like a rock inside him, unwanted, upsetting—and undeniable.

"That's foolish, Charles."

"Hell it is. Hooker's sure to attack Fredericksburg—maybe within a few days. The Army of the Potomac could overrun the whole county."

"Boz and Washington and I can—"

"Hold out against bluebellies who haven't seen a pretty woman for months? Come on."

"You're being quarrelsome."

"So are you. I have good reason. I can't stop worrying."

"You could stop coming here, then you wouldn't have to worry at all."

Cold and flat, the words fell between them. He flung himself out of bed, crossed his arms, furiously scratched his beard in vexation. She rose to her knees on the bed, touched his shoulder.

"Do you think I don't worry about you? Constantly? Sometimes I think I fell in love just when I shouldn't have—with a man I shouldn't have—"

"Then maybe I should stop coming here."

"Is that what you want?"

"I—"

A silence. Then he broke, spun, pulled her naked body up in his arms, hugging her and stroking her hair. "God, no, Gus. I love you so much, sometimes it makes me want to cry for mercy."

Trembling, they held each other, he standing beside the bed, she kneeling. Finally, the searing problem had been exposed. *Sometimes I think I fell in love just when I shouldn't have—with a man I shouldn't have.* She faced the constant threat of loss. He bore a constant concern, one that weighed him down like all the gear carried by the Yankee cavalry. *Lord God, Charlie—*Ab's voice—*you forgotten why we're all here?*

Sometimes he almost did. A lot of men did. For some the burden became too heavy; they put distant wives and sweethearts ahead of duty and deserted. He would never join that company, yet he did recognize that the cancer of worry was in him, too. He

560

knew it while he clasped her body and kissed her clean, soft hair. "Go to Richmond," he pleaded.

She broke the embrace. "Charles, this is my home. I'll not run away."

"It's no admission of cowardice to go for a week or two. Until Hooker moves, and something's decided."

"What if the Yankees came when I wasn't here? What if they looted this place or burned it? It's all I have."

"They can loot it and burn it with you standing in the kitchen."

"Richmond's too crowded. There is no place—"

"My cousin and his wife will take you in. Boz and Washington, too. I stopped to see Orry and Madeline on the way up from Sussex County. They don't have much room, but they'll share what they have."

She sank back on her haunches, bringing her forearms across her breasts as if she were cold. "It would be a great deal of trouble to pack and—"

"Gus, stop. You're a proud woman. Strong. I love that about you. But goddamn it—"

"I wish you wouldn't curse all the time."

The soft words conveyed her anger as nothing had before. He took a breath and grasped the post at the foot of the bed to steady himself.

"I'm sorry. But the point stands. Pride and strength and two nigras aren't enough to protect you against Joe Hooker's army. You need to go to Richmond, if not for your own sake, then for mine."

"For *your* sake—?"

"That's right."

"I see."

"You take that tone, I'll sleep in the other room."

"I think you'd better."

Out he went, wrapped in a blanket, slamming the door.

Just at daylight, he stole back in, whispered her name, started when she sat up, wide awake. From the raw look of her cheeks, he knew she had gotten little sleep.

He held out his hand. "I'm sorry."

They embraced, dismissed the quarrel, and over breakfast she said yes, all right, she'd close up the place and travel to Richmond before the week was out if he could get her a pass. He promised he would. He wrote directions to Orry and Madeline's and went over them with her. Things were all right again. Superficially. For a man and woman to fall in love in times like these was folly, and each had acknowledged it.

Later that morning, he prepared to leave. "I'll stop in Richmond and tell them you'll be coming."

They were standing in the dooryard. She put her arms around him, kissed him, and said, "I love you, Charles Main. You must not worry about me."

"Oh, no, never. And Old Abe will raise the Stars and Bars in Atlanta tomorrow."

He mounted, waved, and cantered to the road. After he had gone a half mile he reined in to look back, but a rattling column of caissons raised dust and forced him to the shoulder. He could see only sweating horses and grinding wheels. At last the column passed. The dooryard was empty.

When he returned to the brigade in Sussex County, he lied to Ab, saying the visit had been a fine one.

75

"Miss Jane, I have got to confess—"

He had walked her to the stoop of her cabin in the dusk, tightening up his nerve along the way. She smiled to encourage him.

"I love you. I pray for the day I'm a free man and can ask for your hand."

He had flirted with the declaration before but never said it outright. The words made her warm and happy. She looked at Andy against a background of cabins and overhanging trees and mist rolling in from the river to fill the spaces between. The hidden sun lit the mist to a dusty rose color. Softly, she said, "The day will come. When it does, I'll be proud to say yes."

He clapped his hands. "Great God! I'd kiss you if there weren't so many people watching."

Laughing, too, she said, "I don't see anyone." She pecked his cheek and ran inside. She leaned against the door, clasping her hands against the cleft of her breast. "Oh, my. Oh, my."

Then the smell assaulted her. The smell of a dirty body and spirits. It wrenched her mind, gripped her attention. He was lounging against the whitewashed wall, his eyes bleary. Where had he gotten whiskey? Stolen it from the house?

"How dare you sneak in here, Cuffey. Get out."

He didn't move. Giving her a sly smile, he reached down and fingered himself. "I heard what that nigger said. He *loves* you." The dark brown hand loosened one button after another until he could show her what was underneath. "He can't do it near as good as me."

"You drunken, foul-minded—"

Cuffey let go of himself and ran at her. Jane cried out and groped for the door latch. He caught her shoulder, yanking her so hard she stumbled. Then someone struck the other side of the door, driving her over to the other wall. She hit with a jolt, dazed, not seeing the door crash back or Andy peering in. Anxious blacks crowded the little porch.

Cuffey said, "Shut that door, nigger. Go do what you do bes'—kiss ol' Meek's backside."

Andy quickly took it in: Jane slumped by the wall, bracing herself with her hands, Cuffey stuffing his dangling organ back into his pants. Andy tilted his head downward slightly and walked into the cabin.

Cuffey picked up an old stool and swept it in an arc, striking Andy's head. One leg of the stool broke; somehow the splintered end drew blood from Andy's temple. The blood streamed into his eye as he jumped at Cuffey and aimed a powerful but mistimed punch. Cuffey easily avoided it, then jabbed at Andy's eye with the splintered leg.

"Let him be. Wait for help," Jane pleaded. If Andy heard, he paid no attention. He walked forward like a soldier in a skirmish line, upright, scared, but never wavering. He laced his hands together to create a double fist. Cuffey kicked him between the legs.

Andy doubled over, letting out a clenched, hurt sound. But he stayed on his feet. He lifted his joined hands and struck Cuffey where his neck met his left shoulder, a sideways blow that shot Cuffey against the wall and made him grunt explosively.

"You been begging somebody to do this," Andy said, looming over the other man, pounding downward with his joined hands. He slammed the top of Cuffey's head. This time Cuffey yelled. Andy began to hammer him like a nail, pushing him down to a crouch, then to his knees, working in sideways blows to the face for good measure. Cuffey's ear bled.

"Watch out, Andy, Mist' Meek comin'," someone called from the street. Jane stood, saw the blacks on the porch disappear and the overseer stride into view, pulling a pistol from his wide belt.

"Who's fighting in here?"

"Cuffey and Andy," a woman answered, just as Andy raised Cuffey by the front of his soiled shirt. Blood leaked from Cuffey's nose as well as his ear. He blew the blood and mucus into Andy's face.

"I kill you, nigger. You an' everybody on this place."

"Let him go, Andy," Meek ordered from the doorway. Andy turned toward the overseer. The blood from his temple blurred his vision a little. Cuffey saw his chance and gave his adversary a shove.

Andy staggered, thrown back against the overseer. Cuffey tore down the flour-sack curtains Jane had tacked over the back window. He flipped one leg over the sill. "Give me room to shoot," Meek shouted, pushing Andy.

Cuffey grabbed Jane and swung her into the line of fire. Meek jerked the pistol upward, and Cuffey dropped down outside the window. He bolted away into rose mist that was deepening to gray.

"Stop, nigger," Meek commanded, discharging one round. Cuffey disappeared behind a live oak. The mist stirred and settled.

Meek swore an uncharacteristic oath. "Andy, what happened?"

"I was outside and—I heard Jane cry out." The words were labored; he was still breathing hard.

"I came inside and found him hiding here," Jane said. "He said dirty things to me, then unbuttoned his trousers."

The listeners outside, especially the women, expostulated and groaned. Still angry at losing the culprit, Meek snorted, "If we gelded all you bucks, things'd be a sight more peaceful."

Andy glared. "Listen here—"

The overseer was too mad to pay much attention. And just then a voice rolled out of the deep rose mist behind the cabin.

"I'll kill ever one of you on this place, you hear me?"

"Get some men," Meek said to Andy. "Eight or ten at least. It's a bad night to chase runaways, but we're going to catch that one. Then I'm going to sell him off."

The pursuit ended three hours later, when the mist had become fog. By the light of a fatwood torch he was carrying, Andy reported the failure to Jane. "I 'spect he's gone for good. Toward Beaufort, most likely."

"Good riddance," she said. The dank night and the memory of Cuffey's wild face made her uneasy. She knew what kind of life Cuffey had led. His hatreds—Mont Royal, its owners, the more docile slaves—were understandable. Yet she nurtured the same hostilities and so did Andy, and neither had been ruined by them.

"Maybe I ought to keep watch here on the porch till morning," he suggested.

"He won't come back."

"You heard what he yelled after he jumped out the window."

"Cuffey's been a braggart ever since I've known him. We'll never see him again."

"Surely hope you're right. Well—good night, then."

"Good night, Andy." She touched his face below the strip of linen tied around his head to protect the clotted cut. "You're a brave man. I meant what I said about being proud to marry you."

His eyes shone in the flaring light. "Thank you."

He walked down the creaking steps into the fog. As soon as her door closed he extinguished his torch, faced about, and quietly lowered himself to the edge of the porch, where he intended to stay until daylight.

Although Jane was awake for some time, she didn't know he was out there. She heard instead the noises of the spring night beyond the window from which Cuffey had torn the curtain. She heard the doglike barks of the frogs, the three-note chant of the chuck-will's-widow, the drone of insects. And, in imagination, she heard a voice promising vengeance. She lay with her hand clenched against her cheek, wishing she didn't hear the voice but unable to silence it.

76

In the early morning of April 28, Billy wrote by the light of a candle pushed into the mounting ring of a borrowed bayonet.

Lije F. and yr. obdt. are detached with a volunteer co. for duty with Gen. Slocum's three corps. We march upstream tomorrow. Some suspect a great sweep around Lee and a strike at his rear. The regulars and vols are cooking rations for 8 days. Pack mules numbering 2,000 will replace most of the supply wagons, further evidence of a desire for speed and surprise.

Weather is better—rains over, though roads & stream banks remain very muddy in some places; we will earn our pay planking the worst spots.

Among the army's current complement of vols, about half are replacements for deserters or the dead, wounded & sick; most of the greenhorns are foolishly excited at the prospect of battle—much happier to march forward than stay behind with those corps which will apparently demonstrate against Lee's works in Fredericksburg, or below the town. One such corps is Howard's XI, the Germans, almost universally detested as radicals, revolutionaries—fugitives from the trouble of 1848 whether they be so or not. Almost without exception, the Dutchmen swear by Old Abe and his proclamation, while the rest of the army swears at them. We have not much tolerance —and I point the finger of conscience first at myself. Yesterday I saw two Negro teamsters in army blue and confess to being unsettled by the sight. Lije prayed twenty mins. longer than

*usual tonight. At supper, while a band played "The Girl I Left
Behind Me," I asked why. He replied, Do not forget who is
over in Fredericksburg. Two of the best—Bob Lee & Old Jack.
Lije said he had implored the Almighty to confuse their minds
and impair their judgment, though he stated this was done
with regret, as both generals are staunch Christians. Wish I
were, Brett. It might ease my soul. I am sick of the dirt and
killing, and cannot take any joy in what's to come, as the vols
do. But they are boys yet. They will be something else before
this spring's over.*

Late the next day, Billy and a detachment of twelve volunteer
engineers found a farmhouse with a sturdy barn and a smaller
outbuilding from which the breeze brought the powerful odor of
chicken droppings.

"What d'you think, sir?" asked the senior noncom with the
group, a youth from Syracuse named Spinnington. He had been
appointed corporal because he seemed less lazy and stupid than
the other replacements; no positive traits recommended him.

From the roadside Billy studied the neatly kept buildings surrounded by a small orchard of peach trees. The detachment had
fallen out around a wagon commandeered from another farm.
Other detachments, with wagons similarly obtained, were roaming the countryside just above the Rapidan. Screened by
Stoneman's horse, the army had marched with great secrecy and
encountered no difficulties until reaching the chosen ford. The
rain-swollen river could still be crossed, but its near bank was a
bog where it should be solid.

"Sir?" Spinnington prodded. Billy continued to stare at the
farmhouse, wishing he could give the order to move on. He felt
tired enough to drop. He knew that had little to do with the
forced march from Fredericksburg and everything to do with the
task at hand.

Billy's beard had grown out during the winter; it was carelessly
trimmed, and matted in places. Despite a natural stockiness, he
had a curiously shrunken appearance. Seen with his brother
George, he might have been picked as the older—or so he thought
on those increasingly rare occasions when he saw himself in the
scrap of polished tin he used as a mirror. The reflected face had a
saggy look, as if it were made of melting candle tallow.

Spinnington fidgeted. Billy said, "All right."

There were whoops as the new replacements charged the house, the low-lying sun gilding an ax blade, the face of a boy with a crowbar. Their elongated shadows climbed up the side of the house.

The front door opened; a man came out. A tiny man with a white tuft of beard but huge strong hands.

Billy approached the porch. Before he could speak, a woman appeared behind the man. She weighed three times what he did and stood a head taller.

"Mr. Tate," she said, "get back inside. General Hooker's men who came by said we'd be shot if we stepped one foot in the open."

"It's a bluff," the old farmer said. "They're afraid we'll slip over the Rapidan and warn Bob Lee. I wouldn't do that. I have to protect this place. That's why I must talk to these boys."

"Mr. Tate—"

"What do you boys want?" the old farmer called over his wife's continuing objection.

Billy pulled off his kepi. "Sir, I regret to inform you that we've been sent to forage for lumber and siding. We need them because the Germanna ford is a mire and must be planked so General Hooker's forces can cross the river. I'll be obliged if you and your wife will go back inside and permit us to do our work."

"What work?" the old man cried, his white tuft twitching in the twilight breeze. "What work?"

He knew. Ashamed to look him in the eye, Billy bobbed his head at Spinnington. "Get them to work, Corporal. Take the barn first, and maybe we'll get enough to fill the wagon. Maybe we can leave the chicken house alone."

"It's taken me all my life to build this place," the old man said, clutching the porch post, angry tears squeezing from the corners of his eyes. "Doesn't that mean anything to you?"

"I'm sorry, sir. Truly sorry."

A nail squealed, a raw, screaming sound. Two volunteers pried off the first piece of siding. Another ran it to the wagon.

The old farmer lurched off the porch. Billy drew his side arm. The farmer hesitated, sat down on the steps, and gave Billy a look he would never forget. Then the farmer stared at his shoes as the engineer volunteers tore the barn apart. They brought out cross-cut saws for the pillars and beams. They had it all down by dark, leaving the unpenned milk cows and plow horses wandering

568

around the chicken house. Billy sat on the seat of the wagon as it rolled away and didn't permit himself to look back.

An entry in his journal, made sometime between sunset that evening and dawn on April 30, read:

I hate what I am becoming because of this war.

"It's the Dutchmen," Spinnington snarled. "The fucking Dutchmen caved in."

"Shut up," Billy said, naked to the waist, swinging the ax two-handed and bracing for the shock when it bit into the five-inch trunk of the elm.

It was just daylight. An hour ago, while the Wilderness burned, set afire by shells, Billy's detachment had been rushed from Slocum's Twelfth Corps to the relatively clear ground at the Chancellorsville crossing. To judge from the heavy presence of headquarters guards and all the couriers riding up and galloping away again, General Hooker was holed up inside the white manor house. No one professed to know what he was doing, but one thing appeared certain: Fighting Joe's great scheme had come to nothing.

Hooker had gained his planned position in the Wilderness, been poised to smash Lee from the rear—and had thrown away the advantage. Why? Billy thought, timing the ax blows to reinforce the raging repetition of the question. *Why?*

Yesterday Fighting Joe had started his men forward to a more advantageous offensive position—higher and more open ground beyond the edge of the Wilderness. When his men encountered enemy fire, he called off the advance. Corps commanders had not concealed their fury. Billy had heard what General Meade said; it had spread everywhere, like the fire in the woods: *"If he can't hold the top of a hill, how can he expect to hold the bottom?"*

But now they were preparing for precisely that. Swing; *why?* Swing back; *why?*

"Stand back," Billy yelled, pushing men as the elm swayed and tilted. The men scattered, the tree crashed, the volunteers leaped forward, stirring the raw, smarting smoke that came partly from the unseen cannon, partly from the fiery forest.

Yesterday, while Hooker shilly-shallied and lost his chance at a superior position, Bob Lee and Old Jack had been busy outfoxing him. Jackson had led his men on one of their famous lightning marches, this one a damnably risky flanking movement. But he had pulled it off without discovery and by nightfall stood ready to savage the Union right. Howard's Dutchmen were at ease there, enjoying their supper. Old Jack's whooping, screaming farm boys took them totally by surprise.

That was the start of the end of Hooker's great plan. Now the rebs were on the offensive throughout the second-growth forest. God knew where they would appear next—which was the reason Union soldiers were frantically preparing rifle pits to defend the open ground at the crossroads, while axmen, including Billy and his detachment, felled trees in front of the lines.

They slashed off branches, bound others together with ropes and vines, sharpened still others and fixed them to point toward the smoke where the rebs might be lurking. The abatis was a defensive fortification, not one employed by troops who meant to march ahead and win. Perhaps Fighting Joe had lost the advantage at the same mysterious spot where he had misplaced his nerve. Even rumors that a stray reb ball had wounded or killed Old Jack last night didn't lift the army's gloom, any more than daylight had lifted the choking smoke.

Chop and chop. Spinnington worked on Billy's left, Lije just beyond. On his right, bent over so as to minimize exposure in case of a sniper attack, was a volunteer whose name he didn't know. The man's posture didn't permit much work. Billy had an impulse to split the coward's head with his ax, but he supposed Lije would object.

White beard gleaming with sweat drops, Lije lifted his heavy ax with his right hand, as if it weighed no more than a straw. He pointed the ax at a tree larger than most, an oak about a foot in diameter.

"That one next, lads. She will fall to the right if we cut her properly. We may then turn her ninety degrees and fix points on some of those topmost branches to torment the enemy." Billy managed an exhausted laugh. What a rock Lije was. Every remark to his men was round and complete as a sermon sentence.

Lije also spoke loudly, which was necessary because of the continual noise: drumming and bugling, men shouting, small arms crackling, strays from the beef herd mooing as they ran down the narrow turnpike or got snared in the forest vines and bled from thorn pricks. Catching a nap at three in the morning, Billy had had his stomach stepped on by a wandering cow.

Now, renewed artillery fire increased the din. The firing came from south of Chancellorsville. Inexplicably, Sickles had been withdrawn from another piece of high ground, a place called Hazel Grove. Had the rebs moved fieldpieces into that favorable position?

Billy and Lije attacked the oak from opposite sides. Lije met his eye, smiled in a weary, fatherly way. Chop and chop. Billy wished he had the older man's faith. If God stood with the Union, why did Old Jack surprise and whip them every time?

They had notched a white vee into the trunk when, above the noise of men, horses, wheels, guns, Billy picked up a more ominous one: the scream of a shell. "Put your heads down," he shouted to those nearby. "That one's coming in mighty—"

The earth blew up around him, hurling him off his feet in a cloud of dirt and grass. He landed on his back, dazed. He breathed the heavy smoke, then coughed. Something lay on his bare chest: a large yellow-white wedge of heartwood blown from the trunk of the oak.

Blinking, he focused on the tree as it started to topple, stirring the smoke. Men as dazed as he struggled to their feet. Lije stood well beyond the tree, and he, too, saw it coming down, directly on Spinnington. Knuckling his eyes, the corporal failed to hear the creak; the bombardment was too loud.

"Spinnington, get out of there," Billy yelled. Spinnington turned, dull-faced, still not comprehending. The rest happened very fast. Lije bowled forward and hit the corporal with his shoulder, intending to push him to safety and fall on top of him. Lije's left boot tangled in a vine. He slammed on his chest, raised his head, clutched handfuls of weedy earth, and said, "Oh," an instant before the oak fell on the small of his back.

"Oh, Lord," Spinnington whispered, standing unhurt a yard beyond Lije's open mouth, closed eyes, fists clenching grass. Billy ran forward, shouting Lije's name. Men hit the ground again; another shell struck twenty yards away. The concussion threw Billy on his rump and hurled bits of earth and stone into his face. Something grazed his left eyeball. Something else cut his cheek.

Up again, he staggered to the fallen oak. Slowly, Lije's eyes opened. Another shell hit to the left and well behind them. Pieces of a man rose up and fell back to the unfinished rifle pits. Cries and moans added to the other noise. Billy knew the pain Lije must be feeling, but only a slight moisture in the older man's eyes betrayed it.

"I'll get you out, Lije." He leaped for the tree, slipped his hands under, pulled. Pain shot through his back. The oak trunk didn't move.

He twisted around. "You men help me!"

"Fruitless," Lije murmured. He closed his eyes, licked his lips, repeated the word, then said, "Withdraw, Lieutenant. The enemy fire is growing too heavy. Withdraw—that is my direct—order."

Though badly frightened, several of the volunteers ran up and attempted to lift the oak. The trunk rose about two inches. Then the hands of one man slipped, and the oak fell again. Billy heard Lije's teeth clench and scrape.

"Withdraw," he whispered.

"No," Billy said, his control breaking down.

"William Hazard, I order—"

"No, no." He was crying. "I can't leave you to die."

" 'What man is he that liveth—and shall not see death?' "

"Don't spout Scripture at me," Billy yelled. "I won't see you left here."

"I will not be." Though Lije's voice was faint, he articulated each syllable. "I trust the Master's promise. 'He that heareth—my word' "—in the shell-struck rifle pit, men shrieked like children, without cease—" '—and believeth in Him that sent me—shall not come into condemnation but—is passed from death unto life.' I was—meant to fall here. You are—meant to live and—take these men—"

Another shell hit in the forest, shredding vines, blasting earth into the smoke, blurring Lije's faint voice with its roar.

"—to safety. I order you."

"Jesus," Billy wept. "Jesus Christ."

"Do not—blaspheme. I *order* you. Live and—fight on. I—loved you like a son. This was—ordained."

It was not, Billy cried in secret places. It isn't God's will but chance and your stupid Christian sacrifice—

"Come on, sir." Hands tugged. "He's dead, sir."

Billy looked down from the smoke to which his gaze had drifted. Lije's eyes were closed, his face smooth. A silver line of saliva trickled from the corner of his mouth nearest the ground. A grasshopper hopped onto his beard and sat there, as if curious about the dead giant.

"Come on, sir," Spinnington repeated. With surprising gentleness, he and another beardless volunteer took hold of Billy's arms. He was dazed, muttering to himself. "We'll come back for his body, don't you worry," said a faraway voice he didn't recognize. He ground a dirty fist into his wet eyes and let them lead him.

Near the headquarters encampment, a surgeon offered a bottle of whiskey. Two swallows jolted Billy awake, made him able to function again. He knew something he hadn't known earlier. God did not rule a war such as this—if indeed He ruled anywhere.

It was dismal to face that truth. Against it, Lije had worn the armor of his faith. It was good armor; it had protected him. Billy felt himself flawed—mean and weak—because he could not don the same armor. But he couldn't. Not after his sojourn in the Wilderness, where the treetops burned through the night, pyres for the dead and dying. Where Billy had watched Lije die. Where Fighting Joe had turned advantage to stalemate, stalemate to defeat.

The retreat to the river began in midmorning, soldiers, cannon, ambulances all pulling out in a mad melee as the reb infantry advanced while the reb artillery kept pounding. Billy, Spinnington, and two others stole forward into the shell-blasted area to retrieve Lije's body. But the guns at Hazel Grove had poured in so much heavy fire and so many trees had ignited and the flames had spread so fast that Lije's body resembled nothing human. None of them, not even Billy, could stand to touch it or look at it for more than a few seconds. They left the charred thing and withdrew.

A realization struck Billy in the midst of the retreat. *Well, at least he went to his rest on Sunday.*

77

Throughout Monday night, the military telegraph remained quiet for long periods. Tired men came and went at the War Department, some keeping vigil for an hour, others intending to stay until some news arrived. Stanley was among the latter, part of a small group whose status permitted waiting in Stanton's office. The President was there for a while, stretched on his favorite couch but turning restlessly every few minutes.

"Where is Hooker now? Where is General Stoneman? Why in thunder don't they send word?"

Stanley held his temples and worked two fingers down to rub his itching eyes. He was sick of the Chief Executive's impatient rhetorical questions. So was Stanton, evidently; his voice rasped as he replied, "They will break silence at the opportune moment, Mr. President. I imagine the generals are busy consolidating our victory."

It was Tuesday, nearly sunrise. For the past twelve hours, as they received only the sketchiest reports and casualty figures on the wire, an unsupported consensus had spread like a bad cold. Hooker had won a victory, though at a high price.

Not everyone had caught the cold. Welles, the bearded curmudgeon who held the Navy portfolio and had once been a newspaperman in Connecticut, had not. "Perhaps they're silent because there is nothing but bad news. If we'd had success, the reports would be coming in volumes, not paragraphs."

The secretary gave him a long look. Lincoln, too, though his, sorrowing, contrasted sharply with the spleen of Stanton's. "I am

574

beginning to believe you're right, Gideon." Lincoln rose, wrinkled and unkempt, and put his plaid shawl around his shoulders. "Send a messenger the instant we have definitive news." The military guards in the antechamber snapped to attention as he shuffled through the door.

Falling asleep even though he had deliberately chosen a hard chair, Stanley hung on till half past eight, by which time the department's daily routine was well started. With permission from the secretary, Stanley entered Stanton's private dressing closet, splashed his face with tepid water from a basin, then some of Stanton's cologne. He stumbled out into the spring morning in search of breakfast.

He hoped to God that Hooker had won a victory. The party needed not one but several. The presidential election was little more than a year away, and if Lincoln went down, he would carry many others with him. Stanley cringed at the possibility. He had acquired a taste for his job and the power it carried. If Isabel had to retire to Lehigh Station for the rest of her life, she would blame him and make his life even more miserable than usual. A pity he didn't have an antidote for Isabel—some younger and less shrewish female who would understand and sympathize with his problems.

Even at this early hour, hawkers were out. One cried the virtues of bars of soap piled on his curbside stand. Another shoved a cheap telescope in George Hazard's face. Military wagons, private carriages, hacks, and horseback riders crowded the avenue, along with pedestrians and the mule-drawn cars of the street railway. Bell clanging, one car blocked George's passage across Pennsylvania. Short-tempered—last night he and William had argued over the boy's poor marks, and George had slept badly—he scowled at the passengers. Most were men, but a few—

A face, glimpsed and then gone, stunned him. A teamster swore at him. Wheel hubs brushed the skirts of his uniform coat. Then two horsemen blocked his view, and when they passed, it was too late for him to do anything unless he wanted to stage a one-man foot race to pursue the car. He shook himself and weaved on across the street like a drunken man.

When Stanley entered Willard's dining room, he saw his brother breakfasting alone at a table half in sunshine, half in

575

shadow. Stanley's first impulse was to leave. He hadn't seen George since Wade's defeat in the Senate, and undoubtedly George would crow about that. Had the situation been reversed, he would have.

But the long vigil had left Stanley in a state not typical for him: he craved the companionship of someone from outside the War Department building. So he ignored the waiter motioning him to another table and proceeded to the one where George sat staring at his fried potatoes with a look Stanley thought odd indeed. George didn't raise his head till his brother cleared his throat.

"Hello, Stanley. Where did you come from?"

"The telegraph room. I've been there all night awaiting news from Virginia."

"Is there any?"

"Very little. May I join you?"

George waved at a chair. Stanley put his tall hat on another, then sat, tugging his waistcoat down over the steadily growing bulge of his paunch. "Is something wrong, George? Trouble with Constance or the children?"

Bastard, George thought. It was Stanley's style to ask such questions with a hopeful tone. "Yes, there is. Ten minutes ago I saw a ghost."

"I beg your—"

"Sir?" said the waiter, who had been hovering to take Stanley's order.

"Come back later," Stanley snapped. "Tell me what you mean, George."

"I saw Virgilia. Riding one of the avenue cars."

Astonished, Stanley didn't speak immediately. "I presumed Virgilia had gone far away from this part of the country. I've not heard from her or about her for two or three years."

"I'm certain it was she—well, virtually certain. You know she never cared for clothes, and this woman was smartly dressed. Her hair was stylish. Even with those differences—"

"Obviously you aren't certain at all," Stanley broke in. "But suppose it was Virgilia. Why are you concerned? What difference would it make? None to me or Isabel, I assure you. I have nothing in common with my sister except a last name and a loathing for the South."

"Don't you ever wonder if she's all right?"

576

"Never. She's a thief and a slut—and those are the kindest descriptions I can apply. I don't care to discuss Virgilia or any other unpleasant topic. I have been up all night, and I want to eat a peaceful breakfast. I can do so at another table if you wish."

"Calm down, Stanley. Order something and I'll keep quiet."

But he didn't. He picked at his potatoes, took a bite of cold beef-steak bathed in greasy gravy, and said, "I do wonder sometimes. Where Virgilia is, I mean."

"That's your prerogative," Stanley said, taking the same tone he would have used with a man thinking of stepping in front of a fifteen-inch columbiad about to be fired. Conversation lagged after that. Stanley ordered and ate a huge breakfast, topped off with the last of seven muffins lathered in plum preserves. George, meantime, saw distorted, sharply angled images of the woman's face sliding away in the street-railway car. In a strange way, the brothers were glad of each other's company.

As they left the dining room, Stanley paused to say hello to a pale, stooped individual just entering with some other men. George recognized Representative Stout, one of the Wade-Stevens gang. He and Stanley whispered like old cronies. George continued to believe that his brother had entrenched himself with the radicals out of expediency rather than conviction.

Stout rejoined his friends, and the brothers went outside. "Going to work now?" Stanley asked. George said no, he planned to walk down three blocks to see whether the *Evening Star* had posted any recent bulletins.

"I've taken to relying on the correspondents for accurate news. You boys in Stanton's office seem to publish what's favorable and quash the rest."

The insult galled Stanley, but he could think of no retort; unfortunately, his brother was right. He fell in step and accompanied him to the *Star* offices, a corner building on the wrong side of the avenue at Eleventh Street. They found a crowd of almost a hundred people reading the long handwritten strips hanging outside.

Latest from the Seat of War

———

General Lee Surprised

———

General Stoneman Playing
the Mischief with His Cavalry
in the Rear of the Rebels

———

Enemy Menaces Fredericksburg;
Our Virginia Correspondents Report
Terrible Fighting Saturday & Sunday
at Chancellorsville

Scowling, George said, "Old hash. I read it all yesterday. I must be going—"

"Wait a moment," Stanley said. "They're bringing out a new one."

The crowd shifted and whispered in anticipation as a man in shirt sleeves appeared with a long sheet trailing from his hand. He moved a ladder, climbed up to the line strung across the building, and attached the hand-printed bulletin.

Thrilling News from the Army!

Hooker All Right!!!

———

Prodigies of Valor Performed
by Our Men—Thousands of
Enemy Prisoners Taken

———

General Stonewall Jackson
Said to Be Severely Wounded

Almost instantly, there was reaction.

"We won! Fighting Joe's done it!"

"Bring those prisoners back, and we'll hang 'em."

"Lookit that—Jackson got what he deserves."

Stanley tapped fingertips against his waistcoat. "If those reports are true—"

George didn't hear. For the second time that morning, he felt as though he had been hit. Blurry pictures swam in his head. He saw the strange, shy Presbyterian boy from the hills of western Virginia who had become his friend. Even in his youth, and de-

578

spite his peculiarities, Jackson had seemed to carry a promise of greatness that was indefinable but very real.

George remembered after-hours hashes and Jackson fastidiously avoiding most of the food because he feared to disrupt his digestion. He remembered calling him Tom and sitting with him, and with Orry and Sam Grant, after the capture of Mexico City. He remembered Jackson ordering a glass of wine and tasting it once, while the rest of them swilled beer.

The bulletin rattled in the breeze. It only said *reported,* and experience reminded George that many such bulletins proved wrong in whole or in part. He had a bad feeling about this one, though.

He realized Stanley had spoken. "What did you say?"

"I remarked that if the rumor about Jackson is true, it will be a blessing for the Union. An even greater one if the wound proves mortal."

"Shut up, Stanley. Save your stupid remarks for that vengeful crowd you're so chummy with."

"I'll say anything about a traitor that I damn well—"

"No, you won't. He was my friend."

Stanley opened his mouth, but just as quickly closed it. Head lowered slightly, George continued to fix him with a baleful stare for another few seconds. Then, stiff-backed, he turned and walked around the corner and out of sight.

Some in the crowd had overheard the exchange. One man thrust his chin toward Stanley. "What did that officer say? That Stonewall was his friend?"

"Anybody who'd admit that oughta be lynched," a fat woman said.

"I share that sentiment," Stanley declared. He regretted his impulse to breakfast with George and again thought of calling him to the attention of Colonel Baker.

78

Virgilia knew she would suffer for going to Washington. When she eventually returned to Aquia Creek, the woman recently installed as head of the hospital nurses would chastise her for leaving when so many wounded were coming in from Chancellorsville. General Hooker's great advance had met with failure there, something not yet widely known in the capital, Virgilia discovered.

Virgilia's conscience had prompted her to stay on duty, and she would have but for several circumstances. She had waited nearly four weeks for an appointment with Miss Dix. Others could pick up her work during an absence of a day and a half. And she had to do something about her situation because it had become intolerable.

The new hospital supervisor, Elvira Neal, was professionally trained. She had, in fact, traveled to Britain before the war to study at one of the Nightingale schools. During her interview on the morning George saw her, Virgilia carefully praised this aspect of Mrs. Neal's background, even though doing so made her gorge rise.

At last she came to the purpose of the appointment. She requested a transfer to another hospital. Choosing words carefully, she said that her personality and that of the widowed Mrs. Neal appeared to clash. She believed each could work more effectively if they worked separately.

"And that is why you left your post at this critical period?" Miss Dix asked. "To seek a personal accommodation?"

Virgilia's temper boiled up. "I see nothing wrong with that, so long as it promotes better—"

"There is a great deal wrong with it, given the importance of the current campaign in Virginia. I shall take your petition under advisement, but not with haste, and, I warn you, not with a positive attitude. You have a good record, Miss Hazard. But this has blemished it. Good morning."

Virgilia left, silently cursing Miss Dix as a damned opinionated cow.

She reboarded the street railway and gradually calmed down. She liked the nursing service. Hence she was glad she hadn't brought up all the accusations she might have made against Mrs. Neal. They were more personal than professional anyway. The woman was a sentimentalist, a peace Democrat who couldn't say enough in praise of McClellan or in criticism of men such as Stevens and Stanton. From the start, the two women had disliked and distrusted each other. Their politics only exacerbated the situation.

I should have expected it would go the way it did, she thought. A small sigh earned her a stare from the man sitting next to her. He noticed her bosom and started to speak. She glared, and he changed seats.

A growling emptiness reminded her she had eaten nothing since waking up in the cheap hotel where she had spent the night. She saw Willard's on the next corner and left the car. She was at the dining-room door when a group of men came out.

"Congressman Stout—"

He turned. She held her breath—did he recognize her?

Yes! He lowered the hat he had been settling on his wavy dark hair. "Gentlemen, excuse me. An old friend. Thank you for your time; we shall pursue the matter."

Sam Stout ignored the faintly lewd chuckles of a couple of his friends and shook her hand. "Miss Hazard. How are you?"

"Pleased that you remember my name."

"Did you think I wouldn't? What are you doing in the city?"

"I had a meeting with Miss Dix on some pressing administrative matters. I hated to leave the hospital, but it couldn't be helped. Is there any news of General Hooker?"

"None but what the papers carry. My friend Stanton guards those telegraph receivers carefully." Stout glanced around, quickly evaluating all the men and women in the busy lobby. He did it casually, without attracting attention, which caused Virgilia to admire him all the more.

She was elated to see him. On a previous visit to Washington, she had made some inquiries about his personal life. He had no children; his wife, a girlhood sweetheart from Indiana, was apparently barren. A description of the woman revealed another tidbit. She was thin, with a chest as flat as a piece of lumber. Virgilia thought it might be useful to know she offered something Stout's wife did not.

His face grave, Stout said, "I would be most interested in hearing about current conditions in the hospitals. Whether you have the equipment you need, drugs in sufficient quantity—"

Clever man. Using the same pretext she had employed the day they met, he was speaking loudly and clearly to offset any suggestion of impropriety. A clerk at the reception counter had recognized Stout and was listening, she noticed. "I believe there's a quiet parlor just up this hallway, Miss Hazard. We could sit and chat there, if it would not interfere with your schedule."

His steady gaze spoke what was really on his mind. Virgilia began to feel light-headed and perspire, constricted by her layers of clothing.

Taking polite hold of her elbow, he guided her along the deserted corridor that had the woolly, musty odor of hotels everywhere. The parlor, with several small tables and chairs scattered about, was empty.

Stout was no fool; he left the door wide open, though he did choose a table where they couldn't be seen unless someone walked into the room.

He laid his hat on the table and his fawn gloves and silver-handled stick beside it. His hair oil had a citrus tang. His skin was whiter than she remembered and his great hooking brows, in contrast, coal black. "I must say, Miss Hazard, you look wonderfully fit." The resonant voice reached deep inside her, stirring—

Be careful. Don't make any casual bargains. He's a married man. He can't be plucked like an apple on a low branch.

"Thank you, Congressman."

An eloquent gesture at a plush chair. "Won't you sit down? How are conditions at Aquia Creek?"

"The work's arduous, but you know how strongly I feel about the cause we serve."

"I well remember," he answered, nodding. "It's one of many

582

reasons I admire you." He studied her mouth, smiled a little. She felt faint. He didn't press.

"Our supplies and food never seem adequate," she continued.

"Even so, the job you ladies do is remarkable."

"It's never good enough to satisfy me, Congressman."

"Sam, if you please."

"All right. My first name is—"

"Virgilia. It's a lovely name."

"You have such a grand voice it makes any name sound splendid."

His gaze moved past her to the parlor door. The corridor remained quiet. He seemed to be pondering his next gambit. Virgilia's eyes encouraged him.

At length he said, "I was sorry that our first meeting ended on a note that was rather discouraging."

"I felt I had to be candid with you, even though I greatly admired your militancy toward the rebels." She was surprised at the ease with which she had put a catch in her voice. She would never be an accomplished flirt like that empty-headed Ashton Main, but she was learning a trick or two.

"Do I detect the past tense, Virgilia?"

She smiled. "A slip of the tongue. My admiration has not abated."

Again he glanced toward the hall. Only the distant murmurs of the lobby filled its dusty spaces. Slowly, his right hand rose from his lap. How languorous the hand seemed, moving toward her bodice like some white bird sailing on currents of air. Beginning to tremble, she pressed her legs together as his thumb came to rest on her left breast, his fingers curled against the swelling side.

She swept her right hand across, closed it on his. She said his first name softly, then shut her eyes. "Oh—"

In the hall, someone rattled a pail. Stout quickly pulled his hand away. The little exchange had lasted no more than five seconds, but it had clarified everything only hinted at before.

An elderly Negro in hotel livery appeared, bucket in hand, and began sifting the contents of a sand urn just outside the parlor door. The old man drew out broken cigar butts, bits of paper, and, when he had them all, smoothed the sand and disappeared.

Virgilia's face felt as if someone had dashed hot water on it.

Stout leaned forward. "I want to see you again."

"I feel the same way."

"Our next meeting should be more private, don't you think?"

For a dizzying moment, she was tempted. Then she remembered what she stood to lose—or gain. She shook her head. Stout's polished veneer cracked.

"You just said—"

"I do feel—a strong attraction, Sam. But I refuse to involve myself in some—some back-street affair."

He draped an arm over his chair and studied her. "Is my wife still the problem?"

"I am afraid so."

Coldly, he said, "If you have a notion that I might throw her over for you or any other woman, you're mistaken."

"I didn't ask—"

"Asking isn't necessary, my dear." Sarcasm and that great resonant voice combined with devastating results. "Your scheme's quite clear. I suppose I can't blame you for hoping, but the hope is misguided. I would never sacrifice what I've achieved in this town —and much more that I want to achieve—by making myself morally notorious. Do you know what some of my constituents in Muncie would do if I became embroiled in a scandal? They'd vote me out—and have bubbling tar and hen feathers waiting at the depot when I came home."

Having gotten the effect he wanted, he softened, grasped her hand. "Why must convention be an obstacle, Virgilia? We have a mutual desire and we can satisfy it discreetly without harming the interests of either party."

"How do you know it would work that way, Congressman? Are you an expert at philandering?"

A chill settled into his eyes. He snatched up his stick, hat, fawn gloves. "I have an appointment. It has been pleasant to visit with you, Miss Hazard. Good-bye."

"Good-bye."

He reached the door. She stood abruptly. "Sam—"

Turning, but giving nothing else, he replied, "Yes?"

How hard it was to say what had to be said. "Nothing. My terms must stand."

"They're too high, I'm afraid. Very much too high." He gave her another smile, this one scornful, meant to wound. His stooping figure vanished down the hall.

She sat again, listening to the faint lobby sounds while a sense of failure consumed her. How stupid she had been to bluff when she held such poor cards. Undoubtedly he could have his pick of half the women in Washington.

And yet, remembering his eyes, she knew he wanted her. *Her* breasts, *her* person—

What did it matter? She had played all her trumps, and she had still lost. Her despair growing worse, she sat counting rosettes in the carpet pattern until she heard a knock. Like someone rousing from sleep, she turned and saw the old black porter with the pail.

"You feelin' all right, ma'am?"

"Fine, thank you. I was merely a bit dizzy and came in here to rest."

Willing herself out of lethargy, she rose. Might it not be a little premature to count failure as a certainty? Setting a high price on her favors could have a reverse effect and make Stout want her all the more. All his back-turning and sneering might be so much sham.

With these thoughts came another, transformed almost at once into a conviction. This would not be the last time she saw Sam Stout. She didn't want it to be the last time, and despite his rhetoric about ambition, constituents, his wife, she felt he didn't either.

Where would they meet? No way to tell. No matter; it would happen. She left the parlor and strode swiftly, confidently, toward the faint sounds. She noticed that she drew covert stares from gentlemen as she crossed the lobby and went out.

79

"It's all there," said the albino. "Where's the money?"

"In due time—in due time!"

Bent's small dark eyes ran over the closely written pages. The albino, a soft, vulnerable-looking boy of eighteen or nineteen, walked away with a petulant expression. He snatched a piece of straw from one of the bales piled in the shed. His right hand drooped in a limp way as he slipped the straw into his mouth and chewed.

Bent continued scanning the pages. "You'll find everything as promised," the albino said. It sounded like a complaint. "Complete inventory of items the Tredegar is manufacturing—cannon, shell casings, gun carriages, rolled plate for Mr. Mallory's ironclads. There's a long list with quantities shown for each. My, uh, friend who got the information together was one of Joe Anderson's top assistants."

Alerted, Bent cleared his throat. "Did you say was?"

"Yes, Mr. Bascom." Daintily, he raised his left hand to brush his pretty white hair off the shoulder of his soiled shirt. "He was discharged last week, I regret to say. Some irregularity about payments."

"What sort of irregularity?"

"Something to do with favoring certain suppliers. It doesn't affect the report. That's a hundred percent reliable."

"Oh, I'm certain it is," Bent said, nodding. He folded the pages and slipped them into a side pocket of his tentlike coat. He resembled a respectable businessman in his new suit of black alpaca, heavy boots, broad-brimmed black hat and cravat of the same color.

His mind sped. The poor warped creature, intending to please, had let slip a piece of damaging information. He was now useless as a contact. Bent knew he must act on that information. He wasn't hesitant about it; Baker had given him wide latitude.

"I have the money." He rooted in another pocket. The albino licked his lips. A bell clanged on a night packet moving down the James River & Kanawha Canal at three miles an hour, its lights visible through gaps in the shed wall. The shed was situated among several others on weedy, deserted ground at the foot of Oregon Hill. A short distance downstream, across the canal but on this side of the river, the sprawling Tredegar foundry reddened the night and filled it with the clatter of machinery.

Bent had not been in the detached service very long, but he already had a grasp of its intricacies, probably because his nature and the nature of the work meshed perfectly. Thus, counting out bills—United States bills, not Confederate; the albino had insisted —he silently ticked off points relative to the situation.

An inactive contact was potentially dangerous. The albino knew Bent was a Union spy. He could report Bent to the authorities if he felt spiteful, and be no poorer for it. Or, after Bent left Richmond, he could talk too freely, making it unsafe for Bent to return.

The albino said, "In regard to my gentleman friend who compiled the information—I have to split the proceeds with him, you know. In hard times like these, an extra dollar's welcome. Also in reference to my friend, I'm not exclusively his, in case—"

"Some other time," Bent said, only briefly tempted. He must keep duty and pleasure separate. Besides, the little sod might be diseased, like some of the pitiful males he had seen offering themselves under the trees of Capitol Square. "I think we can consider our business finished." He handed the money to the albino. "Why don't you leave first? I'll extinguish the lantern and follow in a few minutes."

"All right, Mr. Bascom." The albino sounded disappointed.

"By the way—is your friend still in Richmond?" Bent expected an affirmative answer. It wouldn't alter his decision about the albino, but it might influence the length of his stay in the city.

Unexpectedly, the albino said, "No, sir. He went home to Charlottesville for a few days to collect himself. Being sacked by Joe

587

Anderson was a pretty hard blow. He'd worked at the Tredegar ten years. Began as an apprentice, back when the place built locomotives."

"Sad," Bent declared, injecting as much false sympathy as possible. His heart beat fast now, from nerves and anticipation. The albino gave him a last pleading look.

"Well, then—good night, Mr. Bascom."

"Good night."

While the albino sauntered to the door and reached for the latch, Bent drew the clasp knife from his coat and silently opened it. The six-inch blade flashed under the hanging lantern.

The albino heard the swift, heavy tread of Bent's boots and peeked over his shoulder. Before he could cry out, Bent had his left elbow around the albino's windpipe. He pushed the knife into the albino's back. The blade met resistance. He kept pushing until all the metal had disappeared.

He twisted it one way, then another, to be sure the job was done. The albino pulled at Bent's left arm but lacked strength to loosen it. His torn shoes scraped and twisted in the dirt. Finally the slight body was limp.

Bent extricated the bloody knife and gagged only once. He was astonished and pleased about his suitability for this work. He felt sure that since he had never met the albino's friend, the man would be unable to trace Mr. Bascom or connect him in any way with a Mr. Dayton of Raleigh, North Carolina, who was stopping temporarily at one of the city's cheaper lodging houses.

Taking hold of the collar, he dragged the body. It smelled now. He placed it against a wall and concealed it with straw bales pushed in front of it and stacked on top. Then he remembered something, removed two bales, and dug in the dead boy's pockets till he found the currency. Baker would be glad to have the cash to use again.

He replaced the bales and with his boot smoothed the dirt floor to remove the most conspicuous signs of disturbance. After a careful inspection, he blew out the lantern and went out the door into the balmy May night. The lights of Richmond twinkled on the hilltop and on either hand. Lamps gleamed on the prison island in the river, and the Tredegar spewed red smoke and light. Bent made his way back along the canal for a short distance, then turned left and climbed toward the center of the city that was mourning for a legend.

The next day was Wednesday, May 13. In full-dress uniform, including sash and the Solingen sword, Orry walked with a great many other Confederate officers in the funeral procession.

Behind the officers were hundreds of clerks and minor officials from the statehouse and the city corporation. Directly ahead were Orry's chief, Seddon, his friend Benjamin, and other cabinet members. Ahead of them, hung with great swags of black crepe, was the carriage of President and Mrs. Davis. The Davises followed the most honored mourners—raggedy veterans who had served with the man the procession honored. The veterans walked or dragged themselves on crutches. A few were borne on litters by tired comrades in butternut or fading gray.

Ahead of the veterans walked the official military escort, two companies from George Pickett's division, one of artillery, one of cavalry. Their drummers beat the slow march for the dead.

Ahead of them, led by a single soldier, was the general's favorite war charger, Old Sorrel, saddle empty, stirrups tucked up. Ahead of Old Sorrel, drawn by black-plumed horses and with four generals walking at the corners as a special honor guard, was the black hearse containing the body of Thomas Jonathan Jackson.

Jackson had died on Sunday, after his wound bred pneumonia and bodily poisons and the surgeons lopped off his left arm in a futile attempt to arrest his decline. All day yesterday he had lain in state in the governor's mansion, his coffin draped in the national flag for which he had fought with such loyalty and ferocity. As the body was being readied for the procession to Capitol Square, Jackson's widow had finally broken down and been led away.

On either side of the route of march, Orry saw stricken, tear-stained faces, male and female, soldier and civilian. Even the little children wept. Nothing in recent memory, not even Pelham's fall, had so devastated the Confederacy. Seddon had whispered to Orry as they stood beside the bier yesterday that Lee was almost beyond consolation.

It was difficult to believe that Jackson had been slain not by some Yankee but by one of his own, a Confederate soldier who would remain eternally anonymous. Probably the man didn't know he had fired the fatal bullet.

Ironic, too, that it had happened immediately after Jackson and

589

Lee had once again gambled brilliantly. Faced with Hooker's sudden surprise sweep, they had agreed to split their army a second time and send Jackson's foot cavalry on the swift secret march to the Union right. Jackson had smashed Howard's corps of Dutchmen and by doing so had perhaps drained all the fight out of Fighting Joe. For whatever reason, Hooker had somehow lost his nerve, withdrawn from a strong offensive position at a key moment, and steadily given ground thereafter. Jubal Early had lost Fredericksburg, but the Yanks had lost the battle of Chancellorsville. The roles of winner and loser might be reversed, however, once the full cost of Jackson's death was reckoned. Orry thought the victory a hollow one.

The procession entered Capitol Square through the west gates, where Orry saw his wife in a group of women that included Mrs. Stanard, one of the *grandes dames* of local society. Benjamin had provided an introduction, and Mrs. Stanard had taken to Madeline instantly, favoring her with the information that she had definitely not taken to Orry's sister, Mrs. Huntoon, whom she had invited to her salon once only.

Seeing Madeline cheered him a little. But there wasn't much to be happy about any more, even setting aside this dark day. In the west, Sam Grant was moving relentlessly on the works around Vicksburg. Men no longer lowered their voices when they discussed impeachment of Davis. And General Winder's wardens continued to run the overcrowded prisons cruelly, in defiance of frequent inspections and memorandums of protest from Orry and others.

Cooper was in Richmond, had been for almost a month. His office was in the Mechanics Institute building, so Orry seldom ran into him by accident. Cooper was tragically changed as a result of his son's death, news of which had stunned Orry and his wife. Uncommunicative, totally uninterested in hospitable overtures and dinner invitations from Madeline, he was lost in his work for Navy Secretary Mallory, whom Orry distrusted, as he distrusted anyone and anything connected with the rival service.

In recent days, Orry and Madeline had received a visitor from Spotsylvania County, the stylish, intelligent, occasionally sharp-tongued widow with whom Cousin Charles had formed a romantic attachment. With her two Negroes, Augusta Barclay had come flying from Fredericksburg to take up residence on the parlor sofa until Hooker's withdrawal across the Rapidan became a certainty.

She had left only yesterday, her worry about her farm taking precedence over the public rites for Jackson.

Charles was in love. The widow Barclay didn't say so, but it was evident to Orry from the way she discussed his cousin. Well, that was Charles's affair, though these were hardly the best of times for planning a future.

Nor was Orry enamored of the way Mrs. Barclay sometimes flaunted her learning. She was fond of quoting English poets of the aphoristic school and seemed to have an inexhaustible supply of couplets for all occasions.

Still, his reaction was essentially a favorable one, as was Madeline's. Augusta Barclay was undeniably attractive, and during her stay on Marshall Street she had taken pains to see that her freedmen had adequate food and shelter in the backyard in a tent improvised from blankets. She helped Madeline with the cooking and routine chores. And before departing, she said three times that if she could repay their generosity in any way, they must not hesitate to call on her. Orry believed the offer was sincere.

The hall of the House of Representatives was filled with the sweet fumes of huge floral tributes surrounding the bier and great pyramids of white lilies heaped up beside it. Reluctantly, Orry joined the line of officers shuffling toward the open coffin. When it was his turn to gaze at the bearded head on the satin pillow, he nearly couldn't do it. He saw a callow and oddly likable West Point plebe, not the strange adult from whose convoluted, some said diseased, mind had come victory after victory. Amidst the lilies, Orry bowed his head and cried.

Somehow Madeline worked through the crowd and took his arm and held it tightly against her side until he was himself again.

Like an elephant rousing, Elkanah Bent got out of his disarrayed bed about one that afternoon. He had visited a whorehouse last night and put a black girl to good use. He had returned to the lodging house at dawn, when no one was awake to ask him whether he planned to watch Jackson's funeral parade. He certainly didn't. He had no intention of dignifying a traitor's death with his presence, though he might go take a peek at the body to see how much Jackson had changed since the days when Bent had hazed him. Even then, Jackson had displayed peculiarities; excessive concern for the way his organs hung within his body, for example. More recently, Union officers had jeered at his reluctance to go into battle on Sunday. But the mad old Presbyterian had slaughtered his enemies without pity the other six days of the week. The Union was well shed of him.

Bent lathered his face, opened his razor case, and set about making himself presentable. He was astonished at the ease with which he had accomplished his mission thus far. Of course he had taken precautions—ridden to Richmond with two pistols and a concealed knife—but the rest had been absurdly simple. Whenever he was stopped, he simply showed the pass forged by one of Baker's specialists. His speech caused him no trouble because he was in a part of the South in which the mushy accents of the cotton states sounded foreign. Furthermore, Yankees—whores and speculators, mostly—could be found all over town.

Concerning the female invaders, a barman had given him a piece of advice: "Don't you fret one minute about the safety of Richmond till you see the Baltimore whores trying to buy train tickets. Then you should worry."

Too late for breakfast but in plenty of time to eat a huge midday meal, Bent spent an uncomfortable hour with the minor bureaucrats, traveling men, and low-ranking officers who packed the two communal tables in the dining room. The landlady offered him a strip of black satin, something she was providing for every guest. Inwardly contemptuous, he nevertheless thanked her effusively and tied the armband on his left sleeve.

With the Tredegar information hidden in a special pocket in his coat lining, a pocket he had sewn shut as soon as he filled it, he trudged to Capitol Square and stood in the shuffling line of people who moaned and wept for the dead traitor in a way he found disgusting. When he reached the bier, he hardly recognized the man lying there. But he tried to affect a soulful expression and dabbed at one eye before moving on.

He was jolted by the sight of two people farther back in line: a man with round glasses, nearly as heavy as Bent but in his opinion considerably less handsome, and a woman whose dark beauty sounded chords of familiarity. He approached an officer standing by himself.

"Beg pardon, Major—do you happen to know that couple over there? I think the woman may be a distant relative of my wife."

The officer couldn't help him, but a man with the sleek look of a high-ranking government official overheard and said, "Oh, that's Huntoon. From South Carolina. He has a minor job at Treasury."

Bent almost shook with excitement. "South Carolina, you say? Would his wife's maiden name happen to be Main?"

He asked the question with such intensity that the civilian's suspicions were aroused. "I certainly couldn't tell you that." Nor would he mention to this fat, sweaty fellow, who looked more speculator than Southerner, that he was acquainted with the woman's brother, Colonel Main of the War Department. The civilian excused himself quickly.

Bent hurried into the square and paused by the great statue of Washington, whose birthday those on both sides continued to celebrate. He lingered until the couple emerged and entered a barouche driven by an old Negro. The barouche rolled past Bent where he lounged in the shade of the statue's pedestal. The woman took no notice of him or any of her surroundings; she was busy berating her husband. She struck Bent as arrogant, but she definitely resembled Orry Main. She was worth investigating.

Now that he had accomplished his first mission without a hitch, he was full of confidence. On the spot he decided to risk one more day in the Confederate capital.

In bed that night, he formulated his plan. Next morning he called at the post office as soon as it opened. He introduced himself as Mr. Bell, a native of Louisville, and persuaded the clerk to overlook any deficiencies in his accent by passing a folded bill over the counter. The clerk opened a thick book and found the address of James Huntoon.

Hiring a hack, Bent drove past the Grace Street residence twice. Then, downtown again, he searched the stores till he found some over-priced linen that could be torn up to simulate bandages. He fretted through the next few hours at his lodging house. He planned to call late in the day, before the government offices closed.

Around four, he walked out Grace Street and, when he was unobserved, paused for a swig from a metal flask kept in his side pocket. In an alley two blocks from his destination, he tied the linen into a sling and slid his left forearm through. A few minutes later, the same black man he had seen driving the barouche admitted him to the foyer.

"Yes, Miz Huntoon's at home, but she wasn't expectin' callers."

"I'm a visitor in the city. Tell her it's important."

"Your name again, sar?"

"Bellingham. Captain Erasmus Bellingham, on furlough from General Longstreet's corps." Longstreet was currently far from Richmond, which was the reason for that particular lie. "I must soon return to duty, so kindly ask your mistress to see me at once."

Homer led Bent to a small sitting room, then trudged off. Bent was too nervous to sit. He paced and chewed a clove to cover his whiskey breath. Underneath his white shirt and alpaca suit, sweat soaked him. Just as he had decided to flee, he heard a swish of skirts in the hall. Ashton Huntoon swept in, cross and sleepy-looking.

"Captain Bellingham?"

"Erasmus Bellingham, currently with General—"

"My nigger told me that."

"I dislike interrupting you without prior warning, ma'am—" Her expression made clear that she disliked it as much as he did. Though her resemblance to her brother automatically generated rage, Bent kept his unctuous smile in place as he went on. "However, I haven't much more time in Richmond. I am nearly recovered from this wound I received at the siege of Suffolk. Before I return to Longstreet's command, I wanted to inquire about an old acquaintance."

"You don't sound like a Southerner, Captain."

Bitch. He broadened the smile. "Oh, there are all degrees of Southern speech, I find. You don't sound like a Virginian"—*careful; mustn't let any hostility show*—"and the truth is, I was born and raised on the Eastern Shore of Maryland. I left it the moment I heard the Confederacy's call to arms."

"How interesting." Ashton didn't conceal her boredom.

Bent explained that while on duty in the lower part of the state, he had heard that one of his West Point classmates was stationed in Richmond. "Last evening I was conversing with a gentleman at my lodging house—some chap with friends at the Treasury Department—and when I mentioned my classmate, he brought you and your husband into the conversation. He said you both hailed from South Carolina, as my classmate did, and that your maiden name was the same as his."

594

"Is your classmate Orry Main?"

"Yes."

She acted as if he had dumped a spittoon on her. "He's my older brother."

"Your brother," Bent echoed. "How extraordinary! I haven't seen him in years. Come to think of it, though, I do recall him mentioning you in an affectionate manner."

Ashton dabbed her upper lip with a bit of lace. "I doubt that."

"Please, tell me, is Orry in Richmond?"

"Yes, and so is his wife. I don't see either of them. By choice."

"Is he perchance in the army?"

"He's a lieutenant colonel attached to the War Department." Gathering her skirts, Ashton rose. "Is there anything else?" Her tone said she hoped not.

"Only the location of his residence, if you'd be so kind—"

"They have rooms on Marshall near the White House. I've never been there. Good day, Captain Bellingham."

Rudely dismissed, Bent nevertheless managed to reach the street without displaying his anger. He had brief, dizzy visions of tearing Ashton Huntoon's clothing and subjecting her to punishments that would also yield certain perverse pleasures.

The spiteful mood passed. Turning toward town, he strode along as if there were clouds under his feet. In another alley he stripped off the sling and threw it away. Orry Main was here. Bent was close to one of the objects of his hatred—closer than he had been since Charles Main eluded and disgraced him in Texas. He ought to walk into the War Department, find Main's desk, and shoot him right between—

No. Not only would hasty action imperil his life, it would rob the vengeance of savor. Bent also had the new job to think about. Baker would be expecting him in Washington. He should collect his horse from the stable and leave at once.

Instead, he decided to remain an additional night. He wanted to be thoroughly familiar with the terrain when he returned to Richmond on another mission, as he undoubtedly would. He wanted to know precisely where to look for Orry Main.

Locating the War Department offices next day proved easy. Bent watched the building for half an hour but didn't go in. Finding the flat on Marshall in the fashionable Court End district proved a little harder. He offered three-cent silver pieces to several black children before he found one who knew the colonel and his

595

wife. The youngster pointed out their residence, a large house evidently converted into suites of rental rooms for the duration.

He approached from the opposite side of the street. The brim of his black hat protecting him from the May sunshine, he surveyed the house and got a shock when a lovely woman with a parasol came out and turned left on the walk.

Bent felt as if a thunderbolt had come down to smite him. The woman passing from view was instantly familiar because he often sat gazing at her, or someone very much like her, in the canvas stolen from New Orleans. This woman's mouth, shape of nose, color of eyes and hair were not identical with those in the picture. But the resemblance could not be mistaken.

Sweating, Bent lumbered up the steps of her residence and rang the bell. A wispy old woman answered. He swept his hat off.

"Your pardon, ma'am. I have business with a Mrs. Wadlington, whom I don't know. I was told she lived in this block, and I just passed a lady who fits the sketchy description I was given. The lady came out this door, so I wondered—"

"That's Colonel Main's wife. Never heard of a Mrs. Wadlington, and I know everyone. But I don't know you." *Slam.*

Flushed, elated, and short of breath, Bent went reeling away. His luck had turned at last. First the Baker connection and now this. Orry Main, a high military official, was married to a nigger whore—and he had the evidence. How he would use it, he was too overwrought to determine just now. But use it he would, of that he was—

"Murder! Mysterious stabbing by the canal!"

The shout of the newsboy on Broad Street interrupted the vengeful reverie. He bought a paper and scanned it as he walked. The cold of panic replaced his steamy delirium. They had found the corpse of Bent's informant, though he was not named. *The victim was a white male of the kind commonly called "albino."*

In less than an hour, Elkanah Bent packed his valise, vacated his room, saddled his horse, and took the road north.

80

That same evening, standing knee deep in the James River, Cooper sneezed.

He had caught cold. It didn't matter. Nor did the miserable, weary state of his assistant and two helpers. "One more," he said. "Rig the shell."

"Mr. Main, it's nearly dark," said his assistant, an earnest but fundamentally untalented boy named Lucius Chickering. A Charleston aristocrat, nineteen-year-old Chickering had enrolled in Mallory's Confederate Naval Academy, whose campus consisted of the old side-wheeler *Patrick Henry,* anchored in the river. Chickering had rapidly failed basic astronomy, navigation, and seamanship, and been dismissed, with Lieutenant Parker's regrets. Only his father's influence saved him from absolute disgrace; a job was found for him in the scorned Navy Department. Cooper liked Chickering, but he knew the boy kept quiet about where he worked.

Lucius Chickering had a huge nose with a hump in the middle. His upper teeth jutted over his lower lip, and he had more freckles than anyone deserved. His ugliness somehow contributed to his likability. And he was right about the lateness of the hour. A deep red sunset covered the James with sullen reflections. Birds wheeled against high scarlet clouds, and downstream a barge had already become a blot of shadow dotted yellow by a single lantern.

Replying to his assistant, Cooper said, "We have time. If you're all too lazy, I'll rig it myself."

He hadn't eaten since daybreak. They had been down here in the rushes, a mile from the city limits, struggling with these driftwood torpedoes the entire day. They had not been successful even once, and Cooper knew why. The concept was wrong.

A wood cradle, newly designed within the department, held a metal canister of powder with a small opening in its domed lid. Into the opening went an impact-type percussion fuse. Cradle and canister were painted grayish brown, like the pieces of Atlantic driftwood to which they were lashed. The problem was, the movement of the driftwood in the river current—and therefore on a harbor tide—was uncontrollable. The experimenters found the wrong end of the torpedo bumping against the test target: three barrels anchored in midstream with enough open water on either side for barges and small steam sloops to pass.

To be correct about it, not all of the driftwood torpedoes had even reached the target. By Cooper's count, it was five out of two dozen launched. All had failed to detonate because the fuse and canister were on the side opposite that which struck the barrels.

As Cooper started to work, Chickering exploded. "Mr. Main, I must protest. You've worked us like field bucks all day, and now you want us to continue when we can scarcely see what we're doing."

"Indeed I do," Cooper said, his body a black reed against the red sky. "This is wartime, Mr. Chickering. If you don't care for the hours or the working conditions, submit your resignation and go back to Charleston."

Lucius Chickering glowered at his superior. Cooper Main intimidated and annoyed him. He was a Palmetto State man who acted more like a Yankee. He slopped around in mud and water as if appearances didn't matter. While the others stood by, Cooper carefully screwed the detonator plug into the canister fuse. His trousers and shirt sleeves soaking wet, he launched the driftwood torpedo and watched it turn aimlessly in the water. Five minutes later a flash of flame marked its detonation against the far bank. It had sailed past the target with twenty feet to spare.

Curtly, Cooper said to one of the helpers, "Row out there and tow the barrels in. You"—to the other helper—"load the tools in the wagon." Muttering, the helper picked up a long crosscut saw, which hummed a sad note.

The sun was down, starlight shone, frogs croaked in the sweet Virginia night. The helper grumbled and swore, sneezed again, then said to Chickering, "I'll tell Mallory the design's a failure, like the raft torpedo before it and the keg torpedo before that."

"Sir, with all respect"—having exploded, Chickering was calmer now—"why do we keep on with these fruitless experiments? Our work is so peculiar, we're the butt of jokes in every other department."

"Be thankful, Lucius. Snide remarks will never wound you the way bullets do."

Chickering colored at the suggestion that he might be happy to avoid hazardous duty. But he said nothing because Main's authority was not to be questioned; he and Mallory were close as two peas. Still, more than one person whispered that the new man was unbalanced. Something to do with his son drowning on the voyage from Nassau to Wilmington.

Like a humorless schoolmaster, Cooper continued. "We test these odd devices for one reason: our inferior position vis-à-vis the enemy. As the secretary says so often, we don't outnumber them, we can't out-spend them, so we have to out-think them. That means experimentation, no matter how ludicrous the experiments may seem to the fashionable young ladies and gentlemen you associate with here in Richmond. Mallory wants to win, you see, not merely negotiate an end to the war. I want to win. I want to whip the damn Yankees on the Atlantic and the rivers if we do it nowhere else. Now pick up that hand saw and put it in the wagon."

He sloshed down the bank to help the man who had rowed out to tow the barrels. Together they beached the target and carried the inverted rowboat to the wagon. More water dripped on Cooper's wet shirt, and he sneezed three times, violently, before they stowed the boat and climbed aboard for the homeward trip, four tired men in a world gone dark except for stars.

Cooper began to regret his sharp words. To be influenced by others was the way of the young. Chickering understandably resented a department constantly under attack for mismanagement, overspending, and dalliance with ideas that seemed to be the creations of idiots. Yet the boy, like so many others, simply didn't understand that you had to sift through all that fool's gold if you hoped to discover one nugget—one design, one idea—that might tilt everything in a decisive way.

Cooper had thrown himself into that search with ferocious energy. Mallory had been complimentary about his work in England

and soon took the younger man into his confidence. In Mallory's opinion, the river war was lost. It was now their task to salvage the situation on the Atlantic seaboard. The commerce raiders, including the one Cooper helped launch, had captured or damaged an astonishing number of Yankee merchantmen. Insurance rates had risen, according to plan, to near-prohibitive levels, causing several hundred cargo ships to be transferred to dummy owners in Great Britain. Yet this Confederate success had failed to achieve its final goal—appreciable reduction of the size and effectiveness of the Yankee blockade squadron.

If anything, General Scott's Anaconda was tightening. One point of maximum constriction was Charleston, where Union monitors had attacked in force in April. Harbor and shore batteries had repulsed them, but everyone in the department anticipated further attacks. Not only was Charleston a vital port, but it was the flash point of the war—the city the enemy most wanted to capture and destroy.

If he didn't have the department, Cooper doubted that he could survive. Moreover, he believed in the work; he and Mallory were alike in that and in other ways. Each had started out detesting the idea of secession—early in the war, Mallory had been widely quoted after he said, "I regard it as another name for revolution" —but now both were fierce as hawks in pursuit of the enemy.

The secretary kept everyone busy with schemes. Schemes for new ironclads. Schemes for submersible attack vessels. Schemes for naval torpedoes of every conceivable configuration. Cooper reveled in the frantic effort, because he hated the enemy. But he hated one individual fully as much, though he had said nothing of that to anyone, not even Orry, so far. He wanted to arrange a fitting confrontation. A fitting punishment.

The struggles of the department had one additional benefit. If he worked himself to a stupor every night, his mind was less likely to cast up memories of Judah in the moonlit sea. Judah calling for help. Judah's poor scalded face disintegrating—

As the wagon rattled on toward the lamplit hills, Cooper wondered about the time. It would be quite late when he got home. Judith would be angry. Again. Well, no matter.

In the city, Chickering was first to jump off. Late for a rendezvous with some belle, Cooper assumed. Cooper's nose was dripping. It hurt to swallow. "Be at your desk by seven," he said to his assistant. "I want today's report written and out of the way by the start of regular working hours."

"Yes, sir," Chickering said. Cooper heard him muttering as he disappeared in the dark.

The wagon driver let him off in front of the Mechanics Institute on Ninth Street, bidding him a surly good night. Cooper didn't give a damn about the disapproval; the clod failed to understand the desperate straits of the Confederacy or the problems of the department, which Mallory summed up in two words: "Never enough." Never enough time. Never enough money. Never enough cooperation. They improvised and lived by their wits. That brought a certain pride, but it was killing work.

Cooper presumed Mallory would still be in the department's second-floor offices, and he was. Everyone else had gone except one of the secretary's trio of assistants, the dapper Mr. Tidball, who was locking his desk as Cooper walked in.

"Good evening," Tidball said, tugging each of the desk drawers in turn. He then squared a pile of papers to align it with a corner. Tidball was a drone with no imagination, but with exceptional organizational skills. He complemented the other two members of the triumvirate—Commodore Forrest, a blustery old blue-water sailor who understood the ways of seamen, and Cooper, who served as an extension of Mallory's inventive nature. Those two men preferred "Let us try" over "Here's why we can't."

"He's been waiting for you," Tidball said with a nod at the inner office. Tidball left, and Cooper went in to find the secretary examining engineering drawings by the light of a lamp with a green glass shade. The wick flickered as the scented oil burned. The gas mantles were shut down, and the perimeter of the cluttered office was dark.

"Hallo, Cooper," Mallory said. He was a roly-poly man of fifty, born in Trinidad and reared mostly in Key West by an Irish mother and a Connecticut Yankee father. He had a tilted nose, plump cheeks, and bright blue eyes that often sparkled with excitement. He reminded Cooper of an English country squire.

"What luck?"

Cooper sneezed. "None. The design for the cradle and canister are good enough; the problem is the one we saw when we first examined the plans. A torpedo attached to driftwood will do one thing predictably—drift. Without guidance, it's as likely to blow a hole in Fort Sumter as it is to sink a Yankee. Most probably it would float around Charleston harbor for weeks or months, undetonated and potentially dangerous. I'll put it all in my report."

"You recommend we forget about it?" The secretary looked extremely tired tonight, Cooper observed.

"Absolutely."

"Well, that's definitive, if nothing else. I appreciate your conducting the test."

"General Rains proved the value of torpedoes in land operations," Cooper said, sitting down in a hard chair. "The Yankees may think them inhuman, but they work. They'll work for us if we can find the proper means to deliver them to the target and make certain they fire."

"All true. But we're making precious little progress with them."

"The department's overtaxed, Stephen. Maybe we need a separate group to develop and test them on a systematic basis."

"A torpedo bureau?"

Cooper nodded. "Captain Maury would be an ideal man to head it."

"Excellent thought. Perhaps I can find funds—" Cooper sniffed and Mallory added, "You sound terrible."

"I have a cold, that's all."

Mallory received that skeptically. Perspiration glistened on Cooper's forehead. "Time for you to go home to a hot meal. Speaking of which, Angela remains determined to see you and Judith. When will you take supper with us?"

Cooper slumped farther down in the chair. "We've already refused three invitations from my brother. I'll have to satisfy that obligation first."

"I appreciate your industry, certainly. But you must take more time for yourself. You can't work every moment."

"Why not? I have debts to repay."

Mallory cleared his throat. "So be it. I have something else to show you, but it can wait till morning."

Cooper unbent his long body and stood. "Now will be fine." He circled the desk and peered into the soft oval of lamplight. The top drawing showed a curious vessel indicated as forty feet end to end. In the elevation, it reminded Cooper of an ordinary steam boiler, but in plan the bow and stern showed a pronounced taper, much like a cigar's. The vessel had two hatches, indicated on the elevation as only a few inches high.

"What the devil is it? Another submersible?"

"Yes," Mallory said, pointing to a decorative ribbon in the lower right corner. Elaborate script within the ribbon spelled *H. L. Hunley.* "That's her name. The accompanying letter states that Mr. Hunley, a well-to-do sugar broker, was responsible for the concept and some of the first construction money. She was started at New Orleans. Her developers rushed her away to Mobile before the city fell. These gentlemen are finishing the job." He tapped a line beneath the ribbon: *McClintock & Watson, Marine Engineers.*

"They call her the fish ship," the secretary continued. "She's supposed to be watertight, capable of diving beneath an enemy vessel"—his hand swooped to illustrate—"dragging a torpedo. The torpedo detonates when the fish ship is safe on the other side."

"Ah," Cooper said, "that's how she differs from *David.*" The department had been laboring to develop a submersible for coast and harbor operations. The little torpedo vessel he had just mentioned carried her explosive charge in front, on a long bow boom.

"That and her mode of attack. She is definitely designed to strike while submerged." *David,* though a submersible, was meant to operate on the surface when ramming with her boom.

An underwater boat wasn't a new idea, of course. A Connecticut man had invented one at the start of the Revolution. But few government officials, and certainly not the President, believed that the idea might have a current application. Its only proponents were Mallory and his little cadre of determined dreamers. Brunel would have understood this, Cooper thought. He would have understood us.

After a moment, he said, "Only testing will show us which design's the best, I suppose."

"Quite right. We must encourage completion of this craft. I intend to write the gentlemen in Mobile a warm and enthusiastic letter—and forward copies of all the correspondence to General Beauregard in Charleston. Now go home and get some rest."

"But I'd like to see a little more of—"

"In the morning. Go home. And be careful. I trust you've read about all the murders and street robberies lately." Cooper nodded, unsmiling. The times were dark with trouble. People were desperate.

He bade Mallory good evening and trudged to Main Street,

where he was lucky enough to pick up a hack at one of the hotels. It rattled up to Church Hill, where they had leased a small house at three times the peacetime price. Judith, a book in her lap, raised her head as he came in. Half in sympathy, half in annoyance, she said, "You look wretched."

"We splashed in the James all day. To no purpose."

"The torpedo—?"

"No good. Anything to eat?"

"Calf's liver. You wouldn't believe what it cost. I'm afraid it'll be cold and greasy. I expected you long before this."

"Oh, for God's sake, Judith—you know I have a lot of work."

"Even when you were trying to build *Star of Carolina,* you seldom stayed out this late. At least not every night. And when you came home, you smiled occasionally. Said something pleasant—"

"This is not a pleasant time or a pleasant world," he replied, cold and aloof suddenly. A droplet hung quivering on the end of his nose. He disposed of it with a slash of his soaked sleeve. "As Stephen says, it is no laughing matter to have the fate of the Confederacy in the hands of soldiers with swollen vanities in place of brains."

"Stephen." She snapped the book shut, held it with hands gone white. "That's all I ever hear from you—Stephen—unless you're cursing your sister."

"Where's Marie-Louise?"

"Where do you suppose she'd be at this hour? She's in bed. Cooper—"

"I don't want to argue." He turned away.

"But something's happened to you. You don't seem to have any feeling left for me, your daughter—for anything except that damned department."

One of his slender hands closed on the frame of the parlor door. He sniffed again, head lowered slightly. The way he gazed at her from under his eyebrows frightened her.

"Something did happen to me," he said softly. "My son drowned. Because of this war, my sister's greed, and your refusal to remain in Nassau. Now kindly let me alone so I can eat."

In the kitchen, seated near the cold stove, he cut into the liver, ate three bites, and threw the rest away. He went to their bedroom, lit the gas, and shut the door. After undressing, he piled two coverlets on, but still couldn't get warm.

Presently Judith came in. She undressed, put out the lamp, and climbed in beside him. He lay with his back to her, his face to the wall. She was careful not to touch him. He thought he heard her crying but didn't turn over. He fell asleep thinking of the drawings of the fish ship.

Once a week, Madeline repeated her invitation to dinner. Near the end of May, Judith finally prevailed on Cooper to stay away from the Navy Department for one evening. At four o'clock on the appointed day, he sent a message home saying he would be late. His hack didn't arrive on Marshall Street until half past eight.

In the spacious rooms on the top floor, the brothers embraced. "How are you, Cooper?" Orry smelled whiskey and was dismayed by the sight of his pale, disheveled guest.

"Very busy at the department." The reply made Judith frown.

"What sort of work goes on there?" Madeline asked as she led them in to the table set with lighted candles. She was anxious to serve the meal before it was ruined.

"We're engaged in the job of killing Yankees."

Orry started to laugh, then realized the remark was meant seriously. Judith stared at the floor, unable to conceal a look of distress. Madeline glanced at her husband as if to say, *Is he drunk?*

Murmuring a pretext—"May I help?"—Judith followed her hostess to the hot kitchen.

Madeline raised the lid of a steaming pot. "Can you conceive of greens selling for three and a half dollars a peck?"

The false cheer failed. Judith glanced at the closed door and said, "I must apologize for Cooper. He isn't himself."

Madeline replaced the lid and faced her sister-in-law. "Judith, the poor man acts like he's ready to explode. What's wrong?"

"He's working too hard—the way he did when *Star of Carolina* was on the verge of failure."

"Are you sure that's all it is?"

Judith avoided her eyes. "No. But I mustn't say anything. I promised I wouldn't. He'll tell you when he's ready."

Presently the four were seated with their food—the greens, a few potatoes sliced and fried, and the entree, a stringy saddle of lamb Madeline had purchased at one of the small farmers' markets springing up on the outskirts of the city. "Orry will pour claret, or water, if you prefer that. I refuse to serve that vile concoction of ground peanuts they're selling as coffee."

"They're selling a great many strange things," Judith said. "Pokeberry juice for writing ink—" She stopped as Cooper thrust his glass toward his brother. Orry poured it half full of claret, but Cooper didn't draw his hand back. The goblet sparkled in the candlelight. Orry cleared his throat and filled it full.

"Some—" Cooper gulped half of the claret, dribbling dark drops on his already-stained shirt bosom "—some in this town drink real coffee and write with real ink. Some can pay for those things." He stared at his brother. "Our sister, for one."

"Is that right?" Madeline said with forced lightness. Cooper's stare was sullen, his speech slurred. Something ugly was in the air.

"I'll grant you Ashton lives in a fine house," Orry said. "And on the few occasions when I've seen her on the street, she's always been handsomely dressed—Worth of Paris or something equivalent. I can't imagine how she affords it on Huntoon's salary. Most clerks in the government make a pittance."

Cooper drew a long, raspy breath. Judith clenched her hands beneath the table. The shout of a water seller reached them through open front windows, then the creak of his wagon. "I can tell you how they afford luxuries, Orry. They're profiteers."

Madeline's mouth formed a little o. Orry put down the fork with greens. "That's a serious accusation."

"I was on her ship, God damn it!"

"Dear," Judith began, "perhaps we'd better—"

"It's time they knew."

"What ship do you mean?" Orry said. "The blockade-runner that went down? The one you—?"

"Yes, I mean *Water Witch*. Ashton and her husband owned a substantial interest in it. The owners issued standing orders for the skipper to run the blockade at all hazards. We did, and I lost my son."

He shoved back hair hanging over his forehead, and in the midst of all the shocks, Madeline noticed for the first time that Cooper was going gray. "For Christ's sake, Orry, either pour the wine or pass it here."

Noticeably upset, Orry filled Cooper's glass again. "Who else knows about Ashton and James?"

"The other owners, I suppose. I never heard their names. The only man on the ship who seemed privy to the information was the skipper, Ballantyne, and he went down like—" Cooper's face wrenched. The memory was too hard to articulate.

He drank. Stared at the flame of the candle in front of him. "I'd like to kill her," he said, bringing the empty goblet down so hard the stem snapped.

Everyone stared. "Excuse me," Cooper said, bolting from his chair. It fell backward with a crash. He flung out his hand to prevent a collision with the wall and lurched to the parlor. He managed to reach the settee before he passed out.

They heard a rain shower starting. A sudden breeze set the candle flames in motion. Judith again apologized for Cooper's behavior. Stricken, Orry said apology was unnecessary. "But I hope he didn't mean that last remark."

"I'm sure he didn't. The loss of Judah was grievous for both of us, but it seems to have done special damage to him."

Orry sighed. "All his life he's expected the world to be better than it is. People with that kind of idealism get hurt worst of all. I hope he won't do anything rash, Judith. Ashton has already failed at the one thing she wanted most in Richmond—to belong to the best circles. I expect punishment for the profiteering will find her eventually. If he tries to judge and sentence her"—he glanced over his shoulder at the sad scarecrow figure on the settee—"he'll only harm himself."

The wind gusted, lifting the parlor curtains, stirring the gray-streaked hair on Cooper's forehead. Judith said, "I try to tell him that. It does no good. He's drinking heavily, as you surely noticed. I fear what he might do sometime when he's had too much."

Softly said, the words put dread into Orry. The three sat in silence, listening to the rain come down on the roof and the ruins of the evening.

Copies of the *Richmond Enquirer* reached the Winder Building every week. One issue, which George read with mingled curiosity and sadness, contained several long articles describing Jackson's funeral. On an inside page was a list of high-ranking military officers who had marched in the procession. Among the names he discovered that of his best friend.

"There it is—Colonel Orry Main," he said to Constance, showing her the paper that night. "He's listed with others from the War Department."

"Does that mean he's in Richmond?"

"I assume so. Whatever he's doing, I'm sure it's more important than interviewing lunatics and reading the fine print in contracts."

With a touch of regret, she said, "Your guilt's getting the best of you again."

He folded the paper. "Yes, it is. Daily."

Homer stepped into the dining room, pausing beside the open-fronted cabinet that contained Ashton's fine blue jasperware. *Water Witch* had brought the set from Britain on her penultimate voyage.

Huntoon took off his spectacles. "Mr. Main? Which one? Orry?"

As always, it was Ashton to whom the elderly Negro addressed the reply. "No. The other one."

"Cooper? Why, James, I had no idea he was in Richmond."

Thunder boomed in the northwest; bluish light glittered throughout the downstairs. It was June, muggy, the town astir with rumors of an impending invasion of the North by General Lee.

"He is here, he is very definitely here," said a thick voice from the shadows outside the dining room. Into the doorway stepped a frightening figure—Cooper, right enough, but aged since Ashton had last seen him. Horribly aged and gray. His cheeks had a waxy pallor, and his whiskey stench rolled over the table like a wave, submerging the aroma of the bowl of fresh flowers in the center. "He's here and anxious to see how his dear sister and her husband are enjoying their newfound wealth."

"Cooper dear—" Ashton began, sensing danger, trying to turn it aside with a treacly smile. Cooper refused to let her say more.

"Very fine house you have. Splendid furnishings. Treasury salaries must be larger than those in the Navy Department. Must be enormous."

Trembling, Huntoon clutched the arms of his chair. With a laconic hand, Cooper reached toward the open shelves. Ashton's fist clenched when he plucked out one of the delicately shaded blue plates.

"Lovely stuff, this. Surely you didn't buy it locally. Did it come

608

in on a blockade-runner? In place of guns and ammunition for the army, perhaps—?"

He threw the plate down with great force. Splinters of the white Greek figure embossed in the center rebounded into the light. One struck the back of Huntoon's hand. He muttered a protest no one heard.

Ashton said, "Brother dear, I am at a loss to explain your visit or your churlish behavior. Furthermore, while you're as disagreeable as you ever were, I am astounded to hear what sounds like patriotic maundering. You used to scorn James when he gave speeches in support of secession or states' rights. But here you are, sounding like the hottest partisan of Mr. Davis."

She forced a smile, hoping to hide the fear inside. She didn't know this man. She was in the presence of a lunatic whose intentions she could not guess. Without reacting, she saw Homer edging toward Cooper behind his right shoulder. Good.

Ashton placed her elbows on the table and cushioned her chin on her hands. Her smile became a sneer. "When did this remarkable transformation to patriot occur, may I ask?"

"It occurred," Cooper said above the muttering storm, "shortly after my son drowned."

Ashton's control melted into astonishment. "Judah—drowned? Oh, Cooper, how perfectly—"

"We were aboard *Water Witch*. Nearing Wilmington. The moon was out, the Union blockading squadron present in force. I pleaded with Captain Ballantyne not to risk the run, but he insisted. The owners had issued orders. Maximum risk for maximum earnings."

Ashton's hand fell forward. Her skin felt as if it were frozen.

"You know the rest, Ashton. My son was sacrificed to your intense devotion to the cause—"

"Stop him, Homer," she screamed as Cooper moved. Huntoon started to rise from his chair. Cooper struck the side of his head and knocked his glasses off.

Homer seized Cooper from behind and yelled for help. Using an elbow, Cooper punched him in the stomach, breaking his hold, shouting over a thunderclap, "The cause of profit. Your own fucking, filthy greed." He laid hands on the display cabinet and pulled.

The delicate blue plates and cups and saucers and bowls began to slide. Ashton screamed again as the Wedgwood pieces dropped,

Greek heads exploding, Greek arms and legs breaking. Lightning shimmered. The cabinet fell onto the dining table, where its weight proved too much. The table legs gave way at Huntoon's end. He shrieked as broken jasperware and candle holders and the flower bowl rushed toward him.

The flowers spilled onto his waistcoat. The water soaked his trousers as he kicked and pushed, sliding the chair away, out of danger, while two housemen joined Homer and wrestled the cursing, ranting Cooper to the front door. There they flung him into the rain.

Ashton heard the door slam and said the first thing that came to mind. "What if he tells what he knows?"

"What if he does?" Huntoon snarled. He picked blossoms from his wet crotch. "There was no law against what we did. And we're out of the trade now."

"Did you see how white his hair's gotten? I think he's gone mad."

"He's certainly dangerous," Huntoon said. "We must buy pistols tomorrow in case—in case—"

He couldn't finish the sentence. Ashton surveyed the Wedgwood all over the floor. One cup had survived unbroken. She wanted to weep with rage. Lightning flashed, thunder shook the wet windows, and her mouth set.

"Yes, pistols," she agreed. "For each of us."

81

At seven that same night, Thursday, in the first week of June, Bent reported to Colonel Baker's office as ordered. Baker wasn't there. Another detective said he had gone to Old Capitol Prison to conduct one of his interrogations of an unfriendly journalist who was under detention. "He'll go from there to his hour of pistol practice. He wouldn't let a day pass without that."

Bent settled down to wait, soothing his nerves with one of several apples bought from a street vendor. After two bites, he looked again at a small silver badge pinned to the reverse of his lapel. Baker had awarded the badge, which bore the embossed words NATIONAL DETECTIVE BUREAU, after Bent's return from Richmond. His success there had earned him the token of official acceptance into Baker's organization. The colonel had been especially pleased by the return of the money paid to the albino. Bent stated that he had rendered the spy harmless because he was no longer useful, but he was vague about details and didn't specifically say he had killed him. Baker asked no questions.

Despite the acceptance that the badge signified, Bent had been feeling bad for the past few days. He had caught the moods of the town—apprehension, despondency. Hooker's fighting spirit had proved as substantial as the contents of a glass of water. And while Lee had lost a mighty ally when Jackson fell, he had won not only a splendid victory at Chancellorsville but an ominous supremacy over the minds of many Northerners in and out of the army. There were now daily rumors and alarms out of Virginia. Lee was moving again, but in which direction, no one knew.

Bent was masticating his third apple when Baker reined up outside a window overlooking Pennsylvania Avenue. An orderly took Baker's horse, an unruly bay stallion the colonel had nicknamed Slasher. Humming cheerily, Baker strode into the office. He handed Bent a crudely printed broadside.

"You may find a chuckle or two in that, Dayton."

Fancy type on the front announced that this was the menu for the *Hotel de Vicksburg*. When he opened the piece, he understood the joke. The broadside contained the menu of a city under siege.

Soup: mule tail
Roast: saddle of mule, *à l'armée*
Entrees: mule head, stuffed *à la Reb;*
mule beef, jerked *à la Yankie*
Pastry: cottonwood-berry pie, *à la ironclad*
Liquors: Mississippi water, vintage 1492, very superior

Any diners not satisfied with the starvation fare
are welcome to apply to
JEFF DAVIS & CO., PROPRIETORS

"Very amusing," Bent said because Baker expected it. "Where did this come from, sir?"

"O'Dell brought it back from Richmond last night. He saw large masses of troops moving west of Fredericksburg, by the way. There's truth in those rumors. Lee's up to something—ah!" Among some mail, he found a piece that he immediately tucked in his pocket. "A letter from Jennie." Baker's wife was living with her parents in Philadelphia for the duration.

The man Baker had mentioned, Fatty O'Dell, was another agent. "I didn't realize we had someone else on a mission down there."

"Yes," Baker replied, but didn't elaborate. That was his style. Only he knew all the operatives and what each was doing.

Baker leaned back and clasped hands behind his head. "That broadside is enlightening about attitudes toward Jeff Davis. It helps corroborate something Fatty got wind of from third parties. A Richmond speculator named Powell is agitating very openly against Davis."

Bent picked a bit of apple from his lip. "That sort of thing's been going on for a year or more, hasn't it?"

"Absolutely right. This time, however, there's an unusual wrinkle. Fatty said Mr. Powell's pronouncements include talk of forming an independent Confederate state at some unspecified location."

"God above—that *is* new."

"I wish you would not take the Lord's name in vain. I like it as little as I liked those filthy yellow-backed books I confiscated and burned some months ago."

"Sorry, Colonel," Bent said hastily. "The information surprised me, that's all. What's the speculator's name again?"

"Lamar Powell."

"I never heard it mentioned when I was in Richmond. Nor any new Confederacy, for that matter."

"It may be nothing more than street gossip. If they impeached Davis, it would help our cause. It would help even more if they strung him up. And I'd be the first to applaud. But it's probably a vain hope."

He opened a lower desk drawer and produced one of the folders that contained personal dossiers. Inscribed on the front in a beautiful flowing hand was the name Randolph.

Baker passed the folder across the desk. Bent opened it and discovered several pages of notes in a variety of handwritings, plus a number of news clippings. One of the dispatches carried the words *By Our Capitol Correspondent Mr. Eamon Randolph.*

He closed the folder and waited. When Baker began to speak, he did so in a tone that took Bent into his confidence. Bent's gloom lifted.

"Mr. Randolph, as you'll discover when you read those scurrilous articles, is not a partisan of those for whom we work. Nor is he fond of Senator Wade, Congressman Stevens, or their rigorous program for rehabilitating our Southern brethren after the war. You will find Mr. Randolph's paper, the *Cincinnati Globe,* to be strongly antiadministration and pro-Democratic. Further, only the peace wing of that party earns its admiration. Randolph doesn't go so far as some in the same camp—no advocacy of removal of Mr. Lincoln by violent means, nothing like that. But he definitely favors noninterference with slavery even after the South capitulates. We cannot tolerate the promulgation of that view in a period of crisis. I have been urged by certain administration officials to—shall we say—" Baker stroked his luxuriant beard "—chastise him. Silence him briefly, not only to remove an

613

irritant but to warn his paper, and others of the same persuasion, to have a care lest the same fate befall them. Your work in Richmond impressed me, Dayton. That's why I've chosen you to handle the case."

82

The three contract surgeons in filthy uniforms sat around a rickety table. Their hands were filthy too, stained with dirt and blood, as they were whenever the surgeons examined wounds.

One of the three picked his nose. The second surreptitiously rubbed his groin, an oafish smile spreading over his face. The third doctor drained a bottle of alcohol meant for the wounded. One of these, limping pitifully, was shown in by an orderly, who acted like a mental deficient.

"What have we here?" said the surgeon who had been swilling the alcohol; apparently he was the chief.

"I'm hurt, sir," said the enlisted man. "Can I go home?"

"Not so fast! We must conduct an examination. Gentlemen? If you please."

The surgeons surrounded the soldier, poked, probed, conferred in whispers. The chief stated the consensus: "I'm sorry, but your arms must be amputated."

"Oh." The patient's face fell. But after a moment, he grinned. "Then can I have a furlough?"

"Definitely not," said the surgeon who had been rubbing his privates. "That left leg must come off, too."

"Oh." This time it was a groan. The patient again tried to smile. "But certainly I can have a furlough after that."

"By no means," said the nose picker. "When you get well you can drive an ambulance."

Roars of laughter.

"Gentlemen—another consultation," cried the chief, and back into a huddle they went. It broke up quickly. The chief said, "We have decided one last procedure is necessary. We must amputate your head."

The patient strove to see the bright side. "Well, after that I *know* I'll be entitled to a furlough."

"Absolutely not," said the chief. "We are so short of men, your body must be set up in the breastworks to fool the enemy."

Out of the darkness, massed voices roared again. Seated cross-legged on trampled grass, Charles laughed so hard tears ran from his eyes. On the tiny plank stage lit by lanterns and torches, the soldier playing the patient shrieked and ran in circles while the demented surgeons pursued him with awls, chisels, and saws. Finally they chased him behind a rear curtain rigged from a blanket.

Applause, yelps, and whistling acknowledged the end of the program, which had lasted about forty minutes. All the performers—singers, a banjo player, a fiddler, one of Beverly Robertson's troopers who juggled bottles, and a monologist portraying Commissary General Northrop explaining the healthful benefits of the latest reduction in the meat ration—returned for their bows. Then came the actors from the skit, who got even louder applause. Some anonymous scribe in the Stonewall Brigade had written *The Medical Board,* and it had become a favorite on camp programs.

Shadow masses stood and separated. Charles rubbed his stiff back. The mild June evening and the campfires shining in the fields away toward Culpeper Court House brought images of Barclay's Farm to mind. Barclay's Farm and Gus.

Ab was thinking of less pleasant subjects. "Got to find me some Day and Martin to shine my boots. Damn if I ever thought when I joined the scouts that I'd have to get so fancied up."

"You know Stuart," Charles said with a resigned shrug.

"On some occasions I wish I didn't. This is one. Goddamn if I want to go paradin' for the ladies on Saturday."

The two men crossed the railroad tracks, retrieved their horses from the temporary corral, and started for the field where they had pitched their tents with Calbraith Butler's regiment. A massive movement of forces was under way below the Rappahannock; Ewell and Longstreet were already at Culpeper with infantry.

Charles knew nothing of the army's destination, but lately there had been much talk of a second invasion of the North.

Somewhere above the river there were certain to be Yanks. Yanks who would want to know the whereabouts of Lee's army. So far as Charles could tell, no one was worried about the Yankee presence or its potential threat. Stuart had settled down at Culpeper with more horsemen than he had had in a long time—close to ten thousand. Some of those were on picket duty at the Rappahannock fords, but most were being allowed time to prepare for Stuart's grand review for invited guests on Saturday. Many women would be coming by rail and carriage from Richmond, as well as from the nearer towns. Charles wished he'd had time to invite Gus.

The review was certainly typical of Stuart, but it struck Charles as inappropriate when mass movement of the army was under way, and that army was not in the best of condition. These days he saw many sore, swollen backs among the horses; sixteen or seventeen hours a day was too long for an animal to be saddled. In Robertson's brigade he had seen horses frantically chewing each other's manes and tails—starving even in the season of growth. In the brigade of Old Grumble Jones, the slovenly general whose liking for blue jeans and hickory shirts earned him the dubious honor of being called the Zach Taylor of the Confederacy, Charles had only yesterday spied half a dozen men riding mules. The best replacements they could find, he supposed.

Sweet clover scented the June night. The fires shone along the whole southern horizon. In camp, a few men were resting, writing letters, or playing cards with decks in which the court cards were portraits of generals and politicians. Mr. Davis, popular in the first year of the war, was seldom seen in the newer decks.

Most of the troopers had no time for recreation, however. They were sewing and polishing because Stuart had ordered every man to find or fix up a good uniform for the review. Much as Charles disliked the whole idea, he intended to look as presentable as possible and even unpack the Solingen sword. If Jeb wanted a show, he would do his best to contribute.

Brandy Station had been named for an old stagecoach stop famous for apple brandy served to travelers; the apples grew in orchards close by. Now the Orange & Alexandria line served the place. On Saturday the special trains started rolling in early, the

616

cars packed with politicians and gaily dressed ladies, most of whom would attend both the review and General Stuart's ball at Culpeper that night.

In open meadows near long and relatively flat Fleetwood Hill, just above the village crossroads, Stuart's cavalry performed for the visitors. Columns of horse charged with drawn sabers. Artillery batteries raced, wheeled, loaded, and fired demonstration rounds. Flags and music and the warm smell of summer moved in the breeze that brushed over vistas of tasseled corn and flourishing wheat. Charles and the rest of Hampton's scouts took their turn galloping past the guests and reviewing officers gathered along the rail line. Speeding by, Charles saw the black plume on Stuart's hat dip and flutter; the general had bobbed his head when he recognized his old West Point acquaintance.

After the long and tiring review, Charles returned to his encampment, anticipating a good meal and a sound sleep. Tomorrow he had to scout the river near Kelly's Ford. He was putting up Sport when an orderly appeared.

"Captain Main? General Fitzhugh Lee presents his compliments and requests the captain's company at his headquarters tent this evening. Supper will be served before the ball, which the general may not attend."

"Why not?"

"The general has been sick, sir. Do you know the location of his headquarters?"

"Oak Shade Church?"

"That's correct, sir. May General Lee expect you?"

"I don't plan to go to the ball either. Tell Fitz—the general I accept with pleasure."

That's a damn lie, he thought as the orderly left. Everyone knew Fitz was Stuart's favorite and still jealous of Hampton outranking him because of seniority of appointment. Hampton's partisans, in turn, sneered at Fitz, saying he had risen rapidly solely because he was Old Bob's nephew. Might be something to it. Two of the five brigades of horse were led by Lees—Fitz and the general's son, Rooney.

Uncomfortable about the invitation, Charles spent the next couple of hours cleaning his uniform. At least he had the gift sword to smarten his appearance. Presently he mounted Sport and rode down a lane flanked by fields where bees hummed in the white clover blossoms. The sun was sinking. Northward, the heights of Fleetwood swam in blue haze.

Wish I could get out of here and see Gus, he thought. *Something's mighty wrong about this campaign.*

"Glad you accepted the invitation, Bison. I've been feeling poorly of late. Rheumatism. I need some good company."

Fitz did indeed look pale and unhealthy. His beard was big and bushy as ever, his uniform immaculate, but he lacked his customary vigor; he talked and moved lethargically.

He expressed surprise that his old friend didn't intend to enjoy the company of the ladies gathering at Culpeper. To which Charles replied, "I have a lady of my own now. I'd have invited her, but I couldn't get a message to her soon enough."

"Is it a serious affair of the heart? Going to settle down when this muss is over?"

"Could be, General. I've been thinking about it."

"Let's dispense with general and captain for one evening," Fitz said. He gestured his friend to a camp chair. "The old names will do."

Charles smiled and relaxed. "All right."

The fireball of the sun rested on the low hills in the west. The open tent was breezy and comfortable. One of Fitz's officers joined them for whiskey served by a Negro body servant. Colonel Tom Rosser, a handsome young Texan, had been ready to graduate in the class of May '61 when he resigned to fight for the South. The three cavalrymen chatted easily for fifteen minutes. Rosser twice mentioned a cadet in the later, June, class of '61 who was with the Union.

"Name's George Custer. He's a lieutenant. Aide to Pleasonton. I used to consider him a friend, but I reckon I can't any longer."

Thinking of friendships and Hampton, Charles cast an oblique glance at the general. Why had Fitz invited him? For the reason he gave—company? Or another?

On the subject of Custer, Fitz said, "I hear they call him Crazy Curly."

"Why's that?" Charles asked.

Rosser laughed. "You'd know if you saw him. In fact, you'd recognize him instantly. Hair down to here—" He tapped his shoulder. "Wears a big scarlet scarf around his neck—looks like a damn circus rider gone mad." Softly, more reflectively, he added, "He doesn't lack courage, though."

"I've also heard he doesn't lack for ambition," Fitz remarked. "On the peninsula they called him Pleasonton's Pet."

In the universal fashion of cavalrymen, the three officers fell to discussing the strong and weak points of other opponents. Pleasonton got poor marks, but Fitz and Rosser were impressed by the exploits of a heretofore unknown colonel, Grierson, of Illinois. In late April, to divert attention from Grant at Vicksburg, Grierson had led seventeen hundred horse on a daring ride from LaGrange, Tennessee, to Baton Rouge, tearing up railroad tracks and killing and imprisoning Confederate soldiers along the way.

"Six hundred miles in slightly more than two weeks," Rosser grumbled. "I'd say they've been reading our book."

As the evening went on, Charles found himself growing depressed. He said little and watched his friend Fitz with a feeling amounting to envy. For a young man, Fitz had indeed come a long way—and not solely because of family connections. He had a reputation as a good officer, and he had certainly changed his style since Academy days, when he delighted in thumbing his nose at the rules.

Presently Rosser stood up, putting on his dress hat. "I must go. Pleasure to meet you, Captain Main. Heard good things about you. Hope we'll see you again."

Rosser's final remark seemed to pass some coded message to Fitz. As the general's Negro put tin plates of beef and spoon bread before them, Fitz said, "You're wasting your time with old Hampton, you know. I lost a colonel to gangrene a week ago. His regiment's yours if you want it."

Caught short, Charles stammered, "Fitz, that—well, that's very flattering."

"The devil with that. There are too many problems in this war, right down to and including my rheumatism, for me to squander a minute on flattery. You're a fine cavalryman, an able leader, and if I may say so, you're serving with a commander who is not all he should be—now wait. Don't bristle."

"But I've been with General Hampton for two years. I signed on with him when he raised his legion in Columbia. He has first claim on my loyalty."

"Rightly so. However—"

619

"He's a competent officer and a brave one."

"No one doubts Wade Hampton's courage. But the man is—well—not young. And on occasion he has displayed a certain timidity."

"Fitz, with all due respect, please don't say any more. You're my friend, but Hampton is the best officer I've ever served under."

Fitz cooled noticeably. "Do you include General Stuart in that statement?"

"I'd sooner not elaborate, except on one point. What some call timidity, others call prudence—or wisdom. Hampton concentrates his forces before he attacks. He wants a victory, not casualties or headlines."

Fitz practically bit the spoon bread off his fork. "Amos? Get in here with the whiskey." As the servant poured, Fitz eyed his visitor with disappointment and annoyance. "Your loyalty may be commendable, Charles, but I still insist you're wasting your talents." No more nickname; the reunion had soured. "Most every officer who graduated from West Point when we did is a colonel or a major—at minimum."

That hurt. Charles took a breath. "For what it's worth, I was in the promotion line two years ago. I made some mistakes."

"I know all about what you term your mistakes. They're not as serious as you may imagine. Grumble Jones and Beverly Robertson are disciplinarians, too. Both lost elections to colonel because of it. But new commands were found for—"

"Fitz," he interrupted, "haven't I made myself clear? What I'm doing suits me. I don't want or need a new command."

Silence fell in the tent. Outside, the black servant could be heard pottering at his camp stove. "I'm sorry you feel that way, Charles. If you won't go where you can be most useful, why fight for the South at all?"

The faint scorn angered Charles. "But I'm not fighting for the South if that means slavery or a separate country. I'm fighting for the place where I live. My land. My home. That's why most of the men joined up. Sometimes I wonder if Mr. Davis understands that."

Fitz shrugged and began to eat quickly. "Sorry to hurry you, but I must make an attempt to get to the ball. By the way, General Lee has announced himself available on Monday. General Stuart has ordered a review."

"Another one? What's he thinking of? Today's review tired the horses and put the men in bad temper. We should be watching for Yankees north of the river, not expending more energy on military foppery."

Fitz cleared his throat. "Let us agree those remarks were never uttered. Thank you for coming, Charles. I'm afraid you will have to excuse me now."

The evening taught Charles a gloomy lesson. He and Fitz could no longer be friends. They were divided by rank, by opinion, and by all the political pulling and hauling of command. Next day an incident near Kelly's Ford deepened his gloom. Scouting northeast of the Rappahannock, beyond the picket outposts, he and Ab stopped at a small farm to water their horses and refill their canteens. The householder, a skinny old man, struck up a conversation. With a bewildered air, he told them that his two elderly slaves, husband and wife, had run off the day before yesterday.

"Couldn't get over it. Still can't. They was always so nice. Smiling, biddable darkies—been that way ever since I bought 'em six years ago."

"We had a lot of that in South Carolina," Charles said. "Folks call it puttin' on ol' massa."

"Can't understand it," the farmer said, staring right through him. "I fed 'em. Didn't whip 'em but three or four times. I fixed up presents for 'em ever' Christmas—cakes, little jams and jellies, things like that—"

"Come on, Ab," Charles said wearily, while the old man continued to condemn the ingratitude. Charles mounted, and scratched the inside of his left leg. His case of camp itch was worsening. At least the rash wasn't as bad as the clap that several scouts had caught from camp followers who dignified themselves with the title laundress.

Bound back toward Brandy Station, Charles pictured the foolish farmer with dismay, then disgust. More and more lately, he saw the peculiar institution for what it was and always had been. The reality of it—from the point of view of those enslaved, anyway—could be nothing less than fear and rage behind a deceptive mask. The kind of mask that had to be worn if the slave meant to survive.

Gus would understand his feelings about slavery, though he dared not express them to Ab or anyone else with whom he served. He was beginning to think that whereas he was fighting for his home, the politicians in charge of things were fighting for slogans, rhetoric, a "cause." A wrong one, at that.

No ladies attended the review on Monday; it was a less pleasant event for that reason. Less pleasant, too, because some idiot invited John Hood, and he brought his entire infantry division. The cavalrymen growled threats of what they would do if a foot soldier dared to taunt them with the familiar, "Mister, where's your mule?"

As Charles feared, the review exhausted everyone—and they were supposed to be ready to advance Tuesday morning. He and Ab rode directly from the review field, where they had glimpsed Bob Lee, handsome as ever but graying rapidly, to Hampton's encampment. Charles's sleep was restless, and he woke abruptly, jerking his head off the saddle and rolling out of his blanket to bugling and the drummers pounding out the long roll.

It was just daybreak. The camp was in turmoil. Ab ran up, swirling the fog that had settled during the night. He carried their coffeepot in such a way that Charles knew he hadn't had a chance to heat it.

"Off your ass, Charlie. General Stuart paid too damn much attention to the ladies an' not enough to the bluebellies. A whole cavalry division's across the river at Beverly Ford."

"Whose?"

"They say it's Buford's. He's got infantry an' God knows what else. They may be crossin' at Kelly's, too. Nobody's sure."

The bugler sounded boots and saddles with several sour notes. "They's thousands of 'em," Ab said, dropping the enameled pot. "They come out of the fog an' took the pickets clean by surprise. We're s'posed to go along with Butler to scout an' guard the rear."

Whips cracked. Great ships in a sea of soft gray mist, Stuart's headquarters wagons loomed at the edge of the camp, bound for safety at Culpeper. Damn, Charles thought. Caught napping. But it wouldn't have happened with Hampton in charge. He grabbed his shotgun and blanket, flung his saddle on his other shoulder, and ran like hell after Ab Woolner.

Charles knew Ab must have had a hard night. First he yelled at some hospital rats scurrying to the surgeons with imaginary complaints, a familiar sight whenever cannonading began. Ab cursed a blue storm when he saw two perfectly good boots lying in weeds. Unshod men, like unshod horses, couldn't fight and weren't expected to—and some fucking yellow dog, as Ab characterized him, had shed his boots to escape what looked like a very bad day.

Riding hard in thinning fog, Charles and Ab soon pulled away from the detachment of Butler's sent to screen the southern approaches to Fleetwood Hill, where Stuart's headquarters on high ground was the obvious target of enemy artillery banging away from the southeast. In a small grove of pines above Stevensburg, Charles reined in suddenly. Beyond the trees, half a dozen Union troopers were approaching on a dirt track beside a field of ripening wheat. Alarmingly, Charles saw no sign of the famous mountains of gear the Southern cavalry scornfully termed "Yankee fortifications." The enemy riders carried weapons, nothing else.

"Let's dodge around them, Ab. We'll get to Stevensburg faster."

Haggard, not to say hostile, Ab stared at him. "Let's kill us some Yanks. Then we'll get to Stevensburg for sure."

"Listen, we're only supposed to take a look and see whether—"

"What's wrong with you, Charlie? Lost your nerve 'cause of that gal?"

"You son of a bitch—"

But Ab was already galloping from the pines, double-barrel shotgun booming.

Any Southerner caught with one of those weapons was subject to hanging, the Yankees said. But the two Ab blew from their saddles would never report him. Dry-mouthed, Charles kneed Sport forward.

Bullets buzzed by. As soon as he got in range he gave the Yanks both barrels. That disposed of four. The last two wheeled right and plunged into the wheat to escape. Ab pounded toward Stevensburg without a backward glance. Charles hated his friend because he had stated the truth.

On sunny Fleetwood Hill that afternoon, Jeb Stuart's cavalry waged a new kind of war. They fought Union troopers who swung sabers and handled their mounts as expertly as any Southern boy raised to hunt and spear the hanging rings on lance point. The Yanks drove Stuart off the hill, and by the time Charles and Ab returned from Stevensburg, every available trooper was being pressed into the fight to regain it. Hampton was back from Beverly Ford, where he had been rushed for the unsuccessful attempt to stop Buford. Two more divisions of Union horse had forced Kelly's. No wonder; the untalented Robertson commanded that sector.

Stevensburg, too, had been a disaster. Near there, Frank Hampton had been sabered, then shot to death. Calbraith Butler held his position against the charging Yankees, but at the cost of having a flying shell fragment strike his right foot, nearly blowing it off. The fine troopers of the Fourth Virginia had been routed—a disastrous, confused, angry gallop to the rear—and Charles and Ab had been caught in that for a time.

At Fleetwood, the squadrons rallied, and Stuart shouted, "Give them the saber, boys!" and the buglers blew Trot and Gallop and finally Charge. Up the slopes they went, in sunshine that quickly dimmed behind smoke and dust.

Though Charles couldn't see him, he knew Ab was riding somewhere close by. They had exchanged no words except essential ones since the incident in the pine grove. Charles knew his friend had blurted the accusation because he was tired and tense. But that made it no less telling.

Sport galloped as he always did when riding to the sound of guns—head up, alert and eager. Charles could feel the gray's nervousness—it was his own. Horse and rider fused, centaurlike, in a way old cavalry hands took for granted after they had ridden one animal a long time. Old legion sword raised, Charles screamed the rebel yell, along with thousands around him.

Then they were onto the heights of Fleetwood. Artillery wheeling. Sabers ringing. Pistols flashing. Horses and men tangling. Formations dissolving. Charles fought with a fury he'd never had before. It was necessary to redeem himself in Ab's eyes. It was necessary because the enemy was a new kind of enemy.

Blood drops accumulated in his beard. He gave up the sword for the shotgun, the shotgun for the revolver, then went back to the weapon of last resort when he had no time to reload.

He came upon a dismounted man in gray, reached down to help him. The man struck at him with a rammer staff, nearly took his head off before Charles backed away and thrust his sword into the Yank's chest. Thick dust was graying many a blue uniform that afternoon. A man could die being a moment late to discern the color.

As most battles did, the one for the contested hilltop lost shape and organization and soon swirled into many small, ugly skirmishes. The rebels regained the heights, lost them, rallied to take them again. Riding up a second time, Charles nearly slammed into a knot of Union troopers. He raised his sword in time to parry that of a hot-eyed officer with flowing hair and a red scarf knotted at his throat.

Pushing, pushing down, his sword against Charles's, their horses neighing and shoving, the lieutenant sneered, "Your servant, Reb—"

"I'm not yours." Charles spat in the Yank's face to gain advantage, and would have stabbed him through had not the officer's horse stumbled. *Circus rider gone mad,* said a voice in his memory as the Yank's eyes locked with his for an instant.

The horse fell; the Yank disappeared. Neither man would forget the other.

"Look sharp, Charlie," Ab shouted above the cannonading, the sabers clashing and sparking, the wounded crying out. Through dust clouds, Charles had a blurry view of Ab pointing behind him. He twisted, saw a Yank sergeant raise a huge pistol.

Ab closed in on the Yank. Using his empty revolver as a club, he chopped at the sergeant's arm. The sergeant changed his aim and shot Ab in the chest at a range of two feet.

"Ab!" A scream did no good. Ab was already gone, sliding sideways, his eyes open but no longer comprehending who or where he was—had been—as he sank from sight. The sergeant vanished in the melee.

Teeth clenched, Charles parried a cut from a Union trooper ramming his horse into Sport. *Clang*—the trooper hit a second time. Sparks hissed and leaped where metal edges met.

The trooper fought his bucking horse. He was a redhead, scarcely twenty, with a foolish grin showing under his big red mustaches.

"Lost your nerve?" Ab died thinking that. *Saved me in spite of it—*

"Got you this time," the redhead shouted. With a curse and a skillful dodge, Charles escaped the sword and put his own halfway through the boy's throat. He pulled it out with no remorse. Ab was right: Gus had softened and weakened him. It had taken this bloody June day to reveal the truth.

Driving on up to the heights of Fleetwood again, Charles suddenly realized a riderless horse was running beside Sport. It was Ab's mount, Cyclone. The animal kept on toward the sound of the guns. A bursting grape canister put out one of its eyes and opened a wound in its head. Like any brave, battle-trained war horse, Cyclone didn't neigh or bellow. Cyclone plowed on, slower but still moving forward in blood and silent pain until the wounds and the angle of the slope became too much, and it knelt down on its forelegs, wanting to continue but unable.

Charles sabered like a madman, weaving and feinting so fast, no one could touch him. Then another Yank charged; an ungainly man with the coaly hair and heavy-cream skin and blue eyes of the black Irish. The Yank wore corporal's chevrons and swore at Charles in a tongue he took to be Gaelic. Charles fought him nearly four minutes, blocking cuts, striking the Yank's left shoulder, parrying again, finally running him through the belly. He struck the man's ribs, yanked out the sword, and stabbed again.

The horses bucked and bumped each other. The Irishman swayed. Charles stabbed him a third time. *What keeps him up? Why won't he fall?* Why couldn't the hapless fools be dragged out of the saddle any more? Who had taught them to ride and fight so fiercely?

"Damned pernicious traitor," cried the trebly wounded Irishman, sounding exactly like a Maine cadet Charles had known at West Point. Were the Yanks also making troopers of lobstermen? God help the South if they could accomplish miracles like that.

A fourth stroke sent the corporal down, sliding sideways, unable to free himself from his right stirrup. An artillery limber rolled over his head and pushed it deep in soft brown loam. The man had been a devil; Charles shook with terror for more than a minute.

In the end the Southerners won and held the hill. But the Union reconnaissance in force had achieved its objective. Lee's army was found.

The Yanks achieved a second, unplanned, objective as well. They put a sword deep into the confidence of the Confederate cavalry. Charles knew it when he fought the Irishman with the Down East voice.

Pleasanton ordered a general retreat before dark. As the sun sank and the wind cleared Fleetwood of smoke and dust, legions of glistening bluebottle flies descended on the trampled red grass. The turkey buzzards sailed out of the twilight sky. Charles rode through the detritus of the charges and countercharges he could no longer count or remember separately. He searched until he found Ab's body, a hundred yards beyond the place where he had died. The carrion birds had already reached his face. Charles waved off the birds, but one rose with a piece of pink flesh in its beak. Charles pulled his Colt and killed the bird.

He buried Ab in some woods south of the railroad line, using a borrowed trenching tool. As he dug, he tried to find comfort in the memory of good times he and Ab had shared. There wasn't any.

He put Ab into the hole in the ground, then squatted at the edge, deliberating. A minute passed. He unbuttoned his shirt and lifted the thong over his head. He studied the handmade sack containing the book with the ball embedded in it. The book hadn't protected him, it had emasculated him. He threw the bag in the grave and began to shovel dirt to fill the hole.

He had seen General Hampton a number of times during the fighting, whirling that great Crusader's sword and galloping ahead of his men, as good cavalry generals always did. That night Charles saw him again. The loss of his brother made Hampton look like an old man.

Charles heard that the surgeons didn't think they could save Calbraith Butler's foot. So much had happened on Fleetwood that day—deaths and small heroisms, some noticed, some not. Charles had given up his only good friend and regained something that he had lost.

He rubbed Sport down and fed him and stroked his neck. "We made it through once more, old friend." The gray gave a small shake of his head; he was as spent as Charles.

Brandy Station made the reputation of the Union cavalry. It tarnished Stuart's. And, belatedly, it showed Charles the sharp accuracy of his fear about the relationship with Gus. Such an attachment was wrong in wartime. Wrong for her, wrong for him.

Charles had been observed in action during the assaults on Fleetwood. He received a commendation in general orders from Hampton and a brevet to major. What he got with no official action was a new direction for himself. He must think first of his duty. He loved Gus; that wouldn't change. But speculations about marriage, a future with her, had no place in a soldier's mind.

627

They dulled his concentration. Made him more vulnerable, less effective.

Gus would have to know how he felt. That was only fair. Questions of how and when to tell her, he was too tired to confront just now.

83

"Pack," Stanley said.

Sticky and ill-tempered from the heat of that Monday, June 15, Isabel retorted, "How dare you burst in on me in the middle of the day and start issuing orders."

He mopped his face, but the sweat popped out again. "All right, stay. I'm taking the boys to Lehigh Station via the four o'clock to Baltimore. I paid three times the normal price of the tickets, and I was lucky to be able to do it."

Uneasy all at once—he never spoke sharply to her—she moderated her tone. "What's provoked this, Stanley?"

"What the newsboys are shouting on every corner downtown. 'Washington in danger.' I've heard that Lee is in Hagerstown—I've heard he's in Pennsylvania—the rebs might have the town encircled by morning. I decided it's time for a vacation. If you don't care to go, that's your affair."

There had been rumors of military movement in Virginia, but nothing definite until now. Could she trust his assessment of the situation? She smelled whiskey on him; he had begun to drink heavily of late.

"How did you get permission to leave?"

"I told the secretary my sister was critically ill at home."

628

"Didn't he think the timing—well, a bit coincidental?"

"I'm sure he did. But the department's a madhouse. No one is accomplishing anything. And Stanton has good reason to keep me happy. I've carried his instructions to Baker. I know how dirty his hands are."

"Still, you could damage your career by—"

"Will you stop?" he shouted. "I'd rather be condemned as a live coward than perish as a patriot. You think I'm the only government official who's leaving? Hundreds have already gone. If you're coming with me, start packing. Otherwise keep still."

It struck her then that a remarkable, not altogether welcome change had taken place in her husband in recent months. Stanley's survival of the Cameron purge, his increasing eminence among the radicals, and his new-found wealth from Lashbrook's combined to create a confidence he had never possessed before. Occasionally he acted as if he were uncomfortable with it. A few weeks ago, after gulping four rum punches in an hour and a half, he had bent his head, exclaimed that he didn't deserve his success, and wept on her shoulder like a child.

But she mustn't be too harsh. She was the one who had created the new man. And she liked some aspects of that creation—the wealth, the power, the independence from his vile brother. If she meant to control him, she must change her own style, adopt subtler techniques.

He postured in the doorway, glaring. With feigned meekness and a downcast eye, she said, "I apologize, Stanley. You're wise to suggest we leave. I'll be ready in an hour."

That evening, after dark, a curtained van swung into Marble Alley. The driver reined the team in front of one of the neat residences lining the narrow thoroughfare between Pennsylvania and Missouri avenues. Despite the heat, all the windows of the house were draped, though they had been left open so that gay voices, male and female, and a harpist playing "Old Folks at Home" could be heard outside. The establishment, known as Mrs. Devore's Private Residence for Ladies, was doing a fine business despite the panic in the city.

Looking like a moving mound of lard in his white linen suit, Elkanah Bent climbed down from his seat beside the driver with much wheezing and grunting. Two other bureau men jumped out through the van's rear curtains. Bent signaled one into a passage leading to the back door of the house. The other followed him up the stone steps.

The detectives had debated the best way to take their quarry. They decided they couldn't snatch a noted journalist off the street in daylight. His boardinghouse had been considered, but Bent, who was in charge, finally came down in favor of the brothel. The man's presence there could be used to undermine his inevitable righteous protests.

He rang the bell. The shadow of a woman with high-piled hair fell on the frosted glass. "Good evening, gentlemen," said the elegant Mrs. Devore. "Come in, won't you?"

Smiling, Bent and his companion followed the middle-aged woman into a bright gaslit parlor packed with gowned whores and a jolly crowd of army and navy officers and civilians. One of the latter, a satanic sliver of a man, approached Bent. He had mustaches and a goatee in the style of the French emperor.

"Evening, Dayton."

"Evening, Brandt. Where?"

The man glanced at the ceiling. "Room 4. He's got two in bed tonight. Assorted colors."

Bent's heart was racing now, a combination of anxiety and a sensation close to arousal. Mrs. Devore walked over to speak to the harpist, and from there took notice of the bulge on Bent's right hip, something she had overlooked at the front door.

"You handle things down here, Brandt. Nobody leaves till I've got him." Brandt nodded. "Come on," Bent said to the other operative. They headed for the stars.

Alarm brightened Mrs. Devore's eyes. "Gentlemen, where are you—?"

"Keep quiet," Bent said, turning over his lapel to show his badge. "We're from the National Detective Bureau. We want one of your customers. Don't interfere." The satanic detective produced a pistol to insure compliance.

Lumbering upstairs, Bent threw back his coat and pulled his revolver, a mint-new LeMat .40-caliber, Belgian-made. Used mostly by the rebs, it was a potent gun.

In the upper hall, dim gaslights burned against royal purple wallpaper. Strong perfume could not quite mask the odor of a disinfectant. Bent's boots thumped the carpet as he passed closed doors; behind one, a woman groaned in rhythmic bursts. His groin quivered.

630

At Room 4, the detectives poised themselves on either side of the door. Bent twisted the knob with his left hand and plunged in. "Eamon Randolph?"

A middle-aged man with weak features lay naked in the canopied bed, a pretty black girl astride his loins, an older white woman behind his head, her breasts bobbing a few inches from his nose. "Who in hell are you?" the man exclaimed as the whores scrambled off.

Bent flipped his lapel again. "National Detective Bureau. I have an order for your detention signed by Colonel Lafayette Baker."

"Oh-oh," Randolph said, sitting up with a pugnacious expression. "Am I to be put away like Dennis Mahoney, then?" Mahoney, a Dubuque journalist who held opinions much like Randolph's, had been entertained in Old Capitol Prison for three months last year.

"Something like that," Bent said. The white whore groped for her wrapper. The young black girl, less frightened, watched from a spot near an open window. "The charge is disloyal practices."

"Of course it is," Randolph shot back in a high voice, which Bent instantly loathed. The reporter's receding chin and pop eyes created a false impression of weakness. Instead of cringing, he swung his legs off the bed almost jauntily.

"Ladies, please excuse me. I must dress and accompany these thugs. But you're free to go."

Shooting a look at the black whore, Bent brandished the LeMat. "Everyone stays. You're all getting in the van."

"Oh, God," the white woman said, covering her eyes. The black girl slipped into a gown of ivory-colored silk, then hunched forward, looking like a cornered cat.

"He's bluffing, girls," Randolph said. "Leave."

"Bad advice," Bent countered. "I call your attention to the nature of this weapon. It is what some call a grapeshot revolver. I have merely to move the hammer nose like this and the lower barrel will fire. It is loaded with shotgun pellets. I presume you appreciate what they would do to any face I chose for a target—?"

"You won't shoot," Randolph said, bouncing on his bare feet. "You government boys are all yellow dogs. As for that detention order you say you're carrying, toss it in the same fire in which you and Baker and Stanton burned your copies of the first amendment. Now stand aside and permit me to put on my—"

"Guard the door," Bent growled to his helper. He hauled the LeMat up and across to his left shoulder and slashed down. Unprepared, Randolph took the blow's full force on the right side of his face. His skin opened; blood ran and dripped into white hair on his chest.

The white woman sobbed melodramatically. There were footfalls, oaths, questions from the corridor. Bent jabbed the LeMat into Randolph's bare belly, then struck his head again, and his neck twice after that. Eyes bulging, Randolph pitched onto the bed, bloodying the sheets as he coughed and clutched his middle.

Grabbing Bent's sleeve, the other detective said, "Hold off, Dayton. We don't want to kill him."

Bent jabbed his left arm backward, throwing off the detective's hand. "Shut up. I'm in charge here. As for you, you seditious scum—" He brained Randolph with the butt of his revolver. "You're going to be fresh fish for Old Capitol Prison. We have a special room reserved for—*Watch her!*"

As Randolph writhed, the detective leaped for the black girl. But she already had one bare leg over the sill and quickly vanished. Bent heard a sharp cry as she landed.

Fists beat on the door. The other detective stuck his head out the window. "Harkness! One's getting away."

"Let her go. She's just nigger trash," Bent said. He gave Randolph's shoulder a hard dig with the gun. "Get dressed."

Five minutes later, he and his helper dragged the groggy journalist downstairs. They threw his blanket-bundled body into the back of the van. "You hit him too hard," the other detective said.

"I told you to shut up." Bent was breathing loudly; he felt as if he had just had a woman. "I did the job. That's all Colonel Baker cares about."

Brandt climbed into the van with them. Detective Harkness sat beside the driver. "The coon got away, Dayton," he said. Bent grunted, calming down. On the floor, the prisoner made mewling noises. Bent began to fret; had he really hit him too hard?

Ridiculous to worry. Far worse took place during many of Baker's interrogations. He would be forgiven. He had done the job.

"Let's go or we'll have the metropolitan police on our necks," he yelled. The driver shook the reins; the van lurched forward.

---

*Take the case of the Slaves on American plantations. I dare
say they are worked hard. I dare say they don't altogether like
it. I dare say theirs is an unpleasant experience on the whole;
but, they people the landscape for me, they give it a poetry for
me, and perhaps that is one of the pleasanter objects of their
existence.*

Wonderingly, Brett reread the remarks of Mr. Harold Skimpole
of *Bleak House.* The author of the novel, which she was enjoying,
had toured America, had he not? If he had traveled in the South,
however, and if he had found the slaves merely a form of decoration, his understanding had failed him in that instance. Dickens
was supposed to be a liberal thinker. Surely he understood what
the Negroes really were—human beings converted to parts of an
aging, failing machine. Perhaps the views of the elfin, carefree
Skimpole weren't really those of the author. She hoped they
weren't.

Tired of reading and a little put off by her reaction to Mr.
Skimpole, she laid the novel on top of Frederick Douglass's *Narrative of the Life of an American Slave,* which Scipio Brown had
given her. The book, the most famous of the many in the escaped-
slave genre, had been published a good eighteen years ago. But
she had never seen a copy of it, or any work like it, in South
Carolina. She was alternating Dickens with Douglass, and in the
latter finding not only vestigial guilt but sympathy for the narra-
tor and anger over his travail.

Brett lay in her camisole. Hot yellow twilight filled her room
this twenty-ninth of June. She was exhausted from helping Mrs.
Czorna scrub floors all day. Coming back to Belvedere, she had
deliberately avoided Stanley and Isabel and their obnoxious sons,
who were playing lawn bowls on the grass between the two
houses.

It still surprised her that she was reading—well—differently
from before. It was another result of long and frequent conversations with Brown. She resented the way he constantly thrust the
issue of Negro liberty at her, but she was beginning to grasp why
he did; why he must. She was also beginning to feel herself in the
grip of uncomfortable personal changes.

One of the maids tapped on her door, announcing supper in a

half hour. She rose reluctantly, splashing water on her face and bare arms. The yellow sun, growing red, sank in the west.

She hated to see sunset come. Fears about Billy, and her need of him, affected her most at night. In the last two weeks, coincident with Stanley's unexpected and still-unexplained arrival, Brett's fears had sharpened because of the military threat to the state. For days now, government workers and private citizens had been packing papers and valuables and leaving Harrisburg by rail, horse, or shank's mare. Last Friday, Governor Curtain had issued a plea for sixty thousand men to muster arms and defend Pennsylvania for three months. On Saturday, the invasion had been confirmed. Terrified officials surrendered the town of York to Jubal Early, and Lee's host was sighted at Chambersburg. The whole lower border was afire with panic and rumor, and the smoke blew to every part of the state.

A few minutes later, dressed and sweltering, Brett stepped onto the front veranda. No air was stirring.

"Brett? Hallo! Important news here."

The thickened voice belonged to stuffy Stanley. In shirt sleeves, he brandished a newspaper on the porch of his own residence. She wanted to be rude but couldn't do it. The supper bell would ring soon; she supposed she could put up with him till then.

In the molten light spilling from the west, she walked next door, her shadow three times her size on the brass-colored lawn. "What is it?" she said from the foot of the steps. She smelled gin on him and noticed his glassy look. She could hear the twins cursing and quarreling somewhere upstairs.

Swaying from side to side, Stanley held out a copy of the *Ledger-Union*. "Paper's got a telegraph dispatch from Washington. On Saturday"—his slurred speech injected a *sh* sound—"Pres'dent Lincoln relieved Gen'ral Hooker. Gen'ral Me's now in command."

"General who?"

"Me. M-e-a-d-e. Me."

Drunk, she thought. At the other house, she had overheard some servants' gossip about Stanley's new habit. She said to him, "I'm afraid I don't know either of those men or anything about their qualifications."

"Gen'ral Me is solid. 'F anyone can stop the reb invasion, he

634

can." A nervous glance southward. "By God, wish we'd settle all this."

He struck his leg with the paper. The sudden movement threw him off balance. He prevented a fall by clutching one of the porch posts. For a moment, Brett pitied him. She said, "You don't wish it any more fervently than I."

He blinked, then pulled at his fine linen shirt where it stuck to his armpit. "Know you'd like to see Billy home. So would I. 'Course—family loyalty isn't the only reason I want this blasted war over. Have some political ones, too. Nothing pers'nal, now"—a smarmy grin—"but we Republicans are going to change ol' Dixie Land forever."

She fanned herself with a handkerchief, irked again by his alcoholic smugness, yet curious. "Oh, you are? How is that?"

He put his finger over his lips to signal secrecy, then whispered, "Simple. 'Publican party will pretend to be the friend of all the freed niggers down there. Ignorant lot, niggers. 'F we give 'em the franchise, they'll vote any way we tell 'em. With the niggers voting, our party'll be the majority party before you can say *that.*"

With a broad, almost violent gesture, he managed to snap his fingers. Once more his balance was threatened. Brett caught his arm and steadied him until he lowered his heavy rear into a bent-wood rocker, which sagged and creaked loudly.

"Stanley, that's a very cold-blooded scheme you described. You're not making it up?"

The smarmy smile broadened. "Would I lie to my own rel'tive? Plan's been drawn up a long time. By a certain—inner group." He rolled his eyes. "Better not say any more."

Outraged, Brett retorted, "You said quite enough. You're going to exploit the very people you purport to champion—?"

"Pur-port." He dragged it out, savoring the sound. "*Purrr*-port. Perrr-fect word." He snickered at his own humor. "Niggers wouldn't understand it, an' they won't understand that we're us-ing 'em, either."

"That's utterly unscrupulous."

"No, jus' politics. I—"

"You'll excuse me," she said, her tolerance exhausted. "I must go to supper."

He started to say something else, but a sound much like the bleat of a billy goat came from an upstairs window. Someone had

635

hit someone else. One of the twins screamed, "Get out of my things, you thieving shit."

Sickened by Stanley's drunken statements, Brett walked rapidly back to Belvedere. Though she considered Billy's older brother stupid and venal, she feared that the plan he had described could very well work. The blacks, except for a few of the well-educated ones like Scipio Brown, would logically put their trust in the Republicans. And if they were given the right to vote, they could indeed elect whomever their benefactors chose. Brett had no great liking for the Yankee President, but she couldn't imagine him being party to such a vile scheme.

Hot and angry, she ate supper alone. Maude, one of the serving girls, worked up nerve to say, "Everyone's talking of a great battle. Will they come this far to fight?"

"I don't know," Brett answered. "No one's sure of the whereabouts of either army."

In darkness reddened by the light of Hazard's, Brett walked into the hills, hoping to find cooler air. Where was Billy? She had had no letters for nearly three weeks. He was fighting for what he believed while Stanley cowered in Lehigh Station, sipping gin and boasting of his political plans.

She wandered higher, through the laurel that lay thick and dim on the heights. There was no wind to stir the deep green leaves, and in the hazy night the stars had a red cast.

By chance, her walk took her past the spot where a meteorite had struck one of the slopes. She and Billy had discovered the smoking crater only hours before his departure for Washington in the spring of '61. The crater had seemed to be a warning, and what it had warned of had come to pass. By the light of Hazard's furnaces and chimneys, she saw that the crater was shallower than before. New dirt had washed into its bottom, and the chunk of what Billy called star-iron was no longer visible.

The laurel grew all around the crater, to the very edge. But none grew within the crater itself. Curious, Brett leaned down for a pinch of loose earth from the crater well. It had a gritty, sandy feel. A strange, sour smell.

Was it somehow poisoned, like the nation was poisoned? Poisoned by hatreds, by loss of lives, by the punishment the land deserved because some of its people had chained up so many others for so many years?

Why, they would take a whip to you down on the Ashley if they knew you harbored such thoughts. Yet she wasn't ashamed of them, only surprised. She *had* changed. She preferred the friendship and respect of a Scipio Brown over that of a Stanley Hazard.

Absently, she broke off a sprig of laurel. She remembered Billy likening the laurel to their love. He said both would survive these awful times. But would they?

Where was her husband tonight? Where were the armies? Could Harrisburg be burning and they not know it in this peaceful valley? Shivering under the red stars, she gazed away to the darkness in the southwest, imagining the unseen armies sniffing the hot night for scent of each other.

Upset and frightened, she flung the sprig away and hurried down the hill past the poisoned crater. She didn't fall asleep until the first light of morning.

84

Lee had disappeared into enemy country. A city, a government, a land held its breath in hope of good news.

There was none from the West, Orry told Madeline. Rosecrans was astir in Tennessee, and Grant's hand crushed Vicksburg more tightly by the hour. Orry's work was a blur of conferences, memorandums, constant arguments with Winder and his wardens over the increasing number of deaths among the war prisoners.

In the evenings, he and Madeline read aloud to each other. Now and then they indulged in sad speculations about their inability to conceive a child. "Perhaps Justin wasn't wholly wrong to blame me," she said once.

They studied and responded to occasional letters from

Philemon Meek. And they entertained Augusta Barclay one day, enjoying her company while recognizing how anxious she was about Cousin Charles. She said she had traveled all the way to the capital to find some dress muslin, but she really wanted to inquire about him. She had received no letter in two months and feared he'd been wounded or killed in the cavalry clash at Brandy Station.

Orry assured her that he watched the casualty rolls, and so far the name of Major Charles Main had not appeared. Gus knew nothing of the field promotion. She said she was pleased, but she sounded unenthusiastic.

She accepted their invitation to supper. During the meal, they speculated on Charles's whereabouts. Orry knew that Hampton's horse had gone into Pennsylvania with Lee, but beyond that, he could provide no information. They said good-bye after ten, Gus intending to travel all night on lonely roads with only young Boz to guard her. Just before she left, she again expressed gratitude to the Mains for sheltering her during the Chancellorsville fighting and said she wanted to repay the kindness if ever she could. Madeline thanked her, and the women embraced; they had formed a liking for each other.

After Gus was gone, Madeline said, "Something's wrong between her and Charles, though I'm not sure what it is."

Orry agreed. Like his wife, he had detected a certain sadness in the visitor's eyes.

Something was wrong with Cooper, too. Orry saw his brother occasionally around Capitol Square. Cooper was abrupt in conversation and refused further invitations to dinner with a curt "Too busy right now."

"He's become a stranger to me," Orry told Madeline. "And not a very sane-looking one, at that."

For some months, Orry had known that Beauchamp's Oyster House on Main Street was a postbox for illegal mail to the North. In late June he wrote a long letter to George, addressing it in care of Hazard's of Lehigh Station. He asked how Constance was faring, and Billy and Brett, told of his marriage to Madeline, and mentioned Charles's service with the Iron Scouts. He also described, briefly and somewhat bitterly, his work for Seddon, and his constant conflicts with Winder and the prison wardens. On a sultry evening, wearing the one civilian suit he had brought from Mont Royal, he nervously entered Beauchamp's and handed the wax-sealed envelope to a barman, together with forty dollars of inflated Confederate money. There was no guarantee the letter would get any farther than some trash bin. Still, Orry missed his old friend, and saying it on paper made him feel better.

The June heat continued. And the waiting.

"I'm worried," Ashton said, the same night Orry mailed his letter.

"About what?" Powell said. Naked except for drawers, he sat examining the deed to a small farm he and his associates had purchased. The place was situated on the bank of the James, below the city near Wilton's Bluff. Powell hadn't explained why owning it was advantageous, though Ashton knew it had something to do with the scheme to eliminate Davis.

Powell's perfunctory question made Ashton snap, "My husband." He heard the pique in her voice and laid the deed aside. "Every morning he questions me about my plans for the day. When I was shopping downtown yesterday, I had the queerest feeling I was being watched—and then, from the vestibule of Meyers and Janke, I spied James on the other side of the street, lurking behind a water wagon and trying to look inconspicuous."

A hot breeze blew from the garden, riffling pages of the deed. Far away, heat lightning shimmered. Powell's four-barrel Sharps lay near the document. He placed the gun on the deed like a paperweight and lightly drummed his fingers on the stock.

"Did he question you this evening?"

She shook her head. "He was still at work when I left."

"But you think he knows."

"Suspects. I don't want to say this, Lamar, but I feel I must. It might be better if we stopped these meetings for a while."

His eyes grew glacial. "Do I take that to mean I've become a bore, my dear?"

She ran to him, reached down from behind his chair and pressed her palms to his hard chest. "Oh, my God, no, sweetheart. No! But things are going badly for James. He's—disturbed. No matter how careful you are, he might take you by surprise some night. Harm you." She began to rub slowly, near his waist, her bodice pressing the back of his head as she bent toward the chair. "It would kill me if I were responsible for something like that."

639

Powell guided her hand lower, murmuring, "Well—perhaps you're right."

He allowed her to continue a moment or so, then abruptly took her hand away and nodded at another chair. She sat obediently as he spoke. "My personal safety's the least of my concerns. Momentous work is under way. I wouldn't want it interrupted by some witless and preventable act of violence. To tell you the truth, I have been a bit worried about your husband." He brought his fingertips together and peered over the arch. "Last week I hit on a way to make sure he doesn't threaten us. I've pondered it since then, and I'm convinced it's sound."

"What are you going to do, get him dismissed and sent home?"

Powell ignored the sarcasm. "I propose to recruit him for our group."

"Recruit him?" She jumped up. "That is the most ridiculous, not to say dangerous—"

"Be quiet and let me finish."

His cold voice stilled her. Cowed, she moved back to the chair as he continued. "Of course that is precisely how it sounds—at first. But think a moment. You can find logical and compelling arguments in favor of it."

"I'm sorry, I fail to see them," she countered, though not loudly.

"In any enterprise of this kind, one always needs a certain number of—call them soldiers. Men to carry out the most dangerous phases of the plan. In our case, the men must be more than trustworthy; they must be foursquare against the black vomit of nigger freedom, because only that kind of fervor will beget absolute loyalty. Our soldiers must hate Davis and his coterie of West Point bunglers and Jew bureaucrats, and endorse the formation of our new Confederacy. Except for the last aspect, which he as yet knows nothing about, I submit that your husband meets the specifications in every particular."

"Well, put that way, perhaps he does."

Powell's sly smile broadened. "Finally, would it not be far better to have him close by, where he can be watched, than to have him running about on his own, as he's doing now?" The low-trimmed gas cast his shadow across her as he padded around the table and fingered a lock of her hair. "With your husband actively involved, it would be far easier for you and me to see each other. I don't think he's clever enough to suspect the ruse."

640

"I agree about that—especially now that he's in such a state about the failures of the President."

"You see? It isn't such a crazy notion after all."

He curled the strand of dark hair around his index finger, then moved the finger gently back and forth. "But suppose, despite every precaution against it, he did find us out. Became unbalanced, therefore untrustworthy—" He let the hair fall and laid his hand on the four-barrel Sharps. "That, too, can be dealt with."

Ashton's eyes leaped from his face to the shining gun and back again. Frightened, joyous—aroused suddenly—she flung her arms around his neck, kissed it, and whispered, "Oh, my dearest Lamar. How clever you are."

"Then you don't object to my plan?"

"No."

"Not to any part of it?"

Over his shoulder, she saw the Sharps shining on top of the deed. "No—no. Anything you want is fine, as long as I can stay with you always."

Against her skirt she felt him, large and potent. She felt she was touching more than something physical. She was touching his strength; his ambition; the power they would ultimately share.

"Always," Powell repeated, picking her up as if she weighed no more than a child. "To ensure it, however, we must agree that James Huntoon, Esquire, is expendable."

Her open-mouthed kiss gave him the answer.

Late on Wednesday, July 1, Stanley stepped from the first-class car of the train from Baltimore. Even cushioned by swigs from a bourbon bottle, he could hardly accept all that had happened to him in the past twenty-four hours.

Rumors of an impending battle had reached Lehigh Station. He and Isabel had been packing to retreat to the family's summer home, Fairlawn, in Newport, when Stanton's angry telegram arrived. Stanley had traveled most of last night and all of today, buffeted by crowds talking of nothing but the battle about to begin, if it hadn't already, in the vicinity of the market town of Chambersburg. Exhausted and half drunk, Stanley entered the secretary's sanctum at half past six. He endured ten minutes of Stanton's wrath, then took a hack to the north side of Capitol Square.

Squalid shops and barracks had grown up around the old brick

641

building at First and A. By turns, the building had been a temporary national capitol after the British burned the official one in August 1814, a rooming house for senators and representatives—Calhoun had died there—and, since '61, a prison for a wide variety of inmates. These last included female spies working for the Confederacy; sharps and prostitutes; newsmen; fight-prone officers such as Judson Kilpatrick and George Custer.

Stanley had sent messages ahead. Baker's bay, Slasher, was tethered to the ring post at the First Street entrance. The colonel was waiting outside, truculent but clearly nervous. With him was the prison superintendent, Wood.

"Where is he?" Stanley demanded of Wood.

"Room 16. Same place we put all the editors and reporters."

"Did you clear out the others in the room? It's imperative that no one recognize me. Newsmen certainly would." He was assured it had been done. "You've bungled this, Baker—you know that."

"Not my fault," Baker complained as Stanley started upstairs through the shadows, the stenches, the flicker and play of gaslights spaced wide apart.

"The secretary thinks otherwise. If we can't straighten this out, you may lose your precious toy—those four troops of cavalry you persuaded Mr. Lincoln to give you."

Up they went, past rooms holding inmates, and others where interrogations were conducted, sometimes lasting hours. Room 16 was a long, desolate chamber with a single gas fixture and one filthy window at the end. Spider webs festooned the ceiling corners. Strange stains discolored those portions of the wall that could be seen; bunks piled with dirty blankets and luggage hid the rest.

Packing boxes, empty bottles, items of men's clothing littered the floor. The furniture consisted of two dirty pine tables with benches. The quality of the prison's food could be judged from what was scrawled on the wall in charcoal:

MULE SERVED HERE

"Lower bunk, on the left," Wood whispered.

The floor creaked as they tiptoed toward the small, almost dwarf-like man snoring with his back to the room. The visible side of his face was heavily bruised, his eye a puffy slit yellow with matter. "Good Christ," Stanley said.

Randolph stirred but didn't waken. Stanley shoved Baker aside and walked out. Downstairs, in Wood's office, he slammed the door and said, "Here's the long and short of it. A black whore escaped when Randolph was taken at Mrs. Devore's. The whore telegraphed Cincinnati. The owners of Randolph's paper are Democrats, but they have sufficient influence in Ohio to elicit a response from a Republican administration—I speak particularly of Mr. Stanton. Habeas corpus or no habeas corpus, Randolph goes free first thing in the morning."

Baker sighed. "That clears it up, then."

"The devil it does. Who beat him so badly?"

"That man you sent me. Dayton."

"Get rid of him."

Baker stroked his beard, shrugged. "Easy enough."

"And the witnesses."

"Not so easy."

"Why not? One's in custody—"

"The white prostitute," Wood said. "She's with the other women."

"Get the nigger's name from Mrs. Devore," Stanley ordered Baker. "Find her and get both women out of Washington. Threaten them, bribe them, but I want them five hundred or a thousand miles from here. Tell them to use assumed names if they value their skins." Baker started to raise some objection, but Stanley blustered, "Do it, Colonel, or you'll no longer command the First District of Columbia Cavalry, or any other organization."

With an unintelligible mutter, Baker turned away. Wood scratched his chin. "There's still Randolph to be reckoned with. Nobody cut his tongue out, y'know."

Stanley's glance lashed the warden for joking at such a time. "Randolph is Mr. Stanton's responsibility. The secretary is calling on Senator Wade right now, and it's expected that some well-respected congressmen will soon counsel with Randolph's publishers. The message will be quite simple. It will be to their advantage to keep quiet but infinitely troublesome for them if they don't. I suspect they'll choose the former. Then, if Randolph talks, who'll corroborate his wild statements? Not his paper. Certainly no one here—" Baleful, he eyed the warden and the chief of the Detective Bureau.

"The women won't," he continued. "They'll be gone. Dayton,

too. Many unsubstantiated tales of government excess are circulating these days. One more will hardly cause a ripple."

"I'll speak to Dayton tomorrow," Baker promised.

"Tonight," Stanley said and went down and out to the square, where Union officers, evidently rounded up for disciplinary reasons, stumbled from a newly arrived van while raffish men and women leaned from the prison windows, crying, *"Fresh fish! Fresh fish!"*

"I regret this," Lafayette Baker said to a still-sleepy Elkanah Bent. It was half past eleven. Bent had been wakened and dragged to the office by Detective O'Dell, who professed to know nothing about the reason for the urgent summons.

Baker cleared his throat. "But facts are facts, Dayton. You injured Randolph by repeatedly hitting him."

Bent clutched the arms of his chair, straining forward. "He resisted arrest!"

"Even so, it's evident that you employed more force than was necessary."

Bent struck the desk. "And what do you and Wood employ when you question someone? I've been at the prison. I've heard the screams—"

"That's enough," Baker said, his tone ominous.

"You want a scapegoat—"

"I don't want a thing, Dayton. You're an able agent, and if I could keep you, I would, believe me." Bent spat an oath. Baker colored but kept his voice level. "I am under orders from the War Department. The secretary himself. Some satisfaction must be offered for what happened to Randolph, and I regret—"

"That I'm the bone to be tossed to the wolves," Bent cried, very nearly shrieking. Someone tapped on the door, asked a question.

"Everything's fine, Fatty," Baker called back. Then, more quietly, "I understand your feelings. But it will be to your advantage to take this in good grace."

"The hell I will. I refuse to be thrown on the trash heap by you, by Stanton, or by any other—"

"Shut your mouth!" Baker was on his feet, pointing at the other man. "You have twenty-four hours to remove yourself from Washington. There is no appeal."

Like a sounding whale, Bent came up from his chair. "Is this

644

how the government treats loyal employees? How it repays faithful service—?"

Abruptly, Baker sat again. His hands began to move through dossier folders like busy white spiders. Without raising his eyes, he said, "Twenty-four hours, Mr. Dayton. Or you will be placed under arrest."

"At whose instigation? By whose order?"

Livid, Baker said, "Lower your voice. Eamon Randolph was severely beaten. Much worse will happen to you if you make trouble. You'll disappear into Old Capitol, and you'll be a graybeard before you see daylight again. Now get out of here and out of Washington by this time tomorrow. O'Dell!"

The door flew open. The detective shot in, right hand under his left lapel.

"Show him out. Lock the door after he leaves."

Blinking, panting, Bent was in an instant reduced to helplessness. His shoulders sagged, then his body. He uttered a single, faint, "But—"

"Dayton," Fatty O'Dell said, and stepped aside, leaving the doorway unblocked. Bent lumbered out.

A few hours earlier, an elegant gig open to the night air clipped along the perimeter road of Hollywood Cemetery, west of Richmond. Lights gleamed in distant houses. Shadows of leafy branches flitted over the faces of James Huntoon and the gig's driver, Lamar Powell.

"I can't believe what you've told me, Powell."

"That's precisely why I called for you and brought you out here," Powell replied. "I'd like to recruit you for our group, but I couldn't risk issuing the invitation where we might be overheard."

Huntoon pulled out his pocket kerchief to remove a sudden film of steam from his spectacles. "I certainly understand."

Powell shook the reins to pick up the pace on the straight stretch of road. Monuments, obelisks, great crosses, and anguished stone angels glided by, half seen in the foliage to their right. "I know we didn't begin our, ah, business relationship on the best footing, Huntoon. But, ultimately, *Water Witch* earned you a fine profit."

"That's true. Unfortunately, to obtain it, my wife deceived me."

"I'm sorry about that. Your wife strikes me as a charming person, but I know little about her, so it would be rash as well as rude if I commented on your domestic situation."

He kept his eyes fixed on the starlit road beyond the ears of the horse. He felt Huntoon's suspicious stare for a moment. Then a whistling sigh told him the lawyer's thoughts had jumped back to the plan Powell had described. He probed for a reaction.

"Are you appalled by what I told you a few minutes ago?"

"Yes." More firmly: "Yes—why not? Assassination is—well—not only a crime; it's an act of desperation."

"For some. Not my group. We are taking a carefully planned and absolutely necessary step to reach a desirable end—establishment of the new Confederacy of the Southwest. Properly organized, properly controlled—free and independent of the bungling that has doomed this one. There will be a government, of course. You could play a role. A significant one. You most certainly have the talent. I've inquired about your work at the Treasury Department."

Like a pleased boy, Huntoon said, "Have you really?"

"Do you think I'd be speaking now if I hadn't? You're one of a number of highly competent men King Jeff has misused—wasted in menial posts. It's deliberate, naturally. He downgrades those of us from the cotton states in order to please the damned Virginians. For you, I could envision an important post in our Treasury Department, if that appeals to you. If it doesn't, we can certainly satisfy you with some other high office. Very likely at cabinet level."

Under the wind-rustled branches, Huntoon wondered if he could believe what he was hearing. It was the call of opportunity —the kind of opportunity to which he had aspired in the early days, but which Davis had denied him.

Cabinet level. Wouldn't Ashton be pleased? She might not consider him so inadequate, publicly or—his tongue moved over his damp lip—privately.

But it was dangerous. And Powell spoke of murder so lightly. Hesitating, he said, "Before I decide, I would need more details."

"Details without a commitment on your part? I'm afraid that's impossible, James."

"Some time to consider, then. The risks—"

"They're enormous, no denying it," Powell cut in. "But brave men with vision can meet and master them. You uttered an appropriate word a few moments ago—desperation. But it applies to

646

them far more than it does to us. The Confederacy of Davis and his crowd is already lost, and they know it. The people are beginning to know it, too. The only government that can succeed is a new government. Ours. So the question's quite simple. Will you join it or no?"

Huntoon's mind brimmed with memories: Ashton's adoring eyes at the moment she accepted his proposal; the cheering, clapping crowds to whom he had argued the case for secession from lecture platforms—even tree stumps—throughout his home state. He had starved for both kinds of approval since coming to this wretched city.

"Your answer, James?"

"I'm—inclined to join. But I must think a while before the decision can be final."

"Certainly. Not too long, though," Powell murmured. "Preparations are already going forward."

He shook the reins again; the clip-clop quickened. The breeze lifted Powell's hair and refreshed his face as he swung the gig back toward the city. He was smiling. The fish was securely on the hook.

When Lafayette Baker dismissed him, Elkanah Bent's tenuous self-control broke like a dry twig. He rode straight for the residence of Jasper Dills, passing the *Star* office en route. Swarming crowds read bulletins by torchlight. The armies had engaged or were about to engage near some obscure market town in Pennsylvania.

As he had once done at Starkwether's, Bent pounded the door of the Dills's house. Beat on it until his fist ached and an austere servent answered. "Mr. Dills is out of the city for several days."

"Coward," Bent muttered as the door slammed. Like so many others, the lawyer had fled at the first threat of invasion.

With his sole source of help unavailable, he knew he dared not stay in Washington. An unexpected option suddenly presented itself. Why stay in the North at all? He hated its army for failing to recognize his military talent, thus denying him the career he deserved. He hated its President for favoring the Negroes. Most of all, he hated its government for using him when it was expedient and casting him aside when it was not.

In his rooms, snuffling and cursing those who had conspired against him, he rummaged through a trunk to find the pass he had saved from the Richmond mission. Wrinkled and soiled, it was still too legible to serve his purpose. A sentry would have to be blind not to detect forgery of a new date—which he had neither the materials nor the skills to accomplish anyway.

Use the bureau's regular sources, then? No. Baker might hear of it and guess his destination. He must cross the Potomac without papers, without using any of the bridges. There were ways. The bureau had taught him a lot in a short time.

His damp hair clinging to his forehead and his shirttails flying out of his trousers, he flung clothing and a few possessions into a portmanteau and a small trunk. The last item he packed was the painting from New Orleans. As he worked, the pressure of hatred built again.

He swung to stare at his reflection in the old, speckled pier glass. How ugly he was; gross with fat. With a cry, he seized the china water pitcher and crashed it into the mirror, breaking both.

Moments later, the landlady was pounding on the door. "Mr. Dayton, what are you doing?"

In order to leave, he had to unlock the door and shove the old woman aside. She fell. He paid no attention. Down the stairs he went, trunk on his shoulder, portmanteau in his other hand while the woman bleated about rent in arrears. A sleepy boarder in a nightcap peered at him as he went out.

In the sultry dawn, he rattled south in a hired buggy. Some blustering and a flash of his little silver badge took him through the fortification lines. He went straight on along the roads of Prince Georges and Charles counties toward Port Tobacco, where certain watermen were known to be loyal to the Confederacy provided the loyalty was secured with cash.

Bent scarcely saw the countryside through which the buggy carried him. His mind picked over the decision to which he had been driven, constructing additional justifications for it. Perhaps the Southern leaders weren't as bad as he had always believed. They hated the darkies as much as he did, which was in their favor. And during his time in Richmond, he had found that he could blend in without causing suspicion. There *had* to be a place for him in the Confederacy; there was none in the North any longer.

He was still realistic enough to acknowledge some facts about his defection. The established government—more specifically, the army—probably wouldn't employ him. Put it another way: He did not want to ask *them* for employment. Though he was by no means the first person to change sides in this war, they would still distrust him, hence put him in a menial post if they put him in any at all. Second, he dared not say who he really was or reveal much about his past. To do so would lead to questions, requests for explanations.

He would find some other way to survive. One occurred to him as the morning grew hotter and the road dust thicker. Baker had mentioned a man said to be conspiring to establish a second Confederacy. What was his name? After some minutes, it came to him: Lamar Powell. As Baker said, it was probably just a tissue of rumors. But a question or two wouldn't hurt.

In the drowsy town of Port Tobacco, an old waterman with half his face stiffened from a paralytic seizure said to Bent, "Yes, I can smuggle you over to Virginny for that sum. When will you be comin' back?"

"Never, I hope."

"Then let me buy you a glass to celebrate," the old man said with half a grin. "We'll make the run as soon as the sun's down."

85

"After them," Charles yelled, and spurred Sport down the country lane. Shotgun in his left hand, he closed on the quartet of alarmed Yankees who had ridden out of a grove half a mile distant. "We want to catch one," Charles shouted to his companion, two lengths behind. He was a new-issue replacement, a farmer boy of eighteen who weighed around two hundred and thirty pounds. He was a cheerful, biddable young man with two simple ambitions: "I want to love a lot of Southern girls an' bust a bunch of Yankee heads."

Jim Pickles was his name. He had been posted to the scouts because he was deemed too bulky and inelegant for regular duty. He would probably be on the dead line most of the time, having broken the backs of his mounts because of his weight. He had been sticking close to the senior scout—who insisted on being called Charlie, not Major Main—ever since Stuart and his men began their ride northward out of Virginia and away from the main body of the army, which Longstreet was leading into enemy country.

Three brigades—Hampton's, Fitz Lee's, and that of the wounded Rooney Lee under the command of Colonel Chambers —had crossed the Potomac on the night of June 27. Their route took them almost due north, east of the mountain ranges, under rather vague orders from General Lee. They could, at General Stuart's discretion, pass around the Union army, wherever it might be, collecting information and provisions en route. They had gotten some of the latter already, together with one hundred and twenty-five captured wagons. But of the former they had gotten almost none. They pressed on without knowing the whereabouts of the main Union force.

Charles heard gripes about that, muttered statements that General Jeb was keen to pull off another spectacular stunt—something similar to the ride around McClellan on the peninsula that had brought him fame and turned out crowds to strew flowers before his troops of horse as they rode back into Richmond. Stuart's reputation had been tarnished at Brandy Station when he kept his men so busy with reviews that they failed to detect the Union reconnaissance in force. Maybe he thought a second dash around the Union army would remove the tarnish.

They rode into Pennsylvania on the thirtieth of June. Hunting for Lee, they found the Yanks at Hanover, and after a sharp little fight, read local newspapers for their first solid information about the invasion of the state by Lee and Longstreet.

Familiar history began to repeat. Short rations. Scant sleep or none. Forced marches, with men dozing in the saddle or falling out. And for Charles, contradictory thoughts of Gus. A longing to see her, and doubts about the wisdom of it.

They went on to Dover and Carlisle and then another twenty-odd miles overnight toward Gettysburg, where the army had more or less blundered into an unwanted engagement on ground not of its choosing. It was said this happened because Stuart was off gallivanting—following his vague orders—and was thus unable to provide Lee with accurate reports of the enemy's whereabouts.

Now it was the second of July. About five miles south of the spot where Charles and Jim Pickles had come upon the four Yankees, smoke drifted and cannon roared. Behind the grove from which the blue-clad troopers emerged, there arose a dust cloud of some size. Charles interpreted it as a large body of horsemen on the move—toward Hunterstown, he guessed, after examining a crude map. He wanted to know exactly who was responsible for that dust. He was sure General Hampton would want to know, too. Hence his wish to capture a Yank.

Galloping down on the surprised foursome, he felt his exhaustion slough away. He hadn't slept at all last night, and there had been plenty of excitement while the cavalry rested that morning. General Hampton, riding out alone to survey the terrain, had unexpectedly come upon a soldier from the Sixth Michigan. The enlisted man's carbine had misfired, and, like a gallant Southern duelist, Hampton had allowed him time to reload. While he did, a second Yankee, a lieutenant, approached sneakily from behind. He sabered Hampton on top of the head. Then the enlisted man fired and nicked him. Gallantry wasn't a very useful trait any more.

Even with his hat and thick hair to protect him, the general took a four-inch cut in his scalp and barely escaped. The cut was dressed and so was the light chest graze from the enlisted man's bullet. By noon, he was fully active again, wanting to know, as Stuart did, what was happening north of the main battle site.

So Charles had ridden out with Pickles, and though many times in recent days he had felt he couldn't travel one more mile without falling over, he had gone that mile and many more—and now he was wide awake, tense, and eager to catch one of the bluebellies.

The Yanks milled at the roadside for a minute, then began to snap off carbine shots. Charles heard a buzz to his left in the rows of tasseled corn. He opened his mouth and gave the Yanks one of those wailing yells that scared hell out of them. His beard flew over his left shoulder, spikes of white showing in it now. So many layers of dirt and dried sweat covered him he felt like a mud man.

Pickles closed up behind him, his weight bringing lather to hi roan's flanks. Charles kept going at the gallop, howling. A bulle snapped his hat brim, and then the Yanks started a countercharg with revolvers and drawn sabers.

"Now," Charles shouted when the range was right. He brough up his shotgun, fired both barrels, and veered Sport to the shoul der, slowing a little. In the clear, Pickles fired. Between them they downed two of the Yanks. The other two reined up, wheeled about, and galloped into the safety of the grove.

"I hope one's still alive," Charles yelled as he rode on. The horse of one of the fallen men was trotting away, but the second animal nuzzled its rider where he lay in the road. The troope didn't move. Disgusted, Charles slowed down to a walk.

Soon he could see the flies gathering around the open mouth o the trooper in the road. No information to be gotten there. The other Yank was nowhere in sight.

Charles heard thrashing in some high weeds to his left, then groan. With an eye on the dust clouds billowing perhaps tw miles to the northwest, he dismounted and cautiously advanced t the roadside. Sweat dropped from the end of his nose as he craned over and saw the Union cavalryman, a bearded fellow with hi revolver still in its holster, sitting in the bottom of the ditch Blood soaked his left thigh.

Watching the man, Charles laid his shotgun on the ground with his left hand while drawing his Colt with his right. He cocked the revolver. Wary and scared, the Yank breathed loudly as Charle clambered down to him. Pickles sat watching, an eager pupil.

"What unit are you?"

"General—Kilpatrick's—Third Division."

"Bound where?"

The Yank hesitated. Charles pressed the muzzle of his gun t the perspiring forehead. "Bound where?"

"Lee's left flank—wherever that is."

Quickly, Charles stood and scanned the hazy treetops bendin in the hot wind. Reverberations of cannon fire continued to rol out of the south. With another glance at the wounded man Charles began to back up the side of the ditch. As he leaned dow for his shotgun, his eyes left the Yank for a second. Jim Pickle cried, "Hey, Charlie, watch—"

Pivoting, he sensed rather than saw the downward movemen of the Yank's hand. He fired. The bullet jerked the man sideways

Charles blew into the barrel of his Colt, noting that the Yank had been reaching for his wounded thigh with his left hand, not for his holster with his right.

"All right, Jim. Let's get the word back to Hampton. That dust is Kilpatrick, trying a flanking movement."

As they turned about and started east on the deserted road, Pickles broke into a huge grin. "Lord God, Charlie, you're somethin'. Cool as a block from the icehouse. 'Course, I feel kinda sorry for that Yank. He was only reachin' down because he was hurtin'."

"Sometimes your hand has to move faster than your brain," Charles answered with a shrug. "If I'd waited, he might have pulled the pistol. Better a mistake than a grave."

The younger man chuckled. "Ain't you somethin'. You boys in the scouts, you're regular killin' machines."

"That's the general idea. Every dead man on their side means fewer on ours."

Jim Pickles shivered, not entirely in admiration. To the south, the guns at Gettysburg kept roaring.

Pitch black ahead, pitch black behind. Rain rivered from Charles's hat. It had soaked through his cape hours ago.

In many respects it was the worst night he had ever spent as a soldier. They were bound south to the Potomac, in retreat, a train of confiscated farm wagons, most springless, each hung with a pale lantern. The procession stretched out for miles.

Hampton's men had drawn the honored position of rear guard. To Charles it was more like duty on the perimeter of hell. Full of irony, too. The day now passing into its last hours was July fourth.

Yesterday Hampton had taken a third wound, a shrapnel fragment, in a hot fight with Michigan and Pennsylvania horse, part of a failed effort to sweep around and attack Meade's rear. In some quarters Stuart was being blamed openly for the Gettysburg debacle. Critics continued to say his long ride away from Lee had deprived the army of its eyes and ears.

The Second South Carolina was down to around a hundred effectives. Visiting with his old outfit for an hour, Charles had heard that Calbraith Butler, invalided home after Brandy Station, would spend the rest of his life with a cork foot. The memory stuck with him tonight, and added to it were the outcries of the

653

hurt and maimed packed like fish into the springless wagons whose every roll and lurch increased their pain. The voices filled the rainy dark.

"Let me die. Let me die."

"Jesus Christ, put me out of this wagon. Have mercy. Kill me."

"Please, won't someone come? Take my wife's name and write her?"

That came from the wagon nearest Charles. Feeling Sport stagger and slip in the mud, he tried to shut his mind to the noise. But it went on: the hiss of rain; the squeal of axles; the men crying out like children. It broke his heart to listen to them.

Jim Pickles rode up beside him. "We're stopped. Somebody's mired up the line, I s'pect."

"Won't someone come? I can't make it. I need to tell Mary—"

Bursting with rage, wanting to pull his Colt and blow out the screamer's brains, Charles whipped his right leg over the saddle. He jumped down, splashing deep in mud. He slapped Sport's reins into Pickles's palm.

"Hold him."

He climbed the rear wheel of the ambulance wagon and fought his way under the canvas into the slithering stir and stink. He thought of Christmas in '61. *Snowing then. Raining now. But the same work to be done.*

He was sick in his soul. Sick of the madness and folly of killing men on the other side to save some of his own. Why had they said not one damn word about this kind of thing back at the Academy?

Hands plucked his trousers, the shy, soft touches of frightened children. The rain beat hard on the hooped canvas top. He raised his voice in order to be heard, yet sounded quite gentle.

"Where's the man who needs to write his wife? If he will identify himself, I'll help."

From the parlor window, Orry gazed along Marshall at the rooftops and row houses reddened by the cloudless sunset. An abnormal silence had enveloped the city for several days, for reasons the general populace did not as yet understand. But he did.

"Some of the fools in the department are trying to say Lee was successful—that he did what he set out to do: reprovision the army off the enemy's land." Serious and silent, wearing gray,

Madeline sat waiting till he continued. "The truth is, Lee's in retreat. His casualties may have run as high as thirty percent."

"Dear God," she whispered. "When will that be known?"

"You mean when will the papers get hold of it? A day or two, I suppose." He rubbed his temple, aching suddenly in the broiling heat. "They say Pickett charged the Union positions on Cemetery Hill in broad daylight. With no cover. His men went down like scythed wheat. Poor George—Why did we begin this damned business?"

She went to him, slipped her arms around him, pressed her cheek against his shoulder, wishing she could provide an answer. They held each other in the red light deepening to dark.

In a squalid taproom down by the river basin, Elkanah Bent ordered a mug of beer, which turned out to be warm and flat. Disgusted, he set it down as a white-haired man ran in, tears on his cheeks.

"Pemberton gave up. On the fourth of July. The *Enquirer* just printed an extra. Grant starved him out. The Yanks have got Vicksburg and mebbe the whole goddamn river. We can't even hold our own goddamn territory."

Bent added his sympathetic curse to those of others at the maghogany bar. In the distance, church bells began to toll. Had he slipped into Richmond just when everything was falling apart? All the more reason to locate that fellow Powell.

Mr. Jasper Dills suffered a headache even worse than Orry Main's. The headache started on Independence Day, a Saturday, when word reached the city of a stunning success at Gettysburg. Washington had been waiting for good news for days. Its arrival put some heart into the holiday celebration.

That very morning, he had returned from his vacation cottage on Chesapeake Bay, where he had prudently retired when rumors reached him of a possible rebel invasion. He was soon driven to distraction by the crackling of squibs that youngsters set off outside his house.

To add to the commotion, bands blared patriotic airs in the streets, and jubilant crowds surged through President's Park, serenading at the windows of the Executive Mansion as the news got better and better. Lee whipped; Vicksburg taken; Grant and Sherman and Meade heroes.

The glad tidings couldn't compensate for the debilitating effects of the din on lawyer Dills, nor for the familiar pattern that developed in the steamy days following the celebration. Like all the generals before him, Meade appeared to falter and lose nerve. He failed to pursue Lee aggressively, throwing away the chance to destroy the main Confederate army. The illuminations in the windows of mansions and public buildings went dark. The corner bonfires sparked and subsided into acrid smoke.

Head still pounding, Dills pondered two other pieces of unpleasant information, between which he ultimately perceived a relationship. His butler told him Bent had been at the front door, raving like a madman. And a sharp letter from Stanley Hazard informed Dills that the man he had recommended had nearly precipitated a catastrophe by beating a Democratic newsman when no such treatment had been ordered.

Stanton had demanded someone be held accountable. "Ezra Dayton" was dismissed, ordered out of Washington—and Mr. Dills would be so good as to make no further recommendations to the special service, thank you.

For two days and nights, messengers employed by Dills's firm had been sent out to search the city. It was true—Bent was gone. No one knew where. Dills sat in his office, head throbbing, urgent briefs piling up on his desk while he thought of the stipend, the stipend that would end if he lost track of Starkwether's son. What should he do? What could he do?

"The day has been a disaster," Stanley complained at supper on the Tuesday after Independence Day. "The secretary's furious because Meade won't move, and he blames me for the mess with Randolph."

"I thought you managed to hush that up."

"To a certain extent. Randolph won't publish anything. That is, his paper in Cincinnati won't. But Randolph's on the streets again, and his bruises are a regular advertisement of what was done to him. Then this afternoon, we had more bad news. Laurette?"

He pointed to his empty glass. Isabel touched her upper lip with her handkerchief. "You've had four already, Stanley."

"Well, I want another. Laurette!"

The maid filled the glass with red Bordeaux. He swallowed a third of it while his wife shielded her eyes with her hand. Her husband was undergoing peculiar changes. The responsibilities imposed by his position and the huge sums accumulating in their bank accounts seemed too much for him somehow.

"What else went wrong?" she asked.

"One of Baker's men was in Port Tobacco. He heard that Mr. Dayton, the fellow who brutalized Randolph, apparently deserted to the enemy after Baker drove him out of town. God knows what sensitive information he took with him. The whole business reflects shamefully on the department. No one admits publicly that we control Baker, but everyone knows it. On top of that—" he guzzled the rest of the wine and signaled the maid, who poured another glass after casting an anxious glance at her mistress "—on top of that, as of today, the Conscription Act is officially in force. People hate it. We've already had reports of protests, incidents of violence—"

"Here?"

"New York, mainly."

"Well, my sweet, that's far away from this house—and for once you might reflect on your good fortune. You could be drafted—you're still young enough—if you weren't in the War Department or sufficiently wealthy to pay for a substitute."

Stanley sipped his wine, still looking morose. Isabel ordered Laurette out of the room and came around to his end of the long, shining table. Standing behind her husband, she restrained his hand when he reached for the wine glass again. Resting her long chin on the top of his head, she patted his arm in an unusual display of affection.

"Despite all your troubles, we're very lucky, Stanley. We should be grateful Congress had the wisdom to enact that substitute clause. Thankful that it's a rich man's war but a poor man's fight, as they say."

But he wasn't comforted. He sat contemplating all of the changes in his life during the past couple of years. One was the development of a consuming thirst for strong drink—which could wreck a man's career. On the other hand, that tended to happen less often if you were wealthy. He must do his best to keep the tippling under control and keep selling shoes to the poor fools who were dying for slogans on both sides of the war.

"Constance?" In bed beside George on that sultry Wednesday after Gettysburg, she murmured to signify she was listening. "What will I do?"

The question was one she had been expecting—dreading—for months. She heard the strain in his voice, put there during an evening quarrel with their headstrong son. William had once again absented himself from his late-afternoon dancing class and sneaked off for a game of baseball with some Georgetown boys. Although George championed the game over a quadrille, he nevertheless had to reprimand William. The reprimand led to argument, and the argument ended with shouts from the father, sullen looks of rebellion from the son.

"You mean about the department?" she asked, though it was hardly necessary.

"Yes. I can't abide the stupidity and politicking any longer. And all the money being made from death and suffering—Thank God I have nothing to do with Stanley's contracts. I'd stuff them down his throat till he choked."

A pain started in her left breast. She had experienced many such dull aches lately, in her legs, her upper body, behind her forehead. She suspected the cause was a simple one—worry. She worried about her children, her father in far-off California, her weight creeping up a pound or two each month. She worried about George most of all. Night after night, he brought his troubles home and dwelled on them all evening.

Ripley's obstinacy in particular had become too much to bear. George cited a new example at least once a week. Recently General Rosecrans, hearing that Ordnance had some of those repeating coffee-mill guns in storage, had requested them for his Western command. At first Ripley wouldn't ship a single one; he still disapproved of the design. Finally, forced, he sent ten—and Rosecrans in return sent glowing performance reports to Lincoln. The President urged Ripley to reconsider the purchase of more of the guns. Ripley buried the request.

Constance knew Ripley's crimes by heart. He continued to campaign against breechloaders and repeaters, refusing to issue them to any but the mounted service. He tried to cancel existing contracts for them and wrote *No more wanted* across proposals from manufacturers.

"And yet," George had raged only last night, "not forty-eight hours after poor George Pickett's men were slaughtered charging

658

our positions, I saw a report from a captured reb who fought against Berdan's Sharpshooters at Little Round Top. In twenty minutes, with single-shot breechloaders, Berdan's men fired about a hundred rounds each. The reb said his commander thought they had run into two whole regiments."

"Had they?"

George laughed. "Berdan had one hundred men. And still that old son of a bitch writes 'rejected' or 'tabled' on every plea for better shoulder weapons."

There was nothing new about such complaints from George. What was new was the frequency and the ferocity with which he voiced them. She dated that change from about a month ago, before the fall of Vicksburg, when an angry report on faulty Parrott shells crossed his desk. On investigation, he discovered the shells were part of a shipment from a Buffalo ammunition works whose samples he had inspected and turned back. The casings were pitted with holes resulting from faulty sand casting. How vividly she remembered his rage when he came home that evening.

"The slimy wretches had the gall to try to disguise the defects. They filled the holes with putty colored to match the metal."

Next day there was another blow:

"Ripley countermanded my rejection order. He approved the shipment. Seems the manufacturer's a distant relative of his wife. God, I'd love to lob some of those shells up his rear end. It would be the biggest service anyone could do for the Union."

That was the background, the accumulating bitterness that prompted his question tonight. She lay motionless in the dark of their bed, knowing the inevitable question she was duty-bound to ask by way of reply.

"What would you like to do, George?"

"Which answer do you want, the ideal or the realistic?"

"There are two? The former first, then."

"I'd like to work for Lincoln."

"Honestly? You admire him that much?"

"I do. Since that night we met at the arsenal, I feel I've come to know him well. He's in and out of our offices several times a week, asking questions, prodding, encouraging good ideas in spite of—maybe because of—our departmental dullness. I admit the man's rough-hewn, and it's lucky that campaigns aren't won or lost on the candidate's ability to look and act presentable, or he'd never

659

be elected to anything. He doesn't dissemble, and some say that's a flaw—he never hides his doubts or dark moods. Ward Lamon told me several months ago that Lincoln's convinced he won't live to see Springfield again. But the man has qualities that are in damn short supply in this town. Honesty. Idealism. Strength. Good Lord, Constance, considering all the burdens he bears, from national to domestic, his strength is monumental. Yes, I wish I could work for him in some capacity, but there's no place."

"You inquired?"

"Discreetly. I didn't say anything to you because I felt sure it was an impossibility."

"Then what's the realistic answer?"

"I can go with the military railroads if Herman Haupt will have me. It's a good alternative. And I'm eager."

He said it so promptly she knew he had been ready with the idea for some time. Trying to keep her voice calm, she said, "That's field duty. Close to the battle lines—"

"Sometimes, yes. But what's important is this. It's work I believe I can do and take pride in."

Silence, broken by the inevitable rumbling of the night wagons. Sensing her tension, he rolled on his side—they were sleeping without clothes, as they often did—and caressed her bosom, soft, springy, wonderfully comforting in its familiarity.

"Do you not want me to do it?"

"George, in—" she cleared her throat "—in this marriage, you know neither party ever asks or answers that kind of question."

"I'd still like to know what you—"

"Do what you must," she said, kissing him, one palm against his face. She blinked rapidly, hoping he wouldn't feel the fear-inspired tears that sprang to her eyes.

"So, Herman—will you accept a new man?"

George asked that late the next day as he and the bearded brigadier leaned on Willard's bar. Haupt looked worn out. He had been shunting back and forth to Pennsylvania to get the rail lines from Gettysburg in repair.

"You know the answer to that. Question is, will the secretary release you?"

"By God, he'd better. I can't stand working within a mile of that man." He swallowed a raw oyster from the plate in front of him. "I suppose you've heard of the Randolph scandal—"

"Who hasn't? I gather he's forbidden to write about it, but he recruits listeners and repeats the story every chance he gets."

"He damn well should. It's a disgrace."

"Well, such philosophic reflections aside, I urge you to move fast. I think Stanton wants my head. I dislike him as much as you do, and he knows it. I refuse to put up with his prejudices and arrogance—" Haupt tossed off the rest of his whiskey with a dour smile. "—since I have my own to maintain."

They divided the remaining oysters. After the last one, George belched—one more irksome sign, along with joints that ached in the morning and gray hairs in his mustache, that his time was hurrying by.

Haupt asked how he hoped to effect the transfer. "It won't work if I simply request your services."

"I know. I have an appointment with the general-in-chief in the morning."

"Halleck? The master paper-shuffler? I didn't know you were acquainted with Old Brains."

"I've met him twice socially. He's an Academy man—"

"Class of '39. Four years after mine. West Point takes care of its own—is that what you're counting on?"

"It is," George said. "I've learned a little something about the way this town operates, Herman."

Henry Halleck, who allowed George ten minutes on his schedule, seemed a man of hemispheres: rounded shoulders, convex forehead, bulging eyes. He was more scholar than soldier—some years ago he had translated a work by Jomini—but an able, if pedestrian, administrator.

From the window where he stood in his familiar posture, hands locked behind his spotless, neatly buttoned uniform, he said: "When I noted your name on the appointment calendar, I called for your record, Major. It's exemplary. You are definite about wanting to leave the Ordnance Department?"

"Yes, General. I need to feel more useful. Desk duty has palled."

"I suspect you mean Ripley has palled," Halleck said with a rare show of humor. "He really is your superior, you know. You ought to apply to him for a transfer."

Understanding what he risked, George nevertheless shook his head. "With all respect, sir, I can't do that. General Ripley would

661

almost certainly deny my request. Whereas if I could have your leave to go directly to the adjutant general—"

"No, that isn't permissible."

George knew he had lost. But Halleck kept speaking. "I do understand and sympathize with your predicament, however. I know you came to Washington at Cameron's behest, persuaded only by a strong sense of patriotic duty. I applaud your desire to get more directly into the thick of things. If you're to pull it off, it must be done properly."

Retrieving George from despair with those words, he leaned his great balding head forward till it seemed to float before the junior officer. Lowering his voice, as every good Washingtonian did when arranging some little scheme or favor, Halleck went on.

"Forward your request for a transfer to the adjutant general through channels—being sure to send a copy to General Ripley. Meantime, I shall speak on your behalf—unofficially, you understand. If we are successful, be prepared to do battle with Mr. Secretary Stanton." He extended his hand. "I wish you luck."

George had already prepared the paper to which Halleck referred. He sent them up the line immediately, and received the secretarial summons much sooner than he expected.

The War Department building to which George reported at half past two on Monday had a distinct air of gloom. Meade had dallied; Lee had gotten clean away; the Conscription Act was precipitating more incidents of street violence in New York City. The President was said to have plunged from a period of intensive activity and hope into another of his depressions.

"You wish to work for Haupt? My dear Major," Stanton said sourly, "do you know he has never officially accepted the rank of brigadier after receiving the promotion last September? Who can tell how long he'll remain in charge of the military railroads?"

In the voice of the bearded, Buddha-like man, George heard dislike and a warning. "Nevertheless, sir," he said, "I'm anxious for the transfer. I came to Ordnance at Secretary Cameron's request, and I've tried to carry out my duties faithfully, even though I've never felt fully qualified or very useful. I want to serve in some capacity more directly related to the conduct of the war."

Stanton fingered the earpiece of his spectacles; a trick of the light rendered the lenses opaque. Perhaps he knew how to hold his head to achieve the disquieting effect.

"Would it change your mind if I told you General Ripley may

shortly retire?" An insincere smile. "The general is, after all, sixty-nine years of age."

And has he crossed you once too often? "No, sir, that would have no bearing on my request."

"Let me be frank with you, Major Hazard. Since you came in here, I have detected a measure of hostility in your voice—No, please, spare me the denials." George reddened; he hadn't realized his feelings were so evident. "Your determination to leave is clear from the manner in which you negotiated for the transfer. General Halleck spoke to me personally over the weekend." Stanton removed his spectacles. "I have a feeling you don't like this entire department. Am I correct?"

"Sir—" Better to say nothing, get out and be done. He knew it, yet his nature and his conscience wouldn't settle for that. "With due respect, Mr. Secretary—yes, you are. I am not in accord with some of the policies of the War Department."

Coolly correct, Stanton put on his glasses again. "May I request that you be more specific, sir?"

"There is the Eamon Randolph matter—"

Stanton overrode him with a loud, "I know nothing about that."

"As I understand it, the man was beaten by members of your Detective Bureau, solely for criticizing policies of this administration—which I thought was every citizen's right."

"Not in time of war." Stanton's pursed smile grew cold. He leaned forward, and the light-play turned his lenses to glittering disks again. "May I add, Major, that if you had ever entertained hopes of a permanent career in the military, you would have dashed them by what you just said. You have overstepped."

"I'm sorry," George said, though he wasn't. "The matter's been on my conscience, and it's widely known that Lafayette Baker works for you."

Still the smile, deadly and sly. "Search every item of official correspondence—every scrap of paper in the waste bins of this department, my dear Major—you will find not one scintilla of evidence to support that statement. Now be so kind as to leave this office. I shall be happy to approve your request—you and that madman Haupt are cut from the same bolt."

"Sir—"

Stanton pounded the desk. "Get out."

George heard the door open behind him. Someone rushed in.

"Your brother is just leaving," the secretary said. George turned and saw Stanley hovering, pasty with alarm. "Kindly see that he does it with all due speed."

Stanley grabbed George's sleeve. "Come on."

"Stanley"—George's voice went down half an octave—"I knocked you down once a long time ago. Take your hand off or I'll do it again."

Blinking, his face oozing sweat, Stanley obeyed. *What an ass I am,* thought George. *An opinionated, loud-mouthed ass.* Yet it had given him a sense of pride and relief to say his little piece—which was not quite finished.

"If this government has to win the war by beating or imprisoning every dissident who utters the slightest criticism, God pity us. We deserve to fail."

Gently, so gently, Stanton riffled the underside of his beard. But he was livid. "Major Hazard," he said, "I suggest you remove yourself unless you wish to be court-martialed for sedition."

When the office door was closed, Stanley whispered, "Do you realize who you insulted?"

"Someone who deserves it."

"But do you appreciate how this can harm your career?"

"My so-called career's a farce. They can throw me out of the army tomorrow. I'll cheerfully go back to Lehigh Station and cast cannon."

"You could at least think of me, George—"

"I do," he retorted, still angry. "I hope Stanton roasts you for having a seditious relative. Then you can go to Massachusetts and sell military bootees—to both sides, as I understand it."

"You damned, lying—" Stanley began, trying at the same time to hit George with a wild swing. But Stanley was weak and poorly coordinated. George had only to raise his left hand to block his brother's forearm and push his fist away. He jammed his hat on his head and marched out of the building.

He hurried to Haupt's office, found him gone, and left a note.

Spoke with Secretary S. & ruined my army career. Plan to get drunk to celebrate. Transfer looks certain.   G.H.

86

The work train of two flatcars chugged southwest toward Manassas. The day had grown gray and heavy with the odor of rain.

Pine branches beside the track reached out to brush Billy's face. He sat on the side of one of the cars, legs dangling, carbine resting beside him. Under his shirt was a small copybook, in which he was currently keeping his journal. His dusty trousers partially concealed the legend U.S.M.R. NO. 19 painted in white on the edge of the car.

Against the shuttling rhythm of the slow-moving train, he thought of a number of things: Brett, whom he longed to sleep with for just one night; Lije, whose death seemed such a waste; the disturbing telegraphic news from New York, which they had heard just before pulling out. The city was braced for demonstrations and perhaps widespread rioting when the first names were drawn for the draft.

The engineers had taken part in the Gettysburg campaign, but scarcely in a capacity worth mentioning. They had built the usual Potomac pontoon bridges, then languished on their rumps as part of the headquarters contingent while the main army engaged. Now they were back here in Virginia, and Billy and six enlisted men had been dispatched down the Orange & Alexandria to survey a new spur line proposed near the Bull Run trestle. Guerrillas had recently destroyed the trestle for the sixth or seventh time.

A blond corporal lying on his back hummed "All Quiet Along the Potomac Tonight." Another took up the melody with a small mouth organ, his elbow resting on the lacquered case containing two transits. A third man rested his legs on the folded tripod.

Smoke flowed over the relaxed soldiers riding in the open. Soot and cinders peppered them, but that was the worst of it until the shots exploded. The first rang the locomotive's bell. A volley followed.

"Where the hell are they?" the blond corporal yelled, flopping onto his belly and grabbing his carbine. Billy likewise flattened himself. He heard the enemy before he saw them. They spurred into sight from behind the caboose, eight raggy men with long beards and wiry mounts. Four rode on each side of the train.

Although the train was in territory controlled by the Union, that control was nominal. Right now they were traveling through what was boastfully called Mosby's Confederacy. Were these some of the Gray Ghost's men, Billy wondered, flinging up his carbine. He fired and missed.

A ball tore into the edge of the flatcar where his legs had dangled moments before. A long splintery scar horizontally bisected the letters U.S.M.R. The ragtag attackers whooped and wailed their rebel yells, passing the caboose.

"Stay low, Johnson," Billy shouted as the blond soldier foolishly jumped up, braced his legs, and tried to aim while the flatcar swayed. The rider leading the others on Billy's side, a stick-thin man wearing a fusty black suit, bent to avoid a branch, then fired his revolver and blew Johnson off the other side of the car.

Billy went to one knee, hoping to steady himself that way. The fireman had clambered onto the tender. Holding on with one hand, he leaned out and fired a Colt with the other. Billy felt the train lurch as the engineer opened the throttle. A private picked off a guerrilla on the opposite side, which put an end to the grinning and whooping of the partisans.

The train gained speed. The sky darkened; rain began to patter the flatcar. The guerrillas came up to flank the car on which the engineers were riding. Billy pivoted to shoot toward the far side when something fastened on his arm, dragging him.

Dizzy with fright, he went spinning and tumbling off the car, pulled by the dark-suited man, who had ridden close enough to reach him. Billy struck the shoulder of the roadbed, gasping, the wind knocked out of him. In a daze, he watched the lantern and white numerals on the caboose shrinking.

Billy's carbine lay beside the near rail. Two of the partisans cantered up the center of the right of way. The retreating train slowed, the engineer worried about the men who had fallen off. The partisans fired several volleys at the train, which speeded up again.

On hands and knees, Billy reached for the carbine. "Touch that an' I'll kill you," said a cheerful voice. He raised his head, saw the frail, black-suited man. A huge dragoon pistol filled his right hand.

"We got two, countin' the captain here," Black Suit shouted, controlling his pawing horse. "Is that there one alive?"

"Naw, he's gone," someone called from back along the line. Billy grimaced; Johnson had been anticipating news of the birth of his second child in Albany at any moment.

In the pattering rain, the guerrillas plinked a few last rounds at the train, now no larger than a toy. How dark the morning had become, Billy thought, ringed by men on horseback.

"Gone for sure?" Black Suit asked the man riding up with Johnson's body. The blond volunteer lay over the neck of the horse, head and legs hanging down.

"Deader'n a pickaninny's brain."

"Any val'bles?"

"We can pry the gold out of his teeth, but that's about it."

"Hell," said Black Suit. "This 'pears to be the only real prize we got. Stand up, Yank. Gimme your name an' unit, so we can do a proper job fillin' out the burial papers."

Billy couldn't believe the man meant it. He couldn't believe this had happened—the swift attack, the accidental capture. But then, that was the lesson of war you so often forgot. The bullet that missed you—or killed you—did so by chance.

Rain dampening his hair, Billy stood at the side of the right of way, wondering if these men were who he feared they were. "Name an' unit," Black Suit repeated, testily now.

"Captain William Hazard. Battalion of Engineers, Army of the Potomac. Who are you?"

Snickers, amused whispers, then a bull voice: "He's smack in the middle of Fairfax County an' he's gotta ask who we are."

Ugly and fat, the deep-voiced man rode around where Billy could see him. "Major John S. Mosby's Partisan Rangers, duly authorized for independent action by the 'Federate Congress. That's who we are, you piece of Yankee shit." He swiped at Billy's head with the butt of his shotgun.

Angered, Billy grabbed for the butt. Black Suit reached down and yanked his hair. Billy yelped and let go. He smelled the unwashed men and took notice of their unclean clothes, pieces of cast-off uniforms—and he knew they weren't lying to him. John Mosby had scouted for Stuart for a time but had lately established himself as a guerrilla commander. He came and went by night, ripping up track, burning supply depots, sniping at pickets—all the more feared because he and his small band were seldom seen. Gray ghosts.

Who did not operate by the regular rules of war, Billy remembered with a heavy feeling in his middle. Black Suit gave him another hard shake by the hair and cocked his pistol.

"Hands on your head, boy."

"What?"

"I said lay both hands on top of your head. I want to make this quick."

"Make what quick?"

Jeering laughter. One of those laughing loudest said, "He's real dumb, ain't he?"

"Why, your military execution, Captain Hazard, sir," Black Suit said, with the thick juice of sarcasm in every word. "Now if that's all right with you, mebbe you'll 'low me to get on with the matter and be away to other, more pressing duties."

Disbelieving, Billy stared at the dark figure on horseback. The pines moaned, the wind raced through the boiling dark sky. Why didn't the train come back for him? They must have thought him slain, like Johnson—

"Hands on top of your head!" Black Suit said. "And turn away from me so's I can see your back."

"Under—" Billy struggled to keep his voice from cracking "—under the articles of War, I have the right to be treated as a prisoner and—"

"For Christ's sake, get done with it," another man said, and Billy knew it was all over. *Well, all right,* he thought. *All I can do is take my leave without breaking down in front of them.*

Genuinely angry, Black Suit said, "One last time, Yank—*put your hands where I told you.*"

Billy laid his left palm on his wet hair, his right on top of it. He was ashamed of closing his eyes, but he thought it would be easier to bear it that way. The summer shower pattered in the pines and then, along the track to the north he heard another sound above the snort of horses, the jingle of metal, the creak of harness. A sound he couldn't identify—as if it mattered one damn bit.

Black Suit saluted him with the dragoon pistol. "So long, Captain Engineer. *Sir.*"

"Oh, that's rich. You're a fuckin' sketch." Bull Voice laughed as Billy tightened inside, waiting for the bullet.

At that same moment, a middle-aged man with a bald head and a face that still possessed a certain cherubic aspect, stormed a breastwork. Those storming it with him, howling for blood, were not soldiers, but civilians; about a third were women.

Instead of shoulder and side arms, they attacked with bottles, bricks, sticks, furniture legs looted from wealthy homes, and in the case of the bald man, a wide black belt he had removed from pants of a volunteer fireman knocked unconscious by another rioter. Using the belt like a flail, Salem Jones had already opened the face of one of Mayor Opdyke's policemen with the big brass buckle.

Black smoke rolled over the rooftops of Manhattan. The streets were a silvery sea of glass. The breastwork—overturned carts, hacks, and wagons—stretched across Broadway from curb to curb just below Forty-third Street. Broadway, like most of the main arteries in this city of eight hundred thousand, had been contested since midmorning and held by the rioters since shortly after noon. On Third Avenue, no street-railway cars were moving anywhere from Park Row to One Hundred and Third. Cannon had been placed around City Hall and Police Headquarters on Mulberry. The mob storming the breastwork had just come from torching the Colored Orphan Asylum on Fifth Avenue, where the self-appointed leaders had decided to evacuate the children only moments before lighting the fires.

Salem Jones was not the first to clamber over the wagons to attack a dozen outnumbered police, but neither was he the last. The police scattered and ran. Jones threw a brick, which struck one of the officers in the back of the head. After the man fell, Jones scrambled out from behind a cartwheel that had briefly shielded him. He snatched the policeman's thick locust stick from his limp hand. He hadn't owned a good truncheon since his days as an overseer at Mont Royal. He felt whole again.

Some rioters ran into a restaurant and reappeared with two Negro waiters. A roar went up. A couple of policemen fired futile shots from the next corner, but that did nothing to deter the crowd. Some produced ropes. Others were shinnying up telegraph poles. Within two minutes, both waiters hung from crossarms, turning, turning slowly in the smoke.

The sight brought a smile to Jones's round face. He had been in New York only ten days, drifting there as he had drifted to so many other places after that damned Orry Main had discharged him. He had found a hovel in Mackerelville where he could sleep for nothing, and in grubby Second Avenue saloons he had listened to angry men thrown out of work by a recent dock strike. One of the most effective, a longshoreman by day and a mackerel with three girls working for him at night, had bellowed his grievances at a crowd that included Salem Jones.

All they wanted on the docks was a raise to twenty-five cents an hour for the nine-hour day. Was that too much to ask? The listeners screamed, "No!" and thumped their tin pails on tables and chairs. But what did the bosses do? Locked out the white men and brought in vans of niggers. Was that right? *"No!"*

The following Monday, the draft was to begin dragging these same whites into the army as cannon fodder—hard-working men who couldn't pay three hundred dollars to exempt themselves or hire a substitute. "We have to go to war for the coons, while they stay here and take our jobs, and bust into our houses, and molest our women. Are we going to let the draft people and the coons get away with that?"

"NO! NO! NO!"

Listening to the screaming, Jones could have told the witless police there would be hell to pay on this Monday morning. He had decided to join the fun.

The longshoreman who had exhorted the saloon crowd was one of the organizers of a mammoth parade, which had started early. Carrying banners and placards proclaiming NO DRAFT!, some ten thousand protestors marched up Sixth Avenue to Central Park. There, speeches had incited the mob to less restrained forms of protest. One of the orators, Jones noted, had a pronounced Southern accent. An agent sent to stir things up?

After the rally, the great crowd had divided into smaller ones. Jones ran with rioters who threw glass jars of sulphurous-smelling Greek fire through the windows of mansions on Lexington. He next joined a band that invaded an office where draft names were supposed to be drawn. They found nothing except furniture to

670

wreck; the officials were conveniently absent. Then he was swept into the crowd at the Orphan Asylum, which was now burning briskly. From Broadway, he could glimpse the flames above the intervening buildings.

Around him Jones saw few evidences of anger. After the breastworks were stormed and the waiters hanged, the mob turned sportive. Celebrants swigged from all kinds of bottles. A drunken man snagged the hand of an unkempt woman, equally tipsy, pushed her into the doorway of an abandoned pawnshop, unbuttoned his pants and displayed his stiff member while spectators, including the woman, applauded and whistled. Soon the man was down on her, bouncing busily. The onlookers stayed a short time, but grew bored and went hunting other diversions.

Never much of a drinker, Jones needed no alcohol to stimulate him. He ran with the crowd down Broadway, then toward the East River. A group of them dashed into a tea shop to overturn chairs and tables, hurl cups and pots at the walls, and generally terrify the customers. On the way out he broke a front window with the stolen truncheon.

Near the river, under black smoke-clouds roiling through the hazy white sky, they collided with a herd of milling cows, pushed on through it and discovered the two cowherds, black boys, cowering on a patch of grass down by the water. The boys were fourteen or fifteen. Jones helped lift one and fling him in the river. Others threw in the second one.

"Hep us, hep us! We can't swim—"

Laughter answered the plea, laughter and rocks thrown by the whites. Jones threw one, reached for a second, imagining he was hurling them at that damned, arrogant Orry Main, who had discovered so-called irregularities in the Mont Royal accounts and retaliated by discharging him. Born in New England, Jones had always favored the South because he loathed colored people. But the snobs along the Ashley, and especially the Mains, had given him another target for his hate.

Jones threw another rock, watched with pleasure as it struck one of the gasping cowherds square in the forehead. A minute later the boy sank beneath the water, followed shortly by the second. Laughing, the people around Jones complained that the fun hadn't lasted long enough.

An hour later, he found himself in another saloon in Mackerelville, listening to still another scruffy fellow harangue a crowd.

"We hain't gone where we really should go—over to the Eighth Ward. Over to Sullivan an' Clarkson an' Thompson streets. Over there we can tree some coons right where they live."

Fortified by free beer the owner was serving—his way of demonstrating dislike of the draft—Jones thrust his locust stick in his belt and joined the marchers, who defiantly sang "Dixie" at the top of their lungs as they tramped west.

Arms linked with strangers on either side of him, Jones reflected that he personally liked the conscription law—a sentiment he wouldn't have expressed here, naturally. He liked it because certain states were already paying handsome bounties to men who would enlist and help fill draft quotas. Though he was beyond the age for service, Jones nevertheless believed he could dye his fringe of white hair, lie about the date of his birth, and earn some of that bonus money. Something to think about, anyway—but not till this party was over.

The mob, grown to around one hundred and fifty, brushed with a squad of soldiers, many of whom wore head or arm bandages; the city had even turned out the Invalid Corps for the emergency. The mob easily scattered the invalids and marched on through the glass glitter. The day darkened more rapidly than usual. Heavy smoke, lurid red from all the fires, pressed down on the rooftops. Fire bells tolled from every quarter as the crowd surged into Clarkson Street, a lane of tenements and shacks built from packing boxes.

"Where are they? Where are the niggers?" people shouted. Except for two little girls playing beside an immense garbage heap where fat rats scampered, no human beings could be seen. Jones scanned the tenements. Broken windows, open windows—all were empty.

Some of the rioters vanished behind the packing-box shanties and began tipping outhouses. Most of the whites wanted better sport; they converged on the garbage heap. The rats and the little girls fled. Suddenly Jones spied a head in a third-floor window. "There's one!"

The head vanished. Jones led a party of ten up through the fetid building, kicking open doors in the search. They discovered a young Negro couple and an infant lying on a pallet. A smiling white woman picked up the child, rocked it back and forth a few times, then stepped to the open window, leaned out, and dropped it.

The mother screamed. Jones bashed her head with the truncheon. Outside, in the reddening light of the burning city, they carried the husband and wife to a stunted tree near the garbage heap. Ropes went up, and the two were quickly tied so they hung by their wrists. A shrieking white woman rushed forward with a butcher knife, but a man held her back.

"Don't use that. I found some kerosene."

He doused it on both Negroes; kerosene dripped on the hard-packed ground. Jones shivered, pleasurably imagining the buck was Orry Main. The husband pleaded for the mob to spare his dazed, bleeding wife. That only generated more jeers and jokes. Someone struck a match, tossed it, jumped back—

The fireball erupted with a roar. A smile spread over Jones's cherubic face as he watched the victims burn.

Horsemen. That was the sound he heard. Horsemen cantering through the pines beside the rail line. Hands on top of his head, Billy opened his eyes.

Six men, two in uniform, reined up around the others. The one to whom Black Suit and the rest immediately deferred was a slight, slender officer with sandy yellow hair showing under a hat with an ostrich plume. The man's gray cape, tossed back over both shoulders, displayed a bright red lining. The officer was about thirty. His clean-shaven face looked stern but not unkind. He seemed more interested in Black Suit than in Billy.

"What is happening here?"

"We pulled this Yank off'n a work train that went by a while ago, sir. We were preparing—" Black Suit swallowed, nervously eyeing his comrades.

"To execute the prisoner?" the officer prompted, quieting his dancing horse with a few quick pats.

Black Suit flushed, said faintly, "Yes, sir."

"That is against the rules of civilized warfare, and you know it. No matter what calumnies the Yankee newspapers print about us, we do not engage in murder. You will pay a penalty for this."

Frightened now, Black Suit hastily holstered his dragoon pistol. Billy's heartbeat slowed. "Lower your hands," the officer said to him. Billy obeyed. "Give me your name and unit, please."

"Captain William Hazard, Battalion of Engineers, Army of the Potomac."

"Well, Captain, you are the prisoner of the Partisan Rangers."

Billy caught his breath. "Are you—?"

Gauntlet touched hat brim. "Major John Mosby. At your service." He suppressed a smile. "Pulled you off a train, did they? Well, at least you're in one piece. I will make arrangements to have you transported to the Richmond prison for Union officers."

Mosby's unexpected arrival had left Billy elated and befuddled —so thankful he hadn't stopped to think of the consequences of a reprieve. Prison was better than death, but not much; paroles were becoming fewer as the bitterness of the war intensified.

He should have recognized Mosby at once; after Stuart's, his plume was the most famous in the Confederacy. Mosby addressed the other man in uniform, a sergeant. "See that he's fed and not mistreated. We must move on to—"

"Major?"

Annoyed, Mosby glanced at Billy. "What is it?"

"One of my men was shot to death just before I was captured. He's lying up there in the weeds. Might I ask that he be given a Christian burial?"

"Why, yes, certainly." A hard look at Black Suit. "You're in charge. See that you do it properly."

There was no complaint from Black Suit, not even a flicker of resentment in his eyes as Mosby and his party resumed their canter through the woods. One of their number had been left behind to take charge of the prisoner. While that trooper was loosening the saddle girth to rest his horse, Black Suit managed to whisper to Billy.

"You're going to Libby Prison. When you see how they treat Yankee boys there, you'll wish to God I'd pulled that trigger. You'll wish I'd killed you. Just wait."

87

August infected Richmond with soaring temperatures and humidity, with dusty leaves and still air awaiting a great relieving storm that muttered northwest of the Potomac but never seemed to march farther, and with a pervading despair that followed two realizations: the Mississippi was lost; and Gettysburg had not been the quasi-triumph the high command at first pretended it was. One clear signal was the state of the trade in illegal currency. A Yankee greenback dollar, of which there were thousands in circulation, cost two Confederate dollars before the debacle in Pennsylvania. Now it cost four.

Vicksburg spilled thousands of new captives into the already overcrowded camps and warehouse prisons. Gettysburg sent thousands of new wounded to the overtaxed hospitals. Huntoon absorbed this marginally as he scratched away at work he no longer cared about. Memminger had assigned him the odious task of preparing lists of those business establishments, nearly numberless, engaged in printing and distributing illegal shinplasters.

The Confederacy had no silver for small coins, so the Treasury had authorized states, cities, and selected railroads to issue paper, in denominations from five to fifty cents, for change-making. But hundreds of other businesses took up the idea, and the Confederacy was now suffering a plague of shinplasters more numerous than Biblical frogs and locusts. Huntoon wrote list after list— grogshops, greengrocers, taprooms, short-line railroads. This morning he was copying out names provided by Treasury informants in Florida and Mississippi—hateful work onto which his sweat fell as he hunched over it, blotting it like tears.

What this government did no longer mattered to him. But a new Confederacy—that was tantalizing, that mesmerized him. He lay awake nights thinking about it. Spent long periods daydreaming about it at his desk, until some superior reprimanded him. Finally, one hot noontime, he startled his drone colleagues by seizing his hat and dashing from the office, a kind of crazed exaltation on his face.

He had already made inquiries in saloons. Most barkeeps were well acquainted with Powell, and Huntoon soon learned the Georgian's address. He refused to ask Ashton, for fear she would reveal that she knew it.

Huntoon wanted to put some additional questions to Powell. He needed more details, yet at the same time didn't want to risk offending. So he had delayed a while. Finally, however, his agitated state drove him out of the office that broiling noonday and into a hack.

"Church Hill," he called through the roof slot, rapping with his stick for emphasis. "Corner of Twenty-fourth and Franklin."

Leaves coated with dust hung motionless over the brick wall. Excited, Huntoon lumbered up the steps and knocked. A minute later he knocked again. At last, the door opened.

"Powell, I've decided—"

"What in hell are you doing here?" Powell demanded, giving a yank to tighten the belt of his emerald velvet dressing gown. The vee of flesh showing between his lapels was glittery with sweat.

St. John's Church began to ring the half-hour. Queasy, Huntoon felt that the bell was sounding a knell for his opportunity. "I didn't mean to interrupt—"

"But you have. I'm extremely busy."

Huntoon blinked, overcome with fright. "Please accept my aplogy. I came only because you said you wanted my decision promptly. I made it this morning." A swift look down the street. Then he thought he heard some unseen person stirring behind the door.

"All right, tell me."

"I—I want to join, if you'll have me."

Some of the wrath left Powell's face. "Of course. That's excellent news."

"May we talk about particulars of when and how—?"

"Not now. I'll be in touch." Then, seeing Huntoon react unfavorably to his curtness, Powell smiled. "Very soon. I would be pleased to do it today, but unfortunately I have many other affairs that demand attention. I'm very glad you're with us, James. We need a man of courage and vision in the new Treasury. You'll hear from me in a day or two, I promise."

He closed the door. Huntoon was left in the heat, his heavy coat binding his fat body and his feelings hurt. Of course he had called without an appointment, and Southerners resented such discourtesies. He had no right to harbor resentment, though he did wonder what private matter required Powell to wear a dressing gown in the middle of the day. Huntoon had a suspicion too painful to entertain for very long.

As he went in search of a hack to return him to Capitol Square, he did an emotional turnabout. Powell became the injured party, he the offending one. His mind executed the reversal because he needed to feel himself genuinely a part of Lamar Powell's plan.

And what he wanted most of all was to tell his wife of his brave decision.

"Near thing," Powell said in the foyer, slipping out of the hot velvet robe and hooking it over his shoulder by one finger. It was the closest he had come in many a year to being surprised by a cuckolded husband, and it showed in the tightness of his features. Huntoon waddled away up the sidewalk, and Ashton, buck naked, uncovered her mouth and succumbed to the laughter she had struggled to control while she was hidden behind the door.

"You nearly gave us away."

"But—I had to listen, Lamar." She laughed so hard tears came. "It was—so delicious—my husband on one side of the door—my lover on the other—." She held her sides; her breasts shook.

"I didn't hear you sneak down here while I was answering the door. Seeing you damn near gave me a seizure." He clamped her chin in his left hand and lifted it swiftly, roughly. "Don't ever do such a thing again."

Smile fading: "No, no—I'm sorry—I won't. But I'm elated that he said yes. He's been pondering the decision for days. He hasn't said a word to me, but I could tell it's been on his mind." She took hold of his arm. "You're pleased, aren't you? Now we have him where we can watch him."

"And we don't want him to change his mind. So you must allay any lingering doubts he may have. Make him very proud of his decision by rewarding him." He squeezed her chin; a spasm at the corners of her mouth showed there was pain. "Do you understand, my dear?"

"Yes. Yes. I'll do whatever you say."

"As always." He let go of her. The imprint of his fingers faded. Smiling, he gave her cheek a brief, paternal kiss. "That's why I love you."

That evening, after dismissing the servants and closing the dining-room doors, Huntoon cleared his throat in a way that signaled a pronouncement. Except for a slight scarring of the wallpaper, the room showed no evidence of Cooper's visit. New legs had been installed on the table; new jasperware filled the repaired cabinet.

She felt she must be simpering as she said, "James, what is it? You're so excited—"

"With good reason. Recently I've had some—private conversations with Mr. Lamar Powell—" He pushed aside the tureen of steaming fish bisque, jumped up. "Oh, I can't sit—" He rushed to her end of the table. "He approached me with the most astonishing scheme, Ashton—a proposal I have accepted because I feel it's my patriotic duty, because I believe it's morally right, and also because I think it will work to our very great benefit."

"Dear me," she murmured, trying for precisely the right blend of surprise and reservation. "Does he want money for another vessel?"

"God, no, nothing so mundane. I will tell you what it is, but you must prepare yourself. Open your mind. Not hesitate to think, well, daringly. Unconventionally. Sweetheart—Mr. Powell and some associates I have not met as yet intend to establish—" he gripped her arm, bent down beside her chair "—a new Confederate state."

"What?"

"Please don't raise your voice. You heard me correctly. A new Confederacy. Let me tell you about it."

Giggling inside, Ashton frowned as he pulled a chair from the corner and sat beside her. He fondled her hand, explaining, revealing, persuading while she fluttered her eyelashes to simulate astonishment, pressed a hand to her breast, and at appropriate intervals gasped. Altogether, in her own estimation, she gave a

678

splendid performance—up to and including the dramatic rush of her palm to her open mouth when he first said the word *assassination.*

He took half an hour to pour it all out. The fish bisque had congealed by the time he asked, "Now tell me—did I act improperly? I've withheld none of the facts, including my strong desire to join Powell's group. I want to be his new secretary of the treasury, and I believe that's possible. The Southwest is a long way from our home state, but think of the rewards when we establish a new government. We'll command the attention—the respect—of the entire world."

"I am thinking of that. It's just a trifle—well—overwhelming."

"But you aren't furious with me?"

"James—James!" She began to press little kisses on his flabby face. "Of course not. I'm thrilled by your vision—proud of your courage—gratified to see you exhibit such intelligence and initiative. I've always known you had both qualities, but I also know that working in Richmond has been a miserable, frustrating experience. I'm so happy to learn it hasn't robbed you of your ambition—"

"The principal reason for my ambition is you, Ashton. I want you to be one of the most important women in the new Confederacy."

"Oh, darling—" Steeling herself, she squeezed his slippery face between her palms, kissed him, and pushed her tongue into his mouth. He uttered a groan as she dropped her hand to his right thigh. "I'm so proud of you."

Someone knocked softly—the kitchen, wondering about the overly long soup course. Ashton smoothed her gown, glanced into Huntoon's calf eyes—she knew what was inevitable tonight—and trilled, "Come in, Della."

Huntoon returned to his place. But they had scarcely finished their cups of tasteless fruit ice when he was at her side again, pawing her dress and begging her to go to the bedroom. She pretended to be as breathless as he was, meekly offering her hand for him to lead her.

Undressed, she cooed over his body and manipulated him to a mammoth erection—that was something new, anyway; she couldn't wait to tell Lamar.

North of Richmond was a wayside inn whose faded paint had given the hamlet of Yellow Tavern its name. Some half a mile farther on, at the end of a deserted lane running west from Telegraph Road, rose a large grove of trees. Light from a heat-hazed moon fell all around the grove, illuminating the landscape dimly. But under the trees, where two men talked, neither could see the other.

Over soft sounds of horses moving restlessly, one said, "I must tell you for the good of all of us that you've spoken too freely, too often. They say even that damned Lafayette Baker's heard about us."

"Well, so be it. Men from my state make no secret of their convictions. Governor Brown doesn't, and neither do I."

"But you've drawn attention to yourself. Therefore maybe to the rest of us."

"Oh, I doubt that one more tale of conspiracy will be given much credence—there are so many. Besides, I've no other way to recruit men with the right sort of nerve. I can only put out a baited line and wait. It worked with you."

Grudgingly: "True."

"Are we in any immediate danger?"

"I don't think so. Davis heard some of the talk and sent a letter ordering the general to investigate. I volunteered for the assignment—patriotic zeal, loathing for traitors—the usual claptrap."

"Clever of you. Now you can block the inquiry?"

"Slow it down," the other corrected. "We don't have as much time as we did before."

"We'll move faster. Within a few months, Jeff Davis will be dead and gone."

"If he isn't, the rest of us will be."

"And we'll be enjoying the sunshine and free air of the Southwest. Meanwhile—I deeply appreciate the warning."

"I know it's a long ride out here, but it's the safest spot I could think of, and I thought you'd want to know."

"Absolutely. My thanks. I'll be in touch."

They clasped hands, bid each other good night, and turned their horses in opposite directions. Wan moonlight brushed the face of Lamar Powell as he cantered from one side of the grove and the benign features of the agent of the provost marshal, Israel Quincy, on the other.

680

88

LIBBY & SON
Ship Chandlers & Grocers

Prodded out of the covered wagon at musket point, Billy saw the sign that had identified the block-square structure when it was a warehouse instead of a prison. Some three dozen officers climbed from Billy's wagon and the two behind. Like the others, Billy was exhausted, hungry, and, above all, nervous.

To reach Libby Prison, the wagons had passed through a neighborhood of commercial buildings and vacant lots. Approaching, Billy first noticed the uniformed guards posted at intervals around the brick building.

The prison looked harsh in the morning light. The wagons had parked on the lower side, where the building was four stories high. On the opposite side, at the top of the sloping street, it was three. The warning said to be carved above one of its doors was known throughout the Union Army: *Abandon all hope who enter here.*

"Form up, form up in single file," a bored sergeant said, pushing some of the prisoners, gigging others with his musket. Most of the captives were quietly resolute about their predicament. Inevitably, one or two had insisted on cracking jokes during the ride to Richmond in a filthy freight car. But once the train arrived in the enemy capital, the jokes stopped. In the entire lot, only one prisoner, a portly captain of artillery two or three years older than

681

Billy, seemed genuinely broken by the experience; his eyes were moist as he took his place in line.

"Look there," an officer said, pointing to a barge pulling away from a pier not far from the prison. All the open space on deck was filled by emaciated men in dirty blue uniforms. On the roof of the deckhouse, a white cloth hung from a staff. The barge was headed downriver.

Noticing the prisoners watching, a guard said, "Flag-of-truce boat. Just took a load of you boys out of this yere building for exchange. Not many of them boats leavin' these days. Be a long time 'fore any of you take the trip. Now march."

As they passed through a doorway, Billy searched for the famous inscription and didn't see it; but Libby had many entrances. They shuffled up creaking stairs. Men began to cough because of the odors: fish, tobacco, something acrid.

"What the hell's that stink?"

The prisoner was answered by a sarcastic guard. "Burnin' tar. You Yanks smell so putrid, we got to fumigate the place reg'lar."

Shuffling in line, trying to remember Brett, remember all his many reasons for clinging to hope, Billy reached a large, unfurnished room with high slot windows that admitted only a little daylight. There a private interrogated each prisoner, inscribing name, rank, and unit into a copybook. Then he turned them over to a corporal who stood beneath a window, hands locked behind his back in the rest position. The sight of the stiff-backed noncom made Billy's gut quiver.

"Line up—eight men to a rank—starting here."

The corporal was a boy, pink-faced, wholesome-looking, with blond curls and eyes as brilliant as an October sky. When the prisoners had formed their ranks—Billy was in the second one—the corporal strode to a spot in front of them.

"I am Corporal Clyde Vesey, charged with welcoming you gentlemen to Libby Prison, of whose hospitality you have no doubt heard. You will now strip to the skin so Private Murch and I may conduct a search for money and any other illegal material you may be carrying."

Shirts came off, trousers dropped; dirty hands worked the buttons on sweaty suits of underwear. There were no complaints; guards on the prison train had warned them about a search, saying that whether they were allowed to keep money or personal items frequently depended on the mood of the soldiers doing the searching. Seeing Vesey's blue eyes and listening to his speech, Billy was not encouraged.

"Open your mouth," Vesey snapped to a major in the front row. The major objected. Vesey backhanded his face twice, hard. Two places to the left, the fat artillery captain let out an audible cry of dismay.

"Open," Vesey repeated. The furious major obeyed. Vesey reached in and withdrew a small paper tube, spittle-covered, from its hiding place next to the upper gum. Vesey unrolled the ten-dollar note, wiped it on his blouse, tucked it away and moved on.

When he reached the artilleryman, Vesey smiled, sensing his weakness. After a routine search of mouth and armpits, he stepped back. "Turn around and spread your backside."

"W—what? See here. That isn't decent or—"

Vesey smiled a sweet smile, interrupting. "You have nothing to say about what's decent or indecent in Libby Prison. Such decisions are in the hands of the warden, Lieutenant Turner, and those of us privileged to serve him." His hand flew up, seizing the captain's ear and twisting. The artilleryman shrieked like a girl.

Vesey smiled. "Turn around and grab your backside and spread it."

Enraged looks passed between some of the prisoners, Billy being one of them. Red-faced, the artilleryman turned to face the rank behind him and reached for his buttocks. Billy recalled he had heard about the warden of Libby—a martinet who had resigned from the Academy in his plebe year, just before Sumter fell.

Vesey let the artilleryman stand in that embarrassing position for fifteen seconds—twenty—thirty. The captain began to shake from strain. Vesey reached around and slapped the side of his face. The captain squealed and fell forward. Men in the next rank pushed him back. The captain started to cry. Billy took a half-step forward.

Vesey said to him: "Oh, I wouldn't interfere. It'll go hard with you later."

Billy hesitated, then stepped back to his place. The search went on. Billy's mouth grew dry as the corporal moved along the second row. He bent to rummage through the clothing piled beside Billy's bare feet.

"What's this?" Vesey said, pleased. From Billy's jacket he pulled the copybook.

"That's my journal," Billy said. "It's personal."

Vesey stood and slowly waved the copybook an inch from Billy's nose. "Nothing is personal in Libby unless we declare it so. This is a book. Regular churchgoing has taught me to distrust books, especially novels, and all those who read them. It's my Christian duty not merely to hold you men as prisoners, but to reform your errant ways. 'I will take you from among the heathen,' says the prophet Ezekiel. That's just what you Yankees are, heathen. Here's a fine example. You will just have to get along without your godless books."

He's mad, Billy thought, filled with dread. "Murch?" Vesey flung the copybook to the other soldier, who caught and pocketed it. After a fleeting smile at Billy, Vesey stepped to the next man.

The search continued. Billy's legs started to ache. Finally Vesey finished and returned to the front, hands locked at the small of his back again. At last we can get out of here and sit down, Billy thought.

"It is now my duty and privilege to give you gentlemen some moral instruction." Vesey spread his feet, planting them solidly. One officer swore. Vesey glared. The artilleryman was still weeping softly. "The instruction concerns your status in this prison. As I said to the man with the concealed copybook, we don't consider you merely enemies; we consider you heathen. You—" he lunged forward suddenly, grabbing the fat artilleryman by the hair "—pay attention when I speak." He twisted the hair. The captain's flabby white breasts shook as he struggled to control his sobbing. Breathing loudly through his open mouth, Vesey stepped back, his clean pink face stiff with anger.

"Each of you mark this well. You are no longer officers. You are no longer gentlemen. Your status here is that of a nigger. No, I'm too generous. You are lower than niggers, and you will learn to feel that—sleep and eat that—breathe that every minute you are in my care. Now—"

A long inhalation. Then he smiled.

"Show me that you understand what I just told you. Show me what you are. Get down on your knees."

"What the hell—?" Billy growled. Behind him, another officer said, "You fucking reb ape—"

"Murch?" Vesey gestured. Using his side arm, the private hit the outspoken officer in the back of the head. The man staggered. A second blow laid him on his side, barely conscious.

Vesey smiled again. "I said," he murmured, "kneel down. Heathen niggers. Kneel—*down.*"

The artillery captain dropped first, panting. Someone cursed him. Vesey dashed to the third row and hit the offender, then seized his shoulder and forced him to his knees. Anxious looks flashed between the prisoners, tired men who wanted to save themselves from this lunatic. Slowly, one by one, they knelt, until just three naked officers remained standing. Vesey studied the trio and walked to the nearest—Billy.

"Kneel down," Vesey purred, smiling broadly and fixing him with those October eyes.

Heart hammering, Billy said, "I demand that this group of prisoners be treated according to the rules of war. The rules your superior surely understands even if you do no—"

He saw the hand flying toward his face, tried to jerk aside but was slowed by his fatigue. The open-handed blow hurt more than he anticipated. He lurched sideways, almost fell.

"I told you before. There are no rules here but the ones I make. Get down."

He dug immaculate fingernails into Billy's bare shoulder. "Jesus," Billy said, tears in his eyes. Vesey's nails broke skin; blood oozed as he dug deeper.

"Now you blaspheme. *Get down!*"

Wanting to stay on his feet, Billy felt his legs giving out. His head began to vibrate like some faulty part in a machine. He clenched his teeth, resisting the steady downward pressure—

Unexpectedly, Vesey pulled. The shift unbalanced Billy, and he tumbled over, knees whacking the floor, bare palms skidding along it; a long splinter drove into his right hand.

He raised his head and saw the corporal turn away. "Murch?"

"Sir?"

"What's his name?"

"Hazard. William Hazard. Engineers."

"Thank you. I want to be certain to remember that," Vesey said through lips so tight with rage they had lost all color.

His eyes shifted to the two other officers still standing. First one, then the other, knelt down. "Good," Vesey said.

Billy scrambled up on his haunches. Blood leaked along his forearm from the wounds left by Vesey's nails. He watched the bright October eyes return to him again, marking him.

That day, just at five, the wind strengthened, the sky blackened, the heat broke under an assault of raging rain, pelting hail, thunder loud as massed field guns. Orry started across the capitol rotunda as the storm burst, and, with no gas jets lit as yet, found himself in near-darkness. He blundered into another officer, stepped back, astonished.

"George? I didn't know you were in Richmond."

"Yes," said his old friend Pickett in a peculiar, detached voice. Pickett's long hair was uncombed, his eyes ringed by shadows. "Yes, for a while—I'm temporarily detached. Good to see you. We must get together," he said over his shoulder as he hurried into the dark. Thunder tremors vibrated the marble floor.

He didn't recognize me. What's wrong with him?

But Orry thought he knew. He had heard the stories. Once so courtly and light-hearted, Pickett had gone up Cemetery Hill, leading his boys to a slaughter. He had come down a ruined and a haunted man. Orry stood motionless in the center of the rotunda. The whole building shook, as if the elements wanted to tear it apart.

On the same day, in Washington, George received a bedraggled envelope forwarded by means of a three-cent stamp added at Lehigh Station. So far as he could tell, the envelope bore no other franking. Curious. He opened it, unfolded the letter, saw the signature, and whooped.

Not only was Orry in Richmond, he was with Madeline, who was now his wife. George shook his head in amazement as he read on through the letter obviously sent to Pennsylvania by illegal courier. Fate had ironically shunted the two friends along similar paths. Like George, he could barely tolerate most of his war department duties.

In spite of the letter's tone of melancholy, it brought a smile whenever George read it. And he read it, aloud to Constance and silently to himself, many times before he put it away with his permanent keepsakes.

None of the drinkers in the hotel bar laughed; few raised their voices above a mutter. What was there to be cheerful about? Not even the weather. The heat wave had broken, but relief had come with a storm so fierce it sounded as if it might level all of Richmond.

Trying to shut out the voices of discontent all around him, Lamar Powell worked on a draft of a letter to the foreman of the Mexican Mine. He had chosen a table in a back corner for privacy and was writing to advise the mine foreman that sometime within the next twelve months he would personally appear at the site to take charge.

When he was satisfied with the wording, he began to consider ways to get the letter out of the Confederacy. He distrusted the illegal mail couriers who operated between here and Washington; they were a duplicitous lot, sometimes dumping a pouch of letters into some gully or creek and disappearing with their meager profits. Still, they represented the fastest and most direct means of sending mail across enemy lines. Perhaps he should use a courier but send a copy of the letter by another route. To Bermuda, via Wilmington. That way—

A fraction late, he heard the wet boots squeaking. He quickly folded the draft and glanced at the man whose shadow had fallen on the table. The man was fat, huge, his fusty suit large as a tent. He had dark hair, sly eyes, a conspiratorial air. He licked his lips.

"Have I the honor of addressing Mr. Lamar Powell?"

Powell wished that he had brought his four-barrel Sharps tonight. Could this gross fellow be some spy of Winder's on the prowl for critics of the President?

"What do you want?" Powell retorted.

Put off by the nonanswer, the stranger cleared his throat. "You were pointed out as Mr. Powell. I've been searching for you for several days. I am interested in, ah, certain of your plans. May I sit down and explain? Oh, forgive me—my name is Captain Bellingham."

That night, Bent celebrated by drinking himself into a stupor in his rooming house. Mr. Lamar Powell was shrewd. He had not uttered so much as a syllable to confirm his part in any conspiracy against the government, nor indeed given the slightest indication that such a conspiracy existed. Yet by glance and inflection and gesture, he left no doubt. He was involved, and he could use trustworthy recruits—especially a Maryland-born Southern sympathizer lately wounded in service with General Longstreet.

Not only had it been necessary for Bent to tell those lies, but he had been required to state some fundamental beliefs—extremely risky, but vital if he was to convince Powell of his sincerity. He

687

said he hated to see the South misruled, the war lost, the great principles sullied by King Jeff the First. He wanted the dictator removed, if not by the ballot, then by other means.

Powell had listened, then made a small concession. After further reflection on the captain's story, he would be in touch at the address the captain had provided, if—*if*—there was any reason for contact. He didn't state that there would be, but his manner clearly suggested it.

Powell questioned him hard as to how and where he had heard Powell's name. Bent refused to answer. Being stubborn on that point was a risk, of course. Yet if Powell deemed him too pliable, he might not want his services. So Bent dug in and repeatedly said no, he could reveal nothing about his sources.

He left Powell in the hotel bar, got drunk in his rooming house, and settled down to wait. A week, a month—whatever it took. Meantime, he had another little scheme to occupy him now that he was in the same city as Orry Main. Bent's presence was unknown to him. He could take him by surprise.

Ashton left the house on Grace Street at half past six the next evening. The air felt sharply cooler, though ugly black clouds continued to roll out of the northwest. The storm weather had persisted a long time, but the relief was welcome.

Tugging on her gloves, she hurried down the long front stoop. She was so busy anticipating her evening with Powell that she failed to see the man half concealed behind one of the large brick pillars at the foot of the steps. He hurled himself in front of her.

"Mrs. Huntoon?"

"How dare you startle me that—oh!" She clutched her hat in the stiff wind, recognizing him: a huge heap of dark broadcloth, a fat face beneath a broad-brimmed hat. He had called on her once before, though his name eluded her. He carried an oilskin tube under his arm.

"Excuse me, I didn't mean to frighten you," he said, darting looks at the house. "Is there some spot close by where we might hold a private conversation?"

"Your name again?"

"Captain Erasmus Bellingham."

"That's right. General Longstreet's corps."

"The Invalid Corps now, I'm afraid," Bent replied with his most soulful expression. "I am out of the army."

"When you called the first time, you said you were a friend of my brother's."

"If I left that impression, I regret it. I am not a friend, merely an acquaintance. On that occasion you stated that your feelings toward Colonel Main were—may we say—less than cordial? That is why I came back tonight—my first opportunity to do so since my release from Chimborazo Hospital."

"Captain, I am on my way somewhere, and I'm late. Come to the point."

Tap-tap went his fingers, plump white sausages, on the oilskin tube. "I have a painting here. I should like to show it to you, that's all. I am not trying to sell it, Mrs. Huntoon—I wouldn't part with it. But I think you will find it of great interest all the same."

That same evening, Charles reached Barclay's Farm. He had invited Jim Pickles to come along, explaining en route that he was romantically involved with the widow Barclay. Jim whooped and hollered and waved his hat, which now had a turkey feather stuck in the band; he was imitating Stuart but couldn't find an ostrich plume. Jim thought what Charles had said was fine news, though, curiously, Charles silently questioned his own good sense even as he related how he felt.

Gus hugged and kissed him warmly, and when she went out to supervise the killing of two hens for supper, Jim nudged his fellow scout. "You're a lucky gent, Charlie. She's a dandy." Charles continued to puff his cob pipe in silence and toast his bare feet at the kitchen hearth; the rain through which they had ridden was hard and cold.

Supper was cheerful and boisterous for a while. But talk of the war couldn't be avoided. Everyone expected a new siege of Charleston to begin soon. In the West, Bragg was being pressed by Rosecrans. Brave Morgan, after a twenty-five-day mounted raid through Kentucky and Indiana, had been captured at Salineville, Ohio, the preceding week. Nothing pleasant or consoling in any of that.

Gus remarked that she couldn't feel happy about the recent riots, which had claimed the lives of blacks as well as whites in New York City. Over two million dollars' worth of property had been ruined before units of Meade's army arrived from Pennsylvania to quell the disturbances. Those statements—more specifically, Charles's response to them—started an argument.

"You ought to feel happy about it, Gus. We need help wherever we can find it."

"You can't be serious. That was butchery, not war. Women knifed to death. Little children stoned—"

"Nasty, I'll admit. But we can't be tender hearts any longer. Even when we win, we lose. In every battle, both sides expend men, horses, ammunition. The Yanks can afford it—they have plenty of everything. We don't. If they ever find a general who catches on to that, it will be all over for our side."

She shivered. "You sound so bloodthirsty—"

His temper gave way. "And you sound disapproving."

The old defense, a brittle smile, went into place. "Mr. Pope and I wonder about the cause of your bad disposition."

"My disposition's no concern of—"

But she quoted right on top of that: " 'Perhaps was sick—' " an instant's hesitation. " '—in love, or had not dined?' "

Gnawing a chicken wing, Jim asked, "Who's Mr. Pope? Some farmer around here?"

"A poet Mrs. Barclay favors, you dunce."

"Charles, that's rude," she said.

He sighed, "Yes. I'm sorry, Jim."

"Oh—don't matter," Jim answered, his eye on the bone.

"I'd still like to know why you're so disagreeable, Charles."

"I'm disagreeable because we're losing, goddamn it!" On the last word he knocked his pipe against the hearth so hard the stem snapped.

They smoothed over the quarrel later—she took the initiative—and made love twice between midnight and morning. But damage had been done.

Next afternoon, the clouds cleared as the men started their return ride to camp below the Rapidan, where the infantry had retired behind a cavalry screen. All of the commands in the mounted service were to be evaluated again, and possibly reorganized. As if Charles gave a damn.

The sky, suffused with deep orange as the day waned, had a forlorn quality. Autumnal. Cantering beside the young scout, Charles noticed that the turkey feather in Jim's hat band, bent over behind him a few minutes ago, now bent forward, toward the road in front of them.

Jim noticed his companion's stare. "What's wrong, Charlie?"

"The wind's changed."

So it had, sharp and cold now, from the northwest. Too chilly for summer. Jim waited for further explanation, but none came. He scratched his stubbly beard. Strange man, Charlie. Brave as the devil. But mighty unhappy these days.

Buffeted by the stiff north wind that flattened the grasses of the fields and creaked the trees, they rode on through the orange evening.

BOOK FIVE

THE BUTCHER'S BILL

I cannot describe the change nor do I know when it took place, yet I know that there is a change for I look on the carcass of a man now with pretty much such feeling as I would were it a horse or hog.

A CONFEDERATE SOLDIER, 1862

89

A mild winter softened Virginia's tortured look. Softened but could not erase it. Too many fields lay stripped. Too many trees showed raw circles where limbs had been cut. Too many roads had hoof craters and wheel canyons. Too many farms had walls pitted by musket balls, windows knocked out, a fresh grave that revealed itself like a sugared loaf whenever a light snow fell.

The snow melted and the ditches filled, creating freakish sights. The head of a dead horse appeared to float on tranquil water, resembling some salvered delicacy offered at a medieval feast. The winter soil grew strange crops: shell casings; splintered axles and wheels with spokes missing; thrown-away suits of long underwear patched beyond wearing; broken brown bottles; paper scraps thick as a fall of flower petals.

Haymows were empty. Livestock pens were empty. Larders were empty. So were chairs once occupied by uncles and brothers, fathers and sons.

Three years of asking too much of the earth had inevitably marked it. The fields and glens, the creeks and ponds, the hillsides and blue mountain summits exhaled thin mist in the pale sunshine. It was the breath of a sick land.

In the cavalry of the Army of Northern Virginia, Charles had become a minor legend. His courage and concern for others made him something more than other men, his lack of ambition something less. It was said, behind his back, that the war had done things to his head

He developed odd habits. He spent long hours with his gray gelding, currycombing and brushing him. He was sometimes seen holding lengthy conversations with the animal. Every once in a while during the winter he galloped off to see a girl near Fredericksburg, but always returned in a state of moody silence. He roamed the camps regularly in search of yellow-backed Beadle novels to buy or borrow. He read only one kind, Jim Pickles noticed—those dealing with the Western plains and the scouts and trappers who inhabited them.

"How long was you in that part of the country?" Jim asked over their cook fire on a night in January. They were dining on cush they had prepared themselves from hoarded bacon grease and scraps of leftover beef that they stewed in a little water with week-old corn bread crumbled into it. The dish was a favorite in the army and a lot tastier than the purpling meat and field peas comprising the regular ration.

"Long enough to fall in love with it." Charles used his bowie to lift stew to his mouth. Jim had no implements except a stick and could get none from army sources; the two scouts had taken a canteen off a dead Yankee and split it into a plate for each of them.

After another bite, Charles added, "I'd go back out there tomorrow if we didn't have to fight."

Startled, Jim said, "What about Miss A'gusta?"

"Yes, there's that, too," Charles said. He stared into the fire for a while.

From the darkness, another of the scouts called, "Charlie? I think your gray's loose."

He leaped up, spilling his food. He went charging through leafless underbrush in the direction indicated by the other man. Sure enough, he came on his horse frantically chewing a triangle of gray cloth; Sport had snapped his tether.

Angrily, Charles yanked the blanket out of Sport's mouth. The gray whinnied, peeled back his lips, and nipped at Charles's hand. "Goddamn it, Sport, what's wrong with you?" Of course he knew. There was no longer any forage; the horses were wild with hunger.

As he led Sport back to the customary boards and straw of winter—having publicly threatened to put bullets into the head of anybody who even thought of stealing them—he saw by the light of another fire that the gray's ribs showed regular as rail ties.

He swore again, filthy oaths. He had known for weeks that Sport was losing weight. He guessed the gray was down thirty or forty pounds from his weight at the time of purchase. The wasting away filled Charles with pain and rage, as did, to a lesser degree, the fate of other animals in the cavalry. Many were dying. Why not? The cause was dying, too. Almost every day, Hampton dispatched mounted parties to hunt for fodder, but they seldom found any. Both sides had picked the state clean.

Charles's malaise came to the attention of Hampton, promoted to major general and given a division in the latest reorganization. Fitz Lee had received a similar promotion and the other division. One night Hampton invited Charles to his tent to dine on camp beef, which neither of them would touch.

By the deep gold light of lanterns, Wade Hampton still looked fit, remarkable in view of the severity of the wounds from which he had recovered. His beard, thick and curling, had grown even longer than Charles's, and he waxed his mustaches to points. Yet Charles saw lines that hadn't been there when Hampton raised the legion. A new solemnity draped the general like a mantle.

They gossiped a while. About the unpopularity of Bragg, rewarded for his Western failures by an appointment as military adviser to the President. About the resulting demands from certain newspapers that Mr. Davis be removed in favor of a military dictator; Lee was mentioned. About reports that big John Hood had been ingratiating himself with Davis by frequently going horseback riding with him in Richmond.

Charles had the feeling all this was preparation for something else. He was right.

"I want to say something to you which I know you've heard before, from many others, including your friend Fitz."

Wary, Charles waited. Hampton swirled a little remaining whiskey in his tin cup while his black orderly cleared away battered tin plates and bent forks. "You should be nothing less than a brigadier, Charles. You have the experience. The ability—"

"But not the desire, sir." Why not tell the truth? He was sick of keeping it to himself, and if he could trust anyone to understand, he could trust the general. "I'm coming to detest this war."

Not a trace of reproof; only a brief sigh. "No one wants peace more than I. Why, I wouldn't trade the joys of it for all the military glories of Bonaparte"—points of lantern light showed in his solemn eyes—"but we mustn't deceive ourselves as some do.

696

Vice President Stephens and many others in the government believe peace will simply mean a cessation of the war. It won't. We have come too far. Too much blood has flowed. We'll be fighting as hard afterward, in a different way, as we are fighting right now."

The thought hadn't occurred to Charles. He examined it a few seconds, finding it both realistic and depressing. His response was a shrug, and the playing of a theme only Jim Pickles had thus far heard.

"Then maybe I'll scoot for Texas and find myself a cabin and a patch of farmland."

"I would hope not. The South will need men of strength and sense to look after her interests. In this life, we are called to use our talents responsibly."

Quietly said, it still stung, as Hampton had intended. Having gotten a refusal and answered it, the general let his remarks simmer. He stretched out his powerful booted legs and smiled in the way that won him so many friends; even Stuart had begun to thaw toward him, although everyone knew Fitz Lee would be forever jealous and resentful of the older general.

"Ah, but I suppose we won't have to confront peace for a long time yet," said Hampton presently. "And I do believe we shall win."

Charles kept his face in repose; such lies were required of those belonging to the senior staff. Only occasionally did such men let down. A while back, Charles and Tom Rosser—younger, now a brigadier—had discussed the war over whiskey. After one round too many, the pugnacious Texan opened up and said he saw but one feasible strategy left for the South now: hold Atlanta and hold Richmond and hope to hell that George McClellan ran in the Northern election in the autumn and whipped Old Abe. Then a fair peace could be negotiated.

Hampton, however, continued his discussion of winning. Giving his great brown beard a stroke or two, he mused, "You will go west when we've done it, you say. How does that young lady in Fredericksburg feel about your plans? I have heard your affair of the heart is quite serious."

Somehow, the teasing nettled Charles. "Oh, no, sir. Times like these, I can barely look after my horse. I've got no business trying to look after a woman, too."

Soon they said good night, Hampton shaking his hand warmly,

then accepting his salute and again urging him to think about commanding a brigade. Charles promised he would, but it was only politeness.

Blowing out breath plumes in the dark, he trudged through the eternal mud to see Sport. Although he had spoken about Gus in a joking way, he had said what he believed. Ab and Brandy Station had started the thought process, which had reached a definite conclusion. He loved Gus more than he had ever loved another human being. But he needed to break it off, for both their sakes.

Charles wasn't the only member of his family with a growing sense that the death of the Confederacy was inevitable. Cooper believed it, though he never said it aloud, not even to Judith.

Cooper and his family were in Charleston, sent there the preceding fall by Secretary Mallory. Lucius Chickering had accompanied his superior.

The city to which Cooper had come home was no longer the charming seaport of lamplight, good manners, and chiming church bells with which he had fallen in love after his father exiled him there. Charleston was still scarred from the great fire of '61, exhausted by blockade and siege, menaced by the enemy on water and on land. The graceful old town was hated throughout the North like no other. Above all, the Yankees wanted to recapture Fort Sumter or obliterate it, for purposes more symbolic than military.

Cooper found that the old waterfront complex of the Main family firm, the Carolina Shipping Company, no longer existed as such. The military had taken it over, enlarging the warehouses and permitting the piers to sag and rot because Charleston could not be supplied by sea. The cool, high house on Tradd Street had escaped the fire, although Cooper and Lucius were forced to arm themselves to drive out half a dozen white squatters. It then took brooms, paint, and fumigation to restore the house to something like its former condition. Not that the effort was really worth it, Judith thought scarcely a week after their arrival. Her husband spent every day and a good part of each night in his office or that of General Beauregard, in both places trying to lend needed direction and confidence to the testing and launching of the submersible boat *Hunley.*

A central fact of existence in Charleston was the federal blockade, which took the form of an inner ring of ironclad monitors, a

698

chain barrier, and an outer perimeter of wooden ships. Here, as everywhere, the blockade was proving cruelly effective, and not merely because it continued to isolate the South from sources of essential goods. With the Yankees in virtual control of the Atlantic from the Chesapeake to Florida, it was deemed necessary to spread troops thinly along the entire coast, to cover all points that might be subject to attack. Scott's Anaconda was no longer a theory to be mocked. The coils were crushing the South to death.

A second nerve-wearing reality in the new Charleston was the continuing Yankee pressure to reduce or capture the city. Since coming home, Cooper had heard the terrible story again and again. The preceding spring, Du Pont had tried to take Charleston with a naval assault and failed. After that, the Union had adopted a mixed strategy. Early in July, Federals under Brigadier Quincy Gillmore had established beachheads on Morris Island and begun installation of their batteries among the dunes. Then, on July 18, some six thousand Union infantry had surged forward and surmounted the parapets of Battery Wagner, a Cummings Point fortification whose guns commanded the harbor entrance.

By evening the Yanks had been driven back to their lines, and with particular fury because Shaw's Fifty-fourth Massachusetts Colored Infantry had been in the van of the attack. Black faces swarming over bastions held by white soldiers made the whole town remember old names: Nat Turner; Denmark Vesey.

The failure to keep Battery Wagner galled the Yanks, but it had no significant effect on the siege campaign or the speed with which it took shape. Union artillerists kept working, in scorching sunlight all day and beneath calcium flares all night, to place siege mortars and great breeching guns in their sand batteries. Charleston lived in special dread of one eight-inch, two-hundred-pound Parrott nicknamed "the Swamp Angel." The great monster of a gun was intended to send incendiary shells on a low trajectory of eight thousand yards—right into the city. Cooper had read of the Swamp Angel in Richmond, thinking what an irony it would be if Hazard's had any part in its manufacture.

After days of practice firing, the massed guns opened the bombardment in mid-August. Since that time there had been three periods of heavy shelling, each lasting several days. Sumter now resembled a stone heap, though a garrison of five hundred, manning thirty-eight guns, still held on in the ruins. As for the Swamp

Angel, it had done hardly any damage, had in fact blown up soon after discharging its first rounds.

The city withstood the bombardments and took relatively little damage. Sumter still flew the Confederate and state flags. Yet the enemy had neither given up nor gone away; the Yanks were out there in the haze beyond James Island, where Cooper had started his fledgling shipyard. To boost morale, President Davis had visited the city last November, on his way back to Richmond from the endangered West. Crowds gave Mr. Davis loud and friendly welcomes at each of his appearances. Cooper chose not to attend any of them. Only deeds, not patriotic homilies, could help now. His job was *Hunley*.

The fish-ship had been transported from Mobile last summer and since then had been plagued by misfortune. Docked with one hatch left open, she had been swamped when a much larger vessel passed nearby. All of her eight-man crew, including the skipper, Lieutenant Payne, were aboard. Only Payne escaped drowning.

During a test of the submersible with a replacement crew, five more men lost their lives. Old Bory gave up on *Hunley*, but changed his mind when Mallory reaffirmed his faith in the design, pleaded for patience, and promised that two of his trusted aides would be sent to supervise her testing and operation.

Meanwhile, on October 5, the torpedo boat *David* scored a hit on U.S.S. *New Ironsides*, a bark-rigged steamer with armor plating on her sides. *David*'s spar torpedo successfully detonated six feet below the enemy's waterline, and although the sixty-pound charge was not enough to sink her, it did enough damage to force her to retire to Port Royal for repairs.

Cooper and Lucius arrived then. They pointed out to Beauregard that *Hunley* offered one advantage that *David* did not: silence. The official reports showed that *David*'s engine had alerted *New Ironsides* to danger before the torpedo boat struck. Beauregard protested that he had had no time to scrutinize the reports, else he would have drawn the same conclusion. Cooper suspected the pompous little Creole was lying but settled for the general's promise of encouragement and cooperation. It was needed, he discovered. *Hunley* had already been nicknamed "the Peripatetic Coffin."

Hunley himself reached Charleston a few days later to take charge of the next test, on October 15. He and the entire replacement crew brought from Mobile lost their lives. "She was buried

700

bow first, nine fathoms down, at an angle of roughly thirty-five degrees," Cooper said the night afterward. He hunched before a plate from which he had eaten nothing.

His daughter asked, "How deep is nine fathoms, Papa?"

"Fifty-four feet."

"Brrr. Nothing but sharks in the dark down there."

And that Peripatetic Coffin.

"But you've already raised her—" Judith began.

"Raised her and opened her. The bodies were twisted into horrible postures."

"Marie-Louise," her mother said, "you are excused."

"But, Mama, I want to hear more about—"

"Go."

After their daughter left the room, Judith briefly covered her mouth with her napkin. "Really, Cooper, must you be so graphic in front of her?"

"Why should I sugar-coat the truth? She's practically a young woman. The disaster happened, and it needn't have." He thumped the table. "It needn't have! We studied the bodies carefully. Hunley's, now—his face was black and his right hand was over his head. Near the forward hatch, which he was clearly trying to open when he died. Two others had candles clasped in their hands. They were down by the bolts that secure the iron bars to the bottom of the hull. The bars are extra ballast, unfastened and dropped when the captain wants to come up. But not a single bolt had been removed, though the poor wretches had clearly been trying. It was all a puzzle till we made the important discovery. the seacock for the ballast tank at the bow was still open."

"Telling you what?" Her tone and look said she wasn't sure she wanted to know.

"How she went down! Another crewman was manning the pump that empties the tanks. Panic must have ensured. Perhaps they used up the air, and the candles went out. In that confined space, that would do it. They were trying to bring her up, don't you see? But the seacock was open, and in the dark, with the panic, Hunley failed to order it closed. Or the man responsible was incapable of doing it. That's why they died. Operated properly, the vessel is seaworthy. She can kill plenty of Yankee sailors, and we're going to test her and train a crew until she's ready."

Judith gave him a strange look: sad, yet not submissive. "I'm frankly tired of hearing about your holy crusade to take human lives."

He glared. "Judah means nothing to you?"

"Judah died because of the actions of people on our side. Including your sister."

Cooper shoved his chair away from the table. "Spare me your mealy-mouthed pacifism. I'm going back to the office."

"Tonight? Again? You've been there every—"

"You act as if I go larking off to some bordello or gaming house." He was shouting now. "I go to do work that's urgent and vital. General Beauregard will not, I repeat to you, he will *not* put *Hunley* into service unless we prove her seaworthy and equip her with a bow spar sturdy enough to hold a charge capable of sinking an ironclad, not merely damaging her. The spar must carry at least ninety pounds of powder. We're evaluating materials and designs."

With slow, elaborate movements, he rose. Bowed. "Now if I have once again explained my behavior and motivation to your satisfaction, and if there are no further trivial questions for which you require answers, may I have your permission to leave?"

"Oh, Cooper—"

He pivoted and walked out.

After the Tradd Street door slammed, she continued to sit motionless. His bolting off reminded her of his behavior when he had been struggling to build *Star of Carolina*. But then, living and working in a state of perpetual exhaustion, he had been gentle and affectionate. The man she had married. Now she lived with a vengeful stranger she hardly knew.

Those had been Judith's thoughts last October following the fatal test. As the holidays neared, nothing changed—unless you considered worsening to be a change. Worsening of matters at Tradd Street, worsening of matters in Charleston.

The city continued to resound and shake from enemy shell fire. Pieces of china had to be set well back on a shelf lest the tremors tumble them off. The Parrotts sometimes boomed all night long, and reflected red light on the bedroom ceiling frequently woke her. She wanted to turn and hold her husband, but he usually wasn't there. He seldom stayed in bed longer than two hours.

Curtness became Cooper's way of life. Just before Christmas

702

she suggested that it might be well for them to travel up the Ashley to check on matters at the plantation.

"Why? The enemy is here. Let the place rot."

One night he brought Lucius Chickering home to supper—the purpose was additional time to work, not hospitality—and twelve-year-old Marie-Louise watched the young man adoringly all through the meal. She uttered several sighs impossible to miss or misinterpret.

When she and Judith left the men alone with brandy, Lucius said, "I think your charming daughter's in love with me."

"I am not in the mood to waste time on cheap witticisms."

Nor are you ever, Lucius thought. He found himself possessed of surprising courage as he cleared his throat. "See here, Mr. Main. I know I'm only your assistant. Younger than you, far less experienced. Still, I know how I feel. And I feel a little lightness isn't out of order even in time of war. May help, in fact."

"In your war, perhaps. Not in mine. Finish your brandy so we can get to work."

Now it was January. Old Bory's flagging faith in *Hunley* had been kept alive by Cooper's pleading and by the enthusiasm of the new captain and crew. The former was another army officer, Lieutenant George Dixon, late of the Twenty-first Alabama Volunteers. The crew had been recruited from the receiving ship *Indian Chief,* and each man had been told *Hunley*'s history. General Beauregard insisted.

Cooper knew, absolutely, that the submersible could be effective against enemy vessels blockading the harbor. Beyond that, and more important, if she could operate as designed, she could generate fear out of all proportion to her size. This was Mallory to the letter. Innovation, surprise—the sea route to victory or, barring that, an honorable negotiated peace for the nation whose military adventures were failures.

Thus, morning after morning, Cooper and Lucius stepped into their rowboat at the battery for the long pull out past the fallen casemates of Sumter, within sight of *Catskill* and *Nahant* and the other monitors, to the inlet on the back side of Sullivan's Island where the fish-ship tied up. The trip was hard, but easier than that of Captain Dixon and crew, who marched seven miles from their barracks just to start the day.

The creaky dock jutting from the sandy beach was pleasant in the winter sunshine. The two Navy Department men and Mr. Alexander, the gnarled British machinist who had helped build the vessel, repeatedly watched the crew submerge *Hunley* for short periods, with no mishaps.

Finally, late in January, there came a mellow afternoon when Dixon announced: "We are ready, Mr. Main. Will General Beauregard authorize an attack?"

Cooper's thinning hair fluttered in the wind. His face, normally pale, was the color of pond ice. "I doubt it. Not yet. You've only stayed down a few minutes each time. We must demonstrate that she can stay down much longer."

"Well, sir, how long is much longer?" Alexander asked.

"Till the air runs out. Till the crew has reached the absolute limit of endurance. We must find that limit, Dixon. In fact, I want you to choose one man and put him ashore for the next test. I'll replace him—I got Old Bory's permisssion yesterday. I did it because it will help banish his doubt. I must prove the Navy Department trusts this vessel, that all the deaths have been the result of human error, not faulty design."

"But Mr. Main," Lucius protested, "it could be extremely dangerous for you—"

Then, reddening and realizing he was in the presence of someone else who would face danger, he shut his mouth. He avoided his superior's murderous eye. Dixon's own reaction surprised Cooper.

"Mr. Chickering's right, sir. You are a married man with a family. Is your wife agreeable to—?"

"I need General Beauregard's permission, but I don't need hers. For anything. Keep that in mind, if you please. I want *Hunley* in service, sinking Yankee ships and drowning Yankee seamen, without further delay. I am going to take part in the test dive. We are going to make it tomorrow night."

His hunched posture, compressed lips, furious eyes made argument inadvisable. Seaward, the Parrotts boomed as the day's bombardment started. A dozen big, black-headed gulls lifted from the beach in fright.

90

Approaching the end of his sixth month in Libby Prison, Billy weighed twenty-eight pounds less than he had the day he walked in. His beard hung to the middle of his chest. His face had a gray, sunken appearance. But he had learned how you survived.

You poke your food with your finger, hunting for weevils. Then you smelled the food. Better to starve than swallow some of the spoiled slop fed to prisoners. Bad food could induce the flux and force you to run repeatedly to a trough in one of the odorous wooden closets the keepers dignified with the name bathroom. You could die before you stopped running.

You inserted no angry words or sentiments, no criticism of the prison or its administration, in the letters you were permitted to write. To conserve paper, the allowable length of each letter had been reduced to six lines. Billy took this as a sign of the war going badly for the rebs. You didn't count on any of the letters reaching the North; Billy suspected some or all were burned or dumped in the James.

You slept lightly in case prisoners from another part of the building staged a rat raid, hunting for items to steal. To sleep lightly wasn't difficult. Each of the large rooms of the prison held between three hundred and five hundred men; the place was bursting because exchanges had slowed to a trickle. Billy's room on the top floor was so crowded that everyone slept spoon fashion. Without blankets. That added to the ease of sleeping lightly now that winter had come.

You stayed away from the windows. You did so no matter how

strong your longing for a whiff of fresh air instead of the stinks of fumigation. Guards outside, and even some civilians, occasionally shot at prisoners who appeared at windows. These marksmen received no reprimand from the warden.

You broke the tedium by taking an apple or newspaper or small homemade oatmeal cake from the basket of Crazy Betsy, then chatted with her for a bit about matters of no consequence. Crazy Betsy was a tiny, tense, blue-eyed woman, about forty, addressed formally as Miss Van Lew. Boys loitering outside the building shrieked "witch!" when she entered. Occasionally they threw stones at her. But that didn't deter frequent visits, and the authorities allowed her the run of Libby because she was a lifetime resident of Church Hill and helped keep the inmates pacified with her little gifts.

You did everything possible to avoid depressive thoughts of your situation. You played checkers. Swapped combat stories. Learned French or musical theory in one of the informal classes taught by prisoners. If you had spare paper, you scribbled out an item for the *Libby Chronicle* and handed it to the editor, who stood up and recited an entire newspaper twice weekly to huge crowds jammed into one of the largest rooms.

Above all, if you were Billy Hazard, you avoided contact with Corporal Clyde Vesey.

Throughout the early weeks of Billy's imprisonment, that wasn't hard. Vesey was still posted on the ground floor, where he continued to receive new prisoners and maintain records of those already inside. One night right after Christmas, however, in the freezing room where Billy was trying to sleep amid the restless men around him, Vesey appeared, specterlike, carrying a lantern.

"There you are, Hazard," said he, smiling. "I was anxious to find you and tell you I've been transferred up here, nights. It means half again as much in wages. It also means I shall be able to give you the attention you deserve."

Billy coughed into his fist; he had caught a cold. After the spasm, he said, "Wonderful news. I'll treasure each and every golden moment in your presence, Vesey."

Still sweetly smiling, Vesey glanced at the hand with which Billy braced himself on his bit of floor while he spoke. Quickly Vesey shifted and stepped on the hand with his hobnailed boot.

"I'll have none of your arrogant college ways while I'm on duty." He put more weight on Billy's hand. "Clear, sir?"

Billy clenched his teeth and squinted. Tears filled the corners of his eyes, and a little line of blood ran from under the sole of Vesey's boot. "You son of a bitch," Billy whispered. Fortunately Vesey was talking again.

"What? Do I see the brave Yankee weeping? Excellent. Excellent!" He twisted his boot back and forth. Billy couldn't hold back a low, choked sound. Vesey raised his boot, and Billy saw the gashes, the blood shining in the lantern light. "I must go on my rounds. But I shall be back often from now on. We shall have regular lessons in humility, until you learn your proper station. Lower than the lowest nigger. Good evening, Hazard."

And off he went, humming a hymn.

Billy blinked several times, tore a piece from his ragged shirt, and wrapped his bleeding hand. He sneezed twice. Men lay on either side of him and at his head and foot. He was certain they must be awake, but not one had stirred during Vesey's visit. He didn't blame them. He wasn't sure he would risk his own chances of survival just to defend some other prisoner unlucky enough to draw a guard's wrath.

By early January Billy's hand was infected and his cold much worse. Vesey sought him out at least once every night to abuse him verbally or force him to march up and down the prison staircase for two hours, or stand in a corner on tiptoe while Vesey sat on a stool, a bayonet on his musket and the steel tip held half an inch from Billy's trembling back.

"Confess," Vesey would croon to him, smiling. "By now you must be cognizant of your inferiority. Your heathen nature. Your wrong thinking. Confess that you admire President Davis and consider General Lee the greatest soldier in Christendom."

Billy's legs shook. His toes felt broken. He said, "Fuck you."

Vesey tore Billy's shirt and raked his back once with the bayonet. Luckily the wound didn't fester as his hand had; the hand was all yellow and brown with pus and scabs. "We shall continue this," Vesey promised as his duty sergeant came looking for him. "Be assured of it, heathen."

Billy's attitude about helping other prisoners soon underwent a change. Eight new men arrived in the top-floor room to occupy the space of a captain who had died in his sleep. One of the newcomers, a sallow, curly-haired youth with a high forehead, found space next to Billy. The newcomer's name was Timothy Wann. He had enlisted at the end of his freshman year at Harvard

707

and been brevetted to second lieutenant after three others holding that rank in his unit were killed one by one.

On Wann's second night in Libby, officers from another room conducted a rat raid. Billy woke out of his usual light sleep to see three bearded men carrying the Massachusetts boy toward the communal washroom. A fourth soldier, unbuckling Wann's belt, said, "Skinny little ass on this chicken. But it'll serve."

Billy knew such things went on, though he had never been threatened or been a witness. But he couldn't tolerate such treatment for a young officer who was really just a schoolboy. He wiped his dripping nose, staggered to his feet, and wove his way through dozing prisoners till he caught up with the quartet carrying the round-eyed, terrified Wann.

"Let him go," Billy said. "You can do that in your own room if you must, but not in here."

The gray-haired man who had unbuckled Wann's belt pulled it loose and stroked it, scowling. "Got some claim on this youngster, have you? Is he your pet bird?"

Billy reached out, intending to pull Wann off the shoulders of the three carrying him like a side of beef. The other soldier stepped back for room, then whipped Billy's cheek with the belt.

Sick as he felt—a fever had been on him for the past twenty-four hours—he found strength in his anger. He ripped the belt away from the older man, grasped both ends, looped it over the soldier's head, and crossed his hands. The soldier gagged. Billy pulled harder.

The friends of the strangling man let Wann fall to the floor. "Get back to your place," Billy said to Tim as one of the raiders punched him. In the corridor, he spied a lantern.

"What's the commotion? What's happening in there?"

Vesey appeared, lantern held high, side arm in his other hand. Billy released one end of the belt. The gray-haired officer stepped away, rubbing his red throat. "This crazy loon attacked me. Started to choke me to death—just 'cause we were in here speaking to friends and he said we disturbed his sleep."

"Your accusation doesn't surprise me, sir," Vesey replied with a sympathetic nod. "This officer is a violent man. Constantly provoking trouble. I shall take him in hand. The rest of you go back to your quarters."

"Yessir," two of the raiders muttered. None wasted any time leaving.

708

"What are we to do with you, Hazard?" Vesey managed to speak, sigh, and smile at the same time. "My lessons up here have failed to bring an end to this constant rebellion. Perhaps one conducted in the fresh air would be more effective."

"I want my shoes if we're going out—"

"March," Vesey said, yanking his collar. Billy had a glimpse of heads raised here and there in the room. Then they sank down again, and he wondered why he had been so stupid as to help Tim. The young prisoner started to get up. Billy shook his head and walked out of the room ahead of Vesey.

On the river side of the building, Vesey handed his lantern to the guard at the door, then prodded Billy down the steps and pushed him to his knees. Vesey proceeded to lash Billy's wrists and ankles together behind his back, pulling the ropes steadily tighter until Billy's shoulders bowed with strain. In a matter of seconds, his leg muscles were aching.

Light rain began to fall. Vesey shoved a foul-smelling gag in Billy's mouth and secured it with a second rag tied around his head. While he worked, Vesey hummed "What a Friend We Have in Jesus."

By the time Vesey was finished, the rain was falling hard. Cold rain, freezing rain, Billy realized. He sneezed. Corporal Vesey ran back up to the shelter of the doorway.

"I shall return as soon as I find my overcoat, Hazard. It's nippy out here, but I must watch you undergo your punishment for a while. If we can't break your spirit, perhaps we can break your spine."

That night, miles away in Charleston, Judith said, "I don't understand you any longer, Cooper."

He frowned from the other end of the dining table. Wearing a loose silk shirt, he hunched forward in his customary tense posture. His untouched plate had been pushed aside.

"If this is another of your complaints about my failure to perform my husbandly duties—"

"No, blast you." Her eyes glistened, but she fought herself back to control. "I know you're tired all the time—although it would be nice if you treated me like a wife at least occasionally. That was not the reason I said what I did, however."

A breeze from the walled garden fluttered the candles and played with the curtains of the open French windows. "Then it's the test," Cooper said suddenly. "Damn Lucius for drinking too much claret."

"Don't blame poor Lucius. You invited him again this evening. You poured all that wine. For him and for yourself as well."

He answered that with unintelligible sounds. Out of sight in the parlor, Marie-Louise began to play "The Bonnie Blue Flag" on the pianoforte. At Judith's urging, she had taken the Mains' frequent guest into the other room after he inadvertently blurted a remark about the test now scheduled for Monday of next week. Cooper had withheld all mention of it from Judith, hoping to avoid tiresome reactions—bathetic tears, moralizing—which would in turn require him to waste energy dealing with them.

Looking hostile, he asked, "What did you mean about not understanding me?"

"The sentence was plain English. Is it so difficult to decipher? You're not the man I married. Not even the man with whom I went to England."

His face seemed to jerk with a spastic fury. He locked his hands together, elbows pressing the table so hard it creaked. "And I remind you that this is no longer the world in which either of those events occurred. The Confederacy is in desperate straits. Desperate measures are required. It's my duty to involve myself in this test. My duty. If you lack the wit to appreciate that or the courage to endure it, you're not the woman I married, either."

"Hurrah! Hurrah! For Southern rights—hurrah!" sang the adolescent girl and the guest in the parlor. *"Hurrah for the Bonnie Blue Flag that bears a single star!"*

Judith brushed back the dark blond curls on her forehead. "Oh," she said, with a small bitter twist to her mouth, "how you misunderstand. It isn't the risk to yourself that's upsetting me now, though God knows that kind of upset has become a constant of life here. I object to the callous way you've pushed this infernal fish-boat project. I object to your insistence on another test. I object to your forcing seven innocent men to submerge that iron coffin once more because you think it must be done. There was a time when you hated this war with all your soul. Now, you've become some—some barbarian I don't even recognize."

Icy, he asked, "Are you finished?"

"I am not. Cancel the test. Don't gamble with human lives to fulfill your own warped purpose."

"So now my purpose is warped, is it?"

"Yes." She struck the table.

"Patriotism is warped, is it? Defending my native state is warped? Or preventing this city from being burned and leveled? That's what the Yankees want, you know—nothing left of Charleston but rubble. That's what they want," he shouted.

"I don't care—*I don't care!*" She was on her feet, weeping. The patriotic anthem had ended in mid-phrase. "You are not the sole savior of the Confederacy, despite your attempt to act like it. Well, go ahead, kill yourself in your holy cause if you want. But it's hateful and immoral of you to demand that other lives be sacrificed to appease your anger. The old Cooper would have understood. The Cooper I loved—I loved so very—"

The broken words faded into silence. Out in the garden, palmetto fronds rattled in the wind. Like some long snake uncoiling, Cooper rose from his chair. His face blank, he said, "The test will proceed as scheduled."

"I knew that. Well, commune with yourself about it from now on."

"What does that mean?"

"It means you may take your meals in this house, but don't expect me to be present when you do. It means you may sleep in the extra bedroom. I don't want you in mine."

They stared at each other. Then Cooper walked out.

Judith's façade gave way. Voices reached her from the parlor, the first one—her husband's—curt:

"Lucius, get your coat. We can still accomplish a good deal tonight."

Marie Louise, vexed: "Oh, Papa, Mama said we'd all gather and sing—"

"Keep quiet."

Judith put her head down, pressed her hands to her eyes, and silently cried.

91

For days after his ordeal—Billy had been kept kneeling in the sleet storm till morning—he hobbled rather than walked. Most of the time he curled on the floor, hands locked below his pulled-up knees in a futile effort to stave off chills that would abruptly change to fever and set him raving. And every night Vesey was there—to insult him, to prod with a musket, to lift his boot and nudge the hand that would be forever nail-scarred.

Vesey, a farm boy from Goochland County who had achieved sudden and unexpected importance because of his absolute power over prisoners, reminded Billy of an Academy upperclassman George had mentioned a few times. Some fat fellow from Ohio who had pitilessly deviled his brother and Orry Main and all the other plebes in their class. Billy had never been much for contemplation of philosophic issues, but the fat cadet and Clyde Vesey convinced him that there was indeed such a thing in the world as the person with no redeeming qualities.

On the credit side of the ledger he placed the Tim Wanns.

The Massachusetts boy, though not sturdy, was quick-witted. Under Billy's instruction he rapidly learned the tricks of survival. Because Billy had gone to his rescue, Tim became Billy's devoted friend, eager to share anything he possessed. One thing he possessed, which Billy didn't, was greenback dollars. About twenty of them. The money was in his pocket when he was captured, and two of the dollars had persuaded the check-in guard to let him keep the rest.

With money, little luxuries could be obtained from the more

cooperative guards. Frequently, Tim urged Billy to let him buy him something, whatever he wanted. Tim said it was small payment for the bravery that had earned Billy punishment and a persistent influenza that left him feeble and frequently dizzy.

Billy said no to the offers until one longing grew too strong.

"All right, Tim—a little writing paper, then. And a pencil. So I can start a new journal."

Tim put in the order ten minutes later. Delivery was made at nine that night. Tim objected.

"This is wallpaper! Look at all these bilious blue flowers. How is anyone supposed to write on this side?"

"Ain't," said the guard selling the goods. "But if you do want to write some'pin, you write it on that or nothin'. Jeffy Davis hisself can't get anythin' better these days."

So Billy began.

Jan. 12—Libby Pris. I vow to survive this place. My next, most immed. aim is to send a letter to my dear wife.

He wanted to add that he had been asked to join the escape that was currently being plotted but decided he had better not commit that to paper in case the journal was found. Besides, he had so little to write upon—three sheets a foot square cost Tim three dollars—he must hoard the empty space.

Every night that Vesey was on duty, he continued to show up to harass his favorite prisoner. But Billy managed to endure the pokes with a bayonet, the kicks with a hobnailed boot, the nasty remarks about his friendship with the Harvard boy—he endured it all until he wrote the letter to Brett.

Tim insisted he be allowed to buy an envelope to hold the letter. What was supplied was greasy butcher's paper, folded and held together with paste. Billy addressed it for maximum legibility and enclosed a small square of wallpaper carrying a brief, affectionate message: He was in fine health, he loved her, she shouldn't worry.

The envelope, left open for the censor, was handed to the proper guard at noon. Vesey brought it back that night.

"I am afraid the censor refused to pass this letter." Smiling, he opened his right hand. The envelope and its contents, all in small pieces, fluttered to the floor.

Weak, dizzy, hating the feel and stench of the filthy clothes he

713

removed each morning for the required lice inspection, Billy pushed up from his small section of floor, slowly gained his feet, and stood eye to eye with the corporal.

"There was nothing illegal in that letter."

"Oh, that is for the censor to determine. The censor is a chum of mine. Some weeks ago, I asked him to watch for any letter you might write. I'm afraid none will ever gain his approval for mailing. Your dear wife will just have to go on suffering and grieving —" he winked, smiling "—thinking you dead in a heathen's grave."

"The rules—"

Vesey's hand flew to the back of Billy's head; twisted in his long, matted hair. "I told you—I *told* you," he whispered. "There are no rules here except mine. I hope your wife's grief grows unsupportable. I hope she develops a violent aching in her female parts. A desire so fierce, so insistent—"

He leaned closer, face huge, china-blue eyes gleeful.

"—she'll be driven to fornicate madly to relieve it. Maybe she'll fornicate with some white tramp. Maybe she'll pick a buck nigger."

Billy was shaking, trying to hold back, not see the looming face or hear the whispering.

"Just imagine one of those big coons—your equals, aren't they? Old Abe says they are. Think of him humping and sliding all over your wife's white body. Pushing his blackness into her tender orifice so hard she bleeds. Think of that along with what you'd like to say in all those letters you'll never get past these walls, you heathen, godless—"

With a cry, Billy struck. When three other guards with lanterns rushed in to pull him off, he had Vesey on the floor, pounding his head with both hands. One of the guards hauled Billy up by his jacket. A second kicked him in the crotch, twice. Coughing, he pitched sideways and crumpled. The third guard said, "You all are in for it now, Yank."

92

Although light remained in the west, Cooper saw only darkness and winter stars out toward the Atlantic. Would he see the sight again? His daughter? Judith? The moment the questions came, he drove them out as unworthy sentimentalities.

Lucius Chickering had come down to the dock along with Alexander, the machinist. The young man shook Cooper's hand. "Best of luck, sir. We'll be waiting for your return."

With a brief nod, Cooper glanced at the small crowd of soldiers who had gotten wind of the test and gathered to observe it. Mingled with them were a few villagers from Mount Pleasant. One stared at Cooper in a manner that could only be characterized as pitying.

Alexander went down through *Hunley*'s forward hatch. Once Cooper had secured Bory's permission for the test, the machinist had insisted on taking part. It was his right, he said; it was his submersible.

Stepping from the pier to the hull, Cooper bent over the hatch. "Ready for me to come down, George?"

"Ready, Mr. Main," Lieutenant Dixon replied in his customary drawl. Cooper lifted a long leg over the coaming with its quartet of small, round windows set ninety degrees apart. He lowered himself into the dark interior while a crewman reached up to close the rear hatch with a clang, screwing it down tight. He squeezed past Dixon, who remained at the instruments: a mercury depth gauge and a compass for steering underwater. In a niche between these, in a cup, stood the lighted candle that measured the air supply and provided the sole illumination.

Cooper positioned himself slightly behind and to the side of the skipper, bending and sliding his rear onto a small iron seat attached to the hull. The six crewmen occupied similar seats, three on either side of the fore-to-aft shaft that had been cast with sections offset in the shape of broad, shallow U's. The crewmen grasped these to turn the shaft and propel the submersible at its maximum speed of four knots.

"Mr. Main," said Dixon, "would you be so good as to explain the test procedures to our crew?" As he spoke, he tested two handles. One operated the rudder attached to the propeller housing; the other controlled the angle of port and starboard diving planes.

"Simple enough," Cooper said. His back already ached from bending to the curve of the hull. "Tonight we will not use that candle as the sole determiner of how long this vessel can stay underwater. We shall use you gentlemen. We shall remain submerged an hour—an hour and a half—" some apprehensive murmuring at that "—perhaps more. We will not surface until the first man reaches his limit and announces that he can't continue to function without fresh air. Each man must find that limit for himself, being neither too confident of his own powers of endurance nor too quick to surrender to discomfort."

The final words bore a clear note of scorn, causing Dixon to react. But he was facing the instruments; Cooper didn't see the frown.

"When the first man calls out one word—*up*— that will be our signal to empty the tanks and rise to the surface. Any questions?"

"I just hope we can come up," one man declared with a nervous laugh. "Some of the sojers say this fish ought to be named *Jonah* 'stead of *Hunley*."

"Belay that kind of talk," Dixon said as he climbed the short ladder and poked his head out the forward hatch. From his cramped position, Cooper could glimpse a small section of the hatch opening: an oval of sky decorated with faint stars.

"Cast off the bow and stern lines."

Dockhands ran noisily to obey Dixon's order. Cooper could feel *Hunley* float free all at once. Dixon climbed down again and addressed the mate.

"Airbox shaft open, Mr. Fawkes?"

716

"Open, sir."

"Stand by to reverse crank. Half speed."

"Half speed—crank," the mate repeated. Grunting, the crewmen began to revolve the shaft.

It was awkward work, but Dixon had drilled the men well and developed smooth timing. The candle flickered. Water lapped the hull with a queer hollow sound.

Again Dixon went up the ladder, calling down commands to the mate, who had taken the rudder. As soon as they backed from the dock, they reversed direction and picked up speed. Sweat trickled on Cooper's chin. He felt entombed, wished he were anywhere but here. He fought rising panic.

Still with his head in the open, Dixon looked all around, three hundred and sixty degrees, then came down, reached overhead and secured the hatch.

"Stand by to submerge."

Cooper's heart was tripping so fast his chest hurt. He felt a keen respect for these men who had volunteered for this duty and some sense of the agony of those who had perished in the earlier dives. Then he chided himself. He was indulging in sentimentalities again.

"Close airbox shaft."

"Airbox shaft closed," the mate sang out.

"Opening bow tank seacock."

Cooper heard the gurgle and rush of water. The hull swayed and dipped. He grasped a stanchion mounted above him as *Hunley*'s bow tilted down. He thought of Judith, Marie-Louise. He couldn't help it. They did call this the Peripatetic Coffin, after all.

She settled to the bottom with a shiver and a soft thump. The men relaxed against the hull or leaned on the drive shaft. One fellow said the hardest half of the voyage was over. No one laughed.

Dixon studied the mercury tube in the depth gauge. Cooper fought sudden, terrifying fantasies. Someone tightening a metal band around his head. Someone locking him in a lightless closet whose door had no inside knob—

Alexander patted his waistcoat. "Any of you gents have a timepiece? In the excitement, seems I forgot mine altogether."

"I do." Cooper fumbled for the slim gold watch he always carried. He snapped back the lid. "Ten past seven." The flame of the candle stood straight. Wax ran down to form tiny mountain chains on the sides.

At half past the hour, the candle was visibly dimmer. A man muttered, "Air's growing foul."

"Someone let one go," said another crewman. The snickers were halfhearted. Cooper's eyes began to smart. Dixon kept stroking his side whiskers with index and middle fingers.

"How long?" Alexander asked abruptly. Cooper roused. Either his sight was failing or the candle, half gone, had dimmed still more. He had to lift his watch near his chin to see.

"We've been down thirty-three minutes."

He kept the watch open in his hand. How loudly it ticked. As the light continued to dim, his mind played pranks. The intervals between ticks grew far apart; he seemed to wait a half hour for the next one. When it came, he heard the sound for a long time.

Alexander started to sing softly, some Cockney ditty about wheelbarrows and vegetable marrows. Crossly, Dixon asked him to stop. Cooper longed for Liverpool, Tradd Street, even the deck of *Water Witch*. Thoughts of the blockade-runner led to thoughts of poor Judah, his remains lying somewhere at the bottom of the Atlantic. Cooper felt moisture on his cheeks, averted his head so no one would see—

The candle went out.

A man inhaled, a panicky hiss. Another cursed. Dixon scraped a match on the iron plating, but it produced no light, only a quick fizzing noise and then a smell.

Alexander's voice: "How long, Mr. Main?"

"A few minutes before the candle went out, approximately forty-five minutes."

"The air is still quite breathable," Dixon said. Someone's grumble disputed that.

Without sight, Cooper couldn't judge the passage of time. Nothing remained but a mounting pressure on his temples and devils in the mind, persuading him that he was suffocating, persuading him that he heard the iron plates cracking, persuading him that one thing after another was going wrong. He passed rapidly through dizziness, sleepiness, extreme confidence, the certainty of the imminence of his own death.

He ripped off his cravat, tore loose his collar button. He was strangling—

"Up!"

Laughter then, a rush of conversation. For a moment, wiping his sweaty neck, Cooper nearly convinced himself he had been the one to cry out. Calm, Dixon said, "Mr. Alexander, man the stern pump, if you please. I'll handle this one. Mr. Fawkes, Mr. Billings, unbolt the ballast bars."

Cooper rested his head against the hull, anticipating the sweet night air waiting up above. He heard the squeak and hiss of the pumps, the ring of an iron nut falling to the deck. The sound was repeated several times.

"Ballast bars unfastened, sir."

"The bow's coming up," Dixon grunted, working the pump handle. "We should be lifting momentarily."

Everyone felt the bow rise. The men laughed and whistled, but that didn't last long. One exclaimed, "What's wrong, Alexander? Why ain't the stern coming up, too?"

"Captain Dixon?" The little Englishman sounded frightened. "The tank is still full. It's the pump."

"We'll die," said the man immediately behind Cooper.

Dixon: "What's wrong with it?"

"Fouled, I should suspect. Damn bloody seaweed, probably."

"If we can't fix it, we can't return to the surface." Dixon's words, blurted like a command to Alexander, had a bad effect on the crewman who had spoken a moment before.

"We're going to suffocate. Oh, God, oh, God—I don't want to die that way." His baritone voice ascended to a high register, the words punctuated by the hiccups of his crying. "We're going to die. I know we're going to—"

Cooper twisted and reached into the dark. The watch fell; he heard the crystal smash as he seized the hysterical man's arm. With his free hand he struck the man's face twice.

"Stop that. It will do no one any good."

"Damn you, let go—all of us—we're—"

"I said stop." He struck a third time, so hard the man's head thudded on the hull. Cooper released his arm. The man kept crying, muffling it with his hands. At least he wasn't screaming.

"Thank you, Mr. Main," Dixon said.

Alexander spoke. "Sir? I am going to dismantle the pump a section at a time. I think I can do it in the dark—I know exactly how she's put together. It may be that I can reach and remove whatever's fouling her."

"If you do, the water will rush in."

"Give me another idea, then!"

More softly, Dixon said, "I'm sorry. I have none. Take whatever measures you think will help, Mr. Alexander."

So the nightmare continued, more intense than before. Cooper imagined he couldn't breathe. Not at all. Yet somehow he did: thin breaths, each costing him pain. Or was the pain imagined, too? A silence that was almost sharp settled in the submersible, every man listening for the squeak or chink of a metal part being unscrewed or removed and wondering, *What does that noise mean? That one?*

Cooper groped near his feet for his broken watch. Just as he touched it, he heard a bubbly roar. A man screamed, "God preserve us," and water gushed from the pump, filling the vessel with spray, sloshing along the deck.

Alexander exclaimed, "One minute more—now—*there*. I have a big handful of seaweed, sir. I think that's all of it. Now I must force the pump back together against the pressure—"

The water continued to rush in. Cooper lifted his left foot and tapped it down. Splash. The man he had struck was moaning again. Cooper reached behind and shoved the man's head against the hull. That shut him up.

Almost at once, he felt bad about treating the fellow so brutally. The man was right; they would all die soon. He had a swift and sure sense of that. He fought to draw a little of the malodorous air into his lungs and, with doubt about the outcome removed, settled down to wait for the end.

He began to review his past life quickly, by-passing the shameful moments and dwelling on those of intense pleasure—as when he had first seen Miss Judith Stafford on the deck of the coastal steamer bringing them both to Charleston long ago. He composed a little farewell speech to tell her how grateful he was that she had married hi—

"Done," Alexander shouted. Cooper automatically looked toward the stern, though he could see nothing. He heard the drawn-out squeal of the pump piston. Then Alexander again.

"She's working!"

"Hurrah," Dixon cried. The crew applauded. Tears spilled from Cooper's eyes as he labored to breathe. He thought he felt the stern lift. Dixon confirmed it.

"There she comes!"

Minutes later, *Hunley* broke into the moonlight.

Dixon and Alexander attacked the fore and aft hatch bolts like madmen seeking escape from an asylum. Suddenly Cooper glimpsed stars, felt and inhaled sweet, cold air. In no time, the crewmen were briskly turning the crank as if nothing had happened.

Dixon climbed up to peer over the forward coaming. "Only one person left. Can't see who it is."

Slowly, the submersible nosed back to the pier, where Lucius Chickering jumped up and down and clapped and spun round and round with his arms at shoulder level, like some happy bird. Dixon ordered him to stop capering and help tie up the vessel.

"I'm not capering, I'm celebrating," Lucius exclaimed as Dixon worked his way to the bow and flung a line. "The soldiers and townspeople went home after forty minutes. They all said you were dead, but I had this crazy idea that if I stayed—if I didn't give up—that would prove everybody else was wrong and presently the boat would come up. But Lord Almighty, Lieutenant, you surely tested my faith. Do you realize what time it is?"

Climbing out after Cooper, Alexander asked, "How long were we down?"

Cooper raised his watch to his ear. Good heavens. Still ticking. He jumped to the pier, tilted the watch toward the moon, shook bits of shattered glass from the white face. He thought he had misread the hands, but he hadn't.

"It's fifteen minutes before ten. We were submerged two hours and thirty-five minutes."

"I told you, I told you," Lucius cried, grabbing Cooper's shoulders and whirling him. "Isn't it incredible? You were right. She works." Alexander muttered something; Dixon shushed him. "She can sneak out and kill Yankees any time now—Oh." Lucius stopped his gyrations. "I forgot, Mr. Main. One soldier said he was going to General Beauregard's headquarters to report *Hunley* sunk again. With all hands lost. I'll bet your wife's heard it by now."

"Oh, God. Lieutenant Dixon, well done. I take my leave."

He had begun to do so before the end of the sentence. He rushed toward the rowboat, resembling some great gangly shore bird scurrying on the sand. Lucius jammed his plug hat on his head. "Wait for me, Mr. Main!"

When Cooper reached Tradd Street after his incredible adventure, Judith wept with relief, even though Lucius Chickering's prediction had been incorrect; she had heard no news.

She hugged her husband long and hard. But she still chose to sleep alone that night.

93

"Warden," Vesey said, "that Yank turned on me like a ravening animal. He did so with no provocation but the prompting of his evil disposition. It is your duty, if I may be so bold—your duty as a responsible commander and Christian gentleman to grant me the right to punish him."

Dubious, young Turner thought a while. "I would, but I can't allow that kind of thing inside Libby, for several reasons. One, we've too blasted many Philadelphia lawyers among the inmates. Two, we're getting close scrutiny from that damn busybody who works for Seddon."

"You referring to that one-armed colonel, Warden?"

"That's right. Main. The self-appointed conscience of our prisons. You've seen him nosing around without so much as a by-your-leave from this office." Vesey nodded. "Recently we've been spared his visits—I understand he contracted a bad flux and is confined to his bed. But sure as I say go ahead, he'll recover and pop in here the very day you do."

Vesey looked glum. Then he noticed the slow beginnings of a smile. "Of course, if you could find some way to conduct the, ah, disciplinary lesson away from this building, I could issue a temporary release order, which you could destroy afterward with no one the wiser."

Vesey leaned forward, his smile twice as broad as Turner's.

"Should you need helpers in this—I mean to say, if there are witnesses," the warden continued, "they must be absolutely trustworthy."

"No problem there, sir."

"If you mark him, it must appear to have happened accidentally."

"I guarantee it."

"Then I'll prepare the pass. Before I hand it to you, I'll want to know your plan in detail."

"Yes, sir. Thank you, sir!" Vesey said, fairly clicking his heels as he saluted. "You'll have the information practically right away, I promise. Thank you again, sir."

"Pleasure to help out." Turner was still smiling. "You're an exemplary soldier, Vesey. Wish I had more like you."

That conversation took place on the thirtieth of January. On the first, Vesey returned, glowing with excitement. Catching the corporal's mood, Turner asked, "Well? How are you going to do it?"

"With a caisson borrowed through my cousin in the artillery of the Department of Henrico. A caisson and the roughest road we can find. My cousin's the one who suggested the idea. He told me the Yanks use it on serious offenders all the time. Good enough for them, good enough for us, I say."

He continued speaking for more than a minute. At the end, Turner laughed loudly. "First rate! You'll have the release order in an hour. It will be best if you take him out late at night. Fewer people awake then. We'll say he's being removed to General Winder's office for an urgent interrogation."

"That's perfect, sir." Vesey couldn't suppress his glee. "I must tell you this in candor. We will have a small group at the event— my cousin, some of his pals. But I pledge, Warden, every man can be trusted."

"I'm holding you responsible for that," Turner said with a genial smile. "I wish I could go with you. Get in a few licks for me."

"Yes, sir. We surely will."

"This is General Winder's office?" After the question, Billy spat, but it only dripped down on the spokes because of the awkward angle of his head.

"Shut your face, Yank," said Clyde Vesey's cousin. He pulled

723

Billy's head back, then pushed it forward against the wheel. The horses pranced and snorted. It was a bright, breezy morning, warm for February. Bare trees soughed along both sides of the deserted, heavily rutted road that ran over a succession of little hills.

Billy was spread-eagled against the spare wheel mounted on the rear of the artillery caisson at an angle of about forty-five degrees. His bare back stippled with goose bumps, he lay with the wheel hub jammed into his gut. Normally, six horses pulled the caisson, but taking so many for this kind of excursion might have caused suspicion, so only two had been harnessed. They could handle it; the caisson had been considerably lightened by removal of the ammunition chests.

While four soldiers watched, Vesey inspected the knots of the ropes holding Billy's wrists and ankles to the fellies of the wheel. His body was vertical though tilted forward by the wheel's angle. After brief scrutiny, Vesey said, "Quarter turn, lads. I hear the trip's even better that way."

Snickering, they put their shoulders to it and with effort turned the wheel on its tight hub mount. Vesey called for extra ropes to secure the wheel in that position. Billy's head was now at three o'clock, his feet at nine.

"Crawford?" Vesey's cousin stepped forward. "To you falls the honor of riding postilion." The oafish fellow eagerly mounted the near horse. Cheeks pink in the winter sunshine, Vesey stepped to one side, where the prisoner could see him.

"Gentlemen, are we ready to commence?" Nods, grins. "Ought we to start by singing a hymn? Better still, maybe we should pray for the soul of one about to depart—whether to the nether regions, where all good Yankees go, or merely to the land of the cripples, it is not ours to know just yet."

Following his cousin's example, he seized Billy's hair, yanking his head far back, till he saw Billy grimace. Vesey bent to within three inches of Billy's face.

"One thing sure, boy. You'll never forget the ride."

Billy poked his tongue out between cracked lips and blew spit. This time he didn't miss.

Vesey slammed his head against the spoke, then ran around to the near horse. "Two miles down the road and back, Crawford." He whipped off his cap and lashed the horse, spooking it to

724

greater effort with a long rebel yell that wailed against the noise of the caisson gathering speed.

No matter how determined Billy was, no matter how he braced himself, his body was yanked away from the hub, then hurled back against it as the caisson went over each hump in the road. Being tied horizontally created disorientation; his left eye saw the sky, his right the brown road flying by beneath.

Vesey's cousin whipped the team. "Come on, you nags, do your duty!" Billy's face mashed into a spoke. The inside of his cheek split. Blood began to fill his mouth. A bruise appeared on his temple as it repeatedly hit the wheel. Vesey had known exactly how loosely to tie him, the bastard.

He got a little relief when the team slowed to turn around. But he had been bashed so hard, jerked so violently, that starting up again was twice as bad. His head buzzed. He had a feeling they would break half his bones at least. His emotional control started to slip. He pictured Brett's face. That helped.

The return trip seemed to last much longer. Billy sailed beneath a few winter clouds, watching them expand, shrink, blur. Blood ran from the lower corner of his mouth. Pain spread from his belly, hit repeatedly by the hub, to skull and toes. The caisson slowed, then, mercifully, stopped.

"Well, cousin, what d'ye think?" asked Crawford, scratching himself.

Vesey strutted back and forth where his victim could see him. "Oh, I think he's enjoying himself too much. I see not the slightest sign of repentance for his heathenish behavior. Let's untie him and turn him over with his back next to the hub. And, Crawford, this time go all the way to the covered bridge before you turn. That's at least a mile more each way."

So it started again, Crawford driving up the road as if charging to battle. Billy's middle jackknifed out, then back, the hub battering his spine. Wind-whipped blood trailed away from his upper lip, stringing out behind his head like periods in the air. Finally, ashamed but powerless to stop, he cried out.

And blacked out.

The doctor, a sixty-year-old hack, heavy tippler, and native Virginian, happened to despise the young warden of Libby Prison. He stomped into Turner's office late next day, informing him that prisoners from the third floor had brought him a man, one Hazard, whose body was cruelly battered. A man who could not stand, or speak coherently; a man lying this moment on a cot in the surgery, his life in the balance.

"His back isn't broken, but it's no thanks to whoever beat him."

"Just return that Yank to decent health, and I'll root out the person or persons who did it and discipline them," Turner promised, voice tremoring. "However, Dr. Arnold, we may find it was an accident. A slip on the stairs, a tumble—some of the prisoners get pretty weak, and there isn't much I can do about it. Yes, sir, I'll wager an accidental fall is the answer."

"If you believe that, you're even stupider than I thought. He could have fallen out of one of those reconnaissance balloons and not be hurt this badly." The doctor laid his hands on the desk and pushed his plum nose toward the warden. "You'd better remember one fact, youngster. We may be at war, but we are not on the staff of the Grand Inquisitor of Spain. These are Americans locked up in this building—and Southern honor still stands for something. Find the culprit or I'll go to President Davis personally. I'll see you cashiered."

That might have been the outcome, except for the commotion caused by the great escape.

The escape took place on the ninth of February. A Pennsylvania colonel named Rose had climbed down a prison chimney and discovered an abandoned room in the cellar. There, he and others worked in shifts for several days to tunnel under the wall of the old warehouse. The tunnel they dug was almost sixty feet long. They broke ground and ran, a hundred and nine of them.

Libby was thrown into an uproar, Turner into dire trouble. Special inspectors from Winder's office prowled the area at unexpected hours of the day and night, spying on prisoners for signs of suspicious behavior and insuring that the general's order to double the number of guards on duty had been carried out. Turner, meantime, desperately wrote reports to shift blame for the escape and save himself from charges. All the while, Billy lay on the cot in the surgery, too deep in pain to remember he had been invited to join the escape.

Tim Wann visited at least twice a day. Asked questions of Dr. Arnold, one more than others: "Who did it, Doctor?"

"I can't find out. I've tried like hell, but the guards in this place are a foul breed. They protect one another."

Tim suspected he knew the ringleader. He said, "Someone carried him off in the middle of the night. I was asleep—I never woke up." Pale with guilt, the Massachusetts boy looked at the puffed, discolored face on the thin gray pillow. Even sleeping, Billy occasionally winced in pain.

"No one else in your room saw anything?"

"They say not. It was late. Dark. Those who took him must have worked quietly."

"Goddamn us all for what we do in the name of patriotism. They did a job on him, all right. Something a lot worse than a beating with fists, though I still can't figure out the method."

"Can't Billy tell us? Give us the names or at least the descriptions of those responsible?"

Billy thrashed, arched his back, cried out softly. His left nostril began to ooze blood. The doctor bent to wipe it, giving Tim a bleak look.

"If he lives," he said.

Sunset. Sea birds circling. The air was calm and cold, though in the north massive cloud banks were building rapidly. Over on the Battery, windows glowed and the last daylight touched roof peaks and steeples. Bundled in his caped greatcoat, Cooper noticed mist forming on the water.

George Dixon finished his survey of the harbor and pushed the sections of his brass telescope together. "The mist will help. We have an ebb tide to assist us when we're ready to start back. It's our best opportunity thus far. I think we'll go."

He pivoted and called to the mate. "Mr. Fawkes? Rig the torpedo boom, if you please. I want to get under way promptly."

"Aye, aye, Captain," said the former Alabama soldier. All of the landsmen had learned nautical ways with speed and relish. Having survived the underwater test, they took pride in behaving like experienced tars.

"Which of the ships will be your target?" Cooper asked.

"I think it's best to determine that once we're past the harbor bar."

"I intend to row over to Sumter to watch." He held out his hand. "Godspeed, George. I'll expect you back by midnight."

"By all means," replied the young skipper with a brief smile. "I'm very proud to be taking her out. You should be proud, too. If we succeed, this night will live in history."

"You'll succeed," Lucius said, hovering behind his superior.

"Well—good-bye, then," Dixon said, striding down the pier as confidently as any master who had first gone into the tops as a boy. "Careful with that powder, lads. It's meant to sink a Yankee, not us."

A shiver chased down Cooper's back—a reaction not at all connected with the plunging temperature. This moment made all the peril, the worry, the pleading with Beauregard—even the coldness of his wife, who simply didn't understand him or the importance of his work—worthwhile.

Lucius climbed into the boat first. Through thickening mist, they rowed hard for the landing stage of the shell-blasted fort. Halfway there, Lucius pointed over Cooper's shoulder. "She's heading out." Cooper twisted clumsily on the thwart, barely in time to glimpse a red-orange glitter on the iron hull. Then the dark clouds closed. The slight bulge on the surface of the water disappeared.

From the seaward side of Fort Sumter, they watched darkness and mist rapidly hide the blockade fleet. Only a few signal lanterns showed where the vessels lurked. The night remained very quiet, very cold. Cooper grew nervous. He had just checked his watch once again—8:47 P.M.—when fire and noise erupted in the offshore mist.

Cooper caught his breath. "Which ship is it?"

"*Housatonic,*" said the major from the fort who had come up to watch with them. He passed his telescope, which Cooper peered through just as a sheet of flame carried pieces of timber and rigging skyward. The roar came rolling in over the harbor bar.

"She's hulled on the starboard side," Cooper crowed. "Just forward of the mainmast, I think. I can see men scrambling up the main and mizzen—oh—she's listing already!" He fairly hurled the telescope at his assistant. "Look while you can, Lucius. She's going down."

New lanterns were quickly lit on other ships in the enemy squadron. They heard faint yells through speaking trumpets. The steam warship nearest the sinking vessel put down lifeboats while men from the Sumter garrison rushed out of their quarters, clamoring to know what Confederate battery had fired and mortally wounded the steam sloop.

"None," said Cooper. "She was sunk by our submersible boat, *Hunley.*"

"You mean that coffin ship from Sullivan's Island?"

"She no longer deserves that reputation. Lieutenant Dixon and his crew will be decorated as heroes."

But they were slow to return. At eleven o'clock, Cooper and Lucius rowed back to the pier and kept a vigil that grew colder and grimmer by the hour. At six in the morning, Cooper said, "Let's go back to Charleston."

A haunted man, he trudged up Tradd Street and let himself into the house. No one in the city knew anything about the sinking of *Housatonic,* only that an explosion had occurred on one of the blockade vessels. Of the submersible there was no trace.

A few days later, following the capture of a Union picket boat, Cooper was able to confirm for General Beauregard that *Housatonic* had indeed gone down. He was disappointed to learn she had lost only five hands, thanks to the quick arrival of rescue boats.

"Two less than the number aboard *Hunley,"* he said to Lucius.

In the next few days, Cooper drank large amounts of whiskey and gin, hoping to induce heavy sleep. It refused to come. Every night he roamed the house or sat in a high-backed white-painted wicker chair, staring through the window at the garden drenched by winter rain. Of the garden he saw nothing. He saw instead his drowning son. Dixon's brave face just before *Hunley* sailed at sunset. Strangest of all, he saw the darkness that had surrounded him inside the fish-ship during the test. He saw it, smelled it, tasted it, too, knowing fully, painfully, how Dixon and the rest felt as they died. During these reveries he heard the great bells from the steeple of St. Michael's Church, though the ringing never seemed to coincide with the quarter-hours. All the clocks in the house were set wrong, he decided.

One night, nearly as exhausted as her husband by now, Judith brought a lamp to the room with the white wicker chair.

"Cooper, this can't continue—sitting up, never resting."

"Why should I go to bed? I can't sleep. The night of the seventeenth of February was a milestone in naval warfare. I try to find peace in that thought, and I can't."

"Because you—" She stopped.

"I know what you started to say. I am responsible for that milestone. I wanted it so badly I killed seven men."

She turned her back, unable to withstand his glare. He was right, though. She whispered to herself as much as to him, "You should have left her to rust. But you didn't, and I wouldn't have wished harm on any of those poor boys, but I'm glad *Hunley*'s gone. God forgive me. I'm glad. Perhaps it will finally purge some of the madness that torments you—"

His head jerked up. "What a peculiar choice of words—madness. I performed my duties to the best of my ability, that's all. I did my work. And there's more, much more, waiting. I will do it in the same way."

"Then nothing's changed. I had hoped—"

"What could possibly change?"

She raised her voice. "Won't you even let me finish a sentence?"

"To what purpose? I ask you again, Judith. What could possibly change?"

"You're so full of this awful rage—"

"More than ever. Poor Dixon's life must be paid for, and the life of every man who went down with him." His lips turned white. "Paid for ten times over."

The shudder of her arm rattled the lamp in her hand. "Cooper, when will you understand? The South can't win this war. It cannot."

"I refuse to debate the—"

"Listen to me! This—dedication to slaughter—it's destroying you. It's destroying us."

He turned his head, stiff and silent.

"Cooper?"

No movement. Nothing.

She shook her head and carried her lamp away, leaving him glaring at the rainy garden, the fury on his face digging lines so deep they were becoming permanent.

Passing the head of the stairs, Tim Wann noticed the motionless figure on the landing below. Tim looked a second time to be sure.

"Billy?"

The emaciated prisoner raised his head. Tim saw new streaks of white in the untrimmed hair. "Billy!" With a whoop and a slap of his leg, he bounded down to his friend, who supported himself with a padded crutch under his arm. "You're all right!"

"Well enough to come back to our splendid quarters. There are still some ribs healing, and I'm not steady on my feet—you talk too loudly, you're liable to blow me over. I'm a little slow getting

730

around. It's taken me ten minutes to come from the ground floor."

"Someone should have helped you."

"I guess Turner doesn't believe in coddling his guests. You can help me the rest of the way if you want."

Tim slid his arm around Billy, who put his across the shoulders of the young soldier. Thus they reached their room, where Billy was greeted by exclamations of surprise and shouts of welcome. Even one of the daytime guards said he was happy Billy had pulled through.

A lieutenant thoughtlessly slapped Billy on the back. Billy made a desperate stab with his crutch and prevented a fall. "Jesus, Hazard—I'm sorry," the lieutenant said.

" 'S all right." Sweat showed in Billy's beard suddenly. "I need to sit down. Someone give me a hand—?"

Tim did. Others crowded around. Billy asked, "Is it still February? I lost track downstairs."

"It's the first of March," a man said. "They've doubled the guard force outside. There's a column of our cavalry north of Richmond—practically on the doorsill. Three or four thousand horse. The rebs fear they've come to free us and raze the city."

"Do you know about the escape?" someone else asked. Billy shook his head, and heard about it. More than forty of the prisoners involved had been recaptured; but the rest, presumably, were on their way back to federal lines or already across. He learned next that Vesey, demoted to private, had been transferred to less comfortable duty outside one of the main doors.

They asked questions about his treatment downstairs, how he had gotten hurt. He answered each question with silence or a shake of his head. When he said he needed to visit the lavatory, Tim and another soldier lent a hand.

After Billy gained his feet, Tim said: "It was Vesey, wasn't it? Vesey tortured you and that's why he was demoted and tossed outside. That's right, isn't it?"

Billy's silence was already a matter of pride with him. "Never mind," he said. "I know who did it, and if I get a chance, I'll settle with him."

He wobbled on the crutch, pale and too feeble to settle much of anything. Tim and the other man exchanged looks.

Tim had kept Billy's improvised journal safe. That night, while

731

distant cannon fire reverberated through Libby, Billy wrote with the pencil stub.

Mar. 1—Two remarkable circumstances. I am alive when Dr. Arnold, the old toper in the surgery, expected I'd die. Also— the reb who took it as his duty to injure me taught me a lesson so monumental I do not wholly grasp it yet. In here, forced to obey any order, no matter how humiliating or destructive, I at last understand how the enslaved negro feels. I have dwelt a while in the soul of a shackled black man and taken a little of it into my own, forever.

94

Stanley found it increasingly hard to accept and deal with all the changes in his life. Pennyford continued to send monthly reports of the enormous profits earned by Lashbrook's. Stanley read each with disbelief. The figures could not possibly be real. If they were, no man deserved such wealth. Certainly he didn't.

He found it hard to cope with the swift flow of public events as well. Weariness with the war now infected the entire North, the President having hastened the process with his proclamation of amnesty and reconstruction, announced last December. Lincoln proposed to pardon all rebels except the highest government officials and former army and navy officers who had defected.

The plan was not harsh enough to suit Wade and Stevens and their crowd, therefore not harsh enough for Stanley either. But what other kind of plan could one expect from a negrophile half mad from perpetual sleeplessness and depression? Instead of thinking rigorously about the enemy and the postwar period, Lincoln busied himself with trivialities, pious orations at cemetery dedications and the like. At Gettysburg last November he had delivered himself of one such anthology of homilies, to the monumental boredom of the crowd.

Because of his increasingly pro-Negro position and his failure to bring the war to a successful end, Lincoln was a detested man. The capital seethed with rumors of plots to kidnap or murder him. Stanley heard a new one approximately once a week.

Further, influential Republicans believed the President had done the party great harm by insisting on a new draft of half a million men on the first of February. There would be a call for an additional one or two hundred thousand by mid-March, Stanton had confided. Humans were being ground up like sausage meat in a butcher shop because the generals couldn't win. Thomas had held fast at Chickamauga last autumn—the Rock, the rabble quickly named him—but the engagement itself had been disastrous, redeemed only slightly when Bragg's army was driven from Chattanooga into Georgia in November. Now, flogged to almost insane desperation, Congress had reactivated the grade of lieutenant general and bestowed it on a man Lincoln had chosen—that drunkard, Unconditional Surrender Grant. As general-in-chief, he would soon take charge in the Eastern theater; Old Brains had been demoted to chief of staff.

None of that would save the President, Stanley felt. Lincoln would lose the fall election—no cause for grief there. But the number of Republicans he could drag along to defeat frightened Stanley and his friends.

Increasingly, Stanley felt a desire to leave Washington. He still relished the power that went with his job. But he wasn't comfortable with the philosophies and programs of those with whom he had allied himself in order to survive the Cameron purge. In January, the Senate had proposed a constitutional amendment to abolish slavery—in Stanley's view, far too radical a step, taken too hastily. Too many Negroes were already free and out of hand. Everywhere you looked in the city, black soldiers and freedmen postured and paraded, swollen with new self-importance.

One morning Stanley was summoned by the secretary only moments after arriving at his desk. Stanley's cravat was askew, his hair rumpled, his appearance wild-eyed. Stanton noticed.

"What the devil's biting you?" he asked, brushing the underside of his scented beard. Before leaving home, Stanley had taken some swallows of whiskey on the sly. They loosened his tongue.

"Walking here on the avenue, I had an unbelievable experience. Unbelievable—disgusting—I scarcely know the proper word, it shook me so. I came face to face with seven freedmen who forced me to step into the street to get around them. They would not give me room on the walk!"

The whiskey lent him courage to ignore Stanton's sudden scowl. "I realize they have been downtrodden people, sir. But now they presume too much. They strut about with all the boldness of white men."

Through the little round spectacles, Stanton peered at his assistant. The patient air of the teacher replaced the anger of the zealot. "You must get used to it, Stanley. Like it or not, that's the way it will be henceforth. As Saint Paul wrote to the Corinthians, 'For the trumpet shall sound—and we shall be changed.'"

Not I, Stanley thought, still seething when he and the secretary concluded their business and he left. Not I, Mr. Stanton.

Yet he knew he swam against a flooding tide. When his part of the office was temporarily deserted, he unlocked a bottom drawer and pulled out a bottle of bourbon. He had slipped the first bottle into the drawer on the first business day of the new year; this was the third replacement.

A swift look at his surroundings. Safe. Moted sunlight flashed from the bottle as he tilted it. The loudly ticking clock showed twenty before ten.

The thunder blow—*"Missing in action"*—had fallen on the Hazards late last year. In mid-February, George finally learned something definite about Billy's fate, and with mingled relief and reluctance telegraphed Lehigh Station: YOUR HUSBAND SHOWN ON LATEST ROSTER LIBBY PRISON RICHMOND.

Brett packed the instant she got the news and took the first available train for Washington. When she arrived at the house in Georgetown—thinner now; nervous from months of anxiety—her first question was "What can we do?"

"Officially, the answer is very little," George said. "The mills of the exchange system have nearly ceased to grind. Too much bad feeling on both sides. Each receives reports of the other starving and mistreating prisoners. The War Department's furious because

734

the rebs won't follow protocol when they capture men from Negro regiments. They treat them as runaways and ship them back to slavery. White officers commanding Negro units are threatened with flogging or hanging. It's all gotten very nasty."

Brett flared. "You're right, that isn't much of an answer."

"Did you hear me precede it with the word *officially?*" George retorted. "I do have another suggestion."

Constance stepped behind his chair, reached down, and gently kneaded his shoulders. He was sleeping poorly these days, worrying about his brother and about his transfer to military railroads. It had not come through.

Brett was waiting. He cleared his throat. "In his post in the Richmond War Department, Orry may be able to help us. Old Winder has direct responsibility for Libby and Belle Isle and the rest of those—" he caught himself before saying hellholes "—places. But Seddon oversees Winder. And Orry works for Seddon."

Constance, eagerly: "You think Orry might be able to arrange Billy's release?"

"He's in the central government, and I'm sure he took an oath to serve loyally. I wouldn't ask him to break it. Even more important than that, he's my best friend. I would never risk endangering him by asking him to intervene directly."

Brett struck her skirt with her fist. "Billy's your own brother!"

"And Orry's yours. Be so kind as to let me finish, will you?" George jerked away from his wife's hand, rose, and paced from the breakfast table. "I can ask Orry to find out all he can about Billy's condition, and exactly where he is in Libby."

"How will you do that?" Constance asked, skeptical.

George looked at her. "By doing what he did when he wrote me last year. Break the law."

Out of uniform and wearing a dark overcoat, he rode south through a mid-March snowfall two nights later. He reached Port Tobacco after eight and paid the sly, toothless man who was waiting for him the sum of twenty dollars, gold. He gave the man a letter addressed to Orry, and a warning.

"You must give this to Colonel Main without drawing attention to him or to the act of delivery."

"Don't fret, Major Hazard. It'll be done just that way. I deliver secret mail into offices all around Capitol Square. You'd be astonished at how many."

And with the wink of the experienced profiteer, he slipped out the tavern's back door into the blowing snow.

• Grant had come to Washington at the first of the month. His hard hand was already being felt. A huge campaign would start in the spring, perhaps the final one. Fewer men would be exchanged because slowing paroles or stopping them entirely hurt the South more than it hurt the North.

Meantime, George and Brett and Constance waited. George had said nothing to Stanley about the illegal letter. When informed of Billy's capture last fall, Stanley had expressed only perfunctory sorrow.

George seldom saw his older brother these days. The war had transformed Stanley into a man of enormous personal wealth and a degree of importance in the radical Republican faction. It had also transformed him, incomprehensibly, into a person almost constantly under the influence of spirits. Stanley would have been dismissed, literally and otherwise, as a mere drunkard had he not been rich. Instead, he was tolerated by most and avoided by some, George being among the latter.

George had given up on Virgilia in much the same way. He had sent a letter to her hospital at Aquia Creek, reporting Billy's capture. She didn't reply. Fearing the chaos of the mails, he wrote again. The second time, he decided the silence was deliberate.

As spring drew closer, one of George's worries was relieved. He received orders to report for duty with the Military Railroad Construction Corps on the first of the month.

"I'll be working for old McCallum of the Erie instead of Herman, but at least it's field duty. No more contracts, crazed inventors, water-walkers—Winder Building!" He gave Constance a hug as they lay in bed the night he got the news. He felt her shiver, quickly added, "Don't fret over this. I'll be in no danger."

"Of course you'll be in danger," she said, a certain rare note in her voice, which told him something unusual was happening. He touched her cheek and found it damp.

She took the hand in hers. "But I shall pack up our things, dutifully return to Lehigh Station, and try to pretend otherwise."

Taking him by surprise, she shifted his hand to her breast and pressed it there. "If you'd make love to me, I might be able to sleep tonight."

He laughed softly, nuzzled her neck. "A pleasure, dear lady."

"Portly as I am?"

"Portly is in the eye of the beholder. If you call yourself portly, then portly's perfect."

"Oh, George—you are such a dear man. You can be obstinate. You're short-tempered. Sometimes even a bit vain. And it's impossible for me not to love you."

"Wait now—just a minute—" During the last part of her affectionate little speech, he had done a great lot of rolling and thrashing and flinging of bedclothes, propping himself at last on one elbow. "Since when do I deserve to be called vain?"

"You know as well as I that age is affecting your eyesight. Every evening I watch you bring the *Star* so close to your nose you almost poke a hole in the paper. But you won't admit you need spectacles—George, don't snort or harrumph like Stanley. What I said was all part of paying you a compliment. Heaven knows neither of us is perfect, but I was clumsily trying to say you could have a thousand faults instead of your one or two, and I'd still love you."

He cleared his throat, paused, then did it again. She could hear the smile in his voice as he relaxed and reached for her waist, drawing her in.

"Well," he said, "you'd better. And right away, too."

George exploded when the toothless man showed up in the Winder Building next morning.

"Good God, what possessed you to come here?" He shoved the courier toward the stairs, past the usual collection of contract-seekers and saviors of the Union who continued to treat the department as a second home.

" 'Cause I thought you'd want this right away." The man dangled a soiled and wrinkled envelope in front of his client. "It was waiting at the Richmond drop day 'fore yesterday."

"Not so loud," George whispered, scarlet. A brigadier coming upstairs cast a distrustful eye on the scruffy visitor. "I suppose you also brought it here expecting extra pay."

"Yessir, that did enter my mind. That's what this yere war's all about, ain't it? A chance for the enterprising fellow to make himself comfortable for the future—"

737

"Get out of here," George said, jamming bills in the courier's hand.

"Hey, these are greenbacks. I only take—"

"It's those or nothing." Snatching Orry's letter, he rushed back to his office.

He didn't dare read it there. Allowing time for the courier to leave the building, George put on his hat and escaped to Willard's. Seated at a rear table with beer he didn't want, he opened the letter. His hands shook.

Stump, it began. No names this time, except the old ones from the Academy. Orry was smart as ever, George thought, embarrassing tears in his eyes for a moment. He wiped them away and read on.

> *The party about whom you asked is here in Libby. I saw him day before yesterday, though from a distance only, because I did not want my interest to attract notice. I report to you sorrowfully that he appears to have been ill used by some of the bullies who staff the prison. I would guess he was beaten; he hobbles with the aid of a crutch, and I saw bruises.*
>
> *But he is alive and whole. Take heart at that. I shall attempt to locate a certain trooper of our acquaintance and, between us, we shall see what can be done. Old bonds of affection must count for something, even in these blighted times.*
>
> *It would be unwise for us to risk communication again, unless either finds it absolutely necessary. Do not be alarmed by prolonged silence from here. An effort will be made.*
>
> *My dear wife joins me in sending warmest felicitations to you and your family, and a prayer that we may all survive this terrible struggle. I sometimes fear the nation will be riven for years following a surrender—and if that word startles you, know that I do not employ it carelessly. The South is beaten. Shortages, dissent, wholesale army desertions all witness to the truth of the statement, though I might likely be hung if anyone but you read it.*
>
> *We may succeed in prolonging matters a while yet, inflicting further grief on those directly and indirectly involved, but it is essentially a concluded matter. Your side has won. Now we can only extract a high blood price for that victory. A sad state of affairs.*
>
> *My fondest hope is that whatever gulf exists after a surren-*

der will never be so wide as to keep you and me and our respective families from bridging it once again.

Emotionally shattered by what he was reading, George gulped the beer he didn't want. Flashing images in his head brought back the fiery night in April '61. The ruined house. The charred and swollen bodies. The harm beyond hope of repair. The fear was crawling in him again. Some moments passed before he had the courage to complete the letter.

God preserve you and yours. We shall do our utmost for the person in question.

> Yrs. affectionately,
> Stick

"An effort will be made." Brett clasped the letter between her breasts. "Oh, George, there it is, in Orry's own hand. An effort will be made!"

"Provided he can find Charles. He warns it will take a while."

Her face fell. "I don't know how I'll survive till we hear something."

"If Orry can stand the risk, you can stand the wait," George said, severe as a father chastising a thoughtless child. He had a premonition that it would be a very long time indeed before they heard anything. He prayed that if word did come, it would not be tragic.

95

George kissed his children after delivering a short lecture on how they must behave while he was gone. Then he embraced Constance, who struggled to contain tears. She presented him with a dried sprig of mountain laurel obviously pressed in a book. He kissed her once more, tenderly, by way of thanks. Then he slipped the sprig in his pocket, pulled on his talma, promised he would write soon, and went out to find transportation to Alexandria.

The day was gray and warm. A downpour started as the work train chugged to Long Bridge, which was wide enough to accommodate tracks and a parallel roadway for wagon and foot traffic. Pickets near a sign reading WALK YOUR HORSE waved at George on the rear platform of the caboose. He had chosen to ride there because the interior was stifling.

He touched fingers to his hat to return the greeting, then seized the handgrip and leaned into the rain to look ahead to green hills and the solid brick homes of the riverside town. Forsythia and daffodils, azaleas and apple blossoms colored the somber day. That was Virginia. That was the war. Memory showed him lurid images of Mexico and Manassas and the foreman's burning house. He was still glad to be going.

After searching nearly an hour, he located Colonel Daniel McCallum, Haupt's replacement, in the steamy O&A roundhouse. McCallum, a Scot with a fine reputation as a railway manager, had a fan-shaped beard of the kind common among senior officers. He also struck George as having a bad disposition. George's arrival—the interruption—didn't sit well.

"I've not a lot of time for you," the colonel said, motioning George to follow. They left the busy roundhouse with its great cupola, a local landmark, walked between stacked rails, some of Hazard's, and entered one of the many temporary buildings scattered in the yards. McCallum slammed the door in a way that said much about his frame of mind.

Taking the only chair in the tiny office, he unrolled the pouch containing George's transfer orders and smoothed the papers under rough, big-knuckled hands. He flipped to the second page, the third—too rapidly to be reading. It took no intelligence for George to realize he was unwelcome.

Understandable enough, he supposed; the papers included a letter of recommendation from Haupt. In Washington, it was said that McCallum had intrigued against George's friend, done his utmost to ingratiate himself with Stanton and turn opinion against Haupt so that McCallum would eventually inherit command of the department.

McCallum put the papers in the pouch and handed it back with a slashing motion of his forearm. "You have no practical experience in bridge repair or rail construction, Major. So far as I can determine, your prime qualification for the Construction Corps seems to be your friendship with my predecessor."

George clenched his hand around the pouch, ready to punch the colonel's face. McCallum wrinkled his nose and peered out a small, filthy window. A spring shower was splattering a nearby stack of rails.

Finally he deigned to return his attention to the man standing before him. "General Grant wants the Orange and Alexandria kept open, in good repair, all the way down to Culpeper, his base camp for the spring offensive. It's a tall order because of the Confederate partisans who operate along much of the right of way. The trestle at Bull Run has been rebuilt seven times. What I am saying is, we have not a spare moment for instructing beginners."

"I can swing a pick, Colonel. I can dig with a shovel or pound a spike. No training required." The man offended George because his dislike of Haupt, and therefore Haupt's friends, was not hidden. George wanted no part of such politicking. He wanted to

741

work, and he didn't give a damn if he had to give offense to secure the place to which his orders entitled him.

The rain drummed. A whistle blew, bells rang. McCallum's silence conveyed increasing belligerence. All at once George realized he might be holding a trump or two.

"I know you need officers in the Construction Corps, Colonel. A lot of white men won't command contrabands. I will."

McCallum's sour mouth twitched. "A worthy suggestion, but one our table of organization won't allow, I regret to say. The basic unit of the corps is a ten-man squad. Two such squads are led by one officer. A first lieutenant." The twitch became a smirk. "You are too well educated, laddie—"

George recognized a jibe at the Academy when he heard one. This time he really had to fight the impulse to hit the old bastard.

"—too qualified, if you see what I mean. Have you considered applying for staff duty with General Grant?"

George showed his highest card. "I attended West Point with Sam Grant. I campaigned with him from Vera Cruz to Mexico City. Maybe I should apply to him to straighten out this mess." He shook the pouch. "I was granted a transfer to the military railroads, and now I find I'm refused."

In seconds, McCallum turned gray as the weather. "Nae, nae—there's no need to involve higher-ups in this. No problem's insurmountable. The rules can be bent a wee bit. We can find you a place—"

Seeing George mollified, the older man studied him in a sly way. "If you are indeed willing to lead colored men."

"That's what I said, Colonel. I am."

Twenty-four hours later, in the mustering area, George met his two squads and began to question the certainty with which he had spoken. Tense, he inspected the Negroes while they inspected him. If his scrutiny reflected interest and curiosity, theirs was suspicious. In a few cases, hostile.

They were no more varied, physically, than any randomly gathered group of men except, George quickly observed, in one way: all but one of the blacks were taller than George.

He had dressed for this meeting with special care, though the effect was the opposite. His outfit consisted of old corduroy trousers, non-regulation, stuffed into muddy boots, and a short fatigue jacket of summer-weight linen. He wore no insignia except a turreted-castle-and-wreath device pinned at a careless angle on the stubby collar of the jacket. The silver metal of the device showed he was an officer, but that was all.

At that, he looked better than his men, most of whom were dressed for duty, not show. Their pants were as assorted as their faces, but all had regulation army pullover work shirts without cuffs. At the long-vanished moment of manufacture, the cotton flannel shirts had been white. Three men wore shoes whose uppers had separated from the soles. Products of Stanley's factory, perhaps?

Preparing to address the men, George clasped his hands behind his back and unconsciously raised on tiptoes. Someone caught that and chuckled. George spoke at once, loudly.

"My name is Hazard. I have just transferred to the Construction Corps. Henceforward, you men will be working for me."

"No, sir," said the one Negro shorter than George, a dusky mite with wrists no thicker than saplings. "I'm takin' orders from you, but I'm workin' for me."

The quickness amused George, but he felt he shouldn't show it. "Let me see if I understand. Are you saying you're a free man, therefore this duty is your choice?"

The dusky man grinned. "You're pretty smart—for a white boss."

Laughter. George couldn't help joining in. His tension broke. These men would be all right.

96

Burdetta Halloran had carried her investigation as far as she could. Now she must involve the authorities. But to whom should she give her information?

The question stayed with her, unanswered, during the frightening raid conducted by two bodies of Union horse, led by Brigadier Judson Kilpatrick and Colonel Ulric Dahlgren, son of the Yankee admiral of the same name. Kilpatrick's men had ridden to within two and a half miles of Capitol Square before home guards under Bob Lee's boy Custis drove them back, with assistance from Wade Hampton.

The second attacking force, five hundred horse commanded by Dahlgren, approached Richmond through Goochland County. After Dahlgren died from enemy fire, a thirteen-year-old boy found orders and a memorandum book on the body. The documents, in Dahlgren's handwriting, outlined the purposes of the raid.

Prisoners to be set free. Richmond to be put to the torch. President Davis to be executed, together with all members of his cabinet.

The Confederate capital, which had reeled with fright at the approach of the cavalry, began reeling with rage the moment the contents of Dahlgren's papers were disclosed. The liars in Washington immediately claimed every word a forgery.

During the emergency, there was little outward change in the life of the auburn-haired widow. Burdetta Halloran continued to wage her daily war with escalating prices and the riffraff swarming on the streets and the pervasive certainty that the armies of U.S. Grant would strike at the Confederacy with the onset of warm weather.

Most of all, Mrs. Halloran struggled with the question of greatest emotional importance to her. How to set retribution in motion? If she waited too long and Richmond came under siege, government officials might be too busy to listen to her. The quarry might escape. *To whom should she speak?*

She was still without an answer when a friend boasted that she had been invited to one of the increasingly rare levees at the White House. Pleading, Mrs. Halloran arranged an invitation for herself. She had by this time rejected the idea of going to the most logical person, old Winder.

She did so for several reasons. He was vile-tempered, with a reputation for being contemptuous of women. His staff consisted mostly of illiterate former criminals. And he acted so harshly and precipitously in many cases that he had a long record of overturned arrests and thwarted prosecutions. Gossip said he wouldn't last another three months. Mrs. Halloran wanted to deal with some official who could handle her information properly.

On the evening of the levee—late March—more than a hundred people filled the White House. Wearing her finest dark blue velvet—a trifle heavy, but rich-looking—Mrs. Halloran quickly separated herself from her friend in order to circulate.

She took a cup of sassafras tea—she would drink nothing spirituous tonight; she wanted a clear head—and over the rim surveyed the crowd of government officials and senior military men and their wives. A merry crowd, she thought, considering the circumstances. Then she spied Varina Davis.

Only in her late thirties, the President's wife had the worn appearance of a woman twenty years older. Her husband's burdens had become hers. The President himself, gracious as ever with his guests, was, like his spouse, clearly exhausted. Small wonder, Mrs. Halloran thought as she recovered from the shock of seeing the first lady. Davis was under fire on every front. Under fire because he clung to Bragg and rejected Joe Johnston. Under fire because of worthless money and runaway prices. Under fire because his government and his leadership had failed for three years and continued to fail.

Burdetta Halloran tried not to become depressed as she mingled. She kept her mind on her objective.

She joined a group around Secretary Seddon. Grimly, the secretary was describing how he had nearly lost his Goochland County estate to the torch of Dahlgren's raiders. She moved on to plump, suave Benjamin, who had many more listeners than Mr. Seddon.

"I contend that the Confederacy might do well to steal a leaf from Lincoln's book and adopt his program of emancipation *in toto.*"

The reactions—astonishment, anger—did nothing to perturb Benjamin. Up came one cautioning, well-manicured hands as he continued. "It is, I know, a proposition easy to dismiss as radical. But consider: at one stroke we could augment our depleted army with great numbers of Negroes and instantly undercut all the moralizing that has become a way of life for the black Republicans."

"Nigras will never fight for the people who chained them," someone snorted.

Benjamin first replied with a nod and a rueful smile. "That, of course, is the plan's great flaw. In any case, the President has asked that I do not promote my view to the public at large. I comply. I therefore ask you to regard this conversation as private, among close friends. I endeavor to be, always, a good and faithful servant."

One of his plump hands plucked an oyster from a silver bowl and dispatched it down his throat with gusto. You also endeavor to be a survivor, so I hear, Burdetta said to herself, gliding on.

Across the room, she noticed a tall officer, handsome in a gaunt sort of way. He drew the eye because of his empty left sleeve, pinned up at the shoulder.

She approached cautiously. He was making some point about the military situation to three other people, one a handsome woman with the look of a Spaniard or a Creole. The woman clung to the officer's good arm. His wife?

The man impressed her. She glided away again, inquired here and there, and soon got an answer.

"That's Colonel Main, one of Mr. Seddon's assistants. His duties? Various. I don't know all of them, but one is to act as a watchdog on that beast Winder."

Burdetta Halloran beamed. "Thank you so much for the information. Will you excuse me while I exchange this empty cup for a glass of white wine?"

The search was over.

She was ushered to Orry's desk in the War Department at half past eleven the following morning. Polite and surprisingly graceful despite his handicap, he positioned the visitor's chair for her. "Kindly be seated, Mrs.—Halloran, I believe you said?"

"Yes, Colonel. Is there somewhere we might speak that is more private? I've come on a matter of extreme gravity which is also highly confidential."

Skepticism flickered in Orry's dark eyes. Despite his good manners, he was tense and had been for two weeks. Each morning he awoke with the hope that today he would glance up from his desk to see Cousin Charles striding in. As soon as he had received the letter from George and gone to Libby to see Billy's condition for himself, he had written Charles, in care of Hampton's command, requesting an urgent meeting.

Of course, when the Yanks, the Kilcavalry, struck, Charles had no doubt been occupied, to say the least. But the emergency was over. At minimum, he could have sent a note. Couriers traveled between Richmond and field headquarters frequently. Did the silence mean Charles was hurt? If so, all the responsibility fell on him—

With some struggle, he wrenched his attention back to Mrs. Halloran's question. "Let me see whether our small conference room is free."

It was. He led her in and shut the door. From her reticule she took a folded paper. Spread out, it proved to be a sketch map of the James River below the city. She had indicated several landmarks and drawn four small squares on the riverbank in the Wilton Bluffs area.

She pointed to the squares. "These represent the buildings of an abandoned farm, Colonel. Abandoned, that is, except by those now conducting business on the premises at night. If you investigate, you will find this farm is the headquarters for a cabal led by a certain Mr. Lamar Hugh Augustus Powell, of Georgia."

Orry tap-tapped his long fingers on the gleaming table. What did this attractive woman want? She had a steely, desperate quality he had detected at once. It showed in her posture, her eyes, her controlled voice.

"Powell," he said. "I believe I've heard the name. Speculator, isn't he?"

"By profession. His avocation is treason."

Quickly, she told the rest. Powell's cabal was gathering and storing weapons at the Wilton Bluffs farm. With her nail she touched the rectangle immediately next to the line representing the bluff. "This is the shed that once housed implements. On this side it's a sheer drop, a long one, down to the James. But the shed may be approached safely through this field to the north. Or possibly—"

"Wait, please. I'm sorry to interrupt you, but before we go on, you must tell me the purpose of the cabal. There's nothing illegal about owning and storing weapons, especially if the purpose is home defense."

"The purpose," she said, "is to assassinate President Davis and one or more senior members of the cabinet."

In that deliberate way of his, Orry remained motionless to let his thoughts catch up. After his astonishment passed, he didn't laugh. Didn't even feel like it. "Mrs. Halloran—with all respect for the patriotic impulse that brought you here—do you have any concept of how many reports of threats against the life of Mr. Davis reach these offices every week? One or two—at minimum. Many weeks, the number is much higher."

"I can't help that. My information is correct. If you search this building I'm showing you, I guarantee you will discover rifles, revolvers, infernal devices—"

"Bombs?" That rattled him; it wasn't typical. "What type? How are they to be used?"

"I can't answer either question—I don't know. But I assure you there are explosive devices on the property. Stage a raid; you'll find them. You may even find the plotters. They meet frequently."

"How soon is this attempt to be carried out?"

"I've been unable to learn that."

"All right, then how did you come by the information you do possess?"

The steel was impregnable. He saw it even before she said, "It's impossible for me to tell you that. My refusal involves matters of trust. Promises made—"

"Obviously your inquiry must have taken a great deal of time—"

"Months."

"And determination."

"I am a patriot, Colonel Main."

Somehow he doubted the assertion. Again he said nothing. The attractive Mrs. Halloran struck him as one of those people who had a tightly guarded inner place where true opinions, motives, methods were carefully hidden and permanently unreachable. In that respect, she reminded him of Ashton.

He cleared his throat before resuming. "I don't doubt you for a moment. Nevertheless, it would be extremely helpful if I had some idea of how you came by your information."

"I gathered much of it myself. A person I trust helped with other pieces—actual observation of the farm at night, for example. That is the most I can say. Why do such details matter? What counts the most is the plan. The threat!"

"Agreed. Please allow me another question."

Curiously, the sudden masked look of her eyes reminded him of someone he hadn't thought of in a long time: Elkanah Bent. "All right."

"Didn't it occur to you that the provost marshal is the logical man to hear what you've just told me? Oh, but perhaps you've already—"

"No." She made a face, as if she had bitten into spoiled meat. "I have never met General Winder, but I despise him, like any right-thinking citizen. The civilian population can't find enough food, yet he persists with his ridiculous price decrees that anger the farmers and make the situation worse. I would never deal with a man who's done as much to harm our cause as any general on the other side."

On that point, anyway, Mrs. Halloran had a lot of company. She sounded convincing. His fingers tap-tapped the table. Beyond the closed door, war clerk Jones complained about some error in paperwork.

"Is there anything else?"

"No more facts, Colonel. Only this: I promise that if you investigate, you'll find every word is true. If you fail to investigate—dismiss what I've said, for whatever reason—the death of the President will be on your conscience."

"That's a heavy burden." He sounded unfriendly for the first time.

"Yours now, Colonel. Good day."

"Just a moment."

The command caught her half risen from the chair. "We're not finished. I will take you to one of my clerks. You'll give him your full name, place of residence, and other pertinent information. That is routine with everyone who aids the War Department."

Burdetta Halloran's tension melted under a flood of relief and joy. Main's long, furrowed face, his patient manner—above all, his anger when she tweaked his conscience, and his subsequent display of strength—told her something important. Her intelligence and judgment were all she believed them to be. He was precisely the right man.

She smiled. "Thank you, Colonel. I'll cooperate to the full, so long as I can remain anonymous."

"I'll do my best to respect your wish, but I make no promises."

She hesitated. Thought of Powell. Murmured, "I understand. I agree to the terms. What will you do first?"

"That, I'm not free to say. But I assure you of one thing. The statements you've made won't be ignored."

She saw the iron wall drop in his eyes and knew it was useless to argue or ask more questions. No matter. She had set the machine in motion. Powell was finished.

"Of course I said her statements wouldn't be ignored," he explained to Madeline that night. "What else could I tell someone pretending to be sincere?"

Madeline caught the significance of the word pretending. He went on. "I didn't inform her of the next step because I was damned if I knew what it should be. I still don't. One thing I told her was correct. Reports of assassination schemes are common. Yet this one—How can I properly explain why it feels different? Not because the woman impressed me. I think she's out to get someone. Powell, probably. What bothers me is one question: Why should she invent so many concrete details when it's obvious that an hour's investigation can prove them false? Is she stupid? No. Telling the story may be her way of getting revenge. But maybe the story's also true."

"Powell," Madeline repeated. "The same Powell who was Ashton's investment partner?"

"That's the one."

"If there's a plot, could she be involved?"

Orry reflected only a moment. "No, I don't think so. Ashton isn't precisely a zealot about the cause. Beyond that, it's my im-

750

pression that those who try to change history by killing someone are afflicted with several kinds of lunacy. Condoning murder—being willing to do the deed—that's one, and the most obvious. Another, slightly less obvious, is lack of concern about personal consequences. Ashton never heard of self-sacrifice, or if she did, she laughed. Ashton cares for Ashton. I could believe that James would risk himself in some crazy political scheme, but not my sister."

She nodded. "Does anything else bother you?"

"Yes. The woman's refusal to go to Winder. It was perfect—and perfectly performed. Yet Winder's precisely the man who should be told first. He'd arrest Powell, lock him up, then look into the charges. Instead of doing that, Mrs. Halloran came to the War Department—surely knowing we'd be more deliberate than the provost, though ultimately, if we built a case, it would stand up. Winder's often don't. What I'm saying is, I think she wants results more than she wants quick revenge. Wants them and knows they can be gotten. That bothers me—that and those damn details. We hear of plot after plot, but seldom do we get specifics. Here we have the very center of the cabal pinpointed. She drew the map, which I locked in my desk. One last detail disturbs me most of all."

"What is it?"

"Bombs. It's the first time I've heard infernal devices mentioned in connection with assassination. Knives, pistols, yes. But not bombs."

Raising his hand, Orry slowly squeezed space between thumb and forefinger. "It's the kind of tiny detail that sets my teeth rattling—with or without that prod about bearing the guilt if I do nothing and something happens."

"Will you go to the secretary?"

"Not yet. Nor Winder either. But I may take a ride down the river alone some evening soon."

She knelt at his side, rested her cheek on his right sleeve. "It could be dangerous if you do."

"But disastrous if I don't."

751

97

"And then—"

Charles interrupted the tale to puff his cigar, down to a stub now. The smell grew as the length decreased.

Gus could barely tolerate the smoke. She shifted sideways, away from his bare hip, and pulled the light cover higher on her stomach. The cigar's glow faded, the pale plane of Charles's chest disappeared in the dark.

Though she wouldn't have admitted it, when he failed to say something about her pulling away—didn't even reach for her hand—it was a hurt. Small, but there were so many of them recently. They devastated her. She no longer had the ability to armor herself with words. Once she had lowered the defense, she couldn't seem to raise it again.

"—Hugh Scott and Dan and I slid some logs into the river. We hung onto them and paddled across. The water was cold as sin, and the dark made it worse." He was speaking quietly, reflectively —almost as if he were alone with his thoughts. Which in a sense was not far from the truth.

For most of the winter, he had bivouacked at Hamilton's Crossing. It was no great distance from the farm, but that didn't mean she saw him more often. He was away on duty most of the time. Tonight, as usual, his arrival had taken her by surprise. He rode up just after dark, wolfed the supper she prepared quickly, then grabbed her hand and led her to bed with the same brusqueness he had exhibited at the table. Scarcely a trace of his old politeness remained, though that wasn't the serious issue. The war had wrought a change, and the change had beaten many things out of him, manners being but one.

He was describing events at the time of last month's Richmond raid. She prompted him to go on by saying, "You crossed the river toward the enemy?"

"That's usually how it works when you're a scout. You've been around me long enough to know that much."

"Do forgive my lapse of memory."

Instantly, she regretted the bitterness. The regret was wasted. He just hitched his body higher against the creaky headboard and turned his face away, toward the open window and the slow, stately dance of moonlit curtains. The April night smelled of the earth Washington and Boz had plowed that day. In the pasture behind the barn, where rain had created small ponds in low places, bullfrogs honked.

"We did a lot more than swim the Rappahannock that night—" The memory brought a chuckle, which pleased and relieved her; she hadn't heard him laugh in quite a while. "We went on, soaked through, till we found the Yankee column. It was Kilpatrick, all right. We hid out until we could snag three of his spare horses as they went by. We mounted and rode along for a while, bareback."

"In the middle of the Union cavalry?"

"No one noticed in the dark. And it was easier for us to count noses while we were right among 'em. We even forded the river with General Kilpatrick and his boys. I wish we could have shot some of the sons of bitches, but we had to carry our information back to division. So, south of the river, we split away—the dumb sods didn't notice that, either. We rode like fury, and that's the reason General Hampton was waiting when Little Kil showed up."

She wanted to soothe the hardness from his voice. "That is quite a story," she said, patting his bare arm.

Instantly, he rolled away, lifted the curtain, and flipped the cigar butt into the side yard. An Indian cobra of smoke formed in the moonlight. "Got a few more—" a great loud yawn "—but I'll save them for morning."

He pulled up the cover, pecked her cheek, rolled onto his left side, and within half a minute started to snore.

The curtains leaped and fell back, partners in a moonlit quadrille. Gus pushed the back of her head deeper into the bolster and once again tugged the cover higher, to warm her breasts. She rubbed her right cheek, surprised and angered by what she felt.

I think he's done with me, and I don't know why. I think he wants to end it and hasn't the courage to say so.

The change, whose causes she understood only in a general way, was poisoning every part of their relationship. His love-making had been drained of tenderness; he thrust hard and hastily all the time, with few kisses and no spoken endearments. What was she to do? There were no alternatives. She couldn't stop what was happening to him or stop loving him either.

Facing that quandary and the growing feeling that they were finished, she had been sleepless many a night lately. This promised to be another such night. "Oh God," she said very faintly, continuing to cry in silence.

Later, she opened her eyes and realized she must have slept after all. Freezing there beside him, she burrowed under the cover and called herself a ninny for her earlier behavior. "Oh, God." The tears. The despair.

She had always prided herself on strength, self-sufficiency. And merely because she had lowered her defenses and thereby gotten her emotions trampled, she needn't let it continue. She did love Charles, but if the price of it was perpetual misery, she refused to pay. The wrenchings of the war wouldn't stop—at least not soon enough—so it was up to her to force him to his senses.

He needed a shock. A dose of strong medicine. She would give it to him in the morning. Feeling secure again, she fell asleep.

He had others things on his mind in the morning. He strode into the kitchen soon after sunrise, tucking in his gray shirt and pulling up his galluses. She had scarcely offered her greeting before he announced, "I meant to say my piece about Richmond last night. Any day now—"

"There will be more fighting. You must think I'm an idiot, Charles, always needing instructions from the all-knowing male. I realize the Union forces are at Culpeper Court House and they'll march soon—this way, undoubtedly. But you aren't going to decide when I must look for shelter in the city." She struck her wooden spoon on the edge of the stove, where grits were simmering. "I will decide."

His face grew long above his white-spiked beard. He hooked a stool with his boot, pulled it from under the table, and lit a fresh cigar as he sat down. "What in hell's got into you?"

She threw the spoon on the stove and marched toward him. "A strong desire to settle some things. If you care for me, act like it. I'm tired of your clomping in here whenever you take a notion. Helping yourself to a meal and—whatever else you want, and grumbling and growling like a boor the whole time."

He drew the smoldering cigar from his mouth. "Having me around doesn't suit you, Mrs. Barclay?"

"Don't glare and sneer at me. You treat me like a combination cook, laundress, and whore."

He jumped up. "In the middle of a war, people don't have time for all the little niceties."

"In this house they do, Charles Main. Otherwise they don't set foot in it. Every time you're here, you act as if you'd rather be somewhere else. If that's true, say so and let's be done with it. Believe me—" *no, don't,* said a voice she ignored "—in the state you're in, you're no prize."

In the side yard, her rooster chased two cackling hens. Boz, chopping wood, sang "Kingdom Coming" with la-la's instead of words. Charles stared at Gus, his eyes wide above the dark half-circles that had been there since he came back from Pennsylvania last summer. Suddenly, she saw a startled innocence in his gaze.

Elated, she didn't dare smile. But she had gotten through. Now they could talk. Work it out. Save—

Fierce knocking. Washington on the kitchen stoop.

"Man on horseback jus' turned in. Comin' around back right now."

Hoofbeats and the jingle of metal sounded outside. Charles grabbed for his gun belt hanging on a chair, jerked out the six-shot Colt. He was crouching when the horseman's round face and flop hat passed the side windows.

Charles stood, hung the gun belt over his shoulder, and opened the kitchen door. "What are you doing here, Jim?"

"Hate to roust you out, Charlie, but this here letter come for you 'bout ten o'clock last night. Morning, Miz Barclay." Jim Pickles touched his hat with the crumpled missive, which he then handed to Charles.

"Good morning, Jim." Gus slowly wiped one hand on her apron, then the other. The chance was lost.

Jim pointed to the letter. "Says War Department on it. Personal an' confidential. Mighty fancy."

"Looks like it's been buried under six feet of dirt."

"Well, pretty near. Man who brung it said it was in a bunch of letters an' dispatches somebody come across in the woods near Atlee's Station. They found the courier shot dead—been there some time, I guess—an' his pouch open an' this an' a lot of other stuff strewn about. Mebbe Kilpatrick's sojers did it. Anyway, the letter's been a while in root, as the saying goes."

To Gus, Charles said, "Atlee's Station in the place General Hampton and three hundred of us bushwhacked Kilpatrick on the first of March. We yelled so loud, we made 'em think we were three thousand—"

He was breaking the seals, unfolding the sheet. His beard lifted in the morning breeze. "You're right, Jim; it was written in February. It's from my Cousin Orry, the colonel."

Stunned, he read on. Then he gave Gus the letter. Consisting of one long paragraph, it was inscribed in a fine hand, with all the proper loops and flourishes. As she finished reading, Charles said to Jim, "Billy Hazard is in Libby Prison. Half dead, according to that."

"You talkin' about some Yank?"

"My old friend from West Point. I've told you about him."

"Oh, yeh," said the younger scout, unimpressed. "What are you s'posed to do about it?"

"Go see Orry in Richmond right away. I'll get my gear."

Starting back into the kitchen, Charles had a thought. He turned and pointed at Jim. "And you forget what I just said, understand? You never heard a word."

The swift clump of his boots faded inside. Jim Pickles dismounted, stretched in the sunshine, scratched his armpit, as cardinals swooped in and out of the budding red oaks at the front of the property.

"So Charlie's goin' to Richmond, hah? I s'pect he can get away, all right. Things are still pretty quiet. Guess it's the old calm before the storm. General Hampton's back home in Columbia, tryin' to muster three new regiments so Butler an' some of the old hands will get a little relief. Say, Miz Barclay, may I show you something?"

Reluctantly, she turned her gaze from an empty kitchen. "Surely, Jim."

756

From the pocket of his butternut shirt he took a small, square case of cheap yellow metal. "Mighty proud of this. Came two days ago. My sisters got together an' paid for it." He opened the case on an oval ambrotype of an unsmiling middle-aged woman wearing a black dress. Her face looked like something made from granite, with very little of the granite block removed.

"That's my ma," he said proudly. "Fine likeness, too. She's raised us kids since Pa died. I was only four when he went out shootin' deer with a bunch of boys an' got his leg blowed off. He only lasted two weeks. Ma ain't been in the best of health the last year or so. Worries me. I love her better than any person in this world, an' I ain't ashamed to say it. I'd walk through fire if it'd please her."

"That's commendable, Jim," Gus said, returning the case.

Charles appeared with his hat, patched jacket, and the little cloth bag in which he kept his razor and cigars. He squeezed her arm gently, gave her cheek a peck.

"You mind what I told you about Richmond."

Unhappy because the chance to set things straight had slipped away, she burst out, "I'm not one of your recruits to be ordered about. I told you, I'll make my own decision."

The fiery sunrise filled his eyes. "All right. We'll settle this whole mess next time." It was less plea than warning. She folded her arms over her bosom.

"If I'm here."

"My God, you've got a vinegar tongue this morning."

"So have you. And I'm astonished by your tender concern for your Yankee friend. I thought you wanted to kill every last man on the other side."

"I'll only go to Richmond because it's Orry who's asking. That enough explanation for you? Come on, Jim, let's get my horse."

She stormed inside and kicked the door shut. When she heard the flurry of hoofs at the side of the house, she didn't leave the stove or raise her hand. The grits were burned. Ruined.

As the sounds grew faint, she ran to the side window, the tears born of failure coming again. She strained and squinted, but she could see nothing but dust where the Fredericksburg road vanished into the greening countryside.

Halfway to the capital, a pass in his pocket, Charles rested Sport beside a sunlit creek. While the gray drank, he reread Orry's letter. What business did he have answering such a summons? No more than he had prolonging his involvement with Gus. War changed a lot of things.

He sat on a half-buried rock beside the purling stream and read the letter a third time. Old memories, emotions, began to undercut his rigid sense of duty. Hadn't the Mains and the Hazards— well, most of them—vowed that the bonds of friendship and affection would survive the hammerings of this war? This wasn't simply one more Yank Orry was writing about. This was his best friend. And the husband of his own Cousin Brett.

That was one bond. Another, forged at the Academy, couldn't be broken or dismissed easily either. Many an officer leading troops against an old classmate had learned the truth of that.

He put the letter in his pocket, ashamed of his first impulses to ignore it. He didn't like himself much any more, for that and a lot of other reasons. He smoked another cigar, then galloped on toward Richmond.

98

Afterward, Judith realized she should have been prepared for catastrophe. All the warning signs were there.

Cooper seldom slept more than two hours a night. Often he never came home at all, spreading a blanket on the floor of his office. He was dragging Lucius down, too. The exhausted young man finally got up nerve to appeal to Judith privately—could she not do something, anything, to slow her husband's demented pace?

Lucius hinted that some of the tasks Cooper assigned him were make-work. Judith didn't question that, since it was already clear to her that her husband's fatigued mind was confusing motion with purpose.

She promised Lucius she would try to remedy the situation. She spoke to Cooper in what she considered a gentle and tactful way, but only provoked an outburst that kept him away from Tradd Street for two whole days.

Since his temper erupted without pattern or logic, there was no way to anticipate and avoid circumstances that might trigger it. She could do little more than keep the house calm and quiet whenever he was there. Marie-Louise was forbidden to play or practice her singing, a ban that brought on arguments with her daughter. She issued no social invitations and refused the few they received.

In this way she preserved an uneasy tranquillity until mid-April, when it was announced that General Beauregard would leave to command the Department of North Carolina and Southern Virginia. What was really being thrust on him was responsibility for the Richmond defense lines. A farewell reception at the Mills House was quickly arranged. Cooper announced this fact and said they would go. On the day of the reception, Judith tried to persuade him to change his mind—he had rested less than an hour the night before—but he seized his tall gray hat and matching gloves and his best walking stick, and she knew she was defeated.

They left through the Tradd Street gate. Judith took her husband's arm. His expression bemused, he was listening to the tolling bells of St. Michael's.

At Meeting, they turned north toward the hotel. The mild air, mellow gaslights, and blue shadows of evening created the illusion of a city at peace. She could tell Cooper wasn't at peace. He hadn't spoken since leaving the house. His downturned mouth and vacant eyes, familiar sights, still had the power to inflict great hurt.

They reached the Broad Street intersection and paused beside two soldiers near the steps of St. Michael's. About half a block away, on the other side of Meeting, a group of eighteen or twenty prisoners approached. The Yanks had probably been captured out on Morris Island. Three boys in gray, none older than eighteen, guarded the older men, who were laughing and talking as if they enjoyed their captivity.

759

Gaslight flashed on the bayonets of the young guards and cast bright glints into Cooper's eyes. His head ached from the loud ringing of the bells in the steeple above. He watched the Yanks come shambling and skylarking across Meeting toward the corner where he stood with his wife. A blue-coated sergeant, heavy-bellied, noticed Judith, smiled, and said something to the prisoner next to him.

Cooper flung her hand off his arm and ran into the street. She called his name, but he was already pulling the sergeant out of line. The youthful guard at the head of the column and the two at the rear looked stunned. Cooper shook the astonished prisoner.

"I saw you watching my wife. Keep your eyes and your filthy remarks to yourself."

Voices overlapped. Judith's: "I'm sure the man didn't—"

The guard in charge: "Sir, you must not interfere—"

The Irishman next to the sergeant: "Listen here, he never said a—"

"I know otherwise." Cooper was shrill. He jabbed the sergeant with his stick. "I saw it."

"Mister, you're out of your skull." The sergeant backed up hastily, bumping men behind. "Will someone help me get this crazy reb away from—"

"I saw your expression. You said something filthy about her." Cooper had to speak loudly because of the noise of the other prisoners protesting, the bells pealing.

"Please, sir, stop," pleaded the guard without effect.

"I know you did, and by God, I'll have an apology."

The sergeant had had enough. "You'll get nothing but the back of my hand, you fucking traitor, you—"

The descending stick shimmered in the gaslight. Judith cried out as Cooper struck the sergeant on top of the head, then on the right temple. The sergeant raised his arms to block the blows. "Get him off me!" Cooper dragged one of the Yank's hands down and hit him twice more. The sergeant dropped to one knee, groggily shaking his head.

The Irish prisoner tried to intervene. Cooper's hat fell off as he rammed the cane ferrule into the man's throat, then struck the sergeant again. The blow broke his stick. "Oh, my God, Cooper, stop." Pulling at him, Judith saw spittle on his lips. He threw her off.

He reversed the piece of cane still in his hand. He smashed the

760

sergeant's head with the silver knob. Blood showed in the prisoner's hair. Judith again attempted to take hold of Cooper's arm. He rammed it backward, snorting like an animal. His elbow bruised her breast. She heard obscenities he had never uttered in all the years she'd known him.

A couple of prisoners joined the terrified guards in attempting to block Cooper's renewed attack. Somehow he fought past them, locked both hands on the piece of stick, and raised it over his head. The sergeant, kneeling in the street, pressed a hand to his right eye. Blood flowed down his forehead and ran out between his fingers.

"You killed my son," Cooper screamed, landing one more blow. Finally, enough hands in blue sleeves caught hold of him and were able to restrain him, break his grip, tear the stick loose. The sergeant started to weep with shock. The prisoners and the guard in charge surrounded Cooper, dragging him back. He was pulling, kicking, biting, lunging side to side.

"Let me go—he killed my boy—my son's dead—he killed him."
The mass of men bore Cooper to the sidewalk as the eight steeple bells started tolling the hour. The sound reverberated in Cooper's head as the Yanks loomed over him. One kicked him.

"Please, let me through. He isn't himself—"
They paid no attention to Judith. She watched another prisoner step on Cooper's outstretched hand. She beat and pushed at blue worsted, her desperation rising.

"I'm his wife. Let me through!"
Finally, they opened a way, and she fell on top of him, repeating his name, hoping it might calm him. He rolled his head from side to side, foam in the corners of his mouth. "Stop the bells—they're too loud—I can't stand it."

"What bells?"
"In the steeple," he shouted, his gaze flying up past her shoulder. "There—there."

"The bells are gone, Cooper." She started to shake his shoulders as he had shaken the sergeant. "They took the bells from St. Michael's months ago. They sent them to Columbia so the Yankees would never get hold of them."

His mouth opened and his eyes, too, for a moment's deranged recognition. He stared at her, then the steeple, then at her again. "But I hear them." The cry was like a child's. "I hear them, Judith—"

Groping for her hand, he stiffened suddenly. His eyes closed, and he went limp. His head fell sideways, cheek resting on the sidewalk.

"Cooper?"

99

Andy thought a branch had cracked until he heard the ball buzz past.

The shot came from the thickets on his left, the side of the road away from the Ashley. As he booted the mule with his worn field shoes, Andy tried to spot the person with the gun. The man stood up, well back in the shadowed undergrowth. He snugged a musket against the right shoulder of a uniform jacket of Union blue, worn open to show his black chest. The man's left eye closed while the right slitted down, taking aim. Recognition of the swollen, fat face struck Andy like a ram.

"Go, mule." He kicked the animal again.

The mule sped toward a bend in the road. Andy's pass danced on the piece of twine around his neck. The gun boomed, but the aim was bad. The ball sliced off palmetto fronds ten yards behind the fleeing mule and rider. Moments later, both were safely past the bend.

When Andy reached Mont Royal, he went straight to Meek's office. He found the overseer shuffling bills with a bewildered air, as if wondering which two or three to choose for payment with the plantation's dwindling supply of inflated currency. Dry-mouthed, Andy reported his worst news first.

"He was aiming to kill me, Mr. Meek. And he had two mus-

762

kets. He couldn't have fired off the second round so fast if he had to reload."

Meek's eyes, watery and dismayed, met Andy's over the tops of his half spectacles. The job of trying to run the plantation with crops going to the government for less than full value and essential supplies scarce and the slaves disappearing one or two at a time had bowed his shoulders and furrowed his face. He looked ten years older than he had the day he arrived.

"You're sure it was Cuffey?"

"I wouldn't make a mistake about that face. It was him. I heard he was with that bad lot of runaways, but I didn't believe it till today. He was wearing a Yankee soldier's uniform, and he's fat as a spring toad. That bunch must eat mighty well."

He started to smile, but Meek's anger checked it. "They do. They're thieves. Who do you think carried off those six hens a week ago? Reckon we'd better prepare to give 'em a welcome if they come back. We need to mold some musket balls and inspect those two kegs of powder for dampness."

"I'll do it," Andy promised.

Meek pinched the top of his nose. "You haven't said anything about the curing salt."

Andy shook his head. "Isn't any to be had, Mr. Meek. I even went by Tradd Street in hopes of borrowing some from Mr. Cooper. No one was home. Least, no one answered. I knocked long and hard at the street gate. I'm mighty sorry to come back empty-handed."

"I know you did your best. Tomorrow you can ride over to Francis LaMotte's place. I hate begging favors from that conceited little rooster, but I heard he brought some salt from Wilmington when he came home on leave." He waved in a tired, absent way. "Thank you, Andy. I'm glad you didn't get hurt."

Leaving, Andy saw Meek pick up the Testament he kept on his desk. The overseer opened the book and bent over a page, his lips moving silently. His face had a desperate look. Well, no wonder, Andy thought as he walked down the path. A tense and dismal atmosphere pervaded the district and the plantation. On top of all the other problems, out in the marshes there was that band of runaways, thirty to fifty of them. Including Cuffey.

The swollen face sighting along the gun barrel stuck in Andy's mind as he approached the great house in search of Jane. The runaways left the marshes to steal food or kill and rob travelers unlucky enough to be caught alone on deserted back roads. Two white men from Ashley River plantations had been found dead last month. In January, the band had been seen building cook fires near the abandoned great house at Resolute, where Madeline had lived with Justin LaMotte. Shortly thereafter a blaze had leveled the place.

"Evening, Miss Clarissa," Andy said as he reached the front drive. Orry's mother didn't respond. Motionless on the piazza, she gazed down the lane of arching trees toward the road, her smile sweetly bewildered. She raised her right hand and brushed it past her face as if some of the ubiquitous low-country gnats were bothering her. Andy hadn't seen any this evening.

Shaking his head, he entered the house and followed the sound of hammering till he found Jane. She was helping a houseman nail strips of scrap wood over a downstairs window that had broken in a recent windstorm. Replacement glass couldn't be bought in Charleston, or good lumber either.

She smiled when she saw him, but his expression told her something was wrong. Drawing her aside, he reported the incident on the road, though he minimized the danger. "I'll bet that crazy Cuffey is just waiting to do mischief to this place. Maybe—" he lowered his voice to be certain the houseman wouldn't hear "—maybe we should go ahead and jump over the brooms and steal off together some night."

"No. I gave Miss Madeline my word that I'd stay. And I don't want to jump over the brooms. That's for slave weddings. You and I are going to be married as free people." Taking his hand, she pressed it tightly. "It won't be long. A year. Perhaps even less."

Affection warmed his eyes. "Well, I guess I'll still go along with that, since I haven't met any woman I fancy more than you. Yet."

She batted at his head, and he jumped away, laughing. He hoped the laughter helped hide his gloom. He was sure there'd be a visit from the renegade band one of these days. He was sure because Cuffey was part of it now.

That night he slept badly, dreaming of Cuffey's bloated face. In the morning, as he prepared to leave for Francis LaMotte's place, Philemon Meek took him aside and pushed a small revolver into his brown hand. "That's loaded. Make sure it's out of sight if you meet any white folks on the road. Hide it in the brush while you're on LaMotte's property. You could be hung for carrying it."

"You could be hung for giving it to me, Mr. Meek."

"I'll stand the risk. I'd hate to see something happen to you."

Andy's smile grew stiff. "Don't want to lose your number-one nigger?"

Angered, Meek said, "I don't want to lose a good man. Now get on your mule and get out of here before I boot your uppity backside."

Andy drew a long breath. "Sorry I said that. Old times doing the talking."

"I know."

They shook hands.

Whistling "Dixie's Land," Andy jogged down a dim, overgrown lane, a shortcut to Francis LaMotte's. Old Meek wasn't half bad, he was thinking just as he came upon something dark and misshapen, like a bundle of discarded clothing, in the center of the weedy track.

"Whoa, mule," he whispered. He sat listening. He heard bird cries, the small stirs and rustlings of the low-country forest, but nothing alarming. He climbed off the mule and walked slowly along the track with Meek's revolver in hand.

The bundle was a black man, raggedy and still. The pockets of his pants had been turned out. Two red-edged holes marked his forehead like a second pair of eyes.

Andy shivered, swallowing and studying the brush on both sides of the lane. On his right, he saw a large area trampled down. He walked there, rousing half a dozen noisy salt crows farther back among the trees. Looking that way, Andy invoked the name of Jesus under his breath.

In the humid breeze, something that was not a festoon of Spanish moss swung slowly from a water oak limb around nine feet off the ground. Andy recognized Francis LaMotte, in his Ashley Guards uniform—or the remains of it. LaMotte hung by a rope around his wrists. His top boots had been stolen, and his stockings, too. His feet were bare.

Andy could have been staring at some fantastically colored bird. LaMotte's bright green chasseur's jacket was ripped in many places, creating a feathery effect. The jacket and canary-colored trousers showed patches of red still brilliant because they were still wet.

The sagging limb creaked. LaMotte's body turned slowly,

765

pierced by stab wounds. Andy stopped counting the wounds when he reached thirty.

That same April evening, Orry approached the farm Mrs. Halloran had sketched for him. Thin clouds dulled the moon and stars. That would make it easier for him to cross the unplowed field as his informant had suggested.

Orry wore the black broadcloth suit he had packed away when he arrived in the capital. Into the sheath on the outside of his right boot he had slipped a bowie knife, but he was otherwise unarmed. Should something go wrong, he would claim to be a traveler who had lost his way.

He tied his horse to a fruit tree at the side of the field farthest from the four buildings on the bluff above the James. It was a long way down to the river. By day, the view must be spectacular.

The old house, main barn, and chicken coop all showed as solid black masses. A pronounced V-shaped break in the roof line testified to the barn's disrepair. But the structure Mrs. Halloran called the implement building, perched on the side of the bluff, seemed to have its near side marked with vertical yellow lines—a trick of lantern light shining through gaps in the siding.

On the night wind, Orry heard the whicker of a horse. He drew the back of his hand across his damp upper lip and started a slow, quiet walk toward the lighted building.

There was no cover, no way to remain unseen unless he crawled. When he was halfway across the field, its weedy soil broken here and there by the indentation of rain gullies, he thought he saw a match flare out beyond the house, a good distance to his left. A sentry on the road? More than likely.

Now he heard the horses, softly stamping. A ten-yard strip of thick, tall grass separated the building from the edge of the field where he hunkered down and counted the animals: four saddle horses and a fifth hitched to a covered buggy. Based on this evidence, Mr. Lamar Powell's revolutionary army was minuscule. But Orry had read his *Julius Caesar* as a boy, and he knew it didn't take an armed host to commit a political murder.

Riding out from Richmond, through the picket posts where he had presented his pass like any other traveler, he had begun to feel sheepish, even gulled. At one point he almost turned back. Now he was thankful he hadn't.

Remaining crouched, he started to work his way toward the

siding where the light shone through. He grimaced at all the rustling and crackling of the weeds, struggled to advance more cautiously, minimizing the noise. Halfway to the wall, he heard muted conversation. For a moment he doubted his own senses. Mixed in with the male voices, he detected a woman's.

Because he was surprised, when he moved again, he shifted his weight too quickly. His right boot broke an unseen twig with a loud crack.

"Wait, Powell. I thought I heard a noise outside."

"Probably a rabbit—or a rat. They infest this place."

"Shall I take a look?"

"No. It isn't necessary. Wilbur's on watch at the road." In the voice of the man identified as Powell, Orry heard absolute authority. As fast as he dared, he crept the rest of the way to the wall and pressed his eye to one of the gaps.

Damn. Powell's back was turned. Orry could see nothing but fawn trousers, a dark brown velvet coat, and graying hair, pomaded. Boots stuck into Orry's line of sight to the left—someone seated, legs stretched out.

"Our most important arms shipment arrived yesterday," Powell said, walking toward crates piled on the straw-littered floor. Reaching them, he turned around.

In his late thirties, Lamar Powell had the kind of face Orry supposed most women would term handsome. He posed in a theatrical way, one slim hand clasping the right lapel of his coat. He gestured to a rectangular crate resting on two square ones, both smaller. Painted on the rectangular box was the word WHITWORTH.

"As you can see, we will be equipped with the finest."

"Whitworths are goddamn expensive—" someone began. Powell's eyes showed sudden fury. The speaker mumbled, "Beg your pardon, ma'am."

"Expensive indeed," Powell agreed. "But they're the finest sharpshooting rifles in the world. The .45-caliber Whitworth has a mean radial deviation of one foot or less at eight hundred yards. If there are only a few of us taking aim at the enemy"—a humorless smile jerked his mouth—"each must achieve maximum accuracy."

By uttering just those few sentences, Powell managed to unsettle and alarm Orry. Unlike many fanatics, the man had an air of competence. He would not fail through stupidity, Orry suspected.

Powell continued, "I don't believe any of you would care to hear how many illegalities were necessary—how many costly bribes—to obtain this shipment. The less you know, the safer you are. And we'll be risking the rope soon enough as it is."

"I didn't hazard the long ride out here to joke, Lamar."

Orry's mouth opened, silent shock. The voice belonged to James Huntoon.

"I want to get to the issue," he said. "When and how do we kill Davis?"

Then Orry thought he truly had lost his mind. The next speaker who approached Powell was the woman.

"And who dies along with him?"

There, clearly visible beside Powell, he saw his sister Ashton.

Kneeling by the wall, he shook his head, then again. But of course truth couldn't be banished so easily. Undoubtedly she had become involved through her husband. Madeline had recognized the possibility, but he had dismissed it. He owed her an apology.

He must identify the other conspirators if he could. He changed position, thus able to see a different part of the interior. A man leaned against the wall that overlooked the river. On each side of him, a large window framed a rectangle of darkness dulled by the grime of the glass. The man was a rough, burly sort, unfamiliar to Orry.

Anxious to see more, he put his palm against the wall and pressed his other eye to the crack. The siding creaked under his hand. Huntoon said, "Someone's out there."

Powell ran across Orry's line of vision. Orry scrambled back, almost losing his balance as Powell shouted, "Put the lanterns out."

The verticle slits of yellow turned black. Orry lunged up and ran toward the field, bent low. A door rolled back. He heard voices outside the implement building, Powell's the loudest.

"Wilbur? We need you. We've been spied on."

Orry's chest already hurt from running. Halfway across the field, he heard a horse galloping up the dirt road to the buildings, loud voices again, a confusion of questions and orders. The rider turned into the field, firing a shot.

The bullet slashed through weeds two feet left of Orry. His boot caught the moist earth, and he lost his balance. The shot frightened his own horse, who neighed. Orry slid on his knees, then pushed up so hard he felt a spasm in a muscle in his arm. He ran on, reaching his horse and mounting as his pursuer passed the field's midpoint.

He booted his mount down the lane by which he had approached. Low branches whipped his cheeks and forehead. The man behind him fired a second round. It missed. Orry galloped into the wider main road that curved away from the James. Pulling away from his pursuer and topping a slight rise, he saw the sky glow that identified Richmond.

He breathed deeply of the wind rushing against his face. He was riding away from shock and peril—but toward an inevitable meeting with his conscience. It took place about midnight. Madeline sat on the edge of their bed, arms folded over the bosom of her nightdress, while he paced one way, then other, lumps of mud falling from his boots.

After he told her everything, the first thing she said was: "How in heaven's name did she become involved?"

"Right away I decided it was because of James. But I'm not so sure. Something bothers me about that explanation, though I haven't figured out what it is. Anyway, explanations hardly matter at this point. I'm the one person with knowledge of a direct threat to the President's life. Other lives, too—"

He seized the bedpost. "I must go to Seddon with the information. And Winder. The provost can pick up the conspirators quietly—It's the first time I've ever been thankful Stephens failed in his congressional crusade." In February, despite the politicking of the vice president, suspension of habeas corpus had been reenacted.

"All the conspirators?" Madeline asked. "Does that include your sister?"

"She's one of them. Why does she deserve special consideration?"

"You know, Orry. I don't like her any better than you do. But she's family."

"*Family!* I'd sooner have Beast Butler for a relative. Madeline, my sister tried to have Billy Hazard murdered."

"I haven't forgotten. It doesn't change what I just said. I know you dislike hearing it, but it's true. There's also this: No crime has been committed as yet."

"The very most I could do—and I'm damned if I think she deserves it—is refrain from mentioning her name or the fact that I saw her."

769

"You would have to do the same for James."

"I owe him nothing."

"He's Ashton's husband."

A long silence. Then a disgusted sigh. "All right. But that's as far as I'll compromise for either of them. I'll identify Powell and no one else. If he implicates Huntoon or my sister, so be it."

"We're discovered—we'll be arrested—what in God's name are we to do, Lamar?"

Huntoon's wail sickened Ashton. Outside the implement building, with the others crowding around, Powell shot out his hand, twisting Huntoon's collar. "The one thing we will not do is cry like infants." He shoved Huntoon away as the sentry, Wilbur, came trotting back across the field to report.

"Lost him."

"But you got a look at him—"

"No, I didn't."

"Damn you." Powell turned his back on Wilbur, who tugged his farmer's hat down over his eyes and sat silently.

Powell rubbed his knuckles against the point of his chin, thinking.

Another of the conspirators cleared his throat. "They'll be out here by morning, won't they?"

Huntoon spoke up. "Perhaps not. Suppose it was just some nigger boy hunting chickens to steal." He was trying to reassure himself.

"It was a white man. I seen that much," Wilbur said.

"But maybe he meant us no harm—"

"Are you an imbecile?" Powell said. "He approached by stealth. He observed us through one of the cracks in that wall. But setting that aside, do you seriously imagine I'd sit and wait to find out whether he's harmless?"

He shoved the humiliated Huntoon aside and strode along the weedy strip of ground beside the implement shed. He scanned the bluff, the field, the other buildings. "What we require are sound tactics for meeting the situation. If we think them out carefully and keep our heads, we'll come through this unscathed."

Badly scared, Ashton clung to her faith in Powell's brains and courage. But it was shaken when he returned to them, smiling, and she heard him say, "The first thing we must do is enlist the aid of Mr. Edgar Poe. My favorite author. How many of you know his tale of the purloined letter?"

"You're the one who's an imbecile," Huntoon ranted, "talking of cheap hack writers at a time like this."

For once Ashton silently sided with her husband. Her lover didn't say a word to explain himself, merely gave Huntoon another insulting push and walked past him, laughing.

At daylight, Orry marched up the high stoop of Secretary Seddon's residence and used the knocker so loudly he was sure he woke the whole neighborhood. Within minutes, grumpy Winder was summoned. When he arrived, he resisted for half an hour— Orry was not, after all, one of his most trusted colleagues—but gave in under pressure from Seddon. He would send investigators to Wilton's Bluff before noon.

"I'll go immediately to the President," the secretary said. He was by now largely recovered from the shock of Orry's news. "All cabinet members will be warned. Meanwhile, Colonel Main, yours is the privilege of casting the net for the biggest fish."

"I'll do it with pleasure, sir."

A few minutes past ten, a curtained van raced to Church Hill and wheeled into Franklin Street. Orry jumped out and led an armed squad up the front steps. A second squad, dropped off a block away, had already deployed in the garden. Orry quickly found himself reacting as Seddon had when he first heard the story.

The front door offered no resistance. Dumbfounded, he said to his men, "It's been left unlocked."

Inside, the household furnishings remained, but no clothes or personal belongings.

Lamar Powell had disappeared.

That evening, a second shock. It came in Winder's sanctum, delivered by the man with the long nose, weedy black clothes, and vaguely clerical air.

"I found nothing. No signs of habitation. And, most especially, no trace of those crated weapons you reported, Colonel. In my opinion, no one's been at that farm for months. The neighbors I questioned agree."

Orry jumped up. "That can't be."

Antagonized, the other man said, "Is that so? Well, then—" a

771

gesture to the door, derisive "—question the two operatives I took with me. You've heard my report, and I stand by it. If you don't like it, ride back there and make your own."

"By God, I will," Orry said, as Israel Quincy stepped to the window and gazed at the sunset.

Evening's dark red glinted on the river, lighting Orry's stricken face. He had searched the implement building and found what Quincy and his colleagues predicted: nothing. He had left the building a moment ago, closing its door on the dirt floor, straw-littered and unmarked by any boot prints save those of men. Some were his. Some surely belonged to Winder's operatives—and Powell's crowd. Or did they? Orry hadn't discovered a single imprint of a woman's shoe.

He felt angry, humiliated, baffled. He walked away from the bluff and searched the farmhouse. He found only dust and nesting rats. He searched the barn and chicken coop. Again nothing. By then night had come. He mounted and took a shortcut toward the main road, walking his horse across the same field he had crossed last night. The black of the plowed earth matched his mood exactly.

His meager supper of rice and corn bread untasted, Orry said to Madeline, "Quincy's been bought. Winder, too, for all I know. Mrs. Halloran inadvertently stumbled on a conspiracy that must reach very high. I intend to find out just how high."

"But the President is safe now, isn't he? He's been warned—"

"Yes, but I still have to know! At this moment, I wouldn't be surprised if Seddon and his wife were speculating on my mental condition. Am I a drunkard? Do I take opium? Did I see visions at the farm? I swear to you"—he went to her around the table—"I did *not*."

"I believe you, dearest. But what can you do? It appears they've opened and closed the case all in the same day."

"I haven't. And I know someone who was at the farm. She's still in Richmond—I verified that before I came home tonight. I intend to start some detective work on my sister first thing tomorrow."

But his vow went unfulfilled. In life's strange way of piling one crisis on another when it was least needed, the street bell rang at

772

half past ten. Orry ran downstairs. It had to be for him; the landlady never received callers this late.

Covered with dirt, his head a mountain peak above clouds of cigar smoke, there stood Charles.

"Your letter took a detour to Atlee's Station, but I finally got it. I'm here to do something about Billy."

100

Stephen Mallory arrived in Charleston that same night, after a hard trip in one of the dirty, unheated cars of the decaying Southern rail system. A telegraph message from Lucius Chickering had summoned him.

Cooper didn't know that. Following the incident on Meeting Street, soldiers of the local provost had borne him home, none too gently, and since then he had been in bed, not moving, not speaking, not touching any of the food Judith brought. The pattern with the trays was unvarying: each was left an hour, then removed.

Cooper did rouse a little—turn his head toward the door—when Judith opened it after knocking softly.

"Darling? You have a visitor. Your friend Stephen. The secretary."

He said nothing. He lay beneath blankets layered too deeply for the mild weather. Everything within the dark, sweat-tainted room had a blurred quality. So did sounds from outside—birds in the garden, home guards quickstepping along Tradd Street to the accompaniment of a fife and a snare drum beating time.

"Might I see him alone for a moment, Judith?"

She glanced at her husband. His eyes were round and vacant. As they were every day. She was careful to hide her pain from the visitor.

"Of course. If you need me, there's a small hand bell on that table. Can you see it?"

Mallory nodded and pulled a chair to the bedside. Judith glanced sadly at the bell, which Cooper hadn't used once since being carried home. Mallory sat down. Judith shut the door.

The secretary stared at his assistant. Cooper's eyes fixed on the ceiling. Mallory spoke with the abruptness of a gunshot.

"They say your nerves are gone. Is it true?"

His voice lacked the treacle of conventional sickroom conversation. Cooper acknowledged that by blinking once. But he didn't move or reply.

"See here, Cooper. If you can hear me, have the courtesy to look me in the eye. I didn't ride the train all the way from Richmond to converse with a corpse."

Slowly, Cooper's head tilted over toward the visitor, cheek resting on the feather pillow, graying hair spread above, fine and thin. But the eyes remained empty.

Mallory persisted. "That was a scandalous thing you did. Scandalous—no other word for it. The enemy already considers us a nation of barbarians—regrettably, not without some justification. But for a government official to behave like a demented prison warden, and in public—" He shook his head. "There may be a few brutish Southerners who would condone your behavior, but not many. I'll not pretend, Cooper. You damaged our cause, and you damaged yourself, gravely."

Those words finally produced reaction of a sort: rapid movement of Cooper's eyelids and a compression of his lips. Mallory's face looked nearly as gray as that of the man in bed.

"I couldn't sleep on that wretched train, so I sat up trying to devise some polite way to request your immediate resignation. There is none. Therefore—"

"They killed my son."

The sudden words jerked Mallory like a puppet. "What's that? The prisoners you attacked and fought? Nonsense."

Cooper's hands twitched on the counterpane, aimless white spiders without webs to spin. He blinked rapidly again, said in a hoarse voice, "The profiteers killed my son. The war killed him."

"And it was grievous and tragic; I'll not deny that. But in these

774

times, if you except Judah's extreme youth, neither was it special."

Cooper's head lifted. Anger flooded the holes of his eyes. Mallory pushed him down gently.

"Not special to any but you and your family. Do you know nothing of the figures? How many sons lost to how many fathers? It runs into the hundreds of thousands, all over the South. All over the North, too, for that matter. After a suitable period of mourning, most of those fathers manage to function again. They don't lie abed and weep."

The secretary sagged a little then. The effort was a strain and, worse, unsuccessful. He pulled a handkerchief from his sleeve and wiped his cheeks. He smelled a chamber pot under the bed. One last try.

"You've served the Navy Department more than competently, Cooper. You have served imaginatively and, in the case of *Hunley*, with great bravery. If you're the same man who endured foul air and fear of death at the bottom of Charleston harbor for two and a half hours, I still need your services. We are not yet done with this war. The soldiers and sailors are still fighting, and so am I. Therefore I'd be inclined to substitute a letter of censure for resignation. But, of course, in order to come back to work—" stern as a parent, he stood up "—you would have to get out of bed. Kindly send me word of your decision within seventy-two hours."

He took pains to shut the door more loudly than necessary.

Downstairs with Judith, he mopped his sweating face again. "That is the hardest thing I've ever done—concealing my sympathy for that poor man. It breaks my heart to see him so lost."

"It's been coming for a long time, Stephen. An accumulation of fatigue, frustration, grief—I have no way to bring him out of it. Kind words won't do it; nor will angry ones. I decided some different kind of shock was needed. That's why I begged you to speak as you did."

"I wasn't entirely playacting. I have had demands for his resignation. Strong ones, from important men."

"Oh, I'm sure of that."

"Our resources are depleted, our armies on the brink of starvation—" She wanted to say the civilian population soon would be, but she didn't. "We have little left us but our honor, so a man who behaves as Cooper did isn't easily forgiven." Toying with the hat he picked up from a taboret, he added, "But I'll happily shoulder the criticism and ignore the outcries if I can get him back to work."

She squeezed his hand in silent appreciation. "Would you like something to eat? A cup of coffee? I hit on a way to parch acorns, then roast them in a little bacon fat. It makes a passable substitute."

"Thank you, but I'd rather go back to the hotel and sleep an hour or so."

"I'm the one who owes thanks." She kissed his cheek. Mallory blushed.

"What I said was brutal—at least for me," he said as he walked to the door. "I only hope it may do some good."

When he was gone, Judith looked toward the stairs, then realized she was famished. There was nothing in the house except leftover artificial oysters, fried up from a sticky batter made of grated green corn, one precious egg, and a few other scarce ingredients. But they were less scarce than the oysters themselves, which the Yankees gathered or the greedy oystermen sold directly to civilian customers who would pay an exorbitant price. You couldn't find oysters in the markets any longer. You couldn't find much of anything.

In the kitchen, she discovered her daughter listlessly trying to repair a plate she had broken while helping with the dishes. All they had for glue was a concoction of rice flour simmered in water. As Marie-Louise spread some on one of the broken edges, she gave her mother a dolorous look, as though protesting a sentence of hard labor. Judith's reply was crisp and firm.

"You've begun well. Please finish the same way, clean up, then go to your studies."

"All right, Mama."

Thank heaven their daughter caused them no serious problems, Judith thought, walking through the downstairs with a headache beginning to push at her temples. Cooper in bed day and night, depressed, silent—that was enough.

She wrote a letter to Mont Royal, requesting some rice flour if it could be spared, and a note of congratulations to a cousin in Cheraw who had delivered her first baby last month. On the Mont Royal letter she put a ten-cent rose-colored stamp; on the second, a blue five and one of the older green ones. How tired she was of the face of the President on stamps of every denomination.

She sat down at the pianoforte, her sense of failure deepening as she bent over the keyboard. A few white strands showed in her blond curls. Slowly, expertly, she began to play "The Vacant Chair." Like so many of the war songs published in the North, it was popular on both sides. The lyric suited her mood. Soon she was singing in her fine soprano voice:

> *"We shall meet, but we shall miss him,*
> *There will be one vacant chair—*
> *We shall linger to caress him,*
> *While we breathe our evening prayer."*

A sound startled her. She played the wrong keys, jangly discord, and looked toward the ceiling. Had she imagined—?

No. Faint but unmistakable, the little bell rang again.

Weeping with hope, she ran up the stairs, flung open the door of the stale room. She couldn't see him in the dark, but she heard him clearly.

"Judith, would you mind opening the draperies to let in some light?"

The salt wind reached Tradd Street from the sea, flowing in to cleanse the bedroom. Late that afternoon, Cooper consumed half a bowl of turkey broth and a cup of Judith's imitation coffee. Then he rested with his head turned toward the tall windows, open to show the great live oak just outside and the rooftop of his neighbor's house.

He felt weak, as if he had just thrown off a prolonged high fever.

"But my head's clear. I don't feel—how should I put it?—I don't feel the way I did before Stephen called. I don't feel so angry."

She sat against the headboard and pulled him gently to her small bosom, left arm cradling his shoulders. "Something in you burst like a boil when you attacked that prisoner. You despised slavery and where it was leading the South for so very long, but when you took your stand three years ago, you did it with all the fervor you'd once directed the other way. That was commendable, but I think it started terrible forces warring inside you. Judah's death made it worse. So did long hours at the department, trying to accomplish too much with too little." She hugged him. "Whatever the reason, I thank God you're better. If I were Catholic, I'd ask them to canonize Stephen."

"I hope I'm sane again. I know I'm mightily ashamed. What of that sergeant I attacked?"

"A concussion. But he'll recover."

A relieved sigh. "You're right about the struggle inside. It's still there. I know the war's lost, but I suppose I should go back to work if the department wants me. Where is Stephen, by the way?"

"He's resting at the Mills House. As for working again—I'd think a while. My feelings about the war haven't changed. At the time Sumter fell, they were your feelings, too." His eyes shifted away from her, to the neighbor's rooftop.

"This war's wrong, Cooper. Not only because all war is wrong, but also because it's being fought for an immoral cause—no, please let me finish. I know all the rhetoric and apologetics by heart. So do you. It isn't the tariff or states' rights or Northern arrogance that brought all this suffering. It's what we did—Southerners—either directly or through the complicity of our silence. We stole the liberty of other human beings, we built fortunes from that theft, and we even proclaimed from our pulpits that God approved."

He took her hand, his voice like that of a bewildered child. "I know you're right. But I don't know what to do next."

"Survive the war. Work for Stephen if you must. Whatever you decide, it will be all right. Your head's clear now. But promise yourself—and promise me—that when the South falls, you'll work just as hard for peace. You know how it will be when the shooting stops. Animosity will persist on both sides, but the losers will feel it most. You know that because you went through it. You know what hatred does to a man."

"It feeds on itself. Multiplies. Begets more hate and more pain, and that begets still more—"

Overcome, she let the tears fall, hugging him harder. "Oh, Cooper, how I love you. The man I married—went away for a while—but I think—I found him again—"

He held her while she cried joyously.

Presently she asked if he wanted to talk to Mallory when he returned. Cooper said yes, he thought so. He would put on a fresh nightshirt and dressing gown and join them for supper. She clapped her hands and ran to find Marie-Louise.

Feeling buoyant, free of pain—composed—he returned his gaze to the garden. Above his neighbor's roof he saw a rectangle of clear, brilliant sky; his beloved Carolina sky. He had lost sight of how greatly that kind of simple perception cheered and exalted a man.

Lost sight of a great many other things, too. Including his own nature.

Judith was right: grief for his son had precipitated the worst. That grief would never leave him, just as his loathing for Ashton would not, or the unbecoming wish that she be punished for her greed. But the emotions building and building within him for so long had been purged in that explosion on Meeting Street, purged by his rain of cane strokes on the luckless Yankee.

The aftermath had left him wanting to die—or at least sleep a long time. Was it possible that the emotional desolation was the actual start of healing? He recalled another passage from the pen of the man he most revered, Edmund Burke. *The storm has gone over me, and I lie like one of those old oaks which the late hurricane has scattered about.*

Weakened but not destroyed. Mending; that was his condition. He was no longer the same man who had attacked the sergeant. He could again examine past behavior with objectivity, if not exactly with pride.

He had veered for a time into absolute patriotism—unquestioning acceptance of all things Southern. Before Sumter fell, he knew what was fine and worthy in his homeland. He loved that part, rejecting the rest. But then he had changed, gradually became willing to fight for and accept all of it. Including what was represented by the whitewashed huts three-quarters of a mile from Mont Royal's great house. The attitude was wrong before, and it was wrong now. It was one of the first things he would set right.

He examined his feelings about the war itself. He knew the storm had passed him because he once more felt as he had in the fateful spring of '61. The war was misbegotten because it couldn't be won. The war was an abomination because it pitted American against American. How shameful to grasp now that he had, for a while, become one with those who had pushed the nation into the war. One with the James Huntoons and Virgilia Hazards. One with those who could not or would not find a means to prevent the holocaust.

All right, the war was evil. What then?

He thought it through. He would no longer lend himself to wars except the one of which Judith had spoken, the inevitable one against the political barbarians, whose names he knew well. Wade. Davis. Butler. Stevens. The South would need men to stand against their onslaught. It would be a fierce battle, full of unexpected dangers. Burke, as always, had words to frame the challenge: *The circumstances are in a great measure new. We have hardly any landmarks from the wisdom of our ancestors to guide us.*

Because our ancestors never lost a war on this continent, he thought with a meditative smile empty of humor. Our ancestors were never a conquered people, as we shall be.

He rested a while, and imagination assumed control. He saw himself passing in and out of a dark valley, quite long, which ran from Sumter through Liverpool and Nassau to Richmond and the fateful corner where the Union prisoners passed. In that valley lurked error and the madness of dogmatism. His experience there and the miraculous shock of the street attack that had driven him sane again—there was no other term for it—gave him some grasp of what Catholics must mean by suffering in purgatory.

He had returned from his own purgatory, but the nation was not so blessed. Even if the shooting stopped this instant, America, all of it, would be torn as never before. He knew the dimensions of the hatreds the war had loosed. Within his own heart and mind, one red-handed hater had lived and reigned three years.

So he must rest and prepare. When the formal fighting ended, he would be called to the fiercest fight of all.

Cooper's meditation was interrupted by the firing of distant siege cannon. It shook the house and rattled windowpanes. He got out of bed, poured tepid water from a pitcher to a basin, chose a twig from several in a small glass, scrubbed his teeth with the only dental compound available any more: powdered charcoal.

He rinsed his mouth, winced at the emaciated man in the shaving glass, and wiped gritty black particles from the corners of his lips. His mouth tasted clean enough. A simple pleasure; a welcome one.

He changed nightshirts, put on an old gown, tied it around his shrunken waist, and hunted up slippers. He went downstairs.

Marie-Louise was speechless when she saw him. Then she cried and threw herself into his arms. Judith held Cooper's hand when Mallory arrived and Cooper spoke to him.

"Stephen, I'll be in your debt the rest of my life. Your visit today saved me. From many things, but most of all from my own bad side. You have my highest admiration—you always will. But I can't work for you. I can't build war machinery any longer. Something's changed. I've changed. I want the war to end. I want the dying to stop. Henceforth, I plan to spend my time speaking and writing on behalf of an honorable negotiated peace coupled with emancipation for every Negro still enslaved in the South."

Mallory's open mouth showed a confusion of reactions: disbelief, mockery, anger. At last he muttered, "Oh?" His voice strengthened. "And where do you propose to conduct this new, high-minded crusade?"

"From Mont Royal. My family and I are going home."

101

While the oil in the lamp burned away, Orry and Charles laid plans.

"I can write the order to get him out of Libby—"

"When you say write, you mean forge," Charles interrupted, the cigar stub temporarily out of his mouth. He had taken off his boots and propped his smelly stockinged feet on the edge of the table Orry used for a desk.

"All right, forge. I suppose you're technically right, since the release is illegal."

"What else do we need?"

"A gray coat and trousers to replace his uniform. A horse—"

"I'll arrange for the horse."

Orry nodded. "Finally, he'll need a pass. I can also take care of that. How he gets across the Rapidan is up to him. More whiskey?"

Charles drained his glass and pushed the empty toward his cousin, who was struck by the way time and war had altered their relationship. They were no longer man and boy, mentor and pupil, but adults, and equals. When Orry had poured the refill, and one for himself, he said, "I plan to accompany you to the prison. I won't let you undertake the risk by yourself."

Charles thumped his feet on the floor. "Oh, yes, you will, Cousin. You outrank me, but I'm going alone, and that's that."

"I can't allow—"

"The hell you can't," Charles broke in, flinty. "I'm afraid you forget one pretty important detail. Through no fault of your own, it's too damn easy for guards to remember and describe you later. I don't want the authorities hunting me up a week after they've caught you. This has to be a solo performance."

The notion of saying this had come to him on the ride to Richmond. He could think of no better way to spare Orry any dangers beyond the real ones he would incur by forging the documents. But Charles did his best to hide motives under a cold smile when he glanced at Orry's pinned-up sleeve.

"On this point, Cousin, I insist on having my way." Charles twisted in his chair. "What do you say, Madeline?"

From the sideboard, where she had been standing and listening, she said, "I think you're right."

"Blast," Orry said. "Another conspiracy."

Charles puffed his cigar again. "Another? What's the first one?"

"Just a figure of speech," Orry said, noting Madeline's anxious glance. "We're always hearing of imaginary plots against the government." He had already decided to say nothing of Powell's group or Ashton's involvement. Charles despised Ashton, and rekindling his anger might divert him from the task ahead. For that task he needed every bit of intelligence, nerve, and concentration he possessed.

Only one detail remained to be settled. Charles named it. "When?"

Orry said, "I can get the necessary forms and do the, ah, pen and ink work in the morning."

"Then I'll bring him out tomorrow night."

Charles tied Sport to one of the iron posts on Twenty-first, around the corner from Libby's main entrance. A fishy stench blew from the canal, driven by a stiff wind. He could see a picket standing guard down there. He knew there were others all around the building.

Charles stroked the gray. Without taking the cigar stub from his teeth, he said, "Rest while you can. You'll have a double load to carry pretty soon."

That was his hope, anyway. It was by no means certain, and various parts of him told him so, including his stomach. It had ached for the past hour.

He strode up the sloped walk to Cary, sweat breaking out in his beard. His old army Colt bumped his thigh, most of the holster hidden by the India-rubber poncho borrowed from Jim Pickles. The rubber blanket, which had a practical checkerboard painted on the inside, was hot as hell. But it was a focus, one detail for guards to remember about him, so they would forget everything else. That part, too, was still theoretical, his stomach reminded him.

The wind whirled dust clouds along Cary. Charles bent against it and climbed the prison steps past the armed guard, a red-faced youth with blond curls and china-blue eyes. The soldier gave him a keen stare.

Inside, Charles wrinkled his nose at the stench as he presented the forged order to the corporal on duty. "Prisoner Hazard. William Hazard." He emphasized the name by poking the cold cigar butt at it. He dropped the stub into a spittoon full of brown water. "I'm to remove him to General Winder's office for questioning."

Without a second glance at the order, the corporal laid it on the paperbound book he had been reading with an avid expression. From the yellow front and back, Charles guessed it to be some of the pornography sold in the camps. The corporal picked up a stack of wrinkled pages, leafed through, searching the inked names. Other guards passed. One gave Charles a long look but didn't stop.

"Hazard, Hazard—here 'tis. Y'all find him on the top floor. Ask at the guardroom. Head of the stairs."

The corporal opened the desk drawer, started to put the release order away. Charles snapped his fingers. "Give me that. I don't want to be stopped upstairs."

The noncom reacted before thinking—exactly what Charles

counted on. He thanked the corporal by raising the forged order in a kind of salute, then wheeled and mounted the first flight of creaky steps.

Libby Prison breathed and whispered like some haunted mansion. The dim gas fixtures, widely separated, heightened the effect. So did the sounds. Distant sobbing; laughter with a subterranean echo to it; a sustained low noise like the murmur of disembodied voices. On the outside of the old warehouse, something banged and banged in the fierce wind.

Forlorn prisoners stared at him silently from corridors to the right and left of the landings. He heard a melody on a mouth organ. Smelled unwashed clothes, festering wounds, overflowing latrines. He tugged his hat brim farther down, the better to hide his face, before he reached the top floor.

He stepped into the rectangle of light at the door of the guardroom. Once more he showed the order, repeated what he had said downstairs.

"Should of brung a litter with you," the bored guard told him. "Hazard ain't walkin' so good these days." He turned to the other private in the room. "Go find him, Sid."

"Fuck that. Your turn."

Grumbling, the first soldier stepped past Charles. "Pretty queer to drag him out for questioning at this time of night."

"If you want to make your objection known to General Winder, I'll be happy to convey it, soldier. Together with your name." Charles said it harshly, relying on what long service had taught him: men usually responded automatically to intimidation. It had worked downstairs, and it worked again.

"Never mind, thanks anyway," the guard said with a nervous snicker.

At the entrance to a large room in which hundreds of prisoners sat or lay with hardly an inch between them, the guard halted. "Hazard? Where's William Hazard?"

"Billy," someone said, prodding the prisoner next to him. Charles held his breath as a shrunken figure slowly rose to sitting position, then stood with the help of those closest to him.

A huge silhouette with the corridor light at his back, Charles waited and felt his heartbeat quicken. This was the first critical moment—when the prisoner hobbling on the padded crutch came close enough to recognize him.

A drop of sweat fell from Charles's nose. His mouth felt like a cup of dust. Billy staggered. My God, how wan and weak he looked, all rags and beard. When he was within a few feet of the door, Charles spotted bruises and a healed cut on one ear. His friend had been beaten.

The guard raised a thumb toward Charles. "This yere officer's takin' you down to old Winder's office a while. What did y'do this time?"

"Not a damn thing." Eyes enlarged and darkened by the hollowness of his face, Billy looked at Charles, who was silently crying out, *Don't say anything.*

Billy's mouth hung open a moment. "Bison?" His face showed that he instantly recognized his mistake.

The guard was watching Charles, suspicious. "What'd he call you?"

"Nothing you'd want to repeat to your mother." He grabbed Billy's dirty sleeve. "Don't you say one damn word, or I'll deliver you to the provost in little pieces. I lost a brother at Malvern Hill to you Yankee scum."

Reassured, the guard said, "Don't know why we coddle 'em so. Ought to burn the whole place down—with them inside."

"My sentiments, too." Charles pushed Billy's shoulder too hard. Billy almost fell. He propped himself up with the crutch and a hand against the wall, giving Charles a searching, wary stare. Good, Charles thought. He motioned the prisoner forward.

The guard lingered at the door of his room, watching Charles prod Billy down the first few steps. Billy was slow, much to Charles's annoyance. He was unsteady, too, obviously needing the crutch. The descent to the ground floor would take a hell of a long time. The longer they stayed inside Libby, the greater the risk of discovery.

"Bison?" Billy whispered, leaning against the stained wall beneath a guttering gaslight. "Is it really—?"

"For God's sake shut up," Charles whispered. "If you want to get out of here, act like we don't know each other." Two guards appeared on the landing below, coming up. Charles nudged Billy, said loudly, "Keep moving, bluebelly."

Down they went, one labored step at a time. Billy held fast to the crutch and now and then uttered a little groan. What in hell had they done to him? Charles's anger rapidly grew as strong as his fear of discovery.

The second floor. Billy sweated and breathed hard. More men

watching. Charles yanked his revolver from under the poncho. "Step lively, or I'll blow your sonofabitching head off." He shoved the muzzle in Billy's back, almost tumbling Billy down the stairs headfirst.

Ground floor. The duty corporal stood. Held out his hand. "I'll take back the release order, if you please."

Charles fished it from his pocket, hoping the forged signature would pass muster. They were so close now, just steps away from the doors leading out to Cary, where dust and rubbish rushed on winds of near gale force. The corporal shut the order in the drawer and remained standing, regarding Charles and his prisoner with an unreadable expression.

Six steps to the bottom and the doors.

Four.

Two.

Billy rested his head against the bilious wall. "Give me a minute—"

Hurry, Charles shouted in silence, darting down to the doors so he could turn and observe the duty corporal. The corporal was frowning, sensing something amiss—

"Hurry it up, or I'll drag you by the heels."

Billy gulped, pushed away from the wall, struggled down the next step. Charles thrust the door open, feeling the wind's force on the other side. From under his hat brim he continued to watch the corporal, counting the seconds till they escaped his scrutiny. The corporal represented the maximum threat, Charles felt—discovering his error when he turned in the doorway. There stood the blond guard, musket raised, blue eyes glaring.

"Where are you taking that prisoner?"

"Does everyone have to answer to you, Vesey?" Billy mumbled, immediately conveying to Charles some special animosity between himself and the guard.

"I don't answer to any piss-ant private," Charles said. "One side."

"Hey, Bull, where are they taking this Yank?" Vesey shouted to the duty corporal.

"Provost's office. For questioning."

"Provost?" Vesey repeated, while Charles took Billy's elbow to help him down the first step. "Mr. Quincy was here not an hour ago, while you were at supper. He didn't say anything about springing a prisoner."

The pale eyes widened. "You!" He aimed the musket at Charles. "Hold it right there. I know every one of General Winder's boys, and you aren't one of them. Something's fish—"

Charles smashed the barrel of his Colt against Vesey's head.

102

Vesey yelled and recoiled against the building. His musket tumbled over the stair rail. Inside, the corporal shouted to raise the alarm. "Go on, around the corner," Charles told Billy, an instant before Vesey lunged at him with both hands.

Charles thrust the hands away, flung Vesey against the doors so the corporal, pushing from inside, had trouble opening them. Charles started down the steps. Again Vesey tried to grab him. Two fingernails ripped a bloody track down Charles's cheek. Pain, anger, desperation brought instant response; Charles jammed the Colt into Vesey's stomach and shot him.

Vesey screamed and died toppling. That noise of the shot went rushing away on the wind. Charles saw that Billy had fallen on hands and knees at the foot of the steps. Charles ran down to him. The corporal inside didn't open the doors, though now he could have. He resumed his shouting instead.

"Come on," Charles said, jerking Billy to his feet too roughly; Billy uttered a low cry. Inside Libby, Charles heard more and more voices, a whole baying chorus. At the corner of Twenty-second and Cary, a picket appeared, musket raised. He was young, inexperienced, hesitant. That was worth a few more seconds. Charles forced Billy rapidly to the opposite corner, Twenty-first, where they nearly collided with another picket, who appeared suddenly. Charles pointed the Colt at the boy's face.

"Run or you're dead, youngster."

The picket dropped his musket and ran.

But one more was dashing up the slope of Twenty-first from the river side of the building. Charles hastily untied Sport, shoved his boot in the stirrup, mounted, and fired a shot across his saddle to turn back the running guard. Tightly reining the nervous gray, he pulled his left foot back and thrust his free hand downward.

"Grab hold and use the stirrup. Quick!"

Billy groaned at the exertion, and so did Charles. He fired again to keep the guard cowering. When he felt Billy settle into place behind him, he shouted, "Hang on, Bunk," and spurred the gray the short distance up to Cary. His friend's Academy nickname had come back without thought.

Three pickets gathered on the corner to fire at them as Sport carried them by. Billy wrapped his arms around Charles's poncho and held fast. One shot boomed, then two more. All three missed. The gray galloped away into howling wind.

In an alley a mile from the prison, Billy donned the butternut pants and corduroy shirt unpacked from a blanket roll on the saddle.

"Jesus," Charles said as he handed Billy the gray jacket.

"What's wrong?"

"I killed that guard. Didn't even stop to think about it."

"You deserve a medal."

"For shooting a boy?"

"You did every man in Libby Prison a service. That guard is the bastard who put me in this condition."

"That right? Then I feel better. Glad I did it." Charles smiled in a way that made Billy shiver. He gave Billy the last article from the blanket roll, a kepi. "Let's go."

Billy waited in the darkness with Sport while Charles entered the stable where he had previously arranged to hire a mule for the night. "Get him back by eight in the morning," the sleepy liveryman said. "I got another customer."

"Guaranteed," Charles said, leading the balking animal into the dark.

He had his pass, and Billy had the one Orry had forged, so they traveled north through the defense lines without incident. They dismounted in an orchard, and Charles gave his friend a second, smaller, bundle.

"That's a little hardtack and sliced ham Madeline fixed up. I wish I had a gun for you, or more gear, so you'd look more like a furloughed soldier."

"I'll make it the way I am," Billy promised. "What I wish for is more time for the two of us to catch up on things." Once past the last picket post, they had hardly stopped talking, covering the whereabouts and fortunes of most of the members of both families. Charles learned why the guard at the prison entrance had taken special interest in Billy; the story of the ride on the caisson wheel disgusted him and, as a Southerner, shamed him, too.

Now he said, "I'd like to take you to see Orry and Madeline, but it's better if you put some miles between yourself and Richmond before daylight. With a spot of luck, you should be all right even if you're stopped and questioned. The pass will take you through. When you reach your own lines, don't forget to ditch the cap and jacket."

"I won't—and I'll approach with my hands high in the air, believe me."

Both were trying to minimize what lay ahead for him: hours of riding, patrols on the road, hunger, anxiety. And all of it made worse by his weakened condition. There was plenty to contend with, and Billy knew it. But there was also hope now. A goal. The safety of his own side.

The chance to write Brett with miraculous news.

The wind tore petals from the trees and whirled them around the two friends in the spring dark, each a little awkward with the other because the intervening years had made them near-strangers.

"Bison."

Eyes fixed on the Richmond road, Charles said, "Um?"

"You saved me once before. Now I'll never get out of your debt."

"Just get out of the Confederacy; that's good enough. That'll make me happy."

"My worst problem's liable to be my accent. If I have to answer questions—"

"Speak slowly. Like—this—here. Drop some of your g's and tell 'em you're from out West. Nobody in Virginia really knows how a Missouri reb talks."

Billy smiled. "Good idea. I was stationed in St. Louis—I can pass." More soberly: "You told me about Orry's marriage and a lot of other things, but you haven't said a word about yourself. How have you been getting along? What command are you with?"

"I'm a scout for General Wade Hampton's cavalry, and I'm getting along fine," Charles lied. "I'd be getting along a hell of a lot better if this war was over. I guess it will be soon."

He thought of saying something about Gus. But why mention a relationship that had to end? "I'd like to talk all night, but you ought to go."

"Yes, I guess I should." Billy patted his pocket to be sure he had the pass. Then, with slow, pained movements, he mounted the mule. Charles didn't help him; Billy had to do it himself.

Once Billy was in the saddle, Charles stepped forward. They clasped hands.

"Safe journey. My love to Cousin Brett when you see her."

"Mine to Madeline and Orry. I know what he risked to help me. You, too."

The laugh was dry and forced. "West Point looks after its own, doesn't it?"

"Don't joke, Bison. I'll never be able to repay you."

"I don't expect it. Just stay away from our bullets for the next eight or ten months, and then we can have a good, long visit in Pennsylvania or South Carolina. Now get going."

"God bless you, Bison."

In a surprisingly strong voice, Billy hawed to the mule and rode rapidly out of the orchard. He was soon gone in the darkness.

Petals blew around Charles, a light, sweet cloud, as he thought, *He'll either make it or he won't. I did all I could.* He was unable to forget the dead guard, but it had nothing to do with regrets about killing him.

He felt drained. He wanted whiskey. "Come on," he said to the gray, and mounted.

The clock chimed four. Bare feet stretched to a hassock, Charles swirled the last of the bourbon in the bottom of the glass, then swallowed it.

"I got scared and shot him. Panic—that's the only word for it."

Madeline said, "I imagine killing someone, even an enemy, isn't easy."

790

"Oh, you get used to it," Charles said. She and Orry exchanged swift looks that he didn't see. "Anyway, the guard was the one who tortured Billy. The reason it bothers me is, I lost control. I've seen the elephant often enough. I thought I could handle tight spots."

"But how many prison escapes have you staged?" Orry asked.

"Yes, there's that." Charles nodded, but he remained unconvinced.

"How did Billy look?" Madeline asked.

"White and sickly. Feeble as the devil. I don't know if he can make it even halfway to the Rapidan."

"How is Brett? Did he say?"

Charles answered her with a shake of his head. "He hasn't heard from Brett in months. That guard, Vesey, destroyed every letter Billy wrote, so I'd guess he destroyed any that came in, too. Orry, can you spare some cash for the liveryman? He'll never see his mule again."

"I'll take care of it," Orry promised.

Charles yawned. He was worn out, ashamed of his loss of self-control, and most of all saddened by the reunion with Billy. It seemed to him their talk had been trivial and difficult to carry on. Years of separation, their service on different sides—everything took its toll. They were friends and foes at the same time, and every halting sentence they had spoken expressed that without words.

"One more drink, and I'm going to get some sleep," he announced. "I'd like to be out of Richmond early in the morning. We'll be in the field soon—" He extended his glass to Orry; the liquor trickled noisily from the brown bottle. "Have you heard Grant's bringing a new cavalry commander from the West? Phil Sheridan. I knew him at West Point. Tough little Irishman. Greatest man with a cussword I ever met. I hate to see him in Virginia. Still—"

He tossed off the two inches with a speed that made Madeline frown. "It just means things will wind up that much faster."

Orry watched him a moment. "You don't think we can win?"

"Do you?"

Orry sat still, his gaze wandering through the pattern of the carpet.

Presently Charles stretched and yawned again. "Hell," he said,

"I'm not even sure we can sue for peace on favorable terms. Not with Unconditional Surrender Grant turning the screw."

"I knew him," Orry mused. "We drank beer together in Mexico."

"What's he like?"

"Oh, it's been years since I saw him. Our keen-minded Southern journalists scorn him for being round-shouldered and slovenly. Really important considerations, eh? Ask Pete Longstreet whether he respects Sam Grant. Ask Dick Ewell. Three years ago, Ewell said there was an obscure West Point man somewhere in Missouri whom he hoped the Yankees would never discover. He said he feared him more than all the others put together."

"God help us," Charles remarked, reaching for a blanket. "Would it be all right with you two if I went to sleep now?" Orry turned off the gas, and he and Madeline said good night. Still fully dressed, Charles rolled up in the blanket and shut his eyes.

He found it hard to rest. Too many ghosts had arisen and roamed tonight.

He dragged the blanket against his cheek. He didn't want to think about it. Not about Billy in enemy country, riding for his life. Not about the Union horse already surprisingly good but now with a chance at supremacy under Sheridan. Not about Grant, who preached something called "enlightened warfare," which meant, so far as he could make out, throwing your men away like matchsticks because you always had more.

He fell asleep as some distant steeple rang five. He slept an hour, dreaming of Gus, and of Billy lying in a sunlit field, pierced by bullet holes thick and black with swarming flies.

When he woke, the comforting aroma of the Marshall Street substitute for coffee permeated the flat. In the first wan light, he trudged to the privy behind the building, then returned and splashed water on his face and hands and sat down opposite his cousin over cups of the strong brew Madeline poured for them.

Orry's expression indicated something serious was on his mind. Charles waited till his cousin came out with it.

"We had so much to talk about last night, I never got to the other bad news."

"Trouble back home?"

"No. Right here in the city. I uncovered a plot to assassinate the President and members of his cabinet." Disbelief prompted

Charles to smile; Orry's somber expression restrained him. "Someone well known and close to both of us is involved."

"Who?"

"Your cousin. My sister."

"Ashton?"

"Yes."

"Great balls of Union-blue fire," Charles said, in the same tone he might have taken if someone had told him the paymaster would be late again. He was startled to probe his feelings and find so little astonishment; scarcely more than mild surprise. There was a hardening center in him that nothing much could reach, let alone affect.

Orry described all that had happened thus far, beginning with Mrs. Halloran's visit and ending with the abrupt and mysterious disappearance of the chief conspirator and the arms and ammunition Orry had seen at the farm downriver on the James.

"For a few days after that, I thought I was crazy. I've gotten over it. They may have highly placed friends helping them cover the trail, and I know what I saw. The plot's real, Huntoon's involved, and so is Ashton."

"What are you going to do?"

Orry's stare told Charles he wasn't the only one whose hide had thickened.

"I'm going to catch her."

103

They surprised him on the creek bank at first light, creeping up while he slept. None of the three identified himself. He named them silently—Scars, One Thumb, Hound Face. All of them wore tattered Confederate uniforms.

To allay suspicion, he shared the last of his hardtack and ham. They shared their experiences of the past few days. Not to be sociable, Billy guessed, merely to fill the silence of the May morning.

"Grant put a hundred thousand into the Wilderness 'gainst our sixty or so. It got so fierce, the trees caught on fire, and our boys either choked to death on the smoke or burned up when the branches dropped on 'em." One Thumb, whose left eyelid drooped noticeably, shook his head and laid the last morsel of ham in his toothless mouth.

"How far are the lines?" Billy asked.

Hound Face answered, "Twenty, thirty mile. Would you say that?" His companions nodded. "But we all are goin' the other way. Back to Alabam." He gave Billy a searching look, awaiting reaction; condemnation, perhaps.

"The omens are bad," One Thumb resumed. "Old Pete Longstreet, he was wounded by a bullet from our side, just like Stonewall a year ago. And I hear tell Jeff Davis's little boy fell off a White House balcony a few days ago. Killed him. Like I say—bad omens."

Scars, the oldest, wiped grease from his mouth. "Mighty kind of you to share your grub, Missouri. We ain't got much of anythin' to aid us on our way home"—smoothly, he pulled his side arm and pointed it at Billy—"so we'll be obliged if you don't fuss an' help us out."

They disappeared five minutes later, having taken his mule and his pass.

Lanterns shone on the bare-chested black men. The May dark resounded with shouting, the clang and bang of rails being unloaded from a flatcar, the pound of mallets, the honk of frogs in the marshy lowlands near the Potomac. A group of George's men seized each rail, ran it forward, and dropped it on crossties laid only moments before. The rail carriers jumped aside to make room for men with mauls and buckets of spikes. It was the night of May 9; more accurately, the morning of May 10. Repair work to reopen the damaged Aquia Creek & Fredericksburg line down to Falmouth had been under way since dawn yesterday.

The butcher's bill from the Wilderness had been staggering. Now Lee had entrenched at or near Spotsylvania, and presumably the Union Army was shifting that way to engage. Without being told, George knew why the major portion of the Orange & Alexandria had been abandoned on the very morning Grant started his war machine across the Rapidan and why the Construction Corps had been transferred eastward to this duty. These tracks would soon carry dead and wounded.

George saw one of his best workers, a huge brown youngster named Scow, stumble suddenly. This forced the men behind him to halt. A lantern on a pole reflected in Scow's eyes as he swung to stare at his commander.

" 'M gonna drop."

George slipped in behind him and took the rail on his own shoulder. "Rest for ten minutes. Then come back. After we finish this fourteen miles of track, there's the Potomac Creek bridge to repair."

"You keep givin' ever' one of these niggers ten minutes, you gonna run out of minutes an' fall over yourself."

"You let me worry about that. Get going."

Scow rubbed his mouth, admiration and suspicion mingled on his face. "You're some damn boss," he said, and walked off, leaving George in doubt about which way to take that. With a grim amusement, he wondered what Scow would say if he knew his commander controlled and ran a huge ironworks and a thriving bank.

He took Scow's place in the rail-carrying team. Dizzy and growing sick to his stomach, he strove to hide it. "Come on," he yelled to the other men. He knew they felt as bad as he did, hurt in every muscle as he did. But together they ran the next rail forward, placed it, jumped down off the roadbed as the first mauls arched over and struck, and dashed back for the next one.

On the Brock Road, Billy fell to his knees and crawled into a ditch as a shell whistled in and burst, tossing up a cloud of dirt and stones. Sharp rock fragments rained on his bare neck as he lay in the weeds, the wind and what little strength he possessed knocked out of him.

From the west, the north, the east, he heard the multitudinous sounds of battle. They seemed loudest to the east. He had worked his way through the smoke-filled streets of Spotsylvania Court House and out this far without detection or interference. But as he began to breathe regularly again, and with effort regained the road, staggering from tiredness and hunger and lingering pain, a captain on horseback—from one of Jubal Early's commands, he presumed—loomed through the smoke deepening the gray of the morning.

The bearded officer galloped past Billy before he really took notice of him. He reined in, dismounted swiftly, and wrenched his sword from his sheath. "No straggling," he shouted, hitting Billy's back with the flat of his sword. "The lines are that way."

He pointed eastward with the blade. The ends of a strip of black silk tied around his right sleeve fluttered in the breeze. Mumbling to disguise his voice, Billy said, "Sir, I lost my musket—"

"You won't find another cowering back here." A second stab east. "Move, soldier."

Billy blinked, thinking, *I'll have to try to cross some place. Guess it might as well be here.*

"You and your kind disgust me," the captain said gratuitously. "We lose a great man, and your tribute to his memory is a display of cowardice."

Billy didn't want to speak again but felt he must. "Don't know what you mean, sir." He didn't. "Who's been lost?"

"General Stuart, you damn fool. Sheridan's horse went around our flank to Richmond. They killed the general at Yellow Tavern day before yesterday. Now get moving or you're under arrest."

Billy turned, staggered down the road shoulder, and moved in ungainly fashion through high weeds toward distantly seen entrenchments. A shell burst over him, a black flower. He covered his head and stumbled on, hurting more at every step.

At Potomac Creek, the gap from bluff to bluff was four hundred feet. A deck bridge eighty feet above the water spanned it, but the Confederates had destroyed the bridge. Haupt had rebuilt it; Burnside had destroyed it a second time so the enemy couldn't use it. Now the Construction Corps was building it again.

At the bottom of the chasm, George and his men cut and laid logs for the crib foundation. Haupt was gone, but not his plans and methods. In forty hours, a duplicate of the trestle Mr. Lincoln had wryly referred to as a mighty structure of beanpoles and cornstalks was complete.

They had to rush the work, sacrificing sleep, because men returning from the battle joined around Spotsylvania Court House said the Union and Confederate casualties were piling up like cordwood in the autumn. The temporary hospitals could hold only the worst cases. During the frantic rebuilding of the trestle, eight men fell off from various places. Four died. Their funeral rites consisted of quick concealment beneath tarpaulins.

Now the rails were laid, the huge hawsers rigged across the bridge, the locomotive brought up.

"*Pull,*" the black men and their white officers chanted together, thick ropes running through their hands and over their shoulders and across the trestle to the locomotive spouting steam on the far side. "*Pull—and—pull.*"

As Haupt's Wisconsin and Indiana volunteers had done once before, they pulled the empty locomotive across the trestle while a lurid green twilight came down, presaging storm. Lightning flickered and ran around the horizon. The sky seemed to complain, and so did the bridge. It swayed. It creaked.

But it stood.

Now. Now. *Now.*

He had been saying that to himself for ten minutes to strengthen his nerve because his body was still so weak. Finally he knew he had to obey the silent command. One hand tight on the

Confederate musket they had given him, Billy clawed a hold on the top of the earthwork and labored over while the torrential rain soaked him.

"Hey, Missouri, don't be crazy. You go any closer, you'll get kilt sure."

That was some reb noncom shouting from the earthworks he had just left. He lurched to his feet and limped through long, slippery grass, rapidly using up the small reserve of strength left to him. His kepi did little to shield his face from the hard rain.

He stumbled, sprawled, gagged when he slid into a dead Union vidette gazing at a lightning flash without seeing it. When the glare faded and darkness returned, he dropped his musket and flung off the kepi. The next flash caught him struggling to remove his gray jacket, his mouth opening and closing, silent gasps of pain. He was spotted by the same rebs who had earlier accepted his arrival without much question since the heavy fighting had shattered and mixed different commands all along the Confederate line. The noncom's voice reached him again.

"That dirty scum ain't attackin' nobody. He's runnin' to the other side. Shoot the bastard."

"Running—oh, damn right," Billy panted, trying to beat back fear with mockery. Guns cracked behind him. Lungs hurting, he kept moving, away from them. One shoulder rose and fell in rhythm with his hobbling gait. Thunder rolled in the wake of the last lightning, then in a new burst silhouetted fresh-budded trees and lit a Union bayonet like white-hot metal.

The picket with the bayonet, one of Burnside's men facing the rebel position, spied the filthy figure. Behind the picket, other shoulder weapons started crackling as loudly as those of the rebs. "Don't shoot," Billy yelled in the crossfire, hands raised. "Don't shoot. I'm a Union officer escaped from—"

He tripped on a half-buried stone and twisted, falling. He flapped his arms, losing all sense of direction. So he never knew who fired the shot that hit him and flung him on his face with a muffled cry.

George learned more about the spring offensive from Washington papers than he did from anyone in the war theater. Everyone called it Grant's campaign and praised Grant's brave men, although the actual commander of the Army of the Potomac was Major General Meade. Grant, however, was a general of the armies who took the field. Meade was relegated to a role something like that of a corps commander. It became Grant's war and Grant's plan. Ignore Richmond. Destroy Lee's army. Then the card house would fall.

But the papers also used one more phrase accusingly and often: Grant's casualties. The dispatches took on a sameness as the decimated army refilled its ranks and marched by night in pursuit of the retreating Lee. The repetitious headlines fell like a slow drum cadence: IMMENSE REBEL LOSSES and OUR LOSS TWELVE THOUSAND and HEAVY LOSS ON BOTH SIDES.

George and the youngster named Scow watched one of the death trains traveling north from Falmouth on the reopened Aquia Creek & Fredericksburg. They could always identify the trains of the dead from Falmouth because they traveled noticeably faster than those carrying wounded or prisoners. Hundreds of firefly sparks swarmed above and behind the locomotive, which rapidly vanished. The line of cars was so long that despite its speed it seemed to take forever to pass.

"Twenty, twenty-one—twenty-two," Scow said, watching the last go by. "That's a mighty lot of coffins."

"The general's killing a mighty lot of men, but he'll kill more."

Scow said "Um" in a way that denoted sadness. Then asked, "How many you figure?"

Depressed, George swatted at a floating spark. He missed, and it stung his cheek. "As many as it takes to win." He was proud of the work he and the black men, so diverse in appearance and personality and yet so united in purpose, had accomplished. But he hated the reason for the work.

He clapped Scow on the shoulder in a friendly way that wasn't suitable for an officer, but he didn't give a hang, because the corps was an odd outfit. Odd and proud. "Let's find some food."

Presently George sat cross-legged next to Scow at a campfire built of pieces of broken crossties. He was spooning beans from his tin plate when a whistle signaled the approach of another Falmouth train. He and Scow peered through a maze of stumps toward the track a quarter of a mile away. Northern Virginia was a land of stumps; few uncut trees remained.

George watched the white beam of the headlight sweep around

a bend, stabbing above the stumps and bleaching Scow light tan for a few moments.

"Wounded," George said, having judged the speed. He went back to his beans as the car carrying his brother rattled by.

104

In a thunderstorm, Virgilia and eight other nurses rode the cars from Aquia Creek to Falmouth. There a temporary field hospital had been established to augment the deserted Fredericksburg churches, stables, and private homes used for the same purpose. Casualties were pouring in from the contested ground around Spotsylvania. The worst cases, the ones who couldn't survive even a short rail trip, were treated at Falmouth.

The car in which the nurses traveled had been gutted, the passenger seats replaced by bunks exuding the familiar smells of dirt and wounds. The windows were boarded over, except for one at each end left for ventilation. From these the glass had long ago been smashed. Rain blew in as the train rolled south. A lantern hung by the rear door, but flashes of lightning washed out its glow and lent a corpselike look to the cloaked women attempting to sit decorously on the bunks.

The nurse in charge was Mrs. Neal, from whom Virgilia had three times tried to escape. Each time, Miss Dix had answered her transfer request in the same terse language. Miss Hazard was considered too valuable. Miss Hazard was an asset to her present hospital. Miss Hazard could not be spared for duty elsewhere.

Virgilia suspected Mrs. Neal had a hand in the refusals. The older woman recognized Virgilia's ability but took pleasure in frustrating her. Virgilia, in turn, continued to despise her supervisor, yet could not bring herself to resign. The work was still deeply satisfying. She brought comfort and recovery to scores of men in pain. The sight of the maimed and dying kept her hatred of Southerners at full strength. And when she lost a patient, she was philosophic, remembering *Coriolanus* again. Volumnia saying, "I had rather eleven die nobly for their country than one voluptuously surfeit out of action."

"—they say the Spotsylvania fighting has been fearful." That was a buxom spinster named Thomasina Kisco. The edge of her black travel bonnet cast a sharp shadow across her face. "And the number of casualties enormous."

"That will assure Mr. Lincoln's removal in November," Mrs. Neal said. "He refuses to end the butchery, so the electorate must." She seldom stopped electioneering for McClellan and the Peace Democrats.

"Is it true they're bringing Confederate wounded to this hospital?" Virgilia asked.

"Yes." Mrs. Neal's tone was as cold as her stare. Virgilia was accustomed to both. She shivered. She was chilly because her cloak was damp, but at least the odor of wet wool helped mask those of the car. She considered the supervisor's answer and decided she had to speak.

"I will not treat enemy soldiers, Mrs. Neal."

"You will do whatever you are told to do, Miss Hazard." Her anger drew sympathetic looks from the others—all for Virgilia. Mrs. Neal retreated. "Really, my dear—you're an excellent nurse, but you seem unable to accept the discipline of the service. Why do you continue?"

Because, you illiterate cow, in my own way I'm a soldier, too. Instead of saying that, however, Virgilia merely shifted her gaze elsewhere. Prig and martinet were only two of the terms she applied to Mrs. Neal in the silence of her thoughts.

The past year had been difficult and unhappy because of the supervisor. Many times Virgilia was ready to do exactly what Mrs. Neal wanted—resign. She hung on not only because she drew satisfaction from the work but also because she had become good at it, knowing more than many of the contract hacks who posed as distinguished surgeons. Whenever the need to quit overwhelmed her, she fought it by remembering that Grady had died unavenged—and that Lee, then still a Union officer, had led the detachment that put an end to John Brown's brave struggle. After that, the work always won out.

It did so now. The car swayed, the wind howled, the rain blew in through the shattered windows. Miss Kisco cast an apprehensive eye on the ceiling.

"That thunder is extremely loud."

"Those are the guns at Spotsylvania," Virgilia said.

The storm continued, battering the canvas pavilions of the field hospital. The pavilions were located near the Falmouth station, so that in addition to the outcries of the patients and the swearing of the surgeons and the shouts of the ambulance drivers there was a constant background noise of shunting cars, ringing bells, screeching whistles—war's bedlam.

Virgilia and Miss Kisco were assigned to a pavilion that received men who, though seriously wounded, didn't require immediate surgery. The slicing and sawing went on in the next pavilion, where Mrs. Neal took charge. She inspected Virgilia's about once an hour.

"Over here next, Miss Hazard," said the chief surgeon of the pavilion. A paunchy, wheezy-voiced man, he fairly jerked her along to a cot where orderlies had placed a slim lieutenant with silky brown hair. The young man was unconscious. Though his cot occupied the pavilion's darkest corner, Virgilia clearly saw the color of his uniform.

"This man's a rebel."

"So I assumed from the gray coat," the surgeon said crossly. "He also happens to be shot." He pointed to the right thigh. "Remove that dressing, please."

The surgeon stepped to the left side of the cot, where a large scrap of paper was pinned to the blanket. He ripped it loose to read it. "Bullet lodged near the femoral artery. Vessel torn but not clamped. He's a Mississippi boy. General Nat Harris's brigade. Captured in front of the rifle pits at the Mule Shoe Salient. Can't quite decipher his name—"

He tilted the scrap toward the nearest lantern some yards away. Virgilia, meantime, forced herself to remove the dressing from the torn trouser leg. In the next aisle, a boy gagged and wept. From the operating pavilion, she heard the rasp of saws in bone. So much suffering—and here she was tending one of those who had caused it. Her rage intensified like fire in a dry woods.

The reb's wound had been decently cleaned and dressed by the ambulance orderlies. The bare, pale leg felt slightly cool when she touched it. That explained the lack of bleeding; it had stopped when his temperature dropped.

"O'Grady."

Virgilia's head jerked up. "I beg your pardon?"

"I said," the doctor growled, "his name appears to be O'Grady. Thomas Aloysius O'Grady. Didn't know there were any potato-eaters down in Mississippi. Let me have a look."

The weary doctor waddled around the end of the cot. Virgilia remained where she was, her eyes fixed, unblinking.

"Will you please stand aside?"

Mumbling an apology, she obeyed. Her head hit the sloping canvas; she bent forward to avoid it. O'Grady. She hated the silky-haired boy twice as much for bearing that name. She clutched her apron and began to twist it, gently at first, then with increasing violence.

"Miss Hazard, are you ill?"

His wheezing question wrenched her back from her private anguish. "I'm sorry, Doctor—what did you say?"

"I don't know what you're thinking about, but kindly pay attention to this patient. We must clamp off that artery and try to remove the—"

"Doctor," Miss Kisco called from the other side of the pavilion. "Over here, please—emergency."

Hurrying away, the surgeon said, "I'll tend to him as soon as I can. Put on a new dressing and watch him carefully."

Virgilia withdrew gauze pads from the lacquered box in the center of the pavilion and returned to the cot of Lieutenant O'Grady. How many Union soldiers had the Mississippi boy killed, she wondered. She knew one thing: he wouldn't kill any more. How fitting that his name was so close to that of her dead lover.

She noticed Mrs. Neal at the pavilion entrance, conferring with another of the surgeons. The supervisor, in turn, watched Virgilia for a few seconds. She was always trying to catch her in a mistake, but never could. When Mrs. Neal returned her attention to the doctor, Virgilia carefully and gently rebandaged the wounded thigh.

Without the slightest movement or expression to betray her excitement, she pulled up the wool blanket so it covered the young lieutenant. She found a second blanket and couldn't suppress a little smile as she laid it on top of the first. Softly, soothingly, she stroked the boy's cool forehead, then glided away.

Sudden cannon fire shook the pavilion. All the lanterns swayed. Two more ambulances arrived outside, the horses snorting, the wheels slopping in mud. The rain had diminished to a drizzle. Virgilia decided it must be close to dawn—they had gone to work immediately upon leaving the car—but she felt energetic, renewed. She could hardly keep from glancing at the unconscious reb while she helped with the new cases coming in.

During the next twenty minutes, the chief surgeon didn't have time to return to Lieutenant O'Grady. But Virgilia found time, walking to the cot with fresh gauzes draped over her arm.

Carefully, she raised the blankets. Bright red arterial blood stained the gauzes applied earlier. The soldier's breathing was louder, labored—as expected. She laid the dressings on the cot and felt for his pulse. Stronger, faster—also as expected. The blankets had raised his temperature, and secondary hemorrhaging had begun. As expected.

Drawing the blankets down, she laid two new dressings on top of the first. It would take some time for the pumping blood to soak through all those layers. Should someone raise the blanket, it was doubtful that a problem would be apparent. Once more Virgilia brought the blanket up and tucked it neatly beneath the boy's chin. She felt not the slightest prick of conscience. This was the enemy. She was a soldier. Grady had long cried out to be avenged.

"Miss Hazard!"

The shout of the chief surgeon drew her back to the center of the pavilion. A captain with a serious chest wound was rushed in on a litter. The only vacant cot was that next to O'Grady, back in the poorly lit corner.

Heart racing, she maneuvered herself into the space between O'Grady's bed and that of the new patient, partially blocking the surgeon's view of the reb. Pressed with so many urgent cases, the surgeon did nothing except nod toward O'Grady and ask, "How's that one?"

"Satisfactory the last time I checked, sir."

"Seems to be breathing hard. Have a look."

"Yes, sir." Terrified, she started to turn.

"I mean after you help me here."

Virgilia's tension melted. They worked over the captain for six minutes, until the exhausted surgeon staggered off to answer another appeal from Miss Kisco, who was receiving a new ambulance-load at the entrance. Virgilia snatched fresh gauzes from the storage box and rushed back to O'Grady. She lifted the blanket and saw the small, bright red stars—just two—on the field of white. Her smile was almost sensual.

She applied an additional dressing and once more drew up the blankets. He was bleeding to death unnoticed. Unmourned. Her best estimate was that he would be gone within a half hour. She returned the other dressings to the box and went about her work with a sense of warmth and happiness.

In three-quarters of an hour, carrying a waste pail, she went back to the corner and disposed of the thoroughly soaked dressings, replacing them with a new one, the last that would be needed. She replaced the blankets on the body, put the pail among others with similar contents, and resumed her other work. Despite the clamor and foulness of the pavilion, she floated in a near-euphoric state for twenty minutes. Then she got a jolt.

Unnoticed by Virgilia, Mrs. Neal had returned to inspect various patients. It was her sharp outcry that drew Virgilia's attention. She saw the supervisor back in the dim corner, her squat body silhouetted against the canvas brightened by the light of the new day.

With her right hand, Mrs. Neal held up the blankets that had covered Lieutenant O'Grady. The startled O of her mouth broke.

"Doctor—*Doctor!* This boy is dead. Who was charged with watching him?"

805

105

"Name and rank of the prisoner?"

"Private Stephen McNaughton."

"Caught where?"

"Approximately three miles north of here, sir. He was identified by those." The frog-voiced three-striper hooked his thumb at the prisoner's soiled tartan pantaloons.

The hanging lantern glared in the eyes of the regimental adjutant, a major half the prisoner's age, slight and sandy-haired, with ginger-colored Dundreary whiskers. "Step forward," he ordered, rolling the *r* slightly. Cap in hand, Salem Jones advanced two paces to the field desk.

"Scum of the streets—that's all we get anymore." The major's complaint drew a nod from one of the two corporals who, together with the sergeant, had brought Jones to regimental headquarters. "Such a depraved, vice-hardened, desperate set of human beings never before fouled any army on the face of God's earth."

Worried as he was, Jones had no fundamental disagreement with the major's opinion. When he had signed on as a replacement in his last regiment, a Pennsylvania reserve unit, he had been held in a Philadelphia stockade for three and a half days, constantly watched by armed guards. The other recruits similarly confined terrified him; they were clearly criminals, men who would have knifed or strangled him and looted his pockets if he hadn't already lost his bounty in a high-stakes poker game.

"What was your original occupation, Private McNaughton?"

Cardsharp? Thief? Murderer?" The major's next words sounded like pistol shots. "Never mind, I know the real answers. Opportunist. Coward. You're a disgrace to this regiment, the United States Army, the state of New York, America, and your ancestral homeland."

Pious little prick, Jones thought, envisioning several painful ways he would murder the major, given the chance. Ah, but he mustn't waste time on fantasies. He had to concentrate on saving himself. His was the misfortune of having chosen a Scottish alias, and the adjutant was a Scot. Jones had the feeling this officer wouldn't let him off so lightly as others had.

The major seemed incapable of curbing his temper—understandable, given the great numbers of misfits and jailbirds being shoveled up throughout the North to fuel Grant's war engine. The officer came around the desk and planted himself intimidatingly close to Jones.

"On how many other occasions have you claimed the enlistment bounty, then jumped? Several, I'll wager. Well, McNaughton, if that is your name, which I doubt, it will not be so easy henceforth."

Salem Jones's legs wobbled. His stomach began to slosh as the major said to the sergeant, "Fetch the barber and have him heat the iron. And get this piece of garbage out of my sight."

First the shears, then a razor, the latter applied with little soap and no gentleness. The noncom who functioned as the regiment's unofficial barber twice drew blood as he scraped Jones's skull. Jones didn't dare cry out for fear of provoking him.

He sat on a stool while the barber removed the last of the hair that ringed his bald head. About thirty soldiers had turned out to watch the punishment. He was infuriated by some of the smirking faces. They belonged to men who had enlisted for the bounty under false names, just as he had, with every intention of deserting. Jones had joined up and run away four times during the year since he had conceived the idea at the height of the New York rioting. He knew men who had pulled it off seven or eight times, with never a capture. That kind of luck had eluded him, as luck had eluded him most of his life.

The May night was warm. An owl hooted somewhere. From the great sparking fire, the shirtless three-striper called, "Ready."

The ring of observers opened. Corporals pushed Jones through to the fire as the sergeant reached into it with a right hand protected by a thick gauntlet. The sergeant seized the handle of the branding iron and pulled. The end that slid from the coals was white.

While others held him, someone shoved a bottle of popskull at Jones. They forced him to drink several mouthfuls of the fiery swill. With liquor running down his chin and blood trickling around his left ear from one of the scalp nicks, he was thrust to the fire. The boisterous witnesses closed in behind.

The sweating three-striper lifted the iron. Bastards, Jones screamed in silence. I'll kill you. To those grasping him by the arms and shoulders, the sergeant said, "Hold him steady."

Rising toward his eyes, the white iron grew larger and larger. Jones writhed, began begging. "No—no, *don't.*" A familiar face floated to one side of the intense light. The major had come out to watch.

"I said hold him," the sergeant snarled. Hands clamped Salem Jones's head. He began screaming several seconds before the sergeant pushed the iron against his face.

He flung the firebrand on the tent and ran.

Down a grassy embankment, up the far side, into an apple orchard. There he finally whirled around, clutching an overhanging branch and watching flames ignite the tent. Shouts, oaths came from within. He didn't really suppose he could burn the major to death, but at least he had given him a fright. He turned and ran on.

Three days after the punishment, Jones had been returned to duty, because the army was preparing to march—by night, which seemed to be the rule now—and the fools believed that head shaving and branding had broken him. Besides, they needed bodies to throw into the war machine. His was good enough. Those of immigrants, thugs, physical cripples were good enough. The Union Army was full of splendid specimens these days.

Brimming with rage and a pain that would last far longer than that in his face, Jones met the order to march by stealing some nondescript trousers from another regiment, encamped nearby. He threw away his tartan pantaloons, donned the plain ones, and ripped all the military buttons from his rancid jacket. He had no cash; more gambling had disposed of that. He had no weapon, and he had no identification except the one burned on him. He was preparing for his last desertion.

Even if he could manage to reenlist for another bounty, he wouldn't do it. The war had grown too savage. Lee had withstood Butcher Grant in the Wilderness and bloodied him at Spotsylvania—during the latter action, Jones kept busy straggling or dodging to the safest sectors—but Grant wouldn't quit. The major who had ordered the punishment had once told his assembled regiment about Grant sending a telegraphic dispatch to Washington to express his determination to win in Virginia. The heart of Grant's message was printed in papers all over the North to improve civilian morale, the major said. He could even quote the essence of the message: *"I propose to fight it out on this line if it takes all summer."*

Well, he would do it without Salem Jones, by God. Jones had enjoyed the benefits of the bounty system for a while, but recapture and the ordeal at the fire had put an end to that. He was bound south, as fast and as far as he could travel. He might go as far as South Carolina. He would love to be there when the Confederacy fell, as it surely would now that Grant's bloody engine was rolling. It amused Jones to imagine what he could do to Mont Royal and the people who had discharged him when Carolina became a conquered province—

As he fled through the orchard, the scene behind him— shadowmen running, shouting—convinced him the major had escaped from the burning tent. Too bad, but he had done his best. Now he must worry about slipping through the Union lines and the Confederate ones farther south.

At the adjoining regimental bivouac, he dashed through a gap between picket posts. A few moments later, the May moon sailed from behind a cloud, drenching him with light. Two inches high, the *D* stood out black and clear beneath his right eye.

Within twenty-four hours of the arrival of the nurses, conditions at the field hospital improved. Sanitary Commission wagons with flocks of black youngsters merrily chasing them brought bottled morphine, tinctured opium, chloride of lime. And food. In the first hours, while the hurt, dying, and dead had been shuttled in and out at dizzying speed, only hardtack and coffee had been available.

Amidst the constant activity and occasional confusion, Virgilia managed to marshal her wits and courage for the confrontation that had become inevitable the moment Mrs. Neal raised the dead boy's blanket. She suspected the supervisor would approach her first, rather than go to the surgeon in charge; she would want that satisfaction.

At the end of Virgilia's first full day on duty, there came a lull. No new patients, and nothing more to be done for those already there. Virgilia wiped a tin cup on her apron and ladled hot coffee into it. She was spent, having slept less than an hour in one of the commission wagons that afternoon.

She wandered outside. It was dusk. Fire-blackened stumps and tree trunks surrounding the hospital still gave off the smell of charred wood. Dull pain reached from Virgilia's feet to her lower back, the result of standing for so long. She wandered past the corner of her pavilion, tensing when she heard a rustle of skirts behind her. Without turning, she sat on a stump and brushed away a fly.

"Miss Hazard?"

Her face composed, Virgilia shifted her position to acknowledge the presence of the older woman.

"I have an extremely serious matter to discuss. I fear we both know what it is."

You fear? she thought, wrathful. *You revel in it.* She detected a sparkle of malice in Mrs. Neal's eyes. The supervisor walked to another stump and stopped behind it, facing her subordinate like a presiding judge.

"You allowed that young Southerner to bleed to death, didn't you? In other words, you killed him."

"Of all the ridiculous, insulting—"

"Taking the offensive with protests and bluster will do you no good," Mrs. Neal interrupted. "You told me on the train, very explicitly and before witnesses, that you would not minister to enemy wounded. Your extreme hatred of the South is well known. You covered that young soldier with blankets when you knew full well that warming him would start the damaged vessel bleeding again."

"Yes, I did cover him. I admit to that mistake. In the confusion —so many needing help—the surgeons all yelling at once—"

"Nonsense. You are one of the best nurses I have ever met. I have always disliked you, but I don't minimize your ability. You would not make that sort of mistake unless it was deliberate."

810

Feeling dampness under her arms and a series of tight little convulsions in her middle, Virgilia rose. She had gambled that admission of one mistake might lend credibility to a denial of greater guilt. Mrs. Neal was not taken in. Without looking at the supervisor, Virgilia bluffed. "If I confess to the error in judgment, you'll have a hard time proving it was anything more."

"I can certainly try. I shall report that you put the blankets on the patient, fully understanding the consequences, and you then concealed the hemorrhaging by covering one bloodied bandage with another and another—several, in fact—so that inevitably—"

"Damn you, I didn't!"

Whirling to cry at her tormentor, Virgilia saw two huge black birds perched on the one surviving branch of a scorched tree. She imagined the birds had been drawn by the smell of wounds. Including hers.

Mrs. Neal lifted her several chins, her glare challenging. "If not you, then who?"

"I don't know. One of the orderlies—"

"Again—patent nonsense."

"I admit to the blanket, nothing else."

"In the face of that, further discussion is fruitless. But I know what you did, and I shall take the evidence to Miss Dix. I shall see you punished. I suggest you spend the evening rehearsing your defense. You'll want to have all your lies in order when the investigation begins."

And she swept by with a sideways look of pleasure.

Virgilia stayed outside among the ruined trees as it grew dark. The black birds remained on the charred limb. She took a sip from the cup. Cold. She threw the coffee on the ground. Inside the pavilion, a wounded man began to weep.

She scarcely heard. Given Mrs. Neal's politics and personal animosity, the supervisor would certainly press for an investigation. And it would probably take place. Who besides Miss Dix would be involved? The surgeon general's staff? The civil police in Washington? Exhausted, disheveled, Virgilia saw fantasies in the lowering dark. A barred cell. A man in judicial robes high above her, passing sentence—

"God," she cried softly as something flapped past and brushed her face.

When she recovered, she saw one of the roosting birds sailing above the pavilion. A train whistled. She knuckled her eyes to rid them of tears of fright. *Keep your nerve. Think clearly. What you did isn't a crime. It was for Grady. There are millions who would call it patriotic. He was the enemy.*

All that rationalization did nothing to cancel the other fact. Mrs. Neal would report her. There must be no investigation. It was up to her to prevent it and the possible consequences: prosecution, prison—

How, though? *How?*

"There you are, Virgilia."

The woman's voice startled her. She saw Miss Kisco at the pavilion entrance. Belatedly, she heard something new in the tone of the other nurse: hostility.

"What is it?"

"The chief surgeon wishes to speak to you."

"Tell him I'll be there in a moment. I'm a bit dizzy from all the fumes inside."

"Very well." Miss Kisco vanished.

Virgilia turned and walked the other way into the dark.

Her pass was in order; she had no trouble boarding the first train leaving for Aquia Landing. By sunrise she was on a steamer chugging up the Potomac.

She would never go back to the field hospital, or any other. But neither would she hide. It had come to her outside the pavilion that she had but one hope of aborting an investigation, and that was through the intervention of some person of influence. A person powerful enough to thwart Mrs. Neal and even Miss Dix.

Virgilia sat on deck bundled in her cloak, her valises between her feet. Despite her situation, she had no regrets. The Southerners had been responsible for Grady's death, and she had taken a life in reprisal, as the Confederates themselves did. As the biblical kings did.

She was sorry she could no longer continue as a nurse. The work had given her life a direction it had lacked since the debacle at Harpers Ferry. But at least she had closed out her field career as any good soldier should. By destroying an enemy.

Now she must deal with another. In the cool of the early morning, she debarked at the city pier, her face calm, her course determined. As soon as she found a room and cleaned up, she would set about contacting Congressman Sam Stout.

106

In his bed in Harewood Convalescent Hospital, Billy wrote:

Sun., June 5. Weather warm. At night we must all be co-cooned in mosquito nets or be devoured. Tulip and redbud trees shade this pavilion in the hottest hours, but nothing can relieve the charnel smell which has hung over the city ever since General G. took the field. The dead are everywhere; beyond counting.

Can't get reliable news but am told by orderlies that another great battle is being fought 7–8 mis. from Richmond. Perhaps it will end matters and I can go home to you, my dear wife. If not, will be on my way back to Virginia within a few days—the Minié ball that struck my lower leg passed cleanly through the flesh, doing no permanent damage, though I still walk as awkwardly, for a different reason, as I did on the flight from Richmond.

I do not want to return to duty, and deem myself no coward for that admission. I will go only because if G. fails at Richmond, the effort must continue till this sanguinary business is ended forever.

Old Abe is to be renominated in Baltimore next week as the candidate of something called the National Union party, whose sudden invention is apparently meant to demonstrate a common purpose uniting less radical Republicans and pro-Union Democrats. It is by no means certain that L. will win this time. Many are against him, and more join that company each day. One officer here spoke openly and shockingly on the subject last night. He said the nation would be better served if someone were to slay the President. How far into madness must we sink before this ends?

On the day Lincoln won renomination, joined on the ticket by Governor Johnson of Tennessee, a Democrat, Isabel packed up the twins and left for a long holiday at the house in Newport. Washington had become intolerable. Almost hourly, the trains and steamers carrying the dead rattled over Long Bridge or tied up at the Sixth Street piers. Morticians wandered about with glassy expressions, exhausted from conducting their trade and counting their profits. Eighteen to twenty thousand patients jammed the district's military hospitals. Wounded walked even in the best districts, and pestilential smells overpowered even the strongest scent.

Stanley didn't object to his wife's departure. It enabled him to visit more freely with a young woman whose acquaintance he had made one night in April when he and some Republican cronies, all rip-roaring drunk, visited the Varieties, the big theater on Ninth Street whose front was bedecked with flags and splashed by the rainbow colors of a transparency wheel revolving in front of a calcium light.

The audience for the show was almost entirely male. Before the appearance of the sentimental soloists, Chinese contortionists, black-faced comedians, the scantily clad members of the dancing chorus performed a crowd-pleasing routine set to patriotic airs. The prettiness of one of the dancers, a busty girl of twenty or so, unexpectedly prompted Stanley to leap up on the bench, shouting like dozens of sweaty, tobacoo-chewing soldiers all around him.

A ten-cent whiskey in each hand, Stanley riveted his eye on this particular dancer and, afterward, struck up a conversation backstage—not difficult once the young lady took note of his age and expensive clothing and heard him say he was a confidant of Secretary Stanton, Senator Wade, and Congressman Davis among others.

The last two legislators were much in the news lately. With their Wade-Davis bill, recently passed in the House, they had openly declared war on the President's moderate program for postwar reconstruction. The bill stipulated that civil government would be restored only after fifty percent of a rebelling state's white males took a loyalty oath; Lincoln's plan kept the percentage at ten. Other Wade-Davis provisos were equally harsh, and the President had made it known that he would bury the legislation with a pocket veto if it cleared the Senate.

Enraged, Wade retaliated by saying publicly, "The authority of Congress is paramount. It must be respected by all—and I do not exclude that hag-ridden creature who haunts the Executive Mansion and daily heaps more disgrace upon his office and his nation."

At the reception where Wade first uttered the statement, Stanley clapped and muzzily cried "Hear, hear!" He hadn't gone so far as to attend the splinter nominating convention in Cleveland, where a Republican faction had named General Frémont its candidate. But he was dedicated to Lincoln's overthrow, and this was but one of many facts he conveyed to his new light-of-love.

Miss Jeannie Canary—the last name was something she had adopted to replace the unpronounceable one bestowed by her Levantine father—was impressed by Stanley's friends almost as much as she was by his unlimited cash supply. On the night after the renomination, she and Stanley lay naked in bed in Miss Canary's cheap rooms on the island—quarters from which he had pledged to move her soon.

Pleasantly blurry from bourbon, Stanley rested on his ample stomach, diddling Miss Canary's dark nipples with his fingertips. She usually smiled continually. But not this evening.

"Loves, I want to see the illuminations. I want to hear the Marine Band play 'Tramp! Tramp! Tramp!'"

"Jeannie"—he spoke as if explaining to a slow child—"the celebrations constitute a slap in the face to my closest friends. How dare I attend?"

"Oh, that isn't the reason you're saying no," she retorted, flouncing over and showing him her plump rear. Beyond soiled curtains, a fiery line ran upward in the sky, bursting into a shower of silver spangles. Other rockets, green, yellow, blue, followed. In the direction of Georgetown, many balloons were aloft, dangerously illuminated by lanterns in their baskets.

She poked an index finger into her cheek, as a bad actress might to convey a pensive mood. "The real reason is you don't want to be seen with me."

"You mustn't take offense at that. I am known in this town. I am also a married man."

"Then you've got no business being here, have you? So if you won't take me out, don't bother to rent a new flat for me. Or come backstage again—ever."

Her dark eyes and her pout undid him. He heaved his pale body out of bed, found the bottle, and swigged the last of it. "All right. I suppose we could go for an hour—though I want you to appreciate the risk I'm taking." He reached for his oversized underdrawers.

"Oh, loves, I do, I do," she squealed, scented arms around his neck, breasts mashed flat against his flab. Moments like these somehow canceled Stanley's awareness of his age and banished every thought of Isabel. At such times, he felt like a young man.

The sight Miss Canary wanted to see was the Patent Office, above the avenue on F Street. They caught a hack—Stanley never brought his own carriage and driver to the island—and on the way he attempted to explain why he and his friends despised Lincoln. He started with the different plans for reconstruction, descriptions of which confused her and stiffened her smile, a sure sign she was growing cross again. He immediately tried the military approach.

"The President chose Grant, but Grant's campaign is virtually at a standstill. Cold Harbor was a disaster, the dimensions of which we are just discovering. The general has lost something like fifty thousand men—nearly half the original force with which he advanced across the Rapidan, and almost the same number as you'll find in Lee's entire army. The nation won't tolerate a butcher's bill that high—especially with Richmond still not captured."

"I'm not exactly sure where Richmond is, loves. Down near North Carolina?"

Sighing, he patted her hand and gave up. Jeannie Canary was sweet and droll, but her talents, while delicious, were limited. One shouldn't expect more of actresses, he supposed.

"I want to get out," she insisted when the hack stalled in the crowd at the corner of Seventh and F. He tried to persuade her that they shouldn't, but she opened the door anyway. With a quiver of fear, he followed.

Fireworks exploded overhead, thunderous. The crowd whistled and cheered the red, white, and blue star bursts. On the front of the Patent Office building, great illuminations had been created—huge transparency portraits of Lincoln and the unknown Johnson and tough-jawed Grant blazed in the night. Miss Canary squealed and clung to his arm, and he watched strangers take notice of them. A shiver chased along his spine. The danger had a certain piquant quality, something like the thrill experienced by a soldier, he felt sure.

"Good evening, Stanley."

Paling, he swung sharply and saw Congressman Henry Davis of Maryland tip his hat, skewer Miss Canary with a glance—she was oblivious—and pass on.

Oh, my God, oh, my God, was all that passed through Stanley's head for the next couple of moments. What a fool he was, what an absolute ass. The danger here wasn't piquant; it was deadly.

And he was now a casualty.

Charles wanted to mourn for Beauty Stuart, but no tears would come.

Instead, he examined memories; shining bits of glass in the great bright window of the Stuart legend, a window fashioned partly by Stuart's admirers, partly by his detractors, partly by the man himself. At the end, Charles could forgive Stuart's suspicion and shabby treatment of Hampton early in the war and remember instead how lustily he sang. They said that while he was dying he had asked friends to sing "Rock of Ages" at his bedside.

As senior brigadier, Hampton stood next in line to command the cavalry. He immediately got a large part of the responsibility, but not the promotion. Charles and Jim Pickles and every other veteran knew why. Lee distrusted Hampton's age. Was he fit enough to withstand the rigors of the command?

Charles thought it a ridiculous issue. Hampton had long ago proved himself able to endure hardships, bad weather, long rides, and campaigns that would fell many men who were years younger. Still, those high up seemed determined to test him further. Charles felt bad because he suspected the delay also had something to do with Fitz Lee wanting the promotion for himself.

Once back from Richmond, Charles had no time away from duty, no chance to visit Gus, though he thought of her often. He had decided that the love affair must be cooled off if not ended completely. The war was helping.

At the same time, he worried that harm would come to her as ferocious campaigning started in the Wilderness. He knew the Federals had overrun Fredericksburg again and many of the inhabitants had fled. A note from Orry in answer to one of his said Gus and her freedmen weren't in Richmond or, if they were, they hadn't come to Orry and Madeline for sanctuary. From that, Charles guessed she was still at the farm. He wanted to find out if she was all right but couldn't do it.

Which was better, knowing or not knowing? Jim Pickles received letters from home, and each depressed him for days after it arrived. His mother was bedridden. One doctor suspected she had a cancer and might not last the year.

"I got to go home," Jim announced one day.

"You can't," Charles said with authority.

Jim thought for a while. "I s'pose you're right." But he didn't sound convinced.

Grant's army reeled past its own dead at Cold Harbor, apparently intent on investing the strategic rail junction at Petersburg. Phil Sheridan's cavalry feinted toward Charlottesville; Lee was forced to send Hampton in pursuit. Near Trevilian Station, on the Virginia Central line, Charles briefly saw the curly-haired Yankee, a general now, who had marked him at Brandy Station.

The Federals were about to make off with wagons, ambulances, and around eight hundred horses. Calbraith Butler's brigade was fighting elsewhere, so Hampton sent Texas Tom Rosser galloping in. Charles rode with Rosser's men, and it was then that he spied the boy general, recognizing him first by his scarlet neckerchief. Charles fired one shot, which missed. Custer fired back and rode away. It was doubtful that he recognized Charles, who now resembled a bearded bandit more than a soldier.

The next afternoon, Charles fought dismounted from behind hastily built earthworks on one side of the Virginia Central tracks. He and Jim were back with Butler's troopers. Across the tracks, Sheridan's cavalry formed and advanced on foot while brass instruments dinned "Garryowen."

"D'ja ever hear such noise?" Jim shouted, ducking at the whiz of a Minié ball not far above him. He wasn't referring to the gunfire.

"Little Phil always orders up plenty of music," Charles replied, emptying his revolver at the enemy, then crouching down to reload. "They say he does it to drown out the rebel yells."

Flinging himself up to the fence rails topping the earthworks, he steadied his revolver with both hands, aimed, and slowly squeezed off two shots. A boy in blue crumpled on the tracks.

With a grunt expressing satisfaction, Charles hunted his next target.

"This here's got to be the most tuneful war anybody ever fought," Jim observed. "One thing—it sure ain't the kind of war I expected."

Beyond his gunsight, Charles saw a spectral springtime road where natty gentlemen soldiers trotted their matched bays in smart formation. "It isn't what anybody expected," he said, and blew a hole in another youngster's leg. He found he shot with greater accuracy if he considered the Yanks just so many animated clay targets in a gallery.

On they came, gamely firing carbines braced against their hips. The last assault took place near sunset. When it was repulsed, Sheridan withdrew his men from battle. They began slipping away toward the North Anna during the night. Charles and the other scouts were in the van of the pursuit. Thus they were the ones who discovered the scene of horror.

Jim came upon it first, near an abandoned federal campsite. He galloped to find Charles, told him what he had found. Then, before he could lean out far enough, he threw up all over his own shotgun, saddle, and surprised horse.

Charles rode into the sunny pasture, smelling the slaughter before he saw it. He heard it, too—carrion birds flapping in the weeds, an orchestra of thousands of flies. A couple of minutes later, his mouth set, he turned Sport's head and trotted the starved-looking gray toward the general's temporary headquarters.

Hampton, ever the gentleman, broke that characteristic attitude as he rode bareheaded to the site. The breeze lifted his beard while he stared at the fantastic sculptures of fly-covered horses heaped upon one another.

"Have you counted?" he whispered.

"There are so many of them, so close together, it's hard, General. I figure eighty or ninety, minimum. Jim found as many or more over there near those trees. I searched for wounds—other than those made by the bullets that killed them, I mean—for as long as I could stomach it. I didn't find any. The Yanks must have decided a horse herd would slow down the retreat."

"I've shot injured horses but never foundering ones. To kill fine animals wantonly is even worse. It's a sin."

And no sin to chain a nigra? Aloud, his response was, "Yes, sir."

"Goddamn them," Hampton said.

But as Charles gazed at what men had done and considered what he had become, he felt the general was a mite late with his request. God had already done a pretty good job on most of the population.

Cold Harbor rattled the windowpanes of Richmond again. At night Orry and Madeline lay with their arms around each other, unable to sleep because of the guns.

They had heard them earlier, in May, when Butler pushed up the James to within seven miles of the city. They heard them again on the stifling June nights in the wake of Cold Harbor. Now the fighting raged at Petersburg. After four fruitless days of trying to overcome the fortifications on the old Dimmock Line around the town, the Army of the Potomac halted its attack and settled down to besiege Petersburg instead.

"Lee always said that once the siege starts, we're finished," Orry told Madeline. "If they want, the Federals can keep bringing men and supplies through the river base at City Point till the end of the century. We'll have to capitulate."

"A long time ago, Cooper said it was inevitable, didn't he?"

"Cooper was right," he murmured, and kissed her.

Everywhere, Orry saw signs of the tide flowing the wrong way. Sheridan's horse had ridden almost to the city's north edge, and Butler's infantry had nearly reached the southern one. Joe Johnston—Retreating Joe, people called him hatefully—was withdrawing toward Atlanta in response to Sherman's inexorable advance. Another Union general, Sigel, was loose in the valley.

Few blockade runners got into Wilmington anymore. The nation's money supply was rapidly becoming so much worthless paper. Cold Harbor had brought déjà vu—scenes of panic like those of the Peninsula campaign. But this time there was little heart or martial courage to sustain the resistance. The mighty generals had fallen: Orry's classmate Old Jack; Stuart, the singing cavalier. And the greatest of them all, Marse Bob, couldn't win.

One morning after Cold Harbor, Pickett appeared at the War Department. Dull-eyed and wasted, he resembled a walking casualty. He still wore his scented hair in shoulder-length ringlets, but a great many tiny coils of white showed now. Orry felt sorry for

George, who was gamely trying to maintain an air of youth and jauntiness when every jot of both had been beaten out of him.

In the hot, dusty silence, Orry shared his personal discontentments with his friend. In reply, Pickett said, "There will always be a place on my divisional staff should the time come when a field command suits you." A certain dark undertone in his voice hinted that Orry might think twice about such a decision. Was he remembering the charge at Gettysburg that had failed and aged him in a single day?

"I find myself wanting something like that lately, George. I haven't discussed it with Madeline, but I'll keep the offer in mind. I genuinely appreciate it."

Pickett didn't speak, merely lifted his hand and let it fall. He shambled away through slanting bars of sunshine.

There had been an official inquiry into the escape of a Union prisoner from Libby, abetted by a Confederate officer no one could identify except to say that he was exceptionally tall and heavily bearded, a description that fit several thousand men still in the army. The military threat to Richmond helped reduce the importance of the escape and, slowly, the inquiry. Orry only hoped Billy Hazard had reached and regained the Union lines without harm.

Mallory paid a call, stiffly informing him that Cooper had resigned after declaring his intention to leave Charleston and return to Mont Royal. Orry heard the alarming story of Cooper's attack on the Union prisoner.

"He's undergone a drastic change," Mallory said. "An abrupt and, in my opinion, reprehensible shift to favoring peace at any price."

Irked by the criticism, Orry said, "It was the shift to favoring war that was abrupt and reprehensible, Mr. Mallory. Maybe the brother I used to know has come back."

The secretary didn't like that and promptly left. Orry wrote a letter to Cooper in care of the plantation, posting it with little hope that it would be delivered. He was glad Cooper had gone home. Yet the possible significance of his brother's action depressed him for the same reason he was bothered by an incident the next morning.

"Who is that woman who just applied for a pass?" He asked a departmental clerk.

"Mrs. Manville. Came here from Baltimore in '61 to open a sporting house. She just closed it down."

"She's going back to Maryland?"

"Yes, somehow. She's determined, and we've no reason to stop her."

"Is she the first prostitute wanting a pass?"

"Oh, no, Colonel. There have been a dozen since Cold Harbor."

That night, on Marshall Street, he said to Madeline, "The so-called scarlet women are leaving. There's no more doubt. The curtain is starting down."

One personal problem continued to plague Orry: the mystery of the cabal, which had disappeared as if it never existed. Seddon had warned President Davis, Judah Benjamin, and others in the cabinet, but could do nothing more in the face of lack of evidence. Powell had vanished, or at least hadn't shown up at the farm. Twice, at Orry's insistence, Israel Quincy had returned to survey the place, finding nothing. From his own pocket, Orry paid a departmental clerk to go there at night to verify Merchant's report. Again, nothing.

Orry had seen the crated guns. And James Huntoon. And his sister. But the baffling events that followed his secret visit sometimes made him question his own sanity. Whenever he thought about the puzzle, the result was nothing but frustration. If Ashton had been part of a scheme to kill the President, she must be called to account. But how? The department lacked the manpower to watch her day and night, and he couldn't do it himself. Whenever he expressed the frustration to Madeline, she soothed him and urged him to put the problem away as insoluble. His answer was always the same: "Impossible."

The situation left him angry. Angry with himself, with his sister, with her husband. His feelings finally exploded at an unexpected time and place: an evening reception at the Treasury offices given for Secretary Memminger, who had let it be known that he planned to submit his resignation as soon as he finished a couple of important tasks. He expected to be gone by July.

Several South Carolinians in the capital worked with Treasury staff members to arrange the reception. The guest list included all those in Memminger's department and people from his home state. Huntoon qualified on both counts. He brought Ashton.

And Orry brought Madeline.

The secretary's humorless personality virtually assured a dreary party. So did its location. No spirits could be served in the Treasury Building, just a bowl of rust-colored punch of some indefinable citrus flavor. The wives of clerks and assistant secretaries had provided vegetable sandwiches, mostly carrots or pitiful slices of cucumber.

Munching a sandwich, Orry left Madeline chatting with some ladies and drifted toward his sister. She was, inevitably, the lone woman in a group of five men. It included Huntoon, cheeks puffed big as a toad's as he listened to a senior clerk declare, "Hang Governor Brown and his opinions. I still say recruiting colored troops is the only way we can continue to wage this war."

Huntoon snatched off his spectacles to show the ferocity of his conviction. "Then it's better to surrender."

"Ridiculous," another man said. "The Yankees aren't so stiff-necked. My brother-in-law tells me nigra troops are thick as ticks around Petersburg."

Ashton, fetchingly gowned yet noticeably haggard—she had lost weight, Orry saw immediately—tossed her head in reply to the last comment. "What else would you expect of a mongrel nation? I agree with James. Better to lose everything than compromise. As it is, we're close to seeing the Confederacy legislated —dictated—into disaster."

Dictated was an obvious reference to Davis. Where had she caught the sickness of fanaticism and from whom, Orry wondered as he lounged against a desk near the group. Was it from Huntoon? No; Powell, more likely.

She saw him and broke away while the others continued to argue. "Good evening, Orry. I saw you and your lovely wife come in. How are you?" Ashton's tone and expression said the inquiry was obligatory, nothing more.

"Reasonably well. You?"

"Oh, busy with a thousand things. Did you hear that Cooper resigned from the Navy Department?" He nodded. "They say Secretary Mallory was outraged. Really, Orry—we might as well have the Sphinx for a brother. I would understand it more than I understand Cooper."

"He isn't so hard to figure out." Orry's response was relaxed and cool. He fixed in mind that she was his quarry, not merely his blood relation. "Cooper's always been an idealist. High-minded—"

"Oh, yes, very high-minded—when it comes to disposing of the property of others. He shares that quality with some of our highest officials."

As if she hadn't spoken, Orry finished his sentence: "—fundamentally opposed to demagogues. And deceit."

Ashton was clever enough to realize he had introduced an element that had no bearing on what preceded it. Warned, she immediately raised a defense—a brittle smile—and looped her left arm through his while he finished the limp sandwich. She drew him toward a quieter part of the office, where she spoke to him like a pretty, puzzled child.

"You used the word deceit. Is that a reference I should understand?"

"Possibly. It could apply to your associate Mr. Powell, for instance."

She dropped his arm as if it were spoiled meat. "Cooper told you? I suppose it's logical that he would, the moralistic prig."

"This has nothing to do with Cooper. When I mentioned Powell, I wasn't referring to your little maritime enterprise, but to the group which formerly met at the farm downriver."

Surprise crumpled her composure for a second, before she masked it. Standing as erect as possible so his height would add to the intimidation, he bore in. "Surely you know the place I mean Wilton's Bluff—where the sharpshooting rifles are stored? The .45-caliber Whitworths?"

A laugh of desperation. "Really, Orry, I've never heard such raving. What on earth is it all about?"

"It's about your presence in that gang of conspirators. I went to the farm. I saw James there, and I saw you."

"Nonsense," she snarled through her smile, then darted a step beyond him. "There's Mr. Benjamin arriving."

Orry turned. The plump, suave little man was already surrounded by admirers. He seemed more interested in greeting Madeline. He strolled straight to her side.

Ashton's last words had been quite loud. Huntoon noticed, excused himself from the debate, and approached Orry from the left. Ashton spun back to her brother in the aisle, exclaiming, as if she felt obliged to reinforce her denial, "What you're saying is absurd. Ludicrous."

"Call it what you want," he said, shrugging. "I saw and heard enough to learn the purpose of the gatherings. God knows how you got involved in such business"—Huntoon stopped next to him, goggling with shock as the nature of the conversation sank in —"and I realize most of you have covered your tracks. But it's only temporary. We'll catch you."

Orry had underestimated his sister, never expecting a serious counterattack. She smiled charmingly.

"Not if we catch you first, my dear. I've been meaning to find an opportune moment to discuss the nigger in your own woodpile. Or is it boudoir?"

Orry's palm was ice; his face, too. He peered around the vaulted office. The party grew noticeably quieter, some of the guests realizing a quarrel was in progress, although the only person who could hear particulars was Huntoon. He looked as if he might die within the next few seconds.

Ashton tapped Orry's wrist with her fan. "Let's bargain, brother dear. You maintain a discreet silence and so will I."

A blood vessel appeared under the skin of Orry's temple. "Don't threaten me, Ashton. I want to know the whereabouts of Lamar Powell."

Sweet venom: "You can just go to hell."

Benjamin heard that, Madeline as well. She flashed a surprised, anxious look at her husband. The three women in her conversational circle noticed. Voices began to fade away in mid-sentence. Heads turned.

"Ashton," Orry warned, his voice raw with anger.

"I've been meaning to ask you, dear," she trilled. "How did you manage to conceal the truth so artfully all this time? You certainly hid it from me, you sly fox. But a certain Captain Bellingham showed me indisputable proof. A portrait, which I believe formerly hung in New Orleans—"

Bellingham? Portrait? The first meant nothing, but the second brought a sudden memory, hard as a blow. Madeline's father, Fabray, had told her before he died that a painting of her mother existed, though she had never seen it.

Sensing victory in the making, Ashton grew increasingly animated. Rising on tiptoe, she grasped Orry's forearm and whispered, "You see, I do know all about her. There's more than a touch of the tar brush on your lovely wife. You were a fool to accuse me." She dug her nails into his gray sleeve, then let go.

Whirling and raising her skirts, Ashton ran down the aisle to Madeline, Benjamin, and the circle of women, speaking gaily as a belle prattling of a beau, a hairstyle, an aunt's favorite recipe for conserve:

"Darling, do tell us the truth. When my brother married you, did he know your mother was a New Orleans quadroon?" Benjamin, who had been holding Madeline's hand in both of his, let go. "Employed in a house of ill repute?"

A woman on Madeline's right sidled away from her, frowning. A second woman began to scratch a facial mole nervously. Madeline threw Orry another look. Her dark eyes brimmed with tears. He had never seen her lose control that way. He wanted to run to her and, at the same time, murder his sister on the spot.

"Come, sweet," Ashton persisted. "Confide in us. Wasn't your mother a nigra prostitute?"

Orry seized Huntoon's shoulder. "Get her out of here before I do her bodily harm."

With all the strength of the right arm he had built up to compensate when he lost the left one, he flung Huntoon down the aisle. Huntoon's spectacles fell off. He nearly stepped on them. Ashton was spitting mad; she had been holding the stage and he had taken it away.

Spectacles replaced but not straight, Huntoon lurched up to her. "We're leaving."

"No. I am not ready to—"

"We are *leaving.*" His near-scream piled a new shock on all the others. He pushed Ashton. When she complained, he did it again. That told her Huntoon was hysterical, dangerously so. Refusing him, she could lose all she had gained. She gave Orry a swift, cold smile, flung her shoulder forward to release herself from Huntoon's hand, and walked out.

He hurried after her, frantically rubbing thumbs against the tips of his fingers. "Good evening—excuse us—good evening." And he was gone down the stairs.

Away toward Petersburg, artillery fire began. The office chandelier swayed. Memminger watched Orry with bleak, speculative eyes while Benjamin, once more suave and smiling, comforted Madeline.

"I have never witnessed such shameful behavior. You have my sympathy. I naturally assume that boorish young woman's accusation isn't true—"

Madeline was trembling. Orry strode up the aisle, disgusted by the transformation taking place in Benjamin. The secretary slid from his role of friend to that of government representative by adding two words:

"Is it?"

Orry had never loved or admired his wife more than when she said, "Mr. Secretary, does the law require that I answer your discourteous question?"

"The law? Of course not." Benjamin's eyes resembled those of a stalking cat. "And I certainly meant no discourtesy. Still, refusal may be construed by some as an admission—"

The woman with the mole huffed, "I for one would like to hear an answer. It would be disgraceful if a member of our own War Department was married to a colored woman."

"Damn you and damn your bigotry, too," Madeline exclaimed. The woman stepped away as if stung. Orry reached his wife, somehow managing to bridle all the chaotic, conflicting emotions —surprise, anxiety, wrath, simple confusion—the past few minutes had generated. Quiet and strong, he touched her.

"This way, darling. It's time we went home, too." Gently, he slipped his arm around her. He could tell she was about to collapse.

Somehow they got past the frowsy wives in last year's gowns, the overdressed clerks, Memminger, the assistant comptroller slack-jawed at the punch bowl. A hot, grit-laden wind blew through Capitol Square, whirling paper and other debris. The dust was so thick, the edges of buildings blurred.

"How did she find out?"

"God knows. She said something about a Captain Bellingham. I've never heard of him. The rank could mean army, navy, or it could be self-bestowed. I'll start a search of the records, though they've gotten so jumbled we don't know the names of half of those currently in the services. But you can be sure I'll try. I'd like to find the bastard."

"I didn't have to answer the secretary. He had no right to ask!"

"No, he didn't."

"Will it hurt your position in the department?"

"Of course not," he lied.

"Was it the same as an admission when I refused to answer?"

When he remained silent, she seized him and shook him, her

827

hairpins unfastening, her dark locks streaming and tossing as she cried into the wind, "Was it, Orry? The truth. The truth!"

The wind howled in the silence.

"Yes. I'm afraid it was."

107

Though her money was running out, Virgilia asked for one of the better rooms at Willard's. "We do have less expensive ones," the reception clerk said. "With smaller beds."

"No, thank you. I require a large bed."

To conserve her cash, she avoided the dining room that night. Hunger and nerves made it hard for her to fall asleep, but eventually she did. Next morning she ate no breakfast. About ten, she set out along the wrong side of the avenue, weaving through a throng of Negroes, peddlers, clerks, and the wounded soldiers who were a permanent part of the Washington scenery. Ahead, she observed that the scaffolding had finally been removed from the Capitol dome. The statue of Armed Freedom crowning the dome gleamed in the June sunshine.

The morning was warm, her clothing too heavy. She was awash with perspiration by the time she climbed all the steps, entered the Capitol, and slipped into the House gallery. After some searching, she located Sam Stout at his desk on the floor, lanky legs stretched out while he sorted documents.

Would he come, she wondered as she slipped out again. If he didn't, she was lost.

She left the sealed envelope at his office. On the face, she had inscribed his name and the words *Confidential/To Be Opened*

828

Only by Addressee. Nervous, she strolled on the shabby mall for half an hour. Wandering cows chewed what little grass grew there; pigs rooted in the many mudholes. Finally she returned to Willard's and threw herself on the bed, flinging a forearm over her eyes. But she couldn't doze, couldn't even relax.

At noon she bought two day-old rolls from a street vendor. One served as her midday meal in her room. At three, she undressed and bathed. After drying off, she chose a dark skirt and snug linen blouse with puffed sleeves, buttons down the front, and a stylish tie she could fasten in a bow. She fussed with her hair for three-quarters of an hour, then ate the second roll.

Last night she had bought a *Star,* which she now tried to read. She had trouble concentrating. The official front-page War Department dispatch, dealing with Petersburg and signed by Stanton, might have been printed in Chinese. She was repeatedly distracted by visions of the vindictive Mrs. Neal whispering to government officials.

Sounds in the next room drew her attention: a creaking bed, a woman's strident cry, repeated rhythmically. Virgilia's room seemed hot as a furnace. She dabbed her lip with a handkerchief, which she had tucked into the cuff of her blouse. The cuff was damp.

She picked a roll crumb off the bedspread, pulled and patted until it was perfectly smooth. She paced to the window to look at the wagon and horse traffic on the avenue but never saw it.

In the note, she had asked him to come at seven. At half past nine she was seated by a small table near the gas mantle, slowly rubbing her forehead with her left hand. Despair had eaten away her hope and her energy. She had been an idiot to suppose that—

"What?" she said, her head jerking up. Her heart started racing. She rose, hastily pushed her wrinkled blouse into her waistband, tightening the linen over her breast. She ran to the door, patting her hair.

"Yes?"

"Hurry and let me in. I don't want to be seen."

Weakened by the sound of the rich, deep voice, she fumbled with the door. She finally got it open.

He hadn't changed. His brows were still black hooks on his white face. His wavy hair, dressed carefully with fragrant oil, glistened as he made that unnecessary stooping movement that always accompanied his passage through a doorway; he liked to emphasize his height.

"I do apologize for my tardiness," he said as she closed the door.

"Please don't, Samuel. I can't tell you how much I appreciate this." She could barely keep from touching him.

His gaze lifted from her blouse to her face. "I wanted to see you again. And your note said it was an emergency."

"You didn't show that to—?"

"I read the envelope. No one saw it but me."

He sat down, crossing his thin legs. He smiled at her. She had forgotten how crooked his teeth were. Yet she found him beautiful. Power was never homely.

"I'm late because committee work is so heavy these days. But let me hear about this emergency. Is it something that happened at Aquia Creek?"

"Falmouth. I—" She took a breath; the linen stretched even tighter. He played with the fob of his pocket watch. "There's no way to tell you but straightforwardly. I've left the service. At the field hospital at Falmouth, they brought in a young Confederate officer, badly wounded." She plunged. "I let him die. Deliberately."

He drew out his watch. Opened and glanced at it. Shut it with a snap. Pocketed it again. Even when it was out of sight, she heard, or thought she heard, the maddening *tock-tock* of the movement; that and nothing else. The silence grew unendurable.

"I thought I was doing a good service! He'd only have gone back to kill more of our boys—" She faltered.

"Are you waiting for me to condemn you?" He shook his head. "I commend you, Virgilia. You did the right thing."

She broke then, rushed forward and dropped on her knees beside his chair. "But they're going to punish me." Unconsciously fondling his leg, she poured out the story of Mrs. Neal and her threats. He listened so placidly she was terrified. He wasn't interested.

Just the opposite was true. "Is that all you're worried about, some damned Copperhead widow? There'll be no investigation started by anyone like that. I'll speak to a couple of people I know." His hand crept into her hair. "Put the whole matter out of your mind."

"Oh, Sam, thank you." She rested her cheek on his thigh. "I'd

830

be so grateful if you could prevent trouble." Despite that moment of fright, the scene was playing out exactly as she had hoped. She had felt sad planning it, because circumstances forced her to accept less than what she wanted. But perhaps she could one day turn the compromise to greater advantage.

He cupped her chin and raised it, teasing with his smile but not his eyes. "I'm happy to help, Virgilia. But in politics, as I'm sure you know, the rule is *quid pro quo*. I'm still a family man. Much as I personally might like to alter that, it's impossible if I'm to stay in Congress. I want to stay—I plan to be Speaker of the House before I quit. So if you want my assistance, it must be on my terms, not yours."

What she had once hoped to bargain with, she was now trapped into surrendering. Well, why not? She was confident Sam Stout would rise and wield power and help trample out the weaknesses of Lincoln and his kind. Having part of such a man, like having half of the proverbial loaf, was better than having nothing.

He patted her hand. "Well? What's your answer?"

"It's yes, my darling," she said, rising and reaching to loosen the tie of her blouse.

108

The day after Stanley's philandering was discovered, he wrote a letter to Jeannie Canary saying that urgent business called him out of town. He enclosed a one-hundred-dollar bank draft to soften her grief and fled to Newport.

To his amazement, Isabel showed hardly any surprise when he alighted from an island hackney at the door of Fairlawn. She asked how he managed to get away. He said he had trumped up a story about one of the twins being injured. It might come true; out on the lawn they were attempting to brain each other with horseshoes. How he despised those obnoxious boys.

During the night, he wakened grumpily to see Isabel passing the open door of his bedroom on the way to hers. "Was that someone at the downstairs door?"

"Yes. They mistook this house for another." Her voice had a peculiar, strained quality. The lamp chimney rattled in her hand as she said good night and disappeared.

Early next morning, before breakfast, she handed him his coat. "Please take a walk with me on the beach, Stanley." Though the request was phrased politely, her tone left him no option. Soon they were alone on the seashore. The air was cool, the water calm, the tide running out. A few spotted sandpipers pecked about, hunting tidbits. Sunlight turned the Atlantic into a carpet of silver beads.

Isabel spoke suddenly and with unexpected ferocity. "I would like to discuss your new friend."

A witless smile. "Which friend?"

She bared her teeth. "Your doxy. The performer at the Varieties. The person who came to the house last night had the correct address." She pulled a crumpled flimsy from a pocket of her skirt. "And this telegraph message."

So quickly? "My God, who—who informed—?"

"It isn't important. I've known about the woman for weeks, and I'll give you no explanations there, either. I understand she's hardly talented enough to be called an actress, though I suppose she has other, less public, talents." Except for the moment when she brandished the flimsy, Isabel maintained perfect control, which somehow made her assault all the more threatening.

Stanley bit his knuckle and wandered in an agitated circle, like one of the shore birds. "Isabel, if you know, others must. How many?" She didn't answer. "I'm ruined."

"Nonsense. As usual, you misunderstand the way the world operates. You're dithering over nothing. No one cares if you philander, provided you're discreet and sufficiently well off." She took several steps away from him while, with vacant eyes, he watched the wind ripple sand ribbons along the beach. "It doesn't matter to others, and it doesn't matter to me. You know I loathe

832

that part of marriage anyway. Now I want you to pay particular attention to what I'm going to say next. *Stanley?*"

She raised a fist, then forced it down to her side before continuing. "You may do whatever you wish in private. But if you ever again show yourself in public with that trollop—an hour after you paraded at the Patent Office, it was all over town—I will enlist a regiment of lawyers to strip you of your last penny. I will do it even though every property law in the land favors husbands over wives. Do you understand?"

A fine spray from her mouth struck him. He scrubbed his left cheek with the back of his hand. She had made him angry.

"Yes. I see how it is. You don't care a damn for me. It's only my money that holds you. My money, my position—"

The morning wind became a chorus of eerie voices, whispering. Isabel seemed touched with sadness, although, after a shrug, her reply was firm. "Yes. The war's changed many things. That is all I have to say."

He was too upset to notice the unsteadiness of her step as she left. In a moment she paused to look back, and the sunlight struck her eyes, lending them the brightness of the reflecting sea.

"I did rather like you when we were courting, though."

She turned and walked away through the sand ribbons and scurrying shore birds.

Stanley wandered up and down the beach for a while. With a blink, he realized he was wearing his royal blue frock coat. He groped in the large inner pocket—ah! Shuddering with relief, he pulled out the flask and uncorked it. He swallowed half the remaining bourbon, then staggered to a large rock and sat down.

A fishing smack hove into view, coming around from Narragansett Bay. Scavenging gulls swooped close to the stern. Stanley felt very close to being ill, with a monumental sickness no doctor could name or cure.

A word Isabel had hurled surfaced in his churning thoughts. The changes had done it. There had been too many, too rapidly. Boss Cameron's patronage, unexpected financial opportunity, great personal profit achieved without his brother's help or interference.

Change bestrode the country like a fifth Horseman of the Apocalypse. A mob of free niggers had been loosed in the land to frighten God-fearing white people with their strange dark faces and, worse, to upset the economic order. Just last month a freedman had brazenly applied for a job as floor sweeper at Lashbrook's. Dick Pennyford hired him. After his first day, the Negro was waylaid at the gate and beaten by six white workers. That grieved and angered Pennyford, but he wrote Stanley that it also taught him a lesson. He wouldn't repeat the mistake.

Stanley knew who was responsible for such incidents and for the new assertiveness of Negroes. His friends. It was their program he was forced to pretend to admire if he wanted to preserve and expand his influence in Washington. That pulled him two ways, left his nerves shredded—

There were so many changes he could hardly count them all. He was independently wealthy. He was a confidant of politicians who would control the nation within a very few years. He was in love, or thought so. He was a known philanderer. And he was far along the road to becoming a drunkard and didn't give a damn.

He finished the bourbon and threw the flask at the tide line, a futile gesture of rage. No hiding from the truth any longer. He was incompetent to deal with so much change. On the other hand, his status was such that few, if any, of the problems created by the changes would affect him adversely, provided he conserved his capital and observed a certain hypocritical standard of behavior. That was the most staggering change of all. One so vast and bewildering that he leaned over, elbows on his knees, palms on his eyes, and cried.

Stanley would have been surprised to know that his wife, whom he considered glacial and a shrew, also wept that morning. Safely locked in her rooms at Fairlawn, Isabel cried much longer and harder than he did. Finally, when she had exhausted her tears, she settled down to think and to wait for the redness to leave her eyes, so she could again show herself to the servants.

Her husband was lost to her except in name. Well, so be it. She had used him as an instrument for accumulating new wealth, and with it she could now finance a rise to unprecedented social eminence in Washington, her home state, and the nation. By no stretch of the imagination did Stanley have the ability to become a national political figure. But he already had the money to buy and sell such men. Since she would always guide his choices, that made her the true possessor of the power.

Putting aside her brief and regrettable descent into sentimentality here and on the beach, Isabel contemplated all the days of glory still ahead. She was sure she would experience them if she could only keep Stanley in favor with the Republicans and sober. Success had ruined him, for reasons she could neither understand nor identify.

It didn't matter. Many a strong queen had ruled through a weak king.

109

At the end of the day on which Billy rejoined the Battalion of Engineers, he wrote:

June 16—Petersburg (4 mis. distant). Steamer journey to City Point uneventful but very hot. Saw the great pontoon bridge at Broadway Landing, 1 mi. above the piers where I disembarked. How I wish I'd come back in time to help create such a marvel. Maj. Duane, cordially greeting me upon my arrival at this encampment, said no longer pontoon bridge had ever been built by any army, anywhere. It stretches nearly half a mile, shore to shore, & where the tidal channel runs, a drawbridge section permits the passage of gunboats. Gen. Benham & the 15th & 50th N.Y. Engineers (Vols.) built the bridge in a record 8 hrs. The sight of it renewed my pride in my branch of service.

The battalion crossed the bridge not long before I saw it. Our encampment is at Bryant House, the temporary Second Div. hospital, but we are to move on. Received a warm welcome from many old comrades; all wanted to hear of my escape from Libby, which I said unknown Union sympathizers arranged. Even belatedly, C. might in some way be harmed by the truth; he is such a fine friend & risked himself so greatly for me, I will not permit it to happen through any act of mine.

Thoughts of C. sadden me. My brotherly affection remains unflagging; & I am now twice in debt to him for saving my life. But he is not the laughing fellow I first met in Carolina & came to know at W.P. The war has hurt him somehow. I felt it powerfully. If I were of a literary turn, I might seek metaphors. Some spell has changed the bear cub to a wolf.

Hungry; will continue later.***

Receiving assurances of my fitness for duty—leg is still painful but am walking with less difficulty—Maj. D. said that when we move nearer the enemy works, I shall be doing survey work, practically on top of the rebs. He then went on to enlighten me about the essence of the siege plan:

Through Petersb., a town of less than 18,000, pass all but one of the major Confed. RR's from the S & SW. Thus the P'burg junction is the south end of Richmond's last supply line. Take P.—which U.S.G. has already tried once—& Rich. withers and dies. It cannot happen too soon for me. I have already remarked in these pages about the distressing—***

Interruption. Rushed outside in response to a shattering roar. Was told it is "Dictator," also nicknamed "the Petersburg Express," a great 13" seacoast mortar of 17,000 lbs. From a specially reinforced flatcar, the mortar fires explosive shells into the city from a location on the P'burg-City Pt. RR line. I must note a new & startling change I observed in the Army of the Potomac, viz.—large numbers of negro soldiers, where none were seen before. I hear their bravery & intelligence praised lavishly; just yesterday, the CT (Col. Troops) Div. of E. W. Hinks mounted a successful attack on a sector of the enemy defense line.

My time in Libby did teach me how men long enslaved must feel. I yearned to murder Clyde Vesey and was unashamedly glad when C. shot him during the escape. I now accept emancipation as the only course this country can, in conscience, pursue.

Yet on some things, I hold back. I am thus far unable to look upon negroes in army uniform as the equal of white men in the same uniform. I am ashamed of that reservation—

weakness?—but it is there. The day closed out with an unpleasant incident bearing upon this general subject.

The battalion marched 18 mis. today, in merciless heat, with water in short supply. Despite the cheery reception given me, I could tell the men were cranky. Two negro soldiers, sgt's in some reg't of Gen. Ferrero's 4th (Col.) Div., chanced to pass through with pouches of official papers for City Pt. It was not unusual for them to ask for a drink of water in this hot weather. But they were not allowed it. Three of our worst-tempered led the sgt's to the casks, which two proceeded to block with their bodies while the third danced around dangling the dipper just out of reach of the two colored sgt's, all the while chanting the old tune "Zip Coon" in a derisive manner. The sgt's, who outranked our three, again politely asked for water, were refused, and ordered that it be given—which caused side arms to be drawn by the tormentors and (stupidly) a request to be made that the negroes perform what one of the trio termed "a shuffle step." He fired 2 rounds at the ground to stimulate obedience, at which point the unfortunate sgt's wisely ran away. What stings most is this. A doz. or more of the battalion stood around enjoying the discomfiture of the sgt's, and the few who did not laugh openly condoned the callous actions by saying & doing nothing to stop them. To my shame, I must here confess that I was among the silent.

I could plead tiredness or some other excuse, but in this jrnl. I try to hew to the truth. On this occasion the truth is painful. I looked at those 2 black men as something less than what I am —therefore of no consequence.

I have suffered stinging attacks of conscience ever since. I was wrong today—as thousands in this army who think and behave the same way are wrong. Libby is still working its change upon me. New thoughts and impulses stir—so unsettling, I cannot help wishing they would go away. But they won't, any more than the negro question will go away. Though countless millions might like to do so, we can no longer push the black man through some door & lock him out of sight, content to believe his color renders him unworthy of our concern & relieves us of responsibility to treat him as a fellow human being.

It is a shameful thing I did—rather, did not do this after-

noon. Writing it down helps somewhat. It is a first step, albeit not one which will induce a relaxation of my conscience.

I do have a conviction there will be other steps, however; where they will lead I cannot say, except in a most general way. I think I am starting down a road I have never walked, nor even seen, before.

110

Along the Ashley, those old enough to remember the Mexican War and how Orry Main came home from it thought history had repeated itself with Orry's older brother. Orry had lost an arm, Cooper a son. Hardly the same thing, yet the results were oddly similar. Each man was changed, withdrawn. The less charitable gossiped about severe mental disorder.

Cooper no longer insulted the occasional Mont Royal visitor by forcing him or her to listen to radical opinions. It was presumed that he still held such opinions, though one couldn't be positive. He limited his conversation with outsiders to pleasantries and generalities. And although Sherman's huge army was rumbling down on Atlanta, he refused to discuss the war.

But it remained very much on his mind. That was the case one hot June evening when he sequestered himself in the library after supper.

Cooper loved the library with its aroma of fine leather mingled with inevitable low-country mustiness. There in the corner stood the form holding Orry's old army uniform. Above the mantel spread the realistic mural of Roman ruins, which Cooper had delighted in studying when he sat on his father's knee as a boy.

Although the orange of sunset still painted the wall opposite the half-closed shutters, he lit a lamp and was soon in a chair, using a lap desk to write. The metal nib scratched so loudly he didn't hear the door open. Judith walked in with a newspaper.

"You must look at this *Mercury,* dear. It contains an overseas dispatch that came through Wilmington day before yesterday."

"Yes?" he said, glancing up from the memorial he was drafting to send to the state legislature. It argued for preventing further loss of life any means of a cease-fire and immediate peace negotiations.

His question said he wasn't greatly interested in interrupting the work to read overseas dispatches. So Judith said, "It concerns the *Alabama.* A week ago Sunday, she went down in the English Channel. A Union vessel named *Kearsarge* sank her."

Instantly, he asked, "What of the crew?"

"According to this, many survived. The captain of the *Kearsarge* picked up seventy, and a British yacht that sailed out of Cherbourg harbor to watch the engagement saved another thirty officers and men."

"Anything about Semmes?"

"He was one of those rescued by *Deerhound,* the yacht."

"Good. The men are more important than the ship."

He made the declaration with such feeling that Judith couldn't help rushing to his chair and throwing her arms around him. The *Mercury* fell on crumpled sheets of writing paper discarded on the floor.

"Cooper, I do love you so." She hugged his shoulders. "Everything's in disarray around us. Mont Royal has never looked shabbier. There isn't enough food. Everyone's frightened of those men living in the marshes. Yet I couldn't be more thankful to be here with you. Even with so much uncertainty, Marie-Louise is happier, and I am, too."

"So am I."

"I hope you didn't mind this interruption. I thought you'd want to know about the ship."

He reached up to pat her hand, staring away past the Roman mural to unguessable seascapes of the past. "She was a beautiful vessel. But she served the wrong masters."

Suddenly rising from his chair, he kissed her long and ardently.

The embrace left her gasping, with curls out of place. She was enraptured to see a teasing smile.

"Now, Judith, if you truly do love me, let me return to my labors. I must finish this memorial, even though our heroic legislators will tear it to shreds and dance on it. The ones who've never heard guns fired in anger will tear the most and dance the hardest."

"I'm sure you're right. But I'm proud of you for trying."

"There are no ordained results in this world, I've discovered. The trying is what counts most."

She left him scribbling in the last of the dusty orange daylight. She had worked hard all day—since returning, she had taken on many of Madeline's duties—and in the late afternoon had spent an hour with Clarissa. Though Cooper's mother was unfailingly pleasant, her memory loss made such visits taxing. By supper Judith was exhausted. Yet now, closing the library door, she felt light as a wisp of breeze-blown dandelion seed. Carefree. Sherman's host might be marching across the moon instead of into Georgia.

For the first time since Charleston, she was certain. Her beloved husband was a new, healed man.

It was Benjamin who wielded the velvet ax. After the fact, Orry realized he was the logical choice because of his suave, diplomatic style. The summons came a few days after the reception at Treasury.

"First, I must establish that I am speaking on behalf of the President," Benjamin said to Orry, who sat rigidly on the far side of the desk. "He hoped to see you in person, but the press of duties—" A supple gesture finished the thought.

"The President wanted to express deep gratitude for your concern for his welfare—specifically, your warning of a possible plot against his life. Not to mention the lives of a number of the rest of us," he added with his customary sleek smile.

Orry felt sweat trickling to his collar. In the summer heat, the voices of State Department functionaries sounded sleepy beyond the closed door. That was the moment the image of the velvet ax popped into his head.

"The plot was undoubtedly like many others we hear about—chiefly wishful thinking inspired by barroom bravery. Nevertheless, your loyalty and diligence have been noted and commended by Mr. Davis. He—Is something wrong?"

Orry's tight expression answered that. The government still didn't believe his story. Then and there, he decided to take a step he had only considered until now. Using personal funds, he would hire an agent to carry out a plan he had in mind. He would do it right away.

He forced himself to say, "No. Please go on."

"I have given you the sense of the President's message." Manicured hands folded, the secretary oozed sincerity. "Now I have one or two questions of a personal nature. Are you content with your post in the War Department?" When Orry hesitated, unsure of the purpose of the question, Benjamin prompted him with, "Please be frank. It will go no further."

"Well, then—the answer's no. I think we both know the likely outcome of this war." He expected no agreement with that and got none. "I hate to sit out the final months authorizing passes for prostitutes and monitoring the misdeeds of a martinet."

"Ah, yes, Winder. Are you saying you'd like field duty, then?"

"I've been considering it. Major General Pickett offered me a place on his division staff."

"Poor Pickett. Never have I seen a man so transformed by a single event." Benjamin sounded sincere but immediately slipped back into his official mode. After a slight clearing of his throat, he said, "There is one other subject which I regret I must discuss with you. Your sister's accusation against your charming wife."

The words slid into him like a stiletto of ice. He had been waiting for the matter to come up in some fashion. He had agonized over the best way to deal with it and reached a decision that pained him because it went against his conscience. But Madeline mattered more.

He sat very erect now, his posture a kind of challenge. "Yes? What about it?"

"To put it to you squarely—is it true?"

"No."

Benjamin showed no sign of being relieved, no reaction of any kind. He continued to study his visitor. Am I such a transparent liar? Orry thought.

"You realize I was compelled to ask the question on behalf of the administration," Benjamin said. "The cabinet—indeed, it's fair to say most of the Confederacy—is experiencing a terrible

841

schism on the matter of enlisting our Negroes in the army. The mere statement of the idea drives some of our most influential people to the point of incoherence. So you can see the enormous potential for disruption and embarrassment if it were found that the wife of a high War Department official—"

He could stand no more. "Damn it, Judah, what about Madeline's embarrassment? What about the disruption of her life?"

Unruffled, Benjamin met the attack. "I can appreciate her feelings, certainly. But the charge has implications far beyond the personal. If it were true, it could taint the credibility of the entire government. Mr. Davis, you see, refuses to consider the enlistment of nonwhite—"

"I know how Mr. Davis feels," Orry said, rising. His loud voice momentarily stopped the sleepy conversations outside. "With all due respect, the President's views aren't the issue. An accusation is the issue. My sister made her statement for one reason. She holds a long-standing grudge against me."

Like a prosecutor, Benjamin said, "Why?"

"I see no reason to go into that. It's a family matter."

"And you maintain that this so-called grudge is Mrs. Huntoon's motive for saying what she did? Her sole motive?"

"That's right. May I leave now?"

"Orry, calm yourself. It's better that you hear unhappy news from a friend. I am your friend; please believe that." The supple hand opened outward. "Do sit down again."

"I'll stand, thank you."

Benjamin sighed. There passed a few seconds of silence.

"To minimize potential embarrassment for all concerned, the President requests that Mrs. Main leave Richmond as soon as practicable."

Orry's hand closed on the back of the visitor's chair. His knuckles were the color of chalk. "To keep the administration untouched by the tar brush, is that it? You don't believe my answer—"

"I most certainly do. But I am an official of this government and it remains my duty to accede to the President's wishes, not question them."

"So you can keep your job and enjoy your sherry and your anchovy paste while the Confederacy collapses?"

The olive cheeks lost color. Benjamin's voice dropped, sounding all the more deadly, somehow, because of a small, chill smile.

"I shall pretend I heard no such remark from you. The President expects compliance with his request within a reasonable length of—"

"His order, isn't that what you mean?"

"It is an order courteously framed as a request."

"I thought so. Good day."

"My dear Orry, you must not hold me personally responsible for—"

Slam went the door, well before he finished.

Around noon, Orry's wild anger moderated. He was again able to concentrate, perform routine duties, and answer questions from his colleagues with some coherence. Seddon passed Orry's desk on his way out to dine, but the secretary refused to meet Orry's gaze. *He knows what Davis is demanding. He probably knew before Judah told me.* Instantly, Orry made up his mind to ask Pickett to make good on his offer.

Orry was not in doubt about Madeline's reaction. If they discussed the decision at all, he must be circumspect. Present it as something under consideration, not final. That would spare her worry. Anyway, the first priority wasn't the transfer, but proving to Judah, to Seddon—to the President himself—that the conspiracy was real.

He glanced at a corner desk occupied by a young civilian, Josea Pilbeam, who was handicapped with a club foot. Pilbeam, a bachelor, had undertaken several questionable assignments for the department in the past year. Orry walked over, greeted him affably, and made an appointment to speak with him that evening. Off the premises.

For the rest of the day, although he continued to scrawl his signature on passes and scan the daily quota of self-serving reports from General Winder, his mind wrestled with the presidential fiat and what he should do about it. His first reaction, born of insulted honor, was to dig in and refuse to comply.

On the other hand, suppose Madeline did remain in Richmond. She would be ostracized. And with Grant settling in at Petersburg to the frequent sound of rumbling guns, Richmond was no longer a safe place. Orry definitely didn't want his wife in the city when it surrendered. He believed all signs pointed to such a capitulation relatively soon.

So, much as he hated to admit it, he knew Madeline would be better off—safer—if she left.

Which raised another problem. Where could she go? The most logical answer struck him as far from the best or easiest. He thought carefully on it and by late afternoon had devised a plan that seemed to offer the least risk.

When the office closed, he and Josea Pilbeam left together. At a quiet table in the Spotswood bar, Orry went immediately to the point.

"I suspect my sister Ashton—Mrs. James Huntoon—of treasonous activity. I want to hire you to watch her house on Grace Street in the evenings and follow her if she leaves. I want to know where she goes and a description of whoever she sees. You can report to me each morning. I know it'll tax you to work all day, then stay up most of the night. But you're young and fit"—eyes on the foam on his beer, the clerk scraped his three-inch shoe sole back and forth under the table—"and for good work, carried out in the strictest confidence, I'll pay you from my own pocket. I'll pay you well. Ten dollars a night."

Pilbeam drank some beer. "Thanks for the offer, Colonel. But I have to say no."

"Good Lord, why? You've never objected to a little spying before."

"Oh, it isn't the nature of the work."

"What, then?"

"I have no choice about taking my regular wages in Confederate dollars, but we both know how much those are worth—about as much as the government line saying we can still win the war. I won't do a private job for payment in our currency."

Relieved, Orry said, "I'll get U.S. dollars, somehow—provided you start the surveillance tomorrow night."

"Done," Pilbeam said, shaking his hand.

For supper, Madeline divided a small shad between them, garnishing each plate with two tiny boiled turnips. Nothing else could be bought that day, she said.

He told her he had continued to search departmental records for any mention of an officer named Bellingham. Thus far he had come up with nothing. "It's frustrating as hell. I'd give anything to find out who he is and get my hands on him."

844

After they finished eating, she suggested they read some poetry aloud. Orry shook his head. "We must have a talk."

"My, how portentous that sounds. On what subject?"

"The need for you to leave Richmond while it's still possible."

A fleeting look of hurt crossed her face. "There have been repercussions from the party."

Deeper into the net of lies—for her sake. "No, nothing beyond some snide jokes I've overheard. The two reasons you must leave are mine. First, the city's going to fall. If not this summer, then in the autumn or next winter. It's inevitable, and I don't want you here when it happens. I left Mexico before our army marched into the capital, but later George described some of the atrocities. No matter how good the intentions of the commanders or how stern their warnings to their troops, matters always get out of hand for a while. Homes are looted. Men are killed. As for women—well, you understand. I don't want you to face any of that."

Sitting motionless, she said, "And the second reason?"

"The one I've mentioned before. I'm sick of the department. I'm considering asking for a transfer to George Pickett's staff."

"Oh, Orry—no."

Swift retreat: "Here, not so serious. The word is *considering*. I've done nothing about it."

"Why risk your life for a lost cause?"

"The cause has nothing to do with it. Pickett's a friend, I've had a bellyful of desk work, and officers are desperately needed in the field. Nothing to fret over—it's still in the speculative stage."

"Let's hope it stays there. Even if it does, what you're really doing is banishing me. Well, thank you very much, but I'm not the coward you think I am."

"Now wait, I never implied—"

"You most certainly did. Well, I intend to stay."

"I insist that you go."

"You'll insist on nothing!" She rose abruptly. "Now if you'll excuse me, I must darn your stockings again. There are none to be had in the stores." She stormed out.

Whenever he tried to restart the discussion that evening, she refused to listen. They went to bed barely speaking. But around three, she curled against his back, gently shaking him awake.

"Darling? I feel wretched. I behaved like a harpy. Forgive me? I was mad at myself, not you. I know I've brought shame down on you—"

Sleepy but suddenly lighthearted, he rolled over and touched her cheek. "Never. Not ever while I live. I love you for what you are—everything you are. I just want you safe."

"I feel the same about you. I hate the idea of your going off with George Pickett. The siege lines are dangerous."

"I told you, I've done no more than think about it. Other matters come first."

A low, short sigh. "You want me to go home to Mont Royal, then?"

"That would be ideal, but I think it's impractical as well as too risky. South of here you'd encounter the whole Union Army, stretched from City Point clear to the Shenandoah Valley. The roads and rail lines are constant targets. You might slip through, but I believe I have a safer alternative. It may not sound so at first, but I've thought about it a lot, and I've concluded that it's feasible. I want you to go the other way. To Lehigh Station."

The effect was the same as if he had said Constantinople or Zanzibar. "Orry, our home is South Carolina."

"Now wait. Brett's at Belvedere. She'd be happy to have your company, and I don't believe you'd be there very long. Not even a year, if I read the signs correctly."

"I'd have to cross enemy lines—"

"The country north of Richmond is a no-man's-land. When Grant chased Lee to Petersburg, he took most of his army with him. Our reports show no significant troop concentrations around Fredericksburg, for example. An occasional cavalry or infantry regiment passes through, but that seems to be the extent of it. Furthermore, getting into Washington won't be hard. You simply say you're a Union sympathizer, and they'll think you're a woman of ill repute who decided—"

"What kind of woman?" She sat up, managing to convey mock wrath in the midst of a giggle.

"Now, now—you can stand it. The most you'll suffer are some insults and a brief detention. An hour or two. That bosom of which I'm so fond may be thumped to see if it pings."

"*Pings?* What are you talking about? You've lost your mind."

"No. Women who are, ah, less amply endowed than you resort to metal breast forms."

"Since when have you become a student of metal breast forms?"

"Since those who can't fill them started smuggling medicines and paper money in the, ah, empty spaces. No ping—no search."

He felt like an actor, playing a light role solely because the play demanded it. But he refused to have her know anything about the President's edict, refused to have the woman he loved shamed for something over which she had no control. Tar brush or no, she was worthier, finer, more valuable than a thousand Ashtons—or Davises.

"Best of all," he continued, "unless Augusta Barclay's abandoned her farm, you needn't make the trip to Washington alone. I'll get one of Augusta's freedmen to go with you as far as the Union lines. She promised a favor if we ever needed one, remember."

"When are you going to see her?"

"This weekend."

"A Confederate colonel can't go riding blithely to Fredericksburg. What if you should encounter one of those Yankee units?"

"Believe me, I don't intend to let anyone know I'm a colonel. Stop worrying."

"Easy for you to say—"

He knew an old, conventional, but extremely pleasant way to stop such conversations and allay anxieties. He began to kiss her. Then they made love and fell asleep.

He replaced his uniform with his black broadcloth suit. He donned a wide-brimmed dark hat bought secondhand and tucked Madeline's Bible in one pocket. In another he placed a pass he had written for himself; that is, for the Reverend O. O. Manchester.

He set off on a hired nag at least twenty years old. Badly swollen hock joints indicated a case of bog or bone spavin; Orry hoped the animal could make it the forty-odd miles to Fredericksburg.

He had read reports of the devastation that had struck the town, but reality proved far worse. He saw burned wagons and a decomposing body in ruined fields on the outskirts. He glimpsed a small band of men at a smoky fire back in some woods. Deserters, probably. Fredericksburg itself had an abandoned air; half the houses were empty, and many business establishments boarded up. Some homes and commercial buildings had been blown down by artillery fire. Foundations remained, but the rest lay strewn along the cratered streets, together with shot-away tree limbs, pieces of glass and fragments of furniture.

With his Bible in plain view under his arm, Orry asked an elderly man for directions to Barclay's Farm. He reached it an hour later, appalled by what he found. Charles had described the place in some detail, and its most prominent features, the barn and the two red oaks, were gone, the former razed, the latter cut down. Only stumps remained in the dooryard.

Boz and Washington recognized and hailed him as he climbed down from his quaking mount. The black men were attempting to plow a trampled field. Washington guided the plow; Boz pulled it in place of a horse. That spoke of how completely the farm had been stripped.

He found Gus in the kitchen, listlessly churning butter. Her plain dress, its color gone in repeated launderings, fit her tightly at the waist; she was plumper than he remembered. Haggard, too, especially around her blue eyes.

"More than half the townspeople ran away when the Yankees came," she said after she got over the surprise of his arrival. "A good many who stayed took in enemy wounded. I did. I had one captain here, a polite fellow from Maine who was covered with bandages but acted very lively. He refused to let me help change the dressings. I had Boz watch him. He wasn't hurt. The bandages were borrowed from someone else. I have no idea how he got them, but he must have put them on and run away to avoid fighting. I turned him out and replaced him with a pair of real patients. New York boys. Irish—sweet and gentle and never in battle before. One left after eight days. The other died in my bed." She resumed the slow, tired churning.

"I don't know why we hang on here," she said, sighing. "Stubbornness, I guess. And if I left, Charles wouldn't know where to find me. Have you—have you seen him?" That catch in her voice said much about her emotions.

"Once, before the spring campaign heated up." Seated at the sun-drenched table with a cup of tasteless imitation coffee, he described Billy's escape from Libby.

"Remarkable," she said when he finished. "But Charles would do that. The old Charles." The odd statement puzzled Orry. "I imagine he hasn't had time to ride up this way. Have you had any further word from him since the escape?"

"None. But I'm sure he's fine. I watch the casualty rolls care-

848

fully. I haven't seen his name." There was no reason to add that many of the dead and lost were never identified.

His encouragement lightened her mood a little. "I can't tell you how startled I was to see you on the back porch—Reverend Manchester. You do fit the role."

"Ah, but the reverend is protected against worldly emergencies —and Yankees." He showed her the knife concealed in his boot. "I also have a used but serviceable navy Colt in my saddlebag. Let me tell you why I'm here, Augusta. I need your help—that is, I need the help of one of your men, to escort Madeline to Washington."

Weary astonishment: "Washington? Have you forgotten which side we're on?"

"No, but I must get her out of Richmond, and with Grant entrenching all around Petersburg, it will be much easier and safer to send her to my friend George's home in Pennsylvania, where my sister is—the one married to Billy Hazard—than back to South Carolina."

He explained more of his plan. She readily agreed to help, even insisting that Boz accompany him back to Richmond to assist Madeline with her packing. After Orry ate some stale bread and homemade cheese—the invaders had graciously allowed Gus to keep one milk cow—he and the freedman prepared to leave. "You ride first while I walk," Orry said to Boz. "That nag can't carry two of us."

It was hot. He fanned himself with his hat, then shook Gus's hand. "I'll bring Madeline back as soon as I can prepare the documents she'll need for safe conduct. It may take as long as two weeks."

It took less than one because of continuing pressure from the highest level. Although the department was inundated with work —the news from Georgia was bad; Sherman had advanced to a position near Marietta and at any hour might assault Joe Johnston's Kennesaw Mountain entrenchments—Benjamin wanted Orry to set everything else aside and concentrate on his wife's departure. Seddon told Orry he personally sanctioned it.

The Mains and Boz set out for Barclay's Farm at the end of June, while the war news continued to worsen. Davis, a burned-out man, informed the papers that he had sent Retreating Joe Johnston all the reinforcements that could be spared. Now, whatever happened at the doorstep of Atlanta was the general's responsibility, the general's fault. At the same time, Davis tried to persuade journalists and the public that because Grant had neither crushed Lee nor captured Richmond, the Virginia situation was improving.

No one believed him.

The Reverend Manchester once again traveled to Fredericksburg with Scripture, knife, and .36-caliber navy Colt. He and his companions rode in an old buggy whose cost Orry didn't care to think about. For replacing a broken axle, the wheelwright had charged five times the prewar price.

On a Wednesday, the second-to-last day of the month, Orry and Madeline said good-bye on the front porch of the farmhouse. The weather was appropriate to the occasion. To the northwest, onyx clouds tumbled and spun, speeding over the gutted land through a strange pearly sky. The wind picked up. The first spatters struck the dust of the dooryard. Orry could hardly think of all he must say in a short time.

"—once you're in Washington, use some of the greenbacks to telegraph Brett."

"Yes, we've gone over that, darling. Several times. Boz will see me safely to one of the Potomac bridges—I'll be fine." She touched his face. "Somehow you must send me news about yourself. I'll worry constantly. At least you haven't said anything more about that mad idea of field duty."

"Because I've done nothing about it. There never seems to be time." There was deliberate deceit in the answer, the words chosen and arranged to allay her fear. He hoped she didn't see through the trick. He added quickly, "I'll send a letter by courier when I can."

She came closer, strands of wind-loosened hair blowing around her strangely sad little traveling hat—a sort of cap with a single black-dyed aigrette, which the wind bent and nearly broke. Tears filled her eyes.

"Do you know how much I'll miss you? How much I love you? I know why you're sending me away."

"Because it's unwise for you to stay in—"

"Thousands of other women are staying in Richmond," she broke in. "That isn't the reason—though I love you more than ever for pretending it is. You've been protecting me." Dust blew around them; the landscape whited out in the glitter of lightning. "Your superiors believe Ashton's accusation. Don't bother deny

850

ing it; I know it's true. A War Department official married to a Negress—that's intolerable. So I must be gotten rid of. Except for missing you so terribly, I'm not especially sad to leave. I've never been happy as a lady-in-waiting at a court of bigots."

She gave him a quick, intense kiss. "But I do love you for trying to spare me the truth."

The clouds burst, the rain roared down. Tall and bleak as some Jeremiah, he glowered at her. "Who told you?"

"Mr. Benjamin, when I chanced to meet him on Main Street day before yesterday."

"That slimy, dishonorable—"

"He didn't say a word, Orry."

"Then how—?"

"He cut me dead. Saw me coming and crossed the street to avoid me. Suddenly I understood everything."

He flung his arm around her, wracked by wrath and sorrow. "God, how I hate this damn war and what it's done to us."

"Don't let it do anything worse. To give your life now would be squandering it for nothing."

"I'll be careful. You, too—promise me?"

"Of course." Shining confidence returned to her face as they huddled on the porch, which had grown dark. "I know we'll come through this and be back together at Mont Royal sooner than either of us expects."

"So do I." He eyed the rain beating on the great raw stumps of the vanished trees. "I must go."

"I'll wait until it lets up a little."

"Yes, good idea—" He was wasting time on commonplaces. He swept his arm around her again and kissed her for nearly half a minute, with passion. "I love you, my Annabel Lee."

"I love you, Orry. We'll come through."

"I am sure of it," he said, smiling for the first time.

She stayed on the porch until the falling rain hid the buggy on the road.

On the return trip, Orry started sneezing. By the time he reached the city at noon the next day, his head felt light. Madeline's absence created a gloom in the silent rooms on Marshall Street. As he changed into his uniform to return to the department, he vowed to spend as little time as possible in the flat. He would immerse himself in work till a transfer came through. He could even sleep on one of the office couches if he chose.

It might be wise to do that for the first night or two. He missed Madeline fiercely, and there were too many memories here. Seddon wouldn't object if he stayed in the building. After all, he had proved himself a model bureaucrat by disposing of the troublesome Negress.

God, the bitterness. He couldn't help it. He no longer had the slightest wish to fight or die for any of the bankrupt principles of Mr. Jefferson Davis. He could hardly believe that just three years earlier he had been willing. Joining Pickett was not a matter of patriotism, but of survival. He was answering the drum, as he had when he went to West Point and soldiered in Mexico, because of the drumbeat, not the rhetoric of the drummer. I'd damn near fight for the Yankees to get out of this town, he thought as he left the flat.

He had been at work less than ten minutes when a sound made him look up. Foot scraping, Josea Pilbeam struggled to Orry's desk and whispered, "I must see you at once. It's urgent."

On a staircase heavy with darkness and humidity in the aftermath of the storm, Pilbeam said, "Last night the lady and her spouse left the city for nearly four hours."

"Where did they go?"

"To that location you described. They conferred with a heavyset man I've never seen before."

They were using the farm again. Patience had been repaid. He would show Seddon, Benjamin, the lot of them that he was no lunatic. Excited, he said, "Did you hear the man's name?"

Pilbeam shook his head. "No one used it while I was listening."

"Where exactly did they meet?"

"In the building right at the edge of the bluff. After about a quarter of an hour, they were joined by someone I did recognize. He's been in our office many times."

Orry put a handkerchief to his dripping nose, suppressed a sneeze. "Who was it?"

The marble walls and steps seemed to rumble and quake when Pilbeam said, "Winder's plug-ugly. Israel Quincy."

852

111

_____

So infernally simple, Orry thought as he slipped across the field, following the same route he had taken the first time. Ever since his conversation with Pilbeam, he had marveled at the beauty of the obvious—effective because it was almost always overlooked. The investigator from Winder's office had found no evidence of a plot because he was part of it.

The evening was moonless and still. Orry's broadcloth felt heavy with dampness; his shirt was already soaked through. Halfway to the implement building, he paused to survey the field by the fitful pulses of red light accompanying the federal bombardment to the south.

The earth around him had lately been subjected to digging and trampling. He cast his mind back. His first night here, he remembered, the field was weedy. Then he had ridden out a second time and discovered—

What? He cudgeled his tired mind while sniffing through his dripping nose. He choked off an unexpected sneeze with his hand clapped over his face. He distinctly remembered plowed soil on his second visit. Curious that someone would work the field of an abandoned—

"Stupid. *Stupid!*" The obvious again, and he had missed it. He knew how the Whitworth rifles and ammunition had disappeared. They had been hidden right under everyone's nose.

"Feet," he corrected in a whisper. The trick came straight from Edgar Poe's famous detective tale of the stolen letter. As a Poe fancier, he was doubly humiliated. *And I'll wager Mr. Quincy took*

853

charge of inspecting this part of the farm. Mr. Quincy strolled over the newly plowed field and noticed nothing unusual.

Had Powell himself hidden somewhere on the property all the time? With Quincy involved, it was certainly possible. Orry rubbed his nose with his damp handkerchief while red light ran around the southern horizon and the artillery storm muttered again. He put the handkerchief away, reached across beneath his coat, and drew the navy Colt from the bulky holster tied to his left leg. He pulled the hammer back to half-cock and resumed his cautious advance.

He approached the same light crack through which he had spied before. When close to the building, he discerned a buggy and two saddle horses near the main house. He pressed his cheek to the wood and bit down on his lower lip in a flash of rage. There, perched on one of the dirt-covered Whitworth crates resurrected from the field, James Huntoon.

Gaps showed between the buttons of Huntoon's bulging waistcoat. He had removed his outer coat, rolled up his sleeves, and was holding a large piece of paper by the edges. Some sort of plan or diagram. He tilted it forward, resting it on his paunch so others could see it.

"May I have your attention?" someone else said. "This is the device Mr. Powell described before he was called away for a few days to attend to other details of our campaign." Orry frowned; the speaker was out of his line of sight, but the voice was maddeningly familiar.

He knelt to change position and his angle of vision. Beside Huntoon on the rifle case he now saw a bright lantern. To the right of that, lounging against a beam and picking his teeth with a straw, the benign Mr. Quincy. Orry seethed.

He heard his sister's voice next. "Are you sure it will work, Captain Bellingham?"

Bellingham? Had he found the man who had shown her the painting—?

"My dear Mrs. Huntoon, infernal devices invented by General Rains at the Torpedo Bureau have a notable success record."

A corpulent man waddled into view. Only his back was visible, but something about the shape of his head tantalized Orry as much as his voice did. The man extended his right hand; Orry saw a large lump of coal in his palm. If this was indeed the Bellingham responsible for Madeline's humiliation and flight, Orry was tempted to shoot him in the back.

Lifting his hand slightly to call attention to the coal, the man said, "A device similar to this was placed in the coal bunker of the captured blockade-runner *Greyhound* when she lay at anchor farther down the James. A stoker shoveled it into the boiler with his coal scoop, and if Ben Butler and Admiral Porter had been standing in slightly different locations when the device exploded, there would be two more Yankees in hell."

Orry identified the voice. That is, he put a name to it—the right name—though he could hardly believe it. To the bubbling stew of his anger, the recognition added memories going all the way back to his first summer at the Academy; memories involving George and, later, Charles in Texas, when Charles wrote to express surprise and dismay at the unexplained vendetta of a senior officer of the Second Cavalry.

Israel Quincy made a sucking sound. "Sure is a fooler, Captain. Nobody could tell it from real coal."

"Not unless they handled it." He gave the device to Quincy, whose hands sagged beneath the weight. "Examine the casting. The shape, the texture, the perfect pigmentation of the iron—genius."

That was the moment Orry saw the profile of the former Union officer who had somehow become involved in a Confederate conspiracy. To be positive, he scrutinized the three chins, the receding hair, the one small, dark eye visible to him. There was no doubt. He was looking at Elkanah Bent—alias Bellingham.

If Orry hadn't seen Bent, made the identification, the rest might not have happened as it did; he might have crept away and ridden back to Richmond to turn out a full company of the provost's men, before the Whitworths could be buried again. But the lifelong vendetta of Elkanah Bent of Ohio—a vendetta that had continued down to the present, with the revelation to Ashton—twisted some key in Orry's head. A door that should have remained locked burst open.

There were just three men inside, but in his state of mind it wouldn't have mattered had there been thirty. He stood and strode around the corner of the building. He had the navy Colt on full cock when he booted the door inward.

"Everyone stand still."

Ashton clapped hands over her mouth. Huntoon dropped the

diagram and slid sideways along the edge of the crate. As for Bent —no mistake as to who it was, none—his face was full of bewilderment that swiftly melted into terrified recognition.

"Orry Main—?"

"I'll be a son of a bitch," said the calmly professional Quincy, shooting his right hand beneath his parson's coat. Orry twisted toward him and fired. The bullet flung Quincy backward against the beam. Orry heard his head smack as he dragged out his pepperbox, trigger finger jerking and jerking even as he slid down to land on his rump. The barrels discharged one after another; the last shot blew off the toe of Quincy's left boot as he toppled sideways.

Bent was juggling the coal bomb, shaking like a child caught with a stolen cookie. Orry saw Ashton warn her husband with her eyes. *Attack him, or he'll get us all.* Cringing, Huntoon shook his head. The image was reflected in one of the dirty windows overlooking the river.

"Captain Bellingham, is it?" Orry said in a raw voice. "I sure as hell don't know how you got here, but I know where you're bound, you and your friends. You're going to prison for plotting the murder of the President."

Bent was recovering; his eyes had a sly look. Like Orry, he didn't understand how the astonishing confrontation had come about. But he understood the potential consequences.

Huntoon pressed a fist into his groin and squealed. "Dear God —he knows. He knows everything!"

"So does Secretary Seddon," Orry said, "and the President himself. They've been anxious to catch the culprits with the evidence. You're done for, James. You, too, my dear, treacherous slut of a sist—"

Huntoon snatched the lantern by its bail and threw it.

Orry ducked. The lantern struck the siding behind him, shattering. Droplets of oil splattered the wall and dirt floor. Strewn pieces of straw began to smoke.

Orry had a swift impression of Huntoon passing him, Ashton dragging him by the hand like a child. He could give them no attention because Bent was rushing at him, raising the black iron casting with both hands. *My God, he'll blow us up—*

Bent struck for the top of Orry's head. Orry dodged; the casting raked his left temple. The only explosion was one of pain.

Bent smashed the casting against the outermost point of Orry's left shoulder, the stump of his amputated arm. Orry dropped to one knee. Silent tears of pain ran down his cheeks. There was no mistaking Bent's intention. The trapped animal would kill to escape.

"Bastard," Bent gasped, hitting at Orry's left ear with the casting and nearly knocking him over. Blood ran from a gash in Orry's hair. He had trouble focusing his eyes. The surroundings brightened; he felt heat behind him. The building was afire.

"Arrogant—South Carolina bastard—" Again Bent raised the casting, turning it until he had a sharp point aimed at the top of Orry's skull like some druid's knife. "Waited *years* for this—"

The casting blurred down. Orry aimed the Colt and fired. The ball hit Bent's left wrist, scattering little lumps of flesh and chips of bone. The wound made Bent cry out, jerk the casting to one side, and drop it. The casting grazed the stump of Orry's arm and landed near the fire spreading in the littered straw.

Hatred was powering both men. In all his life, Orry had never felt it so intensely. Scenes clicked in and out of his head like cards in a stereopticon. He saw himself walking an extra tour of guard duty, in a blizzard, thanks to Bent. He saw himself lying in the West Point surgery near death from exposure, courtesy of Bent. He saw the letter from Charles about the officer persecuting him; his sister's face as she spoke of the portrait shown her by a Captain Bellingham—

He came up from his knee, reversing the Colt and leaving it uncocked. He clubbed Bent's head with the base of the butt. Bent shrieked, staggered back.

Orry hit again. Bent's nose squirted blood. He flung his right forearm over his face to protect it, then his left. Bits of flesh were caught in bloody, torn threads of his powder-burned sleeve. Curses poured unconsciously from Orry as he hit again. Bent staggered to the right. Orry hit again. Bent wobbled—

That's enough; he's through.

Above the crackle of flames, he heard traces jingling, wheels creaking, rapid hoofbeats. Huntoon and Ashton in flight. It didn't matter. Only this doughy, cringing coward mattered—and Orry's boundless rage, the reaction to years of Bent's lunatic enmity and his discovery here among people who had driven Madeline away.

Bent continued to wobble. *Take him prisoner; he can't fight anymore.* The faint inner voice inspired no response. Crazed as his adversary, Orry hit again.

857

"Ah-ha." Bent's hurt cry bore a bizarre resemblance to laughter. "Jesus, Main—Jesus Christ, have mercy—"

"When did you?" Orry screamed, driving his right knee into Bent's genitals. Bent went backward, one staggering step, a second, a third—

Too late, Orry jumped to grab him. Bent's back struck one of the windows. For an instant, hundreds of tiny fires burned in the flying fragments. Bent fell through the sawtoothed opening, one side of his face ripped by glass still in the frame. He screamed as he plummeted. Then Orry heard the pulpy thump of a body hitting something.

Hair in his eyes, Orry stuck his head out the window. Bent had grazed an outcrop, spun away, and was still falling. He smashed into another and then bounced like a ball of India rubber, flying out and down and landing in the water with a mighty splash. A bubbling commotion disturbed the river for a moment. Then—nothing.

Orry strained for some sight of Bent's body, but it was gone, already swept underwater and downstream, toward the red lights pulsing on the wooded horizon.

A half-minute passed. Orry grew conscious of the heat and thickening smoke. A section of siding dissolved into fiery debris. Above him, flames ran along dry rafters. Burning straw was within inches of the coal bomb. Orry leaped and flung the bomb through the open doorway.

He wanted to pry open a crate and take two or three Whitworths for evidence. He barely had time to holster the Colt and snatch the diagram Huntoon had been holding—one corner was already smoking—and slip it into his pocket. Hunched over and struggling to breathe, he dragged Israel Quincy's body toward the door.

One of the beams eaten by the flame disappeared. The rafter above him sagged, broke, and rained sparks and flaming splinters on him. He smelled his hair burning as he gasped and strained, finally pulling Quincy's corpse into the open.

A box of cartridges exploded as he snatched the coal bomb and limped to a safe spot away from the building, whose glare washed out the red lights over Petersburg. All the ammunition blew, the reports rolling away through the night like the volleying of regiments in battle.

Bent. Elkanah Bent. By what twisted route had he come from the United States Army to this place? Transformed himself to Captain Bellingham? Embroiled himself in the plot?

He had two pieces of evidence of that plot. He put the bomb on the ground, unrolled the plan, and examined it in the light from the burning building. At first, because he was so shaken, the arrangements of smaller rectangles within larger ones made no sense. Then he realized he was looking at diagrams representing the different floors of the Treasury Building.

He saw inked crosses, each labeled. Those in the cellar said COAL BOMBS. In a suite of second-floor offices identified by the letters J. D., the label was INCIND. DEVICE. The enormity of it left him weak with awe.

He waited long enough to be sure the collapsing implement building wouldn't threaten the other structures. The wind was blowing flame and smoke out above the James, where he envisioned Elkanah Bent's body drifting seaward in the current. He saw an imaginary picture of cockeyed General Butler on a pier at City Point, struck dumb by the sight of a corpse floating by.

Once Orry started to recover from the shock of Bent's death, a different kind of shock set in. It involved Orry's own behavior. He clearly recalled knowing Bent was whipped, able to be taken prisoner without further struggle. Old grudges had driven Orry's arm then, kept him hitting his tormentor unnecessarily, until Bent fell through the window. He had gone far beyond the demands of self-preservation. He had lost control. As he stood in the glare of the fire, he wondered how a human being could feel so glad someone was dead and so guilty and ashamed at the same time.

The exploding ammunition reminded him that people would be drawn by the noise and flames. He didn't want to waste time on explanations to farmers or military patrols in the area. He forced himself from his shock-induced lethargy, starting toward the farmhouse and discovering that in the fight he had twisted his left ankle. It hurt and made him limp.

Nevertheless, he conducted a rapid search of the house. In the attic he found confirmation of something that had come to mind earlier. The attic was arranged with a few furniture pieces and a square of old carpet—a living area. A large crate standing on end served as an open-sided press for three suits. A few books lay on a smaller crate beside a cot: *The Prince, The Prose Romances of Edgar A. Poe,* and his *Tales* as well. Beneath these, Orry found gold-stamped, leather-bound copies of the proceedings of the Georgia and South Carolina secession conventions.

Israel Quincy, then, had also searched the house, intentionally failing to discover Powell or his hideaway. Orry didn't know whether Powell would be caught. Perhaps not. But the conspiracy had been aborted a second time and, more important, Orry could now show proofs of its existence.

He limped down the attic stairs and out the back door. All that remained of the implement building were mounds of bright embers. With no more ammunition exploding, he heard voices and horses from the direction of the road.

As fast as he could, he retrieved his evidence and hobbled back across the plowed field to his horse, tethered in the orchard. Mounting, he saw a farmer's wagon pulled up beside the burned building. Three men sat in the wagon, clear as black-paper stencils against the light. Orry reined his horse's head around and took the road to Richmond.

Wearing a striped nightshirt, a sleepy Seddon stared at the man whose pounding on the street door had awakened him. Orry shoved a roll of heavy paper and a lump of coal into the secretary's hand.

"These prove the whole story—these and Quincy's body. He was one of them. When the fire's out, I'm sure we'll find unmelted pieces of the Whitworth rifles. Enough evidence for any reasonable man," he finished, unable to keep bitterness entirely contained.

"This is astounding. You must come inside and give me a fuller explanation of—"

"Later, sir," Orry interrupted. "I have one more task to do to close the books on this affair. Be careful of that coal. If you try to burn it, you'll blow yourself up."

He limped away, vanishing in the dark.

When he drew the empty navy Colt at the front door of the house on Grace Street, Orry noticed dark speckling on the butt. Bent's blood. With a shiver, he grasped the muzzle and beat on the door with the revolver. The bell had drawn no response.

"Someone open up." He leaned back to roar at the upper story. "If you don't, I'll blow the lock off."

That got immediate response, but it came from the other side of the street where gas lamps shed a pale, misty light. A grumpy householder flung up a window, snatched off his nightcap and shouted, "Do you know the hour, sir? Half past three in the morning. Stop that racket, or I'll come down and horsewhip—" The front door opened. Orry shouldered inside, expecting to see Huntoon's face. Instead, it was Homer's, half illuminated by an upraised lamp.

"Tell them I want to see them, Homer. Both of them."

"Mr. Orry, sir, they aren't—"

He ignored the old man and stalked to the stairs. "Ashton? James? Get down here, damn you."

The wild echo showed him how close he was to losing control again. He gripped the banister post and held tight, calming a little. He sensed Homer behind him; a light pool spread around his feet. Then a second glow, upstairs, preceded Huntoon, who cautiously approached the head of the stairs. Ashton followed, carrying the lamp. Neither was dressed for bed.

Orry looked up as she gripped the white-painted wood of the rail to the left of the landing. It was one of the few times he had ever seen his sister frightened.

"An old scene repeats itself, doesn't it, Ashton? I sent you away once in South Carolina and now I'm doing it in Virginia. This time, however, the stakes are higher. You don't just risk my anger if you stay. You'll be arrested."

Huntoon made a little retching sound and stepped back from the top step. Ashton seized his sleeve. "Stand up, you rotten coward. I said *stand up.*"

She hurt him with her hand. But he steadied. Leaning over and looking down, she fairly spat, "Let's hear the rest, brother dear."

A cold shrug. "Simple enough. I have delivered evidence to Mr. Seddon sufficient to hang you both. I'm referring to a coal bomb and the marked plan of the President's offices. I imagine the provost's men are on their way to the farm, where they'll find the remains of the rifles, Powell's personal belongings, and Israel Quincy's body. Your informant, the one who called himself Bellingham—he's dead, too, drowned in the river."

"You did that?" Huntoon whispered.

Orry nodded. "The one thing I have not yet done is implicate the two of you. I don't know why I should grant you the slightest immunity just because we're related, but I find myself doing it. Although not for long. You have one hour to remove yourselves from the city. If you don't, I'll go straight back to Seddon and charge you with treason and attempted assassination."

"Lord God," Homer said in a shaken voice. Orry had forgotten he was there.

Ashton shrieked at him: "You damned nosy nigger, get out of here. *Get out!*" He did, taking the light with him.

Ashton's effort to smile through her rage was grotesque. "Orry —you must appreciate—even to begin to prepare to leave will take far more time than—"

"One hour." He pointed to a tall clock ticking away, its face a metal shimmer in the gloom. "I'll be back at a quarter to five. You ought to hang, the lot of you—I include your scummy friend Powell, wherever he is. If any of you are in Richmond an hour from now, you will."

He walked out.

When he rode back to Grace Street at half past four, the pre-dawn air was cold. He shivered again, starting to feel genuinely sick from the shocks and exertions of the preceding hours. He reined in before the brick house. The windows were dark. He tied the horse, climbed the stoop, tried the front door. Locked.

On the side terrace, he broke a pane of the French windows with the Colt muzzle, reached through, and let himself in. He roamed the rooms. Empty, every last one.

In their bedrooms—separate ones, he noted—clothes were strewn everywhere. Drawers hung open. Some had been left on the floor, partially emptied. Strangely, he felt no satisfaction, merely tiredness and melancholy as he struggled downstairs again, still favoring the twisted ankle.

What had possessed Ashton? What demons of ambition? He would never know. Somehow, he was thankful.

He started as the tall clock chimed a quarter to five.

By late the following afternoon, several versions of the assassination story were circulating in the offices around Capitol Square. About four, Seddon approached Orry's desk. Orry held a government memorandum and appeared to be reading it—an illusion, Seddon realized, taking note of Orry's blank stare.

He cleared his throat, smiled, and said, "Orry, I have some splendid news. I have just talked with the President, who wants to present you with a written commendation. It's the equivalent of a decoration for gallantry in the field and will be accorded the same treatment. Published in at least one paper in your home state—"

Seddon faltered. On Orry's face there had appeared disbelief and disgust of such ferocity they alarmed the secretary. Avoiding Orry's eyes, he went on, less heartily, "The commendation will also be entered on the permanent Roll of Honor maintained in the adjutant general's office." Cloth and metal couldn't be spared for making decorations; the Roll of Honor was the Confederacy's substitute.

"Mr. Davis would like to award the commendation in his office tomorrow. May we arrange a suitable time?"

"I don't want his damned commendation. He drove my wife out of Richmond."

Seddon swallowed. "Do you mean to say, Colonel—you will—refuse the honor?"

"Yes. That will certainly cause another scandal, won't it? My wife and I have grown used to them."

"Your bitterness is understandable, but—"

Orry interrupted, an uncharacteristic slyness in his eyes. "I'll refuse it, that is, unless you and Mr. Davis also promise me an immediate transfer to General Pickett's staff. I'm tired of this office, this work, this pig-mire of a government—"

He swept all the papers from his desk with one slash of his arm. As the sheets fluttered down, he rose and walked out.

Heads swiveled. Clerks buzzed. Seddon's face lost its conciliatory softness. "I am certain a transfer can be arranged," he said loudly.

112

In the aftermath of the Eamon Randolph case, Jasper Dills began to worry about his stipend. He heard nothing of or from Elkanah Bent. He knew Baker had discharged Starkwether's son because of brutality in the Randolph matter. Beyond that, the record was blank.

Work taxed Dills to the utmost these days. Although some of his employers were Democrats, none wanted a Copperhead or peace candidate elected president; a shortened war meant diminished profits. Nevertheless, he decided he must make time to call on the chief of the special service bureau. He did so in late June. Baker's initial response was curt.

"I don't know what's happened to Dayton. Nor do I care. I followed instructions and dismissed him. Then I forgot about him."

"Blast it, Colonel, you must have some information. Is he still in the city? If not, where is he? Will you force me to pose my questions to Mr. Stanton and tell him you refused to help?"

Instantly, Baker grew cooperative, though Dills wished he hadn't when the bearded man said, "I have it on good authority that Dayton was in Richmond about a month ago."

"Richmond! Why?"

"I don't know. I was only told that he was seen."

"Is it possible he defected to the other side?"

Baker shrugged. "Possible. He was pretty angry when I let him go. He was also, in my opinion, unbalanced. I frankly wish I'd never taken him on. I know your reputation, Mr. Dills. I know you have a lot of friends in this government. But I don't know why you're so interested in Dayton. What's the connection?"

By then Dills had decided he would get no help here and must go higher. "I'm not obliged to answer your questions, Colonel Baker. Good morning."

On Independence Day, a Monday, Dills did go higher, setting out in his carriage for the War Department. While it was technically a holiday, and the Thirty-eighth Congress was rushing to adjourn, many government offices stayed open because of the pressures of war and politics. Things were not going well on any front. The resignation of Treasury Secretary Chase, first submitted to the President last winter, had finally been accepted. Chase, presumed to have been encouraged by the same anonymous radicals who had helped draft the Pomeroy Circular, which called for Lincoln's defeat, was stepping down to become a presidential candidate, so rumor said. Literally overnight, his departure created widespread fear that the government was bankrupt.

Telegraph dispatches from the Shenandoah Valley told of increased guerrilla action—torn-up railroad tracks, burned bridges —and of the steady retreat of Union forces toward Harpers Ferry. No one in the North had quite recovered from the news of the enormous number of casualties in the spring campaign. To this was added the May humiliation at New Market, when Sigel was once again whipped, this time by a rebel force that included two hundred and forty-seven boys—youthful cadets from VMI, the military school where Jackson had taught.

Reaching his destination, Dills alighted on the avenue and wove his way through a large crowd of dusky contrabands, whom he carefully avoided touching in any way. The contrabands loitered on the walks at the edge of President's Park, hungry faces and envious eyes turned toward the picnic in progress on the grounds. Swings hung from the shade trees, and food and drink covered great trestle tables set up between the War Department and the Executive Mansion. With the consent and encouragement of the government, the picnic was being held to raise money for a new District of Columbia school for Negro children. The guests, numbering several hundred already, consisted mostly of well-dressed civilians from the town's colored community. Here and there Dills saw white faces, which disgusted him even more than the cause itself.

Dills had an appointment with Stanton's flunky, Stanley Hazard. Though a mediocrity, Hazard was rich and had somehow acquired a circle of influential friends. Dills supposed he had done it the customary way, by buying them. What made Hazard unusual was his ability to stay balanced at the fulcrum of the wild teeterboard of party politics. He chummed with the politicians who wanted to defeat Lincoln at the polls yet worked for a man considered to be the President's staunchest supporter and friend. Stanley Hazard's survival was doubly remarkable in view of the stories one heard about him, particularly that he was usually drunk by half past nine every morning. When he was extremely busy, no later than ten.

On tiny feet, the tiny lawyer climbed to Stanley's office. In one corner stood a brass tripod holding burning cubes of heavy incense. To mask the odor of spirits?

The incense did nothing to mask the fuzzy expression on Stanley's face as he gestured Dills to a chair. Glancing out the window, Dills allowed himself one pleasantry. "I must say, passing through that mob, I wondered whether I was in the District or the palace gardens of Haiti."

Stanley laughed. "What about a West African village? Did you happen to notice what the darkies are serving down there? I'm guessing it's barbecued effigy of Bob Lee."

Dills pursed his lips, for him the equivalent of hysterical laughter. "I know you're busy, Mr. Hazard, so let me come to the point. Do you recall a man you interviewed for a post with Colonel Baker? A man named Ezra Dayton?"

Stanley sat up straighter. "I do indeed. You recommended him, but he was discharged. Highly unsatisfactory—"

"I deeply regret that. I had no way of anticipating it. What brings me here is the need to learn anything I can about Dayton's whereabouts, for reasons I wish I could divulge to you but cannot."

"Privileged communication with a client?"

"Something like that, yes. In return for assistance from your department, I'm prepared to make a generous contribution to the political candidate of your choice. On the Republican side, I would hope."

"Naturally," Stanley said, not even raising a brow to question the probity of the offer. "Let's see whether we have anything." He summoned an assistant, who was gone for ten minutes, leaving the two men to uneasy conversation punctuated by long silences.

The clerk returned, whispered in Stanley's ear, departed. Stanley sighed.

"Absolutely nothing, I'm afraid. I'm very sorry. I trust the outcome won't affect your pledge, since I accepted your offer in good faith." Dills glimpsed the threat behind the fulsome smile. He reeled when Stanley added, "A thousand would be most generous."

"A thousand! I was thinking of much—" Hastily, Dills swallowed. How could such a puffy, pale creature carry an aura of power? But he did. "Certainly. I'll send my draft in the morning."

Stanley wrote and blotted a slip of paper. "Payable to that account."

"Very good. Thank you for your time, Mr. Hazard." About to close the door from the anteroom side, he observed Stanley bent over a lower drawer of his desk, as if hunting something. Stanley glanced up, scowled, and Dills quickly closed the door.

Bent was gone—and the information had cost him a thousand dollars. Beyond that, unless he could think of some other avenue where he might search for Starkwether's boy, the handsome stipend would disappear. He was in a foul mood as he left the building and crossed the park toward his waiting carriage.

Children at the picnic scampered round and round him, dark leaves whirling. He ran them off with a shout and wave of his cane. Though still angry, he was also bemused by the performance of the nimble Mr. Hazard. Dills had definitely smelled whiskey behind the incense. What a miraculous balancing act.

Ah, but there were many such balancing acts in Washington. It was, as experience had taught him, a city of carnival performers wearing the costumes of patriots.

In Lehigh Station, the cemetery workers dug new graves, arriving freight trains discharged new coffins, arriving cars delivered one or two of the newly injured or permanently maimed. About town there could also be seen the occasional able-bodied male who shouldn't be at home just now. Brett had been a resident long enough to recognize such men.

She chose not to attend the local July fourth celebration—there was little patriotic fervor these days—and instead spent nine hours with Scipio Brown's children, teaching ciphering. It was a time of stifling weather, sinking morale, sudden alarms. Jubal Early's army had encircled Washington and cut rail and telegraph

867

lines to Baltimore. Jubal Early's army had reached Silver Spring, within sight of Union fortifications along Rock Creek. Jubal Early's army had almost pocketed Washington before being driven away toward Pennsylvania. And how far into the state might the rebs come this time?

It was a season of steadily mounting mistrust and hatred of Lincoln. Did he dare do what he said he might—call for another half-million volunteers to feed Grant's red machine before the month was out? It was a season of war-weariness and cynicism. Lute Fessenden's cousin had built up a handsome trade as a substitute broker. Conscription substitutes simply couldn't be found unless one dealt with him; he had cornered all those available in the valley by promising them higher rewards than anyone else. He charged eight hundred to one thousand dollars per substitute, depending on the applicant. The potential draftees raged. But they paid.

All this was a real but somehow immaterial backdrop to the central fact of Brett's life. With the help of Charles Main, Billy had escaped from Libby Prison, dashed through enemy country, and reached the Union lines during the titanic battle at Spotsylvania. A bullet had given him a light leg wound, but his letters said he was completely recovered and back on duty at Petersburg.

The joyous turnabout filled her days with cheer. To a lesser extent, so did the visits of Scipio Brown, who arrived with a new youngster every second or third week. The facility was by now hopelessly overcrowded. But Brown kept bringing more amber or blue-coal or café-au-lait children, and she fell in love with every single one.

Brown himself displayed a growing impatience to join a military unit before the South surrendered. "A commission in a Negro cavalry regiment. It's all I want. I must get it. I'm trying."

"I hope you do get it, Scipio. You're a splendid horseman. How can they not take you?"

Brett had been away from South Carolina three years. It no longer gave her pause to consider that when Brown joined the army, he would have the same status as any white man. She found the fact unremarkable—perfectly natural—because she now saw Brown solely as a man with a singular combination of traits, most of them likable. She knew he was a Negro, but color no longer played a part in how she felt about him.

Constance was a frequently amused and surprised observer of

all this. "I declare, Brett, you're ever so much happier the day before Scipio arrives than you are the day he leaves."

"Am I?" A smile, a lifted shoulder. "I suppose. I like him."

Constance nodded; both women understood it was the only explanation required. But in letters to George, Constance wrote of a marked sea change in the making.

Then came a stunning surprise. A plea by telegraph from Madeline Main. She was in Washington.

"Orry didn't want her trying to reach South Carolina," Constance said after reading the message again to be sure of the contents. "With the help of a black man from Fredericksburg, she reached Fort Du Pont, one of the fortifications along the East Branch, and crossed the lines. She was detained a day for questioning, then released. She wants permission to come here."

At once, Brett said, "I think someone should go to Washington to help her make the journey. I'm willing."

"I won't have you do it alone. We'll both go."

So, while the siege seemed to stall at Petersburg and Sherman seemed to stall before Atlanta, the two women made the long, dirty train trip to the capital, gazing anxiously out the window of the rattling car now and then. Half the passengers did the same thing. There were still wild tales of old Jube Early's men running amok on the lower border.

But they saw no sign of rebs between Lehigh Station and Washington. In a small, dark room on the island, Madeline greeted them from the middle of a pile of ripped clothing she was sorting. With her dark hair bunned and her hot bombazine dress rustling, she looked quite matronly. But still a beauty, Brett saw before they hugged.

"How good to see you," Constance said after she and Madeline embraced. "I'm glad Orry sent you this way instead of down South where there's so much danger."

"We'll take good care of you," Brett promised. "You do look worn out."

"I'm much better now that you two are here."

"Was it an ordeal?" Brett asked.

"Yes, but I'll spare you the details. There you see a few." She pointed to the torn dresses and undergarments. "It took a destructive search to convince one Union officer that I wasn't a smuggler or a spy. I'll have everything repacked in ten minutes. I can't wait to leave. We have big palmetto bugs in South Carolina, but the ones infesting this place make ours look like dwarfs."

Constance laughed, genuinely glad Orry had entrusted his wife to the care of Northerners. It meant that the ties of friendship between the families, though stretched and tenuous, were still intact. Sometimes, she knew, George feared the war would sunder those ties.

All at once Constance noticed a change in Madeline's expression. She was pensive, even pained. She sat down on the bed, hands in her lap, and looked from Brett to Constance. "Before we go, I want to explain why I had to leave Richmond. Other people learned what Orry's known since I ran away from Resolute. I—"

Silence for a moment. She seemed to struggle with some burden, then fling it off, sitting straighter. "I have Negro blood. My mother was a New Orleans quadroon."

Brett's admiration gave way to a rush of dizziness. She held still, not daring to move for fear she would shame Madeline, who continued to speak as calmly as if she were reciting a primer lesson. You know what that means in the Confederacy. One drop of black blood and you're a black person." She paused. "Will that be true in Lehigh Station?"

Constance answered first. "Absolutely not. No one will know. You needn't have told us."

"Oh, no, I felt obligated."

Light-headed, Brett wasn't sure how she felt. Scipio Brown was forgotten as she struggled with the idea that this woman who shared her brother's bed and love—and the family name—was a Negro. Of course she didn't look it, but the truth was exactly as Madeline had stated it. Looks didn't measure blackness; only ancestry. Confusing emotions, childhood-deep, engulfed her.

"Are you positive it makes no difference?" Madeline asked.

"None," Brett said, wishing it were so.

"If I'd stayed on the river road, they'd have caught me sure," Andy said. "They popped out of the palmettos—two of 'em on mules—but I know some of the back paths and they didn't. That's how I got away."

"Well, sit down, rest yourself," Philemon Meek said, giving up his own chair. "I'm thankful you're all right."

The heavy air of a July twilight filled the plantation office. Meek paced, swinging his spectacles from his bent index finger.

How old he's grown, Cooper thought from the shadowed corner where he stood, arms folded.

After Andy came dashing up the lane, sweat and fright on his face, Meek insisted the three of them confer here rather than in the great house. In the office, the overseer explained, they wouldn't be overheard, thus would not alarm Cooper's wife and daughter or the house servants. It was the house people Meek worried about most. He didn't want them to run off.

Cooper went along with Meek, but he had fewer illusions than the overseer. The house people knew the guerrilla band was encamped nearby, its ranks growing weekly. The only person unaware of the danger was Clarissa.

"If I'd known an ordinary errand would be so dangerous, I wouldn't have sent you, Andy," Meek said. "I'm sorry. Hope you believe that."

"Yes, sir. I do." Cooper marveled. The apology and the response demonstrated the immense change the war had wrought on the plantation.

Meek stopped swinging his spectacles. "Now I want to be clear about this. You saw white men this time."

"That's right. Two in regular army gray, three in butternut. Those butternut coats didn't look like much. Still, you could tell they belonged to soldiers—either the ones wearing them or the ones they stole 'em from."

The overseer pronounced the verdict they all knew: "If white deserters are joining the nigras, then we've twice the reason to fear." He swung toward the possessor of final authority. "I have little doubt they'll attack us, Mr. Main. This is the largest plantation still operating in the district. I think we should arm some of the slaves—assuming we can find anything to arm them with. The attack may not come for a while, but we've got to be ready when it does."

"Is that the only way?" Cooper snapped. "Fighting?"

The overseer was momentarily stunned to silence. Andy didn't know what to make of the questioning response. After a few seconds, Meek said, "If you can suggest another, I'll be glad to hear it."

Stillness, filled with insect sounds. Up toward the house, a woman chanted the melody of a hymn. From a great distance they heard the raucous cry of a salt crow, answered by another. Andy peered out the window anxiously.

Cooper recognized defeat, sighed. "All right. I'll go to Charleston to see whether I can find some secondhand guns."

Brusquely and with urgency, Meek said, "Soon, please?"

In Richmond next day, Orry packed the last of the few personal things with which he and Madeline had furnished the rooms on Marshall Street. The items went into a crate he nailed shut with a hammer wielded easily in his powerful right hand. Pounding the precious rusty nails one by one, he wondered if he would ever see the box after he consigned it to a local warehouse. He felt despondent about his negative answer, but comforted when he recalled that it was not an isolated reaction. Throughout the South, expectations sank daily.

He squeezed uniforms and gear into a small dilapidated trunk for which he had paid a barbarous price. He tagged the trunk with appropriate information and set it on the landing. Late in the afternoon, a white-haired Negro teamster appeared. The man's shoulders were round as the top of a question mark. Orry offered him a tip, but the man shook his head, gave him a sadly resentful look, and took the trunk away, making certain Orry heard his groans as he descended the stairs.

At dusk he donned his best gray uniform, locked the flat, and handed the key to the landlady. Carrying a small carpetbag containing items he didn't want to risk losing—his razor, a bar of soap, and two thin books of poetry—he walked to the marshaling yard where his transportation was waiting—a supply wagon bound south, seven and a half miles, to Chaffin's Bluff. There, Pickett's Division anchored the right end of the Intermediate Line, one of the five defense lines ringing the city.

The teamster invited Orry to sit next to him, but Orry preferred to ride in back, along with several unmarked boxes, his trunk and carpetbag, and his thoughts. He was happy to leave Richmond, but the prospect of joining Pickett's staff had not really lifted his spirits the way he had hoped. He was still shamed by Ashton's treachery and shocked by his callous disposal of Elkanah Bent. His loneliness since Madeline's departure could better be termed despondency. He prayed that she had reached Washington and would continue to think he was working in relative safety at the War Department.

Orry had always tried to draw lessons from experience. He had attempted it again after the entire government appeared to turn

872

on his wife solely because she had a Negro ancestor. He found the lesson was familiar. Cooper had preached it for many years, and Orry had just as consistently ignored it until both sides had gone too far down the steep, dark road to war.

To this very day, the South was a stubborn pupil, rejecting the lesson even after the teacher's stick beat the pupil until he bled from mortal wounds. What would bring the Confederacy to an inglorious end was the same thing that had so foolishly created it: a rigidity of thought, a clinging to old ways, a refusal to adapt and change.

That was it, Orry saw with a little *frisson* of revelation. The fatal flaw. Minds of stone—pugnaciously proud of the condition.

Examples abounded. The South needed soldiers in the most desperate way, yet those who urged the enlistment of blacks were still called lunatics.

Were not the rights of states supreme? Of course they were. Thus the governor of Georgia needed no other grounds to exempt three thousand militia officers from army service and five thousand government workers besides. Using the same justification, the governor of North Carolina stockpiled thousands of uniforms, blankets, and rifles under the banner of state defense. Such right-thinking, principled men were more destructive than Sam Grant.

Orry wasn't a strong strategic thinker, but in sorting through probable causes of the inevitable defeat, he thought he had found another important one in newspaper dispatches describing the opposing presidents. At the start of the war, both Davis and Lincoln had personally directed military policy. Lincoln had even told McClellan the precise day on which he had to march to the peninsula.

Bloody losses had somehow taught Lincoln to revise his opinion of himself as a strategist and infallible judge of the capabilities of generals. On Capitol Square, it was widely held that at some point earlier this year, Lincoln had acknowledged his limitations by transferring control of the war engine to a man who ran it his own way: Grant.

Davis, by contrast, had never learned to recognize personal shortcomings, admit mistakes, adapt to new circumstances, change. The wheel revolved to Cooper again. When had Orry first heard him argue scornfully with their father that the South's greatest peril was its inflexibility? Longer ago than he could precisely remember.

Still, Orry reflected as the swaying wagon bore him toward Chaffin's Bluff, he mustn't be too hard on his own kind. Minds of stone were numerous not only inside Dixie but outside, too. There were plenty in the Yankee Congress; even one or two in the Hazard family, the foremost being Virgilia's.

But it was becoming clear to Orry that after the war ended, a new, entirely different world would arise. In that world there would be but one way for the South to survive and rebuild. That way was to accept what had happened. Accept that no black man would ever again labor unwillingly for a white man's profit. In sum—accept change.

He doubted whether most Southerners could do it. Many would undoubtedly go on hating, resisting, insisting they had been morally right, which Orry no longer believed. But again, he supposed just as many Yankees were willingly entrapped in the old modes of enmity and a yearning for reprisals. It was not, perhaps, merely the Southerner who failed to learn lessons, but every man in every epoch.

Trouble was, when you refused to learn, the result was what surrounded the rumbling wagon: soured earth; abandoned homes; imperiled lives.

Ruin.

Ruin and sadness like that on George Pickett's face when the general accepted Orry's salute and welcomed him to division headquarters.

"How good to see you at last."

"It's good to be here, sir."

A melancholy smile. "I hope you'll say that after you've spent a few weeks in close proximity to our old acquaintance from West Point. We have met a man this time who either doesn't know when he's whipped or doesn't care if he loses his whole army to whip us. There is no way effectively to oppose that kind of man for very long."

There is one, Orry thought. But he wasn't foolish enough to bring up the issue of black recruits and spoil the reunion and his first moments in the war zone.

113

Three women dining.

Constance called for candles instead of gaslight, believing it might warm the atmosphere for supper. It did, but that hardly mattered after her first effort to make conversation.

"Well, here we are—" she raised her claret to toast the guests seated on her right and left at the long table "—three war widows."

"I wish you wouldn't say such a thing," Brett exclaimed.

"Oh, my dear, I'm sorry. It was a clumsy attempt to make a light remark. I apologize."

"It's too serious to joke about," Brett said as Bridgit and a second kitchen girl marched in with china tureens of steaming mock turtle soup.

"I understand what you meant," Madeline said to Constance, "but I agree with Brett." She wore a clean, dark dress, and her hair was neatly arranged, but she hadn't lost the haggard air acquired on her long journey. She plied her spoon and tried to comfort Constance with a smile. "This is absolutely delicious."

Straining equally: "Thank you."

Presently, Constance steered the conversation to a safer track. She laughed and spoke ruefully about her continuing weight problem, hoping that jokes at her own expense would enable them to forgive and forget her misplaced flippancy. She saw little sign of success.

She answered Madeline's questions about her father, Patrick Flynn. He was in the pueblo of Los Angeles and busy improving his Spanish so he could serve native-born clients in addition to the settler community.

"And Virgilia?"

"We never hear from her. I presume she's still with the nurse corps."

"I would think she'd be a little more grateful for the shelter and guidance you gave her," Brett said. "Simple politeness would dictate an occasional letter, if nothing else."

Constance reached for the glinting knife on the cutting board. Smiling, she began to slice the hot, fresh loaf. "Alas, I don't think we can count gratitude among my sister-in-law's virtues."

"Does she have any at all?" Brett countered, and with that fell grimly silent, eating her soup.

Dear Lord, Constance thought, did my blunder cause all this? The answer appeared to be yes. The more she considered the dark possibilities wrapped up in her brief, careless remark, the more it depressed her.

Madeline sensed the tension. She said to Brett, "Tell me about this school for black waifs, won't you?"

"If you'd like, I'll take you up there tomorrow."

"Oh, yes, please."

Brett, too, was feeling ashamed of her outburst. Anxiety was the chief cause. The *Ledger-Union* was reporting many lives lost along the Petersburg siege lines. The word *widow* was one she hated to think about in connection with herself.

But she had to be honest; there was another irritant. Madeline's revelation in the rooming house. It had stunned Brett, but more than that, it had loosed an unexpected emotional reaction. As a presumed white woman, Madeline had earned Brett's wholehearted respect and affection. Now—well, she couldn't help it— she regarded Orry's wife differently.

It was a reaction bred into her from childhood. That was an explanation, not an excuse. The reaction shamed her, and yet she seemed powerless to banish it or keep it from affecting her behavior.

Madeline was aware of the new reserve on Brett's part ever since that pivotal moment in Washington. Whenever she felt incensed, she reminded herself that Orry's sister was under great strain, had been living far from her native state for more than three years, had had her husband captured, imprisoned, wounded. That was an immense load for any wife to bear.

876

Brett's response to the revelation was a curious and ironic contrast to her involvement with the colored orphanage, Madeline thought. Her concern for the welfare of the black children was evident from the passion and frequency with which she spoke of them. At least that was a change, and a remarkable one for a young woman bred in the frequently arrogant traditions of the Carolina low country. The war was changing everyone and everything in some fashion; a pity it couldn't alter old attitudes about black blood.

She hoped Brett would eventually be capable of overlooking what she now clearly regarded as a taint. If not—well, it would certainly alter family relationships. It sometimes seemed to Madeline that God had put Americans to a cruel, perhaps impossible test when He permitted the Dutch to land that first shipload of slaves on the Virginia coast so long ago. The black man out of Africa had repeatedly exposed the white man's weaknesses. It was, perhaps, fitting revenge for the moment when the leg irons clinked shut.

There had been unpleasant notes sounded at this table tonight. *Three war widows.* She understood the attempt at lightness but found it disturbing. Thank heaven Orry had done nothing about joining Pickett's staff. He should be relatively safe in Richmond until the city fell. Afterward, he might be interned awhile—even mistreated—but he would survive that; he was a strong, brave man.

Trying to restart conversation, Madeline once more addressed Brett. "This friend of yours—the one who operates the orphanage —will I have a chance to meet him?"

"I think so. I expect he'll pay at least one more visit before he goes into the army. I certainly hope he will." Brett smiled. "You'll like him, I know."

And you like him very much indeed, Madeline said to herself. *You seem able to accept him for what he is, but not me. Is that because you thought I was something you have always been told was better?*

Sensing the onset of more bad feelings, Madeline blocked them by turning back to Constance, this time with a frivolous question about current fashions. The candles burned down, and conversation limped on, but something had gone out of Constance in the past few minutes. Her answers were forced, her efforts at banter unsuccessful. As they were finishing their lemon ices and coconut macaroons, she said abruptly, "I believe I'll go down to town for an hour."

Madeline asked, "Would you like company?"

"Thank you, no. I'm going to church."

It wasn't necessary to tell them she felt the need. Her face made it evident.

She drove the carriage herself down the twisting road in the night glare from Hazard's. Under Wotherspoon's guidance, the entire complex continued to operate twenty-four hours a day—and had never been so profitable.

Reaching the streets of the lower town, Constance felt the night wind rising, blowing dust. Lamps burned late in the army recruiting office. As she drove by, she noticed a sturdy Negro boy, the son of a worker at Hazard's, standing some distance from the entrance. Between the boy and the doorway, Lute Fessenden's cousin and some equally loutish crony whispered and joked.

When a few of the town's black men had attempted to visit the recruiter, there had been incidents of harassment. To prevent another, she slowed the carriage and prepared to speak to the substitute broker. Before she could, the black boy turned and disappeared in a dark alley. The significance of the two men loitering outside the office hadn't been lost on him.

Disgusted, she drove on to the small Catholic chapel that had been named, in a burst of poetic piety, St. Margaret's-in-the-Vale. The river valley, where flying soot and bits of cinder constantly blackened everything, could never live up to the literary connotations of vale, but it was a word very much liked by Lehigh Station's small Catholic community.

Because of the heat of the evening, the front doors of St. Margaret's stood open. Constance tied the horse to a wrought-iron post—Hazard's had donated and installed a row of eight—and slipped in, hoping meditation and prayer might lift the formless anxiety that had settled on her during supper. Inside the entrance, she genuflected, then slipped in to the second pew on the left.

Kneeling, she noticed a heavy, middle-aged woman across the aisle. The woman was poorly dressed, a shawl around her shoulders. Her forehead rested on her clasped hands as she prayed. Constance knew her. Mrs. Waleski's only boy had died in a Cold Harbor medical tent.

Hot wind gusting up the aisle fluttered the votive candles. The seven-foot Christ, painted and gilded, looked down from His cross with pity. Softly, Constance began praying.

Her mind was strangely divided, one part of it on her murmured plea for intercession, another on the great weight crushing her. She knew who had put the weight there. A stupid, thoughtless woman—

Here we are. Three war widows.

Ever since making that remark, she had been possessed by a premonition. For one of the three women at the table, the words would come true.

She was so sure of it, she was consumed with a fear no prayers could allay. Another fierce wind gust blew out half a dozen of the votive lights in their little glass cups red as blood.

114

Charles suffered a ravaging intestinal ailment during the first ten days of July. Still weak, still belonging in bed, he got up on the eleventh morning, obtained a pass, and set off on a dangerous ride around the west of Richmond, then northeast to Fredericksburg. His only guarantees of safe passage were his revolver and shotgun.

It would be his last trip to Barclay's Farm. He had decided that while lying with his knees drawn up against his pain-pierced gut. In bed, he'd had plenty of time to straighten out his thinking. The South would go down fighting, and he would go down with it. That was his sole duty now.

He couldn't deny he loved Gus, but she deserved a man with better prospects. Each day the odds against avoiding a fatal bullet increased. In the short run, he would hurt her. But when she found, as she surely would, a better man—someone whose head had not been oddly twisted by his war experiences—she would thank him.

He reached the farm at the end of a rain shower. The sun was out again, occasionally hidden by the clouds that flew over fields and woods at great speed, exchanging light for shadow, shadow for light. It was half past five in the evening. The clouds, the quality of sunlight at that hour, and the sparkling clarity of the land after the rain helped restore some of the farm's earlier beauty.

"Major Charles!" Washington, mending harness on the back stoop, jumped to his feet as Charles rode up. "Lord save us—old Sport looks about as starved as you do. Didn't expect we'd see you for a while. Wait till I tell Miz Augusta—"

"I'll tell her myself." Unsmiling, Charles yanked the back door open without knocking. "Gus?" He stepped into the kitchen, oblivious to the pained look on the aging freedman's face.

The kitchen was empty. Soup stock containing one large bone simmered on the stove. He shouted, "Gus, where the hell are you?"

She came dashing down the hall, hairbrush in hand. At the sight of him, her face glowed. She flung her arms around his neck. "Sweetheart!"

He pressed his bearded cheek to hers but broke the embrace when she started to kiss him. He flung a shabby butternut trouser leg over a low-backed chair and sat. He fumbled in his shirt for matches and a half-smoked cigar. His lack of emotion worried her.

At the stove, she swirled the long wooden spoon three times around the simmering pot. Then she laid the spoon aside and reluctantly confronted him.

"Darling, you don't look well."

"I caught the intestinal complaint again. I don't know which is worse, lying on a cot wishing my gut would fall out or riding over half of Virginia with General Hampton."

"It's been that bad—?"

"We've lost more men and horses than you'd believe. At least three whole troops of the South Carolina Sixth are in the dead-line camp, without remounts."

She glanced out the window. "You still have Sport."

"Barely." He knocked his knuckles on the table twice.

She brushed at a strand of loose blond hair. "It breaks my heart to see you so thin and white. And discouraged."

"What else can you expect these days?" He found his nervousness increasing. Originally, he had considered staying the night—making love one last time—but he found he didn't have the brass to do that to her. Or the strength to endure it himself. Abruptly, he decided on a quick end.

He bit into the cigar stub, scraped a match on the chair bottom, waved it toward the windows as sulfurous fumes filled the room. "The farm's a wreck."

"Thank the Yankees. Hardly a day goes by without Boz or Washington firing a warning shot at some deserter sneaking around."

"You shouldn't have stayed here. You shouldn't be here now. How can you raise anything? How can you and the niggers survive?"

"Charles, you know I don't like to hear that word. Especially in reference to my freedmen."

He shrugged. "I forgot. Sorry." He didn't sound it.

She tugged at the tight waist of her dress. Charles's head was bent, his eye on the match applied to the cigar. Blue smoke whirled around his beard as he blew the match out.

Frightened, Gus said: "You sound as though you don't really want me to answer the questions you asked. You sound as though you're trying to pick a fight."

He plucked the cigar from his teeth. "Now listen. It was a damned long ride up here "

"May I remind you that no one begged you to make it?" The old defenses were going up again; the tartness, the wry mouth. They hurt him. But he had known for months that pain was necessary if he were to do what was right.

He smoked and stared, saw angry bewilderment in her blue eyes. He nearly relented. Then Ab Woolner came to mind, and Sharpsburg, and a great many other events and changes—so many, it hardly seemed possible that three years could contain them all. Or that any man could withstand them. Yet he had. But he was not unscathed.

More softly: "How long are you able to stay?"

"I have to start back when it's dark."

"Would you like—?" The unfinished question and her slight

turn toward the door leading to the sleeping rooms had an adolescent awkwardness not typical of her. Red appeared in her cheeks.

"I need to water Sport and let him rest," he said, aching to carry her in to bed. She heard the unspoken refusal.

"I'll give you supper when you're finished."

With a bob of his head, he went out.

The dapple of shadow and light from moving clouds continued into the evening. Charles consumed two bowls of the thin beef soup and four pieces of coarse, delicious brown bread baked earlier. She ladled out a small portion of soup for herself but didn't touch it. While he ate, she said little, resting her chin on the backs of her interlocked hands, her elbows on the table on either side of the cooling soup. As she studied his face, she tried to fathom the sad mystery of what was wrong with him. Occasionally she prodded with a brief question.

He said he was sure the war was lost. He spoke of the high rate of desertion and Lee's failure to demonstrate faith in Wade Hampton by promoting him to commander of the cavalry. He mentioned actions whose names were unfamiliar and the escalating hostility.

"When Hunter was in the valley, he burned Governor Letcher's home in Lexington. The Military Institute, too. In Silver Spring, right outside Washington, they say Jube Early looted homes and farms in retaliation. Now he's loose in Pennsylvania—God knows what he's doing there. When this whole business started, it reminded me of a South Carolina tournament: fair ladies, courageous horsemen, games. It's turned into an abattoir, with butchers and cattle on both sides. Good soup," he finished insincerely, pushing the bowl away. *Do it now. Don't prolong it.*

"What I came to say, Gus—" he cleared his throat "—with things going so badly, I don't know when I can get here again."

Gus lifted her head, a swift, fierce movement, like a response to a slap. Bitterly, she said, "Next week or never, the choice is yours. It always has been. I—" There she stopped, shaking her head as if saying no to herself.

"Go ahead, finish."

Her voice strengthened. "I hope you didn't expect a flood of tears in response to your announcement. I'm not sure I want you here in your present frame of mind. It's hardly new or profound to say that war is terrible. And you seem to forget men don't carry the entire burden. Do you think it's any easier to be a woman with a son or husband in the army? Do you think it's easier to sit and watch grown men play soldierboy by tearing up a garden—all the food you have in the world—and ruining a farm with their hooliganism? I know the war's done hard things to you. It's in your eyes, what you say, everything you do. You seem to be filled with rage—"

He rammed the chair back and stood, cigar in his teeth. He had lit a new one after eating, having decided he would go when the cigar was smoked. He might be leaving sooner than that.

"Don't bother to display your truculence," Gus seethed. "I've had my fill. What gives you special dispensation to beat your breast longer and harder than any of the rest of us? I love you, idiot that I am. I'm sorry for you. But I won't be treated like some dumb animal that's misbehaved. I won't be kicked, Charles. If you choose to come here again, let it be as the man I fell in love with. He's the one I want."

Moments ticked by. He drew the cigar from his mouth.

"He died."

She returned his stare. Softly, without wrath, she said, "I think you had better go."

"I think so too. Thanks for the food. Take care of yourself."

He walked out, mounted Sport, and rode away beneath the lowering clouds of night.

For half an hour, Gus did nothing. She sat at the kitchen table, her hands on her stomach, while grief beat at her. Sometime during this period, Washington knocked at the back door. She didn't answer. He went away.

Darkness crept into the kitchen. When she finally stood, it was to light a lamp. She felt much as she had the night her husband died. She couldn't believe it had happened to her.

If she had been more realistic about Charles—less smitten—she would have recognized that something like this could happen. There had been signs, strong ones, during the past year. A couplet from "An Essay on Man" cycled endlessly through her thoughts: *Atoms or systems into ruin hurl'd, And now a bubble burst—*

"And now a world."

The whisper died away. With mental pushes and kicks, she forced herself to move through the dark house. Dusting this. Straightening that. Motion, work—anything to numb the pain.

883

She lit two more lamps in the kitchen, heated water on the stove, pulled all her clean dishes from the shelves and washed each piece, dried them vigorously, and put them back.

Another knock. This time, Washington didn't wait for an answer before stepping inside. "Miz Augusta, it's near onto midnight. Too late for you to be up."

"This floor's filthy. I'm going to scrub it."

Washington's forehead furrowed; such behavior was incomprehensible. "Major Charles didn't look so good—"

"He's been quite ill. Dysentery."

"He didn't stay long."

"No."

"He comin' back soon?"

She had to lie. "I don't know. Perhaps."

Still frowning, Washington chewed on his lower lip. "If you're goin' to wash the floor this time of night, you let me help you."

"I want to do it by myself. I don't feel sleepy." She remembered her manners. "But thank you."

The door closed, shutting out his troubled face.

She filled a pail and found her brush. She couldn't believe how badly she hurt. His leaving was the direct cause, but the deepest guilt was hers. She had let down her defenses. Opened herself to love, whose other Janus face was the possibility of loss.

Would she have changed anything? Refused to love him? It took her no time at all to answer with an emphatic no. But, God above, it did hurt now.

Despite that, she still took pride in being a self-reliant woman. She had endured this damned misbegotten war, and she would continue to endure it. She would endure the pain, too, for as long as it lasted. She knew how long that would be. Till the hour she died.

No matter. She would endure everything because there was always, even amidst the worst, some reason for wanting and needing to survive. She knew her own reason well and only wished she had been able to tell him. But it would have been a cruel and self-serving use of the truth.

Gently, she rested a hand on her waist. Then, as the clock rang midnight, she got down on her knees and began to scrub.

115

The night after the battle of the Crater, Billy wrote:

Sun., Jul. 31. Routine company inspection. All quiet on the siege lines following yesterday's devastation.

Saturday, waking to reveille at 2 a.m., we breakfasted and marched in shirt sleeves to Ft. Meikel, a section of the works from which we witnessed the detonation of 8,000 lbs. of powder in the T-shaped mine shaft, approx. 600 ft. long, dug in complete secrecy by Lt. Col. Pleasants's 48th Penn. Veteran Vol's—chiefly coal miners, from whom came the idea. At first, I regret to say, it was rejected by Gen. Meade & our own chief of engineers, Maj. Duane. But opposition was overcome, and the task accomplished by men working day & night for a month. That the miners did not suffocate was due to a clever scheme which drew foul air from the tunnel by means of a fire & a secret chimney. Company A of our battalion assisted with part of the task, building the covered way protecting the mine entrance & the approach to same. The mine ended at a point 20 ft. beneath the rebel works along Peagram's Salient. The charge went off with a monumental rocking of earth & lighting of the sky such as I have never before witnessed. The scheme was a total success until Gen. Burnside's IX Corps, in line of battle in a nearby ravine, commenced its advance into the smoking crater.

For reasons not yet clear, the advance foundered, with men on the bottom & sides of the crater trapped there as more troops poured in. All were soon entangled—a great writhing human target for deadly rifle & artillery fire from the enemy. This took a huge toll & prepared the way for Gen. Mahone's counterattack, which turned the brilliant effort into a defeat.

What I find singular, beyond the construction of the mine itself, is the courage exhibited by Gen. Ferrero's colored troops. They were to have been sent in first, but Grant feared he would be accused of treating negroes as cannon fodder if the attack failed, so he held them in reserve. When finally committed, they conducted themselves so valorously their praises are being sung by all.

During the battle, the battalion was in readiness for any sudden call—we took a tool wagon to our vantage point—but none was forthcoming, so we returned to our present encampment near the Jerusalem Plank Road, there to resume our routine duties.

Mine have now been expanded, voluntarily, to include campaigning among my fellow soldiers for Mr. Lincoln's re-election. Some men will be enabled by state law to cast votes in the field—Penn. soldiers are among that lucky group—but others will be required to return to their native states. Whatever a man's situation, all but the most phlegmatic are showing a lively, not to say occasionally violent, interest in the coming battle of ballots.

Our President faces a hard fight. Some scorn his shortcomings as a war leader and his policies regarding the colored race. I have listened and argued with avowed loyal Unionists who hope the Democrats nominate Gen. McC. in August because they find L. guilty of so many "crimes"—the draft; promoting growth of centralized federal power; arbitrary arrest & imprisonment of critics of the administration—& so on.

While many feel that way, I do not find the army as "McClellanized" as it was even one year ago. Grant squanders lives almost wantonly, yet there is a rising surety that he has at last fashioned a fighting force which will triumph; along with the expected wailing about the butcher's bill, there is new pride within the Army of the Potomac. Most agree it is only a matter of time until we win. This works in Abe's favor. I will campaign for him to the utmost.

The siege continues without much success. Geo. is now based at City Point in the RR Corps charged with maintaining

our rail supply line, esp. the many trestles which span gullies,
creeks, & other low places along the route. I want to see him
but thus far have not; daily, it seems, there is a new task for
the battalion. Since my arrival, I have led a surveying party
near the reb. siege lines—we drew hot fire for 10 minutes on
that occasion. I have commanded detachments which dug
wells and put up shelters made of boughs for the mules which
pull our wagons. I have twice taught large groups of colored
infantry the techniques of gabion & fascine construction. They
were eager to learn & did, quickly.

We have felled trees for new gun platforms, replaced gabi-
ons ruined by heavy rainstorms, built bombproofs, cut new
embrasures in existing works, & generally added to the siege
line. The line is essentially a series of separate redoubts, or
forts, connected by rifle pits, each fort laid out so its guns may
play not only upon the enemy but on adjoining forts, should
they be attacked.

A great amount of the work is done in close proximity to the
earthworks of the rebels, which calls for extreme care & fre-
quent stealth. We often perform our tasks at night, in complete
silence when that is possible. Every man knows that an im-
proper move, a command uttered too loudly or any inadver-
tent noise can draw the artillery or sharpshooter fire which can
end the war for him a considerable time before an official
surrender. No wonder, then, that we are issued a daily ration
of whiskey. Our job is hard & it is dangerous. I never hesitate
to drink the whiskey. I have every hope of a reunion with my
brother at City Point soon—& many reasons to do my utmost
to live through each new day. Many reasons, but one supreme.
You, my dearest Wife. How I do long to outlast the killing &
hold you in my arms again.

Along with its changing colors, autumn brought better news to
the Lehigh Valley. Sherman had taken Atlanta on the second of
September. That and the successful exploits of Little Phil excited
the entire North. In scornful reply to the pacifists campaigning for
the election of McClellan, Republicans proudly called the Irish
cavalry leader "Peace Commissioner Sheridan."

Autumn also brought Scipio Brown to Belvedere for the last
time. Gleeful as a boy, he pivoted in front of Brett to show off his
light blue trousers with the broad yellow stripe and the dark blue

jacket, without insignia—the means by which junior lieutenants were distinguished from senior ones.

"Lieutenant Brown, Second United States Colored Troops, Cavalry. I'm replacing an officer who was injured when the regiment skirmished at Spring Hill."

"Oh, Scipio—it's exactly what you wanted. You look simply grand."

Constance and Madeline agreed. The three women had gathered in the parlor to welcome and honor Brown with sherry and little sugared cakes. Madeline, who thought the slender-waisted amber-colored man cut a handsome figure, asked him, "Where and when will you report?"

"City Point, next Monday. I hope there won't be as much trouble as there was when I went to take my oath. Ran up against a gang of four white boys, two of them veterans. They didn't care for the idea of colored men entering their army, and they tried to stop me."

Perched on a chair like some long-legged water bird on a nest much too small, he showed them that infectious smile as he pushed outward with his palm. "But I cut a path."

"We have men like that right here in Lehigh Station," Brett said, noticing, as she never had before, that his palm was nearly as white as hers. Brown's chair gave a sudden creak, so he rose—happily, because it allowed him to stand to his full height in the uniform he wore with obvious pride.

Constance asked, "Have you any other late news from the city?"

"They're saying that with Mr. Lincoln's assistance, Nevada Territory will become a state by the first of November. That will provide the last two votes needed to ratify the amendment." It was not necessary for him to explain further; in Brown's lexicon there was but one amendment, the thirteenth.

He bowed to the ladies. "The refreshments were delicious, but I must go up and say good-bye to my children. My train leaves at six." He had arrived at nine that morning, after traveling all night.

"I'll go with you," Brett said immediately. Madeline flashed a glance at Constance, silently remarking on Brett's eagerness and Brown's pleased reaction. Constance smiled to say she saw the same things. Her smile seemed broader these days because her face was fuller; the slim woman George had married had disappeared inside a larger, rounder one. The effect was not unbecoming.

At the school, Mrs. Czorna cried, and the seventeen black waifs hopped and danced around Scipio, admiring the magnificence of his uniform: every button bright, no speck or wrinkle anywhere. He told Mrs. Czorna and her husband that the Christian Commission in Washington would continue to gather strays and route them to Lehigh Station from the temporary shelter in the Northern Liberties.

"It will not be the same," Mrs. Czorna wept. "Oh, never the same, you dear man." She hid her tear-streaked face on her husband's shoulder. She's right, Brett thought with mingled sorrow and pride.

Scipio Brown bid the children good-bye one at a time, leaving each with a hug and kiss. Too quickly, Brett found herself accompanying him down the hill again. Hazard's billowed its smoke into the October sky, dimming the autumn sun. Windblown laurel seethed on both sides of the path. Brown checked his pocket watch.

"Half past five already. I must hurry."

On Belvedere's veranda, she stood with one hand grasping a carved pillar—something she found necessary to steady herself. The western light blazed in her eyes, making it hard to see him. She feared the pitiless light and what it might reveal.

Brown cleared his throat. "I don't know how to begin this good-bye. You have been such a great help to me—"

"Willingly. I don't need thanks. I've loved every one of those children."

"When you feel just as much love for an adult of their color, you'll have made the whole journey. But you've come a long way already. An incredible distance. You are—" there was an uncharacteristic hesitation "—you're a wonderful woman. I can understand why your husband is proud."

His black silhouette loomed against the softly lit mountains across the river. Without conscious thought, Brett reached out to touch him. "You must take good care of yourself. Write to us—"

He stepped away from the hand on his sleeve. Only then did Brett realize what she had done.

"Of course I will, as time permits." He sounded stiff and punctilious suddenly. "I must go, or I'll miss the train."

He untied the hired horse, mounted gracefully, and cantered

down the road toward where it curved between the nearest houses. Light from the west glared above their roof lines; everything below was shadow. She lost the mounted figure in that mass of dark blue and stood with a hand shielding her eyes, trying to find it, for several minutes.

Belatedly, she understood why she had touched him. She had been overcome with emotion: intense sorrow, affection—most stunningly of all, intense attraction. Although she couldn't quite believe it, neither could she deny her memory. For the tiniest moment, lonely and inwardly empty because of Billy's long absence, she had been linked by longing to the tall soldier making his farewell.

And it had not made a whit of difference in that moment that Scipio Brown was a Negro.

By now the emotion had passed. The recollection never would. She had been unfaithful to Billy, and though the infidelity had been silent and brief, her sense of morality generated shame. But it had nothing to do with Brown's color. He was worthy of any woman's love.

Down by the canal, a whistle blew its long, lonely plaint. His train. She wiped tears from her eyes, remembering something he said.

When you feel just as much love for an adult of their color, you'll have made the whole journey.

"Oh," she whispered, and turned and ran into the house. "Madeline? Madeline!" She dashed from room to room till she found her, seated with a book of poems. As Madeline stood up, Brett flung her arms around her, starting to cry.

"Here, what's all this?" Madeline began, her smile tentative, wary.

"Madeline, I'm sorry. Forgive me."

"Forgive you for what? You've done nothing wrong."

"I have. Yes, I have. Forgive me."

The crying continued, and Madeline patted the younger woman to comfort her. At first she felt awkward, then less so. She held her kinswoman close for some length of time, knowing Brett needed absolution, even if she didn't know exactly why.

116

Shelling had partially destroyed the redoubt, forcing the Eleventh Massachusetts Battery to abandon it. For the second moonless night in a row, Billy led a repair and revetting party to the site, working at frantic speed so the redoubt could again be occupied.

It was October, hot for so late in the year. Billy worked without a shirt, his braces hanging down over the hips of sweat-soaked trousers. The wound in his calf had healed cleanly and no longer impaired movement. The bullet's point of entry sometimes ached late in the night, but that was the worst of it.

Billy's laborers were the men of a colored infantry platoon, the same kind of work force he had supervised frequently in the past weeks. The platoon lieutenant and a corporal stationed themselves on a restored section of the parapet to keep watch, a customary procedure.

Not that much was visible. Billy could barely discern the abatis line in front of the redoubt and could see nothing at all of the rebel works, which here ran parallel to those of the Union, with only a couple of hundred yards separating them. Occasionally a match flared on the other side, or someone spoke. The Yankee and rebel pickets talked to one another a lot. They had lately worked out a protocol that helped each side. Neither would open fire unless an advance was about to start. Advances were infrequent, so for much of the time the pickets—and crews like Billy's —were spared anxiety about stray bullets. Unless, of course, they were fired by some hothead, always a possibility—as was a sudden rain of larger projectiles. Soldiers on the front were seldom warned of an artillery bombardment.

The Negro in direct charge of Billy's men was a heavy, placid-looking sergeant. Named Sebastian, he had skin as light as coffee with milk in it, a huge hooked nose, and slightly slanted eyes that didn't fit with the rest of his features. He drove himself hard and expected similiar effort from the rest of the platoon. As he and Billy sweated to raise heavy half-timbers into place, Billy grew curious about him.

After another was set in position, both stepped back. Bits of dirt stuck to Billy's wet skin. He judged the time to be two or three in the morning. He was so tired he wanted to fall down on the spot. He took several deep breaths, then asked, "Where are you from, Sergeant Sebastian?"

"Now or a long time ago?"

"Whichever you want."

"I live in Albany, New York, but way back, my granddaddy ran away from a South Carolina farm where he was the only slave. Granddaddy was what they call a brass ankle. Little bit of white, little bit of black, little bit of Yamasee red all mixed together."

"You mean red as in Indian?" It helped explain the contrasting features.

"Uh-huh. Granddaddy's name was the same as mine. He—"

A scarlet burst in the sky over Petersburg curtailed the conversation. Out by the abatis line, the pickets cursed the sound of the shell whining in. Billy shouted a superfluous command for the men to fall to the ground. Most were already down when he landed on his chest, seconds before the shell made a direct hit on the half-restored parapet.

Billy covered the back of his head with both arms. In the downpour of dirt and splintered wood, he heard someone yell, "Sergeant Sebastian? Lieutenant Buck's hurt or kilt."

Buck was the platoon officer on lookout. Sebastian wasted no time, scrambling up as other guns opened fire in the distant batteries. "I'm going out to get him."

"But it isn't safe while the bombardment—"

"Hell with what's safe. You heard Larkin. Buck's hurt or killed."

Crouched over, Sebastian began to run along the face of the

redoubt, shouting over his shoulder, "Rest of you men back to the rifle pit."

Billy had voiced his objection out of prudence, not cowardice, but he knew Sebastian thought otherwise. He leaped up and raced after the sergeant.

As he ran, some Union picket, spooked by the shelling, fired a round. "Hey, damn you, Billy Yank, what you doin'?" an unseen reb called angrily. The last three words were barely audible as Confederate sharpshooters showed what they thought about the truce violation.

Balls buzzed and thunked into the redoubt inches above Billy; he was on all fours, crawling. Another shell landed six feet behind him, hurling wood and clods of dirt in all directions. Some pelted Billy. Ahead of him, Sebastian caught some, too; Billy heard him groan. Where there had been only heat and silence, now there were pulses of light, reverberating explosions, outcries from wounded pickets, and smoke so thick Billy choked.

"Pass him down, Larkin." Sebastian was on his feet, straining to reach to the crumbling parapet where the black officer lay. Crouching and moving forward again, Billy couldn't quite tell what was happening, but there was some difficulty. He heard Sebastian grunting.

Billy called, "Can you reach him, Sergeant?"

"No."

"I can't hear you. Have you got him?"

"I said no," Sebastian yelled, causing some marksman on the other side to aim for the sound and shoot. Sebastian jerked and exclaimed softly, clawing the dirt of the redoubt's unrepaired face. A shell landed fifty yards to the east. Men in the rifle pits took the burst, started screaming. In the glare, Billy saw Sebastian on his knees, blood running from his shoulder.

Sebastian hooked his fingers into the dirt in front of him. Pain contorting his face, he pulled himself back to a standing position. A bullet nicked a timber on the ground; the splinter hit Billy's neck like a flying nail.

Dry-mouthed with fear, he stepped up beside the sergeant. "Corporal Larkin?"

"Here, sir."

"Where's the lieutenant hit?"

"Chest."

"Let's try again. Lower him feet first. I know you're wounded, Sebastian. You go back right now."

"You can't carry him alone. I'm fine." He didn't sound like it.

"All right. I'll grab his boots. You're taller—you reach over my head and take him under the arms. We mustn't drop him."

"Larkin?" Sebastian gasped. "You hear that?"

"I hear," the scared soldier answered. "Here he comes."

Slowly, they maneuvered the wounded lieutenant down and into a horizontal position, then started to carry him toward the rifle pits. Billy took the lead, facing forward, holding one of Buck's boot heels in each hand. The enemy fire grew heavier. He hunched slightly, which struck him as hilariously futile in view of the number of shells and bullets landing all around. Sweat dripped off his chin. His heart beat hard; the fear persisted. He was ashamed when he thought of the sergeant carrying the wounded man along with a reb ball in his shoulder. Sebastian uttered a short, guttural sound each time he took a step.

"Here we are," Billy whispered at the timbered rim of the rifle pit. "You men down there, take the lieutenant. Gently—gently! That's it—Oh, goddamn it—" He felt Buck's upper body drop as Sebastian let go, fainting on his feet.

Other black soldiers were taking hold of the lieutenant's legs, so Billy pivoted and tried to check Sebastian's fall. But the sergeant slipped sideways, just out of reach, then tumbled into the rifle pit.

Two of Sebastian's men tried to catch him and failed. He landed hard. Billy heard the thump seconds before three more shells exploded. He jumped into the rifle pit, the impact scraping his teeth together. Tears flowed down his cheeks because of the smoke. The bombardment had become steady and thunderous.

He picked one of the black soldiers. "Climb out to the rear and find two litter bearers. Quick, dammit!"

Half the effort was wasted. Surgeons successfully extracted a Minié ball from Lieutenant Buck's chest and patched him up, but Sebastian died at daybreak while the smoke from the final rounds of the bombardment drifted away above the fortifications. Corporal Larkin had stayed flattened on the ledge during the shelling and returned without a scratch.

In his journal that afternoon, Billy put down some thoughts prompted by the sergeant's death.

*The colored troops faced peril as bravely as any white men I
have led. During the bombardment—so senseless in a way,
and so typical of what this war has become—Sebastian exhibited immaculate courage. How wrong I have been to judge
soldiers of his race my inferiors. It does no good to explain that
my opinions and behavior have been the same as those of most
in this army. It is possible, I suppose, for great numbers of
people to be wrong about something—for error to be epidemic.
The death of the "brass ankle" has plunged me into a fury of
doubt about all I previously believed.*

The supply train chugged southwestward. George rode in the
open on a flatcar, huddled in his overcoat. It was a gray Saturday;
Monday would be the first of November. There was a smell of
snow in the air, a sinister look to the barren trees, a sense that the
siege would settle back into lulling quiet after last Thursday's
failed advance. A thrust on the left, its objective the interdiction
of the Southside Railroad, had been repulsed by Heth, Mahone,
and some of Wade Hampton's horse. Hampton had been promoted to full command of the rebel cavalry in August. Was
Charles still scouting for him? Was Orry still in Richmond?

Memories of the fire, of the burned bodies that night in April of
'61 came back again; they were with him often. Another house
had risen to replace the one destroyed, but the new one bore little
resemblance to the old. The war had been long and devastating.
When it was over, could past relationships be restored? Did they
even exist any more? He was not confident.

Among the change rattling in his pocket were some of the new
two-cent pieces authorized by Chase before his resignation and
minted for the first time this year. Each bronze piece bore the
words *In God We Trust,* a motto which had never before appeared
on American coinage. George wondered whether that affirmation
was also an unvoiced cry against the dark times; a declaration of
lack of faith in human ability to find a way through the war's
maze of misery and cupidity and blind chance. In God We Trust
—but not in generals, contractors, even Presidents.

Nevertheless, it did appear that Lincoln would win a second
term. The Republican radicals had decided a splinter candidate
couldn't win and had patched together a sullen truce with the
President. Sherman's capture of Atlanta and Phil Sheridan's
trouncing of Jubal Early at Cedar Creek had completely reversed

895

the political tide. October elections in Pennsylvania, Ohio, and Indiana resulted in strong National Union party majorities. George had voted in camp and, according to the note that had at last arranged a reunion between the brothers, so had Billy. Both cast their ballots for Lincoln and Johnson.

With other states yet to vote, governmental departments, particularly Stanley's, were doing everything possible to influence the outcome. George noticed that officers known to support McClellan were slow to receive promotions to which they were entitled. Each day steamers left City Point packed with men conveniently furloughed home to districts where a Republican victory might be in doubt. George hoped for that victory and believed in the need for it, but he disliked the less than pristine methods being used to achieve it. He had visions of Stanley gleefully inking *Dem.* on promotion authorization and flinging each so labeled into a crackling fireplace.

A few white flakes flurried around George as an artillery colonel clambered aboard to share the edge of the car. They struck up a conversation and were soon discussing a notorious farmer from Dinwiddie County who called himself the Deacon and led a band of mounted partisans—the kind of band the rebel Congress publicly disavowed and secretly praised. The preceding week, Deacon Follywell's men had captured three Union pickets near the left of the siege line and hanged them.

"When we catch them, they should get the same treatment," the colonel declared. His tone left no room for dissent.

The train rounded a curve; shell-blasted trees fell behind, replaced by a vista of a crowded campsite. On frozen ground, among white tents, black infantry drilled, marching to the rear, then to the oblique, while George and his sullen companion rode by.

"Look at that spectacle," the colonel said. "Five years ago, no decent Christian would have believed it possible."

George turned and raised his eyebrows to indicate not merely surprise but disapproval. The colonel mistook it for interest and began proselytizing.

"Any intelligent man knows why it's happened—why the stability and moral fiber of this army and this nation are being undermined." The colonel leaned forward. "It's a conspiracy led by the worst elements of society."

"Oh?" George said above the whistling wind. "Which elements are those?"

"Use your head, man. It's obvious." He ticked them off on gauntleted fingers. "The crackpot editors. The free-love philosophers and perverts from New England. The greenhorn immigrants flooding our shores, and the Jewish usurers who are already here. The radical politicians. The New York banking interests. They're all in it."

"You mean the New York bankers consider Southern field hands to be potential customers? Fancy that."

The colonel was too intense to catch the straight-faced mockery. "They've plotted together to render the white man subservient to the nigger. Well, I tell you what the result will be. Blood in the streets. More blood than has ever been shed in this war, because white people will not permit themselves to be enslaved."

"Is that right?" George said, observing the crossing at the Jerusalem Plank Road coming up ahead. "I thought slavery was ending, not beginning. I do appreciate the enlightenment, sir."

"By God, you're laughing at me. What's your name, Major?"

"Harriet Beecher Stowe," George said, and dropped off the car.

The snow was thickening. He tramped toward the camp of the Battalion of Engineers in low spirits.

The camp rang with the noise of axes. The sudden cold weather had speeded the start of hutting. Three parallel streets had been staked out, and about a dozen timber cottages, no two alike, were already partly finished.

A headquarters orderly said Billy could be found in a work shed at the edge of camp. Welcome heat bathed George as he stepped into the gloomy building where a group of men crouched around a fire burning in a shallow pit in the dirt floor. With a stick or tongs, each man held a tin can near the flames.

Billy saw his brother, grinned and waved, then passed his tongs to the man beside him. As Billy hurried toward him, George thought, Lord, how thin and wan he is. Do I look that terrible? I suppose I do.

The brothers embraced, a hug and several slaps of the back. Billy's grin was huge. "How are you? I couldn't sleep last night thinking you'd be here today."

"Should have paid a visit weeks ago, but the rail line takes a lot

897

of damage, so it always needs repair. Tell me, what in God's name is going on at that fire?"

"We're melting out the solder in the cans before we flatten them into sheets. From the sheets we build stoves. One of the boys in the battalion dreamed up the idea. Got to keep warm somehow. Looks like we'll be in Petersburg all winter. But come along to the mess. We'll find some coffee, and you can give me all the news."

The flurries had stopped, the clouds were breaking. Shafts of sun formed light pools on the bleak landscape. Seated at a grimy trestle table in a cold building made of unpainted lumber, George expressed shock at the sight of Billy's scarred left hand.

"A permanent souvenir of Libby," Billy said with a curious smile. "I have several."

After he described some of his prison experiences, the escape, and his wounding, they fell to discussing other topics: the South's virtually certain defeat, Sherman's brilliant triumphs, the whereabouts of all the members of the family except Virgilia. Then came a chance mention of the barrels of chicken and turkey meat promised for the last Thursday in the month; last year, a presidential proclamation had declared Thanksgiving a national holiday.

"I suppose we have a lot to be thankful for," Billy said. "I could have died in prison. Probably would have except for Charles."

"Any idea where he is?"

Billy shook his head. "Wade Hampton's been in some hot engagements around here, though."

"I gather the cattle raid is still a cause of some embarrassment."

"Some? Try monumental." In September, Texas Tom Rosser and four thousand riders had undertaken an adventure worthy of Stuart. Completely encircling the Union rear, they had rustled twenty-five hundred head of beef cattle from an abatis corral at Coggins Point, on the James, then driven the herd back to the hungry defenders of Petersburg—taking three hundred prisoners along at the same time.

"Some found the whole business pretty funny," Billy said. "Old Jeb's ghost tweaking Grant's nose—that kind of thing. It didn't amuse me much. I can't find humor in this war any more. Nor much enthusiasm for soldiering, either. If I ever get home, I'm not sure I want to come back to the army."

"The last time I saw Herman Haupt, he talked about the West. He predicts a boom in rail construction out there after the war. The idea of a transcontinental line will undoubtedly be revived. He said there would be great opportunities for capable engineers."

"Something to think about." Billy nodded. "Provided we ever get Bob Lee to surrender."

"The siege surely does drag on," George agreed. "It's grim. They say the rebs are starving. Eating a handful of corn once a day, if that. I know they fired the first shot. I know they have to be whipped till they quit. But you're right: knowing you're part of something like that sours you after a while. I wanted duty on the lines. Helping run the military railroads is good, satisfying work. My black crews are fine. But I have days when I'm as low as I've ever been in my whole life."

Billy stared into his empty tin cup, held between hands that looked raw and red; the left one was the ugliest. "So do I. When that happens, I think about a conversation you and I had on the hill behind Belvedere. You talked about some things Mother once said to you. How she believed our family was like the laurel—"

"Hardy. I remember. I hope it's still true."

"Sometimes I wonder, George. So much has changed. Colored men in uniform. Railroads flying up and down the countryside carrying whole regiments. Dead men piled up like kindling—something no one ever expected. I wonder if any of the old things can survive. Including friendship with the Mains—excepting the one I married, of course."

George scratched the stubble on his chin. He had the same fears. Exhaustion sharpened them, exhaustion and depression brought on by the misjudgment and malingering that were as bad in the field as in Washington. By the endless counting of bodies. By the common agreement that the war would probably continue into next year.

Still, he was the older brother, and for some damn reason it was ordained that older brothers were always supposed to be wise and strong. Though he felt his effort was probably transparent and ludicrous, he tried.

"I ask myself the same question when I'm feeling down. My answer has to be yes, or I couldn't keep going. The verities will outlast all the changes—and help winnow the worthless ones. That's the meaning of the laurel, I think. Friendship—the love of our wives and our families and people we cherish, like the Mains

899

—that's more permanent than anything else. That endures and helps us do the same. Otherwise, I'm not sure we could. We'll come through, don't worry."

Billy lifted the tin cup, tilted it to drain the last of the cold coffee. In his brother's eyes George detected a sad skepticism. Billy didn't believe what he had just said.

Well, he didn't, either. He had seen too much of Washington and Petersburg. He had heard the fire bells in April, long ago.

117

The scratch of her pen and the pound of the sea—those were the only sounds in the cramped and wretched stateroom.

Ashton bent over the account book on the tiny table she had pushed against the wall beneath the single flickering lamp. Wearing a loose silk shirt and stained trousers, Huntoon lay in the lower berth, watching her with resentment. During the entire first day after leaving Hamilton, Bermuda, he had puked into a bucket at least every half hour. The second day, he was able to reach the rail, but the earlier stench still tainted the cabin. One more grievance she bore against him.

Ashton weighed nine pounds less than she had on the disastrous night Orry aborted the assassination plot and sent them flying out of Richmond in a closed carriage. She yearned for an opportunity to repay her brother for his ruinous meddling. But at the moment she had more important goals. Surviving. Reaching Montreal, then the Southwest. Restoring her beauty; the way she looked now was loathsome.

Most compelling of all was the need to be with Powell again.

Huntoon sharpened the need because of his constant snuffling and tossing in the berth.

Cresting waves struck and shook the steamer. She was Canadian, the *Royal Albert,* and was presently running as close to the American coastline as she dared, being a neutral. It was the evening of election day in the North. More pertinently, as Ashton's occasionally queasy stomach reminded her, it was November. November meant the onset of this kind of rough sea in the North Atlantic.

From the bunk, Huntoon bleated, "What time is it?"

Writing numbers, Ashton said, "Look at your watch."

He made a pathetic sound to tell her of the suffering induced by the effort. "Almost eleven. Won't you put out the lamp?"

"Not until I'm finished."

"What are you doing?"

"Reckoning our compound interest." The Nassau bank in which, at her insistence, all the *Water Witch* profits had been deposited, wouldn't know where to send quarterly reports until Powell established the new government. In Hamilton, Ashton had been able to cash a draft on the bank, just enough money for minimum traveling expenses. The rest remained safe in their account, in sterling. Sometimes she shuddered, remembering how close she had come to putting it all in a Charleston bank.

Quickly, she toted up the figures and swung around, flourishing a little book at him. "Nearly a quarter of a million dollars, as closely as I can compute it. That's something to compensate us for this misery."

Huntoon's round spectacles misted; he was sweating. "Lamar may ask for some of that money."

"Oh, no." She shut the book and tucked it in her bulging reticule. "He doesn't get the loan of a penny until the new government is in place, and perhaps not even then. In this venture, he hazards the gold from his mine—we hazard ourselves."

"I'd sooner surrender that bank account than our lives," he countered in what she considered a sniveling way. "But if you look at matters honestly, Powell has placed more than his gold at risk. I mean, he faces the same physical dangers we do—"

"He should. It's his scheme."

Ashton loved Powell, but she saw no contradiction of that in her reply to her husband. One plot had foundered; a second might also. Curiously, failure hadn't embittered her lover, even though

901

he had been forced to hide in that filthy attic for weeks, then flee down to Wilmington by himself after he returned to Richmond and found the farm in the hands of the provost's men.

At Ashton's insistence, Huntoon left a sealed letter at one of Powell's drinking haunts. Thus he learned more of what had happened and where the Huntoons were bound. From Wilmington, he had continued on to Nassau before rejoining them in Hamilton. Discovery, hasty flight, fear of pursuit—those had perversely strengthened his determination. It helped convince Ashton that although the possibility of failure was always present, Powell would succeed this time. He would bring the new nation into being.

The need for it was more desperate than ever; that had become clear in the weeks since their flight from Richmond. Lee was stalemated, Sherman was driving to the sea, the old Confederacy was going down. In Nassau, Powell said, some Southerners had begged him to join rebel agents already in Toronto, headquarters for new schemes to throw the North into turmoil, foil Lincoln's election and pave the way for peace negotiations. One plan Powell heard about involved Illinois Copperheads who were supposed to overwhelm Camp Douglas and free great numbers of Confederate prisoners. Another, even more witless in his estimation, called for burning every major hotel in New York City.

"King Jeff is trying eleventh-hour ploys to save the regime he's already destroyed. I'll not help such a mad and desperate man. That's what I told the people in Nassau, and when they didn't like it, I told them to go to hell."

Those were Powell's remarks at luncheon yesterday. Huntoon was in his bunk at the time. To sit opposite her lover and be unable to do so much as clasp his hand frustrated Ashton. They hadn't enjoyed a moment of privacy since leaving Hamilton. Always, there were crewmen close by or passengers. The steamer was carrying several Canadian business travelers and three couples returning from an autumn holiday in the tropics. In the dining saloon, Powell haughtily refused to speak to any of them.

Ashton rose, smoothing her skirt and catching a flash of her image in a small, cracked glass on the wall. The sight was sickening. Her hair was dull, her arms bony, her bosom shrinking. She clung to an imagined future in which she would be attractive again, sharing Powell's bed in the presidential mansion.

From time to time she pressed him for specifics about the new state. Where would he create it? On how much land? How many settlers did he expect, and how many armed men to defend them? He claimed to have all the answers but preferred to keep them to himself—an additional reason Ashton would give him her body but not her money. Not just yet.

"Ohhh." Huntoon clutched his middle. "I think I'm going to die."

I wish you would. She stamped her foot. "I know I'll go insane if you don't stop your childish complaining."

"But I feel so terrible—"

"Believe me, you've made that clear. Whine, whine, whine! You hated the hotel in Wilmington, even after we were lucky enough to get there without being caught and arrested. You complained about the seediness of the man who sold us forged passports for three times what they're worth. You didn't want to sail to Bermuda on a fishing boat, even though there was no other vessel to take us. You hate this steamer, Canadians, the sea—What would make you happy?"

He dragged his legs over the side of the berth and pulled off his glasses. His eyes looked wet and weak. Like a boy's. She could have sunk through the deck when he answered: "To go back to South Carolina—to be done with this business. I've thought it over, endlessly. I can't stand the strain. The possibility of danger, death. It's tearing my nerves to pieces."

"Do you think our poor Southern boys on the battlefield feel any differently? You enlisted when there was glory in the air, but now you want to desert. Well, you can't." He cringed away from the denunciation. "There *will* be a new Confederacy, and we are going to be important in it. Very important."

"Ashton, I just don't know if I have the courage—"

"Yes, you do." She clawed hold of both shoulders and shook him, fairly spitting. "By God, you do or you're no husband of mine. Now go to sleep. I want some air."

She snatched a cape, blew out the lamp, slammed the flimsy slatted door behind her. Hurrying away, she cursed foully when she heard him crying.

Her rage didn't abate as she struggled up the steeply tilting stair to the main deck. Only one passenger was in the saloon, a bald man sleeping with a month-old *London Times* tented on his paunch. Treading softly, Ashton reached the outside door and leaned against the weight of the wind to push it open.

The spill of light revealed Powell at the rail. His hair, much more gray than brown now, tossed in the wild gusts. He had run out of his favorite dye pomade; he had searched the apothecary shops in Nassau, but they had none.

"You shouldn't be out here in this terrible weather, Ashton. Beware the deck—it's wet and slip—"

The warning ended as the *Royal Albert* rolled sharply to port. Ashton's heels flew out from under her. She shrieked, tumbling toward the rail. Only Powell's body, with which she collided painfully, kept her from being flung overboard.

She leaned against him, queasy and terrified by the enormous white-topped waves visible in the glow from the ship's portholes. As a degree of calm returned, the physical contact suddenly aroused her. She pushed her breasts against Powell's sleeve, crushed them, almost to the point of pain. She didn't see him smile when he pulled her head down on his shoulder.

They were motionless a moment, then abruptly separated. A seaman in rubber foul-weather gear rushed by, reiterating the danger of being on deck in a heavy sea.

"I need air; I'll be careful," Ashton called to the disappearing figure. She was; she clutched the varnished rail with both hands. "I do need air," she said to Powell, "but more than that, I need some relief from James. He's driving me insane with his complaining. I can't stand this, I can't stand that—" Her high-pitched voice mimicked him cruelly. "But I'm the one who's breaking, Lamar. I can't come to your stateroom alone. I can't kiss you or even touch you." Half ill and overcome with love, she reached down and closed her hand on him. "This is what I want. Using nothing else, you chained me up as completely as some nigger plantation girl. You made me lose sleep—respectability—my sanity sometimes—just wanting this. You made me a slave to it, and then you took it away."

The whispered tirade delighted him. She lowered her head, realizing what she had done. She let go. He patted her arm in a way that was almost avuncular.

"I took it away, as you so delightfully put it, out of necessity. What's upset you?"

"Wanting *you!*"

"Nothing else? Has James forced himself on you?"

904

"Do you think I'd allow that?" An unsteady laugh. "But, my God—you don't know how resisting him has taxed my capacity for lying. I've gone through the unmentionable monthly complaint, nerves, headaches, the vapors—an encyclopedia of excuses. Can you imagine how happy I was when he got seasick? For a while I even found the smell of the bucket tolerable. Doesn't that tell you how desperate I am?"

"Patience," he murmured, stroking her arm although the seaman was returning. "Patience."

"I don't have any left!" She was almost in her husband's state, ready to cry.

When the crewman was gone, he said, "Patience is vital. We need James awhile longer. Israel Quincy is gone and that Bellingham fellow—he was peculiar, but he had the makings of a splendid aide-de-camp. I need at least one man to go with me to Virginia City and help transport the gold from the mine." They had already argued violently about his plan for Ashton to travel separately to the destination in the Southwest he had not yet revealed. "There are some rough fellows I can enlist in Nevada, but none's as loyal, dependable—or pliable—as your husband."

She started to speak, started to tell him Huntoon's dependability was questionable, his loyalty all but gone. She decided against it. Things were bad enough.

Powell interpreted her silence as agreement. The steamer rolled again; spray burst over them, soaking her hair and streaming down her cheeks. Here with him, she didn't mind. Powell flung a look each way along the deck, then bent quickly and slid his tongue between her lips.

Weak, she grasped the rail again. Seconds passed, then he drew away, smiling. "What you talked of a moment ago, sweet—what you covet—will soon be placed back where it belongs."

"I can't live without you much longer, Lamar. James is more than disgusting—" she tried to warn him then "—he's weak. Things in Richmond changed him. The arrogance of the Virginians. His loss of faith in Davis. Certainly our deteriorating relationship played a big part. In any case, he isn't the man I married or even the windbag who gasconaded bravely so long as he was safe on some lecture platform. Don't put too much faith in him."

"Ashton, my dear, I place no faith in anyone but myself. Remember how I characterized James before I revealed my plans to him? How I described his role? He's a soldier. Useful so long as he obeys orders. Should he prove himself unwilling or unable to do that—well—" He shrugged. "The greatest factor separating the general from the private is the latter's expendability."

"Expendability? You mean you'd—?"

He smiled. "Without a qualm."

"Oh, God, I love you, Lamar." She gripped his arm and leaned her damp cheek against his lapel. That was the moment the purser chose to thrust his knobby head out the saloon door.

"Really, sir—madam—you are taking grave and unnecessary risks by remaining on deck in this weather. I saw you through the porthole. Since I am responsible for the welfare of passengers on this voyage, I really must insist you come inside."

Powell gave the stuffy little man a disdainful look, murmured a good night to Ashton, and sauntered away down the glistening deck without touching anything for support. Tired, wet, but filled with renewed confidence, Ashton went into the saloon.

A few days later, Cooper returned from Charleston along the river road, riding an old nag borrowed from a neighbor. Though he detested firearms, he had traveled with a loaded pocket pistol because Judith insisted.

His overnight visit to the besieged city could hardly be called a success. All he had been able to buy were two badly used Hawkens, twenty years old and caked with rust. Of the .50-caliber ammunition for the muzzle loaders, there was none. But he had found a mold and some bar lead, all of which would be coming up the Ashley on next week's steamer. Powder couldn't be had anywhere; they must make do with the small supply left at Mont Royal.

The afternoon was showery, the natural tunnel through the live oaks darker than usual. The closer Cooper and the plodding horse got to the plantation, the louder and more frequent became the cries of the salt crows. He had never known them to be so numerous this far upriver, but when he peered into the brush or the treetops, he couldn't see a single one. To his left, away from the Ashley, scarcely anything was visible.

In Charleston, he had also searched for little presents for his wife and daughter. Marie-Louise was stricken with girlish grief now that Lucius Chickering had returned to Richmond in the wake of Cooper's resignation. The best gifts he had been able to find in the depleted shops were two crudely made sachets. He took one from his pocket and peeled back part of the brown wrapping paper. He smelled the sachet. "Damn." The scent, weak to begin with, was nearly gone. Cheap goods, profiteer's goods—

A wild burst of crow calls, seeming to surround him, nearly caused him to drop the sachet in the mud. He shoved it in his pocket and heard a disembodied voice. "Mist' Cooper?"

He snatched the pocket pistol from inside his coat. "Who's there?"

"Cain't see me, Mist' Cooper. But I can see you good."

Recognizing the voice brought shock to Cooper's face. Some distance back from the left side of the road, palmetto fronds rattled.

"Cuffey? Is that you?"

There was no denial, so he knew he was right. Unseen crows sent their raucous cries up and down the empty road. Then the voice again. Having gotten over his surprise, Cooper could hear the rage in it.

"They said you was back. Want to tell you som'pin. Bottom fence rail gonna be on top pretty soon."

"If you're a man, Cuffey, show yourself." Silence. "Cuffey?"

CuffeyCuffeyCuffeyCuffey—the shout rolled away into the gloomy distances. The horse shied; Cooper reined him sharply.

"Bottom rail's gonna be on top, and ol' top rail's gonna be broke up. Chopped up. Burned. Gone for good. You count on it—" Word by word, the unseen voice faded till nothing was left but an echo and a final rattle of the fronds.

Sweating, Cooper whirled the pistol muzzle left, then right. There was no target except a bulge-headed blue skink darting across the road in front of the spooked horse. Cooper stared at the pistol he had brandished with abandon. Revulsion on his face, he shoved it back in his pocket with such violence the lining tore.

He forced the nag to gallop up the river road. The salt crows screamed. Why did it sound so much like laughter?

118

Gray wolves slunk into the trenches of the Petersburg line that autumn. Clawed a den in the mud and turned, growling, to wait for their tormentors.

Gray wolves, they lived on burned corn but wanted most of all another drink or two of blood. Cubs of twenty, they had the eyes of predators grown aged from a hundred seasons of killing.

Colder weather bleached many of the faces. Others remained sun-red from the summer. Whether white or red, they looked mean, they looked deadly.

Toting a tin cup, blanket, cartridge box, gun, they had tramped and straggled and fought across the map of the state—plantation boys, farm boys, town boys, feared out of all proportion to their numbers. They had marched to the last rampart on the thickened skin of bare feet, in scarecrow garments, their bellies making wet complaint, their bowels noisy as pipes in a hotel. They crouched in the trenches with nothing left but their nerve and the reputation that was bigger than all of them. Bigger than five times all of them. So big it would outlast all the slogans and speeches and rallying cries they no longer remembered; outlast those who sent them here in an unjust cause; outlast their very bones.

Gray wolves, they were already passed into legend as the first snow fell. They were the Army of Northern Virginia.

The sound came from the right of the ruined plank road, gone before Orry could make sense of it. He reined in. So did the two orderlies, young and inexperienced Virginians from Montague's provisional brigade. The orderlies rode one behind the other on the same horse; because of the scarcity of mounts, doubling up was a common sight on the Petersburg lines.

The road lay east of Richmond. After fronting north of the James, the division had been shifted even farther from Petersburg, to the extreme left of the defense line. They were presently in position from Battery Dantzler, named for a fellow South Carolinian who had fallen, to Swift Creek. It was nine in the morning, Friday, the day before Christmas.

The horses, peculiarly nervous in the thick fog, snorted and refused to stand still. Orry's almost stepped into a gap left by a rotted board; there were many such on the half-demolished road. The woodlands on both sides had an evil look, all black tree trunks, leafless limbs, dark clumps of dormant brush between. The white fog muffled sound and slipped through every tiny space.

"Did you hear that?" Orry asked. His hand rested on the hilt of the Solingen sword. He and the two orderlies were returning from First Corps headquarters when the sound, loud enough to be heard above that made by the animals, brought them to a halt.

Wary eyes shifting from tree to tree, both orderlies nodded. "A holler for help, sir," one said. "Least, I think I heard the word help."

"Want us to look, sir?" asked the other.

Orry's instinct said no. They were late, held at headquarters too long, and the fog afforded perfect concealment. One man might be lying out there—or a dozen, armed for an ambush. He tried to re-create the sound in his mind. Like the orderlies, he did believe there was pain in it.

"I'll lead the way," he said.

The orderlies stepped their horse off the half-demolished planking and walked it to the side so Orry could pass. They drew their revolvers; Orry reached beneath his overcoat and drew his. He nudged his horse forward through the trees at a walk, peering left and ahead and right, then repeating the pattern.

The atmosphere of the morning depressed him. So did the prospect of Christmas without Madeline. Well, he would surely be back at Mont Royal, reunited with her, this time next year. Sherman was advancing to the ocean in Georgia. The next target of the Union Navy was certain to be Fort Fisher, and when that fell, so would the last open port. Bob Lee, stooped and gray and, it was said, atypically grumpy of late, had only sixty-five thousand hungry, worn-out men to defend a line stretching thirty-five miles from the Williamsburg Road here down to Hatcher's Run southwest of Petersburg. No one spoke seriously of winning anymore, only of holding on and ending the sad business without dishonor.

Orry drew a deep, slow breath. Strangely, eerily, the fogbound forest seemed filled with the fragrance of the sweet olive, a scent he associated with South Carolina, and going home.

A sudden whinny alarmed his mount. He controlled the animal, cocked his revolver, circled the next large tree, and saw a fallen cavalry gelding with a great bleeding tear in its side. It raised its head and thrashed its legs feebly. Orry studied the gear and the saddle. A Union horse, no doubt of that.

"Where are you?" he called into the fog.

Silence. Trees dripping moisture. The horse of the orderlies crackling the brush.

Then: "Here."

Orry again walked his mount forward. Over his shoulder he said, "The horse is done for. One of you shoot it." There was murmured acknowledgment, then the cannon-loud boom of a handgun, the echoes rolling away over the noise of the gelding's last great thrash.

Stillness again.

Passing another tree, Orry saw him, blue leg with yellow stripe stuck forward, left leg folded beneath the other to help brace him against the wet bark of the trunk.

Eyes met Orry's. They were full of pain, yet cautious, even cold. The trooper was a heavy-browed, stubble-faced young man, a tough-looking sort. His right hand was wedged near his extended right leg. His left rested on a bloodied rip at the waist of his dark blue coat. A bandage stained brown and yellow encircled his upper left arm. So far as Orry could tell, the Yank had no weapon but his sheathed saber.

"Found him," Orry said without turning. The orderlies rode up. The semiconscious Yank watched them with sullen eyes. "One of you take his sword."

The orderly riding behind dismounted and stepped forward, shifting his revolver to his left hand. The saber slid out with a steely sound. The orderly coughed. "My God, he's dirty. Pus and lice and Lord knows what else." He faced Orry. "Bad wound, Colonel. Belly wound, looks like."

"What's your name and unit, Billy Yank?" the other orderly demanded. The Yank licked his lips while Orry held up his hand.

"Time for that later."

The second orderly registered displeasure as he got down from the saddle. "Might as well shoot him, too, wouldn't you say, sir? Wounded that way, what chance has he got?"

True enough. Stomach wounds were usually mortal. It would save their hard-pressed doctors time and effort if he just put a ball through the soldier's heart and was done with it. That was more humane than leaving him to suffer, and it might be wise from another standpoint as well. Orry distrusted the look in the young trooper's eyes.

Then shame flooded in. What sort of monster was he becoming even to entertain such thoughts? Slowly, he maneuvered the uncocked revolver into the holster on his left hip, beneath the overcoat. He dismounted and took pains to stand erect, a strangely courtly figure in spite of his patched and shabby coat of gray with its pinned-up sleeve.

"We should let the surgeons determine his chances," he said to the Virginia boys. He stepped toward the wounded trooper, who displayed no gratitude, no emotion at all. Well, Orry understood how emotion could be whipped out of a man by war's fatigue and pain. His wariness changed to cool pity as he stared down at the trooper, who stared back, forced by his position to look at Orry with a great deal of white showing in his eyes.

Orry stepped backward two paces to a point between the Yank's outstretched leg and the orderlies. He turned toward the pair, pointing. "See if we can fashion some of those limbs and a saddle blanket into a litter. Then—"

He heard the sounds behind him. Saw, at the same instant, the shock and fear on one orderly's face. Orry's tall body had momentarily prevented the young men from seeing the wounded Yank, who had used the opportunity to slide a concealed Colt from under his right thigh. He aimed at the back of Orry's head and fired.

The booming shot lifted most of the top of Orry's skull. As he dropped to his knees, already dead, the cursing, screaming orderlies began pumping shots into the Yank. The bullets jerked him one way, then another, like some berserk marionette. When the shooting stopped, he leaned to the right with a peculiar, peaceful sigh and lay down as if asleep. The trembling orderlies lowered their smoking pieces as the white silence settled again.

At a few minutes before noon that day, Madeline left Belvedere to walk in the hills. There was an air of jubilation throughout the house, generated by news that had come over the telegraph wire earlier in the morning and spread through all of Lehigh Station within two hours. Three days before, General Sherman had sent an unexpected greeting to the President.

I beg to present you as a Christmas gift the city of Savannah.

Madeline couldn't share the mood of celebration. Constance in particular was sensitive to this, and restrained in her remarks about Sherman's incredible march to the sea. Yet it was easy to detect her delight. Even Brett seemed pleased by the news, though she said nothing to indicate it. All of which made Madeline more than a little resentful.

She wasn't proud of the feeling, which she tried to purge as she adjusted her shawl around her shoulders and climbed a path toward one of the rounded summits covered with laurel. The December sun lent the day a welcome warmth. The weather had been unusually mild recently, almost autumnal. She wondered why she had bothered with the shawl.

From the hilltop, she heard the first clang from a steeple. St. Margaret's-in-the-Vale, she decided. After just a few weeks, she was able to identify the different churches by their bells. She had learned a lot about the industrial town and received a warm welcome there from the Hazards and all the servants. Yet Lehigh Station remained an alien place. Study it as she would, she couldn't create the illusion that she belonged here.

One by one, the other churches began to peal their bells in celebration of the news. Head down, Madeline faced away from the hazy vista of town and factory, obsessed by a single thought: *How I wish Orry were here for Christmas.*

Suddenly, feeling something on her neck, she raised her head and turned around. She studied the sky. A wide gray mass showed in the northwest. What she had felt was the wind shifting to a different quarter. It was chilly now.

She adjusted her shawl again, grateful that she had it. The colder wind began to tug and snap the hem of her skirt. She mustn't resent the bells, but find joy in them. Every Union victory sped the day when Orry would be free to leave Richmond and rejoin her at Mont Royal. Considered that way, the bells pealed a message of hope.

The earlier resentment gone, she lingered beneath the rapidly graying sky to listen to the loud, discordant, yet strangely beautiful music from the steeples. The peace of the season slowly filled her and showed her visions of many other Christmases she would share with her beloved Orry. She was happy when she took the downward path again.

BOOK SIX

THE JUDGMENTS
OF THE LORD

> *My views are, sir, that our people are tired of war, feel themselves whipped, and will not fight. Our country is overrun.*

GENERAL JOE JOHNSTON TO JEFFERSON DAVIS, *after Appomattox*, 1865.

119

Mr. Lonzo Perdue, postal clerk and third-generation resident of Richmond, was a man beset by miseries. Scores of small signs warned that the Confederacy's death agony had begun, which meant the death agony of the city as well. Mr. Perdue wanted to rush his beloved wife and daughters away to safety. But where did safety lie with the Yankees so close? And even if he found sanctuary, how would he provide for his dear ones? The money with which the government paid him was worthless. If an officer on leave was lucky enough to find a pair of secondhand boots these days, he would buy them for fifteen hundred Confederate dollars and tip the clerk another five hundred.

It was January, the coldest in Lonzo Perdue's memory. The upper crust, a section of the social pie in which no one had ever placed Mr. Perdue, even by mistake, continued to hold parties, which the papers dutifully reported. They were called "starvation parties" now. The nobs attending drank lukewarm dandelion coffee and munched bits of James River ice served on dessert plates.

Not only were there snow flurries in the freezing air, there was despair. The brigand Sherman was loose in the Carolinas, burning, raping, and pillaging as he had done while crossing Georgia. Admiral Porter had closed on Fort Fisher with a Union flotilla and would soon force a surrender, if he hadn't already; lately the war news traveled like corn syrup left outdoors overnight.

Mr. Perdue decided this was because all the news was bad and that egotistical, half-blind bungler Davis didn't want any more of it to reach the people than was absolutely necessary. In his bureaucratic post, Mr. Perdue naturally heard rumors. The principal ones concerned the President, who was said to be madly suing for peace in secret. As well he might. The *Enquirer* scathingly asserted that, come spring, not one man in two would be left in the trenches at Petersburg.

There were harbingers of collapse everywhere. Mrs. Perdue, ever a champion of good works, divided her time between the Soup Association, whose kitchens dispensed a watery potato-flavored liquid to the starving, and a ladies' circle from St. Paul's Church that located old pieces of carpet, then sectioned and packed them for shipment to the lines. Each carpet square was intended as a blanket.

On his way to his daily job, Mr. Perdue no longer stopped to visit with acquaintances encountered on the street. His only overcoat had been donated—foolishly, he now realized—to army collection agents last fall. His only pair of woolen gloves, riddled with holes, kept him about as warm as no gloves whatever.

Of course he didn't bump into many acquaintances these days. Wounded soldiers—oh, yes, plenty of those. And roving niggers. But the decent people had deserted the streets. Mr. Perdue no longer ventured out after dark, for those hours now belonged to the sharps who ran the faro banks that were still booming and the plugugliers who made brawls and robberies commonplace and the carriages of the few speculators still enjoying champagne and foie gras—the damned traitors.

An upright and sober man all his life, Mr. Perdue had now become a suspicious and embittered one who whiffed betrayal and conspiracy everywhere. He was sick of a diet of white beans and a once-weekly portion of slightly gamy sliced turkey washed down with a tiny amount of apple brandy. He loved oysters and hadn't tasted one for a year, though he presumed King Jeff still dined on them regularly.

He hated the unseen, unknown powers who had reduced his poor wife and daughters to shabbiness. When they needed pins, they settled for slivers of palmetto. When they needed dress buttons, they dyed small bits of gourd. For his daughter Clytemnestra's eleventh birthday in December, the only present he had been able to find—and afford—angered him and broke his heart, too. It was a cheap little necklace of silvery iridescent flowers made from fish scales; price, thirty dollars.

The newspapers confirmed the approaching end in other ways.

917

Theatrical performances were advertised as sold out, the mobs enjoying a final orgiastic revel. Advertisements for runaway slaves appeared infrequently; some days, there were none. Owners knew they had little chance of recovering their property, thanks to the looming military disaster and the wicked pronouncements of the Original Gorilla.

Mr. Perdue's ears also told him the end was near. It was an unusual day or night that didn't include at least one interval of artillery fire from the defense lines to the south. The cannonading had become such a fact of life that it was worrisome if a day or a night passed without any.

On this particular morning, sunnier than most but still very cold, Mr. Perdue had left his wife in tears. For their daughter Marcelline's thirteenth birthday two days hence, Mrs. Perdue had struggled to find enough scrap satin to re-cover the girl's last pair of shoes. That would be her gift. At half past twelve last night, Mrs. Perdue had broken a needle, then broken down when she realized that her estimate of the amount of material needed was wrong. Half of one shoe could not be finished, and she couldn't buy any more satin to match.

His wife's plight was another stimulus of Mr. Perdue's anger. He looked even sourer than usual when he reached Goddin Hall, the four-story brick structure at Eleventh and Bank streets, just below Capitol Square. The first-floor post office shared the building with the Confederate patent office and various army functionaries. Mr. Perdue stuffed his three-fingered gloves in one pocket and started work next to his old post office colleague, Salvarini, the middle-aged son of a noted meat market proprietor who had lately closed his doors, refusing to butcher and sell dogs and cats.

Salvarini had already dumped two large pouches of incoming mail on the work counter, to be sorted into other crates or cloth and canvas bags lying about. There was little order in the post office anymore and no uniformity in what its employees did or how they did it.

"My wife's jaundiced color is worse," Salvarini said to his friend as they began sorting letters written on brown paper, wallpaper, newspaper—all kinds of paper. "I've got to find a doctor."

"They're all in the trenches," snapped Mr. Perdue. Hands warming at last, he began to whiz letters to the crates and bags or to various Richmond pigeonholes in front of him, with his usual dexterity. "Best thing you can do is consult a leecher."

918

"Is it safe? Are they clean?"

"I can't answer either question, but I know they're available. Read the papers. Dozens of them advertising. I did hear Mrs. Perdue remark that the one opposite the American Hotel is considered among the more reliable—here, what's this?"

He held up an envelope distinguished by the fact that it was exactly that—a genuine envelope, properly sealed with a blob of dark blue wax and addressed in a bold hand. The correspondent had identified himself in the upper corner as *J. Duncan, Esq.*

"The addresses are getting vaguer by the day," Mr. Perdue complained. "Look." He handed the envelope to Salvarini, who studied what was written on it. *Maj. Chas. Main, Hampton's Cavalry Corps, C.S.A.*

Salvarini nodded. "Also, there's no stamp."

"Yes, I saw that." Mr. Perdue scowled. "I'll bet some damn Yankee sent this by illegal courier and the courier didn't bother with a stamp when he posted it locally. I'll be hanged if I'll handle enemy mail."

Salvarini was more charitable. "Perhaps the sender's a Southerner who couldn't afford the stamp."

Lonzo Perdue, respectable husband, worried father, betrayed patriot, stared at the letter while his mouth turned downward still further. There was a distant rumbling, a whine of glass in the windows above them. Salvarini greeted the start of the bombardment with an expression bordering on relief.

"The rules are the rules," declared Mr. Perdue.

"But you don't know what this contains, Lonzo. Suppose it's important. News of some relative's death—something like that?"

"Let this Major Main learn of it some other way," his colleague retorted. With an outward snap of his hand, Mr. Perdue sailed the envelope into a wooden box already half filled with misaddressed letters, small parcels with the inking obliterated by rain or dirt—undeliverable items destined for storage and eventual destruction.

120

Charles felt increasingly alone, taking part in what was now beyond all doubt a losing fight. Even General Hampton no longer expressed confidence, though he swore to expend his last blood before he quit. The general had grown dour and, some said, revenge-crazed since his son and aide, Preston, had been killed near Hatcher's Run last October. Hampton's son Wade had received a wound in the same action.

Charles functioned—he rode and shot—yet his real self lived apart from daily events in some mental netherworld from which associates and friends departed one by one. Following his promotion, Hampton had gone up to staff, and Charles no longer saw him except from afar. Calbraith Butler and his division, after riding all night through the winter's worst sleetstorm to help drive back Gouverneur Warren's augmented Fifth Corps striking at the Weldon Railroad, were now bound for home. In South Carolina the men were to find remounts and, more important, defend the state against Sherman's horde.

All of this and January's cold wrapped Charles in the deepest depression he had ever experienced. The worst of it was a thought that marched into his mind at all hours of the day and night, as unstoppable as Grant's war machine. In leaving Gus, Charles was beginning to believe, he had made the worst mistake of his life.

His beard, white-speared, hung below the midpoint of his chest. His own smell was an offense to his nostrils; the army had run out of soap last autumn. To keep warm in the freezing weather, he used needle and thread from his preciously guarded housewife to fashion a poncho-like garment of rags and pieces of ruined uniforms. As the great robe grew longer and larger, it earned him a new nickname.

He was wearing the robe when he and Jim Pickles crouched beside a small fire one black January night. A bitter wind blew as they enjoyed their meal of the day—one handful of dried and badly burned corn.

"Gypsy?" Charles looked up. Jim groped under his filthy coat with a mittened hand. "Got some mail today."

Charles said nothing. He no longer looked for any for himself, hence never knew when deliveries were made. Jim tugged out a single soiled sheet and held it between index and middle fingers, well away from the fire.

"This was writ at home 'bout six weeks ago. My mama's dyin', if—" he cleared his throat, his breath pluming "—if she ain't gone already." A pause. He watched his friend closely to gauge the impact of what he said next.

"I'm leavin'."

The announcement wasn't unexpected. But Charles's voice was as cold as the weather when he answered it.

"That's desertion."

"So what? There's nobody else to care for the young ones after Mama's gone. Nobody but me."

Charles shook his head. "It's your duty to stay."

"Don't talk about duty when half the army's already took to the southbound roads." Jim's mouth, chapped and raw, grew thinner. "Don't give me that stuff. I know shit when I smell it."

"Makes no difference," Charles said in a strange, dead voice. "You can't go."

"Makes no difference if I stay, either." Jim flung the last of his small ration in the fire; that should have warned Charles to be careful. "We're whipped, Gypsy. Done for! Jeff Davis knows it, Bob Lee knows it, General Hampton—everybody but you."

"Still—" Charles shrugged "—you can't go." He stared. "I won't allow it."

Jim rubbed the palms of his mittens on his stubbled face. Beyond the perimeter of firelight, Sport whickered in hunger. There was no decent forage; the animals were eating wastepaper and each other's tails again.

"Say that again, Gypsy."

"Simple enough. I won't permit you to desert."

Jim jumped to his feet. No longer burly, his body appeared shrunken and frail. "You damn—"

He stopped, swallowed, regained control. Great leafless boughs above him moaned. Scattered through the chasm of the night, other little fires flickered and flared in the wind. "Back off, Charlie. Please. You're my best friend, but I swear to Jesus—you try to stop me, I'll hurt you. I'll hurt you bad."

Feeling heavy and tired as he rested on his haunches, Charles continued to stare from beneath the dirty brim of his old wool hat. Jim Pickles meant it. He really meant it. Charles had his army Colt under the robe, but he didn't reach for it. He remained motionless, the robe's hem dragging in the light snow left from the afternoon's fall.

Sadly: "Somethin's made you crazy, Charlie. You better straighten yourself out 'fore you try workin' on the rest of us."

Charles stared.

Jim curled his mittened fingers against his palms in a tense way. "So long. Take care."

The breath plume vanished as he turned and shuffled away, his step slow and deliberate. In December the sole of his right boot had worn through, requiring him to stuff papers or rags into the bottom to keep out the mud and damp. These always came loose, though, and did so again now. Bits of paper were deposited in Jim's footprints. And red spots, Charles observed. Bright red spots in each print in the new snow.

He heard Jim's horse leave. He stayed crouched by the dying fire, using the tip of his tongue to clean the gooey residue of parched corn from his sore upper gum. *Somethin's made you crazy.* The list was not hard to compile. The war. Loving Gus.

And his final, calamitous, mistake.

Two days later, Charles and five other scouts, all wearing captured Yankee uniforms, rode out once again to observe the Union left, which they reached by passing the Confederate works in front of Hatcher's Run, near the point where the White Oak and Boydton plank roads intersected. In the half-light before dawn, with new snow falling, the scouts bore southeast in a wide arc, pushing toward the Weldon rail line. Presently the snow stopped and the sky cleared. They spread out in order to cover more ground, each man on his own, out of sight of the rest.

Charles gauged his position and headed Sport left, or north-

922

ward, again, intending to scout the Union works built down to a point on Hatcher's Run. He was passing through a deserted stand of trees as the sun rose, bright and surprisingly warm despite the cloud cover. Great shafts of light descended between the thick trunks. In the silence, walking Sport forward with his shotgun resting across his thighs, Charles could almost imagine he had entered some fantastic white cathedral.

Screaming broke the illusion. The screaming of a man in agony. It reached him through thick ground haze directly ahead.

He held Sport back; the bony gelding had heard the outcry, too. Charles listened. No small-arms fire. Odd. He was sure he was near, perhaps even a bit east of, the last Union trenches on the left of the siege line. He had to discover who was doing the screaming —a second man's voice joined the first—but he must go carefully to avoid blundering into videttes.

He murmured a command. The gray started forward at a rapid walk. After about an eighth of a mile, Charles saw orange smudges in the haze. The source was further obscured by the brilliant, sharply defined shafts of sunlight. He heard piercing screams again and a loud crackling. He smelled smoke.

He edged Sport ahead more slowly, began to discern mounted men against a wash of firelight, some structure burning. But why the screams?

A little nearer, halted and partly hidden by a tree, he was able to count ten men, several in gray, the rest in butternut. He saw a white-topped wagon and six more men, in blue uniforms, standing next to it, menaced by the pistols, shotguns, and squirrel rifles of the others. One of the ten—the larger group had captured the smaller, plainly—turned his horse around in order to speak to someone. Charles saw an open officer's coat with gold frogging. Then he saw a clerical collar with geneva bands; a Protestant collar.

Something clicked. He knew of this band of local partisans.

Behind them, a partly demolished farmhouse burned brightly. Charles decided he had better make his presence known. But first he had to get out of the Union blouse and roll it up. That took a minute. He was still struggling with a sleeve when, mouth dropping open, he saw the rider in the clerical collar wave a gauntlet. Two of his men dismounted, strutted around the frightened Union soldiers, then yanked one from the group and shoved him forward at gunpoint. "Walk in there, Yank. Jus' like the other 'uns did."

The prisoner started screaming before the flames touched him. One of the partisans ran a bayonet into the back of both his legs, so that he fell facedown, engulfed by fire, whirling the smoke. His hair ignited; then the smoke hid him.

Shaken, swearing, Charles spurred Sport out of the trees, waving his shotgun. "Major Main, Hampton's Cavalry. Hold your fire!"

It was well that he shouted that last, because the partisans turned and leveled their weapons at the first sound of his coming. He reined up among the unwashed, mean-looking civilians, the kind of irregular unit whose depredations had become a scandal in the Confederacy. This bunch was led by the gaunt, graying rascal wearing the parson's collar, confiscated dress sword, and gray coat with dirty frogging.

"What in the name of hell is going on here?" Charles demanded, although the billowing smoke and the screams and a sickening smell something like that of burned meat told him.

"Colonel Follywell, sir," said the leader. "And just who are you to ask such a question of us, and so arrogantly?"

"Deacon Follywell," Charles said, suspicions confirmed. "I've heard of you. I told you who I am. Major Main. Scout for General Hampton."

"Have you the means to prove that?" Follywell shot back.

"I have my word. And this." Charles lifted his shotgun with his gloved hand. "Who are these prisoners?"

"Party of enemy engineers, according to their commanding officer." Charles didn't follow the deacon's pointing finger. "We came across them desecrating this abandoned property—"

"Taking the lumber, that's all, you murdering bastard," one of the prisoners yelled. A partisan on horseback clubbed him with the butt of a squirrel rifle. The Yank fell to his knees, clutching the spokes of a wagon wheel.

"—and so, as is our custom, we are extracting recompense for numerous Yankee atrocities, including those of the Dahlgren raid, while we fulfill, at the same time, the apostle Paul's promise to the good Christians of the church at Thessaly: 'The Lord Jesus shall be revealed from heaven with His mighty angels' "—the deacon shook a ministerial finger at Charles—" 'in flaming fire taking vengeance on them that know not God and that obey not the gospel of Our Lord Jesus Christ.' "

Charles's tightened lips showed his disgust. Deacon Follywell was indifferent. With a hint of threat in his watery brown eyes, he said, "We trust we have satisfactorily explained ourselves. We will therefore, with your kind permission, continue our work."

Again Charles smelled the vile odor from the blazing house. He would just as soon shoot a Yankee as spit on him, but if the South had to rely on this kind of defender—this kind of tactic—then her cause richly deserved to fail.

Sport raised and gently plopped his right forefoot in the snow. Charles shook his head. "You sure as hell don't have my permission, Deacon. Not to burn people alive. If Dahlgren was sent to commit atrocities in Richmond, he was killed before he had the opportunity. I'll take charge of these prisoners."

He counted on the partisans responding to commands of a regular army officer; Follywell's colonelcy was undoubtedly self-conferred. He realized his mistake when Deacon Follywell pulled his saber and shoved the point against Charles's chest.

"You try, Major, and you will be next into the flames."

Charles grew genuinely frightened then. He couldn't order or shout this band into obedience. Nor, he suspected, could he ride away from the scene easily, even if his conscience would have allowed it, which it didn't. Instantly, he saw his only means of saving the Yanks and preventing more murders. He had to form a temporary alliance.

He looked at the remaining prisoners for the first time. His stomach wrenched. The stocky, bearded officer in charge of the party was Billy Hazard.

Billy recognized him; Charles saw it in his friend's shocked eyes. But Billy was careful to give no sign.

What about the rest of the Yanks? Would they fight? Considering the alternative, he suspected they would. Could they overcome twice their number? Might—if Charles evened the odds slightly. What he contemplated was a departure from the road he had traveled since Sharpsburg, but somehow, in this weary winter, he had come to understand too late where that road led.

Only a moment had passed since the partisan leader spoke. Charles lowered his head and returned Follywell's stare. "Don't threaten me, you ignorant farmer. I'm a duly commissioned officer of the Confederacy, and I am taking these men to—"

"Pull him out of the saddle." Follywell waved a couple of his louts. The horseman on Charles's right reached for him. Charles gave him the shotgun point-blank.

The pellets sieved the man's face; blood streamed from his eye sockets and all the other holes. Follywell roared and pulled his sword arm back for a killing thrust. He got the other shotgun barrel. The blast lifted him from his saddle with his head tilting forward over his tornaway neck.

"Billy—the bunch of you—run!"

Charles had pared the odds to eight against five. But the eight had weapons, and the prisoners were dazed, slow to react. The wagon horses stamped and whinnied as a partisan turned his roan toward Charles, who was hurriedly dragging his Colt from the holster. Two of the Yanks leaped on another partisan while the one near Charles kneed his mount to steady it, raised his left forearm, and laid the muzzle of his revolver across it, all within seconds.

Shouts, oaths, struggle erupted just as the partisan fired. Charles would have been hit but for the stupidity of another of Follywell's men, who rode up from the rear and smacked Charles's head with the barrel of his long squirrel gun.

Knocked sideways, Charles started to slip off the left side of his saddle. He kicked his right boot free of the stirrup. The partisan with the squirrel gun coughed hard; the shot fired by the other man had gone in and out of his right shoulder.

The snowy landscape and towering fire tilted. Falling backward, Charles tried to free his left boot and couldn't. He felt a sharp twist in his thigh as his shoulder and the back of his head thumped the ground. He shot upward at the first partisan, missing. Sport was stamping and shying, feeling the unnatural drag on the left stirrup.

The rest happened swiftly, yet to Charles each action seemed harrowingly slow. Another partisan, dismounted, stamped on Charles's outstretched right arm. His hand opened. He lost the revolver.

The partisan flung himself on top of Charles, left hand choking, right hand pressing a pistol muzzle against Charles's body, up high near his armpit. He braced for the shot, seeing against a backdrop of misty sun shafts the first partisan, still on horseback, still maneuvering so that he, too, could shoot.

With no warning, weight and shadow crashed in from the left, knocking away the partisan kneeling on Charles. The man's pistol discharged; someone cried out. Only then did Charles understand that Billy had come on the run and dived and bowled the partisan back, taking the bullet himself.

The partisan on horseback fired. The blast was followed by an animal's bellow. Charles screamed, *"Sport!"*

Billy, wounded, wrestled the other partisan underneath the belly of the gray gelding. Punching, thrashing, kicking dirt and snow, the men struggled until Billy turned the partisan's own gun back on him by pressuring his wrist. Billy's finger slipped over the other man's, forcing him to fire into his own stomach.

Charles stared at Sport's left shoulder where the partisan's bullet had entered. The angle of fire would carry the bullet rearward and down. Not deep, he thought. God, don't let it be deep—

He retrieved his Colt, rolling to the left again. The mounted partisan tried to shoot him but was slow. Charles clasped his revolver in both hands. Two rounds killed the partisan and sent his horse galloping away through the shafts of sunshine. The dead man hung forward over the animal's neck.

Breathing hard, Billy scrambled from underneath the gray. The other engineers were locked hand-to-hand with Follywell's men and were by no means out of danger. Charles lurched to his feet. So did Billy, whose uniform had a moist patch of brilliant red on the upper left front. Beyond his friend, Charles saw more blood; it streamed down Sport's elbow and forearm to his left knee.

"Go on—while you can." Billy's breath plumed out. For a moment he locked his teeth against pain. "That's—one less I owe you."

"The slate's clean." Reaching out quickly, Charles squeezed his friend's sleeve. "Take care of yourself."

He put his boot in the stirrup and, when Sport took his weight, felt the gray's foreleg almost buckle. He had to escape—the firing would bring nearby Union videttes—but first he had to do a little more to ensure survival of the Yankees. He shot twice; two partisans dropped, one killed, one injured. As a couple of the Union engineers took possession of fallen weapons, the remaining partisans turned their horses, abandoned their dead leader, and thundered away in the vapor rising from the warming ground.

The gelding began to trot. "Can you do it, Sport?" Charles asked in a dry, strained voice. They passed over a patch of clean snow and, looking behind, he saw the trail of bloodstains, splashes at regular intervals. He knew what the end would be and began to curse.

In the melee he had dropped his shotgun and forgotten it, he realized. Didn't matter. Nothing mattered but this beautiful brave horse that had carried him so far, so faithfully, only to be hit by chance in a meaningless little fray that wouldn't even merit a footnote in official records. "Jesus," he said, squeezing his eyelids shut till he could barely see. "Jesus, Jesus."

Sport seemed to know they had a good distance to travel to safety. He galloped with the strength and exuberance of a colt, hoofs rifling out snow and mud beneath his tail, then rat-tatting along a stretch of plank road and through a covered bridge. They turned west again, into denuded pasture. Charles heard a drumming that grew louder. There was pursuit.

Over his shoulder he saw a pair of Deacon Follywell's partisans riding down on him. One dropped his rein and fired his carbine. The bullet dug a ditch in front of Sport, who veered with the sureness of an experienced war-horse and left the ditch stained red.

The thin, cool sunshine cast pale shadows of the riders in the field, one ahead, two behind. Charles breathed almost as hard as his horse, wanting the sanctuary of some woods directly ahead yet knowing that every bit of extra exertion pumped more blood from Sport's wound. The gray's mane stood out horizontally, fringe petrified by the wind. The eye Charles could see had the wild cast of battle, pain, both.

Another shot from the pursuers. It thunked a tree as horse and rider plunged into the woods. Abruptly, an ice-covered brook loomed. A shot broke a limb three feet behind, dropping it with a crash. Charles applied spurs. Up and over the stream Sport flew, leaving a misty red ribbon in the air behind him.

Branches whipped Charles's cheeks and laid one open. He could hear the gelding's labored breathing now, sense his strength faltering. Sport couldn't jump Hatcher's Run; they had to gallop through, tossing up fans of water. A moment more, and Charles saw the Confederate works.

He waved his hat, yelled the countersign. He indicated his pursuit, and the boys behind the earthworks began pinking away. The partisans wheeled and retreated. One shook a fist, then both vanished.

Charles reined in, dismounted, wiped his bleeding cheek, and walked Sport past the end of the earthworks, bending to murmur a gratitude so profound he could scarcely find words for it. A lot of men had joshed him about treating a horse as if it were human, but Sport had acted that way these past fifteen minutes, understanding Charles was in peril, giving everything—everything—to save him if he could. He owed as much to the gray as he did to Billy.

Sport stumbled, almost fell. Charles led him into a natural semicircle of bare shrubbery, let the rein drop, and watched as the gray slowly toppled onto his right side and lay there, heaving. Pink lather covered his left side from withers to belly.

A couple of mangy pickets tiptoed up. Without looking around, Charles said, "Find me a blanket."

"Sir, they ain't no blankets out here on—"

"Find me a blanket."

Within five minutes, a piece of sewn-together carpet square was passed over his left shoulder. Charles laid it gently on Sport. The gray kept trying to raise his head, as if he wanted to see his master. Charles knelt, the wet ground soaking his knees. His hand moved up and down Sport's neck, up and down.

"Best horse in the world," he whispered. "Best horse in the world." Twenty minutes later, Sport died.

On his knees next to the gray, Charles pressed dirty palms tight against his eyes. He wanted to cry, but he was unable, as he had been ever since Sharpsburg. He remained motionless a long time. Faces of gaunt, starving boys peeked from the door of a nearby bombproof. There was no comment, no mockery of the tall man with the bleeding cheek kneeling bareheaded by the horse.

Presently Charles struggled to his feet. He put his hat back on. He felt different inside. Purged. Dead. He walked slowly to the bombproof and said to one of the starving boys, "Now I need a shovel."

"So I buried him," Charles told Fitz Lee. "Dug the pit myself, put him in, and covered him. Then I piled up a few stones for a marker. Not a very fitting memorial to the best horse I ever rode."

Fitz had heard of the loss and invited Charles to his tent for whiskey. The burly, bearded general now looked far older than his years. He gestured to the tin cup on the field desk.

"Why don't you drink that? You'll feel better."

Charles knew he wouldn't, but he took some to be courteous. It was poor stuff, scalding to the throat.

"So it was Bunk Hazard who saved you?"

A nod. "But for him, I'd be dead right this minute. I hope he's all right. Looked to me as if he was hit pretty badly."

Fitz shook his head. "You've had one blow after another lately. First your cousin—"

Frozen, Charles repeated, "Cousin?"

"Colonel Main. Pickett's Division. It happened two or three weeks ago. I assumed you knew."

Knew what?

"That he came across a wounded Yank in the woods and stopped to help him, but the Yankee had a hide-out gun."

"Is Orry—?"

"Gone. Almost instantly, according to the orderlies who were with him."

Once, at West Point, Charles had fought bare-knuckled. It was a challenge, a contest—no animosity. After twenty minutes, his opponotet, shorter but more experienced and agile, began leaping through his guard time and again to land blows. There had been a point at which every blow hurt exquisitely—and then a sudden crossing into another state in which he could still feel each one but only its weight; he was beyond his own capacity for pain.

So it was now. He stared down between his scarred boots and thought of all he owed Orry, who had seen something worth saving in a scapegrace boy. Orry had urged him to try for the Academy, had even arranged for a tutor to prepare him for the entrance examinations. Charles loved his tall, slow-spoken cousin. Madeline loved him, too. What would they do?

"Charles, I am deeply sorry to break tragic news in such a blundering way. Had I understood—"

A vague wave. "It's all right. Never mind."

After a moment Fitz asked, "Do you have any present plans?"

"I'm not going to the dead-line camp, that I can promise you. I want to get a pass, head south, and hunt for a remount."

"Doubt you'll find one in all of Virginia."

"North Carolina, then."

"There, either."

A listless shrug. "Maybe General Butler will have an extra. He's in South Carolina."

"So is Cump Sherman."

"Yes." It had no power to alarm him. Nothing did. With a sigh and a stretch of his aching bones—he was falling victim to rheumatism—he rose from the camp chair, then picked up the scrap-and-rag cloak, which by now had developed a fringe from heavy wear. He poked his head through the slit in the center and settled the garment on his shoulders. He could still smell horse on it. He wished that tears were not mysteriously locked up inside him.

"Thank you for the drink, Fitz. You be careful now that we're so close to winding things up."

Fitz didn't care for the admission of defeat implicit in the remark. Annoyance flickered in his eyes. But he checked it, shaking Charles's hand and saying, "Again, my most sincere condolences about your cousin. I'm also sorry you lost the gray."

"I'm sorry I lost them both for nothing."

"For nothing? How can you say—?"

Without rancor, Charles interrupted, "Please don't use that superior-officer tone with me, Fitz. We fought for nothing. We lost family, friends—hundreds of thousands of good men—for what? We never had a chance. The best men in Dixie said so, but no one listened. It's a pity."

The friend insisted on being the general. "That may be true. But it remains every Southerner's sacred duty—"

"Come on, Fitz. There's nothing sacred about killing someone. Have you taken a close look at a dead body lately? Or a dead horse? It's goddamn near blasphemy, that's what it is."

"Nevertheless, duty demands—"

"Don't worry, I'll do my duty. I'll do my fucking duty until your uncle or Davis or someone with sense realizes it's time to run up the surrender flag and stop the dying. But there's no way you can make me feel good or noble about it. Good evening. Sir."

Two nights later, on foot, he reached the contested Weldon Railroad line south of Petersburg. A raggedy figure with a revolver on his hip, the oilskin-wrapped light cavalry sword tucked under his arm and a piece of cigar smoldering between clenched teeth, he climbed aboard a slow-moving freight car. Shells had ripped two huge holes in the car, windows on the moonlit countryside and the bitter white stars above. He wasn't interested in scenic views. They could blow up the whole state of Virginia for all he cared. They damn near had.

Ratlike stirrings and rustlings from the head end told him there

931

were others in the southbound car. They might have passes; they might be deserters. He was indifferent.

He stood in the open door as the train chugged slowly through a way station where army signalmen waved dim lanterns at several switch points. He smoked his cigar to a stub and threw it away. Night air bathed him, cold as he felt inside.

The fringe of his rag cape fluttered. One of the boys huddled in a front corner thought he should speak to the new passenger. Then he got a look at the fellow's bearded face by the light of a waving lantern and thought again.

121

Ashton ached from sleeping in strange beds and straining to avoid contact with her husband's lardlike body beside her. How sick she was of all the dissembling—with James and with strangers who continually asked about their accents.

"Why, yes, sir—yes, madam—we are Southerners of a sort. We are Kentuckians, but of the loyal Union breed."

How galling to repeat that lie over and over, to be forced to endure the graceless remarks and cramped quarters offered by inn and hotel keepers along the route of their long, seemingly endless pilgrimage. With their forged papers, they had traveled from Montreal to Windsor and Detroit, then on to Chicago, and now, in early February, to St. Louis, where their paths would diverge. Powell and her husband would head due west on the overland stage; she was to take the twice-weekly service for Santa Fe.

On the afternoon before her departure, Powell sensed Ashton's malaise and risked inviting her for a walk on the levee while

Huntoon napped, Ashton's husband had been in a stupor all day, having consumed far too much bourbon the night before.

"I'm sorry we're forced to part for a while," Powell said. Without touching, they strolled by a gang of noisy, laughing stevedores; the black men were putting cargo aboard a river steamer. "I know the journey has been difficult."

"Vile." Ashton jutted her lower lip. "I have no words to describe how sick I am of unclean beds and cheap food."

Assuming that no one on the busy river front could identify them, Powell took her hand and slipped it around his left arm. Their squalid hotel lay two blocks behind, and Huntoon had been asleep when they left.

"I understand," Powell murmured. "And some hard days are still ahead." He reached over to caress her right hand. She wondered why that produced such an uneasy feeling.

The back of her neck itched, too. But then, she was presently passing through those few days that were womankind's monthly burden; she had learned to suffer debilitating aches and peculiar moods as part of the experience.

"Once those are behind us, we can begin to build our enclave for people of true merit. Those who believe in the only genuine aristocracy—that of money and property. No egalitarians or negrophiles need apply."

She didn't smile; nothing was amusing today. "I really don't relish going on by myself."

"You will be perfectly safe in the coach. You have emergency funds—"

"That isn't the point. It's another long, miserable trip."

He flared. "Do you think mine will be easier? To the contrary. In Virginia City, I must load two wagons with secret cargo—remaining constantly on watch for thieves all the while. Then I must bring those wagons several hundreds of miles to the New Mexico Territory, through a wilderness infested with hostile savages. If I consider the potential rewards worthy of such risk, I should think you could curb your complaints about a relatively tame ride in a stagecoach."

Pain cramped her middle abruptly; the corners of her mouth whitened. A crude plainsman swaggered by, running his eyes over her bosom. The greasy fringe of his hide shirt brushed her arm. She felt as though a leper had touched her.

And Powell was still glaring. Everything angered him lately;

he, too, must be feeling great strain. Realizing that moderated Ashton's cross feelings.

"Yes, you're right—I apologize." She lowered her head briefly to acknowledge his authority. "I just don't think you understand what a trial it's been to get in bed with James night after night and wish it were you."

A whistle sounded from a packet churning upstream in the broad river. "Never forget what I said on the *Royal Albert*. James is necessary. James is"—a pointed look—"a good soldier."

Some color appeared in her face, which had grown pale over the winter and gaunt because she had refused so much bad food. She had quite forgotten the military metaphor.

Powell's eyes brightened. Sometimes, seeing that particular glint in them, Ashton questioned whether her lover was altogether sane. Not that it mattered; a conventional mind was not an attribute of a man with epic dreams.

"I also remind you," he continued softly, "that it's a very long way from the Comstock to our destination. With miles of waterless waste to traverse, and the Indian threat, something could happen to any of the soldiers accompanying me."

She laughed then, feeling relieved, buoyant in spite of her feminine complaint. She did experience a twinge of pity for James. *Poor soldier; about to start his last campaign.* But it was brief.

Half a block away, hidden in shadow by the high wall of a mercantile building, Huntoon shook his head, reached under his spectacles with a kerchief, and vigorously wiped each eye. He then continued toward the river, following his wife and Powell until they disappeared behind a pyramid of casks.

Tears welled again. He blinked them away, dazed and angry. This was no surprise. He had suspected for more than a year and, since rejoining Powell, had caught more than one furtive glance between the lovers.

He didn't blame Lamar, whom he still advised. He blamed the bitch he had married. He had pretended to nap, then came skulking after them, because he wanted absolute proof, which he had obtained by spying. He must now write a second letter, telling her about the first one.

He faced about and walked swiftly back to the cheap hotel where they were staying. His expression was so odd—maniacal—

that two blanket-wrapped Indians seated against the wheel of a wagon watched him long after he sped by.

In the clamor before departure, Huntoon kissed Ashton's cheek, then pressed a sealed envelope into her hand. Passengers were already boarding the elegant egg-shaped Abbot-Downing coach that rested on wide, thick leather thorough braces. The manufacturers in Concord, New Hampshire, had painted it to order—lustrous dark blue—and decorated the doors with identical sentimental portraits of a beautiful girl admiring a dove on the back of her hand. Ashton cared less for aesthetics than for the availability of good seats, all of which would soon be taken. Crossly, she said, "What is this?"

"Just some—personal sentiments." His smile was limp; he avoided her eye. "If anything should happen to me, open it. But not before. You must swear you'll honor that request, Ashton."

Anything to humor the fat fool and get aboard. "Of course, darling. I swear."

She presented her cheek for a parting kiss. Huntoon buried his head on her shoulder, giving her a chance to cast a final longing look at Powell, very elegant and ebullient this morning. He twirled his stick and regarded the loving couple from a polite distance.

The coach driver poked his head into the vehicle while Ashton was engaged in her prolonged farewell. He had a big fan-shaped beard, white, and a beaded vest that looked as if it had once been rinsed in vegetable soup.

"How many of you folks rid in a Concord 'fore this?" Only one hand went up. "Wal, she's mighty comfortable, as you'll soon find out. But if you're travelin' the whole way to Santa Fe, I got to warn you that we hit some mighty twisty roads. Gits so bad some places, the horses kin eat out of the luggage boot."

Having delivered his standard joke for tourists, he tipped his hat, climbed to the box, and began separating the various reins of the four-mustang hitch.

Impatiently, Ashton pushed Huntoon away. "I must go."

"Godspeed, my love," he said, handing her into the coach. She managed to squeeze into the last place on the rear-facing front seat, leaving two laggards, a middle-aged drover in poor but clean clothes and a sleazy drummer with a sample case, to take the hard drop seats in the middle.

She examined the envelope. He had written *Ashton* on the front and closed it with three large drops of wax. He certainly did want his request honored if he sealed it that carefully. She dropped the letter in her reticule and then, despite the prospect of the rough roads, foul food, and verminous sleeping accommodations en route, began to feel quite cheerful. She suspected it wouldn't be long before circumstances required her to open the letter.

Handlers flung the last valises in the boot and lashed down the tarpaulin. The dispatcher blew a final sour call on his dented trumpet. Lamar Powell linked his arm with Huntoon's and waved with his lacquered stick.

Ashton waved back merrily. From Powell's jaunty air and confident smile, she knew she was absolutely right about the letter.

On several occasions George had reason to step down into a rifle pit or enter a bombproof. Each time the muck and stench nearly made him sick. Along the lines he frequently saw ears plugged with wadding, protection against the noise of the seige guns. He saw illness, boredom, fear all stewed together, with the dirt of Virginia sprinkled on for garnish. If the filth and squalor were this bad on the Union side, what must conditions be like on Orry's? And if this was Professor Mahan's newstyle warfare, he pitied his son's generation and those beyond.

The siege wore away men's sanity and decency. Occasionally he heard reports of acts of friendliness between those on opposing sides; some trading of coffee, tobacco, newspapers. But most of the time, only two things passed between the facing enemies: small-arms fire and vicious taunts. He was glad he had joined the Military Railroad Corps. He doubted he could have withstood a post on the line—the responsibility for ordering seventeen-year-olds to picket duty in the contested, shell-pocked strip between the rifle pits, there perhaps to die.

A morning in January found him underneath a trestle spanning a gully on the City Point line. He was surveying repairs his crew had made on one of the trusses. Well satisfied, he suddenly noticed the icicles along the edge of the trestle. They were dripping.

"So," he muttered to himself. The winter was ending. Maybe the spring would bring a surrender. He prayed that would be the case. He had come to hate the regular letters from Wotherspoon, cheerfully reporting the enormous profits Hazard's was still earning from war production. The bank was doing equally well.

Above him, mauls rapped steadily. His head started to ache. He climbed the muddy side of the gully, shielding his eyes against the sunshine till he found the man he wanted.

"Scow? I'm going over to that creek for a drink. Be right back."

"Good enough, Major," the black said to George's retreating back.

George unhooked his tin cup from his belt, using his other hand to loosen the flap of his holster. The creek, out of sight of the rail line, meandered within a few hundred yards of the Confederate salient. But it was Sunday—early—so he didn't anticipate any danger.

Patches of snow were melting and shrinking on both sides of the creek. The water rushed with a frothy, springlike sound. George thought he heard a suspicious noise in thick woods on the far side, so he waited behind a big maple for a moment or two. Seeing nothing, he moved down the bank, there squatting to dip his cup. He had it at his mouth when a man stepped from behind a tree on the other side.

George dropped the cup, spilling the water. His hand flew toward his side arm. The reb, in a kepi and torn butternut coat, swiftly raised his right hand, palm outward.

"Hold on, Billy. All I want is a drink, like you."

Holding his breath, George remained crouched with his hand near his revolver. The reb was about his age, though considerably taller, with a sickly mien enhanced by raw sores on his close-shaven white cheeks. The reb held his rifle carelessly, the barrel pointed toward the sky.

"Just a drink?" The reb nodded. "Here." George picked up his cup and tossed it across the creek. The impulse was so sudden he didn't quite understand it.

"Thank you very much." The reb walked, or, rather, limped, down to the water's edge. Shooting one more swift glance at his enemy—the reb's eyes were greenish, like a cat's, George observed—he laid his rifle on the ground. He crouched, dipped the cup, whirled it around to rinse it, threw the contents out, and refilled it to the brim. George smiled a little.

Loudly, greedily, the reb drank. The thudding mauls of the work crew seemed miles away. If this turned out to be some kind of ambush—more men lurking in the trees—George doubted he would survive it. Unexpectedly, that served to relax him. He pushed his forage cap back while trying to spot an insignia or any

937

indication of rank on the reb's uniform. He couldn't. He assumed the man was a picket.

Suddenly, flashing in the sun, the cup came sailing back. "Thank you once again, Billy." George caught the cup, dipped it, and drank. The reb stood up and fastidiously wiped his lips with one finger. "Where is your home?"

Rising, too, George hooked the cup on his belt again. "Pennsylvania."

"Oh. I was hoping it might be Indiana."

George thought he detected an accent, though it was an indefinable one, not heavily Southern. "Why's that?"

"My brother lives there. He moved from Charlottesville to a small farm outside Indianapolis eight years ago. He belongs to a volunteer infantry regiment; I do not know which one. I thought perhaps you might be acquainted with him. Hugo Hoffman, two *f*'s."

"Afraid not. The Union Army's pretty big."

Hoffman didn't respond to George's smile. "Much bigger than ours."

"It must be hard, having a brother on our side. But I know it isn't uncommon. There are cousins fighting each other—and friends. My best friend in the whole world is a colonel in your army, as a matter of fact."

"What is his name?"

"Oh, you wouldn't know him. He's in Richmond, at your War Department."

"What is his name?"

Stubborn Dutchman, George thought. "Main, as in Main Street. His first name is Orry."

"But I do know him. That is, I have heard of him." George was openmouthed. "I remember because it is not a common name. There was a Colonel Orry Main on General Pickett's staff throughout most of last fall."

George could barely speak. "Was?"

"He was ambushed and shot by a wounded man he was trying to succor—a cavalryman from your side." Resentment crept in; Hoffman's green eyes were less friendly. "The incident has been widely circulated as proof of the barbarity of General Grant's troops."

"You say he was shot. You don't mean he was—?"

"Killed? Of course he was. Why else would anyone repeat the

938

story? Well, Billy, the drink was refreshing, and I have enjoyed the conversation. I regret I am the one to inform you about your friend. I must go now. This business won't last much longer, I think. I hope I am not hurt before it stops. I hope you are not either. I am sorry about your friend." He tipped his grease-blackened kepi. "Good-bye."

George said good-bye, but so faintly the reb couldn't possibly have heard him above the bubble of the stream. He turned slowly toward the railroad. Sunshine poured over his face, blinding him. Stick, he thought. Stick.

He walked a less than straight course toward the sound of the hammering, stumbling twice. Just as the trestle came in sight, he had to turn back into the trees, where he hid and cried for five minutes, remembering his friend and the April fire.

Work on the trestle was finished before noon. In the mess where George stopped for Sunday dinner, he sat apart, not bothering to introduce himself to other officers, as he usually did. The mess was located behind one of several redoubts he had passed on his way to get this food he found he didn't want. The redoubts and adjoining trenches, packed with bored, yawning men, gave off increasingly noxious odors as the temperature climbed. He could smell the reek as he stared at his plate. It was the stench of ruin. Of a loss he could not yet accept or even believe.

Dully, he raised his head in response to faint music from the siege lines. A fife or piccolo, soon joined by a cornet, then by an improvised drum—it sounded to George like a stick on a large tin can. The melody was "Dixie's Land."

"There they go again," a captain complained to others at his table.

Out in the rifle pits, someone yelled: "Hey, Johnny, turn off that tune. Go home and beat your niggers if you have any left."

The response was a series of mocking rebel yells, more amusing than frightening today. George covered his face with both hands, then quickly dropped his hands to his lap when he realized others might be staring. They were. He didn't look at any of them straight on. He was too miserable.

"Here they come. Let the boys through with their instruments—"

That, too, came from outside, as did a general commotion. Several officers hastily finished their meals, grabbed their hats, and hurried out. He wondered why as "Dixie" continued to ring merrily over the Union lines.

Suddenly a second musical group, larger and including, from God knew where, a glockenspiel, began "John Brown's Body." Applause and cheers greeted the opening bars of the retaliation.

Singly or in groups, more and more officers left, until George was the last man seated at the stained trestle tables. Wearily, he picked up his cap and trudged outside. Both bands played at maximum volume, each trying to drown out the other. George was astonished to see soldiers in shirt sleeves on the parapets of the redoubts. Others were leaning over the forward edges of the rifle pits, enjoying the sunshine or a puff on a cob pipe or some raillery exchanged with the other side.

He walked slowly toward the stinking trenches. Looking beyond them, across the strip of scarred and trampled ground, he saw other soldiers, toy figures in gray and butternut, emerge from the fortifications; the lines were close here.

The musical conflict quickly became mere noise, one melody canceling the other. Then, abruptly, George heard men repeating a word to one another. "Hush. Hush." Someone else said, *"Listen."* Both bands fell silent.

Raising his hand over his eyes again, he tried to see the source of the sweet, piercing cornet notes. At last he did. The player was a small, dim figure on the other side—a musician of very small stature or, more likely, quite young. He had climbed to the top of a half-destroyed redoubt, his tattered shirt fluttering at the elbows, his horn flashing like an exploding star whenever the sun struck the metal at a certain angle.

George recognized the song before he heard the voices of the enemy soldiers who were climbing out of the rifle pits around the cornetist. It was the piece played and sung most frequently on both sides. Near George, an ugly top sergeant began to sing.

> " 'Mid pleasures and palaces
> Though we may roam,
> Be it ever so humble,
> There's no place like home."

A baritone joined in, a tenor added harmony. The voices swelled, on the Union side and the Confederate side, and reached out and fused to form a single, strong-throated chorus.

"A charm from the skies
Seems to hallow us there.
Which, seek through the world,
Is ne'er met with elsewhere."

Johnny Reb and Billy Yank, they sat or stood in full view of those who, at other hours and other places, were devoted to killing them. One or two Union men waved to soldiers on the other side. Here and there the waves were returned. But mostly it was just singing—austere, sober, loud as a hymn from a fervent congregation—as though both groups of Americans charged with shooting down other Americans were saying there was a deep and private place in each of them where dwelled a resistance to that awful idea. They said it with the clichéd words of a sentimental ballad—and with tears, George saw suddenly. He counted at least a dozen men weeping while they sang.

"Home, home,
Sweet, sweet home.
There's no place like home,
Oh, there's no place like home."

The voices died away and then the last held note of the cornet. George donned his cap, giving it a smart tug. He felt a little more like himself again, conscious of his responsibilities. The song had reminded him of Belvedere. Madeline. He doubted she knew of her husband's death.

He loathed the thought of being the one to send the news. But it would be greater cruelty to refrain. No message from Richmond would ever reach her in Pennsylvania. He wasn't even sure she would be informed if she were living in the South. He heard that all the amenities were breaking down on the other side. The task was his.

As he set out to rejoin his men—they had taken their meal with one of the Negro regiments—he decided he must write immediately. He would send the letter to Constance, relying on her to know the best way to approach both Madeline and Brett.

Laughing, joshing, the Union soldiers continued to sun themselves in the mild afternoon air. A shot rang out.

"Damn you, Johnny," someone shouted. "That's a rotten thing to do."

941

Scrambling, men dropped out of sight with remarkable speed. The intermission was over. The concert of the guns was ready to resume.

122

February. In the dark over Washington, a freak electrical storm boomed and blazed. The intermittent lightning lent an eerie glow to a large diamond pendant Jeannie Canary wore between her small pink-pointed breasts. She lay nude in the sweaty bed, happily playing with her new jewel.

Stanley tied the sash of his dressing gown of royal blue velvet. Then he poured from the whiskey decanter. There was only a small amount left. In plush slippers, he walked to the pantry of the five-room flat in which he had installed his mistress. He returned with a fresh bottle of sour mash and topped off his glass.

Miss Canary bounced the big stone in her palms; another lightning burst made it twinkle. "You're drinking a lot tonight, loves."

"Oil for the machinery of the mind." And defense against constant fear that all of this—the little dancer, the six million dollars that had accumulated in the profit column of Lashbrook's, his power in Republican circles—would be snatched away because he was undeserving. He took a hefty swallow, a third of the glass.

Miss Canary knew better than to be overly critical of the source of her security. She dropped the subject of drinking, substituting a familiar and, to Stanley, annoying complaint.

"I do so wish you'd let me attend Mr. Lincoln's inaugural with you."

"I've told you before, it's impossible." Isabel was returning from a long stay in Newport for the event. She had spent lavishly to convert Fairlawn into a year-round residence and had moved in without asking permission of anyone else in the family. The three brothers shared ownership of the property, but that fact was ignored when Isabel took it over last fall, just after she placed their incorrigible sons in a small Massachusetts boarding school. The school earned huge fees for catering to parents who wanted their offspring out of sight and mind. Aping their father, neither of the twins had any desire to don a uniform; resort to the school was unavoidable.

Stanley and Miss Canary had argued several times about the inaugural, which was scheduled for the first Saturday in March. To compensate for his refusal to take her, Stanley had given her the pendant—paste, but she didn't know the difference. Out of gratitude, she had an hour ago performed a certain act whose mere mention would have rendered Isabel catatonic.

Now, however, he found the girl back on the subject again, whining.

"But I have such a longing to see the President up close. I haven't, ever."

"You've missed nothing, believe me."

"You talk to him often, don't you?" Stanley nodded and drank more whiskey. He liked to maintain a slight blurring of his vision, a slight dulling of his senses, through all of the waking hours. "Is it true he doesn't bathe?"

"The statement's highly exaggerated."

Miss Canary reached down to scratch herself. "But they say women avoid him because he smells."

"Some women avoid him because he tells an occasional off-color story. It's the Western taste in humor. Farmerish," he said with a disdainful shrug. "But the chief reason he's avoided is his wife. Mary Lincoln is a jealous harpy. It prostrates her if her husband is alone with another woman for so much as five seconds."

"You don't mean alone the way we're alone?" Miss Canary giggled.

What a pathetic mind she has, he thought. Her last name suits her. "No, my dear." He slipped out of the velvet gown and began to dress. "I was referring to speaking with women at presidential levees. Public functions."

"Oh, that reminds me. Last night at the theater, I heard a

943

terrible thing about the President. I heard that some actors are planning to kidnap or kill him. They're all supposed to be Southern sympathizers, but I didn't hear any names."

Buttoning his shirt, Stanley belched softly. "My sweet, if I had a penny for every such story circulating in this town, we'd soon amass enough money for a sea voyage to Egypt."

Miss Canary sat up, the diamond bobbing in her cleavage. "Are you thinking of taking me to Egypt?"

Stanley quickly raised a hand. "Merely an example." The poor child really taxed his patience sometimes. But he always forgave her when she demonstrated her sexual precocity.

"Must you go, loves?"

"I must. I'm receiving a guest at half past nine."

"Speaking of receiving—the draft for this month's rent hasn't arrived."

"No? I'll slap the wrist of my bookkeeper. You shall have it tomorrow, first thing."

She gave him a long, deep taste of her tongue to show her appreciation. After one more stiff drink of whiskey, he donned his overcoat and slipped out the door, his last impression a vivid picture of her on her knees on the bed, left hand caressing the diamond, right-hand fingers flexing in a tiny, childlike wave.

His waiting carriage bore him through rainy streets to the large house on I Street. With Isabel gone, he spent little time there. Sometimes, alone in the emptiness, he even missed the twins. He never let that foolish sentiment best him for long, though.

Servants had the gas burning and had set out refreshments. But the guest didn't arrive until quarter to eleven.

Ben Wade flung off his wet cape. The butler retrieved it from the floor. Stanley gestured sharply. The man left, closing the door.

Wade paced to the hearth to warm himself. "Sorry I'm late. I waited until the *River Queen* returned." He rubbed his hands, clearly pleased. "Mr. Seward and our beloved leader received the Confederate commissioners at Hampton Roads, all right. However, I was told there will be no armistice."

"Still the same sticking place—?"

Wade nodded. "The question of two nations or one. The President continues to insist on unconditional acceptance of the latter. Davis continues to refuse. That means you'll have a few more months to sell footwear to the army," he concluded with a sly smile. He left the hearth, took a plate and fork, and plucked a slice of turkey breast from the silver tray. "I have one more item of news."

"I hope it's the news I've been waiting to hear."

"Not quite. I can't get you the appointment as chief of the Freedmen's Relief Bureau."

"You mean Congress won't establish the agency?"

"Oh, no. That will be done this month—next month at the latest." The bureau had been under discussion since last year, when it became clear that the Confederacy would ultimately fall. The bureau's proposed mission was the regulation of all matters affecting the millions of newly freed Negroes in the South. Everything from land distribution to resettlement. It was an avenue to immense power, but if Stanley correctly read Wade's behavior—the senator seemed more interested in food than conversation—not only was the avenue closed, but the subject as well.

This was to Stanley what the inaugural was to Miss Canary. "Ben, I've given the party a hell of a lot of money. Thousands last fall alone, just to defeat the incumbent—until it became evident that we couldn't do it. I think my contributions should at least entitle me to the answer to one question. Why can't I have the job?"

"They—ah—" Wade seemed mesmerized by a morsel of turkey on his fork.

"A straight answer, Ben."

Wade whacked the fork down on the plate. A pinhead-sized speck of Isabel's precious gilt vanished from the edge. Wade jolted Stanley with the impact of his stare. "All right. They want a man with more administrative experience. They're considering a general. Oliver Howard's high on the list."

Stanley knew what the senator was really telling him. The radical cadre, which decided every important matter these days—the men who privately bragged that they needed no assassin to render the President powerless because they had already done it—had decided he was incompetent.

Of course the word *they* was inappropriate, and both men knew it. Wade belonged to the cadre. He had cast a vote. No matter how much black ink filled the profit columns of Lashbrook's, no matter how frantically Stanley diverted himself with variety-hall dancers or how much whiskey he consumed, he could never escape the truth of what he was. It hurt. He poured another glass of sour-mash medicine.

945

"General Jake Cox is also in the running," Wade said. "God help the rebs if he gets it. You've heard what he and Sam Stout propose, haven't you?"

"I don't think so," Stanley said in a dead voice.

Trying to jolly him out of his disappointment, Wade went on. "They propose we create a sort of American Liberia from the entire state of South Carolina. This new principality, or whatever the hell you want to call it, would be colonized and ruled by the niggers—whom we, of course, would diligently encourage to move there. Something in it, I'd say," he finished, adding a chuckle, to which Stanley didn't respond.

Wade tried a more direct approach, crossing to his wealthy host and laying a companionable arm across his shoulders. "Look, Stanley. It was never guaranteed that I could obtain the post for you. I can and I will make certain you're named one of the senior assistants, if you wish. The true power will reside on that level anyway—with the men who write the policy documents and operate the bureau on a daily basis. A Christian namby-pamby like Howard will be a mere figurehead. For that reason, I'm banking on him to get the job. When he does, those of us behind the scenes will be the ones who really make the colored people dance a Republican tune on Election Day. We'll have the whole country dancing before we're through. In a year, we can change our status from minority party to the only party—*if* we give the niggers the franchise but maintain control of it."

The glitter of Wade's gaze, the quiet fervor of his words, soothed and convinced Stanley. Even lifted his spirits a little, much as alcohol did.

"All right, Ben. I'll take the highest bureau post offered to me."

"Good—splendid!" Wade started to clap his shoulder a second time, but Stanley was already in motion toward the sideboard and the decanters. "Old friend—" Wade cleared his throat "—forgive me for saying this, but I can't help noticing you're drinking a lot lately. Frankly, there's been some talk."

Stanley pushed the stopper in, turned, and raised the brimming glass. He gazed at Wade across the shimmery disk of whiskey.

"So I've heard. But if a man has money and distributes enough of it in the right places, no one listens to that kind of talk. No one wants to risk disturbing the flow of generosity. Isn't that right, Ben?"

Challenged, Wade chose to lose. He laughed. "Indeed it is," he said, and toasted Stanley with his empty glass.

As Cuffey had grown, so had his guerrilla band. It now numbered fifty-two, nearly a third of them white deserters. They inhabited two acres of heavily wooded, relatively solid ground at the edge of a salt marsh near the Ashley. They carried firearms taken from murdered whites caught on the roads, and they lived well on food and drink stolen from homes, small farms, and the rice plantations of the district.

Three times Cuffey had personally led parties that pilfered hens from Mont Royal. The plantation itself he was saving for a special day. He watched the skies for telltale smoke and regularly sent one of his white boys to Charleston to report on the situation there.

During the past year, Cuffey had discovered within himself a certain instinctive ability to lead men, whatever their color. He was assertive, foxy, and implacable because of his years in slavery. He took special delight in stuffing himself with the food of the local white people. For that reason he was always hunting for new clothes. His stomach had grown huge, his face round as a cheese wheel.

In the short, cool days of early February, he scanned the skies with increasing impatience. He knew that Sherman, the general whose style and reputation he worshiped, had passed through Beaufort and Pocataligo and was now marching northward, his ultimate destination presumed to be Columbia. Soon, Cuffey reasoned the Confederate general in Charleston would have to rush most of his troops to the defense of the capital. When he did, the whole Ashley River district would lie open, unprotected—awaiting Cuffey's pleasure.

One night in the second week of the month, he lolled by his fire, roasting a dove on a stick and recollecting the pale thrashing legs of the woman from whom he had taken pleasure an hour ago. The band had recruited two white slatterns, both over forty, and a pair of younger mulatto girls to look after that aspect of the men's needs. Cuffey was fingering himself, wondering if the wench carried vermin, when shouts arose in the dark beneath some live oaks on the far side of the encampment.

He threw the impaled dove on the ground and jumped up. "Wha's all that racket over there?"

947

"Prisoner," called a yellow-bearded Georgia boy in a gray jacket. "Caught him on the road." The Georgia boy was one of Cuffey's best, a deserter with a fine love of killing. Hands on his paunch, Cuffey watched the boy and two blacks drag a small, bald, frightened man from the shadows.

"Bring him over here, Sunshine," he ordered, with the authority he had learned to invoke through voice and gesture. Something about the stumbling captive in grimy clothing struck him as peculiar. The boy nicknamed Sunshine gave the prisoner a prod with a bayonet he carried like a knife. At that moment, Cuffey's jaw went slack.

"Lord God—Mr. Jones."

"Is it—? Why, I think—" Salem Jones could hardly believe his good fortune. "Cuffey? *Cuffey!*" He almost slobbered with glee. At another fire, half a dozen men started singing the refrain Sherman's host had chanted all the way from Savannah:

> *"Hail, Columbia, happy land—*
> *If I don't burn you, I'll be damned!"*

"Yes, sir, it's me," Cuffey replied, with a grin intended to lull his prisoner. Suddenly his hand shot out. He twisted Jones's right ear savagely. "The nigger boy you used to cuss and beat and work half to death. I'm the boss now. Boss of this whole damn bunch. I like you t'show me some respeck."

One more twist and Jones dropped to his knees, howling. The singing stopped. Jones rubbed his reddened ear; blood oozed from the lobe. Cuffey snickered, retrieved the dove on the stick, and with some difficulty, resulting from his girth, squatted to resume the cooking.

"What you doin' away down here in South Carolina, Mist' Jones? I figured you ran off to jine up with the Yankees."

"He ran away from them, too," Sunshine said, with a giggle and a queer glitter in his blue eyes. With the tip of the bayonet, he touched the dark red *D* that disfigured Jones's right cheek. "I know what this yere brand means. *D* fer deserter'."

"I heard there was a band like yours somewhere in these marshes," Jones said, gasping between almost every word. "I was hunting for it, but I never imagined I'd find you in charge."

Again Cuffey smiled. "No, sir. Bet you didn't." He rotated the bird in the fire. "Well, Mist' Jones, you cast your lot with a mighty fine group. We livin' off the fat of the land here—yes, sir, the fat of the land. Tell you somethin' else you might like to know. Soon as Gen'ral Hardee leave Charleston, we gonna have a real festivity down along the river." His smile dazzled. "Gonna visit a plantation name of Mont Royal. You 'member that place, don't you? You white son of a bitch." He whipped the stick around and touched Jones's neck with the smoking-hot dove. Jones screamed and fell over sideways.

Cuffey chuckled and put the bird back in the fire. He was jolly again. "I been savin' Mont Royal till we could pay a call an' not worry about reb sojers. Gonna be soon now. Gonna be a grand visit. Mr. Cooper's there—an' his wife an' little girl an' a stuck-up free nigger wench name Jane. I got a whole bunch of randy boys gonna like meetin' up with them. Meantime—"

Cuffey ran his tongue over his rotting upper teeth. "We got you to fool with, Mist' Jones. Ain' that right, Sunshine?"

The Georgia boy giggled again. "Sure is, boss."

Suddenly, frantically, Jones flung himself at Cuffey's legs and clasped them. Only his pleading cry kept Sunshine from running the bayonet through his back.

"Please don't hurt me. Let me join up."

"What's that? Wha'd you say?" Cuffey lumbered to his feet with the white man dragging on him.

"I hate those people, Cuffey. Hate that whole family as much as you do. I hate Cooper Main like poison. His brother disgraced me —discharged me—Look, I know I mistreated you. God, how I know that. But times have changed. Things are all turned around anymore—"

"Damn if they ain't," Cuffey agreed. "Bottom rail's on top."

"Let me join up," Jones pleaded. "I'm good with a gun. I'll follow orders, I swear. Please—let me."

Cuffey gazed at the man clutching his leg. He smiled a lazy, quizzical smile and glanced at Sunshine, who touched three fingers to his wet lips and shrugged, giggling. One of the mulatto wenches ran through the encampment, shrieking with laughter. Two men chased her; one had his pants open. Out in the marsh, a salt crow called.

"Well—" Cuffey greatly prolonged the word, tormenting his prisoner "—I might. But you gonna have to beg me some more, Mist' Jones. You gonna have to beg me a mighty lot before I say yes."

He knew he would, though. The prospect of marching on Mont Royal, razing it, obliterating it forever with the former overseer in his little army was just too fine to pass up.

123

Next morning, about ten, Charles arrived at the place where the river road intersected the moss-hung lane leading to the great house. His rag robe, infernally hot, weighed heavily on him. His little bit of cigar—the last he had—went out while he stared up the lane at the familiar roof line, the upper and lower piazzas, the thick wisteria vines climbing the chimney.

Smoke rose from the kitchen building. He saw a Negro girl leave it and hurry to the main house. A crow went swooping across in front of him, and if he had been less tired, he would have laughed. He was home.

Not in a good season, though. Evening before last, he had passed near the route of march of General Sherman's vast army and seen fire in the heavens—Kilpatrick's horse leading the way and signaling its position to the infantry in the rear, a frightened farmer told him. Little Kil's riders were advancing toward Columbia through an avenue of burning pines. It was that conflagration filling the night sky with a furnace glow and that of the day with plumes of resinous smoke.

"I heard what them boys is sayin'," the frightened farmer declared as Charles drank from his well. "They say they're gonna wipe this hellhole of secession off the earth. The say here's where treason began and here's where it's gonna end."

"I wouldn't take that lightly," Charles advised. "I'd watch

your womenfolk and expect the worst. This war's turned mean. Many thanks for the water."

It now appeared that Sherman, who had vowed to make Georgia howl, then done it, had kept on going due north, bypassing the Ashley district. Charles walked slowly up the lane with a weary wonder in his eyes; the place appeared untouched by the war. Then he began to change his mind. He saw noticeable wear on the buildings and a marked absence of slaves. How many of them had run away?

The signs increased as he drew closer. Tall weeds grew where lawn had spread before. A wagon without front wheels and axle lay abandoned near the office. He went all the way to the house, a dirty, bearded, ragged specter with a revolver on his hip, and no one opened a door or raised a window.

A few azalea bushes around the wisteria-clad chimney showed early buds; the weather had been unusually warm. He passed the chimney and continued along the half-oval of the hard-packed drive, spying a woman previously hidden by a pillar. She rose from her chair with a vague smile as he approached.

He stopped, thankful that he could soon pull off his boots and bathe his blisters. To the small, stout woman on the piazza he said politely, "Hello, Aunt Clarissa."

She frowned, studied him—especially the revolver and the wrapped sword under his arm—a few seconds more. Then she raised her palms to her cheeks and screamed in mortal fright to announce his homecoming.

That brought people all right. Two of the house servants ran out to take charge of Clarissa. How grizzled and stooped they looked, Charles thought as he waited to be recognized. It took them a minute—they were hovering around his aunt, who struggled—and during the interval he wondered whether none but the old, tired blacks had stayed.

"Charles? Charles Main?"

He tilted his hat back but couldn't manage a smile, even though he was nearly as astonished as Clairssa had been. "Yes, Judith, it's me. What are you doing here?"

"I'm dying to ask the same of you." She rushed to embrace him; felt his arms and torso stiffen at her touch. His garments were filthy. They reeked.

The two servants, one so old he hobbled, helped Clarissa inside.

951

The hobbling Negro gave Charles a curious stare but no greeting. Charles knew the man recognized him. In the old days, a stern master would have laid on the cane to punish such disrespect. Things had surely changed.

To answer Judith, he said, "I lost my horse up at Petersburg. I came all the way down here hunting a remount."

"Are the trains running?"

"Some. Mostly I walked. When I left North Carolina, I figured I'd find a horse—or a mule, anyway—before I got this far. Guessed wrong," he finished soberly, as Orry's older brother stepped onto the piazza. In shirt sleeves, a ledger under one arm, Cooper recognized Charles and let out his name with a whoop. Husband and wife shepherded the new arrival into the well-loved, well-remembered house, but Charles hardly saw it. One thought obsessed him. *Do they know about Orry?*

On the curve of the drive opposite the one where Charles had approached, motion stirred a tall, thick row of untended ileagnus. The motion suggested birds squabbling in the dense foliage. In the excitement of Charles's arrival, no one noticed.

On the other side of the shrubbery, after the front door closed, a narrow-faced young man with a smooth beige complexion crawled away through the weeds. He was barefoot, and his old jeans pants had a yellowing star on the rump. When the seat of his pants had worn through, his mother, who later died, had patched the hole with white flannel and imagination. The star was the North Star—the freedom star—and when his mama had sewn it on, he had still been property.

He had been sent to Mont Royal to estimate the number of men still present on the plantation. He had been born there and spent most of his life in the slave community. Now he had some real news to report.

Charles bathed in a big zinc tub in Cooper and Judith's bedroom—the same spacious chamber that once had belonged to Tillet and Clarissa and then, he presumed, to Orry and Madeline.

He had forgotten how it felt to have his long hair so clean it squeaked when he rubbed his palms over it. He put on a shirt and pair of pants borrowed from Cooper and went downstairs. His arrival had caused a great stir. There were nigras swarming all over the house—damn near as if they were Cooper and Judith's equals, he thought without animosity, just recognition of another remarkable change. He met a muscular, well-proportioned driver named Andy and a handsome black woman named Jane, who shook his hand in a grave way as she said, "I've heard of you."

Her steady stare, not hostile but not friendly either, conveyed meaning with perfect clarity. What it said was, *I've heard you're in the army that's fighting to keep my people shackled.*

Maybe he was being too thin-skinned, but he thought that was what she meant. Despite her attitude and her reserve, she still impressed him in a positive way.

Philemon Meek, the new and elderly overseer, shuffled in to join them for the midday meal—the most bounteous they could provide, Judith said with embarrassment. Each plate held a bit of saffroned rice, a few field peas, a one-inch square of corn bread, and two strips of chicken cooked for the second or third time.

"Don't apologize," Charles said. "Compared to the fare up North, this is a feast."

The dining room, its rich woods gleaming, was both familiar and comforting. He started eating rapidly. Meek watched him over his half-glasses, and it was from the overseer that Charles presently heard of the guerrilla band operating in the neighborhood. Runaway slaves and army deserters, they were like the bummers traveling on the fringes of Sherman's army.

"But this bunch has stayed put in the low country," Meek said. "I'm told the leader is an old chum of yours—nigra named Cuffey."

Mildly startled, Charles finished the field peas and started to wipe his mouth with the back of his hand. He noticed Marie-Louise, grown now and quite pretty, staring at him. The skin above his beard turned pink as he snatched his napkin from his lap.

"Cuffey," he repeated. "Imagine that. Think Mont Royal might be in for some trouble?"

"We've been preparing for that eventuality," Meek said.

"It appears to me you don't have many men left on the plantation. Except for your driver, those I've seen are gray as the moss outside that window."

"We're down to thirty-seven people," Cooper admitted. "Barely enough to run the place. I thought of closing the rice mill entirely for a while, but how would we survive? I don't mean just Judith

953

and Marie-Louise and Mother; I mean everyone. Especially the older nigras. They're too worn out and frightened to run away."

"Which is what the rest did, I presume?"

Cooper nodded. "Liberty's a magnet for human beings. One of the strongest in creation. That's a point I frequently made to my father, to no avail. For a while I also forgot it myself, I'm ashamed to say. Ah, well. Why rake up the past? I want to hear the news from Virginia. Have you been in Richmond at all? Seen Orry or Madeline?"

To Charles's left, Clarissa sat with her meager meal untouched. Hands folded under the table, she studied him with the eyes of a threatened child. She had been doing so ever since they sat down. Those eyes held the kind of awe and fright with which long-ago European folk must have watched the pony-mounted Mongols storm out of Asia.

The thrice-boiled chicken pieces, so flavorful a moment earlier, suddenly had the taste of chewed paper. Well, he thought as he returned Clarissa's sad, alarmed stare, there's at least one blessing in a broken mind. She won't understand.

Cooper was awaiting an answer. Slowly, Charles placed his napkin to the left of his plate.

"I didn't expect to be the bearer of the bad news."

Judith leaned forward. "Oh, dear—is one of them ill? It is Madeline?"

Silence. Memories flashed by, including one from the time when Orry had been educating him for the West Point examinations. The hired German tutor had forced Charles to read Scripture for its literary value as well as its religious content. He remembered a passage he had never fully appreciated before: the moment during the Crucifixion when Christ asked His Father to let a cup pass.

"Charles?" Cooper said, almost inaudibly.

But of course it wouldn't pass, and he told them.

On his knees, Salem Jones heard the commotion beyond the blanket hung on a length of wisteria vine to afford a little privacy. He withdrew from the grimy, drunken white woman, who rolled her head from side to side and whimpered for him to start again. He was already buttoning his pants.

Picking up his shirt, he stepped around the great live oak to which he had spiked one end of the vine. The usual evening fires sent smoke and sparks toward the winter stars. He spied Cuffey seated on the stump he liked to occupy—as if he were some damn nigger chief in Africa, Jones thought with a flash of resentment. He put the bad feeling aside in order to learn the reason for all the excitement.

Men crowded around Cuffey while two tried to talk at the same time. One was Sunshine, who had been away scouting around Charleston. The other was a light tan Negro whose name Jones didn't know.

Hurrying to the group, Jones heard Sunshine say, "Hardee marched out. I seen it. By now the troops are all gone from the city."

"There ain' but a few protectin' my old home place," Cuffey mused, smiling. "Now they's no sojers to come help, either. That's what I been waitin' on. Hey there, Jones—you hear?"

A vigorous nod. "Yes, sir."

"Well, that ain' the only good part. Lon—" he poked a thumb at the beige boy with the flannel star on his pants "—he spied an old friend at Mont Royal this mornin'. Cousin Charles."

"Invalided home from Hampton's cavalry?"

Cuffey prompted Lon with a look. The boy shook his head. "Didn't see any sign of him bein' hurt. But he was walkin', not ridin'."

Jones nodded. "That's enough to bring him home."

A meditative look spread over Cuffey's face. "Cousin Charles an' me useta be friends. Useta fish together. Wrestle, too."

He spat in the flames. Men smirked and nudged each other, sensing the end of boring inactivity. Cuffey arose and hooked his thumbs over the bulging waist of his trousers. Like a king, he paraded around the huge sparkling fire. Jones loathed the ignorant oaf, but Cuffey had spared him and allowed him to join the band in anticipation of their next big raid. He had to be grateful for that, he supposed, reaching up to scratch the itching *D*.

"We wait one more day—maybe two," Cuffey announced. "Till we sure the sojers are gone." He peered past the leaping flames at Salem Jones. "Then we go to Mont Royal an' take it clean down to the ground. Kill every living thing."

In the raw amiability of the moment, Jones rashly said, "Young Charles may give you quite a fight."

Cuffey's face drained of good humor. "I'm waitin' for that. I'm jus' waitin'. Maybe we wrestle one las' time. We do, I know who gonna lose."

124

Invalided home with a chest wound, Billy slept a good deal. He wasn't awake when Constance, ashen, brought the letter to Brett in the library.

"It's from George. Come sit down before you read it."

The news about Orry fell on Brett with the force of a sledge. Seated, she felt her whole body sag, and for a moment she labored to get her breath. Constance dropped to her knees beside the chair while Brett swallowed and made queer gulping sounds. She lifted the two sheets, gestured with them in a forlorn way, laid them down again, shaking her head.

"I don't understand. Madeline said he was still in Richmond."

"We all thought that."

Brett started to cry then, heaving sobs. Constance was startled because the manifestation of grief lasted such a short time. Less than a minute. Then a stark look came onto Brett's face. Constance saw the object of her sister-in-law's fierce stare: the prized meteorite in its place on the library table.

"Damn them. Damn their oratory and their precious rights and their generals"—Brett was up then, lunging—"and their weapons —" Constance was too slow to prevent her from snatching the meteorite, whose significance all those in the household understood. Spinning, Brett threw it like a discus at the nearest window.

It shattered glass and sailed away over the sunlit lawn. In panic, Constance thought, *He'll never forgive me if it's lost. I must go find it this minute.* She was immediately ashamed of the reaction; staying with Orry's sister was far more important.

Brett collapsed on an ottoman, the pages of the letter fluttering to the floor. She crossed her arms on her knees and bent her head, crying again. Constance barely heard the words amid the sobs.

"I'm—sorry. I'll—hunt for the star iron. I know it's—George's treasure. It's just—just that—"

Constance could make out nothing else.

What an admirable woman Billy had married, she thought half an hour later. In the face of a smiliar responsibility, would she be as strong? Brett had dried her puffy eyes, put back a few undone strands of hair, and recovered the letter, saying, "I must go up to Madeline. Is she in her sitting room?"

Constance nodded. "She wanted to read awhile. Would you like me to go with you?"

"Thank you, but I think it's best if I'm alone."

Slowly, Brett walked past the library table. After a ten-minute search, the meteorite had been found by the gardener and returned to its place on the gleaming wood. But Billy's wife, in a matter of an instant, had conceived a hatred of the object—what it meant, what it made possible—that would last until she died.

In the foyer, she reached out to grasp the freshly oiled banister, gazing upward. She fought back more tears and images of Orry. She lifted her foot to the first step.

It seemed to require hours to go up the staircase; she had never taken a longer or harder journey. At last she turned down the hall to the door of Madeline's sitting room, which was ajar. Through the opening Brett saw sunshine flooding the carpet; the room overlooked the laurel-covered hilltops behind the mansion. Her hand shook as she knocked.

"Yes, come in," Madeline called cheerily.

Go on, Brett thought. It became a silent scream. *Go on.* She wanted to run.

"Who's there?"

Underskirts rustling, Madeline walked to the door and opened it. The index finger of her other hand held her place in a slim, gold-stamped book. Her dress today was one of her favorites, a blue silk so deep and rich it almost looked black.

"Brett! Do come in. I was just rereading a few of Poe's poems. One is Orry's very favor—my dear, what's the matter?" She had been slow to note the signs that Brett had been crying. "Has Billy taken a bad turn?"

"It isn't Billy. It's Orry."

Madeline's dark eyes showed apprehension. So did her fading smile. She took her finger from the book, drew it against her breast like a shield. She saw the letter in Brett's right hand.

"Is there some problem in Richmond?"

"Orry isn't—wasn't—in Richmond." Why was she so slow to tell it? Delay would only prolong the anguish for both of them. "This is from George. I'm afraid it's very bad news."

With a forced look of skepticism, Madeline took the letter to the sunlit window bay. Brett waited near the door, noting the way Orry's wife moved the first page away from her face; her eyesight had begun to trouble her. She was turned toward the window.

She finished the first page and began the second. The initial indication of a reaction was a ripple of the dress material across her shoulders.

Her head whipped around. Angry, she said, "The Petersburg lines? How did he get to the Petersburg lines?"

"I wish I could tell you."

Madeline forced her eyes back to the letter. Watching her in profile, Brett saw the light glisten on a tear. The book dropped from Madeline's hand, striking the carpet with a soft thump. She seemed to tense and grow taller, as if straining on tiptoe for some reason.

Her hand crushed the letter. "Orry," she cried out and tumbled sideways in a spill of silk and petticoats.

"Kathleen," Brett exclaimed in the hall. "Kathleen—someone —bring the sal ammonia. Hurry!"

Voices downstairs said she had been heard. Brett turned around in the doorway, stricken by the sight of Madeline sprawled on the fine Persian rug. She was awake after the brief fainting spell, but she didn't get up. She lay on her side, awkwardly supporting herself with both hands. She trembled, her mouth half open. When she looked at Brett, there was no recognition.

The effect was overpowering. Brett was paralyzed, unable to move or help her sister-in-law for the next few moments. She couldn't even speak. Billy had been spared, but her brother was gone. The pain was unmerciful. How much worse it must be for Madeline. How would she find the strength to survive?

Or even a reason to try?

125

Charles woke at daybreak on Sunday, the nineteenth of February. He had been dreaming of Gus.

It happened often. Opening his eyes didn't relieve the melancholy of the dreams or banish her image. She was a constant presence, stealing into his thoughts at intervals every day.

Yawning, he picked up the light cavalry saber and trudged downstairs. In the kitchen building, he found a fresh pot of imitation coffee, concocted of God knew what, and not a single Negro. He drank half a cup of the stuff—all he could stomach; it tasted like wood shavings. He poured the rest out the door and hunted for a rag.

He walked back to the weathered plantation house and braced an old chair against the wall on the piazza. From there he could watch the tree-sheltered lane leading to the river road and the road itself, brightened by winter sun. He pulled the rag out of his back pocket and reached down at the end of the piazza for a pinch of sandy soil. He dropped it on the rag and moistened it with spit till its consistency suited him. He sat down in the chair, drew the Solingen sword from its scabbard, and began to polish the dulled blade.

The stillness had a quality of expectancy. It had been present since yesterday, when wild rumors swept the river district. Rumors that Columbia had been burned night before last.

About eight o'clock, traffic on the river road began to pick up, men and an occasional military wagon coming from the direction of Charleston. Some butternut boys turned in, begging for a drink. Charles agreed to direct them to the well in return for information.

"What's going on in the city?"

"A lot of it's burned down. The mayor surrendered the whole place to some damned Dutchman, General Schimmel-something, right about this time yesterday. We are all going home. The South's licked."

Could have told you that a year ago. He didn't say it. They looked miserable enough—as did Cooper, who stepped onto the piazza wearing ragged slippers and a dressing gown with a large hole in one elbow.

"What's become of Sumter?" he asked one of the ragged soldiers.

"Nothing left but a pile of rock." The boy added bitterly, "That's what the Yanks wanted more'n anything."

"I have a house on Tradd Street. Do you think it survived the fire?"

"Couldn't say, but I wouldn't count on it. Is it all right if we stop talkin' and find the well?"

After they left, Cooper went inside, shaking his head. Charles returned to his chair and kept rubbing the steel. The engraved flowers. The medallion containing the letters C. S. The legend on the other side: *To Charles Main, beloved of his family, 1861.* That was another man. From another life, not this one.

A dilapidated shay pulled in about noon. The driver was Markham Bull, a neighbor and member of the large and distinguished Bull family. Fifty-five or so, Markham was in a state. He had been in Columbia attending to the affairs of a lately deceased sister when Sherman arrived. He had barely escaped in the aftermath of Friday night's fire, which he confirmed as fact.

"Whole town's gone, just about. The damn Yankees are claiming Wade Hampton lit the first match, to destroy the cotton rather than let them get hold of it. You can't imagine the behavior of Sherman's men. By comparison, the Goths and the Vandals were courtly. They even burned Millwood."

Charles raised his eyebrows. "Hampton's Millwood?"

960

"Yes, sir. All of his family portraits—his fine library—everything."

"Where's the general now?"

"I don't know. I heard he planned to ride west of the Mississippi to continue the fight, but that may not be true."

The fighting part could be true, Charles thought as Bull climbed into his shay and rattled off. The death of his son had embittered Hampton. If beautiful old Millwood was gone as well, that would only enhance the bitterness. Charles had a dark feeling that much the same process would be taking place within a lot of people in Dixie during the next weeks and months. Whether you construed it as punishment or suffering depended on your loyalties, but either way he was damn sure there would be plenty of bad blood left after the war.

The stragglers on the road became fewer as the day wore on. Light clouds moved in, hazing the sun, then hiding it. Charles kept polishing. By four o'clock he had restored most of the blade's original brilliance. He spat into an azalea bush, stretched and sniffed the wind's marshy odor. A salt crow squawked somewhere on the river behind the house. It struck him that he had heard a lot of crows during the last hour.

Around five, Cooper reappeared, gray-faced and tense. "Charles, you'd better come inside."

In the library, he discovered Andy and a twelve-year-old Negro boy who was excited and perspiring. "This is Jarvis, Martha's son," Cooper said to his cousin, thus identifying the youth as part of the Mont Royal population. "Tell us again what you saw, Jarvis."

"I seen a bunch of white an' black men in the marsh about a mile beyond the cabins. They was comin' this way."

"How many is a bunch?" Charles asked.

"Forty. Maybe fifty. They got guns. But they was laughin' and larkin' a lot. Sure not in any hurry. One buck, he was fat as a papa coon in the summertime. He was ridin' an old mule and singin' and joshin' with everybody—"

Andy scowled. "Got to be that damn Cuffey."

"Thank you," Charles said to the boy.

Cooper repeated the words, then abruptly added, "Wait." He reached in his pocket and gave Jarvis a coin, which delighted the youngster. Charles was astonished at the persistence of old patterns, even in a man as free-thinking as Cooper. The little exchange was seen by the woman named Jane, who had appeared silently at the library door. She looked at Cooper with contempt as Jarvis ran out.

Charles felt an old tension in his middle, the kind that always preceded a scrap. At the same time, there came an unexpected buoyancy. The waiting was over.

Cooper said, "Wonder when they'll come?"

"If I were Cuffey," Charles said, "I'd wait till first thing tomorrow—when we're dog-tired from staying up all night keeping watch. Better break out those two Hawkens and anything else that can be put to lethal use."

Andy frowned, as if considering whether he dared speak his mind. He did. "Might make more sense to pack up and leave, Mr. Cooper."

"No," Cooper said in a voice so firm and calm Charles was startled a second time. "This is my home. My family built Mont Royal, and I won't see it lost without a fight."

"My sentiments, too," Charles said. A tired smile. "Not very intelligent but nevertheless my sentiments."

Jane spoke. "And are the others supposed to risk their lives to save a place where you kept them like chattels?"

"Jane," Andy began, stepping forward. She ignored him.

Cooper scowled but quickly controlled his feelings. "No one is forced to stay. Not you or any of the people."

"But most will," Andy said. "I will. There are some good things on Mont Royal."

"Oh, yes," Jane said, though the assent was canceled by her tone. Walking past Charles, she ran a finger along a row of gilt-lettered book spines, rich embossed leathers dyed green, deep maroon, royal blue. "A few. Here's one—Mr. Jefferson's *Notes on the State of Virginia*—" She faced Cooper, defiant. "He made some wise observations about slaves and slavery. If the South had heeded them, you could have saved yourselves all of this."

"You can lecture us later, Miss Jane," Charles said, overly sharp because he privately agreed with her. "Right now we must call the men together."

"And bring the women and youngsters to one safe place," Cooper added. "Andy, will you get started?"

Nodding, Andy took Jane's arm and guided her out of the library—too firmly for her taste. She reacted by pulling away. Charles could hear them arguing as they left the house.

Cooper cast a glance at the stand holding Orry's old uniform, then sank into a chair. He regarded his cousin with gloomy eyes. "We're in a bad spot, aren't we?"

"Afraid so. The numbers are against us. Best we can do is maybe try an old Plains Indian trick I learned in Texas—" Frowning, he examined the saber he had brought in from the outdoors. One of the strands of fine brass wire that wrapped the hilt was broken.

He realized Cooper was waiting for him to finish. "Kill the leader, and sometimes the rest of the war party will turn back."

Cooper pulled at his lower lip. "Sounds like a pretty faint hope to me."

"It is. Do we have another?"

"Pack and run."

"I thought you said—"

"I did. I want to save this place, and not merely for sentimental reasons. I think we'll need it for survival once there's a surrender. If we run, we can be sure they'll spare nothing."

"All right, it's settled. We stay."

"You needn't."

"What?"

"I mean it, Charles. You came here hunting a remount, not more fighting."

"Hell, Cousin, fighting's all I know how to do. The current unpleasantness has rendered me unfit for a civilized occupation."

They stared at each other, neither man smiling. Charles felt anxious, impatient. The buoyancy returned, more intense than before. There was a battle coming, all right. In the distance, a salt crow screamed and a second one answered.

126

Each time Virgilia heard a carriage on Thirteenth Street, she rushed to the front window and was disappointed. Why was Sam so late? Something wrong at home?

Once more she let the curtain fall. Outside, February dusk deepened over the Northern Liberties. Virgilia's cottage in that outlying village—not the best location, but adequate—was a tidy four-room place, freshly painted after Sam bought it for her. The small lot was enhanced by two giant oaks and a bordering fence of new white pickets.

As the mistress of a congressman, Virgilia found herself constantly experimenting with roles she couldn't have imagined herself playing even a year ago. Tonight the cottage smelled of succulent roast duckling. She had always loathed kitchen work and would never be an accomplished cook. But she was learning. Her lover liked good food and wine.

She was also dressing properly and not just occasionally. Sam liked women well-groomed everywhere but the bedroom. For this visit, she had spent forty minutes arranging her hair, perfumed herself, and put on her best burgundy bombazine over a merciless corset that minimized her waist and emphasized her breasts.

To her immense satisfaction, Virgilia had also been cast as her lover's unofficial adviser. He discussed congressional business with her and had even started to ask her advice on certain matters. On the parlor desk lay a stack of closely written sheets he had left with her last time—the draft of a speech he was to deliver to a Republican caucus a few days after the inaugural. Sam wanted to use the occasion to put distance between himself and the Chief Executive. He had asked for her opinion of what he had written.

He got no such help from his wife, nor did he want any. He would stay married to the woman, though, as he confided to Virgilia, he considered her a sexless nonentity. He suspected his wife knew about the liaison with Virgilia, but he was confident she would never make trouble. His strategy for assuring this was a simple one. He frequently hinted that her situation was precarious and that he might leave her at any moment, although neither was true.

By half past seven the duckling was overdone, and Virgilia was upset. Pacing, she whirled toward the door at the sound of a horse. She flung the door open.

"Sam? Oh, I was so worried—"

It puzzled her that he didn't immediately climb down from the covered seat of the buggy. "I had to rush Emily to the train. Her father's ill in Muncie. She took the children. She'll be away at least a week." Light from the doorway illuminated his smile. "I can stay the night if I'm invited."

"Darling, that's wonderful. Of course you are."

"Then I'll put the horse up. He's been fed. It will take me a few minutes."

While he drove around to the small outbuilding behind the cottage, she warmed the duckling, the yams and snap beans. He came tramping across the backyard, knocking dust from the sleeves of his black frock coat.

"The traffic near the depot was unbelievable. It's the same downtown. I think half the country's here for the inauguration. At Willard's this noon, my waiter said they're putting cots and mattresses in the hall for the overflow." He bussed her cheek. "If you offer tent space in the yard, you might get rich."

Laughing, she put her arms around his neck and kissed him. He liked her tongue in his mouth and elsewhere. At the end of the long embrace, she asked, "Shall we eat now or later? I'm afraid the duckling is nearly black—"

"Let's have some anyway. Then we'll have the entire evening to do whatever we please."

She gave him a warm, slightly bawdy smile before he went down to the cellar for one of the several dozen bottles of wine with which he kept the place furnished. He was expert with a waiter's corkscrew; while she prepared the serving platters, he opened and decanted the wine.

Seated, they toasted each other. As Virgilia admired him over the rim of her goblet, she reflected that in many ways she was more fortunate than a wife. The illicit nature of their relationship lent all their times together a spice surely absent from most marriages. She had experienced the same kind of wicked and defiant excitement living with a black man.

The wine was a heavy-bodied Bordeaux; superb and not cheap. After he savored a sip, he said, "Damn big fuss over the inaugural ball—have you heard?"

She shook her head. "What's wrong? It sounds grand—just ten dollars for supper and dancing at the Patent Office, the *Star* said."

"But a number of our darker brethren expressed a desire to attend. Some of the congressional wives, mine included, were nearly prostrated by the news. Emily raved for an hour about the possibility of being asked to waltz by Fred Douglass or some other baboon. The ball committee had to rush out a statement of reassurance. The phrasing was polite, but the message was clear. No ticket sales to niggers."

"I find that disgraceful."

"Don't confuse liberty with equality, Virgilia. The former's all right. It's a tool for gathering votes. The latter will never be tolerated. At least not in our lifetime."

They talked on more pleasant subjects for a few minutes. The wine relaxed Virgilia and induced a playful mood not typical of her. "May I ask about the seat for the inaugural ceremony?"

"I have it for you. Reserved section near the platform for dignitaries in front of the east portico."

"Oh, that's grand, Sam. Thank you."

"But that's not all. I also managed to get you into the Senate gallery at noon, when that clod Johnson will be sworn in. Lincoln will be seated on the floor of the chamber, and his wife in a special section near your seat. You'll get to see the whole lot close up. When everyone moves outside for the swearing-in and the President's address, Emily and I will have places on the platform."

The giddiness brought words she herself didn't expect. "Perhaps when I see you and your wife, I'll wave."

He had been fondling her hand on the table. He let go, surprising her with his severity.

"I don't appreciate that kind of remark."

966

"Sam, I was only teasing—"

"I'm not."

Frightened and sobered, she hastily said, "I'm sorry, darling." The apology didn't come easy for her, but it was mandatory if she meant to keep him, which she did. "I know that in public we can't acknowledge that we're acquainted. I would never do the slightest thing to jeopardize your name or career. They've become as important to me as they are to you." She squeezed his hand. "You do believe me?"

An alarming silence. When he decided she had been punished sufficiently, he let his face soften. "Yes."

Virgilia was anxious to redirect the conversation. "I don't care a snap for hearing the Gorilla deliver a speech, but I am anxious to see him at close range. Does he look as bad as they say?"

"The man looks embalmed. He's thirty pounds underweight, and I've heard he suffers from almost constant chills. People are whispering that he's mortally ill. Unfortunately, his ailments have done nothing to reduce his mulish dedication to pushing his own opinions and programs. If the rumors of impending death were true, we'd be lucky." He sliced into the crackly duck and tasted a morsel. "Very good, this."

"I know it isn't, but it's kind of you to lie."

That got him smiling again. "I do it well, don't I? I practice every time I write or speak to constituents. Did you read the draft?" She nodded. "What do you think?"

Virgilia laid down her fork. "You told me you thought Lincoln's inaugural address would be conciliatory toward the South—"

"So far as I can find out, that's the tone, yes."

"I'm afraid the draft sounds much the same."

"Really? Too mild?"

"Not only that, too indefinite in terms of what you stand for." Here was one area in which she felt totally confident. So she pressed:

"The text wanders away from its purpose. The President has one approach to reconstruction, you and your friends quite another. You must do more than just establish the difference and identify your wing of the party. You must promote yourself more clearly and forcefully as a member of an elite group that should and will dominate reconstruction and rebuff the President's plan as the maundering of a moral coward. The public must know your name, Sam. They must identify it with absolute commitment to a hard peace. No forgiveness for traitors. You mustn't merely march in the right parade—you must show yourself leading it."

"I thought my draft did that."

"You want me to be honest, don't you? It's much too generalized and polite. For instance, it contains nothing remotely resembling Sherman's remark that he would make Georgia howl. The public needs to perceive *you* as the man who will make the whole South howl for years to pay for its crimes. It's that kind of simple, vivid concept you must put into the speech, then repeat at every opportunity. If you do, when people think of congressmen, yours will be the first name to come to mind."

He chuckled. "That's an ambitious goal."

"It's what you want, isn't it?' He sobered. "Of course it is. But you won't get it unless you go after it. What if you fall short? All right, yours will be the *second* name people think of. But if you try for anything less than first, you'll be nothing."

Low laughter again. He took her right hand in his left, began stroking her palm with his thumb. "You are a remarkable woman. I'm lucky to have you for a friend."

"For as long as you want, darling. Shall we look at the draft?"

His thumb pressed and stroked, pressed and stroked. "Not just yet."

"More food, then?"

"No."

"The dinner will be cold if—"

"It may be, but we shan't." He nearly overturned the table in his haste to stand and embrace her from behind her chair. She remained seated, pressed against the stiff bulge.

She reached around and squeezed the great strong thickness of it, moaning a little. His hand came over and down to grope her breasts. They stumbled toward the bedroom, pulling frantically at each other's clothing. Hair undone, Virgilia sprawled on the bed's edge and let him work at untying the side laces on her corset with one hand while he teased her lace-covered nipples with the other. Her breasts came free and sagged. He knelt at the bedside, kissing them. Then he kissed other places while she clasped her arms around his head.

She would never let him go. She would help him, comfort him, guide him—be a wife in every way but legally.

He flung her on her back, still with her petticoats around her ankles. She was yelling for him, arms extended. His sex felt huge as a Parrott rifle when he thrust it inside her. He was a potent, potent man, and not just physically. With him—through him— she would take revenge for poor Grady and the millions like him. She would exorcise her deepest hate.

She would make the South howl.

In the lassitude afterward, a curious new thought occurred to her. The war had worked a change in much more than her appearance and the way she regarded herself. Her loathing for the South was as deep as ever, punishment of Southerners her abiding cause.

Yet there, too, she had changed. She now coveted the means as well as the end; the raw power to prosecute her cause or any other. Because of a chain of events, seemingly disconnected but which were not—they had a pattern, an inevitability she could clearly follow—the power was within her grasp. It was as near as the body of her lover slumbering beside her.

If this change in her prospects was the result of war, then war wasn't hell, as someone said Sherman had remarked, but one of God's greatest miracles. For perhaps the first time in her adult life, Virgilia fell asleep content.

127

Next morning, as clock hands at Mont Royal reached the final minute before six, a fiery light described a high arc out in the darkness, then descended, trailing sparks. "They've come," Philemon Meek exclaimed.

Thoughtlessly, he lifted the low-trimmed lamp from the dining table and rushed to one of the tall windows. Charles pushed his chair back. The scabbarded Solingen sword lay on the tablecloth. "Get away from there with that light!"

Frightened and excited, the overseer either didn't hear or ignored the warning. He lifted the swagged drapery for a better view. "They've torched the kitchen building. I can see them moving toward—" A gun blast broke the window, scattered glass, and hurled Meek backward over some chairs. The shattered lamp spilled oil that ignited instantly. Charles jumped up, swearing.

Shouts and taunts drifted from the darkness. Charles ran to the overseer, a pointless effort. The entire front of Meek's shirt bore oozing red spots left by the shotgun charge that had killed him.

Charles tore down a large section of drape and flung it over the oil fire eating the gleaming wood floor. Then he stamped on the drape, quenching the flames. A shot; the unseen bullet buried in the wall opposite the broken window.

The scorched drapes exuded a foul smell. Crouching down, he saw capering figures silhouetted by the fire consuming the kitchen building. Andy rushed in, then Cooper with one of the old Hawkens in hand. The other, Meek's, still lay on the table. Charles pointed to it.

"That's yours now, Andy. Take it upstairs, find a good vantage point, and start shooting. But make sure it's a place you can get out of quickly if they torch the house."

"Yes, Major," Andy said, snatching the old rifle and two of the small flannel bags Judith had sewn for powder and ball. Charles wasted no time pondering how remarkable it was to be arming a slave on a Carolina rice plantation. He had other things on his mind, chief among them survival.

"One more thing, Andy. You know what Cuffey looks like. Watch for him. He's the one we want taken out of action."

" 'Deed I do know him. They say he's all gone to fat and got himself a mule. Should make him easy to spot. I hope I'm the one who gets him."

He left. Charles crept to the window. A second fire was burning. The office.

"We'd better post ourselves in the hall," he said to Cooper. "You watch the door on the river side; I'll take the one by the drive." From these locations they would also be able to cover the locked doors of the parlor, where they had put all the women and children about five o'clock.

His face showing fear and strain, Cooper followed his younger cousin into the broad foyer that crossed the ground floor from front to back. "We had no warning, Charles. What happened to all those bucks you sent out as pickets?"

"Who the hell knows? They either got killed, ran off, or joined Cuffey's army." As any competent commander would have in a similar situation, he had spent most of the night outdoors, roaming from man to man, encouraging alertness in the pickets, jacking up their spirits. He had come inside the house half an hour ago to rest and collect himself, and this was the result. No warning.

"One side," he whispered suddenly, crouching again. A shadow passed a narrow vertical panel of glass at the left side of the driveway door. He drew his army Colt. A fire-limned figure appeared in the matching panel on the right side. Charles put a bullet into it. The figure sank down amid the tinkling of glass.

"That's one."

Behind him, a bolt rattled. He heard a child crying as the parlor door opened. Judith called, "Cooper? How many are—"

"Too many," Charles shouted. "Stay in there, goddamn it." The door slammed. The bolt shot home again.

In a flat, unemotional voice, Cooper said, "I don't think we'll live through this."

"Shut up with that kind of talk." Charles ran to the door on his side; he had seen a mounted figure fly past the narrow window lights. Smoke was drifting into the house. A defiant voice startled him.

"Hey, Charles Main, you in there? This here's one of your niggers come back to get you. Gonna burn you out, Mist' Charles Main. Roast you alive an' fuck your womenfolk."

"Cuffey, you son of a bitch—" Charles rammed his right arm through the broken window and fired. "Come in here and try."

Winged by the bullet, someone yelped. Charles heard the mule's hoofs rattling out there in the smoke and glare.

Then Cuffey's voice: "Pretty soon now. Pretty soon—"

Someone else had taken the bullet meant for him. Damn. It was a shot Charles could ill afford to waste.

"Over here," Cooper cried, an instant before the bolted door on the river side split apart, pounded by the butt ends of garden

971

implements the raiders had found. As Charles waited for the door to give completely, brighter light outside the dining room drew his attention. There, beyond the trees, the whole sky glared.

He uttered a low, despairing syllable. They had fired the slave cabins. The sick house and probably the little chapel, too. They were warring on their own; the color of their victims no longer mattered. They were scum. Before they finished him, he would send some more down to tell Old Nick he was coming.

The river door burst apart. Four men crowded in, one with a fatwood torch that lit two white faces and two black ones. Cooper was struggling to aim the Hawken. Charles shot and hit no one. Three of the men leaped to one side, but one of the whites, a dumpy fellow with a pitchfork, lost his balance and lurched on toward the center of the foyer. The fatwood torch, thrown down, revealed the intruder's face, with a deserter's brand on the right cheek. Charles thought his mind had snapped.

"Salem Jones?"

"Paying a call long overdue, you arrogant—" The rest was lost as Jones rushed him with the pitchfork.

Cooper fired. So did Charles, simultaneously throwing himself sideways to avoid the stabbing tines. Both shots missed. The momentum of Salem Jones's lunge carried him all the way to the other side of the foyer. The pitchfork tore through the fine flocked wallpaper, buried to a depth of two inches.

Charles ran at the former overseer, confused impressions assaulting him as they did in every battle. In the dining room, torches sailed through smashed windows, spreading fire again. In the parlor, breaking glass, frightened screams. The women had kitchen knives and cleavers for defense. Two of the men who had destroyed the river door beat at the doors of the parlor and yanked the knobs. All of this and a general background of gunfire, yelling, celebration registered during the seconds in which Charles dashed at Jones, who ranted incoherently while trying to free the pitchfork from the wall.

Charles knew he should shoot Jones in the back but couldn't. The men at the parlor doors succeeded in separating one door from the hardware of the bolt on the inside. Cooper's Hawken boomed. One man fell as Charles looped his free hand around Jones's waist and dragged him from the wall and the pitchfork. He saw a small, stout figure in the parlor doorway.

"Mother—Jesus Christ, get back in there," Cooper cried at

972

Clarissa, who was smiling in a puzzled way. Still pulling Jones, Charles failed to see the knife the panting man snatched from his belt. But he felt it when Jones slashed downward and back, stabbing his thigh.

Charles uttered a low cry, tears of pain momentarily blinding him. Without thinking, he pushed the former overseer away. Jones tore the pitchfork from the wall, and with his reach thus extended, ran back at Charles, who had shifted his Colt to his left hand so he could grip his bleeding leg.

The firelit tines flashed toward Charles's eyes. "You first, then your high and mighty cousin," Jones screamed. Charles had to try a shot with his left hand, though he had never been able to fire effectively that way. He was done—

A roar. Jones rose as if huge invisible hands had seized his middle. Legs and chest folded toward each other; then the vee reopened, and he came down, dead but still bleeding. The skittering of the pitchfork behind Charles told him it had sailed past his head.

As he turned to verify that, he saw several things: Cooper with the smoking Hawken, with which he had shot Jones after managing to reload; Jane at the open parlor door, urging Clarissa back into the room; one of the door-breakers fallen on his side, holding his face, which bled from a stroke of the red cleaver in Jane's hand. The fourth man had fled.

With a nod toward the light and heat filling the dining room, Cooper gasped, "Got to get everyone out before the whole place goes." Remembering, Charles yelped and dashed in there. He snatched the scabbarded sword from the smoldering tablecloth with his red-smeared right hand.

Back in the foyer, he leaned against the wall. Blood ran down his leg into his boot. He supposed he should have expected something this bad. He really hadn't believed that all the Negroes he had armed with lengths of lumber or implements and posted around the house would stay and fight for Mont Royal. He wouldn't have, in their position.

Something struck the door on the driveway side. A bullet? No, louder. A post wielded as a ram? Hastily, he limped toward his cousin, who was again reloading.

The door burst in. Charles pivoted too fast and fell on his face—which saved his life. Shots whined through the space where he

973

had been standing. Recovering, he fired until the revolver was empty. The attackers withdrew.

Sweat glazed his face above his beard. He struggled to his feet, noticing the glistening blood his leg left on the inlaid squares of wood. "We have to get the women out," Cooper said.

"All right, but you stay with them from now on."

"We're done for, aren't we?"

"Not if—" Charles swallowed. Trying to reload, he found his fingers numb and thick-feeling. He couldn't grasp the shells properly. He dropped two. Kneeling to hunt for them, he finished, "—not if I can find Cuffey."

"You foun' him, white man. He foun' you, too."

Charles looked up to the head of the staircase and for the second time thought his mind had given way. Swollen with weight, there stood Cuffey. He shimmered in a ball gown of bright yellow satin.

Charles remembered hearing that Sherman's bummers and some of the freed slaves had donned women's clothing snatched from the closets of homes in Georgia. Cuffey must have heard it, too. He acted drunk and was an even more bizarre sight because of what he held in his right hand—a wide-bladed knife for cutting brush. The blade was two feet long.

Charles stared and stared, searching for the boy hidden inside the man. The boy with whom he had wrestled, fished, talked about women, and done most all the other things boys did. He couldn't find that lost friend, seeing only an apparition in yellow with a brush knife and insane eyes.

"You foun' him, an' he's obliged to kill you," Cuffey said, descending the stairs while Cooper and Charles watched with unloaded guns in their hands and the great house began to blaze on the second floor. Charles felt heat from the ceiling, saw curls of smoke like an evil halo near Cuffey's head.

"Get the women out," Charles whispered.

"I can't leave you to—"

"*Go, Cooper.*"

"Yeh, go on," Cuffey said, slurring it. "It's Mist' Charles I wan' right now." To men crowding the driveway piazza, he screamed, "You all stay out till I'm finished, hear me? Stay out!"

Slowly, Charles slid the Colt back in its holster. He wiped his red hand on his shirtfront to dry it, then picked up the scabbard from the small table where he had laid it. The dress sword was too fine and slim to be of great use. But he had no time to get the fallen pitchfork, and Cooper, darting out of sight in the parlor, needed the Hawken.

Cuffey waddled on down the stairs, the yellow satin rustling. He held the flat of the long knife tight against his side, grinning.

"We useta be frens, din we?"

Taunting him, Cuffey slid the knife back and forth over the yellow satin, as if to burnish the metal. Charles stared at the blotched and bloated face touched with firelight.

"Used to. No more."

Two men, one a giggling blond boy wearing a frock coat of Cooper's and on top of that a petticoat, slipped through the door from the serving pantry, bringing a cloud of smoke with them. Both carried stacks of china plates topped by red-glinting heaps of silverware. Cuffey shrieked at them from the bottom of the stairs. They staggered outdoors, the giggling boy spilling silver pieces, one after another, a continuous clatter.

A moment before they left, Charles saw a familiar figure pass in the driveway, walking in a slow, stately fashion, as if on a morning stroll.

"Aunt Clarissa!"

She was already out of sight.

The slight turn of Charles's head gave Cuffey the advantage he wanted. He ran at Charles, both hands clasped on the brush knife. He brought it down from above, a whistling cut that would have cleaved Charles's head if he hadn't jerked aside.

Chop, the small table where the sword had rested split in half. Charles struggled to draw the saber but, God help him, it had somehow gotten stuck. Cuffey slashed horizontally, straight toward his neck. Charles staggered back out of the way. Cuffey's blade hit an ornamental mirror, which exploded fragments of glass, all reflecting the fire a moment, hundreds of skyrocketing sparks—

His right leg muscles starting to spasm because of the wound, Charles at last managed to pull the too-fragile sword. Cuffey again raised arms over his head; huge sweat spots discolored the armpits of the dress. The brush knife jangled the pendants of the foyer chandelier.

Unreasonably enraged, Cuffey flailed at the chandelier, two great angry slashes. Pendants broke and the bits fell, a brief pris-

975

matic rain. Unable to think but one thought—at the Academy he had been graceless in fencing class—Charles lunged in, sword arm fully extended.

His boot skidded on a pendant. Cuffey kicked him in the groin, hard enough to make him grunt and lean forward sharply. His right leg gave out. He crashed down on that knee, an impact that hurt even more than the kick. The brush knife blurred down toward his exposed neck.

Charles brought the Solingen blade over and cut Cuffey's right wrist on the inside. Blood spurted. Cuffey released the knife, which sailed past Charles's ear, so close he felt metal touch the lobe.

Charles was still kneeling. Cuffey kicked his left arm. He tipped the other way and sprawled. With his heavy boot, Cuffey stomped on Charles's outstretched right arm. His hand opened. He lost the wired hilt of the saber.

Grimacing—it couldn't be termed a smile—Cuffey dropped on Charles's chest with both knees. Charles grappled with him. They rolled in a litter of pendants, prisms, table splinters, mirror chips. Cuffey clawed for his eyeballs. Charles held him back, but it took two white hands on the bleeding black wrist. Charles could feel his strength draining fast.

"Gonna—kill—you—white man." Panting, Cuffey wrenched his arm back. Slippery blood on Charles's fingers enabled him to get loose. He fastened both hands on Charles's neck. Charles felt the drip of Cuffey's blood on his throat.

"You—all finished. Jus' like—this place—"

And so it seemed. Charles was succumbing to shock and pain. His vision blurred. His right hand flopped out, scurrying desperately around the floor like a sightless white spider. He wanted a shard of mirror, a piece of prism to attack Cuffey's face.

The hands choked tighter, steadily tighter. Charles's red fingers touched and closed on something he couldn't immediately identify because of its ridged texture—

The wired hilt.

From the corner of his eye Cuffey saw it coming. Charles rammed the light cavalry saber into Cuffey's left side under his arm. Simultaneously, Cuffey let go of Charles's bloodied throat and reared away from the sword. It had already pierced the yellow satin and now slid in two inches. Four. Six—

976

Charles felt the blade scrape bone and slide on. Twelve inches. Fifteen—

Cuffey shrieked then, leaping and writhing with the killing steel stuck through him. Charles held fast. Cuffey continued his violent contortions. The blade snapped below the hilt, three inches from the dress.

Still impaled on the part that was deep inside him, Cuffey plucked wildly at the stub of steel, teetering and twirling into the burning dining room. The belling yellow skirt caught. Flames encircled the hem, ran upward like a fringe going the wrong way. Turning, weaving, Cuffey completed the figure of his death waltz and dropped into the consuming fire.

Finding something to feast on, it rose higher. Charles saw no more of him.

The smoking ceiling creaked and sagged. Charles struggled to his feet, the remaining part of the sword—it resembled a metal cross—gripped in his right hand. Most of the engraved inscription was gone. All that remained was *amily, 1861.*

Blood soaked his right pants leg and squished in his boot when he walked. He spied his fallen Colt and retrieved it. He found the parlor as yet largely untouched by the fire. The windows had been knocked out, presumably so Cooper and the others could escape. He had to find them. The great house was lost.

He ripped down another drapery, cut it by stabbing and sawing with the stub end of the sword until he had a strip long enough to wind around his thigh several times. He snapped off the leg of a taboret, broke that in two, and used half to finish the tourniquet, hoping it would suffice.

His lungs hurt, an abrasive feeling throughout his chest. Smoke grew thicker every moment. He ducked through a window to the piazza, the empty revolver in his left hand, the broken sword in his right.

Daylight was coming. Cuffey's followers had managed to find most everything of value before the fire claimed the house. The evidence littered the drive. They had emptied the wine and spirit racks, the wardrobes, the kitchen cabinets. He saw seedy, bearded men, white and black, slipping away in the smoke between the trees, arms laden with loot.

Not all of them had been equally successful. The blond boy wearing Cooper's frock coat and the petticoat lay facedown amid silver and smashed plates. A bullet hole showed between his shoulder blades.

There was little shooting now. But all it took was one bullet, so Charles cautiously remained behind one of the white pillars as he shouted, "Cooper?"

Silence.

"Cooper!"

"Charles?"

The distant voice provided the guidance he needed. They were hiding in the mazy plantings of the formal garden by the river. He crept along the side of the house, careful to avoid touching it; the walls were hot. He turned the corner, passed the chimney, and scrutinized the lawn.

No one. He readied himself to make a dash, then remembered to announce something important with another shout.

"Cuffey's dead, Cooper. Cuffey—is—dead. I killed him."

The sounds of Mont Royal burning filled the stillness. But no voices. Yet he knew they had heard him. He drew air into his pained lungs, stepped away from the house, and ran as fast as he could on his injured leg down the grassy slope toward the Ashley.

Someone shot at him. He heard the bullet splat the dewy grass to his right, but no second report followed. In the garden he found himself surrounded by familiar faces. Without so much as a word to anyone, he fell forward in a faint.

They hid all day in one of the rice squares, resting with their backs against the dirt embankment that held back the river until the wood gates were opened to let it flow in. The band of survivors consisted of Cooper, his wife and daughter, Clarissa, Jane, Andy, a young kitchen wench named Sue and her two small boys, and Cicero, the elderly, arthritic slave with curly white hair. Cicero had managed to fill his two big coat pockets with rice. He passed it around as the sun approached noon. It was their only food.

Others, including Cooper, frequently spoke of wanting to go back to assess the damage. Clarissa was the most insistent. Charles was adamant.

"Not until dusk. Then I'll go first, alone. No use risking any more lives."

The tourniquet had helped. The thigh cut had clotted. He

978

didn't feel good, but he was able to stay awake. He did wish he had some bourbon for the pain.

Cooper seemed prone to argue with his last remark. Charles forestalled it. "Look at the sky. That tells you what's happened." Above the embankment and the live oaks and palmettos bordering the rice acreage, black smoke banners flew.

Cicero was visibly affected by it. After watching the smoke for a length of time, his tension evident in the set of his lips and the glint of his eye, he exploded. "What happened to those boys we put on guard?"

"They didn't stay there," Cooper replied. It was a statement, not an accusation. But it enraged the old Negro.

"Cowards. Wouldn't fight for their home—"

Squatting and drawing patterns in the dirt with a stick, Andy said, "Wasn't their home by choice, remember."

Cicero glared. "Damn skunk-belly cowards, that's what they are. Nigger trash."

"Don't be so hard on them," Charles said. "They knew the South's beaten—that they'll have their liberty the minute it becomes official. Why should they stay here and die when all they had to do was run a mile or so and be free men right away? Tell you one thing. Thousands and thousands of fine, high-principled white Southern boys ran away from the army with a lot less reason." He put two grains of rice in his mouth and chewed.

Clarissa was particularly displeased by the need to stay in the field most of the day. Shortly after noon, she had to relieve herself and cried because there was no privacy. Jane bent close to her ear, whispered, then gently helped her all the way across the square and over the next embankment. She waited on the near side until the elderly woman reappeared.

Clarissa's familiar cheery smile had returned. When Jane brought her back, she said, "How sweet the air smells. Spring's coming. Isn't that lovely?"

"Yes," said Judith, putting an arm around her mother-in-law and patting her. "Yes, it is." Andy gave Jane a swift, almost chaste kiss on the cheek. Charles thought he heard the black man whisper, "Thank you."

Charles drowsed awhile during the afternoon. Eyes half closed, he visualized bits of the writhing struggle with Cuffey. His eyes flew open and he shuddered, reminded of another day, at the slave cabins, when they had both been only six or seven. Friends, they had wrestled for possession of a fishing rod. This time it had been two enemies contesting one life. My God, how far the wheel had turned.

Toward sunset, Cooper again declared that he wanted to go back to inspect the property. No shots had been heard for more than four hours, or any unusual sound at all. The smoke kept drifting, thinner but still strong-smelling. Why Clarissa no longer noticed, Charles couldn't imagine, unless it was because she dwelled so much of the time in the safer, softer landscape of her own mind and had retreated there again. She was a lucky woman in some respects.

"I don't believe anybody should go up there alone," Andy said. "I'm goin' with whoever decides to do it."

"I suggest the three of us go," Cooper said. Charles was by now too tired to continue the argument. He gave in with a shrug.

Unarmed, they trudged along the bank of the Ashley. The water shone red-gold in the lowering light. They passed the last rice square and advanced cautiously through the belt of big trees separating the fields from the formal garden and riverside lawn. From their angle of approach, the first visible damage was the broken planking and debris on the bank. The dock no longer existed.

Pale, Cooper wiped his lips and walked out of the garden. Following him, Charles saw pieces of two gold-edged platters on the grass and a ripped dress with a mound of excrement on it. Human, he presumed.

Cooper's attention was on the house. He whispered, "Oh, God above." Even Andy appeared stricken. Charles didn't want to look, but he did.

Mont Royal had been burned to its tabby foundation. Nothing stood in the ashes and rubble except a few canted black beams and the great chimney, soot-marked but with all of its thick wisteria vines intact. Charles supposed the vines were dead.

"How could they?" Cooper said, wrath in his voice. "How could they, the damned ignorant barbarians—"

Softly, Charles said, "You used to tell me South Carolinians were fools because they were inviting war. They were eager for one. We just got what you predicted. The war paid us a call."

He touched his cousin's trembling shoulder to console him, then began to limp up the grassy incline. When he was still a good distance away, he felt the oven heat of the rubble. Here and there coals gleamed like imp's eyes. Slowly, wonderingly, he circled around the great chimney.

Cooper and Andy approached more slowly. Charles disappeared beyond the chimney. Suddenly Cooper and Andy exchanged alarmed looks. They heard Charles laughing like a crazy man.

"Hurry up," Cooper said, already running.

They dashed around the chimney to the darkening, tree-lined driveway. A few limbs near the house still smoked. Some others had burned away completely. Charles stood near the corpse of the blond boy, pointing and howling like a lunatic. The object of his mirth stood further down the drive: a flop-eared mule with rope halter and rein.

"Cuffey's mule," Charles gulped between bursts of laughter. "Mont Royal is wiped off the earth, but I've got a remount. Praise God and Jeff Davis! The war can go on and on and—"

The crazed voice broke off. He gave them a shamed glance and stalked away to the nearest live oak. He braced his forearm against it and hid his face.

128

That Sunday morning, the second of April, Mr. Lonzo Perdue and his wife and daughters were kneeling in prayer when the messenger rushed up the aisle of St. Paul's to whisper to the President. Mr. Perdue watched the Chief Executive, white-haired now, leave the church with an unsteady step. Mr. Perdue leaned close to his wife's ear.

"The defenses have broken. Did you see his face? It can't be anything else. We must pack and get on a train."

After the service, they wasted no time conversing with friends. They went straight home, packed three portmanteaus, and set out for the depot. They found all outbound trains were being held, though no official would explain why. During the afternoon the crowds grew steadily larger and more unruly, milling, pushing, overflowing the platforms and waiting room. Ultimately Mr. Perdue and his family found themselves encamped just outside the station entrance.

They heard glass smashing in nearby streets. Mr. Perdue trembled. "Looting."

"It must be the niggers," said his wife.

By dusk, the streets surrounding the depot were packed with more people than Mr. Perdue had seen for months. As night came, rumors flew. Lee had pulled out of the Petersburg and Richmond defense lines. He was in wild and confused retreat to the west.

Tempers shortened. There were incidents of pushing, fistfighting, rough treatment of the civilians when squads of soldiers had to quick-march into the mob to restore order. Then came the first explosion.

"Oh, Papa," cried Mr. Perdue's daughter Clytemnestra, cringing against her equally terrified father. "What are they doing?"

"Demolishing buildings. I think that was the Tredegar Works."

His daughter Marcelline began to shriek and babble as if taking leave of her senses. Without hesitation, Mr. Perdue slapped her several times. That took care of that.

By eleven, the city was an asylum lit by spreading fires. Davis arrived in a carriage surrounded by heavily armed soldiers. In the smoky lamplight, Mr. Perdue watched him pass into the depot. A train for Danville was waiting, someone said.

Mr. Perdue began to smell betrayal as he glimpsed certain other persons entering the station, each escorted by at least one soldier. He saw the scoundrel Mallory, who had wasted so many precious dollars on his worthless naval schemes. Trenholm, who had replaced Memminger at Treasury, arrived in an ambulance. Then came the damned Jew, Benjamin, sleek and cheery as ever. The privileged were to be carried to safety, away from the steady detonations of gunpowder, the brightening light of fires, the threat of hooligans looting—

"The boxcars of the special train will be opened," a railroad official shouted from the depot steps. "I repeat, the boxcars will be opened, but no baggage will be allowed. None!"

Screaming, shoving, the crowd surged forward. Not everyone could squeeze through the station doors at once. People began striking and clawing one another like enemy soldiers. Mr. Perdue saw a child fall, trampled, a short distance to his left. He didn't try to assist the girl; he was busy dragging his wife relentlessly toward the platform.

"Oh, but Lonzo—no baggage? I can't leave these few precious things—"

"Then you'll stay here without me. Girls, kick those women if they won't move." Thus the family won a place on the 11:00 P.M. out of Richmond.

As the train started up slowly, chugging and jerking, desperate laggards trampled and pushed one another, still trying to climb into boxcars already filled to capacity. In his car, Mr. Perdue and several other men manned the open door and protected their families by booting the faces and stamping on the hands of those attempting to board.

Marcelline tugged her father's coattail and pointed to a waving, yelling group on the platform. "Papa, it's Mr. Salvarini and his family."

"Yes, too bad," said Mr. Perdue as he reached down to a soft hand with two wedding rings on the fourth finger. Like some tenacious deep-sea creature, the hand had emerged from the mob to fasten on his trouser leg. He gripped the middle finger and bent it backward. As the hand released, he heard a bone pop. A stout woman sank from sight.

The tangle of bodies fell away at a faster rate; the train gathered speed and moved onto the trestle. Mr. Perdue's coat and cravat were in shreds. He was exhausted but happy—very satisfied and pleased by his untypical display of heroism in the face of danger.

Upriver, great light pylons showed where other James River bridges had been set afire. Perhaps I should have gone into the army after all, Mr. Perdue thought as the train bore him away into the night.

The soldiers, chiefly wounded veterans, had organized a rear guard to sweep through the government warehouses on Thirteenth and Fourteenth, putting matches to the cartons and crates of official records. One grizzled man, who was twenty-five but looked forty, pried open a wooden box and exclaimed, "Here's something new—undelivered mail."

"Burn it," said his sergeant, whose pant legs, like those of his men, were soaked with whiskey. They had waded through gutters filled with it. The looters were breaking open everything.

The soldier stuck in his match. When a few letters caught, he plucked them from the box and used them to fire a second one, then a third and fourth. With the blaze roaring nicely, he dropped the original packet of letters on the plank floor, already hot, and hurried away to safety.

129

Outside the *Ledger-Union,* an office boy hung up a summary of a new telegraphic dispatch almost hourly. Each piece of information from the distant Petersburg-Richmond line was greeted with cheers from a crowd becoming steadily larger.

By midday on Monday, the third of April, the excitement brought work to a standstill at Hazard's and swept through Belvedere like fire in a dry spell. Madeline was the only one who retreated from it, going to her suite of rooms and shutting the door.

She was thankful the end seemed near. The dispatches did not say positively that General Lee had abandoned his hopeless position in front of Petersburg and the Richmond lines as well, but that presumption was being accepted throughout the mansion—and the ironworks and the town. Everyone felt the Confederate capital would soon fall. If all of this meant the bloodletting would stop, she was grateful.

Yet the news raised a less welcome consideration. After a surrender, she would have no excuse for not returning to Mont Royal.

She hated the thought. The place would only remind her of Orry. Yet she knew she had an obligation to go back as soon as it was possible to travel to South Carolina. There was a great deal of Washington talk about confiscating all the property of the largest slaveholders. She must be home to fight against that if it happened. If the love she and Orry shared had any monument at all, it was Mont Royal, tainted by black slavery though it was.

So her duty was unavoidable. She must remember and take courage from her father's words. *We are all dying of life.* She must make the journey and stand in Orry's stead, maintaining the home they had occupied together such a short time. Assuming, of course, that the plantation still existed. Northern journalists wrote long articles about the advance of General Sherman's army and the activities of his foragers operating on the flanks. So lurid and gleeful were these pieces, it was possible to imagine half of the state of South Carolina put to the torch, exactly like the city of Columbia.

But she wouldn't know Mont Royal's fate until she got there, and she couldn't get there without preparation. She was tired of imagining scenes of destruction. One antidote was physical activity.

From the closet where she had stored it, she brought a small trunk, in which she had carried her things from Richmond. She opened it and savored the aroma of a few cedar chips in the bottom. From the wardrobe, she took two dresses she seldom wore. One by one, she folded them and laid them in the trunk.

When it was about half full of items seldom used or worn since her arrival, her gaze fell on the half-dozen slender books on her bedside table. She picked out the third from the top, opened it at the ribbon marker, and gazed at the poem without seeing a word.

Don't, a silent voice warned. She shut the book, clasping it tight to her breast. Tears ran down her cheeks as she stared through the window at the hillsides of sunlit mountain laurel.

"It was many and many a year ago—in a kingdom—by the sea —that a maiden there lived whom you may know—by the name of—"

Shuddering, she bowed her head.

"By the name of—"

She couldn't say the rest. The poem had meant too much to both of them. She leaned over the trunk and laid the volume of Poe on a neatly folded shawl, then closed the trunk lid with a small, final click. It was all the packing she could manage at the moment.

When the conquerors marched into Richmond that day, Mrs. Burdetta Halloran was ready. She had spent nearly all her remaining money on one of the old flags, which cost dearly because the speculator selling them said many people wanted them. She burned her Confederate national flag in her fireplace.

In the morning the Yankees paraded past her home, led by the black horsemen of the Fifth Massachusetts Colored Cavalry—incredible sight. She concealed her sick scorn and cheered and waved her handkerchief beneath the Stars and Stripes she had hung above her front veranda. Many of her neighbors openly wept, but not all. She didn't give a damn for what the weepers thought of her behavior.

By the hundreds the conquerors came, fifing, drumming, grinning, celebrating beneath a sky painted by fires that still burned. On the flanks of the riding and marching men, Negroes skipped and danced and taunted the whites watching from porches and upper windows.

She saw a white officer notice her and cheered all the louder. Perhaps such a man would be taken with her appearance, stop, introduce himself. She had to survive somehow. She would.

"Oh, thank God, thank God," she cried beneath the grand old flag, waving her hanky so hard her arm ached. Her acting was so fine, tears coursed down her cheeks. Presently a chubby colonel reined his horse out of column and slowly approached the picket fence, to which she rushed and was waiting to speak as he smiled and removed his hat.

"No more slavery—and soon no more war, doesn't it seem so, Captain?"

"Yes, there's every indication that Lee is on the run," Billy agreed. Pinckney Herbert's small, bright eyes rejoiced as he tied a bit of string around the rolled-up razor strop. Billy had let his beard grow since coming home, but he kept the upper edges trimmed, and his old strop was worn out.

It was about an hour after Madeline had shut herself in her room—a mild bright Monday afternoon. Billy was mending. The wound frequently filled the upper half of his body with a diffuse but severe pain, though he always managed to overcome it when he and Brett snuggled in bed together. She said he had never been so passionate in all the relatively short times they had been together during four years of marriage. She told him that with great pleasure. He liked to reply, "Been living on army rations a mighty long time. You know—coffee, corn bread, and continence."

He thanked Herbert, took his change and the strop, and left the dim, dust-moted store with its wonderful homey smells of cloth, crackers, and onion sets. Though his chest was starting to ache again, he felt a renewed and joyful sense of life returning to normal. In recognition of it, he no longer wore his side arm.

The storekeeper was right, certainly. It was a new day for the whole land. The Thirteenth Amendment had gone to the individual states for ratification, and Illinois had been the first to do so. Even the pathetic Confederate President had acknowledged a need for change, though in his case Billy assumed the motive to be desperation, not principle. Davis, who would probably be hanged when the war ended—if he were caught, that is; any sensible man would flee the country—had in mid-March signed a law admitting blacks to the Confederate Army. Billy found it a gesture both sad and contemptible.

Doing his best to ignore the mounting chest pain, he strolled toward the *Ledger-Union* office to see whether there was more late news. His route took him past a lager beer saloon crowded with men who would soon trudge up the hill to start the afternoon shift at Hazard's. Beyond that, he approached a corner where bunting decorated the front of the recruiting office.

Three doors this side of the office, he stopped, studying an odd little scene in progress. A trio of loutish men hovered around the hitch rail, between the recruiting office entrance and a broad-shouldered Negro boy in the street. One of the whites wore a soiled army uniform. Billy recognized Fessenden, the man who had once harassed Brett. The black youth had an apprehensive expression.

"Scat, coon," one of the men said. He picked up a good-sized pebble. Laughing, he lobbed it at the boy's old shoes. The stone

987

landed an inch in front of a cracked leather toe. The soft plop was exaggerated by the silence.

"Yeh, get on back up to the mill and go to work," Fessenden said, equally amused. He relaxed and leaned back, resting his elbows on the rail and cocking one leg over the other like a standing stork. "Bob Lee's on the run. War's nearly over. We don't want colored boys fighting for us."

Billy stood quietly beside the brick wall of the café, which closed up during this part of the afternoon. The sloping wooden covering built over the sidewalk placed him in heavy shadow, but the Negro boy, facing the buildings, saw him. Fessenden and his cronies didn't. Watching the shabbily dressed boy, Billy began rubbing his thumb back and forth over the oiled strop leather.

The boy was clearly frightened, yet he swallowed hard and said, "I don't want trouble. I just want to join up while there's time." He stepped forward.

The young, pimply white man to Fessenden's left jerked something from a pocket in his checked pants. A snap—a flash—the boy held perfectly still at the sight of the long blade of the clasp knife.

"D'ja hear what the soldier said? No niggers from this town wanted in the You-nited States Army. Now you turn around and shuffle back to your shanty, boy, or they'll be pickin' pieces of your black balls outa this here dirt for weeks." A pause. *"Boy? You hear me?* Don't just stand there when a white man—"

"Let him pass."

The voice out of blue shadow spun all three of them. Billy stepped to the sunlit walk, halting just short of the recruiting office door. He couldn't see who was inside, but clearly they had no heart for intervening. Damn fool, Billy called himself, conscious of the absence of a side arm. A crawl of sweat reached his beard from under his left eye.

Fessenden was the only member of the trio to recognize him. "This is no damn affair of yours, Hazard."

"He has a right to present himself for enlistment if he wants."

"A right?" The knife carrier guffawed. "Since when's a coon got any—?"

Billy overlapped him, louder. "So let him pass."

"Tell him to go fuck, Lute," the third man said.

Fessenden scratched his stubbly chin, mumbling, "Shit, I dunno, boys. He's a wounded veteran like me."

988

"I've been told you were wounded in the tail," Billy said. "While you were running."

"You son of a bitch," Fessenden yelled, but it was the pimply one with the knife who took action, loping at Billy. Hastily, Billy backed against the building, broke the string on the strop, unrolled the leather, and laid it full force across the attacker's face.

"Oh, my God." Shrieking, he dropped the knife. A purpling welt striped him from brow to chin. The leather had drawn blood as well.

Under the heavy bandages, Billy's wound throbbed. Dizziness assailed him suddenly. Bending and watching Billy at the same time, the pimply young man groped for his knife. Billy kicked it off the wooden walk into the dust. Fessenden gave him an outraged look, heaved an aggrieved sigh.

"Shit," he said again. "Next thing, you'll be tellin' us this nigger oughta vote—just like white men."

"If he's allowed to die for the government, I guess he should be allowed to vote for it, wouldn't you say, Lute?"

Snickers of disbelief. "Jesus," Fessenden said, shaking his head. "What'd they do to you in the army? You've turned into one of them goddamn radicals."

It was nearly as surprising to Billy as to them. He had spoken out of conviction, one that had been growing without full awareness on his part until this contretemps demanded the translation of conviction to deed. He rippled the strop against his leg.

"Have I? Well—so be it."

He looked at the pimply lout and, summoning his best West Point upperclassman's voice, bellowed, "Get the hell away from me, you garbage." He raised the strop. *That's an order.*"

The pimply young man ran like a deer, nearly knocking Pinckney Herbert from his observation place in front of his store.

Billy glanced at the Negro boy. "You can go on inside."

The boy walked toward Lute Fessenden. He didn't hurry, but neither did he waste time while he was within Fessenden's reach. But Fessenden just watched him, turning as he passed, repeatedly shaking his head.

Before the boy entered the office, he gave Billy a smile. He said, "Thank you, sir," and was gone.

Billy raised the strop, intending to roll it up again. The sudden motion made Fessenden's other companion flinch visibly. Though Billy felt a mite guilty about it, he milked the moment, drawing

989

the strop ever so slowly and provocatively across his open left palm. Fessenden's companion drew back.

"Good day, gentlemen," Billy barked. The frightened man jumped, grabbing Fessenden's arm.

"Let go of me, for Chrissake." Fessenden shook him off, and the two shamed whites quickly disappeared around the corner.

Shameless, Billy said to himself. Absolutely shameless, that last part. It relieved his guilt to recall that the two were deserving.

Pinckney Herbert ran down the sidewalk to shake his hand. Billy had all but forgotten about the painful wound. He felt fine: wickedly amused, unexpectedly proud, gloriously alive.

130

Rain fell on the low country that same afternoon. Charles sat at the foot of a great water oak, reasonably well protected from the drizzle as he read an old Baltimore paper that had somehow found its way to Summerville, the village where he and Andy had gone in search of food.

Charles had stayed at Mont Royal much longer than he should have, and much longer than he had planned. But every hand was needed to put up a new house—little more than an oversized cabin—on the site once occupied by the plantation summerhouse, which had been smashed and leveled but not burned. All the lumber in the new place was either broken, scorched, or both. The result was a crazy-quilt structure, but at least it sheltered the survivors, black and white, in separately curtained areas.

The food situation was desperate. Their neighbor Markham Bull had shared some hoarded flour and yeast. Thus they had bread and their own rice, but little else. Occasional visitors who appeared on the river road said the whole state was starving.

The visit to Summerville confirmed it. Even if they had been carrying bags of gold, it would have done no good. There was nothing to buy. Just the paper left behind by some refugee in flight.

Wishing for a cigar—he hadn't enjoyed one since the day he came home—Charles finished reading the lengthy account of Abe Lincoln's second inaugural. The war might last a while longer, but Charles assumed Lincoln would soon take charge of a conquered South. Therefore he ought to know what the man was thinking.

Mr. Lincoln sounded forgiving—on the surface. There was much in his address about *malice toward none* and *charity for all.* He wanted to *bind up the nation's wounds,* to *care for him who shall have borne the battle and for his widow, and his orphan.* He wanted to achieve *a just and lasting peace.*

All very fine and humane, Charles thought. But certain other passages suggested that while Mr. Lincoln might forgive Southerners as individuals, he could not forgive the sin of slavery. And so long as the institution survived, he would prosecute the war.

. . . *if God wills that it continue until all the wealth piled by the bondman's two hundred and fifty years of unrequited toil shall be sunk, and until every drop of blood drawn with the lash shall be paid by another drawn with the sword . . . it must be said, "The judgments of the Lord are true and righteous altogether."*

The judgments of the Lord. Charles kept returning to the phrase, staring at the five words on the yellowing newsprint. They summed up and reinforced what had been with him ever since the fire. A positive, guilt-tainted conviction that the war was ending in the only fitting and proper way.

Still, resting the back of his head against the tree and closing his eyes—speculation—he did recognize that it might have come out differently had not chance betrayed the South on so many occasions.

If the copy of Lee's order had not been found wrapped around the cigars before Sharpsburg.

If Jackson had not been wounded by a North Carolina rifleman.

If Stuart hadn't disappeared off the map, riding to repair his reputation, before Gettysburg.

If the Commissary Department had been run by a competent man instead of a bungler.

If Davis had cared more for common folk and the land and less for the preservation of philosophic principles.

If, if, *if*—what the hell was the use? They would lose. They had lost.

Up in Virginia, however, the war went on. And he had a remount. The war had done things to his head. Burned him out, used him up, like a piece of fatwood kindling. But he still had to go back. West Point taught duty above all.

He crumpled the newspaper and threw it away. He sat staring into the rain where he imagined he saw Gus standing, smiling at him.

He put his hand over his eyes, held it there half a minute, lowered it.

She was gone.

He climbed to his feet feeling as if he weighed seven hundred pounds. Still limping slightly from the healing leg wound, he went off to search for his mule. He collected his old army Colt, for which he had no ammunition, the cross-shaped sword fragment, which might in an emergency serve as a dagger, and his gypsy cloak of scraps and rags. He said good-bye to everyone and rode away north before dark.

131

On Palm Sunday evening, Brett and Billy walked up through the laurel above Belvedere. Hazard's was shut down, customary on the Sabbath, though some of the banked fires still fed smoke traceries out of the chimneys. The air was warm and fragrant with spring. Behind them, the tiered streets of the town, the peaceful river, the sunset over the mountains created a landscape of grays and mauves and small patches of pale, dusty orange.

That morning they had attended church, then partaken of a huge noonday meal, at which Mr. Wotherspoon had been a welcome guest. Ever since, Brett had silently rehearsed the two things she wanted to say to her husband. One was directly related to the impending end of the war, the other less so.

She knew the essence of each statement and some of the words, but she wanted a proper setting, too. So she had suggested the stroll. Now she found herself anxious and strangely unable to begin.

Billy seemed content to walk in silence, relishing the spring dusk and the feel of her hand in his. They came to the meteorite crater they had discovered the night before he returned to duty in the spring of '61, a night followed by so many changes in Brett herself and in the country that it sometimes resembled a series of tableaux on a stage, viewed from a balcony, rather than events in which she had taken part.

She noticed that weeds had at last begun to grow in the crater, covering about two-thirds of the surface of the sloping sides. But the poisoned earth at the bottom remained bare.

They strolled toward the next summit. Should she start with the second subject? No, it was better to dispose of the difficult one first. She forced herself.

"How soon do you think Madeline will be able to travel to South Carolina?"

He thought a moment. "They say there's almost nothing left of Lee's army. Or Joe Johnston's. I can't imagine that either can hold out more than a few weeks longer. I would guess she could start home sometime in May, if not sooner."

She took his other hand. Holding both, she faced him in the fading, dusty light.

"I'd like to go with her."

A smile. "I suspected you might."

"It isn't entirely for the reason you think. I do want to see how Mont Royal fared, but I have another motive. One which—" steadily, she looked at him "—which I'm not sure you'll approve of. I want to go back and stay awhile. The nigras will be free, and they'll need help adjusting to the change."

"You'll forgive me, but that sounds faintly like the benevolent mistress of the plantation speaking."

His wry smile angered her unexpectedly. "It may be, but don't you dare patronize me for it."

Billy put his arm around her. "Here, I didn't mean to upset you—"

She sighed. "And I didn't mean to snap. But I've been away so long—I admit I'm homesick. And I'm not patronizing the people at Mont Royal when I say they need help. Protection. They're in danger of being transferred from one kind of slavery to another. It was your own brother, Stanley, who warned me."

"Stanley? What do you mean?"

As accurately as she could, she repeated Stanley's remarks of a couple of years ago concerning the Republican scheme to befriend the freed Negroes, the better to manipulate them as voters.

"Stanley said that?"

"Indeed he did. He was drunk at the time, else he wouldn't have spoken so freely. He declared that the party, or one faction anyway, had already agreed on the strategy. I believe him. That's why I want to go home and stay for a time. The slavery of ignorance is as wicked as any other kind. Perhaps it's the cruelest slavery of all, because any man can see an iron cuff on his own leg, but it's hard to detect an invisible one."

She watched for a reaction. He lowered his head slightly, the dark hair, so like his brother George's, tossing in the strengthening breeze. A few bright stars shone against the mauve now. She could only interpret his silence as disapproval.

She refused to be so easily defeated. Not after Scipio Brown and his brood of lost children had worked such changes in the way she viewed people. She snapped off a bit of laurel, twirling it in her fingers.

"Do you remember your last night at home when the war started?" A nod. "We walked up here, and I said I was frightened. You reassured me by talking about this." She held out the sprig. "You told me what your mother had taught—that the laurel is like a man and woman's love for each other. It can endure anything. Well, I made a discovery while you were gone. I discovered it in the eyes and faces of those children at Mr. Brown's school. If the kind of love your mother described doesn't touch everyone— embrace everyone—if it can't be given freely and equally to everyone, it's meaningless. It doesn't exist."

"And going home—helping the nigras in whatever way you have in mind—that's an expression of love?"

Very softly: "To me it is."

"Brett—" he cleared his throat—"I met hundreds of men in the army who finally accepted emancipation because it was government policy, but they would choke on what you just said. There are a lot of them in that town right down there. They'd reach for a club or a gun to defend their right to be superior to Negroes."

"I know. But how can love be the property of a favored few? Or freedom, either? I was raised to believe they could. Then I came here to this state, this town, an utter stranger—and I learned."

"Changed, I would say."

"Use any term you like. I gather you object to my wish to—?"

His palm touched her cheek. "I object to nothing. I love you. I'm proud of you. I believe every word of what you just said."

"Is that really true?"

"You're not the only one this war affected," he said. He hadn't described the incident outside the recruiting office and didn't do so now. It struck him as too much like bragging. But his next statement touched the core of the incident. "I'm not the same soldier boy who stood here four years ago. I didn't realize what a distance I've traveled until—well, lately."

His smile warmed. Bending in the starlight, he kissed her mouth.

"I love you, Brett. What you are and what you believe. You're right about going home. Your help will probably be needed. I'll be proud and honored to escort you and Madeline back to Mont Royal. And since I'll have to return to duty sometime soon, there isn't any reason you can't stay as long as you wish."

"There's one."

The soft words startled him. Was that scarlet in her cheek? The lowering dark made him unsure.

"Sweetheart," she said, "you've been so ardent despite the wound—well, I'm not entirely certain yet—I haven't seen the doctor—but I believe we're going to have a child."

Wonderstruck, he could find no words. New life after so much loss—there was magic in it. Something miraculous. He looked at the laurel sprig in her hand, took it from her gently and studied it while she said, "You see, if I stay at Mont Royal, there's a possibility our child could be born there."

"I don't care where it happens, just so long as it happens. I don't care!" Exuberantly, he tossed the laurel in the air and hugged her, exclaiming his joy. The whoop rose up and echoed back from clear across the river.

That same Sunday evening, April 9, George was in Petersburg, having spent the afternoon assembling and loading construction materials on two flatcars. The Petersburg & Lynchburg line that ran west from town was under repair to supply the army pursuing Lee. George had to be up before daylight and on his way toward Burkeville.

Tired, he walked in the direction of the tents assigned to visiting officers. Off in the darkness, several horns, two fifes, and a snare drum struck up "The Battle Cry of Freedom." Yells and whistling accompanied the music.

"Damned strange hour for a concert," he muttered. He jumped back suddenly as a horseman galloped by, shouting, "Surrender! Surrender!"

An officer with his galluses down and his chest bare stumbled sleepily from a nearby tent. "Surrender? My God, I didn't even know we were under attack—"

Grinning, George said, "I think someone else may have surrendered. Hear the music? Come on, let's find out."

Away he went on his stocky legs. The other officer snapped his suspenders over his naked shoulders and ran after him. They soon came upon a whole mob of men piling out of tents. George could barely make sense of their noise:

"—sometime today—"

"—old Gray Fox asked Ulysses for terms—"

"—out by Appomattox Court House someplace—"

In an hour, Petersburg was bedlam. It was true, apparently; the Army of Northern Virginia was laying down its arms to stop the shedding of more blood in a war that couldn't be won. Under the Southern stars, George snatched off his kepi, tossed it in the air, and caught it, then began to take brain-pummeling swallows of busthead from bottles shoved into his hand by officers and enlisted men he had never seen before and never would again, but who were fine friends, closest of comrades, in this delirious moment of lifting burdens and spirits.

Pistols and rifles volleyed into the dark. Large and small musical groups blared patriotic airs. It occurred to George that, once he got home, he could sleep next to Constance every night for the rest of his life, with no one to tell him otherwise. He jammed his fists on his hips and danced a jig without knowing how.

Men swirled around him, jumping, dancing, staggering, drinking, cheering. He helped himself to more stiff drinks from the bottles being passed. He threw his cap in the air again, bellowing like a schoolboy.

"—rally round the flag, boys, rally once again, shouting the battle cry of—"

Singing lustily, jigging madly, he didn't notice the sink in the dark behind him, though he had certainly whiffed it. Luckily he only sank to his knees, though that was bad enough.

He cleaned up on the bank of the calm Appomattox River. Returning to the celebration, he noticed that other revelers didn't come as close to him as they had earlier. Still, he managed to get a few more drinks and, thus fortified, could regard what had happened as a humorous cap on an already glorious night. A night men would forever recall to fellow veterans, wives, sweethearts, children, and grandchildren, in terms of where they were and what they were doing when they heard the news. George could not quite picture himself being truthful:

I was in Petersburg, gathering crossties and spikes to reopen a section of the military railroad.

"Were you happy when you heard the news, Grandpa?"
"You can't believe how happy."
"What did you do to celebrate?"
"I started dancing and fell in a trench full of shit."

132

Peace had its own unique strains, Stanley realized late in the week. Washington streets mobbed with drunken celebrants extended a ten-minute trip to an hour—or made it impossible. Isabel said the patriotic illuminations glaring from the windows of most houses and public buildings gave her bad headaches, though why this should be so when she stayed home and saw very few of them, Stanley couldn't explain.

He was bothered by the loud reports of fireworks all night long, by the tolling bells, the endlessly parading bands, and the hoots and merrymaking of gangs of whites and blacks roaming at will, even in the best neighborhoods. Add to that Stanton's tense air and repeated expressions of fear of plots to kill Grant or the President, and it added up to a miserable week for Stanley.

Stanton wanted to see him to go over matters pertaining to his departure from the War Department to take up the new post Wade had arranged. Stanley was ready with his files at nine Friday morning, but Stanton was too busy. At eleven the secretary had to rush to the Executive Mansion for a cabinet meeting. It lasted several hours, during which time Stanley didn't leave the department. He was hungry and out of sorts when, late in the day, he was finally summoned to Stanton's office.

Even then, the stout man with the scented whiskers and round spectacles was preoccupied with his fear of murder plots.

"The Grants aren't going to Ford's, anyway. That's half the battle won."

"Ford's?" Stanley repeated, blank because of fatigue.

Stanton was irritable. "What's the matter with your memory? Ford's on Tenth Street. The theater!"

"Oh. The President is going to see Miss Keene—?"

"Tonight. He seems to regard the appearance as some sort of patriotic obligation. He has completely disregarded my warnings. Grant listened. He was only too happy for an excuse to whisk his wife out of town on a train for New Jersey."

He stumped to the window, hands locked behind his back. "It's been a queer day. In that long meeting, we spent nearly as much time discussing the President's latest dream as we did on the pressing issue of practical steps to restore the Union."

Lincoln's strange dreams were a subject frequently gossiped about in Washington. "Which one this time?" Stanley asked, since some of them were known to recur.

"The boat," Stanton replied, staring out the window. "The boat in which he sees himself drifting. He says the dream always comes on the eve of some great happening. Before Antietam he dreamed of the boat. Before Gettysburg, too. It's curious that he can describe the boat vividly but not the destination. It's merely a dark, indefinite shore. His words," Stanton added, returning to his desk.

"It seems to me there's nothing indefinite about the future," Stanley observed while the secretary settled himself. "The war's over." That was the consensus, even though General Johnston's army remained in the field somewhere in the Carolinas. "What lies ahead is a period of intensive reconstruction—including, I trust, punishment for the rebels."

"Yes, definitely punishment," Stanton said. Stanley smiled. It would be his pleasure to help mete it out to former slaveowners.

They ran rapidly through the agenda Stanley had prepared. Stanton made notes—these records to be transferred here, those responsibilities assigned there. Stanley was thankful the secretary was overburdened and therefore impatient. It allowed Stanley to finish and leave the office two hours earlier than expected. He knew he should go home, but went instead, despite the traffic, to Jeannie Canary's.

It proved a bad decision. It was the wrong day for a carnal romp. And she was whiny.

"Won't you take me out this evening, loves? Surely we wouldn't be bothered, with so many drunken people everywhere. I'd love to see the play at Ford's." She no longer performed at the Varieties. She much preferred lazing about and spending the allowance Stanley furnished.

"They say the President and his wife are to appear in the state box," she went on. "You know I've never seen Mrs. Lincoln. Is she as squat and beady-eyed as they say?"

"Yes, dreadful," he retorted, made cross himself by her inability to make love just now.

"Couldn't you get tickets?"

"Not this late. Even if I could, we'd spent most of the time squeezed in crowds and wilting in the heat—on top of which, Tom Taylor's play is old and creaky. It would be a very disagreeable evening. A thoroughly dull one, too."

It was as if a perverted Nature had brought forth a black spring. Crepe blossomed everywhere that Easter weekend: on coat sleeves, the President's pew at the York Avenue Presbyterian Church, the marble façades of public buildings. Stores remained open extra hours to sell it by the yard and by the bolt.

Booth had escaped. Stanton proclaimed that the whole South must be prosecuted. Even Grant spoke of retaliatory measures of *extreme rigor.* In preparation for the state funeral on Wednesday, dry-goods stores quickly fashioned black-wrapped batons, sable sashes, ebony rosettes. Portraits of the slain President appeared in windows. Groups of stunned, grieving Negroes appeared on street corners. Paroled Confederate prisoners turned their coats inside out or threw them away for fear of being lynched.

Early on Tuesday, using a special pass provided by Sam Stout, Virgilia was able to cut into the double line of waiting mourners, as many diplomats and public officials were doing. Only in that way could she be assured of getting into the East Room of the mansion.

The slow-shuffling lines were extremely long. A guard told her an estimated fifteen thousand waited outside. Most would be disappointed when night came. The President was to lie in state this day only.

Carpenters had built a catafalque now covered in black silk.

1000

The silk matched the outside of the white-lined canopy high above the casket, which was embossed with silver stars and shamrocks and bedecked with silver ropes and tassels. A silver plate mounted on a shield read:

Abraham Lincoln
Sixteenth President of the United States
Born Feb. 12, 1809
Died April 15, 1865

Black drapes, windings, covers, concealed nearly every touch of color normally visible in the room. White cloth hid the glass of every black-edged mirror. Waiting her turn on black-painted steps which led up to the right side of the casket, Virgilia tugged at one black mitten, then the other, and smoothed her mourning dress. Finally her turn came. She stepped past the army officer at rigid attention at the end of the coffin—another guarded the opposite end—and gazed down at Abraham Lincoln.

Not even the techniques and cosmetics of the mortician could do much to improve his crude, wasted look. She had come here more out of curiosity than anything else, and she studied the corpse with half-lidded eyes. He had been too lenient and forgiving. Too much of a threat to the high purpose of men such as Sam and Thad Stevens.

The newly sworn President, Andrew Johnson, would pose no similar threat. Sam dismissed him as a dull-witted bumpkin. Along with Ben Wade and Congressman Dawes, Sam had already paid a courtesy call on Johnson. He reported to Virgilia that Wade, through pointed indirection, had left no doubt about what he and legislators of like mind expected of the new man.

"Mr. Johnson, I thank God you're here," Wade had said. "Lincoln had too much of the milk of human kindness to deal with these damned rebels. Now they'll be dealt with according to their deserts."

As the hunt for Wilkes Booth went on, even moderate politicians and newspapers throughout the North were blaming the entire South for the deed. Hinting at a Davis-inspired conspiracy. Demanding vengeance, Sam reported with glee. "By giving his life, Virgilia, our direst philosophical foe has been of infinite aid to our cause."

The conspiracy theory intrigued Virgilia. But she skewed her version slightly. Booth's murder ring had included others; a hulk named Payne or Paine had broken into Secretary Seward's house on the same night Lincoln was shot and would have stabbed Seward to death had not the secretary's son and a male nurse intervened. Others were said to be involved as well. Was Booth the sole motivator of the group? Suppose some radical Republican had inspired and encouraged him, hoping to produce the very result that had now occurred—a renewed cry for Southern blood?

It certainly wasn't beyond the realm of possibility, though she supposed the truth of it would never be known. Still, the truth mattered less than what had happened these past couple of days. Ordinary citizens were demanding the same harsh measures men such as Sam had long advocated.

"Madam? You will have to move on. Many others are waiting."

The usher spoke from the East Room floor, near some chairs hastily painted black and set out for the hacks from the press. The usher's whisper focused attention on Virgilia, embarrassing her. She almost called him a name. But this was no place to create a scene.

Besides, she felt good. The sight of the dead Chief Executive was not at all depressing. The program of Sam's group could now be carried forward with less obstruction. The great majority, converted overnight by a bullet, wanted that program. Virgilia gave the usher a scathing look and walked decorously to the steps leading down. She glanced back once and fought to suppress a smile.

Sam was right. In death, the ugly prairie lawyer served his country far better than he ever had in life. His murder was a blessing.

133

Huntoon wanted to die. At least once daily, he was positive he would within the hour. He had lost something like twenty-five pounds and all his fervor. Would he never sleep in a regular bed again? Eat food cooked on a stove? Be able to relieve himself in privacy?

Each section of the long road from St. Louis had had its own distinctive frights and travails. On the journey in the overland coach, they had been accompanied and guarded more than half the way by a Union cavalry detachment. The Plains Indians were raiding, they were told.

Huntoon quaked when informed of that. Powell, on the other hand, seemed stimulated to broaden his performance as the loyal, fearless Kentuckian. Huntoon's loathing grew.

Virginia City, with its looming mountains, belching smokestacks, ruffian miners, was as strange and threatening as China or the steppes. He and Powell had to load the bullion at night at the refinery, laying the half-inch-thick tapered ingots in rows, according to a plan Powell had sketched. The ingots measured five by three inches. Each wagon bed carried ninety of them, for a total weight of around four hundred and fifty pounds. The worth at the prevailing price of twenty dollars and sixty-seven cents an ounce was just short of one hundred fifty thousand dollars. The arrangement and value of the gold loaded in the second wagon was identical.

"This is but the first shipment," Powell reminded him. "There'll be more, though not right away. The lode's rich, but most laymen don't appreciate the time and the immense ore tonnage needed to produce this much bullion. I've been readying this one shipment for over a year. But I was working in secret, through couriers, over a long distance. It will go faster from now on."

Because of the added weight, the underside of each wagon had been reinforced with special braces. After wooden wedges were placed inside to keep the ingots from shifting, the two men nailed a false floor into each wagon, covering them with dirty blankets. On top of the blankets, boxes and barrels of provisions as well as some crates of Spencer rifles were loaded next day. A six-horse hitch was required to pull each wagon.

Powell then hired his teamsters—two as regular drivers, a third as relief man. They were all thuggish, illiterate young fellows who spoke little and collectively carried a total of seven weapons. This trio constantly intimidated Huntoon with beetling stares and smirks. They would receive a hundred dollars apiece at the end of the trip. The guide, even cruder and more brutish, would be paid double that sum.

The journey had its own horrors: insects, bad water, freezing nights as they climbed to the Sierra passes, then descended to hazy, empty valleys. Huntoon suffered sneezes and ague for a week.

Bearing south through what the guide assured them was California, they were soon broiling and quarreling over the need to drink sparingly from the water casks while they crossed a frightful stretch of desert. Huntoon became so dizzy from the heat he was barely able to reply coherently when anyone spoke to him.

Eventually they turned southeast, whereupon Powell's hired men started to bedevil Huntoon with tales of Indian signs, which he, of course, could never see. Powell eavesdropped on some of these recitations with a straight face, suppressing amusement bordering on the hysterical. Huntoon took note of Powell's grave expression and concluded that the warnings were true—which terrified him even more.

He lost track of the days. Was it early May or the last of April? Was there really a Confederacy? A Richmond, a Charleston—an Ashton? He doubted it with increasing frequency as they pushed deeper into sinister mountains and arid, windblown valleys where strange, thorny vegetation grew.

The guide had quickly sensed Huntoon's weakness and joined

1004

in to exploit it for the sake of relieving the boredom. Banquo Collins was about forty, a brawny Scot with mustaches he had let grow down long and pointed, like those of some of the Chinese on the Comstock. His first name had been bestowed by his father, an itinerant actor born in Glasgow, trained in London, and buried, penniless, in the pueblo of Los Angeles. Collins didn't know his mother's name.

He did know he enjoyed making the bespectacled Southron squirm. Collins's employer, Powell, was something of a hard case. Collins thought him demented but not to be trifled with. Huntoon, however, was born for bullying.

Nearly every day, he would say pathetically, "Where are we?" To which Collins liked to reply, after a number of suitable obscenities to register his annoyance, "Aren't you tired of asking that question, laddie? I am tired of answering it, for we're exactly where we were yesterday and last week and two weeks previous. On the trail to bonny Santa Fe. And that's that."

And away he would gallop, up alongside the lumbering wagons, leaving Huntoon on foot, swallowing dust.

Bonny, did he say? Sweet Christ, there was nothing bonny about this part of America. Why had Powell chosen it? Why had the Confederacy tried to occupy it? It was as forlorn as the moon, and full of menace. The teamsters delighted in warning him to watch out for coral and giant bull snakes—they neglected to mention the latter were harmless—or tarantulas and the allegedly venomous vinegarroons. "What the greasers call sun spiders. Real poison, those suckers." Another lie.

Huntoon was uninterested in the occasional sight of hairy buffalo, prairie-dog towns, orioles and hummingbirds and swooping duck hawks, the taste of roasted piñon nuts or the fact that crushed yucca root made excellent suds for washing. "Thass why they call it soapweed down this way, reb."

He hated all the verbal jabbing, but he was even more frightened when, one day, it stopped. The teamsters kept their eyes on the jagged horizon. Collins began to deluge Huntoon with warnings about red Indians, and not entirely for sport. He wanted to exorcise some of his own mounting worry.

"We're in the country of the Apaches now. Fiercest warriors God ever made—though some claim it was Satan who whelped them. Got no respect whatsoever for flesh, be it human or horse. The braves ride their animals till they get hungry, then they eat 'em. Makes no difference in their fighting—they always do that on foot. They like to sneak up, and it doesn't endanger them all that much. In a pinch, many an Apache lad can outrun a mustang."

"Do—" Huntoon gulped "—do you think there are Apaches close by, Collins?"

"Aye. A party from the Jicarilla tribe, if I read the sign properly. They're out there somewhere right now, watching."

"But surely we have enough guns to frighten them off—?"

"Nothing frightens off the Apaches, laddie. They go out of their way to plague white men and each other. Year or two ago, some of your Southron soldier boys rode into this country. The Apaches made a treaty of friendship at Fort Stanton, then endorsed it by ambushing and massacring a party of sixteen. They don't take sides, though—altogether neutral, they are. In a Union settlement they killed forty-six, including youngsters."

"Stop telling me that kind of thing," Huntoon protested. "What good does it do?"

"It prepares you for what we may run into. If we have bad luck and the Jicarilla decide to do more than watch, you'll have to fight like the rest of us." He sniffed. "Doesn't appear to me that you've ever done much fighting. But you'll learn fast, laddie. Mighty fast if you like living."

Taunting Huntoon with a laugh more like a dog's bark, he booted his horse forward toward the first six-horse hitch.

After years in the Southwest, Collins had adopted many Indian ways and devices. He didn't ride with a saddle, only a soft ornamented pad of supple hide stuffed with grass and buffalo hair. His pony had a war bridle: the rope of braided buffalo hair tied around the animal's lower jaw was the bit, the ends of the rope the reins. Collins had lived with a squaw wife for a while. Despite all this, he hated red men, the lot of them, and now began to regret hiring on with this crowd.

One possibility of profit offset the danger. Banquo Collins knew the two wagons contained something besides guns and provisions. Powell hadn't told him so, of course. But he suspected from the moment he saw the six powerful horses straining against the traces of the first wagon back in Virginia City. He confirmed the suspicion by discovering the special cross-bracing on the underside of both wagons. The extra weight was not visible, but it was there.

How much precious metal the wagons carried, he didn't know.

1006

But it had to be a goodly amount. Gold bullion, probably. As to its purpose, its ultimate use, he presumed that was Powell's secret. Maybe it had a connection with the Confederate cause, for which the man was openly keen. All the Southrons Collins had met were fanatics of one sort or another.

The secret cargo prodded him to prepare for various eventualities, for he did fear they were being followed. Had been for three days. Or at least that was when Collins first observed the sign, which he pointed out to no one else until he was sure he was right about it.

He estimated the number of Jicarilla as between ten and twenty. In the event of a hot brush with them, Collins intended to behave like the glass snake, a natural oddity he had discovered down this way. The glass snake was not a snake at all but a legless lizard with the ability to shake off part of its tail when attacked. The tail kept twitching after it separated from the body, and while the attacker was being distracted by the sight, the creature writhed away to safety.

Collins was not only determined to escape with his skin and his hair but with part of the gold. He certainly couldn't get away with several hundred pounds of it, but even a little would allow him to live handsomely and have fun for a while.

Aye, he would play the glass snake, all right. Having of course made sure, either by observing the Apaches at work or by taking action himself, that Mr. Powell and the lawyer were in no state to tell tales of his thievery, ever.

That evening they encamped among tall standing rocks near a deep gully, part of a line of eroded breaks above a stream they must ford. Collins assured Powell of an easy descent to be found three miles due south, but he preferred this campsite because of the natural fortifications the rocks provided.

"Better here tonight than in the open."

"You think the Apaches are close?"

"I'm certain of it."

"How much longer to reach Santa Fe? Three days?"

"Or a wee bit more." Collins never risked a lie with Powell. The man's eyes and barely controlled tension warned against it. "Now, sir, I suggest we build a fire and stay close to it. If you take a stroll, make sure it isn't far."

"All right."

"I must go ha' my dinner now."

"And we'll have ours."

Powell, Huntoon, and the teamsters ate biscuits and jerky, both of which helped relieve the boredom because it took so much time to soften the food with chewing. Collins preferred his own fare, pit-roasted pieces of mescal, an Apache delicacy of which Powell wanted no part.

Powell rubbed a slim hand over his hair. It felt dry, scratchy. He had run out of pomade weeks ago. He disliked hats. The result was more and more gray apparent. He must resemble a scarecrow. An old one, at that. Would Ashton laugh, he wondered. He imagined her naked as he leaned against a wagon wheel.

Huntoon rose, his apologetic expression explaining the reason. He stepped behind a rock. Two teamsters snickered at the sound of water.

Three days to Santa Fe. Apache in the vicinity. Powell decided he had better wait no longer. Huntoon had been useful, performing menial chores and dutifully twitching each time Powell reminded him that no matter how onerous his task, he must carry it out to prove his mettle. The stupid cuckold had done it, too.

Twilight came on rapidly in this craggy, lonesome land, which resembled nothing Lamar Powell had ever seen. He found it magically beautiful if taken on its own terms. As a teamster stood, stretched, and rubbed his rump, Powell left the fire and threaded through the stones to the gully rim, where he looked down. The gully bottom was already hidden in cool black shadow.

He gazed east, toward clouds that picked up the fiery light slanting from the opposite direction. Eastward, Ashton was waiting. He was disarmed and amazed to realize how much he missed her. In his own way, he loved her. She was intensely physical and warm, something her pitiful husband undoubtedly hadn't appreciated during his short span on earth. She would be an ideal first lady for the new state he would rule and guard from harm for the rest of his life.

He had planned the first steps months ago. Locate an appropriate site, near Santa Fe but not too near. Hire workers to erect a small ranch house and sink a well. Find some Confederate sympathizer to travel into Texas, spreading the word—rallying the disaffected soldiers, who, if not already paroled after a surrender, soon would be.

At first they would ride to Santa Fe singly or in pairs. But before the year was out, they'd be arriving by platoons and companies, shaking the earth with the sound of their coming. He would devise a new flag for them to carry against potential enemies, and write a proclamation establishing the new government on an equal basis with that of mongrelized Washington and all the nations of Europe.

It would be convenient to employ Huntoon as his first herald in Texas, but Ashton made it impossible. Powell meant to live with her from the moment they were reunited. Therefore—

A contented sigh signaled his decision.

Powell shivered; the evening air was cooling rapidly. Tonight was not only suitable; it was ideal, he thought, gazing east. He felt close to Ashton all at once.

Perhaps she, too, was growing excited as he drew near. He had sent a letter from Virginia City, which he presumed she had received by now; the mail surely traveled faster than his overburdened wagons. In the letter, he had described the contents of the wagons, their probable route of travel and approximate timetable. Was she poring over his words at this moment, thinking of the two of them romping on sheets of presidential satin? Delightful vision—

About an hour later, with night settling, he examined his four-barrel Sharps to be certain it was fully loaded. He tucked the gun away inside his frock coat, yellowed by travel dust, and sought Huntoon at the smoky fire. Collins was napping against a boulder on the far side. Two of the hired men still squatted next to each other, chewing jerky. The third had gone to take the first turn at picket duty.

"James, my friend?" Powell said, touching his shoulder. Huntoon's spectacles flashed with firelight as he turned.

"What is it?"

"Would you come for a short stroll? I have a matter to discuss."

Pettish, Huntoon said, "Is it important?"

A charming smile. "I wouldn't ask otherwise."

"I'm infernally tired."

A level stare, once more demanding that he prove his mettle. "Just five minutes. Then you can have a long rest."

"Oh, all right." Sounding like a cranky child, Huntoon wiped biscuit crumbs from the corners of his mouth. He had grown slovenly on the journey. Powell distastefully noted black dirt under the lawyer's nails.

They moved off among the rocks as the fire crackled beneath the black sky. From the near distance came the cry of an animal, half yelp, half growl. Banquo Collins sat up instantly, raising the brim of his buckskin hat. One of the teamsters glanced at the guide.

"Mountain lion?"

"No, laddie. That animal has two legs."

134

Earlier that day, Charles rode north in the Carolina springtime, through green rolling land where bowers of azalea blew to and fro in the warm wind and wisteria bloomed in purple brilliance. He saw little except Gus.

He saw her in the face of a much older farm woman who gave him a dipper of water when he asked politely. He saw her in a cloud formation. He saw her on the backs of his eyelids when he tethered the mule and rested by a roadside tree.

In all the muddle and madness of the past four years, he was trying to find something of worth. She was all there was. His memory held scores of small, touching portraits of her racing across the grass to greet him, cooking in the kitchen, scrubbing his back in the zinc tub, bending to embrace him in bed.

He had found one thing of value in the war, and out of confusion and some stupid, contradictory sense of duty—the same duty still driving him along these unfamiliar dirt roads—he had thrown it away. The hurt and regret that followed the dawning realization were immense. His physical wound was healing nicely, but the other one—that never would.

While still in his home state, he had chanced upon a rural store on whose counter stood a glass jar containing four old, dry cigars. He had the remainder of one in his clenched teeth at this moment; he had smoked the first half last night. The other three protruded from the pocket of his cadet gray shirt.

He was riding in hot sunshine, the gypsy robe rolled and tied behind him. Suddenly he saw a mounted man crest the next rise in the road and come cantering in his direction. Alarm gripped him until he realized he was still in North Carolina, though damned if he knew where. And the emaciated horseman raising dust in the afternoon wore gray.

Charles reined in the mule and waited. Birds sang and wheeled over nearby meadows. The rider approached, slowing his mount while he took Charles's measure and decided he was all right, though the man—an officer—still kept his hand near his side arm.

Charles chewed the cigar nervously, a glassy look in his eyes. The officer walked his skeletal roan closer and stopped.

"Colonel Courtney Talcott, First Light Artillery Regiment of North Carolina, at your service, sir. I gather from that shirt and your revolver that you're a soldier?" He scrutinized the scrap of sword in Charles's belt and his peculiar, dazed expression. The tone of the colonel's question hinted at lingering doubt.

Almost as an afterthought, Charles muttered, "Yes, sir. Major Main, Hampton's cavalry scouts. Where's the army?"

"The Army of Northern Virginia?" Charles nodded. "Then you haven't heard?"

"Heard what? I've been down on the Ashley, finding this remount."

"General Lee requested terms from General Grant more than three weeks ago. At Appomattox Court House, in Virginia."

Charles shook his head. "I didn't know. I've been taking my time riding back there."

"You certainly have," Talcott replied, not hiding his disapproval. "You needn't continue. The army has disbanded. The last I knew, General Johnston and his men were still in the field, though he, too, may have surrendered by now. If he hasn't, he soon will. The war's over."

Silence. A tan female cardinal fussed in a bush when a jay swooped too near her nestlings. The artillery officer looked askance at Charles, who showed no emotion. The colonel said again, more emphatically, "Over."

Charles blinked. Then he nodded. "I knew it would be. I just didn't know when." The officer scowled. "Thanks for the information."

Frostily: "You're welcome. I would turn around and go home if I were you, Major. There's nothing more to be done in Virginia." *Yes, there is.*

The artilleryman cantered past, raising dust. He had no intention of riding beside the listless and slightly mad-eyed junior officer even for a few miles. The fellow had even forgotten to salute. Disgraceful.

The dust settled. Charles sat on his mule in the middle of the road, slumped, as the news sank in. It was official. They had lost. So much blood, suffering, effort, hope—wasted. For a few blindly wrathful moments, it made no difference that the cause was misbegotten. He hated every goddamn Yankee in creation.

Quickly, that passed. But to his surprise, the defeat hurt more than he would have expected, even though it was inevitable. He had known it was inevitable for at least a year. Seen portents, read prophecies, long before that. The horses slowly starving in Virginia. Articles in brown old newspapers about Southern governors defying Davis with his own sacred doctrine of states' rights. A Union carbine that fired seven shots—

Feelings of relief and despair overwhelmed him. He plucked the fragment of the light cavalry saber from his belt and studied it. Suddenly, while light glanced off the stub of blade, his eyes brimmed with rage. A savage outward lash of his arm sent the metal cross whirling over the meadow, there to drop and vanish.

He knew the only course left to him if he were to stay remotely sane. He must ride on to Virginia and try to repair the damage done by his own foolishness. But first there was duty. Duty always came first. He had to make sure those at Mont Royal were not threatened by occupying troops or other dangers whose nature he couldn't guess. He would cover the distance to the plantation much faster than he had when riding north. Then, the moment he was finished at home—Virginia.

He lifted the rein, turned the mule's head and started him rapidly back the way they had come.

135

Under a brilliant full moon, Huntoon and Powell reached the edge of the gully. Huntoon was glad to stop. His feet hurt. Powell slipped his right hand in his coat pocket.

Huntoon took off his spectacles, pinched up a bit of shirt bosom and polished one lens, then the other, saying finally, "What is it you want to discuss?"

With a cryptic, "Look down there," Powell bobbed his head toward the gully bottom. Huntoon leaned forward, peered down. Powell pulled out the four-barrel Sharps and shot him in the back.

The lawyer uttered a short, gasping cry. He spun and reached for Powell's lapel. Powell smacked him with his free hand. Huntoon's spectacles flew off and sailed into the dark below.

Blinking like a newborn animal, Huntoon tried to focus his eyes on the man who had shot him. Pain blazing through his body, he understood the betrayal. It had been meant to happen on this journey. Planned from the start.

How stupidly naïve he had been. Of course he had suspected Ashton and Powell were lovers. For that reason he had mailed the letter to his Charleston law partner. But later, filled with renewed hope of regaining Ashton's affection through a display of courage, he had regretted the instructions in the letter. But he had done nothing to countermand them, always assuming there would be ample time later. And what he'd seen in St. Louis had prompted the second letter; the one he'd given her—

Now, as if he could somehow cancel both past and present pain by will and action, he seized Powell's sleeve. Formed in his throat a plea for mercy and help. But the fiery wound and saliva rendered the words gibberish.

"Let go of me," Powell said with disgust, and shot him a second time.

The ball went straight into Huntoon's stomach, forcing him to step back. He stepped into space. Powell had a last brief vision of the poor fool's wet eyes and mewling mouth. Then Huntoon dropped.

Powell blew into the barrels of his pistol and put it away. Over the strident barking of coyotes across the gully, he heard the clump and thump of Huntoon's body striking, rebounding into space, falling and rebounding again.

Then it grew quiet. He could hear Collins and the others shouting to him. Was he all right?

With a smile, he stood regarding the high-riding moon. Despite the alarms from the campfire, he lingered a moment, studying the sky above the wind-scoured land and congratulating himself. He imagined Ashton's dark-tipped breasts, his alone now, together with the wild thatch below. He felt youthful. Content. Refreshed.

Over a hump of rock behind him, a small, skinny man with stringy hair and a waist clout appeared, bathed in brilliant moonlight for a moment. In his right hand he held a buckskin-covered war club consisting of a wood handle connected by sinew to a round stone head. Powell didn't see the man, or the second one, who rose into sight as the first man jumped.

He heard the man land and turned, terror clogging his throat. He clawed for the Sharps, but it caught in his pocket lining. The stone struck his head, one powerful and correctly aimed blow that broke open his left temple and killed him by the time he dropped to his knees, open-mouthed. Blood rushed down the left side of his face as he toppled forward.

The little Apache grinned and thrust the dripping club over his head, triumphant. His companion leaned down and landed beside him. Half a dozen others glided from behind other rocks, barefoot and light as dancers. All of them stole toward the voices and the fire glow.

The moment Banquo Collins heard the two shots and the teamsters started hollering, he quietly but quickly looked to his own gear. One of the teamsters said, "Who fired? 'Paches?"

1014

"I doubt it. Sometimes they carry stolen pieces, but customarily it's a club—or a wee knife to slit your throat. Also, they'll not risk a fight and possible death at night. They believe conditions existing when they die follow them to the spirit world, and they want to rest forever in pleasant sunshine. Nothing to fear, see?"

Throughout the speech, Collins had finished gathering his gear. He tugged his hat over his eyes, turned and started away from the fire at a brisk walk. The teamster was too tense and stupid to compare the guide's statements with reality: the full moon lent the landscape a clarity and whiteness almost like that of a wintry noonday.

But Collins's rapid stride woke up the teamster. "Where the hell you goin'?" he yelled.

Head down, the guide kept moving. A few more steps, and he would have cover among the big—

"Collins, you yella dog, you come back here!"

Not a dog, a glass snake, he thought, recognizing hysteria in the voice and flinging himself sideways while reaching for his revolver. The wild shot fired by the teamster missed by two yards, pinging off rock. He didn't waste a bullet of his own—he might need every one—but his leap threw him against a boulder, bruising his shoulder. Recovering, he lunged on.

After a few steps he turned again, glimpsed part of the clearing between tall stones. He saw the Jicarillas swarm out of the dark beyond the fire and surround the three hired men. Genuinely frightened, Collins fled, leaving behind the capering Apaches and the wild, sharp barks with which they imitated a coyote. The barks were not quite loud enough to drown out the screams.

Running, stumbling often, Collins drove himself until pain and shortness of breath forced him to slow down. His chest felt close to bursting. After a brief rest he pushed on until he found a place where he thought he could descend. Hand over bloodied hand, he went down the rock wall. He misjudged one hold and fell the last twenty feet, knocked nearly unconscious.

Dust-covered, his hands and face red from cuts and scrapes, he rested again, then lurched to the edge of the stream, which he crossed with a minimum of noise. Not that the Apaches would hear the splashes. They were whooping and yelling to celebrate.

Collins knew they would take the horses to ride awhile, then butcher. They would also break open the gun crates and take the

Spencers. He wanted to learn the fate of the two heavy wagons, the object of the late Mr. Powell's attention. The moment Collins saw the Apaches at the fire he knew they had disposed of his half-crazy employer and that worm of a lawyer. Neither man mattered to him, nor any of the teamsters. The teamsters were the tail of the glass snake.

What mattered was his own skin and, secondarily, the wagons. When he reached the shallows on the other side, he headed upstream until he located a good observation point in some twisted junipers. He was almost directly opposite the mouth of the deep gully near the campsite. The Apaches had added fresh wood to the fire. He saw flames leap above the tall rocks occasionally.

He was wrong about the source of the fire, he quickly discovered. It came from one of the wagons, which appeared between the rocks, pushed by fifteen or twenty angry Indians. The whole forward third of the wagon was burning. The front wheels blazed brightly.

The Apaches pushed it to the gully rim and with grunts and exclamations tipped it over. The emptied wagon—if indeed it was completely empty, which Collins doubted—stood perpendicular a moment, tailgate toward the moon. Then it dropped, the front end decorated with two swiftly spinning disks of fire, like the Catherine wheels he remembered dimly from a childhood visit to his pa's home city of Glasgow.

Wood splintered. The fire separated into several gaudy sections, each of which hit a different place on the bottom. The Apaches disappeared, returning soon with the second burning wagon, which they also sent into the gully. Then they howled and shook their clubs and lances.

To Collins they sounded angry. Maybe they had expected some greater prize from the wagons than rifles and provisions. Maybe, he speculated, fingering an oozing gash in his left cheek, they didn't know where to look. The heaviness of both wagons in relation to their appearance had long ago convinced him of the existence of false floors.

He would investigate, though he certainly wouldn't remain here through the night to do so. He wanted no contact with the Jicarillas. It wasn't wise to buck the odds. A man won a pot with a pair only once in a while.

Merely by surviving the night, he would win plenty. He would win the chance to come back to the gully. He doubted these particular Apaches would ever come back to it, and they would be gone by daylight. The debris in the gully was safe for a while; this was not a heavily traveled route. He could return weeks, even months later, and be confident of finding whatever the burned wagons had concealed. Especially if it were gold.

Banquo Collins didn't know a lot about metallurgy, but he knew some. Gold could change its form. Mingle with other elements in the earth—that was gold ore. But it couldn't be destroyed. So long as no one chanced on the gully or examined the ashes, any gold that was there would remain there, his for the claiming.

Feeling good, he slipped away from the junipers by the stream. The red light down in the gully faded as he limped east beneath the huge full moon, wetting his lips occasionally as he imagined himself a wealthy tourist swallowing raw oysters and bouncing a San Francisco whore on each knee.

136

Homebound soldiers stopped occasionally at Mont Royal, bringing the Mains vivid word pictures of the ruin in the state. These they traded for water from the well. Cooper had no food to offer the travelers.

Although no partisan of the South, especially of the reasons it had waged war, Judith broke down and cried when she heard descriptions of the huge swathes of burned forest, trampled fields, looted homes that marked the passage of Sherman's juggernaut.

Columbia was scorched earth, whole blocks gone except for a fragment of wall or an isolated chimney standing amid acres of rubble. The new statehouse, roofless and unfinished, had been spared, though its west wall had been marked forever by four Union cannonballs fired during a bombardment from Lexington Hills, across the Congaree.

Bands of blacks clogged the roads, the visitors said, free but generally baffled by their new status and, for the most part, starving. There was no food available for white or black, and many village storekeepers had closed and boarded up their places. Altogether, the picture was one of desolation.

Since the danger of crop damage from the spring rice birds was past, Cooper decided to plant three squares for a June crop, something his father always did in case the earlier planting was ruined by the birds or by a storm-summoned infusion of salty water. To help him prepare the ground with a few rusty, unbroken implements remaining, he had only Andy, Cicero—too old for the work—Jane, and his daughter. Judith helped when she wasn't cooking or tending the small house built of raw pine.

Unused to physical labor, Cooper stumbled back to the house every night insect-bitten and hurting from his ankles to his neck. He would eat whatever tiny portion of food was offered, saying little, and go straight to his pallet. Often he moaned or exclaimed in his sleep.

Questions without answers tormented him during his waking hours. Could they raise enough rice to sell off a little, retaining the rest to help them survive the coming winter? Would the South be occupied by hostile troops for years now that the North was reportedly set on harsh reprisal because of Lincoln's murder? How would he ever learn what had happened to Orry's body since Richmond had been burned and, presumably, many army records destroyed? One soldier who had stopped described the mass graves around Petersburg, hundreds of corpses dumped in each with little regard for identification.

Questions hammered at his head till it ached as much as his body while he scratched the Carolina soil in the steaming sun. He was bent at the task one afternoon when Andy called his name sharply. He raised his head, wiped his sweaty eyelids to clear his vision, saw Judith dashing along the embankments separating the squares.

From her haste and her reddened face, he could tell something was wrong. He ran to meet her.

"Cooper, it's your mother. I went in during her nap, as I usu-

1018

ally do, and found her. If I can judge from her expression, her passing was peaceful. Perhaps painless. I'm so sorry, darling—"

She stopped, cocking her head, puzzled and a little frightened by his queer half-smile. He didn't explain the momentary recollection that produced the strange reaction. Memories of Clarissa airily wandering about in the midst of the guerrilla attack. She had walked where guns were firing and never been scratched.

The odd smile disappeared; practical matters intruded. "Do you suppose we can find any ice at all for the body?"

"I doubt it. We'd better bury her right away."

"Yes, I think you're right." He slipped a throbbing arm around her, tears filling his eyes. They returned to the yellow-pine house for the rest of the day.

Cooper had discovered long ago that life had a perverse way of surprising you with the unexpected when you least needed it. He was sweating with Andy in the dusk, hammering together a coffin for Clarissa, when Jane appeared.

"We have three visitors."

Cooper swabbed his wet brow with his forearm. "More soldiers?"

She shook her head. "They came by railroad as far as they could—they say it's been reopened part of the way. Then they managed to buy an old mule and a wagon, both about done for—"

Testy, he said, "Well, whoever they are, you know what to tell them. They're welcome to camp and use the well. But we have no food."

"You'll have to feed these people," Jane said. "It's your sister and her husband and Miss Madeline."

When he thought it reasonably safe, Jasper Dills went down to occupied Richmond.

He was appalled at the destruction that had accompanied the collapse and flight of the Confederate government. A Union officer told him that while the fires raged, small-arms ammunition and more than eight hundred thousand shells had detonated over a period of several hours. A few substantially fireproofed buildings remained standing, but there were blocks and blocks destroyed. It was the heart of springtime, and the air should have smelled of flowers and new greenery. In Richmond it smelled of smoke.

1019

The rutted streets were dumps for broken and abandoned furnishings, clothing, rags, bottles, books, personal papers. Even more distasteful to the little attorney was the human litter. Destitute white families roaming. Confederate veterans, many as young as fourteen, sitting in the sun with starved faces and vacant eyes. Crowds of Negroes, some strutting outrageously. And everywhere —on foot, astride saddle horses, driving wagons—soldiers in the blue of the conqueror. They were the only whites in the city who smiled, Dills noticed.

He was in a high state of nerves when he reached the sutlers' tents set up, complete with outdoor tables and cheap chairs, on the lawns of Capitol Square. At one such establishment, identified by its canvas banner as Hugo Delancy's, he met his contact, a former operative of Lafayette Baker's whom Dills had hired at a high price, dispatching him to Virginia to attempt to pick up a trail that was, perhaps, nonexistent.

The operative, a burly fellow with a cocked eye, took Dills to an outdoor table at Delancy's. He swilled lager while Dills drank a pitiful watery concoction passed off as lemonade.

"Well, what do you have to report?"

"Didn't think I'd have a blessed thing till six days ago. Tramped up and down the James almost three weeks before I turned up something. And it still isn't much."

The operative signaled a waiter to bring another beer. "Early in July last year a farmer saw a body floating in the James. Civilian clothes. The body was too far from shore to be retrieved, but the description—an obese man; dark-haired—roughly matches the one you provided for Captain Dayton."

"Last July, you say—?" Dills licked his lips. The stipend had continued during the intervening months. "Where did this happen?"

"The farmer was on the east bank of the river, about half a mile above the Broadway Landing pontoon bridge the army built later in the autumn. I spent another three days in the neighborhood, asking questions, but I didn't turn up anything else. So I'll take my money."

"Your report's inconclusive. Unsatisfactory."

The operative seized the lawyer's frail wrist. "I did the job. I want the pay."

Dills's strategy to save some money failed. He surrendered the bank draft from inside his jacket. The operative gave it a moment's suspicious scrutiny to embarrass him, then pocketed it, gulped the rest of his beer, and departed, leaving Dills between two tables of noisy whores, not far from the magnificent statue of George Washington.

Had Starkwether's son deserted to the enemy after Baker discharged him? If he had been killed, was it the result of a military mission or something more sinister? Was the body in the river actually Bent's? He had to know. If his periodic reports stopped, so would the stipend. He thumped his fist on the table.

"What happened?"

Two of the sluts to his right heard the loud expression of turmoil and made remarks. Dills composed himself. The trail had run out. Starkwether's son was dead, merely another casualty of the long, distasteful, and ultimately purposeless war.

On reflection, the lawyer decided that an inconclusive report was better than none at all. Was valuable, in fact, if interpreted correctly. Since it said nothing to the contrary, it allowed him to continue writing the periodic memoranda, confidently asserting that Bent was still alive. It permitted him to continue to generate income indefinitely with those little pieces of paper—a huge return on a minuscule investment.

Less upset, he relaxed in the sunshine, ignored the odors of smoke and cheap perfume, and ordered a second glass of lemonade.

137

They buried Clarissa Gault Main in the half-acre of fenced ground that had received Mont Royal's dead, white and black, for three generations. Jane cried longest and loudest of any of the small band of mourners. She had developed a great affection for the gentle little woman whose aging mind had long ago freed her of ordinary human burdens. Jane had always taken special pains to see to Clarissa's needs, as she would those of a child. Aunt Belle Nin had once told her that for many people the process of growing old was one of reversal, a return to the state of the child, who needed a special kind of care, patience, love.

Andy stood at Jane's side and wept with her. Brett and Madeline were more controlled in their grief. Their greatest shock and emotional catharsis had come immediately after Billy escorted them up the lane, when Madeline saw that Orry's home was gone, and they learned about Clarissa.

Cooper showed the least emotion. He felt it his duty to remain steady, an example in a difficult time. Before the burial, he read verses from the New Testament—Christ's dialogue with Nicodemus on everlasting life from the gospel of John. Following the reading, Andy and Billy lowered the coffin into the ground, and each mourner tossed in a handful of sandy soil. For the closing prayer Cooper deferred to Andy, who praised Clarissa as a kind and generous woman, and movingly commended her to God's care.

A moment of silence followed the murmured amens. Then Andy said, "I'll finish the rest. You all needn't stay." Billy put his arm around Brett and walked out through the gate in the badly rusted fence. Wrought iron, he noted. Hazard's iron would have lasted longer. He was momentarily embarrassed by the thought.

Cooper and the others trudged after the young couple. Suddenly Brett stopped, gazing through the live oaks to the black ash heaps where the house had stood. Tears came again, but only briefly. She shook her head and turned to Billy.

"Mother's passing just now—it's a kind of watershed, isn't it? The end of something. That house, this plantation—it never was quite what it seemed to be. But whatever it seemed to be is gone forever."

Madeline overheard and nodded melancholy agreement. It was Cooper who replied, quietly but with a fervor surprising to his younger sister.

"We have let the worst go, but we'll rebuild the best. And fight for it with every breath."

Who is he? Brett asked herself in wonderment. *I hardly know him. The old Cooper wouldn't have said such a thing. I am not the only one the war changed.*

Three days later, following the arrival of a soiled letter misdelivered to the nearest neighbor, Charles reappeared in the lane riding his mule. Brett ran to greet and embrace him. He pressed his bearded cheek against hers, but it was perfunctory. She found him sullen and withdrawn; alarmingly so. When she tried to ask him about his experiences with Hampton's cavalry, he brushed the questions aside with terse, empty answers.

Before the evening meal, Madeline found an opportunity to speak to him. "How is Augusta Barclay?"

"I don't know. I haven't seen her in some time."

"Is she still in Fredericksburg?"

"I hope so. I'm going there in a few days to find out."

After dark, he and Cooper strolled the riverbank near the site of the ruined dock, at Charles's request. Before they got down to their talk, Cooper reported a piece of news.

"We've received specific information about Orry. It came day before yesterday, in a letter from General Pickett, much delayed. Orry's body was not put in a mass grave. It was shipped south together with a number of others when it became possible to locate enough draft horses to portage the coffins around a break in some rail line below Petersburg."

"The Weldon," Charles said with a nod.

"That took place many weeks ago. Unfortunately, there was an accident."

"What kind of accident?" Cooper told him. "Jesus." Charles shook his head. "Jesus Christ."

They walked on in silence for five minutes. Charles collected himself and informed his cousin that he wanted to leave for Virginia as soon as he felt those on the plantation were safe from danger.

"Oh, we're safe enough," Cooper said with an empty laugh. "Starving, perhaps, but safe. May I ask what takes you back to Virginia?"

"Something personal."

How closed and somber he's become, Cooper thought. "Will you be returning here?"

"I hope not. The trip involves a lady."

"Charles—I had no idea—that's wonderful. Who is she?"

"I'd rather not discuss it, if you don't mind."

Mystified and a little hurt by the rebuff from the cold stranger Charles had become, Cooper bobbed his head to signal acceptance, then fell silent.

It was their season for callers, it seemed. The following Monday, as Charles prepared to leave, Wade Hampton arrived on horseback. He was bound for Charleston but stopped off because he had heard of the burning of Mont Royal and Clarissa's death. Though never close, the Hampton and Main families had known each other for three generations. Most of the great planters of the piedmont and low country had at least a nodding acquaintance, but in this case it was Charles who had strengthened the ties.

Besides visiting Clarissa's grave alone and expressing his sympathy to the family, he had another reason for calling, he said. He hoped to hear something about one of his best scouts. To his surprise, they met face-to-face. Hampton was visibly appalled to find Charles in such a scruffy state, and so dour.

No longer in uniform and grayer than Charles remembered, Hampton wore a holstered side arm beneath his coat. His favorite, Charles observed. The revolver with ivory handle grips.

Because of his high military rank, Hampton had been denied

1024

the amnesty given the majority of Confederate soldiers after the surrender. The general carried this burden openly. Bitterness was particularly apparent when he stalked all around the rubble that had once been the great house.

"As bad as Millwood," he said, shaking his head. "We should take a photograph and mail it to Grant. Perhaps it might teach him the real meaning of what he calls 'enlightened war.'"

Later, in the hot May dusk, the men sat on crates and small casks on the grass in front of the pine house; it had no piazza. Hampton had brought a bottle of peach brandy in his saddlebag. They shared it, using a collection of unmatched cups and glasses.

Hampton questioned Charles about his last days in the cavalry. Charles had little to say. Hampton told them briefly of his own experiences. He had indeed wanted to continue the fight west of the Mississippi. "What they did to my son and my brother and my home persuaded me that I was not morally bound by the surrender." So he had ridden on in pursuit of the fleeing President and his party.

"I would have escorted Mr. Davis all the way to Texas. Even Mexico. I had a small company of loyal men, or so I thought. But they dropped away, gave up, one by one. Finally I was alone. At Yorkville, I chanced to meet my wife, Mary. She and Joe Wheeler —General Wheeler—persuaded me that trying to find the President was futile. I was tired. Ready to be persuaded, I suppose. So I stopped."

Cooper asked, "Do you know where Davis is now?"

"No. I suppose he's in jail somewhere—perhaps even hanged. What a disgraceful end to the whole business." He tossed off the last of his brandy, which seemed to calm him.

Hampton went on to say he was living in a house belonging to a former overseer. "My daughter Sally's to be married in June. I have that happy event to anticipate, along with the work of rebuilding this poor, wracked state. I'm glad you're on Mont Royal again, Cooper. I remember where you stood at the time of the secession convention. We're going to need men like you. Men of sanity and good will. Patience, strength—I think the Yankees will press us hard. Try us—punish us—severely. Booth did us incredible harm."

"Has there been any word of him?" Billy said.

"Oh, yes. He was caught and shot to death a couple of weeks ago on a farm near the Rappahannock."

"Well, gentlemen—" Charles stood up and set the fruit jar from which he had been drinking on the log that had been his chair "—I'll excuse myself with your permission. I have business in Virginia, and I want to be on the road by daylight. I leave you to your high ideals and the reconstruction of our glorious state."

Billy was baffled by this sourness. His old friend stood out in memory as lighthearted, quick to laugh. This shabby, bearded skeleton wasn't Bison Main, but someone much older, of much darker temperament.

"Someone must champion the South," Cooper declared. "We must defend her with every peaceful means, or there'll be nothing left for generations but burned earth and despair."

Charles stared at him. "That isn't what you used to say, Cousin."

"Nevertheless, he's right," Hampton said, some of the old authority in his voice. "The state will need many good men. Including you, Charles."

With a bow toward the visitor, Charles smiled. "No, thank you, General. I did my job. Killed God knows how many fellow human beings—fellow Americans—on behalf of the high-minded principles of the high-minded Mr. Davis and his high-minded colleagues. Don't ask me to do anything else for the South or its misbegotten cause."

Hampton leaped to his feet, his stocky frame silhouetted against fading light in the west. "It is your land, too, sir. *Your* cause—"

"Correction, sir. It was. I obeyed orders until the surrender. But not a moment longer. Good evening, gentlemen."

Charles left before dawn, while Billy and Brett were still asleep with their arms around each other, squeezed onto the rickety cot provided for them. Billy had gone to bed saddened because his best friend had said so little to him. Charles had withheld something of great personal importance and had walked away every time Billy tried to mention his heroic behavior during the Libby escape. He had ridden off without a word of farewell, as Billy discovered soon after he awoke.

Smelling imitation coffee brewing, he gently touched Brett's middle—it was now certain that she was pregnant—kissed her warm throat, and slipped off the creaky cot. He lifted the cloth partition and found Andy at the stove. Andy confirmed that Charles had gone.

"Strange fella," he said. "Was he always so moody and glum?"

"No. Something happened to him in Virginia. Something other than the war. He was courting a woman. A widow. He cared for her very much—"

"Never heard a thing about any woman."

"He didn't tell me, either. Madeline did."

"Maybe that's it," Andy said, nodding. "If he thinks he lost her, that could account for it. A woman can tear up a man almost as much as goin' to war, I guess."

He smiled, but Billy didn't.

The passing days showed Brett how radically conditions and relationships had changed in four short years. Cooper toiled in the rice fields like one of their father's people. Madeline, who had been the chatelaine for a time, tied up her skirts, wrapped her black hair in a bandanna, and sweated right alongside him. Despite Billy's protests, Brett did, too. She insisted it would be a few months yet before she was unable to do her share.

Despite the joy of the new life growing within her, Mont Royal disappointed Brett because there were no blacks who wanted or needed her help. The kind of teaching Jane had done for a while, for example.

"There's an entire state in need of help," Cooper said when she expressed her feeling. "You've seen all the people camped in the fields and along the roads—"

But she wasn't persuaded. Everything was different and, except for her life with Billy, unhappily so.

George felt much the same way on the thirteenth of May. It was Saturday, the end of a week that saw Davis and his small party captured at a woodland bivouac near Irwinville, Georgia. George was shocked at the widespread ruin in Charleston, to which a coastal steamer from Philadelphia had brought him, with Constance. He was grieved by the sight of so many burned homes and buildings, and even more saddened by the great numbers of Negroes everywhere. Rather than happy, they seemed uneasy and occasionally sullen in their new state of freedom.

"It's entirely fitting and right that they have it," he said to Constance as they boarded the ancient sloop *Osprey,* which would

1027

take them up the Ashley. George wore a dark broadcloth suit; though not yet mustered out, he refused to wear his uniform. Nor did he need it to generate plenty of hostile stares and rude treatment.

"But there are practical problems," he went on. "How is freedom going to feed them? Clothe them? Educate them?" Even if practical answers could be found, would Northerners allow them to be implemented now that the military victory was won? Some would, of course; his sister, Virgilia, for example. But he believed such people were in a minority. The majority's turn of mind was illustrated by the telegraphic flimsy still folded in his pocket.

The message from Wotherspoon had been delivered to the pier in Philadelphia an hour before the coastal steamer weighed anchor: SIX MEN QUITTING TO PROTEST HIRING TWO COLORED.

He had immediately wired back: LET THE SIX GO. HAZARD. But that didn't alter the larger picture, and he knew it. His attitude was an atypical drop in the Yankee ocean.

Answering his questions of a moment ago, Constance said, "That's the purpose of the Freedmen's Bureau, isn't it? General Howard is supposed to be a decent, capable man—"

"But look who wormed into the bureau as one of his assistants. Do you really believe Stanley did it for humanitarian reasons? There's some secret agenda—political, probably. We're in for a bad time for a few years, I'm afraid. It may last even longer if the wounds don't heal. Aren't *permitted* to heal—"

But the Ashley was smooth, and their short journey upriver on *Osprey* uneventful—until they had their first glimpse of the plantation. George exclaimed softly. Constance clutched the rail.

"My God," he said. "Even the pier's gone."

"That's right, sir," the master of the sloop called from the wheel. There was a slyly exaggerated politeness to the last word, saying the captain didn't really believe his passenger deserved the appellation. The overused, overblown *sir* was a common Southernism, George was discovering.

"You'll have to cross a plank to shore," the man added. His eyes indicated that he might be pleased if husband and wife fell in the muddy water.

They had sent no advance word of their visit. They piled their valises on the grassy bank, including one old satchel that George had not let out of his sight since leaving Lehigh Station. As the

1028

whistle blew and the sloop chugged away, an unfamiliar black man appeared from behind the ruins of the great house. While Constance waited, George walked up the lawn. The Negro hurried down to meet him, introducing himself as Andy.

"George Hazard." They shook hands. Andy recognized the name and dashed off to carry the news to Cooper and the others, who were apparently at work in the rice fields.

George's shock deepened as he again studied the ruins, seeing in imagination the glittering ball the Mains once gave in honor of the visiting Hazards. The hanging lanterns, the swelling music, the laughing gentlemen and soft-shouldered women.

And here came Cooper, bare-chested and sweaty, a look of exhaustion on his face. He was followed by Billy, Brett, and Madeline, all grubby as farmers and giving off strong odors in the afternoon heat.

George silently reproved himself for the negative reaction. The Mains had always been farmers, though of a very elegant and special kind. Now it appeared that they had—to twist it a little—no hands but their own. Billy's were wet from the ooze of broken blisters, George noticed.

He wasn't surprised to find his brother here. Constance had reported Billy's departure with Brett and Madeline when George came home on furlough late in April. Once George had decided on this trip, he had shamelessly telegraphed Stanley and asked him to secure an extension of his leave.

Cooper and Judith, however, were astonished by the arrival of the visitors. They pretended elation, but their tiredness showed. So did an unmistakable reserve, a tension. George could scarcely believe he had ever heard the music at that lovely ball. The sight of the impoverished Mains left him full of despair. He hoped he had a partial remedy, brought up with the luggage and placed near his feet on the brilliant spring lawn.

Madeline and Judith led the visitors to the substitute porch—logs, boxes, and barrels arranged in front of the new pine house—then went inside to prepare some refreshments.

There was a half hour of halting exchanges of information about the two families. George expressed his sympathy to Madeline, then asked Cooper, "Where is Orry's grave? I'd like to pay my respects."

"I'll show you the marker we erected. The grave itself is empty."

1029

"They didn't send the body home?"

"Oh, yes, they put it on a train, finally. Somewhere in North Carolina there was an accident on our splendid transportation system. The train derailed. A terrible smash-up. Forty pine coffins burned. George Pickett wrote to say there was nothing left."

George hurt as he seldom had in all his life. He heard April's fire bells dinning in his mind. He struggled to get the words out. "I'd still—like to see the marker and spend some time there alone."

"When would you like to do it?" Cooper asked.

"Now, if you don't mind. But first I must get something from my luggage."

Cooper described the route to the graveyard. Finding the marker, George drew from his pocket the letter he had kept in the satchel in his desk for four years. The letter to Orry. He knelt and dug a shallow hole in the sandy soil six inches in front of the marker. He folded the letter once and placed it in the hole, which he refilled, smoothing the sand afterward. Then, though never a deeply religious man, he clasped his hands and bowed his head. He stayed thirty minutes, making his farewell.

The afternoon was a trial. The Mains seemed a company of strangers. Or was that merely their plight distorting his own vision?

No, he decided, much had changed as a result of the destruction. It was most noticeable in Cooper, who had a certain forbidding politeness new to George. Orry's brother said he was glad to have an excuse to leave the fields for half a day, but his exhausted, anxious eyes belied that. Much had changed; did that mean everything had changed?

Supper lifted his spirits a bit. Although the meal was scanty—chiefly rice—the conversation was slightly livelier, less strained, than before. The exception was Cooper. He said little. George's anxiety deepened. Staring at Cooper was like trying to read a page of some Oriental language. Nothing could be deciphered.

When all of them had finished, they once again took places on the improvised furniture while the evening cooled and darkened around them. Madeline asked George about conditions in Charleston.

"Terrible," he replied. "I felt guilty because I couldn't hand a few dollars to each of the people on the streets."

"Black people," Jane said, not as a question.

"Whites, too. They all looked destitute—and hungry. On the docks, we saw dozens trying to catch fish with string. We saw scores tenting under blankets in vacant lots. What happened down here is dreadful."

"So was slavery, Mr. Hazard."

"Jane," Andy said, but her eyes defied him. George was dismayed to see brief anger on Cooper's face. Judith observed it, too, her mouth drawing into a tight line.

George's anxiety deepened. He had better say the rest, or he might never get it said.

"Of course you're right, Jane. I believe no person of conscience would assert any other view. But this is also true: there's been terrible damage to everyone. I don't mean loss of property. I mean damage to feelings. What's left, in the North as well as the South, is anger. Confusion. Bereavement—"

He and Madeline exchanged looks. Then he rose and walked a few steps down the lawn, locking hands at the small of his back as he struggled to focus his thoughts into the right words.

"The day Lincoln was shot, according to my brother Stanley, he told his cabinet about a dream he had the night before. He was in a boat rowing toward what he termed a dark, indefinite shore."

He turned, facing the semicircle of listeners, white and black, in front of the pine house not yet whitewashed. In the distance, the wisteria on the great chimney splashed the dusk with color.

"A dark, indefinite shore," he repeated. "It strikes me as an apt metaphor to describe our situation. Ours personally, and that of the country, too. It is one country again. Slavery's gone, and I say thank God. It was evil, and it was also brandished as a club over Northern heads for a long time."

"And when the club was finally put to use, it hurt us as much as you," Brett said.

George noticed another sharp look from Cooper. Had he indeed become someone else? Had the loss of his boy on the voyage from Liverpool destroyed the passionate convictions—the humanity—of his earlier days? George hoped this prickly new defensiveness, a trait he had seen in other Southerners but never before in Orry's brother, was a temporary aberration.

Self-conscious, George cleared his throat. "Anyway, we were

friends, my family and yours, long before this terrible time." Brett leaned against Billy, who was standing behind her left shoulder. "More than friends, in some cases," he amended with a gentle smile.

Encouraged by a loving look from Constance, he went on, with a steadily strengthening voice. "We must remain so. Steadfastly. Four years ago, I believed we all faced a time of severe testing. Orry and I pledged to keep the bonds of friendship and affection between ourselves and our families intact despite a war—"

Then the fire came, and I feared we couldn't.

"We did—" he turned more directly to Cooper "—at least in my estimation."

Orry's brother stayed silent. With effort, George resumed. "Now I fear something else. The shore ahead is new but darker and more indefinite than ever. I think we're destined to pass through a second period of animosity and struggle which may, in its own way, be worse than war. How can we avoid it, with so much grief and loss on both sides? With a whole people newly freed but still justifiably enraged by the past? With venal men—I can name some, but I won't—waiting to take advantage of any misstep or show of weakness? We must be ready to weather all that. We must once again—"

A simple lift of his right hand; a glance slowly moving from face to face. Then, quietly: "Keep the bonds strong."

No one moved. No one spoke. God above, he had failed. He had failed personally, but, far worse, he had failed Orry. If only he knew how to speak properly, the way skilled politicians—

It was Brett who reacted first, reaching up and across to find and clasp Billy's hand. It was Madeline, her eyes tear-filled, who gave a single strong nod of agreement. But it was Cooper who gravely spoke for them all.

"Yes."

Almost dizzy from the sudden relief of his tension, George saw the Mains smiling, rising, starting forward. Hastily he held up both hands. "Just humor me a moment longer. One of the chief reasons I wanted to visit Mont Royal was to bring you a small token of my belief in what we have all reaffirmed."

He walked back to his log stool and the small satchel on the ground beside it. He slid the polished toe of his right boot forward, nudging the satchel.

"Does anyone recognize this?"

With a faint, puzzled smile, Cooper scratched his chin. "Wasn't it my brother's?"

"Exactly. In this bag Orry brought money to repay the loan I made to help finance the *Star of Carolina*. Orry traveled all the way to Lehigh Station at a very perilous time in the spring of '61, carrying over six hundred thousand dollars in cash—all he could raise of the sum I invested in your project. I never forgot that or —" again he cleared his throat "—or how much Orry himself meant to me. I came here to repay a debt of honor and friendship, just as he did. To put some of my resources into your hands, to help you rebuild."

He picked up the satchel and handed it to Cooper. "Before leaving home, I wasn't able to get reliable information about the banking situation in this state. I imagined it was still chaotic, however—"

Cooper nodded.

"Well, I am majority stockholder in the Bank of Lehigh Station, which I formed at the start of the war. Inside the satchel is a letter of credit drawn on my bank. The initial amount is forty thousand dollars"—Madeline gasped—"but there's more available. As much as you need. Now—"

He reddened unexpectedly. "I wonder if I might have some of that delicious berry punch you served this afternoon? I find my throat very dry all at once."

For a prolonged moment, nothing interrupted the twilight quiet but the rasp and hum of insects. Suddenly, with a swirl of sunfaded skirt, Madeline ran to him. She threw her arms around his neck. "I love you, George Hazard." He felt her tears as she pressed her cheek to his and hugged him. "And don't misconstrue the reason. If you were penniless, I would love you just as much."

Then they were all moving forward, closing around the two visitors. Judith kissed each of them twice. Andy spoke a few words of admiration and gratitude. Jane said a soft thank you to both. Brett embraced them in turn. Last of all, Cooper shook George's hand, so overcome he could barely speak.

"God bless you, George."

Shamefully, George wished it were Orry standing there instead. He turned away so none of them would see his eyes.

1033

138

Santa Fe was fly-infested and revoltingly Latin-Catholic. Ashton was sure the caverns of hell, if they existed, could be no hotter.

She had a clean but cramped second-floor room on a narrow street of yellow walls, just a few steps from a cantina and the cathedral square beyond. Three weeks of waiting, mostly in that room, made her feel old as a crone. The parched air created new wrinkles, especially around her eyes. At least twice daily she examined her wrecked face in a triangle of broken mirror hanging on the adobe wall beside the hard bed. Would Lamar be displeased by her dry, sun-reddened skin? The possibility agitated her every day and spoiled her rest every night. But no more than the waiting.

Even now she found it unbelievable that a woman of her background and breeding had endured all that was necessary to reach this benighted place. The unspeakably long, occasionally terrifying coach trip. Poor sleep. Foul food at filthy way stations. Crude Westerners for traveling companions. An escort of scruffy Yankee cavalry for a couple of hundred miles because of the Indian threat. Mercifully, there had been no incidents.

When she reached Santa Fe, she found Powell's letter and thus expected his two wagons within a week. The week passed, and so did another, then a third. Her optimism began to dwindle along with her funds. Only a few dollars remained in her reticule—barely enough for another week's lodging and the barbarically spicy food the owner's wife brought up from the cantina.

On Saturday at the end of the third week, a commotion drew

her to the spacious, sunlit plaza along with several dozen other people. A cavalry patrol had arrived, causing great excitement because the blue-clad troopers brought the body of a young man stabbed three times before he died.

"Picked him up at Winslow's trading station, west of here on the Rio Puerco," explained the Yankee lieutenant in response to the questions of a paunchy, self-important man Ashton presumed to be some town official. *Mighty pompous for a greaser,* she thought as the lieutenant went on: "He crawled that far—two, three miles—with these wounds after the Jicarillas massacred the rest of his party."

Ashton's flesh froze. Above a great roaring in her ears, she heard the lieutenant's voice continuing faintly.

"Winslow cleaned and dressed the stab wounds, but even so, the lad didn't last twelve hours." *No,* Ashton thought, queasy. *Surely it couldn't be Powell's party.*

She was wild to ask questions but feared the troopers would be suspicious of her accent. They were the sorriest, most villainous-looking soldiers she had ever seen, far worse than those who had escorted the stage. There was a private with only one thumb. A corporal wearing an eye patch. One bearded man sounded like an Irish comic from a variety hall, and two others jabbered in some foreign tongue—Hungarian, perhaps. On the coach trip, a passenger had told her the hard-pressed Union government was having trouble filling the ranks of its Western army, hence would take the physically handicapped, immigrants who knew little or no English—even Confederates.

Finally, unable to contain her curiosity, she approached the cleanest of the lot, a sergeant. She asked the question of greatest importance to her.

"Can you tell me whether there were wagons with this party?"

The sergeant was from Indiana, but he was courteous and helpful in spite of that. "Yes, ma'am, the trader did say the dead boy mentioned wagons. Two, burned and pushed into a gully where the massacre took place."

She swayed, dizzy. The sergeant's eyes narrowed. What did it matter if he were suspicious? The questions must be answered; she asked the second most important one.

"Was the leader of the party a man named Powell?"

1035

"That's right. Some reb."

"And he's—?"

A nod. Only then did Ashton think of her husband.

"The rest, too?"

"Every one. Did you know any of them?"

"Mr. Powell—by reputation, not personally."

The answer clearly bothered the sergeant. If she had no connection with the victims, why had she asked about wagons? She knew it was a blunder and turned away before he could interrogate her. The lieutenant was talking to others about the wagons. She listened, haughtily ignoring the sergeant's scrutiny.

"After the young man died, Winslow and his two sons armed themselves and rode to the site. The 'Paches were long gone. Winslow saw pieces of a wagon wheel and a lot of ashes at the bottom of the gully, but that's all. The birds and the big cats got the other bodies."

She wheeled and set off up the street to her room, increasingly weak from shock. The Hoosier trooper watched her, asking himself questions about the puzzling behavior of the beautiful young woman in the gray summer dress. One thing sure; she obviously didn't hail from this part of the country.

In her room, Ashton sat on the bed, trembling. Two wagons containing three hundred thousand in gold—gone. And Powell, too. She had cared for Lamar Powell more than she had ever cared for any man. Her affection derived in part from his amazing sexual prowess, in part from his implacable ambition and where it could take both of—

No. That was over, and she had to face it. She was alone and abandoned in a wilderness, with no funds except those on deposit in Nassau. Her money and her dead husband's. All hers now.

A lot of good that would do her for the next two or three months. It would take at least that much time to supply the Bahamian bankers with evidence of Huntoon's death and proof of her right to the money. Could the funds be sent to her in Santa Fe? She couldn't answer all the questions arising from this newest, cruel turn.

But she knew one thing. She would live on that Bahamian money for as long as it took to locate the gully containing what was left of the wagons. The trader and his son hadn't investigated the wreckage, probably because it would never occur to any ordinary person that the ashes might conceal gold ingots.

What if the savages had carried the ingots away? It was a disturbing possibility, but not one that would alter her course. A fortune in gold that would double her personal worth could be waiting in that gully to the west, unknown to anyone except herself. The prospect helped soften her sadness about Powell. And the more she thought of the treasure, the faster her grief dwindled.

Concerning James, she could summon no grief at all. He had always been spineless, only marginally a man. Thinking of him did jog her memory. She dug in the bottom of her reticule for the sealed letter. Presuming it to be filled with sentimental twaddle, she had put it away in St. Louis and hadn't thought of it until this moment.

The letter was anything but sentimental. After a brusque salutation—just her name, followed by a dash—and a short paragraph of unflattering preamble, it said:

I joined Mr. Powell's adventure not only out of loyalty to the founding principles of the first Confederacy and the hope of reestablishing them as the keystones of a second one, but also to regain your respect and those favors which were always mine by right as your legal husband.

You have continually and cruelly refused me those rights, Ashton. You have repeatedly humiliated me despite my great love for you, and ruined me, both professionally and as a man. I admire Mr. Powell's view of Southern rights and ideals, though I here confess that I have come to despise him personally because of what I suspect about him and you. Although I lack evidentiary proof, I am sure the two of you are, and have been for some time, lovers.

So in case some untimely fate should befall me, the least I can do is make certain you are not rewarded for harlotry. To this end, before leaving Richmond, I directed a duly witnessed letter to my old partner at the firm of Thomas & Huntoon, Charleston. In Detroit I received word of its arrival and confirmation of its legality as a will replacing my earlier one drawn in your favor. Now your ill-gotten Water Witch money, wholly mine under existing marital law, will be disbursed in the event

1037

*of my death to such cousins and other distant relatives of mine
as can be located. The balance will go to charitable causes.
You will not have a pennyworth of it.*

*This is my small retribution for the many wrongs you have
done me.*

James

Ashton staggered up, crushing the letter between her clammy
palms. "Not true," she whispered.

She seized her reticule and flung it against the slats of the shutters. *"Not true."* She overturned the bed. Hurled the chair against
the wall. The landlady ran upstairs and pounded on the door,
which was secured on the inside by a metal hook and eye.

"¿Señora, qué pasa ahí adentro?"

The chair broke. She smashed the clay wash bowl—pieces flew
like shrapnel—and the drinking gourd, then dashed the scrap of
mirror on top of them, screaming now.

"Not true—not true—NOT TRUE!"

"¿Señora, está enferma? ¡Conteste o tumbaré la puerta!"

The last words went whirling into a windy void as Ashton's
eyes rolled up in her head and she fainted.

The landlady pushed until the hook broke away from the door.
She shook and slapped Ashton awake. Gasping, Ashton explained
her behavior in terms of a vaguely described seizure. She promised to pay for all the damages—a lie—if just the woman would
help her into bed; she was ill. Muttering, the landlady did so.

Wearing only her chemise, Ashton lay rigid throughout the
afternoon and into the hot hours of the night. Her brain was a
cauldron of fear, anxiety, speculation. Finally, toward early morning, the air began to cool. She fell asleep and woke shortly before
noon. The mariachi, which seemed to inhabit the cantina on a
permanent basis, had resumed its dolorous violin and guitar music.

She sat up and held her head. There wasn't a dollar to be had
from Nassau. But there was gold out here. She was not defeated.
Far from it. She rummaged in her luggage until she found the
lacquered Japanese box, which hadn't been opened since she deposited her memento from Powell. She lifted the lid slowly, gazed
at the happily copulating couple and studied the assortment of
buttons. After nearly four years, it was time to resume her collect-

ing. And not merely for pleasure. She lowered the lid, confident that survival lay in what her box represented.

She put on her best cool dress, mauve lawn. It was in sorry condition after so much traveling, but a tiny triangle of mirror retrieved from the floor showed her that it would pass, especially with her bosom made prominent by her corset. In this heat the stays felt like implements of torture, but no matter. The effect was everything.

She left the room, descended the squeaky stairs with a regal air, and walked the short distance to the cantina entrance. She had been told the landlord was a Yankee, a former fur trapper who had left Kit Carson's company for a more settled existence.

When she pushed the doors back and entered the cool blue place, the mariachi men stopped in mid-squeak and mid-twang. Their mustaches went up as their jaws went down. Some elderly customers, Mexicans or Spaniards or whatever they were, clearly disapproved of her presence, but she didn't give a damn. Neither did the fellow in the apron behind the bar. He was a burly, strong-looking sort, with plenty of white in his blond hair.

Ashton smiled at him. "You are an American, I understand?"

"That's right."

"So am I." She worked to minimize her accent. "Unexpectedly stranded here by circumstance."

"I noticed you on the street. Wondered about your situation—"

"Might I ask you a question? In confidence?"

"Sure." She didn't miss the way his eyes touched her breast a moment.

"I would like to know the names of the two or three wealthiest men in the area."

"The two or three—?"

"Wealthiest."

"I thought I heard right." Amused, he added, "Hitched or single?"

Damn him. He thinks I'm nothing but a feather-headed female, to be made sport of. He'll find out. I'll come through this, survive this, the way I've survived everything else. And when I do, I'll have every man in this part of the country groveling for two minutes of my time.

"Ma'am? Hitched or single?"

Ashton's smile was dazzling.

"That really doesn't matter."

139

In the calm, starry hour after sunset, Andy and Jane walked along the Ashley, talking quietly and searching for their answer to a question Madeline had posed.

Of Cicero's future, there was no doubt. He was too old, too lacking in skills to do anything except stay on. He actually seemed displeased with the outcome of the war, complaining that the liberty Father Abraham had bestowed on him was unwanted, because it upset the routine of his life. Jane had started to reprove him on one occasion, but held back. Cicero was past seventy; she understood that any change was a threat.

Not so with her or with Andy. So they talked, their arms around each other's waist. The conversation was occasionally interrupted by some kissing and affectionate touching. After an hour, holding hands, they returned to the pine house where the lamps gleamed.

Everyone was still up because George and Constance were leaving tomorrow when *Osprey* came downriver again. As Jane and Andy entered the large, plain room that was a parlor in name only, they heard George saying he was anxious to get back to Lehigh Station and resume the role of full-time parent. Madeline smiled at the black couple from a barrel chair Cooper had made the week before. "Hello, Andy—Jane. Come in."

Jane began, "If this is a bad time to speak to you—"

"Not at all. Join us."

Andy cleared his throat. "We just wanted to answer your question about our plans."

Not a sound followed those words; they had everyone's attention. Jane spoke for both of them.

"We thought we'd stay a little longer in South Carolina."

"As free people," Andy added.

"It's our state now, too," Jane said. "Our land as much as it is the white man's."

Her words carried a faint challenge. Perhaps that was why Cooper hesitated a moment before he said, "Of course it is. I'm pleased by your decision. I'd be glad to have you stay here, unless you have something else in mind."

Jane shook her head, then glanced at the strong, proud man standing beside her. "Mont Royal's been good to me. Better than I ever expected."

"But we can't work without wages," Andy said. "Not now."

Cooper and Madeline exchanged looks signifying mutual consent. "I agree," Cooper said. "It's possible now, thanks to George."

"Then we'll stay," Andy said. "If we decide we made the wrong choice—if either of us decides that—we'll tell you and go. We don't answer to anyone but each other anymore."

Cooper responded with a small, quick nod of agreement. "I hope you won't ever reach that decision. I need you both very much."

Jane smiled. Relieved expressions showed on the faces of the others. Andy stepped forward.

"One other thing—"

"Yes?" Judith said.

"We want to get married."

There was a burst of congratulations, abruptly stilled when Andy went right on in a level voice. "But not the old way. Not by jumping over brooms. And we're both going to change our names. Jane and Andy are slave names. They were given to us. We want to pick our own."

Tense silence. Then Cooper simply raised his hand.

"Fine."

Madeline smoothed her skirt as she rose. "Can't we find something for a toast to the engaged couple?"

Smiling broadly, Andy put his arm around Jane again. "I'm so happy I'd settle for water out of the well."

"I think I remember something better," Judith said, raising the curtain that screened the kitchen. "Yes, here it is," she called from the attached pantry closet. She emerged smiling. "You gentlemen didn't finish Wade Hampton's peach brandy—thank goodness."

She poured a tiny amount for each of them as they fell into relaxed, companionable conversation. George, who had drawn the fruit jar, raised it to salute Andy and Jane.

"I wish you both the best. It won't be easy for you down here, at least not in the immediate future. But I'm not certain it would be much better up North."

With a touch of sadness, Jane said, "I know. Black faces do threaten people somehow. Scare them. Well, I can't help that. We'll come through just fine. You fought to free us, Major Hazard, so now we must take up the fight. I do expect many more battles before white people even start to accept us."

In the uneasy silence that followed, Cooper frowned and Billy admitted to himself that Jane was right. He need only examine his own attitudes of a couple of years ago. Though one war was over, he shared his brother's belief that another was just starting.

140

OPIN AGIN said the sign hanging crookedly on the front of a large log building just outside Goldsboro, North Carolina. Charles reached it right before dark. The weather was surprisingly cool for May. Rain had started an hour ago, and he had wrapped himself in the robe of rags and scraps.

A smaller line on the sign proclaimed, *Confedrate Bills Prodly Acepted Here!* Charles had nine hundred dollars' worth of those— back pay—stuffed in his shirt and pants pockets. He pitied a man who would try to run a business on pride and worthless currency, but he would accept that kind of lunatic hospitality tonight. He didn't want to sleep in the open again, especially with the rain, and hunt for an orchard or coop to rob for food

A black boy led his mule away, promising a good rubdown and feed. Charles entered the main room of the roadside tavern, a drab place with a few desolate-looking men sitting about, talking, or lazily clicking pieces across a checkerboard. A fire brightened the stone hearth.

Charles ordered whiskey, a plate of lamb barbecue, and purchased a cigar from the innkeeper. He discovered the man had several rusty guns for sale and a few old boxes of ammunition. One contained shells that would fit his .48 army Colt. Elated, he bought the whole box for fifty Confederate dollars.

While he was eating, a man of about forty came noisily downstairs from the sleeping rooms under the eaves. He rubbed his hands at the fire while Charles tried to avoid his eye.

But the man forced conversation on him. He had a pink face, curly hair gone prematurely white, and a mouth downcast in a curve of perpetual suffering. He introduced himself as Mordecai Woodvine, itinerant salesman of Bibles and Christian tracts.

"Sure hope business picks up soon. Sure has been terrible the past couple of years. I hate traveling anymore. Too many uppity free niggers all over the place. But the work I do is God's work, so I guess I oughtn't complain." So saying, he continued to look miserable.

He sat down without invitation and insisted on knowing Charles's name and whether he had been in the army.

"Yes, I was. I scouted for Hampton's cavalry."

"The cavalry! There's plenty on that subject in Revelations. 'And I looked, and behold a pale horse, and his name that sat on him was Death, and Hell followed with him.'" Through the smoke of his cigar, Charles could be seen scowling. Woodvine poked a finger at heaven, intoning, "'And power was given unto them over the fourth part of the earth, to kill with sword, and with hunger, and with death, and with the beasts of the earth—'"

With intentional rudeness, Charles interrupted. "I'd say that describes our work pretty well." He wanted to strangle the man for prompting memories of Sport.

The fool went right on. "My cousin Fletcher was a cavalryman out west. Rode with Bedford Forrest—there's one good old rebel

1043

who won't tolerate this nigger freedom, I'll tell you. Fletcher got captured, and do you know what happened to him?"

Charles was on his feet. He indicated no interest in the answer, but got it anyway.

"They offered him a choice. Prison—or the Yankee cavalry. That's right, they shipped him to a regiment out on the plains somewhere. To fight Indians. There are a goodly number of our boys doing that, I'm told. They're called galvanized Yankees."

He leaned forward. "You understand, don't you? Galvanized metal is iron coated with zinc to keep out rust. A galvanized Yankee is a Confederate wearing a blue—"

"I know the meaning of galvanized."

"Oh. Oh, well—I thought maybe you didn't. Anyway, if you hanker to stay in some army, you might keep it in mind. That is, if you could stand to serve with men who brought this plague of emancipation upon us. I couldn't stand it. I'd puke my guts out, if you'll pardon the indelicacy."

"Surely," Charles said, an almost malevolent glint in his eye. "Galvanized Yankees. Think of that. Tell me, Mr. Woodvine, in which branch did you serve?"

"Me? Why—uh—I didn't. I'm too old."

"You're over forty-five? You don't look it."

"But there are reasons—a physical impairment—"

"And you probably spent most of the war in the woods, selling Testaments to the trees and quoting Scripture to the saplings—where they couldn't find you. Am I right, Mr. Woodvine?"

"What? What's that?"

"Good night, Mr. Woodvine."

He walked away, heading for his room. On the stairs, he heard the parting shot.

"Drunken veterans—that's all you see anymore. The army taught them to love whiskey. Issued regular rations of it. Disgraceful, that's my opinion."

Charles wanted to turn, go back, and beat Woodvine bloody. Instead, he shut the door of his room and leaned against it. He was a fool to react angrily. He had no interest in the Bible salesman or his cousin. Much as he had come to love Texas while he was with the Second, he had no interest in continuing as a cavalryman. He had no interest in anything but reaching Spotsylvania County as quickly as possible.

Rain tapped the roof as he stretched out and pulled up the

1044

cover. He heard the rain leaking with a steady drip near the foot of the bed. Downstairs, made boisterous with drink, some of the desolate men started to sing.

Charles recognized the piece. He had heard "O I'm a Good Old Rebel" several times since leaving South Carolina. It was sung with great fervor now that Johnston's army had surrendered to Sherman near Durham Station.

> *"I hates the Yankee nation*
> *And everything they do.*
> *I hates the Declaration*
> *Of Independence, too.*
> *I hates the glorious Union.*
> *'Tis dripping with our blood.*
> *I hates their striped banner.*
> *I fit it all I could."*

"Christ," Charles groaned, pulling the thin pillow over his head. It didn't shut out the rhythmic thumping of tin cups on the bar, the stamp of boots, or the splendid choir baritone of Mordecai Woodvine joining in.

> *"I can't take up my musket*
> *And fight 'em now no more,*
> *But I ain't got to love 'em,*
> *Now that is sarten sure.*
> *And I don't want no pardon*
> *For what I wus and am,*
> *I won't be reconstructed,*
> *And I don't care a damn!"*

Weeds and wild grasses tossed in the warm wind, high as the hamstrings of his mule. The wind snapped the gypsy cloak as Charles turned into the dooryard, an ominous feeling on him. The fields hadn't been prepared for planting. On such a pleasant day, when fresh air would have broomed the house, every window was shuttered. Around the rear stoop, wild violets showed where none had grown before. The open door of the barn revealed a rectangle of darkness.

"Washington? Boz?"

The wind blew.

"Anyone here?"

Sunflowers swayed in what had been the garden. Why was he awaiting an answer? Hadn't he gotten it when he came over the last hump in the scarred road and seen the house so still, the surrounding fields empty in the sunshine?

She had locked the place before going wherever she had gone. Using his elbow, he broke the window of the kitchen door, reached through, and let himself in. The furniture was there, chairs neatly squared up beneath the table. Pots and the iron skillet hung from their pegs in their remembered places. He jerked open cabinets. Dishes there, too.

He ran to her bedroom, his boots thudding the pegged floor. The bed was neatly made and on the table next to it he spied her book of Pope, a place marked with a pale blue ribbon. Surely she wouldn't leave that if she were planning to be gone for any length of time. She must be away for just a day or two, with the freedmen.

To confirm it, he bore down on the wardrobe, expecting to find most of her clothing. He yanked the doors open.

Empty.

He stood still, frowning, worried. How to explain the contradiction—all the clothes missing and her favorite book left behind?

He had left the porch door open; a strong gust of wind blowing through the hall caught a wardrobe door and hurled it shut with a bang. That roused him and broke the grip of his panic. He carried the book to the kitchen, laid it on the table, then hurried to the barn, where the freedmen stored their tools. All were still in place.

He sawed some boards, nailed them on the inside of the broken window, took the book, and tied the door shut with a length of rope. It would be one of the things for which he would ask her forgiveness the moment he saw her. One of many.

About to mount the mule, he paused and opened the book at the place marked by the ribbon. He discovered a small, unfamiliar flower, its blossom pressed flat, most of the yellow gone. He swallowed.

The poem was "Ode to Solitude." Gus had bracketed four lines with delicate strokes of an inked pen.

Thus let me live, unseen, unknown,
Thus unlamented let me die;

> *Steal from the world, and not a stone*
> *Tell where I lie.*

He cursed and shut the book. A shudder ran down his spine. He booted the mule all the way into Fredericksburg.

Although most of the population had come back, he saw few signs that repair of the destruction had begun. He inquired at two stores, without success. The proprietor of the third, a hefty butcher, gave him some information after he introduced himself.

"She let both her free nigras go. The younger, Boz, passed through town and told me. A few nights later, she disappeared without a word to anybody. That made me recall she had come in the day before and settled her account."

"How long ago was all this?"

"Several months."

"And you haven't seen her since?"

"That's right."

"But where the hell did she go?"

"Who do you think you're talking to, soldier? I'm a Union man." His hand slid across the moist red block to a boning knife. "I were you, I'd be more polite to the people that whipped you, else they might do it again."

Reddening, Charles restrained his anger. "I'm sorry. It's just that I rode a long way to find her."

The butcher saw his opportunity and smirked. "Maybe she didn't want you to find her. Ever think of that? Mrs. Barclay left her place without telling a soul in Fredericksburg or the county where she was headed. You don't believe me, you ask anybody."

He picked up his cleaver and began chopping a slab of faintly shiny meat with hard, swift strokes. Charles walked out, leaving a trail of boot prints in the sawdust. He leaned on the store front, stricken by the truth in the butcher's nastiness.

She hadn't wanted him to come back, else she would have waited. Or at least left word of her destination. Instead, she left a poem about death. The end of everything. He understood the positioning of the ribbon and the inked brackets. They were meant for him.

He walked around the iron hitching post, rested a hand on his worn saddle, and said something broken-sounding under his breath. The mule flicked his ears. Flies landed anyway. The pain, the uncertainty of loss, beat at Charles harder and harder by the second. He didn't try to quell the feelings. He couldn't have done it if he had wanted.

141

The corporal in charge of the two-man detail hailed from Illinois. He had been educated at Indiana Asbury, a tiny college in the next state, then returned to Danville, the home town of Mr. Lincoln's great companion Ward Lamon, where he taught in a one-room school for two years before mustering for war. He was twenty-four. The private helping him was four years younger. Their detail was one of many assigned to sift through the rubble of Richmond, with shovels and by hand, to locate and retrieve any unburned government documents.

The corporal and the private worked in the skeletal ruins of what had been a warehouse. Part of the roof remained, and two walls. The soldiers started early each day; this morning there was a slight fog, not yet burned off. The sun shafts around the fragment of roof seemed to hold smoke.

"Here's a box hardly touched, Sid," the private said. In this part of the warehouse yesterday they had discovered batches of undelivered letters, most of them at least partly scorched. When they pried open the new box, they found bundles that appeared untouched.

Since their assignment was to recover and mark any mail that could be forwarded, they thought their search, thankless thus far, had finally borne fruit. They were disappointed. The private showed Sid the top letter of a stack he was holding.

"Must've had a heavy rain. Guess the box leaked. Spoilt the address."

The corporal studied the letter. Saw faint handwriting indecipherable because of blots and water streaks.

"The rest like that?"

The private fanned the stack. "Ever' one."

Pleased, Sid said, "Then I guess we should open them. The address might be repeated before the salutation." That was an excuse; he was bored and wanted to sit down awhile. Opening mail beat pawing through wet ashes that stuck to your uniform and made it stink.

Besides, reading the mail of strangers appealed to his sense of drama. He had always loved *Othello* and *Romeo and Juliet* and the novels of Dickens. He dreamed of writing a piece of fiction of his own one of these days. Might be some stories worth remembering in these letters.

They sat on fallen beams and opened them one by one. The private did it mechanically, unmoved by anything he read. Sid rapidly grew disgusted. Contrary to his expectations, he found little except bad spelling, worse grammar, and fragmentary, wholly uninteresting observations about homesickness, mother's dearly remembered cooking, or the absolute perfection of every girl to whom a letter was addressed. In twenty minutes he was bored again. But orders were orders.

An hour had passed when he sat up suddenly. "Hold on, here's an interesting one. Signed J. B. Duncan—one of our own officers."

He showed the private the abbreviations and initials following the name. "Brigadier General, United States Volunteers. But it's addressed to someone he calls 'My dear Major Main.' You suppose that's a reb, Chauncey?"

"Pretty likely if the letter's here, don't you think?"

Sid nodded. "Seems to concern some female named Augusta— Oh, my Lord, listen to this. *She became pregnant with your child, and although she knew of her condition at the time of your last visit, she would say nothing, not wishing to exert moral coercion—*" With new enthusiasm, Sid said, "This is an educated man. Telling quite a story."

"Sounds like a hot one," Chauncey observed.

Sid kept reading. *"The pregnancy was fully as difficult, not to say dangerous, as that which occurred while she was married to*

1049

Mr. Barclay. You know the unfortunate outcome that time, I believe. Fearing for her well-being and also her safety on that isolated farm where she foolishly remained throughout much of the worst fighting, I arranged to smuggle my niece over the Potomac and on to my present home in Washington. Here, on December 23 last, she delivered your son, a fine healthy infant to whom she gave the name Charles. But I regret to say the birth—"

The corporal's voice had dropped. He shot the private a melancholy look.

"What's wrong, Sid?"

". . . the birth was not without its tragic aspect. One hour after delivering, poor Augusta succumbed. She passed away with your name upon her lips. I know she loved you more than life itself, for she told me so."

Sid wiped his nose. "My God." He went on. *"I have written twice before and paid to have each missive borne to Richmond by private messenger. I hasten to write yet a third time because I know postal service is disrupted, and I wish to do all that I can to make certain at least one of the letters reaches you. Regrettably, each letter bears the skimpiest of addresses, but I have none better."*

A gulp of breath. "New paragraph. *The divisive holocaust, perhaps ordained by God but tragic for His children nonetheless, shows every aspect of an imminent conclusion. When it is over, it is your right to claim your son. I will keep him, providing proper care, until you come for him, or, if you do not, for as long as is practicable for an old bachelor bent upon continuing his military career. I bear you no enmity. I pray this finds you whole and glad of the good portion of my news. Respectfully—"*

Sid rested the last sheet on his knee. "That's all except for the signature."

"That ought to be delivered for sure," Chauncey said. He was subdued now, sitting motionless in a smoky shaft of light.

"Yes." The corporal thrust the envelope into the sun. Tilted and peered at it. "Hello, that's better. Here's the name again. Main. And the word *Major*. The first name's gone, along with the address. Still, that may be enough."

He folded the two pages, replaced them in the envelope, and slipped it in his pocket. "I'll bring this one to the lieutenant's attention myself."

"Good," said Chauncey, staring at Sid. Sid stared back. When the government of that damned Davis had torched so many of its records, how did you find one reb soldier among the hundreds of thousands wandering homeward on the roads of the South—or lying dead in mass graves, thickets, fields, from Virginia and the Pennsylvania mountains to the bluffs of Vicksburg and the hills of Arkansas?

Both knew you didn't; not easily. Sid would try, but he felt it was hopeless.

142

After leaving Fredericksburg, Charles wandered aimlessly for three days. Lay rigid each night, unable to sleep. Lost his temper without provocation and almost got knifed for it in another wayside tavern. Wanted to cry and could not.

In the scarred country above the Rapidan, he came to a four-way crossroads and dismounted. While the mule cropped grass, he took off his gypsy robe and lay down at the roadside. He hoped the mule kept eating for hours. He had no destination. No reason to go on.

Out of the bright north, three men approached on foot. All three wore filthy remnants of butternut uniforms. One, a towhead of eighteen or nineteen, hobbled on a handmade crutch. His right leg ended in a stump three inches above the road.

He was the one who greeted Charles with a wave and a smile. "Howdy. You're one of our boys, aren't you?"

Charles took the cigar out of his mouth. "I'm not one of anybody's boys anymore."

Giving him surly stares, the soldiers muttered among themselves, swung to the other side of the road, and continued on south. To homes that probably don't exist any longer, Charles thought.

Down the road, he heard noises suggesting a vehicle. He turned on his left elbow, squinted, saw the soldiers pass a group coming the other way. The soldiers went by without speaking. The group consisted of four people: a man, a woman, and two small girls. Black.

When they came closer, he saw their clothes were clean but threadbare. The cart, which carried the girls and some possessions bundled in croker sacks, had solid wheels but otherwise looked flimsy, obviously built by someone not trained as a wheelwright.

Nor did the family own an animal. The father pulled the cart. The mother walked barefoot beside him.

Yet neither parent seemed unhappy. They smiled and sang right along with their children. The mother and two girls clapped the beat. Charles stared at them as they started to go by. The sight of him reclining in the grass made them tense. The singing softened. He could hear no words except one: *"Jubilo."*

A grimace twisted his mouth. The father took note of that and of Charles's gray shirt. He took a firmer grip on the handles of the cart, pulling it as quickly as he could through the crossroads and away down the northern road. The children looked back at Charles, but not the adults.

Too tired and despondent to move, he tethered the mule to a tree branch. He wriggled back against the trunk, intending to doze a few minutes. There was no hurry about anything. She was gone for good.

He woke with a start. The slant of the light told him it was late afternoon. Something hanging above him tickled his face.

Half the tether, still tied to a branch. It had been chewed apart. The mule was gone, saddle gear and all. Luckily he still had his army Colt in the holster.

From the crossroads, he walked about half a mile in each of four directions. The road to the west faded away around a bend; the western landscape blended into the backdrop of the Blue Ridge. He stared at the mountains a moment, recalling his fondness for Texas.

He trudged back to the crossroads. No sign of the mule anywhere. Damn.

The sun slanted lower, casting spears of light between thick trees at the southwest corner of the crossroads. Charles started suddenly. Out toward the Shenandoah, past the woodlands, he heard a wailing rebel yell—

He shook his head. It was only the whistle of a train speeding through the countryside. A Yankee-operated train, more than likely. They had so many of them. And so many guns. And so many men who had come out of mills and stockyards and barns and offices and saloons to make war as nobody had ever made war before.

He walked into the center of the empty crossroads and surveyed it, and then the dead, empty land. For one strange moment, he felt as if all of the might of the Union had been directed against him personally.

It had beaten him, too.

He stood at the crossroads in the lowering dusk, tired desperation in his eyes. He just wanted to lie down. Stop. For good.

But pictures kept intruding. The Bible salesman he had met in Goldsboro who said they wanted cavalrymen on the plains. He had the right experience. It would be a way to survive. Start over. Maybe find a scrap of hope someday.

Hope in a world like this? Stupid idea. He'd do better to lie down in the roadside grass and never get up.

But more pictures came. Men with whom he had served. Ab Woolner. Calbraith Butler. Wade Hampton. Lee—imagine how he must have felt, once the superintendent of West Point and the country's finest soldier, forced to ask a fellow Academy graduate for terms. They said Old Marse Bob had conducted himself with dignity, rebuffing a few hotheads who wanted to continue guerrilla war from the hills and woodlands.

Although the men Charles remembered had, in his opinion, fought for the wrong reasons, they weren't quitters. Gus wasn't a quitter either. He dwelled on her memory awhile. It summoned a detail he had forgotten. A name.

Brigadier Duncan.

He wiped his mouth with the back of his hand. Gus had unmistakably signaled that their love affair was over, but he could at least satisfy himself as to her whereabouts and her well-being. Duncan might be able to help, if Charles could locate him.

Only one place to start. Not the safest place, either. But he didn't worry too much, because suddenly recalling Duncan infused him with the kind of energy he hadn't felt in a long time. His head started to clear, and his chin came up. Still a lot of daylight left. He had time to walk awhile. He picked up the gypsy robe and left the crossroads, northbound.

In half an hour he caught up with the black family, resting at the roadside. The moment the adults recognized him, they looked alarmed. Stopping in the center of the road, Charles took off his hat and tried to smile. It came hard. It had nothing to do with who or what they were. It just came hard.

"Evening."

"Evening," the father said.

Less suspicious than her husband, the woman said, "Are you going north?"

"Washington."

"That's where we're going. Would you like to sit down and rest?"

"Yes, I would, thank you." He did. One of the girls giggled and smiled at him. "I lost my mule. I'm pretty tired."

At last the father smiled. "I was born tired, but lately I've been feeling better."

Charles wished he could say the same. "If you're willing, I'll be glad to help you pull that cart."

"You're a soldier." He didn't mean a Union soldier.

"Was," Charles said. *"Was."*

143

Brigadier Jack Duncan, a stocky officer with crinkly gray hair, a drink-mottled nose, and a jaw like a short horizontal line, strode into the War Department, shoulders back, left hand resting on the hilt of his gleaming dress sword. When he emerged half an hour later, he was beaming.

He had enjoyed a brief but highly satisfactory chat with Mr. Stanton, who commended him for his performance of Washington staff work throughout the war and for his patience when repeated requests for field duty were denied because General Halleck wanted his administrative skills. Now, with the war concluded, his wish could be honored. Duncan had new orders and travel vouchers in his pocket.

He was being posted to the plains cavalry, where experienced men were needed to confront and overcome the Indian threat. He was to depart immediately, and would not even see the grand parade of Grant's army, scheduled for a few days hence. Special reviewing platforms and miles of patriotic bunting were already in place for the event.

Musing on how it would feel to ride regularly again—for the past couple of years, he had managed only an occasional Sunday canter along Rock Creek on some livery-stable plug—the brigadier prepared to cross crowded, noisy Pennsylvania Avenue. He noticed a slender, tough-looking fellow with a long beard, cadet gray shirt, and holstered army Colt. Obviously nervous, the man chewed a cigar and studied the building Duncan had just left.

The stride—better, the swagger—suggested the man might be a cavalryman. A reb, to judge from his shirt and threadbare appearance. Union boys were keeping themselves trim and neat in preparation for the grand review.

There seemed to be hundreds of ex-Confederates swarming around town, though if that wild-looking specimen had indeed fought on the other side, he was risking a lot carrying a side arm. Stepping off the walk, Duncan nimbly dodged a dray, then an omnibus, and forgot about the man. There was really just one reb with whom he was concerned: a brevetted major named Main.

Would he ever hear from the fellow? He was beginning to doubt it. He had written three letters, paid exorbitantly to have each smuggled to Richmond, and received no answer to any of them. It seemed likely that Main was dead.

In a guilty way, the brigadier was grateful for the silence. Of course Main deserved to have his son with him. But Duncan was enjoying the responsibility of caring for young Charles. He had his housekeeper and more recently had hired a fine Irish girl to wet-nurse the infant and take care of certain other odious duties.

She was expert at her job. The housekeeper must be given notice and a month's wages—no, two, he decided—but Duncan had obtained the Irish girl's promise that she would accompany him to any new post where duty took him. She might well refuse to go out among the Indians, however.

If she did, he would find someone else. He was determined to take the child with him. Being a great-uncle and de facto parent had added an unexpectedly rich dimension to Duncan's lifelong bachelorhood. The one girl he had adored as a young man had died of consumption before they could be married, and none other had ever been fine or sweet enough to replace her. Now the void where love belonged was filled again.

He soon reached the small rented house a few blocks from the avenue. Jaunty as a boy, he took the steps two at a time and roared through the door into the dim lower hall.

"Maureen? Where's my grandnephew? Bring him here. I have splendid news. We're leaving town tonight."

Few things in life had ever intimidated Charles. For a day or two, the newness of West Point had. Sharpsburg had. Washington did now. So many damn Yankees. Whether soldier or civilian, most were hostile as reptiles when he asked a polite question in his distinctly Southern voice. The bunting everywhere depressed him further by reminding him of defeat. He felt like some scruffy animal just out of the woods and surrounded by hunters.

With an air of confidence he didn't feel, he walked through President's Park and up the steps of the War Department. He had left his gypsy cloak at the squalid island rooming house and fastened the throat button of his faded cadet gray shirt for neatness, though the effect was lost because of his chest-length beard. Nothing could do much to improve his wolfish appearance, and he knew it.

Nervously fiddling with a fresh cigar, he entered the ground-floor lobby and walked through the first open doors he saw. In a large room, he found a great many noncommissioned soldiers and civilian clerks shuffling piles of paper at desks on the other side of a counter. This was worse than setting yourself up for battle.

But he had to go through with it. Any humiliation or scrap was worth it, if only he could find Duncan and satisfy himself about Gus.

One of the clerks in blue, bald as the knob of a cane although he barely looked thirty, approached the counter after making Charles wait three minutes. The clerk stroked his huge oiled mustaches, first the right, then the left, as he scrutinized the lean visitor.

The clerk took note of Charles's patched shirt of cadet gray. He eyed the army Colt and the cigar held between wind-browned thumb and forefinger almost as if it were a second weapon. He found the visitor vaguely menacing and barely worth the time of an offhand "Yes?"

"I'm trying to locate an army officer. Is this the right place for—"

"Haven't you got the wrong city?" the clerk broke in. He had reacted visibly before Charles finished his first sentence. "The United States War Department maintains no files on rebels. And in case no one's told you, if you were paroled, you're carrying that gun illegally." He turned away.

"Excuse me," Charles said. "The officer belongs to your army." As the words came out, he knew it was a bad slip, caused by nerves. He had confirmed his former loyalty. Tense, he continued, "His name is—"

"I am afraid we can't help you. We aren't in business to look up records for every paroled traitor who walks in the door."

"Private," Charles said, seething, "I am asking you as politely as I know how. I need help. It's urgent that I find this man. If you'll just tell me which office—"

"No one in this building can help you," the clerk retorted loudly. The raised heads, suspended pens, sharp stares said he spoke for all those in the room. "Why don't you go ask Jeff Davis? They locked him up in Fort Monroe this morning."

"I'm not interested in the whereabouts of Jeff—" Again the clerk turned away.

Charles dropped his cigar, shot his hand across the counter and grabbed the clerk's collar. "Listen to me, damn you."

Consternation. Men running. Shouts—Charles's the loudest. "You can at least do me the courtesy of—"

Voices:

"He has a gun."

"Take it away from him."

"Watch out, he might—"

In the confusion, hands seized him from behind. Two other noncoms, one formidably large, had dashed around the end of the counter. "You'd better get out of here, boy," the big man said while the clerk puffed out his cheeks in a series of gasps, to demonstrate his outrage. He fingered his collar as if it had been permanently soiled. "Start trouble and you'll have your lunch in Old Capitol Prison. Maybe your Christmas dinner, too."

Charles wrenched free of their hands, glaring. They weren't hostile—at least the big one wasn't—but they were determined. His impulse was to start throwing punches. Behind him, in the lobby, spectators had gathered. He heard the questions and muttering as the big noncom gripped his arm.

"Come on, reb. Be sensible. Hightail it before—"

"What the devil is going on here?"

The barked words sent the noncoms to attention. They released Charles, who turned to see a stern, middle-aged officer with white hair and three fingers of his right hand missing. One shoulder of his dark blue coat-cloak was thrown back far enough to show an epaulet with an eagle of silver embroidery.

"Colonel," the clerk began, "this reb marched in here and made insulting demands. He wouldn't accept a polite refusal. Instead, he tried—"

The words went whirling away through Charles's mind, unheard as he stared at the Union officer and saw a farm in northern Virginia, in another year, in another lifetime.

"What is it exactly that he demanded?" the officer said with an angry glance at Charles, then a second, swift and astonished, one. *My God*, Charles thought, *he isn't an old man at all. He only looks it.*

His voice unexpectedly hoarse, he said, "Prevo?"

"That's right. I remember you. Hampton's cavalry. West Point before that."

Someone in the office mumbled, "Oh, we're to have an Academy reunion, are we?"

Prevo's glance silenced the speaker. Then, more temperately, he said to Charles, "What's the trouble here?"

"I came to ask for help. I desperately need to locate a Brigadier Duncan in the Union Army."

"Nothing so hard about that," Prevo said, his eye and his testiness directed toward the flushed clerk. "However, you shouldn't walk around with that revolver. Especially in this building. Take it off and give it to me, and we'll see what we can do."

Calming, Charles unfastened his gun belt. Prevo buckled it and

1058

hung it over his shoulder. To the bald clerk he said, "I want your name, soldier. Why didn't you do the decent thing and direct this man to the personnel clerks in the adjutant general's office?" To Charles: "They would have the brigadier's current address. I don't know him."

"Sir," the clerk stammered, "I explained—This man's a reb. Look at him. Arrogant, dirty—"

"Shut your mouth," Prevo said. "The war's over. It's time to quit fighting. Generals Grant and Lee seem to have assimilated that fact, even if you can't."

The humiliated clerk stared at the floor. To the big noncom, Colonel Prevo said, "I want his name on my desk in an hour."

"Yes, sir."

"Come on, Main. I remember your name now, too. I'll show you to the right office." As they started out, he paused and pointed to the counter. "I think you dropped your cigar."

The lobby crowd dispersed, though Charles continued to draw stares as he and Prevo walked up to the next floor. "Thank you, Prevo," Charles said. "I recognized you right away. Georgetown Mounted Dragoons—"

"And several other units since. Every one was decimated in Virginia, so they finally retired me to duty here. I'll be out in a couple of months. Here we go—turn right. We'll soon know the whereabouts of this General Duncan."

"I'm immensely grateful, Prevo. I really do need to see him about a serious matter."

"Professional?"

"Personal."

Prevo paused at a closed door. "Well, here's the office. Let's see what we can do." All of the wrinkles in his exhausted face moved when he tried to smile. "Even though I only lasted my plebe year, I have fond memories of the Academy. And the Academy does take care of its own. By the way—are you in a rush?"

"No. Finding Duncan is important, but there's no hurry."

"Excellent. I'll buy you a drink afterward. And," he added, lowering his voice, "return your gun." He opened the door as effortlessly as if he had all his fingers instead of one and a thumb.

144

Maureen, the plump, potato-plain young woman, brought the baby from the kitchen in response to Duncan's shout. The infant had been resting on a blanket in a patch of sunshine while Maureen opened pea pods for the evening meal. He had dark hair and a merry round face and wore a tiny shirt, trousers, and snug slippers, all of navy blue flannel. Maureen had sewn the garments herself.

"You say *tonight*, sir? Where are we going?"

The infant recognized his great-uncle and cooed when the brigadier swung him expertly into the curve of his left arm. "To the frontier—to see red Indians." Anxiously: "Will you still come along?"

"Indeed I will, General. I have read about the West. There is great opportunity there—and not nearly so much crowding as here in the East."

To ensure the arrangement, he added with a cagey smile, "Also, in the United States Cavalry there are many men of good character—single men—desirous of finding attractive, decent young women to marry."

Maureen's eyes sparkled. "Yes, sir. I have read that, too."

Mrs. Caldwell, the buxom, middle-aged housekeeper, came downstairs as the brigadier held out his right index finger. "Ah, sir, it is you. I was in the attic, but I thought I heard you arrive."

"Only to announce a permanent departure, this very evening." While he said that, Maureen wiped the extended finger with her apron. Duncan then put the finger into the baby's mouth. Up came one small, clutching hand, to find the knuckle and close.

Duncan explained matters to his housekeeper and entertained the baby at the same time. White spots, hints of teeth, had appeared on the infant's gums, and he loved teething on the brigadier's finger. He chewed it hard, grimacing and drooling happily.

"Then it's a promotion, is it, sir?"

"Yes, Mrs. Caldwell."

"My most sincere congratulations." She touched a corner of one eye. "I shall be sorry to see you go. The past five years have passed swiftly. And pleasurably, I might add."

"Thank you. Now we must discuss your future."

Mrs. Caldwell was happy about the generous settlement and even found a positive side to the sudden departure. "My widowed sister in Alexandria has been begging me to come for a visit. I may stay a week or two—"

"By all means. I can handle storage of the furniture and close out the lease by letter. We needn't bother with those things today. We have quite enough to do."

"What time is your train, General?"

"Six sharp."

"Then I'll definitely go to my sister's this evening. I'll hire a cab."

"Take the horse and buggy. I make you a present of it. I won't be needing it again."

"Oh, sir, that's extremely generous—"

"No more so than you have been," he said, remembering certain nights, lonely for both of them, when she was far more than a conventional housekeeper. Their gazes met, held a moment. Then, blushing, she looked elsewhere.

"You must at least permit me to drive you to the depot," she said.

"No, we'll hire a cab. That way, you can reach your sister's before dark."

"Very well, sir. Will you excuse me so I can see to your packing?" A great deal of it had to be squeezed into the next few hours.

But even little Charles seemed to approve of the abrupt redirection of their lives. He chewed harder than ever on his great-uncle's finger.

Charles continued to draw stares in Willard's saloon bar, but Prevo's presence forestalled trouble. The gun belt on the table had some effect as well.

They started with a whiskey each. That led to three more as the hours slipped by in an increasingly pleasant and easygoing exchange of reminiscences. Charles felt a euphoria of a kind he hadn't experienced since before Sharpsburg. Not only did he have Duncan's address on a slip of paper in his pocket, but it was in Washington, close by. The brigadier had been on the general staff throughout the war.

Slightly bleary, Prevo held his pocket watch near his face. "I have an appointment back at the department at a quarter past five. That leaves us twenty minutes for one farewell drink. Game?"

"Absolutely. Then I'll take a leisurely stroll to Duncan's." Prevo nodded, signaling the waiter. Charles went on, "Having another gives me a chance to mention something that bothered me for a long time. I'm also just drunk enough."

Puzzled, the colonel smiled and waited.

"You recall the day we met? I gave you my word that the female smuggler wasn't in the house."

The colonel nodded. "Your word as an officer and West Point man. I accepted it."

"But what I said was a trick. Oh, I was telling the strict truth. She wasn't in the house—" The waiter arrived with two fresh drinks. Charles waited until he set them down and left. "She was hiding in the woods."

"I know."

Glass at his lips, Charles started so hard he spewed a spray of whiskey, some of which landed on Prevo. The colonel produced a handkerchief and used it, explaining, "I spied the buggy. Fortunately, none of my men did."

Charles put the glass down. Shook his head. "I don't understand. Why—?"

"I had to pursue her, but nothing said I had to catch her. I didn't like making war on women, and I still don't."

With an owlish blink, Charles replied, "Damn shame some of your boys didn't feel the same way. Sherman and his stinking bummers. The damage done to South Carolina went beyond all bounds of—"

Abruptly, he stopped. A new flintiness showed in Prevo's eyes.

He hadn't touched his whiskey. Charles drew a hand across his mouth.

"I apologize. What you told that clerk applies to me, too. The war's over. Sometimes I forget."

Prevo glanced at his mutilated right hand, resting beside his glass. "So do I, Charles. We all paid. We'll all remember for years."

At ten past five, on the street outside the hotel, they parted with a firm handshake, friends.

At the Baltimore & Ohio terminal on New Jersey Avenue, amid a great crowd of departing passengers, Brigadier Duncan and Maureen, carrying the baby, boarded the cars. Duncan settled the Irish girl in her seat in second class—he had first-class accommodations—then returned to the platform to find his porter and make certain every piece of luggage was loaded.

The platform clock showed 5:35 P.M.

145

Studying house numbers, Charles moved along the block with a slight unsteadiness left over from Willard's. Should be one of these, he thought, a second before his eye fell on the tin numeral matching that written on the paper. Something choked in his throat a moment, and he began to sober quickly.

The house had a dark, abandoned appearance. Every drapery closed. No lights showing in the spring dusk. Panicky, he bounded up the steps to the door, knocking hard.

"Hello? Anyone in there?" *What if he's moved? What if I can't find him?* "Hello?"

More pounding, attracting the unfriendly notice of a couple rocking on their porch across the street. Behind the house, he heard sounds. Wheels and traces, a horse. He ran to the end of the porch just as a buggy passed, driven by a stout middle-aged woman with a portmanteau on the seat beside her.

"Ma'am? May I speak to you?" A glance had told him the buggy had come from the shed in back of the house.

She turned her head, eyes widening at the sight of the bearded, threatening figure leaning over the porch rail. Mrs. Caldwell's instinctive reaction was fright. She whipped up the horse.

"Wait! I have to ask you something—"

She turned into the street. Charles vaulted over the rail, landed in the side drive with a jolt, raced in pursuit of the buggy, which was gathering speed. The man and woman rose from their rockers, their expressions showing fear of the deranged-looking man chasing the vehicle.

Panting, Charles pumped his arms until he drew abreast of the buggy. "Please stop. It's urgent that I locate—"

"Get away from me!" Mrs. Caldwell flailed at him with the buggy whip, stung his cheek. Charles's instinct for defense took over. He shot his hand across to clamp and drag on her wrist.

"Stop! I don't mean you any harm, but—"

Struggling with him, she was forced to rein the buggy to a halt. "The law," she cried. "Someone call the law."

"Damn it, woman, listen to me," Charles said, breathing hard. "I need to find General Duncan."

Releasing her, he stepped back. The whip in her right hand shook, but she acted less alarmed. "I didn't mean to scare you—I apologize for grabbing you that way. But it's extremely important that I locate the brigadier. That's his house back there, isn't it?"

Guardedly: "It was."

"Was?"

"The general has left for a new military post."

Charles's stomach knotted. "When?"

"He is at the B & O station at this moment, departing at six. Now, sir, I insist on knowing who you are and the reason for this alleged urgency."

"Six," Charles repeated. "It must be almost that now—"

"Your name, sir, or I shall drive on immediately."

"Charles Main."

She acted as if he'd hit her. "Late of the Confederate Army?" He nodded, thinking. "Then you are the one—"

"Move over," he said suddenly, climbing up and practically shoving her to the far side of the seat. "Better hold the rail. I'm going to catch that train. *Hah!*"

He slapped the reins over the horse. Mrs. Caldwell screeched, clutching both her hat and the rail as the buggy shot forward like a bolt released from a crossbow.

Mrs. Caldwell was convinced she would die on the breakneck ride to the depot. The bearded man, the one Brigadier Duncan had sought so diligently, then given up for lost or dead, rammed the buggy through impossibly narrow spaces in evening traffic, causing pedestrians to scatter, hackney drivers to swear, dray horses to rear up and whinny. Rounding the corner into New Jersey, driver and passenger saw a water wagon looming ahead. Charles hauled on the reins, braked, veered, and stood the buggy on its left wheels for a moment. Mrs. Caldwell uttered a scream as the right ones came crashing down, the buggy missing the back end of the water wagon by inches.

Axles howling, wheel hubs smoking, the buggy jerked to a stop directly in front of the station, whose outdoor clock showed a minute after six. Leaping out, Charles flung the reins at the stunned woman, remembering to shout, "Thank you." He plunged into the depot like a distance runner.

"Train for Baltimore?" he yelled at a uniformed man rolling an iron gate shut.

"Just left," the man said, pointing down the platform toward an observation car receding behind billows of steam. Charles turned sideways to squeeze through the opening. "Here, you can't—"

Almost at once, he had three station officials in pursuit. They were older and in poor condition; he was lean and desperate. Still, his lungs quickly began to hurt from the exertion. And he was losing the race. The train was already out of the roofed shed.

He saw the end of the passenger platform ahead. It was too late to brake his momentum. He jumped for the tracks.

He landed crookedly. His wounded leg twisted, hurling him onto the ties. "Get that man!" one of the pursuers howled.

Hurt and panting, Charles pushed up, gained his feet, and ran

1065

again, harder than he had ever run in his life. His beard flew over his shoulder. He thought of Sport. Sport could do it. Sport would have the stamina—

That drove him to greater effort. He came within a hand's length of the rear car. Reached for the handrail of the steps. Missed his stride again and almost fell—The rail receded. Concentrating on a memory of Gus's face, he put everything into a last long step.

He caught hold of the step rail with both hands. The train dragged him, his boots bouncing and bumping. He kicked upward with both legs, knowing that if he didn't, his legs might be pulped under the train.

One boot slipped on the metal step. He nearly fell off. His wrists and forearms felt fiery, tortured by the strain. But he pulled—

Pulled—

Weak and gasping, he staggered upright on the rear platform, only to see the car door open and a broad-shouldered conductor step through, barring him. The trainman saw the pursuers staggering down the track, understood their shouts and gestures.

"Please," Charles said, "let me go inside."

"Get off this train."

"You don't understand. It's an emergency. One of your passengers—"

"Get off or I'll throw you off," the conductor said, starting to push. Charles lurched backward, his left boot finding just empty air above the second step. Frantically, he grabbed the handrail and only in that way kept himself from tumbling into space.

"Get off!" the conductor yelled, raising his hands for a second, final, shove. Something hard rammed the center of his vest. He looked down and went rigid at the sight of Charles's army Colt pressed into his stomach.

"You have ten seconds to stop this train."

"I can't possibly—"

Charles drew the hammer back to full cock.

"Ten seconds."

With a flurry of signal flags and alarm whistles, the train stopped.

146

Only Brigadier Duncan's intervention and influence prevented Charles's immediate arrest and imprisonment. At half past ten that night, the two men sat in the parlor of the reopened house, their faces grim as those of opponents still at war. The Irish wet nurse was upstairs with the child Charles had looked at twice, the second time with feelings of confusion and even revulsion. After returning from the depot, Duncan had told him the whole story, and Charles wished he hadn't.

The evening had grown sultry, with rumbles of an approaching storm in the northwest. His neck button still fastened, Charles sat in a plush chair, an untasted shot of whiskey on a small table to his right. His lamplit eyes looked dead. As dead as he felt inside.

Suddenly, with fury, he leaned forward. "Why didn't she tell me?"

"Major Main," the brigadier replied with icy correctness, "that is the third, possibly the fourth time you have asked the same question. She loved you very much—as I stated in the letters you never received. She grieved because the war had—damaged you, to use her phrase. Damaged you to the point where you mistakenly believed you could not continue your relationship with her. But my niece was a decent and honorable young woman." Unmistakably, there was the suggestion that Charles had neither of those characteristics.

Duncan continued, "She refused to hold her—condition as a club over your head. Now I shall not explain all that again. Indeed, I am beginning to regret you found me. I cannot understand your coldness toward your own flesh and blood."

"The baby killed her."

"There is indeed something wrong in your head, Main. Circumstance killed her. Her frailness killed her. She wanted the child. She wanted to bear your son—she named him after you. Do you seriously mean to tell me you want nothing to do with him?"

Anguished, Charles said, *"I don't know."*

"Well, I have no intention of remaining in Washington while you undertake your bizarre deliberations on the matter. I thought that if I ever found you, the reunion would be a joyous moment. It is anything but that."

"Give me just a little time—"

"Hardly worth my while, Major—having heard your remarks of a moment ago. I shall be on tomorrow evening's six o'clock express for Baltimore and the West. If you do not want your son, I do."

A dazed blink. "The West—?"

"Duty with the plains cavalry, if it's any of your affair. Now, if you will excuse me, I find this conversation odious. I shall retire." He stalked to the parlor door, where strained politeness made him pause and say, "There is an unused bedroom at the second floor rear. You may spend the night if you wish." Duncan's eyes flayed him. "Should your son cry out, you needn't trouble yourself. Maureen and I will look after him."

"Goddamn you, don't take that tone with me," Charles yelled, on his feet. "I loved her! I never loved anyone so much! I thought I should break things off for her sake, so I could do my job and she wouldn't worry constantly. Now if that's a crime in your estimation, the hell with you. When I stopped your train and found you inside, I didn't know I had a son. All I wanted was to learn where she is—was—"

"She is buried in the private cemetery in Georgetown. There is a marker. I shall ask you tomorrow, Major, before my departure, to give me your decision about young Charles."

"I can't. I don't know what it is."

"God pity any man who must say words like those."

The brigadier marched up the stairs. On the upper landing, he heard the front door slam, then a rumble of thunder, then silence. White light glittered through the house. Duncan raised his head

1068

as the hard pelting rain hit the roof. He heard no further sound from below.

With a shake of his head and a sudden sag of his shoulders, he continued to his room, a grieving and dismayed man.

Charles walked all the way to Georgetown in the lightning and thunder and rain. Knocking at a cottage, rousing the owners, he obtained directions to the private cemetery. The sleepy couple with the lamp were too frightened to deny him an answer. He was a hellish apparition on their wet porch, a nightmare man with furnace eyes and a soaked gray shirt and rain dripping from his beard and his holstered gun.

Hurrying on, he reached the cemetery in an interval of pitch darkness. He slipped in wet grass, falling forward and nearly impaling himself on the spikes of the low fence. On his knees next to it, he felt the metal. Wrought iron.

Was it Hazard's? He uttered a crazed laugh. He was losing his mind. Everything was slipping, fusing, jumbling together. He wanted to scream. He wanted to die.

He kicked the gate open and lurched into the cemetery, searching by lightning flash. Granite angels spread granite arms and granite wings, imploring him to heaven with granite eyes. *No thank you, I'm at my proper destination already.*

In the dark he stumbled repeatedly over low headstones or crashed painfully into cold marble. Jagged lightning ran through the sky. He saw a towering obelisk against the glare and a name carved huge on the pedestal. STARKWETHER.

After a long period of wandering one way, then another, he found the grave. The headstone was small and rectangular, with a slightly sloping top upon which Duncan had put her name and the years of her birth and death, nothing more.

Charles sank to his knees, every inch of him soaked by the rain that still poured down. He didn't feel it or the cold. Only the misery, the awful, mind-destroying misery. He knelt beside the grave, careful not to kneel on it, and without conscious volition closed his fists and began to beat them on his thighs.

He pounded harder. To hurt, to punish. The undersides of his fists ached, but he kept pounding. The thunder cannonaded like the guns at Sharpsburg. The lightning flashed again and again, revealing a spot of blood on the right leg of his pants. The rhythm of the pounding quickened.

What was he to do, now that he bore this guilt? What was he to do with the child for whom he was responsible, thereby making himself responsible for this headstone? *What was he to do?*

A short, strange cry came from his throat; animal grief. Then, deep inside, a force began to build, its outlet impossible to deny. He opened his throbbing fists. Raised his right hand to his wet face and felt beneath his eye. That was not rain.

He threw himself forward on the grave, wet body to wet earth, and for the first time since Sharpsburg, wept.

Charles kept vigil at Augusta Barclay's grave until well past dawn, when the storm abated. Shivering, teeth chattering, he walked the long distance back to the central part of town, reaching the brigadier's house about ten.

Exhausted from the physical and emotional strain of the night before, Duncan had slept late and was only just starting his breakfast when the unbelievably sorry sight named Charles Main appeared in the door of the dining room. From somewhere above came the bawling of Charles's son and Maureen's comforting voice in counterpoint.

Clenching his jaw, Duncan strove to control himself. It was difficult. Red-faced, he said, "Christ. What did you do, drink and wallow in some gutter all night long?"

It looked like it. Charles's right pants leg showed a large blood spot. Dirt clung to his beard and every part of his soaked shirt.

"I spent the night at her grave. I spent the night thinking of my son. Trying to decide what to do."

Slowly, Duncan straightened to his most erect posture, his back no longer touching the chair. His eyes were full of hostile challenge.

"Well?"

147

"Next stop Lehigh Station. Lehigh Station will be the next stop—"

The conductor's voice faded as he left the car. The local had pulled out of Bethlehem at half past six. That meant they should be stepping through Belvedere's front door in less than an hour. George was thankful; he was spent. So was Constance, to judge from the way she leaned against him, silent.

He occupied the seat beside the window, watching twilight burnish the river and the blue-mantled slopes on the western side. He turned to say something to his wife but didn't. Her eyes were closed, her head sagging forward, creating three rounded chins in place of one.

George's tired face smoothed out as he lovingly studied her. Then his eye was caught by movement beyond the window on the other side of the aisle. As the train slowed down before a curve, he saw a cemetery and, in the foreground, three rows of five crosses, new and white. The movement drawing his attention was that of two elderly workers shoveling earth onto an unseen coffin in an open grave. A middle-aged man and woman stood beside the grave, the man with something red and white folded in his crossed arms. A flag.

The cemetery disappeared. Carefully, George put his arm around Constance so as not to wake her. But he wanted the comfort of touching her.

He felt an immense surge of love for the plump woman dozing beside him. Love for her and for his children, whose lives he must begin to supervise again, changing from soldier back to father. Love was really all that had pulled him through the past four years, he reflected. His eyes drifted across the river again, to the profusion of mountain laurel on the hillsides. *Nothing else will pull us through the years just ahead, either.*

"—gone too fast. With too many changes."

"Oh, definitely. I'm sorry Lincoln was martyred, but he can certainly be faulted for his policies."

George frowned, overhearing the travelers in the seat immediately behind. The first speaker sounded old, his voice full of the cranky negativism that inevitable state too often produced. The second speaker, female, sounded young. It was she who continued.

"The darkies deserve their liberty, I suppose. But at that point it should stop."

"So far as I'm concerned, it does. Let any nigger try to step through my front door like a white man, and I'll be there to deny him with my old horse pistol."

The woman sighed. "Some of our politicians aren't as courageous as you. They're actually promoting the franchise for the colored."

"Ridiculous. Why would anyone encourage such a change in the order of things? It's insanity."

Having endorsed each other's convictions, they settled into a period of quiet, leaving George to meditate amid the smells of dusty upholstery and the overflowing spittoon at the head of the car. Now the western hills were higher, their summits intermittently blocking the direct rays of the low sun. Changing patterns of shadow and light flickered over his face as he pondered.

Changes indeed. He thought of the slain President, whose unbelievably stark photograph—a recent one—they had seen in a black-draped shop window after they docked in Philadelphia. In 1860, Abraham Lincoln's party had nominated him because he was the least-known, therefore least-offensive candidate available. A strong man with strong views might have stirred strong reactions, which was dangerous to any organized group in pursuit of votes.

But once in office—the furnace of war—Lincoln, like iron, had been heated and hammered, melted and molded and transformed into something wholly new. Out of the corn-country politician of unknown views, presumably safe views—or no views or insane

1072

views, depending on the speaker—there emerged with the aid of the pricking of conscience and the whipping of expedience a President who propounded a definition of freedom so new and sweeping the nation would be years finding and deciphering all its meanings.

Lincoln's burdens of party leadership, governmental leadership, war leadership wrought radical physical changes as well. They cut gullies in the pain-eroded landscape of his face and drowned his eyes in lakes of perpetual shadow. The photographic portrait in the Philadelphia shop barely resembled those of a few years earlier.

In the hearts of the black people of the nation, Lincoln had changed from a man to a god by means of his own pen stroke. But in one way, George reflected, the man had never changed at all. He remembered Executive Mansion aides gossiping that Lincoln often lost his patience and sometimes his good humor and on rare occasions his compassion for the enemy. But it seemed to George that the man had never lost sight of his own North Star. He loved humanity, Southern as well as Northern, with a great heart. But he loved the Union more.

To preserve it, he had sorrowfully led a people to war. He had suffered mental depression and haunted sleep, fought the demons of ineptitude and incompetence and innuendo, hectored and joked, preached and cajoled, dreamed and wept for it. And then he had been chosen as the last sacrifice at the site where its continuity had been assured: the blood altar.

At least Abraham Lincoln had known for five days that his North Star still shone bright and pure, above the cooling embers of fires first kindled in that long-lost spring George remembered vividly, frighteningly, to this hour. The Union stood—profoundly altered but fundamentally unchanged.

George recognized but couldn't fully understand the paradox. It was simply *there,* mighty, majestic, and mysterious, like the murdered President himself. It was there—Lincoln was there—and would be forever, George suspected.

Closing his eyes, he rested a moment. Then he drew a circle of thought of much smaller diameter and meditated on the changes within that.

Orry dead—and his widow making no secret that she was, at least in the strictest view of Southerners, a Negress. He had heard

1073

it first from his brother Billy, but Madeline had candidly discussed it before the Hazards left Mont Royal.

And Charles. Everyone agreed Charles had been burned out by the war. Become a sullen, angry man. Brett, by contrast, was eagerly anticipating motherhood and, amazingly, often sounded more like Virgilia than a Southerner.

Cooper occasionally displayed a new, almost reactionary streak, as if he had turned about and finally accepted the Southern inheritance his father had always wanted to bequeath to him, and he had scorned for such a long time. In Cooper's case, anyway, George could identify the causes of the transformation. Cooper had lost his son, and he was growing older. Age brought a man more conservative thoughts and opinions. As George well knew.

Billy's views about blacks had changed, too, although his plan for his life was one of the few things that hadn't. Saying good-bye to George in South Carolina—he had two more weeks of leave and planned to spend it working for and with the Mains—he had stated his intention to remain with the Army Engineers. Unless, of course, something impeded his advancement, in which case there was always that railroad construction he and George had discussed. Trains were the coming thing. People had a nickname to certify it. The iron horse.

How intimately the process of change accelerated by the war had touched all of them, and the country. How deeply it had affected them and the country. No one was spared, neither those who accepted it nor those who denied it. Witness the pair on whom he had eavesdropped. The hardening of attitudes was in itself a change, in response to change.

Why did so many deny the universal constancy of the process, he wondered. Through some quirk of temperament or upbringing, George had embraced it early, within the framework of the family business. He had been open to innovation and had fought Stanley, who was not. Gradually, his perceptions had widened until he saw the benefit—or at least the inevitability—of change outside the gates of Hazard's as well.

Why did people ignore the lessons of history and their own senses, deny a law of life immutable as the seasons, and erect twisted barriers against it in their minds? He didn't know why, but they did. They wept for the goodness of half-imaginary yesterdays, yesterdays beyond altering, instead of anticipating and helping to shape the good of possible tomorrows. They found

1074

things to blame for the flow of events they wanted to stop and could not. They blamed God, their wives, government, books, fanciful combinations of unnamed men—sometimes even voices in their own heads. They lived tortured and unhappy lives, trying to dam Niagara with a teacup.

But he doubted anyone could change people of that stamp. They were the curse and burden of a race laboring forward up a mountain in half-darkness. They were—it brought a weary smile —constant as the very change they hated.

Which reminded him of a certain small but important change he wanted to make at Belvedere. Ever since finding the fragment of iron-rich meteorite in the hills above West Point, he had kept it on the library table as a symbol of the power and potency of the metal that had created the Hazard fortune. For many years he had been seduced by iron's wide application in weaponry, and thus by its potential to change the fate of nations, the globe itself.

But in Virginia, he had begun to think that a certain adjustment or balance was required. During the last four years, Americans had fallen on other Americans like ravening animals. The full impact of the blood-letting—the ultimate shock when all the casualties, tangible and otherwise, were at last enumerated—lay in the future. When the shock set in, it would not soon pass, he was convinced. So it was wise to prepare, identify a balancing force.

When they reached Belvedere, he surprised Constance by what he did immediately after he spent a half hour hugging and talking with his son and daughter. He went out through the kitchen and up the hill, bringing back a green sprig of laurel, which he laid beside the piece of star-iron in the library.

"I should like a fresh sprig to be kept there at all times," he said. "Where all of us can see it."

That same night, on the 6:00 P.M. train bound for the transfer point at Baltimore, Brigadier Duncan and Charles sat opposite each other in a first-class car. Charles hardly looked as though he belonged there, smoking cigars and wearing that disreputable rag robe. Duncan insisted they take time on the trip west to obtain a decent suit until he was issued a new uniform.

Several times since Charles's return from the cemetery, Duncan had tried to draw him out on the subject of his vigil, particularly the thoughts and emotions that had led to his decision. But it was impossible for Charles to describe or even be open about the various alternatives that had flowed through his mind during that long night of rain, uncertainty, guilt, despair.

There was the possibility of sailing for Egypt to serve in the khedive's army, as he had heard in a Washington barroom that some Confederate officers were doing. There was the possibility of taking to the hills to continue guerrilla action against the Yankees. There was going home and wasting away in drink and idleness.

There was suicide.

There was also the West, where Duncan was bound. He had always loved the West, and Duncan reiterated the need for cavalrymen out there. Charles was trained for nothing else.

But all of that was peripheral to the central issue he confronted during the vigil: Gus's death and his son's life. They were not separate but one, inextricably interlocked.

It was Gus who had shown him the way. At the grave he had remembered their best times together. Remembered her strength, her will. No miraculous transformation had occurred while the rain fell on him in Georgetown and washed against his own flooding tears. He had never hurt so badly as he did then and now, and he knew the uncertainty and pain would persist for a long time. But he had learned, keeping vigil with the guilt and grief undammed at last, one truth above all: he still loved Augusta Barclay beyond life itself. So he must love the boy. He must live for the boy as well as for her, because they were one.

Seeing Charles's somber expression as he stared out the window into the sunlit meadows of evening, Duncan frowned. He was not yet comfortable in the Confederate officer's presence and wondered if he ever would be. Further, he wondered if Charles understood the ramifications of his decision. While the train was passing through one of the many small hamlets dotting the right of way in Maryland—Charles saw two demolished houses and a shell-blasted barn—Duncan cleared his throat.

"You know, my boy, this duty you plan to take on—serving in the regular army again—it won't be easy for a man of your background."

That drew blood. Charles chewed hard on his unlit cigar stub.

"I went through the Academy the same way you did, General. I'm a professional. I changed uniforms once. I can change a second time. It's all one country again, isn't it?"

"That's true. Still, not everyone will treat you as we both would

1076

wish. I'm only trying to warn you against the inevitable. Discourtesies. Insults—"

In a hard voice, Charles said, "I'll handle it." A flash of sunlight between low hills illuminated his ravaged face, unsmiling.

Duncan looked up, gratefully. "Ah—here's Maureen—"

The wet nurse appeared in the aisle, gently cradling the baby she had brought from her seat in second class. "He's awake, General. I thought perhaps you might like—" She stopped, plainly uncertain about which man to address.

"Give him to me." Then, catching himself, Charles said in a gentler way, "Thank you, Maureen."

With extreme care, he took the bundled shape into his arms, while Duncan leaned across to raise the corner of blanket with which Maureen had covered the infant's face while carrying him between cars. Duncan beamed, the picture of the proud greatuncle.

The pink-faced child regarded his father with wide eyes. Awed and fearful of somehow damaging him, Charles tried a tentative smile. The younger Charles grimaced and bawled. "Rock him, for God's sake," Duncan said.

That worked. Charles had never rocked a child, but he quickly caught on. The train passed through fields where a farmer walked behind his mule and plow in the dying daylight, turning new earth.

"Frankly, my boy," Duncan said, "although I'm extremely pleased the three of us are here together and headed where we are, I continue to admit to some astonishment. I felt that if you took your son, you would undoubtedly want to return to South Carolina and raise him as a Southerner."

The father stared at the older man. "Charles is an American. That's how I'll raise him."

Duncan harrumphed to signify acceptance, if not understanding. "He has a middle name, by the way."

"You didn't tell me that."

"It slipped my mind. This has hardly been an ordinary day. His full name is Charles Augustus. My niece chose it just before—"

He pressed a closed hand to his lips. Remembering was hard for him, too, Charles realized.

"Before her confinement. She said she had always loved the nickname Gus."

Feeling tears, Charles blinked several times. He gazed down at his son, whose face had mysteriously reddened, and taken on a puzzling appearance of strain. Duncan peeked at the infant. "Oh, I think we shall need the assistance of Maureen. Excuse me while I fetch her."

He stepped into the aisle. With great care, Charles touched his son's chin. The baby reached out and grasped his index finger. He drew it into his mouth and gnawed vigorously.

Duncan had already lectured Charles about the need for cleanliness. So far today, he had scrubbed his hands three times—something of a record in his adult life. He wiggled his finger. Charles Augustus gurgled. Charles smiled. With all of his attention on his son, he didn't see the rail fence that suddenly appeared beside the track or the feasting buzzards disturbed by the train and swirling upward, away from the rotting remains of a black horse.

> *The war has left a great gulf between what happened before it in our century and what has happened since. . . . It does not seem to me as if I am living in the country in which I was born.*

GEORGE TICKNOR *of Harvard,* 1869

AFTERWORD

All changed, changed utterly:
A terrible beauty is born.

So wrote Yeats in "Easter 1916." His nine words are the underpinning of this novel.

Love and War was not written to demonstrate, again, that war is hell, though it is; or to show slavery, again, as our most heinous national crime, though arguably it is. Both ideas figure in the story, and not in a small way. But this is meant to be a tale about change as a universal force and constant, told in terms of a group of characters living through the greatest redefinition of America, in the shortest time, that we have ever experienced: the Civil War.

In his book *Ordeal by Fire: The Civil War and Reconstruction,* Professor James McPherson of Princeton splendidly characterizes the war as "the central event in the American historical consciousness. . . . [It] preserved this nation from destruction and determined, in large measure, what sort of nation it would be. The war settled two fundamental issues . . . whether [the United States] was to be a nation with a sovereign national government, or a dissoluble confederation of sovereign states; and whether this nation, born of a declaration that all men are created with an equal right to liberty, was to continue to exist as the largest slaveholding country in the world."

Beyond the essential element of a strong narrative, I felt the book needed three things if it were to do its job.

First, it needed detail. And not the detail of the more familiar events, either. As the book developed from a first draft on my typewriter through the final draft on my IBM PC, a new mental signboard was hung where I couldn't miss it. (The permanent signboard, very old now, reads: *Storytelling first.)* The new one said: *Not Gettysburg again.*

The details I wanted were many from what I call the byways: the fascinating places novels about the Civil War seldom go. To the bottom of Charleston harbor, for instance, where the astonishing and astonishingly small, submersible *Hunley* forecast a dramatic change in naval warfare. Into the bureaucracy and the cavalry camps. To the work sites of an engineer battalion and a military railroad track crew. Inside Libby Prison, over to Liverpool, and back to the Ordnance Department in Washington, with its permanent parade of inventors, some sane, many mad. I even wanted to go onto a camp stage to show a bit of the Civil War equivalent of a USO show; the skit that Charles and Ab watch is authentic.

Hoping that what interests me would interest readers, I chose a number of these lesser-known byways and began the search, which took a year. There is certainly no shortage of material. Quoting McPherson again, "Perhaps it is simply because the conflict was so astonishingly rich and varied that it is inexhaustible." Historian Burke Davis observed that "more than 100,000 volumes of [Civil War literature] have failed to tell the tale to the satisfaction of . . . readers." Or of writers, for that matter. I could see no way to include a relatively recent, fascinating finding that in England, in the desperate late hours of the Confederacy, operatives may have developed a primitive two-stage guided missile. The device was allegedly shipped to a site in Virginia, then tested and fired at Washington. The burning of records in Richmond consumed whatever report may have been made of the missile's performance, and we have no evidence that it struck or even came close to its target or, indeed, any evidence that it existed at all. No room for that story. And many more.

But I hope there are enough specifics, for only by means of them is it possible to take a stab at suggesting what it was like to serve in, and live through, the struggle.

Librarian-scholar Richard H. Shryock aptly stated the case for detail fifty years ago: "Political and military traditions, plus the apparent necessity for abstraction, rob historical writings of that realism which alone can convey a sense of the suffering involved in a great war. An historian's description of the battle of Gettysburg is likely to tell of what occurred to Lee's right wing, or to Longstreet's corps, but rarely of what happened to [the bodies of] plain John Jones and the thousands like him. . . . The historians might, however, picture reality and convey a sense of the costs involved if, in describing campaigns, they gave less space to tactics in the field and more to . . . the camps and hospitals."

Amen. That is the reason Charles encounters the first land mines on the peninsula, and Cooper experiments with "torpedoes" (confusingly, that term at the time meant naval mines). That is one reason Cooper descends in *Hunley*, whose full-size replica stands outside the entrance of the Museum of the City of Charleston today. That is why there is less here about generals than about soldiers of lower rank tending their horses, losing company elections, getting ill, feeling homesick, reading tracts and pornography, scrounging food, sewing clothes, scratching lice.

One problem with some of the details of the war is their tendency to strain credulity because we gaze at them through a modern lens flawed by the circumstances and skepticism of our own time. Thus it may be hard to accept the virtual absence of presidential security even in the Executive Mansion, or the fact that Lincoln got his first solid news of the Fredericksburg defeat from an angry field correspondent frustrated by military censors, or that the unsteady General Burnside, in connection with the same engagement, consulted his personal chef for strategic advice. The reader must take particulars like these on faith; they are not invented, no matter how odd they may seem.

Some of the details that are fictional have a sound and reasoned base in possibility. Powell's scheme, for one—no more unlikely than the real plan to establish a "third nation" by joining the Upper South—the so-called border states—with the Middle West. This idea was afloat in Richmond during the winter of '62–'63. A Pacific Confederacy, also mentioned in the novel, was widely rumored early in the war.

The assassination plot against Davis is an invention, but it, too, seems logical in view of two givens. One, if Lincoln was constantly considered an assassin's target, why not his Confederate counterpart? Especially since—two—Davis was just as passionately hated, most notably by some from his own cotton South. I sometimes wonder if the few present-day Southerners who ride around in pickups adorned with crass license plates declaring *Hell no I ain't fergittin'!* have ever heard of Messrs. Brown and Vance —the war governors of Georgia and North Carolina respectively

—surely two of the most venomous enemies a Chief Executive ever had. Furiously waving the banner of states' rights, they damned and defied the central government, withheld men, uniforms, and shoes the army desperately needed, and generally did as much, or more, damage as many a Union field commander.

Neither governor is here accused of sinister plotting. But a man such as Powell, whose remedy for grievance is bullets, is not that far removed from those like Brown and Vance who continually screamed "dictator" and "despot" at Jefferson Davis.

The second ingredient I needed, also mentioned in the Afterword of *North and South,* was accuracy.

I don't mean infallibility. In a novel this long and complex, it's impossible to be perfect. But it's absolutely necessary to try. I had a sharp lesson on the point during the early stages of work.

Always a fan of Errol Flynn films, I taped and watched one I hadn't seen for years—*Santa Fe Trail.* It was released by Warner Brothers in 1940 and is still shown frequently on television. It includes the following men as members of the West Point class of 1854. Jeb Stuart, played by Flynn—that, at least, is correct. There is also Longstreet (class of '42), Pickett ('46), Hood ('53), and Stuart's best pal, George Custer ('61). Young Custer is portrayed by young Ronald Reagan.

During the course of the muddled plot—Flynn devotees consider it one of his lesser efforts for Warner's—we meet a silver-haired actor cast as a familiar character type, the Distinguished Businessman. This Distinguished Businessman possesses a Kansas railroad and a daughter whom Jeb marries. In other words, Jeb doesn't come anywhere close to doing what he really did: wed the daughter of Philip St. George Cooke, the career officer who became his sworn foe in the war and the man he attempted to humiliate as part of his ride around McClellan.

Stuart's endlessly grinning sidekick Custer is forced to settle for an insipid blond, the daughter of Jeff Davis. Davis is made up to look like a bargain-basement Lincoln; the girl resembles a chorine from a Betty Grable musical.

Even worse, it's a curiously spineless film when dealing with the slave question. The cavalrymen at one point fight John Brown in "bloody"—*sic*—Kansas, but Stuart and Custer mutually declare that "others" must "decide" about slavery. They just "carry out orders" and presumably have no opinions on national issues.

Well, not many, anyway. At one point Custer makes a mild

statement on behalf of the abolitionist position. He is at once reprimanded. The script then requires Reagan to grin sheepishly and say, "Sorry."

The film is relevant to the matter of accuracy in this way. Since people, not machines, write novels—and screenplays—the re-creation of any chunk of the past will more than likely result in at least a few mistakes. (I made a dandy in connection with coinage in the first book of this trilogy.) But unintentional errors are not quite the same as gross revisions of the record, perpetrated for heaven knows what reason, and obviously tolerated in many novels, but most notoriously in motion pictures. The technique is what I call "History à la Polo Lounge." I hope readers have found none of it here.

In fairness, it must be said that film producers are not the only individuals guilty of doctoring the past. As a people, we all tend to be mythmakers as the generations pass. Thus our icon version of Lincoln is forever the all-knowing, eternally calm idealist and humanitarian, rather than the doubt-ridden, depressive, and widely hated political pragmatist who was lifted to greatness by necessity and his own conscience. Our Lee is the eternally benign hero seated on Traveller, not a soldier whose ability was suspect, whose decisions were often questioned, and who received the scorn of many fellow Confederates through nicknames such as "Granny" and "Retreating" Lee.

We mythologize not only individuals but also the war itself. Perhaps the Polo Lounge effect, the remove of most serious historians from the personal elements—there are splendid exceptions, such as the late Bell I. Wiley—and our own quite natural human tendency to prefer the glamorous to the grimy, have combined to put a patina on the war. To render it romantic. It was—for about ninety days. After that came horror. And the horror grew.

Yet the dewy visions persist.

Although *Gone With the Wind* is a film deserving of all the admiration and honor it has received, the reason is not its faithful re-creation of history; the picture is a romance. Sanitized battles occur—briefly—in montages, or on title cards. Atlanta burning is a grand action spectacle, but says little about personal tragedy. Slavery is never an issue; the house blacks at Tara are happy, cute, and apparently content. And despite a few hospital scenes, genuine suffering is never depicted, except in the famous depot shot with the camera crane rising and rising to reveal, gradually and with devastating power, more and more and more maimed men.

It may be unfair to judge a classic by standards other than those of its own time. On the other hand, most of the social views of Charles Dickens hold up today. Those of *GWTW* don't.

In 1939, white Americans considered it all right for Butterfly McQueen and Hattie McDaniel to be cute though enslaved, just as it was all right for Mantan Moreland to play a stereotyped succession of railway porters and other servitors in Charlie Chan pictures; the black actor was usually required to demonstrate Comical Negro Cowardice by trembling, exhibiting saucer eyes, and speaking lines such as the famous "Feet, don't fail me now!"

My problems with the magisterial *GWTW*, which I love with shameless emotion despite its clear negative aspects, are two. First, it is the major film representation of the war, thus an implicit validation of its own dubious morality. Second, only one recent picture that I can recall—David L. Wolper's landmark production of *Roots*—comes close to matching it for popular stature and impact. Yet that enduring acclaim may be valuable as a continuing reminder of the difference between the standards of the thirties and a newer America; the difference between the myth and the truth.

Occasionally there are works of fiction—Stephen Crane's *Red Badge of Courage*, the landmark *Andersonville*, the wonderful *The Killer Angels*—that cut to the bone and expose the truth about the war. The truth that the legends of perpetual chivalry and decency at all levels, beginning to end, are false. Along with correct detail, I sought this larger sense of truth throughout the book. Whether I found it is not a judgment that is mine to make.

On the trail of accuracy, I rewalked every one of the eastern battle sites and historical parks. I had visited most before, but not all. I saw little Brandy Station on a beautiful spring day in 1982. That same week, I spent the whole of a foggy wet Saturday at Antietam. There were few present beyond those the markers and monuments conjured. It was a dark and moving day.

In passages dealing with battles and campaigns, readers may have noticed that there is little use of the names and numbers of military units. An army table of organization is always complex, but that's doubly true in the Civil War, since the armies on both sides were restructured several times to suit the ideas of the particular general in command. I believe the alpha-numerical hash of armies and corps, divisions and regiments is chiefly of interest to the specialist. When used, as it is so often, as the backbone of an account of a battle, it leaves me confused and irritated. That is why I avoided it. Nevertheless, I endeavored to put units important to the story in the right place at the right time.

A couple of other points must be mentioned to keep the record straight.

Wade Hampton did have "Iron Scouts," but the ones whose exploits are described are fictitious.

Remarks of senators taking part in the 1863 debate over H.R. 611—the West Point appropriation bill—are excerpted from the Congressional *Globe* for January 15, 1863. Although my version of the content and general flow of the floor fight is accurate, the actual debate was far more windy. In transcript it runs ten pages, three columns per page, in miniature type. I have also chosen widely separated sentences from long statements by Ben Wade and other speakers and arranged these into shorter pieces of oratory. Where I've taken liberties, I have abridged the factual record, not invented a new one.

To one deliberate long step from the true path, I plead guilty. I voted against trying to duplicate what Douglas Southall Freeman rightly termed the period's "ornate conversational style." For a reason. "Even the casual conversation . . . was, by present-day usage, deliberate and stiff." Billy's fellow engineering officer, Farmer, is a character meant to give a flavor of this style, but only a flavor.

The third ingredient I needed was help. Help from experts who knew the answers to specific questions. Help from individuals who assisted in areas not directly connected with research. And help from those who gave support just by being there. I want to thank them all publicly and at the same time absolve them of all responsibility for possible mishandling of any reference material they provided. Nor are they responsible for my interpretations of fact, or the story, in part or in total.

I begin with Ruth Gaul, of the Hilton Head Island Library, who patiently processed and kept track of my long list of requests for interlibrary loan materials. The secondary source books, the diaries, letter collections, monograph and training manual photocopies, maps, and other references consulted approach three hundred. There's even a slim but fascinating collection of Confederate wartime recipes, many of them food substitutes. Without Ruth and the equally helpful people at the Beaufort County and South Carolina State libraries, the research job would have been all but impossible.

I also owe much, as does every Civil War student, to *The War of the Rebellion: A Compilation of the Official Records of the Union and Confederate Armies*—the O.R., as it's commonly called. This monumental and justly famed work was begun in 1864 and completed in 1927. It runs to 128 volumes, not counting the separate atlases. I have a friend who owns one of the very few complete sets in private hands in this country. For invaluable help, I hereby thank him, though not by name, because he prefers to remain anonymous.

In Liverpool, K. J. Williams, honorable secretary of the Merseyside Confederate Navy History Society, and Cliff Thornton, curator of the Williamson Museum and Art Gallery, Birkenhead, became new friends while proving themselves expert guides to the various sites connected with the Confederacy. To Jerry, my thanks are almost inexpressible. And I shall never forget the windy summer afternoon Cliff and my wife and I received dispensation to enter a fenced patch of land on the bank of the Mersey, where we gazed down, at low tide, on some slipways Cliff himself had never seen before—perhaps the very ways where *Alabama* was built. No one knows exactly which ways held her, but the abandoned land is the site of Laird's in the 1860s. That is a thrill of discovery to be remembered always.

Senator Ernest Hollings and Ms. Jan Buvinger and her staff at the Charleston Public Library helped me track down a copy of the fascinating, if prolix, West Point appropriation bill debate.

My friend Jay Mundhenk, whose Civil War expertise is matched only by his skill as chef and host, solved several difficult problems about operations in northern Virginia when I was at a dead end.

Robert E. Schnare, chief, Special Collections Division of the Library at the U.S. Military Academy, was generous and helpful in matters as diverse as the daily whereabouts of the Army of the Potomac's Battalion of Engineers throughout the war and the contents of the cavalry tactics manual in use at the beginning. As with *North and South,* the cooperation of the West Point library has been all an author could wish for.

Arnold Graham Smith, M.D., was invaluable on medical matters. Other special questions were answered with the help of

Belden Lee Daniels; Peggy Gilmer; Dr. Thomas L. Johnson, of the South Caroliniana Library; Bob Merritt, of the *Richmond Times-Dispatch;* Donna Payne, president of the Rochester, New York, Civil War Roundtable; John E. Stanchak, editor of *Civil War Times;* and Dan Starer. Two of my daughters, Dr. Andrea Jakes-Schauer and Victoria Jakes Montgomery, helped with work on special topics.

In addition to the gratitude expressed to my editor in the dedication, I cannot overlook a number of other people in publishing.

Julian Muller's assistant, Joan Judge, handled quite literally reams of computer-printed manuscript with her customary efficiency and good cheer. Rose Ann Ferrick brought her speed and fine judgment to preparation of the fine typescript, which then benefited from the talents of Roberta Leighton, copy editor nonpareil.

My old friend and colleague classmate Walter Meade, of Avon Books, contributed in a special way he understands.

And my publisher, Bill Jovanovich, continued to stand behind the project.

My attorney, adviser, and friend, Frank Curtis, was along during every step of the two-year journey to this point of completion.

So, too, were all the members of my family, but especially my wife, Rachel, to whom I once again tender my gratitude and love.

JOHN JAKES

Hilton Head Island
April 30, 1984

John Jakes

Hailed by the *Los Angeles Times* as "the godfather of historical novels," John Jakes' masterfully researched Civil War trilogy follows the lives and times of the Mains of South Carolina and the Hazards of Pennsylvania, two American families torn by the fiery politics that divided North and South.

The epic TV mini-series...
- ☐ **HEAVEN AND HELL**   20170-5 $6.99

The epic TV mini-series...
- ☐ **NORTH AND SOUTH**
  (A Dell/HBJ Book)   16205-X $6.99

- ☐ **LOVE AND WAR**   15016-7 $6.99

At your local bookstore or use this handy page for ordering:
DELL READERS SERVICE, DEPT. DNS
2451 South Wolf Road, Des Plaines, IL. 60018

Please send me the above title(s). I am enclosing $_____.
(Please add $2.50 per order to cover shipping and handling.) Send check or money order—no cash or C.O.D.s please.

Ms./Mrs./Mr. _____

Address _____

City/State _____ Zip _____

DNS—3/94
Prices and availability subject to change without notice. Please allow four to six weeks for delivery.